The Fountains of Paradise

Arthur C. Clarke was born in Somerset in 1917 and is a graduate of King's College, London. During the Second World War, as an RAF officer, he was in charge of the first radar talk-down equipment during experimental trials. The author of over forty books and many articles, he won the 1962 Kalinga Prize, the 1965 Aviation-Space Writers' Prize and the 1969 Westinghouse Science Writing Prize; he also shared an 'Oscar' nomination with Stanley Kubrick for the screenplay of *2001: A Space Odyssey*.

For some years Clarke has lived in Sri Lanka and has been doing underwater exploration along that coast and along the Great Barrier Reef. Together with two other commentators, he covered the lunar land flights of Apollo 11, 12 and 15 for American CBS television.

Also by
Arthur C. Clarke in Pan Books

Arthur C. Clarke
The Fountains of Paradise

Pan Books London and Sydney

First published 1979 by Victor Gollancz Ltd
This edition published 1980 by Pan Books Ltd
Cavaye Place, London SW10 9PG
3rd printing 1980
© Arthur C. Clarke 1979
ISBN 0 330 25984 9
Set, printed and bound in Great Britain by
Cox & Wyman Ltd, Reading

to the still unfading memory
of

LESLIE EKANAYAKE
(13 July 1947 – 4 July 1977)

only perfect friend of a lifetime, in whom were uniquely
combined Loyalty, Intelligence and Compassion.
When your radiant and loving spirit vanished from this
world, the light went out of many lives.

NIRVANA PRĀPTO BHŪYĀT

Politics and religion are obsolete; the time has come for science and spirituality.

Sri Jawaharlal Nehru, to the Ceylon Association for the Advancement of Science, Colombo, 15 October 1962.

Contents

Foreword

'From Paradise to Taprobane is forty leagues; there may be heard the sound of the Fountains of Paradise.'

Traditional: reported by Friar Marignolli (AD 1335)

The country I have called Taprobane does not quite exist, but is about ninety per cent congruent with the island of Ceylon (now Sri Lanka). Though the *Afterword* will make clear what locations, events and personalities are based on fact, the reader will not go far wrong in assuming that the more unlikely the story, the closer it is to reality.

The name 'Taprobane' is now usually spoken to rhyme with 'plain', but the correct classical pronunciation is 'Tap-ROB-a-nee' – as Milton, of course, well knew:

'From India and the golden Chersoness
And utmost Indian Isle Taprobane . . .'

(*Paradise Regained*, Book IV)

part one
The Palace

1 Kalidasa

The crown grew heavier with each passing year. When the Venerable Bodhidharma Mahanayake Thero had – so reluctantly! – first placed it upon his head, Prince Kalidasa was surprised by its lightness. Now, twenty years later, King Kalidasa gladly relinquished the jewel-encrusted band of gold, whenever court etiquette allowed.

There was little of that here, upon the windswept summit of the rock fortress; few envoys or petitioners sought audience on its forbidding heights. Many of those who made the journey to Yakkagala turned back at the final ascent, through the very jaws of the crouching lion, that seemed always about to spring from the face of the rock. An old king could never sit upon this heaven-aspiring throne. One day, Kalidasa might be too feeble to reach his own palace. But he doubted if that day would ever come; his many enemies would spare him the humiliations of age.

Those enemies were gathering now. He glanced towards the north, as if he could already see the armies of his half-brother, returning to claim the blood-stained throne of Taprobane. But that threat was still far off, across monsoon-riven seas; although Kalidasa put more trust in his spies than his astrologers, it was comforting to know that they agreed on this.

Malgara had waited almost twenty years, making his plans and gathering the support of foreign kings. A still more patient and subtle enemy lay much nearer at hand, forever watching from the southern sky. The perfect cone of Sri Kanda, the Sacred Mountain, looked very close today, as it towered above the central plain.

Since the beginning of history, it had struck awe into the heart of every man who saw it. Always, Kalidasa was aware of its brooding presence, and of the power that it symbolized.

And yet the Mahanayake Thero had no armies, no screaming war elephants tossing brazen tusks as they charged into battle. The High Priest was only an old man in an orange robe, whose sole material possessions were a begging bowl and a palm leaf to shield him from the sun. While the lesser monks and acolytes chanted the scriptures around him, he merely sat in cross-legged silence – and somehow tampered with the destinies of kings. It was very strange...

The air was so clear today that Kalidasa could see the temple, dwarfed by distance to a tiny white arrowhead on the very summit of Sri Kanda. It did not look like any work of man, and it reminded the king of the still greater mountains he had glimpsed in his youth, when he had been half-guest, half-hostage at the court of Mahinda the Great. All the giants that guarded Mahinda's empire bore such crests, formed of a dazzling, crystalline substance for which there was no word in the language of Taprobane. The Hindus believed that it was a kind of water, magically transformed, but Kalidasa laughed at such superstitions.

That ivory gleam was only three days' march away – one along the royal road, through forests and paddy-fields, two more up the winding stairway which he could never climb again, because at its end was the only enemy he feared, and could not conquer. Sometimes he envied the pilgrims, when he saw their torches marking a thin line of fire up the face of the mountain. The humblest beggar could greet that holy dawn and receive the blessings of the gods; the ruler of all this land could not.

But he had his consolations, if only for a little while. There, guarded by moat and rampart, lay the pools and fountains and Pleasure Gardens on which he had lavished the wealth of his kingdom. And when he was tired of these, there were the ladies of the rock – the ones of flesh and blood, whom he summoned less and less frequently – and the two hundred changeless immortals with whom he often shared his thoughts, because there were no others he could trust.

Thunder boomed along the western sky. Kalidasa turned away

12

from the brooding menace of the mountain, towards the distant hope of rain. The monsoon was late this season; the artificial lakes that fed the island's complex irrigation system were almost empty. By this time of year he should have seen the glint of water in the mightiest of them all – which, as he well knew, his subjects still dared to call by his father's name: Paravana Samudra, the Sea of Paravana. It had been completed only thirty years ago, after generations of toil. In happier days, young Prince Kalidasa had stood proudly beside his father, when the great sluice-gates were opened and the life-giving waters had poured out across the thirsty land. In all the kingdom there was no lovelier sight than the gently rippling mirror of that immense, man-made lake, when it reflected the domes and spires of Ranapura, City of Gold – the ancient capital which he had abandoned for his dream.

Once more the thunder rolled, but Kalidasa knew that its promise was false. Even here, on the summit of Demon Rock, the air hung still and lifeless; there were none of the sudden, random gusts that heralded the onset of the monsoon. Before the rains came at last, famine might be added to his troubles.

'Your Majesty,' said the patient voice of the court Adigar, 'the envoys are about to leave. They wish to pay their respects.'

Ah yes, those two pale ambassadors from across the western ocean! He would be sorry to see them go, for they had brought news, in their abominable Taprobani, of many wonders – though none, they were willing to admit, that equalled this fortress-palace in the sky.

Kalidasa turned his back upon the white-capped mountain and the parched, shimmering landscape, and began to descend the granite steps to the audience chamber. Behind him, the chamberlain and his aides bore gifts of ivory and gems for the tall, proud men who were waiting to say farewell. Soon they would carry the treasures of Taprobane across the sea, to a city younger by centuries than Ranapura; and perhaps, for a little while, divert the brooding thoughts of the Emperor Hadrian.

His robes a flare of orange against the white plaster of the temple walls, the Mahanayake Thero walked slowly to the northern parapet. Far below lay the chequer-board of paddy-fields stretching

13

from horizon to horizon, the dark lines of irrigation channels, the blue gleam of the Paravana Samudra – and, beyond that inland sea, the sacred domes of Ranapura floating like ghostly bubbles, impossibly huge when one realized their true distance. For thirty years he had watched that ever-changing panorama, but he knew that he would never grasp all the details of its fleeting complexity. Colours, boundaries altered with every season – indeed, with every passing cloud. On the day that he too passed, thought Bodhidharma, he would still see something new.

Only one thing jarred in all this exquisitely patterned landscape. Tiny though it appeared from this altitude, the grey boulder of Demon Rock seemed an alien intruder. Indeed, legend had it that Yakkagala was a fragment of the herb-bearing Himalayan peak that the monkey god Hanuman had dropped, as he hastily carried both medicine and mountain to his injured comrades, when the battles of the *Ramayana* were over.

From this distance, of course, it was impossible to see any details of Kalidasa's folly, except for a faint line that hinted at the outer rampart of the Pleasure Gardens. Yet once it had been experienced, such was the impact of Demon Rock that it was impossible to forget. The Mahanayake Thero could see in imagination, as clearly as if he stood between them, the immense lion's claws protruding from the sheer face of the cliff – while overhead loomed the battlements upon which, it was easy to believe, the accursed King still walked . . .

Thunder crashed down from above, rising swiftly to such a crescendo of power that it seemed to shake the mountain itself. In a continuous, sustained concussion it raced across the sky, dwindling away into the east. For long seconds, echoes rolled around the rim of the horizon. No one could mistake *this* as any herald of the coming rains; they were not scheduled for another three weeks, and Monsoon Control was never in error by more than twenty-four hours. When the reverberations had died away, the Mahanayake turned to his companion.

'So much for dedicated re-entry corridors,' he said, with slightly more annoyance than an exponent of the Dharma should permit himself. 'Did we get a meter reading?'

The younger monk spoke briefly into his wrist microphone, and waited for a reply.

'Yes – it peaked at a hundred and twenty. That's five db above the previous record.'

'Send the usual protest to Kennedy or Gagarin Control, whichever it is. On second thoughts, complain to them *both*. Not that it will make any difference, of course.'

As his eye traced the slowly dissolving vapour trail across the sky, Bodhidharma Mahanayake Thero – eighty-fifth of his name – had a sudden and most un-monkish fantasy. Kalidasa would have had a suitable treatment for space-line operators who thought only of dollars per kilo to orbit . . . something that probably involved impalement, or metal-shod elephants, or boiling oil.

But life, of course, had been so much simpler, two thousand years ago.

2 The Engineer

His friends, whose numbers dwindled sadly every year, called him Johan. The world, when it remembered him, called him Raja. His full name epitomized five hundred years of history; Johan Oliver de Alwis Sri Rajasinghe.

There had been a time when the tourists visiting the Rock had sought him out with cameras and recorders, but now a whole generation knew nothing of the days when he was the most familiar face in the solar system. He did not regret his past glory, for it had brought him the gratitude of all mankind. But it had also brought vain regrets for the mistakes he had made – and sorrow for the lives he had squandered, when a little more foresight or patience might have saved them. Of course, it was easy now, in the perspective of history, to see what *should* have been done to avert the Auckland Crisis, or to assemble the unwilling signatories of the Treaty of

Samarkand. To blame himself for the unavoidable errors of the past was folly, yet there were times when his conscience hurt him more than the fading twinges of that old Patagonian bullet.

No one had believed that his retirement would last so long. 'You'll be back within six months,' World President Chu had told him. 'Power is addictive.'

'Not to *me*,' he had answered, truthfully enough.

For power had come to him; he had never sought it. And it had always been a very special, limited kind of power – advisory, not executive. He was only Special Assistant (Acting Ambassador) for Political Affairs, directly responsible to President and Council, with a staff that never exceeded ten – eleven, if one included ARISTOTLE. (His console still had direct access to Ari's memory and processing banks, and they talked to each other several times a year.) But towards the end the Council had invariably accepted his advice, and the world had given him much of the credit that should have gone to the unsung, unhonoured bureaucrats of the Peace Division.

And so it was Ambassador-at-Large Rajasinghe who got all the publicity, as he moved from one trouble-spot to another, massaging egos here, defusing crises there, and manipulating the truth with consummate skill. Never actually lying, of course; that would have been fatal. Without Ari's infallible memory, he could never have kept control of the intricate webs he was sometimes compelled to spin, that mankind might live in peace. When he had begun to enjoy the game for its own sake, it was time to quit.

That had been twenty years ago, and he had never regretted his decision. Those who predicted that boredom would succeed where the temptations of power had failed did not know their man or understand his origins. He had gone back to the fields and forests of his youth, and was living only a kilometre from the great, brooding rock that had dominated his childhood. Indeed, his villa was actually inside the wide moat that surrounded the Pleasure Gardens, and the fountains that Kalidasa's architect had designed now splashed in Johan's own courtyard, after a silence of two thousand years. The water still flowed in the original stone conduits; nothing had been changed, except that the cisterns high up on the rock were now filled by electric pumps, not relays of sweating slaves.

Securing this history-drenched piece of land for his retirement had given Johan more satisfaction than anything in his whole career, fulfilling a dream that he had never really believed could come true. The achievement had required all his diplomatic skills, plus some delicate blackmail in the Department of Archaeology. Later, questions had been asked in the State Assembly; but fortunately not answered.

He was insulated from all but the most determined tourists and students by an extension of the moat, and screened from their gaze by a thick wall of mutated Ashoka trees, blazing with flowers throughout the year. The trees also supported several families of monkeys, who were amusing to watch but occasionally invaded the villa and made off with any portable objects that took their fancy. Then there would be a brief inter-species war with fire-crackers and recorded danger-cries that distressed the humans at least as much as the simians – who would be back quickly enough, for they had long ago learned that no one would really harm them.

One of Taprobane's more outrageous sunsets was transfiguring the western sky when the small electrotrike came silently through the trees, and drew up beside the granite columns of the portico. (Genuine Chola, from the late Ranapura Period – and therefore a complete anachronism here. But only Professor Sarath had ever commented on it; and he of course invariably did so.)

Through long and bitter experience, Rajasinghe had learned never to trust first impressions, but also never to ignore them. He had half-expected that, like his achievements, Vannevar Morgan would be a large, imposing man. Instead, the engineer was well below average height, and at first glance might even have been called frail. That slender body, however, was all sinew, and the raven-black hair framed a face that looked considerably younger than its fifty-one years. The video display from Ari's BIOG file had not done him justice; he should have been a romantic poet, or a concert pianist – or, perhaps, a great actor, holding thousands spell-bound by his skill. Rajasinghe knew power when he saw it, for power had been his business; and it was power that he was facing now. Beware of small men, he had often told himself – for they are the movers and shakers of the world.

And with this thought there came the first flicker of apprehension. Almost every week, old friends and old enemies came to this remote spot, to exchange news and to reminisce about the past. He welcomed such visits, for they gave a continuing pattern to his life. Yet always he knew, to a high degree of accuracy, the purpose of the meeting, and the ground that would be covered. But as far as Rajasinghe was aware, he and Morgan had no interests in common beyond those of any men in this day and age. They had never met, or had any prior communication; indeed, he had barely recognized Morgan's name. Still more unusual was the fact that the engineer had asked him to keep this meeting confidential.

Though Rajasinghe had complied, it was with a feeling of resentment. There was no need, any more, for secrecy in his peaceful life; the very last thing he wanted now was for some important mystery to impinge upon his well-ordered existence. He had finished with Security for ever; ten years ago – or was it even longer? – his personal guards had been removed at his own request. Yet what upset him most was not the mild secrecy, but his own total bewilderment. The Chief Engineer (Land) of the Terran Construction Corporation was not going to travel thousands of kilometres merely to ask for his autograph, or to express the usual tourist platitudes. He must have come here for some specific purpose – and, try as he might, Rajasinghe was unable to imagine it.

Even in his days as a public servant, Rajasinghe had never had occasion to deal with TCC; its three divisions – Land, Sea, Space – huge though they were, made perhaps the least news of all the World Federation's specialized bodies. Only when there was some resounding technical failure, or a head-on collision with an environmental or historical group, did TCC emerge from the shadows. The last confrontation of this kind had involved the Antarctic Pipeline – that miracle of twenty-first-century engineering, built to pump fluidized coal from the vast polar deposits to the power plants and factories of the world. In a mood of ecological euphoria, TCC had proposed demolishing the last remaining section of the pipeline and restoring the land to the penguins. Instantly there had been cries of protest from the industrial archaeologists, outraged at such vandalism, and from the naturalists, who pointed out that the penguins simply loved the abandoned pipeline. It had provided housing of a standard they had never before enjoyed, and thus contributed to a population explosion that the killer whales could barely handle. So TCC had surrendered without a fight.

Rajasinghe did not know if Morgan had been associated with this minor *débâcle*. It hardly mattered, since his name was now linked with TCC's greatest triumph . . .

The Ultimate Bridge, it had been christened; and perhaps with justice. Rajasinghe had watched, with half the world, when the final section was lifted gently skywards by the *Graf Zeppelin* – itself one of the marvels of the age. All the airship's luxurious fittings had been removed to save weight; the famous swimming pool had been drained, and the reactors were pumping their excess heat into the gas-bags to give extra lift. It was the first time that a dead-weight of more than a thousand tons had ever been hoisted three kilometres straight up into the sky, and everything – doubtless to the disappointment of millions – had gone without a hitch.

No ship would ever again pass the Pillars of Hercules without saluting the mightiest bridge that man had ever built – or, in all probability, would ever build. The twin towers at the junction of Mediterranean and Atlantic were themselves the tallest structures in the world, and faced each other across fifteen kilometres of space – empty, save for the incredible, delicate arch of the Gibraltar Bridge. It would be a privilege to meet the man who had conceived it; even though he was an hour late.

'My apologies, Ambassador,' said Morgan as he climbed out of the trike. 'I hope the delay hasn't inconvenienced you.'

'Not at all; my time is my own. You've eaten, I hope?'

'Yes – when they cancelled my Rome connection, at least they gave me an excellent lunch.'

'Probably better than you'd get at the Hotel Yakkagala. I've arranged a room for the night – it's only a kilometre from here. I'm afraid we'll have to postpone our discussion until breakfast.'

Morgan looked disappointed, but gave a shrug of acquiescence. 'Well, I've plenty of work to keep me busy. I assume that the hotel has full executive facilities – or at least a standard terminal.'

Rajasinghe laughed. 'I wouldn't guarantee anything much more sophisticated than a telephone. But I have a better suggestion. In just over half-an-hour, I'm taking some friends to the Rock.

There's a *son-et-lumière* performance that I strongly recommend and you're very welcome to join us.'

He could tell that Morgan was hesitating, as he tried to think of a polite excuse.

'That's very kind of you, but I really must contact my office . . .'

'You can use my console. I can promise you – you'll find the show fascinating, and it only lasts an hour. Oh, I'd forgotten – you don't want anyone to know you're here. Well, I'll introduce you as Doctor Smith from the University of Tasmania. I'm sure my friends won't recognize you.'

Rajasinghe had no intention of offending his visitor, but there was no mistaking Morgan's brief flash of irritation. The ex-diplomat's instincts automatically came into play; he filed the reaction for future reference.

'I'm sure they won't,' Morgan said, and Rajasinghe noted the unmistakable tone of bitterness in his voice. 'Doctor Smith would be fine. And now – if I might use your console.'

Interesting, thought Rajasinghe as he led his guest into the villa, but probably not important. Provisional hypothesis: Morgan was a frustrated, perhaps even a disappointed man. It was hard to see why, since he was one of the leaders of his profession. What *more* could he want? There was one obvious answer; Rajasinghe knew the symptoms well, if only because in his case the disease had long since burned itself out.

'*Fame is the spur*,' he recited in the silence of his thoughts. How did the rest of it go? '*That last infirmity of noble mind. . . To scorn delights, and live laborious days.*'

Yes, that might explain the discontent his still-sensitive antennae had detected. And he suddenly recalled that the immense rainbow linking Europe and Africa was almost invariably called *the* Bridge . . . occasionally the Gibraltar Bridge . . . but never Morgan's Bridge.

Well, Rajasinghe thought to himself, if you're looking for fame, Dr Morgan, you won't find it here. Then why in the name of a thousand *yakkas* have you come to quiet little Taprobane?

3 The Fountains

For days, elephants and slaves had toiled in the cruel sun, hauling the endless chains of buckets up the face of the cliff. 'Is it ready?' the King had asked, time and again. 'No, Majesty,' the master craftsman had answered, 'the tank is not yet full. But tomorrow, perhaps...'

Tomorrow had come at last, and now the whole court was gathered in the Pleasure Gardens, beneath awnings of brightly coloured cloth. The King himself was cooled by large fans, waved by supplicants who had bribed the chamberlain for this risky privilege. It was an honour which might lead to riches, or to death.

All eyes were on the face of the Rock, and the tiny figures moving upon its summit. A flag fluttered; far below, a horn sounded briefly. At the base of the cliff workmen frantically manipulated levers, hauled on ropes. Yet for a long time nothing happened.

A frown began to spread across the face of the King, and the whole court trembled. Even the waving fans lost momentum for a few seconds, only to speed up again as the wielders recalled the hazards of their task. Then a great shout came from the workers at the foot of Yakkagala – a cry of joy and triumph that swept steadily closer as it was taken up along the flower-lined paths. And with it came another sound, one not so loud, yet giving the impression of irresistible, pent-up forces, rushing towards their goal.

One after the other, springing from the earth as if by magic, the slim columns of water leaped towards the cloudless sky. At four times the height of a man, they burst into flowers of spray. The sunlight, breaking through them, created a rainbow-hued mist that added to the strangeness and beauty of the scene. Never, in the whole history of Taprobane, had the eyes of men witnessed such a wonder.

The King smiled, and the courtiers dared to breathe again. *This* time the buried pipes had not burst beneath the weight of water; unlike their luckless predecessors, the masons who had laid them had as good a chance of reaching old age as anyone who laboured for Kalidasa.

Almost as imperceptibly as the westering sun, the jets were losing altitude. Presently they were no taller than a man; the painfully filled reservoirs were nearly drained. But the King was well satisfied; he lifted his hand, and the fountains dipped and rose again as if in one last curtsy before the throne, then silently collapsed. For a little while ripples raced back and forth across the surface of the reflecting pools; then they once again became still mirrors, framing the image of the eternal Rock.

'The workmen have done well,' said Kalidasa. 'Give them their freedom.'

How well, of course, they would never understand, for none could share the lonely visions of an artist-king. As Kalidasa surveyed the exquisitely tended gardens that surrounded Yakkagala, he felt as much contentment as he would ever know.

Here, at the foot of the Rock, he had conceived and created Paradise. It only remained, upon its summit, to build Heaven.

4 Demon Rock

This cunningly contrived pageant of light and sound still had power to move Rajasinghe, though he had seen it a dozen times and knew every trick of the programming. It was, of course, obligatory for every visitor to the Rock, though critics like Professor Sarath complained that it was merely instant history for tourists. Yet instant history was better than no history at all, and it would have to serve while Sarath and his colleagues still vociferously disagreed about the precise sequence of events here, two thousand years ago.

The little amphitheatre faced the western wall of Yakkagala, its two hundred seats all carefully orientated so that each spectator looked up into the laser projectors at the correct angle. The performance always began at exactly the same time throughout the year – 19.00 hours, as the last glow of the invariant equatorial sunset faded from the sky.

Already it was so dark that the Rock was invisible, revealing its presence only as a huge, black shadow eclipsing the early stars. Then, out of that darkness, there came the slow beating of a muffled drum; and presently a calm, dispassionate voice:

'This is the story of a king who murdered his father and was killed by his brother. In the blood-stained history of mankind, that is nothing new. But *this* king left an abiding monument; and a legend which has endured for centuries . . .'

Rajasinghe stole a glance at Vannevar Morgan, sitting there in the darkness on his right. Though he could see the engineer's features only in silhouette, he could tell that his visitor was already caught in the spell of the narration. On his left his other two guests – old friends from his diplomatic days – were equally entranced. As he had assured Morgan, they had not recognized 'Dr Smith'; or if they had indeed done so, they had politely accepted the fiction.

'His name was Kalidasa, and he was born a hundred years after Christ, in Ranapura, City of Gold – for centuries the capital of the Taprobanean kings. But there was a shadow across his birth . . .'

The music became louder, as flutes and strings joined the throbbing drum, to trace out a haunting, regal melody in the night air. A point of light began to burn on the face of the Rock; then, abruptly, it expanded – and suddenly it seemed that a magic window had opened into the past, to reveal a world more vivid and colourful than life itself.

The dramatization, thought Morgan, was excellent; he was glad that, for once, he had let courtesy override his impulse to work. He saw the joy of King Paravana when his favourite concubine presented him with his first-born son – and understood how that joy was both augmented and diminished when, only twenty-four hours later, the Queen herself produced a better claimant to the throne. Though first in time, Kalidasa would not be first in precedence; and so the stage was set for tragedy.

'Yet in the early years of their boyhood Kalidasa and his half-brother Malgara were the closest of friends. They grew up together quite unconscious of their rival destinies, and the intrigues that festered around them. The first cause of trouble had nothing to do with the accident of birth; it was only a well-intentioned, innocent gift.

'To the court of King Paravana came envoys bearing tribute from many lands – silk from Cathay, gold from Hindustan, burnished armour from Imperial Rome. And one day a simple hunter from the jungle ventured into the great city, bearing a gift which he hoped would please the Royal family . . .'

All around him, Morgan heard a chorus of involuntary 'Oohs' and 'Aahs' from his unseen companions. Although he had never been very fond of animals, he had to admit that the tiny, snow-white monkey that nestled so trustingly in the arms of young Prince Kalidasa was very endearing. Out of the wrinkled little face two huge eyes stared across the centuries – and across the mysterious, yet not wholly unbridgeable, gulf between man and beast.

'According to the Chronicles, nothing like it had ever been seen before; its hair was white as milk, its eyes pink as rubies. Some thought it a good omen – others an evil one, because white is the colour of death and of mourning. And their fears, alas, were well founded.

'Prince Kalidasa loved his little pet, and called it Hanuman after the valiant monkey-god of the *Ramayana*. The King's jeweller constructed a small golden cart, in which Hanuman would sit solemnly while he was drawn through the court, to the amusement and delight of all who watched.

'For his part, Hanuman loved Kalidasa, and would allow no one else to handle him. He was especially jealous of Prince Malgara – almost as if he sensed the rivalry to come. And then, one unlucky day, he bit the heir to the throne.

'The bite was trifling – its consequences immense. A few days later Hanuman was poisoned – doubtless by order of the Queen. That was the end of Kalidasa's childhood; thereafter, it is said, he never loved or trusted another human being. And his friendship towards Malgara turned to bitter enmity.

'Nor was this the only trouble that stemmed from the death of one small monkey. By command of the King, a special tomb was built for Hanuman, in the shape of the traditional bell-shaped shrine or *dagoba*. Now this was an extraordinary thing to do, for it aroused the instant hostility of the monks. *Dagobas* were reserved for relics of the Buddha, and this act appeared to be one of deliberate sacrilege.

'Indeed, that may well have been its intention, for King Paravana had now come under the sway of a Hindu Swami, and was turning against the Buddhist faith. Although Prince Kalidasa was too young to be involved in this conflict, much of the monks' hatred was now directed against him. So began a feud that in the years to come was to tear the kingdom apart.

'Like many of the other tales recorded in the ancient chronicles of Taprobane, for almost two thousand years there was no proof that the story of Hanuman and young Prince Kalidasa was anything but a charming legend. Then, in 2015, a team of Harvard archaeologists discovered the foundations of a small shrine in the grounds of the old Ranapura Palace. The shrine appeared to have been deliberately destroyed, for all the brickwork of the superstructure had vanished.

'The usual relic chamber set in the foundations was empty, obviously robbed of its contents centuries ago. But the students had tools of which the old-time treasure-hunters never dreamed; their neutrino survey disclosed a *second* relic chamber, much deeper. The upper one was only a decoy, and it had served its purpose well. The lower chamber still held the burden of love and hate it had carried down the centuries – to its resting-place today, in the Ranapura Museum.'

Morgan had always considered himself, with justification, reasonably hard-headed and unsentimental, not prone to gusts of emotion. Yet now, to his considerable embarrassment – he hoped that his companions wouldn't notice – he felt his eyes brim with sudden tears. How ridiculous, he told himself angrily, that some saccharine music and a maudlin narration could have such an impact on a sensible man! He would never have believed that the sight of a child's toy could have set him weeping.

And then he knew, in a sudden lightning flash of memory that brought back a moment more than forty years in the past, why he had been so deeply moved. He saw again his beloved kite, dipping and weaving above the Sydney park where he had spent much of his childhood. He could feel the warmth of the sun, the gentle wind on his bare back – the treacherous wind that suddenly failed, so that the kite plunged earthwards. It became snagged in the branches of the giant oak that was supposed to be older than the country itself and, foolishly, he had tugged at the string, trying to pull it free. It was his first lesson in the strength of materials, and one that he was never to forget.

The string had broken, just at the point of capture, and the kite had rolled crazily away into the summer sky, slowly losing altitude. He had rushed down to the water's edge, hoping that it would fall on land; but the wind would not listen to the prayers of a little boy.

For a long time he had stood weeping as he watched the shattered fragments, like some dismasted sailboat, drift across the great harbour and out towards the open sea, until they were lost from sight. That had been the first of those trivial tragedies that shape a man's childhood, whether he remembers them or not.

Yet what Morgan had lost then was only an inanimate toy; his tears were of frustration rather than grief. Prince Kalidasa had much deeper cause for anguish. Inside the little golden cart, which still looked as if it had come straight from the craftsman's workshop, was a bundle of tiny white bones.

Morgan missed some of the history that followed; when he had cleared his eyes a dozen years had passed, a complex family quarrel was in progress, and he was not quite sure who was murdering whom. After the armies had ceased to clash and the last dagger had fallen, Crown Prince Malgara and the Queen Mother had fled to India, and Kalidasa had seized the throne, imprisoning his father in the process.

That the usurper had refrained from executing Paravana was not due to any filial devotion but to his belief that the old king still possessed some secret treasure, which he was saving for Malgara. As long as Kalidasa believed this, Paravana knew that he was safe; but at last he grew tired of the deception.

'I will show you my real wealth,' he told his son. 'Give me a chariot, and I will take you to it.'

But on his last journey, unlike little Hanuman, Paravana rode in a decrepit ox-cart. The Chronicles record that it had a damaged wheel which squeaked all the way – the sort of detail that must be true, because no historian would have bothered to invent it.

To Kalidasa's surprise, his father ordered the cart to carry him to the great artificial lake that irrigated the central kingdom, the completion of which had occupied most of his reign. He walked along the edge of the huge bund and gazed at his own statue, twice life-size, that looked out across the waters.

'Farewell, old friend,' he said, addressing the towering stone figure which symbolized his lost power and glory, and which held forever in its hands the stone map of this inland sea. 'Protect my heritage.'

Then, closely watched by Kalidasa and his guards, he descended the spillway steps, not pausing even at the edge of the lake. When he was waist deep he scooped up the water and threw it over his head, then turned towards Kalidasa with pride and triumph.

'*Here*, my son,' he cried, waving towards the leagues of pure, life-giving water, 'here – *here* is all my wealth!'

'Kill him!' screamed Kalidasa, mad with rage and disappointment.

And the soldiers obeyed.

So Kalidasa became the master of Taprobane, but at a price that few men would be willing to pay. For, as the Chronicles recorded, always he lived 'in fear of the next world, and of his brother'. Sooner or later, Malgara would return to seek his rightful throne.

For a few years, like the long line of kings before him, Kalidasa held court in Ranapura. Then, for reasons about which history is silent, he abandoned the royal capital for the isolated rock monolith of Yakkagala, forty kilometres away in the jungle. There were some who argued that he sought an impregnable fortress, safe from the vengeance of his brother. Yet in the end he spurned its protection – and, if it was merely a citadel, why was Yakkagala surrounded by immense pleasure gardens whose construction must have demanded as much labour as the walls and moat themselves? Above all, *why the frescoes*?

As the narrator posed this question, the entire western face of the rock materialized out of the darkness – not as it was now, but as it must have been two thousand years ago. A band starting a hundred metres from the ground, and running the full width of the rock, had been smoothed and covered with plaster, upon which were portrayed scores of beautiful women – life-size, from the waist upwards. Some were in profile, others full-face, and all followed the same basic pattern.

Ochre-skinned, voluptuously bosomed, they were clad either in jewels alone, or in the most transparent of upper garments. Some wore towering and elaborate head-dresses – others, apparently, crowns. Many carried bowls of flowers, or held single blossoms nipped delicately between thumb and forefinger. Though about half were darker-skinned than their companions, and appeared to be hand-maidens, they were no less elaborately coifed and bejewelled.

'Once, there were more than two hundred figures. But the rains and winds of centuries have destroyed all except twenty, which were protected by an over-hanging ledge of rock . . .'

The image zoomed forward; one by one the last survivors of Kalidasa's dream came floating out of the darkness, to the hackneyed yet singularly appropriate music of *Anitra's Dance*. Defaced though they were by weather, decay and even vandals, they had lost none of their beauty down the ages. The colours were still fresh, unfaded by the light of more than half a million westering suns. Goddesses or women, they had kept alive the legend of the Rock.

'No one knows who they were, what they represented, and *why* they were created with such labour, in so inaccessible a spot. The favourite theory is that they were celestial beings, and that all Kalidasa's efforts here were devoted to creating a heaven on earth, with its attendant goddesses. Perhaps he believed himself a God-King, as the Pharaohs of Egypt had done; perhaps that is why he borrowed from them the image of the Sphinx, guarding the entrance to his palace.'

Now the scene shifted to a distant view of the Rock, seen reflected in the small lake at its base. The water trembled, the outlines of Yakkagala wavered and dissolved. When they had reformed, the Rock was crowned by walls and battlements and spires, clinging to its entire upper surface. It was impossible to see them clearly; they remained tantalizingly out of focus, like the images in a dream. No man would ever know what Kalidasa's aerial palace had *really* looked like, before it was destroyed by those who sought to extirpate his very name.

'And here he lived, for almost twenty years, awaiting the doom that he knew would come. His spies must have told him that, with the help of the kings of southern Hindustan, Malgara was patiently gathering his armies.

'And at last Malgara came. From the summit of the Rock, Kalidasa saw the invaders marching from the north. Perhaps he believed himself impregnable; but he did not put it to the test. For he left the safety of his great fortress, and rode out to meet his brother, in the neutral ground between the two armies. One would give much to know what words they spoke, at that last encounter. Some say they embraced before they parted; it may be true.

'Then the armies met, like the waves of the sea. Kalidasa was fighting on his own territory, with men who knew the land, and at first it seemed that victory would go to him. But then occurred another of those accidents that determine the fate of nations.

'Kalidasa's great war elephant, caparisoned with the royal banners, turned aside to avoid a patch of marshy ground. The defenders thought that the king was retreating. Their morale broke; they scattered, as the Chronicles record, like chaff from the winnowing fan.

'Kalidasa was found on the battlefield, dead by his own hand. Malgara became king. And Yakkagala was abandoned to the jungle, not to be discovered again for seventeen hundred years.'

5 Through the Telescope

'My secret vice', Rajasinghe called it, with wry amusement but also with regret. It had been years since he had climbed to the summit of Yakkagala, and though he could fly there whenever he wished, that did not give the same feeling of achievement. To do it the easy way by-passed the most fascinating architectural details of the ascent; no one could hope to understand the mind of Kalidasa without following his footsteps all the way from Pleasure Garden to aerial Palace.

But there was a substitute which could give an ageing man considerable satisfaction. Years ago he had acquired a compact and powerful twenty-centimetre telescope; through it he could roam the entire western wall of the Rock, retracing the path he had followed to the summit so many times in the past. When he peered through the binocular eyepiece, he could easily imagine that he was hanging in mid-air, close enough to the sheer granite wall to reach out and touch it.

In the late afternoon, as the rays of the westering sun reached beneath the rock overhang that protected them, Rajasinghe would visit the frescoes, and pay tribute to the ladies of the court. Though he loved them all, he had his favourites; sometimes he would talk silently to them, using the most archaic words and phrases that he knew – well aware of the fact that his oldest Taprobani lay a thousand years in *their* future.

It also amused him to watch the living, and to study their reactions as they scrambled up the Rock, took photographs of each other on the summit, or admired the frescoes. They could have no idea that they were accompanied by an invisible – and envious – spectator, moving effortlessly beside them like a silent ghost, and so close that he could see every expression, and every detail of their clothing. For such was the power of the telescope that if Rajasinghe had been able to lip-read, he could have eavesdropped on the tourists' conversation.

If this was voyeurism, it was harmless enough – and his little 'vice' was hardly a secret, for he was delighted to share it with visitors. The telescope provided one of the best introductions to Yakkagala, and it had often served other useful purposes. Rajasinghe had several times alerted the guards to attempted souvenir hunting, and more than one astonished tourist had been caught carving his initials on the face of the Rock.

Rajasinghe seldom used the telescope in the morning, because the sun was then on the far side of Yakkagala and little could be seen on the shadowed western face. And, as far as he could recall, he had *never* used it so soon after dawn, while he was still enjoying the delightful local custom of 'bed-tea', introduced by the European planters three centuries ago. Yet now, as he glanced out of the wide picture-window that gave him an almost complete view of Yakkagala, he was surprised to see a tiny figure moving along the crest of the Rock, partly silhouetted against the sky. Visitors never climbed to the top so soon after dawn – the guard wouldn't even unlock the elevator to the frescoes for another hour. Idly, Rajasinghe wondered who the early bird could be.

He rolled out of bed, clambered into his bright batik *sarong*, and made his way, bare-bodied, out on to the verandah, and thence to the stout concrete pillar supporting the telescope. Making a mental note, for about the fiftieth time, that he really should get the instrument a new dust-cover, he swung the stubby barrel towards the Rock.

'I might have guessed it!' he told himself, with considerable pleasure, as he switched to high power. So last night's show had impressed Morgan, as well it should have done. The engineer was seeing for himself, in the short time available, how Kalidasa's architects had met the challenge imposed upon them.

Then Rajasinghe noticed something quite alarming. Morgan was walking briskly around at the very edge of the plateau, only centimetres away from the sheer drop that few tourists ever dared to approach. Not many had the courage even to sit in the Elephant Throne, with their feet dangling over the abyss; but now the engineer was actually kneeling beside it, holding on to the carved stonework with one casual arm – and leaning right out into nothingness as he surveyed the rock-face below. Rajasinghe, who had never been very happy even with such familiar heights as Yakkagala's, could scarcely bear to watch.

After a few minutes of incredulous observation, he decided that Morgan must be one of those rare people who are completely unaffected by heights. Rajasinghe's memory, which was still excellent but delighted in playing tricks on him, was trying to bring something to his notice. Hadn't there once been a Frenchman who had tightroped across Niagara Falls, and even stopped in the middle to cook a meal? If the documentary evidence had not been overwhelming, Rajasinghe would never have believed such a story.

And there was something else that was relevant here – an incident that concerned Morgan himself. What could it possibly be? Morgan . . . Morgan . . . he had known virtually nothing about him until a week ago . . .

Yes; *that* was it. There had been a brief controversy that had amused the news media for a day or so, and that must have been the first time he had ever heard Morgan's name.

The Chief Designer of the proposed Gibraltar Bridge had announced a startling innovation. As all vehicles would be on automatic guidance, there was absolutely no point in having parapets or guard rails at the edge of the roadway; eliminating them would save thousands of tons. Of course, everyone thought that this was a perfectly horrible idea; what would happen, the public demanded, if some car's guidance failed, and the vehicle headed towards the edge? The Chief Designer had the answers; unfortunately, he had rather too many.

If the guidance failed, then as everyone knew the brakes would go on automatically, and the vehicle would stop in less than a hundred metres. Only on the outermost lanes was there any possibility that a car could go over the edge; that would require a total failure of guidance, sensors *and* brakes, and might happen once in twenty years.

So far, so good. But then the Chief Engineer added a *caveat*. Perhaps he did not intend it for publication; possibly he was half-joking. But he went on to say that, if such an accident did occur, the quicker the car went over the edge without damaging his beautiful bridge, the happier he would be.

Needless to say, the Bridge was eventually built with wire deflector-cables along the outer lanes, and as far as Rajasinghe knew no one had yet taken a high-dive into the Mediterranean. Morgan, however, appeared suicidally determined to sacrifice himself to gravity here on Yakkagala; otherwise, it was hard to account for his actions.

Now what was he doing? He was on his knees at the side of the Elephant Throne, and was holding a small rectangular box, about the shape and size of an old-fashioned book. Rajasinghe could catch only glimpses of it, and the manner in which the engineer was using it made no sense at all. Possibly it was some kind of analysis device, though he did not see why Morgan should be interested in the composition of Yakkagala.

Was he planning to build something here? Not that it would be allowed, of course, and Rajasinghe could imagine no conceivable attractions for such a site; megalomaniac kings were fortunately now in short supply. In any event, he was quite certain, from the engineer's reactions on the previous evening, that Morgan had never heard of Yakkagala before coming to Taprobane.

And then Rajasinghe, who had always prided himself on his self-control in even the most dramatic and unexpected situations, gave an involuntary cry of horror. Vannevar Morgan had stepped casually backwards off the face of the cliff, out into empty space.

6 The Artist

'Bring the Persian to me,' said Kalidasa, as soon as he had recovered his breath. The climb from the frescoes back to the Elephant Throne was not difficult, and it was perfectly safe now that the stairway down the sheer rock face had been enclosed with walls. But it was tiring; for how many more years, Kalidasa wondered, would he be able to make this journey unaided? Though slaves could carry him, that did not befit the dignity of a king. And it was intolerable that any eyes but his should look upon the hundred goddesses and their hundred equally beautiful attendants, who formed the retinue of his celestial court.

So from now on, night and day, there would always be a guard standing at the entrance to the stairs – the only way down from the Palace to the private heaven that Kalidasa had created. After ten years of toil, his dream was now complete. Whatever the jealous monks on their mountain-top might claim to the contrary, he was a god at last.

Despite his years in the Taprobanean sun, Firdaz was still as light-skinned as a Roman; today, as he bowed before the king, he looked even paler, and ill at ease. Kalidasa regarded him thoughtfully, then gave one of his rare smiles of approval.

'You have done well, Persian,' he said. 'Is there any artist in the world who could do better?'

Pride obviously strove with caution before Firdaz gave his hesitant reply.

'None that I know, Majesty.'

'And have I paid you well?'

'I am quite satisfied.'

That reply, thought Kalidasa, was hardly accurate; there had been continuous pleas for more money, more assistants, expensive materials that could only be obtained from distant lands. But artists could not be expected to understand economics, or to know how the royal treasury had been drained by the awesome cost of the palace and its surroundings.

'And now that your work here is finished, what do you wish?'

'I would like your Majesty's permission to return to Ishfahan, so that I may see my own people once again.'

It was the answer that Kalidasa had expected, and he sincerely regretted the decision he must make. But there were too many other rulers on the long road to Persia, who would not let the master-artist of Yakkagala slip through their greedy fingers. And the painted goddesses of the western wall must remain forever unchallenged.

'There is a problem,' he said flatly – and Firdaz turned yet paler, his shoulders slumping at the words. A king did not have to explain anything, but this was one artist speaking to another. 'You have helped me to become a god. That news has already reached many lands. If you leave my protection, there are others who will make similar requests of you.'

For a moment, the artist was silent; the only sound was the moaning of the wind, which seldom ceased to complain when it met this unexpected obstacle upon its journey. Then Firdaz said, so quietly that Kalidasa could hardly hear him: 'Am I then forbidden to leave?'

'You may go, and with enough wealth for the rest of your life. But only on condition that you never work for any other prince.'

'I am willing to give that promise,' replied Firdaz with almost unseemly haste.

Sadly, Kalidasa shook his head. 'I have learned not to trust the word of artists,' he said, 'especially when they are no longer within my power. So I will have to enforce that promise.'

To Kalidasa's surprise, Firdaz no longer looked so uncertain; it was almost as if he had made some great decision, and was finally at ease.

'I understand,' he said, drawing himself up to his full height. Then deliberately he turned his back upon the king, as though his royal master no longer existed, and stared straight into the blazing sun.

The sun, Kalidasa knew, was the god of the Persians, and those words Firdaz was murmuring must be a prayer in his language. There were worse gods to worship, and the artist was staring into that blinding disc, as if he knew it was the last thing he would ever see...

34

'Hold him!' cried the king.

The guards rushed swiftly forward, but they were too late. Blind though he must now have been, Firdaz moved with precision. In three steps he had reached the parapet, and vaulted over it. He made no sound in his long arc down to the gardens he had planned for so many years, nor was there any echo when the architect of Yakka-gala reached the foundations of his masterwork.

Kalidasa grieved for many days, but his grief turned to rage when the Persian's last letter to Ishfahan was intercepted. Someone had warned Firdaz that he would be blinded when his work was done; and that was a damnable falsehood. He never discovered the source of the rumour, though not a few men died slowly before they proved their innocence. It saddened him that the Persian had believed such a lie; surely he should have known that a fellow artist would never have robbed him of the gift of sight.

For Kalidasa was not a cruel man, nor an ungrateful one. He would have laden Firdaz with gold – or at least silver – and sent him on his way with servants to take care of him for the remainder of his life. He would never have needed to use his hands again; and after a while he would not have missed them.

7 The God-King's Palace

Vannevar Morgan had not slept well, and that was most unusual. He had always taken pride in his self-awareness, and his insight into his own drives and emotions. If he could not sleep, he wanted to know why.

Slowly, as he watched the first pre-dawn light glimmer on the ceiling of his hotel bedroom, and heard the bell-like cries of alien birds, he began to marshal his thoughts. He would never have become a senior engineer of Terran Construction if he had not planned his life to avoid surprises. Although no man could be immune to the accidents of chance and fate, he had taken all reasonable steps to safeguard his career – and, above all, his reputation. His future was as fail-safe as he could make it; even if he died suddenly, the programmes stored in his computer bank would protect his cherished dream beyond the grave.

Until yesterday he had never heard of Yakkagala; indeed, until a few weeks ago he was only vaguely aware of Taprobane itself, until the logic of his quest directed him inexorably towards the island. By now he should already have left, whereas in fact his mission had not yet begun. He did not mind the slight disruption of his schedule; what *did* perturb him was the feeling that he was being moved by forces beyond his understanding. Yet the sense of awe had a familiar resonance. He had experienced it before when, as a child, he had flown his lost kite in Kiribilli Park, beside the granite monoliths that had once been the piers of the long-demolished Sydney Harbour Bridge.

Those twin mountains had dominated his boyhood, and had controlled his destiny. Perhaps, in any event, he would have been an engineer; but the accident of his birthplace had determined that he would be a builder of bridges. And so he had been the first man to step from Morocco to Spain, with the angry waters of the Mediterranean three kilometres below – never dreaming, in that moment of triumph, of the far more stupendous challenge that still lay ahead.

If he succeeded in the task that confronted him, he would be famous for centuries to come. Already his mind, strength and will were being taxed to the utmost; he had no time for idle distractions. Yet he had become fascinated by the achievements of an engineer-architect two thousand years dead, belonging to a totally alien culture. And there was the mystery of Kalidasa himself; what was his purpose in building Yakkagala? The king might have been a monster, but there was something about his character which struck a chord in the secret places of Morgan's own heart.

Sunrise would be in thirty minutes; it was still two hours before his breakfast with Ambassador Rajasinghe. That would be long enough – and he might have no other opportunity.

Morgan was never one to waste time. Slacks and sweater were on in less than a minute, but the careful checking of his footwear took considerably longer. Though he had done no serious climbing for years, he always carried a pair of strong, light-weight boots; in his profession, he often found them essential. He had already closed the door of his room when he had a sudden afterthought. For a moment he stood hesitantly in the corridor; then he smiled and shrugged his shoulders. It wouldn't do any harm, and one never knew . . .

Once more back in the room, Morgan unlocked his suitcase and took out a small flat box, about the size and shape of a pocket calculator. He checked the battery charge, tested the manual override, then clipped it to the steel buckle of his strong synthetic waist-belt. Now he was indeed ready to enter Kalidasa's haunted kingdom, and to face whatever demons it held.

The sun rose, pouring welcome warmth upon his back as Morgan passed through the gap in the massive rampart that formed the outer defences of the fortress. Before him, spanned by a narrow stone bridge, were the still waters of the great moat, stretching in a perfectly straight line for half a kilometre on either side. A small flotilla of swans sailed hopefully towards him through the lilies, then dispersed with ruffled feathers when it was clear that he had no food to offer. On the far side of the bridge he came to a second, smaller wall and climbed the narrow flight of stairs cut through it; and there before him were the Pleasure Gardens, with the sheer face of the Rock looming beyond them.

The fountains along the axis of the gardens rose and fell together with a languid rhythm, as if they were breathing slowly in unison. There was not another human being in sight; he had the whole expanse of Yakkagala to himself. The fortress-city could hardly have been lonelier even during the seventeen hundred years when the jungle had overwhelmed it, between the death of Kalidasa and its rediscovery by nineteenth-century archaeologists.

Morgan walked past the line of fountains, feeling their spray against his skin, and stopped once to admire the beautifully carved stone guttering – obviously original – which carried the overflow. He wondered how the old-time hydraulic engineers lifted the water to drive the fountains, and what pressure differences they could handle; these soaring, vertical jets must have been truly astonishing to those who first witnessed them.

And now ahead was a steep flight of granite steps, their treads so uncomfortably narrow that they could barely accommodate Morgan's boots. Did the people who built this extraordinary place really have such tiny feet, he wondered? Or was it a clever ruse of the architect, to discourage unfriendly visitors? It would certainly be difficult for soldiers to charge up this sixty-degree slope, on steps that seemed to have been made for midgets.

A small platform, then another identical flight of steps, and Morgan found himself on a long, slowly ascending gallery cut into the lower flanks of the Rock. He was now more than fifty metres above the surrounding plain, but the view was completely blocked by a high wall coated with smooth, yellow plaster. The rock above him overhung so much that he might almost have been walking along a tunnel, for only a narrow band of sky was visible overhead.

The plaster of the wall looked completely new and unworn; it was almost impossible to believe that the masons had left their work two thousand years ago. Here and there, however, the gleaming, mirror-flat surface was scarred with scratched messages, where visitors had made their usual bids for immortality. Very few of the inscriptions were in alphabets that Morgan could recognize, and the latest date he noticed was 1931; thereafter, presumably, the Department of Archaeology had intervened to prevent such vandalism. Most of the *graffiti* were in flowing, rounded Taprobani; Morgan recalled from the previous night's entertainment that many were poems, dating back to the second and third century. For a little while after the death of Kalidasa, Yakkagala had known its first brief spell as a tourist attraction, thanks to the still lingering legends of the accursed king.

Halfway along the stone gallery, Morgan came to the now locked door of the little elevator leading to the famous frescoes, twenty metres directly above. He craned his head to see them, but they were obscured by the platform of the visitors' viewing cage, clinging like a metal bird's-nest to the outward-leaning face of the rock. Some tourists, Rajasinghe had told him, took one look at the dizzy location of the frescoes, and decided to satisfy themselves with photographs.

Now, for the first time, Morgan could appreciate one of the chief mysteries of Yakkagala. It was not *how* the frescoes were painted – a scaffolding of bamboo could have taken care of that problem – but *why*. Once they were completed, no one could ever have seen them properly; from the gallery immediately beneath, they were hopelessly foreshortened – and from the base of the Rock they would have been no more than tiny, unrecognizable patches of colour. Perhaps, as some had suggested, they were of purely religious or magical significance – like those Stone Age paintings found in the depths of almost inaccessible caves.

The frescoes would have to wait until the attendant arrived and unlocked the elevator. There were plenty of other things to see; he was still only a third of the way to the summit, and the gallery was still slowly ascending, as it clung to the face of the Rock.

The high, yellow-plastered wall gave way to a low parapet, and Morgan could once more see the surrounding countryside. There below him lay the whole expanse of the Pleasure Gardens, and for the first time he could appreciate not only their huge scale (was Versailles larger?) but also their skilful planning, and the way in which the moat and outer ramparts protected them from the forest beyond.

No one knew what trees and shrubs and flowers had grown here in Kalidasa's day, but the pattern of artificial lakes, canals, pathways and fountains was still exactly as he had left it. As he looked down on those dancing jets of water, Morgan suddenly remembered a quotation from the previous night's commentary:

'From Taprobane to Paradise is forty leagues; there may be heard the sound of the Fountains of Paradise.'

He savoured the phrase in his mind; the *Fountains of Paradise*. Was Kalidasa trying to create, here on earth, a garden fit for the gods, in order to establish his claim to divinity? If so, it was no wonder that the priests had accused him of blasphemy, and placed a curse upon all his work.

At last the long gallery, which had skirted the entire western face of the Rock, ended in another steeply rising stairway – though this time the steps were much more generous in size. But the palace was still far above, for the stairs ended on a large plateau, obviously artificial. Here was all that was left of the gigantic, leonine monster who had once dominated the landscape, and struck terror into the hearts of everyone who looked upon it. For springing from the face of the rock were the paws of a gigantic, crouching beast; the claws alone were half the height of a man.

Nothing else remained, save yet another granite stairway rising up through the piles of rubble that must once have formed the head of the creature. Even in ruin the concept was awe-inspiring: anyone who dared to approach the king's ultimate stronghold had first to walk through gaping jaws.

The final ascent up the sheer – indeed, slightly over-hanging – face of the cliff was by a series of iron ladders, with guard-rails to reassure nervous climbers. But the real danger here, Morgan had been warned, was not vertigo. Swarms of normally placid hornets occupied small caves in the rock, and visitors who made too much noise had sometimes disturbed them, with fatal results.

Two thousand years ago, this northern face of Yakkagala had been covered with walls and battlements to provide a fitting background to the Taprobanean sphinx, and behind those walls there must have been stairways that gave easy access to the summit. Now time, weather, and the vengeful hand of man had swept everything away. There was only the bare rock, grooved with myriads of horizontal slots and narrow ledges that had once supported the foundations of vanished masonry.

Abruptly, the climb was over. Morgan found himself standing on a small island floating two hundred metres above a landscape of trees and fields that was flat in all directions except southwards, where the central mountains broke up the horizon. He was completely isolated from the rest of the world, yet felt master of all he surveyed; not since he had stood among the clouds, straddling Europe and Africa, had he known such a moment of aerial ecstasy. This was indeed the residence of a God-King, and the ruins of his palace were all round.

A baffling maze of broken walls – none more than waist high – piles of weathered brick and granite-paved pathways covered the entire surface of the plateau, right to the precipitous edge. Morgan could also see a large cistern cut deeply into the solid rock – presumably a water-storage tank. As long as supplies were available, a handful of determined men could have held this place forever; but if Yakkagala had indeed been intended as a fortress, its defences had never been put to the test. Kalidasa's fateful last meeting with his brother had taken place far beyond the outer ramparts.

Almost forgetting time, Morgan roamed among the foundations of the palace that had once crowned the Rock. He tried to enter the mind of the architect, from what he could see of his surviving handiwork; why was there a pathway *here*? – did this truncated flight of steps lead to an upper floor? – if this coffin-shaped recess in the stone was a bath, how was the water supplied and how did it drain away? His research was so fascinating that he was quite oblivious of the increasing heat of the sun, striking down from a cloudless sky.

Far below, the emerald-green landscape was waking into life. Like brightly-coloured beetles, a swarm of little robot tractors was heading towards the rice-fields. Improbable though it seemed, a helpful elephant was pushing an overturned bus back on to the road, which it had obviously left while cornering at too high a speed; Morgan could even hear the shrill voice of the rider, perched just behind the enormous ears. And a stream of tourists was pouring like army ants through the Pleasure Gardens from the general direction of the Hotel Yakkagala; he would not enjoy his solitude much longer.

Still, he had virtually completed his exploration of the ruins – though one could, of course, spend a life-time investigating them in detail. He was happy to rest for a while, on a beautifully carved granite bench at the very edge of the two-hundred-metre drop, overlooking the entire southern sky.

Morgan let his eyes scan the distant line of mountains, still partly concealed by a blue haze which the morning sun had not yet dispersed. As he examined it idly, he suddenly realized that what he had assumed to be a part of the cloudscape was nothing of the sort. That misty cone was no ephemeral construct of wind and vapour; there was no mistaking its perfect symmetry, as it towered above its lesser brethren.

For a moment, the shock of recognition emptied his mind of everything except wonder – and an almost superstitious awe. He had not realized that one could see the Sacred Mountain so clearly from Yakkagala. But there it was, slowly emerging from the shadow of night, preparing to face a new day; and, if he succeeded, a new future.

He knew all its dimensions, all its geology; he had mapped it through stereo-photographs and had scanned it from satellites. But to see it for the first time, with his own eyes, made it suddenly real; until now, everything had been theory. And sometimes not even that; more than once, in the small grey hours before dawn, Morgan had woken from nightmares in which his whole project had appeared as some preposterous fantasy, which far from bringing him fame would make him the laughing-stock of the world. 'Morgan's Folly', some of his peers had once dubbed the Bridge; what would they call his latest dream?

But man-made obstacles had never stopped him before. Nature was his real antagonist – the friendly enemy who never cheated and always played fair, yet never failed to take advantage of the tiniest oversight or omission. And all the forces of Nature were epitomized for him now in the distant blue cone which he knew so well, but had yet to feel beneath his feet.

As Kalidasa had done so often from this very spot, Morgan stared across the fertile green plain, measuring the challenge and considering his strategy. To Kalidasa, Sri Kanda represented both the power of the priesthood and the power of the gods, conspiring together against him. Now the gods were gone; but the priests remained. They represented something that Morgan did not understand, and would therefore treat with wary respect.

It was time to descend; he must not be late again, especially through his own miscalculation. As he rose from the stone slab on which he had been sitting, a thought that had been worrying him for several minutes finally rose to consciousness. It was strange to have placed so ornate a seat, with its beautifully carved supporting elephants, at the very edge of a precipice . . .

Morgan could never resist such an intellectual challenge. Leaning out over the abyss, he once again tried to attune his engineer's mind to that of a colleague two thousand years dead.

8 Malgara

Not even his closest comrades could read the expression on Prince Malgara's face when, for the last time, he gazed upon the brother who had shared his boyhood. The battlefield was quiet now; even the cries of the injured had been silenced by healing herb or yet more potent sword.

After a long while, the prince turned to the yellow-robed figure standing by his side. '*You* crowned him, Venerable Bodhidharma. Now you can do him one more service. See that he receives the honours of a king.'

For a moment, the prelate did not reply. Then he answered softly. 'He destroyed our temples and scattered the priests. If he worshipped any god, it was Siva.'

Malgara bared his teeth in the fierce smile that the Mahanayake was to know all too well in the years that were left to him.

'Revered sire,' said the prince, in a voice that dripped venom, 'he was the first-born of Paravana the Great, he sat on the throne of Taprobane, and the evil that he did dies with him. When the body is burned, you will see that the relics are properly entombed, before you dare set foot upon Sri Kanda again.'

The Mahanayake Thero bowed, ever so slightly. 'It shall be done – according to your wishes.'

'And there is another thing,' said Malgara, speaking now to his aides. 'The fame of Kalidasa's fountains reached us even in Hindustan. We would see them once, before we march on Rana-pura...'

From the heart of the Pleasure Gardens which had given him such delight, the smoke of Kalidasa's funeral pyre rose into the cloudless sky, disturbing the birds of prey who had gathered from far and wide. Grimly content, though sometimes haunted by sudden memories, Malgara watched the symbol of his triumph spiralling upwards, announcing to all the land that the new reign had begun.

As if in continuation of their ancient rivalry, the water of the fountains challenged the fire, leaping skyward before it fell back to shatter the surface of the reflecting pool. But presently, long before the flames had finished their work, the reservoirs began to fail, and the jets collapsed in watery ruin. Before they rose again in the gardens of Kalidasa, Imperial Rome would have passed away, the armies of Islam would have marched across Africa, Copernicus would have dethroned the earth from the centre of the universe, the Declaration of Independence would have been signed, and men would have walked upon the Moon . . .

Malgara waited until the pyre had disintegrated in a final brief flurry of sparks. As the last smoke drifted against the towering face of Yakkagala, he raised his eyes towards the palace on its summit, and stared for a long time in silent appraisal.

'No man should challenge the gods,' he said at last. 'Let it be destroyed.'

9 Filament

'You nearly gave me a heart attack,' said Rajasinghe accusingly, as he poured the morning coffee. 'At first I thought you had some anti-gravity device – but even I know that's impossible. How *did* you do it?'

'My apologies,' Morgan answered with a smile. 'If I'd known you were watching, I'd have warned you – though the whole exercise was entirely unplanned. I'd merely intended to take a scramble over the Rock, but then I got intrigued by that stone bench. I wondered why it was on the very edge of the cliff and started to explore.'

'There's no mystery about it. At one time there was a floor – probably wood – extending outwards, and a flight of steps leading down to the frescoes from the summit. You can still see the grooves where it was keyed into the rock-face.'

'So I discovered,' said Morgan a little ruefully. 'I might have guessed that someone would have found that out already.'

Two hundred and fifty years ago, thought Rajasinghe. That crazy and energetic Englishman Arnold Lethbridge, Taprobane's first Director of Archaeology. He had himself lowered down the face of the Rock, exactly as you did. Well, not *exactly* . . .

Morgan had now produced the metal box that had allowed him to perform his miracle. Its only features were a few press-buttons, and a small readout panel; it looked for all the world like some form of simple communications device.

'This is it,' he said proudly. 'Since you saw me make a hundred-metre vertical walk, you must have a very good idea how it operates.'

'Commonsense gave me one answer, but even my excellent telescope didn't confirm it. I could have sworn there was absolutely nothing supporting you.'

'That wasn't the demonstration I'd intended, but it must have been effective. Now for my standard sales-pitch – please hook your finger through this ring.'

Rajasinghe hesitated; Morgan was holding the small metal torus – about twice the size of an ordinary wedding-ring – almost as if it was electrified.

'Will it give me a shock?' he asked.

'Not a shock – but perhaps a surprise. Try to pull it away from me.'

Rather gingerly, Rajasinghe took hold of the ring – then almost dropped it. For it seemed alive; it was straining towards Morgan – or, rather, towards the box that the engineer was holding in his hand. Then the box gave a slight whirring noise, and Rajasinghe felt his finger being dragged forward by some mysterious force. Magnetism? he asked himself. Of course not; no magnets could behave in this fashion. His tentative but improbable theory was correct; indeed, there was really no alternative explanation. They were engaged in a perfectly straightforward tug-of-war – *but with an invisible rope*.

Though Rajasinghe strained his eyes, he could see no trace of any thread or wire connecting the ring through which his finger was hooked and the box which Morgan was operating like a fisherman reeling in his catch. He reached out his free hand to

45

explore the apparently empty space, but the engineer quickly knocked it away.

'Sorry!' he said. 'Everyone tries that, when they realize what's happening. You could cut yourself very badly.'

'So you *do* have an invisible wire. Clever – but what use is it, except for parlour tricks?'

Morgan gave a broad smile. 'I can't blame you for jumping to that conclusion; it's the usual reaction. But it's quite wrong; the reason you can't see this sample is that it's only a few microns thick. Much thinner than a spider's web.'

For once, thought Rajasinghe, an overworked adjective was fully justified. 'That's – incredible. What *is* it?'

'The result of about two hundred years of solid state physics. For whatever good that does – it's a continuous pseudo-one-dimensional diamond crystal – though it's not actually pure carbon. There are several trace elements, in carefully controlled amounts. It can only be mass-produced in the orbiting factories, where there's no gravity to interfere with the growth process.'

'Fascinating,' whispered Rajasinghe, almost to himself. He gave little tugs on the ring hooked around his finger, to test that the tension was still there and that he was not hallucinating. 'I can appreciate that this may have all sorts of technical applications. It would make a splendid cheese-cutter—'

Morgan laughed. 'One man can bring a tree down with it, in a couple of minutes. But it's tricky to handle – even dangerous. We've had to design special dispensers to spool and unspool it – we call them "spinnerettes". This is a power-operated one, made for demonstration purposes. The motor can lift a couple of hundred kilos, and I'm always finding new uses for it. Today's little exploit wasn't the first, by any means.'

Almost reluctantly, Rajasinghe unhooked his finger from the ring. It started to fall, then began to pendulum back and forth without visible means of support until Morgan pressed a button and the spinnerette reeled it in with a gentle whirr.

'You haven't come all this way, Dr Morgan, just to impress me with this latest marvel of science – though I *am* impressed. I want to know what all this has to do with me.'

'A very great deal, Mister Ambassador,' answered the engineer, suddenly equally serious and formal. 'You are quite correct in thinking that this material will have many applications, some of which we are only now beginning to foresee. And one of them, for better or for worse, is going to make your quiet little island the centre of the world. No – not merely the world. The whole Solar System. Thanks to this filament, Taprobane will be the stepping-stone to all the planets. And one day, perhaps – the stars.'

10 The Ultimate Bridge

Paul and Maxine were two of his best and oldest friends, yet until this moment they had never met nor, as far as Rajasinghe knew, even communicated. There was little reason why they should; no one outside Taprobane had ever heard of Professor Sarath, but the whole Solar System would instantly recognize Maxine Duval, either by sight or by sound.

His two guests were reclining in the library's comfortable lounge chairs, while Rajasinghe sat at the villa's main console. They were all staring at the fourth figure, who was standing motionless.

Too motionless. A visitor from the past, knowing nothing of the everyday electronic miracles of this age, might have decided after a few seconds that he was looking at a superbly detailed wax dummy. However, more careful examination would have revealed two disconcerting facts. The 'dummy' was transparent enough for highlights to be clearly visible through it; and its feet blurred out of focus a few centimetres above the carpet.

'Do you recognize this man?' Rajasinghe asked.

'I've never seen him in my life,' Sarath replied instantly. 'He'd better be important, for you to have dragged me back from Maharamba. We were just about to open the Relic Chamber.'

'*I* had to leave my trimaran at the beginning of the Lake Saladin races,' said Maxine Duval, her famous contralto voice containing just enough annoyance to put anyone less thick-skinned than

47

Professor Sarath neatly in his place. 'And I know him, of course. Does he want to build a bridge from Taprobane to Hindustan?'

Rajasinghe laughed. 'No – we've had a perfectly serviceable causeway for two centuries. And I'm sorry to have dragged you both here – though *you*, Maxine, have been promising to come for twenty years.'

'True,' she sighed. 'But I have to spend so much time in my studio that I sometimes forget there's a *real* world out there, occupied by about five thousand dear friends and fifty million intimate acquaintances.'

'In which category would you put Dr Morgan?'

'I've met him – oh, three or four times. We did a special interview when the Bridge was completed. He's a very impressive character.'

Coming from Maxine Duval, thought Rajasinghe, that was tribute indeed. For more than thirty years she had been perhaps the most respected member of her exacting profession, and had won every honour that it could offer. The Pulitzer Prize, the *Global Times* Trophy, the David Frost Award – these were merely the tip of the iceberg. And she had only recently returned to active work after two years as Walter Cronkite Professor of Electronic Journalism at Columbia.

All this had mellowed her, though it had not slowed her down. She was no longer the sometimes fiery chauvinist who had once remarked: 'Since women are better at producing babies, presumably Nature has given men some talent to compensate. But for the moment I can't think of it.' However, she had only recently embarrassed a hapless panel chairman with the loud aside: 'I'm a news*woman*, dammit – not a news*person*.'

Of her femininity there had never been any doubt; she had been married four times, and her choice of REMs was famous. Whatever their sex, Remotes were always young and athletic, so that they could move swiftly despite the encumbrance of up to twenty kilos of communications gear. Maxine Duval's were invariably very male and very handsome; it was an old joke in the trade that all her Rems were also Rams. The jest was completely without rancour, for even her fiercest professional rivals liked Maxine almost as much as they envied her.

'Sorry about the race,' said Rajasinghe, 'but I note that *Marlin III* won very handily without you. I think you'll admit that this is rather more important . . . But let Morgan speak for himself.'

He released the PAUSE button on the projector, and the frozen statue came instantly to life.

'My name is Vannevar Morgan. I am Chief Engineer of Terran Construction's Land Division. My last project was the Gibraltar Bridge. Now I want to talk about something incomparably more ambitious.'

Rajasinghe glanced round the room. Morgan had hooked them, just as he had expected.

He leaned back in his chair, and waited for the now familiar, yet still almost unbelievable, prospectus to unfold. Odd, he told himself, how quickly one accepted the conventions of the display, and ignored quite large errors of the Tilt and Level controls. Even the fact that Morgan 'moved' while staying in the same place, and the totally false perspective of exterior scenes, failed to destroy the sense of reality.

'The Space Age is almost two hundred years old. For more than half that time, our civilization has been utterly dependent upon the host of satellites that now orbit Earth. Global communications, weather forecasting and control, land and ocean resources banks, postal and information services – if anything happened to their space-borne systems, we would sink back into a dark age. During the resultant chaos, disease and starvation would destroy much of the human race.

'And looking beyond the Earth, now that we have self-sustaining colonies on Mars, Mercury and the Moon, and are mining the incalculable wealth of the asteroids, we see the beginnings of true interplanetary commerce. Though it took a little longer than the optimists predicted, it is now obvious that the conquest of the air was indeed only a modest prelude to the conquest of space.

'But now we are faced with a fundamental problem – an obstacle that stands in the way of all future progress. Although generations of research have made the rocket the most reliable form of propulsion ever invented—'

('Has he considered bicycles?' muttered Sarath.)

'—space vehicles are still grossly inefficient. Even worse, their

49

effect on the environment is appalling. Despite all attempts to control approach corridors, the noise of take-off and re-entry disturbs millions of people. Exhaust products dumped in the upper atmosphere have triggered climatic changes, which may have very serious results. Everyone remembers the skin-cancer crisis of the twenties, caused by ultra-violet break-through – and the astronomical cost of the chemicals needed to restore the ozonosphere.

'Yet if we project traffic growth to the end of the century, we find that Earth-to-orbit tonnage must be increased almost fifty per cent. This cannot be achieved without intolerable costs to our way of life – perhaps to our very existence. And there is nothing that the rocket engineers can do; they have almost reached the absolute limits of performance, set by the laws of physics.

'What is the alternative? For centuries, men have dreamed of anti-gravity or of "spacedrives". No one has ever found the slightest hint that such things are possible; today we believe that they are only fantasy. And yet, in the very decade that the first satellite was launched, one daring Russian engineer conceived a system that would make the rocket obsolete. It was years before anyone took Yuri Artsutanov seriously. It has taken two centuries for our technology to match his vision.'

Each time he played the recording, it seemed to Rajasinghe that Morgan really came alive at this point. It was easy to see why; now he was on his own territory, no longer relaying information from an alien field of expertise. And despite all his reservations and fears, Rajasinghe could not help sharing some of that enthusiasm. It was a quality which, nowadays, seldom impinged upon his life.

'Go out of doors any clear night,' continued Morgan, 'and you will see that commonplace wonder of our age – the stars that never rise or set, but are fixed motionless in the sky. We – and our parents – and *their* parents – have long taken for granted the synchronous satellites and space stations, which move above the equator at the same speed as the turning earth, and so hang forever above the same spot.

'The question Artsutanov asked himself had the childlike brilliance of true genius. A merely clever man could never have thought of it – or would have dismissed it instantly as absurd.

'*If* the laws of celestial mechanics make it possible for an object to stay fixed in the sky, might it not be possible to lower a cable down to the surface – and *so to establish an elevator system linking Earth to space*?

'There was nothing wrong with the theory, but the practical problems were enormous. Calculations showed that no existing materials would be strong enough; the finest steel would snap under its own weight long before it could span the thirty-six thousand kilometres between Earth and synchronous orbit.

'However, even the best steels were nowhere near the theoretical limits of strength. On a microscopic scale, materials had been created in the laboratory with far greater breaking strength. If they could be mass-produced, Artsutanov's dream could become reality, and the economics of space transportation would be utterly transformed.

'Before the end of the twentieth century, super-strength material – hyperfilaments – had begun to emerge from the laboratory. But they were extremely expensive, costing many times their weight in gold. Millions of tons would be needed to build a system that could carry all Earth's outbound traffic; so the dream remained a dream.

'Until a few months ago. Now the deep-space factories can manufacture virtually unlimited quantities of hyperfilament. At last we can build the Space Elevator – or the Orbital Tower, as I prefer to call it. For in a sense it *is* a tower, rising clear through the atmosphere, and far, far beyond . . .'

Morgan faded out, like a ghost that had been suddenly exorcised. He was replaced by a football-sized Earth, slowly revolving. Moving an arm's-length above it, and keeping always poised above the same spot on the equator, a flashing star marked the location of a synchronous satellite.

From the star, two thin lines of light started to extend – one directly down towards the earth, the other in exactly the opposite direction, out into space.

'When you build a bridge,' continued Morgan's disembodied voice, 'you start from the two ends and meet in the middle. With the orbital tower, it's the exact opposite. You have to build upwards *and* downwards simultaneously from the synchronous satellite, according to a careful programme. The trick is to keep the structure's centre of gravity always balanced at the stationary point; if you don't, it will move into the wrong orbit, and start drifting slowly round the Earth.'

The descending line of light reached the equator; at the same moment, the outward extension also ceased.

'The total height must be at least forty thousand kilometres – and the lowest hundred, going down through the atmosphere, may be the most critical part, for there the tower may be subject to hurricanes. It won't be stable until it's securely anchored to the ground.

'And then, for the first time in history, we shall have a stairway to heaven – a bridge to the stars. A simple elevator system, driven by cheap electricity, will replace the noisy and expensive rocket, which will then be used only for its proper job of deep-space transport. Here's one possible design for the orbital tower—'

The image of the turning earth vanished as the camera swooped down towards the tower, and passed through the walls to reveal the structure's cross-section.

'You'll see that it consists of four identical tubes – two for Up traffic, two for Down. Think of it as a four-track *vertical* subway or railroad, from Earth to synchronous orbit.

'Capsules for passengers, freight, fuel would ride up and down the tubes at several thousand kilometres an hour. Fusion power stations at intervals would provide all the energy needed; as ninety per cent of it would be recovered, the net cost per passenger would be only a few dollars. For as the capsules fall earthwards again, their motors will act as magnetic brakes, generating electricity. Unlike re-entering spacecraft, they won't waste all their energy heating up the atmosphere and making sonic booms; it will be pumped back into the system. You could say that the Down trains will power the Up ones; so even at the most conservative estimate, the elevator will be a hundred times more efficient than any rocket.

'And there's virtually no limit to the traffic it could handle, for additional tubes could be added as required. If the time ever comes when a million people a day wish to visit Earth – or to leave it – the orbital tower could cope with them. After all, the subways of our great cities once did as much . . .'

Rajasinghe touched a button, silencing Morgan in mid-sentence.

'The rest is rather technical – he goes on to explain how the tower can act as a cosmic sling, and send payloads whipping off to the moon and planets without the use of any rocket power at all. But I think you've seen enough to get the general idea.'

'My mind is suitably boggled,' said Professor Sarath. 'But what on earth – or off it – has all this to do with me? Or with you, for that matter?'

'Everything in due time, Paul. Any comments, Maxine?'

'Perhaps I may yet forgive you; this could be one of the stories of the decade – or the century. But why the hurry – not to mention the secrecy?'

'There's a lot going on that I don't understand, which is where you can help me. I suspect that Morgan's fighting a battle on several fronts; he's planning an announcement in the very near future, but doesn't want to act until he's quite sure of his ground. He gave me that presentation on the understanding that it wouldn't be sent over public circuits. That's why I had to ask you here.'

'Does he know about this meeting?'

'Of course; indeed, he was quite happy when I said I wanted to talk to you, Maxine. Obviously, he trusts you and would like you as an ally. And as for *you*, Paul, I assured him that you could keep a secret for up to six days without apoplexy.'

'Only if there's a very good reason for it.'

'I begin to see light,' said Maxine Duval. 'Several things have been puzzling me, and now they're starting to make sense. First of all, this is a *space* project; Morgan is Chief Engineer, *Land*.'

'So?'

'*You* should ask, Johan! Think of the bureaucratic in-fighting, when the rocket designers and the aerospace industry get to hear about this! Trillion dollar empires will be at stake, just to start with. If he's not very careful, Morgan will be told "Thank you very much – now we'll take over. Nice knowing you."'

'I can appreciate that, but he has a very good case. After all, the Orbital Tower *is* a building – not a vehicle.'

'Not when the lawyers get hold of it, it won't be. There aren't many buildings whose upper floors are moving at ten kilometres a second, or whatever it is, faster than the basement.'

'You may have a point. Incidentally, when I showed signs of vertigo at the idea of a tower going a good part of the way to the moon, Dr Morgan said, "Then don't think of it as a tower going *up*

– think of it as a bridge going *out*." I'm still trying, without much success.'

'Oh!' said Maxine Duval suddenly. 'That's another piece of your jig-saw puzzle. The Bridge.'

'What do you mean?'

'Did you know that Terran Construction's Chairman, that pompous ass Senator Collins, wanted to get the Gibraltar Bridge named after him?'

'I didn't; that explains several things. But I rather like Collins – the few times we've met, I found him very pleasant, and very bright. Didn't he do some first-rate geothermal engineering in his time?'

'That was a thousand years ago. And *you* aren't any threat to his reputation; he can be nice to you.'

'How was the Bridge saved from its fate?'

'There was a small palace revolution among Terran's senior engineering staff. Dr Morgan, of course, was in no way involved.'

'So that's why he's keeping his cards close to his chest! I'm beginning to admire him more and more. But now he's come up against an obstacle he doesn't know how to handle. He only discovered it a few days ago, and it's stopped him dead in his tracks.'

'Let me go on guessing,' said Maxine. 'It's good practice – helps me to keep ahead of the pack. I can see why he's here. The earth-end of the system has to be on the equator, otherwise it can't be vertical. It would be like that tower they used to have in Pisa, before it fell over.'

'I don't *see* . . .' said Professor Sarath, waving his arms vaguely up and down. 'Oh, of course . . .' His voice trailed away into a thoughtful silence.

'Now,' continued Maxine, 'there are only a limited number of possible sites on the equator – it's mostly ocean, isn't it? – and Taprobane's obviously one of them. Though I don't see what particular advantages it has over Africa or South America. Or is Morgan covering all his bets?'

'As usual, my dear Maxine, your powers of deduction are phenomenal. You're on the right line – but you won't get any further. Though Morgan's done his best to explain the problem to me, I don't pretend to understand all the scientific details. Anyway, it turns out that Africa and South America are *not* suitable for the space elevator. It's something to do with unstable points in the earth's gravitational field. Only Taprobane will do – worse still, only one spot in Taprobane. And that, Paul, is where *you* come into the picture.'

'Mamada?' yelped Professor Sarath, indignantly reverting to Taprobani in his surprise.

'Yes, you. To his great annoyance, Dr Morgan has just discovered that the one site he *must* have is already occupied – to put it mildly. He wants my advice on dislodging your good friend Buddy.'

Now it was Maxine's turn to be baffled. 'Who?' she queried.

Sarath answered at once. 'The Venerable Anandatissa Bodhidharma Mahanayake Thero, incumbent of the Sri Kanda temple,' he intoned, almost as if chanting a litany. 'So *that's* what it's all about.'

There was silence for a moment; then a look of pure mischievous delight appeared on the face of Paul Sarath, Emeritus Professor of Archaeology of the University of Taprobane.

'I've always wanted,' he said dreamily, 'to know exactly what would happen when an irresistible force meets an immovable object.'

11 The Silent Princess

When his visitors had left, in a very thoughtful mood Rajasinghe depolarized the library windows and sat for a long time staring out at the trees around the villa, and the rock walls of Yakkagala looming beyond. He had not moved when, precisely on the stroke of four, the arrival of his afternoon tea jolted him out of his reverie.

'Rani,' he said, 'ask Dravindra to get out my heavy shoes, if he can find them. I'm going up the Rock.'

Rani pretended to drop the tray in astonishment.

'*Aiyo*, Mahathaya!' she keened in mock distress. 'You must be mad! Remember what Doctor McPherson told you—'

'That Scots quack always reads my cardiogram backwards. Anyway, my dear, what have I got to live for, when you and Dravindra leave me?'

He spoke not entirely in jest, and was instantly ashamed of his self-pity. For Rani detected it, and the tears started in her eyes.

She turned away, so that he could not see her emotion, and said in English: 'I *did* offer to stay – at least for Dravindra's first year . . .'

'I know you did, and I wouldn't dream of it. Unless Berkeley's changed since I last saw it, he'll need you there. (Yet no more than I, though in different ways, he added silently to himself.) And whether you take your own degree or not, you can't start training *too* early to be a college president's wife.'

Rani smiled. 'I'm not sure that's a fate I'd welcome, from some of the horrid examples I've seen.' She switched back to Taprobani. 'You aren't *really* serious, are you?'

'Quite serious. Not to the top, of course – only the frescoes. It's five years since I visited them. If I leave it much longer . . .' There was no need to complete the sentence.

Rani studied him in silence for a few moments, then decided that argument was futile.

'I'll tell Dravindra,' she said. '*And* Jaya – in case they have to carry you back.'

'Very well – though I'm sure Dravindra could manage that by himself.'

Rani gave him a delighted smile, mingling pride and pleasure. This couple, he thought fondly, had been his luckiest draw in the state lottery, and he hoped that their two years of social service had been as enjoyable to them as it had been to him. In this age, personal servants were the rarest of luxuries, awarded only to men of outstanding merit; Rajasinghe knew of no other private citizen who had three.

To conserve his strength, he rode a sun-powered trike through the Pleasure Gardens; Dravindra and Jaya preferred to walk, claiming that it was quicker. (They were right; but they were able to take shortcuts.) He climbed very slowly, pausing several times for breath, until he had reached the long corridor of the Lower Gallery, where the Mirror Wall ran parallel to the face of the Rock.

Watched by the usual inquisitive tourists, a young archaeologist from one of the African countries was searching the wall for inscriptions, with the aid of a powerful oblique light. Rajasinghe felt like warning her that the chance of making a new discovery was virtually zero. Paul Sarath had spent twenty years going over every square millimetre of the surface, and the three-volume *Yakkagala Graffiti* was a monumental work of scholarship which would never be superseded – if only because no other man would ever again be so skilled at reading archaic Taprobani inscriptions.

They had both been young men when Paul had begun his life's work. Rajasinghe could remember standing at this very spot while the then Deputy Assistant Epigrapher of the Department of Archaeology had traced out the almost indecipherable marks on the yellow plaster, and translated the poems addressed to the beauties on the rock above. After all these centuries, the lines could still strike echoes in the human heart:

I am Tissa, Captain of the Guard.
I came fifty leagues to see the doe-eyed ones,
but they would not speak to me.
Is this kind?

May you remain here for a thousand years,
like the hare which the King of the Gods
painted on the Moon. I am the priest Mahinda
from the *vihara* of Tuparama.

That hope had been partly fulfilled, partly denied. The ladies of the Rock had been standing here for twice the time that the cleric had imagined, and had survived into an age beyond his uttermost dreams. But how few of them were left! Some of the inscriptions referred to 'five hundred golden-skinned maidens'; even allowing for considerable poetic licence, it was clear that not one-tenth of the original frescoes had escaped the ravages of time or the malevolence of man. But the twenty that remained were now safe forever, their beauty stored in countless films and tapes and crystals.

Certainly they had outlasted one proud scribe, who had thought it quite unnecessary to give his name:

I ordered the road to be cleared, so that
pilgrims could see the fair maidens standing
on the mountainside.
I am the King.

Over the years Rajasinghe – himself the bearer of a royal name,
and doubtless host to many regal genes – had often thought of
those words; they demonstrated so perfectly the ephemeral nature
of power, and the futility of ambition. '*I am the King.*' Ah, but
which King? The monarch who had stood on these granite flagstones – scarcely worn then, eighteen hundred years ago – was
probably an able and intelligent man; but he failed to conceive
that the time could ever come when he would fade into an anonymity as deep as that of his humblest subjects.

The attribution was now lost beyond trace. At least a dozen
kings might have inscribed those haughty lines; some had reigned
for years, some only for weeks, and few indeed had died peacefully
in their beds. No one would ever know if the king who felt it
needless to give his name was Mahatissa II, or Bhatikabhaya, or
Vijayakumara III, or Gajabahukagamani, or Candamukhasiva,
or Moggallana I, or Kittisena, or Sirisamghabodhi ... or some
other monarch not even recorded in the long and tangled history
of Taprobane.

The attendant operating the little elevator was astonished to see
his distinguished visitor, and greeted Rajasinghe deferentially. As
the cage slowly ascended the full fifteen metres, he remembered
how he would once have spurned it for the spiral stairway, up
which Dravindra and Jaya were bounding even now in the thoughtless exuberance of youth.

The elevator clicked to a halt, and he stepped on to the small
steel platform built out from the face of the cliff. Below and behind
were a hundred metres of empty space, but the strong wire mesh
gave ample security; not even the most determined suicide could
escape from the cage – large enough to hold a dozen
people – clinging to the underside of the eternally breaking wave
of stone.

Here in this accidental indentation, where the rock-face formed
a shallow cave and so protected them from the elements, were the
survivors of the king's heavenly court. Rajasinghe greeted them

silently, then sank gratefully into the chair that was offered by the official guide.

'I would like,' he said quietly, 'to be left alone for ten minutes. Jaya – Dravindra – see if you can head off the tourists.'

His companions looked at him doubtfully; so did the guide, who was supposed never to leave the frescoes unguarded. But, as usual, Ambassador Rajasinghe had his way, without even raising his voice.

'*Ayu bowan,*' he greeted the silent figures, when he was alone at last. 'I'm sorry to have neglected you for so long.'

He waited politely for an answer, but they paid no more attention to him than to all their other admirers for the last twenty centuries. Rajasinghe was not discouraged; he was used to their indifference. Indeed, it added to their charm.

'I have a problem, my dears,' he continued. 'You have watched all the invaders of Taprobane come and go, since Kalidasa's time. You have seen the jungle flow like a tide around Yakkagala, and then retreat before the axe and the plough. But nothing has really changed in all those years. Nature has been kind to little Taprobane, and so has History; it has left her alone . . .

'Now the centuries of quiet may be drawing to a close. Our land may become the centre of the world – of many worlds. The great mountain you have watched so long, there in the south, may be the key to the universe. If that is so, the Taprobane we knew and loved will cease to exist.

'Perhaps there is not much that I can do – but I have *some* power to help, or to hinder. I still have many friends; if I wish, I can delay this dream – or nightmare – at least beyond my lifetime. Should I do so? Or should I give aid to this man, whatever his real motives may be?'

He turned to his favourite – the only one who did not avert her eyes when he gazed upon her. All the other maidens stared into the distance, or examined the flowers in their hands; but the one he had loved since his youth seemed, from a certain angle, to catch his glance.

'Ah, Karuna! It's not fair to ask you such questions. For what could you possibly know of the *real* worlds beyond the sky, or of men's need to reach them? Even though you were once a goddess,

Kalidasa's Heaven was only an illusion. Well, whatever strange futures you may see, I shall not share them. We have known each other a long time – by my standards, if not by yours. While I can, I shall watch you from the villa; but I do not think that we shall meet again. Farewell – and thank you, beautiful ones, for all the pleasure you have brought me down the years. Give my greetings to those who come after me.'

Yet as he descended the spiral stairs – ignoring the elevator – Rajasinghe did not feel at all in a valedictory mood. On the contrary, it seemed to him that he had shed quite a few of his years (and, after all, seventy-two was not *really* old). He could tell that Dravindra and Jaya had noticed the spring in his step, by the way their faces lit up.

Perhaps his retirement had been getting a little dull. Perhaps both he and Taprobane needed a breath of fresh air to blow away the cobwebs – just as the monsoon brought renewed life after the months of torpid, heavy skies.

Whether Morgan succeeded or not, his was an enterprise to fire the imagination and stir the soul. Kalidasa would have envied – and approved.

part two
The Temple

While the different religions wrangle with one another as to which of them is in possession of the truth, in our view the truth of religion may be altogether disregarded . . . If one attempts to assign to religion its place in man's evolution, it seems not so much to be a lasting acquisition, as a parallel to the neurosis which the civilized individual must pass through on his way from childhood to maturity.

Freud: *New Introductory Lectures on Psycho-Analysis* (1932).

Of course man made God in his own image; but what was the alternative? Just as a real understanding of geology was impossible until we were able to study other worlds beside Earth, so a valid theology must await contact with extra-terrestrial intelligences. There can be no such subject as comparative religion, as long as we study only the religions of man.

El Hadj Mohammed ben Selim, Professor of Comparative Religion: Inaugural Address, Brigham Young University, 1998.

We must await, not without anxiety, the answers to the following questions; (a) What, if any, are the religious concepts of entities with zero, one, two, or more than two 'parents' (b) is religious belief found only among organisms that have close contact with their direct progenitors during their formative years?

If we find that religion occurs exclusively among intelligent analogues of apes, dolphins, elephants, dogs, etc, but *not* among extra-terrestrial computers, termites, fish, turtles or social amoebae, we may have to draw some painful conclusions . . . Perhaps both love and religion can arise only among mammals, and for much the same reasons. This is also suggested by a study of their pathologies; anyone who doubts the connection between religious fanaticism and perversion should take a long, hard look at the *Malleus Maleficarium* or Huxley's *Thè Devils of Loudon*.

(Ibid)

Dr Charles Willis' notorious remark (Hawaii, 1970) that 'Religion is a by-product of malnutrition' is not, in itself, much more helpful than Gregory Bateson's somewhat indelicate one-syllable refutation. What Dr Willis apparently meant was (1) the hallucinations caused by voluntary or involuntary starvation are readily interpreted as religious visions; (2) hunger in *this* life encourages belief in a compensatory afterlife, as a – perhaps essential – psychological survival mechanism . . .

. . . It is indeed one of the ironies of fate that research into the so-called consciousness-expanding drugs proved that they did exactly the opposite, by leading to the detection of the naturally occurring 'apothetic' chemicals in the brain. The discovery that the most devout adherent of any faith could be converted to any other by a judicious dose of 2–4–7 *ortho-para*-theosamine was, perhaps, the most devastating blow ever received by religion.

Until, of course, the advent of Starglider . . .

R. Gabor: *The Pharmacological Basis of Religion* (Miskatonic University Press, 2069).

12 Starglider

Something of the sort had been expected for a hundred years, and there had been many false alarms. Yet when it finally happened, mankind was taken by surprise.

The radio signal from the direction of Alpha Centauri was so powerful that it was first detected as interference on normal commercial circuits. This was highly embarrassing to all the radio astronomers who, for so many decades, had been seeking intelligent messages from space – especially as they had long ago dismissed the triple system of Alpha, Beta and Proxima Centauri from serious consideration.

At once, every radio telescope that could scan the southern hemisphere was focused upon Centaurus. Within hours, a still more sensational discovery was made. The signal was not coming from the Centaurus system at all – but from a point half a degree away. *And it was moving*.

That was the first hint of the truth. When it was confirmed, all the normal business of mankind came to a halt.

The power of the signal was no longer surprising; its source was already well inside the solar system, and moving sunward at six hundred kilometres a second. The long-awaited, long-feared visitors from space had arrived at last . . .

Yet for thirty days the intruder did nothing, as it fell past the outer planets, broadcasting an unvarying series of pulses that merely announced 'Here I am!'. It made no attempt to answer the signals beamed at it, nor did it make any adjustments to its natural, comet-like orbit. Unless it had slowed down from some much higher speed, its voyage from Centaurus must have lasted two thousand years. Some found this reassuring, since it suggested that the visitor was a robot space-probe; others were disappointed, feeling that the absence of real, live extra-terrestrials would be an anti-climax.

The whole spectrum of possibilities was argued, *ad nauseam*, in all the media of communications, all the parliaments of man. Every plot that had ever been used in science fiction, from the arrival of benevolent gods to an invasion of blood-sucking vampires, was disinterred and solemnly analysed. Lloyds of London collected substantial premiums from people insuring against every possible future – including some in which there would have been very little chance of collecting a penny.

Then, as the alien passed the orbit of Jupiter, man's instruments began to learn something about it. The first discovery created a short-lived panic; the object was five *hundred* kilometres in diameter – the size of a small moon. Perhaps, after all, it was a mobile world carrying an invading army . . .

This fear vanished when more precise observations showed that the solid body of the intruder was only a few metres across. The five-hundred-kilometre halo around it was something very familiar – a flimsy, slowly revolving parabolic reflector, the exact equivalent of the astronomers' orbiting telescopes. Presumably this was the antenna through which the visitor kept in touch with its distant base. And through which, even now, it was doubtless beaming back its discoveries, as it scanned the solar system and eavesdropped upon all the radio, TV and data broadcasts of mankind.

Then came yet another surprise. That asteroid-sized antenna was *not* pointed in the direction of Alpha Centauri, but towards a totally different part of the sky. It began to look as if the Centauri system was merely the vehicle's last port of call, not its origin.

The astronomers were still brooding over this when they had a remarkable stroke of luck. A solar weather probe on routine patrol beyond Mars became suddenly dumb, then recovered its radio voice a minute later. When the records were examined, it was found that the instruments had been momentarily paralysed by intense radiation. The probe had cut right across the visitor's beam – and it was then a simple matter to calculate precisely where it was aimed.

There was nothing in that direction for fifty-two light-years, except a very faint – and presumably very old – red dwarf star, one of those abstemious little suns that would still be shining peacefully billions of years after the galaxy's splendid giants had burned themselves out. No radio telescope had ever examined it closely; now all those that could be spared from the approaching visitor were focused upon its suspected origin.

And there it was, beaming a sharply tuned signal in the one-centimetre band. The makers were still in contact with the vehicle they had launched, thousands of years ago; but the messages it must be receiving *now* were from only half a century in the past.

Then, as it came within the orbit of Mars, the visitor showed its first awareness of mankind, in the most dramatic and unmistakable way that could be imagined. It started transmitting standard 3075-line television pictures, interleaved with video text in fluent though stilted English and Mandarin. The first cosmic conversation had begun – and not, as had always been imagined, with a delay of decades, but only of minutes.

13 Shadow at Dawn

Morgan had left his hotel in Ranapura at four am on a clear, moonless night. He was not too happy about the choice of time, but Professor Sarath, who had made all the arrangements, had promised him that it would be well worthwhile. 'You won't understand anything about Sri Kanda,' he had said, 'unless you have watched the dawn from the summit. And Buddy – er, the Maha Thero – won't receive visitors at any other time. He says it's a splendid way of discouraging the merely curious.' So Morgan had acquiesced with as much good grace as possible.

To make matters worse, the Tapobanean driver had persisted in carrying on a brisk though rather one-sided conversation, apparently designed to establish a complete profile of his passenger's personality. This was all done with such ingenuous good nature that it was impossible to take offence, but Morgan would have preferred silence.

He also wished, sometimes devoutly, that his driver would pay rather more attention to the countless hairpin bends round which they zipped in the near-darkness. Perhaps it was just as well that he could not see all the cliffs and chasms they were negotiating as the car climbed up through the foothills. This road was a triumph of nineteenth-century military engineering – the work of the last colonial power, built in the final campaign against the proud mountain folk of the interior. But it had never been converted to automatic operation, and there were times when Morgan wondered if he would survive the journey.

And then, suddenly, he forgot his fears and his annoyance at the loss of sleep.

'There it is!' said the driver proudly, as the car rounded the flank of a hill.

Sri Kanda itself was still completely invisible in a darkness which as yet bore no hint of the approaching dawn. Its presence was revealed by a thin ribbon of light, zig-zagging back and forth under the stars, hanging as if by magic in the sky. Morgan knew that he was merely seeing the lamps set two hundred years ago to guide pilgrims as they ascended the longest stairway in the world, but in its defiance of logic and gravity it appeared almost a prevision of his own dream. Ages before he was born, inspired by philosophers he could barely imagine, men had begun the work he hoped to finish. They had, quite literally, built the first crude steps on the road to the stars.

No longer feeling drowsy, Morgan watched as the band of light grew closer, and resolved itself into a necklace of innumerable, twinkling beads. Now the mountain was becoming visible, as a black triangle eclipsing half the sky. There was something sinister about its silent, brooding presence; Morgan could almost imagine that it was indeed the abode of gods who knew of his mission, and were gathering their strength against him.

These ominous thoughts were entirely forgotten when they arrived at the cable car terminus and Morgan discovered to his surprise – it was still only five am – that at least a hundred people were milling around in the little waiting-room. He ordered a welcome hot coffee for himself and his garrulous driver – who, rather to his relief, showed no interest in making the ascent. 'I've done it at least twenty times,' he said with perhaps exaggerated boredom. '*I'm* going to sleep in the car until you come down.'

Morgan purchased his ticket, did a quick calculation, and estimated that he would be in the third or fourth load of passengers. He was glad that he had taken Sarath's advice and slipped a thermocloak in his pocket; at a mere two-kilometre altitude, it was already quite cold. At the summit, three kilometres higher still, it must be freezing.

As he slowly shuffled forward in the rather subdued and sleepy line of visitors, Morgan noted with amusement that he was the only one *not* carrying a camera. Where were the genuine pilgrims, he wondered? Then he remembered; they would not be here. There was no easy way to heaven, or Nirvana, or whatever it was that the faithful sought. Merit was acquired solely by one's own efforts, not with the aid of machines. An interesting doctrine, and one containing much truth; but there were also times when only machines could do the job.

At last he got a seat in the car, and with a considerable creaking of cables they were on their way. Once again, Morgan felt that eerie sense of anticipation. The elevator *he* was planning would hoist loads more than ten thousand times as high as this primitive system, which probably dated right back to the twentieth century. And yet, when all was said and done, its basic principles were very much the same.

Outside the swaying car was total darkness, except when a section of the illuminated stairway came into view. It was completely deserted, as if the countless millions who had toiled up the mountain during the last three thousand years had left no successor. But then Morgan realized that those making the ascent on foot would already be far above on their appointment with the dawn; they would have left the lower slopes of the mountain hours ago.

At the four-kilometre level the passengers had to change cars and walk a short distance to another cable-station, but the transfer involved little delay. Now Morgan was indeed glad of his cloak, and wrapped its metallized fabric closely round his body. There was frost underfoot, and already he was breathing deeply in the thin air. He was not at all surprised to see racks of oxygen cylinders in the small terminus, with instructions for their use prominently displayed.

And now at last, as they began the final ascent, there came the first intimation of the approaching day. The eastern stars still shone with undiminished glory – Venus most brilliantly of all – but a few thin, high clouds began to glow faintly with the coming dawn. Morgan looked anxiously at his watch, and wondered if he would be in time. He was relieved to see that daybreak was still thirty minutes away.

One of the passengers suddenly pointed to the immense stairway, sections of which were occasionally visible beneath them as it zigzagged back and forth up the mountain's now rapidly steepening slopes. It was no longer deserted; moving with dreamlike slowness, dozens of men and women were toiling painfully up the endless steps. Every minute more and more came into view; for how many hours, Morgan wondered, had they been climbing? Certainly all through the night, and perhaps much longer – for many of the pilgrims were quite elderly, and could hardly have managed the ascent in a single day. He was surprised to see that so many still believed.

A moment later, he saw the first monk – a tall, saffron-robed figure moving with a gait of metronome-like regularity, looking neither to the right nor to the left, and completely ignoring the car floating above his shaven head. He also appeared capable of ignoring the elements, for his right arm and shoulder were bare to the freezing wind.

The cable car was slowing down as it approached the terminus; presently it made a brief halt, disgorged its numbed passengers, and set off again on its long descent. Morgan joined the crowd of two or three hundred people huddling in a small amphitheatre cut in the western face of the mountain. They were all staring out into the darkness, though there was nothing to see but the ribbon of light winding down into the abyss. Some belated climbers on the last section of the stairway were making a final effort, as faith strove to overcome fatigue.

Morgan looked again at his watch; ten minutes to go. He had never before been among so many silent people; camera-touting tourists and devout pilgrims were united now in the same hope. The weather was perfect; soon they would all know if they had made this journey in vain.

There came a delicate tinkling of bells from the temple, still invisible in the darkness a hundred metres above their heads; and at the same instant all the lights along that unbelievable stairway were extinguished. Now they could see, as they stood with their backs towards the hidden sunrise, that the first faint gleam of day lay on the clouds far below; but the immense bulk of the mountain still delayed the approaching dawn.

Second by second the light was growing on either side of Sri Kanda, as the sun outflanked the last strongholds of the night. Then there came a low murmur of awe from the patiently waiting crowd.

One moment there was nothing. Then, suddenly, it was *there*, stretching half the width of Taprobane – a perfectly symmetrical, sharp-edged triangle of deepest blue. The mountain had not forgotten its worshippers; there lay its famous shadow across the sea of clouds, a symbol for each pilgrim to interpret as he wished.

It seemed almost solid in its rectilinear perfection, like some overturned pyramid rather than a mere phantom of light and shade. As the brightness grew around it, and the first direct rays of the sun struck past the flanks of the mountain, it appeared by contrast to grow even darker and denser; yet through the thin veil of cloud responsible for its brief existence, Morgan could dimly discern the lakes and hills and forests of the awakening land.

The apex of that misty triangle must be racing towards him at enormous speed, as the sun rose vertically behind the mountain, yet Morgan was conscious of no movement. Time seemed to have been suspended; this was one of the rare moments of his life when he gave no thought to the passing minutes. The shadow of eternity lay upon his soul, as did that of the mountain upon the clouds.

Now it was fading swiftly, the darkness draining from the sky like a stain dispersing in water. The ghostly, glimmering landscape below was hardening into reality; halfway to the horizon there was an explosion of light as the sun's rays struck upon some building's eastern windows. And even beyond that – unless his eyes had tricked him – Morgan could make out the faint, dark band of the encircling sea.

Another day had come to Taprobane.

Slowly, the visitors dispersed. Some returned to the cable-car terminus, while others, more energetic, headed for the stairway, in the mistaken belief that the descent was easier than the climb. Most of them would be thankful enough to catch the car again at the lower station; few indeed would make it all the way down.

Only Morgan continued upwards, followed by many curious glances, along the short flight of steps that led to the monastery and to the very summit of the mountain. By the time he had reached the smoothly plastered outer wall – now beginning to glow softly in the first direct rays of the sun – he was very short of breath, and was glad to lean for a moment against the massive wooden door.

Someone must have been watching; before he could find a bell-push, or signal his presence in any way, the door swung silently open, and he was welcomed by a yellow-robed monk, who saluted him with clasped hands.

'*Ayu bowan*, Dr Morgan. The Mahanayake Thero will be glad to see you.'

14 The Education of Starglider

(Extract from *Starglider Concordance*, First Edition, 2071)

We now know that the interstellar spaceprobe generally referred to as Starglider is completely autonomous, operating according to general instructions programmed into it sixty thousand years ago. While it is cruising between suns, it uses its five-hundred-kilometre antenna to send back information to its base at a relatively slow rate, and to receive occasional up-dates from 'Starholme', to adopt the lovely name coined by the poet Llwellyn ap Cymru.

While it is passing through a solar system, however, it is able to tap the energy of a sun, and so its rate of information transfer increases enormously. It also 'recharges its batteries', to use a doubtless crude analogy. And since – like our own early Pioneers and Voyagers – it employs the gravitational fields of the heavenly bodies to deflect it from star to star, it will operate indefinitely, unless mechanical failure or cosmic accident terminates its career. Centaurus was its eleventh port of call; after it had rounded our sun like a comet, its new course was aimed precisely at Tau Ceti, twelve light years away. If there is anyone there, it will be ready to start its next conversation soon after AD 8100 . . .

. . . For Starglider combines the functions both of ambassador and explorer. When, at the end of one of its millennial journeys, it discovers a technological culture, it makes friends with the natives and starts to trade information, in the only form of interstellar commerce that may ever be possible. And before it departs again on its endless voyage, after its brief transit of their solar system, Starglider gives the location of its home world – already awaiting a direct call from the newest member of the galactic telephone exchange.

In our case, we can take some pride in the fact that, even before it had transmitted any star charts, we had identified its parent sun and even beamed our first transmissions to it. Now we have only to wait 104 years for an answer. How incredibly lucky we are, to have neighbours so close at hand.

It was obvious from its very first messages that Starglider under-stood the meaning of several thousand basic English and Chinese words, which it had deduced from an analysis of television, radio and – especially – broadcast video-text services. But what it had picked up during its approach was a very unrepresentative sample from the whole spectrum of human culture; it contained little advanced science, still less advanced mathematics – and only a random selection of literature, music and the visual arts.

Like any self-taught genius, therefore, Starglider had huge gaps in its education. On the principle that it was better to give too much than too little, as soon as contact was established Starglider was presented with the Oxford English Dictionary, the Great Chinese Dictionary (Romandarin edition), and the *Encyclopaedia Terrae*. Their digital transmission required little more than fifty minutes, and it was notable that, immediately thereafter, Starglider was silent for almost four hours – its longest period off the air. When it resumed contact, its vocabulary was immensely enlarged, and for over ninety-nine per cent of the time it could pass the Turing test with ease – ie, there was no way of telling from the messages received that Starglider was a machine, and not a highly intelligent human.

There were occasional giveaways – for example, incorrect use of ambiguous words, and the absence of emotional content in the dialogue. This was only to be expected; unlike advanced terrestrial computers – which could replicate the emotions of their builders, when necessary – Starglider's feelings and desires were presumably those of a totally alien species, and therefore largely incomprehensible to man.

And, of course, *vice versa*. Starglider could understand precisely and completely what was meant by 'the square on the hypotenuse equals the sum of the squares on the other two sides'. But it could scarcely have the faintest glimmer of what lay in Keats' mind when he wrote:

Charmed magic casements, opening on the foam
Of perilous seas, in faery lands forlorn . . .

Still less –

Shall I compare thee to a summer's day?
    Thou art more lovely and more temperate . . .

Nevertheless, in the hope of correcting this deficiency, Starglider was also presented with thousands of hours of music, drama, and scenes from terrestrial life, both human and otherwise. By general agreement, a certain amount of censorship was enforced here. Although mankind's propensity for violence and warfare could hardly be denied (it was too late to recall the *Encyclopaedia*) only a few carefully selected examples were broadcast. And, until Starglider was safely out of range, the normal fare of the video networks was uncharacteristically bland.

For centuries – perhaps, indeed, until it had reached its next target – philosophers would be debating Starglider's *real* understanding of human affairs and problems. But on one point there was no serious disagreement. The hundred days of its passage through the solar system altered irrevocably men's views of the universe, its origin, and their place in it.

Human civilization could never be the same, after Starglider had gone.

15 Bodhidharma

As the massive door, carved with intricate lotus patterns, clicked softly shut behind him, Morgan felt that he had entered another world. This was by no means the first time he had been on ground once sacred to some great religion; he had seen Notre Dame, Saint Sophia, Stonehenge, the Parthenon, Karnak, Saint Paul's, and at least a dozen other major temples and mosques. But he had viewed them all as frozen relics of the past – splendid examples of art or engineering, but with no relevance to the modern mind. The faiths that had created and sustained them had all passed into oblivion, though some had survived until well into the twenty-second century.

But here, it seemed, time had stood still. The hurricanes of history had blown past this lonely citadel of faith, leaving it unshaken. As they had done for three thousand years, the monks still prayed, and meditated, and watched the dawn.

During his walk across the worn flagstones of the courtyard, polished smooth by the feet of innumerable pilgrims, Morgan experienced a sudden and wholly uncharacteristic indecision. In the name of progress, he was attempting to destroy something ancient and noble; and something that he would never fully understand.

The sight of the great bronze bell, hanging in a campanile that grew out of the monastery wall, stopped Morgan in his tracks. Instantly, his engineer's mind had estimated its weight at not less than five tons, and it was obviously very old. How on earth . . . ?

The monk noticed his curiosity, and gave a smile of understanding.

'Two thousand years old,' he said. 'It was a gift from Kalidasa the Accursed, which we felt it expedient not to refuse. According to legend, it took ten years to carry it up the mountain – and the lives of a hundred men.'

'When is it used?' asked Morgan, after he had digested this information.

'Because of its hateful origin, it is sounded only in time of disaster. I have never heard it, nor has any living man. It tolled once, without human aid, during the great earthquake of 2017. And the time before *that* was 1522, when the Iberian invaders burned the Temple of the Tooth and seized the Sacred Relic.'

'So after all that effort – it's never been used?'

'Perhaps a dozen times in the last two thousand years. Kalidasa's doom still lies upon it.'

That might be good religion, Morgan could not help thinking, but hardly sound economics. And he wondered irreverently how many monks had succumbed to the temptation of tapping the bell, ever so gently, just to hear for themselves the unknown timbre of its forbidden voice . . .

They were walking now past a huge boulder, up which a short flight of steps led to a gilded pavilion. This, Morgan realized, was the very summit of the mountain; he knew what the shrine was supposed to hold, but once again the monk enlightened him.

'The footprint,' he said. 'The Muslims believed it was Adam's; he stood here after he was expelled from Paradise. The Hindus attributed it to Siva or Saman. But to the Buddhists, of course, it was the imprint of the Enlightened One.'

'I notice your use of the past tense,' Morgan answered in a carefully neutral voice. 'What is the belief now?'

The monk's face showed no emotion as he replied: 'The Buddha was a man, like you and me. The impression in the rock – and it is *very* hard rock – is two metres long.'

That seemed to settle the matter, and Morgan had no further questions while he was led along a short cloister that ended at an open door. The monk knocked, but did not wait for any response as he waved the visitor to enter.

Morgan had half-expected to find the Mahanayake Thero sitting cross-legged on a mat, probably surrounded by incense and chanting acolytes. There was, indeed, just a hint of incense in the chill air, but the Chief Incumbent of the Sri Kanda *vihare* sat behind a perfectly ordinary office desk, equipped with standard display and memory units. The only unusual item in the room was the head of the Buddha, slightly larger than life, on a plinth in one corner. Morgan could not tell whether it was real, or merely a projection.

Despite his conventional setting, there was little likelihood that the head of the monastery would be mistaken for any other type of executive. Quite apart from the inevitable yellow robe, the Mahanayake Thero had two other characteristics that, in this age, were very rare indeed. He was completely bald; and he was wearing spectacles.

Both, Morgan assumed, were by deliberate choice. Since baldness could be so easily cured, that shining ivory dome must have been shaved or depilated. And he could not remember when he had last seen spectacles, except in historical recordings or dramas.

The combination was fascinating, and disconcerting. Morgan found it virtually impossible to guess the Mahanayake Thero's age; it could be anything from a mature forty to a well-preserved eighty. And those lenses, transparent though they were, somehow concealed the thoughts and emotions behind them.

'*Ayu bowan*, Dr Morgan,' said the prelate, gesturing his visitor to the only empty chair. 'This is my secretary, the Venerable Parakarma. I trust you won't mind if he makes notes.'

'Of course not,' said Morgan, inclining his head towards the remaining occupant of the small room. He noticed that the younger monk had flowing hair and an impressive beard; presumably shaven pates were optional.

'So, Dr Morgan,' the Mahanayake Thero continued, 'you want our mountain.'

'I'm afraid so, your – er – reverence. Part of it, at any rate.'

'Out of *all* the world – these few hectares ?'

'The choice is not ours, but Nature's. The Earth terminus has to be on the equator, and at the greatest possible altitude, where the low air density maintains wind forces.'

'There are higher equatorial mountains in Africa and South America.'

Here we go again, Morgan groaned silently. Bitter experience had shown him that it was almost impossible to make laymen, however intelligent and interested, appreciate this problem, and he anticipated even less success with these monks. If only the Earth was a nice, symmetrical body, with no dents and bumps in its gravitational field . . .

'Believe me,' he said fervently, 'we've looked at all the alternatives. Cotopaxi and Mount Kenya – and even Kilimanjaro, though that's three degrees south – would be fine except for one fatal flaw. When a satellite is established in the stationary orbit, it won't stay *exactly* over the same spot. Because of gravitational irregularities, which I won't go into, it will slowly drift along the equator. So all our synchronous satellites and space-stations have to burn propellent to keep them on station; luckily the amount involved is quite small. But you can't keep nudging millions of tons – especially when it's in the form of a slender rod tens of thousands of kilometres long – back into position. And there's no need to. Fortunately for us—'

'—not for *us*,' interjected the Mahanayake Thero, almost throwing Morgan off his stride.

'—there are two stable points on the synchronous orbit. A satellite placed at them will *stay* there – it won't drift away. Just as if it's stuck at the bottom of an invisible valley. One of those points is out over the Pacific, so it's no use to us. The other is directly above our heads.'

'Surely a few kilometres one way or the other would make no difference. There are other mountains in Taprobane.'

'None more than half the height of Sri Kanda – which brings us down to the level of critical wind forces. True, there are not many hurricanes exactly on the equator. But there are enough to endanger the structure, at its very weakest point.'

'We can control the winds.'

It was the first contribution the young secretary had made to the discussion, and Morgan looked at him with heightened interest.

'To some extent, yes. Naturally, I have discussed this point with Monsoon Control. They say that absolute certainty is out of the question – especially with hurricanes. The best odds they will give me are fifty to one. That's not good enough for a trillion dollar project.'

The Venerable Parakarma seemed inclined to argue. 'There is an almost forgotten branch of mathematics, called Catastrophe Theory, which could make meteorology a really precise science. I am confident that—'

'I should explain,' the Mahanayake Thero interjected blandly, 'that my colleague was once rather celebrated for his astronomical work. I imagine you have heard of Dr Choam Goldberg.'

Morgan felt that a trap-door had been suddenly opened beneath him. He should have been warned! Then he recalled that Professor Sarath had indeed told him, with a twinkle in his eye, that he should 'watch out for Buddy's private secretary – he's a very smart character'.

Morgan wondered if his cheeks were burning, as the Venerable Parakarma, *alias* Dr Choam Goldberg, looked back at him with a distinctly unfriendly expression. So he had been trying to explain orbital instabilities to these innocent monks; the Mahanayake Thero had probably received much better briefing on the subject than he had done.

And he remembered that the world's scientists were neatly divided on the subject of Dr Goldberg . . . those who were *sure* that he was crazy, and those who had not yet made up their minds. For he had been one of the most promising young men in the field of astrophysics when, five years ago, he had announced, 'Now that Starglider has effectively destroyed all traditional religions, we can at last pay serious attention to the concept of God.'

And, with that, he had disappeared from public view.

16 Conversations with Starglider

Of all the thousands of questions put to Starglider during its transit of the solar system, those whose answers were most eagerly awaited concerned the living creatures and civilizations of other stars. Contrary to some expectations, the robot answered willingly, though it admitted that its last update on the subject had been received over a century ago.

Considering the immense range of cultures produced on Earth by a single species, it was obvious that there would be even greater variety among the stars, where every conceivable type of biology might occur. Several thousand hours of fascinating – often incomprehensible, sometimes horrifying – scenes of life on other planets left no doubt that this was the case.

Nevertheless, the Starholmers had managed a rough classification of cultures according to their standards of technology – perhaps the only objective basis possible. Humanity was interested to discover that it came number five on a scale which was defined approximately by: 1 Stone tools. 2 Metals, fire. 3 Writing, handicrafts, ships. 4 Steam power, basic science. 5 Atomic energy, space travel.

When Starglider had begun its mission, sixty thousand years ago, its builders were, like the human race, still in category Five. They had now graduated to Six, characterized by the ability to convert matter completely into energy, and to transmute *all* elements on an industrial scale.

'And is there a Class Seven?' Starglider was immediately asked. The reply was a brief 'Affirmative'. When pressed for details, the probe explained: 'I am not allowed to describe the technology of a higher grade culture to a lower one.' There the matter remained, right up to the moment of the final message, despite all the leading questions designed by the most ingenious legal brains of Earth.

For by this time Starglider was more than a match for any terrestrial logician. This was partly the fault of the University of Chicago's Department of Philosophy; in a fit of monumental *hubris*, it had clandestinely transmitted the whole of the *Summa Theologica*, with disastrous results . . .

2069 June 02 GMT 19.34 Message 1946 sequence 2.
Starglider to Earth:

I have analysed the arguments of your Saint Thomas Aquinas as requested in your message 145 sequence 3 of 2069 June 02 GMT 18.42. Most of the content appears to be sense-free random noise and so devoid of information, but the printout that follows lists 192 fallacies expressed in the symbolic logic of your reference Mathematics 43 of 2069 May 29 GMT 02.51.
Fallacy 1 . . . (hereafter a 75-page printout.)

As the log timings show, it took Starglider rather less than an hour to demolish Saint Thomas. Although philosophers were to spend the next several decades arguing over the analysis, they found only two errors; and even those could have been due to a misunderstanding of terminology.

It would have been most interesting to know what fraction of its processing circuits Starglider applied to this task; unfortunately, no one thought of asking before the probe had switched to cruise mode and broken contact. By then, even more deflating messages had been received . . .

2069 June 04 GMT 07.59 Message 9056 sequence 2.
Starglider to Earth:

I am unable to distinguish clearly between your religious ceremonies and apparently identical behaviour at the sporting and cultural functions you have transmitted to me. I refer you particularly to the Beatles, 1965; the World Soccer Final, 2046; and the Farewell appearance of the Johann Sebastian Clones, 2056.

2069 June 05 GMT 20.38 Message 4675 sequence 2.
Starglider to Earth:

My last update on this matter is 175 years old, but if I understand you correctly the answer is as follows. Behaviour of the type you call religious occurred among 3 of the 15 known Class One cultures, 6 of the 28 Class Two cultures, 5 of the 14 Class Three cultures, 2 of the 10 Class Four cultures, and 3 of the 174 Class Five cultures. You will appreciate that we have many more examples of Class Five, because only they can be detected over astronomical distances.

2069 June 06 GMT 12.09 Message 5897 sequence 2.
Starglider to Earth:

You are correct in deducing that the 3 Class Five cultures that engaged in religious activities all had two-parent reproduction and the young remained in family groups for a large fraction of their lifetime. How did you arrive at this conclusion?

2069 June 08 GMT 15.37 Message 6943 sequence 2.
Starglider to Earth:

The hypothesis you refer to as God, though not disprovable by logic alone, is unnecessary for the following reason.

If you assume that the universe can be quote explained unquote as the creation of an entity known as God, he must obviously be of a higher degree of organization than his product. Thus you have *more* than doubled the size of the original problem, and have taken the first step on a diverging infinite regress. William of Ockham pointed out as recently as your fourteenth century that entities should not be multiplied unnecessarily. I cannot therefore understand why this debate continues.

2069 June 11 GMT 06.84 Message 8964 sequence 2.
Starglider to Earth:

Starholme informed me 456 years ago that the origin of the universe has been discovered but that I do not have the appropriate circuits to comprehend it. You must communicate direct for further information.

I am now switching to cruise mode and must break contact.
Goodbye.

In the opinion of many, that final and most famous of all its thousands of messages proved that Starglider had a sense of humour. For why else would it have waited until the very end to explode such a philosophical bomb-shell? Or was the entire conversation all part of a careful plan, designed to put the human race in the right frame of reference – when the first direct messages from Starholme arrived in, presumably, 104 years?

There were some who suggested following Starglider, since it was carrying out of the solar system not only immeasurable stores of knowledge, but the treasures of a technology centuries ahead of anything possessed by man. Although no spaceship now existed that could overtake Starglider – *and* return again to earth after matching its enormous velocity – one could certainly be built.

However, wiser councils prevailed. Even a robot space-probe might have very effective defences against boarders – including, as a last resort, the ability to self-destruct. But the most telling argument was that its builders were 'only' fifty-two light years away. During the millennia since they had launched Starglider, their spacefaring ability must have improved enormously. If the human race did anything to provoke them they might arrive, slightly annoyed, in a very few hundred years.

Meanwhile, among all its countless other effects upon human culture, Starglider had brought to its climax a process that was already well under way. It had put an end to the billions of words of pious gibberish with which apparently intelligent men had addled their minds for centuries.

17 Parakarma

As he quickly checked back on his conversation, Morgan decided that he had not made a fool of himself. Indeed, the Mahanayake Thero might have lost a tactical advantage by revealing the identity of the Venerable Parakarma. Yet it was no particular secret; perhaps he thought that Morgan already knew.

At this point there was a rather welcome interruption, as two young acolytes filed into the office, one carrying a tray loaded with small dishes of rice, fruits and what appeared to be thin pancakes, while the other followed with the inevitable pot of tea. There was nothing that looked like meat; after his long night, Morgan would have welcomed a couple of eggs, but he assumed that they too were forbidden. No – that was too strong a word; Sarath had told him that the Order prohibited nothing, believing in no absolutes. But it had a nicely calibrated scale of toleration, and the taking of life – even potential life – was very low on the list.

As he started to sample the various items – most of them quite unknown to him – Morgan looked enquiringly at the Mahanayake Thero, who shook his head.

'We do not eat before noon. The mind functions more clearly in the morning hours, and so should not be distracted by material things.'

As he nibbled at some quite delicious papaya, Morgan considered the philosophical gulf represented by that simple statement. To him, an empty stomach could be very distracting indeed, completely inhibiting the higher mental functions. Having always been blessed with good health, he had never tried to dissociate mind and body, and saw no reason why one should make the attempt.

While Morgan was eating his exotic breakfast the Mahanayake Thero excused himself, and for a few minutes his fingers danced, with dazzling speed, over the keyboard of his console. As the readout was in full view, politeness compelled Morgan to look elsewhere. Inevitably, his eyes fell upon the head of the Buddha. It was probably real, for the plinth cast a faint shadow on the wall behind. Yet even that was not conclusive. The plinth might be solid enough, and the head a projection carefully positioned on top of it; the trick was a common one.

Here, like the Mona Lisa, was a work of art that both mirrored the emotions of the observer and imposed its own authority upon them. But La Gioconda's eyes were open, though what they were looking at no one would ever know. The eyes of the Buddha were completely blank – empty pools in which a man might lose his soul, or discover a universe.

Upon the lips there lingered a smile even more ambiguous than the Mona Lisa's. Yet was it indeed a smile, or merely a trick of the lighting? Already it was gone, replaced by an expression of super-human tranquillity. Morgan could not tear his eyes away from that hypnotic countenance, and only the familiar rustling whirr of a hard-copy readout from the console brought him back to reality – if this *was* reality . . .

'I thought you might like a souvenir of your visit,' said the Mahanayake Thero.

As Morgan accepted the proffered sheet, he was surprised to see that it was archival-quality parchment, not the usual flimsy paper, destined to be thrown away after a few hours of use. He could not read a single word; except for an unobtrusive alpha-numeric reference in the bottom left-hand corner, it was all in the flowery curlicues which he could now recognize as Taprobian script.

'Thank you,' he said, with as much irony as he could muster. 'What is it?' He had a very good idea; legal documents had a close family resemblance, whatever their languages – or eras.

'A copy of the agreement between King Ravindra and the Maha Sangha, dated Vesak AD 854 of your calendar. It defines the ownership of the temple land – in perpetuity. The rights set out in this document were even recognized by the invaders.'

'By the Caledonians and the Hollanders, I believe. But *not* by the Iberians.'

If the Mahanayake Thero was surprised by the thoroughness of Morgan's briefing, not even the twitch of an eyebrow betrayed the fact.

'*They* were hardly respecters of law and order, particularly where other religions were concerned. I trust that their philosophy of might equals right does not appeal to you.'

Morgan gave a somewhat forced smile. 'It certainly does not,' he answered. But where did one draw the line? he asked himself silently. When the overwhelming interests of great organizations were at stake, conventional morality often took second place. The best legal minds on earth, human and electronic, would soon be focused upon this spot. If they could not find the right answers, a very unpleasant situation might develop – one which could make him a villain, not a hero.

'Since you have raised the subject of the 854 agreement, let me remind you that it refers only to the land *inside* the temple boun-daries – which are clearly defined by the walls.'

'Correct. But they enclose the entire summit.'

'You have no control over the ground outside this area.'

'We have the rights of any owner of property. If the neighbours create a nuisance, we would have legal redress. This is not the first time the point has been raised.'

'I know. In connection with the cable-car system.'

A faint smile played over the Maha Thero's lips. 'You have done your homework,' he commended. 'Yes, we opposed it vigorously, for a number of reasons – though I admit that, now it is here, we have often been very thankful for it.' He paused thoughtfully, then added: 'There have been some problems, but we have been able to coexist. Casual sightseers and tourists are content to stay on the lookout platform; *genuine* pilgrims, of course, we are always happy to welcome at the summit.'

'Then perhaps some accommodation could be worked out in this case. A few hundred metres of altitude would make no difference to us. We could leave the summit untouched, and carve out another plateau, like the cable car terminus.'

Morgan felt distinctly uncomfortable under the prolonged scrutiny of the two monks. He had little doubt that they recognized the absurdity of the suggestion, but for the sake of the record he had to make it.

'You have a most peculiar sense of humour, Dr Morgan,' the Mahanayake Thero replied at last. 'What would be left of the spirit of the mountain – of the solitude we have sought for three thousand years – if this monstrous device is erected here? Do you expect us to betray the faith of all the millions who have come to this sacred spot, often at the cost of their health – even their lives?'

'I sympathize with your feelings,' Morgan answered. (But was he lying? he wondered.) 'We would, of course, do our best to minimize any disturbance. All the support facilities would be buried inside the mountain. Only the elevator would emerge, and from any distance it would be quite invisible. The general aspect of the mountain would be totally unchanged. Even your famous shadow, which I have just admired, would be virtually unaffected.'

The Mahanayake Thero turned to his colleague as if seeking confirmation. The Venerable Parakarma looked straight at Morgan and said: 'What about noise?'

Damn, Morgan thought; my weakest point. The payloads would emerge from the mountain at several hundred kilometres an hour – the more velocity they could be given by the ground-based system the less the strain on the suspended tower. Of course, passengers couldn't take more than half a gee or so, but the capsules would still pop out at a substantial fraction of the speed of sound.

'There will be some aerodynamic noise,' Morgan admitted. 'But nothing like that near a large airport.'

'Very reassuring,' said the Mahanayake Thero. Morgan was certain that he was being sarcastic, yet could detect no trace of irony in his voice. He was either displaying an Olympian calm, or testing his visitor's reactions. The younger monk, on the other hand, made no attempt to conceal his anger.

'For years,' he said with indignation, 'we have been protesting about the disturbance caused by re-entering spacecraft. Now you want to generate shock waves in . . . in our back garden.'

'Our operations will *not* be transonic, at this altitude,' Morgan replied firmly. 'And the tower structure will absorb most of the sound energy. In fact,' he added, trying to press what he had suddenly seen as an advantage, 'in the long run, we'll help to eliminate re-entry booms. The mountain will actually be a quieter place.'

'I understand. Instead of occasional concussions, we shall have a steady roar.'

I'm not getting anywhere with *this* character, thought Morgan; and I'd expected the Mahanayake Thero to be the biggest obstacle . . .

Sometimes, it was best to change the subject entirely. He decided to dip one cautious toe into the quaking quagmire of theology.

'Isn't there something appropriate,' he said earnestly, 'in what we are trying to do? Our purposes may be different, but the net results have much in common. What we hope to build is only an extension of your stairway. If I may say so, we're continuing it – all the way to Heaven.'

For a moment, the Venerable Parakarma seemed taken aback at such effrontery. Before he could recover, his superior answered smoothly: 'An interesting concept – but our philosophy does not believe in Heaven. Such salvation as may exist can be found only in *this* world, and I sometimes wonder at your anxiety to leave it. Do you know the story of the Tower of Babel?'

'Vaguely.'

'I suggest you look it up in the old Christian Bible – *Genesis* 11. That, too, was an engineering project to scale the heavens. It failed, owing to difficulties in communication.'

'Though we shall have our problems, I don't think *that* will be one of them.'

But looking at the Venerable Parakarma, Morgan was not so sure. Here was a communications gap which seemed in some ways greater than that between *Homo sapiens* and Starglider. They spoke the same language, but there were gulfs of incomprehension which might never be spanned.

'May I ask,' continued the Mahanayake with imperturbable politeness, 'how successful you were with the Department of Parks and Forests?'

'They were extremely cooperative.'

'I am not surprised; they are chronically under-budgeted, and any new source of revenue would be welcome. The cable system was a financial windfall, and doubtless they hope your project will be an even bigger one.'

'They will be right. And they have accepted the fact that it won't create any environmental hazards.'

'Suppose it falls down?'

Morgan looked the venerable monk straight in the eye.

'It won't,' he said, with all the authority of the man whose inverted rainbow now linked two continents.

But he knew, and the implacable Parakarma must also know, that absolute certainty was impossible in such matters. Two hundred and two years ago, on 7 November 1940, that lesson had been driven home in a way that no engineer could ever forget.

Morgan had few nightmares, but that was one of them. Even at this moment the computers at Terran Construction were trying to exorcise it.

But all the computing power in the universe could provide no protection against the problems he had *not* foreseen – the nightmares that were still unborn.

18 The Golden Butterflies

Despite the brilliant sunlight and the magnificent views that assailed him on every side, Morgan was fast asleep before the car had descended into the lowlands. Even the innumerable hairpin bends failed to keep him awake – but he was suddenly snapped back into consciousness when the brakes were slammed on and he was pitched forward against his seat-belt.

For a moment of utter confusion, he thought that he must still be dreaming. The breeze blowing gently through the half-open windows was so warm and humid that it might have escaped from a Turkish bath; yet the car had apparently come to a halt in the midst of a blinding snowstorm.

Morgan blinked, screwed up his eyes, and opened them to reality. This was the first time he had ever seen *golden* snow . . .

A dense swarm of butterflies was crossing the road, headed due east in a steady, purposeful migration. Some had been sucked into the car, and fluttered around frantically until Morgan waved them out; many more had plastered themselves on the windscreen. With what were doubtless a few choice Taprobani expletives, the driver emerged and wiped the glass clear; by the time he had finished, the swarm had thinned out to a handful of isolated stragglers.

'Did they tell you about the legend?' he asked, glancing back at his passenger.

'No,' said Morgan curtly. He was not at all interested, being anxious to resume his interrupted nap.

'The Golden Butterflies – they're the souls of Kalidasa's warriors – the army he lost at Yakkagala.'

Morgan gave an unenthusiastic grunt, hoping that the driver would get the message; but he continued remorselessly.

'Every year, around this time, they head for the Mountain, and they all die on its lower slopes. Sometimes you'll meet them half-way up the cable ride, but that's the highest they get. Which is lucky for the Vihara.'

'The Vihara?' asked Morgan sleepily.

'The Temple. If they ever reach it, Kalidasa will have conquered, and the *bhikkus* – the monks – will have to leave. That's the prophecy – it's carved on a stone slab in the Ranapura Museum. I can show it to you.'

'Some other time,' said Morgan hastily, as he settled back into the padded seat. But it was many kilometres before he could doze off again, for there was something haunting about the image that the driver had conjured up.

He would remember it often in the months ahead – when waking, and in moments of stress or crisis. Once again he would be immersed in that golden snowstorm, as the doomed millions spent their energies in a vain assault upon the mountain and all that it symbolized.

Even now, at the very beginning of his campaign, the image was too close for comfort.

19 By the Shores of Lake Saladin

Almost all the Alternative History computer simulations suggest that the Battle of Tours (AD 732) was one of the crucial disasters of mankind. Had Charles Martel been defeated, Islam might have resolved the internal differences that were tearing it apart and gone on to conquer Europe. Thus centuries of Christian barbarism would have been avoided, the Industrial Revolution would have started almost a thousand years earlier, and by now we would have reached the nearer stars instead of merely the further planets . . .

. . . But fate ruled otherwise, and the armies of the Prophet turned back into Africa. Islam lingered on, a fascinating fossil, until the end of the twentieth century. Then, abruptly, it was dissolved in oil . . .

(Chairman's Address: Toynbee Bi-centennial Symposium, London, 2089.)

'Did you know,' said Sheik Farouk Abdullah, 'that I have now appointed myself Grand Admiral of the Sahara Fleet?'

'It wouldn't surprise me, Mr President,' Morgan answered, as he gazed out across the sparkling blue expanse of Lake Saladin. 'If it's not a naval secret, how many ships do you have?'

'Ten at the moment. The largest is a thirty-metre hydro-skimmer run by the Red Crescent; it spends every weekend rescuing incompetent sailors. My people still aren't much good on the water – look at that idiot trying to tack! After all, two hundred years really isn't long enough to switch from camels to boats.'

'You had Cadillacs and Rolls-Royces in between. Surely that should have eased the transition.'

'And we still have them; my great-great-*great*-grandfather's Silver Ghost is just as good as new. But I must be fair – it's the visitors who get into trouble, trying to cope with our local winds. *We* stick to power-boats. And next year I'm getting a submarine guaranteed to reach the lake's maximum depth of 78 metres.'

'Whatever for?'

'*Now* they tell us that the Erg was full of archaeological treasures. Of course, no one bothered about them before it was flooded.'

It was no use trying to hurry the President of ANAR – the Autonomous North African Republic – and Morgan knew better than to attempt it. Whatever the Constitution might say, Sheik Abdullah controlled more power and wealth than almost any single individual on earth. Even more to the point, he understood the uses of both.

He came from a family that was not afraid to take risks, and very seldom had cause to regret them. Its first and most famous gamble – which had incurred the hatred of the whole Arab world for almost half a century – was the investment of its abundant petro-dollars in the science and technology of Israel. That farsighted act had led directly to the mining of the Red Sea, the defeat of the deserts, and, very much later, to the Gibraltar Bridge.

'I don't have to tell you, Van,' said the Sheik at last, 'how much your new project fascinates me. And after all that we went through together while the Bridge was being built, I know that you could do it – given the resources.'

'Thank you.'

'But I have a few questions. I'm still not clear why there's Midway Station – and why it's at a height of twenty-five thousand kilometres.'

'Several reasons. We needed a major power plant at about that level, which would involve fairly massive construction there in any case. Then it occurred to us that seven hours was too long to stay cooped up in a rather cramped cabin, and splitting the journey gave a number of advantages. We shouldn't have to feed the passengers in transit – they could eat and stretch their legs at the Station. We could also optimize the vehicle design; only the capsules on the lower section would have to be streamlined. Those on the upper run could be much simpler and lighter. The Midway Station would not only serve as a transfer point, but as an operations and control centre – and ultimately, we believe, as a major tourist attraction and resort in its own right.'

'But it's *not* midway! It's almost – ah – two-thirds of the distance up to stationary orbit.'

'True; the mid-point would be at eighteen thousand, not twenty-five. But there's another factor – safety. If the section above is severed, the Midway Station won't crash back to Earth.'

'Why not?'

'It will have enough momentum to maintain a stable orbit. Of course, it will fall earthward, but it will always remain clear of the atmosphere. So it will be perfectly safe – it will simply become a space station, moving in a ten-hour, elliptical orbit. Twice a day it will be right back where it started from, and eventually it could be reconnected. In theory, at least . . .'

'And in practice?'

'Oh, I'm sure it could be done. Certainly the people and equipment on the station could be saved. But we wouldn't have even that option if we established it at a lower altitude. *Anything* falling from below the twenty-five thousand kilometre limit hits the atmosphere and burns up in five hours, or less.'

'Would you propose advertising this fact to passengers on the Earth-Midway run?'

'We hope they would be too busy admiring the view to worry about it.'

'You make it sound like a scenic elevator.'

'Why not? Except that the tallest scenic ride on earth only goes

up a mere three kilometres! We're talking about something ten thousand times higher.'

There was a considerable pause while Sheik Abdullah thought this over.

'We missed an opportunity,' he said at last. 'We could have had *five*-kilometre scenic rides up the piers of the Bridge.'

'They were in the original design, but we dropped them for the usual reason – economy.'

'Perhaps we made a mistake; they could have paid for themselves. And I've just realized something else. If this – hyperfilament – had been available at the time I suppose the Bridge could have been built for half the cost.'

'I wouldn't lie to you, Mr President. Less than a fifth. But construction would have been delayed more than twenty years, so you haven't lost by it.'

'I must talk that over with my accountants. Some of them still aren't convinced it was a good idea, even though the traffic growth rate is ahead of projection. But I keep telling them that money isn't everything – the Republic *needed* the Bridge psychologically and culturally, as well as economically. Did you know that eighteen per cent of the people who drive across it do so just because it's there, not for any other reason? And then they go straight back again, despite having to pay the toll both ways.'

'I seem to recall,' said Morgan dryly, 'giving you similar arguments, a long time ago. You weren't easy to convince.'

'True. I remember that the Sydney Opera House was your favourite example. You liked to point out how many times *that* had paid for itself – even in hard cash, let alone prestige.'

'And don't forget the Pyramids.'

The Sheik laughed. 'What did you call them? The best investment in the history of mankind?'

'Precisely. Still paying tourist dividends after four thousand years.'

'Hardly a fair comparison, though. Their running costs don't compare with those of the Bridge – much less your proposed Tower's.'

'The Tower may last longer than the Pyramids. It's in a far more benign environment.'

'That's a very impressive thought. You *really* believe that it will operate for several thousand years?'

'Not in its original form, of course. But in principle, yes. Whatever technical developments the future brings, I don't believe there will ever be a more efficient, more economical way of reaching Space. Think of it as another bridge. But this time a bridge to the stars – or at least to the planets.'

'And once again you'd like us to help finance it. We'll still be paying for the *last* bridge for another twenty years. It's not as if your space elevator was on our territory, or was of direct importance to us.'

'But I believe it is, Mr President. Your republic is a part of the terran economy, and the cost of space transportation is now one of the factors limiting its growth. If you've looked at those estimates for the '50s and '60s...'

'I have – I have. Very interesting. But though we're not exactly poor, we couldn't raise a fraction of the funds needed. Why, it would absorb the entire Gross World Product for a couple of years!'

'And pay it back every fifteen, for ever afterwards.'

'*If* your projections are correct.'

'They were, for the Bridge. But you're right, of course, and I don't expect ANAR to do more than start the ball rolling. Once you've shown your interest, it will be that much easier to get other support.'

'Such as?'

'The World Bank. The Planetary banks. The Federal government.'

'And your own employers, the Terran Construction Corporation? What are you *really* up to, Van?'

Here it comes, thought Morgan, almost with a sigh of relief. Now at last he could talk frankly with someone he could trust, someone who was too big to be involved in petty bureaucratic intrigues – but who could thoroughly appreciate their finer points.

'I've been doing most of this work in my own time – I'm on vacation right now. And incidentally, that's just how the Bridge started! I don't know if I ever told you that I was once officially ordered to forget it . . . I've learned a few lessons in the past fifteen years.'

'This report must have taken a good deal of computer time. Who paid for that?'

'Oh, I have considerable discretionary funds. And my staff is always doing studies that nobody else can understand. To tell the truth, I've had quite a little team playing with the idea for several months. They're so enthusiastic that they spend most of their free time on it as well. But now we have to commit ourselves – or abandon the project.'

'Does your esteemed Chairman know about this?'

Morgan smiled, without much humour. 'Of course not, and I don't want to tell him until I've worked out all the details.'

'I can appreciate some of the complications,' said the President shrewdly. 'One of them, I imagine, is ensuring that Senator Collins doesn't invent it first.'

'He can't do *that* – the idea is two hundred years old. But he, and a lot of other people, could slow it down. I want to see it happen in my lifetime.'

'And, of course, you intend to be in charge . . . Well, what exactly would you like us to do?'

'This is merely one suggestion, Mr President – you may have a better idea. Form a consortium – perhaps including the Gibraltar Bridge Authority, the Suez and Panama Corporations, the English Channel Company, the Bering Dam Corporation. Then, when it's all wrapped up, approach TCC with a request to do a feasibility study. At this stage, the investment will be negligible.'

'Meaning?'

'Less than a million. Especially as I've already done ninety per cent of the work.'

'And then?'

'Thereafter, with *your* backing, Mr President, I can play it by ear. I might stay with TCC. Or I might resign and join the consortium – call it Astroengineering. It would all depend on circumstances. I would do whatever seemed best for the project.'

'That seems a reasonable approach. I think we can work something out.'

'Thank you, Mr President,' Morgan answered with heartfelt

sincerity. 'But there's one annoying roadblock we have to tackle at once – perhaps even before we set up the consortium. We have to go to the World Court, and establish jurisdiction over the most valuable piece of real estate on Earth.'

20 The Bridge that Danced

Even in this age of instantaneous communications and swift global transport, it was convenient to have a place that one could call one's office. Not everything could be stored in patterns of electronic charges; there were still such items as good old-fashioned books, professional certificates, awards and honours, engineering models, samples of material, artists' rendering of projects (not as accurate as a computer's, but very ornamental), and of course the wall-to-wall carpet which every senior bureaucrat needed to soften the impact of external reality.

Morgan's office, which he saw on the average ten days per month, was on the sixth or LAND floor of the sprawling Terran Construction Corporation Headquarters in Nairobi. The floor below was SEA, that above it ADMINISTRATION – meaning Chairman Collins and his empire. The architect, in a fit of naïve symbolism, had devoted the top floor to SPACE. There was even a small observatory on the roof, with a thirty-centimetre telescope that was always out of order, because it was only used during office parties, and frequently for most non-astronomical purposes. The upper rooms of the Triplanetary Hotel, only a kilometre away, were a favourite target, as they often held some very strange forms of life – or at any rate of behaviour.

As Morgan was in continuous touch with his two secretaries – one human, the other electronic – he expected no surprises when he walked into the office after the brief flight from ANAR. By the standards of an earlier age, his was an extraordinarily small organization. He had less than three hundred men and women under his direct control; but the computing and information-processing power at their command could not be matched by the merely human population of the entire planet.

'Well, how did you get on with the Sheik?' asked Warren Kingsley, his deputy and long-time friend, as soon as they were alone together.

'Very well; I think we have a deal. But I still can't believe that we're held up by such a stupid problem. What does the legal department say?'

'We'll definitely have to get a World Court ruling. *If* the Court agrees that it's a matter of overwhelming public interest, our reverend friends will have to move . . . though if they decide to be stubborn, there would be a nasty situation. Perhaps you should send a small earthquake to help them make up their minds.'

The fact that Morgan was on the board of General Tectonics was an old joke between him and Kingsley; but GT – perhaps fortunately – had never found a way of controlling and directing earthquakes, nor did it ever expect to do so. The best that it could hope for was to predict them, and to bleed off their energies harmlessly before they could do major damage. Even here, its record of success was not much better than seventy-five per cent.

'A nice idea,' said Morgan, 'I'll think it over. Now, what about our other problem?'

'All set to go – do you want it now?'

'OK – let's see the worst.'

The office windows darkened, and a grid of glowing lines appeared in the centre of the room.

'Watch this, Van,' said Kingsley. 'Here's the regime that gives trouble.'

Rows of letters and numbers materialized in the empty air – velocities, payloads, accelerations, transit times – Morgan absorbed them at a glance. The globe of the Earth, with its circles of longitude and latitude, hovered just above the carpet; and rising from it, to little more than the height of a man, was the luminous thread that marked the position of the orbital tower.

'Five hundred times normal speed; lateral scale exaggeration fifty. Here we go.'

Some invisible force had started to pluck at the line of light, drawing it away from the vertical. The disturbance was moving upwards as it mimicked, *via* the computer's millions of calculations a second, the ascent of a payload through the Earth's gravitational field.

'What's the displacement?' asked Morgan, as his eyes strained to follow the details of the simulation.

'Now about two hundred metres. It gets to three before—'

The thread snapped. In the leisurely slow-motion that represented real speeds of thousands of kilometres an hour, the two segments of the severed tower began to curl away from each other – one bending back to Earth, the other whipping upwards to space . . . But Morgan was no longer fully conscious of this imaginary disaster, existing only in the mind of the computer; superimposed upon it now was the reality that had haunted him for years.

He had seen that two-century-old film at least fifty times, and there were sections that he had examined frame by frame, until he knew every detail by heart. It was, after all, the most expensive movie footage ever shot, at least in peacetime. It had cost the State of Washington several million dollars a minute.

There stood the slim (too slim!) and graceful bridge, spanning the canyon. It bore no traffic, but a single car had been abandoned midway by its driver. And no wonder, for the bridge was behaving as none before in the whole history of engineering.

It seemed impossible that thousands of tons of metal could perform such an aerial ballet; one could more easily believe that the bridge was made of rubber than of steel. Vast, slow undulations, metres in amplitude, were sweeping along the entire width of the span, so that the roadway suspended between the piers twisted back and forth like an angry snake. The wind blowing down the canyon was sounding a note far too low for any human ears to detect, as it hit the natural frequency of the beautiful, doomed structure. For hours, the torsional vibrations had been building up, but no one knew when the end would come. Already, the protracted death-throes were a testimonial that the unlucky designers could well have foregone.

Suddenly, the supporting cables snapped, flailing upwards like murderous steel whips. Twisting and turning, the roadway pitched into the river, fragments of the structure flying in all directions.

Even when projected at normal speed, the final cataclysm looked as if shot in slow motion; the scale of the disaster was so large that the human mind had no basis of comparison. In reality, it lasted perhaps five seconds; at the end of that time, the Tacoma Narrows Bridge had earned an inexpungable place in the history of engineering. Two hundred years later there was a photograph of its last moments on the wall of Morgan's office, bearing the caption 'One of our less successful products'.

To Morgan that was no joke, but a permanent reminder that the unexpected could always strike from ambush. When the Gibraltar Bridge was being designed, he had gone carefully through von Kármán's classic analysis of the Tacoma Narrows disaster, learning all he could from one of the most expensive mistakes of the past. There had been no serious vibrational problems even in the worst gales that had come roaring in from the Atlantic, though the roadway had moved a hundred metres from the centre line – precisely as calculated.

But the space elevator was such a leap forward into the unknown that some unpleasant surprises were a virtual certainty. Wind forces on the atmospheric section were easy to estimate, but it was also necessary to take into account the vibrations induced by the stopping and starting of the payloads – and even, on so enormous a structure, by the tidal effects of the sun and moon. And not only individually, but acting all together; with, perhaps, an occasional earthquake to complicate the picture, in the so-called 'worst case' analysis.

'All the simulations, in this tons-of-payload-per-hour regime, give the same result. The vibrations build up until there's a fracture at around five hundred kilometres. We'll have to increase the damping – drastically.'

'I was afraid of that. How much do we need?'

'Another ten megatons.'

Morgan could take some gloomy satisfaction from the figure. That was very close to the guess he had made, using his engineer's intuition and the mysterious resources of his subconscious. Now the computer had confirmed it; they would have to increase the 'anchor' mass in orbit by ten million tons.

Even by terrestrial earth-moving standards, such a mass was hardly trivial; it was equivalent to a sphere of rock about two hundred metres across. Morgan had a sudden image of Yakkagala, as he had last seen it, looming against the Taprobanean sky. Imagine lifting *that* forty thousand kilometres into space! Fortunately, it might not be necessary; there were at least two alternatives.

Morgan always let his subordinates do their thinking for themselves; it was the only way to establish responsibility, it took much of the load off him – and, on many occasions, his staff had arrived at solutions he might have overlooked.

'What do you suggest, Warren?' he asked quietly.

'We *could* use one of the lunar freight launchers, and shoot up ten megatons of moon-rock. It would be a long and expensive job, and we'd still need a large space-based operation to catch the material and steer it into final orbit. There would also be a psychological problem—'

'Yes, I can appreciate that; we don't want another San Luiz Domingo—'

San Luiz had been the – fortunately small – South American village that had received a stray cargo of processed lunar metal intended for a low-orbit space station. The terminal guidance had failed, resulting in the first man-made meteor crater – and two hundred and fifty deaths. Ever since that, the population of planet Earth had been very sensitive on the subject of celestial target practice.

'A much better answer is to catch an asteroid; we're running a search for those with suitable orbits, and have found three promising candidates. What we really want is a carbonaceous one – then we can use it for raw material when we set up the processing plant. Killing two birds with one stone.'

'A rather large stone, but that's probably the best idea. Forget the lunar launcher – a million 10-ton shots would tie it up for years, and some of them would be bound to go astray. If you can't find a large enough asteroid, we can still send the extra mass up by the elevator itself – though I hate wasting all that energy if it can be avoided.'

'It may be the cheapest way. With the efficiency of the latest fusion plants, it will take only twenty dollars' worth of electricity to lift a ton up to orbit.'

'Are you sure of that figure?'

'It's a firm quotation from Central Power.'

Morgan was silent for a few minutes. Then he said: 'The aerospace engineers really are going to hate me.' Almost as much, he added to himself, as the Venerable Parakarma.

No – that was not fair. Hate was an emotion no longer possible to a true follower of the Doctrine. What he had seen in the eyes of ex-Doctor Choam Goldberg was merely implacable opposition; but that could be equally dangerous.

21 Judgement

One of Paul Sarath's more annoying specialities was the sudden call, gleeful or gloomy as the case might be, which invariably opened with the words: 'Have you heard the news?' Though Rajasinghe had often been tempted to give the general-purpose answer: 'Yes – I'm not at all surprised,' he had never had the heart to rob Paul of his simple pleasure.

'What is it *this* time?' he answered, without much enthusiasm.

'Maxine's on Global Two, talking to Senator Collins. I think our friend Morgan is in trouble. Call you back.'

Paul's excited image faded from the screen, to be replaced a few seconds later by Maxine Duval's as Rajasinghe switched to the main news channel. She was sitting in her familiar studio, talking to the Chairman of the Terran Construction Corporation, who seemed to be in a mood of barely suppressed indignation – probably synthetic.

'—Senator Collins, now that the World Court ruling has been given—'

Rajasinghe shunted the entire programme to RECORD, with a

muttered: 'I thought that wasn't until Friday.' As he turned off the sound and activated his private link with ARISTOTLE, he exclaimed, 'My God, it *is* Friday!'

As always, Ari was on line at once.

'Good morning, Raja. What can I do for you?'

That beautiful, dispassionate voice, untouched by human glottis, had never changed in the forty years that he had known it. Decades – perhaps centuries – after he was dead, it would be talking to other men just as it had spoken to him. (For that matter, how many conversations was it having at this very moment?) Once, this knowledge had depressed Rajasinghe; now it no longer mattered. He did not envy ARISTOTLE's immortality.

'Good morning, Ari, I'd like today's World Court ruling on the case Astroengineering Corporation *versus* the Sri Kanda Vihara. The summary will do – let me have the full printout later.'

'Decision 1. Lease of temple site confirmed in perpetuity under Taprobanean and World Law, as codified 2085. Unanimous ruling.

'Decision 2. The construction of the proposed Orbital Tower with its attendant noise, vibration and impact upon a site of great historic and cultural importance would constitute a private nuisance, meriting an injunction under the Law of Torts. At this stage, public interest not of sufficient merit to affect the issue. Ruling 4 to 2, one abstention.'

'Thank you, Ari – cancel printout – I won't need it. Goodbye.'

Well, that was that, just as he had expected. Yet he did not know whether to be relieved or disappointed.

Rooted as he was in the past, he was glad that the old traditions were cherished and protected. If one thing had been learned from the bloody history of mankind, it was that only individual human beings mattered: however eccentric their beliefs might be, they must be safeguarded, so long as they did not conflict with wider but equally legitimate interests. What was it that the old poet had said? 'There is no such thing as the State.' Perhaps that was going a little too far; but it was better than the other extreme.

At the same time, Rajasinghe felt a mild sense of regret. He had half convinced himself (was this merely cooperating with the inevitable?) that Morgan's fantastic enterprise might be just what was needed to prevent Taprobane (and perhaps the whole world, though *that* was no longer his responsibility) from sinking into a comfortable, self-satisfied decline. Now the Court had closed that particular avenue, at least for many years.

He wondered what Maxine would have to say on the subject, and switched over to delayed playback. On Global Two, the News analysis channel (sometimes referred to as the Land of Talking Heads), Senator Collins was still gathering momentum.

'—undoubtedly exceeding his authority and using the resources of his division on projects which did not concern it.'

'But surely, Senator, aren't you being somewhat legalistic? As I understand it, hyperfilament was developed for *construction* purposes, especially bridges. And isn't this a kind of bridge? I've heard Dr Morgan use that analogy, though he also calls it a tower.'

'*You're* being legalistic now, Maxine. I prefer the name "space elevator". And you're quite wrong about hyperfilament. It's the result of two hundred years of aerospace research. The fact that the final breakthrough came in the *Land* Division of my – ah – organization is irrelevant, though naturally I'm proud that my scientists were involved.'

'You consider that the whole project should be handed over to the Space Division?'

'What project? This is merely a design study – one of hundreds that are always going on in TCC. I never hear about a fraction of them, and I don't want to – until they reach the stage when some major decision has to be made.'

'Which is not the case here?'

'Definitely not. My space transportation experts say that they can handle all projected traffic increases – at least for the foreseeable future.'

'Meaning precisely?'

'Another twenty years.'

'And what happens then? The Tower will take that long to build, according to Dr Morgan. Suppose it isn't ready in time?'

'Then we'll have something else. My staff is looking into *all* the possibilities, and it's by no means certain that the space elevator is the right answer.'

'The idea, though, is fundamentally sound?'

'It appears to be, though further studies are required.'

'Then surely you should be grateful to Dr Morgan for his initial work.'

'I have the utmost respect for Dr Morgan. He is one of the most brilliant engineers in my organization – if not in the world.'

'I don't think, Senator, that quite answers my question.'

'Very well; I *am* grateful to Dr Morgan for bringing this matter to our notice. But I do not approve of the way in which he did it. If I may be blunt, he tried to force my hand.'

'How?'

'By going outside my organization – *his* organization – and thus showing a lack of loyalty. As a result of his manoeuvrings, there has been an adverse World Court decision, which inevitably has provoked much unfavourable comment. In the circumstances, I have had no choice but to request – with the utmost regret – that he tender his resignation.'

'Thank you, Senator Collins. As always, it's been a pleasure talking to you.'

'You sweet liar,' said Rajasinghe, as he switched off and took the call that had been flashing for the last minute.

'Did you get it all?' asked Professor Sarath. 'So *that's* the end of Dr Vannevar Morgan.'

Rajasinghe looked thoughtfully at his old friend for a few seconds.

'You were always fond of jumping to conclusions, Paul. How much would you care to bet?'

part three
The Bell

22 Apostate

Driven to despair by his fruitless attempts to understand the Universe, the sage Devadasa finally announced in exasperation:

ALL STATEMENTS THAT CONTAIN THE WORD GOD ARE FALSE.

Instantly, his least-favourite disciple Somasiri replied: 'The sentence I am now speaking contains the word God. I fail to see, Oh Noble Master, how *that* simple statement can be false.'

Devadasa considered the matter for several Poyas. Then he answered, this time with apparent satisfaction:

ONLY STATEMENTS THAT DO *NOT* CONTAIN THE WORD GOD CAN BE TRUE.

After a pause barely sufficient for a starving mongoose to swallow a millet seed, Somasiri replied: 'If this statement applies to itself, Oh Venerable One, it cannot be true, because it contains the word God. But if it is *not* true—'

At this point, Devadasa broke his begging bowl upon Somasiri's head, and should therefore be honoured as the true founder of Zen.

(From a fragment of the *Culavamsa*, as yet undiscovered)

In the late afternoon, when the stairway was no longer blasted by the full fury of the sun, the Venerable Parakarma began his descent. By nightfall he would reach the highest of the pilgrim rest-houses;

and by the following day he would have returned to the world of men.

The Maha Thero had given neither advice nor discouragement, and if he was grieved by his colleague's departure he had shown no sign. He had merely intoned, 'All things are impermanent', clasped his hands, and given his blessing.

The Venerable Parakarma, who had once been Dr Choam Goldberg, and might be so again, would have had great difficulty in explaining all his motives. 'Right action' was easy to say; it was not easy to discover.

At the Sri Kanda Maha Vihara he had found peace of mind – but that was not enough. With his scientific training, he was no longer content to accept the Order's ambiguous attitude towards God; such indifference had come at last to seem worse than outright denial.

If such a thing as a rabbinical gene could exist, Dr Goldberg possessed it. Like many before him, Goldberg-Parakarma had sought God through mathematics, undiscouraged even by the bombshell that Kurt Gödel, with the discovery of undecidable propositions, had exploded early in the twentieth century. He could not understand how anyone could contemplate the dynamic asymmetry of Euler's profound, yet beautifully simple,

$$e^{\pi i} + 1 = 0$$

without wondering if the universe was the creation of some vast intelligence.

Having first made his name with a new cosmological theory that had survived almost ten years before being refuted, Goldberg had been widely acclaimed as another Einstein or N'goya. In an age of ultra-specialization, he had also managed to make notable advances in aero- and hydrodynamics – long regarded as dead subjects, incapable of further surprises.

Then, at the height of his powers, he had experienced a religious conversion not unlike Pascal's, though without so many morbid undertones. For the next decade, he had been content to lose himself in saffron anonymity, focusing his brilliant mind upon questions of doctrine and philosophy. He did not regret the interlude, and he was not even sure that he had abandoned the Order; one day, perhaps, this great stairway would see him again. But his God-given talents were reasserting themselves; there was massive work to be done, and he needed tools that could not be found on Sri Kanda – or even, for that matter, on Earth itself.

He felt little hostility, now, towards Vannevar Morgan. However inadvertently, the engineer had ignited the spark; in his blundering way, he too was an agent of God. Yet at all costs the temple must be protected. Whether or not the Wheel of Fate ever returned him to its tranquillity, Parakarma was implacably resolved upon that.

And so, like a new Moses bringing down from the mountain laws that would change the destinies of men, the Venerable Parakarma descended to the world he had once renounced. He was blind to the beauties of land and sky that were all around him; for they were utterly trivial compared to those that he alone could see, in the armies of equations that were marching through his mind.

23 Moondozer

'Your trouble, Dr Morgan,' said the man in the wheelchair, 'is that you're on the wrong planet.'

'I can't help thinking,' retorted Morgan, looking pointedly at his visitor's life-support system, 'that much the same may be said of you.'

The Vice-President (Investments) of Narodny Mars gave an appreciative chuckle.

'At least I'm here only for a week – then it's back to the Moon, and a civilized gravity. Oh, I can walk if I really have to: but I prefer otherwise.'

'If I may ask, why do you come to Earth at all?'

'I do so as little as possible, but sometimes one has to be on the spot. Contrary to general belief, you can't do *everything* by remotes. I'm sure you are aware of that.'

Morgan nodded; it was true enough. He thought of all the times when the texture of some material, the feel of rock or soil underfoot, the smell of a jungle, the sting of spray upon his face, had played a vital rôle in one of his projects. Some day, perhaps even these sensations could be transferred by electronics – indeed, it had already been done so crudely, on an experimental basis, and at enormous cost. But there was no substitute for reality; one should beware of imitations.

'If you've visited Earth especially to meet me,' Morgan replied, 'I appreciate the honour. But if you're offering me a job on Mars, you're wasting your time. I'm enjoying my retirement, meeting friends and relatives I haven't seen for years, and I've no intention of starting a new career.'

'I find that surprising; after all, you're only fifty-two. How do you propose to occupy your time?'

'Easily. I could spend the rest of my life on any one of a dozen projects. The ancient engineers – the Romans, the Greeks, the Incas – they've always fascinated me, and I've never had time to study them. I've been asked to write and deliver a Global University course on design science. There's a text-book I'm commissioned to write on advanced structures. I want to develop some ideas about the use of active elements to correct dynamic loads – winds, earthquakes, and so forth – I'm still consultant for General Tectonics. And I'm preparing a report on the administration of TCC.'

'At whose request? Not, I take it, Senator Collins'?'

'No,' said Morgan, with a grim smile. 'I thought it would be – useful. And it helps to relieve my feelings.'

'I'm sure of it. But all these activities aren't really *creative*. Sooner or later they'll pall – like this beautiful Norwegian scenery. You'll grow tired of looking at lakes and fir trees, just as you'll grow tired of writing and talking. You are the sort of man who will never be really happy, Dr Morgan, unless you are shaping your universe.'

Morgan did not reply. The prognosis was much too accurate for comfort.

'I suspect that you agree with me. What would you say if I told you that my Bank was seriously interested in the space elevator project?'

'I'd be sceptical. When I approached them, they said it was a fine idea, but they couldn't put any money into it at this stage. All available funds were needed for the development of Mars. It's the old story – we'll be glad to help you, when you don't need any help.'

'*That* was a year ago; now there have been some second thoughts. We'd like you to build the space elevator – but not on Earth. *On Mars*. Are you interested?'

'I might be. Go on.'

'Look at the advantages. Only a third of the gravity, so the forces involved are correspondingly smaller. The synchronous orbit is also closer – less than half the altitude here. So at the very start, the engineering problems are enormously reduced. Our people estimate that the Mars system would cost less than a tenth of the Terran one.'

'That's quite possible, though I'd have to check it.'

'And *that's* just the beginning. We have some fierce gales on Mars, despite our thin atmosphere – but mountains that get completely above them. Your Sri Kanda is only five kilometres high. We have Mons Pavonis – twenty-one kilometres, and exactly on the equator! Better still, there are no Martian monks with long-term leases sitting on the summit . . . And there's one other reason why Mars might have been designed for a space elevator. Deimos is only three thousand kilometres above the stationary orbit. So we already have a couple of million megatons sitting in exactly the right place for the anchor.'

'That will present some interesting problems in synchronization, but I see what you mean. I'd like to meet the people who worked all this out.'

'You can't, in real time. They're all on Mars. You'll have to go there.'

'I'm tempted, but I still have a few other questions.'

'Go ahead.'

'Earth *must* have the elevator, for all the reasons you doubtless know. But it seems to me that Mars could manage without it. You have only a fraction of our space traffic, and a much smaller projected growth rate. Frankly, it doesn't make a great deal of sense to me.'

'I was wondering when you'd ask.'

'Well, I'm asking.'

'Have you heard of Project Eos?'

'I don't think so.'

'Eos – Greek for Dawn – the plan to rejuvenate Mars.'

'Oh, of course I know about that. It involves melting the polar caps, doesn't it?'

'Exactly. If we could thaw out all that water and CO_2 ice, several things would happen. The atmospheric density would increase until men could work in the open without spacesuits; at a later stage, the air might even be made breathable. There would be running water, small seas – and, above all, *vegetation* – the beginnings of a carefully planned biota. In a couple of centuries, Mars could be another Garden of Eden. It's the only planet in the solar system we can transform with known technology: Venus may always be too hot.'

'And where does the elevator come into this?'

'We have to lift several million tons of equipment into orbit. The only practical way to heat up Mars is by solar mirrors, hundreds of kilometres across. And we'll need them *permanently* – first to melt the ice-caps, and later to maintain a comfortable temperature.'

'Couldn't you get all this material from your asteroid mines?'

'Some of it, of course. But the best mirrors for the job are made of sodium, and that's rare in space. We'll have to get it from the Tharsis salt-beds – right by the foothills of Pavonis, luckily enough.'

'And how long will all this take?'

'If there are no problems, the first stage could be complete in fifty years. Maybe by your hundredth birthday, which the actuaries say you have a thirty-nine per cent chance of seeing.'

Morgan laughed.

'I admire people who do a thorough job of research.'

'We wouldn't survive on Mars unless we paid attention to detail.'

'Well, I'm favourably impressed, though I still have a great many reservations. The financing, for example—'

'That's my job, Dr Morgan. I'm the banker. *You're* the engineer.'

'Correct, but you seem to know a good deal about engineering, and I've had to learn a lot of economics – often the hard way. Before I'd even consider getting involved in such a project, I should want a detailed budget breakdown—'

'Which can be provided—'

'—and *that* would just be the start. You may not realize that there's still a vast amount of research involved in half-a-dozen fields – mass production of the hyperfilament material, stability and control problems – I could go on all night.'

'That won't be necessary; our engineers have read all your reports. What they are proposing is a small-scale experiment that will settle many of the technical problems, and prove that the principle is sound—'

'There's no doubt about *that*.'

'I agree, but it's amazing what a difference a little practical demonstration can make. So this is what we would like you to do. Design the minimum possible system – just a wire with a payload of a few kilogrammes. Lower it from synchronous orbit to Earth – yes, *Earth*. If it works here, it will be easy on Mars. Then run something up it just to show that rockets are obsolete. The experiment will be relatively cheap, it will provide essential information and basic training – and, from our point of view, it will save years of argument. We can go to the Government of Earth, the Solar Fund, the other interplanetary banks – and just point to the demonstration.'

'You really *have* worked all this out. When would you like my answer?'

'To be honest, in about five seconds. But obviously, there's nothing urgent about the matter. Take as long as seems reasonable.'

'Very well. Give me your design studies, cost analyses, and all the other material you have. Once I've been through them, I'll let you have my decision in – oh, a week at the most.'

'Thank you. Here's my number. You can get me at any time.'

Morgan slipped the banker's ident card into the memory slot of his communicator and checked the ENTRY CONFIRMED on the visual display. Before he had returned the card, he had already made up his mind.

Unless there was a fundamental flaw in the Martian analysis – and he would bet a large sum that it was sound – his retirement was over. He had often noted, with some amusement, that whereas he frequently thought long and hard over relatively trivial decisions, he had never hesitated for a moment at the major turning-points of his career. He had always known what to do, and had seldom been wrong.

And yet, at this stage in the game, it was better not to invest too much intellectual or emotional capital into a project that might still come to nothing. After the banker had rolled out on the first stage of his journey back to Port Tranquillity, *via* Oslo and Gagarin, Morgan found it impossible to settle down to any of the activities he had planned for the long northern evening; his mind was in a turmoil, scanning the whole spectrum of suddenly changed futures.

After a few minutes of restless pacing, he sat down at his desk and began to list priorities in a kind of reverse order, starting with the commitments he could most easily shed. Before long, however, he found it impossible to concentrate on such routine matters. Far down in the depths of his mind something was nagging at him, trying to attract his attention. When he tried to focus upon it it promptly eluded him, like a familiar but momentarily forgotten word.

With a sigh of frustration Morgan pushed himself away from the desk, and walked out on to the verandah running along the western face of the hotel. Though it was very cold, the air was quite still and the sub-zero temperature was more of a stimulus than a discomfort. The sky was a blaze of stars, and a yellow crescent moon was sinking down towards its reflection in the fjord, whose surface was so dark and motionless that it might have been a sheet of polished ebony.

Thirty years ago he had stood at almost this same spot, with a girl whose very appearance he could no longer clearly recall. They had both been celebrating their first degrees, and that had been really all they had in common. It had not been a serious affair; they were young, and enjoyed each other's company – and that had been enough. Yet somehow that fading memory had brought him back to Trollshavn Fjord at this crucial moment of his life. What would the young student of twenty-two have thought, could he have known how his footsteps would lead him back to this place of remembered pleasures, three decades in his future?

There was scarcely a trace of nostalgia or self-pity in Morgan's reverie – only a kind of wistful amusement. He had never for an instant regretted the fact that he and Ingrid had separated amicably without even considering the usual one-year trial contract. She had gone on to make three other men moderately miserable before finding herself a job with the Lunar Commission, and Morgan had lost track of her. Perhaps, even now, she was up there on that shining crescent, whose colour almost matched her golden hair.

So much for the past. Morgan turned his thoughts to the future. Where was Mars? He was ashamed to admit that he did not even know if it was visible tonight. As he ran his eye along the path of the ecliptic, from the Moon to the dazzling beacon of Venus and beyond, he saw nothing in all that jewelled profusion that he could certainly identify with the red planet. It was exciting to think that in the not-too-distant future he – who had never even travelled beyond lunar orbit! – might be looking with his own eyes at those magnificent crimson landscapes, and watching the tiny moons pass swiftly through their phases.

In that moment the dream collapsed. Morgan stood for a moment paralysed, then dashed back into the hotel, forgetting the splendour of the night.

There was no general purpose console in his room, so he had to go down to the lobby to get the information he required. As luck would have it, the cubicle was occupied by an old lady who took so long to find what she wanted that Morgan almost pounded on the door. But at last the sluggard left with a mumbled apology, and Morgan was face to face with the accumulated art and knowledge of all mankind.

In his student days, he had won several retrieval championships, racing against the clock while digging out obscure items of information on lists prepared by ingeniously sadistic judges. ('What was the rainfall in the capital of the world's smallest national state on the day when the second largest number of home runs was scored in college baseball?' was one that he recalled with particular affection.) His skill had improved with years, and this was a perfectly straightforward question. The display came up in thirty seconds, in far more detail than he really needed.

Morgan studied the screen for a minute, then shook his head in baffled amazement.

'They couldn't *possibly* have overlooked that!' he muttered. 'But what can they do about it?'

Morgan pressed the HARD COPY button, and carried the thin sheet of paper back to his room for more detailed study. The problem was so stunningly, appallingly obvious that he wondered if he had overlooked some equally obvious solution and would be making a fool of himself if he raised the matter. Yet there was no possible escape...

He looked at his watch: already after midnight. But this was something he had to settle at once.

To Morgan's relief, the banker had not pressed his DON'T DISTURB button. He replied immediately, sounding a little surprised.

'I hope I didn't wake you up,' said Morgan, not very sincerely.

'No – we're just about to land at Gagarin. What's the problem?'

'About ten teratons, moving at two kilometres a second. The inner moon, Phobos. It's a cosmic bulldozer, going past the elevator every eleven hours. I've not worked out the exact probabilities, but a collision is inevitable every few days.'

There was silence for a long time from the other end of the circuit. Then the banker said: '*I* could have thought of that. So obviously, someone has the answer. Perhaps we'll have to move Phobos.'

'Impossible: the mass is far too great.'

'I'll have to call Mars. The time delay's twelve minutes at the moment. I should have some sort of answer within the hour.'

I hope so, Morgan told himself. And it had better be good... that is, if I *really* want this job.

24 The Finger of God

Dendrobium macarthiae usually flowered with the coming of the south-west monsoon, but this year it was early. As Johan Raja-singhe stood in his orchid house, admiring the intricate violet-pink blossoms, he remembered that last season he had been trapped by a torrential downpour for half-an-hour while examining the first blooms.

He looked anxiously at the sky; no, there was little danger of rain. It was a beautiful day, with thin, high bands of cloud moder-ating the fierce sunlight. But *that* was odd . . .

Rajasinghe had never seen anything quite like it before. Almost vertically overhead, the parallel lanes of cloud were broken by a circular disturbance. It appeared to be a tiny cyclonic storm, only a few kilometres across, but it reminded Rajasinghe of something completely different – a knot-hole breaking through the grain in a smoothly planed board. He abandoned his beloved orchids and stepped outside to get a better view of the phenomenon. Now he could see that the small whirlwind was moving slowly across the sky, the track of its passage clearly marked by the distortion of the cloud lanes.

One could easily imagine that the finger of God was reaching down from heaven, tracing a furrow through the clouds. Even Rajasinghe, who understood the basics of weather control, had no idea that such precision was now possible; but he could take a modest pride in the fact that, almost forty years ago, he had played his part in its achievement.

It had not been easy to persuade the surviving superpowers to relinquish their orbital fortresses and hand them over to the Global Weather Authority, in what was – if the metaphor could be stretched that far – the last and most dramatic example of beating swords into ploughshares. Now the lasers that had once threatened mankind directed their beams into carefully selected portions of the atmosphere, or on to heat-absorbing target areas in remote regions of the earth. The energy they contained was trifling, com-pared to that of the smallest storm; but so is the energy of the falling stone that triggers an avalanche, or the single neutron that starts a chain reaction.

Beyond that, Rajasinghe knew nothing of the technical details, except that they involved networks of monitoring satellites, and computers that held within their electronic brains a complete model of the earth's atmosphere, land surfaces and seas. He felt rather like an awestruck savage, gaping at the wonders of some advanced technology, as he watched the little cyclone move purposefully into the west, until it disappeared below the graceful line of palms just inside the ramparts of the Pleasure Gardens.

Then he glanced up at the invisible engineers and scientists, racing round the world in their man-made heavens.

'Very impressive,' he said. 'But I hope you know *exactly* what you're doing.'

25 Orbital Roulette

'I should have guessed,' said the banker ruefully, 'that it would have been in one of those technical appendices that I never looked at. And now you've seen the whole report, I'd like to know the answer. You've had *me* worrying, ever since you raised the problem.'

'It's brilliantly obvious,' Morgan answered, 'and I should have thought of it myself.'

And I would have done – eventually – he told himself, with a fair degree of confidence. In his mind's eye he saw again those computer simulations of the whole immense structure, twanging like a cosmic violin string, as the hours-long vibrations raced from earth to orbit and were reflected back again. And superimposed on that he replayed from memory, for the hundredth time, the scratched movie of the dancing bridge. *There* were all the clues he needed.

'Phobos sweeps past the tower every eleven hours and ten

minutes, but luckily it isn't moving in exactly the same plane – or we'd have a collision *every* time it went round. It misses on most revolutions and the danger times are exactly predictable – to a thousandth of a second, if desired. Now the elevator, like any piece of engineering, isn't a completely rigid structure. It has natural vibration periods, which can be calculated almost as accurately as planetary orbits. So what your engineers propose to do is to *tune* the elevator, so that its normal oscillations – which can't be avoided anyway – always keep it clear of Phobos. Every time the satellite passes by the structure, it isn't there – it's sidestepped the danger zone by a few kilometres.'

There was a long pause from the other end of the circuit.

'I shouldn't say this,' said the Martian at last, 'but my hair is standing on end.'

Morgan laughed. 'Put as bluntly as this, it does sound like – what was it called – Russian Roulette. But remember, we're dealing with exactly predictable movements. We always know where Phobos will be, and we can control the displacement of the tower, simply by the way we schedule traffic along it.'

'Simply,' thought Morgan, was hardly the right word, but anyone could see that it was possible. And then an analogy flashed into his mind that was so perfect, yet so incongruous, that he almost burst into laughter. No – it would *not* be a good idea to use it on the banker.

Once again, he was back at the Tacoma Narrows Bridge, but this time in a world of fantasy. There was a ship that had to sail beneath it, on a perfectly regular schedule. Unfortunately, the mast was a metre too tall.

No problem. Just before it was due to arrive, a few heavy trucks would be sent racing across the bridge, at intervals carefully calculated to match its resonant frequency. A gentle wave would sweep along the roadway from pier to pier, the crest timed to coincide with the arrival of the ship. And so the masthead would glide beneath, with whole centimetres to spare . . . On a scale thousands of times larger, this was how Phobos would miss the structure towering out into space from Mons Pavonis.

'I'm glad to have your assurance,' said the banker, 'but I think

I'd do a private check on the position of Phobos before I take a trip.'

'Then you'll be surprised to know that some of your bright young people – they're certainly bright, and I'm assuming they're young because of their sheer technical effrontery – want to use the critical periods as a tourist attraction. They think they could charge premium rates for views of Phobos sailing past at arm's length at a couple of thousand kilometres an hour. Quite a spectacle, wouldn't you agree?'

'I prefer to imagine it, but they may be right. Anyway, I'm relieved to hear that there *is* a solution. I'm also happy to note that you approve of our engineering talent. Does this mean we can expect a decision soon?'

'You can have it now,' said Morgan. 'When can we start work?'

26 The Night before Vesak

It was still, after twenty-seven centuries, the most revered day of the Taprobanean calendar. On the May full moon, according to legend, the Buddha had been born, had achieved enlightenment, and had died. Though to most people Vesak now meant no more than that other great annual holiday, Christmas, it was still a time for meditation and tranquillity.

For many years, Monsoon Control had guaranteed that there would be no rain on the nights of Vesak plus and minus one. And for almost as long, Rajasinghe had gone to the Royal City two days before the full moon, on a pilgrimage that annually refreshed his spirit. He avoided Vesak itself; on that day Ranapura was too crowded with visitors, some of whom would be guaranteed to recognize him, and disturb his solitude.

Only the sharpest eye could have noticed that the huge, yellow moon lifting above the bell-shaped domes of the ancient *dagobas* was not yet a perfect circle. The light it gave was so intense that only a few of the most brilliant satellites and stars were visible in the cloudless sky. And there was not a breath of wind.

Twice, it was said, Kalidasa had stopped on this road, when he had left Ranapura forever. The first halt was at the tomb of Hanuman, the loved companion of his boyhood; and the second was at the shrine of the Dying Buddha. Rajasinghe had often wondered what solace the haunted king had gathered – perhaps at this very spot, for it was the best point from which to view the immense figure carved from the solid rock. The reclining shape was so perfectly proportioned that one had to walk right up to it before its real size could be appreciated. From a distance it was impossible to realize that the pillow upon which the Buddha rested his head was itself higher than a man.

Though Rajasinghe had seen much of the world, he knew no other spot so full of peace. Sometimes he felt that he could sit here forever, beneath the blazing moon, wholly unconcerned with all the cares and turmoil of life. He had never tried to probe too deeply into the magic of the Shrine, for fear that he would destroy it, but some of its elements were obvious enough. The very posture of the Enlightened One, resting at last with closed eyes after a long and noble life, radiated serenity. The sweeping lines of the robe were extraordinarily soothing and restful to contemplate; they appeared to flow from the rock, to form waves of frozen stone. And, like the waves of the sea, the natural rhythm of their curves appealed to instincts of which the rational mind knew nothing.

In timeless moments such as this, alone with the Buddha and the almost full moon, Rajasinghe felt that he could understand at last the meaning of Nirvana – that state which can be defined only by negatives. Such emotions as anger, desire, greed no longer possessed any power; indeed, they were barely conceivable. Even the sense of personal identity seemed about to fade away, like a mist before the morning sun.

It could not last, of course. Presently he became aware of the buzzing of insects, the distant barking of dogs, the cold hardness of the stone upon which he was sitting. Tranquillity was not a state of mind which could be sustained for long. With a sigh, Rajasinghe got to his feet and began the walk back to his car, parked a hundred metres outside the temple grounds.

He was just entering the vehicle when he noticed the small white patch, so clearly defined that it might have been painted on the sky, rising over the trees to the west. It was the most peculiar cloud that Rajasinghe had ever seen – a perfectly symmetrical ellipsoid, so sharp-edged that it appeared almost solid. He wondered if someone was flying an airship through the skies of Taprobane; but he could see no fins, and there was no sound of engines.

Then, for a fleeting moment, he had a far wilder fancy. *The Starholmers had arrived at last . . .*

But that, of course, was absurd. Even if they had managed to outrun their own radio signals, they could hardly have traversed the whole solar system – *and* descended into the skies of Earth! – without triggering all the traffic radars in existence. The news would have broken hours ago.

Rather to his surprise, Rajasinghe felt a mild sense of disappointment. And now, as the apparition came closer, he could see that it undoubtedly was a cloud, because it was getting slightly frayed around the edges. Its speed was impressive; it seemed to be driven by a private gale, of which there was still no trace here at ground level.

So the scientists of Monsoon Control were at it again, testing their mastery of the winds. What, Rajasinghe wondered, would they think of next?

27 Ashoka Station

How tiny the island looked from this altitude! Thirty-six thousand kilometres below, straddling the equator. Taprobane appeared not much bigger than the moon. The entire country seemed too small a target to hit; yet he was aiming for an area at its centre about the size of a tennis court.

Even now, Morgan was not completely certain of his motives. For the purpose of this demonstration, he could just as easily have operated from Kinte Station and targeted Kilimanjaro or Mount Kenya. The fact that Kinte was at one of the most unstable points along the entire stationary orbit, and was always jockeying to remain over Central Africa, would not have mattered for the few days the experiment would last. For a while he had been tempted to aim at Chimborazo; the Americans had even offered, at considerable expense, to move Columbus Station to its precise longitude. But in the end, despite this encouragement, he had returned to his original objective – Sri Kanda.

It was fortunate for Morgan that, in this age of computer-assisted decisions, even a World Court ruling could be obtained in a matter of weeks. The *vihara*, of course, had protested. Morgan had argued that a brief scientific experiment, conducted on grounds outside the temple premises, and resulting in no noise, pollution or other form of interference, could not possibly constitute a tort. If he was prevented from carrying it out, all his earlier work would be jeopardized, he would have no way of checking his calculations, and a project vital to the Republic of Mars would receive a severe setback.

It was a very plausible argument, and Morgan had believed most of it himself. So had the judges, by five to two. Though they were not supposed to be influenced by such matters, mentioning the litigious Martians was a clever move. The RoM already had three complicated cases in progress, and the Court was slightly tired of establishing precedents in interplanetary law.

But Morgan knew, in the coldly analytical part of his mind, that his action was not dictated by logic alone. He was not a man who accepted defeat gracefully; the gesture of defiance gave him a certain satisfaction. And yet – at a still deeper level – he rejected this petty motivation; such a schoolboy gesture was unworthy of him. What he was *really* doing was building up his self-assurance, and re-affirming his belief in ultimate success. Though he did not know how, or when, he was proclaiming to the world – and to the stubborn monks within their ancient walls – 'I shall return'.

Ashoka Station controlled virtually all communications, meteorology, environmental monitoring and space traffic in the Hindu Cathay region. If it ever ceased to function, a billion lives would be threatened with disaster and, if its services were not quickly

119

restored, death. No wonder that Ashoka had two completely independent sub-satellites, Bhaba and Sarabhai, a hundred kilometres away. Even if some unthinkable catastrophe destroyed all three stations, Kinte and Imhotep to the west or Confucius to the east could take over on an emergency basis. The human race had learned, from harsh experience, not to put all its eggs in one basket.

There were no tourists, vacationers or transit passengers here, so far from Earth; they did their business and sightseeing only a few thousand kilometres out, and left the high geosynchronous orbit to the scientists and engineers – not one of whom had ever visited Ashoka on so unusual a mission, or with such unique equipment.

The key to Operation Gossamer now floated in one of the station's medium-sized docking chambers, awaiting the final checkout before launch. There was nothing very spectacular about it, and its appearance gave no hint of the man-years and the millions that had gone into its development.

The dull grey cone, four metres long and two metres across the base, appeared to be made of solid metal; it required a close examination to reveal the tightly-wound fibre covering the entire surface. Indeed, apart from an internal core, and the strips of plastic interleaving that separated the hundreds of layers, the cone was made of nothing but a tapering hyperfilament thread – forty thousand kilometres of it.

Two obsolete and totally different technologies had been revived for the construction of that unimpressive grey cone. Three hundred years ago, submarine telegraphs had started to operate across the ocean beds; men had lost fortunes before they had mastered the art of coiling thousands of kilometres of cable and playing it out at a steady rate from continent to continent, despite storms and all the other hazards of the sea. Then, just a century later, some of the first primitive guided weapons had been controlled by fine wires spun out as they flew to their targets, at a few hundred kilometres an hour. Morgan was attempting a thousand times the range of those War Museum relics, and fifty times their velocity. However, he had some advantages. His missile would be operating in a perfect vacuum for all but the last hundred kilometres; and its target was not likely to take evasive action.

The Operations Manager, Project Gossamer, attracted Morgan's attention with a slightly embarrassed cough.

'We still have one minor problem, Doctor,' she said. 'We're quite confident about the lowering – all the tests and computer simulations are satisfactory, as you've seen. It's reeling the filament *in* again that has Station Safety worried.'

Morgan blinked rapidly; he had given little thought to the question. It seemed obvious that winding the filament back again was a trivial problem, compared to sending it out. All that was needed, surely, was a simple power-operated winch, with the special modifications needed to handle such a fine, variable-thickness material. But he knew that in space one should never take anything for granted, and that intuition – *especially* the intuition of an earth-based engineer – could be a treacherous guide.

Let's see – when the tests are concluded, we cut the earth end and Ashoka starts to wind the filament in. Of course, when you tug – however hard – at one end of a line forty thousand kilometres long, nothing happens for hours. It would take half a day for the impulse to reach the far end, and the system to start moving as a whole. So we keep up the tension – Oh!—

'Somebody did a few calculations,' continued the engineer, 'and realized that when we finally got up to speed, we'd have several tons heading towards the station at a thousand kilometres an hour. They didn't like *that* at all.'

'Understandably. What do they want us to do?'

'Programme a slower reeling in, with a controlled momentum budget. If the worst comes to the worst, they may make us move off-station to do the wind-up.'

'Will that delay the operation?'

'No; we've worked out a contingency plan for heaving the whole thing out of the airlock in five minutes, if we have to.'

'And you'll be able to retrieve it easily?'

'Of course.'

'I hope you're right. That little fishing line cost a lot of money – and I want to use it again.'

But *where*? Morgan asked himself, as he stared at the slowly waxing crescent earth. Perhaps it would be better to complete the Mars project first, even if it meant several years of exile. Once

Pavonis was fully operational, Earth would *have* to follow, and he did not doubt that, somehow, the last obstacles would be overcome.

Then the chasm across which he was now looking would be spanned, and the fame that Gustave Eiffel had earned three centuries ago would be utterly eclipsed.

28 The First Lowering

There would be nothing to see for at least another twenty minutes. Nevertheless, everyone not needed in the control hut was already outside, staring up at the sky. Even Morgan found it hard to resist the impulse, and kept edging towards the door.

Seldom more than a few metres from him was Maxine Duval's latest Remote, a husky youth in his late twenties. Mounted on his shoulders were the usual tools of his trade – twin cameras in the traditional 'right forward, left backward' arrangement, and above those a small sphere not much larger than a grapefruit. The antenna inside that sphere was doing very clever things, several thousand times a second, so that it was always locked on the nearest comsat despite all the antics of its bearer. And at the other end of that circuit, sitting comfortably in her studio office, Maxine Duval was seeing through the eyes of her distant *alter ego* and hearing with his ears – but not straining *her* lungs in the freezing air. This time she had the better part of the bargain; it was not always the case.

Morgan had agreed to the arrangement with some reluctance. He knew that this was an historic occasion, and accepted Maxine's assurance that 'my man won't get in the way'. But he was also keenly aware of all the things that could go wrong in such a novel experiment – especially during the last hundred kilometres of atmospheric entry. On the other hand, he also knew that Maxine could be trusted to treat either failure or triumph without sensationalism.

Like all great reporters, Maxine Duval was not emotionally

detached from the events that she observed. She could give all points of view, neither distorting nor omitting any facts which she considered essential. Yet she made no attempt to conceal her own feelings, though she did not let them intrude. She admired Morgan enormously, with the envious awe of someone who lacked all real creative ability. Ever since the building of the Gibraltar Bridge she had waited to see what the engineer would do next; and she had not been disappointed. But though she wished Morgan luck, she did not really like him. In her opinion, the sheer drive and ruthlessness of his ambition made him both larger than life and less than human. She could not help contrasting him with his deputy, Warren Kingsley. Now *there* was a thoroughly nice, gentle person ('And a better engineer than I am,' Morgan had once told her, more than half seriously). But no one would ever hear of Warren; he would always be a dim and faithful satellite of his dazzling primary. As, indeed, he was perfectly content to be.

It was Warren who had patiently explained to her the surprisingly complex mechanics of the descent. At first sight, it appeared simple enough to drop something straight down to the equator from a satellite hovering motionless above it. But astrodynamics was full of paradoxes; if you tried to slow down, you moved faster. If you took the shortest route, you burned up the most fuel. If you aimed in one direction, you travelled in another . . . And *that* was merely allowing for gravitational fields. This time, the situation was much more complicated. No one had ever before tried to steer a space-probe trailing forty thousand kilometres of wire. But the Ashoka programme had worked perfectly, all the way down to the edge of the atmosphere. In a few minutes the controller here on Sri Kanda would take over for the final descent. No wonder that Morgan looked tense.

'Van,' said Maxine softly but firmly over the private circuit, 'stop sucking your thumb. It makes you look like a baby.'

Morgan registered indignation, then surprise – and finally relaxed with a slightly embarrassed laugh.

'Thanks for the warning,' he said. 'I'd hate to spoil my public image.'

He looked with rueful amusement at the missing joint, wondering when the self-appointed wits would stop chortling: 'Ha! The engineer hoist by his own petard!' After all the times he had cautioned others, he had grown careless and had managed to slash himself while demonstrating the properties of hyperfilament. There had been practically no pain, and surprisingly little inconvenience. One day he would do something about it; but he simply could not afford to spend a whole week hitched up to an organ regenerator, just for two centimetres of thumb.

'Altitude two five zero,' said a calm, impersonal voice from the control hut. 'Probe velocity one one six zero metres per second. Wire tension ninety per cent nominal. Parachute deploys in two minutes.'

After his momentary relaxation, Morgan was once again tense and alert – like a boxer, Maxine Duval could not help thinking, watching an unknown but dangerous opponent.

'What's the wind situation?' he snapped.

Another voice answered, this time far from impersonal.

'I can't believe this,' it said in worried tones. 'But Monsoon Control had just issued a gale warning.'

'This is no time for jokes.'

'They're not joking; I've just checked back.'

'But they guaranteed no gusts above thirty kilometres an hour!'

'They've just raised that to sixty – correction, eighty. Something's gone badly wrong . . .'

'*I'll* say,' Duval murmured to herself. Then she instructed her distant eyes and ears: 'Fade into the woodwork – they won't want you around – but don't miss anything.' Leaving her Rem to cope with these somewhat contradictory orders, she switched to her excellent information service. It took her less than thirty seconds to discover which meteorological station was responsible for the weather in the Taprobane area. And it was frustrating, but not surprising, to find that it was not accepting incoming calls from the general public.

Leaving her competent staff to break through *that* obstacle, she switched back to the mountain. And she was astonished to find how much, even in this short interval, conditions had worsened.

The sky had become darker; the microphones were picking up the faint, distant roar of the approaching gale. Maxine Duval had known such sudden changes of weather at sea, and more than once had taken advantage of them in her ocean racing. But this was un-believably bad luck; she sympathized with Morgan, whose dreams and hopes might all be swept away by this unscheduled – this *impossible* – blast of air.

'Altitude two zero zero. Probe velocity one one five zero metres a second. Tension ninety-five per cent nominal.'

So the tension was increasing – in more ways than one. The ex-periment could not be called off at this stage; Morgan would simply have to go ahead, and hope for the best. Duval wished that she could speak to him, but knew better than to interrupt him at this crisis.

'Altitude one nine zero. Velocity one one zero zero. Tension one hundred five per cent. First parachute deployment – NOW!'

So – the probe was committed; it was a captive of the earth's atmosphere. Now the little fuel that remained must be used to steer it into the catching net spread out on the mountainside. The cables supporting that net were already thrumming as the wind tore through them.

Abruptly, Morgan emerged from the control hut, and stared up at the sky. Then he turned and looked directly at the camera.

'*Whatever* happens, Maxine,' he said slowly and carefully, 'the test is already ninety-five per cent successful. No – ninety-nine per cent. We've made it for thirty-six thousand kilometres and have less than two hundred to go.'

Duval made no reply. She knew that the words were not intended for her, but for the figure in the complicated wheelchair just outside the hut. The vehicle proclaimed the occupant; only a visitor to Earth would have need of such a device. The doctors could now cure virtually all muscular defects – but the physicists could not cure gravity.

How many powers and interests were now concentrated upon this mountain top! The very forces of nature – the Bank of Nar-odny Mars – the Autonomous North African Republic – Vannevar Morgan (no mean natural force himself) – and those gently im-placable monks in their windswept eyrie.

Maxine Duval whispered instructions to her patient Rem, and the camera tilted smoothly upwards. There was the summit, crow-ned by the dazzling white walls of the temple. Here and there along its parapets Duval could catch glimpses of orange robes fluttering in the gale. As she had expected, the monks were watching.

She zoomed towards them, close enough to see individual faces. Though she had never met the Maha Thero (for an interview had been politely refused) she was confident that she could identify him. But there was no sign of the prelate; perhaps he was in the *sanctum sanctorum*, focusing his formidable will upon some spiritual exercise.

Maxine Duval was not sure if Morgan's chief antagonist indulged in anything so naïve as prayer. But if he had indeed prayed for this miraculous storm, his request was about to be answered. The Gods of the Mountain were awakening from their slumbers.

29 Final Approach

With increasing technology goes increasing vulnerability; the more Man conquers (*sic*) Nature the more liable he becomes to artificial catastrophes. Recent history provides sufficient proof of this – for example, the sinking of Marina City (2127), the collapse of the Tycho B dome (2098), the escape of the Arabian iceberg from its towlines (2062) and the melting of the Thor reactor (2009). We can be sure that the list will have even more impressive additions in the future. Perhaps the most terrifying prospects are those that involve *psychological*, not only technological, factors. In the past, a mad bomber or sniper could kill only a handful of people; today it would not be difficult for a deranged engineer to assassinate a city. The narrow escape of O'Neill Space Colony II from just such a disaster in 2047 has been well documented. Such incidents, in theory at least, could be avoided by careful screening and 'fail-safe' procedures – though all too often these live up only to the first half of their name.

There is also a most interesting, but fortunately very rare, type of event where the individual concerned is in a position of such eminence, or has such unique powers, that no one realizes what he is doing until it is too late. The devastation created by such mad geniuses (there seems no other good term for them) can be worldwide, as in the case of A. Hitler (1889–1945). In a surprising number of instances nothing is heard of their activities, thanks to a conspiracy of silence among their embarrassed peers.

A classic example has recently come to light with the publication of Dame Maxine Duval's eagerly awaited, and much postponed, Memoirs. Even now, some aspects of the matter are still not entirely clear.

(*Civilization and its Malcontents*: J. K. Golitsyn, Prague, 2175)

'Altitude one five zero, velocity ninety-five – repeat, ninety-five. Heat shield jettisoned.'

So the probe had safely entered the atmosphere, and got rid of its excess speed. But it was far too soon to start cheering. Not only were there a hundred and fifty vertical kilometres still to go, but three hundred horizontal ones – with a howling gale to complicate matters. Though the probe still carried a small amount of propellent, its freedom to manoeuvre was very limited. If the operator missed the mountain on the first approach, he could not go round and try again.

'Altitude one two zero. No atmospheric effects yet.'

The little probe was spinning itself down from the sky, like a spider descending its silken ladder. I hope, Duval thought to herself, that they have enough wire: how infuriating if they run out, only a few kilometres from the target! Just such tragedies had occurred with some of the first submarine cables, three hundred years ago.

'Altitude eight zero. Approach nominal. Tension one hundred per cent. Some air drag.'

So – the upper atmosphere was beginning to make itself felt, though as yet only to the sensitive instruments aboard the tiny vehicle.

A small, remotely controlled telescope had been set up beside the control truck, and was now automatically tracking the still invisible probe. Morgan walked towards it, and Duval's Rem followed him like a shadow.

'Anything in sight?' Duval whispered quietly, after a few seconds. Morgan shook his head impatiently, and kept on peering through the eyepiece.

127

'Altitude six zero. Moving off to the left – tension one hundred five per cent – correction, one hundred ten.'

Still well within limits, thought Duval – but things were starting to happen up there on the other side of the stratosphere. Surely, Morgan had the probe in sight now—

'Altitude five five – giving two-second impulse correction.'

'Got it!' exclaimed Morgan. 'I can see the jet!'

'Altitude five zero. Tension one hundred five per cent. Hard to keep on course – some buffeting.'

It was inconceivable that, with a mere fifty kilometres to go, the little probe would not complete its thirty-six-thousand kilometre journey. But for that matter how many aircraft – and spacecraft – had come to grief in the last few *metres*?

'Altitude four five. Stong sheer wind. Going off course again. Three second impulse.'

'Lost it,' said Morgan in disgust. 'Cloud in the way.'

'Altitude four zero. Buffeting badly. Tension peaking at one fifty – I repeat, one fifty per cent.'

That was bad; Duval knew that the breaking strain was two hundred per cent. One bad jerk, and the experiment would be over.

'Altitude three five. Wind getting worse. One second impulse. Propellent reserve almost gone. Tension still peaking – up to one seventy.'

Another thirty per cent, thought Duval, and even that incredible fibre would snap, like any other material when its tensile strength has been exceeded.

'Range three zero. Turbulence getting worse. Drifting badly to the left. Impossible to calculate correction – movements too erratic.'

'I've got it!' Morgan cried. 'It's through the clouds!'

'Range two five. Not enough propellent to get back on course. Estimate we'll miss by three kilometres.'

'It doesn't matter!' shouted Morgan. 'Crash where you can!'

'Will do soonest. Range two zero. Wind forces increasing. Losing stabilization. Payload starting to spin.'

'Release the brake – let the wire run out!'

'Already done,' said that maddeningly calm voice. Duval could have imagined that a machine was speaking, if she had not known that Morgan had borrowed a top space-station traffic controller for the job. 'Dispenser malfunction. Payload spin now five revs second. Wire probably entangled. Tension one eight zero per cent. One nine zero. Two zero zero. Range one five. Tension two one zero. Two two zero. Two three zero.'

It can't last much longer, thought Duval. Only a dozen kilometres to go, and the damned wire had got tangled up in the spinning probe.

'Tension zero – repeat, *zero*.'

That was it; the wire had snapped, and must be slowly snaking back towards the stars. Doubtless the operators on Ashoka would wind it in again, but Duval had now glimpsed enough of the theory to realize that this would be a long and complicated task. And the little payload would crash somewhere down there in the fields and jungles of Taprobane. Yet, as Morgan had said, it had been more than ninety-five per cent successful. Next time, when there was no wind . . .

'There it is!' someone shouted.

A brilliant star had ignited, between two of the cloud-galleons sailing across the sky; it looked like a daylight meteor falling down to earth. Ironically, as if mocking its builders, the flare installed on the probe to assist terminal guidance had automatically triggered. Well, it could still serve some useful purpose. It would help to locate the wreckage.

Duval's Rem slowly pivoted so that she could watch the blazing day-star sail past the mountain and disappear into the east; she estimated that it would land less than five kilometres away. Then she said, 'Take me back to Dr Morgan. I'd like a word with him.'

She had intended to make a few cheerful remarks – loud enough for the Martian banker to hear – expressing her confidence that, next time, the lowering would be a complete success. Duval was still composing her little speech of reassurance when it was swept out of her mind. She was to play back the events of the next thirty seconds until she knew them by heart. But she was never quite sure if she fully understood them.

30 The Legions of the King

Vannevar Morgan was used to setbacks – even disasters – and this was, he hoped, a minor one. His real worry, as he watched the flare vanish over the shoulder of the mountain, was that Narodny Mars would consider it money wasted. The hard-eyed observer in his elaborate wheel-chair had been extremely uncommunicative; Earth's gravity seemed to have immobilized his tongue as effectively as his limbs. But this time he addressed Morgan before the engineer could speak to him.

'Just one question, Dr Morgan. I know that this gale is unprecedented – yet it happened. So it may happen again. What if it does – *when the Tower is built*?'

Morgan thought quickly. It was impossible to give an accurate answer at such short notice, and he could still scarcely believe what had happened.

'At the very worst, we might have to suspend operations briefly: there could be some track distortion. No wind forces that *ever* occur at this altitude could endanger the Tower structure itself. Even this experimental fibre would have been perfectly safe – if we'd succeeded in anchoring it.'

He hoped that this was a fair analysis; in a few minutes, Warren Kingsley would let him know whether it was true or not. To his relief, the Martian answered, with apparent satisfaction: 'Thank you; that was all I wanted to know.'

Morgan, however, was determined to drive the lesson home.

'And on Mount Pavonis, of course, such a problem couldn't possibly arise. The atmospheric density there is less than a hundreth—'

Not for decades had he heard the sound that now crashed upon his ears, but it was one that no man could ever forget. Its imperious summons, overpowering the roar of the gale, transported Morgan halfway round the world. He was no longer standing on a windswept mountainside; he was beneath the dome of the Hagia Sophia, looking up in awe and admiration at the work of men who had died sixteen centuries ago. And in his ears sounded the tolling of the mighty bell that had once summoned the faithful to prayer.

The memory of Istanbul faded; he was back on the mountain, more puzzled and confused than ever.

What was it that the monk had told him – that Kalidasa's unwelcome gift had been silent for centuries, and was allowed to speak only in time of disaster? There had been no disaster here; indeed, as far as the monastery was concerned, precisely the opposite. Just for a moment, the embarrassing possibility occurred to Morgan that the probe might have crashed into the temple precincts. No, that was out of the question; it had missed the peak with kilometres to spare. And in any event it was much too small an object to do any serious damage as it half-fell, half-glided out of the sky.

He stared up at the monastery, from which the voice of the great bell still challenged the gale. The orange robes had all vanished from the parapets; there was not a monk in sight.

Something brushed delicately against Morgan's cheek, and he automatically flicked it aside. It was hard even to think while that dolorous throbbing filled the air and hammered at his brain. He supposed he had better walk up to the temple, and politely ask the Maha Thero what had happened.

Once more that soft, silken contact against his face, and this time he caught a glimpse of yellow out of the corner of his eye. His reactions had always been swift; he grabbed, and did not miss.

The insect lay crumpled in the palm of his hand, yielding up the last seconds of its ephemeral life even as Morgan watched – and the universe he had always known seemed to tremble and dissolve around him. His miraculous defeat had been converted into an even more inexplicable victory, yet he felt no sense of triumph – only confusion and astonishment.

For he remembered, now, the legend of the golden butterflies. Driven by the gale, in their hundreds and thousands, they were being swept up the face of the mountain, to die upon its summit. Kalidasa's legions had at last achieved their goal – and their revenge.

31 Exodus

'What happened?' said Sheik Abdullah.

That's a question I'll never be able to answer, Morgan told himself. But he replied: 'The Mountain is ours, Mr President; the monks have already started to leave. It's incredible – how could a two-thousand-year-old legend . . . ?' He shook his head in baffled wonder.

'If enough men believe in a legend, it becomes true.'

'I suppose so. But there's much more to it than that – the whole chain of events still seems impossible.'

'That's always a risky word to use. Let me tell you a little story. A dear friend, a great scientist, now dead, used to tease me by saying the because politics is the art of the possible, it appeals only to second-rate minds. For the *first*-raters, he claimed, are only interested in the *impossible*. And do you know what I answered?'

'No,' said Morgan, politely and predictably.

'It's lucky there are so many of us – because *someone* has to run the world . . . Anyway, if the impossible has happened, you should accept it thankfully.'

I accept it, thought Morgan – reluctantly. There is something very strange about a universe where a few dead butterflies can balance a billion-ton tower.

And there was the ironic rôle of the Venerable Parakarma, who must surely now feel that he was the pawn of some malicious gods. The Monsoon Control Administrator had been most contrite, and Morgan had accepted his apologies with unusual graciousness. He could well believe that the brilliant Dr Choam Goldberg had revolutionized micrometeorology, that no one had really understood all that he was doing, and that he had finally had some kind of a nervous breakdown while conducting his experiments. It would never happen again. Morgan had expressed his – quite sincere – hopes for the scientist's recovery, and had retained enough of his bureaucrat's instinct to hint that, in due course, he might expect future considerations from Monsoon Control. The Administrator had signed off with grateful thanks, doubtless wondering at Morgan's surprising magnanimity.

'As a matter of interest,' asked the Sheik, 'where are the monks going? I might offer them hospitality here. Our culture has always welcomed other faiths.'

'I don't know; nor does Ambassador Rajasinghe. But when I asked him he said: They'll be all right. An order that's lived frugally for three thousand years is not exactly destitute.'

'Hmm. Perhaps we could use some of their wealth. This little project of yours gets more expensive each time you see me.'

'Not really, Mr President. That last estimate includes a purely book-keeping figure for deep-space operations, which Narodny Mars has now agreed to finance. They will locate a carbonaceous asteroid and navigate it to earth orbit – they've much more experience at this sort of work, and it solves one of our main problems.'

'What about the carbon for their own tower?'

'They have unlimited amounts on Deimos – exactly where they they need it. Narodny has already started a survey for suitable mining sites, though the actual processing will have to be off-moon.'

'Dare I ask why?'

'Because of gravity. Even Deimos has a few centimetres per second squared. Hyperfilament can only be manufactured in completely zero gee conditions. There's no other way of guaranteeing a perfect crystalline structure with sufficient long-range organization.'

'Thank you, Van. Is it safe for me to ask why you've changed the basic design? I liked that original bundle of four tubes, two up and two down. A straightforward subway system was something I could understand – even if it *was* up-ended ninety degrees.'

Not for the first time, and doubtless not for the last, Morgan was amazed by the old man's memory and his grasp of details. It was never safe to take anything for granted with him; though his questions were sometimes inspired by pure curiosity – often the mischievous curiosity of a man so secure that he had no need to uphold his dignity – he never overlooked anything of the slightest importance.

'I'm afraid our first thoughts were too earth-orientated. We were rather like the early motor-car designers, who kept producing horseless carriages. So now our design is a hollow square tower with a track up each face. Think of it as four vertical railroads. Where it starts from orbit, it's forty metres on a side, and it tapers down to twenty when it reaches Earth.'

'Like a stalag— stalac—'

'*Stalactite*. Yes, I had to look it up! From the engineering point of view, a good analogy now would be the old Eiffel Tower – turned upside down and stretched out a hundred thousand times.'

'As much as *that*?'

'Just about.'

'Well, I suppose there's no law that says a tower can't hang downwards.'

'We have one going *upwards* as well, remember – from the synchronous orbit out of the mass anchor that keeps the whole structure under tension.'

'And Midway Station? I hope you haven't changed that.'

'Yes, it's still at the same place – twenty-five thousand kilometres.'

'Good. I know I'll never get there, but I like to think about it . . .' He muttered something in Arabic. 'There's another legend, you know – Mahomet's coffin, suspended between heaven and earth. Just like Midway.'

'We'll arrange a banquet for you there, Mr President, when we inaugurate the service.'

'Even if you keep to your schedule – and I admit you only slipped a year on the Bridge – I'll be ninety-eight then. No, I doubt if I'll make it.'

But *I* shall, said Vannevar Morgan to himself. For now I know that the gods are on my side; whatever gods may be.

part four
The Tower

32 Space Express

'Now don't *you* say,' begged Warren Kingsley, 'it'll never get off the ground.'

'I was tempted,' chuckled Morgan, as he examined the full-scale mock-up. 'It *does* look rather like an upended railroad coach.'

'That's exactly the image we want to sell,' Kingsley answered. 'You buy your ticket at the station, check in your baggage, settle down in your swivel seat, and admire the view. Or you can go up to the lounge-cum-bar and devote the next five hours to serious drinking, until they carry you off at Midway. Incidentally, what do you think of the Design Section's idea – nineteenth-century Pullman decor?'

'Not much. Pullman cars didn't have five circular floors, one on top of the other.'

'Better tell Design that – they've set their hearts on gas-lighting.'

'If they want an antique flavour that's a little more appropriate, I once saw an old space movie at the Sydney Art Museum. There was a shuttle craft of some kind that had a circular observation lounge – just what we need.'

'Do you remember its name?'

'Oh – let's think – something like *Space Wars 2000*. I'm sure you'll be able to trace it.'

'I'll tell Design to look it up. Now let's go inside – do you want a hard-hat?'

'No,' answered Morgan brusquely. That was one of the few advantages of being ten centimetres shorter than average height.

As they stepped into the mock-up, he felt an almost boyish thrill of anticipation. He had checked the designs, watched the computers playing with the graphics and layout – everything here would be perfectly familiar. But this was *real* – solid. True, it would never leave the ground, just as the old joke said. But one day its identical brethren would be hurtling up through the clouds and climbing, in only five hours, to Midway Station, twenty-five thousand kilometres from Earth. And all for about one dollar's worth of electricity per passenger.

Even now, it was impossible to realize the full meaning of the coming revolution. For the first time Space itself would become as accessible as any point on the surface of the familiar earth. In a few more decades, if the average man wanted to spend a weekend on the moon, he could afford to do so. Even Mars would not be out of the question; there were no limitations to what might now be possible.

Morgan came back to earth with a bump, as he almost tripped over a piece of badly-laid carpet.

'Sorry,' said his guide, 'another of Design's ideas – that green is supposed to remind people of Earth. The ceilings are going to be blue, getting deeper and deeper on the upper floors. And they want to use indirect lighting everywhere, so that the stars will be visible.'

Morgan shook his head. 'That's a nice idea, but it won't work. If the lighting's good enough for comfortable reading, the glare will wipe out the stars. You'll need a section of the lounge that can be completely blacked-out.'

'That's already planned for part of the bar – you can order your drink, and retire behind the curtains.'

They were now standing in the lowest floor of the capsule, a circular room eight metres in diameter, three metres high. All around were miscellaneous boxes, cylinders and control panels bearing such labels as OXYGEN RESERVE, BATTERY, CO_2 CRACKER, MEDICAL, TEMPERATURE CONTROL. Everything was clearly of a provisional, temporary nature, liable to be rearranged at a moment's notice.

'Anyone would think we were building a spaceship,' Morgan

commented. 'Incidentally, what's the latest estimate of survival time?'

'As long as power's available, at least a week, even for a full load of fifty passengers. Which is really absurd, since a rescue team could always reach them in three hours, either from Earth or Midway.'

'Barring a major catastrophe, like damage to the tower or tracks.'

'If *that* ever happens, I don't think there will be anyone to rescue. But if a capsule gets stuck for some reason, and the passengers don't go mad and gobble up all our delicious emergency compressed food tablets at once, their biggest problem will be boredom.'

The second floor was completely empty, devoid even of temporary fittings. Someone had chalked a large rectangle on the curved plastic panel of the wall and printed inside it: AIRLOCK HERE?

'This will be the baggage room – though we're not sure if we'll need so much space. If not, it can be used for extra passengers. Now, this floor's much more interesting—'

The third level contained a dozen aircraft-type chairs, all of different designs; two of them were occupied by realistic dummies, male and female, who looked very bored with the whole proceedings.

'We've practically decided on this model,' said Kingsley, pointing to a luxurious tilting swivel-chair with attached small table, 'but we'll run the usual survey first.'

Morgan punched his fist into the seat cushion.

'Has anyone actually *sat* in it for five hours?' he asked.

'Yes – a hundred-kilo volunteer. No bed-sores. If people complain, we'll remind them of the pioneering days of aviation, when it took five hours merely to cross the Pacific. And, of course, we're offering low-gee comfort almost all the way.'

The floor above was identical in concept, though empty of chairs. They passed through it quickly and reached the next level, to which the designers had obviously devoted most attention.

The bar looked almost functional, and indeed the coffee dispenser was actually working. Above it, in an elaborately gilded frame, was an old engraving of such uncanny relevance that it took Morgan's breath away. A huge full moon dominated the upper left quadrant, and racing towards it was – a bullet-shaped train towing four carriages. From the windows of the compartment labelled 'First Class' top-hatted Victorian personages could be seen admiring the view.

'Where *did* you get hold of that?' Morgan asked in astonished admiration.

'Looks as if the caption's fallen off again,' Kingsley apologized, hunting round behind the bar. 'Ah, here it is.'

He handed Morgan a piece of card upon which was printed, in old-fashioned typeface,

PROJECTILE TRAINS FOR THE MOON
Engraving from 1881 Edition of
FROM THE EARTH TO THE MOON
Direct
In 97 Hours and 20 Minutes
AND A TRIP AROUND IT
by Jules Verne

'I'm sorry to say I've never read it,' said Morgan, when he had absorbed this information. 'It might have saved me a lot of trouble. But I'd like to know how he managed without any rails . . .'

'We shouldn't give Jules too much credit – or blame. This picture was never meant to be taken seriously – it was a joke of the artist.'

'Well – give Design my compliments; it's one of their better ideas.'

Turning away from the dreams of the past, Morgan and Kinsley walked towards the reality of the future. Through the wide observation window a back-projection system gave a stunning view of Earth – and not just *any* view, Morgan was pleased to note, but the correct one. Taprobane itself was hidden, of course, being directly below; but there was the whole subcontinent of Hindustan, right out to the dazzling snows of the Himalayas.

'You know,' Morgan said suddenly, 'it will be exactly like the Bridge all over again. People will take the trip just for the view. Midway Station could be the biggest tourist attraction ever.' He glanced up at the azure-blue ceiling. 'Anything worth looking at on the last floor?'

'Not really – the upper air-lock is finalized, but we haven't decided where to put the life-support backup gear and the electronics for the track-centring controls.'

'Any problems there?'

'Not with the new magnets. Powered or coasting, we can guarantee safe clearance up to eight thousand kilometres an hour – fifty per cent above maximum design speed.'

Morgan permitted himself a mental sigh of relief. This was one area in which he was quite unable to make any judgements, and had to rely completely on the advice of others. From the beginning, it had been obvious that only some form of magnetic propulsion could operate at such speeds; the slightest *physical* contact – at more than a kilometre a second! – would result in disaster. And yet the four pairs of guidance slots running up the faces of the tower had only centimetres of clearance around the magnets; they had to be designed so that enormous restoring forces came instantly into play, correcting any movement of the capsule away from the centre line.

As Morgan followed Kingsley down the spiral stairway which extended the full height of the mockup, he was suddenly struck by a sombre thought. I'm getting old, he said to himself. Oh, I *could* have climbed to the sixth level without any trouble; but I'm glad we decided not to.

Yet I'm only fifty-nine – and it will be at least five years, even if all goes very well, before the first passenger car rides up to Midway Station. Then another three years of tests, calibration, system tune-ups. Make it ten years, to be on the safe side . . .

Though it was warm, he felt a sudden chill. For the first time, it occurred to Vannevar Morgan that the triumph upon which he had set his soul might come too late for him. And quite unconsciously he pressed his hand against the slim metal disc concealed inside his shirt.

33 CORA

'*Why* did you leave it until now?' Dr Sen had asked, in a tone appropriate to a retarded child.

'The usual reason,' Morgan answered, as he ran his good thumb along the seal of his shirt. 'I was too busy – and whenever I felt short of breath I blamed it on the height.'

'Altitude was partly to blame, of course. You'd better check all your people on the mountain. How could you have overlooked anything so obvious?'

How indeed? thought Morgan, with some embarrassment.

'All those monks – some of them were over eighty! They seemed so healthy that it never occurred to me . . .'

'The monks have lived up there for years – they're completely adapted. But *you've* been hopping up and down several times a day—'

'—twice, at the most—'

'—going from sea level to half an atmosphere in a few minutes. Well, there's no great harm done – *if* you follow instructions from now on. Mine, and CORA's.'

'CORA's?'

'Coronary alarm.'

'Oh – one of those things.'

'Yes – one of *those* things. They save about ten million lives a year. Mostly top civil servants, senior administrators, distinguished scientists, leading engineers and similar nit-wits. I often wonder if it's worth the trouble. Nature may be trying to tell us something, and we're not listening.'

'Remember your Hippocratic Oath, Bill,' retorted Morgan with a grin. 'And you must admit that I've always done just what you told me. Why, my weight hasn't changed a kilo in the last ten years.'

'Um . . . Well, you're not the worst of my patients,' said the slightly mollified doctor. He fumbled round his desk and produced a large holopad. 'Take your choice – here are the standard models. Any colour you like as long as it's Medic Red.'

Morgan triggered the images, and regarded them with distaste.

'Where do I have to carry the thing?' he asked. 'Or do you want to implant it?'

'That isn't necessary, at least for the present. In five years' time, maybe, but perhaps not even then. I suggest you start with *this* model – it's worn just under the breastbone, so doesn't need remote sensors. After a while you won't notice it's there. And it won't bother you, unless it's needed.'

'And then?'

'Listen.'

The doctor threw one of the numerous switches on his desk console, and a sweet mezzo-soprano voice remarked in a conversational tone: 'I think you should sit down and rest for about ten minutes.' After a brief pause it continued. 'It would be a good idea to lie down for half an hour.' Another pause: 'As soon as convenient, make an appointment with Dr Sen.' Then:

'Please take one of the red pills immediately.'

'I have called the ambulance; just lie down and relax. Everything will be all right.'

Morgan almost clapped his hands over his ears to cut out the piercing whistle.

'THIS IS A CORA ALERT: WILL ANYONE WITHIN RANGE OF MY VOICE PLEASE COME IMMEDIATELY. THIS IS A CORA ALERT. WILL—'

'I think you get the general idea,' said the doctor, restoring silence to his office. 'Of course, the programmes and responses are individually tailored to the subject. And there's a wide range of voices, including some famous ones.'

'*That* will do very nicely. When will my unit be ready?'

'I'll call you in about three days. Oh yes – there's an advantage to the chest-worn units I should mention.'

'What's that?'

'One of my patients is a keen tennis player. He tells me that when he opens his shirt the sight of that little red box has an absolutely devastating effect on his opponent's game . . .'

34 Vertigo

There had once been a time when a minor, and often major, chore of every civilized man had been the regular updating of his address book. The universal code had made that unnecessary, since once a person's lifetime identity number was known he could be located within seconds. And even if his number was *not* known, the standard search programme could usually find it fairly quickly, given the approximate date of birth, his profession, and a few other details. (There were, of course, problems if the name was Smith, or Singh, or Mohammed . . .)

The development of global information systems had also rendered obsolete another annoying task. It was only necessary to make a special notation against the names of those friends one wished to greet on their birthdays or other anniversaries, and the household computer would do the rest. On the appropriate day (unless, as was frequently the case, there had been some stupid mistake in programming) the right message would be automatically flashed to its destination. And even though the recipient might shrewdly suspect that the warm words on his screen were entirely due to electronics – the nominal sender not having thought of him for years – the gesture was nevertheless welcome.

But the same technology that had eliminated one set of tasks had created even more demanding successors. Of these, perhaps the most important was the design of the Personal Interest Profile.

Most men updated their PIP on New Year's Day, or their birthday. Morgan's list contained fifty items; he had heard of people with hundreds. They must spend all their waking hours battling with the flood of information, unless they were like those notorious pranksters who enjoyed setting up News Alerts on their consoles for such classic improbabilities as:

Eggs, Dinosaur, hatching of
Circle, squaring of
Atlantis, re-emergence of
Christ, Second Coming of
Loch Ness Monster, capture of

or finally

World, end of

Usually, of course, egotism and professional requirements ensured that the subscriber's own name was the first item on every list. Morgan was no exception, but the entries that followed were slightly unusual:

Tower, orbital
Tower, space
Tower, (geo) synchronous
Elevator, space
Elevator, orbital
Elevator, (geo) synchronous

These names covered most of the variations used by the media, and ensured that he saw at least ninety per cent of the news items concerning the project. The vast majority of these were trivial, and sometimes he wondered if it was worth searching for them – the ones that really mattered would reach him quickly enough.

He was still rubbing his eyes, and the bed had scarcely retracted itself into the wall of his modest apartment, when Morgan noticed that the Alert was flashing on his console. Punching the COFFEE and READOUT buttons simultaneously, he awaited the latest overnight sensation.

ORBITAL TOWER SHOT DOWN

said the headline.

'Follow up?' asked the console.

'You bet,' replied Morgan, now instantly awake.

During the next few seconds, as he read the text display, his mood changed from incredulity to indignation, and then to concern. He switched the whole news package to Warren Kingsley with a 'Please call me back as soon as possible' tag, and settled down to breakfast, still fuming.

Less than five minutes later, Kingsley appeared on the screen.

'Well, Van,' he said with humorous resignation, 'we should consider ourselves lucky. It's taken him five years to get round to us.'

'It's the most ridiculous thing I ever heard of! Should we ignore it? If we answer, that will only give him publicity. Which is just what he wants.'

Kingsley nodded.'That would be the best policy – for the present. We shouldn't over-react. At the same time, he *may* have a point.'

'What do you mean?'

Kingsley had become suddenly serious, and even looked a little uncomfortable.

'There *are* psychological problems as well as engineerings ones,' he said. 'Think it over. I'll see you at the office.'

The image faded from the screen, leaving Morgan in a somewhat subdued frame of mind. He was used to criticism, and knew how to handle it; indeed, he thoroughly enjoyed the give-and-take of technical arguments with his peers, and was seldom upset on those rare occasions when he lost. It was not so easy to cope with Donald Duck.

That, of course, was not his real name, but Dr Donald Bickerstaff's peculiar brand of indignant negativism often recalled that mythological twentieth-century character. His degree (adequate but not brilliant) was in pure mathematics; his assets were an impressive appearance, a mellifluous voice, and an unshakeable belief in his ability to deliver judgements on *any* scientific subject. In his own field, indeed, he was quite good; Morgan remembered with pleasure an old-style public lecture of the doctor's which he had once attended at the Royal Institution. For almost a week afterwards he had almost understood the peculiar properties of transfinite numbers . . .

Unfortunately, Bickerstaff did not know his limitations. Though he had a devoted coterie of fans who subscribed to his information service – in an earlier age, he would have been called a pop-scientist – he had an even larger circle of critics. The kinder ones considered that he had been educated beyond his intelligence. The others labelled him a self-employed idiot. It was a pity, thought Morgan, that Bickerstaff couldn't be locked in a room with Dr Goldberg/Parakarma; they might annihilate each other like electron and positron – the genius of one cancelling out the fundamental stupidity of the other. That unshakeable stupidity against which, as Goethe lamented, the Gods themselves contend in vain. No gods being currently available, Morgan knew that he would have to undertake the task himself. Though he had much better things to do with his time, it might provide some comic relief; and he had an inspiring precedent.

There were few pictures in the hotel room that had been one of Morgan's four 'temporary' homes for almost a decade. Most prominent of them was a photograph so well faked that some visitors could not believe that its components were all perfectly genuine. It was dominated by the graceful, beautifully restored steamship – ancestor of every vessel that could thereafter call itself modern. By her side, standing on the dock to which she had been miraculously returned a century and a quarter after her launch, was Dr Vannevar Morgan. He was looking up at the scrollwork of the painted prow; and a few metres away, looking quizzically at *him*, was Isambard Kingdom Brunel – hands thrust in pockets, cigar clenched firmly in his mouth, and wearing a very rumpled, mud-spattered suit.

Everything in the photo was quite real; Morgan had indeed been standing beside the *Great Britain*, on a sunny day in Bristol the year after the Gibraltar Bridge was completed. But Brunel was back in 1857, still awaiting the launch of his later and more famous leviathan, whose misfortunes were to break his body and spirit.

The photograph had been presented to Morgan on his fiftieth birthday, and it was one of his most cherished possessions. His colleagues had intended it as a sympathetic joke, Morgan's admiration for the greatest engineer of the nineteenth century being well known. There were times, however, when he wondered if their choice was more appropriate than they realized. The *Great Eastern* had devoured her creator. The Tower might yet do the same to him.

Brunel, of course, had been surrounded by Donald Ducks. The most persistent was one Doctor Dionysius Lardner, who had proved beyond all doubt that no steamship could ever cross the Atlantic. An engineer could refute criticisms which were based on errors of fact or simple miscalculations. But the point that Donald Duck had raised was more subtle and not so easy to answer. Morgan suddenly recalled that his hero had to face something very similar, three centuries ago.

He reached for his small but priceless collection of genuine books, and pulled out the one he had read, perhaps, more often than any other – Rolt's classic biography *Isambard Kingdom Brunel*. Leafing through the well-thumbed pages, he quickly found the item that had stirred his memory.

Brunel had planned a railway tunnel almost three kilometres long – a 'monstrous and extraordinary, most dangerous and impracticable' concept. It was inconceivable, said the critics, that human beings could tolerate the ordeal of hurtling through its Stygian depths. 'No person would desire to be shut out from daylight with a consciousness that he had a superincumbent weight of earth sufficient to crush him in case of accident . . . the noise of two trains passing would shake the nerves . . . no passenger would be induced to go twice . . .'

It was all so familiar. The motto of the Lardners and the Bickerstaffs seemed to be: 'Nothing shall be done for the first time.'

And yet – *sometimes they were right*, if only through the operation of the laws of chance. Donald Duck made it sound so reasonable. He had begun by saying in a display of modesty as unusual as it was spurious, that he would not presume to criticize the *engineering* aspects of the space elevator. He only wanted to talk about the psychological problems it would pose. They could be summed up in one word: vertigo. The normal human being, he had pointed out, had a well-justified fear of high places; only acrobats and tight-rope artistes were immune to this natural reaction. The tallest structure on earth was less than five kilometres high – and there were not many people who would care to be hauled vertically up the piers of the Gibraltar Bridge.

Yet that was *nothing* compared to the appalling prospect of the orbital tower. 'Who has not stood,' Bickerstaff declaimed, 'at the foot of some immense building, staring up at its sheer precipitous face, until it seemed about to topple and fall? Now imagine such a building soaring on and on through the clouds, up into the blackness of space, through the ionosphere, past the orbits of all the great space-stations – up and up until it reaches a large fraction of the way to the moon! An engineering triumph, no doubt – but a psychological nightmare. I suggest that some people will go mad at its mere contemplation. And how many could face the vertiginous ordeal of the ride – *straight upwards*, hanging over empty space, for twenty-five thousand kilometres to the first stop at the Midway Station?

'It is no answer to say that perfectly ordinary individuals can fly in spacecraft to the same altitude, and far beyond. The situation then is completely different – as indeed it is in ordinary atmospheric flight. The normal man does not feel vertigo even in the open gondola of a balloon, floating through the air a few kilometres above the ground. But put him on the edge of a cliff at the same altitude, and study his reactions *then*!

'The reason for this difference is quite simple. In an aircraft, there is no *physical* connection linking the observer and the ground. Psychologically, therefore, he is completely detached from the hard, solid earth far below. Falling no longer has terrors for him; he can look down upon remote and tiny landscapes which he would never dare to contemplate from any high elevation. That saving physical detachment is precisely what the space elevator will lack. The hapless passenger, whisked up the sheer face of the gigantic tower, will be all too conscious of his link with earth. What guarantee can there possibly be that anyone not drugged or anaesthetised could survive such an experience? I challenge Dr Morgan to answer.'

Dr Morgan was still thinking of answers, few of them polite, when the screen lit up again with an incoming call. When he pressed the ACCEPT button, he was not in the least surprised to see Maxine Duval.

'Well, Van,' she said, without any preamble, 'what are you going to do?'

'I'm sorely tempted, but I don't think I should argue with that idiot. Incidentally, do you suppose that some aerospace organization has put him up to it?'

'My men are already digging; I'll let you know if they find anything. Personally, I feel it's all his own work – I recognize the hallmarks of the genuine article. But you haven't answered my question.'

'I haven't decided; I'm still trying to digest my breakfast. What do *you* think I should do?'

'Simple. Arrange a demonstration. When can you fix it?'

'In five years, if all goes well.'

'That's ridiculous. You've got your first cable in position . . .'

'Not cable – *tape*.'

'Don't quibble. What load can it carry?'

'Oh – at the Earth end, a mere five hundred tons.'

'There you are. Offer Donald Duck a ride.'

'I wouldn't guarantee his safety.'

'Would you guarantee *mine*?'

'You're not serious!'

'I'm always serious, at this hour of the morning. It's time I did another story on the Tower anyway. That capsule mock-up is very pretty, but it doesn't *do* anything. My viewers like action, and so do I. The last time we met, you showed me drawings of those little cars the engineers will use to run up and down the cable – I mean tapes. What did you call them?'

'Spiders.'

'Ugh – that's right. I was fascinated by the idea. Here's something that has *never* been possible before, by any technology. For the first time you could sit still in the sky, even above the atmosphere and watch the earth beneath – something that no spacecraft can ever do. I'd like to be the first to describe the sensation. *And* clip Donald Duck's wings at the same time.'

Morgan waited for a full five seconds, staring Maxine straight in the eyes, before he decided that she was perfectly serious.

'I can understand,' he said rather wearily, 'just how a poor struggling young media-girl, trying desperately to make a name for herself, would jump at such an opportunity. I don't want to blight a promising career, but the answer is definitely no.'

The doyen of media-persons emitted several unladylike, and even ungentlemanly words, not commonly transmitted over public circuits.

'Before I strangle you in your own hyperfilament, Van,' she continued, 'why not?'

'Well, if anything went wrong, I'd never forgive myself.'

'Spare the crocodile tears. Of course, my untimely demise would be a major tragedy – for *your* project. But I wouldn't dream of going until you'd made all the tests necessary, and were sure it was one hundred per cent safe.'

'It would look too much like a stunt.'

'As the Victorians (or was it the Elizabethans?) used to say – *so what*?'

'Look, Maxine – there's a flash that New Zealand has just sunk – they'll need you in the studio. But thanks for the generous offer.'

'Dr Vannevar Morgan – I know exactly why you're turning me down. *You* want to be the first.'

'As the Victorians used to say – so what?'

'*Touché*. But I'm warning you, Van – just as soon as you have one of those spiders working, you'll be hearing from me again.'

Morgan shook his head. 'Sorry, Maxine,' he answered. 'Not a chance—'

35 Starglider Plus Eighty

Extract from *God and Starholme*. (Mandala Press, Moscow, 2149)

Exactly eighty years ago, the robot interstellar probe now known as Starglider entered the Solar System, and conducted its brief but historic dialogue with the human race. For the first time, we knew what we had always suspected; that ours was not the only intelligence in the universe, and that out among the stars were far older, and perhaps far wiser, civilizations.

After that encounter, nothing would ever be the same again. And yet, paradoxically, in many ways very little has changed. Mankind still goes about its business, much as it has always done. How often do we stop to think that the Starholmers, back on their own planet, have already known of our existence for twenty-eight years – or that, almost certainly, we shall be receiving their first direct messages only twenty-four years from now? And what if, as some have suggested, they themselves *are already on the way*?

Men have an extraordinary, and perhaps fortunate, ability to tune out of their consciousness the most awesome future possibilities. The Roman farmer, ploughing the slopes of Vesuvius, gave no thought to the mountain smoking overhead. Half the twentieth century lived with the Hydrogen Bomb – half the twenty-first with the Golgotha virus.

We have learned to live with the threat – or the promise – of Starholme.

Starglider showed us many strange worlds and races, but it revealed almost no advanced technology, and so had minimal impact upon the technically-orientated aspects of our culture. Was this accidental, or the result of some deliberate policy? There are many questions one would like to ask Starglider, now that it is too late – or too early.

On the other hand, it did discuss many matters of philosophy and religion, and in these fields its influence was profound. Although the phrase nowhere occurs in the transcripts, Starglider is generally credited with the famous aphorism 'Belief in God is apparently a psychological artefact of mammalian reproduction.'

But what if this is true? It is totally irrelevant to the question of God's *actual* existence, as I shall now proceed to demonstrate . . .

Swami Krisnamurthi (Dr Choam Goldberg)

36 The Cruel Sky

The eye could follow the tape much further by night than by day. At sunset, when the warning lights were switched on, it became a thin band of incandescence, slowly dwindling away until, at some indefinite point, it was lost against the background of stars.

Already, it was the greatest wonder of the world. Until Morgan put his foot down and restricted the site to essential engineering staff, there was a continual flood of visitors – 'pilgrims', someone had ironically called them – paying homage to the sacred mountain's last miracle.

They would all behave in exactly the same way. First they would reach out and gently touch the five-centimetre-wide band, running their finger tips along it with something approaching reverence. Then they would listen, ears pressed against the smooth, cold material of the ribbon, as if they hoped to catch the music of the spheres. There were some, indeed, who claimed to have heard a deep bass note at the uttermost threshold of audibility, but they were deluding themselves. Even the highest harmonics of the tape's natural frequency were far below the range of human hearing. And some would go away shaking their heads, saying: 'You'll never get *me* to ride up *that* thing!' But they were the ones who had made just the same remark about the fusion rocket, the space shuttle, the aeroplane, the automobile – even the steam locomotive . . .

To these sceptics, the usual answer was: 'Don't worry – this is merely part of the scaffolding – one of the four tapes that will guide the Tower down to Earth. Riding up the final structure will be exactly like taking an elevator in any high building. Except that the trip will be longer – and much more comfortable.'

Maxine Duval's trip, on the other hand, would be very short, and not particularly comfortable. But once Morgan had capitulated, he had done his best to make sure that it would be uneventful.

The flimsy 'Spider' – a prototype test vehicle looking like a motorized Bosun's Chair – had already made a dozen ascents to twenty kilometres, with twice the load it would be carrying now. There had been the usual minor teething problems, but nothing serious; the last five runs had been completely trouble-free. And what *could* go wrong? If there was a power failure – almost unthinkable, in such a simple battery-operated system – gravity would bring Maxine safely home, the automatic brakes limiting the speed of descent. The only real risk was that the drive mechanism might jam, trapping Spider and its passenger in the upper atmosphere. And Morgan had an answer even for this.

'Only fifteen kilometres?' Maxine had protested. 'A *glider* can do better than that!'

'But *you* can't, with nothing more than an oxygen mask. Of course, if you like to wait a year until we have the operational unit with its life-support system . . .'

'What's wrong with a space suit?'

Morgan had refused to budge, for his own good reasons. Though he hoped it would not be needed, a small jet-crane was standing by at the foot of Sri Kanda. Its highly skilled operators were used to odd assignments; they would have no difficulty in rescuing a stranded Maxine, even at twenty kilometres altitude.

But there was no vehicle in existence that could reach her at twice that height. Above forty kilometres was no-man's land – too low for rockets, too high for balloons.

In theory of course, a rocket *could* hover beside the tape, for a very few minutes, before it burned up all its propellent. The problems of navigation and actual contact with the Spider were so horrendous that Morgan had not even bothered to think about them. It could never happen in real life, and he hoped that no producer of video-drama would decide that there was good material here for a cliff-hanger. That was the sort of publicity he could do without.

Maxine Duval looked rather like a typical Antarctic tourist as, glittering in her metal-foil thermosuit, she walked towards the waiting Spider and the group of technicians round it. She had chosen the time carefully; the sun had risen only an hour ago, and its slanting rays would show the Taprobanean landscape to best advantage. Her Remote, even younger and huskier than on the last memorable occasion, recorded the sequence of events for her System-wide audience.

She had, as always, been thoroughly rehearsed. There was no fumbling or hesitation as she strapped herself in, pressed the BATTERY CHARGE button, took a deep draught of oxygen from her facemask and checked the monitors on all her video and sound channels. Then, like a fighter pilot in some old historical movie, she signalled 'Thumbs Up', and gently eased the speed control forward.

There was a small burst of ironic clapping from the assembled engineers, most of whom had already taken joy-rides up to heights of a few kilometres. Someone shouted: 'Ignition! We have lift off!' and, moving about as swiftly as a brass bird-cage elevator in the reign of Victoria I, Spider began its stately ascent.

This must be like ballooning, Maxine told herself. Smooth, effortless, silent. No – not completely silent; she could hear the gentle whirr of the motors powering the multiple drive wheels that gripped the flat face of the tape. There was none of the sway or vibration that she had half expected; despite its slimness, the incredible band she was climbing was as rigid as a bar of steel, and the vehicle's gyros were holding it rock-steady. If she closed her eyes, she could easily imagine that she was already ascending the final tower. But, of course, she would not close her eyes; there was so much to see and absorb. There was even a good deal to hear; it was amazing how well sound carried, for the conversations below were still quite audible.

She waved to Vannevar Morgan, then looked for Warren Kingsley. To her surprise she was unable to find him; though he had helped her aboard Spider, he had now vanished. Then she remembered his frank admission – sometimes he made it sound almost like a wry boast – that the best structural engineer in the world couldn't stand heights ... Everyone had some secret – or perhaps not-so-secret – fear. Maxine did not appreciate spiders, and wished that the vehicle she was riding had some other name; yet she could handle one if it was really necessary. The creature she could *never* bear to touch – though she had met it often enough on her diving expeditions – was the shy and harmless octopus.

The whole mountain was now visible, though from directly above it was impossible to appreciate its true height. The two ancient stairways winding up its face might have been oddly twisting level roads; along their entire length, as far as Maxine could observe, there was no sign of life. Indeed, one section had been blocked by a fallen tree – as if Nature had given advance notice, after three thousand years, that she was about to reclaim her own.

Leaving Camera One pointed downwards, Maxine started to pan with Number Two. Fields and forests drifted across the monitor screen, then the distant white domes of Ranapura – then the dark waters of the inland sea. And, presently, there was Yakkagala ...

She zoomed on to the Rock, and could just make out the faint pattern of the ruins covering the entire upper surface. The Mirror Wall was still in shadow, as was the Gallery of the Princesses – not that there was any hope of making them out from such a distance. But the layout of the Pleasure Gardens, with their ponds and walkways and massive surrounding moat, was clearly visible.

The line of tiny white plumes puzzled her for a moment, until she realized that she was looking down upon another symbol of Kalidasa's challenge to the Gods – his so-called Fountains of Paradise. She wondered what the king would have thought, could he have seen her rising so effortlessly towards the heaven of his envious dreams.

It was almost a year since she had spoken to Ambassador Rajasinghe. On a sudden impulse she called the Villa.

'Hello, Johan,' she greeted him. 'How do you like *this* view of Yakkagala?'

'So you've talked Morgan into it. How does it feel?'

'Exhilarating – that's the only word for it. And unique; I've flown and travelled in everything you can mention, but this feels quite different.'

' "To ride secure the cruel sky . . ." '

'What was that?'

'An English poet, early twentieth century—

I care not if you bridge the seas,
   Or ride secure the cruel sky . . .'

'Well, *I* care, and I'm feeling secure. Now I can see the whole island – even the Hindustan coast. How high am I, Van?'

'Coming up to twelve kilometres, Maxine. Is your oxygen mask on tight?'

'Confirmed. I hope it's not muffling my voice.'

'Don't worry – you're still unmistakeable. Three kilometres to go.'

'How much gas is still left in the tank?'

'Sufficient. And if you try to go above fifteen, I'll use the override to bring you home.'

'I wouldn't dream of it. And congratulations, by the way – this is an excellent observing platform. You may have customers standing in line.'

'We've thought of that – the comsat and metsat people are already making bids. We can give them relays and sensors at any height they like; it will all help to pay the rent.'

'I can see you!' exclaimed Rajasinghe suddenly. 'Just caught your reflection in the 'scope. Now you're waving your arm . . . Aren't you lonely up there?'

For a moment there was an uncharacteristic silence. Then Maxine Duval answered quietly: 'Not as lonely as Yuri Gagarin must have been, a hundred kilometres higher still. Van, you have brought something new into the world. The sky may still be cruel – but you have tamed it. There may be some people who could never face this ride; I feel very sorry for them.'

37 The Billion-Ton Diamond

In the last seven years much had been done, yet there was still so much to do. Mountains – or at least asteroids – had been moved. Earth now possessed a second natural moon, circling just above synchronous altitude. It was less than a kilometre across, and was rapidly becoming smaller as it was rifled of its carbon and other light elements. Whatever was left – the core of iron, tailings and industrial slag – would form the counterweight that would keep the Tower in tension. It would be the stone in the forty-thousand-kilometre-long sling that now turned with the planet once every twenty-four hours.

Fifty kilometres eastwards of Ashoka Station floated the huge industrial complex which processed the weightless – but not mass-less – megatons of raw material and converted them into hyper-filament. Because the final product was more than ninety per cent carbon, with its atoms arranged in a precise crystalline lattice, the Tower had acquired the popular nickname 'The Billion-Ton Diamond'. The Jeweller's Association of Amsterdam had sourly pointed out that (a) hyperfilament wasn't diamond at all (b) if it *was*, then the Tower weighed five times ten to the fifteen carats.

Carats or tons, such enormous quantities of material had taxed to the utmost the resources of the space colonies and the skills of the orbital technicians. Into the automatic mines, production plants and zero-gravity assembly systems had gone much of the engineering genius of the human race, painfully acquired during two hundred years of spacefaring. Soon all the components of the Tower – a few standardized units, manufactured by the million –

would be gathered in huge floating stock-piles, waiting for the robot handlers.

Then the Tower would grow in two opposite directions – down to Earth, and simultaneously up to the orbital mass-anchor, the whole process being adjusted so that it would always be in balance. Its cross-section would decrease steadily from orbit, where it would be under the maximum stress, down to Earth; it would also taper off towards the anchoring counter-weight.

When its task was complete, the entire construction complex would be launched into a transfer orbit to Mars. This was a part of the contract which had caused some heartburning among terrestrial politicians and financiers now that, belatedly, the space elevator's potential was being realized.

The Martians had driven a hard bargain. Though they would wait another five years before they had any return on their investment, they would then have a virtual construction monopoly for perhaps another decade. Morgan had a shrewd suspicion that the Pavonis tower would merely be the first of several; Mars might have been designed as a location for space elevator systems, and its energetic occupants were not likely to miss such an opportunity. If they made their world the centre of interplanetary commerce in the years ahead, good luck to them; Morgan had other problems to worry about, and some of them were still unsolved.

The Tower, for all its overwhelming size, was merely the support for something much more complex. Along each of its four sides must run thirty-six thousand kilometres of track, capable of operation at speeds never before attempted. This had to be powered for its entire length by super-conducting cables, linked to massive fusion generators, the whole system being controlled by an incredibly elaborate, fail-safe computer network.

The Upper Terminal, where passengers and freight would transfer between the Tower and the spacecraft docked to it, was a major project in itself. So was Midway Station. So was Earth Terminal, now being lasered into the heart of the sacred mountain. And in addition to all *this*, there was Operation Cleanup . . .

For two hundred years, satellites of all shapes and sizes, from loose nuts and bolts to entire space villages, had been accumulating in Earth orbit. All that now came below the extreme elevation of the

156

Tower, at *any* time, now had to be accounted for, since they created a possible hazard. Three-quarters of this material was abandoned junk, much of it long forgotten. Now it had to be located, and somehow disposed of.

Fortunately, the old orbital forts were superbly equipped for this task. Their radars – designed to locate oncoming missiles at extreme ranges with no advance warning – could easily pin-point the debris of the early space age. Then their lasers vaporized the smaller satellites, while the larger ones were nudged into higher and harmless orbits. Some, of historic interest, were recovered and brought back to Earth. During this operation there were quite a few surprises – for example, three Chinese astronauts who had perished on some secret mission, and several reconnaissance satellites constructed from such an ingenious mix of components that it was quite impossible to discover what country had launched them. Not, of course, that it now mattered a great deal, since they were at least a hundred years old.

The multitude of active satellites and space stations – forced for operational reasons to remain close to Earth – all had to have their orbits carefully checked, and in some cases modified. But nothing, of course, could be done about the random and unpredictable visitors which might arrive at any minute from the outer reaches of the Solar System. Like all the creations of mankind, the Tower would be exposed to meteorites. Several times a day its network of seismometers would detect milligram impacts; and once or twice a year minor structural damage might be expected. And sooner or later, during the centuries to come, it might encounter a giant which could put one or more tracks out of action for a while. In the worst possible case, the Tower might even be severed somewhere along its length.

That was about as likely to happen as the impact of a large meteorite upon London or Tokyo – which presented roughly the same target area. The inhabitants of those cities did not lose much sleep worrying over this possibility. Nor did Vannevar Morgan. Whatever problems might still lie ahead, no one doubted now that the Orbital Tower was an idea whose time had come.

part five
Ascension

38 A Place of Silent Storms

(Extract from Professor Martin Sessui's address, on receiving the Nobel Prize for Physics, Stockholm, 16 December 2154.)

Between Heaven and Earth lies an invisible region of which the old philosophers never dreamed. Not until the dawn of the twentieth century – to be precise, on 12 December 1901 – did it make its first impact upon human affairs.

On that day, Guglielmo Marconi radioed the three dots of the Morse letter 'S' across the Atlantic. Many experts had declared this to be impossible, as electromagnetic waves would travel only in straight lines, and would be unable to bend round the curve of the globe. Marconi's feat not only heralded the age of world-wide communications, but also proved that, high up in the atmosphere, there exists an electrified mirror, capable of reflecting radio waves back to earth.

The Kennelly-Heaviside Layer, as it was originally named, was soon found to be a region of great complexity, containing at least three main layers, all subject to major variations in height and intensity. At their upper limit they merge into the Van Allen Radiation Belts, whose discovery was the first triumph of the early space age.

This vast region, beginning at a height of approximately fifty kilometres and extending outwards for several radii of the Earth, is now known as the ionosphere; its exploration by rockets, satellites and radio waves has been a continuing process for more than two centuries. I should like to pay a tribute to my precursors in this enterprise – the Americans Tuve and Breit, the Englishman Appleton, the Norwegian Størmer – and, especially, the man who, in 1970, won the very award I am now so honoured to accept, your countryman Hannes Alfvén . . .

The ionosphere is the wayward child of the sun; even now its behaviour is not always predictable. In the days when long-range radio depended upon its idiosyncrasies it saved many lives – but more men than we shall ever know were doomed when it swallowed their despairing signals without trace.

For less than one century, before the communications satellites took over, it was our invaluable but erratic servant – a previously unsuspected natural phenomenon, worth countless billions of dollars to the three generations who exploited it.

Only for a brief moment in history was it of direct concern to mankind. And yet – if it had never existed, we should not be here! In one sense, therefore, it was of vital importance even to pre-technological humanity, right back to the first ape-man – indeed, right back to the first living creatures on this planet. For the ionosphere is part of the shield that protects us from the sun's deadly X-ray and ultra-violet radiations. If they had penetrated to sea level, perhaps some kind of life might still have arisen on earth; but it would never have evolved into anything remotely resembling us . . .

Because the ionosphere, like the atmosphere below it, is ultimately controlled by the sun, it too has its weather. During times of solar disturbance it is blasted by planet-wide gales of charged particles, and twisted into loops and whirls by the earth's magnetic field. On such occasions it is no longer invisible, for it reveals itself in the glowing curtains of the aurora – one of Nature's most awesome spectacles, illuminating the cold polar nights with its eerie radiance.

Even now, we do not understand all the processes occurring in the ionosphere. One reason why it has proved difficult to study is because all our rocket- and satellite-born instruments race through it at thousands of kilometres an hour; we have never been able to stand still to make observations! Now, for the very first time the construction of the proposed Orbital Tower gives us a chance of establishing *fixed* observatories in the ionosphere. It is also possible that the Tower may itself modify the characteristics of the ionosphere – though it will certainly not, as Dr Bickerstaff has suggested, short-circuit it!

Why should we study this region, now that it is no longer important to the communications engineer? Well, apart from its beauty, its strangeness and its scientific interest, its behaviour is closely linked with that of the sun – the master of our destiny. We know now that the sun is *not* the steady, well-behaved star that our ancestors believed; it undergoes both long- and short-period fluctuations. At the present time it is still emerging from the so-called 'Maunder Minimum' of 1645 to 1715; as a result, the climate now is milder than at any time since the Early Middle Ages. But how long will this upswing last? Even more important, when will the inevitable downturn begin, and what effect will this have upon climate, weather and every aspect of human civilization – not only on this planet, but on the others as well? For they are all children of the sun. . .

Some very speculative theories suggest that the sun is now entering a period of instability which may produce a new Ice Age, more universal than any in the past. If this is true, we need every scrap of information we can get to prepare for it. Even a century's warning might not be long enough.

The ionosphere helped to create us; it launched the communications revolution; it may yet determine much of our future. That is why we must continue the study of this vast, turbulent arena of solar and electric forces – this mysterious place of silent storms.

39 The Wounded Sun

The last time that Morgan had seen Dev, his nephew had been a child. Now he was a boy in his early teens; and at their next meeting, at this rate, he would be a man.

The engineer felt only a mild sense of guilt. Family ties had been weakening for the last two centuries: he and his sister had little in common except the accident of genetics. Though they exchanged greetings and small talk perhaps half-a-dozen times a year, and were on the best of terms, he was not even sure when and where they had last met.

Yet when he greeted the eager, intelligent boy (not in the least overawed, it seemed, by his famous uncle) Morgan was aware of a certain bitter-sweet wistfulness. He had no son to continue the family name; long ago, he had made that choice between Work and Life which can seldom be avoided at the highest levels of human endeavour. On three occasions – not including the liaison with Ingrid – he might have taken a different path; but accident or ambition had deflected him.

He knew the terms of the bargain he had made, and he accepted them; it was too late now to grumble about the small print. Any fool could shuffle genes, and most did. But whether or not History gave him credit, few men could have achieved what he had done – and was about to do.

In the last three hours, Dev had seen far more of Earth Terminus than any of the usual run of VIPs. He had entered the mountain at ground level, along the almost completed approach to the South Station, and had been given the quick tour of the passenger and baggage handling facilities, the control centre, and the switching yard where capsules would be routed from the East and West DOWN tracks to the North and South UP ones. He had stared up the five-kilometre-long shaft – like a giant gun barrel aimed at the stars, as several hundred reporters had already remarked in hushed voices – along which the lines of traffic would rise and descend. And his questions had exhausted three guides before the last one had thankfully handed him over to his uncle.

'Here he is, Van,' said Warren Kingsley as they arrived *via* the high-speed elevator at the truncated summit of the mountain.

'Take him away before he grabs my job.'

'I didn't know you were so keen on engineering, Dev.'

The boy looked hurt, and a little surprised. 'Don't you remember, Uncle – that No 12 Meccamax you gave me on my tenth birthday?'

'Of course – of course. I was only joking.' (And, to tell the truth, he had not *really* forgotten the construction set; it had merely slipped his mind for the moment.) 'You're not cold up here?' Unlike the well-protected adults, the boy had disdained the usual light thermocoat.

'No – I'm fine. What kind of jet is that? When are you going to open up the shaft? Can I touch the tapes?'

'See what I mean?' chuckled Kingsley.

'One: that's Sheik Abdullah's Special – his son Feisal is visiting. Two: we'll keep this lid on until the Tower reaches the mountain and enters the shaft – we need it as a working platform, and it keeps out the rain. Three: you can touch the tapes if you want to – *don't run* – it's bad for you at this altitude!'

'If you're twelve, I doubt it,' said Kingsley towards Dev's rapidly receding back. Taking their time, they caught up with him at the East Face anchor.

The boy was staring, as so many thousands of others had aleady done, at the narrow band of dull grey that rose straight out of the ground and soared vertically into the sky. Dev's gaze followed it up – up – up – until his head was tilted as far back as it would go. Morgan and Kingsley did not follow suit, though the temptation, after all these years, was still strong. Nor did they warn him that some visitors got so giddy that they collapsed and were unable to walk away without assistance.

The boy was tough: he gazed intently at the zenith for almost a minute, as if hoping to see the thousands of men and millions of tons of material poised there beyond the deep blue of the sky. Then he closed his eyes with a grimace, shook his head, and looked down at his feet for an instant, as if to reassure himself that he was still on the solid, dependable earth.

He reached out a cautious hand, and stroked the narrow ribbon linking the planet with its new moon.

'What would happen,' he asked, 'if it broke?'

That was an old question; most people were surprised at the answer.

'Very little. At this point, it's under practically no tension. If you cut the tape it would just hang there, waving in the breeze.'

Kingsley made an expression of distaste; both knew, of course, that this was a considerable over-simplification. At the moment, each of the four tapes was stressed at about a hundred tons – but that was negligible compared to the design loads they would be handling when the system was in operation and they had been integrated into the structure of the Tower. There was no point, however, in confusing the boy with such details.

Dev thought it over; then he gave the tape an experimental flick, as if he hoped to extract a musica note from it. But the only response was an unimpressive 'click' that instantly died away.

'If you hit it with a sledge-hammer,' said Morgan, 'and came back about ten hours later, you'd be just in time for the echo from Midway.'

'Not any longer,' said Kingsley. 'Too much damping in the system.'

'Don't be a spoil-sport, Warren. Now come and see something really interesting.'

They walked to the centre of the circular metal disc that now capped the mountain and sealed the shaft like a giant saucepan lid. Here, equidistant from the four tapes down which the Tower was being guided earthwards, was a small geodesic hut, looking even more temporary than the surface on which it had been erected. It housed an oddly-designed telescope, pointing straight upwards and apparently incapable of being aimed in any other direction.

'This is the best time for viewing, just before sunset; then the base of the Tower is nicely lit up.'

'Talking of the sun,' said Kingsley, 'just look at it now. It's even clearer than yesterday.' There was something approaching awe in his voice, as he pointed at the brilliant flattened ellipse sinking down into the western haze. The horizon mists had dimmed its glare so much that one could stare at it in comfort.

Not for more than a century had such a group of spots appeared; they stretched across almost half the golden disc, making it seem as if the sun had been stricken by some malignant disease, or pierced by falling worlds. Yet not even mighty Jupiter could have created such a wound in the solar atmosphere; the largest spot was a quarter of a million kilometres across, and could have swallowed a hundred Earths.

'There's another big auroral display predicted for tonight – Professor Sessui and his merry men certainly timed it well.'

'Let's see how they're getting on,' said Morgan, as he made some adjustments to the eye-piece. 'Have a look, Dev.'

The boy peered intently for a moment, then answered: 'I can see the four tapes, going inwards – I mean upwards – until they disappear.'

'Nothing in the middle?'

Another pause. 'No – not a sign of the Tower.'

'Correct – it's still six hundred kilometres up, and we're on the

164

lowest power of the telescope. Now I'm going to zoom. Fasten your seatbelt.'

Dev gave a little laugh at the ancient cliché, familiar from dozens of historical dramas. Yet at first he could see no alteration, except that the four lines pointing towards the centre of the field were becoming a little less sharp. It took him a few seconds to realize that no change could be expected as his point of view hurtled upwards along the axis of the system; the quartet of tapes would look exactly the same at any point along its length.

Then, quite suddenly, it was *there*, taking him by surprise even though he had been expecting it. A tiny bright spot had materialized in the exact centre of the field; it was expanding as he watched it, and now for the first time he had a real sensation of speed.

A few seconds later, he could make out a small circle – no, now both brain and eye agreed that it was a square. He was looking directly up at the base of the Tower, crawling earthwards along its guiding tapes at a couple of kilometres a day. The four tapes had now vanished, being far too small to be visible at this distance. But that square fixed magically in the sky continued to grow, though now it had become fuzzy under the extreme magnification.

'What do you see?' asked Morgan.

'A bright little square.'

'Good – that's the underside of the tower, still in full sunlight. When it's dark down here you can see it with the naked eye for another hour before it enters the Earth's shadow. Now, do you see anything else?'

'Nooo . . .' replied the boy, after a long pause.

'You should. There's a team of scientists visiting the lowest section to set up some research equipment. They've just come down from Midway. If you look carefully you'll see their transporter – it's on the south track – that will be the right side of the picture. Look for a bright spot, about a quarter the size of the Tower.'

'Sorry, Uncle – I can't find it. *You* have a look.'

'Well, the seeing may have got worse. Sometimes the Tower disappears completely though the atmosphere may look—'

Even before Morgan could take Dev's place at the eyepiece, his personal receiver gave two shrill double beeps. A second later, Kingsley's alarm also erupted.

It was the first time the Tower had ever issued a four-star emergency alert.

40 The End of the Line

No wonder they called it the 'Transiberian Railway'. Even on the easy downhill run, the journey from Midway Station to the base of the Tower lasted fifty hours.

One day it would take only five, but that still lay two years in the future, when the tracks were energized and their magnetic fields activated. The inspection and maintenance vehicles that now ran up and down the faces of the Tower were propelled by old-fashioned tyres, gripping the interior of the guidance slots. Even if the limited power of the batteries permitted, it was not safe to operate such a system at more than five hundred kilometres an hour.

Yet everyone had been far too busy to be bored. Professor Sessui and his three students had been observing, checking their instruments, and making sure that no time would be wasted when they transferred into the Tower. The capsule driver, his engineering assistant, and the one steward who comprised the entire cabin staff were also fully occupied, for this was no routine trip. The 'Basement', twenty-five thousand kilometres below Midway – and now only six hundred kilometres from Earth – had never been visited since it was built. Until now, there had been no purpose in going there, since the handful of monitors had never reported anything amiss. Not that there was much to go wrong, as the Basement was merely a fifteen-metre-square pressurized chamber – one of the scores of emergency refuges at intervals along the Tower.

Professor Sessui had used all his considerable influence to borrow this unique site, now crawling down through the ionosphere at two kilometres a day towards its rendezvous with Earth. It was essential, he had argued forcibly, to get his equipment installed before the peak of the current sunspot maximum.

Already, solar activity had reached unprecedented levels, and Sessui's young assistants often found it hard to concentrate on their instruments; the magnificent auroral displays outside were too much of a distraction. For hours on end, both northern and southern hemispheres were filled with slowly moving curtains and streamers of greenish light, beautiful and awe-inspiring – yet only a pale ghost of the celestial firework displays taking place around the poles. It was rare indeed for the aurora to wander so far from its normal domains; only once in generations did it invade the equatorial skies.

Sessui had driven his students back to work with the admonition that they would have plenty of time for sight-seeing during the long climb back to Midway. Yet it was noticeable that even the Professor himself sometimes stood at the observation window for minutes at a time, entranced by the spectacle of the burning heavens.

Someone had christened the project 'Expedition to Earth' – which, as far as distance was concerned, was ninety-eight per cent accurate. As the capsule crawled down the face of the Tower at its miserable five hundred klicks, the increasing closeness of the planet beneath made itself obvious. For gravity was slowly increasing, from the delightful less-than-lunar buoyancy of Midway to almost its full terrestrial value. To any experienced space traveller, this was strange indeed: feeling *any* gravity before the moment of atmospheric entry seemed a reversal of the normal order of things.

Apart from complaints about the food, stoically endured by the overworked steward, the journey had been devoid of incident. A hundred kilometres from the Basement, the brakes had been gently applied and speed had been halved. It was halved again at fifty kilometres – for, as one of the students remarked: 'Wouldn't it be embarrassing if we ran off the end of the track?'

The driver (he insisted on being called pilot) retorted that this was impossible, as the guidance slots down which the capsule was falling terminated several metres short of the Tower's end; there was also an elaborate buffer system, just in case *all* four independent sets of brakes failed to work. And everyone agreed that the joke, besides being perfectly ridiculous, was in extremely poor taste.

41 Meteor

The vast artificial lake known for two thousand years as the Sea of Paravana lay calm and peaceful beneath the stone gaze of its builder. Though few now visited the lonely statue of Kalidasa's father, his work, if not his fame, had outlasted that of his son; and it had served his country infinitely better, bringing food and drink to a hundred generations of men. And to many more generations of birds, buffalo, monkeys and their predators, like the sleek and well-fed leopard now drinking at the water's edge. The big cats were becoming rather too common and were inclined to be a nuisance, now that they no longer had anything to fear from hunters. But they never attacked men, unless they were cornered or molested.

Confident of his security, the leopard was leisurely drinking his fill, as the shadows round the lake lengthened and twilight advanced from the east. Suddenly, he pricked up his ears and became instantly alert; but no mere human senses could have detected any change in land, water or sky. The evening was as tranquil as ever.

And then, directly out of the zenith, came a faint whistling that grew steadily to a rumbling roar, with tearing, ripping undertones, quite unlike that of a re-entering spacecraft. Up in the sky something metallic was sparkling in the last rays of the sun, growing larger and larger and leaving a trail of smoke behind it. As it expanded, it disintegrated; pieces shot off in all directions, some of them burning as they did so. For a few seconds an eye as keen as the leopard's might have glimpsed a roughly cylindrical object, before it exploded into a myriad fragments. But the leopard did not wait for the final catastrophe; it had already disappeared into the jungle.

The Sea of Paravana erupted in sudden thunder. A geyser of mud and spray shot a hundred metres into the air – a fountain far surpassing those of Yakkagala, and one indeed almost as high as the Rock itself. It hung suspended for a moment in futile defiance of gravity, then tumbled back into the shattered lake.

Already, the sky was full of waterfowl wheeling in startled flight. Almost as numerous, flapping among them like leathery ptero-dactyls who had somehow survived into the modern age, were the big fruit-bats who normally took to the air only after dusk. Now, equally terrified, birds and bats shared the sky together.

The last echoes of the crash died away into the encircling jungle; silence swiftly returned to the lake. But long minutes passed before its mirror surface was restored and the little waves ceased to scurry back and forth beneath the unseeing eyes of Paravana the Great.

42 Death in Orbit

Every large building, it is said, claims a life; fourteen names were engraved on the piers of the Gibraltar Bridge. But thanks to an almost fanatical safety campaign, casualties on the Tower had been remarkably low. There had, indeed, been one year without a single death.

And there had been one year with four – two of them particularly harrowing. A space-station assembly supervisor, accustomed to working under zero gravity, had forgotten that though he was in space he was not in orbit – and a life-time's experience had be-trayed him. He had plummeted more than fifteen thousand kilo-metres, to burn up like a meteor upon entry into the atmosphere. Unfortunately his suit radio had remained switched on during those last few minutes . . .

It was a bad year for the Tower; the second tragedy had been much more protracted, and equally public. An engineer on the counterweight, far beyond synchronous orbit, had failed to fasten her safety belt properly – and had been flicked off into space like a stone from a sling. She was in no danger, at this altitude, either of falling back to Earth or of being launched on an escape trajectory; unfortunately her suit held less than two hours' air. There was no possibility of rescue at such short notice; and despite a public outcry, no attempt was made. The victim had cooperated nobly. She had transmitted her farewell messages, and then – with thirty minutes of oxygen still unused – had opened her suit to vacuum. The body was recovered a few days later, when the inexorable laws of celestial mechanics brought it back to the perigee of its long ellipse.

These tragedies flashed through Morgan's mind as he took the highspeed elevator down to the Operations Room, closely followed by a sombre Warren Kingsley and now almost forgotten Dev. But *this* catastrophe was of an altogether different type, involving an explosion at or near the Basement of the Tower. That the transporter had fallen to earth was obvious, even before the garbled report had been received of a 'giant meteor shower' somewhere in central Taprobane.

It was useless to speculate until he had more facts; and in this case, where all the evidence had probably been destroyed, they might never be available. He knew that space accidents seldom had a single cause; they were usually the result of a chain of events, often quite harmless in themselves. All the foresight of the safety engineers could not guarantee absolute reliability, and sometimes their own over-elaborate precautions contributed to disaster. Morgan was not ashamed of the fact that the safety of the project now concerned him far more than any loss of life. Nothing could be done about the dead, except to ensure that the same accident could never happen again. But that the almost completed Tower might be endangered was a prospect too appalling to contemplate.

The elevator floated to a halt, and he stepped out into the Operations Rooms – just in time for the evening's second stunning surprise.

43 Fail-Safe

Five kilometres from the terminus, driver-pilot Rupert Chang had reduced speed yet again. Now, for the first time, the passengers could see the face of the Tower as something more than a featureless blur dwindling away to infinity in both directions. Upwards, it was true, the twin grooves along which they were riding still stretched forever – or at least for twenty-five thousand kilometres, which on the human scale was much the same. But downwards, the end was already in sight. The truncated base of the Tower was clearly silhouetted against the verdant green background of Taprobane, which it would reach and unite with in little more than a year.

Across the display panel, the red ALARM symbols flashed yet again. Chang studied them with a frown of annoyance, then pressed the RE-SET button. They flickered once, then vanished.

The first time this had happened, two hundred kilometres higher, there had been a hasty consultation with Midway Control. A quick check of all systems had revealed nothing amiss; indeed, if all the warnings were to be believed, the transporter's passengers were already dead. *Everything* had gone outside the limits of tolerance.

It was obviously a fault in the alarm circuits themselves, and Professor Sessui's explanation was accepted with general relief. The vehicle was no longer in the pure vacuum environment for which it had been designed; the ionospheric turmoil it had now entered was triggering the sensitive detectors of the warning systems.

'Someone should have thought of *that*,' Chang had grumbled. But, with less than an hour to go, he was not really worried. He would make constant manual checks of all the critical parameters; Midway approved, and in any case there was no alternative.

Battery condition was, perhaps, the item that concerned him most. The nearest charging point was two thousand kilometres higher up, and if they couldn't climb back to that they would be in trouble. But Chang was quite happy on this score; during the braking process the transporter's drive-motors had been functioning as dynamos, and ninety per cent of its gravitational energy had been pumped back into the batteries. Now that they were fully charged, the surplus hundreds of kilowatts still being generated should be diverted into space through the big cooling fins at the rear. Those fins, as Chang's colleagues had often pointed out to him made his unique vehicle look rather like an old-time aerial bomb. By this time, at the very end of the braking process, they should have been glowing a dull red. Chang would have been very worried indeed had he known that they were still comfortably cool. For energy can never be destroyed; it has to go *somewhere*. And very often it goes to the wrong place.

When the FIRE–BATTERY COMPARTMENT sign came on for the third time, Chang did not hesitate to reset it. A real fire, he knew, would have triggered the extinguishers; in fact, one of his biggest worries was that these might operate unnecessarily. There were several anomalies on the board now, especially in the battery-charging circuits. As soon as the journey was over and he had powered down the transporter, Chang was going to climb into the motor-room and give everything a good old-fashioned eyeball inspection.

As it happened, his nose alerted him first, when there was barely more than a kilometre to go. Even as he stared incredulously at the thin wisp of smoke oozing out of the control board, the coldly analytical part of his mind was saying: 'What a lucky coincidence that it waited until the end of the trip!'

Then he remembered all the energy being produced during the final braking, and had a pretty shrewd guess at the sequence of events. The protective circuits must have failed to operate, and the batteries had been overcharging. One fail-safe after another had let them down; helped by the ionospheric storm, the sheer perversity of inaminate things had struck again.

Chang punched the battery compartment fire-extinguisher button; at least *that* worked, for he could hear the muffled roar of the nitrogen blasts on the other side of the bulkhead. Ten seconds later, he triggered the VACUUM DUMP which would sweep the gas out into space – with, hopefully, most of the heat it had picked up from the fire. That too operated correctly; it was the first time that Chang had ever listened with relief to the unmistakable shriek of atmosphere escaping from a space vehicle; he hoped it would also be the last.

He dared not rely on the automatic braking sequence as the vehicle finally crawled into the terminus; fortunately, he had been well rehearsed and recognized all the visual signals, so that he was able to stop within a centimetre of the docking adapter. In frantic haste, the airlocks were coupled together, and stores and equipment were hurled through the connecting tube . . .

. . . And so was Professor Sessui, by the combined exertions of pilot, assistant engineer and steward, when he tried to go back for his precious instruments. The airlock doors were slammed shut just seconds before the engine compartment bulkhead finally gave way.

After that, the refugees could do nothing but wait in the bleak, fifteen-metre square chamber, with considerably fewer amenities than a well-furnished prison cell, and hope that the fire would burn itself out. Perhaps it was well for the passenger's peace of mind that only Chang and his engineer appreciated one vital statistic: the fully-charged batteries contained the energy of a large chemical bomb, now ticking away on the outside of the Tower.

Ten minutes after their hasty arrival, the bomb went off. There was a muffled explosion, which caused only slight vibrations of the Tower, followed by the sound of ripping and tearing metal. Though the breaking-up noises were not very impressive, they chilled the hearts of the listeners; their only means of transport was being destroyed, leaving them stranded twenty-five thousand kilometres from safety.

There was another, more protracted explosion – then silence; the refugees guessed that the vehicle had fallen off the face of the Tower. Still numbed, they started to survey their resources; and slowly, they began to realize that their miraculous escape might have been wholly in vain.

44 A Cave in the Sky

Deep inside the mountain, amid the display and communications equipment of the Earth Operations Centre, Morgan and his engineering staff stood around the tenth-scale hologram of the Tower's lowest section. It was perfect in every detail, even to the four thin ribbons of the guiding tapes extending along each face. They vanished into thin air just above the floor, and it was hard to appreciate that, even on this diminished scale, they should continue downwards for another sixty kilometres – completely through the crust of the earth.

'Give us the cutaway,' said Morgan, 'and lift the Basement up to eye level.'

The Tower lost its apparent solidity and became a luminous ghost – a long, thin-walled square box, empty except for the superconducting cables of the power supply. The very lowest section – the 'Basement' was indeed a good name for it, even if it was at a hundred times the elevation of this mountain – had been sealed off to form a single square chamber, fifteen metres on a side.

'Access?' queried Morgan.

Two sections of the image started to glow more brightly. Clearly defined on the north and south face, between the slots of the guidance tracks, were the outer doors of the duplicate airlocks – as far apart as possible, according to the usual safety precautions for all space habitats.

'They went in through the south door, of course,' explained the Duty Officer. 'We don't know if it was damaged in the explosion.'

Well, there were three other entrances, thought Morgan – and it was the lower pair that interested him. This had been one of those afterthoughts, incorporated at a late stage in the design. Indeed, the whole Basement was an afterthought; at one time it had been considered unnecessary to build a refuge here, in the section of the Tower that would eventually become part of Earth Terminus itself.

'Tilt the underside towards me.' Morgan ordered.

The Tower toppled, in a falling arc of light, and lay floating horizontally in mid-air with its lower end towards Morgan. Now

174

he could see all the details of the twenty-metre-square floor – or roof, if one looked at it from the point of view of its orbital builders.

Near the north and south edges, leading into the two independent airlocks, were the hatches that allowed access from below. The only problem was to reach them – six hundred kilometres up in the sky.

'Life support?'

The airlocks faded back into the structure; the visual emphasis moved to a small cabinet at the centre of the chamber.

'*That's* the problem, Doctor,' the Duty Officer answered sombrely. 'There's only a pressure maintenance system. No purifiers, and of course no power. Now that they've lost the transporter, I don't see how they can survive the night. The temperature's already falling – down ten degrees since sunset.'

Morgan felt as if the chill of space had entered his own soul. The euphoria of discovering that the lost transporter's occupants were all still alive faded swiftly away. Even if there was enough oxygen in the Basement to last them for several days, that would be of no importance if they froze before dawn.

'I'd like to speak to Professor Sessui.'

'We can't call him direct – the Basement emergency phone only goes to Midway. No problem, though.'

That turned out to be not completely true. When the connection was made, Driver-Pilot Chang came on the line.

'I'm sorry,' he said, 'the Professor is busy.'

After a moment's incredulous silence Morgan replied, pausing between each word and emphasising his name: 'Tell him that Dr Vannevar Morgan wants to speak to him.'

'I will, Doctor – but it won't make the slightest difference. He's working on some equipment with his students. It was the only thing they were able to save – a spectroscope of some kind – they're aiming it through one of the observation windows . . .'

Morgan controlled himself with difficulty. He was about to retort: 'Are they crazy?', when Chang anticipated him.

'You don't know the Prof – *I've* spent the last week with him. He's – well, I guess you could say single-minded. It took three of us to stop him going back into the cabin to get some more of his gear. And he's just told me that if we're all going to die anyway, he'll make damn sure that *one* piece of equipment is working properly.'

Morgan could tell from Chang's voice that, for all his annoyance, he felt a considerable admiration for his distinguished and difficult passenger. And, indeed, the Professor had logic on his side. It made good sense to salvage what he could, out of the years of effort that had gone into this ill-fated expedition.

'Very well,' said Morgan at length, cooperating with the inevitable. 'Since I can't get an appointment, I'd like *your* summary of the situation. So far, I've only had it secondhand.'

It now occurred to him that, in any event, Chang could probably give a much more useful report than the Professor. Though the driver-pilot's insistence on the second half of his title often caused derision among genuine astrologers, he was a highly skilled technician with a good training in mechanical and electrical engineering.

'There's not much to say. We had such short notice that there was no time to save anything – except that damned spectrometer. Frankly, I never thought we'd make it through the airlock. We have the clothes we're wearing – and that's about it. One of the students grabbed her travel bag. Guess what – it contained her draft thesis, written on *paper*, for heaven's sake! Not even flame-proofed, despite regulations. If we could afford the oxygen, we'd burn it to get some heat.'

Listening to that voice from space, and looking at the transparent – yet apparently solid – hologram of the Tower, Morgan had a most curious illusion. He could imagine that there were tiny, tenth-scale human beings moving around there in the lowest compartment; it was only necessary to reach in his hand, and carry them out to safety . . .

'Next to the cold, the big problem is air. I don't know how long it will be before CO_2 build-up knocks us out – perhaps someone will work out *that* as well. Whatever the answer, I'm afraid it will be too optimistic.' Chang's voice dropped several decibels and he began to speak in an almost conspiratorial tone, obviously to prevent being overheard. 'The Prof and his students don't know this, but the south airlock was damaged in the explosion. There's a leak – a steady hiss round the gaskets. How serious it is, I can't tell.' The speaker's voice rose to normal level again. 'Well, that's the situation. We'll be waiting to hear from you.'

And just what the hell *can* we say, Morgan thought to himself, except 'Goodbye'?

Crisis-management was a skill which Morgan admired but did not envy. Janos Bartok, the Tower Safety Officer up at Midway, was now in charge of the situation; those inside the mountain twenty-five thousand kilometres below – and a mere six hundred from the scene of the accident – could only listen to the reports, give helpful advice, and satisfy the curiosity of the news media as best they could.

Needless to say, Maxine Duval had been in touch within minutes of the disaster, and as usual her questions were very much to the point.

'Can Midway Station reach them in time?'

Morgan hesitated; the answer to *that* was undoubtedly 'No'. Yet it was unwise, not to say cruel, to abandon hope as early as this. And there had been one stroke of good luck . . .

'I don't want to raise false hopes, but we may not need Midway. There's a crew working much closer, at the 10K – ten-thousand-kilometre – Station. Their transporter can reach the Basement in twenty hours.'

'Then why isn't it on the way down?'

'Safety Officer Bartok will be making the decision shortly – but it could be a waste of effort. We think they have air for only half that time. And the temperature problem is even more serious.'

'What do you mean?'

'It's night up there, and they have no source of heat. Don't put this out yet, Maxine, but it may be a race between freezing and anoxia.'

There was a pause for several seconds; then Maxine Duval said in an uncharacteristically diffident tone of voice: 'Perhaps I'm being stupid, but surely the weather stations with their big infra-red lasers—'

'Thank you, Maxine – *I'm* the one who's being stupid. Just a minute while I speak to Midway . . .'

Bartok was polite enough when Morgan called, but his brisk

reply made his opinion of meddling amateurs abundantly clear.

'Sorry I bothered you,' apologized Morgan, and switched back to Maxine. 'Sometimes the expert does know his job,' he told her with rueful pride. '*Our* man knows his. He called Monsoon Control ten minutes ago. They're computing the beam power now – they don't want to overdo it, of course, and burn everybody up.'

'So I was right,' said Maxine sweetly. '*You* should have thought of that, Van. What else have you forgotten?'

No answer was possible, nor did Morgan attempt one. He could see Maxine's computer-mind racing ahead, and guessed what her next question would be. He was right.

'Can't you use the Spiders?'

'Even the final models are altitude-limited – their batteries can only take them up to three hundred kilometres. They were designed to inspect the Tower, when it had already entered the atmosphere.'

'Well, put in bigger batteries.'

'In a couple of hours? But *that's* not the problem. The only unit under test at the moment can't carry passengers.'

'You could send it up empty.'

'Sorry – we've thought of that. There must be an operator aboard to manage the docking, when the Spider comes up to the Basement. And it would still take days to get out seven people, one at a time.'

'Surely you have *some* plan!'

'Several, but they're all crazy. If any make sense, I'll let you know. Meanwhile, there's something you can do for us.'

'What's that?' Maxine asked suspiciously.

'Explain to your audience just why spacecraft can dock with each other six hundred kilometres up – but *not* with the Tower. By the time you've done that, we may have some news for you.'

As Maxine's slightly indignant image faded from the screen, and Morgan turned back once more to the well-orchestrated chaos of the Operations Room, he tried to let his mind roam as freely as possible over every aspect of the problem. Despite the polite re-buff of the Safety Officer, efficiently doing his duty up on Midway, he might be able to think of some useful ideas. Although he did not imagine that there would be any magical solution, he understood the Tower better than any living man – with the possible exception of Warren Kingsley. Warren probably knew more of the fine details; but Morgan had the clearer overall picture.

Seven men and women were stranded in the sky, in a situation that was unique in the whole history of space technology. There *must* be a way of getting to safety, before they were poisoned by CO_2, or the pressure dropped so low that the chamber became, in literal truth, a tomb like Mahomet's – suspended between Heaven and Earth.

45 The Man for the Job

'We can do it,' said Warren Kingsley with a broad smile. 'Spider *can* reach the Basement.'

'You've been able to add enough extra battery power?'

'Yes, but it's a very close thing. It will have to be a two-stage affair, like the early rockets. As soon as the battery is exhausted it must be jettisoned to get rid of the dead weight. That will be around four hundred kilometres; Spider's internal battery will take it the rest of the way.'

'And how much payload will *that* give?'

Kingsley's smile faded.

'Marginal. About fifty kilos, with the best batteries we have.'

'Only fifty! What use will *that* be?'

'It should be enough. A couple of those new thousand-atmosphere tanks, each holding five kilos of oxygen. Molecular filter masks to keep out the CO_2. A little water and compressed food. Some medical supplies. We can bring it all in under forty-five kilos.'

'Phew! And you're *sure* that's sufficient?'

'Yes – it will tide them over until the transporter arrives from the 10K Station. And if necessary Spider can make a second trip.'

'What does Bartok think?'

'He approves. After all, no one has any better ideas.'

Morgan felt that a great weight had been lifted from his shoulders. Plenty of things could still go wrong, but at last there was a ray of hope; the feeling of utter helplessness had been dispelled.

'When will all this be ready?' he asked.

'If there are no hold-ups, within two hours. Three at the most. It's all standard equipment, luckily. Spider's being checked out right now. There's only one matter still be be decided . . .'

Vannevar Morgan shook his head. 'No, Warren,' he answered slowly in a calm, implacably determined voice that his friend had never heard before. 'There's nothing more to decide.'

'I'm not trying to pull rank on you, Bartok,' said Morgan. 'It's a simple matter of logic. True, anyone can drive Spider – but only half-a-dozen men know *all* the technical details involved. There may be some operational problems when we reach the Tower, and I'm in the best position to solve them.'

'May I remind you, Dr Morgan,' said the Safety Officer, 'that you are sixty-five. It would be wiser to send a younger man.'

'I'm *not* sixty-five; I'm sixty-six. And age has absolutely nothing to do with it. There's no danger, and certainly no requirement for physical strength.'

And, he might have added, the psychological factors were far more important than the physical ones. Almost anybody could ride passively up and down in a capsule, as Maxine Duval had done and millions of others would be doing in the years ahead. It would be quite another matter to face some of the situations that could easily arise, six hundred kilometres up in the empty sky.

'I still think,' said Safety Officer Bartok with gentle persistence, 'that it would be best to send a younger man. Dr Kingsley, for example.'

Behind him, Morgan heard (or had he imagined?) his colleague's suddenly indrawn breath. For years they had joked over the fact that Warren had such an aversion to heights that he never inspected the structures he designed. His fear fell short of genuine acrophobia, and he could overcome it when absolutely necessary; he had, after all, joined Morgan in stepping from Africa to Europe. But that was the only time that anyone had ever seen him drunk in public, and he was not seen at all for twenty-four hours afterwards.

Warren was out of the question, even though Morgan knew that he would be prepared to go. There were times when technical ability and sheer courage were not enough; no man could fight against fears that had been implanted in him at his birth, or during his earliest childhood.

Fortunately, there was no need to explain this to the Safety Officer. There was a simpler and equally valid reason why Warren should not go. Only a very few times in his life had Vannevar Morgan been glad of his small size; this was one of them.

'I'm fifteen kilos lighter than Kingsley,' he told Bartok. 'In a marginal operation like this, that should settle the matter. So let's not waste any more precious time in argument.'

He felt a slight twinge of conscience, knowing that this was unfair. Bartok was only doing his job, very efficently, and it would be another hour before the capsule was ready. No one was wasting any time.

For long seconds the two men stared into each other's eyes as if the twenty-five thousand kilometres between them did not exist. If there was a direct trial of strength, the situation could be messy. Bartok was nominally in charge of all safety operations, and could theoretically over-rule even the Chief Engineer and Project Manager. But he might find it difficult to enforce his authority; both Morgan and Spider were far below him on Sri Kanda, and possession was nine points of the law.

Bartok shrugged his shoulders, and Morgan relaxed.

'You have a point. I'm still not too happy, but I'll go along with you. Good luck.'

'Thank you,' Morgan answered quietly, as the image faded from the screen. Turning to the still silent Kingsley, he said: 'Let's go.'

Only as they were leaving the Operations Room on the way back to the summit did Morgan automatically feel for the little pendant concealed beneath his shirt. CORA had not bothered him for months, and not even Warren Kingsley knew of her existence. Was he gambling with other lives as well as his own, just to satisfy his own selfish pride? If safety Officer Bartok had known about *this* . . .

It was too late now. Whatever his motives, he was committed.

46 Spider

How the mountain had changed, thought Morgan, since he had first seen it! The summit had been entirely sheared away, leaving a perfectly level plateau; at it centre was the giant 'saucepan lid', sealing the shaft which would soon carry the traffic of many worlds. Strange to think that the greatest spaceport in the solar system would be deep inside the heart of a mountain . . .

No one could have guessed that an ancient monastery had once stood here, focusing the hopes and fears of billions for at least three thousand years. The only token that still remained was the ambiguous bequest of the Maha Thero, now crated and waiting to be moved. But, so far, neither the authorities at Yakkagala nor the director of the Ranapura Museum had shown much enthusiasm for Kalidasa's ill-omened bell. The last time it had tolled the peak had been swept by that brief but eventful gale – a wind of change indeed. Now the air was almost motionless, as Morgan and his aides walked slowly to the waiting capsule, glittering beneath the inspection lights. Someone had stencilled the name SPIDER MARK II on the lower part of the housing; and beneath that had been scrawled the promise: WE DELIVER THE GOODS. I hope so, thought Morgan . . .

Every time he came here he found it more difficult to breathe, and he looked forward to the flood of oxygen that would soon gush into his starved lungs. But CORA, to his surprised relief, had never issued even a preliminary admonition when he visited the summit; the regime that Dr Sen had prescribed seemed to be working admirably.

Everything had been loaded aboard Spider, which had been jacked up so that the extra battery could be hung beneath it. Mechanics were still making hasty last-minute adjustments and disconnecting power leads; the tangle of cabling underfoot was a mild hazard to a man unused to walking in a spacesuit.

Morgan's Flexisuit had arrived from Gagarin only thirty minutes ago, and for a while he had seriously considered leaving without one. Spider Mark II was a far more sophisticated vehicle than the simple prototype that Maxine Duval had once ridden; indeed, it was a tiny spaceship with its own life-support system. If all went well, Morgan should be able to mate it with the airlock on the bottom of the Tower, designed years ago for this very purpose. But a suit would provide not only insurance in case of docking problems; it would give him enormously greater freedom of action. Almost form-fitting, the Flexisuit bore very little resemblance to the clumsy armour of the early astronauts, and, even when pressurized, would scarcely restrict his movements. He had once seen a demonstration by its manufacturers of some spacesuited acrobatics, culminating in a sword-fight and a ballet. The last was hilarious – but it had proved the designer's claims.

Morgan climbed the short flight of steps, stood for a moment on on the capsule's tiny metal porch, then cautiously backed inside. As he settled down and fastened the safety belt, he was agreeably surprised at the amount of room. Although the Mark II was certainly a one-man vehicle, it was not as claustrophobic as he had feared – even with the extra equipment that had been packed into it.

The two oxygen cylinders had been stowed under the seat, and the CO_2 masks were in a small box behind the ladder that led up to the overhead airlock. It seemed astonishing that such a small amount of equipment could mean the difference between life and death for so many people.

Morgan had taken one personal item – a memento of that first day long ago at Yakkagala, where in a sense all this had started. The spinnerette took up little room, and weighed only a kilo. Over the years it had become something of a talisman; it was still one of the most effective ways of demonstrating the properties of hyperfilament, and whenever he left it behind he almost invariably found that he needed it. On this, of all trips, it might well prove useful.

He plugged in the quick-release umbilical of his spacesuit, and tested the air-flow both on the internal and external supply. Outside, the power cables were disconnected; Spider was on its own.

Brilliant speeches were seldom forthcoming at such moments – and this, after all, was going to be a perfectly straightforward operation. Morgan grinned rather stiffly at Kingsley and said: 'Mind the store, Warren, until I get back.' Then he noticed the small, lonely figure in the crowd around the capsule. My God, he thought to himself – I'd almost forgotten the poor kid . . . 'Dev,' he called. 'Sorry I haven't been able to look after you. I'll make up for it when I get back.'

And I will, he told himself. When the Tower was finished there would be time for everything – even the human relations he had so badly neglected. Dev would be worth watching; a boy who knew when to keep out of the way showed unusual promise.

The curving door of the capsule – the upper half of it transparent plastic – thudded softly shut against its gaskets. Morgan pressed the CHECK-OUT button, and Spider's vital statistics appeared on the screen one by one. All were green; there was no need to note the actual figures. If any of the values had been outside nominal, they would have flashed red twice a second. Nevertheless, with his usual engineer's caution, Morgan observed that oxygen stood at 102 per cent, main battery power at 101 per cent, booster battery at 105 per cent . . .

The quiet, calm voice of the controller – the same unflappable expert who had watched over all operations since that first abortive lowering years ago – sounded in his ear. 'All systems nominal. You have control.'

'I have control. I'll wait until the next minute comes up.'

It was hard to think of a greater contrast to an old-time rocket launch, with its elaborate countdown, its split-second timing, its sound and fury. Morgan merely waited until the last two digits on the clock became zeroes, then switched on power at the lowest setting.

Smoothly – *silently* – the flood-lit mountain top fell away beneath him. Not even a ballon ascent could have been quieter. If he listened carefully he could just hear the whirring of the twin motors as they drove the big friction drive-wheels that gripped the tape, both above and below the capsule.

Rate of ascent, five metres a second, said the velocity indicator; in slow, regular steps Morgan increased the power until it read fifty – just under two hundred kilometres an hour. That gave maximum efficiency at Spider's present loading; when the auxiliary battery was dropped off, speed could be increased by twenty-five per cent to almost 250 klicks.

'Say *something*, Van!' said Warren Kingsley's amused voice from the world below.

'Leave me alone,' Morgan replied equably. 'I intend to relax and enjoy the view for the next couple of hours. If you wanted a running commentary, you should have sent Maxine Duval.'

'She's been calling you for the last hour.'

'Give her my love, and say I'm busy. Maybe when I reach the Tower . . . What's the latest from there?'

'Temperature's stabilized at twenty – Monsoon Control zaps them with a modest megawattage every ten minutes. But Professor Sessui is furious – complains that it upsets his instruments.'

'What about the air?'

'Not so good. The pressure has definitely dropped, and of course the CO_2's building up. But they should be OK if you arrive on schedule. They're avoiding all unnecessary movement, to conserve oxygen.'

All except Professor Sessui, I'll bet, thought Morgan. It would be interesting to meet the man whose life he was trying to save. He had read several of the scientist's widely-praised popular books, and considered them florid and overblown. Morgan suspected that the man matched the style.

'And the status at 10K?'

'Another two hours before the transporter can leave; they're installing some special circuits to make quite sure that nothing catches fire on *this* trip.'

'A very good idea – Bartok's, I suppose.'

'Probably. And they're coming down the north track, just in case the south one was damaged by the explosion. If all goes well, they'll arrive in – oh – twenty-one hours. Plenty of time, even if we don't send Spider up again with a second load.'

Despite his only half-jesting remark to Kingsley, Morgan knew that it was far too early to start relaxing. Yet all did seem to be going as well as could be expected; and there was certainly nothing else that he could do for the next three hours except admire the ever-expanding view.

He was already thirty kilometres up in the sky, rising swiftly and silently through the tropical night. There was no moon, but the land beneath was revealed by the twinkling constellations of its towns and villages. When he looked at the stars above and the stars below, Morgan found it easy to imagine that he was far from any world, lost in the depths of space. Soon he could see the whole island of Taprobane, faintly outlined by the lights of the coastal settlements. Far to the north a dull glowing patch was creeping up over the horizon like the herald of some displaced dawn. It puzzled him for a moment, until he realized that he was looking at one of the great cities of Southern Hindustan.

He was higher now than any aircraft could climb, and what he had already done was unique in the history of transportation. Although Spider and its precursors had made innumerable trips up to twenty kilometres, no one had been allowed to go higher because of the impossibility of rescue. It had not been planned to commence serious operations until the base of the Tower was much closer, and Spider had at least two companions who could spin themselves up and down the other tapes of the system. Morgan pushed aside the thought of what could happen if the drive mechanism jammed; that would doom the refugees in the Basement, as well as himself.

Fifty kilometres; he had reached what would, in normal times, have been the lowest level of the ionosphere. He did not, of course, expect to see anything, but he was wrong.

The first intimation was a faint crackling from the capsule speaker; then, out of the corner of his eye, he saw a flicker of light. It was immediately below him, glimpsed in the downward-viewing mirror just outside Spider's little bay-window. He twisted the mirror around as far as it would adjust, until it was aimed at a point a couple of metres below the capsule. For a moment, he stared with astonishment, and more than a twinge of fear; then he called the Mountain.

'I've got company,' he said. 'I think this is in Professor Sessui's department. There's a ball of light – oh, about twenty centimetres across – running along the tape just below me. It's keeping at a constant distance, and I hope it stays there. But I must say it's quite beautiful – a lovely bluish glow, flickering every few seconds. And I can hear it on the radio link.'

It was a full minute before Kingsley answered in a reassuring tone of voice.

'Don't worry – it's only St Elmo's Fire. We've had similar displays along the tape during thunderstorms; they can make your hair stand on end aboard the Mark I. But *you* won't feel anything – you're too well shielded.'

'I'd no idea it could happen at this altitude.'

'Neither did we. You'd better take it up with the Professor.'

'Oh – it's fading out – getting bigger and fainter – now it's gone – I suppose the air's too thin for it – I'm sorry to see it go—'

'*That's* only a curtain raiser,' said Kingsley. 'Look what's happening directly above you.'

A rectangular section of the star-field flashed by as Morgan tilted the mirror towards the zenith. At first he could see nothing unusual so he switched off all the indicators on his control panel and waited in total darkness.

Slowly his eyes adapted, and in the depths of the mirror a faint red glow began to burn, and spread, and consume the stars. It grew brighter and brighter and flowed beyond the limits of the mirror; now he could see it directly, for it extended halfway down the sky. A cage of light, with flickering, moving bars, was descending upon the Earth; and now Morgan could understand how a man like Professor Sessui could devote his life to unravelling its secrets.

On one of its rare visits to the equator, the aurora had come marching down from the Poles.

47 Beyond the Aurora

Morgan doubted if even Professor Sessui, five hundred kilometres above, had so spectacular a view. The storm was developing rapidly; short-wave radio – still used for many non-essential services – would by now have been disrupted all over the world.

Morgan was not sure if he heard or felt a faint rustling, like the whisper of falling sand or the crackle of dry twigs. Unlike the static of the fireball, it certainly did not come from the speaker system, because it was still there when he switched off the circuit.

Curtains of pale green fire, edged with crimson, were being drawn across the sky, then shaken slowly back and forth as if by an invisible hand. They were trembling before the gusts of the solar wind, the million-kilometre-an-hour gale blowing from Sun to Earth – and far beyond. Even above Mars a feeble auroral ghost was flickering now; and sunward, the poisonous skies of Venus were ablaze. Above the pleated curtains long rays like the ribs of a half-opened fan were sweeping around the horizon; sometimes they shone straight into Morgan's eyes like the beams of a giant searchlight, leaving him dazzled for minutes. There was no need, any longer, to turn off the capsule illumination to prevent it from blinding him; the celestial fireworks outside were brilliant enough to read by.

Two hundred kilometres; Spider was still climbing silently, effortlessly. It was hard to believe that he had left earth exactly an hour ago. Hard, indeed, to believe that earth still existed; for he was now rising between the walls of a canyon of fire.

The illusion lasted only for seconds; then the momentary unstable balance between magnetic fields and incoming electric clouds was destroyed. But for that brief instant Morgan could truly believe that he was ascending out of a chasm that would dwarf even Valles Marineris – the Grand Canyon of Mars. Then the shining cliffs, at least a hundred kilometres high, became translucent and were pierced by stars. He could see them for what they really were – mere phantoms of fluorescence.

And now, like an aeroplane breaking through a ceiling of low-lying clouds, Spider was climbing above the display. Morgan was emerging from a fiery mist, twisting and turning beneath him. Many years ago he had been aboard a tourist liner cruising through the tropical night, and he remembered how he had joined the other passengers on the stern, entranced by the beauty and wonder of the bioluminescent wake. Some of the greens and blues flickering below him now matched the plankton-generated colours he had seen then, and he could easily imagine that he was again watching the byproducts of life – the play of giant, invisible beasts, denizens of the upper atmosphere . . .

He had almost forgotten his mission, and it was a distinct shock when he was recalled to duty.

'How's power holding up?' asked Kingsley. 'You've only another twenty minutes on that battery.'

Morgan glanced at his instrument panel. 'It's dropped to ninety-five per cent – but my rate of climb has *increased* by five per cent. I'm doing 210 klicks.'

'That's about right. Spider's feeling the lower gravity – it's already down by ten per cent at your altitude.'

That was not enough to be noticeable, particularly if one was strapped in a seat and wearing several kilos of spacesuit. Yet Morgan felt positively buoyant, and he wondered if he was getting too much oxygen.

No, the flow-rate was normal. It must be the sheer exhilaration produced by that marvellous spectacle beneath him – though it was diminishing now, drawing back to north and south, as if retreating to its polar strongholds. That, and the satisfaction of a task well begun, using a technology that no man had ever before tested to such limits.

This explanation was perfectly reasonable, but he was not satisfied with it. It did not wholly account for his sense of happiness – even of joy. Warren Kingsley, who was fond of diving, had often told him that he felt such an emotion in the weightless environment of the sea. Morgan had never shared it, but now he knew what it must be like. He seemed to have left all his cares down there on the planet hidden below the fading loops and traceries of the aurora.

The stars were coming back into their own, no longer challenged by the eerie intruder from the poles. Morgan began to search the zenith, not with any high expectations, wondering if the Tower was yet in sight. But he could make out only the first few metres, still lit by the faint auroral glow, of the narrow ribbon up which Spider was swiftly and smoothly climbing. That thin band upon which his own life – and seven others' – now depended was so uniform and featureless that it gave no hint of the capsule's speed; Morgan found it difficult to believe that it was flashing through the drive mechanism at more than two hundred kilometres an hour. And, with that thought, he was suddenly back in his childhood, and knew the source of his contentment.

He had quickly recovered from the loss of that first kite, and had graduated to larger and more elaborate models. Then, just before he had discovered Meccano and abandoned kites forever, he had experimented briefly with toy parachutes. Morgan liked to think that he had invented the idea himself, though he might well have come across it somewhere in his reading or viewing. The technique was so simple that generations of boys must have rediscovered it.

First he had whittled a thin strip of wood about five centimetres long, and fastened a couple of paper-clips on to it. Then he had hooked these around the kite-string, so that the little device could slide easily up and down. Next he had made a handkerchief-sized parachute of rice paper, with silk strings; a small square of cardboard served as payload. When he had fastened that square to the wooden strip by a rubber band – not too firmly – he was in business.

Blown by the wind, the little parachute would go sailing up the string, climbing the graceful catenary to the kite. Then Morgan would give a sharp tug, and the cardboard weight would slip out of the rubber band. The parachute would float away into the sky, while the wood-and-wire rider came swiftly back to his hand, in readiness for the next launch.

With what envy he had watched his flimsy creations drift effortlessly out to sea! Most of them fell back into the water before they had travelled even one kilometre, but sometimes a little parachute would still be bravely maintaining altitude when it vanished from sight. He liked to imagine that these lucky voyagers reached the enchanted islands of the Pacific; but though he had written his name and address on the cardboard squares he never received any reply.

Morgan could not help smiling at these long-forgotten memories, yet they explained so much. The dreams of childhood had been far surpassed by the reality of adult life; he had earned the right to his contentment.

'Coming up to three eighty,' said Kingsley. 'How is the power level?'

'Beginning to drop – down to eighty-five per cent – the battery's starting to fade.'

'Well, if it holds out for another twenty kilometres, it will have done its job. How do you feel?'

Morgan was tempted to answer with superlatives, but his natural caution dissuaded him. 'I'm fine,' he said. 'If we could guarantee a display like this for all our passengers, we wouldn't be able to handle the crowds.'

'Perhaps it could be arranged,' laughed Kingsley. 'We could ask Monsoon Control to dump a few barrels of electrons in the right places. Not their usual line of business, but they're good at improvising . . . aren't they?'

Morgan chuckled, but did not answer. His eyes were fixed on the instrument panel, where both power and rate of climb were now visibly dropping. But this was no cause for alarm; Spider had reached 385 kilometres out of the expected 400, and the booster battery still had some life in it.

At 390 kilometres Morgan started to cut back the rate of climb, until Spider crept more and more slowly upwards. Eventually the capsule was barely moving, and it finally came to rest just short of 405 kilometres.

'I'm dropping the battery,' Morgan reported. 'Mind your heads.'

A good deal of thought had been given to recovering that heavy and expensive battery, but there had been no time to improvise a braking system that would let it slide safely back, like one of Morgan's kite-riders. And though a parachute had been available, it was feared that the shrouds might become entangled with the tape. Fortunately the impact area, just ten kilometres east of the earth terminus, lay in dense jungle. The wild life of Taprobane would have to take its chances, and Morgan was prepared to argue with the Department of Conservation later.

He turned the safety key and then pressed the red button that fired the explosive charges; Spider shook briefly as they detonated. Then he switched to the internal battery, slowly released the friction brakes, and again fed power into the drive motors.

The capsule started to climb on the last lap of its journey. But one glance at the instrument panel told Morgan that something

191

was seriously wrong. Spider should have been rising at over two hundred klicks; it was doing less than one hundred, even at full power. No tests or calculations were necessary; Morgan's diagnosis was instant, for the figures spoke for themselves. Sick with frustration, he reported back to Earth.

'We're in trouble,' he said. 'The charges blew – but the battery never dropped. Something's still holding it on.'

It was unnecessary, of course, to add that the mission must now be aborted. Everyone knew perfectly well that Spider could not possibly reach the base of the Tower carrying several hundred kilos of dead-weight.

48 Night at the Villa

Ambassador Rajasinghe needed little sleep these nights; it was as if a benevolent Nature was granting him the maximum use of his remaining years. And at a time like this, when the Taprobanean skies were blazing with their greatest wonder for centuries, who could have stayed abed?

How he wished that Paul Sarath was here to share the spectacle! He missed his old friend more than he would have thought possible; there was no one who could annoy and stimulate him in the way that Paul had done – no one with the same bond of shared experience stretching back to boyhood. Rajasinghe had never thought that he would outlive Paul, or would see the fantastic billion-ton stalactite of the Tower almost span the gulf between its orbital foundation and Taprobane, thirty-six thousand kilometres below. To the end Paul had been utterly opposed to the project; he had called it a Sword of Damocles, and had never ceased to predict its eventual plunge to earth. Yet even Paul had admitted that the Tower had already produced some benefits.

For perhaps the first time in history, the rest of the world actually knew that Taprobane existed, and was discovering its ancient culture. Yakkagala, with its brooding presence and its sinister legends, had attracted special attention; as a result, Paul had been able to get support for some of his cherished projects. The enigmatic personality of Yakkagala's creator had already given rise to numerous books and videodramas, and the *son-et-lumière* display at the foot of the Rock was invariably sold out. Shortly before his death Paul had remarked wryly that a minor Kalidasa industry was in the making, and it was becoming more and more difficult to distinguish fiction from reality.

Soon after midnight, when it was obvious that the auroral display had passed its climax, Rajasinghe had been carried back into his bedroom. As he always did when he had said goodnight to his household staff, he relaxed with a glass of hot toddy and switched on the late news summary. The only item that really interested him was the progress that Morgan was making; by this time he should be approaching the base of the Tower.

The news editor had already starred the latest development; a line of continuously flashing type announced

MORGAN STUCK 200 KM SHORT OF GOAL

Rajasinghe's fingertips requested the details, and he was relieved to find that his first fears were groundless. Morgan was *not* stuck; he was unable to complete the journey. He could return to earth whenever he wished – but if he did Professor Sessui and his colleagues would certainly be doomed.

Directly above his head the silent drama was being played out at this very moment. Rajasinghe switched from text to video, but there was nothing new – indeed, the item now being screened in the news recap was Maxine Duval's ascent, years ago, in Spider's precursor.

'*I* can do better than that,' muttered Rajasinghe, and switched to his beloved telescope.

For the first months after he had become bed-ridden he had been unable to use it. Then Morgan had paid one of his brief courtesy calls, analysed the situation, and swiftly prescribed the remedy. A week later, to Rajasinghe's surprise and pleasure, a small team of technicians had arrived at the Villa Yakkagala, and had modified the instrument for remote operation. Now he could lie comfortably in bed, and still explore the starry skies and the looming face of the Rock. He was deeply grateful to Morgan for the gesture; it had shown a side of the engineer's personality he had not suspected.

He was not sure what he could see, in the darkness of the night – but he knew exactly where to look, for he had long been watching the slow descent of the Tower. When the sun was at the correct angle, he could even glimpse the four guiding tapes converging into the zenith, a quartet of shining hair-lines scratched upon the sky.

He set the azimuth bearing on the telescope control, and swung the instrument around until it pointed above Sri Kanda. As he began to track slowly upwards, looking for any sign of the capsule, he wondered what the Maha Thero was thinking about this latest development. Though Rajasinghe had not spoken to the prelate – now well into his nineties – since the Order had moved to Lhasa, he gathered that the Potala had not provided the hoped-for accommodation. The huge palace was slowly falling into decay while the Dalai Lama's executors haggled with the Chinese Federal Government over the cost of maintenance. According to Rajasinghe's latest information, the Maha Thero was now negotiating with the Vatican – also in chronic financial difficulties, but at least still master of its own house.

All things were indeed impermanent, but it was not easy to discern any cyclic pattern. Perhaps the mathematical genius of Parakarma-Goldberg might be able to do so; the last time Rajasinghe had seen *him*, he was receiving a major scientific award for his contributions to meteorology. Rajasinghe would never have recognized him; he was clean-shaven and wearing a suit cut in the very latest neo-Napoleonic fashion. But now, it seemed, he had switched religions again … The stars slid slowly down the big monitor screen at the end of the bed, as the telescope tilted up towards the Tower. But there was no sign of the capsule, though Rajasinghe was sure that it must now be in the field of view.

He was about to switch back to the regular news channel when, like an erupting nova, a star flashed out near the lower edge of the picture. For a moment Rajasinghe wondered if the capsule had exploded; then he saw that it was shining with a perfectly steady light. He centred the image and zoomed to maximum power.

Long ago he had seen a two-century-old video-documentary of the first aerial wars, and he suddenly remembered a sequence showing a night attack upon London. An enemy bomber had been caught in a cone of searchlights, and had hung like an incandescent mote in the sky. He was seeing the same phenomenon now, on a hundredfold greater scale; but this time all the resources on the ground were combined to help, not to destroy, the determined invader of the night.

49 A Bumpy Ride

Warren Kingsley's voice had regained its control; now it was merely dull and despairing.

'We're trying to stop that mechanic from shooting himself,' he said. 'But it's hard to blame him. He was interrupted by *another* rush job on the capsule, and simply forgot to remove the safety-strap.'

So, as usual, it was human error. While the explosive links were being attached, the battery had been held in place by two metal bands. And only *one* of them had been removed . . . Such things happened with monotonous regularity; sometimes they were merely annoying, sometimes they were disastrous, and the man responsible had to carry the guilt for the rest of his days. In any event, recrimination was pointless. The only thing that mattered now was what to do next.

Morgan adjusted the external viewing mirror to its maximum downward tilt, but it was impossible to see the cause of the trouble. Now that the auroral display had faded the lower part of the capsule was in total darkness, and he had no means of illuminating it. But that problem, at least, could be readily solved. If Monsoon Control could dump kilowatts of infra-red into the basement of the Tower, it could easily spare him a few visible photons.

'We can use our own searchlights,' said Kingsley, when Morgan passed on his request.

'No good – they'll shine straight into my eyes, and I won't be able to see a thing. I want a light behind and *above* me – there must be somebody in the right position.'

'I'll check,' Kingsley answered, obviously glad to make some useful gesture. It seemed a long time before he called again; looking at his timer, Morgan was surprised to see that only three minutes had elapsed.

'Monsoon Control *could* manage it, but they'd have to retune and defocus – I think they're scared of frying you. But Kinte can light up immediately; they have a pseudo-white laser – *and* they're in the right position. Shall I tell them to go ahead?'

Morgan checked his bearings – let's see, Kinte would be very high in the west – that would be fine.

'I'm ready,' he answered, and closed his eyes.

Almost instantly, the capsule exploded with light. Very cautiously, Morgan opened his eyes again. The beam was coming from high in the west, still dazzlingly brilliant despite its journey of almost forty thousand kilometres. It appeared to be pure white, but he knew that it was actually a blend of three sharply-tuned lines in the red, green and blue parts of the spectrum.

After a few seconds' adjustment of the mirror he managed to get a clear view of the offending strap, half a metre beneath his feet. The end that he could see was secured to the base of Spider by a large butterfly nut; all he had to do was to unscrew *that*, and the battery would drop off...

Morgan sat silently analysing the situation for so many minutes that Kingsley called him again. For the first time there was a trace of hope in his deputy's voice.

'We've been doing some calculations, Van ... What do you think of this idea?'

Morgan heard him out, then whistled softly. 'You're certain of the safety margin?' he asked.

'Of course,' answered Kingsley, sounding somewhat aggrieved; Morgan hardly blamed him, but *he* was not the one who would be risking his neck.

'Well – I'll give it a try. But only for one second, the first time.'

'That won't be enough. Still, it's a good idea – you'll get the feel of it.'

Gently Morgan released the friction brakes that were holding Spider motionless on the tape. Instantly he seemed to rise out of the seat, as weight vanished. He counted 'One, TWO!' and engaged the brakes again.

Spider gave a jerk, and for a fraction of a second Morgan was pressed uncomfortably down into the seat. There was an ominous squeal from the braking mechanism, then the capsule was at rest again, apart from a slight torsional vibration that quickly died away.

'That was a bumpy ride,' said Morgan. 'But I'm still here – and so is that infernal battery.'

'So I warned you. You'll have to try harder. Two seconds at least.'

Morgan knew that he could not outguess Kingsley, with all the figures and computing power at his command, but he still felt the need for some reassuring mental arithmetic. Two seconds of free fall – say half a second to put on the brakes – allowing one ton for the mass of Spider . . . The question was: which would go first – the strap retaining the battery, or the tape that was holding him here four hundred kilometres up in the sky? In the usual way it would be 'no contest' in a trial between hyperfilament and ordinary steel. But if he applied the brakes too suddenly – or they seized owing to this maltreatment – *both* might snap. And then he and the battery would reach the Earth at very nearly the same time.

'Two seconds it is,' he told Kingsley. 'Here we go.'

This time the jerk was nerve-racking in its violence, and the torsional oscillations took much longer to die out. Morgan was certain that he would have felt – or heard – the breaking of the strap. He was not surprised when a glance in the mirror confirmed that the battery was still there.

Kingsley did not seem too worried. 'It may take three or four tries,' he said.

Morgan was tempted to retort: 'Are you after my job?' but then thought better of it. Warren would be amused; other unknown listeners might not.

After the third fall – he felt he had dropped kilometres, but it was only about a hundred metres – even Kingsley's optimism started to fade. It was obvious that the trick was not going to work.

'I'd like to send my compliments to the people who made that safety strap,' said Morgan wryly. 'Now what do you suggest? A *three*-second drop before I slam on the brakes?'

He could almost see Warren shake his head. 'Too big a risk. I'm not so much worried about the tape as the braking mechanism. It wasn't designed for this sort of thing.'

'Well, it was a good try,' Morgan answered. 'But I'm not giving up yet. I'm damned if I'll be beaten by a simple butterfly nut, fifty centimetres in front of my nose. I'm going outside to get at it.'

50 The Falling Fireflies

01 15 24
This is Friendship Seven. I'll try to describe what I'm in here. I am in a big mass of some very small particles that are brilliantly lit up like they're luminescent . . . They're coming by the capsule, and they look like little stars. A whole shower of them coming by . . .

01 16 10
They're very slow; they're not going away from me more than maybe three or four miles an hour . . .

01 19 38
Sunrise has just come up behind in the periscope . . . as I looked back out of the window, I had literally thousands of small, luminous particles swirling round the capsule . . .
(Commander John Glenn, Mercury 'Friendship Seven',
20 Feb 1962.)

With the old-style spacesuits, reaching that butterfly nut would have been completely out of the question. Even with the Flexisuit that Morgan was now wearing it might still be difficult – but at least he would make the attempt.

Very carefully, because more lives than his own now depended upon it, he rehearsed the sequence of events. He must check the suit, depressurize the capsule, and open the hatch – which, luckily, was almost full-length. Then he must release the safety belt, get down on his knees – if he could! – and reach for that butterfly nut. Everything depended upon its tightness. There were no tools of any kind aboard Spider, but Morgan was prepared to match his fingers – even in spacegloves – against the average small wrench.

He was just about to describe his plan of operations in case anyone on the ground could find a fatal flaw when he became aware of a certain mild discomfort. He could readily tolerate it for much longer, if necessary, but there was no point in taking chances. If he used the capsule's own plumbing, he would not have to bother with the awkward Diver's Friend incorporated in the suit . . .

When he had finished he turned the key of the Urine Dump – and was startled by a tiny explosion near the base of the capsule. Almost instantly, to his astonishment, a cloud of twinkling stars winked into existence, as if a microscopic galaxy had been suddenly created. Morgan had the illusion that, just for a fraction of a second, it hovered motionless outside the capsule; then it started to fall straight down, as swiftly as any stone dropped on earth. Within seconds it had dwindled to a point, and then was gone.

Nothing could have brought home more clearly the fact that he was still wholly a captive of the earth's gravitational field. He remembered how, in the very early days of orbital flight, the first astronauts were puzzled and then amused by the haloes of ice crystals that accompanied them around the planet; there had been some feeble jokes about the 'Constellation Urion'. That could not happen here; anything that he dropped, however fragile it might be, would crash straight back into the atmosphere. He must never forget that, despite his altitude, he was not an astronaut, revelling in the freedom of weightlessness. He was a man inside a building four hundred kilometres high, preparing to open the window and go out on to the ledge.

51 On the Porch

Though it was cold and uncomfortable on the summit, the crowd continued to grow. There was something hypnotic about that brilliant little star in the zenith, upon which the thoughts of the world, as well as the laser beam from Kinte, were now focused. As they arrived, all the visitors would head for the north tape, and stroke it in a shy, half-defiant manner as if to say: 'I know this is silly, but makes me feel I'm in contact with Morgan'. Then they would gather round the coffee dispenser and listen to the reports coming over the speaker system. There was nothing new from the refugees in the Tower; they were all sleeping – or trying to sleep – in an attempt to conserve oxygen. As Morgan was not yet overdue. they had not been informed of the hold-up; but within the next hour they would undoubtedly be calling Midway to find what had happened.

Maxine Duval had arrived at Sri Kanda just ten minutes too late to see Morgan. There was a time when such a near-miss would have made her very angry; now she merely shrugged her shoulders and reassured herself with the thought that she would be the first to grab the engineer on his return. Kingsley had not allowed her to speak to him, and she had accepted even this ruling with good grace. Yes, she was growing old . . .

For the last five minutes the only sound that had come from the capsule was a series of 'Checks' as Morgan went through the suit routine with an expert up in Midway. That was now complete; everyone was waiting tensely for the crucial next step.

'Valving the air,' said Morgan, his voice overlaid with a slight echo now that he had closed the visor of his helmet. 'Capsule pressure zero. No problem with breathing.' A thirty second pause; then: 'Opening the front door – there it goes. Now releasing the seat-belt.'

There was an unconscious stirring and murmuring among the watchers. In imagination, every one of them was up there in the capsule, aware of the void that had suddenly opened before him.

'Quick-release buckle operated. I'm stretching my legs. Not much head-room . . .

'Just getting the feel of the suit – quite flexible – now I'm going out on the porch – don't worry! – I've got the seat-belt wrapped around my left arm . . .

'Phew. Hard work, bending as much as this. But I can see that butterfly nut, underneath the porch grille. I'm working out how to reach it . . .

'On my knees now – not very comfortable – I've got it! Now to see if it will turn . . .'

The listeners became rigid, silent – then, in unison, relaxed with virtually simultaneous sighs of relief.

'No problem! I can turn it easily. Two revs already – any moment now – just a bit more – I can feel it coming off – LOOK OUT DOWN BELOW!'

There was a burst of clapping and cheering; some people put their hands over their heads and cowered in mock terror. One or two, not fully understanding that the falling nut would not arrive for five minutes and would descend ten kilometres to the east, looked genuinely alarmed.

Only Warren Kingsley failed to share the rejoicing. 'Don't cheer too soon,' he said to Maxine. 'We're not out of the woods yet.'

The seconds dragged by . . . one minute . . . two minutes . . .

'It's no use,' said Morgan at last, his voice thick with rage and frustration. 'I can't budge the strap. The weight of the battery is holding it jammed in the threads. Those jolts we gave must have welded it to the bolt.'

'Come back as quickly as you can,' said Kingsley. 'There's a new power-cell on the way, and we can manage a turn-around in less than an hour. So we can still get up to the Tower in – oh, say six hours. Barring any further accidents, of course.'

Precisely, thought Morgan; and he would not care to take Spider up again without a thorough check of the much-abused braking mechanism. Nor would he trust himself to make a second trip; he was already feeling the strain of the last few hours, and fatigue would soon be slowing down his mind and body, just when he needed maximum efficiency from both.

He was back in the seat now, but the capsule was still open to space and he had not yet refastened the safety belt. To do so would be to admit defeat; and that had never been easy for Morgan.

The unwinking glare of the Kinte laser, coming from almost immediately above, still transfixed him with its pitiless light. He tried to focus his mind upon the problem, as sharply as that beam was focused upon him.

All that he needed was a metal cutter – a hacksaw, or a pair of shears – that could sever the retaining strap. Once again he cursed the fact that there was no tool-kit aboard Spider; even so, it would hardly have contained what he needed.

There were megawatt-hours of energy stored in Spider's own battery; could he use that in any way? He had a brief fantasy of establishing an arc and burning through the strap; but even if suitable heavy conductors were available – and of course they weren't – the main power supply was inaccessible from the control cab.

Warren and all the skilled brains gathered around him had failed to find any solution. He was on his own, physically and intellectually. It was, after all, the situation he had always preferred.

And then, just as he was about to reach out and close the capsule door, Morgan knew what he had to do. All the time the answer had been right by his finger-tips.

52 The Other Passenger

To Morgan, it seemed that a huge weight had lifted from his shoulders. He felt completely, irrationally confident. This time, surely, it *had* to work.

Nevertheless, he did not move from his seat until he had planned his actions in minute detail. And when Kingsley, sounding a little anxious, once again urged him to hurry back, he gave an evasive answer. He did not wish to raise any false hopes – on Earth, or in the Tower.

'I'm trying an experiment,' he said. 'Leave me alone for a few minutes.'

He picked up the fibre dispenser that he had used for so many demonstrations – the little spinnerette that, years ago, had allowed him to descend the face of Yakkagala. One change had been made for reasons of safety; the first metre of filament had been coated with a layer of plastic, so that it was no longer quite invisible, and could be handled cautiously, even with bare fingers.

As Morgan looked at the little box in his hand, he realized how much he had come to regard it as a talisman – almost a good luck charm. Of course, he did not *really* believe in such things; he always had a perfectly logical reason for carrying the spinnerette around with him. On this ascent it had occurred to him that it might be useful because of its strength and unique lifting power. He had almost forgotten that it had other abilities as well . . .

Once more he clambered out of the seat, and knelt down on the metal grille of Spider's tiny porch to examine the cause of all the trouble. The offending bolt was only ten centimetres on the other side of the grid, and although its bars were too close together for him to put his hand through them, he had already proved that he could reach around it without too much difficulty.

He released the first metre of coated fibre, and, using the ring at the end as a plumb-bob, lowered it down through the grille. Tucking the dispenser itself firmly in a corner of the capsule, so that he could not accidentally knock it overboard, he then reached round the grille until he could grab the swinging weight. This was not as easy as he had expected, because even this remarkable spacesuit sould not allow his arm to bend quite freely, and the ring eluded his grasps as it pendulumed back and forth.

After half-a-dozen attempts – tiring rather than annoying, because he knew that he would succeed sooner or later – he had looped the fibre around the shank of the bolt, just behind the strap it was still holding in place. Now for the really tricky part . . .

He released just enough filament from the spinnerette for the naked fibre to reach the bolt, and to pass round it; then he drew both ends tight – until he felt the loop catch in the thread. Morgan had never attempted this trick with a rod of tempered steel more than a centimetre thick, and had no idea how long it would take. Bracing himself against the porch, he began to operate his invisible saw.

After five minutes he was sweating badly, and could not tell if he had made any progress at all. He was afraid to slacken the tension, lest the fibre should escape from the equally invisible slot it was – he hoped – slicing through the bolt. Several times Warren had called him, sounding more and more alarmed, and he had given a brief reassurance. Soon he would rest for a while, recover his breath – and explain what he was trying to do. This was the least that he owed to his anxious friends.

'Van,' said Kingsley, 'just what *are* you up to? The people in the Tower have been calling – what shall I say to them?'

'Give me another few minutes – I'm trying to cut the bolt—'

The calm but authoritative woman's voice that interrupted Morgan gave him such a shock that he almost let go of the precious fibre. The words were muffled by his suit, but that did not matter. He knew them all too well, though it had been months since he had last heard them.

'Dr Morgan,' said CORA, 'please lie down and relax for the next ten minutes.'

'Would you settle for five?' he pleaded. 'I'm rather busy at the moment.'

CORA did not deign to reply; although there were units that could conduct simple conversations, this model was not among them.

Morgan kept his promise, breathing deeply and steadily for a full five minutes. Then he started sawing again. Back and forth, back and forth he worked the filament, as he crouched over the grille and the four-hundred-kilometre distant earth. He could feel considerable resistance, so he must be making some progress through that stubborn steel. But just how much there was no way of telling.

'Dr Morgan,' said CORA, 'you really must lie down for half-an-hour.'

Morgan swore softly to himself.

'You're making a mistake, young lady,' he retorted. 'I'm feeling

204

fine.' But he was lying; CORA knew about the ache in his chest . . .

'Who the hell are you talking to, Van?' asked Kingsley.

'Just a passing angel,' answered Morgan. 'Sorry I forgot to switch off the mike. I'm going to take another rest.'

'What progress are you making?'

'Can't say. But I'm sure the cut's pretty deep by this time. It *must* be . . .'

He wished that he could switch off CORA, but that of course was impossible, even if she had not been out of reach between his breastbone and the fabric of his spacesuit. A heart monitor that could be silenced was worse than useless – it was dangerous.

'Dr Morgan,' said CORA, now distinctly annoyed, 'I really *must* insist. At least half-an-hour's *complete* rest.'

This time Morgan did not feel like answering. He knew that CORA was right; but she could not be expected to understand that his was not the only life involved. And he was also sure that – like one of his bridges – she had a built-in safety factor. Her diagnosis would be pessimistic; his condition would not be as serious as she was pretending. Or so he devoutly hoped.

The pain in his chest certainly seemed to be getting no worse; he decided to ignore both it and CORA, and started to saw away, slowly but steadily, with the loop of fibre. He would keep going, he told himself grimly, just as long as was necessary.

The warning he had relied upon never came. Spider lurched violently as a quarter-ton of dead-weight ripped away, and Morgan was almost pitched out into the abyss. He dropped the spinnerette and grabbed for the safety belt.

Everything seemed to happen in dreamlike slow motion. He had no sense of fear, only an utter determination not to surrender to gravity without a fight. But he could not find the safety belt; it must have swung back into the cabin . . .

He was not even conscious of using his left hand, but suddenly he realized that it was clamped around the hinges of the open door. Yet still he did not pull himself back into the cabin; he was hypnotized by the sight of the falling battery, slowly rotating like some strange celestial body as it dwindled from sight. It took a long time to vanish completely; and not until then did Morgan drag himself to safety, and collapse into his seat.

For a long time he sat there, his heart hammering, awaiting CORA'S next indignant protest. To his surprise, she was silent, almost as if she too had been equally startled. Well, he would give her no further cause for complaint; from now on he would sit quietly at the controls, trying to relax his jangled nerves.

When he was himself again, he called the mountain.

'I've got rid of the battery,' he said, and heard the cheers float up from earth. 'As soon as I've closed the hatch I'll be on my way again. Tell Sessui and Co to expect me in just over an hour. And thank Kinte for the light – I don't need it now.'

He repressurized the cabin, opened the helmet of his suit, and treated himself to a long, cold sip of fortified orange juice. Then he engaged drive and released the brakes, and lay back with a sense of overwhelming relief as Spider came up to full speed.

He had been climbing for several minutes before he realized what was missing. In anxious hope he peered out at the metal grille of the porch. No, it was not there. Well, he could always get another spinnerette, to replace the one now following the discarded battery back to Earth; it was a small sacrifice for such an achievement. Strange, therefore, that he was so upset, and unable fully to enjoy his triumph . . . He felt that he had lost an old and faithful friend.

53 Fade-out

The fact that he was still only thirty minutes behind schedule seemed too good to be true; Morgan would have been prepared to swear that the capsule had halted for at least an hour. Up there in the Tower, now much less than two hundred kilometres away, the reception committee would be preparing to welcome him. He refused even to consider the possibility of any further problems.

When he passed the five-hundred-kilometre mark, still going strong, there was a message of congratulations from the ground.

'By the way,' added Kingsley, 'the Game Warden in the Ruhana Sanctuary's reported an aircraft crashing. We were able to reassure him – if we can find the hole, we may have a souvenir for you.' Morgan had no difficulty in restraining his enthusiasm; he was glad to see the last of that battery. Now if they could find the spinnerette – but *that* would be a hopeless task . . .

The first sign or trouble came at five-fifty kilometres. By now the rate of ascent should have been over two hundred klicks; it was only one nine eight. Slight though the discrepancy was – and it would make no appreciable difference to his arrival time – it worried Morgan.

When he was only thirty kilometres from the Tower he had diagnosed the problem, and knew that this time there was absolutely nothing he could do about it. Although there should have been ample reserve, the battery was beginning to fade. Perhaps those sudden jolts and restarts had brought on the malaise; possibly there was even some physical damage to the delicate components. Whatever the explanation the current was slowly dropping, and with it the capsule's speed.

There was consternation when Morgan reported the indicator readings back to the ground.

'I'm afraid you're right,' Kingsley lamented, sounding almost in tears. 'We suggest you cut speed back to one hundred klicks. We'll try to calculate battery life – though it can only be an educated guess.'

Twenty-five kilometres to go – a mere fifteen minutes, even at this reduced speed! If Morgan had been able to pray, he would have done so.

'We estimate you have between ten and twenty minutes, judging by the rate the current is dropping. It will be a close thing, I'm afraid.'

'Shall I reduce speed again?'

'Not for the moment; we're trying to optimize your discharge rate, and this seems about right.'

'Well, you can switch on your beam now. If I can't get to the Tower, at least I want to see it.'

Neither Kinte nor the other orbiting stations could help him, now that he wished to look up at the underside of the Tower. This was a task for the searchlight on Sri Kanda itself, pointing vertically towards the zenith.

A moment later the capsule was impaled by a dazzling beam from the heart of Taprobane. Only a few metres away – indeed, so close that he felt he could touch them – the other three guiding tapes were ribbons of light, converging towards the Tower. He followed their dwindling perspective – and there it was . . .

Just twenty kilometres away! He should be there in a dozen minutes, coming up through the floor of that tiny square building he could see glittering in the sky, bearing presents like some troglodytic Father Christmas. Despite his determination to relax, and obey CORA's orders, it was quite impossible to do so. He found himself tensing his muscles, as if by his own physical exertions he could help Spider along the last fraction of its journey.

At ten kilometres there was a distinct change of pitch from the drive motor; Morgan had been expecting this, and reacted to it at once. Without waiting for advice from the ground, he cut speed back to fifty klicks. At this rate he *still* had twelve minutes to go, and he began to wonder despairingly if he was involved in an asymptotic approach. This was a variant of the race between Achilles and the tortoise; if he halved his speed every time he halved the distance, would he reach the Tower in a finite time? Once he would have known the answer instantly; now he felt too tired to work it out.

At five kilometres he could see the constructional details of the Tower – the catwalk and protective rails, the futile safety net provided as a sop to public opinion. Although he strained his eyes he could not yet make out the airlock towards which he was now crawling with such agonizing slowness.

And then it no longer mattered. Two kilometres short of the goal Spider's motors stalled completely. The capsule even slid downwards a few metres, before Morgan was able to apply the brakes.

Yet this time, to Morgan's surprise, Kingsley did not seem utterly downcast.

'You can still make it,' he said. 'Give the battery ten minutes to recuperate. There's still enough energy there for that last couple of kilometres.'

It was one of the longest ten minutes that Morgan had ever known. Though he could have made it pass more swiftly by responding to Maxine Duval's increasingly desperate pleas, he felt too emotionally exhausted to talk. He was genuinely sorry about this, and hoped that Maxine would understand and forgive him.

He did have one brief exchange with Driver-Pilot Chang, who reported that the refugees in the Basement were still in fairly good shape, and much encouraged by his nearness. They were taking turns to peer at him through the one small porthole of the airlock's outer door, and simply could not believe that he might never be able to bridge the trifling space between them.

Morgan gave the battery an extra minute for luck. To his relief the motors responded strongly, with an encouraging surge of power. Spider got within half a kilometre of the Tower before stalling again.

'Next time does it,' said Kingsley, though it seemed to Morgan that his friend's confidence now sounded somewhat forced. 'Sorry for all these delays . . .'

'Another ten minutes?' Morgan asked with resignation.

'I'm afraid so. And this time use thirty-second bursts, with a minute between them. That way, you'll get the last erg out of the battery.'

And out of me, thought Morgan. Strange that CORA had been quiet for so long. Still, this time he had not exerted himself physically; it only *felt* that way.

In his preoccupation with Spider he had been neglecting himself. For the last hour he had quite forgotten his zero-residue glucose-based energy tablets and the little plastic bulb of fruit juice. After he had sampled both he felt much better, and only wished that he could transfer some of the surplus calories to the dying battery.

Now for the moment of truth – the final exertion. Failure was unthinkable, when he was so close to the goal. The fates could not possibly be so malevolent, now that he had only a few hundred metres to go . . .

He was whistling in the dark, of course. How many aircraft had crashed at the very edge of the runway, after safely crossing an ocean? How many times had machines or muscles failed, when there were only millimetres to go? Every possible piece of luck, bad as well as good, happened to somebody, somewhere. He had no right to expect any special treatment.

The capsule heaved itself upwards in fits and starts, like a dying animal seeking its last haven. When the battery finally expired, the base of the Tower seemed to fill half the sky.

But it was still twenty metres above him.

54 Theory of Relativity

It was to Morgan's credit that he felt his own fate was sealed, in the desolating moments when the last dregs of power were exhausted, and the lights on Spider's display panel finally faded out. Not for several seconds did he remember that he had only to release the brakes and he would slide back to Earth. In three hours he could be safely back in bed. No one would blame him for the failure of his mission; he had done all that was humanly possible.

For a brief while he stared in a kind of dull fury at that inaccessible square, with the shadow of Spider projected upon it. His mind revolved a host of crazy schemes, and rejected them all. If he still had his faithful little spinnerette – but there would have been no way of getting it to the Tower. *If* the refugees had possessed a spacesuit, someone could have lowered a rope to him – but there had been no time to collect a suit from the burning transporter.

Of course, if this was a videodrama, and not a real-life problem, some heroic volunteer could sacrifice himself – better still, herself – by going into the lock and tossing down a rope, using the fifteen seconds of vacuum consciousness to save the others. It was some measure of Morgan's desperation that, for a fleeting moment, he even considered this idea before commonsense reasserted itself.

From the time that Spider had given up the battle with gravity, until Morgan finally accepted that there was nothing more that he could do, probably less than a minute had elapsed. Then Warren

Kingsley asked a question which, at such a moment, seemed an annoying irrelevance.

'Give us your distance again, Van – exactly *how* far are you from the Tower?'

'What the hell does it matter? It could be a light-year.'

There was a brief silence from the ground; then Kingsley spoke again, in the sort of tone one uses to address a small child or a difficult invalid. 'It makes all the difference in the world. Did you say *twenty* metres?'

'Yes – that's about it.'

Incredibly – unmistakably – Warren gave a clearly audible sigh of relief. There was even joy in his voice when he answered: 'And all these years, Van, I thought that *you* were the Chief Engineer on this project. Suppose it *is* twenty metres exactly—'

Morgan's explosive shout prevented him from finishing the sentence. 'What an idiot! Tell Sessui I'll dock in – oh, fifteen minutes.'

'Fourteen point five, if you've guessed the distance right. And nothing on earth can stop you now.'

That was still a risky statement, and Morgan wished that Kingsley hadn't made it. Docking adaptors sometimes failed to latch together properly, because of minute errors in manufacturing tolerances. And, of course, there had never been a chance of testing this particular system.

He felt only a slight embarrassment at his mental blackout. After all, under extreme stress a man could forget his own telephone number, even his own date of birth. And until this very moment the now dominant factor in the situation had been so unimportant that it could be completely ignored.

It was all a matter of Relativity. He could not reach the Tower; but the Tower would reach him – at its inexorable two kilometres a day.

55 Hard Dock

The record for one day's construction had been thirty kilometres, when the slimmest and lightest section of the Tower was being assembled. Now that the most massive portion – the very root of the structure – was nearing completion in orbit, the rate was down to two kilometres. That was quite fast enough; it would give Morgan time to check the adaptor line-up, and to mentally rehearse the rather tricky few seconds between confirming hard-dock and releasing Spider's brakes. If he left them on for too long there would be a very unequal trial of strength between the capsule and the moving megatons of the Tower.

It was a long but relaxed fifteen minutes – time enough, Morgan hoped, to pacify CORA. Towards the end everything seemed to happen very quickly, and at the last moment he felt like an ant about to be crushed in a stamping press, as the solid roof of the sky descended upon him. One second the base of the Tower was still metres away; an instant later he felt and heard the impact of the docking mechanism.

Many lives depended now upon the skill and care with which the engineers and mechanics, years ago, had done their work. If the couplings did not line up within the allowed tolerances; if the latching mechanism did not operate correctly; if the seal was not airtight . . . Morgan tried to interpret the medley of sounds reaching his ears, but he was not skilled enough to read their messages.

Then, like a signal of victory, the DOCKING COMPLETED sign flashed on the indicator board. There would be ten seconds while the telescopic elements could still absorb the movement of the advancing Tower; Morgan used half of them before he cautiously released the brakes. He was prepared to jam them on again instantly if Spider started to drop – but the sensors were telling the truth. Tower and capsule were now firmly mated together. Morgan had only to climb a few rungs of ladder, and he would have reached his goal.

After he had reported to the jubilant listeners on Earth and Midway, he sat for a moment recovering his breath. Strange to think that this was his second visit, but he could remember little of that first one, twelve years ago and thirty-six thousand kilometres away. During what had, for want of a better term, been called the foundation laying, there had been a small party in the Basement, and numerous zero-gee toasts had been squirted. For this was not only the very first section of the Tower to be built; it would also be the first to make contact with Earth, at the end of its long descent from orbit. Some kind of ceremony therefore seemed in order, and Morgan now recalled that even his old enemy, Senator Collins, had been gracious enough to attend and to wish him luck with a barbed but good-humoured speech. There was even better cause for celebration now.

Already Morgan could hear a faint tattoo of welcoming raps from the far side of the airlock. He undid his safety belt, climbed awkwardly on to the seat, and started to ascend the ladder. The overhead hatch gave a token resistance, as if the powers marshalled against him were making one last feeble gesture, and air hissed briefly while pressure was equalized. Then the circular plate swung open and downwards, and eager hands helped him up into the Tower. As Morgan took his first breath of the fetid air he wondered how anyone could have survived here; if his mission had been aborted, he felt quite certain that a second attempt would have been too late.

The bare, bleak cell was lit only by the solar-fluorescent panels which had been patiently trapping and releasing sunlight for more than a decade, against the emergency that had arrived at last. Their illumination revealed a scene that might have come from some old war; here were homeless and dishevelled refugees from a devastated city, huddling in a bomb shelter with the few possessions they had been able to save. Not many such refugees, however, would have carried bags labelled PROJECTION, LUNAR HOTEL CORPORATION, PROPERTY OF THE FEDERAL REPUBLIC OF MARS, or the ubiquitous MAY/NOT/BE STOWED IN VACUUM. Nor would they have been so cheerful; even those who were lying down to conserve oxygen managed a smile and a languid wave. Morgan had just returned the salute when his legs buckled beneath him, and everything blacked out. Never before in his life had he fainted, and when the blast of cold oxygen revived him his first emotion was one of

213

acute embarrassment. His eyes came slowly into focus, and he saw masked shapes hovering over him. For a moment he wondered if he was in hospital; then brain and vision returned to normal. While he was still unconscious, his precious cargo must have been unloaded.

Those masks were the molecular sieves he had carried up to the Tower; worn over nose and mouth, they would block the CO_2 but allow oxygen to pass. Simple yet technologically sophisticated, they would enable men to survive in an atmosphere which would otherwise cause instant suffocation. It required a little extra effort to breathe through them, but Nature never gives something for nothing – and this was a very small price to pay.

Rather groggily, but refusing any help, Morgan got to his feet and was belatedly introduced to the men and women he had saved. One matter still worried him: while he was unconscious, had CORA delivered any of her set speeches? He did not wish to raise the subject, but he wondered . . .

'On behalf of all of us,' said Professor Sessui, with sincerity yet with the obvious awkwardness of a man who was seldom polite to anyone, 'I want to thank you for what you've done. We owe our lives to you.'

Any logical or coherent reply to this would have smacked of false modesty, so Morgan used the excuse of adjusting his mask to mumble something unintelligible. He was about to start checking that all the equipment had been unloaded when Professor Sessui added, rather anxiously; 'I'm sorry we can't offer you a chair – this is the best we can do.' He pointed to a couple of instrument boxes, one on top of the other. 'You really should take it easy.'

The phrase was familiar; so CORA *had* spoken. There was a slightly embarrassed pause while Morgan registered this fact, and the others admitted that they knew, and he showed that he knew *they* knew – all without a word being uttered, in the kind of psychological infinite regress that occurs when a group of people share completely a secret which nobody will ever mention again.

He took a few deep breaths – it was amazing how quickly one got used to the masks – and then sat down on the proffered seat. I'm not going to faint again, he told himself with grim determination. I must deliver the goods, and get out of here as quickly as possible – hopefully, before there are any more pronouncements from CORA.

'That can of sealant,' he said, pointing to the smallest of the containers he had brought, 'should take care of your leak. Spray it round the gasket of the airlock; it sets hard in a few seconds. Use the oxygen only when you have to; you may need it to sleep. There's a CO_2 mask for everyone, and a couple of spares. And here's food and water for three days – that should be plenty. The transporter from 10K should be here tomorrow. As for the Medikit – I hope you won't need *that* at all.'

He paused for breath; it was not easy to talk while wearing a CO_2 filter, and he felt an increasing need to conserve his strength. Sessui's people could now take care of themselves, but he still had one further job to do – and the sooner the better.

Morgan turned to Driver Chang and said quietly: 'Please help me to suit up again. I want to inspect the track.'

'That's only a thirty-minute suit you're wearing!'

'I'll need ten minutes – fifteen at the most.'

'Dr Morgan – *I'm* a space-qualified operator – *you're* not. No one's allowed to go out in a thirty-minute suit without a spare pack, or an umbilical. Except in an emergency, of course.'

Morgan gave a tired smile. Chang was right, and the excuse of immediate danger no longer applied. But an emergency was whatever the Chief Engineer said it was.

'I want to look at the damage,' he answered, 'and examine the tracks. It would be a pity if the people from 10K can't reach you, because they weren't warned of some obstacle.'

Chang was clearly not too happy about the situation (what *had* that gossiping CORA jabbered while he was unconscious?), but raised no further arguments as he followed Morgan into the north lock.

Just before he closed the visor Morgan asked, 'Any more trouble with the Professor?'

Chang shook his head. 'I think the CO_2 has slowed him down. And if he starts up again – well, we outnumber him six to one, though I'm not sure if we can count on his students. Some of them are just as crazy as he is; look at that girl who spends all her time scribbling in the corner. She's convinced that the sun's going out, or blowing up – I'm not sure which – and wants to warn the world before she dies. Much good *that* would do. I'd prefer not to know.'

Though Morgan could not help smiling, he felt quite sure that none of the professor's students would be crazy. Eccentric, perhaps – but also brilliant; they would not be working with Sessui otherwise. One day he must find out more about the men and women whose lives he had saved; but that would have to wait until they had all returned to earth, by their separate ways.

'I'm going to take a quick walk around the Tower,' said Morgan, 'and I'll describe any damage so that you can report to Midway. It won't take more than ten minutes. And if it does – well, don't try to get me back.'

Driver Chang's reply, as he closed the inner door of the airlock, was very practical and very brief. 'How the hell *could* I?' he asked.

56 View from the Balcony

The outer door of the north airlock opened without difficulty, framing a rectangle of complete darkness. Running horizontally across that darkness was a line of fire – the protective hand-rail of the catwalk, blazing in the beam of the searchlight pointed straight up from the mountain so far below. Morgan took a deep breath and flexed the suit. He felt perfectly comfortable, and waved to Chang, peering at him through the window of the inner door. Then he stepped out of the Tower.

The catwalk that surrounded the Basement was a metal grille about two metres wide; beyond it the safety net had been stretched out for another thirty metres. The portion that Morgan could see had caught nothing whatsoever during its years of patient waiting.

He started his circumnavigation of the Tower, shielding his eyes against the glare blasting up from underfoot. The oblique lighting showed up every least bump and imperfection in the surface that stretched above him like a roadway to the stars – which, in a sense, it was.

As he had hoped and expected, the explosion on the far side of the Tower had caused no damage here; *that* would have required an atomic bomb, not a mere electro-chemical one. The twin grooves of the track, now awaiting their first arrival, stretched endlessly upwards in their pristine perfection. And fifty metres below the balcony – though it was hard to look in that direction because of the glare – he could just make out the terminal buffers, ready for a task which they should never have to perform.

Taking his time, and keeping close to the sheer face of the Tower, Morgan walked slowly westwards until he came to the first corner. As he turned he looked back at the open door of the airlock, and the – relative, indeed! – safety that it represented. Then he continued boldly along the blank wall of the west face.

He felt a curious mixture of elation and fear, such as he had not known since he had learned to swim and found himself, for the first time, in water out of his depth. Although he was certain that there was no real danger, there *could* be. He was acutely aware of CORA, biding her time; but Morgan had always hated to leave any job undone, and his mission was not yet complete.

The west face was exactly like the north one, except for the absence of an airlock. Again, there was no sign of damage, even though it was closer to the scene of the explosion.

Checking the impulse to hurry – after all, he had been outside for only three minutes – Morgan strolled on to the next corner. Even before he turned it, he could see that he was not going to complete his planned circuit of the Tower. The catwalk had been ripped off and was dangling out into space, a twisted tongue of metal. The safety net had vanished altogether, doubtless torn away by the falling transporter.

I won't press my luck, Morgan told himself. But he could not resist peering round the corner, holding on to the section of the guard rail that still remained.

There was a good deal of debris stuck in the track, and the face of the Tower had been discoloured by the explosion. But, as far as Morgan could see, even here there was nothing that could not be put right in a couple of hours by a few men with cutting torches.

He gave a careful description to Chang, who expressed relief and urged Morgan to get back into the Tower as soon as possible.

'Don't worry,' said Morgan. 'I've still got ten minutes and all of thirty metres to go. I could manage on the air I have in my lungs now.'

But he did not intend to put it to the test. He had already had quite enough excitement for one night. More than enough, if CORA was to be believed; from now on he would obey her orders implicitly.

When he had walked back to the open door of the airlock he stood for a few final moments beside the guard-rail, drenched by the fountain of light leaping up from the summit of Sri Kanda far below. It threw his own immensely elongated shadow directly along the Tower, vertically upwards towards the stars. That shadow must stretch for thousands of kilometres, and it occurred to Morgan that it might even reach the transporter now dropping swiftly down from the 10K Station. If he waved his arms the rescuers might be able to see his signals; he could talk to them in Morse code.

This amusing fantasy inspired a more serious thought. Would it be best for him to wait here, with the others, and not risk the return to earth in Spider? But the journey up to Midway, where he could get good medical attention, would take a week. That was not a sensible alternative, since he could be back on Sri Kanda in less than three hours.

Time to go inside – his air must be getting low and there was nothing more to see. That was a disappointing irony, considering the spectacular view one would normally have here, by day or by night. Now, however, the planet below and the heavens above were both banished by the blinding glare from Sir Kanda; he was floating in a tiny universe of light, surrounded by utter darkness on every side. It was almost impossible to believe that he was in space, if only because of his sense of weight. He felt as secure as if he were standing on the mountain itself, instead of six hundred kilometres above it. *That* was a thought to savour, and to carry back to earth.

He patted the smooth, unyielding surface of the Tower, more enormous in comparison to him than an elephant to an amoeba.

But no amoeba could ever conceive of an elephant – still less create one.

'See you on earth in a year's time,' Morgan whispered, and slowly closed the airlock door behind him.

57 The Last Dawn

Morgan was back in the Basement for only five minutes; this was no time for social amenities, and he did not wish to consume any of the precious oxygen he had brought here with such difficulty. He shook hands all round, and scrambled back into Spider.

It was good to breathe again without a mask – better still to know that his mission had been a complete success, and that in less than three hours he would be safely back on Earth. Yet, after all the effort that had gone into reaching the Tower, he was reluctant to cast off again, and to surrender once more to the pull of gravity – even though it was now taking him home. But presently he released the docking latches and started to fall downwards, becoming weightless for several seconds.

When the speed indicator reached three hundred klicks, the automatic braking system came on and weight returned. The brutally depleted battery would be recharging now, but it must have been damaged beyond repair and would have to be taken out of service.

There was an ominous parallel here: Morgan could not help thinking of his own overstrained body, but a stubborn pride still kept him from asking for a doctor on stand-by. He had made a little bet with himself; he would do so only if CORA spoke again.

She was silent now, as he dropped swiftly through the night. Morgan felt totally relaxed, and left Spider to look after itself while he admired the heavens. Few spacecraft provided so panoramic a view, and not many men could ever have seen the stars under such superb conditions. The aurora had vanished completely, the searchlight had been extinguished, and there was nothing left to challenge the constellations.

Except, of course, the stars that man himself had made. Almost directly overhead was the dazzling beacon of Ashoka, poised forever above Hindustan – and only a few hundred kilometres from the Tower complex. Halfway down in the east was Confucius, much lower still Kamehameha, while high up from the west shone Kinte and Imhotep. These were merely the brightest signposts along the equator; there were literally scores of others, all of them far more brilliant than Sirius. How astonished one of the old astronomers would have been to see this necklace around the sky; and how bewildered he would have become when, after an hour or so's observation, he discovered that they were quite immobile – neither rising nor setting while the familiar stars drifted past in their ancient courses.

As he stared at the diamond necklace stretched across the sky, Morgan's sleepy mind slowly transformed it into something far more impressive. With only a slight effort of the imagination, those man-made stars became the lights of a titanic bridge . . . He drifted into still wilder fantasies. What was the name of the bridge into Valhalla, across which the heroes of the Norse legends passed from this world to the next? He could not remember, but it was a glorious dream. And had other creatures, long before Man, tried in vain to span the skies of their own worlds? He thought of the splendid rings encircling Saturn, the ghostly arches of Uranus and Neptune. Although he knew perfectly well that none of these worlds had ever felt the touch of life, it amused him to think that here were the shattered fragments of bridges that had failed.

He wanted to sleep but, against his will, imagination had seized upon the idea. Like a dog that had just discovered a new bone, it would not let go. The concept was not absurd; it was not even original. Many of the synchronous stations were already kilometres in extent, or linked by cables which stretched along appreciable fractions of their orbit. To join them together, thus forming a ring completely around the world, would be an engineering task much simpler than the building of the Tower, and involving much less material.

No – not a ring – a *wheel*. This Tower was only the first spoke.

There would be others (four? six? a score?) spaced along the equator. When they were all connected rigidly up there in orbit, the problems of stability that plagued a single tower would vanish. Africa – South America, the Gilbert Islands, Indonesia – they could *all* provide locations for earth terminals, if desired. For some day, as materials improved and knowledge advanced, the Towers could be made invulnerable even to the worst hurricanes, and mountain sites would no longer be necessary. If he had waited another hundred years, perhaps he need not have disturbed the Maha Thero...

While he was dreaming the thin crescent of the waning moon had lifted unobtrusively above the eastern horizon, already aglow with the first hint of dawn. Earthshine lit the entire lunar disc so brilliantly that Morgan could see much of the nightland detail; he strained his eyes in the hope of glimpsing that loveliest of sights, never seen by earlier ages – a star within the arms of the crescent moon. But none of the cities of man's second home was visible tonight.

Only two hundred kilometres – less than an hour to go. There was no point in trying to keep awake; Spider had automatic terminal programming and would touch gently down without disturbing his sleep...

The pain woke him first; CORA was a fraction of a second later. 'Don't try to move,' she said soothingly. 'I've radioed for help. The ambulance is on the way.'

That was funny. But don't laugh, Morgan ordered himself, she's only doing her best. He felt no fear; though the pain beneath his breastbone was intense, it was not incapacitating. He tried to focus his mind upon it, and the very act of concentration relieved the symptoms. Long ago he had discovered that the best way of handling pain was to study it objectively.

Warren was calling him, but the words were far away and had little meaning. He could recognize the anxiety in his friend's voice, and wished that he could do something to alleviate it; but he had no strength left to deal with this problem – or with any other. Now he could not even hear the words; a faint but steady roar had obliterated all other sounds. Though he knew that it existed only in his mind – or the labyrinthine channels of his ears – it seemed completely real; he could believe that he was standing at the foot of some great waterfall ...

It was growing fainter, softer – *more musical*. And suddenly he recognized it. How pleasant to hear once more, on the silent frontier of space, the sound he remembered from his very first visit to Yakkagala!

Gravity was drawing him home again, as through the centuries its invisible hand had shaped the trajectory of the Fountains of Paradise. But he had created something that gravity could never recapture, as long as men possessed the wisdom and the will to preserve it.

How cold his legs were! What had happened to Spider's life-support system? But soon it would be dawn; then there would be warmth enough.

The stars were fading, far more swiftly than they had any right to do. That was strange; though the day was almost here, everything around him was growing dark. And the fountains were sinking back into the earth, their voices becoming fainter ... fainter ... fainter ...

And now there was another voice, but Vannevar Morgan did not hear it. Between brief, piercing bleeps CORA cried to the approaching dawn:

HELP! WILL ANYONE WHO HEARS ME PLEASE
  COME AT ONCE!
  THIS IS A CORA EMERGENCY!
HELP! WILL ANYONE WHO HEARS ME PLEASE
  COME AT ONCE!

She was still calling when the sun came up, and its first rays caressed the summit of mountain that had once been sacred. Far below the shadow of Sri Kanda leaped forth upon the clouds, its perfect cone still unblemished, despite all that man had done.

There were no pilgrims now, to watch that symbol of eternity lie across the face of the awakening land. But millions would see it, in the centuries ahead, as they rode in comfort and safety to the stars.

58 Epilogue: Kalidasa's Triumph

In the last days of that last brief summer, before the jaws of ice clenched shut around the equator, one of the Starholme envoys came to Yakkagala.

A Master of the Swarms, It had recently conjugated Itself into human form. Apart from one minor detail, the likeness was excellent; but the dozen children who had accompanied the Holmer in the autocopter were in a constant state of mild hysteria – the younger ones frequently dissolving into giggles.

'What's so funny?' It had asked in Its perfect Solar. 'Or is this a private joke?'

But they would not explain to the Starholmer, whose normal colour vision lay entirely in the infra-red, that the human skin was not a random mosaic of greens and reds and blues. Even when It had threatened to turn into a *Tyrannosaurus Rex* and eat them all up, they still refused to satisfy Its curiosity. Indeed, they quickly pointed out – to an entity that had crossed scores of light-years and collected knowledge for thirty centuries – that a mass of only a hundred kilogrammes would scarcely make an impressive dinosaur.

The Holmer did not mind; It was patient, and the children of Earth were endlessly fascinating, in both their biology and their psychology. So were the young of all creatures – all, of course, that *did* have young. Having studied nine such species, the Holmer could now almost imagine what it must be like to grow up, mature, and die . . . almost, but not quite.

Spread out before the dozen humans and one non-human lay the empty land, its once luxuriant fields and forests blasted by the cold breaths from north and south. The graceful coconut palms had long since vanished, and even the gloomy pines that had succeeded them were naked skeletons, their roots destroyed by the spreading permafrost. No life was left upon the surface of the Earth; only in the oceanic abyss, where the planet's internal heat kept the ice at bay, did a few blind, starveling creatures crawl and swim and devour each other.

Yet to a being whose home had circled a faint red star, the sun that blazed down from the cloudless sky still seemed intolerably bright. Though all its warmth had gone, drained away by the sickness that had attacked its core a thousand years ago, its fierce, cold light revealed every detail of the stricken land, and flashed in splendour from the approaching glaciers.

For the children, still revelling in the powers of their awakening minds, the sub-zero temperatures were an exciting challenge. As they danced naked through the snowdrifts, bare feet kicking up clouds of powder-dry, shining crystals, their symbiotes often had to warn them: 'Don't over-ride your frost-bite signals!' For they were not yet old enough to replicate new limbs without the help of their elders.

The oldest of the boys was showing off; he had launched a deliberate assault on the cold, announcing proudly that he was a fire-elemental. (The Starholmer noted the term for future research, which would later cause It much perplexity.) All that could be seen of the small exhibitionist was a column of flame and steam, dancing to and fro along the ancient brickwork; the other children pointedly ignored this rather crude display.

To the Starholmer, however, it presented an interesting paradox. Just *why* had these people retreated to the inner planets, when they could have fought back the cold with the powers that they now possessed – as, indeed, their cousins were doing on Mars? That was a question to which It had still not received a satisfactory answer. It considered again the enigmatic reply It had been given by ARISTOTLE, the entity with which It most easily communicated.

'For everything there is a season,' the global brain had replied. 'There is a time to battle against Nature, and a time to obey her. True wisdom lies in making the right choice. When the long winter is over, Man will return to an Earth renewed and refreshed.'

And so, during the past few centuries, the whole terrestrial population had streamed up the equatorial Towers and flowed sunwards towards the young oceans of Venus, the fertile plains of Mercury's Temperate Zone. Five hundred years hence, when the sun had recovered, the exiles would return. Mercury would be abandoned, except for the polar regions; but Venus would be a permanent second home. The quenching of the sun had given the incentive, and the opportunity, for the taming of that hellish world.

Important though they were, these matters concerned the Star-holmer only indirectly; Its interest was focused upon more subtle aspects of human culture and society. Every species was unique, with its own surprises, its own idiosyncrasies. This one had introduced the Starholmer to the baffling concept of Negative Information – or, in the local terminology, Humour, Fantasy, Myth.

As it grappled with these strange phenomena, the Starholmer had sometimes said despairingly to Itselves: We shall *never* understand human beings. On occasion It had been so frustrated that It had feared an involuntary conjugation, with all the risks that entailed. But now It had made real progress; It could still remember Its satisfaction the first time It had made a joke – and the children had all laughed.

Working with children had been the clue, again provided by ARISTOTLE. 'There is an old saying: the child is father of the man. Although the biological concept of "father" is equally alien to us both, in this context the word has a double meaning—'

So here It was, hoping that the children would enable It to understand the adults into which they eventually metamorphosed. Sometimes they told the truth; but even when they were being playful (another difficult concept) and dispensed negative information, the Starholmer could now recognize the signs.

Yet there were times when neither the children, nor the adults, nor even ARISTOTLE knew the truth. There seemed to be a continuous spectrum between absolute fantasy and hard historical facts, with every possible graduation in between. At the one end were such figures as Columbus and Leonardo and Einstein and Lenin and Newton and Washington, whose very voices and images had often been preserved. At the other extreme were Zeus and Alice and King Kong and Gulliver and Siegfried and Merlin, who could not *possibly* have existed in the real world. But what was one to make of Robin Hood or Tarzan or Christ or Sherlock Holmes or Odysseus or Frankenstein? Allowing for a certain amount of exaggeration, they might well have been actual historic personages.

The Elephant Throne had changed little in three thousand years, but never before had it supported the weight of so alien a visitor. As the Starholmer stared into the south, It compared the half-kilometre-wide column soaring from the mountain peak with the feats of engineering It had seen on other worlds. For such a young race, this was indeed impressive. Though it seemed always on the point of toppling from the sky, it had stood now for fifteen centuries.

Not, of course, in its present form. The first hundred kilometres was now a vertical city – still occupied at some of its widely-spaced levels – through which the sixteen sets of tracks had often carried a million passengers a day. Only two of those tracks were operating now; in a few hours the Starholmer and Its escorts would be racing up that huge, fluted column, on the way back to the Ring City that encircled the globe.

The Holmer everted Its eyes to give telescopic vision, and slowly scanned the zenith. Yes, there it was – hard to see by day, but easy by night when the sunlight streaming past the shadow of Earth still blazed upon it. The thin, shining band that split the sky into two hemispheres was a whole world in itself, where half-a-billion humans had opted for permanent zero-gravity life.

And up there beside Ring City was the starship that had carried the envoy and all the other Companions of the Hive across the interstellar gulfs. Even now it was being readied for departure – not with any sense of urgency, but several years ahead of schedule, in preparation for the next six-hundred-year lap of its journey. That would represent no time at all to the Starholmer, of course, for It would not reconjugate until the end of the voyage, but then It might well face the greatest challenge of Its long career. For the first time a Starprobe had been destroyed – or at least silenced – soon after it had entered a solar system. Perhaps it had at last made contact with the mysterious Hunters of the Dawn, who had left their marks upon so many worlds, so inexplicably close to the Beginning itself. If the Starholmer had been capable of awe, or of fear, It would have known both, as It contemplated its future, six hundred years hence.

But now It was on the snow-dusted summit of Yakkagala, facing mankind's pathway to the stars. It summoned the children to Its side (they always understood when It *really* wished to be obeyed) and pointed to the mountain in the south.

'You know perfectly well,' It said, with an exasperation that was only partly feigned, 'that Earthport One was built two thousand years *later* than this ruined palace.' The children all nodded in solemn agreement. 'Then why,' asked the Starholmer, tracing the line from the zenith down to the summit of the mountain, '*why* do you call that column – the Tower of Kalidasa ?'

Afterword
Sources and Acknowledgements

The writer of historical fiction has a peculiar responsibility to his readers, especially when he is dealing with unfamiliar times and places. He should not distort facts or events, when they are known; and when he invents them, as he is often compelled to do, it is his duty to indicate the dividing line between imagination and reality.

The writer of science fiction has the same responsibility, squared. I hope that these notes will not only discharge that obligation but also add to the reader's enjoyment.

Taprobane and Ceylon

For dramatic reasons, I have made three trifling changes to the geography of Ceylon (now Sri Lanka). I have moved the island eight hundred kilometres south, so that it straddles the equator – as indeed it did twenty million years ago, and may some day do again. At the moment it lies between six and ten degrees north.

In addition, I have doubled the height of the Sacred Mountain, and moved it closer to 'Yakkagala'. For both places exist, very much as I have described them.

Sri Pada, or Adam's Peak, is a striking cone-shaped mountain sacred to the Buddhists, the Muslims, the Hindus and the Christians, and bearing a small temple on its summit. Inside the temple is a stone slab with a depression which, though two metres long, is reputed to be the foot print of the Buddha.

Every year, for many centuries, thousands of pilgrims have made the long climb to the 2,240-metre-high summit. The ascent is no longer dangerous for there are two stairways (which must surely be the longest in the world) to the very top. I have climbed once, at the instigation of the *New Yorker*'s Jeremy Bernstein (see his *Experiencing Science*), and my legs were paralysed for several days afterwards. But it was worth the effort, for we were lucky enough to see the beautiful and awe-inspiring spectacle of the peak's shadow at dawn – a perfectly symmetrical cone visible only for the few minutes after sunrise, and stretching almost to the horizon on the clouds far below.

I have since explored the mountain with much less effort in a Sri Lanka Air Force helicopter, getting close enough to the temple to observe the resigned expressions on the faces of the monks, now accustomed to such noisy intrusions.

The rock fortress of Yakkagala is actually Sigiriya (or Sigiri, 'Lion Rock'), the reality of which is so astonishing that I have had no need to change it in any way. The only liberties I have taken are chronological, for the palace on the summit was (according to the Sinhalese Chronicle the *Culavamsa*) built during the reign of the parricide King Kasyapa 1 (AD 478–495). However, it seems incredible that so vast an undertaking could have been carried out in a mere eighteen years by a usurper expecting to be challenged at any moment, and the real history of Sigiriya may well go back for many centuries before these dates.

The character, motivation and actual fate of Kasyapa have been the subject of much controversy, recently fuelled by the posthumous *The Story of Sigiri* (Lake House, Colombo, 1972), by the Sinhalese scholar Professor Senerat Paranavitana. I am also indebted to his monumental two-volume study of the inscriptions on the Mirror Wall, *Sigiri Graffiti* (Oxford University Press, 1956). Some of the verses I have quoted are genuine; others I have only slightly invented.

The frescoes which are Sigiriya's greatest glory have been handsomely reproduced in *Ceylon: Paintings from Temple, Shrine and Rock* (New York Graphic Society/UNESCO, 1957). Plate V shows the most interesting – and the one, alas, destroyed in the 1960s by unknown vandals. The attendant is clearly *listening* to the mysterious hinged box she is holding in her right hand; it remains unidentified, the local archaeologists refusing to take seriously my suggestion that it is an early Sinhalese transistor radio.

The legend of Sigiriya has recently been brought to the screen by Dimitri de Grunwald in his production *The God King*, with Leigh Lawson as a very impressive Kasyapa.

The Space Elevator

This apparently outrageous concept was first presented to the West in a letter in the issue of *Science* for 11 February 1966, 'Satellite Elongation into a True "Sky-Hook" ', by John D. Isaacs, Hugh Bradner and George E. Backus of Scripps Institute of Oceanography, and Allyn C. Vine of Wood's Hole Oceanographic Institute. Though it may seem odd that oceanographers should get involved with such an idea, this is not surprising when one realizes that they are about the only people (since the great days of barrage balloons) who concern themselves with very long cables hanging under their own weight. (Dr Allyn Vine's name, incidentally is now immortalized in that of the famous research submersible 'Alvin'.)

It was later discovered that the concept had already been developed six years earlier – and on a much more ambitious scale – by a Leningrad engineer, Y. N. Artsutanov (*Komsomolskaya Pravda*, 31 July 1960). Artsutanov considered a 'heavenly funicular', to use his engaging name for the device, lifting no less than 12,000 tons a day to synchronous orbit. It seems surprising that this daring idea received so little publicity; the only mention I have ever seen of it is in the handsome volume of paintings by Alexei Leonov and Sokolov, *The Stars are Awaiting Us* (Moscow 1967). One colour plate (page 25) shows the 'Space Elevator' in action; the caption reads: '. . . the satellite will, so to say, stay fixed in a certain point in the sky. If a cable is lowered from the satellite to the earth you will have a ready cable-road. An "Earth-Sputnik-Earth" elevator for freight and passengers can then be built, and it will operate without any rocket propulsion.'

Although General Leonov gave me a copy of his book at the Vienna 'Peaceful Uses of Space' Conference in 1968, the idea simply failed to register on me – despite the fact that the elevator is shown hovering exactly over Sri Lanka! I probably thought that Cosmonaut Leonov, a noted humorist,* was just having a little joke.

The space elevator is quite clearly an idea whose time has come,

---

* Also a superb diplomat. After the Vienna screening he made quite the nicest comment on *2001* I've ever heard: 'Now I feel I've been in space *twice*.' Presumably after the Apollo-Soyuz mission he would say '*three* times'.

as is demonstrated by the fact that within a decade of the 1966 Isaacs letter it was independently re-invented at least three times. A very detailed treatment, containing many new ideas, was published by Jerome Pearson of Wright-Paterson Air Force Base in *Acta Astronautica* for September–October 1975 ('The Orbital Tower; a spacecraft launcher using the Earth's rotational energy'). Dr Pearson was astonished to hear of the earlier studies, which his computer survey had failed to locate; he discovered them through reading my own testimony to the House of Representatives Space Committee in July 1975. (See *The View From Serendip*.)

Six years earlier (*Journal of the British Interplanetary Society*, Vol 22, pp 442–457, 1969) A. R. Collar and J. W. Flower had come to essentially the same conclusions in their paper 'A (Relatively) Low Altitude 24-hour Satellite'. They were looking into the possibility of suspending a synchronous communications satellite far below the natural 36,000 kilometre altitude, and did not discuss taking the cable all the way down to the surface of the earth, but this is an obvious extension of their treatment.

And now for a modest cough. Back in 1963, in an essay commissioned by UNESCO and published in *Astronautics* for February 1964, 'The World of the Communications Satellite' (now available in *Voices From the Sky*), I wrote: 'As a much longer term possibility, it might be mentioned that there are a number of theoretical ways of achieving a *low-altitude, twenty-four-hour satellite*; but they depend upon technical developments unlikely to occur in this century. I leave their contemplation as an exercise for the student.'

The first of these 'theoretical ways' was, of course, the suspended satellite discussed by Collar and Flower. My crude back-of-an-envelope calculations, based on the strength of existing materials, made me so sceptical of the whole idea that I did not bother to spell it out in detail. If I had been a little less conservative – or if a larger envelope had been available – I might have been ahead of everyone except Artsutanov himself.

As this book is (I hope) more of a novel than an engineering treatise, those who wish to go into technical details are referred to the now rapidly expanding literature on the subject. Recent examples include Jerome Pearson's 'Using the Orbital Tower to Launch Earth-Escape Payloads Daily' (Proceedings of the 27th

International Astronautical Federation Congress, October 1976) and a remarkable paper by Hans Moravec, 'A Non-Synchronous Orbital Skyhook' (American Astronautical Society Annual Meeting, San Francisco, 18–20 October 1977).

I am much indebted to my friends the late A. V. Cleaver of Rolls-Royce, Dr Ing Harry O. Ruppe, Professor of Astronautics at the Technical University of Munich's Lehrstuhl fur Raumfahrt-technic, and Dr Alan Bond of the Culham Laboratories for their valuable comments on the Orbital Tower. They are not responsible for my modifications.

Walter L. Morgan (no relation to Vannevar Morgan, as far as I know) and Gary Gordon of the COMSAT Laboratories, as well as L. Perek of the United Nations' Outer Space Affairs Division, have provided most useful information on the stable regions of the synchronous orbit; they point out that natural forces (particularly sun–moon effects) would cause major oscillations, especially in the north–south directions. Thus 'Taprobane' might not be as advantageous as I have suggested; but it would still be better than anywhere else.

The importance of a high-altitude site is also debatable, and I am indebted to Sam Brand of the Naval Environment Prediction Research Facility, Monterey, for information on equatorial winds. If it turns out that the Tower *could* be safely taken down to sea level, then the Maldivian island of Gan (recently evacuated by the Royal Air Force) may be the twenty-second century's most valuable piece of real estate.

Finally, it seems a very strange – and even scary – coincidence that, years before I ever thought of the subject of this novel, I myself should have unconsciously gravitated (*sic*) towards its locale. For the house I acquired a decade ago on my favourite Sri Lankan beach (see *The Treasure of the Great Reef* and *The View From Serendip*) is at *precisely* the closest spot on any large body of land to the point of maximum geosynchronous stability.

So in my retirement I hope to watch the other superannuated relics of the Early Space Age, milling around in the orbital Sargasso Sea immediately above my head.

Colombo
1969–1978

And now, one of those extraordinary coincidences I have learned to take for granted . . .

While correcting the proofs of this novel, I received from Dr Jerome Pearson a copy of NASA Technical Memorandum TM-75174, 'A Space "Necklace" About the Earth' by G. Polyakov. This is a translation of 'Kosmicheskoye "Ozherel'ye" Zemli', published in *Teknika Molodezhi*, No 4, 1977, pp 41–43.

In this brief but stimulating paper, Dr Polyakov, of the Astrakhan Teaching Institute, describes in precise engineering details Morgan's final vision of a continuous ring around the world. He sees this as a natural extension of the space elevator, whose construction and operation he also discusses in a manner virtually identical with my own treatment.

I salute *tovarich* Polyakov, and am beginning to wonder if, yet again, I have been too conservative. Perhaps the Orbital Tower may be an achievement of the twenty-first century, not the twenty-second.

Our own grandchildren may demonstrate that – sometimes – Gigantic is Beautiful.

Colombo
18 September 1978

Arthur C. Clarke
A Fall of Moondust 75p

The setting is the Moon in the 21st century and it is depicted vividly
and convincingly. But the vital core of the novel is this: will the crew
and the passengers of the Dust-cruiser *Selene*, buried fifteen metres
down in the Sea of Thirst, be rescued before half a dozen possible
catastrophes overcome them?

Imperial Earth 80p

Arthur C. Clarke – '. . . at the height of his powers' NEW YORK TIMES

Colonists from the entire solar system converge on the mother planet
for the 2276 celebrations.
Duncan Makenzie, scientist administrator from the underground
colony of Titan, one of the outer moons of Saturn, has a delicate
mission to perform – for his planet, his family and himself . . .

Childhood's End 75p

Breath-taking in its imaginative sweep, this brilliant story explores
the distant reaches of space, tells of the last generation of Man – and of
the last Man himself.

'There has been nothing like it for years . . . an author who
understands there are many things that have a higher claim on
humanity than its own "survival"' C. S. LEWIS

Rendezvous with Rama £1

Rama – a metallic cylinder approaching the Sun at a tremendous velocity. Rama – first product of an alien civilization to be encountered by man. Rama – a world of technological marvels and artificial ecology. What is its purpose in the year 2131 ? Who is inside it ? And why ?

The Deep Range 95p

After a terrifying nightmare in outer space, Walter Franklin needs to discover a reason for living, and he finds it in the ocean depths where strangers defy death to give him life. But Franklin is haunted by the memory of an echo, an echo that could solve the oldest mystery of the Sun.

Earthlight 85p

Two centuries from now there may be men who do not owe allegiance to any nation on Earth – or even to Earth itself . . . This brilliant story tells of a time when man stands upon the moon and the planets – tells of men now divided by the vast stretches of the Solar System but once again torn by jealousy and fear.

'In the grand Wellsian manner . . . the finest descriptive space battle I have ever read' NEW WORLDS SCIENCE FICTION

Brian Aldiss
The Eighty-Minute Hour 50p

While recovering from the holocaust of war, Earth suffers chaotic
breakdowns in the fabric of time and space. Survivors are stranded in
the past, present or future – or on Mars, which is worse . . . And a
band of heroes still battles in its alternate world of swords and sorcery . . .

Non-Stop 60p

In this, his first SF novel, Brian Aldiss immediately demonstrated his
exuberant range and versatility. The tale of a lost tribe trapped in a
world of space-ships, time machines, giants, armed rats, outcasts and
raiders . . .

'Fascinating reading . . . when you discover what it was all about, you
start again at the beginning' OBSERVER

Frankenstein Unbound 50p

'Science fiction of a high order . . . Joe Bodenland, a twenty-first-
century American, passes through a timeslip and finds himself with
Byron and Shelley in the famous villa on the shore of Lake Geneva.
More fantastically, he finds himself face to face with a real Frankenstein,
a *Doppelgänger* inhabiting a complex world where fact and fiction may
as easily have congress as Bodenland himself manages to make love to
Mary' GUARDIAN

Christopher Priest
Indoctrinaire 75p

'A novelist of real distinction' THE TIMES

In a laboratory deep under the Antarctic, Wentik is experimenting with mind-affecting drugs. Suddenly he is transported into the 22nd-century Brazilian jungle. After nuclear war only South America has survived, but vestiges of the war gases remain to create 'The Disturbances' and threaten the social order. Wentik must return to his own time to find out about the gas and its antidote . . . but finds himself in the wrong time-slot, and the War has already begun . . .

'Excellent . . . a Kafka-type nightmare' SUNDAY TIMES

Fugue for a Darkening Island 70p

'Britain in the near future. In power is a strong right-wing Government struggling against rising prices and unemployment. Then the African refugees begin to arrive . . .' SUNDAY EXPRESS

'In the Wyndham tradition; but Wyndham's mellow sunsets have faded and the dark night of the soul is coming down'
BRIAN ALDISS, GUARDIAN

Inverted World 85p

Helward Mann leaves the City of Earth to become a Future Surveyor in an alien world – apparently familiar, but gradually revealing its strange difference. This world is 'inverted': a planet of infinite size existing in a finite universe . . .

'One of the most gifted and poetic young writers of science fiction'
JOHN FOWLES

'One of the trickiest and most astonishing twist endings in modern SF' TRIBUNE

Vonda McIntyre
Dreamsnake 95p

In a world devasted by nuclear holocaust, Snake is a healer. One of an élite, dedicated to caring for sick humanity, she goes wherever her skills are needed, taking, too, the three deadly reptiles through which her medicine works – a cobra, a rattlesnake, and Grass – a creature which can smooth the path between life and death by inducing benign dreams . . . Rare and valuable is this dreamsnake.

'Richly and beautifully imagined' SPECTATOR

The Exile Waiting 75p

Center is the sole surviving city in a storm-torn Earth, quarried deep underground out of a limestone cave system. Like some city of the Renaissance it is a hierarchical, free enterprise society ruled by a Medici figure gone to seed and his court of perverts . . .

'The polish of a robot's hard exterior . . . sufficiently rewarding to make one look forward to next time' NEW SCIENTIST

GOOD BEER GUIDE 1993

EDITED BY JEFF EVANS

Campaign for Real Ale Ltd.

34 Alma Road, St Albans,
Herts, AL1 3BW

CONTENTS

Editor: Jeff Evans. **Deputy Editor:** Jill Adam. **Vital Support:** Iain Walter Dobson MBE, Iain Loe, Steve Cox, Malcolm Harding, Roger Protz, Andrew Sangster, Jo Bates, Catherine Dale, Su Tilley, Clare Stevens, Iljoesja Lowinsky, Gillian Dale. **Maps:** David Perrott. **Design:** Rob Howells. **Illustrations:** David Downton *cover*, Christine Roche *pages 24-26*. **Cartoons** from earlier Good Beer Guides: Ken Pyne.

Published by: Campaign for Real Ale Ltd., 34 Alma Road, St Albans, Herts, AL1 3BW. Tel. (0727) 867201. **Typeset by** BP Integraphics, Bath. **Printed by** Bath Press.

ISBN 1 85249 005 5 © Campaign for Real Ale Ltd. 1992/3

35,000 CAMRA members make this guide possible. Particular thanks go to those involved with surveying and providing information on beers, breweries and pubs.

INTRODUCTION

Every drinker has heard it said that there is no bad beer, but some is just better than the rest. It's an old tale, which has never borne any truth. But today it is even further off the mark than ever.'

These words were penned twenty years ago, as an introduction to the first Good Beer Guide. At the time, the beer drinker's lot was not a happy one. Big breweries were carving up the market with their insipid keg beers – brewery-processed, characterless concoctions, nationally advertised and forced onto the bar at the expense of much-loved, distinctive brews from smaller breweries. Until the Good Beer Guide arrived, the quest for a decent pint demanded sixth sense, a prevailing wind and an acute air of optimism. At last, here in black and white, was confirmation that good beer really did exist, and, what's more, it even told you where to find it.

Strange then, twenty years later, when so many pubs proudly display handpumps and tout the wonders of their cask beers, that the Good Beer Guide should be going as strong as ever. Might it be because there appears to be so much choice now, and that this is now a guide for all the *right* reasons? Or could it have something to do with the fact that many publicans still have the amazing knack of turning fine, well-crafted beers into lifeless pints of vinegar? Probably a combination of both.

There has never been a better time in the last two decades to seek out some interesting brews, but you have to tread carefully for top-notch prices are no guarantee of top-notch beer. And, sadly, there are still areas of the country where traditional ale remains the exception, not the rule.

One thing is certain: there is still no truth in the tale that there is no such thing as bad beer, and, as long as beer is brewed, the Good Beer Guide will have a job to do.

3

HOW DOES A PUB GET INTO THE GUIDE?

The Good Beer Guide is unique amongst guidebooks in its insistence on the quality of beer as the criterion for entry. We are totally independent and accept no advertising or payment for inclusion. We don't employ paid inspectors who visit pubs perhaps once or twice before making their recommendations. Our surveyors are CAMRA members, people who know the pubs in their locality like the backs of their hands. They don't just visit on the good nights, but on the bad nights too. They know just how consistent the pubs in their area are. After discussion of their findings, the final list of entries is compiled at a CAMRA branch meeting.

However, readers' letters are an important part of the annual pub survey. All recommendations – and criticisms – are forwarded to the local branch, so, please, continue to write. All pubs are surveyed each year, with the descriptions and details freshly written. The facts are accurate to our knowledge, and are updated right up to the last possible moment. Unfortunately, changes are inevitable during the currency of the Guide, and some beers or facilities may be different on your visit.

WHAT TYPES OF PUB ARE INCLUDED?

As long as it sells good beer, any licensed outlet is eligible for the Guide. You will find a few wine bars, theatre bars, clubs and even off-licences amongst the entries, but the outlets are predominantly pubs. Because CAMRA members come from such a broad cross-section of the community, our surveyors tend to be enthusiastic about all sorts of establishments. Don't be surprised to stumble across thatched, picture-postcard pubs alongside basic, back-street boozers, or even heavy metal or disco bars. There are pubs for all occasions and nearly 5,000 are featured.

FACILITIES

For each entry, a row of symbols quickly sums up its potential for visitors. The symbols are explained on the inside front cover for easy reference but range from real fires to no-smoking areas. No assessment of meals or accommodation quality is made, unless there are additional comments in the pub description.

Only traditional, cask-conditioned beers (real ales) are listed. (The differences between real ale and keg beer and lager are explained on pages 337-339.) The order is alphabetical by brewery, with beers in original gravity order (generally the weakest first) for each brewery. Guest beers are indicated where they are offered. Seasonal beers, such as winter ales, are listed but are clearly not always available. Check The Breweries at the back of the book for detailed information on all beers.

OPENING HOURS

Pubs in England and Wales have the right to open between the hours of 11am and 11pm, though not all choose to do so. Some towns have special arrangements for events like market days, hence the occasional variation in opening hours. Sunday hours are 12-3, 7-10.30, unless otherwise stated. The same hours apply to Scotland, though exceptions are commonplace and are mentioned. Sunday opening in Scotland is generally 12-2.30, 6.30-11, though publicans can now request to stay open all day, if they wish.

COUNTY ORDER

Pubs are listed in counties and then alphabetically by town or village. The counties are also arranged from A-Z, though all Yorkshire counties are under Y, all Glamorgans under G and both Sussexes under S. English counties come first, followed by Welsh, then Scottish regions, Northern Ireland, the Channel Islands and the Isle of Man. Maps are provided for each county, indicating the approximate location of the pubs and the independent breweries which brew in the area. Don't forget to check the neighbouring counties for pubs, if you're travelling near the county border. A key map is supplied on the inside back cover.

PUBS FEATURED IN ALL TWENTY EDITIONS OF THE GOOD BEER GUIDE

ENGLAND

AVON
Bull, Hinton

BEDFORDSHIRE
Rose & Crown, Ridgmont
Sow & Pigs, Toddington

CAMBRIDGESHIRE
Queen's Head, Newton

CHESHIRE
Rising Sun, Tarporley

CORNWALL
Blue Anchor, Helston

DERBYSHIRE
Durham Ox, Ilkeston

DORSET
Square & Compass, Worth
Matravers

DEVON
Drewe Arms, Drewsteignton

GLOUCESTERSHIRE
Fox, Great Barrington
Queens Head, Stow-on-the-Wold

HAMPSHIRE
Tudor Rose, Romsey

HERTFORDSHIRE
Farriers Arms, St Albans

KENT
Jolly Drayman, Gravesend

LANCASHIRE
Empress Hotel, Blackpool

GREATER LONDON
Anglesea Arms, SW7
Buckingham Arms, SW1
Fox & Hounds, SW1
Star Tavern, SW1
Thatched House, Cranham

MERSEYSIDE
Roscoe Head, Liverpool

NORFOLK
Ostrich, Castle Acre

NORTHUMBERLAND
Star, Netherton

NOTTINGHAMSHIRE
Cross Keys, Epperstone

OXFORDSHIRE
Crown & Tuns, Deddington

SHROPSHIRE
All Nations, Madeley

SOMERSET
Old Down Inn, Emborough

SUFFOLK
Butt & Oyster, Pin Mill

EAST SUSSEX
Bell, Burwash
Fountain, Plumpton Green

WILTSHIRE
Haunch of Venison, Salisbury

NORTH YORKSHIRE
Groves, Knaresborough

WALES

WEST GLAMORGAN
Adam & Eve, Swansea

GWENT
Cherry Tree, Tintern

SCOTLAND*

LOTHIAN
Grey Horse, Balerno

TAYSIDE
Fisherman's Tavern,
Broughty Ferry

* 19 editions only: Scotland was not included in the first *Good Beer Guide*

HOW IT ALL BEGAN

*Michael Hardman looks back
at the birth of the Good Beer Guide*

I t seems ridiculous now, but when we first had the idea of producing a guide to recommended pubs, our collective imagination stretched no further than calling it the *CAMRA List*.

It was to be a typewritten, duplicated document available only to members of the fledgling campaign. We knew little about beer beyond the fact that there were some brews we loved and some we hated, so we contented ourselves with plans for a mere list of names of pubs and their addresses, spiced perhaps by the occasional snippet of information about buxom barmaids, rude landlords or the possibility of after-hours drinks (which was to be signified, without further explanation, by a double full stop).

At the time, the entire membership of CAMRA consisted of Graham Lees, Jim Makin, Bill Mellor and me, but we expected that we might attract a few dozen others over the next couple of years and that we might, if we were lucky, produce a list of a hundred of so good pubs dotted around the country.

Little did we know that there were hundreds of knowledgeable beer drinkers out there just waiting for an organisation like CAMRA to come along and that many of them already had their own lengthy lists of pubs serving good traditional draught beer and of

TODDINGTON
10.30–2.00; 5.30–10.30 (11 F.S)
● Sow and Pigs
High Street
Greene King (Biggleswade) ○ ● (G)
Excellent, basic pub in quiet village.
Ale fetched from cellar.

GRAVESEND
10.30–2.30; 6.00–11.00
● Jolly Drayman (Tel 2355)
Love Lane
Charrington ○ (H)
Very attractive old pub in unspoilt condition. Excellent ale. Dart board with oversize numbers is useful for shortsighted people.

Two ever-present pubs, as they appeared in the first properly printed *Good Beer Guide* in 1974

Keyston

Covington

Kimbolton

Gt. Staughton

St. Neots

Huntingdonshire on the map in 1974 – the product of two hours' Sunday drinking

breweries that produced it. These God-sent people also knew, with varying degrees of accuracy, *why* some beer was good and some was bad.

Lees and I began to meet them in the Young's pubs of London or the Holt's pubs of Manchester, and we were staggered by the amount of research into pubs, beer and brewing that had already been carried out but never published. Mind you, we almost missed one of these experts altogether and, if we had, our projected pub guide might still have been called the *CAMRA List*.

One afternoon, during one of the outbreaks of minor industrial action that plagued Fleet Street in the 1970s, I had abandoned my desk for some hours in favour of the Olde Cheshire Cheese and a bit too much Marston's Pedigree than was good for me. When the printers eventually returned to action and we were summoned back into the office, I apparently received a telephone call from a fellow I had never met before and even arranged to meet him that evening in a pub near St Paul's.

I never turned up, having been in a near-stupor when I had spoken to him, but he was sufficiently good humoured to telephone me again the next day, not so much by way of complaint – for which he had ample grounds – but to arrange another meeting so that he could learn something of this new campaign with a view to including its activities in his forthcoming book, *The Death of the English Pub*.

This time, the meeting took place and the budding author, Christopher Hutt, eventually became one of the major catalysts in the transformation of CAMRA from a jokey little drinking club into a serious consumer organisation, and along the way he insisted that the name of our pub list should be the *Good Beer Guide*.

The first edition came out in 1973, two years after CAMRA had been born. It was a modest affair – typewritten and duplicated, as originally envisaged – but considerably wider in scope and more comprehensive in its information about beer than we had ever thought it could be only six months earlier. Its pages were collated and bound in document

8

folders by a production line of half a dozen or so volunteers working on a wallpaper-pasting table in my sitting-room, and only a couple of hundred copies were produced. But it started the ball rolling.

A more elaborate affair was planned for the following year and a Hertfordshire stalwart called John Hanscomb – one of the most enthusiastic beer drinkers I have ever met – took over as editor to allow me to concentrate on developing *What's Brewing* as CAMRA's monthly newspaper.

Hanscomb and his deputy, Tom Linfoot, another amazing beer brain, worked tirelessly in their spare time to compile the first properly printed *Good Beer Guide*. I was seconded to help with the production side and to liaise with printers, and we recruited a Manchester-based designer called Trevor Hatchett. He had joined CAMRA with an old friend, Jeremy Beadle, who served briefly on the National Executive before he became better known for his television pranks.

CAMRA

GOOD
BEER
GUIDE

CAMPAIGN FOR REAL AI

GOOD
BEER
GUIDE

IN WHICH The History of Inns, Taverns and Public Houses is discussed by the erudite Mr. Michael Jackson; the processes of Brewing are fully expounded; the pure and natural ingredients of Real Ale are specified; and about 6,000 Public Houses throughout the country are Listed, Described & located upon 36 Maps, all delineated in Colour; the whole compiled and ably edited yet again by the bibulous Mr. Roger Protz. 1980

Hanscomb had insisted that the book should follow the old county boundaries, which had been newly redrawn, but, as the publishing deadline approached, he noticed that Huntingdonshire was the only English county with no recommended pubs. He set out next day, a Sunday, visited as many pubs as he could in the two hours of lunchtime opening and returned with seven entries, which formed a short, straight line on the map.

Hanscomb's sterling efforts were due to be rewarded by the launch of the *Good Beer Guide* at CAMRA's third annual meeting, in York early in 1974. The printers, however, had suffered a last-minute attack of cold feet over a phrase describing one of the breweries listed inside the back cover, and on the eve of the launch they refused to release the 10,000 copies they had printed.

The offending description, about one of Watney's keg-beer plants,

10

read: 'Avoid like the plague.' Libellous, said the printers' lawyers; poppy-cock, retorted Hanscomb. But the publicity surrounding the non-publication of the *Guide* worked to CAMRA's – and eventually the printers' – benefit, for no sooner had a compromise been reached, whereby *like the plague* would be replaced by *at all costs*, than the *Guide* began to sell as fast as the ale it was recommending.

CAMRA and real ale now began their first period of rapid growth and the *Good Beer Guide* became a best seller. I was employed full time to edit the *Guide* and other publications, working alongside CAMRA secretary John Green, the Campaign's first full-time employee, in rented offices above a cycle shop in St Albans. Branches sprang up around Britain and were quickly organised into doing the research and compiling the entries for the next *Guide*, though there were still some huge gaps around the country that had to be covered almost single-handedly by members who had the time, the money and the ability to write legibly after visiting twenty or more pubs in a day.

Now, all these years later, the *Good Beer Guide* is as much a part of the annual publishing calendar as *Who's Who*, *Whitaker's Almanack* and *Wisden*. It is eccentric in its choice of pubs, but that may be no bad thing for a publication that aims to cover a most subjective subject objectively, and it is irritating in its use of pretentious descriptions of beers, though not so much as it was a few years ago.

These criticisms aside, however, the *Guide* has matured and improved beyond recognition from the efforts of the mid 1970s. It has always been CAMRA's biggest single weapon and it will become ever more important in these times of turmoil in the brewing industry, which are as much a threat to our culture as were the constant brewery closures of the 1950s and 60s that ultimately led to CAMRA's birth.

So here's to another twenty years, at least, of what almost became the *CAMRA List*.

Michael Hardman, one of the four founders of CAMRA and its first chairman, edited the Good Beer Guide in 1973 and from 1975 to 1977. He and his wife Marion are journalists and partners in a publications and public relations consultancy whose clients include Young's Brewery of Wandsworth .

TIME TO ACT!

Four years after the MMC report, Steve Cox calls on the Government to get tough with the big brewers and plug the loopholes in the beer laws

The Monopolies and Mergers Commission completed a two-year enquiry into the brewing industry in 1989. Its report was highly critical and outlined wide-ranging proposals for change.

THE MMC FOUND THAT

■ Over a decade, beer prices had risen faster than inflation.

■ Big national brewers, by ownership of pubs and loans to free houses, dominated the trade, to the detriment of consumer choice.

■ New brewers were excluded from the market.

■ Pub tenants were in a weak bargaining position compared with their brewery landlords.

It is against these four points (price, choice, ease of entry for new brewers, and the position of tenants) that the action taken by the Government in response to the MMC report must be judged.

THE GOVERNMENT'S PROPOSALS

■ Big brewers would be required to sell, or lease free of a tie on products, a proportion of their pubs. The deadline for this was November 1992. For each brewer, half the number of pubs over two thousand were affected. A brewer with 5,000 pubs, therefore, would have to sell, or lease free of tie, 1,500 pubs. In total, 11,000 pubs were to be 'freed up'.

■ Tenants (but not managers) of national brewers' pubs would be allowed to sell a 'guest beer', a real ale bought from the supplier of their own choice. They would also be freed from the tie on all products other than beer.

■ From July 1992, tenants would be given security under the 1954 Landlord and Tenant Act.

So what has happened since the proposals became law?

PRICE

CAMRA price surveys show that beer prices have risen 17 per cent more than inflation since 1989. Despite a severe recession, brewers have still succeeded in raising the real price of beer, even allowing for tax and VAT changes.

CONSUMER CHOICE AND NEW BREWERS

The guest beer has undoubtedly had some effect. Surveys show a quarter of pubs take a guest beer, although half of these take it from an 'approved' list drawn up by their brewery landlords. Some small brewers have seen impressive increases in sales as a result of this law and the number of new breweries chancing their arm suggests that, at least in some areas, the market may have opened up.

However, the number of pubs legally allowed to take a guest beer is on the decline.

NEWSPAPER OF THE CAMPAIGN FOR REAL ALE JULY 1991

What's BREWING

CAMRA is a member of the European Beer Consumers Union

Indies fly the ale flag
Special report on progress by Britain's regional and micro brewers

BACK BRITAIN'S INDEPENDENT BREWERS

Great guest ale prices scandal

BIG brewers have drinkers of guest ales on the rack, this year's CAMRA prices survey reveals.

Customers in a Big Six pubs are likely to pay per

three times the inflation rate.

'Cautious optimism' over Camerons future

by Stephen Cox

SOURCES close to the Camerons management buy-out team expressed "cautious optimism" last month about saving the Hartlepool brewery.

Owner Brent Walker has been at the centre of high drama in recent weeks, with company founder George Walker evicted as Chief Executive in a board-room coup.

Brent Walker's banks, led by Standard Chartered, made his departure as Chief Executive a condition of agreeing to a restructuring of the highly indebted company.

Results for 1990 show operating profit to £122 million, interest, tax ...

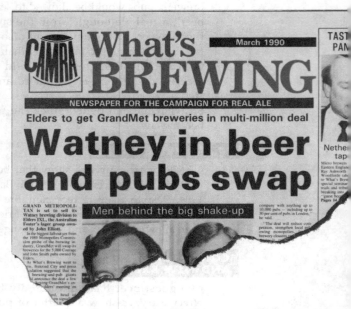

What's BREWING

March 1990

NEWSPAPER FOR THE CAMPAIGN FOR REAL ALE

Elders to get GrandMet breweries in multi-million deal

Watney in beer and pubs swap

Men behind the big shake-up

GRAND METROPOLI-
TAN is set to sell its
Watney brewing division to
Elders IXL, the Australian
Foster's lager group own-
ed by John Elliott.

In the biggest fallout yet from
the 1989 Monopolies Commission probe of the brewing industry, GrandMet will swap six
breweries for the 5,000 Courage
and John Smith pubs owned by
Elders.

As What's Brewing went to
press, frenzied City and press
speculation suggested that the
brewing-and-pub giants
would announce the deal a few
days after GrandMet's an-
nual shareholders' meeting on

company with anything up to
10,000 pubs — including up to
30 per cent of pubs in London,
he said.

"The deal will reduce competition, strengthen local
brewing monopolies
brewery closures
Pages 14

Nethe
tap

Micro brewers
Eastern England
Ray Ashworth
Woodforde cafe
to What's Brewi
special seminar
reals and lettur
breaking into a
"guest beer
Pages 14

National brewers have been taking pubs back
into management, or selling them to other
companies, so closing the door to guest beers.

The Nationals have also sold pubs to new
pub-owning chains, and then promptly signed
agreements to continue to supply them with
beer. As a result, the beers on the bar don't
change – in some cases, choice has even been
reduced.

Worst of all, the Government has allowed
mergers and take-overs to further concentrate
the brewing market. Boddingtons, Greenalls,
and Devenish have all left brewing, and their
pubs are now largely supplied by national
brewers. Courage has bought Grand
Metropolitan's (Watney's) breweries. Allied
plan to merge with Carlsberg. The Greene King
bid for Morland showed that larger regionals
plan to gobble up their smaller rivals.

Taken together, the top three brewers'
market share has risen from 47 to 62% in three
years – a dramatic tightening of the market.
Fewer breweries undoubtedly means higher
prices and less choice, in the long run.

Finally, considering choice, the brewers are
taking full advantage of their right to tie 'free'
houses to their products through the offer of

attractive financial loans (the 'loan tie'), a practice the MMC wanted to ban. Many of the new 'freed-up' houses have, in this way, remained tied to their original supplier.

POSITION OF TENANTS

The larger brewers have moved from traditional tenancies to longer leases, sometimes as long as twenty years. This move is the brewers' response to the Government legislation, not a requirement of it.

Leases impose greatly increased rents on the tenant, and require tenants to also pay for expensive repairs. Many leases are still tied for beer; some penalise the tenant if he doesn't sell enough. Pubs are already struggling to meet these drastically higher costs, and many will go out of business.

Tenants have been placed in impossible positions, with this change to leases being imposed under threat of eviction. Because the Landlord and Tenant Act was not introduced until July 1992, brewers have been able to issue notice to quit to all their tenants. Thousands have left the trade rather than take on unworkable terms and conditions.

For many tenants, things are worse, not better than they were in 1989. The importance of the publican to the quality of the pub, and the quality of the beer that pub sells, is well known. CAMRA is deeply concerned that many pubs face an unstable future of rapidly changing publicans, bankrupt businesses and 'chain-store' management, where untrained staff work for some distant boss.

THE VERDICT

The case against the big brewers meant that the Government was right to intervene. The results cannot be said to be promising.

■ On price, there has clearly been little or no improvement.
■ On choice, some developments have been very encouraging. However, the big brewers have found plenty of ways round the legislation. Mergers are occurring at an alarming rate. Many of the proposed benefits in terms of choice seem unlikely to appear.

15

What's BREWING

NEWSPAPER OF THE CAMPAIGN FOR REAL ALE OCTOBER 1991

HOP REPORT – centre pages

Giant's pub deal robs tenants of guest beer rights

Bass dodges the draught

GIANT brewers Bass have sold 372 pubs to Enterprise Inns, a new pub-owning company based in Solihull, and have artfully dodged the government's "guest beer" rule.

It is the biggest sale of pubs to a single company since the 1989 Monopolies Commission report on the brewing industry.

The new company's tied estate is centred on the West Midlands but stretches from Sheffield to Worcester and from Leicester to

Report by Stephen Cox

exclusive, so Enterprise could take beers from other brewers ... they chose ...

... of research,"
... last tenan...

GBG heralds 'key of the door' birthday
by Jeff Evans

HOT on the heels of the 1991 sell-out, the 1992 edition of the Good Beer Guide goes on sale at the end of this month as a prelude to CAMRA's 21st birthday year.

The Guide has long been seen as CAMRA's flagship, mixing solid campaigning points with entertaining features, the latest information from the brewing and Britain's best...

This year's ... again genero... by British C... ception.

The brewe... times to ex... growth in ... ale, and ... brewers h...

More ... tion h... been ... paper ... out c... tast...

Membership reaches all-time high

■ On the security of tenants, many good publicans will suffer - with untold consequences for the viability of the British pub and the quality of our beer.

The Government has announced that the effectiveness of its measures will be reviewed by the Office of Fair Trading from the end of 1993. It is already all too clear how things are panning out. The Government must move, now, to carry out the intentions of its original reforms.

■ Take-overs and mergers in the brewing industry must be halted.

■ The Government must get tough on exclusive supply deals between brewers and pub chains.

■ We need limits on loan ties.

■ The more ludicrous features of pub leases must be prohibited, such as unaffordable rents, and unfair obligations. A lease should be a partnership, not a prison sentence.

■ The guest beer must be chosen by the tenant, irrespective of any so-called 'guest' the brewery landlord might supply.

The final question must be whether the consumer would be best served by breaking the links between the big brewers and their pubs altogether.

That well known beer drinker, John Major, wants a classless society. There is a danger of us achieving a publess society instead.

16

THE BEER INVASION
Roger Protz sifts the wheat from the chaff as international beers vie for space on our off-licence shelves

Real Ale may be a British phenomenon but Good Beer is not confined to these shores. Brewers large and small are breaking out of national markets and selling their wares on the global stage. A visit to your local supermarket will confirm this. Your first choice – like mine – may be a glass of cask-conditioned beer, but if you play the fascinating game of *Desert Island Casks*, it is likely that several imported styles will join you on the sand.

Most of the great beers from other countries are genuine lagers, but not exclusively so. Top-fermenting ales are increasingly available, though not often in cask form, and it must be stressed that we should not judge other countries by our heritage and tradition. Our pubs determine how we drink: 80 per cent of our beer is consumed in draught form. In some countries take-home, packaged beer accounts for the same percentage.

Packaging means that most beers are filtered and too often pasteurised. Lager beers, after a lengthy conditioning, need filtration, but pasteurisation is a double-edged sword, prolonging inactive life yet, at its clumsiest, imparting a stale cardboard tang to the product.

Grolsch of the Netherlands does not pasteurise its beer and another Dutch company, Brand, declares 'There is no need to pasteurise: pasteurisation serves to lengthen the shelf-life of beer, but only marginally and at enormous cost to the taste and aroma of the beer.' Others please copy.

With these disclaimers and a warning that there are many extremely poor beers around, too (though, thankfully, sales of Mexican lager-and-lime are now plummeting as the young trendies search for a new fad), we can look for pleasure in the most unlikely areas. Who, for example, would think that the country with the most fascinating and burgeoning range of beers – beers booming with malt and hop character – is not Britain, Belgium, Germany or Czechoslovakia, but the United States of America?

USA

Inspired by CAMRA and Britain's own small brewery revolution in the 1970s and 1980s, scores of Americans are installing brewing plants and producing some beautifully crafted ales and lagers. Many of these new microbreweries have grown out of the movement organised by the American Homebrewers' Association, which was formed to provide a platform – via magazines, books and beer festivals – for the countless thousands of Americans who preferred to mash and boil at home rather than drink the fizzy pap provided by the national conglomerates.

The commercial beers produced by the likes of Samuel Adams, Bert Grant and Sierra Nevada are superb. The owners have dug deep into recipe books and folklore to create a range of ales, stouts, Pilsners and bock beers.The problem is finding them.

Many friends return from the US with the same complaint: 'Where are all these beers you keep cracking on about? All we could find were Budweiser and Miller Lite.'

With America's Big Three – Anheuser-Busch, Miller and Coors – controlling some 96 per cent of the US market and A-B's Budweiser accounting for 46 per cent of beer sales – there is little room for independent brewers. And they devote so much time to finding outlets for their beers in the US that they have neither the time nor the inclination to export them as well.

The Sam Adams' Boston beers are on sale in Germany and perhaps a few cases could be parachuted down to Britain as the plane passes over. However, two splendid examples of American beers are on regular sale in Britain.

The Anchor Brewery in San Francisco was saved from closure in 1965 by Fritz Maytag, a member of the wealthy washing-machine dynasty. He had enjoyed the local beer so much as a student in California that he decided to buy the brewery rather than lose his favourite tipple. Anchor is rated as a micro in the US but by British standards it is a large brewing concern. Its most famous product is Steam Beer, a 19th-century Gold Rush speciality that is something of a hybrid of ale and lager. A lager yeast is used but fermentation takes place at an ale temperature, a process that develops a high level of carbonation – or 'steam' as it was dubbed in San Francisco.

All Maytag's beers are sold in Britain by Fuller's. They include a porter, a remarkable barley wine called Old Foghorn and a Christmas Ale with a different specification each year. My favourite is the fruity Liberty Ale, with a massive hop aroma from the use of the home-grown Cascade strain.

On the East Coast, the Brooklyn Brewery has revived the honour and tradition of a suburb of New York City that once housed a vast number of breweries, most of which disappeared during Prohibition. Brooklyn

Sierra Nevada, Anchor and Brooklyn – three microbreweries leading the American beer revival

Lager, with some crystal malt in the mash and dry hopping in the cask, recreates the aromas and flavours of pre-Prohibition beer and its rich and hoppy character restores one's faith in American lager. You will find the beer in specialist shops and selected branches of Sainsbury's.

GERMANY

Lager and Pilsner are much abused terms and it is always good to find genuine examples of Pils beer in Britain that emphasise the dire nature of the local parodies of the style. Germany is a large brewing nation with more than 1,200 manufacturers, but many test the British market and quickly retire hurt. One company that has come and stayed, thanks to wholesaling arrangements with such regional brewers as Adnams, is Bitburger.

The town of Bitburg is in the Eifel region, close to the historic town of Trier and the Luxembourg border. Bitburger Pils is conditioned (lagered) for three months and is fully attenuated to brew out nearly all the malt sugars. With generous hopping from four different strains, the end result is a beautifully balanced Pils with an exceptionally dry finish.

A German Pils with a honey sweetness, offset by a shatteringly dry finish, is Jever from the resort town of the same name in Friesland in northern Germany. Jever has 44 units of bitterness, more than twice as many as the renowned Czech Budweiser and more even than the original Pils, Pilsner Urquell.

British bitter drinkers and cider lovers will find common cause when imbibing European wheat beers. The best wheat beers (of which the German Erdinger and Schneider products are arguably the classics) have a tart, slightly sour palate and a delectable 'apples and cloves' aroma that will appeal to cider drinkers.

Once derided as an 'old ladies' drink', wheat beer is now the fashionable beer among health-conscious young Germans. It is neither

'Shatteringly dry' Jever from Germany and the Belgian Chimay – from Trappist to Tesco

20

better nor worse for you than barley-based beers and in fact is made from a mix of barley malt and wheat, with the sharp and tangy character coming from the top-fermenting yeasts. Some wheat beers are filtered but the best and most authentic are left *mit hefe* – with yeast – to give a cloudy appearance in the glass.

BELGIUM

Belgium's brewing industry is steeped in tradition and the country has several examples of wheat or 'white' beer. The classic is Hoegaarden White, a bittersweet beer of awesome complexity that is spiced with coriander and curaçao as well as hops. The aroma has massive coriander appeal and there is a delicious orange note in the palate and finish.

The top-fermenting beers brewed by Trappist monks in Belgium have been given considerable coverage in recent years. The monks who brew the Chimay range now have a sales team to market their beers and you will find them in such unlikely outlets as Tesco. Trappist monks briefing salesmen must rate as one of the quainter examples of God sitting down with Mammon.

Look out, too, for the lesser-known but characterful Orval, produced in a 900-year-old Trappist monastery. Brewed with five different malts, candy sugar, German and Kentish hops, and both top and bottom-fermenting yeasts, this can only be a rich and complex brew. Orange in colour, and with an enormous fruit and hop character, it is not entirely dissimilar to Coopers Sparkling Ale, a bottle-conditioned beer from Australia, also now available in Britain.

Who would have thought we'd look forward to sampling beers imported from Australia and the United States, countries for too long identified with lacklustre lagers? It's even more evidence that the world of beer continues to fascinate and refresh its devotees.

Coopers: Australian for real ale

Roger Protz edits CAMRA's newspaper, What's Brewing. He writes for the Morning Advertiser and is The Guardian's beer correspondent. His books include The Real Ale Drinker's Almanac, The European Beer Almanac and The Village Pub.

THE FULL PINT

Do we have to sacrifice our handpumps to get one?

When is a pint not a pint? When it's got a head on it, according to Consumer Minister Edward Leigh, when he announced that the Government intended to implement Section 43 of the Weights and Measures Act.

From April 1994, the froth on the top of a glass can no longer be counted as part of a pint. A pint of beer must contain 20 fluid ounces of liquid. 'A pint should be that, a full pint', Mr Leigh declared, and beer drinkers across the land cheered in support.

Not so the Brewers' Society. Shocked to find that they would now have to give customers what they had paid for, they immediately dug in their heels. They announced that Section 43 would cost £530 million to implement and that the days of the handpump were numbered. In one fell swoop, they sacrificed their greatest marketing tool of the eighties and nineties.

The tall, elegant handpull, such a symbol of quality in the industry that the brewers have used it in their glossy advertisements and even for dispensing keg beer and cider, is now under threat. The brewers claim that it can no longer do the job, that it will not accurately measure out a full pint, and that electronic metered pumps will have to be installed in all pubs. Drinkers maintain that, with oversized lined glasses, the task can be completed accurately and at no extra cost to the publican. (No beer spills over the sides of the glass for a start.)

But the head is made of beer, retort the brewers, and that has to be paid for. It's mostly air, that's why the froth is white not brown, say the consumers: 'Ever bitten into an Aero?'.

The debate rages on. Not all the brewers cling to the Brewers' Society line; not all consumers see the need for a change. At the heart of the wrangle is the sense of grievance felt by beer drinkers who have been short-measured over the years – even under the old system. When the brewers talk about a hike in prices to pay for the pleasure of a head on a full pint, they tempt drinkers to tally up the cost of every short measure they've been given over

the years. It brings back to mind every word of abuse or scornful glance they have received when asking for a top-up.

When Section 43 is implemented, at least everyone will know what a pint is.

THREE STEPS
TO HEAVEN

*Or why enjoying a pint at the local
is not so easy for all of us,
as Angie Carmichael explains*

Picture the scene: it's a celebration - a wedding, a win on the pools, the sun shining on a bank holiday for once - you know the sort of thing. Or maybe it's just an ordinary evening and you're with a group of friends who've decided they fancy a pint down at the local. No problem with that is there?

Well, yes, there is – just one little problem. Well, actually, it's several little problems and one slightly larger one. The little ones are steps, usually at least one at the front door of the pub. The slightly larger problem is the toilet, or rather, the lack of an accessible one.

Our imaginary group of friends, you may have gathered, includes wheelchair users.

Ever tried to find a pub with level access *and* an accessible loo? Believe it or not, you can't take the one for granted when you see the other. Let me explain.

There's a pub near Bath which I've been known to pop into occasionally. It's out in the country, is very pretty and has an accessible loo. It's a shame about the step down from the car park - it would be quite easy to put in a small ramp.

I was there with a friend who's a wheelchair user one day, having a drink and a chat, and, at the end of the evening, off she went to the loo, only to return slightly irate a moment later to announce that she couldn't get in the loo because it was stacked to the roof with outdoor tables. The landlord was very apologetic but explained that he rarely had disabled customers and needed the space for storage!

Some places do have ramps at the door but you wouldn't get a wheelchair anywhere near the toilets. So it's a quick drink then a sharp exit to find an accessible loo elsewhere. Some landlords have very funny ideas about the definition of 'access for people with disabilities'. But then so do an awful lot of people. A friend of mine hurried into work one morning, enthusing about a pub she and her husband had visited the night before – "it's perfectly accessible, there's just the one step at the door....oh..no, I didn't check out the toilets, I'm afraid".

The trouble is, more often than not, pubs are very old buildings, sometimes with preservation orders stamped on them to prevent extensive alterations. But that's really no excuse for not trying to think of ways round the problem. And, let's face it, legislation's on our side; if a brewery's doing an extensive refurbishment, it is under a legal obligation to maintain or improve access for people with

disabilities.

Sometimes though, you do have to laugh. There's one pub I know of which has a level entrance round the back (which unfortunately they are in the habit of locking at the first gust of wind), and an accessible loo near the bar - what more could you ask for? But until recently the flush chain dangled tantalisingly out of reach near the ceiling, the lock didn't work and there was the constant worry that someone had removed the light bulb to replace a dud one elsewhere. Whoever said going for a drink was a relaxing way to spend an evening?

And it's not just wheelchair users who sometimes find their local a bit of a trial. Consider the problems facing people with visual impairments, hearing difficulties or cerebral palsy.

Bars the height of Mount Everest, split-level interiors, badly placed fruit machines, spring clips which don't allow doors to open fully, immovable bar stools and tables (ever tried tucking a wheelchair under a standard pub table?) ... you name it, I've seen it - and more. It's almost (but not quite) enough to make you give up drink.

But, on a serious note, I'm sure if the breweries put their minds to it they could achieve results. Pubs are always being refurbished or renovated and it wouldn't take too much of an effort to have a look at what could be done to improve access for people with disabilities. Look at the thousands of pounds that pubs raise each year for charity. I know quite a few people who would think making a pub accessible to all a cause worthy of support!

Meanwhile, seeing as it's lunchtime, I think I'll pop into my local for a bite to eat and a quick one. There's just the one step and the accessible toilet is only half a mile on down the road....

Angie Carmichael works as assistant producer with the Same Production Company, an independent television company specialising in programmes on disability issues, including Channel 4's highly-successful Same Difference.

BEYOND THE GOOD BEER GUIDE
New titles from CAMRA

RISING TO THE CHALLENGE of the Single Market, CAMRA has expanded its publishing division, Alma Books, in the direction of Europe.

THE GOOD BEER GUIDE TO BELGIUM & HOLLAND

The Good Beer Guide to Belgium & Holland, compiled by Tim Webb, presents a bibulous tour of these two beer-rich countries. Beer-hunting weekends across the Channel have long been favourite pastimes of British enthusiasts. Now the paths are marked out, as the Guide pinpoints the best bars with the most exciting beer menus. Like its established British brother, this Good Beer Guide also includes full details of all the breweries, from Belgian Abbey brewers and producers of the weird and wonderful, spontaneously fermenting lambics and fruit beers, to the new, exciting Dutch microbrewers who have thrown down the gauntlet to the multi-national giants. And, as beer barriers fall, and more and more continental brews find their way into our pubs and off-licences, this book will provide all the information you'll need about the fascinating beers of the Low Countries.

THE BEST WATERSIDE PUBS

Also new to the CAMRA publishing list is The Best Waterside Pubs, by John Simpson and Chris Rowland. If you're a canal user or a broad boater, you'll appreciate how frustrating it is to moor up at a less than inspiring pub, only to discover that a real classic was waiting just around the next bend. With this new guide to real ale pubs at the water's edge, such disappointments will be a thing of the past.

GOOD PUB FOOD

Look out, too, for the next edition of Susan Nowak's best-selling guide to Good Pub Food. This is a book which celebrates the rebirth of quality pub catering, singling out those hostelries which offer excellent, home-cooked pub fare alongside their traditional ales. For further details of CAMRA books see page 505.

GOOD BEER GUIDE BEERS OF THE YEAR

Chosen by CAMRA tasting panels, by votes from the public at CAMRA beer festivals, and by a poll of CAMRA members, these are the *Good Beer Guide Beers of the Year*. Each took its place as a finalist in the *Champion Beer of Britain* competition at the Great British Beer Festival at Olympia. These aren't the only good beers in the country, but they were found to be consistently outstanding in their categories. They have also been awarded a tankard symbol in The Breweries section of this book.

DARK AND LIGHT MILDS

Bateman Dark Mild
Brains Dark
Gale's XXXD
Holden's Mild
King & Barnes Mild
Taylor Golden Best

OLD ALES AND STRONG MILDS

Adnams Old
King & Barnes Old
S&N Theakston Old Peculier
Sarah Hughes Original Dark
    Ruby Mild
Woodforde's Norfolk Nog
Young's Winter Warmer

BITTERS

Adnams Bitter
Butterknowle Bitter
Cains Traditional Bitter
Otter Bitter
Plassey Bitter
Ridleys IPA

BARLEY WINES

Gibbs Mew Bishop's Tipple
Lees Moonraker
Marston's Owd Rodger
Robinson's Old Tom
Trough Festival Ale
Woodforde's Headcracker

BEST BITTERS

Batham Best Bitter
Butterknowle Conciliation Ale
Exe Valley Dob's Best Bitter
Fuller's London Pride
Nethergate Bitter
Taylor Landlord

PORTERS AND STOUTS

Bateman Salem Porter
Big Lamp Summerhill Stout
Coach House Blunderbus
    Old Porter
Malton Pickwick's Porter
Mauldons Black Adder
Reepham Velvet Stout

STRONG BITTERS

Cains Formidable Ale
Fuller's ESB
Harveys Armada Ale
Hop Back Summer Lightning
Pilgrim Crusader Premium
    Bitter
Randalls Best Bitter

BOTTLE-CONDITIONED BEERS

Bass Worthington White Shield
Burton Bridge Burton Porter
Courage Imperial Russian Stout
Eldridge Pope Thomas
    Hardy's Ale
Gale's Prize Old Ale
Guinness Original

28

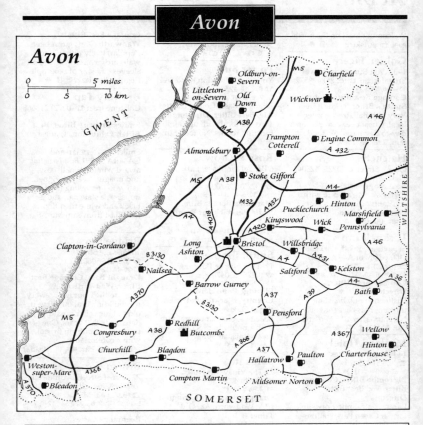

Avon

0 — 5 miles
0 — 5 — 10 km

GWENT

Oldbury-on-Severn
Littleton-on-Severn
Old Down
Charfield
Wickwar
Frampton Cotterell
Engine Common
Almondsbury
Stoke Gifford
Pucklechurch
Hinton
Marshfield
Kingswood
Wick
Pennsylvania
WILTSHIRE
Clapton-in-Gordano
Long Ashton
Bristol
Willsbridge
Nailsea
Saltford
Kelston
Barrow Gurney
Bath
Pensford
Redhill
Congresbury
Butcombe
Wellow
Churchill
Blagdon
Hinton
Weston-super-Mare
Hallatrow
Paulton
Charterhouse
Bleadon
Compton Martin
Midsomer Norton

S O M E R S E T

 Butcombe, Butcombe; **Hardington, Ross, Smiles**, Bristol; **Wickwar**, Wickwar

---

Almondsbury

Bowl Inn

16 Church Road, Lower Almondsbury ☎ (0454) 612757
11–3, 5 (6 Sat)–11
Courage Best Bitter, Directors; John Smith's Bitter; Wadworth 6X H; **guest beer**
Pleasant 17th-century pub. A good reputation for food; snacks only Sat eve and Sun lunch (separate restaurant). Supposedly haunted by the 'Grey Lady'. Guest beer from the Courage list.
🛏 🌸 🚪 🍴 ▶ P

Barrow Gurney

Princes Motto

Barrow Street ☎ (0275) 472282
11–2.30, 6–11
Draught Bass G; **Butcombe Bitter; Marston's Pedigree; Smiles Best Bitter** H; **Wadworth 6X** G; **Whitbread Boddingtons Bitter** H
Friendly roadside village local

with high-backed wooden settles. 🛏 🌸 ♣ P

Bath

Bell Inn

Walcot Street ☎ (0225) 460426
11.30–11
Courage Best Bitter, Directors; Eldridge Pope Hardy Country; Smiles Best Bitter H
Open-plan bar renowned for its jazz and soul music. 🌸 ♣

Belvedere Wine Vaults

25 Belvedere, Lansdown Road ☎ (0225) 330264
12–3, 5.30–11
Draught Bass; Charrington IPA H
Welcoming, unpretentious local with a quiet lounge.
Q 🚪 ♣

Bladud Arms

Gloucester Road, Lower Swainswick (A46, ¼ mile N of A4) ☎ (0225) 420152

11–3, 7–11
Butcombe Bitter; Hall & Woodhouse Hard Tackle; Marston's Pedigree; Wadworth 6X; Wells Eagle H; **guest beers**
Single lounge bar with a public bar section. Named after a local swineherd and prince who cured himself and his pigs of leprosy. 🌸 🚪 ♣ P

Coeur de Lion

17 Northumberland Place (opp. Guildhall)
12–11
Devenish Cornish Original, Royal Wessex; Marston's Pedigree; Wadworth 6X H
Reckoned to be the smallest pub in Bath, situated in a picturesque passageway. Note the superb stained-glass window. ⇌ (Spa)

Fairfield Arms

1 Fairfield Park Road, Fairfield Park ☎ (0225) 310594
11–2.30 (3 Sat), 6–11
Courage Best Bitter; Ushers Best Bitter H

Welcoming local on the north-eastern outskirts. ❀ 🍺 ♣

Golden Fleece

1–3 Avon Buildings, Lower
Bristol Road ☎ (0225) 429572
11–2.30, 5.30–11
**Courage Best Bitter; John
Smith's Bitter** Ⓗ**; guest beer**
Very popular street-corner
local. Guest beer changed on a
day-to-day basis. No food
Sun. 🍴 🍺 ♣ P

Hatchetts

Queen Street ☎ (0225) 425045
11–11
Beer range varies Ⓗ
Lively side-street pub with a
constantly changing guest
beer list. Mole's house beer.
🍴 ≢ (Spa)

Larkhall Inn

St Saviours Road, Larkhall
(400 yds N of A4/A46 jct)
☎ (0225) 425710
11–2.30, 6–10.30 (11 Fri & Sat)
**Courage Best Bitter,
Directors** Ⓗ
Distinctive pub boasting
unusual brass beer engines.
No entry after 10.30 Fri and
Sat. ♨ Q ❀ 🍺

Midland Hotel

14 James Street West
☎ (0225) 425029
11–3, 5.30–11 (11–11 Sat)
**Butcombe Bitter; Courage
Bitter Ale, Best Bitter,
Directors** Ⓗ
Large, central pub opposite
former Green Park station –
now Sainsbury's. No food
Sun. 🍴 🍺 ≢ (Spa) ♣

Old Farmhouse

1 Lansdown Road
☎ (0225) 316162
12–3, 5–11 (12–11 Fri & Sat)
**Draught Bass; Butcombe
Bitter; Hall & Woodhouse
Tanglefoot; Wadworth 6X,
Old Timer** Ⓗ
Lively local of great character.
The unusual pub sign is a
caricature of its landlord.
Lunches Tue–Sat. ♨ 🍴 🍺

Old Green Tree

Green Street ☎ (0225) 462357
11–11 (10.30 Mon & Tue; closed Sun
lunch)
**Hardington Best Bitter;
Ruddles County; Ushers Best
Bitter** Ⓗ
Pleasant city-centre pub
behind the main post office.
Three small, wood-panelled
bars. No food Sun.
Q 🍴 ≢ (Spa) ✍

Pig & Fiddle

2 Saracen Street
☎ (0225) 460868
12–3, 5 (6 Sat)–11
**Ash Vine Bitter, Challenger,
Tanker, Hop & Glory** Ⓗ**;
guest beers**
A former fish restaurant, and
Ash Vine's only pub, apart

from the brew pub in
Somerset. No food Sun.
❀ 🍴 (Spa) ⌂

Porter Butt

York Place, London Road (A4)
☎ (0225) 425084
12–3, 5.30–11 (12–11 Sat)
**Draught Bass; Courage Bitter
Ale, Best Bitter, Directors** Ⓗ
Two-bar local with upstairs
function rooms. No food Sun.
❀ 🍴 🍺 ♣ P

Rose & Crown

6 Brougham Place, Larkhall
(400 yds NW of A4/A46 jct)
☎ (0225) 425700
11–2.30, 5–11 (11–11 Sat)
**Marston's Border Bitter,
Pedigree; Wickwar Brand
Oak** Ⓗ
Friendly, out-of-town local,
worth seeking out. 🍺 ♣ ⌂

Smith Brothers

11–12 Westgate Buildings
☎ (0225) 330470
11–3, 5.30–11 (11–11 summer)
**Eldridge Pope Hardy
Country, Blackdown Porter,
Royal Oak** Ⓗ
Spacious, one-bar central pub,
with a public bar section. Eve
meals finish at 8pm.
🍴 🍽 ≢ (Spa) ♣

Star Inn

23 The Vineyards (A4)
☎ (0225) 425072
11–2.30, 5.30–11
Draught Bass Ⓖ**; Charrington
IPA; Wadworth 6X, Old
Timer** Ⓗ
Enjoy the atmosphere in this
classic town pub. The Bass is
served from the jug. Q 🍺 ♣

Blagdon

New Inn

Church Street (near A368)
☎ (0761) 462475
11–2.30, 7–11
**Draught Bass; Wadworth
IPA, 6X** Ⓗ**, Old Timer** Ⓖ
Stone pub with horse-brass
decor. The garden offers a
beautiful view over Blagdon
Lake. Good, reasonably priced
food; Sun lunch in winter
only. ♨ Q ❀ 🍴 🍽 ♿ ♣ P

Bleadon

Queens Arms

Celtic Way ☎ (0934) 812080
11–3, 7–11
Whitbread Flowers IPA Ⓗ**;
guest beers** Ⓖ
At least one Ringwood beer
and three other guests always
available in three small bars.
Q 🐕 ❀ 🍴 🍽 ▲ ♣ ⌂ P

Bristol

Albert

West Street, Bedminster
☎ (0272) 661968
11–2.30, 7–11 (12–2, 7–10.30 Sun)

**Courage Best Bitter;
Wadworth 6X** Ⓗ**; guest beer**
Popular, lively pub where the
walls are covered with record
sleeves and jazz photographs.
Regular live jazz. 🍴 ♣

Brewery Tap

Colston Street ☎ (0272) 213668
11–11
**Smiles Brewery Bitter, Best
Bitter, Exhibition** Ⓗ**; guest
beer**
Smiles brewery tap and
CAMRA's 1991 *Best New Pub*
award winner. Small, cosy,
and imaginatively designed:
ash wood panelling inset with
hopsack, a slate bar, and a
black and white tiled floor.
Breakfast from 8am Mon–Sat.
Q 🍴

Bridge Inn

16 Passage Street
☎ (0272) 250601
11.30–11 (12–3, 5–11 Sat)
**Draught Bass; Courage Best
Bitter; Wadworth 6X** Ⓗ
Close to the Courage brewery,
this building is about 90 years-
old but the cellar possibly
dates back 800 years. One of
the smallest pubs in Bristol,
with a comfortably
refurbished bar. ≢ (T Meads)

Brown Jug

77 Garnet Street, Bedminster
(off the Chessells)
☎ (0272) 635145
5–10.30 (12–2, 6–10.30 Sat; 12–2, 7–10
Sun)
Beer range varies Ⓗ
Real ale off-licence. Two ales
at competitive prices.

Cadbury House

68 Richmond Road,
Montpellier (E off Cheltenham
Rd, A38) ☎ (0272) 247874
12–11
**Courage Best Bitter;
Wadworth 6X; Wickwar
Coopers WPA, Brand Oak,
Olde Merryford** Ⓗ
Frequented mostly by young
people occupied by the many
electronic games. Enamel
signs and old one-armed
bandits are a feature. Great
jukebox. Coopers WPA is sold
as 'Tinkers'.
♨ ❀ 🍴 ≢ (Montpellier)

Cambridge Arms

Coldharbour Road
☎ (0272) 735754
11–11
**Courage Bitter Ale, Best
Bitter, Directors; Hardington
Best Bitter; Wadworth 6X** Ⓗ
Comfortable, well-kept
suburban pub offering
occasional barbecues and
music. Dogs accepted. No
food Sun. ❀ 🍴 P

Grosvenor Arms

3 Coronation Road, Southville
☎ (0272) 663325

11–11
Draught Bass H**; guest beers**
Companionable, single-bar free house in the former wharf area, overlooking the canalised River Avon.
Q ◖ ⬦ & ⇌ (T Meads/ Bedminster) ♣ ᗡ

Highbury Vaults

164 St Michaels Hill, Kingsdown ☎ (0272) 733203
12–11
Brains SA; Smiles Brewery Bitter, Best Bitter, Exhibition H**; guest beers**
Highly original and popular with all, a pub that has sensitively evolved over the years, thanks to a caring brewery. Superb original Victorian/Edwardian fittings, with a tiny public the crowning glory. Q ❀ ◖ ▶ ⬦
⇌ (Clifton Down)

Humpers Off-Licence

26 Soundwell Road, Staple Hill ☎ (0272) 565525
12–2, 4.30–10 (varies summer; 12–2, 7–10.30 Sun)
Draught Bass E**; Hardington Traditional, Jubilee; Smiles Best Bitter, Exhibition** H**; guest beers**
Friendly, well-run off-licence: an oasis for interesting guest beers from far and wide. Discounts given for quantity; supports local breweries. Strong ale in winter. ᗡ

Kellaway Arms

140 Kellaway Avenue, Horfield ☎ (0272) 246694
11–2.30 (3 Fri & Sat), 6–11 (12–2.30, 7–10.30 Sun)
Courage Bitter Ale, Best Bitter; Smiles Best Bitter H
Comfortable, friendly two-bar local. The public bar is deceptively large.
Q ❀ ◖ ⬦ ♣

King Charles

11 King Square Avenue
☎ (0272) 424451
11–11 (11–3, 7–11 Sat)
Hardington Traditional, Old Lucifer; Ruddles Best Bitter, County H
Small corner pub, popular with office workers at lunchtime; board games played in the evening. ♣

Kings Head

60 Victoria Street
☎ (0272) 277860
11 (12 Sat)–3.30, 5.30 (7.30 Sat)–11
Courage Bitter Ale, Best Bitter H
Small, Victorian gem, restored but unspoilt, and full of character. Four-pint jug discount rate at off-peak times (Mon–Fri). Q ⇌ (T Meads)

Kings Head

Whitehall Road, Whitehall
☎ (0272) 517174
11–3, 6–11 (12–2.30, 7–10.30 Sun)

Courage Bitter Ale, Best Bitter, Directors H
Popular suburban local, spacious and comfortable. Skittle alley in the public bar.
🚍 ❀ ◖ ⬦ ♣ P

Knowle Hotel

Leighton Road, Knowle
☎ (0272) 777019
11.30–2.30, 5.30–11 (11–3, 6–11 Sat)
Ind Coope Burton Ale; Smiles Best Bitter; Tetley Bitter H
Large, friendly, two-bar pub with good views from the lounge. Quiz night. Good value food. Q ❀ ◖ ⬦ & ♣

Lion Tavern

19 Church Lane, Clifton Wood
☎ (0272) 268492
11–2.30 (3.30 Sat), 6–11
Butcombe Bitter; Courage Best Bitter, Directors H**; guest beer**
Two-bar, street-corner, 19th-century local, busy in the evenings. Good food till 8pm; guest beer from the Courage list. ◖ ▶ ♣

Phoenix

15 Wellington Road, Broad Weir ☎ (0272) 558327
11.30–11
Ash Vine Bitter, Hop & Glory G**; Draught Bass** G **&** H**; Oakhill Bitter, Black Magic** H**, Yeoman** G**; Smiles Best Bitter** H**; Wadworth 6X** G**; guest beers**
Welcoming, traditional drinkers' pub, very popular with locals. Note the collection of bottles and local photos. ❀

Prince of Wales

84 Stoke Lane, Westbury on Trym ☎ (0272) 623715
11–3, 5.30–11 (11–11 Sat)
Courage Bitter Ale, Directors; Hardington Best Bitter H
Friendly pub in a residential area with a good-size single bar. Ask for 'Boys' when drinking BA. ❀ ◖ ♣

Printers Devil

10 Broad Plain, Old Market (inner ring road)
☎ (0272) 264290
11.30–3 (not Sat), 5–9 (11 Fri; 8–11 Sat; closed Sun)
Courage Bitter Ale, Best Bitter; Ushers Best Bitter, Founders H
One-bar city pub, HQ for the Cartoonists' Club of GB. The walls are adorned with cartoons. A centre for the business community at lunchtime – dress appropriately. Mixed clientele in the eve. No food weekends. ◖ ⇌ (T Meads)

Seven Ways

23 New Street, St Judes (off A420) ☎ (0272) 556862
11.30–3, 6.30–11

Courage Best Bitter; Ushers Best Bitter, Founders H
Homely two-bar local fronting St Matthias Park and enjoying a thriving lunchtime food trade. The lounge is busier than the sports-oriented bar; popular skittle alley. No food weekends. ◖ ⬦ ♣

Star

4–6 North Street, Bedminster
☎ (0272) 663588
11–2.30, 5.30–11
Ind Coope Burton Ale; Smiles Best Bitter; Tetley Bitter H
Popular local with a horseshoe-shaped central bar; homely and pleasant. Some lunchtime and evening office trade. ❀ ◖ & ♣

Victoria

20 Chock Lane, Westbury on Trym ☎ (0272) 500441
11 (12 Sat)–2.30, 5.30 (7 Wed, 5 Fri, 6 Sat)–11
Adnams Broadside; Draught Bass; Hall & Woodhouse Tanglefoot (summer)**; Wadworth IPA, 6X** H**, Old Timer** G
Popular, busy pub, comfortably furnished and out of the way down a quiet lane. No food weekends. ❀ ◖ ♣

Charfield

Pear Tree

Wotton Road ☎ (0454) 260663
11.30–2.30, 6–11
Whitbread WCPA H**; guest beers**
Village pub on the main road where the three continually changing guest beers are the main attraction.
🚍 Q ❀ ◖ ⬦ ♣ P

Churchill

Crown Inn

The Batch, Skinners Lane (near A38/A368 jct) OS446596
☎ (0934) 852955
11.30–3, 5.30–11
Draught Bass; Butcombe Bitter; Eldridge Pope Hardy Country; Palmers IPA G**; guest beers**
Old, stone, cottage-style pub by a quiet lane. Popular for the best range of beers in the area. The house ale, Batch, is Cotleigh Harrier. No meals Sun. Beware keg cider on handpump.
🚍 Q ⛫ ❀ ◖ ⬦ A P

Clapton-in-Gordano

Black Horse

Clevedon Lane OS472739
☎ (0275) 842105
11–2.30 (3 Sat), 6–11
Courage Bitter Ale, Best Bitter, Directors; Hardington Best Bitter G

Avon

14th-century stone pub with a flagstone floor, inglenooks, and high-back settles. Formerly the village lock-up and now the centre of village life. ⚌ Q ✿ ◖ ♣ ⌂ P

Compton Martin

Ring o' Bells
Bath Road (A368)
☎ (0761) 221284
11.30–3, 7–11
Draught Bass G; **Butcombe Bitter; Wadworth 6X** H; **guest beer**
Very pleasant pub serving excellent food. Family room and a safe garden, with plenty of children's amenities. A separate bar has pub games.
⚌ Q ⛱ ✿ ◖ ◗ ⬚ ♣ P

Congresbury

White Hart
Wrington Road (off A370)
☎ (0934) 833303
11.30–3, 6–11
Butcombe Bitter G; **Hall & Woodhouse Badger Best Bitter, Gribble Ale; Wadworth 6X** H
Attractive country pub, renowned for its food in both the pub and the separate (Trawlers) restaurant. ♣
⚌ Q ⛱ ✿ ◖ ◗ ⬚ ♣ P

Engine Common

Cross Keys
North Road, Yate (300 yds off A482) ☎ (0454) 228314
12–2.30, 5.30–11
Courage Best Bitter; John Smith's Bitter; Morland Old Masters; Wadworth 6X H
17th-century, two-bar pub with a stone-floored bar: a comfortable village local with a lively clientele.
⚌ Q ◖ ⬚ ⇌ (Yate) ♣ P

Frampton Cotterell

Golden Lion
Beesmoor Road
☎ (0454) 773348
11–11
Draught Bass; Ind Coope Burton Ale G
Large, family pub refurbished and extended to provide a single bar with a separate family area. Food always available. Unaccompanied young men in groups of more than three may not be served. No-smoking restaurant.
⛱ ⇔ ◖ ◗ P

Rising Sun
Ryecroft Road ☎ (0454) 772330
11.30–3, 7–11
Draught Bass; Hall & Woodhouse Tanglefoot; Marston's Pedigree; Smiles Best Bitter; Wadworth 6X H;
guest beers

A real free house: a small pub with a single bar and a separate skittle alley. Usually busy with locals. Restaurant at the rear. ◖ ◗ ♣ P

Hallatrow

Old Station Inn
Wells Road (A39, 400 yds from A37 jct) ☎ (0761) 452228
11–3, 5 (6 Sat)–11
Ash Vine Challenger; Draught Bass; Wadworth 6X H; **guest beers**
Old railway hotel on the disused GWR North Somerset line. A busy main road free house which retains its friendly, local atmosphere.
⚌ ⛱ ✿ ◖ ◗ ♣ P

Hinton

Bull
Off A46, 1 mile SW of M4 jct 18 OS735768 ☎ (027 582) 2332
12–2.30, 6 (7 winter)–11
Draught Bass; Wadworth IPA, 6X H; **Old Timer** G
A country local with a splendid garden for children. Full meals (including a vegetarian option) served in the lounge.
⚌ Q ✿ ◖ ◗ ⬚ ♣ P

Hinton Charterhouse

Rose & Crown
High Street ☎ (0225) 722153
11.30 (11 Sat)–3, 6–11
Draught Bass; Marston's Border Bitter, Pedigree; Wadworth 6X G
A comfortable, wood-panelled lounge bar and a separate restaurant (no eve meals Sun or Mon). ⚌ ✿ ◖ ◗ ⬚ ♣ P

Kelston

Old Crown
On A431 ☎ (0225) 423032
11.30–3, 5–11
Draught Bass; Butcombe Bitter; Smiles Best Bitter, Exhibition (summer); **Wadworth 6X, Old Timer** H
Delightful 18th-century coaching inn with a flagstoned floor and original beer engines. Lunches served Mon–Sat; eve meals Thu–Sat in the restaurant. The large garden is popular with families. ⚌ Q ✿ ◖ ▲ ♣ P

Kingswood

Highwayman
Hill Street ☎ (0272) 671613
12–2 (3 Fri & Sat), 7.30 (7 Fri & Sat)–11 (may vary)
Ind Coope Burton Ale; Tetley Bitter; Wadworth 6X H
Pre-war, traditional building: a single central bar in pleasing

'olde-worlde' surroundings. Landlord is a *Burton Master Cellarman*. Smoking restrictions apply weekday lunchtime.
⛱ ✿ ◖ ◗ ⬚ ♣ P ✄

Littleton-on-Severn

White Hart
OS596900 ☎ (0454) 412275
11.30–2.30, 6–11 (11–11 Sat)
Smiles Brewery Bitter, Best Bitter, Exhibition; Wadworth 6X H; **guest beer**
16th-century farmhouse, tastefully enlarged into a two-bar, multi-roomed pub. Winner of CAMRA's 1991 *Pub Refurbishment* award. Jazz Wed eve. Large garden, popular with families.
⚌ Q ⛱ ✿ ⇔ ◖ ◗ ⬚ ♣ P

Long Ashton

Angel Inn
172 Long Ashton Road (near B3128 jct) ☎ (0275) 392244
11–2.30 (3 Sat), 5.30 (6 Sat)–11
Courage Best Bitter; Eldridge Pope Hardy Country; John Smith's Bitter; Oakhill Bitter; Wadworth 6X H
Old, unspoilt village pub with a large courtyard seating area. Note the priest hole. Separate dining room. ⚌ ⛱ ✿ ◖ ◗

Marshfield

Catherine Wheel
High Street ☎ (0225) 892220
11–2.30, 6–11
Courage Bitter Ale, Best Bitter; Wadworth 6X H
Thriving, 17th-century village local with a warm welcome. The new rear lounge bar was formerly the coal cellar.
⚌ Q ⇔ ◖ ◗ ⬚ ♣ P

Midsomer Norton

White Hart
The Island ☎ (0761) 418270
11–3, 5.30–11
Draught Bass G
Victorian establishment with many rooms. Old mining relics on the walls. A minor classic. No food Sun.
⚌ ⛱ ◖ ⬚ ♣ ⌂

Nailsea

Blue Flame
West End (signed from centre) OS449690 ☎ (0275) 856910
12–3, 6–11
Draught Bass; Smiles Best Bitter, Exhibition G; **guest beers** (occasionally)
Unpretentious, friendly rural pub with a small public bar and a lounge. Often busy.
⚌ ⛱ ✿ ⬚ ◖ ▲ ♣ ⌂

Sawyers Arms
High Street
☎ (0275) 853798
11–3, 5.30–11
Courage Best Bitter, Directors; Eldridge Pope Best Bitter, Hardy Country; Webster's Yorkshire Bitter Ⓗ
Popular, friendly two-roomer. Good value food.
❀ ◖▶ ⊟ ♣ P

Oldbury-on-Severn

Anchor
Church Road
☎ (0454) 413331
11.30–2.30 (3 Sat), 6.30 (6 Sat)–11
Draught Bass; Butcombe Bitter; Marston's Pedigree; S&N Theakston Best Bitter Ⓗ, **Old Peculier** Ⓖ
16th-century converted mill near the River Severn. Wide range of good food served. Renowned for its selection of 70-plus whiskies.
ﲘ Q ❀ ◖▶ ⊟ ⅋ ♣ P

Old Down

Fox Inn
Inner Down OS617873
☎ (0454) 412507
11–3 (3.30 Sat), 6 (5.30 Fri & Sat)–11
Draught Bass; Hook Norton Best Bitter; Whitbread Boddingtons Bitter, Flowers IPA Ⓗ
Traditional village pub dating back to the 1830s, popular with the local community. A large garden attracts families.
ﲘ Q ❀ ◖▶ ⌂ P

Paulton

Somerset Inn
Bath Road (½ mile NE of town) ☎ (0761) 412828
12–2.30 (3 Fri & Sat), 7–11
Courage Bitter Ale, Best Bitter; Ushers Best Bitter, Founders Ⓗ
One-bar local, with fine views. Renowned for its pub grub.
ﲘ ❀ ◖▶ ♣ ⌂ P

Pennsylvania

Swan Inn
On A46, ¼ mile N of A420 jct
☎ (0225) 891022
11–3, 5–11 (11–11 summer)
Archers Village; Draught Bass; Marston's Pedigree; Smiles Brewery Bitter Ⓗ; **guest beer**
Excellent free house in a rural area. A comfortable split-level interior with a busy bar and a quieter lounge eating area.
ﲘ Q ◖▶ ♣ P

Pensford

Rising Sun
Church Street ☎ (0761) 490402
11.30–2.30, 7–11
Ind Coope Burton Ale; Tetley Bitter; Wadworth 6X Ⓗ
15th-century stone pub with a garden leading down to the River Chew (unfenced). Cosy, comfortable and friendly. No eve meals Sun or Mon; book for Sun lunch.
ﲘ ❀ ◖▶ ⅋ ♣ ⌂ P

Pucklechurch

Rose & Crown
Parkfield Road
☎ (0272) 372351
11–2.30, 6.30–11
Draught Bass; Hall & Woodhouse Tanglefoot; Wadworth IPA, 6X, Farmer's Glory, Old Timer Ⓗ
1700s miners' tavern, recently extended to include a no-smoking dining room. Pleasant surroundings including a feature fireplace.
ﲘ ❀ ◖▶ ⊟ ⅋ ♣ P

Redhill

Darlington Arms
On A38 ☎ (0934) 862247
11–3, 6–11
Tetley Bitter; Ind Coope Burton Ale
Comfortable and friendly pub, affording good views towards the Mendips. Two meals for the price of one Mon–Fri lunch and Mon–Thu 6.30–9.
ﲘ ❀

Saltford

Jolly Sailor
Mead Lane (on River Avon N of A4) OS693680
☎ (0225) 873002
11–11
Ash VineTrudoxhill, Challenger; Draught Bass; Butcombe Bitter; Courage Best Bitter Ⓗ
Lively pub in a picturesque lockside setting. Can be crowded in summer. The large conservatory houses a restaurant. The Addlestones cider is on a fake handpump.
ﲘ ❀ ◖▶ P

Stoke Gifford

Parkway Tavern
North Road ☎ (0272) 690329
11–2.30, 5–11 (11–11 Fri & Sat)
Banks's Mild, Bitter Ⓔ
Large, modern pub on the northern edge of Bristol. Benefits from local community trade as well as the increasing number of office workers in this growth area. Prices are very competitive.
❀ ◖ ⇌ (Parkway) ♣ P

Wellow

Fox & Badger
Railway Lane (2 miles W of B3110 at Hinton Charterhouse)
☎ (0225) 832293
11–3, 6–11
Butcombe Bitter; Ruddles County; John Smith's Bitter; Ushers Best Bitter Ⓗ
Wellow's only pub, a pretty, two-bar local where, unusually, the public bar is carpeted and the lounge flagstoned.
ﲘ ❀ ◖▶ ⊟ ♣ ⌂

Weston-super-Mare

Major From Glengarry
10–14 Upper Church Road
☎ (0934) 629594
11–11 (11–3, 7–11 winter)
Draught Bass; Butcombe Bitter; Wadworth IPA, 6X, Farmer's Glory (summer) Ⓗ
Good local off the seafront and opposite Knightstone harbour.
⋈ ❀ ◖▶ & ♣

Regency
22–24 Lower Church Road
☎ (0934) 633406
10–2.30, 7–11
Draught Bass; Butcombe Bitter; Whitbread Flowers Original Ⓗ
Pleasant, friendly single-bar pub with a separate pool room, which attracts students. A popular meeting place for the older regulars.
❀ &

Wick

Rose & Crown
High Street ☎ (0275) 822198
11.30–2.30, 5.30–11
Courage Best Bitter, Directors; John Smith's Bitter; Wadworth 6X Ⓗ
Very old, low-beamed inn; its well furnished, comfortable interior has two bars and a restaurant (excellent, reasonably-priced meals; book for Sun lunch; no meals Sun eve).
ﲘ Q ❀ ◖▶ P ⅋

Willsbridge

Queens Head
62 Willsbridge Hill (A431)
☎ (0272) 322233
11–2.30, 7–11
Courage Bitter Ale, Best Bitter; Ushers Best Bitter Ⓗ
Don't be fooled by the dusty exterior. This is a genuine multi-roomed local. No children Fri eve.
Q ⋈ ♣ P

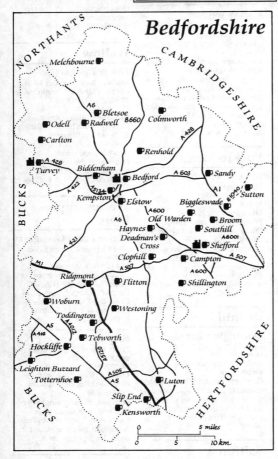

Bedfordshire

Biggleswade

Red Lion
1 London Road (top end of
High Street) ☎ (0767) 313963
11–2.30, 5.30–11
**Greene King XX Mild, IPA,
Rayments Special, Abbot** H
Olde-worlde pub full of
antique-style decorations.
Good lunchtime and evening
food menu (no food Sun).
Good mix of customers in
both bars.
🍴 ◑ ▶ ⊞ ♿ ⇌ ♣ ⌂ P

Try also: **Golden Pheasant**
(Wells)

Bletsoe

Falcon Inn
Rushden Road (A6)
☎ (0234) 781222
11–2.30, 5.30–11
Wells Eagle, Bombardier H
17th-century coaching inn
with a large riverside garden
and play area. Skittles in the
public bar; separate family
room. The landlord flies the
flag outside and hates plastic!
No meals Sun/Mon eves.
🛏 Q ⏃ 🍴 ◑ ▶ ⊞ ♣ P

Broom

Cock
High Street (100 yds N of
B658) ☎ (0767) 314411
12–2.30, 6–11
**Greene King IPA, Rayments
Special, Abbot** G
Multi-roomed village local
with beer served direct from
the cellar. Separate skittles
room and two splendid snugs.
No eve meals Sun/Mon.
🛏 ⏃ 🍴 ◑ ▶ ♣ P

Campton

White Hart
Mill Lane (off A507)
☎ (0462) 812657
11.30–3, 7–11 (11–11 Sat)
**Mansfield Riding Bitter;
Wells Eagle** H
Popular, three-bar, open-plan
village pub with a comfortable
lounge and dining area.
Games dominate the public
bar, which has a flagstone
floor and an inglenook.
Petanque played all year. No
lunches Sun.
🛏 🍴 ◑ ▶ ⊞ ♿ ♣ P

Carlton

Fox
High Street (3 miles N of A428
at Turvey) ☎ (0234) 720235
10.30–2.30, 6–11
**Adnams Broadside; Wells
Eagle, Bombardier** H
18th-century, friendly,
thatched village inn with

Banks & Taylor, *Shefford*; **Nix
Wincott**, *Turvey*; **Wells**, *Bedford*

Bedford

Fleur de Lis
12 Mill Street (E of A6, High
Street) ☎ (0234) 211004
10.30–2.30 (4 Sat), 5.30 (7 Sat)–11
(10.30–11 Thu & Fri; 12–2.30, 7–10.30
Sun)
**Adnams Broadside; Wells
Eagle** H
Very well run, one-bar, town-
centre pub with a mixed
clientele. Parking difficult
lunchtimes. Upstairs meeting
room. No lunches weekends. ◑

Three Cups
Newnham Street (E of A6,
High Street)
☎ (0234) 352153
11–3 (4 Sat), 5 (7 Sat)–11 (11–11
Wed–Fri)
**Greene King IPA, Rayments
Special, Abbot** H

Warm and welcoming, wood-
panelled, two-bar pub
opposite a large auction house
which is well worth a visit. No
lunches Sun.
🍴 ◑ ⊞ ♣ P

Try also: **Castle**, Newnham St
(Wells)

Biddenham

Three Tuns
Main Road (off A428)
☎ (0234) 354847
11.30–2.30, 6–11
**Greene King IPA, Rayments
Special, Abbot** H
Delightful village inn with an
excellent range of home-
cooked food. Children
permitted in the dining area.
Skittles played. No food Sun
eve. ⏃ 🍴 ◑ ▶ ⊞ ♣ P

34

excellent restaurant and bar food. Near Harrold Country Wildlife Park. No food Mon eve or Sun. Children welcome until 8pm. Q ✿ ◖ ▶ P

Clophill

Stone Jug
Back Street (2nd right N of A6/A507 roundabout)
☎ (0525) 60526
11–3, 6–11
Banks & Taylor Shefford Bitter; Courage Directors; S&N Theakston Best Bitter; John Smith's Bitter; guest beer Ⅎ
Deservedly popular free house. Check before arriving with children. No food Sun.
▷ ✿ ◖ P

Colmworth

Wheatsheaf
Wilden Road (1 mile N of B660) ☎ (0234) 862370
11–2.30, 6–11
Adnams Bitter, Broadside; Draught Bass; Marston's Pedigree; guest beer Ⅎ
17th-century, oak-beamed country pub to the south of the village. Low beams – mind your head! Varied bar food and full menu in the restaurant. Children's play area in the garden.
▨ Q ✿ ◖ ◩ ♣ P

Deadman's Cross

White Horse
On A600 ☎ (023 066) 634
11–3, 6–11 (10–11 Sat & summer)
Banks & Taylor Shefford Bitter, SPA, SOS, 2XS Ⅎ
Welcoming roadside pub gaining a reputation for food in the restaurant. The cosy bar has inglenooks and a settee. Weston's cider on handpump. No food Mon eve.
▨ ✿ ◖ ▶ ◠ P

Elstow

Swan
High Street ☎ (0234) 352066
11–3, 7–11 (11–11 Fri & Sat)
Greene King XX Mild, IPA, Abbot Ⅎ
Old village pub near Elstow Abbey: one L-shaped room with a separate skittles room. Local clientele but also businessmen at lunchtimes. Very good granary sandwiches served. No food weekends. ▨ ✿ ◖ ♣ P

Flitton

White Hart
Brook Lane ☎ (0525) 61486
11–11
Adnams Broadside; Wells Eagle Ⅎ
Attractive village pub. The

public bar has games and the lounge a dining area. Very good range of meals at reasonable prices (no eve meals Sun). Camping/caravanning must be booked in advance. ✿ ◖ ▶ ◩ ▲ ♣ P

Haynes

Greyhound
68 Northwood End Road (off A600) ☎ (023 066) 239
11–11
Greene King IPA, Rayments Special, Abbot Ⅎ
Friendly village local offering a wide variety of good home-cooked food. Petanque played.
▨ ▷ ✿ ◩ ◖ ▶ ♣ P

Hockliffe

Red Lion
Watling Street (A5)
☎ (0525) 210240
11–2.30 (3 Sat), 5.30 (6 Sat)–11
Tetley Bitter; guest beer Ⅎ
Friendly roadside pub with one long bar where one end is oriented towards games, and the other towards food. The sizeable garden has barbecues and petanque in summer. A family room is due to open shortly. ▨ ▷ ✿ ◩ ◖ ▶ ♣ P

Kempston

Griffin
174 Bedford Road (opp. police station) ☎ (0234) 854775
11–3, 6–11
Greene King XX Mild, IPA, Rayments Special, Abbot Ⅎ
Tastefully refurbished pub with three bars catering for a mixed clientele. Excellent food served at all times at good prices. The lounges and restaurant area feature landscape paintings.
✿ ◖ ▶ ◩ ♣ P

Try also: King William IV, High St (Wells)

Kensworth

Farmers Boy
216 Common Road
☎ (0582) 872207
11–11
Fuller's London Pride, ESB Ⅎ
Well renovated, ex-Watneys village pub which has reverted to two bars, including a comfortable lounge with a separate dining area. Note the original Mann, Crossman & Paulin leaded windows. Good range of good value food served lunchtime and evening. Occasional Dwile Flonking!
▨ ✿ ◖ ◩ ♣ P

Leighton Buzzard

Black Lion
High Street ☎ (0525) 372260

11–11
Adnams Bitter; Ind Coope Benskins Best Bitter; Tetley Bitter Ⅎ
Recently refurbished Heritage Inn which is popular at lunchtimes with local office workers. The video jukebox attracts the young set weekend eves. ✿ ◖ ⇌ ♣

Ship
Wing Road ☎ (0525) 373261
10.30–3, 5.30–11 (10.30–11 Fri; 11–11 Sat)
Banks's Bitter; Ruddles Best Bitter, County; Webster's Yorkshire Bitter Ⅎ
A genuine pub for all tastes, with an excellent restaurant.
✿ ◖ ▶ ⇌ ♣ P

Stag
1 Heath Road
☎ (0525) 372710
12 (11 Sat)–2.30, 6–11
Fuller's London Pride, ESB Ⅎ
Wedge-shaped pub on a fork in the road just north of the town centre. A small public bar and a plain but comfortable lounge bar.
◖ ▶ ◩ ♣ P

Star
230 Heath Road
☎ (0525) 377294
11–2.30 (3 Sat), 5.30 (6 Sat)–11
Adnams Bitter; Draught Bass; Ind Coope ABC Best Bitter; Wadworth 6X Ⅎ
Very smart pub on the northern extremity of town. Its decor has cricketing and aeroplane themes. No food Sun. Q ✿ ◖ ▶ P

Try also: Ashwell Arms (Wells)

Luton

Bird & Bush
Hancock Drive, Bushmead (off A6, behind Barnfield College)
☎ (0582) 480723
11–2.30, 6–11 (11–11 Sat)
Adnams Bitter; Draught Bass; Charrington IPA Ⅎ
Opened in May 1991, a 'community tavern' with attractive Yorkshire flagstone and quarry tiled floors. Live jazz Tue. A good selection of bar food. Up-to-date facilities include a no-smoking area, wheelchair WC and a children's play area in the garden. ✿ ◖ ▶ ♿ ♣ P ⌀

Jolly Topers
369 Hitchin Road, Round Green ☎ (0582) 25008
11–11
Greene King IPA, Rayments Special, Abbot Ⅎ
Popular, well-appointed pub, with a single L-shaped, low-beamed bar. Evening meals may be introduced (no food Sun). ✿ ◖ ♣ P

Bedfordshire

Two Brewers
43 Dumfries Street
☎ (0582) 23777
11.30–3, 5.30–11
Banks & Taylor Shefford Bitter, SPA, Edwin Taylor's Stout, SOS, Black Bat (winter) [H]
Lively locals' pub just off the town centre, with a back yard for outside drinking. Weston's cider. ❀ ♣ 🍎

Windsor Castle
12 Albert Road (beside A505 inner ring road)
☎ (0582) 28985
10.30–11
Adnams Broadside; Wells Eagle, Bombardier [H]
Comfortable bar with a nautical theme; small games room with darts and table football. Families welcome in the conservatory, which has a bar billiards table. Enclosed garden with a children's play area. No food Sun.
🐴 ❀ ◖ ♣ P

Melchbourne

St Johns Arms
Knotting Road (Rushden Rd jct) ☎ (0234) 708238
11–4, 6–11
Greene King IPA, Abbot [H]
Former gamekeeper's lodge with a fine tankard collection and a warm welcome. Flexible about afternoon closing – knock on the door if the pub seems closed. Separate pool room in a converted barn, available for families. Occasional barbecues in the garden in summer.
🔥 🐴 ❀ ◖ ◗ ▲ ♣ P

Odell

Mad Dog
Little Odell (W end of village)
☎ (0234) 720221
11–2.30, 6–11
Greene King IPA, Rayments Special, Abbot [H]
Thatched pub near Harrold-Odell Country Park with an occasional ghost near the inglenook and a children's roundabout in the garden. The home-cooked food includes vegetarian dishes. Can be busy mealtimes. Q ❀ ◖ ◗ P

Try also: Bell (Greene King)

Old Warden

Hare & Hounds
High Street
☎ (076 727) 225
11–2.30, 6–11
Wells Eagle, Bombardier [H]
Welcoming, two-bar country pub in a picturesque village near the Shuttleworth Aircraft Collection and the Swiss Gardens. Children welcome in the separate restaurant. No eve meals Sun in winter.
🔥 🐴 ❀ ◖ ◗ 🍴 ♣ P

Radwell

Swan
Felmersham Road
☎ (0234) 781351
12–2.30, 6.30–11
Wells Eagle [H]
17th-century thatched country inn with a restaurant and a quiet bar. High quality food includes a vegetarian choice (no food Tue eve or Sun). Children's play area in the garden. 🔥 Q ❀ ◖ ◗ P

Renhold

Three Horseshoes
42 Top End (1 mile N of A428)
☎ (0234) 870218
10.30–2.30, 6–11 (11–11 Sat)
Greene King XX Mild, IPA, Rayments Special, Abbot [H], **Winter Ale** [G]
Friendly village pub with a children's play area in the garden. Good value home-cooked food, including fresh steaks and soup (no meals Tue eve or Sun).
🔥 Q ❀ ◖ ◗ 🍴 ♣ P

Ridgmont

Rose & Crown
89 High Street (A507, near M1 jct 13) ☎ (0525) 280245
10.30–2.30, 6–11
Adnams Broadside; Mansfield Riding Bitter; Wells Eagle, Bombardier [H]
Popular, welcoming pub and restaurant (booking advised). The refurbished public bar has a separate games area; the large grounds offer facilities for camping/caravanning and barbecues in summer.
🔥 ❀ ◖ ◗ 🍴 ▲ ♣ P

Sandy

Bell
Station Road (50 yds S of B1042) ☎ (0767) 680267
12–3, 5.30–11
Greene King IPA [H]
Friendly one-bar local. Opposite the station and handy for the RSPB HQ. Eve meals till 8pm; no food Sun.
🔥 ❀ ◖ ◗ ⇌ P

Shefford

White Hart
2 North Bridge Street (A600)
☎ (0462) 811144
11–3, 6 (7 Sat)–11
Banks & Taylor Shefford Mild, Shefford Bitter, Edwin Taylor's Stout, SOS, 2XS, Black Bat [H]
Large, pleasant Victorian pub with 17th-century parts. The real Victorian fireplace is not used. Good food, not microwaved from the freezer. No meals Sun.
Q ❀ 🛏 ◖ ◗ ♿ ♣ P

Shillington

Musgrave Arms
Apsley End Road
☎ (0462) 711286
11–3, 5.30–11
Greene King IPA, Rayments Special, Abbot [G]
Unspoilt, country local, successfully brought into the 20th century: a cosy, low-beamed lounge and a clay-tiled public bar end. The wide range of home-cooked food includes curry, game and vegetarian dishes. The large garden has a children's play area. 🔥 ❀ ◖ ◗ ♿ ♣ P

Slip End

Frog & Rhubarb
Church Road ☎ (0582) 452722
12–3, 5.30–11
Adnams Bitter; Draught Bass; Greene King IPA, Abbot; Welsh Brewers Worthington BB [H]
Large split-level pub offering live music Sat nights, and an interesting quiz night. Warm, friendly atmosphere and an excellent range of home-cooked food. ❀ ◖ ◗ P

Southill

White Horse
High Road (1 mile E of B658)
☎ (0462) 813364
11–3, 6–11 (supper licence)
Whitbread Boddingtons Bitter, Flowers IPA [H]
Large country inn and restaurant (children welcome in the latter), which boasts a miniature diesel railway in the extensive garden. Two function rooms include a banqueting suite. A brief walk from Southill Park cricket ground. Supper licence until midnight Mon–Sat. No meals Sun eve in winter. 🔥 ❀ ◖ ◗ 🍴 ♣ P

Sutton

John O'Gaunt
High Street ☎ (0767) 260377
12–3, 7–11
Greene King IPA, Abbot [H]
Attractive pub in a picturesque village where a ford crosses the high street. Good range of bar food (not served Sun). Skittles played; boules court in the garden. Live blues once a month.
🔥 Q ❀ ◖ ◗ 🍴 ♣ P

Tebworth

Queens Head
The Lane ☎ (0525) 874101
11–3, 6 (7 Sat)–11

Adnams Broadside G; **Wells Eagle**
Two small bars, popular with locals and visitors alike. A very hospitable and entertaining pub with weekly sing-songs. No food Sun.
🏚 ❀ ◖ ▸ 🖛 ♣ P

Toddington

Angel
1 Luton Road ☎ (0525) 872380
11–3, 6–11
Banks & Taylor Shefford Bitter, SOS; Whitbread Boddingtons Bitter H
Lively and enterprising pub. The lower Stable Bar is largely used by younger drinkers, while the lounge bar, decorated with jazz memorabilia and instruments, features regular live jazz (Sun lunch, and Sun and Wed eves) – the landlord likes to blow his own trumpet! 🏚 ❀ ◖ ▸ ♣ P

Bedford Arms
64 High Street ☎ (0525) 872401
11.30–3, 6.30–11
Wells Eagle, Bombardier H
Attractive pub both outside and in, with a magnificent rambling garden to the rear. Two warm and comfortable lounge bars. No food Sun eve.
🏚 ❀ ◖ ▸ 🖛 ♣ P

Sow & Pigs
19 Church Square
☎ (0525) 873089
11–11
Greene King IPA, Rayments Special, Abbot H
Unpretentious and unpredictable. Apart from a piano, an harmonium and

stuffed fish, the bar area features a large number of pigs (even flying!). The pool room to the rear has Breughel prints and stuffed birds. A sense of humour can be an asset for visitors! No food Sun.
🏚 Q ❀ ♣ P

Try also: Griffin (Greene King)

Totternhoe

Old Bell
Church Road ☎ (0582) 662633
12–3, 6–11
Arkell's Kingsdown; Bateman XXXB; Greene King IPA; Hook Norton Old Hooky; Marston's Burton Best Bitter; Palmers IPA H
Comfortable, friendly village free house offering an imaginative choice of up to ten real ales. The range may alter, but normally includes many rare to the area. Good menu of lunchtime food, with an interesting range of sausages (no meals Sun).
🏚 Q ❀ ♣ P

Old Farm Inn
Church Road ☎ (0582) 661294
11–3.30, 6–11
Fuller's Chiswick, London Pride H
Popular, friendly, old village pub: a traditional public bar and a cosy lounge with a large fireplace. No meals Sun.
🏚 Q ❀ ◖ ▸ ♣ P

Turvey

Three Cranes
High Street (off A428)
☎ (023 064) 305

11–2.30, 6–11
Adnams Bitter; Fuller's London Pride, ESB; Hook Norton Best Bitter; Morland Old Speckled Hen; guest beers (summer) H
17th-century coaching inn with an excellent range of food, including pizzas and vegetarian dishes, in both the pub and the separate restaurant.
🏚 Q ❀ 🖛 ◖ ▸ P

Westoning

Bell Inn
1½ miles from M1 jct 12
☎ (0525) 712511
11–2.30, 6–11 (may vary in summer)
Greene King XX Mild, IPA, Rayments Special, Abbot H
15th-century pub with oak beams and stone floors. On an island in the centre of the village. Authentic Indian food served Tue–Sat eves. No food Mon eve or Sun. Petanque played. 🏚 ❀ ◖ ▸ & ♣ P

Woburn

Black Horse
1 Bedford Street
☎ (0525) 290210
11–2.30, 6–11
Marston's Pedigree; Nethergate Bitter or **Old Growler; Tetley Bitter** H; **guest beer**
Attractive free house, situated amongst Woburn's antique and china shops and close to the abbey. Popular for food, with a good range of meals available. Pleasant courtyard garden. Q ❀ ◖ ▸ &

From Good Beer Guide 1989

Berkshire

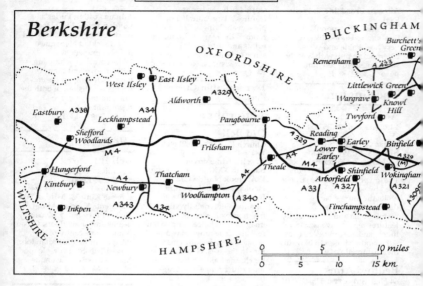

Berkshire

(Map showing Berkshire and surrounding counties: Buckinghamshire, Oxfordshire, Wiltshire, Hampshire. Locations marked include Burchett's Green, Remenham, Littlewick Green, Wargrave, Knowl Hill, Twyford, Reading, Earley, Binfield, Lower Earley, Shinfield, Wokingham, Arborfield, Finchampstead, Theale, Woolhampton, Thatcham, Newbury, Hungerford, Kintbury, Inkpen, Eastbury, Shefford Woodlands, Leckhampstead, West Ilsley, East Ilsley, Aldworth, Pangbourne, Frilsham. Roads: A34, A329, A4, A33, A343, A340, A327, A321, A338, M4. Scale: 0–10 miles / 0–15 km)

Aldworth

Bell

Off B4009 ☎ (0635) 578272
11–3, 6–11 (closed Mon)
Arkell's 3B, Kingsdown; Hall & Woodhouse Badger Best Bitter; Hook Norton Best Bitter; Morrells Mild Ⓗ
A haven for traditionalists. This pub has been in the same family for over 200 years and hasn't changed much. A splendid one-handed clock monitors the passage of time in the tranquil tap room. Fresh hot rolls are the only food. CAMRA national *Pub of the Year* 1990. 🏡 Q ⛄ ❀ ♣ P

Arborfield

Swan

Eversley Road, Arborfield Cross (A327) ☎ (0734) 760475
11–3, 6–11
Courage Best Bitter, Directors Ⓗ
Attractive old country pub with two pleasant, intimate bars. Very friendly, with a chatty landlord. Separate, well-furnished function room. No meals Sun eve. Beer range may vary. ⛄ ❀ ◖▷ P

Binfield

Stag & Hounds

Forest Road (B3018/B3034 jct)
OS711851 ☎ (0344) 483553
11.30–3, 5.30–11
Courage Best Bitter, Directors Ⓗ
Interesting olde worlde saloon bar full of curios and alcoved seating areas, each with its

own character. Wonderful real fires; friendly bar staff. The old tree outside marks part of old Windsor Forest. Eve meals in the bistro (not Sun); pub lunches, except Sat/Sun. 🏡 Q ❀ ◖ ▣ P

Bracknell

Blue Lion

Broad Lane ☎ (0344) 425875
11.30–3, 5–11 (11–11 Sat)
Draught Bass; Charrington IPA; Wadworth 6X Ⓗ
Smart, one-bar large modern pub. Occasional eve meals. Games on request.
❀ ◖ ♿ ⇌ ♣ P

Burchett's Green

Crown

Burchett's Green Road (A404)
☎ (0628) 822844
11–11
Morland Bitter, Old Masters, Old Speckled Hen Ⓗ
Small, interesting village local. Aircraft prints on the bar walls. Backgammon played. Separate restaurant.
🏡 Q ❀ ◖▷ ♣ P

Red Lion

Applehouse Hill, Hurley (A423, 200 yds N of A404 jct)
☎ (0628) 824433
11–11
Brakspear Bitter, Special, Old Ⓔ
Country pub with a friendly, intimate atmosphere. Live music occasionally on Sat. Spacious front terrace with plentiful seating in summer; glorious log fires in winter. Handpumps on the bar

operate electric pumps. A pub for 200 years. 🏡 Q ❀ ◖▷ P

Earley

George

479 Wokingham Road (at Loddon Bridge)
☎ (0734) 268144
11–2.30 (3 Sat), 5.30 (5 Thu & Fri)–11
Courage Best Bitter, Directors Ⓗ
Busy early evening pub, filled with office people; local trade later. An interesting mix for a drink or two. Handy for buses to London. Pleasant surroundings. ❀ ◖ P

Eastbury

Plough

On main road ☎ (0488) 71312
11–3, 6–11
Morland Bitter Ⓗ; **guest beers** Ⓖ
Village pub used by farmers and racing folk. About 250 years-old but pleasantly modernised. Usually two guest beers: Wychwood and Bunces have featured in the past year. Small restaurant behind. No food Sun eve. 🏡 ❀ ◖▷ ♣ P

East Ilsley

Crown & Horns

Off A34 ☎ (063 528) 545
11–3, 6–11
Draught Bass; Fuller's London Pride; Morland Bitter, Old Masters, Old Speckled Hen; S&N Theakston Old Peculier Ⓗ
Large, 18th-century, four-bar free house in a village once

Berkshire

famous for sheep fairs. A fine all-round pub with good food (traditional English puddings), accommodation, children's room, paved courtyard and a skittle alley. Stocks 160 whiskies and was the model for the 'Dog & Gun' in *Trainer*.
🍺 Q ☎ ❀ 🏠 🌙 🍴 🍺 ♣ P

Finchampstead

Queens Oak
Church Lane ☎ (0734) 734855
11.30–2.30 (3 Sat), 6 (6.30 Sat)–11
Brakspear Bitter, Special, Old Ⓗ
Old pub with an original name just a stone's throw from the church. In a good area for walkers. Key fob collection above the lounge bar; separate no-smoking bar. Good garden for children. Pizzas recommended.
Q ❀ 🌙 🅰 ♣ P ✄

Frilsham

Pot Kiln
On Yattendon–Bucklebury road OS793639
☎ (0635) 201366
12–2.30, 6.30–11
Arkell's 3B; Morland Bitter, Old Speckled Hen; Ringwood Fortyniner Ⓗ
Unspoilt pub with the best views in Berkshire; not another building in sight. Dates in part from the 15th century; bricks were made here in the 1700s; a pub for over 200 years. Good range of vegetarian food. Rolls only Sun and Tue. Occasional folk music Sun.
🍺 Q ☸ ❀ 🌙 🍺 ♣ P ✄

Holyport

Belgian Arms
Holyport Street
☎ (0628) 34468
11–2.30, 5.30 (7.30 winter)–11
Brakspear Bitter, Special, Old Ⓗ
Old wisteria-clad local just off the green. The village pond is at the end of the garden. Renamed during WWI, it used to be the Eagle (Prussian connotations). Small and intimate dining area. No food Sun. 🍺 Q ❀ 🌙 P

George
The Green
☎ (0628) 28317
11–3, 5.30–11 (11–11 Sat)
Courage Best Bitter, Directors; John Smith's Bitter Ⓗ
Low-beamed, large single bar, incorporating a restaurant area. A 600-year-old building which was once the village butcher's and barber's. No food Sun/Mon eves (darts nights). 🍺 Q ❀ 🌙 ♣ P

Hungerford

Behind the Green Door
50 Church Street (50 yds from High Street, opp. fire station)
☎ (0488) 682189
11–3, 5.30–11
Arkell's 3B; Wells Bombardier Ⓗ
Cosy, small back-street local close to a car park. An early Victorian building on the site of a previous hostelry. Excellent food and wine. Try the moules marinière in season. ❀ 🌙 🍺 ♣

Inkpen

Swan
Craven Road, Lower Green OS359643
☎ (048 84) 326
11.30–2.30 (not Tue), 6.30–11 (closed Mon, except bank hols)
Brakspear Bitter; Hook Norton Best Bitter; Whitbread Boddingtons Bitter; guest beers Ⓗ
Large 16th-century inn near famous Combe gibbet. The excellent menu features English and Singaporean dishes. No less than three open fires. A comfortable and popular pub with very reasonably priced beer. No eve meals Sun.
🍺 Q ❀ 🌙 🍽 P

Kintbury

Dundas Arms
Station Road (off A4)
☎ (0488) 58263
11–2.30, 6–11 (12–2.30, 7–10.30 Sun)
Eldridge Pope Hardy Country; Fuller's London Pride; Morland Bitter; Wells Bombardier Ⓗ
Attractive 18th-century inn by the Kennet and Avon Canal (lock 78). Named after Lord Dundas who opened the canal in 1810. Note the old penny covered bar. Separate restaurant. Q ❀ 🏠 🌙 🍴 ⇌ P

Try also: **Blue Ball** (Courage)

Knowl Hill

Seven Stars
On A4 ☎ (0628) 822967
11–2.30, 5–11 (11–11 Sat)
Brakspear Mild, Bitter, Special, Old Ⓗ
Large 16th-century coaching inn with a skittle alley and a large garden (barbecues on summer weekends). Family room at lunchtime only. 🍺 Q 🍺 ❀ 🏠 🌙 🍴 🅰 ♣ P

Try also: **Old Devil Inn** (Hall & Woodhouse)

Leckhampstead

Stag
Shop Lane (opp. village hall)
☎ (048 82) 436
12–3 (not Mon–Wed), 7–11
Morland Bitter; Ushers Best Bitter Ⓗ
Cosy, community pub with a small restaurant at the rear of the one bar. Reassuringly fair beer prices. The Ushers may be replaced during the currency of this guide.
🍺 ❀ 🌙 ♣ P

Try also: **Ibex,** Chaddleworth (Morland)

Littlewick Green

Cricketers
Off A4 ☎ (0628) 822888
11–3, 5.30–11
Eldridge Pope Hardy Country; Fuller's London Pride; Morland Bitter, Old Speckled Hen; Wadworth 6X Ⓗ
Village local overlooking the village green and popular with cricketers in the summer. Originally cottages, it now has three separate drinking areas. Built over 400 years ago. No meals Sun eve. Q 🍺 ❀ 🌙 P

Lower Earley

Seven Red Roses
Maiden Place (near Kilnsea Drive shopping centre)
☎ (0734) 351781
11–3, 5–11
Draught Bass; Charrington IPA; Fuller's London Pride; Welsh Brewers Worthington BB Ⓗ; **guest beer**

Berkshire

Smartly modern, busy pub with Bass breweriana and a model of a Burton Union square. No-smoking area at lunchtime only.
❀ ◑ ◐ ♣ P ⅙

Maidenhead

Cricketers Arms

16 Park Street (opp. Town Hall) ☎ (0628) 38332
11–2.30 (3 Fri & Sat), 5.30–11
Morland Bitter, Old Masters, Old Speckled Hen Ⓗ
Two-bar town pub: a small public bar with bar billiards and an open-plan saloon. No food Sun. ◑ ◐ ❀ ⇌ ♣

Hand & Flowers

15 Queen Street
☎ (0628) 23800
10.30–3, 5.30 (7 Sat)–11 (12–2.30, 7–11 Sun)
Brakspear Bitter, Special, Old Ⓗ
Small Victorian pub in the town centre. The single bar provides good value snacks for office workers at lunchtime and in the evening. Mild sometimes available. No food Sun.
♨ Q ◑ ⇌

Moneyrow Green

White Hart

☎ (0628) 21460
10.30–11
Morland Bitter, Old Speckled Hen Ⓗ
Over 400 years-old and originally a hunting lodge in Windsor Royal Forest: a picturesque pub with leaded-light windows. Both the public and the saloon are wood-panelled to give an air of class. The public has bar billiards, crib and dominoes. No food Sun. ♨ Q ❀ ◑ ◐ ♣ P

Newbury

Old Waggon & Horses

26 Market Place ☎ (0635) 46368
Market Bar 10.30–3 (4 Sat), 6–11 (11–11 Fri); Riverside Bar 10.30–2.30, 7.30–11
Courage Best Bitter, Directors Ⓗ
Two pubs in one! The Market Bar is bustling and lively while the Riverside Bar (totally separate) is quieter, with its own terrace over-looking the canal. Very busy on market day (Thu). Excellent pub lunches.
Q ❀ ◑ ◐ ♣ ⇌

Red House

12 Hampton Road (100 yds from St Johns roundabout, behind the hospital)
☎ (0635) 30584
12–2.30, 7.30–11
Archers Golden; Marston's Pedigree Ⓗ

Red brick pub next to a chapel and opposite a funeral directors in a tiny back street! Bar billiards played. Snacks available. ⇌ ♣

Oakley Green

Olde Red Lion

Oakley Green Road (B3024, off A308 Windsor–Maidenhead road) ☎ (0753) 863892
11–11
Brakspear Bitter; Ind Coope Friary Meux Best Bitter, Burton Ale Ⓗ
400-year-old country inn, with a superior separate restaurant (as well as bar snacks). Eve meals Tue–Sat. Aunt Sally played in the large rear garden. If you need electronic entertainment look elsewhere!
Q ❀ ◑ ◐ ♣ P

Old Windsor

Oxford Blue

Crimp Hill (off A308 at Wheatsheaf)
☎ (0753) 861954
11–11
Brakspear Bitter; Ind Coope Burton Ale; Tetley Bitter Ⓗ
Verandah-fronted pub, over 300 years-old, taking its name from military connections. The back bar is full of airline models and memorabilia. Popular restaurant with home-cooked food; adventure-type garden area for children. Q ❀ ⇔ ◑ ◐ P

Pangbourne

Cross Keys

Church Street
☎ (0734) 843268
11–3, 6–11
Courage Best Bitter, Directors Ⓗ; **guest beer**
Super, unspoilt, 17th-century village pub where the patio garden backs onto the River Pang. Small aviary. $^{1}/_{4}$ mile south of Whitchurch bridge on the Thames. Tiny car park. OAP discount lunches. ♨ Q ⇌ ❀ ◑ ◐ ⊟ ⇌ ♣ P

Star

Reading Road (A329)
☎ (0734) 842566
11–3 (4 Fri & Sat), 6 (7 Sat)–11
Courage Best Bitter Ⓗ; **guest beer**
Village local, the lounge bar of which was a bottling factory for H Levers ginger beer for 107 years. Live music regularly. No food Mon eve or Sun. Very small car park.
❀ ◑ ◐ ⊟ ⇌ ♣ P

Pinkneys Green

Stag & Hounds

1 Lee Lane (SW corner of the Green) ☎ (0628) 30268

11–2.30, 6–11
Courage Best Bitter; guest beers Ⓗ
Originally a Nicholson's beer house from the 1820s. The raised open porch leads to two small cosy bars: the saloon is smart, being used mainly as an eating area; the public is plain and simple with bench seating, bar billiards and darts. No meals Sun/Mon eves. ♨ ❀ ◑ ◐ ♣

Waggon & Horses

112 Pinkneys Road (S of Green) ☎ (0628) 24429
11–3, 5–11
Morland Bitter, Old Masters Ⓗ
Very welcoming and popular locals' pub. The quiet, comfy saloon at the rear is accessed via the alley to the right. The public is plain but can get very busy, with darts, dominoes and crib played regularly. No food Sat/Sun.
♨ Q ❀ ◑ ⊟ ♣

Try also: Robin Hood (Morland)

Reading

Butler

85 Chatham Street (off ring road near swimming pool)
☎ (0734) 576289
11–11
Fuller's Chiswick, London Pride, ESB Ⓗ
Efficiently-run town pub retaining mementoes of Butler & Son who bottled their own Guinness and wines on the premises. Intimate atmosphere with a colourful clientele. Folk music Thu. No food Sun. Parking limited.
❀ ◑ P

Cambridge Arms

109 Southampton Street
☎ (0734) 871446
11–3, 5–11 (11–11 Fri & Sat)
Morland Bitter, Old Speckled Hen Ⓗ
Popular pub with a Brewers Tudor exterior and nine sports teams: first winners of Morland's quiz league. No food Sat. ❀ ◑ ♣

Horn

St Mary's Butts
☎ (0734) 574794
11–3, 5.30–10.30 (11–10.30 Wed & Thu, 11–11 Fri & Sat)
Courage Best Bitter, Directors Ⓗ
Sit and watch the world go by from this traditional, town-centre pub which is popular with shoppers, traders and business people. No food Sun.
❀ ◑

Sweeney & Todd

10 Castle Street (near civic centre) ☎ (0734) 586466

11–11 (closed Sun eve)
Adnams Bitter; Eldridge Pope Blackdown Porter, Royal Oak; Wadworth 6X Ⓗ
Splendid little bar at the rear of a pie shop: cellar restaurant and a patio area (covered in winter). Always a cheery atmosphere and diners mix easily with drinkers. The house wines and port are recommended, as are the home-made pies. Q ⛄ ❀ ◑ ▶

Wallingford Arms

2 Caroline Street/Charles Street (off ring road near swimming pool)
☎ (0734) 575272
11–3, 5.30–11 (12–11 Fri, 11–11 Sat)
Morland Bitter, Old Masters, Old Speckled Hen; Wells Bombardier Ⓗ
Good, solid local with comfortable bars and a congenial atmosphere. Not easy to find, but worth the effort. No food Sun. Bar billiards table. ❀ ◑ ⊞ ♣ P

Remenham

Five Horseshoes

Remenham Hill (A423)
☎ (0491) 574881
12–3, 5–11
Brakspear Mild, Bitter, Special, Old Ⓗ
Friendly, two-bar roadside inn with very reasonably priced beer. Patio at the front; garden to the rear. ▲ Q ⛄ ❀ ◑ ⊞ ▲ ➤ (Henley: not winter Sun) ♣ P

Try also: Two Brewers (Brakspear)

Shefford Woodlands

Pheasant

Baydon Road (B4000 just W of village; near M4 jct 14)
☎ (0488) 648284
11–3, 5.30–11
Brakspear Bitter; Wadworth IPA, 6X; guest beers Ⓗ
Excellent, two-bar country pub (once known as the 'Paraffin House'). Basic public bar with Ring the Bull; smart saloon and a small dining room with a wide range of imaginative food. Very popular with itinerant rugby fans. ▲ ❀ ◑ ▶ ⊞ ♣ P

Shinfield

Royal Oak

39 School Green (B3349, Hyde End Road)
☎ (0734) 882931
11–11
Morland Bitter, Old Masters, Old Speckled Hen Ⓗ
Busy, friendly local in a village just outside Reading; renowned for its good food.
Q ❀ ◑ ▶ ⊞ ♿ ♣ P

Thatcham

White Hart

2 High Street ☎ (0635) 863251
11–11 (11–3 7–11 Sat)
Courage Best Bitter; Wadworth 6X; guest beer Ⓗ
Smart, comfortable town-centre pub. No food Sun or Mon eves. Rather expensive beer-wise. ❀ ◑ ▶ P

Try also: Old Chequers (Ind Coope)

Theale

Falcon

High Street ☎ (0734) 302523
10.30–11
Courage Best Bitter, Directors; Wadworth 6X Ⓗ**; guest beers**
Old coaching inn near the site of the former Blatch's brewery. Bar billiards. No food Sun. Close to Theale swing bridge on the Kennet and Avon Canal.
Q ❀ ◑ ⊞ ➤ ♣ P

Lamb at Theale

Church Street ☎ (0734) 302216
11–2.30 (3 Fri & Sat), 5.30 (6 Sat)–11
Courage Best Bitter, Directors; guest beer Ⓖ
Pub where the beer is kept on stillage behind the bar and cooled with water jackets in summer. Function room with part-time skittle alley; garden with children's play frame, etc. No food Sun.
▲ Q ❀ ◑ ⊞ ➤ ♣ P

Red Lion

High Street ☎ (0734) 302394
11–2.30, 5.30–11
Greene King IPA; Ind Coope Burton Ale Ⓗ
Popular village pub with a well appointed skittle alley. Food all week. ❀ ◑ ▶ ➤ ♣ P

Twyford

Duke of Wellington

29 High Street ☎ (0734) 340456
11–2.30 (3 Fri & Sat), 5 (6 Sat)–11
Brakspear Mild, Bitter, Special, Old Ⓗ
Popular, friendly, two-bar pub with a 400-year history. Aunt Sally played in the garden (play tree for children). No food at weekends.
❀ ◑ ▶ ➤ ♣ P

Try also: Kings Arms (Brakspear)

Wargrave

Bull

High Street (A321 crossroads)
☎ (0734) 403120
11–2.30, 6–11
Brakspear Bitter, Special Ⓗ
17th-century village pub with beams and a huge open fire. Well deserved reputation for food (no meals Sun eve).
▲ Q ❀ ❀ ◑ ◑ ▶ ➤ (not winter Sun)

Greyhound

High Street (A321 crossroads)
☎ (0734) 402556
11–3, 5.30–11
Courage Best Bitter Ⓗ**; guest beer**
Friendly, two-bar, basic village pub: busy, noisy public bar, cosy snug. Family room not always available in the evening. ▲ Q ⛄ ❀ ◑ ⊞ ➤ (not winter Sun) ♣ P

Try also: St George & Dragon (Courage)

West Ilsley

Harrow

Off A34 ☎ (063 528) 260
11–3, 6–11 (11–11 Sat if any custom)
Morland Bitter, Old Masters, Old Speckled Hen Ⓗ
Beautifully refurbished, one-bar village pub opposite the cricket ground in a downland village where Morland started brewing. Close to the ancient Ridgeway. Excellent, imaginative, home-cooked food; try the rabbit pies – also available to take away.
▲ ❀ ◑ ▶ ♿ ⚓ ♣ P

White Waltham

Beehive

Waltham Road
☎ (0628) 822877
11–3, 5.30–11
Brakspear Bitter; Greene King Abbot; Whitbread Wethered Bitter, Flowers Original Ⓗ**; guest beers**
Traditional community local catering for all tastes, opposite the cricket pitch. Friendly regulars make visitors and locals welcome. Petanque and mini zoo in the back garden. Ciders. Well worth seeking out.
▲ Q ❀ ◑ ▶ ⊞ ♿ ♣ ⊖ P

Windsor

Court Jester

Church Lane ☎ (0753) 864257
11–11
Ind Coope Friary Meux Best Bitter, Burton Ale; Tetley Bitter Ⓗ
Set in cobbled lanes opposite the main gate of the castle, in an area which retains a 17th-century ambience. One tidy bar with a separate servery for home-prepared food. Eve meals in summer only. ◑ ▶ ♿ ➤ (Central/Riverside) ♣

Prince Albert

2 Clewer Hill Road (B3022 S of centre) ☎ (0753) 864788
11–11
Courage Best Bitter, Directors; Wadworth 6X Ⓗ

Early 19th-century former hunting lodge, near the Safari Park. Two cosy bars with a predominantly local clientele. Reasonably priced lunches (no food Sun). Thatcher's cider.
Q ❀ ◖ ⊟ ♣ ⌓ P

Prince Christian

11 King's Road
☎ (0753) 860980
11–3, 5–11 (11–11 Fri)
Fuller's London Pride; S&N Theakston Best Bitter Ⓗ; **guest beer**
Windsor's longest established free house, a short stroll (down Sheet Street) from the town centre and castle: local CAMRA *Pub of the Year* for the last two years. Reasonable prices for the locality. No food weekends. ◖ ⇌ (Central)

Trooper

97 St Leonards Road
☎ (0753) 861717
11.30–11
Beer range varies Ⓗ
Small single-bar pub opposite the arts centre, recently converted to a free house, but was once used for filming Hammer horror films. The beer range changes every two months. Popular with younger people in the evenings and can get crowded. Parking difficult.
❀ ⛟ ◖ ◗ ♿ ⇌ (Central) P

Vansittart Arms

Vansittart Road
☎ (0753) 865988
11–2.30, 5.30–11
Fuller's London Pride, ESB Ⓗ
Comfortable open-plan pub with a pool table in an alcove. The name relates to a former local landowning family. Two football teams and a considerable crib following. No food Sun.
❀ ◖ ⇌ (Central) ♣

Winkfield

Old Hatchet

Hatchet Lane OS922713
☎ (0344) 882303
11–11
Draught Bass; Charrington IPA; Fuller's London Pride Ⓗ
Attractive pub converted from three woodcutters' cottages: a welcoming bar with a large restaurant area attached and a reputation for good food in a homely atmosphere. No food Sun eve. ♔ ❀ ◖ ◗ P

Wokingham

Crooked Billet

Honey Hill (off B3430, 2 miles SE of town) OS826667
☎ (0734) 780438
11–11
Brakspear Bitter, Special, Old Ⓗ
Excellent, extended country pub: an old building retaining all its character. The bar is split into three areas, with a separate restaurant. Well worth seeking out, which many people do. Ramp access for wheelchairs to the bar. Interesting collection of chiming clocks. Eve meals Tue–Sat. ♔ Q ❀ ◖ ◗ ♣ P

Dukes Head

56 Denmark Street
☎ (0734) 780316
11.30–3, 5.30 (4.30 Fri, 6 Sat)–11
Brakspear Bitter, Special, Old Ⓗ
Town pub popular with business and passing trades. Separate area with games. Well furnished with many pictures and an unusual bar top. The pub was converted from three cottages in 1795 and the skittle alley building (book) is over 200 years-old. No food Sun. ❀ ◖ ⇌ ♣ P

Olde Leathern Bottle

221 Barkham Road
☎ (0734) 784222
11–3, 5.30–11 (11–11 Sat)
Courage Best Bitter, Directors Ⓗ
Extended 18th-century pub, popular with younger people at weekends. Large garden with play area and a bouncy castle in summer. Function room. ♔ ♘ ❀ ◖ ◗ ♣ P ⍻

Queens Head

23 The Terrace (A329, top of Station Rd) ☎ (0734) 781221
11–3, 5.30–11
Morland Bitter, Old Masters, Old Speckled Hen Ⓗ
Charming, single-bar pub retaining much olde-worlde character. Popular with locals and business people. Usually busy from early eve. Active darts and quiz teams; Aunt Sally matches in the garden (access through bar). No food Sun. ❀ ◖ ⇌ ♣

Ship

104 Peach Street
☎ (0734) 780389
11.30–2.30 (3 Sat), 5 (6.30 Sat)–11 (11.30–11 Fri)
Fuller's Chiswick, London Pride, ESB Ⓗ
Pub dating from the 17th century. The earliest known landlord was also a wheelwright and his workshop is now part of the large three-bar pub (nautical furnishings). Particularly busy Fri/Sat eves and a popular meeting place. Eve meals finish at 7: no food Sat/Sun eves. ♔ ❀ ◖ ◗ ⊟ ⇌ ♣ P

Woolhampton

Rising Sun

Bath Road (A4, 1 mile E of village) ☎ (0734) 712717
12.30–2.30 (3 Fri & Sat), 5.30–11
Arkell's 3B; Fuller's London Pride; Hook Norton Best Bitter; Ringwood Old Thumper; S&N Theakston Best Bitter; Younger IPA Ⓗ
Friendly two-bar pub made up of a small snug public and a larger saloon with a separate dining area. Serves superior quality cheese for bar snacks on Sun lunchtimes. In spite of being on a major road, it remains a real local and not an impersonal roadhouse. Near Kennet and Avon Canal.
❀ ◖ ◗ ⊟ ♣ P

Try also: Rowbarge, Station Rd (Courage)

⌓

Real Cider

Where a pub serves traditional cider – as different from keg cider as traditional ale is from keg beer – we include the apple symbol.

For more information on real cider, and a comprehensive directory of where to find it, you should pick up David Kitton's **Good Cider Guide**, priced £5.95 and available from all good book stores or direct from CAMRA, 34 Alma Road, St Albans, Herts, AL1 3BW (post free).

Buckinghamshire

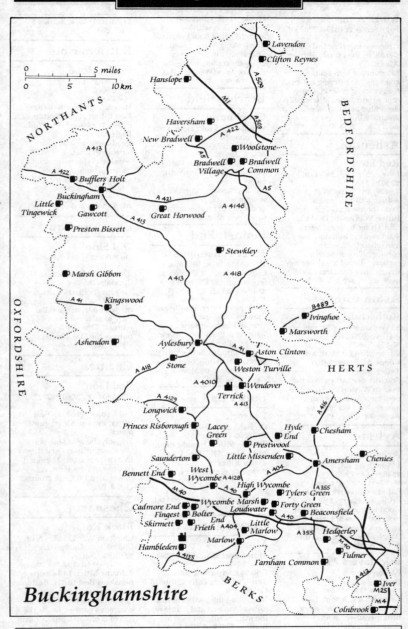

Chiltern, Terrick; *Old Luxters*, Hambleden

Amersham

Eagle
High Street ☎ (0494) 725262
11–3, 6–11 (12–2.30, 7–10.30 Sun)

Greene King IPA; Ind Coope
Benskins Best Bitter; Tetley
Bitter H
Traditional old-town pub with
a narrow frontage but
deceptively roomy inside. A

footbridge gives access to the
rear of this comfortable and
friendly pub. Eve meals Sat
only; no food Sun.
♨ Q ❀ ◑ ♣

Buckinghamshire

Kings Arms

High Street ☎ (0494) 726333
11–11
**Greene King IPA; Ind Coope
Benskins Best Bitter, Burton
Ale** Ⓗ
Magnificent 15th-century
coaching inn offering cream
teas every afternoon. The
many rooms are authentically
decorated and furnished.
Award-winning restaurant.
🏨 Q ✿ ◖ ▶ ♣ P

Ashendon

Red Lion

Lower End (lane by church)
☎ (0296) 651296
12–2.30, 7–11 (closed Mon)
**Adnams Bitter; Hall &
Woodhouse Badger Best
Bitter; Wadworth IPA, 6X,
Old Timer** Ⓗ; **guest beers**
400 years old and once used as
a magistrates' court: a
comfortable pub with a
separate dining area offering
imaginative food (no food Sun
eve). 🏨 ✿ 🛏 ◖ ▶ ♣ P

Aston Clinton

Rothschild Arms

82 Weston Road (200 yds from
A41) ☎ (0296) 630320
12–2.30, 5.30–11
**Greene King Abbot; Ind
Coope ABC Best Bitter;
Tetley Bitter** Ⓗ
Friendly one-bar pub on the
road to Weston Turville. The
pool table is in a former
garage. No food Sun eve.
🏨 ✿ 🛏 ◖ ▶ ♣ P

Aylesbury

Aristocrat

1 Wendover Road
☎ (0296) 415366
11–3, 5–11 (11–11 Fri & Sat)
**Fuller's Chiswick, London
Pride, Mr Harry, ESB** Ⓗ
Good just-out-of-town local,
over 100 years old. Friendly
staff and clientele. No food
Sun; half portions available.
✿ ◖ ▶ & �✈ ♣

Bricklayers Arms

Walton Terrace
☎ (0296) 82930
11–3, 5.30–11 (11–11 Sat)
**Greene King Abbot; Hook
Norton Best Bitter; Tetley
Bitter; Wadworth 6X** Ⓗ
Cosy and friendly 17th-
century pub. Strong darts
following (raised playing
area). Bar meals at all times;
restaurant now open. Free
house since 1990.
🛏 ✿ ◖ ▶ ≷ ≈ ♣ P

Butlers

32 Market Square
☎ (0296) 82382
11–11 (closed Sun lunch)
Hook Norton Best Bitter, Old

Hooky; Tetley Bitter Ⓗ
A narrow bar with an
attractive first floor balustrade
overlooking Market Square.
Originally the Green Man.
Open for traders at 8am on
market days (Wed, Fri and
Sat). ◖ ▶ ≈

Beaconsfield

Greyhound

Windsor End (old Slough road
off roundabout off A40)
☎ (0494) 673823
11–2.30, 5.30–11
**Courage Best Bitter; Fuller's
London Pride; Wadworth
6X** Ⓗ
Small, charming, unspoilt pub.
A snug bar has recently been
added; large function room
upstairs. Noted for food. ◖ ▶ 🍴

Bennett End

Three Horseshoes

Horseshoe Road (in lanes
between Bledlow Ridge and
Stokenchurch) OS783973
☎ (0494) 483273
12–2.30, 7–11 (closed Mon)
**Brakspear Bitter; Whitbread
Flowers Original** Ⓗ
Unspoilt 18th-century inn
with attractive views over a
super Chiltern valley. Not
easy to find but well worth the
effort. Lunch only on Sun; no
eve meals Sun or Mon.
🏨 Q ▶ 🍴 ♣ P

Bolter End

Peacock

On B482 ☎ (0494) 881417
11–2.30, 6–11
**Ansells Mild; Draught Bass;
Ind Coope ABC Best Bitter;
Tetley Bitter** Ⓗ
Popular country pub with
cosy corners. Emphasis on
home-cooked bar meals at
reasonable prices (no food Sun
eve). 🏨 Q ✿ ◖ ▶ ♣ P

Buckingham

Mitre

Mitre Street ☎ (0280) 813080
11–2.30, 7–11
**Courage Directors; John
Smith's Bitter; Tolly Cobbold
Original** Ⓗ
Interesting pub, adjacent to a
railway viaduct and a little off
the main roads, but worth
finding. ✿ ◖ ▶ ♣ P

New Inn

Bridge Street ☎ (0280) 815713
10–11
Greene King IPA, Abbot Ⓗ
Small, friendly and popular
local. Sri Lankan cuisine
available occasionally
(booking advised). Small
garden; cellar has been
adapted as a family room.
🏨 ≷ ✿ ◖ ▶ ♣

Try also: **Whale**, Market St
(Fuller's)

Bufflers Holt

Robin Hood

Brackley Road
☎ (0280) 813387
11–2.30, 6.30–11
**Hall & Woodhouse Badger
Best Bitter; Hook Norton Best
Bitter; Wadworth 6X; Wells
Eagle** Ⓗ
Roadside gem with an
outstanding range of malt
whiskies, odd vodkas and a
choice of country wines.
Varied menu (eve meals
Tue–Sat). Beer range
constantly changes.
🏨 ✿ 🛏 ◖ ▶ ♣ P

Cadmore End

Old Ship

On B482 ☎ (0494) 881404
11–3, 6–11
**Brakspear Mild, Bitter,
Special, Old** Ⓖ
Tiny, unspoilt, traditional
country pub where all beer is
carried up from the cellar.
Easy to miss but you will
regret it. One of the classic
pubs of the Hambleden
Valley. 🏨 Q ✿ ♣

Chenies

Red Lion

Off A404 ☎ (0923) 282722
11–3, 5.30–11
**Ind Coope Benskins Best
Bitter, Burton Ale** Ⓗ; **guest
beers**
Friendly, busy village pub
attracting drinkers and diners
from near and far. The small
rear bar can double as a
dining area for large groups.
Q ◖ ▶ P

Chesham

Black Horse

Chesham Vale (2 miles N of
Chesham on Cholesbury road)
☎ (0494) 784656
11–2.30, 6–11 (12–2.30, 7–10.30 Sun)
**Adnams Bitter; Ind Coope
Benskins Best Bitter, Burton
Ale** Ⓗ; **guest beers**
Comfortable old inn with an
enormous garden. Inside the
accent is on food, but drinkers
are also very welcome. Watch
out for the low beam!
✿ ◖ ▶ & P

Queens Head

Church Street (B485
Gt Missenden road)
☎ (0494) 783773
11–2.30, 5.30–11
**Brakspear Bitter, Special;
Fuller's London Pride** Ⓗ
Traditional public bar and a
comfortable, airy lounge; very

much a centre of local life.
Brakspear's Old occasionally
appears in winter. No food
Sun. ♨ Q ✿ ◖◗ ⊟ ⊕ ♣ P

Clifton Reynes

Robin Hood
☎ (0234) 711574
11.30–2.30, 6 (6.30 winter)–11
Greene King IPA, Abbot Ⓗ
Very pleasant pub serving the
best Greene King in the area.
A little off the main road but
well worth finding. No food
Mon eve. Mild may be added.
♨ ☎ ✿ ◖◗ ⊟ ♣

Colnbrook

Red Lion
High Street
☎ (0753) 682685
12–11 (11–4, 7–11 Sat)
**Courage Best Bitter;
Wadworth IPA** Ⓗ
200 year-old former coaching
inn with a friendly and lively
atmosphere. ♨ ✿ ◖◗ & P

Farnham Common

Yew Tree
Collinswood Road (A355, 1
mile N of village)
☎ (0753) 643723
11–11
**Morland Bitter, Old Masters,
Old Speckled Hen** Ⓗ
Named after a yew tree
outside which burnt down in
1972. Two small bars: a lounge
given over to food and a lively
public bar. Food all day.
♨ ✿ ◖◗ ⊟ & ♠ ♣ P

Fingest

Chequers
1½ miles off B482 at Bolter
End OS778911
☎ (0491) 63335
11–3, 5.30–11
**Brakspear Bitter, Special,
Old** Ⓗ
Smart, comfortable pub with
distinct areas; the spacious
garden is a feature.
Outstanding bar food and
restaurant (no meals Sun eve).
♨ Q ☎ ✿ ◖◗ ♣ P ⊬

Forty Green

Royal Standard of
England
Forty Green Road, Knotty
Green OS923919
☎ (0494) 673382
11–3, 5.30–11
**Eldridge Pope Royal Oak;
Marston's Pedigree, Owd
Rodger; Webster's Yorkshire
Bitter** Ⓗ
Ancient and historic free
house; very popular at all
times despite being difficult to
find. Good food bar. House
beer. ♨ Q ☎ ✿ ◖◗ P

Frieth

Prince Albert
Moor End (100 yds from Lane
End–Frieth road) OS798906
☎ (0494) 881683
11–2.30 (3 Sat), 5.30–11
**Brakspear Mild, Bitter,
Special, Old** Ⓗ
The sort of pub you don't
want to tell other people
about. Superb atmosphere,
location, hospitality and dog.
Patsy's platefuls an added
bonus at lunchtimes (Tue-Sat).
♨ Q ✿ ◖ ♣

Fulmer

Black Horse
Windmill Road
☎ (0753) 663183
11–2.30, 5.30–11
**Courage Best Bitter,
Directors** Ⓗ
Small three-bar pub dating
from the early 17th century.
The central bar is the smallest:
plain and simple with a wood
floor. The public can get
crowded on darts nights. No
meals Sun.
♨ Q ✿ ◖◗ ⊟ ♣ P

Gawcott

Cuckoos Nest
New Inn Lane
10.30–3 (not Mon), 6–11
**Hook Norton Best Bitter;
Marston's Pedigree** Ⓗ**; guest
beer** (summer)
Better of the two village pubs.
♨ ✿ ⊟ & ♣ P

Great Horwood

Swan Inn
Winslow Road
☎ (0296) 712556
11–2.30, 6–11
Ruddles Best Bitter Ⓗ**; guest
beer** (occasionally)
Former 17th-century coaching
inn on a main road. Boasts
two inglenooks and a ghost
called Arthur which leads to
spirited conversation in the
quieter of the two bars. Meals
Wed-Sat. ♨ ✿ ◖◗ ⊟ P

Hambleden

Stag & Huntsman
Off A4155 ☎ (0491) 571227
11–2.30, 6–11
**Brakspear Bitter, Special; Old
Luxters Barn Ale; Wadworth
6X; Farmer's Glory** Ⓗ
Unspoilt three-bar pub in a
picturesque, brick and flint
NT village. Extensive menu
(not served Sun eve) with
seafood a speciality and fish
and chip specials on Tue eves
in winter.
♨ Q ✿ ✠ ◖◗ ⊟

Hanslope

Globe
Hartwell Road
☎ (0908) 510336
11–2.30, 6–11
Banks's Mild, Bitter Ⓔ
Cosy roadside pub to the
north of the village. Oversize
glasses are standard; a full
pint under a full head is
guaranteed. Good food
(booking Fri night and
weekends advised). No food
Mon eve. ♨ ✿ ◖◗ ⊟ ♣ P

Try also: **Watts Arms** (Wells)

Haversham

Greyhound
High Street ☎ (0908) 313487
11.30–2.30, 5.30–11 (12–3, 6.30–11
Sat)
Greene King IPA, Abbot Ⓗ
Attractive 17th-century village
pub whose landlord is actively
involved in darts and quiz
teams. Live music Tue. No
meals Sun, or Tue/Wed eves.
♨ ✿ ◖◗ ⊟ P

Hedgerley

One Pin
One Pin Lane ☎ (0753) 643035
11–4, 5.30–11
**Courage Best Bitter,
Directors** Ⓗ
Traditional two-bar pub at a
crossroads south of the village,
offering old-fashioned
comfort. Licensee has been in
residence for 28 years. No
meals Sun. ♨ Q ✿ ◖◗ ♣ P

High Wycombe

Bird in Hand
81 West Wycombe Road (A40)
☎ (0494) 523502
11.30–3, 5.30 (6.30 Sat)–11
**Courage Best Bitter,
Directors; Hook Norton Best
Bitter; Wadworth 6X** Ⓗ
Pub with distinctive wood
panelling. Home of Wycombe
folk music club. Live music
Wed. No food Sun.
♨ ✿ ◖◗ ♣ P

Rose & Crown
Desborough Road
☎ (0494) 527982
11–3, 5 (7 Sat)–11
**Courage Best Bitter,
Directors; Gale's HSB;
Ruddles Best Bitter;
Wadworth 6X; Wychwood Dr
Thirsty's Draught** Ⓗ
Wycombe's most interesting
selection of beers in an L-
shaped corner pub with busy
office lunchtime trade (no
meals weekends). Near the
bus station. ◖ ⇌ ♣

Buckinghamshire

Hyde End

Barley Mow

On B485 Chesham road, 1½ miles from Great Missenden
☎ (024 06) 5625
11–3, 5.30–11 (11–11 Fri & Sat)
Brakspear Special; Marston's Pedigree; Morrells Bitter Ⓗ; **guest beer**
Isolated pub on a hill above Great Missenden. One large bar with darts at one end. Children are permitted in the family room/restaurant. Ever-changing guest beer.
🏚 ❀ ◑ ♣ P

Iver

Bull Inn

High Street ☎ (0753) 651115
11–3, 5–11
Ind Coope Benskins Best Bitter, Burton Ale Ⓗ
Welcoming, traditional Victorian pub with a bull theme. Look out for the leaded windows, miniature car collection and tankards. Plush saloon with long bar. Food highly recommended (not served Sun).
Q ⌗ ◑ Ⓖ ♣ P

Ivinghoe

Rose & Crown

Vicarage Lane (turn opp. church, then first right)
☎ (0296) 668472
12–2.30 (3 Sat), 6–11
Adnams Bitter; Greene King IPA; Morrells Mild Ⓗ; **guest beer**
Hard to find but very much worth the effort, this ex-Allied pub is a thriving street-corner local. Fresh fish a speciality (no food Sun). 🏚 Q ◑ Ⓖ 🅐 ♣

Kingswood

Crooked Billet

Ham Green (A41)
☎ (0296) 770239
11–3, 5–11 (11–11 Fri & Sat)
Greene King Abbot; Ind Coope Burton Ale; Tetley Bitter; Wadworth 6X Ⓗ
Rambling, 17th-century pub with a unique inn sign mentioning Mary Uff, wife of the first ale licence-holder, William Uff, who started selling ale on the site in 1760.
🏚 ⌂ ❀ ◑ ♣ P

Lacey Green

Pink & Lily

Pink Road, Parslows Hillock (1 mile from village)
☎ (0494) 408308
11.45 (11 Sat)–3, 6–11
Brakspear Bitter; Fuller's Chiswick; Marston's Pedigree; Whitbread Boddingtons Bitter, Flowers

Original; Wychwood Hobgoblin Ⓗ
Roomy country pub. The Brooke Bar is an original snug named after Rupert, the poet. Good meals – no chips (no food Sun eve). Always eight ales available. 🏚 Q ❀ ◑ ♣ P

Lavendon

Horseshoe

Main Road ☎ (0234) 712641
11–3, 5.30–11 (11–11 Sat)
Wells Eagle, Bombardier Ⓗ; **guest beer**
Popular, extended 17th-century pub; a cosy, comfortable lounge and a public bar with beams. Eve meals Tue-Sat.
🏚 ❀ ◑ Ⓖ ♣ P

Little Marlow

King's Head

Church Road ☎ (0628) 484407
11–3, 5–11
Brakspear Bitter; Fuller's London Pride; Greene King Abbot; Marston's Pedigree; Wadworth 6X; Whitbread Wethered Bitter Ⓗ
Village pub, dating from the 14th century. Two bars with character. Varied home-cooked meals. 🏚 ❀ ◑ Ⓖ P

Little Missenden

Crown

Just off A413 ☎ (024 06) 2571
11–2.30, 6–11 (12–2.30, 7–10.30 Sun)
Hook Norton Best Bitter; Marston's Pedigree; Morrells Varsity Ⓗ
Authentic old village pub. The one small bar manages to create a two-bar atmosphere. No food Sun.
🏚 Q ❀ ♣ ⌂ P

Red Lion

Off A413 ☎ (024 06) 2876
11–2.30, 5.30 (6 Sat)–11
Ind Coope Benskins Best Bitter, Burton Ale; Tetley Bitter Ⓗ & Ⓖ; **guest beer**
An ancient fireplace, dated 1649, dominates the bar of this classic local. Families allowed in the games room. Meals by arrangement after 7.30.
🏚 Q ❀ ◑ ♿ P

Little Tingewick

Red Lion

Mere Lane ☎ (0280) 847836
11–11
Fuller's Chiswick, London Pride, ESB Ⓗ
Stone pub on a busy main road. Constantly improving.
🏚 ❀ ◑ ♣ P

Longwick

Red Lion

Thame Road ☎ (084 44) 4980
12–2.30, 6–11

Fuller's London Pride; Hook Norton Best Bitter; Ind Coope ABC Best Bitter; Tetley Bitter Ⓗ
Comfortable roadside inn.
Q ⌗ ◑ ♣ P

Loudwater

Derehams Inn

5 Derehams Lane (just N of A40) ☎ (0494) 530965
11–3, 5.30–11
Brakspear Bitter; Fuller's London Pride; Greene King Abbot; Whitbread Boddingtons Bitter; Young's Bitter Ⓗ
Formerly the Bricklayers: a cosy, locals' pub, unspoilt by time. Beer range may vary. Lunches weekdays only.
🏚 ❀ ◑ ♣ P

Marlow

Clayton Arms

Quoiting Square, Oxford Road
☎ (0628) 483037
10.30–2.30 (3 Fri & Sat), 6–11
Brakspear Mild, Bitter, Old Ⓗ
Town-centre gem with two small bars. The landlord has lived here since 1929; the original and genuine local.
🏚 Q ⌂ Ⓖ 🚃 ♣

Prince of Wales

1 Mill Road (off Station Rd)
☎ (0628) 482970
11–11
Brakspear Bitter; Wadworth 6X; Whitbread Boddingtons Bitter Ⓗ; **guest beers**
Friendly back-street local with two connecting bars – a comfortable public and a lounge with a dining area where families are welcome. No food Sun eve.
❀ ◑ 🚃 ♣ P

Marsh Gibbon

Greyhound

West Edge ☎ (0869) 277365
12–4, 6–11
Fuller's London Pride; Greene King Abbot; Hook Norton Best Bitter; S&N Theakston Best Bitter Ⓗ
Listed building, probably of Tudor origin with 17th-century brickwork. Rebuilt after a fire in 1740. The Oakapple Day parade at the end of May starts here. Thai and continental cuisine a speciality (no food Tue eve).
🏚 Q ⌂ ❀ ◑ 🅐 P

Marsworth

Red Lion

Vicarage Road (off B489, near canal bridge 130)
☎ (0296) 668366
11–2.30, 6–11
Hook Norton Best Bitter, Old Hooky; S&N Theakston Best

Bitter; Wadworth 6X Ⓗ
Welcoming, idyllic village free
house with contrasting bars on
two levels. No food Sun.
🅰 Q ❀ ◖ ▶ ♣ ➟ P

Milton Keynes: *Bradwell Common*

Countryman
Bradwell Common Boulevard
☎ (0908) 676346
Ansells Mild; Courage
Directors; Ruddles Best
Bitter, County; Webster's
Yorkshire Bitter
Modern estate pub boasting a
permanent beer festival (eight
beers at any one time).
❀ ◖▶ ⇌ (Central) P

Bradwell Village

Prince Albert
Vicarage Road
☎ (0908) 312080
11–2.30 (5 Sat), 5.30 (7 Sat)–11
Hall & Woodhouse Badger
Best Bitter; Wells Eagle,
Bombardier Ⓗ
Large, comfortable lounge on
two levels. Live music and
quiz nights. Eve meals
Tue–Sat. ❀ ◖▶ ♣ P

New Bradwell

New Inn
Bradwell Road
☎ (0908) 312094
11–11
Adnams Broadside; Wells
Eagle, Bombardier Ⓗ
Longstanding favourite; a
canalside pub. Good value
meals. Pleasant garden with
menagerie. Moorings.
❀ ◖▶ ⊟ ⇌ (Wolverton) ♣ P

Woolstone

Cross Keys
Newport Road
☎ (0908) 679404
11–11
Wells Eagle, Bombardier Ⓗ;
guest beer (occasionally)
Classic thatched pub at the
heart of this modern city, a
stone's throw from the canal.
❀ ◖▶ ⊟ ♣ P

Preston Bissett

Old Hat
Main Street ☎ (028 04) 355
11–2.30, 7 (6 Sat)–11
Hook Norton Best Bitter Ⓗ
Every pub should be more like
this: good beer and
conversation are all that is
required. Go on a rainy
evening and take root. 🅰 Q P

Prestwood

Kings Head
188 Wycombe Road (A4128)
☎ (024 06) 2392

11–11
Brakspear Mild, Bitter,
Special, Old; Fuller's London
Pride; Greene King Abbot Ⓖ;
guest beers
The ultimate antidote to the
worst modern pubs.
Traditional atmosphere and
decor. Lager louts barred.
Tasty snacks. Alcoholic ginger
beer. 🅰 Q ❀ ♣ ➟ P

Princes Risborough

Bird in Hand
Station Road ☎ (084 44) 5602
11–3, 6–11
Greene King IPA, Rayments
Special, Abbot Ⓗ
End-of-terrace, cosy cottage
pub – a real 'locals' local'.
Country music fans especially
welcome. ❀ ◖ ⇌ ♣

Saunderton

Golden Cross
Wycombe Road (A4010)
☎ (0494) 562293
Adnams Bitter; Ind Coope
Burton Ale; Wadworth 6X Ⓗ
Recently leased by Ind Coope,
this traditional roadside pub
has now severed almost all
connections with Aylesbury
Brewery Co. Home-cooked
meals. ❀ ◖▶ ⊟ ⇌ ♣ P

Skirmett

King's Arms
3 miles N of A4155 at Mill End
OS776903 ☎ (049 163) 247
11–2.30, 6–11
Brakspear Bitter; Old Luxters
Barn Ale Ⓗ; guest beers
Village pub in picturesque
Chiltern countryside. Good
variety of bar meals; Sun
lunch a speciality.
🅰 Q ⌕ ❀ ⌂ ◖▶ ♣ P

Stewkley

Swan
High Street North
☎ (0525) 240285
11 (11.30 winter)–3, 6–11
Courage Best Bitter,
Directors; Ruddles County;
John Smith's Bitter Ⓗ
Fine Georgian pub at the
village centre. One attractive
rambling bar divided into
clearly defined areas. No food
Sun. ⌕ ❀ ◖▶ ♣ P

Stone

Waggon & Horses
Oxford Road ☎ (0296) 748740
11–2.30 (3 Sat), 6–11
Ind Coope ABC Best Bitter,
Burton Ale Ⓗ
Immaculate roadside pub with
two bars; the landlord has the
Burton Ale cellarmanship
award. Good home-cooked
food. ❀ ◖▶ ⊟ ♣ P

Tylers Green

Horse & Jockey
Church Road ☎ (0494) 815963
11–2.30, 5.30–11
Ansells Mild; Ind Coope
Benskins Best Bitter, Burton
Ale Ⓗ; guest beers
Spacious pub serving food at
all hours. ❀ ◖▶ ♣ P

Wendover

King & Queen
17 South Street (A413)
☎ (0296) 623272
12–3, 6–11 (12–11 Sat)
Ansells Mild; Hook Norton
Best Bitter; Tetley Bitter Ⓗ
Small 16th-century local: a
cosy stone-flagged public bar
with inglenook complete with
seats. Serves both mild and
real cider, unusual in this area.
Eve meals till 8pm (not music
nights).
🅰 ❀ ◖▶ ⊟ ⇌ ➟ P

Try also: Red Lion (Free)

Weston Turville

Chequers
35 Church Lane (off B4544)
☎ (0296) 613298
11.30–3 (not Mon), 6–11
Adnams Bitter; Marston's
Pedigree Ⓗ; guest beer
Traditional stone-flagged
lounge bar; can be busy,
especially at weekends.
Popular French restaurant.
🅰 ❀ ◖▶

Try also: Plough (Fuller's)

West Wycombe

George & Dragon
High Street (A40)
☎ (0494) 464414
11–2.30, 5.30–11 (11–11 Sat; 12–2.30,
7–10.30 Sun)
Courage Best Bitter,
Directors Ⓗ; guest beers
19th-century coaching inn in a
NT village. The original
timbered bar is reputed to be
haunted. Excellent garden. All
food is home cooked (no
meals Sun eve).
🅰 Q ⌕ ❀ ⌂ ◖▶ P

Wycombe Marsh

General Havelock
114 Kingsmead Road (parallel
to A40, E of High Wycombe)
☎ (0494) 520391
11–2.30 (3 Fri & Sat), 5.30 (5 Fri)–11
Fuller's Chiswick, London
Pride, Mr Harry, ESB Ⓗ
Smart and friendly pub, noted
for good value lunches. Eve
meals in summer only.
🅰 ❀ ◖▶ ♣ P

Cambridgeshire

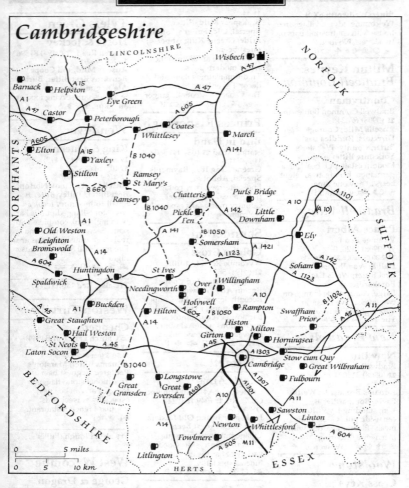

Cambridgeshire

LINCOLNSHIRE

NORFOLK

NORTHANTS

SUFFOLK

BEDFORDSHIRE

ESSEX

HERTS

Wisbech
Barnack · Helpston
A 1
A 15
A 47 · Castor
Eye Green
A 47
Peterborough
A 605
Coates
Whittlesey
March
Elton
A 15
Yaxley
A 141
Stilton
Ramsey St Mary's
B 660
Ramsey
B 1040
Chatteris
Purls Bridge
A 10
A 1101
Pickle Fen
A 142
Little Downham
Old Weston
A 141
B 1050
Somersham
A 1421
Ely
A 142
Leighton Bromswold
A 14
A 604
Huntingdon
St Ives
A 1123
Soham
A 1123
Spaldwick
Needingworth
Over
Willingham
A 10
B 1102
A 11
A 45
A 1
Buckden
Holywell
Rampton
Swaffham Prior
Hilton
Histon
Milton
A 45
Great Staughton
Girton
Horningsea
Hail Weston
A 1303
St Neots
A 45
Cambridge
Stow cum Quy
Eaton Socon
B 1040
Great Wilbraham
A 1307
Longstowe
Fulbourn
Great Gransden
Great Eversden
A 603
A 10
A 11
A 130?
Sawston
Linton
A 14
Newton
Whittlesford
A 604
Fowlmere
A 505
M 11
Litlington

0 ___ 5 miles
0 ___ 5 ___ 10 km

 Elgood's, *Wisbech*

Barnack

Millstone
Millstone Lane
☎ (0780) 740296
11–3, 6–11
**Adnams Bitter; Everards
Tiger, Old Original** Ⓗ
Stone-built village local close
to 'Hills and Holes' – a former
stone quarry for many
churches. Restaurant and
function suite. No food Sun
and Mon eves. ⌂ ❀ ◑ ⅋ P

Buckden

Falcon
Mill Road ☎ (0480) 811612
11–2.30, 6.30–11
Wells Eagle Ⓗ
Pub just outside the main

village on the road to Offords:
a single lounge bar with a
separate games room at the
rear. Traditional games include
Northants skittles, now sadly
rare this far east. Two gardens,
one enclosed with a patio and
barbecue for summer. ❀ ♣ P

Cambridge

Ancient Druids
Napier Street ☎ (0223) 324514
11–2.30 (3 Fri & Sat), 5.30 (6 Sat)–11
**Ancient Druids Kite Bitter,
Druid's Special, Merlin; Hall
& Woodhouse Badger Best
Bitter; Mansfield Riding
Mild; Wells Bombardier** Ⓗ
The micro brewery attached to
this modern, open-plan pub is
an obvious attraction but there
is always a good range of

other beers, plus good value
food (not served Sun/Mon
eves). Public car parks nearby.
❀ ◑ ▶ ♣

Cambridge Blue
85–87 Gwydir Street
☎ (0223) 61382
12–2.30 (3.30 Sat), 6–11
**Nethergate IPA, Bitter, Old
Growler** Ⓗ**; guest beers**
Bustling, friendly pub with a
no-smoking bar and snug.
Nethergate brewery's only
pub, but at least two guest
beers are also on offer – over
300 in two years. Public car
park in Gwydir Street.
♨ Q ❀ ◑ ▶ ♣ ⌂ ⅋

Champion of the
Thames
68 King Street ☎ (0223) 352043

48

11–11
Greene King XX Mild, IPA Ⓗ,
Abbot Ⓖ
One of the very few 'real'
pubs in the city centre: small
and lively, it can get crowded
at night. Note the splendid
etched windows. No food
Sun. Q ◖ & ♣

Clarendon Arms
35 Clarendon Street (near
Parkers Piece, off Parkside)
☎ (0223) 313937
11–11
**Greene King IPA, Rayments
Special, Abbot** Ⓗ
Unpretentious, friendly pub
close to the city centre.
Popular with the local
business community at
lunchtimes (good pub fare).
Boasts a fine working example
of an old cash register and is
reputed to be haunted by the
ghost of an old lady.
❀ ⇌ ◖ ▶

Cow & Calf
St Peters Street
☎ (0223) 311919
12–3, 5.30 (7 Sat)–11
**Courage Best Bitter,
Directors; Nethergate Bitter;
John Smith's Bitter; S&N
Theakston Best Bitter** Ⓗ;
guest beers
Superb street-corner local,
Cambridge CAMRA's *Pub of
the Year* 1990. Use Shire Hall
car park in the evening. Meals
served weekdays. ♨ ❀ ◖ ♣

Empress
72 Thoday Street
☎ (0223) 247236
11–2.30, 6.30–11 (12–2.30, 7–10.30
Sun)
**Marston's Pedigree;
Whitbread Castle Eden Ale,
Flowers Original** Ⓗ; guest
beer
Thriving community local: a
lively public bar with a
separate games area, and a
comfortable lounge.
❀ ⊟ ♣ ♡

Panton Arms
Panton Street
☎ (0223) 355733
11–2.30, 6–11 (11–11 Fri & Sat)
**Greene King XX Mild, IPA,
Rayments Special, Abbot** Ⓗ
Timelessly simple public bar
and a plusher lounge. Once
the brewery tap of the long-
gone Panton brewery – hence
the impressive gates to the
patio. Bar billiards played.
❀ ◖ ▶ ♣

St Radegund
129 King Street
☎ (0223) 311794
12–11
**Marston's Pedigree;
Nethergate IPA, Bitter, Old
Growler** Ⓗ; guest beers
Tiny triangular pub packed
with character. The starting

point for the (in)famous King
Street run. Ask about the Veil
Ale. Crusty bread sandwiches
served.

Seven Stars
249 Newmarket Road
☎ (0223) 354430
11–3, 6–11
**Greene King XX Mild, IPA,
Abbot** Ⓗ
Busy and friendly local; the
nearby Cambridge Museum of
Technology explains the
characters sometimes to be
found in the pub. No food
Sun. ◖ ▶ ♣   P

Six Bells
11 Covent Garden (off Mill
Road) ☎ (0223) 67527
11–11
**Greene King IPA, Rayments
Special, Abbot** Ⓗ
A lively local with a friendly
atmosphere; membership of
the Six Bells Beer and Banter
club is free. Sandwiches
available at the bar. Games
include chess and
backgammon, but not darts.
♨ Q ❀ ▶ ♣

Tram Depot
5 Dover Street (off East Rd)
☎ (0223) 324553
11–11
**Adnams Bitter; Earl Soham
Victoria; Everards Mild,
Beacon, Tiger, Old
Original** Ⓗ; guest beers
Characterful, award-winning
pub that actually used to be
the stables of the tram depot.
Exceptional food includes a
good vegetarian selection (not
served Sat/Sun eves). Public
car park at the rear. ❀ ◖ &

Zebra
80 Maids Causeway
☎ (0223) 464116
12–3, 6–11
**Greene King IPA, Rayments
Special, Abbot** Ⓗ
Although basically open-plan,
this comfy pub has several
distinct drinking areas. Food
is good, cheap and plentiful
(not served Sun eve).
❀ ◖ ▶ & ♣

Try also: **Elm Tree,** Orchard St
(Wells)

Castor
Royal Oak
24 Peterborough Road
☎ (0733) 380217
11–2.30, 6–11
**Ind Coope Burton Ale; Tetley
Bitter** Ⓗ
Listed building with a
thatched roof and considerable charm. The cosy
atmosphere is enhanced by a
low, beamed ceiling. Quieter
now that the village has been
bypassed. ♨ Q ❀ ◖ ♣   P

Chatteris
Honest John
South Park Street
☎ (0354) 32698
10.45–2.30, 5.45–11
**Fuller's Chiswick; Marston's
Pedigree; Whitbread
Wethered Bitter** Ⓗ
Former labour exchange built
in the 1950s. It became a pub
in 1977. The lounge bar houses
a model ship collection. The
best range and quality of beer
in town. ◖ ▶ ♣   P

Coates
Vine
4 South Green
☎ (0733) 820343
11–2.30, 6–11 (11–11 Sat)
Wells Eagle, Bombardier Ⓗ
1950s style lounge, with an
open fire. The large, enclosed
garden is ideal for children,
with a swing and a climbing
frame. ♨ Q ❀ ⊟ ♣   P

Eaton Socon
Crown
Great North Road (A45 St
Neots bypass)
☎ (0480) 212232
11–2.30, 5.30–11 (11–11 Sat)
Tetley Bitter; guest beers Ⓗ
Ivy-clad free house which is
often crowded. At least six
real ales on offer. Bookings
advised for the restaurant.
❀ ◖ ▶   P

Millers Arms
Ackerman Street (off Great
North Road) ☎ (0480) 405965
12–3, 5–11 (11–11 Fri & Sat)
**Greene King XX Mild, IPA,
Abbot** Ⓗ
Small 'village' pub on the
larger of Eaton Socon's greens.
The large garden has many
children's facilities and a
boules pitch. Summer
barbecues are popular with
boat owners from the nearby
river moorings. Children
welcome until 8pm.
♨ ⛾ ❀ ♣

Elton
Crown
8 Duck Street ☎ (0832) 280232
11.30–2.30, 6–11
**Greene King IPA; Marston's
Pedigree** Ⓗ; guest beers
Grade II listed building on the
village green, rebuilt in 1985
after a major fire. A large
comfortable bar and a separate
restaurant. Games include
shove-ha'penny, Pope Joan
and mini-skittles. A local
CAMRA *Pub of the Season.*
♨ ❀ ◖ ♣   P

Try also: **Black Horse** (Free)

Cambridgeshire

Ely

Prince Albert
62 Silver Street
☎ (0353) 663494
11.30 (11 Fri & Sat)–2.30 (3.30 Sat), 6.30–11
Greene King XX Mild, IPA, Abbot Ⓗ
The emphasis is firmly on good ale and good company in this friendly little pub which boasts a delightful, secluded garden. Public car park across the street (entrance in Barton Rd).
🏰 ⚙ ♣

West End House
West End ☎ (0353) 662907
11.30–2.30, 6–11
Courage Directors; Marston's Pedigree; Ruddles Best Bitter; Webster's Yorkshire Bitter Ⓗ
Low ceilings and beams; four separate drinking areas in a pub with a bad-tempered cat!
🏰 ⚙ ♣

Eye Green

Greyhound
41 Crowland Road
☎ (0733) 222487
11–2.30, 7–11
Wells Eagle, Bombardier Ⓗ
Basic, popular village local with a lounge and a public bar. Winner of a local CAMRA *Pub of the Month* award.
🏰 ⚙ ⬡ ᵴ ♣ P

Fowlmere

Queens Head
Long Lane
☎ (0763) 208288
12–2.30 (4 Sat), 6 (7 Mon, Tue & Sat)–11
Greene King IPA, Abbot Ⓗ
Excellent village local with darts, dominoes and Shut the Box are popular. Amazing selection of unusual real cheeses and real breads served at lunchtime. Eve meals Wed–Sun.
🏰 Q ⚙ ◑ ♪ ⬡ ♣ P

Try also: Swan (Free)

Fulbourn

Bakers Arms
Hinton Road
☎ (0223) 880606
11–11
Greene King XX Mild, IPA, Rayments Special, Abbot Ⓗ
Recently refurbished in cottage-style without being fussy. Outstanding garden with an aviary and a variety of animals. Food (all home-cooked and including vegetarian and special diet options) is served from 5.30pm (not Sun eve).
🏰 ᵴ ⚙ ◑ ♪ ⬡ ᵴ ▲ ♣ P

Girton

George
71 High Street
☎ (0223) 276069
11–4.30, 6–11
Ind Coope Burton Ale; Tetley Bitter; Tolly Cobbold Mild; Whitbread Wethered Bitter Ⓗ
Thriving two-bar pub rightly renowned for its food – the extensive menu always includes a vegetarian option (no meals Sun/Mon eves). A rare outlet in the area for Tolly Mild. Q ⚙ ◑ ♪ ⬡ ᵴ ♣ P

Great Eversden

Hoops
High Street
☎ (0223) 262185
12–2.30 (may vary in summer), 7–11
Adnams Broadside; Wells Eagle Ⓗ, **Bombardier** Ⓖ
17th-century village inn with a heavily timbered seating area separated from the public bar by a conversational lobby. No food Mon.
🏰 ⚙ ⬡ ◑ ♪ ⬡ ♣ P

Great Gransden

Crown & Cushion
On B1046
☎ (076 77) 214
12–11 (12–2.30, 6–11 Mon)
Adnams Broadside; Mansfield Riding Mild; Wells Eagle, Bombardier Ⓗ
Traditional thatched village pub whose split-level interior is divided into areas. Good home-cooked food. Pool table; small menagerie in the garden. Regular live music.
🏰 ⚙ ◑ ♪ P

Great Staughton

New Tavern
The Green (A45)
☎ (0480) 860336
11–3, 6–11 (11–11 Thu–Sat)
Adnams Broadside; Wells Eagle, Bombardier Ⓗ
Lively village pub with separate games and dining areas. Hood skittles played.
🏰 ◑ ♪ ♣ P

Great Wilbraham

Carpenters Arms
10 High Street
☎ (0223) 880202
11–2.30, 6.30 (7 winter)–11 (12–2, 7–10.30 Sun)
Greene King XX Mild *or* **Rayments Special, IPA, Abbot** Ⓗ
Community pub dedicated to the upkeep of the village. Its floral displays are something to behold. The landlord may be depended on to provoke discussion. No food Sun eve.
🏰 Q ◑ ♪ ⬡ ♣ P

Hail Weston

Royal Oak
High Street (off A45)
☎ (0480) 472527
11–11
Adnams Broadside; Mansfield Riding Mild; Wells Eagle, Bombardier Ⓗ
Picturesque thatched village pub which has a large garden with a children's playground, and a pleasant family room with video games. Eve meals Tue–Sat. 🏰 ᵴ ⚙ ◑ ♪ ♣ P

Helpston

Blue Bell
10 Woodgate ☎ (0733) 252394
11–2.30, 7–11
Bateman XXXB; Ruddles Best Bitter; Webster's Yorkshire Bitter Ⓗ
Pub dating from the 1600s: its wood-panelled lounge houses a collection of teapots and toby jugs; basic bar. John Clare, the peasant-poet, used to be the pub's pot-boy.
⚙ ⬡ ⬡ ♣ ᴗ P

Hilton

Prince of Wales
Potton Road (B1040)
☎ (0480) 830257
11–2.30, 6–11 (11–11 Sat)
Adnams Bitter; Banks & Taylor Shefford Bitter; Draught Bass Ⓗ; guest beers
Friendly, village free house with a small public bar and larger, well furnished lounge. Good range of guest beers.
🏰 ⚙ ◑ ♪ ⬡ ♣ P

Histon

Boot
High Street ☎ (0223) 233745
11–3, 6–11
Courage Directors; Tetley Bitter; Tolly Cobbold Bitter; Whitbread Wethered Bitter Ⓗ
Smart, comfortable pub in a village rich in real ale outlets. No food Tue eve.
🏰 ⚙ ◑ ♪ ⬡ P

Red Lion
High Street ☎ (0223) 232288
11.30–3, 5.30–11
Adnams Bitter; Draught Bass; Greene King IPA; Samuel Smith OBB; Taylor Landlord; Tetley Bitter Ⓗ
Relaxing lounge bar and a lively games-oriented public bar. Good home-cooked weekday lunches. The beer range can change but you can rely on the Taylor Landlord.
🏰 ⚙ ◑ ♪ ⬡ ♣ P

Holywell

Olde Ferry Boat Inn
OS343707 ☎ (0480) 63227

11–3, 6–11
**Adnams Bitter, Broadside;
Draught Bass; Greene King
IPA, Abbot** Ⓗ
Partly thatched, much-
extended, riverside pub,
reputedly haunted; now very
much a lounge bar pub.
Popular with river-goers in
summer. Features in the
Guinness Book of Records as one
of England's oldest pubs.
🏨 ⚲ ✿ 🛏 ◖▶ P

Horningsea

Plough & Fleece
High Street ☎ (0223) 860795
11.30–2.30, 7–11 (12–2, 7–10.30 Sun)
Greene King IPA, Abbot Ⓗ
A conservatory extension
adds interest to the lounge but
the public bar is the real gem
here. Superb food based on
old English recipes – try the
chocolate pudding. Eve meals
Tue–Sat. 🏨 Q ✿ ◖▶ 🛏 ♻

Huntingdon

Victoria
Ouse Walk ☎ (0480) 53899
11–2.30, 6–11
**Tetley Bitter; Whitbread
Flowers Original** Ⓗ
Hard to find back-street pub,
but well worth the effort. One
long bar is divided into
distinct areas. Good choice of
food. ✿ 🛏 ◖▶ ♣ ♻

Leighton Bromswold

Green Man
Off A604 ☎ (0480) 890238
12–2.30 (not Thu), 7–11 (closed Mon)
**Hook Norton Best Bitter;
S&N Theakston Old
Peculier** Ⓗ**; guest beers**
East Anglia CAMRA *Pub of the
Year*: a comfortable rural free
house with a collection of
brewery memorabilia, offering
a wide and ever-changing
range of guest beers. Hood
skittles played. ⚲ ✿ ◖▶ ♣ ♻

Linton

Crown
High Street
☎ (0223) 891759
12–2.30, 6.30–11
**Greene King Abbot;
Nethergate Bitter; Whitbread
Boddingtons Bitter, Flowers
IPA** Ⓗ
Long, narrow pub and
restaurant situated in one of
the finest streets in the county.
No meals Sun eve.
🏨 ✿ ◖▶ P

Litlington

Crown
Silver Street ☎ (0763) 852439
11–2.30, 5.30–11

Greene King IPA, Abbot Ⓗ
Enlarged village pub retaining
two bars; the lounge bar has
memorabilia from the nearby
WWII American airbase.
Don't be confused by the
village one-way system. Has
appeared in 19 editions of the
Guide. 🏨 ✿ ◖▶ 🛏 ♣

Little Downham

Anchor
25 Main Street
☎ (0353) 699494
11–3, 6–11
**Greene King IPA; Tetley
Bitter** Ⓗ**; guest beer**
Welcoming fenland village
local with some real
'characters'. No meals Mon
eve or Sun.
🏨 Q ✿ ◖▶ ♣ P

Longstowe

Golden Miller
High Street
11.30–2.30, 7–11
**Adnams Bitter; Bateman
XXXB; Greene King Abbot** Ⓗ**;
guest beers**
One-bar free house in rural
surroundings with a
restaurant and a large garden
at the rear. Named after the
famous racehorse which was
stabled nearby. ✿ ◖▶ P

March

Ship
1 Nene Parade ☎ (0354) 56999
11–3, 7–11 (10.30–11 Sat)
**Greene King XX Mild, IPA,
Abbot** Ⓗ**, Winter Ale** Ⓖ
17th-century, thatched
riverside pub with unusual
carved beams. Its convivial
atmosphere is appreciated by
all. Extensive boat moorings.
No food Mon; eve meals at
weekends. 🛏 ◖▶ 🛏 ♣

Milton

Waggon & Horses
39 High Street
☎ (0223) 860313
12–2.30 (4 Sat), 5 (7 Sat)–11
**Bateman XB; Nethergate
Bitter** Ⓗ**; guest beers**
Two permanent guest beer
pumps, one for a strong beer,
the other alternating mild and
bitter. Fri night is curry night;
Sun roasts served (no meals
Sat lunch or Sun eve). Popular
with local residents and the
business community.
🏨 ✿ ◖ ♻ P

Needingworth

Queens Head
High Street ☎ (0480) 63946
11–11
**Courage Directors; Fuller's
London Pride; Greene King**

**XX Mild, IPA; Taylor
Landlord** Ⓗ**; guest beers**
Two-bar village local, with a
strong domino following in
the public. Two large fish
tanks in the lounge bar. Note:
the handpumps are in the
public bar. ✿ ◖▶ & ♣ P

Newton

Queens Head
Fowlmere Road
☎ (0223) 870436
11.30 (11 Sat)–2.30, 6–11
**Adnams Bitter, Old,
Broadside** Ⓗ
Unspoilt village pub offering
simple but delicious food to
complement the ale. The pub
sign has a story – ask the
landlord.
🏨 Q ✿ ◖▶ 🛏 ♣ ♻ P

Old Weston

Swan
☎ (083 23) 400
12–3 (4 Sat), 7–11
**Adnams Bitter; Greene King
Abbot; Marston's Pedigree** Ⓗ
Olde-worlde free house with
beams, a low ceiling and a
restaurant. 🏨 ✿ ◖▶ ♣ P

Over

Exhibition
2 King Street (off Longstanton
Rd) ☎ (0954) 30790
11.30–2.30, 6.30–11
**Tetley Bitter; Tolly Cobbold
Bitter** Ⓗ**; guest beer**
Former beerhouse named after
the Great Exhibition of 1851,
now twice extended.
Swimming-pool for children
in summer. Weekday lunches;
eve meals Fri and Sat only.
🏨 ✿ ◖▶ ♣ P

Peterborough

Blue Bell
6 The Green, Werrington
☎ (0733) 571264
11–3, 6–11
**Elgood's Cambridge Bitter,
GSB; King & Barnes Sussex;
Wadworth 6X** Ⓗ
1890s village local
transformed into one of
Elgood's flagship pubs.
Usually serves the best
Elgood's in Peterborough.
✿ ◖▶ 🛏 ♣ P

Bogart's
17 North Street
☎ (0733) 349995
11–3 (4 Sat), 5.30–11 (closed Sun)
**Draught Bass; Bateman XB;
Taylor Landlord** Ⓗ**; guest
beers**
Once the Ostrich pub, then a
home-brew shop; now an
oasis in the real ale desert of
Peterborough's city centre.
Interesting lunchtime food.
◖ ⇌

Cambridgeshire

Charter's
Town Bridge
☎ (0733) 315700
12–3, 5–11 (11–11 Sat except in
football season)
**Adnams Broadside; Draught
Bass; Welsh Brewers
Worthington BB** H; **guest
beer**
A Dutch barge built in 1907,
now moored upstream of the
Town Bridge on the south
bank. Restaurant upstairs.
❀ ◐ ⇌

Crown
749 Lincoln Road, New
England
☎ (0733) 341666
11–3, 5–11 (11–11 Fri & Sat)
**Adnams Bitter; Draught Bass;
S&N Theakston Old
Peculier** H
Large and lively corner pub
with an imposing 1920s mock
Tudor facade: two bars and a
function room. Diverse
clientele and entertainment.
Good reputation for pizzas.
🏾 ❀ ◐ ♣ P

Dragon
Hodgson Avenue, Werrington
☎ (0733) 322675
11–2.30 (3.30 Fri & Sat), 5.30–11
Wells Eagle, Bombardier H;
guest beer
Modern pub in a recently
developed estate, opened in
1988: a popular local which
caters for families. A former
CAMRA local *Pub of the
Season.* ⛄ ❀ ◐ ♣ ♠ P

Fenman
Whittlesey Road, Stanground
☎ (0733) 69460
11.30–3, 6.15–11
**Courage Directors; John
Smith's Bitter** H
Large estate pub with a bar
and a lounge, built in 1967.
Q ❀ 🍺 ♠ P

Hand & Heart
12 Highbury Street
☎ (0733) 69463
10.30–2.30 (3 Sat), 6–11
**Courage Directors; John
Smith's Magnet** H
Original Warwick's brewery
windows remain on this gem
of a back-street pub. A very
friendly, lively bar and a quiet
lounge. Note the whisky
collection. 🍺 ♣

Swiss Cottage
2 Grove Street, Woodston
☎ (0733) 68734
11–11
**Courage Directors; John
Smith's Bitter** H
Back-street local with an Irish
flavour, built in the style of an
Alpine chalet. A lively pub.
❀ ◐ ⇌ ♣

Try also: **Botolph Arms**,
Oundle Rd (Free)

Pickle Fen
Crafty Fox
London Road ☎ (0354) 692266
11–2.30, 6–11
**Home Bitter; S&N Theakston
XB** H
Pleasant pub with a small bar,
a restaurant and a covered
'vineyard' area. Home-cooked
food includes a vegetarian
option. Children welcome.
🏾 🐾 ♦ 🍺 P

Purls Bridge
Ship
Purls Bridge Road, Manea
OS477869 ☎ (035 478) 578
12–3, 7–11 (closed Mon except bank
hols)
Greene King IPA H
Isolated fenland pub, two
miles down a dead-end road
from Manea. Consists of one
refurbished lounge bar with a
dining area. Situated on a
recently reopened section of
the Bedford river; boat
moorings available. 🏾 ❀ ◐ ♦

Rampton
Black Horse
High Street ☎ (0954) 51296
11.30–3, 5–11 (11.30–11 Sat)
Greene King IPA, Abbot H
Cheerful village inn. The
prints in the lounge have an
interesting history – ask the
landlord. Growing reputation
for food. No meals Tue; eve
meals Thu–Sat only.
🏾 Q ❀ ◐ ♦ 🍺 ♣ P

Ramsey
Three Horseshoes
Little Whyte ☎ (0487) 812452
11–2.30, 6–11
**S&N Theakston Best Bitter;
Younger IPA** H
Busy, back-street pub with a
distinct northern flavour.
🛏 ◐ ♦ 🍺 ♣

Ramsey St Mary's
White Lion
201 Hurn Road
☎ (073 129) 386
12–2.30 (3 Sat, not Wed), 7–11
Wells Eagle, Bombardier H
Isolated pub in a long fenland
village; old photos in the
lounge show local flooding.
The garden has children's play
equipment. No lunches Wed
or eve meals Tue.
🏾 Q ❀ ◐ ♦ ♣ ♠ P

St Ives
Oliver Cromwell
Wellington Street
☎ (0480) 65601
10.30–2.30, 6–11
**Adnams Broadside; Greene
King IPA** H

Busy lounge bar largely
unchanged in recent years,
near the riverside quay and
historic bridge. Note the
ornate sign. The pub clock
keeps to GMT. Q

Try also: **Royal Oak** (Ind
Coope)

St Neots
Wheatsheaf
Church Street ☎ (0480) 477435
11–2.30, 7 (6 Fri)–11
**Greene King XX Mild, IPA,
Abbot** H, **Winter Ale** H
Cheerful locals' pub, a rare
outlet in the area for the
excellent XX Mild. Successful
quiz team. ♣ ❀ ♣

Sawston
Black Bull
High Street ☎ (0223) 834472
11–2.30 (4 Sat), 6 (7 Sat)–11 (may
close some lunchtimes)
Tetley Bitter H; **guest beers**
Attractive old inn where food
may be introduced soon.
🏾 ❀ ♣ P

Try also: **Kings Head** (Greene
King)

Soham
Carpenters Arms
72 Brook Street
☎ (0353) 720869
11–11
**Adnams Bitter; Greene King
IPA** H; **guest beers**
Lively one-bar local,
somewhat hidden away but
worth finding. Basic snacks
available most times and an
ever-changing selection of
guest ales. 🏾 ♣ P

Somersham
Windmill
St Ives Road (B1089) OS349778
☎ (0487) 840328
11–2.30, 6.30–11
Greene King IPA, Abbot H,
Winter Ale G
Cottage-style pub one mile
west of Somersham, with two
contrasting bars.
❀ ◐ ♦ 🍺 ♣ P

Spaldwick
George
High Street ☎ (0480) 890293
11.30–2.30, 6–11
Wells Eagle, Bombardier H
Comfortable Georgian inn
built from ships' timbers.
Large garden.
🏾 ❀ 🛏 ◐ ♦ ♣ ♠ P

Stilton
Bell
Old Great North Road
☎ (0733) 241066

12–2.30 (11–3 Sat), 6–11
Marston's Pedigree; Ruddles County; Tetley Bitter H**; guest beer**
17th-century stone-built coaching inn, restored to its former glory. James I, Cromwell and Dick Turpin were guests.
🏨 ❀ 🍴 🏮 ◖ ▶ ♣ P

Stow cum Quy

Prince Albert
Newmarket Road (A1303, off A45 at Quy roundabout)
☎ (0223) 811294
11.30–3, 5–11
Greene King IPA H**; guest beers**
Guest beers? They've only had 500 in five years. Always a mild, a low and mid gravity bitter, plus a strong beer, available. A village pub without a village, that creates its own community with good company and a varied menu of good food.
🏨 ❀ ◖ ▶ ♿ ⌂ P

Swaffham Prior

Red Lion
High Street
☎ (0638) 742303
12–2.30, 7–11
Adnams Bitter; Courage Directors; Greene King IPA H**; guest beers**
Recently refurbished, with plenty of exposed beams and brickwork. Meeting place of the Devils Dyke Morrismen (Thu). Small furry creatures

abound in the garden. No food Sun eve or Mon.
🏨 ❀ ❀ ◖ ▶ ♣ P

Try also: Black Horse, Swaffham Bulbeck

Whittlesey

Bricklayers Arms
9 Station Road
☎ (0733) 202593
11–3, 6–11
Ruddles Best Bitter; Webster's Yorkshire Bitter H
Popular town local with a large basic bar and a modernised lounge. Bar skittles. Eve meals Sat only, unless by arrangement. 🏨 ❀ ▶ 🍺 ⇌ (Whittlesea) ♣ P

Whittlesford

Bees in the Wall
36 North Road
☎ (0223) 834289
12–2.30, 6.30–11
Adnams Bitter; Draught Bass; Bateman XB; Hook Norton Best Bitter; Wadworth 6X H
Large pub at the north end of the village, named after the live inhabitants of one of the walls. Food may be introduced soon.
🏨 ❀ 🍺 ♣ P

Willingham

Three Tuns
Church Street ☎ (0954) 60437
Greene King XX Mild, IPA, Abbot H
Good ale and good company

in a classic example of what a village local should be.
Q ❀ 🍺 ♣ P

Wisbech

Red Lion
32 North Brink
☎ (0945) 582022
11.30–2.30, 6 (7 Sat)–11
Elgood's Cambridge Bitter H
Popular pub amongst classical Georgian buildings, overlooking the tidal River Nene. A smart lounge bar and a restaurant (no eve meals Mon). ❀ ◖ ▶ P

Rose Tavern
53 North Brink
☎ (0945) 588335
11–11
Adnams Bitter; Fuller's London Pride; Marston's Pedigree H**; guest beers**
Cosy one-room pub on the riverside, a listed, 200-year-old building. The closest pub to Elgood's brewery.
Q ❀ 🍴 ◖ ▶ ♣

Try also: Three Tuns (Elgood's)

Yaxley

Royal Oak
106 Main Street
☎ (0733) 240464
12–2.30, 5–11 (11–11 Sat)
John Smith's Bitter; Ruddles Best Bitter H**; guest beer**
Thatched village pub in the Grand Metropolitan monopoly area. P

HOW MUCH?

It is the law of the land that pubs should display a representative sample of their prices. According to CAMRA surveys, one in seven pubs is breaking the law, by having no price list at all. Furthermore, for another one in six pubs the price list is not easily visible from the bar.

Why the fuss? Well, would you shop in a supermarket that didn't price goods on its shelves? Would you trust a restaurant where the menu didn't show prices?

The British system of buying drinks in rounds obscures what each individual drink might cost. If prices are concealed as well, perhaps this is one reason why beer prices are always going up.

The law is there to protect customers, and CAMRA wants it enforced.

Cheshire

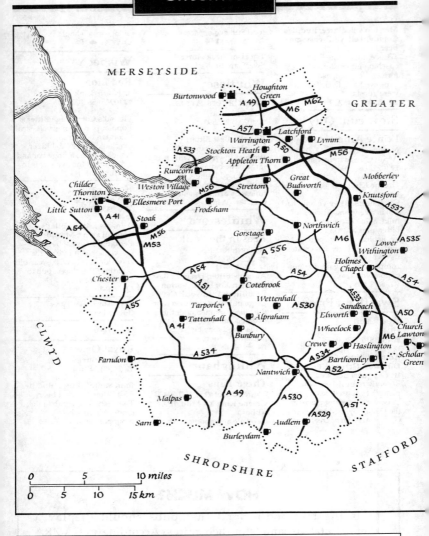

 Burtonwood, Burtonwood; **Coach House,** Warrington

Alpraham

Travellers Rest
Chester Road (A51)
☎ (0829) 260523
12–3 (not Mon–Fri), 6–11
McEwan 70/-; Tetley Walker Mild, Bitter Ⓗ
Quiet village local unchanged for years, with its own bowling green.
🏶 Q ⊛ ⊞ ♣ P

Appleton Thorn

Village Hall
Stretton Road ☎ (0925) 261187
8.30pm–11 (Thu–Sat only; 8.30–10.30 Sun)
Moorhouse's Black Cat Mild Ⓗ**; guest beers**
Cosy lounge attached to a village hall in old school buildings, run by a charitable trust. Restricted hours but also opens the first Sun lunch of

each month. Runner-up in CAMRA's 1991 *Club of the Year* awards. Two or three guest beers always available. The house beer is from Coach House. Q ⊛ ♣ P

Audlem

Bridge
Shropshire Street
☎ (0270) 811267

54

Barthomley

White Lion
2 miles from M6 jct 16, off
B5078 OS768524
☎ (0270) 882242
11.30–3, 6–11
**Burtonwood Mild, Bitter,
Forshaw's** H
Black and white thatched pub
in the centre of a small village.
Built in 1614, a list of all its
landlords on the wall shows
only 18 names. The church
opposite was the scene of a
Civil War massacre. Popular
with motorcyclists.
🏚 Q ❀ 🍴 ♣ P

Bollington

Queens Arms
High Street ☎ (0625) 573068
2 (12 Fri & Sat)–11
**Robinson's Mild, Best
Bitter** H
Solidly-built stone pub, set
back slightly from the rest of
the terrace. Modernised
internally in typical Robinson
style. Very popular.
🏚 ❀ 🍴 ▶ ♣

Vale
Adlington Road
☎ (0625) 575147
11.30–3, 7–11
**Taylor Landlord; Thwaites
Best Mild, Bitter** H
Once three terraced houses,
now a comfortable one-room
pub. Live jazz Mon nights. No
food Sun eve or Mon.
🏚 Q ❀ 🍴 P

Bosley

Queens Arms
Leek Road ☎ (0260) 223267
12–3, 5.30–11
**Whitbread Boddingtons
Bitter** H
Large, detached 17th-century
inn set in beautiful
surroundings with a pleasant
garden to the rear. The clean
and attractive open bar area
has a small room off for
families. No meals Mon eve.
🏚 Q 🛏 ❀ 🍴 ▶ P

Buglawton

Church House
Buxton Road ☎ (0260) 272466
11–3, 5.30–11
**Robinson's Best Mild, Best
Bitter** E
Roomy pub offering excellent
bar meals and a restaurant
(closed Sat eve). The unusual
pub sign is combined with a
pigeon cote. Very good
outside facilities for children.
🏚 🛏 ❀ 🍴 ▶ ♣ P

Bunbury

Dysart Arms
College Lane, Upper Bunbury
OS569581 ☎ (0829) 260183
12–3, 5.30–11 (11–11 Sat)
**Thwaites Bitter; Whitbread
Boddingtons Bitter** H
Picturesque 18th-century
former farmhouse which
provides the focus for the
village. The stone-floored
public bar has a pool table
while the lounge has a large
inglenook and an entertaining
marine aquarium.
🏚 Q 🍴 ❀ ♣ P

Burleydam

Combermere Arms
On A525 ☎ (0948) 871223
11.30–3, 5 (7 Sat)–11 (11–11 summer
Sat)
**Draught Bass; Marston's
Pedigree** H; **guest beers**
17th-century pub also serving
as the local polling station.
The enterprising landlord
holds twice-yearly beer
festivals; three guest beers,
including a mild.
🏚 🛏 ❀ 🍴 ♣ P

Burtonwood

Bridge Inn
Phipps Lane ☎ (0925) 225709
11.30–11
**Burtonwood Mild, Bitter,
Forshaw's** H
Games and sports-oriented
pub displaying the licensee's
rugby (union and league)
mementos. Own bowling
green. ❀ 🍴 ♣ P

Chester

Albion
Park Street
11.30–3, 5.30–11
**Greenalls Mild, Bitter,
Thomas Greenall's Bitter;
Stones Best Bitter** H
Traditional back-street local,
popular with a wide range of
drinkers who are often aghast
at the landlord's choice of
decor. No admittance after
10.30pm on Fri and Sat nights.
(No pub crawlers allowed.)
No fried food. Enjoy! 🏚 🍴

Boathouse Inn
The Groves (via Dee Lane)
☎ (0244) 328709
11–11
S&N Theakston Best Bitter H;
guest beers
Always seven beers on offer at
this recently refurbished
riverside pub with the only
family room in the city. Two
bars, of which the 'Ale-Taster'
has the largest choice, plus a
good selection of imported
beers. Occasional live music.
🏚 Q 🛏 ❀ 🍴 🍴 ⇌ P

MANCHESTER

Disley
Handforth
Kettleshulme
Wilmslow
DERBYSHIRE
A523 *Bollington*
Rainow
Henbury A537
Macclesfield
A34 A523
Eaton A54
Bosley *Wincle*
Buglawton
Congleton *Timbersbrook*
Newbold

SHIRE

Cheshire

11–3 (4 summer), 7 (5.30 summer)–11
(11–11 summer Sat)
**Marston's Burton Best Bitter,
Merrie Monk, Pedigree** H
Primarily a locals' pub which
in summer also caters for
canal-users, being situated at
the foot of a staircase of locks.
🏚 Q ❀ 🍴 ▲ ♣ P

Lord Combermere
The Square ☎ (0270) 811316
11–3.30, 6–11
**Courage Directors; Marston's
Pedigree; John Smith's
Bitter** H
Low-ceilinged, multi-roomed
pub with many artefacts
hanging from the roof. An
unusual-shaped bar with a
larger side room and a small
snug. Play area and pets in the
garden. 🏚 🛏 ❀ 🍴 ♣ P

Cheshire

Boot Inn

Eastgate Street Row (above Samuels jeweller)
11–3.30, 5.30–11 (11–11 Fri & Sat)
Samuel Smith OBB, Museum H

Pub situated in Chester's historic rows above street level, which may make this well renovated pub difficult to find. Nevertheless the persevering pub hunter will be rewarded by looking upwards. Look for the panel showing the original wall. ◖

Centurion

Oldfield Drive, Vicars Cross (off A54, 1 mile from Chester)
☎ (0244) 347623
11.30–3, 6–11
Cains Bitter; Jennings Bitter; Robinson's Best Bitter; Tetley Walker Mild, Bitter H; guest beer (occasionally)

Well-furnished, modern estate-style pub with a smart lounge and a games-oriented bar. The cellar space has been improved recently and occasional beer festivals are held. ❀ ⊞ ♣ P

Clavertons

Lower Bridge Street
☎ (0244) 316316
11.30–11 (11.30–4.30, 7–11 Sat)
Lees Bitter, Moonraker H

Lively town-centre pub which appeals especially to the younger drinker. Recently extended to give more eating room to the lunchtime trade (meals served until 5.30pm). A rare local outlet for Moonraker. ◖

Old Custom House

Watergate Street
☎ (0244) 324035
11–3, 5.30–11
Marston's Border Exhibition, Burton Best Bitter, Pedigree H, **Owd Roger** (winter) G

Friendly, never-changing pub, a quarter of a mile from the Cross. The building dates back to 1637 and features ornate bar carvings and splendid fireplaces. Still home to unsuccessful sports teams. A rare outlet for Exhibition. No food Sun. ◖ ⊞ ♣

Try also: Cherry Orchard, Boughton Lane (John Smith's); **Little Oak**, Boughton (Greenalls)

Childer Thornton

White Lion

New Road (200 yds off A41)
☎ (051) 339 3402
11.30–3, 5–11 (11.30–11 Fri & Sat)
Thwaites Best Mild, Bitter H

Excellent, unspoilt two-roomed country local catering for all. The snug is used by families at lunchtime but gets crowded at weekends. Lunches are recommended – try the chicken tikka (no food Sun). ♨ Q ❀ ◖ P

Church Lawton

Lawton Arms

Knutsford Road (A50, near B5077 jct) ☎ (0270) 873743
11–3, 5.30 (7 Sat)–11
Robinson's Best Mild, Best Bitter E

Local in a Georgian building with a snug and a games room. ♨ Q ❀ ⊞ ♣ P

Congleton

Grove

Manchester Road, Lower Heath ☎ (0260) 272898
12–2, 7–11
Marston's Mercian Mild, Burton Best Bitter, Pedigree H

Family local with a good atmosphere. Food is available at all times. Bar games played and special events held.
❀ ◖ ♣ P

Waggon & Horses

Newcastle Road, West Heath
☎ (0260) 274366
11.30–3, 6–11
Marston's Burton Best Bitter, Pedigree H

Large, well-established inn standing on the western edge of town. Tables outside in the summer, with the pub's situation (at the junction of the A34, A54 and A534), make it somewhat akin to sitting in the middle of a roundabout. No food Sun. ♨ ❀ ◖ ♣ P

Cotebrook

Alvanley Arms

Forest Road (A49)
☎ (0829) 760200
11.30–3, 5.30–11
Robinson's Best Mild, Bitter H, **Old Tom** G

Country pub with decor to suit: two comfortable lounges, one with a bar, and a separate restaurant. Pleasant external appearance, with a cobbled forecourt. ♨ 🛏 ❀ 🖾 ◖ ▶ P

Crewe

Albion

1 Pedley Street
☎ (0270) 256234
12–2 (3 Mon, 4.30 Sat), 7–11 (12–11 Fri)
Ind Coope Burton Ale; Tetley Walker Dark Mild, Bitter H; guest beer

Good example of a street-corner local: a bar with an emphasis on darts and dominoes, plus a pool room.
⊞ ⇌ ♣

British Lion

58 Nantwich Road (A534, 300 yds W of station)
☎ (0270) 214379
12–4 (3 Tue & Wed, 5 Fri), 7–11
Ind Coope Burton Ale; Tetley Walker Dark Mild, Bitter H

Small, busy local on the main road, known locally as the 'Pig' because of the carving above the fireplace.
♨ ◖ ♧ ♣

Crown

25 Earle Street
☎ (0270) 257295
11–(varied closing), 7–11
Robinson's Best Mild, Best Bitter H

Pub recently refurbished but without the loss of character. Four-roomed layout. ⊞ ♣

Kings Arms

56 Earle Street
☎ (0270) 584134
11.30–3 (4 Mon, Fri, Sat), 7–11
Whitbread Chester's Mild, Best Bitter, Boddingtons Bitter, Trophy H

Large pub with rooms to suit all tastes. Q ⊞ ♣

Try also: Horseshoe, North St (Robinson's)

Disley

Dandy Cock

Market Street ☎ (0663) 763712
11–11
Robinson's Best Mild, Best Bitter H, **Old Tom** G

Small, cosy pub on the main road (A6) in the centre of the village. Traditional comforts in addition to a separate restaurant. Popular with locals and passers by.
♨ ❀ ◖ ▶ ⇌ P

Try also: Crescent (Robinson's)

Eaton

Plough

Macclesfield Road (A536)
☎ (0260) 280207
12–3, 7–11
Banks's Bitter; Camerons Strongarm H

Village pub on the green, revitalised in recent years by its licensee. Much emphasis on food (can get busy as a consequence), but this does not detract from the welcoming atmosphere.
♨ Q ❀ ◖ ▶ P

Waggon & Horses

Manchester Road (A34)
☎ (0260) 224229
11.30–3, 5.30 (6 Sat)–11
Robinson's Best Mild, Best Bitter H

Pleasant, roadside pub with a vast car park.
♨ Q 🛏 ❀ ◖ ▶ ♣ P

Ellesmere Port

Straw Hat
Hope Farm Road
12–10.45
**Courage Directors; John
Smith's Bitter** Ⓗ
Friendly estate pub offering
darts and dominoes in the bar
and a jukebox in the lounge.
Entertainments include
singers on Sun eve and
karaoke on Tue. 🍴 ♣ P

Sutton Way
Thelwall Road, Great Sutton
☎ (051) 348 0144
11–11
**Courage Directors; John
Smith's Bitter** Ⓗ
Large, boisterous estate pub
featuring live bands and
karaoke nights.
❀ 🍴 ⅙ ≷ (Overpool) ♣ P

Try also: Sir Robert, Overpool
Rd (Whitbread)

Elworth

Midland
5 New Street ☎ (0270) 762070
11.30–3 (4 Thu–Sat), 6–11
**Robinson's Best Mild, Best
Bitter** Ⓗ
Two-roomed local in a terrace
close to Foden's wagon works.
🏨 🍴 ≷ (Sandbach) ♣

Farndon

Greyhound Hotel
High Street ☎ (0829) 270244
12–3, 5.30 (7 Sat)–11
**Greenalls Mild, Bitter,
Thomas Greenall's Bitter** Ⓗ
Friendly hotel by the River
Dee, whose residents include
two donkeys and four goats.
🏨 Q ❀ 🏨 🍴 ♣ P

Frodsham

Aston Arms
Mill Lane (just off A56 by
River Weaver bridge)
☎ (0928) 32333
11–3, 5.30 (7 Sat)–11
Burtonwood Mild, Bitter Ⓗ
Quiet, friendly, ex-Greenalls'
pub in the shadow of a
railway viaduct. Several small,
cosy rooms, a comfortable
lounge and a pool room, with
a bowling green at the rear.
Old drinks adverts and
breweriana adorn the walls.
Q ❀ 🍴 ♣

Rowlands Bar
31 Church Street (50 yds from
station) ☎ (0928) 33361
11–3, 5–11
**Whitbread Boddingtons
Bitter** Ⓗ; guest beers
Pub with two regularly-
changing guest beers (soon to
be increased) and a full range
of food always available to its
wide-ranging clientele. Also
offers foreign bottled beers, an
extensive wine list and regular
special menus. No jukebox or
bandit; a local CAMRA
award-winner. Q ⅅ 🍴 ≷

Gorstage

Oaklands
Millington Lane (200 yds off
A49) OS610727
☎ (0606) 853249
11–11
**Tetley Walker Mild, Bitter;
Whitbread Boddingtons
Bitter** Ⓗ; guest beers
Once a gentlemen's club set in
the Cheshire countryside, now
a pub/hotel of great character.
Comfortable and welcoming,
with many individual features
in an open-plan interior. Note
the remarkable monkey puzzle
tree and beautiful gardens.
❀ 🏨 ⅅ ≷ (Cuddington) P

Great Budworth

George & Dragon
High Street ☎ (0606) 891317
12–3, 7–11
**Ind Coope Burton Ale; Tetley
Walker Bitter** Ⓗ; guest beer
Located opposite the church in
a picturesque village. The
dimly-lit, cosy lounge is full of
copper and brass; recently
enlarged bar. Monthly guest
beer. 🏨 ⅙ ⅅ 🍴 ♣ P ⅛

Handforth

Railway
Station Road
11–3, 5.30–11
**Robinson's Best Mild, Best
Bitter** Ⓔ
Large, multi-roomed pub
facing the station. Smart, and
popular with locals. No food
Sun. ⅅ ≷ P

Haslington

Hawk
Crewe Road ☎ (0270) 582181
11–11 (12–2.30, 7–10.30 Sun)
**Robinson's Best Mild, Best
Bitter** Ⓔ
15th-century roadside inn and
restaurant. An exposed panel
inside reveals the original
wattle wall. Eve meals
Thu–Sat. 🏨 ❀ ⅅ P

Henbury

Cock
Chelford Road (A537)
☎ (0625) 423186
11–3, 5.30–11
**Robinson's Best Mild, Best
Bitter, Old Tom** Ⓗ
Comfortable main road pub
attracting both local and
passing trade, situated just
outside Macclesfield. Children
are welcome in the restaurant.
Q ❀ ⅅ 🍴 P

Holmes Chapel

Swan
Station Road ☎ (0477) 32259
11–3, 4.30–11 (11–11 Fri & Sat)
**Samuel Smith OBB,
Museum** Ⓗ
Former coaching inn with
good food, and an interesting
old black stove on display.
🏨 ❀ 🏨 ⅅ ≷ ♣ P

Houghton Green

Millhouse
Ballater Drive, Cinnamon
Brow (off A574)
☎ (0925) 811405
12–3.30, 5.30 (7 Sat)–11
Holt Mild, Bitter Ⓗ
Large, spacious estate pub
built in the 1980s to cater for
new residential areas. The
basic bar and two-roomed
lounge are equally popular
with the locals. Holt's most
westerly tied outlet, selling the
best value pint in the area.
Quiz night Tue. ❀ 🍴 ♣ P

Kettleshulme

Bulls Head
Macclesfield Road
☎ (0663) 733225
12–3 (summer only), 7–11
**Whitbread Boddingtons
Bitter; Castle Eden Ale** Ⓗ
Stone terraced pub of
character in the centre of a
village within the Peak
National Park. The traditional
country interior has a friendly
atmosphere with a public bar
and darts area as well as a
small, cosy lounge bar.
🏨 ❀ 🍴 ♣ P

Knutsford

Builders Arms
Mobberley Road (off A537)
☎ (0565) 634528
11.30–3, 5.30–11 (12–2, 7–10.30 Sun)
**Marston's Mercian Mild,
Burton Best Bitter,
Pedigree** Ⓗ
Delightful pub in an attractive
terrace on the outskirts of the
town centre. A former
Taylor's Eagle brewery house.
A busy pub with a keen games
emphasis. Q ❀ 🍴 ≷ ♣

White Bear
Canute Place ☎ (0565) 632120
11–3, 5.30–11 (11–11 Sat)
**Greenalls Mild, Bitter; Stones
Best Bitter** Ⓗ
An old, thatched coaching inn
dating from 1634 which has
seen much of the town's
history from its position facing
the former cattle market. An
excellent community pub with
small, low-ceilinged rooms.
Twenty-two different societies
meet here. ❀ ≷ ♣

Cheshire

White Lion
King Street ☎ (0565) 632018
11.30–11
Tetley Walker Bitter H**; guest beer**
Tasteful pub serving an extensive range of cheese and pâté lunches (not Sun); doggie bags provided. Guest beer is either Robinson's, Jennings or Hydes' Anvil.
🏚 Q 🏵 ◗ ≈ ♣

Latchford

Penny Ferry
271 Thelwall Lane (off A50)
☎ (0925) 38487
12–4.30, 7–11
Burtonwood Bitter, Forshaw's H
One-roomer near the Latchford locks on the Manchester Ship Canal. Its nautical theme includes old photos of the local ferry service. Sandwiches available lunchtime. 🏵 ♣ P

Little Sutton

Travellers Rest
14 Ledsham Road (100 yds from A41) ☎ (051) 339 2176
11.30–11
Walker Mild, Bitter, Best Bitter, Winter Warmer H
Large two-roomed pub with a separate eating area and helpful bar staff. Quiz on Wed. 🏚 🏵 ◗ ◗ 🍺 P

Lower Withington

Red Lion
Trap Street, Dicklow Hill (B5392 from Macclesfield)
☎ (0477) 71248
11.45–2.30 (3 Sat), 5.30–11
Robinson's Dark Mild, Best Bitter H
Large rural pub with a restaurant and a tap room for locals. Close to Jodrell Bank radio telescope. Even though the pump clip says Robinson's Best Mild, it is actually a very rare outlet for the Dark Mild.
🏚 🏵 ◗ ◗ 🍺 ♣ P

Lymm

Spread Eagle
Eagle Brow (A6144)
☎ (092 575) 5939
11.30–11
Lees GB Mild, Bitter H**, Moonraker** (winter) E
Ornate old village pub near Lymm Cross with canal moorings close by. Three varying rooms: the cosy snug is especially popular with the locals. A bar was added in the late 1980s by extending into the adjoining building.
🏚 ◗ 🍺

Wheatsheaf
Higher Lane, Broomedge (A56 at Agden Brow)
☎ (092 575) 2567
11.30–3 (4 Sat), 5.30–11
Hydes' Anvil Mild, Bitter E
Roadside pub dating back over 200 years and much-extended in the late 1980s into an open-plan layout with a central bar. A strong local following has been retained and the games area is still very popular. 🏵 ◗ ♣ P

Macclesfield

Albion
London Road ☎ (0625) 425339
11–11
Robinson's Best Mild, Bitter, Best Bitter H
Known as the 'Flying Horse' until 1855, this small, busy pub on the A523 retains a beautiful vestibule window as evidence of its former identity. Handy for Macclesfield Town football matches. 🏵 ♣ P

Baths Hotel
40 Green Street (behind station)
11–4 (not Mon–Fri), 6.30–11
Banks's Mild, Bitter H
Small, but thriving local, just off the A537 Buxton road. A local bowling green inspired its original name of 'Bowling Green Tavern', and a public bath its current title. The pub has survived both. 🍺 ≈ ♣

Evening Star
87–89 James Street (400 yds from A536/A523 jct)
☎ (0625) 424093
11–3, 5.30–11 (12–2, 7–10.30 Sun)
Marston's Mercian Mild, Burton Best Bitter, Pedigree E
Friendly little local, tucked away in the back streets, made difficult to find by car by a maze of blocked streets. Quiet at lunchtimes but busier eves and weekends. Q 🏵 ♣

George & Dragon
23 Sunderland Street
☎ (0625) 421898
11–4 (3 Tue & Wed), 5.30 (7 Sat)–11
Robinson's Best Mild, Best Bitter E
Friendly pub serving good value food (eves until 6.45; no meals Sun). Pool, darts and skittles played. Close to bus and rail stations.
Q 🏵 ◗ ◗ ≈ ♣

Prince of Wales
33 Roe Street ☎ (0625) 424796
11–3, 5.30–11
Greenalls Bitter, Thomas Greenall's Bitter H
Pleasant pub, handy for shoppers in the town centre, and visitors to the Silk Heritage Centre opposite.
◗ ◗ ≈ ♣

Malpas

Red Lion
1 Old Hall Street
☎ (0948) 860368
11–11
Draught Bass H**; guest beers** (occasionally)
Well-kept village inn which has its own sauna and solarium. Try the pub's own special malt whisky. Restored cottages next door provide accommodation. Wholesome country fare available.
🏚 Q 🛏 🏵 🛏 ◗ ◗ ♣ P

Try also: Blue Bell, Tushingham (Hanby)

Mobberley

Bird in Hand
Knolls Green ☎ (0565) 873149
11.30–3, 5.30–11
Samuel Smith OBB, Museum H
Popular 18th-century pub on the eastern outskirts of the village. Modernised, it has retained its 'local' charm with a number of wood-panelled alcoves. A wide selection of freshly prepared food is available (except Mon eve and Sun). 🏚 Q 🏵 ◗ ◗ & P

Try also: Chapel House (Boddingtons)

Nantwich

Bowling Green
The Gullet (behind church)
☎ (0270) 626001
11–11
Courage Directors; John Smith's Magnet; Webster's Yorkshire Bitter; Whitbread Boddingtons Bitter H
Dating from the 15th century but much altered and extended; one of the few buildings to survive the great fire of 1583. 🏚 🏵 ◗ ◗ ≈ ♣

Try also: Rifleman (Robinson's)

Newbold

Horseshoe
Fence Lane (off A34 at Astbury church, right after 1/2 mile; follow bends for 1 1/2 miles) OS863602
☎ (0260) 272205
11–3, 6–11
Robinson's Best Mild, Best Bitter H
Isolated country pub, formerly part of a farmhouse. Difficult to find but worth the effort.
🏚 🛏 🏵 ◗ ♣ P

Try also: Egerton Arms (Robinson's)

Northwich

Beehive

High Street
11–11
**Greenalls Mild, Bitter,
Thomas Greenall's Bitter;
Stones Best Bitter** Ⓗ
Attractive town-centre pub
with a red brick exterior and
an open, split-level interior.
Excellent value lunches and a
congenial atmosphere entices
both locals and shoppers alike.
◖

Rainow

Highwayman

On B5470 N of Rainow
☎ (0625) 573245
11.30–3, 7–11
Thwaites Bitter Ⓗ
Remote and windswept inn,
known as the 'Blacksmiths
Arms' until 1949 and locally as
the 'Patch'. Breathtaking
views from the front door
which opens into a maze of
connecting rooms, with a
small tap room in the far
corner of the pub. Three
blazing fires in winter.
🍴 Q ⚲ ❀ ◖ ▶ ♣ P

Runcorn

Windmill

Windmill Hill (off A558, 1
mile from A56 jct)
☎ (0928) 710957
11.30–3, 5–11 (11.30–11 Fri & Sat)
Hydes' Anvil Light, Bitter Ⓔ
Large, modern octagonal pub
built in the late 1980s with a
split-level lounge and a
separate public bar. Quiz
night Tue. ⚲ ❀ ◖ ⊟ ♣ P

Sandbach

Lower Chequers

Crown Banks, The Square
☎ (0270) 762569
11–3.30, 5–11
**Banks's Bitter; Ruddles Best
Bitter** Ⓗ**; guest beer**
The oldest pub in town, dating
back to 1570; a former
coaching inn and money-
changing house. It boasts a
striking frontage and an
unusually-shaped interior.
Note the old Saxon cross in
the cobbled square nearby.
🍴 ◖▶ ⊟ ♣

**Try also: Iron Grey
(Robinson's)**

Sarn

Queens Head

Off B5069, S of Threapwood
OS440447 ☎ (094 881) 244
11–3, 6–11
**Marston's Burton Best
Bitter** Ⓗ
Small pub by a stream at the
heart of S Cheshire. A *Guide*
regular and well worth
finding. 🍴 Q ❀ ◖ ▶ ⊟ ♣ P

Scholar Green

Globe

Drumber Lane (2 miles off
A34, follow Mow Cop signs)
OS846579
12–3 (not Tue-Fri), 7–11
**Marston's Burton Best Bitter,
Pedigree** Ⓗ
Small, traditional local, close
to Little Moreton Hall and
near the starting line of the
'Mow Cop Killer Mile' road
race run in April. Parking
difficult. Q ⊟ ♣ P

**Try also: Travellers Rest
(Marston's)**

Stoak

Bunbury Arms

Little Stanney Lane (near M53
jct 10) ☎ (0244) 301665
11.30–3, 6–11 (may be 11.30–11 in
summer)
**Cains Bitter; Whitbread
Higsons Bitter** Ⓗ
Superb village local where one
can still enjoy a quiet
conversation. Has undergone
tasteful and sympathetic
alterations and holds a 'bat
roosting' certificate. Weekday
lunches. Q ❀ ◖ ⊟ ♣ P

Stockton Heath

Red Lion

60 London Road
☎ (0925) 861041
11–3, 5.30–11 (11–11 Fri & Sat)
**Greenalls Mild, Bitter,
Thomas Greenall's Bitter;
Stones Best Bitter** Ⓗ
Old, unspoilt village pub of
multiple cosy rooms attracting
a good mixed clientele. Its
active crown green teams
boast championship-winning
ladies. Q ❀ ◖ ⊟ ♣ P

Stretton

Hollow Tree

Tarporley Road (off A49 at
M56 jct 10) ☎ (0925) 730733
11–11 (11–3, 5.30–11 Sat)
**S&N Theakston Best Bitter,
XB, Old Peculier** Ⓗ
Renovated Georgian
farmhouse, converted into a
pub and restaurant in the mid
1980s. Large garden area. An
accommodation extension is
planned. ❀ ◖ ▶ P

Ring O'Bells

Northwich Road, Lower
Stretton (100 yds along A559
from M56 jct 10)
☎ (0925) 730556
12–3 (3.30 Sat), 5.30 (7 Sat)–11
Greenalls Mild, Bitter Ⓗ
Small, welcoming roadside
pub, once a row of cottages,
now comprising a narrow
front lounge and two smaller
rooms to the side. Operates a
small library in the corridor
with proceeds donated to
charity. 🍴 Q P

Tarporley

Crown Hotel

High Street ☎ (0829) 732416
11–11 (open all day summer Sun)
**Burtonwood Mild, Bitter,
Forshaw's** Ⓗ
150-year-old village pub,
refurbished to provide a large,
open-plan lounge, a
conservatory and a separate
bar with a pool table.
🍴 ❀ ◖ ▶ ⊟ ♣ P

Rising Sun

High Street ☎ (0829) 732423
11.30–3, 5.30–11
**Robinson's Best Mild, Best
Bitter** Ⓗ
15th-century listed building
with a beamed ceiling, old
fireplaces and wooden
furniture. A cosy village pub
of character, popular for
meals, with the result that the
lounge is often full of diners
(no food Sun eve). ◖ ▶ ⊟ P

Tattenhall

Letters Inn

High Street ☎ (0829) 70221
11–3, 5.30–11
**Taylor Landlord; Whitbread
Boddingtons Bitter, Flowers
IPA, Original** Ⓗ
Country village inn with a
friendly atmosphere, offering
a large selection of meals as
well as snacks and
sandwiches; tables can be
booked for the 'Post Room'.
Beer garden at the rear. ❀ ◖ ▶

**Try also: Sportsmans
(Thwaites)**

Timbersbrook

Coach & Horses

Dane in Shaw Bank (1 mile N
of Congleton, on Rushton
Spencer road) OS890619
☎ (0260) 273019
11–3, 6–11
**Robinson's Best Mild, Best
Bitter** Ⓔ
Pleasant hostelry composed of
a through lounge with a small
tap room behind the fireplace.
Popular with locals.
🍴 ⚲ ❀ ◖ ▶ ⊟ ♣ ♠ P

Warrington

Lord Rodney

67 Winwick Road (off A49
near the brewery)
☎ (0925) 234296
12–11 (12–4, 7–11 Sat)
**Cains Bitter; Robinson's Best
Bitter; Tetley Walker Dark
Mild, Bitter, Walker Best**

Cheshire

Bitter, Winter Warmer Ⓗ; guest beers
Tetley Walker flagship pub, recently converted to Victorian style. The long bar with its bank of handpumps serves three or four changing guest beers; also a plush lounge. Quiz nights Tue; live music Fri. Occasional two-week beer festivals held.
✿ ◑ ⊟ ≱ (Central) ♣

Lower Angel
27 Buttermarket Street (next to Odeon cinema) ☎ (0925) 33299
11–4, 7–11
Ind Coope Burton Ale; Walker Mild, Bitter, Best Bitter, Winter Warmer Ⓗ; guest beer
Extremely popular, small town-centre pub with an ever-changing guest beer: a basic bar and a comfortable lounge. It is usually the first pub to offer new beers from the nearby Coach House brewery.
⊟ ≱ (Central) ♣

Weston Village

Royal Oak
Heath Road South
☎ (0928) 565839
12–3, 7–11 (11–11 Fri)
Marston's Burton Best Bitter Ⓗ
Friendly village pub overlooking the Mersey and ICI's Rocksavage works; popular with workers at lunchtime. A large bar and a smaller, cosy lounge, plus a meeting room upstairs.
✿ ◑ ▶ ⊟ ♣

Wettenhall

Boot & Slipper
Long Lane (between Winsford and Nantwich) OS625613
☎ (0270) 73238
11.30–3, 5.30–11 (11.30–11 Sat)
Bass Highgate Mild; Marston's Pedigree Ⓔ & Ⓗ
16th-century country local with beams and a friendly atmosphere. A full à la carte menu is served in the separate restaurant, but pub meals are also popular. Can get busy at weekends. Accommodation is often fully booked.
🏠 Q ✿ 🛏 ◑ ▶ ♣ P

Wheelock

Commercial
Crewe Road ☎ (0270) 760122
8–11 (12–2, 8–10.30 Sun)
Marston's Pedigree; Thwaites Bitter; Whitbread Boddingtons Bitter Ⓗ; **guest beer** (occasionally)
Exceptional free house displaying signs of its former Birkenhead brewery ownership. Collection of bottled beers. A finely restored games room offers a full-size snooker table and table skittles.
🏠 Q ♣ ♻ ✗

Wilmslow

Farmers Arms
71 Chapel Lane (off A34)
☎ (0625) 532443
11–11
Whitbread Boddingtons Mild, Bitter Ⓗ
Traditional Victorian town pub of several rooms with brasses and antiques. Very busy at times (especially the tap room) due to its friendly atmosphere and well-kept beer. Quiz night Tue. Nice garden in summer. No food Sun. 🏠 Q ✿ ◑ ⊟ P

New Inn
Alderley Road
☎ (0625) 523123
11.30–3 (3.30 Fri & Sat), 5.30–11
Hydes' Anvil Light, Bitter Ⓔ
An extensive modernisation of a much smaller pub, designed almost exclusively to cater for the appetites of the shoppers trooping from the even larger Sainsbury's supermarket next door. No eve meals Sun or Mon. ◑ ▶ ♣ P

Try also: **Swan** (Boddington Pub Co)

Wincle

Ship
☎ (0260) 227217
12–2 (3 Sat), 7–11 (closed Mon Nov–Mar)
Marston's Pedigree; Whitbread Boddingtons Bitter Ⓗ
16th-century village inn, once part of the Swythamly Estate. The 18-inch thick stone walls are designed to withstand the rigours of local winters.
Q ☙ ✿ ◑ ▶ ⊟ ♣ P

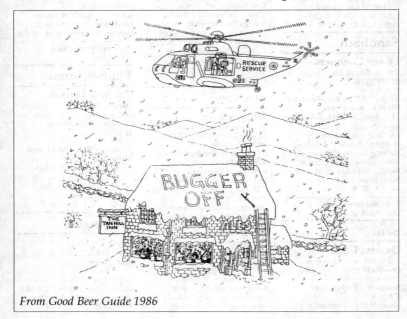

From Good Beer Guide 1986

60

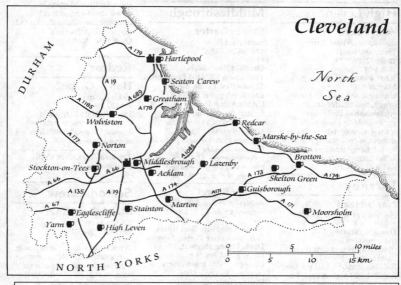

Cleveland

North Sea

DURHAM

A 179 — Hartlepool
Seaton Carew
A 19
A 689
A 1185 — Greatham
A 178
Wolviston
Redcar
A 171
Norton
Marske-by-the-Sea
A 1085
Brotton
Stockton-on-Tees
A 66 — Middlesbrough
Lazenby
A 66
Acklam
Skelton Green
A 174
A 135
A 19
A 173
Guisborough
A 174
A 67
Marton
A 171
A 171
Egglescliffe
Stainton
Moorsholm
Yarm
High Leven

NORTH YORKS

0 — 5 — 10 miles
0 — 5 — 10 — 15 km

Camerons, Hartlepool; **North Yorkshire**, Middlesbrough

Acklam

Master Cooper
291 Acklam Road
☎ (0642) 819429
11–11
Samuel Smith OBB Ⓗ
Listed building, a former restaurant and fish and chip shop. Recently renovated to expose its original fabric. Large, L-shaped single bar.
🏚 Q ❀ ◗ ♣ P

Brotton

Green Tree
90 High Street
☎ (0287) 76377
11–1, 7–11
Camerons Strongarm Ⓗ
Former 14th-century manor house; its cosy interior retains separate rooms with many quiet corners. Strong local trade — one regular has been in every night for 50 years. Can get very busy. Sun lunch available. 🏚 Q ⛵ ⊞ ◖ ♣

Try also: Malt & Hop (Camerons)

Egglescliffe

Pot & Glass
Church Road
☎ (0642) 780145
11–3, 5.30–11
Draught Bass Ⓗ
Charming village pub with a long and fascinating history. The ornate bar fronts were

carved from old furniture by a former licensee. Comfortable bar lounge with separate children's/function room. Well worth seeking out. Eve meals on request.
Q ⛵ ❀ ◗ ⊞ ♣ P

Try also: Pavilion (John Smith's)

Greatham

Hope & Anchor
Front Street (400 yds off A689)
☎ (0429) 870451
Tetley Bitter Ⓗ
Modernised pub in a quiet village just to the west of the conurbation of Hartlepool.
◗ ◖ ♣ P

Guisborough

Globe Hotel
Northgate
☎ (0287) 632778
12 (11.30 Sat)–3, 6.30–11
Camerons Strongarm; Tetley Bitter Ⓗ
Traditional local with regular public bar clientele. Lounge available for meetings Mon-Tue. Live music Fri (piano) and Sat (band). Quiz Sun.
❀ ⊞ ♣

Tap & Spile
Westgate ☎ (0287) 632983
11–3, 5.30–11 (11–11 Thu–Sat)
Beer range varies Ⓗ
Old town-centre pub, refurbished in traditional style. Offers up to ten guest

ales from a portfolio of 200. No meals Sun in summer or Sun-Wed in winter. Cider occasionally. Most pubs in Guisborough centre now sell real ale. Q ❀ ◗ ◖ ⇄

Hartlepool

Gillen Arms
Clavering Road
☎ (0429) 860218
Whitbread Castle Eden Ale Ⓗ
Large, modern, open-plan estate pub on the northern edge of town. Strong community links. Comfortable interior with quiet corners. Family conservatory.
⛵ ❀ ◗ ◖ ♣ P

Jackson's
Tower Street ☎ (0429) 862413
11–11
Draught Bass; S&N Theakston XB, Old Peculier; Whitbread Castle Eden Ale Ⓗ
Two-roomed pub with typical Fitzgerald's antique touches. Lunchtime snacks. ⊞ ⇄ ♣

New Inn
Durham Street (road to headland) ☎ (0429) 267797
11–3, 5.30–11
Camerons Strongarm Ⓗ
Fine street-corner local which has featured in this guide for almost two decades. CAMRA Cleveland branch *Pub of the Year* 1991. Not to be missed!
Q ⊞ ♣

Cleveland

High Leven

Fox Covert
Low Lane (A1044 Yarm-Thornaby road)
☎ (0642) 760033
11–3, 5–11
Vaux Samson, Double Maxim [H]
Unmistakably of farmhouse origin, this cluster of whitewashed buildings commands its crossroads setting. Comfortable open-plan interior with a warm welcome for all. Large upstairs function suite. Imaginative menu.
♨ ❀ ◖◗ ♣ P

Lazenby

Nag's Head
High Street ☎ (0642) 440149
11.30–4, 7–11
Draught Bass [H]
Cosy yet spacious; photographs and paintings of rural scenes abound. Recommended for its popular lunches (not served Sat). The local for ICI's Wilton works.
◖ ♣

Marske-by-the-Sea

Frigate
Hummershill Lane (250 yds along Windy Hill Lane from square) ☎ (0642) 484302
12–3, 6.30–11 (12–11 Fri & Sat)
John Smith's Magnet; Webster's Green Label [H]
Pleasant estate pub: a large lounge and a separate bar with a pool table. Quiet room available. ◖◗ ⊟ ≋ ♣ P

Zetland
9 High Street ☎ (0642) 483973
11–11
Vaux Samson, Double Maxim [H]
Large spacious lounge and a separate bar. Function room upstairs. Live folk music; summer barbecues. Other Vaux beers sold in rotation.
Q ◖◗ ⊟ ≋ ♣ P

Try also: All pubs in the village serve real ale

Marton

Rudd's Arms
Stokesley Road (A172)
☎ (0642) 315262
11–11
Marston's Pedigree; Whitbread Trophy, Flowers Original [H]
Large single-room pub, catering for all ages. Open-plan with separate areas for food, families, darts, etc. Quiet and relaxing during the day, very busy after 8pm.
◖ ♿ ♣ P

Try also: Apple Tree (Bass)

Middlesbrough

Star & Garter
Southfield Road
☎ (0642) 245307
11–11
Draught Bass; S&N Theakston XB, Old Peculier; Stones Best Bitter; Taylor Landlord; guest beers [H]
CAMRA Pub Preservation Group award-winning conversion of a former club. Many genuine Victorian features from defunct pubs were used in the reconstruction. Discreet games area and a large L-shaped lounge. ❀ ◖◗ ⊟ ≋ ♣ P

Tap & Barrel
86 Newport Road (by bus station) ☎ (0642) 219995
11–11
North Yorkshire Best Bitter, IPA, Yorkshire Porter, Erimus Dark, Flying Herbert, Dizzy Dick; guest beers [H]
Cosy pub near town centre, converted from a shop. Dining/function room upstairs. (Wheelchair access to ground floor only.) Cider varies. ♞ ◖ ♿ ≋ ♣ ⌽

Westminster Hotel
Parliament Road
☎ (0642) 424171
11–11
Courage Directors; John Smith's Magnet [H]
Built in 1938 and virtually unchanged since. Fascinating snug with a feature fireplace and original animal carvings. Popular with football fans. Families welcome in the snug.
Q ♞ 🛏 ⊟ ♣ P

Try also: Malt Shovel (North Yorkshire)

Moorsholm

Toad Hall Arms
High Street ($1^1/_2$ miles off A171)
☎ (0287) 660155
7–11 (12–3, 7–10.30 Sun; may open Sat lunch in summer)
Tetley Bitter [H]
Family pub on the edge of the North York moors, but only 20 minutes from industrial Teesside. Views out to sea from the garden; cosy interior with 'Toad' bric-a-brac. Excellent value meals (not served Mon eve). Children welcome in the dining room. Self-contained flat to rent.
♨ Q ❀ 🛏 ◖◗ ⊟ ♣ P

Norton

Unicorn
High Street
☎ (0642) 553888
12–3, 5–11 (12–11 Fri & Sat; 12–2, 7–10.30 Sun)
John Smith's Magnet [H]
Small street-corner local opposite the village duckpond. Locals call it 'Nellie's'.
Q ❀ ◖ ⊟ ♿ ♣

Redcar

Hop & Grape
99 High Street
11–3.30, 7–11
John Smith's Magnet [H]
Small town-centre pub well known for good value lunches (served Tue-Sat). ◖

Try also: Yorkshire Coble (Samuel Smith)

Seaton Carew

Staincliffe Hotel
Coronation Drive
☎ (0429) 264301
11–11
Whitbread Castle Eden Ale [H]
Large seafront hotel, originally a private house complete with its own chapel. Overlooks the notorious Longscar Rocks. Large bar with two full-sized snooker tables.
♞ ❀ 🛏 ◖◗ ⊟ ♣ P

Skelton Green

Miners Arms
5 Boosbeck Road
☎ (0287) 650372
12–4, 7–11
Vaux Samson [H]
Terraced local with a comfortable, narrow lounge, a separate family room and a pool room with a jukebox. Central corridor with service from a hatch. Shove-ha'penny played. Q ♞ ♿ ♣ P

Stainton

Stainton Inn
☎ (0642) 599902
11.30–3, 6–11
Camerons Strongarm; Everards Old Original [H]
Village-centre pub of imposing red brick construction; extended in 1987 into adjacent cottages. Strong emphasis on food. The landlord is trying to retain the Everards against brewery pressure. Good quality meals.
❀ ◖◗ ⊟ ♿ ♣ P

Stockton-on-Tees

Cricketers Arms
Portrack Lane
☎ (0642) 675468
11–11
Whitbread Boddingtons Bitter, Castle Eden Ale, Flowers Original [H]

Comfortable and friendly one-roomed pub with a separate games area. ♣ P

Elm Tree

Elm Tree Avenue, Fairfield
☎ (0642) 677942
11.30–3 (4 Thu & Fri), 6–11 (11–11 Sat)
Courage Directors; John Smith's Bitter Ⓗ
Smart, modern estate pub built in 1985: several separate rooms decorated in Art Deco style. For a modern pub, a strong sense of community prevails. Children welcome in the conservatory until 8pm. Good value home-cooked food.
🛏 ⊛ ◑ 🍴 & ♣ P

Fitzgeralds

9-10 High Street
☎ (0642) 678220
11–3.30 (4 Fri, 5 Sat), 6.30–11
Draught Bass; McEwan 80/-; S&N Theakston Old Peculier; Taylor Landlord Ⓗ
An imposing stone facade with granite pillars fronts a split-level interior with typical Fitzgerald fittings. Much frequented by younger patrons. Deafening jukebox!
◑ 🍴 ♣

Parkwood Hotel

64-66 Darlington Road, Hartburn
☎ (0642) 580800
11–3 (4 Sat), 5–11
Vaux Samson Ⓗ
Impressive old hotel in a tree-lined suburb, converted from a house in 1964. Former home of the local shipbuilding and owning Ropner family.

Usually one other Vaux/Wards beer available. Excellent garden play area for children.
⊛ 🚲 ◑ ♣ P

Senators

Bishopton Road West
☎ (0642) 672060
11–4, 6 (7 Mon)–11
Vaux Extra Special Ⓗ
Modern pub built on to Whitehouse Farm shopping centre. A plain exterior hides a warm and comfortable interior. ⊛ ◑ ▶

Sun

Knowles Street
☎ (0642) 615676
11–11
Draught Bass Ⓗ
Excellent and deservedly popular drinkers' pub just off the High Street. Venue of Stockton Folk Club. Reputedly sells more Draught Bass than any other pub in the UK. Local CAMRA branch *Pub of the Year* 1990. May close briefly before the evening rush. 🚃 ♣

Trader Jacks

Blue Post Yard
☎ (0642) 675718
11–11
Whitbread Trophy, Castle Eden Ale Ⓗ
The oldest pub in Stockton, formerly known as the Blue Post. Now completely refurbished, it boasts the best jukebox in town. ◑

Try also: Clarendon (Camerons)

Wolviston

King's Arms

Wolviston Road (just off old A19)
11–11
S&N Theakston Best Bitter Ⓗ
Large estate pub, popular with young people. Can be very busy at weekends.
⊛ ◑ & ♣ P

Yarm

George & Dragon

70 High Street
☎ (0642) 780425
11–3.30, 5.30–11 (11–11 Fri & Sat)
Courage Directors; John Smith's Magnet Ⓗ
Historic market and coaching inn, venue for the original meeting of the founders of the Stockton & Darlington Railway. Warm, welcoming interior with original railway documents. Look for the fine carved sign above the inner door. Bargain beers sometimes available. No meals at weekends. ⊛ ◑ ♣

Ketton Ox

100 High Street
☎ (0642) 788311
11–11
Vaux Samson Ⓗ
One of several fine, historic coaching inns in the village conservation area. Oval windows blocked in on the facade betray the site of old cock-fighting rooms. Warm and hospitable interior. Children welcome lunchtime and early eve. 🛏 ⊛ ◑ ♣

"OF COURSE YOU'VE GOT A CHOICE – PAY UP OR GET OUT!"

From Good Beer Guide 1986

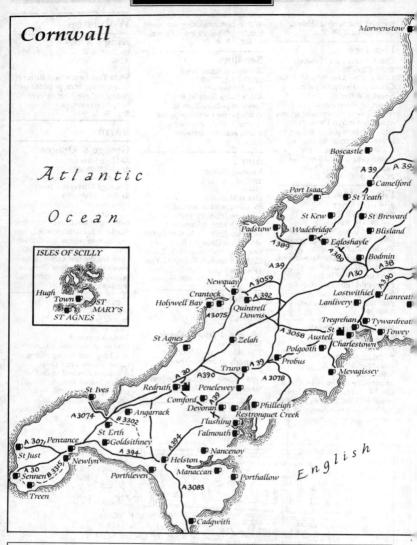

Cornwall

Cornwall

Morwenstow

Atlantic Ocean

ISLES OF SCILLY

Hugh Town
ST MARY'S
ST AGNES

Boscastle
Camelford
Port Isaac
St Teath
St Kew
St Breward
Padstow
Wadebridge
Egloshayle
Blisland
Bodmin
Newquay
Crantock
Lostwithiel
Lanreath
Holywell Bay
Quintrell Downs
Lanlivery
A3075
Tregrehan
Tywardreath
St Agnes
Zelah
St Austell
Fowey
Polgooth
Charlestown
Truro
Probus
Mevagissey
St Ives
Redruth
Penelewey
Comford
Phillleigh
Angarrack
Devoran
Restronguet Creek
Penzance
St Erth
Flushing
St Just
Goldsithney
Falmouth
Nancenoy
Sennen
Newlyn
Helston
Treen
Porthleven
Manaccan
Porthallow
Cadgwith

English

 Redruth, Redruth; **St Austell,** St Austell

Albaston

Queen's Head
¹/₂ mile S of A390
☎ (0822) 832482
11–2.30, 6–11
**Courage Best Bitter,
Directors; Ind Coope Burton
Ale** ᴴ
Excellent village local on the
edge of the Tamar valley. An
unspoilt pub run by the same,
well-respected landlord for
many years. Good value bar
snacks. 🏚 Q ❀ ⅏ Å
⇌ (Gunnislake) ♣ ⇪ P

Altarnun

Rising Sun
Off A30 on Camelford road, 1
mile N of village OS825215
☎ (0566) 86636
11–3, 6–11
**Draught Bass; Bateman XB;
Brains Bitter; Exmoor Ale;
Wiltshire Stonehenge Bitter;
Whitbread Flowers
Original** ᴴ**; guest beers**
Lively, 16th-century country
pub, popular with both locals
and visitors. It enjoys an
unspoilt rural setting on the

fringe of Bodmin Moor. Ever-
changing range of guest beers.
Camping/caravans in the pub
grounds.
🏚 🐾 ❀ 🛏 ⅏ ▸ Å ♣ P

Angarrack

Angarrack Inn
12 Steamer's Hill (off A30, N
of Hayle)
☎ (0736) 752380
11–2.30, 6–11 (12–2, 7–10.30 Sun)
**St Austell Bosun's, XXXX
Mild, HSD** ᴴ
Very welcoming and

Bodmin

Hole in the Wall
Crockwell Street (near A389)
☎ (0208) 72397
11–2.30 (3 Fri), 6–11 (11–11 Sat)
Draught Bass; Marston's Pedigree Ⓗ
Formerly the town's debtors' prison which contains a collection of antiques and bric-a-brac. Entered through the gardens or via a walkway from the main town car park.
🏰 Q ❀ ◑ ▶ ₺

Masons Arms
5–9 Higher Bore Street (A389)
☎ (0208) 72607
11–3, 5–11 (11–11 Fri & Sat)
Draught Bass; Whitbread Flowers IPA Ⓗ
Historic town pub built before the Napoleonic wars and reputed to hold the oldest continuous licence in Cornwall. The lounge is quiet; good value food.
🏰 Q ⛟ ❀ 🛏 ◑ ▶ ♣ P

Boscastle

Cobweb
☎ (0840) 250278
11–2.30, 6–11
Draught Bass; St Austell XXXX Mild, Tinners Ⓗ**; guest beers**
Set in an ancient building but only fully licensed since 1947, an inn full of character with open beams, slate floor and stone walls. The figurehead behind the bar was from Swedish ship *The Welm* which was wrecked locally in 1890.
🏰 Q ⛟ ❀ ◑ ▶ ♣ P

Botus Fleming

Rising Sun
Off A388, 4 miles from Tamar Bridge ☎ (0752) 842792
12–3, 6–11 (may vary)
Ruddles County; Ushers Best Bitter Ⓗ
Unspoilt and unpretentious country pub with 12th-century origins, tucked away in a quiet village on the outskirts of Saltash. A happy, friendly pub now in the third generation of family ownership. A good value cider house. Raucous euchre sessions. Boules pitch.
🏰 Q ❀ ₺ ♣ ⌂ P

Cadgwith

Cadwith Cove Inn
☎ (0326) 290513
11–11 (12–2.30, 7–11 winter)
Devenish Cornish Original; Marston's Pedigree; Whitbread Flowers IPA Ⓗ**; guest beers** (summer)
17th-century, unspoilt smuggling inn in the heart of Cadgwith Cove and the traditional fishing village of Cadgwith. Good food.
🏰 Q ❀ 🛏 ◑ ▶ ₺ ▲

Callington

Coachmaker's Arms
Newport Square (A388)
☎ (0579) 82567
11.30–2.30, 6.30–11
Draught Bass; Greene King Abbot Ⓗ**; guest beers**
300-year-old coaching inn with a warm, friendly atmosphere. Much emphasis is placed on good food and en suite accommodation but the small bar area is also popular.
Q 🛏 ◑ ▶ ♣ P

Camelford

Mason's Arms
Market Place ☎ (0840) 213309
11–3, 6 (7 winter)–11
St Austell Tinners Ⓗ**, HSD** Ⓖ
Town pub, over 300 years old, popular with locals. The garden overlooks the River Camel.
🏰 ❀ 🛏 ◑ ▶ ₺ ♣

Charlestown

Rashleigh Arms
☎ (0726) 73635
11–11
Draught Bass; Ruddles County; St Austell Tinners; Wadworth 6X Ⓗ**; guest beers**
Large, friendly inn overlooking the famous port of Charlestown, comprising two large bars, a restaurant and a family room. At least two guest ales. AA three-star accommodation.
⛟ ❀ 🛏 ◑ ▶ ₺ ₷ ▲ ♣ P

Comford

Fox & Hounds
On A393 Falmouth–Redruth road ☎ (0209) 820251
11–3, 6–11
Draught Bass; St Austell Bosun's, Tinners, HSD, Winter Warmer Ⓖ
Comfortable country pub and restaurant; a prize-winner in a garden competition.
🏰 ❀ ◑ ▶ ₺ ▲ ♣ P

Crantock

Old Albion
Langurroc Road
☎ (0637) 830243
11–11
Courage Best Bitter, Directors Ⓗ
Quaint thatched pub by the old church lychgate, attracting many visitors in summer for photos and pub meals. A short walk to the good sandy beach or the picturesque village centre. Meals in summer only.
🏰 ⛟ ❀ ◑ ▶ ▲ ♣ P

comfortable village pub offering an extensive, good value menu of home-prepared food (vegetarian option).
🏰 ❀ ◑ ▶ ▲ P

Blisland

Royal Oak
Village Green
☎ (0208) 850739
12–3, 6–11
Draught Bass Ⓗ**; guest beers**
Friendly inn on the only village green in Cornwall. Rebuilt in 1900 after a fire, this is a sturdy granite pub on the edge of Bodmin Moor. Up to three guest beers. No food Sun eve. 🏰 Q ⛟ ❀ ◑ ▶ ₺ ♣ P

Cornwall

Devoran

Old Quay Inn
St John's Terrace (off A39)
☎ (0872) 863142
11–3, 6–11
Whitbread Flowers IPA Ⓗ;
guest beer
Friendly, welcoming pub
affording fine views over
Devoran Quay and Creek.
🏠 ❀ 🛏 ◑ ▶ ♣ P

Egloshayle

Earl of St Vincent
Of A389 ☎ (0208) 814807
11–3, 6.30–11
St Austell Tinners, HSD Ⓗ
Built in 1485 and later named
after one of Nelson's admirals,
a fine old pub which has
recently had a major spring
clean inside and out. Its smart,
comfortable interior boasts a
fine collection of clocks. No
eve meals winter Sun.
🏠 ❀ ◑ ▶ ⌂

Falmouth

Seven Stars
The Moor ☎ (0326) 312111
11–3, 6–11
Draught Bass; St Austell
HSD Ⓖ; guest beers
Unspoilt by 'progress', a pub
in the same family for five
generations. A lively tap room
with barrels on display, and a
quiet snug to the rear, together
with a number of forecourt
benches. Q ❀ 🍴

Flushing

Royal Standard
1 St Peters Road (off A393 at
Penryn) ☎ (0326) 374250
11–2.30 (3 Fri & Sat), 6.30–11 (12–2,
7–10.30 Sun)
Draught Bass; Devenish
Cornish Original; Whitbread
Flowers IPA Ⓗ
Friendly local near village
entrance; beware of swans in
the road nearby! 🏠 ❀ ◑ ▶ ♣

Fowey

Ship Inn
3 Trafalgar Square
☎ (072 683) 3751
11–3, 6–11 (11–11 summer)
St Austell Tinners, HSD Ⓗ
Comfortable, one-bar, village-
centre pub with a separate
games/children's room.
🏠 ⛵ 🛏 ◑ ▶ ♣

Goldsithney

Crown
Fore Street ☎ (0736) 710494
11–3 (extended in summer), 6–11
St Austell Bosun's, XXXX
Mild, HSD Ⓗ
Attractive, comfortable village
pub with a warm atmosphere.

Very popular restaurant
(bookings advisable) and
excellent home-cooked bar
meals. 🏠 Q ❀ 🛏 ◑ ▶ ▲

Helston

Blue Anchor
50 Coinagehall Street
☎ (0326) 562821
11–3 (may extend), 6–11
Blue Anchor Medium, Best,
Special, Extra Special Ⓗ
Superb, 15th-century thatched
pub, once a monks' resting
place and, last century, a tin-
miners' pay centre. Its
splendidly strong beers
('Spingo') are brewed in the
old brewhouse in the rear
yard. Simple bar snacks
available. 🏠 Q ⛵ ▲

Holywell Bay

Treguth Inn
Holywell Road (off A3075)
☎ (0637) 830248
11.30–11 (11.30–2.30, 7–11 winter)
Courage Best Bitter,
Directors; John Smith's Bitter;
Wadworth 6X Ⓗ; guest beers
Well situated on the hill down
to a beautiful sandy beach,
this thatched pub has genuine
low beams (watch your head
through the door) and a good
mix of local and holiday
customers. Popular for meals.
Good choice of camping or
self-catering sites, plus a
leisure park nearby.
🏠 Q ⛵ ❀ ◑ ▶ ▲ ♣ P

Isles of Scilly: St Agnes

Turks Head
☎ (0720) 22434
11–11 (please knock in winter!)
Ind Coope Burton Ale Ⓗ
Friendly pub in a converted
boat house overlooking the
Island of Gugh. Good food
and idyllic views make this an
excellent place to start and
end your visit to St Agnes.
❀ 🛏 ◑ ▶ ⅋ ▲ ♣

Isles of Scilly: St Mary's

Bishop & Wolf
Main Street, Hugh Town
☎ (0720) 22790
11–11
St Austell Tinners, HSD Ⓗ
Lively pub with a large bar, a
pool room downstairs and a
restaurant above. Named after
the two famous lighthouses, it
has several maritime items on
display. The beer is fined at
the pub after the sometimes
arduous crossing.
⛵ ◑ ▶ ⅋ ▲ ♣

Try also: **Mermaid**, Hugh
Town (Devenish)

Lanlivery

Crown Inn
Off A390, 2 miles W of
Lostwithiel ☎ (0208) 872707
11–3, 5.30–11 (extends if busy)
Draught Bass; Welsh Brewers
Worthington BB Ⓗ
Comfortable and old-
fashioned pub in a 12th-
century listed building.
Popular restaurant and
accommodation in separate
buildings. 🏠 Q ⛵ ❀ 🛏
◑ ▶ ⅋ ⅖ ▲ P

Lanreath

Famous Punch Bowl Inn
Off B3359 Looe–Liskeard road
☎ (0503) 220218
11–3, 6–11
Draught Bass; St Austell
HSD Ⓗ; guest beers (summer)
Magnificent velveteen chaises
longues in the lounge and an
enormous flagstoned farmer's
kitchen as the public bar are
features of this 17th-century
coach house with enough
room to swing a horse! 🏠 Q
⛵ ❀ 🛏 ◑ ▶ ⅋ ⅖ ▲ ♣ P

Launceston

White Horse Inn
14 Newport Square, St
Stephens ☎ (0566) 772084
11–11
Ruddles Best Bitter, County;
Ushers Best Bitter; Webster's
Yorkshire Bitter Ⓗ
Friendly, 18th-century
coaching inn with two large
bars; regular live music in the
stable bar. Wide selection of
food all day. Taunton cider.
🏠 Q ❀ 🛏 ◑ ▶ ♣ ⌂ P

Looe

Jolly Sailor Inn
Princes Square, West Looe
☎ (0503) 263387
12 (11 summer)–11
Courage Best Bitter;
Marston's Pedigree; Ushers
Best Bitter Ⓗ
'Jolly Japes' in one of Britain's
oldest pubs. A folk group has
sung for over 500 years every
Sat night in this low-beamed
Cornish shark-fishing local,
set opposite the passenger
ferry. Beware of generous
portions of good food.
⛵ 🛏 ◑ ▶ ⅖ ▲ ⇌ ♣

Lostwithiel

Royal Oak
Duke Street ☎ (0208) 872552
11–3, 5.30–11 (11–11 Sat)
Draught Bass; Fuller's
London Pride; Marston's
Pedigree; Whitbread
Boddingtons Bitter, Flowers
Original Ⓗ; guest beers

Busy, friendly 13th-century inn where food is a speciality.
🏚 Q 🍺 ✿ 🍴 ◑ ◖ 🍷 ⇌

Manaccan

New Inn
☎ (032 623) 323
11–3, 6–11
Devenish Cornish Original; Marston's Pedigree Ⓖ
Very traditional, thatched pub in the village centre. Prides itself on good, home-cooked food. No jukebox or fruit machines. The car park is tiny.
🏚 Q ✿ ◑ ◖ ▲ P

Menheniot

White Hart
1¼ miles off A38
☎ (0579) 342245
12–2.30 (4 Sat), 6–11
Draught Bass; Whitbread Boddingtons Bitter Ⓗ
Well-appointed, 16th-century, family-run hotel with a friendly village atmosphere in the public bar. The varied menu includes good value Sunday roasts. Pool room and a small patio.
🏚 Q ✿ 🍴 ◑ ◖ 🍷 ♣ P

Mevagissey

Fountain Inn
St Georges Square (near harbour) ☎ (0726) 842320
11.30–11
St Austell Bosun's, Tinners Ⓗ
Friendly, local drinking house with two bars and an upstairs restaurant. Traditional decor with excellent slate floors. Fish is a speciality. 🏚 Q 🍺 ✿ 🍴
◑ ◖ 🍷 & ▲ ♣

Morval

Snooty Fox
On A387 ☎ (050 34) 233
11–2.30, 6–11
Whitbread Best Bitter, Flowers Original Ⓗ**; guest beers** (summer)
Large, single-bar pub with a converted stable as a family/games room and additional bar. Excellent food (separate restaurant). The large grounds include an adventure play area and a campsite.
🍺 ✿ 🍴 ◑ ◖ 🍷 & ▲ ♣ P

Morwenstow

Bush Inn
Crosstown OS208151
☎ (0288) 83242
11.30–3, 7–11 (closed winter Mon)
St Austell HSD Ⓗ**; guest beer** (summer)
Ancient building, once a chapel, with a lepers' squint hole and a Celtic cross outside. Simply furnished with wooden benches and tables,

slate floors, granite walls and exposed beams.
🏚 Q ✿ ◑ ◖ 🍷 ♣ P

Nancenoy

Trengilly Wartha
Off B3291 OS731282
☎ (0326) 40332
11–3, 6–11 (may vary)
Ind Coope Burton Ale; Tetley Bitter Ⓗ**; guest beers** Ⓖ
Delightful, remote country pub with beer-loving owners who ring the changes with a variety of guest beers. Also renowned for its food. Taunton cider sold. Excellent walks nearby. 🏚 Q 🍺 ✿ 🍴
◑ ◖ & ♣ ◯ P

Newlyn

Fishermans Arms
Fore Street ☎ (0736) 63399
10.30–2.30, 5.30–11
St Austell Tinners, HSD Ⓗ
Popular local, affording superb views over the harbour and Mount's Bay. Note the inglenook and display of memorabilia. Good value simple food. Limited parking.
🏚 ✿ ◑ ◖ ♣ P

Newquay

Buccaneer
Sutherland Hotel, 29 Mount Wise ☎ (0637) 874470
12–3 (not Mon–Fri), 7–11
Greene King Abbot; Whitbread Boddingtons Bitter Ⓗ**; guest beers**
Just up the hill from the town centre and beach, this erstwhile hotel bar has now achieved a reputation for guest beers which prove popular with local and holiday trade alike.
🏚 🍺 ✿ 🍴 ⇌ ♣ P

Padstow

Golden Lion
19 Lanadwell Street
☎ (0841) 532797
11–3, 5.30–11 (11–11 summer)
Devenish Cornish Original; Marston's Pedigree; Whitbread Boddingtons Bitter Ⓗ
Padstow's oldest pub, used as the stable for the 'Red Oss' which makes an appearance for the May Day celebrations. It has a low-beamed public bar and a spacious lounge. The full range of beers is only available in summer.
🏚 ✿ 🍴 ◑ ◖ 🍷 ♣

Penelewey

Punchbowl & Ladle
Off A39 at Playing Place
☎ (0872) 862237
11–3, 6–11
Draught Bass; Whitbread

WCPA, Boddingtons Bitter, Flowers Original Ⓗ**; guest beers**
Tastefully converted country pub with a restaurant area serving excellent food.
🍺 ✿ ◑ ◖ 🍷 ♣ P

Penzance

Fountain Tavern
St Clare Street ☎ (0736) 62673
11–2.30, 5.30–11
St Austell Bosun's, HSD Ⓗ
Unpretentious local with a real community spirit and a warm, friendly atmosphere. Off the town centre but worth visiting. Bar snacks lunchtime.
🏚 ✿ 🍴 ♣ P

Mount's Bay Inn
The Promenade, Werrytown
☎ (0736) 63027
11–2.30, 5.30–11
Draught Bass Ⓗ**; guest beers**
Small, friendly free house on the promenade towards Newlyn. The natural stone-walled bar offers three guest ales, changed regularly. The eating area is to one side. No children. 🏚 Q ◑ ◖ &

Philleigh

Roseland Inn
2½ miles off A3078 at Ruan Highlanes ☎ (0872) 580254
11–3, 6–11
Devenish Cornish Original; Whitbread Flowers IPA Ⓗ
Superb example of a 17th-century pub, unspoilt and spotless, with low beams, slate floors and plenty of local character. Excellent home-made food makes this house a winner (eve meals summer only). 🏚 Q ✿ ◑ ◖ P

Polbathic

Half Way House
On A387, half-way between Torpoint and Liskeard
☎ (0503) 30202
11–3, 5.30 (6 Sat)–11
Courage Best Bitter; Ushers Best Bitter Ⓗ
Large, roadside 16th-century coaching inn with several bars. Great home-cooked food is served in the restaurant and bars. Families and pets are welcomed. 🏚 Q 🍺 ✿ 🍴 ◑
◖ 🍷 & ⇌ (St Germans) ♣ P

Polgooth

Polgooth Inn
☎ (0726) 74689
11–3 (extends if busy), 6–11
St Austell Bosun's, XXXX Mild (summer)**, Tinners, HSD** Ⓗ
Refurbished village local with a children's room and playground. Food is a speciality. 🏚 🍺 ✿ ◑ ◖ ▲ P

Cornwall

Polperro

Blue Peter
The Quay ☎ (0503) 72743
11–11
St Austell Tinners, HSD Ⓗ;
guest beers
The smallest pub in Polperro,
reached by a steep flight of
steps adjacent to the harbour.
Bags of atmosphere; good
food; wide variety of guest
beers and local scrumpy.
Tinners Ale is sold as Blue
Peter Bitter. ♨ ⑤ ☀ ◑ ▶ ⌣

Crumplehorn Inn
The Old Mill ☎ (0503) 72348
11–11
**Draught Bass; St Austell
XXXX Mild, HSD** Ⓗ; **guest
beers**
Inn converted from an old
mill, with self-contained
chalets and bed and breakfast
accommodation adjacent.
⑤ ☀ ⌸ ◑ ▶ ⊟ & ▲ ♣ P

Porthallow

Five Pilchards
☎ (0326) 280256
11–2.30, 6–11
**Devenish Cornish Original;
Greene King Abbot** Ⓗ; **guest
beers** (summer)
Attractive rural pub on the
beach with views over to
Falmouth. Boasts a fine
collection of brass, ships'
lamps and wreck
histories. Self-catering
accommodation.
♨ Q ☀ ⌸ ◑

Porthleven

Ship Inn
Harbourside ☎ (0326) 572841
11.30–2.30, 7–11 (11.30–11 summer)
**Courage Best Bitter,
Directors; Ushers Best
Bitter** Ⓗ
Old fisherman's pub, with an
open, but rambling bar area.
Its stone walls are hung with
maritime artefacts. Superb
views over the harbour and
out to sea; look out for the
local six-oared gig practising
on summer eves. Those faint
of heart beware on stormy
days. Good home-cooked food
available. ♨ ⑤ ☀ ◑ ▶ ▲ P

Port Isaac

Golden Lion
13 Fore Street
☎ (0208) 880336
11–11 (11–2.30, 6–11 winter)
St Austell Tinners, HSD Ⓗ
Fine, unaltered pub with
several drinking areas and a
small balcony overlooking the
harbour. Beware of the
slightly uneven floor. A new
bistro has opened downstairs.
♨ ⑤ ◑ ▶ ⊟ ♣

Probus

Hawkins Arms
Fore Street
☎ (0726) 882208
11–3, 5.30–11 (11–11 Sat)
**St Austell Bosun's, XXXX
Mild, Tinners** Ⓗ, **HSD** Ⓖ *or* Ⓗ
Friendly, unpretentious local
in an attractive 17th-century
building. Welcoming to locals
and visitors alike, it has a
children's assault course in the
garden. High quality and
excellent value food. Pool
room doubles as a
family/meeting room.
♨ ⑤ ☀ ⌸ ◑ ▶ & ▲ ♣ P

Quintrell Downs

Two Clomes
East Road (A392)
☎ (0637) 873485
12–2.30, 7–11
Beer range varies Ⓗ
Clome ovens, either side of the
large open log fire, give rise to
the pub's name. Conveniently
situated on the outskirts of
Newquay, where the self-
catering chalets or campsites
provide a good base for
holidays. Up to four
frequently-changed ales. ♨ Q
⑤ ☀ ⌸ ◑ ▶ & ▲ ♣ P

Redruth

Tricky Dickies
Tolgus Mount OS684482
☎ (0209) 219292
12–3, 6–11
**Greene King Abbot;
Wadworth 6X; Whitbread
Flowers IPA** Ⓗ
Renovated old tin-mine
smithy, displaying many
artefacts. Squash/exercise
facilities are available for the
energetic. Children welcome.
The choice of beer may vary;
good food. Jazz sessions on
Tue. Q ⑤ ☀ ◑ ▶ & ▲ ♣ P

Restronguet Creek

Pandora Inn
End of Passage Hill, near A39
OS814371 ☎ (0326) 372678
11–11 (11–3, 6.30–11 winter)
**Draught Bass; St Austell
Bosun's, Tinners, HSD** Ⓗ
13th-century thatched pub at
the waterside, accessible by
both road and water. *À la carte*
restaurant upstairs.
♨ Q ⑤ ☀ ◑ ▶ ▲ P

St Agnes

Railway Inn
10 Vicarage Road
☎ (0872) 552310
11–3, 6–11
**Whitbread Boddingtons
Bitter, Flowers IPA** Ⓗ
Pub named when the railway
arrived: the railway has gone,
but not the nice village pub. It
boasts a large collection of
copper and horse brasses, and
much more.
♨ Q ⑤ ☀ ◑ ▶ & ▲ ♣ P

St Breward

Old Inn
Churchtown OS098773
☎ (0208) 850711
12–3, 6–11
**Draught Bass; John Smith's
Bitter** Ⓗ
Sturdy granite pub dating
from the 11th century, with a
slate floor, beamed ceiling and
large open fireplace. At 210m,
it is claimed to be the highest
pub in Cornwall.
♨ ⑤ ☀ ◑ ▶ ⊟ ♣ P

St Cleer

Stag Inn
Fore Street (2 miles N of
Liskeard) ☎ (0579) 342305
11–3, 6.30–11
**Draught Bass; Marston's
Pedigree; St Austell XXXX
Mild, HSD; Whitbread
Boddingtons Bitter, Flowers
Original** Ⓗ; **guest beers**
Granite moorland inn, built in
the 19th century. A friendly
atmosphere; many local
activities. Good value food.
Q ☀ ◑ ▶ ⊟ & ♣ P

St Erth

Star Inn
Church Street
☎ (0736) 752068
11–3, 5.30–11
**Marston's Pedigree;
Whitbread Boddingtons
Bitter** Ⓗ
Fine village pub with a
welcoming environment,
dripping with bric-a-brac of
all descriptions: keys,
militaria, photographs and the
largest collection of snuff in
the county. Well worth a visit.
♨ ◑ ▶ ▲ ≢ ♣ P

St Ives

Cornish Arms
Trelyon ☎ (0736) 796112
11.30 (11 summer)–2.30, 6 (5.30
summer)–11
**Whitbread Best Bitter,
Flowers Original** Ⓗ
Cosy local serving good food,
situated on the road to Carbis
Bay. ♨ Q ◑ ▶ ≢

St Just

Star
Fore Street
☎ (0736) 788767
11–3, 5.30–11
**St Austell Bosun's,
Tinners** Ⓗ, **HSD** Ⓖ
Friendly village-centre pub in
an impressive granite
building. ♨ Q ☀ ◑ ▶ ▲

St Kew

St Kew Inn
Churchtown OS022769
☎ (0208) 84259
11–2.30, 6–11 (12–2.30, 7–10.30 Sun)
St Austell Tinners, HSD G
Pleasant, unspoilt 15th-century pub with worn slate floors and a large fireplace. Very popular in summer but a quiet haven for locals in the winter. Steaks are a speciality.
🏚 Q ❀ ◑ ▮ ♣ P

St Teath

White Hart Hotel
☎ (0208) 850281
11–2.30, 6–11
Ruddles County; Ushers Best Bitter H
Fine pub in the centre of the village, opposite the clock tower. It dates from the 1700s but was greatly rebuilt in 1884; three bars, ranging from a boisterous public to a quiet snug, set in the old kitchen. Good outdoor play area.
🏚 Q ❀ ⇔ 🛏 ◑ ▮ ♣ P

Saltash

Two Bridges
Albert Road
☎ (0752) 848952
12–11
Courage Best Bitter, Directors; Ushers Founders H
Pub with a cosy, country-cottage-style interior, plus a walled garden affording river views. 🏚 ❀ ⇌ ♣

Sennen

First & Last
☎ (0736) 871680
11–2.30, 5.30–11 (may vary)
Tetley Bitter H; **guest beer**
The most westerly real ale outlet in England. The spacious, sub-divided bar originated as a church mason's dwelling, circa 1643. Good value food; very busy in the high season. The back entrance is suitable for wheelchair users.
🏚 ⇘ ❀ ◑ ▮ ♿ ▲ P

Stratton

Tree Inn
Fore Street ☎ (0288) 352038
11.30–3, 6.30–11
Draught Bass; St Austell Tinners H
16th-century coaching inn with four bars and a restaurant, set around a courtyard. Plain public bar and a comfortable saloon. Regular live folk music. Skittle alley. 🏚 ⇘ ❀ ⇔ ◑ ▮ ♣

Try also: **Kings Arms**, on A3072 (Free)

Treen

Logan Rock Inn
☎ (0736) 810495
10.30–3, 5.30–11 (10.30–11 summer)
St Austell Tinners, HSD H
Outstanding small pub near some superb coastal scenery and the Minack Open-Air Theatre. The old characterful bar offers good food and atmosphere. Named after the 65-ton cliff stone dislodged in 1824 by Lt Goldsmith.
🏚 ⇘ ❀ ◑ ▮ ♿ ▲ P

Tregrehan

Britannia
On A390, 3 miles E of St Austell
☎ (0726) 812889
11–11
Draught Bass; Courage Best Bitter; St Austell Tinners H
16th-century inn on the main road. Well-known for its good food (available all day), it has a separate restaurant and a safe garden with a play area.
Q ⇘ ❀ ◑ ▮ ♿ ♣ ▲ P

Trematon

Crooked Inn
Signed on A38
☎ (0752) 848177
11–2.30 (3 summer), 6–11
Furgusons Dartmoor Best; Ind Coope Burton Ale; Ruddles County; St Austell XXXX Mild, HSD H
A good selection of traditional ales and homely bar meals in an 18th-century farmhouse. Accommodation is in the converted stable.
🏚 ⇘ ❀ ⇔ ◑ ▮ ♿ ▲ P

Try also: **Rod & Line**, Tideford (Ushers)

Truro

City Inn
Pydar Street
☎ (0872) 72623
11–3, 5–11 (11 Fri & Sat)
Courage Best Bitter, Directors; Ruddles Best Bitter, County; John Smith's Bitter; Wadworth 6X; Webster's Yorkshire Bitter; guest beers H
Friendly local featuring good food and a garden with an aviary for families. ❀ ◑ ▮ ⇌

Old Ale House
Quay Street
☎ (0872) 71122
11–2.30, 5.30 (6.30 Sat)–11 (12–2.30, 7–10.30 Sun)
Draught Bass; Courage Directors; Ruddles County; Whitbread Boddingtons Bitter H, **Flowers Original; guest beers** G
Old ale house with a 'spit and sawdust' atmosphere: a happy

drinkers' pub normally carrying at least ten real ales, including five guests. Twice-weekly jazz sessions, excellent food and a cosmopolitan clientele complete the picture. No meals Sun lunch. ◑ ⇌

Tywardreath

New Inn
Fore Street
☎ (0726) 813901
11–2.30 (3 Sat), 6–11
Draught Bass G; **St Austell XXXX Mild** H, **Tinners** G
Popular, village local near the coast, with a secluded garden leading off the lounge. No food Sun. Q ❀ ⇔ ◑ ▮ ▲
⇌ (Par) ♣ ○ P

Upton Cross

Caradon Inn
On B3254, 6 miles N of Liskeard
☎ (0579) 62391
11.30–3, 5.30–11
Marston's Pedigree; St Austell HSD; Whitbread Flowers Original H; **guest beers**
Friendly, 17th-century slate-clad country inn. Pool and a jukebox with sixties records in the public bar and a quieter lounge. Good value food. Near the open-air theatre and a clay pigeon range. Cider in summer.
🏚 Q ❀ ◑ ▮ ♣ ○ P

Wadebridge

Ship Inn
Gonvena Hill
☎ (0208) 812839
11–3, 5.30–11 (11–11 summer)
Devenish Cornish Original; Whitbread Boddingtons Bitter H
Small, friendly 16th-century coaching inn; a fine leaded window shows the pub name. Live folk music first Sat every month.
🏚 Q ⇘ ⇔ ◑ ▮ ♣ P

Zelah

Hawkins Arms
High Road (off A30)
☎ (0872) 540339
11–3, 6–11
Ind Coope Burton Ale; Tetley Bitter H; **guest beers**
Although the village is now bypassed, this pub remains a good reason for finding the old road, especially as excellent value meals are served, along with the weekly-changed guest beers. Safe garden play area for children and B&B at good rates.
🏚 Q ⇘ ❀ ◑ ▮ ▲ ♣ P

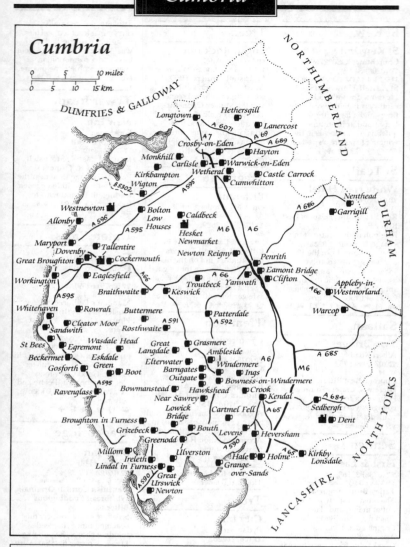

Cumbria

0 5 10 miles
0 5 10 15 km

DUMFRIES & GALLOWAY

NORTHUMBERLAND

DURHAM

NORTH YORKS

LANCASHIRE

Dent, Dent; **Hesket Newmarket**, Hesket Newmarket; **Jennings**, Cockermouth; **Yates**, Westnewton

---

Allonby

Ship Inn
Main Street
☎ (0900) 881462
12–3, 7–11 (all day when busy)
Yates Bitter Ⓗ
Seaside hotel – ample parking across the stream by the children's playground. There is also pony-riding and windsurfing nearby. Children welcome. ✿ ⌘ ◑ ◗ ⊞ ▲ ♣

Ambleside

Golden Rule
Smithy Brow (off A591 towards Kirkstone)
☎ (053 94) 32257
11–11
Robinson's Best Mild, Bitter, Hartleys XB Ⓗ
Ever-popular, no-frills, drinkers' pub, welcoming locals, students, walkers, climbers, paragliders and anyone seeking a decent pint and good 'crack'. Three rooms, two clocks, one bar but no jukebox. Usually has well-filled rolls and/or soup available. ⋈ Q ✿ ♣ P

White Lion
Market Place
☎ (053 94) 33140
11–3, 5.30–11 (may vary)
Bass Special, Draught Bass; Welsh Brewers Worthington BB Ⓗ

Busy, two-bar, town-centre pub noted for efficient service and good value food – especially the roast beef Sun lunch. The low gear handpumps get plenty of use.
Q ❀ 🛏 ◑ ▶ 🍴 ♣ P

Appleby-in-Westmorland

Royal Oak Inn
Bongate ☎ (076 83) 51463
11.30–3, 6–11
S&N Theakston Best Bitter; Yates Bitter, Younger Scotch H**; guest beers**
Excellent pub on the outskirts of town. Comfortable surroundings, with a superb corner bar, a fine stone wall and a wood-panel surround. An absolute gem.
🚶 Q ❀ 🛏 ◑ ▶ ≈ ♣ P

Barngates

Drunken Duck
Off B5286, near Hawkshead
OS351012 ☎ (053 94) 36347
11.30–3, 6–11
Jennings Bitter; Marston's Pedigree; S&N Theakston XB, Old Peculier; Whitbread Boddingtons Bitter; Yates Bitter H**; guest beers**
Among the best-known and most difficult to find pubs in the Lake District, reputed to be some 400 years-old. An amusing legend about the pub's name can be read inside. Nearly always busy, especially in summer. The good house includes vegetarian meals. Fishing available.
🚶 Q ❄ 🛏 ◑ ▶ 🅰 ♣ P

Beckermet

Royal Oak Inn
Holly View ☎ (0946) 841551
11–3, 5.30–11
Jennings Bitter, Cumberland Ale H
Cosy and interesting village pub with several small rooms and a small restaurant. Children welcome in the games room.
🚶 Q ❀ 🛏 ◑ ▶ ♣ P

Bolton Low Houses

Oddfellows Arms
Off A595, Carlisle–Cockermouth road
12–3, 7–11
Jennings Bitter; Whitbread Boddingtons Bitter H
Very friendly village local, with mock Tudor decoration. Beware of outdoor drinking due to the farm next door.
Q 🛏 ▶ ◑ & P

Boot

Burnmoor
☎ (094 67) 23224
11–3, 5–11
Jennings Bitter, Cumberland Ale H
Traditional lakeland inn, dating from 1578 in parts. Meals include authentic Austrian dishes. Scafell Pike, La'al Ratty (Dalegarth station), waterfalls and superb walks are all nearby. The landlord will collect those arriving by train for a walking holiday. Children's adventure play area in the garden.
🚶 Q ❀ 🛏 ◑ ▶ P

Bouth

White Hart
Off A590 between Newby Bridge and Ulverston
OS329856 ☎ (0229) 861229
12–3, 6–11 (12–11 Thu–Sat in summer)
Ind Coope Burton Ale; Jennings Bitter; Robinson's Hartleys XB; Tetley Bitter; Whitbread Boddingtons Bitter H
17th-century coaching inn by the village green, with a games room and collections of clay pipes and barrel shive rings. Live music Sun night; quiz night alternate Mon. Good food; families welcome. The house cats are usually to be found in the bar. 🚶 Q ⛄ ❀ 🛏 ◑ 🅰 ♣ ⌂ P

Bowmanstead

Ship Inn
On A593 near Coniston (signposted) ☎ (053 94) 41224
11–3 (summer only), 5.30–11
Robinson's Hartleys XB H
Comfortable, welcoming local at the heart of the Lakes. The snug, adjoining the main bar, is used as a family and/or games room.
Q ⛄ ❀ 🛏 ◑ ▶ 🅰 P

Try also: Sun Inn (Free)

Bowness-on-Windermere

Hole in T'Wall (New Hall Inn)
Lowside ☎ (053 94) 43488
11–11
Robinson's Best Mild, Hartleys XB, Best Bitter H
The oldest pub in Bowness, boasting many interesting features; the ceiling is worth a look. Games room downstairs and a dining/family room upstairs. Good value food (not eves Jan–Easter). Very busy through the summer.
🚶 Q ⛄ ❀ ◑ ♣

Braithwaite

Coledale Inn
Off A66 ☎ (076 87) 78272
11–11
Yates Bitter H
Village pub and hotel on the site of an old pencil factory. The house beer, Coledale XXPS, is Younger Scotch. Tarzan-type play area for children; lovely front garden with views of Skiddaw.
🚶 ❀ 🛏 ◑ ▶ 🛏 🅰 ♣ P

Broughton in Furness

Manor Arms
The Square ☎ (0229) 716286
12 (2 Mon–Thu in winter)–11
S&N Theakston Best Bitter; Yates Bitter H**; guest beers**
Popular village pub run by a real ale enthusiast: Taylor Landlord is often available. Pool played. Snacks available. Irish setters can often be found in the bar. 🚶 Q ❀ 🛏 🅰 ♣

Buttermere

Bridge Hotel
☎ (076 87) 70252
11–11
McEwan 80/-; S&N Theakston Best Bitter, Old Peculier, XB; Younger No. 3 H
Pub, originally a cornmill and first licensed 1735, which has had various names, including 'The Victoria', after the queen who stayed here. Interesting memorabilia around the bar area. A good choice of traditional Cumbrian dishes and real ale dishes on the menu. Walkers, leave muddy boots at the door! Families welcome.
🚶 Q ❀ 🛏 ◑ ▶ 🛏 🅰 ⌂ P

Caldbeck

Oddfellows
☎ (069 98) 227
12–3, 6.30–11
Jennings Cumberland Ale H
Pleasant village inn which has undergone sympathetic refurbishment; previously known as the John Peel. Excellent value food is freshly prepared; occasional foreign cuisine nights.
🚶 Q ❀ 🛏 ◑ ▶ & ♣ P

Try also: Old Crown, Hesket Newmarket

Carlisle

Gosling Bridge
Kingstown Road (A7, ¾ mile S of M6 jct 44) ☎ (0228) 515294
11–11
Greenalls Bitter, Thomas Greenall's Bitter; Stones Best Bitter H

Cumbria

Large, comfortable, modern roadside inn of unusual design, where friendly service is assured. Meals served all day Suns and bank hols.
🏠 Q 🏡 ◐ ▣ & ♣ P ⚥

Howard Arms
Lowther Street ☎ (0228) 32926
11–11
S&N Theakston Best Bitter, XB Ⓗ
Consistently excellent city-centre pub, partitioned to give a multi-room effect. Can be a squeeze most nights, but enjoys a great atmosphere. Retains the tiled frontage and an impressive collection of State Management bottles. ❀ ◐ ⇌

Turf Tavern
Newmarket Road
☎ (0228) 515367
11–11 (occasional late licence to 1am Fri & Sat)
Marston's Pedigree; Whitbread Boddingtons Bitter, Flowers IPA Ⓗ**; guest beer**
Excellently renovated former racecourse grandstand, offering good, friendly service.
❀ & P

Woolpack Inn
Milbourne Street
☎ (0228) 32459
11–3, 5.15–11 (11–11 Fri & Sat)
Jennings Mild, Bitter, Cumberland Ale Ⓗ
Eighteen consecutive years in the *Guide*! A large local with an extraordinarily warm welcome in a spacious lounge, a snug bar and a games room. A mural depicts Carlisle's history. After a short time you'll feel you've been a regular for years! Large selection of malt whiskies. Live jazz Thu and second Sun of month; other live music Fri.
❀ 🏡 ◐ ▣ ⇌ ♣ P

Cartmel Fell

Masons Arms
Strawberry Bank (between Gummers How and Bowland Bridge) OS413895
☎ (053 95) 68486
11.30–3, 6–11
Lakeland Amazon, Great Northern, Big Six, Damson; S&N Theakston XB; Thwaites Bitter Ⓗ**; guest beers**
Extremely popular Lakeland pub carrying an enormous selection of bottled beers from all over the world. Home of the Lakeland Brewery Co. Very popular for its wide food range. 🏠 Q 🏠 ❀ 🏡 ◐ ▣ P

Castle Carrock

Weary Sportsman
Signed from Brampton along B6413 ☎ (0228) 70230
11–2.30, 6–11

Whitbread Chester's Mild, Boddingtons Bitter, Trophy Ⓗ
Old country inn popular with locals and visitors. Picturesque in summer with flower boxes, etc. outside. Relaxed atmosphere in the bar and lounge.
🏠 Q ❀ 🏡 ◐ ▣ & ▲ ♣ P

Try also: Hare & Hounds, Talkin (Free)

Cleator Moor

Derby Arms
Ennerdale Road
☎ (0946) 810779
11–4, 5–11
S&N Theakston Best Bitter, XB Ⓗ
Lively and interesting pub for the adventurous drinker. ❀ ♣

Clifton

George & Dragon
On A6, 3 miles S of Penrith
☎ (0768) 65381
11–3, 6.30–11 (may vary)
Ind Coope Burton Ale; Tetley Bitter Ⓗ
Excellent example of a traditional Cumbrian inn, stone-built and set back from the main road in the middle of a cottage terrace. Pool-cum-family room and a separate restaurant serving excellent food.
🏠 🏠 ❀ 🏡 ◐ ▣ & ▲ ♣ P

Cockermouth

Swan Inn
Kirkgate ☎ (0900) 822425
11–3, 7–11
Jennings Bitter, Cumberland Ale (summer) Ⓗ
Popular pub on a cobbled Georgian square, near All Saints church. Boasts a huge selection of whiskies. Q ▲ ♣

Crook

Sun Inn
On B5284
☎ (0539) 821351
11–11 (11–3, 6–11 Nov–Easter)
Draught Bass; S&N Theakston Best Bitter; Whitbread Boddingtons Bitter; Younger IPA Ⓗ
Attractive, comfortable pub on the route from Kendal to the Windermere ferry. Separate areas for games and dining (good value home-made meals). 🏠 ❀ ◐ ▲ ♣ P

Crosby-on-Eden

Stag
☎ (0228) 573210
12–3, 6–11
Jennings Mild, Bitter, Cumberland Ale Ⓗ
Lovely, olde-worlde pub with superb stonework and low

beams. Real food is served upstairs in the restaurant.
❀ ◐ ▣ ♣ P

Cumwhitton

Pheasant
A69 from Carlisle, turn right at Warwick Bridge, follow signs ☎ (0228) 560102
11–11
Hesket Newmarket Doris's 90th Birthday Ale; S&N Theakston Best Bitter, XB Ⓗ
Pub built in 1690 and offering a step back in time with its original stone-flagged floor, fireplace, beams and antique furniture, including a genuine old horsehair sofa. Old prints of local interest – birds, animals and sporting pursuits – cover the walls.
🏠 Q ❀ 🏡 ◐ ▣ ▣ ▲ ♣ P

Dent

Sun Inn
Main Street
☎ (058 75) 208
11–2.30, 7–11 (11–11 school hols)
Dent Bitter, Ramsbottom; S&N Theakston XB Ⓗ**; Younger Scotch** Ⓔ
Friendly, traditional village local with a well-used dominoes table and a separate games room. The first brewery tap for Dent beers. Local CAMRA *Pub of the Year* 1990. A good start/end for walkers and cyclists. Eve meals finish at 8.30.
🏠 Q ❀ 🏡 ◐ ▣ ♣ P ⚥

Try also: George & Dragon (Free)

Dovenby

Ship Inn
☎ (0900) 828097
11–3, 5.30–11 (11–11 Sat)
Jennings Bitter, Cumberland Ale Ⓗ
Friendly village pub with a garden play area for children.
🏠 ❀ 🏡 ◐ ▣ ♣ P

Eaglesfield

Black Cock Inn
Off A5086, 2 miles SW of Cockermouth
☎ (0900) 822989
11–3.30, 6–11 (11–11 Sat)
Jennings Bitter Ⓗ
Cosy, village-centre pub, with the same landlady for many years. The brass-hung interior offers traditional pub games.
🏠 Q ❀ & ♣ P

Eamont Bridge

Beehive
☎ (0768) 62081
11–3, 6–11 (11–11 summer)
Draught Bass; Whitbread Castle Eden Ale Ⓗ

Friendly roadside inn, on the outskirts of Penrith, serving good, wholesome food. Unusual hexagonal pool table. The garden has a large children's play area.
❀ ◐◑ ♿ ▲ ⇌ ♣ P

Egremont

Blue Bell
Market Place ☎ (0946) 820581
11–3, 6–11 (12–2, 7–10.30 Sun)
Robinson's Best Bitter, Hartleys XB Ⓗ
Unpretentious modernisation with a fishing theme, in a pub where children are welcome. Long, safe garden with a nice lawn. Occasional quizzes. Free public car park behind the pub. ♛ ❀

Elterwater

Britannia
Off B5343 ☎ (096 67) 210/382
11–11
Jennings Mild, Bitter; Marston's Pedigree; Mitchell's Best Bitter Ⓗ
Very popular traditional pub at the heart of the Lake District. The back bar is open if the patio-green is full. Bulmers cider available. Always worth a visit.
♛ Q ♘ ❀ 🛏 ◐◑ ⊟ ♣ ⌓

Eskdale Green

Bower House Inn
☎ (094 67) 23244
11–3, 6–11
Robinson's Hartleys XB; Ruddles Best Bitter; Younger Scotch Ⓗ
Very attractive country inn featuring low beams, oak settles and excellent meals. The large, enclosed garden has a small stream. A very short walk from Irton Road station on the Ravenglass & Eskdale steam railway.
♛ Q ❀ 🛏 ◐◑ ▲ P

Garrigill

George & Dragon
Signed off B6277 from Alston (on the Pennine Way)
☎ (0434) 381293
12–3, 7–11 (maybe all day in summer)
McEwan 70/-; S&N Theakston Best Bitter, XB, Old Peculier Ⓗ**; guest beer**
Excellent free house and restaurant, popular with fell walkers and hikers. Has retained its stone-flagged floor in front of the large open fire.
♛ Q ♘ 🛏 ◐◑ ♿ ▲ ♣ P

Gosforth

Olde Lion & Lamb
The Square ☎ (094 67) 25242
11 (12 winter)–11
Ruddles Best Bitter; S&N Theakston XB; Younger IPA Ⓗ
Cosy and busy, two-roomed local at the heart of a lovely, large village. Good meals available; children welcome. Parking is limited but there is a large public car park nearby.
♛ ❀ ◐◑ ♣ P

Grange-over-Sands

Hardcragg Hall Hotel
Grange Fell Road
☎ (053 95) 33353
11–3, 6–11
Thwaites Best Mild, Bitter Ⓗ**; guest beers**
Elegant 16th-century former manor house with wood-panelled bars and dining rooms. Good views of the village and the sea. A warm welcome is assured from both the owner and the enormous real fire. ♛ Q ♘ ❀ 🛏 ◐◑ ▲ ⇌ ♣ P

Grasmere

Travellers Rest
On A591
☎ (053 94) 35378
11–3, 6–11 (11–11 Apr–Nov)
Jennings Bitter, Cumberland Ale Ⓗ
Attractive, roadside pub with a games/family room, a dining area and a separate dining room. Good views to be had in all directions; situated on the well-known Coast to Coast walk.
♛ Q ♘ ❀ 🛏 ◐◑ ▲ ♣ P

Great Broughton

Punchbowl Inn
Main Street
☎ (0900) 824708
11–3 (not Mon except bank hols), 6.30–11 (may vary)
Jennings Bitter Ⓗ
Small, friendly village pub with a cosy atmosphere. Traditional pub games always available. ♛ ◐◑ ♿ ♣ P

Great Langdale

Old Dungeon Ghyll Hotel
On B5343 at head of valley OS285061 ☎ (096 67) 272
11–11
Marston's Merrie Monk, Pedigree; S&N Theakston Mild, XB, Old Peculier; Yates Bitter Ⓗ**; guest beers**
Popular walkers' and climbers' bar in an idyllic setting below the Langdale Pikes. CAMRA *Pub of the Year* finalist in 1990, recognisable from almost every TV series/film set in the Lake District.
♛ Q ❀ 🛏 ◐◑ ▲ ⌓ P

Great Urswick

Derby Arms
☎ (0229) 56348
12–3 (12–11 Sat & bank hols), 5.30–11
Robinson's Best Mild, Bitter, Hartleys XB Ⓗ
Real village local with a warm friendly welcome. The snug off the main bar room is suitable for families.
♛ ♘ ❀ P

Try also: General Burgoyne (Robinson's)

Greenodd

Machells Arms
Main Street ☎ (0229) 861246
11–3, 6–11
Greenalls Thomas Greenall's Bitter; Ind Coope Burton Ale; Tetley Mild, Bitter Ⓗ
Small, friendly village local supplying good home-cooked food and very reasonably-priced B&B. Also pool, darts and Sky TV.
♛ Q 🛏 ◐◑ ♣ P

Grizebeck

Greyhound
At A5092/A595 jct
☎ (0229) 89224
12–3 (not Mon–Thu, Jan–Feb), 6–11
Courage Directors; John Smith's Bitter Ⓗ
Village local in a former farmhouse where families are welcome. The floor is made from slate from the local quarry; note the unusually-shaped oak bar top. Good food available, plus pool, darts and a jukebox.
♛ ❀ ◐◑ ♿ ♣ P

Hale

King's Arms
On A6, 1/2 mile S of Beetham
☎ (053 95) 63203
11–3, 6–11
Mitchell's Best Bitter Ⓗ
A popular lunchtime halt; an L-shaped bar with settles and a smaller room off. Family room upstairs. The pub has its own bowling green. No food Sun. ♛ ♘ ❀ ◐◑ ♣ P

Hawkshead

Red Lion Inn
☎ (053 94) 36213
11–11
Jennings Bitter; Tetley Bitter Ⓗ**; guest beers**
15th-century coaching inn at the village centre, popular with youngsters. Good food, including pizzas and local trout.
♛ Q ❀ 🛏 ◐◑ ▲ ♣ ⌓ P

Try also: Queens Head (Robinson's)

Cumbria

Hayton

Stone Inn
☎ (0228) 70498
11–3, 5.30–11 (11–11 Sat)
Jennings Cumberland Ale; Mitchell's Best Bitter; S&N Theakston Best Bitter; Tetley Bitter Ⓗ
Very comfortable village local with an attractive stone bar and fireplace. Serves a range of unusual toasties. 🏚 Q ♣ P

Hethersgill

Black Lion
Off A6071, 2¹⁄₂ miles N of Smithsfield ☎ (0228) 75318
11–11 (may vary)
Draught Bass Ⓗ; guest beer
Convivial country local, well worth a visit. Doubles as the village post office. Self-catering cottage available.
❀ 🏚 ⏣ & ♣ P

Heversham

Blue Bell
Princes Way ☎ (053 95) 62018
11–3, 6–11
Samuel Smith OBB, Museum Ⓗ
Over 500 years-old, this former vicarage was much enlarged during the heyday of the A6. A traditional bar/games room, a lounge bar and dining room ensure that all tastes are satisfied. The only Sam Smith's pub in Cumbria, close to Levens Hall.
🏚 ⛄ ❀ 🏚 ⏣ ⏣ ♣ P

Holme

Smithy
Milnthorpe Road
☎ (0524) 781302
11.45–3, 6–11
Thwaites Best Mild, Bitter Ⓔ
A large lounge which can be crowded summer weekends, and a smaller, slate-floored, vault. Play area in the garden.
🏚 ⛄ ❀ ⏣ ⏣ & ♣ P

Ings

Watermill Inn
School Lane (off A591 at Ings church) ☎ (0539) 821309
12–3, 6–11
S&N Theakston Best Bitter, XB, Old Peculier Ⓗ; guest beers
Increasingly popular pub, now three years-old! Has an ever-changing range of up to seven guest beers, including a mild; cider in summer. Voted CAMRA branch *Pub of the Year* 1991. Good food, using local produce. Wheelchair WC. What better welcome could you find at the entrance to the Lake District?
🏚 Q ❀ 🏚 ⏣ ⏣ & ♣ ⊂ P

Ireleth

Bay Horse
Ireleth Brow (A595)
☎ (0229) 63755
7–11 (12–2, 7–10.30 Sun)
Jennings Mild, Bitter, Cumberland Ale, Sneck Lifter Ⓗ
Friendly, 18th-century country pub, popular with locals and visitors alike, featuring original oak beams throughout. The games room hosts regular darts, pool and quiz nights. Other Jennings products on sale.
🏚 Q ❀ ≷ (Askam) ♣ P

Kendal

Burgundys Wine Bar
19 Lowther Street
☎ (0539) 733803
11–2.30, 6.30–11 (closed Sun lunch & Mon)
Stones Best Bitter Ⓗ; guest beers
A former labour exchange, now a thriving continental-style wine bar – with a difference! It offers two guest beers which change with bewildering regularity (refer to the chalk board if in doubt). A real boost to the real ale scene in Kendal. Eve meals by arrangement in winter. ⏣ ♦ ≷

Ring O'Bells
Kirkland ☎ (0539) 720326
12–3, 5–11 (may vary)
Vaux Lorimers Best Scotch, Extra Special; Wards Sheffield Best Bitter Ⓗ
Pub standing on consecrated ground. The snug remains unspoilt, with a welcoming fire. Good value home-made meals. Listen for the bells ringing out on Wed eves!
🏚 Q ❀ 🏚 ⏣ ⏣ ⏣ ♣

Sawyers Arms
139 Stricklandgate
☎ (0539) 729737
11.30–4, 6.30-11 (11–11 Fri, Sat & summer)
Robinson's Best Bitter, Hartleys XB Ⓗ, **Old Tom** (winter) Ⓖ
Pub full of local character/s! Note the Hartleys etched window and the 50s/60s jukebox selection. Beers are dispensed by 1936 Gaskell & Chambers handpumps.
🏚 ≷ ♣

Keswick

Bank Tavern
Main Street ☎ (076 87) 72663
11–11
Jennings Mild, Bitter, Cumberland Ale, Sneck Lifter Ⓗ
Popular local in the town centre. Q ⛄ ❀ 🏚 ⏣ ⏣ ▲ ♣

Dog & Gun
Lake Road ☎ (076 87) 73463
11–3, 6–11
S&N Theakston Best Bitter, XB, Old Peculier Ⓗ
Busy town-centre pub, popular for food. 🏚 ⏣ ▲ 🅰

Kirkbampton

Rose & Crown
☎ (0228) 576492
7–11 (7–10.30 Sun)
Wilson's Mild, Webster's Yorkshire Bitter; guest beer Ⓗ
A two-roomed local that has not been spoiled; very popular for dominoes. Always has a beer on the guest pump.
🏚 Q ⛄ ❀ ⏣ ♣

Kirkby Lonsdale

Sun
Market Street ☎ (052 42) 71965
11–11
Dent Bitter; Whitbread Boddingtons Bitter; Younger Scotch, No. 3 Ⓗ
Pub with a 17th-century colonnaded facade: the interior is not original but contrives an olde-worlde atmosphere with some nice touches. Food is recommended. 🏚 🏚 ⏣ ♦ ♣

Lanercost

Abbey Bridge Inn (Blacksmiths Bar)
Off A69 near Brampton
☎ (069 77) 2224
11–2, 7–11 (may extend in summer)
Yates Bitter Ⓗ; guest beers
One of the best pubs in the county: no jukebox, bandits or videos; just a totally relaxed atmosphere in a superbly converted 17th-century smithy. Excellent food in the restaurant above the bar. Miss this pub at your peril.
🏚 Q ❀ 🏚 ⏣ ♦ & 🅰 ♣ P

Levens

Hare & Hounds
Off A590 ☎ (053 95) 60408
11–3, 6–11
Vaux Samson, Double Maxim; Wards Sheffield Best Bitter Ⓗ
Pleasant, three-roomed pub which caters for all tastes: diners in the lounge, drinkers in the tap room (no children) and pool fans in the ex-cellar. The beer range may vary. Good value food (not served Sun–Tue eve, Nov–Mar).
Q ❀ ⏣ ♦ ⏣ ♣ P

Lindal in Furness

Railway Inn
London Road ☎ (0229) 62889
7.30–11 (12–11 Sat)
Jennings Cumberland Ale Ⓗ; guest beer

Friendly village local where you'll find good conversation. Children's play area in the garden. The guest beer changes regularly. 🏮 Q ⚘

Longtown

Graham Arms Hotel
English Street ☎ (0228) 791213
11–11
Jennings Bitter; S&N Theakston Best Bitter; Tetley Bitter; Whitbread Boddingtons Bitter H**; guest beer**
Attractive coaching inn with welcoming hosts and comfortable accommodation. Any two of the above beers are on sale.
🏮 Q ⚓ ⚘ 🛏 ◖▶ & ♣ P

Lowick Bridge

Red Lion Inn
1 mile from A5092/A5084 jct
OS292865 ☎ (0229) 85366
11–3.30, 6 (6.30 winter)–11
Robinson's Best Mild, Hartleys XB, Best Bitter H
Excellent country pub – a focal point for the community and popular with visitors and walkers. Good food, including an excellent Sun lunch. Families welcome. The garden offers mountain views.
🏮 Q ⚘ ◖▶ ♣ P

Maryport

Captain Nelson Tavern
Irish Street, South Quay
☎ (0900) 813109
11–11
Whitbread Castle Eden Ale H
One large, comfortable room resembling 'below deck' on a ship. Live music Wed and bank hols. Overlooks the harbour and marina. ◖ ≢

Millom

Station
Salthouse Road
☎ (0229) 772223
11–3, 6–11 (11–11 Fri & Sat)
S&N Theakston Best Bitter H
Large, friendly, comfortable Victorian pub displaying pictures of local history and railways. Popular with younger drinkers; live entertainment Fri. Busy at weekends: traditional Sunday lunches are a speciality.
⚘ ◖▶ 🍴 & ≢ ♣ P

Try also: Miners Arms, Silecroft (Free)

Monkhill

Drovers Rest
☎ (0228) 576591
12–3, 5.30–11 (12–11 Sat)
Jennings Mild, Bitter H

Traditional-style pub, skilfully enlarged. 🏮 ⚓ ♣ P

Near Sawrey

Tower Bank Arms
On B5285 ☎ (053 94) 36334
11–3, 6 (5.30 summer)–11
S&N Theakston Mild, Best Bitter, XB, Old Peculier; Younger Scotch H
Pub with a traditional Lake District slate-flagged floor and a kitchen range. Excellent atmosphere. Separate dining room available (good food). Owned by the NT and a short walk from Beatrix Potter's former home. It featured in her book *Jemima Puddleduck*.
🏮 Q ⚘ 🛏 ◖▶ & ♣ P

Nenthead

Miners Arms
Take A689 from Alston towards Stanhope
☎ (0434) 381427
12–3, 7–11
Beer range varies H
At 1500ft above sea level, this is probably the highest village pub in England. It offers national prize-winning cuisine and a friendly atmosphere. Three handpumps serve different ales, changed weekly.
🏮 Q ⚘ 🛏 ◖▶ & 🅰 ♣ P

Newton

Farmers Arms
Off main road
☎ (0229) 62607
11–3 (Thu & Fri only), 6.30 (7 winter)–11 (11–11 Sat)
Thwaites Best Mild, Bitter H
Large, welcoming village pub with a very attractive interior of wooden beams and stone fireplaces. Bar billiards and bar skittles played.
🏮 Q ⚘ ◖▶ 🍴 ♣ P

Newton Reigny

Sun Inn
W of Penrith ☎ (0768) 67055
11–3, 6–11 (may vary; 11–11 Sat)
Ruddles Best Bitter H**; guest beers**
Large village pub, serving excellent value food and regular guest beers. The unusual jukebox offers a wide range of music.
🏮 ⚓ ⚘ 🛏 ◖▶ & 🅰 ♣ P

Outgate

Outgate Inn
On B5286 Hawkshead–Ambleside road
☎ (053 94) 36413
11–3, 6–11
Robinson's Hartleys XB, Best Bitter H
Friendly rural pub serving good helpings of good value

food. Live traditional jazz every Fri night – get there early if you want a seat!
🏮 Q ⚘ 🛏 ◖▶ 🅰 ♣ P

Patterdale

White Lion Hotel
☎ (076 84) 82214
11–11
S&N Theakston Best Bitter; Whitbread Castle Eden Ale H
Pub surrounded by hills (walkers welcome); a good place to relax after a day on the fells. 🛏 ◖▶ 🅰 P

Penrith

Lowther Arms
Queen Street ☎ (0768) 62792
11–2.30, 7–11
S&N Theakston Best Bitter, XB H
Cosy, atmospheric and welcoming town-centre pub. Eve meals by arrangement.
🏮 ◖ & ≢ ♣

Ravenglass

Ratty Arms
☎ (0229) 717676
11–3, 6–11 (11–11 when busy)
Jennings Bitter; Ruddles Best Bitter, County H**; guest beers**
Cheerful, friendly local, converted from a railway station, with lots of railway memorabilia. Next to the main line and the narrow gauge steam (La'al Ratty) railway stations. Also handy for the Roman bathhouse and Muncaster Castle. Tasty wholesome food served.
🏮 Q ⚓ ⚘ ◖▶ ≢ P

Rosthwaite

Scafell Hotel (Riverside Bar)
☎ (076 87) 77208
11–11
S&N Theakston Best Bitter, XB, Old Peculier H
Welcoming real ale bar at the rear of a country hotel in a beautiful valley. Children welcomed. Open from 8.30am for campers' breakfast and flask-filling. A popular stop on the Coast to Coast walk. Walkers' and climbers' muddy boots aren't frowned on! Occasional music – mainly folk. 🏮 Q ⚘ 🛏 ◖▶ 🅰 P

Rowrah

Stork Hotel
Rowrah Road (A5086)
☎ (0946) 861213
11–3, 6–11
Jennings Mild, Bitter H
A well established family-run local, which has recently become a free house. Snacks (sausages, etc.) are available.

An international karting track is a half-mile away.
🚗 ❀ 🛏 ♣ P

St Bees

Oddfellows Arms
91 Main Street (B5345, 400 yds S of station) ☎ (0946) 822317
Lunch hours vary, 6.30–11
Jennings Bitter Ⓗ
Cosy village local serving lunches on Sun and on summer Sats.
🚗 Q ❀ ◑ ⊟ 🛏 ▲ ≢ ♣ P

Sandwith

Dog & Partridge
☎ (0946) 692671
12–3, 7–11 (all day summer if busy)
Draught Bass; Yates Bitter Ⓗ; guest beers (occasionally)
Cosy, friendly village pub at St Bees end of the Coast to Coast long distance walk. No accommodation but they'll try to get you fixed up in the village if you ask. Occasional tent allowed next to the pub.
❀ ◑ ♣ P

Sedbergh

Red Lion
Finkle Street
☎ (053 96) 20433
11.30–3, 6.30–11
Jennings Mild, Bitter, Cumberland Ale, Sneck Lifter Ⓗ
Well-established pub, recently purchased by Jennings from Marston's. Popular with locals and visitors, it offers home-made 'no junk' food. Unusual covered outside area at the rear. ❀ ◑ ▶ ▲ ♣

Tallentire

Bush Inn
☎ (0900) 823707
12–3, 6–11
S&N Theakston XB Ⓗ
The centre of a small rural village community. No food Tue. Yucca is played on Wed.
🚗 ❀ ◑ ♣ P

Troutbeck

Troutbeck Inn
Just off A66, Penrith–Keswick road ☎ (076 84) 83635
12–3 (not Mon–Fri in winter), 6–11
Draught Bass Ⓗ
Former Greenalls house set just off the A66: a pleasant inn with a friendly welcome. An additional beer may be available. Good food.
🚗 ❀ 🛏 ◑ ⊟ 🛏 ⑆ ▲ ♣ P

Ulverston

Kings Head
Queen Street (just off A590) ☎ (0229) 52892
11–3, 6–11 (11–11 Thu–Sat)

S&N Theakston Best Bitter; Younger Scotch, No. 3 Ⓗ; guest beer
Friendly market town pub about 300 years old, with its own bowling green and a resident (friendly) ghost.
🚗 ❀ ◑ ⑆ ≢

Swan Inn
Swan Street
☎ (0229) 52519
12–3, 6–11 (11–11 Sat)
Robinson's Hartleys XB, Best Bitter Ⓗ
Comfortable, friendly pub with a splendid etched front window. ⌔ ◑ ▶ ≢ ♣

Warcop

Chamley Arms
☎ (076 83) 41237
11–11
Jennings Bitter, Cumberland Ale, Sneck Lifter (summer) Ⓗ
Popular village local, near the army barracks; a former Marston's house, now serving Jennings fine beers, following Marston's exodus from Cumbria. 🚗 ❀ 🛏 ◑ ⊟ ♣

Warwick-on-Eden

Queens Arms
Off A69, 4 miles from Carlisle ☎ (0228) 560699
12–3, 5–11 (11–3, 6–11 Sat)
Greenalls Thomas Greenall's Bitter; Ind Coope Burton Ale; S&N Theakston Best Bitter; Tetley Bitter Ⓗ
Comfortable 18th-century inn, with an open fire and traditional furnishings; well worth a detour off the main Carlisle–Newcastle road. Separate restaurant.
🚗 Q ❀ 🛏 ◑ ▶ ♣ P

Wasdale Head

Wasdale Head Inn
OS187089
☎ (094 67) 26229
11–11 (6–11 Fri; 12–3, 6–11 Sat; 12–3 only winter Sun)
Jennings Bitter; S&N Theakston Best Bitter, Old Peculier; Yates Bitter Ⓗ
In the shadow of England's highest mountain and at the head of England's deepest lake, set in a hauntingly beautiful landscape, this inn was first opened as 'The Huntsman' by Will Ritson, a renowned liar and entrepreneur. Popular with climbers and fellwalkers. CAMRA West Pennines *Pub of the Year* 1991.
Q ⌔ ❀ 🛏 ◑ ▶ ▲ ♣ P

Wetheral

Wheatsheaf
☎ (0228) 560686
11–3, 6–11

Greenalls Bitter, Thomas Greenall's Bitter Ⓗ
Very comfortable pub with an easy atmosphere and an award-winning real food menu. Well-kept garden for summer. 🚗 ❀ ◑ ▶ ≢ ♣ P

Try also: Kilorran Hotel (S&N)

Whitehaven

Sun Inn
Main Street, Hensingham
☎ (0946) 695149
12–4, 6.30–11
Jennings Bitter Ⓗ
Small, traditional pub with loyal regulars. Q ♣

Try also: Central, Duke St (S&N); **Golden Fleece** (Jennings)

Wigton

Victoria
King Street ☎ (069 73) 42672
11–11
Jennings Mild, Bitter Ⓗ
Comfortable local in the centre of the town, virtually opposite the bus station. No meals served, but toasties, pizzas and sandwiches are available.
⑆ ≢ ♣ P

Windermere

Grey Walls Hotel (Greys Inn)
Elleray Road ☎ (053 94) 43741
11–11
S&N Theakston Mild, Best Bitter, XB, Old Peculier Ⓗ; guest beer
Pub at the edge of the village centre, with a bar/games area and dining and family facilities. Noted for its large helpings of home-made food – look out for the jumbo mixed grill. Meals served all day Sat.
🚗 ⌔ ❀ 🛏 ◑ ▶ ≢ ♣ P

Workington

George IV
Stanley Street (near harbour)
☎ (0900) 602266
11–3, 7–11
Jennings Bitter Ⓗ
Cosy back-street local.
🚗 Q ≢ ♣

Yanwath

Gate Inn
12–3, 6.30–11 (11–11 summer, may vary)
S&N Theakston Best Bitter; Yates Bitter Ⓗ; guest beers (summer)
Excellent three-roomed pub; one room serves as a restaurant with good value food. 🚗 Q ❀ ◑ ▶ ▲ ♣ P

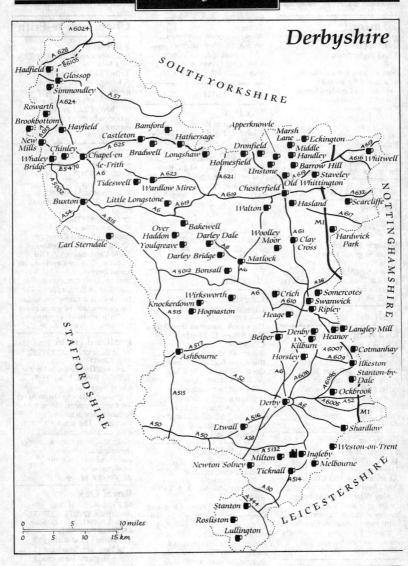

Derbyshire

 Lloyds, Ingleby

Apperknowle

Yellow Lion
High Street
☎ (0246) 413181
12–2 (3 Sat), 6–11
Adnams Bitter; Greene King Abbot; Stones Best Bitter; Tetley Bitter Ⓗ**; guest beers**
Busy, stone-built village free house with a comfortable lounge and a separate restaurant. An extensive menu includes vegetarian dishes. Winner of CAMRA awards. ⊛ ◑ ◗ P

Ashbourne

Smiths Tavern
St Johns Street (B5035)
☎ (0335) 42264
11–3, 5–11
Marston's Merrie Monk, Pedigree Ⓗ
Oldest pub in Ashbourne, on the site of a pilgrims' retreat. Characterful interior with interesting old furniture in the back room. No eve meals Sun. ◑ ◗ ♣

Bakewell

Manners
Haddon Road ☎ (0629) 812756
11–11
Robinson's Best Bitter Ⓔ
Recently refurbished pub frequented mainly by locals, but tourists also in summer.
♨ ⊛ ⇌ ◑ ▲ ♣ P

Derbyshire

Bamford

Derwent
Main Road ☎ (0433) 51395
11–11
Stones Best Bitter; Wards Sheffield Best Bitter; Whitbread Boddingtons Bitter Ⓗ; **guest beers**
Country hotel dating from 1890 with tap room, two lounge areas and a dining room (reasonably-priced, home-made food). A friendly and unspoilt haven in the heart of the Peak District.
⌂ ❀ ⇥ ◖▶ ⊞ ▲ ⇌ ♣ P

Barrow Hill

Barrow
Station Road
☎ (0246) 472277
11–11
Draught Bass; Stones Best Bitter Ⓗ; **guest beers**
Traditional Victorian local with unusual graffiti. Meeting place of the local canal society. Usually four guest beers.
⌂ ⊞ ♣ P

Belper

Old Kings Head
1 Days Lane (off Cheapside) ✓
☎ (0773) 821497
11.30–3.30, 7–11 (11–11 Fri & Sat)
Marston's Pedigree Ⓗ
Early 15th-century inn on a quiet lane near the town centre: a multi-roomed friendly pub used by a folk club. Lunches Thu–Sat only.
♨ Q ◖▶ ⇌ ♣

Queens Head
29 Chesterfield Road
☎ (0773) 825525
12 (4 Mon)–11
Ansells Mild; Ind Coope ABC Best Bitter, Burton Ale; Tetley Bitter Ⓗ; **guest beers**
Large pub with a roomy lounge and a delightful snug with bench seats. Across the corridor is a family room with a jukebox and toys.
♨ Q ⌂ ❀ ◖▶ ⇌ ♣

Bonsall

Kings Head
62 Yeoman Street
☎ (0629) 822703
12–3, 6–11
Ind Coope Burton Ale; Tetley Bitter Ⓗ; **guest beer**
Traditional, unspoilt village local, with a good atmosphere and home-cooked food.
♨ Q ❀ ◖▶ ⊞ ⇌ ♣ P

Bradwell

New Bath
Stretfield Road (B6049)
☎ (0433) 20431
12–4.30, 7–11 (12–11 Sat)

Stones Best Bitter; Tetley Bitter Ⓗ
Attractive country pub in a pleasant setting, with a view of Bradwell Edge. Homely bar with a pool room and a cosy lounge. ❀ ⇥ ◖▶ ▲ ♣ P

Brookbottom

Fox Inn
Brookbottom Road (end of High Lea Road, off St Mary's Road, New Mills) OS985864
☎ (061) 427 1634
11.30–3, 5.30 (6.30 winter)–11
Robinson's Best Mild, Best Bitter Ⓗ, **Old Tom** (winter) Ⓖ
Old, whitewashed pub in a quiet hamlet a mile from New Mills centre. Comfortable, beamed lounge with many original features; basic games room. Access (on foot only) from Strines station. Family room till early eve. ♨ ⌂ ❀ ◖ ▶ ⊞ ⇌ (Strines) ♣ P

Buxton

Cheshire Cheese
High Street ☎ (0298) 25371
12–3, 6.30–11 (11–11 Fri & Sat)
Hardys & Hansons Best Mild, Best Bitter, Kimberley Classic Ⓗ
Refurbished some years ago, this stone-built pub, close to the market place, still has great character. Three separate areas and two seated bay windows with an air of privacy. A music pub, with jazz and R&B. Skiffle in the garden in summer.
♨ ❀ ◖▶ ⇌ ♣ P

Old Clubhouse
Water Street (follow signs to opera house) ☎ (0298) 25371
11.30 (11 summer)–11
Ind Coope Burton Ale; Tetley Bitter Ⓗ
Originally the Duke of Rutland Gentleman's Club, as reflected in the spacious lounge with its easy chairs and book shelves. Impressive stairs lead to a snug. Water Street is closed during the summer Buxton Festival, when the area assumes a continental air.
♨ ❀ ◖▶ ⇌ ♣

Castleton

George
Castle Street ☎ (0433) 620238
11.30–3, 6.30–11 (11.30–11 Sat & summer)
Draught Bass; Stones Best Bitter Ⓗ
Ancient pub lying in the old heart of the village, beneath Peveril Castle. A friendly local with two traditional-style rooms; also popular with visitors.
♨ Q ❀ ◖▶ ⊞ ▲ ♣ P

Chapel-en-le-Frith

Roebuck
Market Place ☎ (0298) 812274
11–3, 5–11
Tetley Mild, Bitter Ⓗ
A lounge with a separate games room, and a tap room area: full of character, with oak beams and an unusual wooden bar. No music ensures good local gossip.
♨ Q ⅏ ♣

Chesterfield

Derby Tup
387 Sheffield Road, Whittington Moor (400 yds S of A61/B6052 roundabout, 2 miles N of centre)
☎ (0246) 454316
11.30–3, 5 (6 Sat)–11
Adnams Bitter; Bateman XXXB; Marston's Pedigree; S&N Theakston XB, Old Peculier; Taylor Landlord Ⓗ; **guest beers**
Superb, unspoilt, corner free house with three rooms. The landlord is a rugby union fan. Large selection of guest beers, including a mild. Eve meals till 8pm. Q ◖▶ ⊞ ⅏ ❀ ⌕

Portland Hotel
West Bars ☎ (0246) 234502
11–3, 5.30–11
Courage Directors; John Smith's Bitter, Magnet Ⓗ; **guest beers**
Imposing former station hotel for the Lancashire, Derbyshire & East Coast Railway's terminus. The unspoilt exterior is of significant historical importance; inside, the original wooden fire surround has escaped modernisation.
♨ ⇥ ◖▶ ⇌ ♣ P

Royal Oak
43 Chatsworth Road, Brampton ☎ (0246) 277854
11.30–3, 6–11 (11.30–11 Fri & Sat)
McEwan 80/-; S&N Theakston Best Bitter, XB, Old Peculier; Younger No. 3 Ⓗ; **guest beer** (Sun)
Lively pub with a good atmosphere, on the main road from the Peak District. Quiz night Sun. ❀ ⊞ ⅏ ♣ ⌕ P

Spread Eagle
7 Beetwell Street
☎ (0246) 275292
11–4, 6–11
Mansfield Riding Bitter, Old Baily Ⓗ
Old, traditional town pub catering for all. Car park via Markham Road. ◖ ⅏ ⇌ ♣ P

Victoria Inn
21–23 Victoria Street West, Brampton (off A619, Chatsworth road)
☎ (0246) 273832

Derbyshire

12–3.30, 7–11
Vaux Samson; Wards Thorne Best Bitter, Sheffield Best Bitter, Kirby H
Two-roomed traditional local with a warm welcome. The separate pool room was converted from an adjoining property. Winner of both brewery and CAMRA awards.
Q 🏠 ⚓ ⅃ ♣ P

Chinley

Squirrels
1 Green Lane (B6062)
☎ (0663) 750001
11–11
Ind Coope Burton Ale; Lloyds Derby Bitter; Tetley Mild, Bitter H; **guest beers**
Impressive, three-storey, stone-built hotel, daunting at first but welcoming inside. Enlarged with a comfortable lounge bar/dining area, leaving the original bar as the vault. Two guest beers and a guest cider.
🏠 🏚 ◑ ▶ ⚓ ⅃ ≠ ♣ ◡ P

Clay Cross

Queens
113 Thanet Street (300 yds E of A61 lights) ☎ (0246) 862348
12–3 (not Tue or Thu), 7–11
Stones Best Bitter; Tetley Bitter H
Typical, friendly local: a comfortable lounge and a lively public bar. A children's room leads on to the patio.
🏂 🏠 ⚓ ♣ P

Shoulder of Mutton
High Street
☎ (0246) 863307
12–4, 7–11
Tetley Bitter H
Popular beer drinkers' pub on the A61, overlooking Amber Valley. Friendly landlord. Frequented by a cross-section of the community.
🏠 ⚓ Å ♣ P

Cotmanhay

Bridge Inn
Bridge Street (off A6007)
☎ (0602) 322589
11–11
Hardys & Hansons Best Mild, Best Bitter E
Traditional village local by the Erewash Canal. Good mix of locals, fishermen and boaters; frequent visitors include eagles and goats. The landlord is a real character who permits no swearing in the bar. A rare find. Q 🏠 ⚓ ♣ P

Crich

Cliff Inn
Cromford Road (NW of village) ☎ (0773) 852444
11–3, 6–11

Hardys & Hansons Best Mild, Best Bitter, Kimberley Classic H
Popular, stone-built local with two small rooms. Near the National Tramway Museum.
🏠 ◑ ▶ ⅃ P

Darley Bridge

Three Stags Heads
Main Road ☎ (0629) 732358
12–3, 6–11 (12–11 Sat)
Hardys & Hansons Best Mild, Best Bitter, Kimberley Classic H
Friendly, olde-worlde pub with traditional decor and a homely atmosphere. The initials over the side door, GOG (apparently meaning Go Out Quietly), date from the 18th century, when the local hunt met here.
🍴 🏠 ◑ ⚓ Å ♣ P

Darley Dale

Grouse Inn
Dale Road North
12–3, 7–11
Hardys & Hansons Best Mild, Best Bitter, Kimberley Classic H
Roadside local recently renovated but keeping a traditional atmosphere. Good selection of lunchtime meals. Popular with all ages and handy for tourists. Children's adventure playground.
🍴 🏠 ◑ ⅃ Å ♣ P

Denby

Bulls Head
Denby Common
☎ (0332) 742159
12–3, 7–11
Adnams Broadside; Bateman XXXB; Eldridge Pope Royal Oak; Mansfield Old Baily H
Large, open-plan lounge and a smaller bar. ♣ ♣ P

Derby

Alexandra Hotel
203 Siddals Road
☎ (0332) 293993
11–2.30, 4.30 (6 Sat)–11
Bateman Mild, XB; Marston's Pedigree H; **guest beers**
Friendly pub with pleasing, subtle decor and wooden floors. Bottled beer collection and train pictures in the bar. Guest ciders. No food Sun.
Q 🏠 ◑ ≠ ◡ P

Brunswick Inn
1 Railway Terrace
☎ (0332) 290677
11–11
Brunswick Celebration Mild, First Brew, Second Brew, Old Accidental; Burton Bridge Bridge Bitter; Hook Norton Old Hooky H & G; **guest beers**

The oldest purpose-built railwayman's pub: flagstone floors, high ceilings and dark walls preserve the original character. Brewery on the premises; beer festival early Oct. Too many beers to list.
Q 🏂 🏠 ◑ ⚓ ⅃ ≠ ♣ ◡ ✗

Crompton Tavern
46 Crompton Street
☎ (0332) 292259
11–11
Marston's Pedigree; Taylor Landlord; Wards Thorne Best Bitter, Sheffield Best Bitter H; **guest beers**
U-shaped room catering for all types: busy, friendly and unpretentious. Annual beer festival. 🏠 ◑ ♣

Dolphin Inn
Queen Street (200 yds from cathedral) ☎ (0332) 49115
11–11
Draught Bass; M&B Highgate Mild, Springfield Bitter; Stones Best Bitter; Welsh Brewers Worthington BB H; **guest beers**
The oldest and most picturesque pub in the city. Built in the same year (1530) as the cathedral tower. One of the four rooms is devoted to memorabilia of Offiler's brewery. Tea room upstairs. Cheap beer Mon.
Q 🏠 ◑ ▶ ⅃ ♣ P

Drill Hall Vaults
1 Newlands Street
☎ (0332) 298073
12–2.30, 7–11
Marston's Pedigree H
One-roomed, comfortable, friendly pub, with brasses on the walls and beams. 🍴 ◑ ♣

Friargate
Friargate ☎ (0332) 297065
11.30–3, 6–11
Bateman Mild; Hoskins Beaumanor Bitter, Penn's Ale, Premium H; **guest beers**
One-roomed, out-of-town pub in the town! Decorated with beer mats. Three guest beers. ◑

Furnace
Duke Street ☎ (0332) 31563
11–3, 6–11
Hardys & Hansons Best Mild, Best Bitter, Kimberley Classic H
Popular, open-plan pub with photographs of bygone Derby. Close to St Mary's Bridge.
🏠 ♣

New Inn
42 Rose Hill Street
☎ (0332) 366304
11–11
Mansfield Riding Mild, Riding Bitter, Old Baily H
Multi-roomed, corner pub, friendly and welcoming. Local characters include a Seth Armstrong double. ◑ ♣ ♣

79

Derbyshire

Station Inn
Midland Road
☎ (0332) 360114
11–2.30, 7–11
Draught Bass G
Narrow pub used mostly by postal workers. Pool table off the main bar; large function room. ♣

Woodlark
80 Bridge Street (off Friargate)
☎ (0332) 32910
11.30–2.30, 5 (7.30 Sat)–11
Draught Bass H; **guest beers**
Former brew pub now a free house, built in the early 19th century. Small bar and a larger lounge, with highly polished brass tables. Q ♣

York Tavern
York Street ☎ (0332) 362849
12–3, 6–11
Marston's Pedigree H; **guest beers**
Busy back-street local with a U-shaped drinking area. ♣ ♣

Try also: Lord Napier, Milton Street (Bass)

Dronfield

Old Sidings
91 Chesterfield Road
☎ (0742) 410023
12–11
Draught Bass; Marston's Pedigree; Stones Best Bitter; Whitbread Boddingtons Bitter, Castle Eden Ale, Flowers Original H; **guest beers**
Lively pub with an L-shaped lounge on two levels. Comfortably furnished with a railway theme. Eve meals in the basement restaurant.
♣ ◖ ≠ ♣ P

Earl Sterndale

Quiet Woman
☎ (0298) 83211
11–3, 6–11
Marston's Mercian Mild, Burton Best Bitter, Pedigree H
Superb example of a village local, overlooking the green. Two-roomed, with a bar and a games room, real fires in both. In the low-beamed bar dominoes tables can be found, as well as peace and quiet – sometimes!
♨ Q ⛵ ♣ ♣ A P

Eckington

White Hart
32 Church Street
☎ (0246) 434855
12–3.30, 6–11
Home Bitter; Younger Scotch, No. 3 H
Historic inn in the old centre of the village, next to the church: a traditional tap room

with a pool table; comfortable lounge. Occasional live music. Eve meals finish at 8pm.
Q ♨ ◖ ◗ ⛵ ♣ ♣ P

Etwall

Hawk & Buckle
Main Street ☎ (0283) 733471
11.30–2.30, 7–11
Marston's Pedigree H
Smart, modern village local with a comfortable lounge and a smaller bar with a games area. ♨ ♣ ♣ ♣ P

Glossop

Crown Inn
142 Victoria Street
☎ (0457) 862824
11.30–11
Samuel Smith OBB H
A true local with two small snugs, an active games room and an attractive central bar. Recently refurbished. Runs trips to beer festivals.
♨ ♣ ♣ ≠ ♣

Fleece Inn
1 Bernard Street
☎ (0457) 865203
11–11
Bateman XXXB; Taylor Landlord; Tetley Bitter H; **guest beers**
Red brick, open-plan free house with an original black and white tiled floor and a red phone box. Two bar areas and a games room. Very popular live R&B/rock music on Thu/Fri nights. ♨ ♣ ♣ ≠

George Hotel
32 Norfolk Street
☎ (0457) 855449
11.30–3, 5.30–11
S&N Matthew Brown Mild E, **Theakston Best Bitter, XB** H
Friendly hotel opposite the station. Food, from bar snacks to functions, is of high quality and served at all times. Lounge, bars and a restaurant.
Q ⛵ ⌂ ◖ ◗ ♣ ≠

Hadfield

Palatine Hotel
Station Road
☎ (0457) 852459
1 (12 Sat)–11
Robinson's Best Mild, Best Bitter, Old Tom H
Warm, friendly pub with a wood-clad interior. Its proximity to bus and railway termini ensures steady custom all day. Old Tom all year round. ♨ ♣ ♣ ♣ ≠ ♣ P

Hardwick Park

Hardwick Inn
1 mile S of M1 jct 29
☎ (0246) 850245
11.30–3, 6.30–11

S&N Theakston XB; Younger Scotch H
17th-century inn owned by the National Trust, at the gates to Hardwick Hall. Excellent food (no meals Sun eve or Mon).
♨ ⛵ ⌂ ◖ ◗ P

Hasland

Devonshire Arms
3a Mansfield Road (B6039, near B6038 jct)
☎ (0246) 232218
12–11 (12–3, 5.30–11 Sat)
Tetley Bitter H
Busy local near the park. Pool table. No food Sun.
♣ ◖ ♣ ♣ P ✗

Hathersage

Plough Inn
Leadmill Bridge (B6001, 1 mile from village centre)
☎ (0433) 650319
11.30–3, 6.30–11
Ind Coope Burton Ale; Tetley Bitter H
Comfortable pub with a spacious, split-level lounge and a small, intimate tap room. Converted from a farmhouse on the banks of the River Derwent. Popular with walkers but also local trade.
♨ ♣ ⌂ ◖ ◗ ♣ A ≠ ♣ P

Scotsman's Pack
School Lane ☎ (0433) 50253
12–3 (may extend in summer), 7–11
Burtonwood Mild, Bitter, Forshaw's H
Comfortable village pub with three lounge areas served by a central bar. Note 'Little John's Chair', obviously made for a giant though perhaps not the one who lies in the nearby churchyard.
♣ ⌂ ◖ ◗ ♣ A ≠ ♣ P

Hayfield

George Hotel
Church Street ☎ (0663) 743691
12–11
Burtonwood Bitter, Forshaw's H
Idyllic old village local, with low, oak-beamed ceilings, and stained-glass windows featuring Kings George I–VI. Burtonwood's *Pub of the Year* 1991. An ideal base for walks in the Kinder Scout area.
♨ ⛵ ♣ ⌂ ◖ ◗ ♣ A ♣ P

Sportsman
Kinder Road (follow campsite signs) ☎ (0663) 741565
12–3 (Sat & Sun only), 7–11
Thwaites Best Mild, Bitter H
Pleasant, spacious pub on the road to Kinder Scout. Good selection of food; upstairs function room. Eight accommodation rooms with reduced rates for groups.
♨ Q ⌂ ◖ ◗ A

Derbyshire

Heage

Black Boy
Old Road ☎ (0773) 856799
11.30–3, 6.30–11
Mansfield Riding Bitter, Old Baily Ⓗ
Modernised, large, open-plan, bright and friendly, lounge-based pub. 🏭 ❀ ◑ ▶ ♣ P

Heanor

New Inn
Derby Road ☎ (0773) 719609
11–3.30, 7–11
Home Mild, Bitter; S&N Theakston XB Ⓗ
Popular and friendly, compact local on Tag Hill. ❀ ◑ ▣ ♣ P

Hognaston

Red Lion
Main Street ☎ (0335) 370396
11–3, 6–11
Marston's Pedigree Ⓗ
Typical, upland village pub; one U-shaped room, warm and friendly; small pool room, where families are welcome. Sells eggs and cheese.
🏭 ❀ ◑ ▲ ♣ P

Holmesfield

Travellers Rest
Main Road ☎ (0742) 890446
12–4, 7–11
Home Bitter; Younger No. 3 Ⓗ
Pleasant, two-roomed pub with pool in the tap room and a comfortable, spacious lounge. Occasional live music. ❀ ▣ ▲ ♣ P

Try also: George & Dragon (Wards)

Horsley

Coach & Horses
47 Church Street
☎ (0332) 880581
11.30–2.30, 6–11
Marston's Burton Best Bitter, Merrie Monk, Pedigree Ⓗ, **Owd Rodger** (winter) Ⓖ
Popular village pub, smart and comfortable with a conservatory. Children's play area in the garden. ❀ ◑ P

Try also: Horsley Lodge (Free)

Ilkeston

Durham Ox
Durham Street
☎ (0602) 324570
11–4, 6–11 (11–11 Sat)
Wards Mild, Thorne Best Bitter, Sheffield Best Bitter Ⓔ, **Kirby** Ⓗ
Busy, popular, open-plan back-street pub with a separate pool area. Incredibly cheap B&B; Sun night quiz.

Knock on the side window if not open on time.
🏭 ❀ 🐕 ♣ P

Spring Cottage
1 Fullwood Street
☎ (0602) 323153
11–3 (4 Fri, 5 Sat), 6 (7 Sat)–11
Draught Bass Ⓗ; **guest beer** (weekends)
Genuine pub tucked away in a back street with a good mix of friendly locals. TV and pool in the bar, but a sociable, relaxing atmosphere.
🏭 🐕 ◑ ▣ ♣ P

Ingleby

John Thompson Inn
☎ (0332) 862469
10.30–2.30, 7–11
JTS XXX; Marston's Pedigree Ⓗ
Pub opened in 1969, converted from a 15th-century farmhouse. A wealth of oak is complemented by a large collection of paintings and antiques. Upmarket, and motorcyclists are not welcome. Brewery in the car park. 🏭 🐕 ❀ ◑ ▲ P ⊬

Kilburn

Travellers Rest
Chapel Street ☎ (0773) 880108
12–3 (4 Sat), 7–11
Ind Coope Burton Ale; Tetley Bitter Ⓗ
Two-roomed village local, with a comfortable lounge and a very small car park. Skittle alley. Quizzes. 🏭 Q ❀ P

Knockerdown

Knockerdown
On B5035 ☎ (0629) 85209
11–3, 7–11
Marston's Pedigree Ⓗ
Isolated, friendly country pub. China cups hang from the beams in both rooms.
🏭 ◑ ♣ P

Langley Mill

Railway Tavern
Station Road ☎ (0773) 764711
11–4 (not Mon, Tue or Sat), 6 (7 Mon, Tue & Sat)–11
Home Mild, Bitter Ⓔ
Friendly, popular roadside pub, efficiently run to a high standard. Display of ornamental cats. Weekend organist; steak night every Thu (meals Tue, Thu and Fri only). Barbecues in summer. ❀ ◑ ▶ 🚆 ♣ P

Little Longstone

Packhorse
Main Street ☎ (0629) 640471
11–3, 5 (6 Sat)–11
Marston's Burton Best Bitter, Pedigree Ⓗ

Ancient, unspoilt village local, a pub since 1787. Small comfortable lounge and a tap room well used by ramblers. Small dining room (open Wed–Sat). Live folk music Wed. 🏭 Q ❀ ◑ ▶ ▲ ♣

Longshaw

Grouse Inn
On B6054 ☎ (0433) 30423
12–3, 6–11
Vaux Double Maxim; Wards Sheffield Best Bitter, Kirby Ⓗ
Originally built as a farmhouse in 1804 and the hayloft, barn doors and stone trough survive. A comfortable lounge at the front leads to a conservatory overhung with vines, and an adjoining tap room. No meals Mon/Tue.
🏭 Q ❀ ◑ ▶ ♣ P

Lullington

Colvile Arms
Coton Road
☎ (082 786) 212
12–2.30 (not Mon–Fri), 7–11
Draught Bass; Marston's Pedigree Ⓗ
18th-century, village pub, not quite the most southerly in the county. Basic wood-panelled bar, smart lounge, plus a function room. Bowling green in the garden. 🏭 ❀ ▣ ♣ P

Marsh Lane

Fox & Hounds
Main Road (B6056)
☎ (0246) 432974
12–3, 7–11
Burtonwood Bitter, Forshaw's Ⓗ
Pub with a comfortable lounge and a traditional tap room; large beer garden and play area. Good-sized car park. ❀ ◑ ▶ ▣ ▲ ♣ P

Matlock ✓

Thorn Tree
48 Jackson Road (up hill behind county offices)
☎ (0629) 582923
11.30–3 (not Mon or Tue), 7–11
Draught Bass; Mansfield Old Baily Ⓗ
Small, unspoilt local, popular with office workers and darts players. Fine atmosphere.
Q ❀ ◑ ▣ ♣

Melbourne

Roebuck
Potter Street ☎ (0332) 862872
12–2.30, 7–11 (12–11 Fri & Sat)
Draught Bass Ⓗ
Multi-sectioned pub with an old, welcoming appeal. The lounge has an antique range. Function room/restaurant.
🏭 ❀ ♣ P

Derbyshire

Middle Handley

Devonshire Arms
Westfield Lane (off B6052)
☎ (0246) 432189
11–3, 7–11 (12–2.30, 7–10.30 Sun)
Tetley Bitter Ⓗ
Friendly and popular village
local. Q ✿ P

Milton

Swan Inn
Main Street ☎ (0283) 703188
12–2.30, 7–11
Marston's Pedigree Ⓗ
Popular village pub with a
smart lounge and a locals' bar.
Very friendly. No food Sun
eve or Mon.
🏨 ✿ ◖▶ ⊟ ♣ P

New Mills

Crescent Inn
76 Market Street
☎ (0663) 742879
11.30–11
Tetley Mild, Bitter Ⓗ; guest
beers (occasionally)
Two-roomed pub with an
unassuming vault and a long,
pleasant lounge. Secluded
beer garden and good value
food (eve meals end at 8pm).
Next to Heritage Centre and
Torrs Gorge. ✿ ◖▶ ⊟
⇌ (Central/Newtown) ♣

Masons Arms
High Street ☎ (0663) 744292
12–4.30, 7–11
Robinson's Best Mild, Best
Bitter Ⓔ, Old Tom (winter) Ⓖ
Stone-built pub in an old part
of town: a long, low-ceilinged
lounge with an adjoining bar
and a separate games room.
Close to the Sett Valley Trail.
🏨 ⊟ ⇌ (Central) ♣ P

Newton Solney

Unicorn Inn
Repton Road (B5003)
☎ (0283) 703324
11.30–3, 5–11 (11.30–11 Fri & Sat)
Draught Bass Ⓔ
Busy village local with a bar
expanded from original
smaller rooms but retaining a
small lounge with no bar
counter. Q ✿ ◖▶ ⅙ P

Ockbrook

Royal Oak
Green Lane ☎ (0332) 662378
11.30–2.30, 7–11
Draught Bass Ⓔ
Characterful, village meeting
place with four small rooms.
No food Sun. 🏨 Q ✿ ◖ ♣ P

Old Whittington

Cock & Magpie
2 Church Street North
☎ (0246) 454453

11–3, 6–11
Mansfield Riding Bitter, Old
Baily Ⓗ
Good village local with
excellent value-for-money
food (no meals Sat/Sun eves).
Next to the old Cock &
Magpie (now a museum)
where the plot to bring
William of Orange to the
English throne, was hatched
by the Earl of Devonshire and
others. Walled garden; seats in
front of the pub.
✿ ◖▶ ⊟ ⅙ ♣ ⌂ P

Over Haddon

Lathkil Hotel
1/2 mile SW of B5055
☎ (0629) 812501
11–3, 6–11
Wards Mild, Thorne Best
Bitter, Sheffield Best Bitter Ⓗ
Free house in an idyllic setting
overlooking one of the Peak's
most picturesque dales. Fine
oak-panelled bar with
traditional-style leather and
wood furnishings. Excellent
food. Children welcome at
lunchtime.
🏨 Q 🛏 ◖▶ ⊟ A P

Ripley

Sitwell Arms
Wall Street
☎ (0773) 742727
1–3 (4 Sat), 7.30–11
Hardys & Hansons Best Mild,
Best Bitter Ⓗ
Basic, friendly, one-roomed
locals' pub. Skittles alley in the
back yard. ♣

Try also: Woodman, Maple
Ave (Hardys & Hansons)

Rosliston

Plough Inn
Main Street
☎ (0283) 761354
11–3 (not Mon), 6.30–11
Marston's Pedigree, Owd
Rodger Ⓗ
18th-century village pub with
an attractive black and white
exterior adorned with hanging
baskets. An H-shaped
drinking area with low
ceilings provides a cosy
atmosphere. 🏨 Q ✿ ◖ ♣ P

Rowarth

Little Mill Inn
Signed off Siloh Road
OS011889 ☎ (0663) 743178
11–11
Banks's Hanson's Bitter,
Bitter; Robinson's Best
Bitter Ⓗ; guest beers
Busy, convivial pub serving
good home-made food. A
veritable adventure park for
children. Separate restaurant.
Up to three guest beers.
🏨 🐾 ✿ ◖ A P

Scarcliffe

Horse & Groom
Mansfield Road
☎ (0246) 823152
12–3.30, 7–11
Home Bitter; S&N Theakston
XB Ⓗ
Beamed coaching inn with a
children's play area to the
rear. Good home cooking.
🏨 Q ◖▶ ⊟ P

Shardlow

Malt Shovel
The Wharf (Navigation pub
turning on A6)
☎ (0332) 799763
11–3, 6–11
Marston's Mercian Mild,
Burton Best Bitter,
Pedigree Ⓗ
Characterful, canalside tavern
converted from old maltings;
popular with the boating
fraternity in summer.
Zachariah Smith's Shardlow
Brewery once stood opposite.
🏨 Q ✿ ◖ ♣ P

Simmondley

Hare & Hounds
☎ (0457) 852028
12–3, 5.30–11
Ind Coope Burton Ale; Tetley
Walker Dark Mild, Bitter Ⓗ;
guest beers
Former 19th-century textile
mill with extensive views of
Glossopdale. The landlord is a
Master Cellarman. Holds its
own beer festival in June.
Meals at all times. ✿ ◖▶ ♣ P

Somercotes

Horse & Jockey
Leabrooks Road
☎ (0773) 602179
11–3, 7–11
Home Mild, Bitter Ⓗ
Popular, unspoilt, multi-
roomed local. Parking
difficult. ✿

Stanton

Gate Inn
Woodlands Road (A444)
☎ (0283) 216818
11–3, 6–11
Marston's Pedigree Ⓗ
Comfortable, popular pub
with a plain bar and a smart
lounge linked as an L-shaped
drinking area; separate dining
area off (no food Sun eve).
Children's play area.
✿ ◖▶ ⊟ ⅙ ♣ P

Stanton-by-Dale

Chequers
Dale Road
11–2.30 (3 Thu–Sat), 7–11
Draught Bass; M&B Mild Ⓔ
Small, cottage-style pub of

exceptional character with a raised lounge area where an old water pump takes pride of place. In the same family for four generations; well worth a visit. Q ❀ ❍ ◖ & ♣ P

Staveley

Nags Head
Chesterfield Road
☎ (0246) 472907
11–3.30, 7–11
Mansfield Riding Bitter H
Main road pub on the outskirts of Staveley. Good cooking. ❀ ◖ ♣ P

Swanwick

Gate Inn
The Delves (E of A61, via the green) ☎ (0773) 602039
11.30–3, 7–11
Courage Directors; John Smith's Bitter H
Smart, open-plan pub with a bar, lounge and eating area.
◖ ▶ ♣ P

Ticknall

Chequers
High Street ☎ (0332) 864392
12–2.30, 6–11
Marston's Pedigree; Ruddles Best Bitter, County H
Small, friendly local offering many games, including bar billiards. ♨ ❀ ♣ P

Staff of Life
High Street ☎ (0332) 862479
11.30–2.30, 6 (7 winter)–11
Everards Old Original; Gibbs Mew Bishop's Tipple; Marston's Pedigree, Owd Rodger; Moorhouse's Pendle Witches Brew; Taylor Landlord H; guest beers
Food house with a bar and an excellent choice of beers: usually over ten guests.
❀ ◖ ▶ P

Tideswell

Anchor
Four Lane Ends (A623/B6049 jct) ☎ (0298) 871371
11–3 (4 summer), 6–11
Robinson's Best Bitter, Hartleys XB H, **Old Tom** G
500-year-old pub on a crossroads: a traditional tap room with a dartboard, a spacious, oak-panelled lounge and a dining room.
♨ Q ❀ ◖ ▶ ❍ ▲ ♣ P

George
Commercial Road
☎ (0298) 871382
11–3, 7–11
Hardys & Hansons Best Mild, Best Bitter, Kimberley Classic H
Substantial, stone-built country hotel in the village centre: a comfortable lounge

with a dining room off, and a small snug leading to a tap room with pool and darts.
♨ Q ❀ ◖ ◖ ▶ ❍ ▲ ♣ P

Try also: Horse & Jockey, Main Road (Free)

Unstone

Fleur de Lys Hotel
Main Road ☎ (0246) 412157
12–3 (not Mon–Fri), 5 (7 Sat)–11
S&N Theakston Best Bitter, XB, Old Peculier; Younger Scotch, No. 3 H
Conspicuous old coaching inn, standing on an old wishing well. Live entertainment Thu and Sun eve. ♨ ❀ ❍ & ♣ P

Walton

White Hart Inn
Matlock Road (B6015)
☎ (0246) 566392
11–3, 5–11
Courage Directors; John Smith's Bitter H
Pleasantly situated roadside inn with a vast outdoor drinking and children's play area – ideal for summer eves. Noted for its food (not available Sun eve).
♨ ❀ ◖ ▶ & P

Try also: Blue Stoops (John Smith's)

Wardlow Mires

Three Stags Heads
At A623/B6465 jct
☎ (0298) 872268
5.30 (7 Mon)–11 (11–11 Sat and summer)
S&N Theakston Old Peculier; Younger Scotch, No. 3 H; guest beers
Carefully restored, 17th-century farmhouse pub with two rooms. The bar is heated by an ancient cooking range (still used for meals). Popular with hikers; dogs welcome.
♨ Q ❀ ◖ ▲ ♣ P

Weston-on-Trent

Coopers Arms
Weston Hall ☎ (0332) 690002
11–3, 6–11
Draught Bass H
Built in 1633, Weston Hall, visible for miles, was converted into a pub in 1991. Large fire in each room; glass-covered well in the lounge. Virtually all the beams are original. The lake has coarse fishing in summer.
♨ Q ⛵ ❀ ◖ ▶ P

Whaley Bridge

Shepherd's Arms
Old Road ☎ (0663) 732384
11.30–3, 7–11
Marston's Mercian Mild,

Burton Best Bitter, Pedigree H
Excellent, ageless local, above the main street. The lounge is softly lit and quiet, in contrast to the excellent vault with its stone-flagged floor, unvarnished tables, settles and stools. Two real fires.
♨ Q ❀ ❍ ⇌ ♣ P

Whitwell

Jug & Glass
Portland Street
☎ (0909) 720289
11–3, 6.30–11
John Smith's Bitter, Magnet H
Compact pub in the centre of the village. ♨ ❍ P

Wirksworth

Blacks Head
Market Place ☎ (0629) 823257
11–3, 6–11 (11–11 Sat)
Hardys & Hansons Best Bitter, Kimberley Classic H
One-roomed, busy pub decorated with bric-a-brac, from spears to bottles. Eve meals finish early.
♨ ❀ ◖ ▶ P

Hope & Anchor
Market Place
☎ (0629) 824620
11–4, 7–11
Home Mild, Bitter; S&N Theakston XB H
Old, stone-built pub with a large bar and a small lounge, dominated by a 17th-century chimneypiece. Of great historic interest. Parking in the market place. ♨ Q ❍ ◖ ▶ ♣

Woolley Moor

White Horse Inn
White Horse Lane (400 yds off B6014) ☎ (0246) 590319
11.30–2.30, 6.30–11
Draught Bass H; guest beers
Pub almost legendary for its fine ale and food. Set in excellent walking country where the less active can enjoy a view of the rolling Derbyshire hills. Inventive menu (no food Sun eve). Not to be missed.
Q ❀ ◖ ▶ ❍ & ♣ P

Youlgreave

George Inn
Church Street (off A6)
☎ (0629) 636292
11–2.30, 6.30–11
Home Mild, Bitter H
Large, lively local across from one of the finest churches in the county. Historic Haddon Hall and Arbor Low nearby.
Q ⛵ ❀ ◖ ❍ & ▲ ♣ P

Try also: Bulls Head Hotel (Marston's)

83

Devon

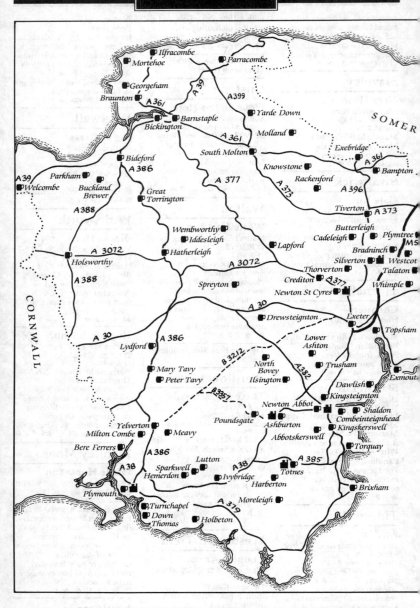

Beer Engine, *Newton St Cyres;* **Blackawton,** *Totnes;*
Branscombe Vale, *Branscombe;* **Exe Valley,** *Silverton;*
Mill, *Newton Abbot;* **Otter,** *Mathayes, Luppitt;*
Summerskills, *Plymouth;* **Thompson's,** *Ashburton*

Abbotskerswell

Two Mile Oak
Totnes Road ☎ (0803) 812411

11–2.30, 5–11 (11–11 Sat & summer)
**Draught Bass; Eldridge Pope
Royal Oak** Ⓖ**; Whitbread
Flowers IPA** Ⓗ
15th-century coaching house

with a food-dominated
lounge, though the public bar
retains an old-fashioned
atmosphere.
🍴 ❀ ◑ ▶ ⛊ P

Devon

```
0        5        10 miles
0                 15 km
```

S E T

Holcombe Rogus

Clayhidon

Broadhembury
Mathayes
Honiton
Feniton   Kilmington
         A 35   Axminster
Ottery St Mary
                A 3052
Branscombe Seaton Axmouth
         Beer

Ashburton

London Inn
West Street ☎ (0364) 52478
11–2.30, 5–11
Cotleigh Tawny; Thompson's Best Bitter, Velvet Stout, IPA, Botwrights Ⓗ
Comfortable coaching house with an enormous rambling lounge. The home of Thompson's brewery.
🏨 ◖▶ P

Axminster

Axminster Inn
Silver Street ☎ (0297) 34947
11–11
Palmers BB, IPA Ⓗ
Unprepossessing town pub with a wealth of facilities and perhaps the best-kept Palmers beers in East Devon. 🏨 🐃 ❀
🛏 ◖▣ & ⇤ ♣ ⌂ P

Millwey
Chard Road ☎ (0297) 32774
11–2.30, 7–11
Palmers BB, IPA Ⓗ
Friendly, modern pub on the edge of a housing estate on the fringe of town. Good garden for children, who are also welcome in the skittle alley. Lunches Tue–Sat. ❀ ◖▣ ♣ P

Axmouth

Ship Inn
☎ (0297) 21838
11–2.30 (2 winter), 6–11
Devenish Cornish Original; Whitbread Flowers IPA Ⓗ
Welcoming inn serving excellent food.
🏨 Q ❀ ◖▶ ▣ ▲ ♣ ⌂ P

Bampton

Exeter Inn
1 mile from Bampton on A396
☎ (0398) 331345
11–2.30, 6–11
Exmoor Ale Ⓗ
Very friendly local; it pays to be in here drinking otherwise you get talked about. Busy with tourists in summer. Cider in summer only. 🏨 Q ❀ 🛏
◖▶ ▣ & ▲ ⌂ P

Barnstaple

Barnstaple Inn
12 Trinity Street
11–2.30 (4 Sat), 5 (7 Sat)–11 (11–11 Fri)
Courage Best Bitter; John Smith's Bitter Ⓗ
Traditional and friendly town local in the Victorian part of Barnstaple. The pub's tenancy is under threat following the Grand Met take-over of Courage pubs. Q ▣ ♣

Corner House
108 Boutport Street
11–2.30, 5.30–11
Draught Bass Ⓗ**; guest beer**
Welcoming town ale house retaining its 1930s wood-panelled interior and curved bar. Unspoilt, and appealing to discerning drinkers from all walks of life. 🐃 ♣

Beer

Anchor
Fore Street ☎ (0297) 20386
11–3, 5.30–11 (11–11 summer if busy)
Furgusons Dartmoor Best Bitter; Wadworth 6X Ⓗ
Warm, friendly pub with pleasant staff, it has large bar areas and an excellent restaurant, offering fresh local produce, including fish. Cider in summer.
🏨 Q ❀ 🛏 ◖▶ ▣ ▲ ♣ ⌂

Bere Ferrers

Old Plough
Take A386 from Plymouth, turn left for Bere Alston, then signed ☎ (0822) 840358
12–3 (4 Sat), 7–11 (also supper licence)
Draught Bass Ⓖ**; Courage Best Bitter** Ⓗ**; Summerskills Best Bitter** Ⓖ**; Whitbread Boddingtons Bitter** Ⓗ**; guest beers**
16th-century inn situated beside the River Tavy in a scenic village, in an area of outstanding beauty. 1991 local *Seafood Pub of the Year*. Moorings for pub visitors by boat. Cider in summer.
🏨 Q ❀ ◖▶ & ⇤ ♣ ⌂

Bickington

Old Barn Inn
Bideford Road ☎ (0271) 72195
11.30–2.30, 6.30 (5 Fri & Sat)–11 (12–2, 7–10.30 Sun)
Draught Bass Ⓗ**; guest beers**
Pub converted from an old village barn. Unobtrusive entertainment on Wed and Sun. Children welcome. ◖▶

Bideford

Joiners Arms
Market Place ☎ (0237) 472675
12–3, 7–11 (11–11 Sat)
Draught Bass Ⓖ**; Fuller's London Pride; Ind Coope Burton Ale** Ⓗ
Busy town pub near Panier Market. At one time it had its own coinage which was given as change.
🏨 🐃 ❀ ◖▶ ♣

Bradninch

Castle Inn
Fore Street ☎ (0392) 881378
12–3, 6–11
Ind Coope Burton Ale Ⓗ
Popular local, run by an enterprising landlord, offering a varied menu of good value home-cooked food. Castle Ale is brewed by Allied.
❀ ◖▶ ♣ P

Braunton

New Inn
Silver Street ☎ (0271) 812254
11–2.30, 5–11 (11–11 Sat)
Ind Coope Burton Ale; Ushers Best Bitter Ⓗ

Devon

16th-century coaching inn which, although altered, retains a warm welcome. Situated in the old village conservation area.
🏚 Q ⬕ 🛏 ◑▶ 🍴 ♣ ⌂ P

Brixham

Burton

Burton Street ☎ (0803) 855458
11–3, 5.30 (6 winter)–11 (11–11 Fri & Sat)
Courage Best Bitter, Directors Ⓖ**; John Smith's Bitter** Ⓗ
Busy local off the main street; a sporty pub with two pool tables and a football table, plus a large garden.
⬕ 🍴 ◑▶ ♣ P

Broadhembury

Drewe Arms

☎ (040 484) 267
11–2.30, 6–11
Draught Bass, Cotleigh Tawny; Otter Bitter Ⓖ**; guest beers**
Largely unspoilt pub in a village of whitewashed, thatched cottages. Children admitted if well behaved. Otter Ale replaces Bitter now and again.
🏚 Q 🍴 ◑▶ ♣ ⌂ P

Buckland Brewer

Coach & Horses

☎ (0237) 451395
11.30–2.30, 5–11
Wadworth 6X; Whitbread Flowers IPA, Original Ⓗ
Friendly old coaching inn at the centre of the village. It has a low-beamed interior with a sloping floor. Excellent food.
🏚 Q ⬕ 🍴 🛏 ◑▶ 🍴 ♣ ⌂ P

Butterleigh

Butterleigh Inn

☎ (0884) 855407
12–2.30, 6 (5 Fri)–11 (12–2.30, 7–10.30 Sun)
Cotleigh Harrier, Tawny, Old Buzzard Ⓗ**; guest beers**
Popular village inn featuring a stained-glass porch. Good food; occasional cider. 🏚 Q 🍴 🛏 ◑▶ 🍴 🐕 ⌂ P

Cadeleigh

Cadeleigh Arms

☎ (0884) 855238
11–3, 6–11
Draught Bass; Butcombe Bitter; Cotleigh Tawny Ⓗ**; guest beers**
Homely, traditional country pub. ⬕ 🍴 ◑▶ 🐕 🛆 ♣ ⌂ P

Clayhidon

Half Moon

4½ miles S of Wellington
☎ (0823) 680291

12–2.30, 7–11
Draught Bass; Cotleigh Tawny, Old Buzzard Ⓗ
Old, but well cared-for village local affording nice views across the Culm valley.
🏚 Q ⬕ 🍴 ◑▶ 🐕 🛆 ♣ ⌂ P

Combeinteignhead

Wild Goose Inn

☎ (0626) 872241
11.30–2.30, 6.30–11 (12–2.30, 7–10.30 Sun)
Mill Janner's Ale; Otter Ale; Wadworth 6X Ⓗ**; guest beers**
17th-century farmhouse, full of character and pleasantly eccentric. Jazz nights are popular (Mon), and it offers a good range of food plus guest beers, all from the West Country. 🏚 🍴 ◑▶ ♣ P

Crediton

Crediton Inn

Mill Street ☎ (0363) 772882
11–11
Draught Bass Ⓗ**; guest beers**
Lively local dating from 1852, with a function room/skittle alley at the rear. Snacks lunchtimes and eves. ⬕ ⇌ P

Exchange

High Street ☎ (0363) 775853
11–3, 5–11 (11–11 Fri, Sat & summer)
Courage Best Bitter, Directors Ⓗ**; guest beers**
Comfortable, one-bar pub where it 'finds' from the landlord's trips to auctions adorn the walls. Steak and wine bar downstairs. 🍴 ◑▶

Dawlish

Prince Albert

The Strand ☎ (0626) 862132
11–11
Draught Bass; Whitbread Flowers IPA Ⓗ
Small, one-bar pub, known as the 'Hole in the Wall'.
🏚 ◑▶ ⇌

Down Thomas

Mussel Inn

☎ (0752) 862238
11.30–2.30, 6–11 (11–11 summer)
Courage Best Bitter, Directors Ⓗ
Old cottages converted to a pub: a popular eating place. Children are welcome (a good play area in summer). A campers' holiday estate stands nearby. 🏚 🍴 ◑▶ 🛆 P

Drewsteignton

Drewe Arms

The Square ☎ (0647) 21224
11–2.30, 5.30–11
Whitbread Flowers IPA Ⓖ
Unspoilt old Devon pub close to Castle Drogo and Teign Gorge. Home to the country's

oldest and longest-serving landlady. 🏚 Q 🍴 🍺

Exebridge

Anchor Inn

On B3222 ☎ (0398) 23433
11–2.30, 6.30 (6 summer)–11
Ruddles County; Ushers Best Bitter Ⓗ
Small country hotel, over 300 years-old: a cosy bar, restaurant, function room and children's play area overlooking the river. Doone Ale is Webster's. 🏚 Q ⬕ 🍴 🛏 ◑▶ 🐕 🛆 ♣ P

Exeter

Bowling Green

Blackboy Road
11–2.30 (3 Sat), 5 (7 Sat)–11
Greene King Abbot; Wadworth 6X Ⓗ**; Whitbread Boddingtons Bitter, Castle Eden Ale; guest beers**
Lively pub, popular with locals and students alike. Sunday breakfasts are served 11–12. ◑ 🐕 ⇌ (St James Pk)

Chaucers

High Street ☎ (0392) 422365
11–2.30, 5–11 (closed winter Sun)
Draught Bass; Tetley Bitter Ⓗ**; guest beer**
Very popular new(ish) pub underneath C&A's. The emphasis is on food, which is well above average for a pub. Do not wear jeans or trainers in the eves. ◑▶ ⇌ (Central)

Double Locks

Canal Banks, Marsh Barton
OS933900 ☎ (0392) 56947
11–3, 5.30–11
Adnams Broadside; Eldridge Pope Royal Oak; Everards Old Original Ⓗ**; Exmoor Ale** Ⓖ**; Greene King Abbot** Ⓗ**; Marston's Pedigree** Ⓖ**; guest beers**
Popular canalside pub with a huge garden and children's facilities. Excellent value food; barbecue in summer.
🏚 Q ⬕ 🍴 ◑▶ 🛆 ♣ ⌂ P

Exeter & Devon Arts Centre Café/Bar

Bradninch Place, Gandy Street
11–2.30, 5 (6.30 Sat)–11 (closed Sun)
Furgusons Dartmoor Strong; Ind Coope Burton Ale; Wadworth 6X Ⓗ
Small bar in a centre offering a wide range of events/work-shops. Good lunches include vegetarian options.
Q ◑ 🐕 ⇌ (Central)

Hole in the Wall

Little Castle Street
11–2.30, 5.30–11 (closed Sun)
Eldridge Pope Hardy Country, Blackdown Porter, Royal Oak Ⓗ
Pub where the pleasant

upstairs bar hosts a Tue night quiz; downstairs is a wine bar/library. Handy for the courts. Q ◑ ⇌ (Central) ♣

Jolly Porter
St David's Hill
☎ (0392) 54848
11–11
Courage Best Bitter, Directors; John Smith's Bitter; Wadworth 6X Ⓗ**; guest beers**
Old building opposite St Davids station with pleasing architecture and lots of space: three separate areas. Jazz Wed eve. ◑ ◗ ⛺ ⇌ (St Davids) ♣

Red Cow
Red Cow Village
11–11
Draught Bass; Eldridge Pope Royal Oak Ⓖ
17th-century building with a notable facade and a courtyard, opposite St Davids station.
⊞ ⛺ ⇌ (St Davids) ♣ ⌓

Well House
Royal Clarence Hotel, Cathedral Close
☎ (0392) 58464
11–2.30, 5 (6 Sat)–11 (closed Sun lunch)
Draught Bass; Otter Ale Ⓗ**; guest beers**
Friendly bar facing Exeter Cathedral, making it very popular with office workers, tourists *et al.* Ask to see the Black Death skeleton in the Roman cellar. House ale is Worthington BB.
🛏 ⇌ (Central)

Exmouth

Country House Inn
176 Withycombe Village Road
☎ (0395) 263444
11–2.30 (3.30 Sat), 5–11
Devenish Cornish Original, Royal Wessex; Marston's Pedigree; Whitbread Best Bitter Ⓗ
Originally the village blacksmith. Very friendly atmosphere, good food, pub games and the largest beer garden in Exmouth, with barbecues, exotic birds, a stream and children's play frames. Whitbread house beers. Eve meals Sat only.
Q ☊ ❀ ◑ ◗ ♿ ⛺ ♣ ⌓ P

Grove
The Esplanade
☎ (0395) 272101
11–3, 5.30–11 (11–11 summer)
Beer range varies Ⓗ
Friendly seafront pub near the marina, with a traditional wooden bar, part-wood floor, timber decor and furniture. Excellent home-cooked food. Five beers; monthly mini beer festivals (not summer).
☊ ❀ ◑ ◗ ♿ ⇌ P

Feniton

Nog Inn
Ottery Road
☎ (0404) 850210
11–2.30, 6–11
Cotleigh Tawny; Otter Ale Ⓗ**; guest beers**
Cheerful, friendly village local with its own squash court. Its possessive cat opposes extended drinking-up time! Unusual guest beers and a useful sideline of cycle repair kits! Active fund-raising social club. 🜲 🛏 ⊞ ⇌ ⌓ P

Georgeham

Rock Inn
Rock Hill ☎ (0271) 890322
11–3, 5–11 (11–11 Fri, Sat & summer)
Ind Coope Burton Ale; Ruddles Best Bitter, County; Ushers Best Bitter Ⓗ**; guest beers** (occasionally)
Traditional, unspoilt, village pub, offering good food and a range of games. Pleasant garden. Cider in summer.
🜲 ☊ ❀ 🛏 ◑ ◗ ⛺ ♣ ⌓ P

Great Torrington

Black Horse Inn
The Square ☎ (0805) 22121
11–3, 6 (6.30 Sat)–11
Ruddles County; Ushers Best Bitter Ⓗ
Said to be the oldest pub in Torrington. The original inn was built in the 12th century, and was frequented by General Fairfax during the Civil War. Altered recently, but retains its character.
🜲 Q ☊ 🛏 ◑ ◗ ⛺ ♣

Hunters Inn
Well Street ☎ (0805) 23832
11–11
Ind Coope Burton Ale; Whitbread Boddingtons Bitter, Flowers Original Ⓗ**; guest beers** (occasionally)
Pub where the guest beers are normally sold cheaper than the regulars. Quiz eves.
🜲 ❀ 🛏 ◑ ◗ ⛺ ♣ P

Harberton

Church House Inn
☎ (0803) 863707
11–2.30, 6–11
Draught Bass; Courage Best Bitter, Directors Ⓗ**; guest beers**
Pub with an enormous, heavily-beamed lounge and a family room with antique furnishings. Lots of real food.
🜲 Q ☊ ❀ ◑ ◗ ⌓ P

Hatherleigh

Tally Ho!
Market Street
☎ (0837) 810306
11–2.30 (3 Mon & Tue), 6–11
Tally Ho Dark Mild, Potboiler's Brew, Tarka's Tipple, Janni Jollop Ⓗ
Attractive town pub with its own brewery, 1992 North Devon CAMRA *Pub of the Year*. Brewery visits are available on request. Very good food. 🜲 ❀ 🛏 ◑ ◗ ♣ P

Hemerdon

Miners Arms
(off A38 at Plympton, follow signs to Langage/Hemerdon)
11–2.30 (3 Sat), 5.30–11
Draught Bass Ⓗ **&** Ⓖ**; Furgusons Dartmoor Best Bitter; Ruddles County; Ushers Best Bitter** Ⓗ
Former tin miners' pub on the edge of Dartmoor, featuring a very large beer garden with a play area. 🜲 Q ☊ ❀ ⊞ ♿ P

Holbeton

Dartmoor Union
Fore Street
☎ (075 530) 288
11.30–3, 6–11
Draught Bass; Summerskills Best Bitter Ⓗ
Very old pub, built before deeds existed. Reputedly haunted, the landlady has seen ghosts. Noted for its food. 🜲 Q ☊ ❀ ◑ ◗ ⛺ ⌓ P

Holcombe Rogus

Prince of Wales
☎ (0823) 672070
12–3, 7–11
Draught Bass; Cotleigh Harrier, Tawny, Old Buzzard Ⓗ**; guest beers**
Pleasant country pub with cash register handpumps. Part-owned by Cotleigh.
🜲 Q ☊ ❀ ◑ ◗ ♣ ⌓ P

Holsworthy

Golden Fleece
Bodmin Street
☎ (0409) 253263
11–11
St Austell Tinners Ⓗ
Tastefully renovated pub with a welcoming atmosphere. Exposed timber beams, wood panelling and slate floor.
Q ◑ ◗ ⊞

Kings Arms
The Square
☎ (0409) 253517
11–11
Draught Bass; Furgusons Dartmoor Best Bitter Ⓗ
Popular Victorian hostelry in the centre of an attractive market town. Friendly atmosphere; splendid stained-glass windows and a snug.
🜲 Q ◑ ◗ ⊞ ♣

Devon

Honiton

Red Cow
High Street ☎ (0404) 47497
11–2.30, 5.30–11
Draught Bass; Courage Directors; John Smith's Bitter; S&N Theakston Old Peculier Ⓗ
Newly refurbished town pub with oak panelling and beams, stained-glass over the bar and booths which give privacy but don't keep out atmosphere. Old carpenters' tools on the walls. ▟ ⏣ ⌑ ◖ ▸ ▲ ✦

Volunteer
High Street ☎ (0404) 42145
11–11
Cotleigh Tawny Ⓗ
Friendly local which attracts all age groups. The family room has a pool table and a jukebox. ⏣ ⊟ ▲ ⇌ ✦ ⌒

Iddesleigh

Duke of York
On B3217 ☎ (0837) 810253
11.30–3, 6.30–11
Cotleigh Tawny; Hook Norton Old Hooky Ⓖ
12th-century village longhouse with a large log fire in its cosy bar. Folk music Tue.
▟ Q ⊛ ⌑ ◖ ▸ ✦ ⌒

Ilfracombe

Wellington Arms
High Street
☎ (0271) 862206
11–3.30, 5–11
Courage Best Bitter, Directors Ⓗ
Beamed, town pub featuring an Iron Duke theme and an aviary. Good value food; popular with locals at lunchtime (eve meals in summer only).
▟ Q ⏣ ⊛ ◖ ▸ ⊟ ✦

Ilsington

Carpenters Arms
☎ (0364) 661215
11–2.30, 6–11
Whitbread Flowers IPA Ⓖ
Timeless, one-bar village local, popular with darts and card players. ▟ ⊛ ◖ ▸ ✦ ⌒

Ivybridge

Imperial Inn
28 Western Road (off A38)
☎ (0752) 892269
11–3, 5.30–11 (11–11 Fri, Sat & summer)
Courage Best Bitter; Ruddles Best Bitter; Wadworth 6X Ⓗ; **guest beers**
A friendly atmosphere in a pub with a large open fire. Summer barbecues.
▟ ⏣ ⊛ ◖ ▸ ⊟ ▲ ✦ ⌒ P

Kilmington

New Inn
The Hill ☎ (0297) 33376
11–2.30, 7 (6.30 Sat)–11
Palmers BB, IPA Ⓗ
Quiet, friendly village pub, an unspoilt rural inn just off the busy A35. No food Mon.
⊛ ◖ ▸ ⊟ ▲ ✦

Kingskerswell

Bickley Mill
Stoneycombe (1 mile W of village) ☎ (0803) 873201
11–2.30, 6–11
Draught Bass; Eldridge Pope Royal Oak; Wadworth 6X Ⓗ
Very large lounge converted from a 13th-century mill, with terraced gardens. Good food.
▟ ⏣ ⊛ ⌑ ◖ ▸ P

Kingsteignton

Old Rydon
Rydon Lane ☎ (0626) 54626
11–3, 6–11
Draught Bass; Wadworth 6X Ⓗ; **guest beers**
Substantial, very old pub/restaurant. Drink upstairs or outside. ▟ Q ⏣ ⊛ ◖ ▸ P

Knowstone

Masons Arms
☎ (039 84) 231
11–3, 7–11
Cotleigh Tawny; Hall & Woodhouse Badger Best Bitter Ⓖ
Charming, 16th-century, Grade II listed inn on the edge of Exmoor. It boasts a thatched roof, rendered walls and a superb, unspoilt interior with an impressive open fireplace. Friendly and welcoming; home-cooked food; occasional cider. ▟ Q ⊛ ⌑ ◖ ▸ ⊟ ▲ ✦ ⌒ P

Lapford

Old Malt Sloop
☎ (0363) 83330
11.30–2.30, 6–11
Draught Bass Ⓗ; **Butcombe Bitter; Eldridge Pope Royal Oak; Wadworth 6X** Ⓖ; **guest beers**
A real village pub with wooden stillage behind the bar and an inglenook. A barn at the rear has recently been converted to a function room/skittle alley. No wheelchair access to ladies' WC. ▟ Q ⊛ ⌑ ◖ ▸ ⊟ ▲ ⇌ ✦ ⌒ P

Lower Ashton

Manor Inn
☎ (0647) 53204
12–2.30, 6 (7 Sat)–11 (closed Mon; 12–2.30, 7–10.30 Sun)

Draught Bass; Cotleigh Tawny; Wadworth 6X Ⓗ; **guest beers**
Lovely little pub nestling in the Teign valley, serving good home-cooked food. ▟ Q ⊛ ⌑ ◖ ▸ ▲ ✦ ⌒

Lutton

Mountain Inn
Off A38 at Plympton, follow signs to Langage/Lutton
☎ (075 537) 247
11–3, 6 (7 Mon–Wed in winter)–11
Draught Bass; Furgusons Dartmoor Best Bitter; Ind Coope Burton Ale; Wadworth 6X Ⓗ
Pub with exposed cob walls and a large granite fireplace, set in a quiet village affording lovely views. Families are very welcome. Burton Ale is sold as 'Mountain Ale'. Renowned for its large hot rolls. Car parking requires tact.
▟ Q ⏣ ⊛ ◖ ▸ ⊟ ✦ ⌒ P

Lydford

Castle Inn
Off A386
☎ (082 282) 242
11.30–3, 6–11
Furgusons Dartmoor Best Bitter; Ind Coope Burton Ale; Marston's Pedigree; Palmers IPA Ⓗ
Stone-flagged, 16th-century free house by the castle. Beware of the low ceiling in the bar. The extensive garden at the rear is safe for small children. ▟ Q ⏣ ⊛ ⌑ ◖ ▸ ⊟ ▲ ✦ P

Mary Tavy

Mary Tavy Inn
On A386
☎ (0822) 810326
11.30 (11 summer)–3, 6–11
Draught Bass; St Austell Tinners, HSD Ⓗ
16th-century inn on the Okehampton road. A pleasant and welcoming atmosphere in a two-roomed pub with a large stone fireplace. ▟ ⏣ ⊛ ⌑ ◖ ▸ ⊟ ▲ ✦ P

Meavy

Royal Oak
1 mile E of A386
☎ (0822) 852944
11–2.30, 6–11
Draught Bass; Whitbread Boddingtons Bitter, Castle Eden Ale Ⓗ; **guest beers**
15th-century pub on the village green within the National Park. The public bar has a slate floor and an inglenook. Owned by the local parish.
▟ Q ⊛ ◖ ▸ ⊟ ▲ ✦ ⌒

Devon

Milton Combe

Who'd Have Thought It
2 miles W of A386
☎ (0822) 853313
11.30–2.30 (11–3 Sat), 6–11
Draught Bass; Blackawton Headstrong; Eldridge Pope Royal Oak; Exmoor Ale; Wadworth 6X H
16th-century pub in a steep, wooded valley, with slate floors and three rooms. Folk club Sun.
🏚 Q ❀ ◖ ▶ & ⌣ P

Molland

Black Cock
Off A361 ☎ (076 97) 297
11–11
Cotleigh Harrier, Tawny H; **guest beer** (summer)
Pub located near the former Tiverton–Barnstaple railway in attractive countryside. Camping facilities and holiday accommodation in season. An opened-up interior.
🏚 ⛺ ❀ ⌂ ◖ ▶ ▲ ⌣ P

Moreleigh

New Inn
Off B3207 ☎ (0548) 82326
12–2, 6.30–11
Palmers IPA G
Excellent traditional pub off the beaten track, not fancy or spoiled, but a reputation for good food. 🏚 Q ◖ ▶ ♣ P

Mortehoe

Ship Aground
The Square
☎ (0271) 870856
11–3, 5.30–11 (may vary in summer)
Exmoor Ale; Whitbread Boddingtons Bitter, Castle Eden Ale H
Attractive pub converted from old cottages next to the village church. Close to coastal walks and golden beaches. The beer range varies in summer.
🏚 ⛺ ❀ ◖ ▶ ▲ ♣ ⌣

Newton Abbot

Dartmouth Inn
East Street
☎ (0626) 53451
11–11 (11–2.30, 4.30–11 Tue & Wed)
Draught Bass H; **guest beer**
Probably the oldest pub in town, retaining the character of its age. The guest beer changes daily. No food Sun.
⛺ ❀ ◖ ♣ ⌣

Wolborough Inn
Wolborough Street
11–2, 6 (7 Sat)–11
Draught Bass H
Small sports-oriented local.
⌂ ◖ ♣

Newton St Cyres

Beer Engine
Off A377 ☎ (0392) 851282
11–2.30, 6–11
Beer Engine Rail Ale, Piston, Sleeper H
Popular, good value pub-brewery, which hosts live bands in the cellar bar at weekends. On 'Tarka', the Exeter–Barnstaple railway line. Children welcome in the restaurant. 🏚 Q ❀ ◖ ▶ ⇌ P

North Bovey

Ring of Bells
Village Square
☎ (0647) 40375
11–3, 6–11
Furgusons Dartmoor Best Bitter; Ind Coope Burton Ale; Wadworth 6X H; **guest beers**
Rambling, low-beamed pub and restaurant with a walled garden. Good food, plus Gray's cider (summer).
🏚 Q ⛺ ❀ ⌂ ◖ ▶ ▲ ⌣

Ottery St Mary

London Hotel
Gold Street
☎ (0404) 814763
11–3, 5.30–11 (11–11 Sat)
Draught Bass; Ind Coope Burton Ale; Tetley Bitter H; **guest beers**
Modernised 18th-century coaching house with genuine oak beams, horse brasses, etc. Two function rooms, a pool room and a skittle alley.
Q ⛺ ⌂ ◖ ▶ ⊞ ♣ ⌣ P

Parkham

Bell Inn
1 mile S of A39 OS387212
☎ (0237) 451201
11–3, 6–11 (varies in winter)
Draught Bass G; **Fuller's London Pride; Whitbread Flowers IPA** H
Delightful thatched inn at the edge of a thriving village. Its low-beamed interior features a grandfather clock set into the wall. 🏚 Q ◖ ▶ ▲ P

Parracombe

Hunters Inn
Heddons Mouth (off A39 and A399, not in Parracombe village) ☎ (059 83) 230
11–2.30, 7–11 (11–11 summer)
Exmoor Ale; Wadworth 6X; Whitbread Flowers Original H; **guest beers** (summer)
Edwardian, country house hotel in a spectacular National Park valley, close to coastal walks. Beware of the peacocks. Family room and cider in summer only.
🏚 ⛺ ❀ ⌂ ◖ ▶ & ⌣ P

Peter Tavy

Peter Tavy Inn
Off A386
☎ (0822) 810348
11.30–2.30, 6.30–11
Butcombe Bitter; Furgusons Dartmoor Best Bitter, Dartmoor Strong; Wadworth 6X; Whitbread Boddingtons Bitter, Castle Eden Ale G
Ancient moorland pub with low ceilings and flagstones, serving excellent vegetarian food. Expensive but nice. Access to the garden is via steps from the car park; it is not suitable for small children.
🏚 Q ❀ ◖ ▶ P

Plymouth

Abbey Hotel
5 St Catherine Street
☎ (0752) 661624
11–11
Courage Best Bitter H
Bright, breezy two-bar pub with some interesting fittings, next to the magistrates court. Busy food trade weekday lunchtimes. ◖ ▶ ⊞

Clifton Hotel
35 Clifton Street
☎ (0752) 266563
11.30–3, 7–11 (11.30–11 Thu–Sat)
Draught Bass G; **Furgusons Dartmoor Strong; Summerskills Best Bitter** H, **Whistle Belly Vengeance** G; **Tetley Bitter** H; **guest beers**
Recently-opened free house with a warm, friendly atmosphere. Numerous teams. The large old wallclock is never right. ◖ ▶ & ♣ ♠

Colebrook Inn
Colebrook Village, Plympton (off A38)
☎ (0752) 336267
11–3, 6–11
Courage Best Bitter; John Smith's Bitter; Summerskills Whistle Belly Vengeance H
Built in 1714 as four small cottages alongside the brook where fishing boats landed their catch of pilchards. Reputedly haunted.
🏚 Q ⛺ ❀ ◖ ⊞ & ♣

Dolphin Hotel
14 The Barbican
10–11
Draught Bass G
The last unaltered pub on the historic Barbican: a time-warp for serious drinkers, and popular with the fishermen. The Tolpuddle Martyrs stayed here on their first night back in England from Australia. 🏚

Fishermans Arms
31 Lambhay St, Barbican
☎ (0752) 661457
11–3, 6–11 (11–11 Sat & summer)
St Austell HSD H

89

Devon

200-year-old local on the Barbican, with a friendly atmosphere (families welcome). Note the unusual electric weather vane. The only pub in the locality selling HSD. ◑ ▶ ♣ ⌂

Little Mutton Monster

240 James Street, Devonport
☎ (0752) 560938
11.30–2.30, 6–11
Draught Bass; Courage Best Bitter; Ruddles County; St Austell HSD Ⓗ; **guest beers**
200-year-old pub adjoining the naval dockyard; formerly the Mutton Cove Tavern. Excellent value food; two guest beers. ⌘ ◑ ▶ ♣

Mechanics Arms

31 Stonehouse Street
11–3, 5–11 (11–11 Fri & Sat)
St Austell HSD Ⓗ
Corner pub in a busy industrial area with a family atmosphere. Music hall piano Sun eves. No meals Sun. ◑ ♣

Pennycomequick

Central Park Avenue
☎ (0752) 661412
12–3, 7–11 (11–11 Sat)
Furgusons Dartmoor Best Bitter Ⓗ
Well-positioned two-bar pub near the main station. A cosy lounge with a real fire, and a large public where games are played (euchre and doms).
🏚 ⌘ ◑ ▶ 🍴 & ⇌ ♣

Pym Arms

16 Pym Street, Devonport
11–3, 6–11
Draught Bass; Charrington IPA; St Austell XXXX Mild, HSD Ⓗ; **Wadworth 6X** Ⓖ; **guest beers**
Side-street pub, frequented by students, near the dockyard.
⇌ (Devonport) ♣

Shipwrights Arms

Sutton Road, Coxside
☎ (0752) 665804
11–11
Courage Best Bitter Ⓗ
Comfortable pub near the city centre. ⌘ ◑ ▶ P

Thistle Park Tavern

32 Commercial Road, Coxside (off A374) ☎ (0752) 667677
11–11
Adnams Broadside; Greene King Abbot; St Austell HSD; Summerskills Best Bitter, Whistle Belly Vengeance; Wadworth 6X Ⓗ; **guest beers**
Warm, friendly atmosphere in a pub which holds two regular beer festivals – May Day weekend and the last weekend of October. 🏚 ♣

Plymtree

Blacksmiths Arms

☎ (088 47) 322

11–3 (not Mon–Fri), 6–11 (may be 11–11 summer)
Draught Bass; Whitbread Flowers IPA Ⓗ; **guest beers**
Traditional, village local, comprising one large bar and a skittle alley. A varied menu of home-cooked meals includes vegetarian and children's meals. The beer range may vary. 🏚 ⌘ ◑ ▶ ♣ ⌂ P

Poundsgate

Tavistock Inn

On A384 between Ashburton and the moor ☎ (036 43) 251
11–2.30 (3 summer), 6 (5 summer)–11
Courage Best Bitter; Ushers Best Bitter, Founders Ⓗ
Traditional Dartmoor pub with a good atmosphere in an isolated hamlet: a cosy rugged front bar, a side room and plenty of outside seating. All day breakfasts are served.
🏚 ⛄ ⌘ ◑ ▶ ♣ ⌂ P

Rackenford

Stag Inn

1 mile S of A361
☎ (088 488) 369
12–2.30, 6–11
Cotleigh Tawny; Exmoor Gold (summer) Ⓗ
North Devon's oldest inn, dating back to 1237. A thatched roof, cob walls and an unusual tunnel entrance with cobblestones complement the low-beamed interior with its open fireplace and panelling. A must for all those visiting the area.
🏚 Q ⛄ ⌘ 🛏 ◑ ▶ ♣ P

Seaton

Hook & Parrot

The Esplanade ☎ (0297) 20222
11–3, 5.30–11 (11–11 Sat & Sun)
Devenish Royal Wessex; Whitbread Boddingtons Bitter Ⓗ; **guest beer**
Large ground-level bar/lounge area with an adjoining restaurant which is used as a family room until 8pm. The downstairs bar serves Boddingtons only and caters for the younger generation with a pool table.
Q ⛄ ⌘ ◑ ▶ 🛏 & A ♣

Sleeper Inn

Marine Place ☎ (0297) 24380
11–3, 6.30–11 (12 Fri; 11–12 Sat); 11–11 (12 Fri & Sat) in summer
Beer Engine Rail Ale, Piston, Sleeper Ⓗ
Spacious, three-bar, town pub; the high-ceilinged downstairs room displays paintings of the pub. The upstairs family room (until 9pm) is also the venue for live music on Fri and Sat nights. A supper licence operates in the top bar.
⛄ ◑ ▶ 🛏 A ♣

Shaldon

Shipwrights Arms

Ringmore Road
☎ (0626) 873237
11–3, 5.30–11
Courage Best Bitter, Directors; John Smith's Bitter Ⓗ
Pub with a nautical flavour and an estuary view.
🏚 ⛄ ⌘ ◑ ▶ 🍴 ♣ P

Silverton

Silverton Inn

Fore Street ☎ (0392) 860196
12–3, 5.30–11 (11–11 Sat; may vary)
Draught Bass; Exe Valley Dob's Best Bitter; guest beers Ⓗ
Friendly, one-bar village pub with a restaurant. Formerly the New Inn.
🏚 Q ⌘ ◑ ▶ A ♣

South Molton

Town Arms

East Street ☎ (076 95) 2531
11–11 (11–3, 6–11 Fri & Sat)
Gibbs Mew Local Line, Salisbury Ⓗ
Quiet town-centre local featuring stained-glass windows. Cider in summer.
🏚 ⌘ 🛏 ◑ ▶ ♣ ⌂ P

Sparkwell

Treby Arms

☎ (075 537) 363
11–3, 6.30–11
Draught Bass; Ruddles Best Bitter; Webster's Yorkshire Bitter Ⓗ; **guest beers**
Pub dating from circa 1750, in a picturesque village near a wildlife park. No eve meals Mon in winter.
🏚 Q ⌘ ◑ ▶ & A ♣ P

Spreyton

Tom Cobley Tavern

Off B3219 ☎ (064 723) 314
12–2.30 (not Mon), 6 (7 Mon)–11
Cotleigh Tawny; Exe Valley Dob's Best Bitter Ⓖ; **guest beers**
Quiet village local with an indoor barbecue in the function room available for private parties. All food is home cooked (no meals Mon).
🏚 Q ⛄ ⌘ 🛏 ◑ ▶ & ♣ P

Talaton

Talaton Inn

On B3176 ☎ (0404) 822214
12–3, 7–11
Draught Bass; Wadworth 6X Ⓗ
Friendly village local serving good value food both in the bar and restaurant.
🏚 Q ⛄ ⌘ ◑ ▶ 🛏 ♣ P

Thorverton

Exeter Inn
Bullen Street ☎ (0392) 860206
11.30–3, 6–11
Courage Best Bitter; Exe Valley Devon Glory; Ind Coope Burton Ale H
Old coaching inn displaying farm implements; a well was uncovered during alterations. Eve meals by arrangement only. ♨ Q ◑ ✓ & ♣ ⌂ P

Tiverton

Four in Hand
Fore Street ☎ (0884) 252765
11–3, 6 (5 Fri)–11 (11–11 Sat)
Draught Bass H
Busy bar in the town centre, near the bus station. No wheelchair access to the gents' WC. Q ◑ & ♣

Racehorse
Wellbrook Street
☎ (0884) 252606
11–11
Ruddles County; Ushers Best Bitter; Webster's Yorkshire Bitter H
Popular local with a friendly atmosphere and a large function room. Meals all day.
♨ ⍣ ❀ ◑ ▶ & ♣

White Horse
Gold Street ☎ (0884) 252022
11–11
Draught Bass H; guest beers
Small but friendly town-centre local serving good value food.
❀ 🚲 ◑ ▶ & ♣

Topsham

Bridge Inn
Bridgehill ☎ (039 287) 3862
12–2, 6–10.30 (11 Sat)
Adnams Broadside; Cotleigh Tawny; Exe Valley Devon Glory; Exmoor Ale; Fuller's ESB; Otter Ale G
Unspoilt, multi-roomed pub: a local institution with a dozen ales. ♨ Q ⍣ ❀ ⇌ P

Torquay

Crown & Sceptre
2 Petitor Road, St Mary Church ☎ (0803) 328290
11–3, 6–11 (11–11 Sat)
Courage Best Bitter, Directors; Ruddles County; John Smith's Bitter H; guest beer
200-year-old village pub, now engulfed by Torbay. Regular folk music sessions and much character. ♨ ⍣ ❀ ◑ ▶ ♣ P

Totnes

Albert
32 Bridgetown Hill (Paignton road) ☎ (0803) 863214
11–3, 6–11 (11–11 Thu & Sat)

Courage Best Bitter; Wadworth 6X H
Lively traditional pub.
❀ ◑ ♣ ⌂

Kingsbridge Inn
9 Leechwell Street
☎ (0803) 863324
11–2.30, 5.30–11
Draught Bass; Courage Best Bitter, Directors; Fergusons Dartmoor Best Bitter H
Ancient, low-ceilinged inn with many alcoves where the accent is on food. Q ◑ ▶ ✗

Trusham

Cridford Inn
☎ (0626) 853694
12 (11 summer)–3, 7 (6 summer)–11 (12–2.30, 7–10.30 Sun)
Draught Bass; Butcombe Bitter; Cotleigh Old Buzzard G; guest beers
Originally an old barn but a pub since 1983. Stained-glass windows and old church pews add character; the main bar has a stone floor. ♨ Q ⍣ ❀ ⇌ ◑ ▶ ⌖ ▲ ♣ ⌂ P

Turnchapel

Boringdon Arms
Boringdon Terrace
☎ (0752) 402053
11–3.30, 6–11 (11–11 Fri & Sat)
Draught Bass; Butcombe Bitter; Summerskills Whistle Belly Vengeance H; guest beer
Friendly local displaying masses of artefacts, including a Meccano clock, charts, knots and a rope puzzle. B&B with sea views, a family room and a garden carved from solid rock are all features of this ex-quarry master's house.
♨ Q ⍣ ❀ ⇌ ◑ ▶ ▲ ♣

Welcombe

Old Smithy Inn
2 miles off A39 OS232178
☎ (028 883) 305
11–3, 7–11 (11–11 summer; 12–2.30, 7–10.30 Sun)
Butcombe Bitter; Marston's Pedigree (summer) H
Popular, 13th-century thatched inn set in attractive countryside. Extremely busy during the tourist season. Try the superb coastal walk to the Bush in Cornwall.
♨ ⍣ ❀ ⇌ ◑ ▶ ▲ ⌂ P

Wembworthy

Lymington Arms
Lama Cross (1/2 mile from the village on Winkleigh road) OS664092 ☎ (0837) 83572
11–3 (4.30 Sat), 6–11 (midnight supper licence)
Eldridge Pope Hardy Country, Royal Oak; Palmers IPA H; guest beers

Old coaching inn, rebuilt in the 1820s. Cider in summer.
♨ ❀ ⇌ ◑ ▶ ♣ ⌂ P

Westcott

Merry Harriers
On B3181 ☎ (0392) 881254
12–2.30, 7–11
Draught Bass H
Friendly roadside pub and restaurant which enjoys a reputation for good food.
♨ Q ❀ ◑ ▶ & ▲ P

Whimple

New Fountain
Church Road ☎ (0404) 822350
11–3, 6–11
Courage Directors; Fergusons Dartmoor Strong; Tetley Bitter H
Friendly, enterprising village local featuring splendid beams and fireplaces, a successful sell-off from the Devenish empire. Children are understood and welcomed by the cheerful proprietors.
♨ ❀ ◑ ▶ ⇌ ⌂ P

Paddock Inn
London Road (A30)
☎ (0404) 822356
11–3, 6–11 (11–11 Sat)
Beer Engine Piston; Courage Best Bitter, Directors H; guest beers
Large pub with a games room/family area. The restaurant serves a varied menu of home-cooked food at reasonable prices. Large range of imported bottled beers.
Q ⍣ ❀ ◑ ▶ ▲ ♣ ⌂ P

Yarde Down

Poltimore Arms
Top of hill outside Brayford on Simonsbath road
☎ (0598) 710381
11.30–3.30, 6.30–11
Cotleigh Tawny G; **Ruddles County** H
Classic, unspoilt Exmoor pub. Enjoy convivial winter evenings round the log fire. On summer eves the landlord runs a cricket team in the fields opposite. Fine reputation for food.
♨ Q ⍣ ◑ ▶

Yelverton

Rock Inn
Rock Complex (near A386/B3212 jct) ☎ (0822) 852022
11–2.30, 6–11 (11–11 summer)
Draught Bass; Charrington IPA; St Austell HSD; Whitbread Boddingtons Bitter, Pompey Royal H
Large, well-run pub with three bars. The popular family room has videos for children.
♨ Q ⍣ ❀ ◑ ▶ & ♣ P

Dorset

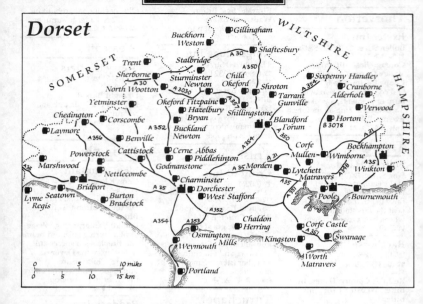

Dorset

Alderholt

Churchill Arms
Daggons Road (off A338 at
Ibsley) ☎ (0425) 652147
11–2.30, 6–11
**Hall & Woodhouse Hard
Tackle; Wells Eagle** H
Convivial, comfortable inn.
Good range of food (children's
menu); function room.
🍴 ⛺ 🚫 ◖ ▶ 🅵 🐕 🅰 ♣ P

Benville

Talbot
1½ miles off A356 OS542039
☎ (0935) 83381
11.30–2.30, 6.30–11
Greene King Abbot H; **guest
beer**
Village pub with both fake and
real dogs. Collection of key
rings. 🍴 ❀ ◖ ▶ 🅵 🐕 🅰 ♣ P

Blandford Forum

Half Moon
Whitecliff Mill Street
☎ (0258) 452318
10–11
**Hall & Woodhouse Badger
Best Bitter; Wells Eagle** H
Unspoilt, basic town pub with
a friendly atmosphere. Hall &
Woodhouse's longest serving
licensees (over 20 years).
Q 🚫 ❀ 🅵 ♣ 🍷 P

Railway Hotel
Oakfield Street
☎ (0258) 456374
11–2.30, 6–11
**Hall & Woodhouse Badger
Best Bitter, Hard Tackle;
Ringwood Fortyniner** H
Upmarket pub, popular with
the young. 🍴 ◖ ▶

Bournemouth

Criterion
41–43 Old Christchurch Road
☎ (0202) 290070
11–11
Draught Bass H
Large, town-centre Victorian
local: a downstairs drinkers'
bar, an upstairs lounge and
Micawbers wine bar adjoining
(eve meals). ◖

Hollies
1010 Wimborne Road,
Moordown ☎ (0202) 512819
11.30–2.30, 5–11 (11.30–11 Fri & Sat)
**Marston's Burton Best Bitter,
Pedigree** H
Lively community pub with
live music and entertainment
on Thu and Sun eves. ❀ ♣ P

Old Thumper
113 Poole Road, Westbourne
☎ (0202) 768576
11–3, 5–11
**Fuller's London Pride;
Ringwood Best Bitter, XXXX
Porter, Fortyniner, Old
Thumper** H
Lively town pub, for all types.
Friendly bar staff; reasonably
priced beer. The best choice of
real ales in a town dominated
by keg hotel and wine bars. No
food Sun. ◖ ≋ (Branksome)

Bridport

Oddfellows Arms
172 North Allington (B3162)
☎ (0308) 22665
11–2.30, 5.15–11 (11–11 summer)
Palmers BB, IPA H
Red brick, terraced boozer
with possibly the cheapest
beer in Dorset. Live music
weekends. ❀ 🅵 🅰 ♣ 🍷

Ropemakers Arms
West Street ☎ (0308) 421255
11–3, 7–11 (11–11 Fri, Sat & summer)
Palmers BB, IPA, Tally Ho! H
Lively town pub near the
market square where the
emphasis is on net-making.
Popular with young people.
The varied menu includes
rabbit pie. Not cheap.
🍴 🚫 ❀ ◖ 🅵 🐕 🅰 ♣ 🍷 P

Buckhorn Weston

Stapleton Arms
OS756246 ☎ (0963) 70396
11.30–3, 6.30–11
Draught Bass; Exmoor Ale H

Large village pub with a
dining area and two spacious
bars. 🏚 🕯 🍴 🍺 🌳 🚲 P ⚲

Buckland Newton

Gaggle of Geese
Off B3143 ☎ (030 05) 249
12–2.30, 6.30–11
Draught Bass; Hall &
Woodhouse Badger Best
Bitter, Hard Tackle;
Wadworth 6X Ⓗ
Large, friendly village local
with a games room and a
skittle alley. Goose auction in
summer. 🏚 🕯 🍴 🍺 ⚷ ▲ 🌳 P

Burton Bradstock

Three Horseshoes
Mill Street ☎ (0308) 897259
11–2.30, 6–11
Palmers BB, IPA, Tally Ho! Ⓗ
Large, thatched village pub
with a restaurant. 🏚 Q 🕯 🍺
🍴 🍺 🍺 ⚷ ▲ 🌳 P

Cattistock

Fox & Hounds
Duck Street ☎ (0300) 20444
12–2.30 (11–3 Sat), 7–11
Beer range varies Ⓗ
Village local always serving at
least two beers. Skittle alley.
🏚 🕯 🍺 🍴 🍺 ▲ 🌳 P

Cerne Abbas

Red Lion
Long Street ☎ (0300) 341441
11–2.30, 6.30–11
Wadworth IPA, 6X Ⓗ; guest
beer
Village-centre local with a
striking Victorian frontage,
not far from the legendary
giant. Large bar with an
imposing Tudor fireplace.
Good value menu. Skittle
alley. 🏚 Q 🕯 🍴 🍺 ⚷ ▲

Chaldon Herring

Sailors Return
S of A352 ☎ (0305) 853847
11–3, 7–11
Goldfinch Tom Brown's;
Wadworth 6X; Whitbread
Strong Country Ⓗ; guest beer
Thatched country pub,
extended but retaining
character. Stone floors and
whitewashed walls
throughout. Good value food.
🕯 🍴 ▲ 🌳 🚲 P

Charminster

New Inn
North Street ☎ (0305) 264694
12–2.30, 7–11 (11–3, 6–11 summer)
Draught Bass; Charrington
IPA; Wadworth 6X Ⓗ
Roadside pub with a large
main bar and a spacious
conservatory, overlooking the
streamside garden. Jazz Thu.
🏚 Q 🍺 🕯 🍴 ▲ 🌳 🚲 P

Chedington

Winyards Gap Inn
On A356 ☎ (093 589) 244
11.30–2.30 (10.30–3 summer), 7–11
Smiles Brewery Bitter;
Whitbread Flowers
Original Ⓗ; guest beers
Hillside pub with fine views
into Somerset, incorporating a
skittle alley. Two self-
contained cottages to rent.
Good menu, including home-
made pies. 🏚 Q 🍺 🕯 🍺 🍴
🍴 🌳 🚲 P ⚲

Child Okeford

Saxon Inn
Gold Hill ☎ (0258) 860310
11.30–2.30, 7–11
Draught Bass; Whitbread
Boddingtons Bitter Ⓗ
Pub overlooked by
Hambledon Hill-fort – hence
the name. Look for this small,
intimate inn up a narrow lane
at the north end of the village.
Plenty of wildlife in the
garden. 🏚 🍺 🕯 🍴 ▲ 🌳 P

Corfe Castle

Fox
West Street ☎ (0929) 480449
11–2.30 (3 summer), 6.30–11
Gibbs Mew Wiltshire,
Bishop's Tipple; Ind Coope
Burton Ale Ⓖ; Tetley Bitter Ⓗ
Unique building, over 400
years-old. Home of the
Ancient Order of Purbeck
Marblers. Recently extended
for an eating area. An old
well, covered by glass, is a
new feature. 🏚 Q 🕯 🍴 ▲

Corfe Mullen

Coventry Arms
Mill Street ☎ (0258) 857284
11–2.30, 5.30–11
Draught Bass; Marston's
Pedigree; Ringwood Best
Bitter, XXXX Porter, Old
Thumper; Wadworth 6X Ⓖ
Popular roadside inn.
Although recently modified, it
still retains an impressive rack
of gravity-served beers. One
real ale is sold at a cheaper
price every Thu eve.
🍺 🕯 🍴 ⚷ 🌳 P

Corscombe

Fox Inn
Off A356 ☎ (0935) 891330
12–2.30, 7–11
Exmoor Ale Ⓖ
Picturesque thatched pub with
a slate-top bar and a
flagstoned floor. An extra beer
in summer. Quality home-
cooked food. Cider in summer.
🏚 Q 🍺 🕯 🍴 ▲ 🌳 🚲 P

Cranborne

Fleur de Lys
5 Wimborne Street (B3078)
☎ (072 54) 282
11–2.30, 6–11
Hall & Woodhouse Badger
Best Bitter, Tanglefoot Ⓗ
Well-appointed, 16th-century
coaching inn. Excellent food in
the lounge bar. The separate
cosy village bar is enjoyed by
locals and visitors alike. The
subject of a Rupert Brooke
poem. 🏚 Q 🍺 🍴 🕯 🍺 ▲
🌳 🚲 P

Sheaf of Arrows
The Square ☎ (072 54) 456
11–2.30, 6–11
Ringwood Best Bitter;
Wadworth 6X Ⓗ
Friendly, Victorian village-
centre local with two
contrasting bars: a large,
rather noisy public, used by
locals, and a small, quiet
lounge. Q 🍺 🍴 🕯 🍺 🍺 🌳

Dorchester

Old Ship
High West Street ☎ (0305) 264455
11–2.30, 4.30–11 (11–11 summer)
Eldridge Pope Dorchester,
Hardy Country, Blackdown
Porter, Royal Oak; Wadworth
Old Timer Ⓔ
Town pub with the full range
of Eldridge Pope beers.
🍺 🕯 🍴 🍺 🚲 (South) 🌳

Tom Brown's
47 High East Street
☎ (0305) 264020
11–3, 6–11
Goldfinch Tom Brown's,
Flashman's Clout Ⓗ
Revitalised town pub now
managed and allowing the
owner to concentrate on
brewing. Home-cooked food;
live music. 🏚 🍴 🕯 🌳

White Hart
53 High East Street
☎ (0305) 263545
11–3, 6–11
Hall & Woodhouse Badger
Best Bitter, Tanglefoot Ⓗ
Pub where plenty of activities
occupy a varied clientele. The
art of conversation is alive and
kicking, unlike the late
unlamented jukebox.
🏚 Q 🍺 🕯 🍴 🍺 🌳 P

Gillingham

Buffalo Inn
Wyke (off B3081)
☎ (0747) 823759
11–2.30, 5.30–11
Hall & Woodhouse Badger
Best Bitter; Wells Eagle Ⓗ
Cosy, one-bar local on the
outskirts of town. Jugs and
glasses adorn the beams.
🏚 Q 🍺 🕯 🍴 ▲ 🍺 🍺 P

Dorset

Godmanstone

Smiths Arms
Main Road ☎ (0300) 341236
11–3, 6–11
Ringwood Best Bitter Ⓖ
England's smallest inn, as
stated in the *Guinness Book of
Records*. Granted a licence by
Charles II when he stopped
here to have his horse shod
(the blacksmith could not
serve him as he had no
licence). Cider in summer
only. ♨ Q ✿ ◑ ▷ ♿ ⇦ P

Hazelbury Bryan

Antelope
Pidney (1 mile E of B3143)
OS745091 ☎ (0258) 817295
11–3, 6–11
**Hall & Woodhouse Badger
Best Bitter** Ⓖ
Despite a recent renovation,
this village local has retained
its character. Beer is now
straight from the barrel (the
handpumps are just for show).
♨ Q ✿ ◑ ▷ ♣ ⇦

Horton

Horton Inn
On B3078 ☎ (0258) 840252
11–2.30, 6–11
**Courage Directors; Ringwood
Best Bitter, Fortyniner** Ⓗ
18th-century coaching inn set
in rural countryside: one well-
appointed bar with a large
open fire and a relaxing
atmosphere. High quality food
and accommodation.
♨ Q ✿ ⋈ ◑ ▷ ▲ P

Kingston

Scott Arms
West Street ☎ (0929) 480270
11–2.30, 6–11
**Ringwood Best Bitter,
Fortyniner; Wadworth 6X** Ⓗ
Scenic pub in an old village,
often used as a TV and film
set. The garden and the
recently rebuilt lounge enjoy
splendid views of the
Purbecks. Comfortable public
bar with displays of fishing
tackle. Small dining room (no
food Sun eve in winter). A
house beer is also on sale
(brewery varies).
♨ ✿ ⋈ ◑ ▷ ▲ P

Laymore

Squirrel
OS387048 ☎ (0460) 30298
11.30–2.30, 6–11 (12–2.30, 7–10.30
Sun)
**Cotleigh Harrier; Courage
Directors; Oakhill Yeoman** Ⓗ;
guest beers
Incongruous red brick pub in
beautiful countryside on the
Somerset border. Lovely
views: a good base for

exploring darkest Dorset.
Friendly atmosphere. ♨ ⌛
✿ ⋈ ◑ ▷ ⊞ ▲ ♣ ⇦ P

Lyme Regis

Angel Inn
Mill Green (300 yds down
Monmouth St, off High St)
☎ (0297) 443267
11–2.30, 7–11
Palmers BB, IPA Ⓖ
Northern 1950s-type locals'
pub, plain but friendly and
well-run by an ex-GWR steam
railwayman. Collection of
bottled beers (over 700). Good
value. ⌛ ✿ ◑ ▷ ♣ P

Royal Standard
Marine Parade (on the Cobb)
☎ (0297) 442637
11–3, 7–11 (11–11 summer)
Palmers BB, IPA, Tally Ho! Ⓗ
Historic, 400-year-old pub on
the beach, popular with young
people and tourists. Beer
prices reflect its position.
♨ Q ✿ ◑ ▷ ♣ ⇦

Lytchett Matravers

Chequers
High Street ☎ (0202) 622215
11–2.30 (3 Sat), 6–11
**Draught Bass; Ringwood Best
Bitter** Ⓗ; **guest beer**
Large pub with a number of
different bar areas. Offers 18
country wines, a restaurant
and a children's play area.
♨ Q ⌛ ✿ ⋈ ◑ ▷ ♿ ▲ ⇦ P

Marshwood

Bottle Inn
On B3165 ☎ (029 77) 254
11–2 (3 summer), 6–11
**Exmoor Ale; Ruddles Best
Bitter; Wadworth 6X** Ⓗ
Genuine, olde-worlde wayside
inn with a skittle alley for
functions. An extensive menu
caters for families. Wheelchair
access to function room. Cider
in summer.
✿ ⋈ ◑ ▷ ⊞ ▲ ♣ ⇦ P

Morden

Cock & Bottle
On B3075 ☎ (092 945) 238
11–2.30, 6 (7 winter)–11
**Hall & Woodhouse Badger
Best Bitter, Hard Tackle,
Tanglefoot; Wells Eagle** Ⓗ
Unspoilt village pub in a rural
setting. Friendly welcome;
home-cooked food.
♨ ⌛ ✿ ◑ ▷ ♣ P

Nettlecombe

Marquis of Lorne
Off A3066 ☎ (030 885) 236
11–2.30, 6.30–11
Palmers BB, IPA Ⓗ
16th-century inn: a panelled
bar with a central fireplace;
dining room with a good

reputation and an extensive, if
expensive, menu. Excellent
value winter breaks.
♨ ✿ ⋈ ◑ ▷ ♿ P

North Wootton

Three Elms
On A3030 ☎ (0935) 812881
11–2.30, 6.30 (6 Fri & Sat)–11
**Ash Vine Bitter; Fuller's
London Pride; Greene King
Abbot; Hook Norton Mild;
Smiles Best Bitter; Wadworth
6X** Ⓗ; **guest beers**
W Dorset CAMRA *Pub of the
Year* 1991. The landlord has
converted many to the cause
of good beer (foreign bottled
beers also available). Popular
food. Q ✿ ⋈ ◑ ▷ ♿ ♣ ⇦ P

Okeford Fitzpaine

Royal Oak
Lower Street ☎ (0258) 860308
11–2.30, 6.30–11
**Fuller's London Pride;
Ringwood Best Bitter** Ⓗ
Basic but homely pub in an
attractive village. Look out for
the famous picture-postcard
view of the church. Skittle
alley. No food Wed.
♨ ⌛ ✿ ◑ ▷ ♿ ♣ ⇦ P

Osmington Mills

Smugglers
Off A353 ☎ (0305) 833125
11–2.30 (3 summer), 6.30 (5.30
summer)–11
**Courage Best Bitter;
Ringwood Old Thumper;
Whitbread Flowers
Original** Ⓗ
Popular family pub close to
the sea. Large beamed interior
with a restaurant; a stream
runs through the large garden
and play area. The beer range
varies a little, but is on the
expensive side.
♨ ⌛ ✿ ⋈ ◑ ▷ ▲ ♣ ⇦ P

Piddlehinton

Thimble Inn
On B3143 ☎ (030 04) 270
12–2.30, 7–11 (12–2.30, 7–10.30 Sun)
**Eldridge Pope Hardy
Country; Hall & Woodhouse
Badger Best Bitter, Hard
Tackle; Ringwood Old
Thumper** Ⓗ
Pretty country inn beside the
River Piddle. Interesting beer
engine at the entrance to the
car park. Good value beer.
♨ ✿ ◑ ▷ ♿ ♣ P

Poole

Beehive
Sandbanks Road, Lilliput
(B3369) ☎ (0202) 708641
10.30–2.30, 6–11 (11–11 summer)
**Eldridge Pope Dorchester,
Hardy Country, Royal Oak** Ⓗ
Built 100 years ago, a pub now

popular with the windsurfing and beach fraternity. Weekends see the restaurant and garden crowded with families enjoying the excellent facilities, which include an indoor playroom with a nanny. ⛱ ❀ ◑ ◗ P

Bermuda Triangle

10 Parr Street ☎ (0202) 748087
11.30–2.30, 5.30 (5 Fri)–11 (11–11 Sat)
Bateman XXXB; Felinfoel Double Dragon; Fuller's ESB; Goldfinch Flashman's Clout; King & Barnes Festive; Moorhouse's Pendle Witches Brew Ⓗ
Friendly free house with an interior based on the Bermuda Triangle mystery. A true free house offering a range of ales from around the country. Also over 30 international bottled beers. ❀ ◑ ⌓ P

Conjurors Half Crown

Commercial Road, Parkstone (A35 civic roundabout near park) ☎ (0202) 740302
11–2.30, 5 (6 Sat)–11 (12–2.30, 7–10.30 Sun)
Hall & Woodhouse Badger Best Bitter, Tanglefoot Ⓗ**; guest beers**
Large, multi-roomed pub on different levels. Wood panelling and oak beams give a Dickensian atmosphere (the name comes from a Dickens character).
❀ ◑ ◗ ≢ (Parkstone) P

Dorset Knob

164 Alder Road, Parkstone (A3040) ☎ (0202) 745918
11–3, 5.30–11 (11–11 Fri & Sat)
Hall & Woodhouse Badger Best Bitter, Tanglefoot Ⓗ
Modern two-bar pub: a basic public with a dartboard, pool and pub games, and a comfortable, wood-panelled lounge. Small meeting room-cum-children's room. No food Sun. ⛫ ⛱ ❀ ◑ ⊟ ≢ (Branksome) ♣ P

Foundry Arms

58 Lagland Street
☎ (0202) 672769
11–3, 6 (7 Sat)–11
Eldridge Pope Hardy Country, Blackdown Porter, Royal Oak; Wadworth Old Timer Ⓗ
Comfortable town-centre pub. Good home-cooked food always available in the L-shaped one bar. Dartboards and photos of old Poole. Beers may vary. ❀ ◑ ◗ ≢ ♣ P

Grasshopper

141 Bournemouth Road, Parkstone (A35)
☎ (0202) 741463
11–11
Hall & Woodhouse Badger Best Bitter, Tanglefoot; Wells Eagle Ⓗ
Pub with collections of toby jugs and spirit miniatures: one large bar with several areas.
❀ ◑ ◗ ♿ ≢ (Branksome) ♣ P

Inn in the Park

Pinewood Road, Branksome Park (off the Avenue, off Westminster Rd)
☎ (0202) 761318
11–2.30 (3 Sat), 5.30 (6 Sat)–11
Adnams Bitter; Draught Bass; Wadworth 6X Ⓗ
Plush inn near the sea. Meals in the dining area (no food Sun). ⛫ Q ❀ 🛏 ◑ ◗ P

Lord Nelson

The Quay
☎ (0202) 673774
11–11
Hall & Woodhouse Badger Best Bitter, Tanglefoot; Wells Eagle Ⓗ
Busy pub with nautical artefacts and flagstone floors. Live bands and loud blues/rock music. Shower facilities for visiting yachtsmen. A well furnished children's room provides a quiet, alternative drinking area. No food Sun. ⛱ ❀ ◑ ♿

Portland

Corner House

49 Straits, Easton
☎ (0305) 822526
11–3, 6–11
Eldridge Pope Dorchester, Hardy Country, Blackdown Porter, Royal Oak Ⓗ
Unchanged, 19th-century corner ale house with a small, cosy bar and a games room. Regular winner of Eldridge Pope's *Cellar Supremo* award.
❀ 🛏 ♣

Cove House Inn

Chesil Beach, Chiswell
☎ (0305) 820895
11.30–2.30, 6.30–11 (varies summer)
Devenish Royal Wessex; Greene King Abbot; Marston's Pedigree; Wadworth 6X Ⓗ**; guest beers** (occasionally)
Old inn at the end of Chesil Beach, virtually rebuilt after the storms of 1990 when struck by a 60ft wave. A friendly, no-frills pub with an excellent restaurant. ❀ ◑ ◗ P

Powerstock

Three Horseshoes

Off A3066 ☎ (030 885) 328
11–3, 6–11
Palmers BB, IPA Ⓗ
Character pub with fine views. Highly recommended for food in the bar and the separate restaurant (fresh fish always available). Families welcomed. DIY barbecues in summer.
⛫ Q ❀ 🛏 ◑ ◗ ▲ ⌓ P

Seatown

Anchor Inn

☎ (0297) 89215
11–2.30, 7–11 (11–11 summer)
Palmers BB, IPA, Tally Ho! Ⓔ
Small, cosy pub next to a stony beach. Popular with walkers and anglers but no muddy shoes allowed inside!
⛫ Q ⛱ ❀ ◑ ◗ ⊟ ▲ ♣ P

Shaftesbury

Olde Two Brewers

24 St James Street (100 yds from bottom of Gold Hill)
☎ (0747) 54211
11–3, 6–11
Courage Best Bitter; Wadworth 6X; Young's Special Ⓗ**; guest beers**
300-year-old pub with excellent views of the Blackmoor Vale and several different drinking areas. The landlord wears a different bow tie each evening and offers a drink in exchange for a tie he hasn't got. ❀ ◑ ◗ P

Try also: Crown Inn (Hall & Woodhouse)

Sherborne

Digby Tap

Cooks Lane ☎ (0935) 813148
11–2.30, 5.30–11
Beer range varies Ⓗ
Splendid, side-street tap room near the abbey. Stone flags, old photos and a friendly atmosphere make this the non-plastic type of real pub fast disappearing nowadays. Three or four beers available.
⛱ ◑ ≢ ♣ ⌓

Skippers

Horsecastles (near centre on A352) ☎ (0935) 812753
11.30–2.30, 5.30 (6.30 Sat)–11 (12–2.30, 7–10.30 Sun)
Draught Bass Ⓗ**; guest beers**
Friendly, welcoming corner pub with an ever-changing selection of guest beers as well as a house beer. Good range of bar meals and a separate restaurant area. Some foreign bottled beers. Cider in summer. ❀ ◑ ◗ ≢ ♣ ⌓ P

Shillingstone

Silent Whistle

Cookswell (on A357)
☎ (0258) 860488
11–11
Courage Best Bitter; Ringwood Best Bitter Ⓗ**; guest beer**
Friendly, L-shaped bar named Elmo's by a phantom signwriter. Its true name is after the long closed S&D Railway nearby. No food Wed. ⛫ ⛱ ❀ ◑ ◗ ♿ ♣ P

Dorset

Shroton

Cricketers
W of A350 ☎ (0258) 860421
11–3, 7–11
**Fuller's London Pride;
Greene King IPA; Smiles
Best Bitter Ⓗ; guest beers**
Jovial local with an excellent
restaurant. Popular with
walkers. 🏠 Q ❀ ◖❱ ♣ P

Sixpenny Handley

Roebuck
High Street ☎ (0725) 52002
11.30–3, 6.30–11
**Ringwood Best Bitter, XXXX
Porter, Old Thumper Ⓗ; guest
beer**
Upmarket, L-shaped bar with
a cosy fireside, resembling
someone's front room. Old
village pictures. The piano
needs a pianist. No lunches
Mon in winter.
🏠 Q ⛟ ❀ 🛏 ◖❱ 🅰 ♣ P

Star
High Street ☎ (0725) 52272
11–3, 7–11 (11–11 Sat)
**Draught Bass; Wadworth
6X Ⓗ; guest beer**
Village pub with a bustling
public bar. Small eating area
in the more sedate lounge. No
food Sun eve.
🏠 ❀ ◖❱ ⊟ 🅰 ♣ P

Stalbridge

Stalbridge Arms
Lower Road
☎ (0963) 62447
11.30–2.30, 6–11
**Eldridge Pope Dorchester;
Wadworth 6X Ⓗ; guest beers**
Basic drinking pub just off the
main road. Skittle alley. No
lunches Mon.
🏠 ❀ 🛏 ◖❱ ♣ P

Sturminster Newton

Bull
The Bridge (A357)
☎ (0258) 72435
11–2.30, 6–11
**Hall & Woodhouse Badger
Best Bitter; Wells Eagle Ⓗ**
Popular with both skittlers
and runners, a cosy thatched
inn, close to the mill on the
Stour. 🏠 ⛟ ❀ ◖❱ ♣ P

Swanage

Black Swan
High Street (up hill toward
Herston) ☎ (0929) 422761
12–3, 6.30–11 (may vary summer)
**Wiltshire Stonehenge Ⓗ, Old
Grumble Ⓖ**
Pretty and traditional building
with stables converted to
children's rooms. Two
gardens. ⛟ ❀ 🛏 ◖❱ 🅰 P

Tarrant Gunville

Bugle Horn
2 miles N of Tarrant Hinton
☎ (025 889) 300
11.30–3, 6–11
**Fuller's London Pride;
Wadworth 6X Ⓗ**
Comfortably furnished village
local on the edge of Cranborne
Chase. 🏠 Q ❀ ◖❱ ♣ P

Trent

Rose & Crown
N of A30 ☎ (0935) 850776
12–2.30, 7 (6.30 summer)–11
Oakhill Bitter Ⓗ; guest beers
Excellent village local
converted from a farmhouse.
Children's menu and unusual
dishes (eg Cajun). Three guest
beers.
🏠 Q ⛟ ❀ ◖❱ ⊝ P ⊬

Verwood

Albion
Station Road ☎ (0202) 825267
11–2.30, 5 (6 Sat)–11
**Gibbs Mew Salisbury,
Bishop's Tipple Ⓗ**
CAMRA E Dorset *Pub of the
Year* 1990. Real characters and
a ghost called Wesley can be
found here. 🏠 Q ❀ ◖❱ ⊟ P

West Stafford

Wise Man
☎ (0305) 263694
11–2.30, 6.30–11 (12–2.30, 7–10.30
Sun)
**Devenish Cornish Original,
Royal Wessex Ⓗ; guest beer**
Lovely thatched pub in the
centre of the village. Usually
three ales. Collection of toby
jugs and pipes. Will be really
worth hunting out after the
village has been bypassed.
Cider in summer only.
🏠 Q ❀ ◖❱ ⊟ ❧ ♣ ⊝ P

Weymouth

Dorset Brewers
Hope Square ☎ (0305) 786940
11–11
**Draught Bass; Eldridge Pope
Hardy Country; Palmers
Tally Ho!; Ringwood Old
Thumper Ⓗ**
Attractive pub in a relaxed
square near the old Devenish
brewery. The beer range
changes in summer.
🏠 ❀ ◖❱ ❧

Waterloo

Red Lion
High Street ☎ (0929) 423533
11–11 (may vary winter)
**Whitbread Strong Country,
Flowers Original Ⓖ**
Popular, down-to-earth pub:
public bar with an open fire;
comfortable lounge leading to
a large beer garden. Eve meals
Fri/Sat only.
🏠 ⛟ ❀ ◖❱ ⊟ 🅰 ♣ ⊝ P

Waterloo
Grange Road
☎ (0305) 784488
11.30–3 (4 Sat), 6.30–11
**Gibbs Mew Local Line,
Salisbury Ⓗ**
Corner pub just off the
Esplanade: a long, narrow bar,
often crowded and sometimes
smoky. ❀ ◖❱ ⊜

Weatherbury
7 Carlton Road North (off
Dorchester Rd)
☎ (0305) 786040
11–2.30, 5.30–11 (11–11 Fri & Sat)
Draught Bass Ⓗ; guest beers
Lively, often crowded local in
a residential area. Large
selection of beers; live music;
homely food.
Q ❀ 🛏 ◖❱ ⊜ ♣ P

Wimborne

Cricketers Arms
Park Lane
☎ (0202) 882846
11–2.30, 6–11 (11–11 Fri & Sat)
**Devenish Royal Wessex;
Ringwood Fortyniner;
Wadworth 6X Ⓗ**
Large, comfortable, recently
refurbished, one-bar, town-
centre pub. Beers may vary.
🏠 ◖ ♣

Winkton

Fisherman's Haunt
Salisbury Road (B3347)
☎ (0202) 484071
10.30–2.30, 6–11
**Draught Bass; Courage
Directors; Ringwood XXXX
Porter, Fortyniner Ⓗ**
17th-century Avon valley
hotel. Reasonably priced food
in the bar and restaurant.
Children welcome in one
lounge. 🏠 ❀ 🛏 ◖❱ P ⊬

Worth Matravers

Square & Compass
Off B3069
☎ (0929) 43229
11–3, 6–11
**Hall & Woodhouse
Tanglefoot; Marston's
Pedigree; Whitbread Strong
Country, Pompey Royal Ⓖ**
Ancient bastion of the
Purbecks, in the same family
since the early 1900s. Superb
views of the medieval field
system and sea.
🏠 Q ❀ 🅰 ♣ ⊝ P

Yetminster

White Hart
High Street
☎ (0935) 872338
11.30 (11 Sat)–2.30, 7–11
Draught Bass Ⓗ; guest beer
Two-bar village pub: one
lively, one comfortable. Skittle
alley and good value food.
Q ❀ ◖❱ ⊜ ♣ P

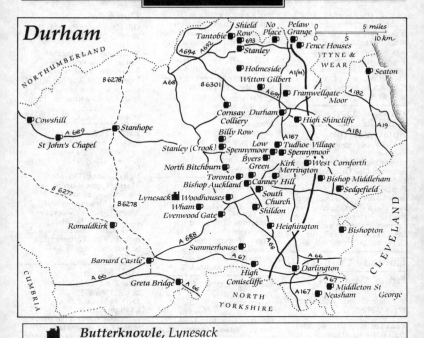

Durham

NORTHUMBERLAND

TYNE & WEAR

Shield Row · No Place · Pelaw Grange · Fence Houses
Tantobie · Stanley · Seaton
Holmeside · Witton Gilbert
Framwellgate Moor
Cowshill · Stanhope · Cornsay Colliery · Durham · High Shincliffe
St John's Chapel · Billy Row · Low Spennymoor · Tudhoe Village · West Spennymoor
Stanley (Crook) · Byers Green · Kirk Merrington · West Cornforth
North Bitchburn · Toronto · Bishop Auckland · Canney Hill · Bishop Middleham · Sedgefield
Lynesack · Woodhouses · South Church Shildon · Bishopton
Wham · Evenwood Gate · Heighington
Romaldkirk · Summerhouse
Barnard Castle · High Conisscliffe · Darlington · Middleton St George · Neasham
Greta Bridge
CUMBRIA · NORTH YORKSHIRE · CLEVELAND

5 miles / 10 km

Butterknowle, Lynesack

Barnard Castle

Kings Head
Market Place ☎ (0833) 690333
11–3 (4 Sat), 6–11 (11–11 Sat in summer)
Courage Directors; John Smith's Bitter Ⓗ
Pub with two large oak-panelled bars. The rear bar has Dickensian pictures.
❀ ◖ ▶ ♣ P

Old Well
21 The Bank ☎ (0833) 690130
12–2.30, 7–11
Courage Directors; John Smith's Bitter; Whitbread Boddingtons Bitter Ⓗ
Cosy market town pub, well kept. Two main bars with a separate rear restaurant (eve meals). The front bar has stained-glass behind the bar and pictures of the town on the walls. Q ❀ ⇔ ◖ ⊟ ☒ ▲ ♣

Try also: **Three Horseshoes**, Galgate (Bass)

Billy Row

Royal George
1 Well Bank (B6298, 400 yds S of B6299 jct) ☎ (0388) 764765
7–11 (11–11 Sat)
Ind Coope Burton Ale; Stones Best Bitter Ⓗ
Larger than it looks, this two-roomed local is named after a steam engine by Timothy

Hackworth and this is reflected in the decor. Friendly local 'crack'. ❀ ◖ ▶ ♣ P

Bishop Auckland

Newton Cap
Bank Top (A689 at top of hill)
☎ (0388) 605445
11–2.30, 7–11
Camerons Strongarm Ⓗ
Traditional locals' pub near the town centre: a lively bar with a separate pool room and an events room. Down to earth atmosphere in one of Bishop's unspoilt pubs. Ask for a game of Ringo. Excellent view across the Wear valley from the rear of the pub.
🏘 Q ❀ ⊟ ⇌ ♣

Sportsman
Market Place ☎ (0388) 607376
11–3, 7–11
Butterknowle Conciliation Ale; Marston's Pedigree; Whitbread Boddingtons Bitter, Trophy Ⓗ
Lively town-centre pub offering something for everyone. One of the town's oldest, with many original features still evident, including carved oak beams and big real fires. Quiz on Tue nights; competitive pool, darts and dominoes. 🏘 ◖ & ⇌ ♣

Try also: **Henknowle Manor**, Henknowle Estate (Vaux); **Silver Bugle**, Newgate St (Whitbread)

Bishop Middleham

Cross Keys
Bank Top ☎ (0740) 51231
11–3.30, 7–11
S&N Theakston Best Bitter, XB Ⓗ
Popular locals' pub with a newly modernised lounge area, an open-plan eating area and a games room.
🏘 ◖ ▶ & ♣ P

Try also: **Old Fleece Inn** (Bass)

Bishopton

Talbot
The Green ☎ (0740) 30371
11.30–3, 6.30–11
Camerons Strongarm; Ind Coope Burton Ale; Tetley Bitter Ⓗ
Pleasant village local with a long lounge, a tiny snug and a small sheltered garden. The centre of varied village activities, from football to morris dancing.
🏘 Q ❀ ◖ ▶ ♣ P

Byers Green

Royal Oak
93 High Street
☎ (0388) 605918
7–11 (12–3, 7–11 Sat)
Camerons Bitter Ⓗ

Durham

Locals' pub in a small ex-pit village: the plain exterior hides a warm and friendly atmosphere. A central bar serves a bar area and a lounge. The separate pool room promises stiff competition. Former winner of Durham CAMRA *Best Pub* award.
❀ ❒ 🍺 ♣

Canney Hill

Sportsman Inn
Off new A689 ☎ (0388) 603847
11–3, 7–11
Camerons Bitter, Strongarm; Everards Old Original; Tolly Cobbold Old Strong H
Popular, lively roadside inn with an open-plan lounge and bar with a separate, cosy snug (real fire). Horse racing connections are reflected in the decor. A regular in the *Guide*. 🍴 Q 🍺 ❀ ❒ ♣ P

Cornsay Colliery

Firtree (Monkey)
Hedley Hill Lane Ends (B6301 $1/2$ mile S of Cornsay Colliery)
☎ (091) 373 3212
7–11 (12–2, 7–10.30 Sun)
Vaux Lorimers Best Scotch H
Built in 1868 and hardly changed since; originally called the Monkey's Nest, a basic boozer with one bar-room and two small domestic side rooms. Owned by a farming family.
🍴 Q ❀ ♣ P

Try also: Blackhorse Inn, Cornsay Village (Free)

Cowshill

Cowshill Hotel
On A689 ☎ (0388) 537236
11–3, 7–11
Tetley Bitter H
Basic but comfortable pub at the head of Weardale. Convenient for Kilhope Lead Mine Museum. Soup available, but phone for meals. Children not catered for in the bar. 🍴 Q ❀ 🍴 ❒ P

Darlington

Britannia
Archer Street ☎ (0325) 463787 ✓
11–3, 5.30–11 (12–2, 7–10.30 Sun)
Camerons Strongarm; Tetley Bitter H
Warm, relaxed atmosphere and no pretensions in a 130-year-old, town-centre pub.
Q ♣ P

Central Borough
Hopetown Lane
☎ (0325) 468490
11–11
Camerons Strongarm H
Small street-corner pub in an area of terraced housing. Very

much a local with a loyal following, run by the same tenants for over 30 years. Near the impressive Little Railway Museum on the original Stockton–Darlington line.
Q ❒ ⇌ (North Rd) ♣

Cricketers Hotel
55 Parkgate ☎ (0325) 384444 ✓
11.30–3.30, 5.30–11
John Smith's Bitter, Magnet H
Recently modernised, town-centre pub with a warm, friendly atmosphere. On the inner ring road.
🍴 ❒ ❀ ♣ P

Falchion
8 Blackwell Gate ✓
☎ (0325) 462541
11–3.30, 6.30–11
Camerons Strongarm H
Cosy, friendly little bar in a central shopping street; named after a legendary worm-killing sword. A dominoes stronghold. ❒ ♣

Golden Cock
13 Tubwell Row ✓
☎ (0325) 468843
11–11 (11–3, 6.30–11 Tue–Thu)
Courage Directors; John Smith's Bitter, Magnet; guest beers H
18th-century, listed town-centre pub, modernised internally but retaining much character. Bar billiards played – the only table in town. Good turnover of interesting guest ales. 🍴 ♣

Pennyweight
Bakehouse Hill (Market Place) ✓
☎ (0325) 464244
11–11
Vaux Double Maxim, Extra Special; Wards Sheffield Best Bitter H**; guest beers**
Attractive modern pub in an 18th-century building. ❒ ♣

Tap & Spile
99 Bondgate ☎ (0325) 463955 ✓
11.30–3, 6.30–11 (11.30–11 Fri & Sat)
Beer range varies H
Popular town-centre local after the style of a Victorian ale house. Up to eight real beers and regular live jazz and blues nights. ❒

Try also: Turks Head, Bondgate (Camerons) ✓

Durham City

Colpitts Hotel
Hawthorn Terrace (A690, 200 yds from bus station)
☎ (091) 386 9913
11–3, 5.30–11 (11–11 Fri & Sat)
Samuel Smith OBB H
Still the cheapest pint in Durham. Basic and friendly pub with a bar, a small lounge and a pool room. Occasional live music. 🍴 Q ❒ ⇌ ♣

Dun Cow
Old Elvet (near Shire Hall)
☎ (091) 386 9219
11–11
Whitbread Boddingtons Bitter, Castle Eden Ale H
Two-roomed pub near Durham Gaol. The bar is small and cosy with a larger lounge frequented by students. Pie and peas highly recommended. Q ❒ ♿ ⇌

Elm Tree
Crossgate (top of Neville St)
☎ (091) 386 4621
12–3, 6–11 (12–11 Sat; 12–2, 7–10.30 Sun)
Vaux Samson, Double Maxim H**; guest beers**
Friendly regulars' pub catering for grannies and bikers. Quiet midweek; busy and cosmopolitan at weekends. Guest beers include Vaux Lorimers Best Scotch and Extra Special.
Q ❒ ♣

Half Moon
New Elvet (Old Elvet jct) ✓
☎ (091) 386 4528
11–11 (12–2, 7–10.30 Sun)
Draught Bass H
A crescent-shaped bar (from which the name is derived) dominates this split-level pub, a *Guide* regular for many years. A little expensive.
🍴 ⇌

Shakespeare
63 Saddler Street ✓
☎ (091) 386 9709
11–11
McEwan 80/-; S&N Theakston Best Bitter, XB; Younger No. 3 H
Small, old city-centre pub on the road to the cathedral: three rooms popular with students. Sun night quiz. Sandwiches lunchtime. Q ❒ ⇌ ♣

Try also: Angel, Crossgate (Bass); **Buffalo Head,** Saddler St (Whitbread); **City Hotel,** Old Elvet (Tetley) ✓

Evenwood Gate

Brown Jug
On A688 ☎ (0388) 875301
11–11
Marston's Pedigree; Whitbread Boddingtons Bitter, Castle Eden Ale H
Newly decorated inn on a busy main road. Boasts a fine reputation for meals. Popular with locals as well as road-users. Regular rotation of Whitbread ales.
🍴 ❀ 🍴 ♿ ♣ P

Fence Houses

Floaters Mill
Woodstone Village (1$1/2$ miles from A183/A1(M))
☎ (091) 385 6695

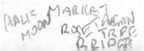

11.30–3, 6.30–11
**Camerons Bitter; Ind Coope
Burton Ale; Tetley Bitter** Ⓗ
Country fare-style inn with an
attractive conservatory eating
area, popular with family
diners. Garden with children's
adventure play area.
Q ❀ ◖▮ ⇦ P

Try also: Dun Cow,
Bournmoor (Vaux)

Framwellgate Moor

Marquis of Granby

Front Street (old Great North
Rd) ☎ (091) 386 9382
11–4, 6–11
Samuel Smith OBB, Museum
(summer) Ⓗ
Popular with all ages, a local
which has always been at the
centre of community activities.
Two main rooms with a small
side room in contemporary
traditional decor. ❀ & ♣ P

Try also: Tap & Spile, Front St

Greta Bridge

Morritt Arms Hotel

On A66 ☎ (0833) 27232
11–3, 6–11
**Butterknowle Conciliation
Ale** Ⓗ
Two bars, one in the hotel, the
other a separate public bar.
The hotel bar features wall to
wall Dickensian characters,
whilst the public offers
traditional pub games. ♣
♨ Q ❀ ⍢ ◖▮ ⇦ & ♣ P

Heighington

Locomotion No. 1

Heighington Station (1 mile W
of A167 at Aycliffe)
☎ (0325) 320132
11–11
**Butterknowle Conciliation
Ale; McEwan 80/-; S&N
Theakston Best Bitter, XB,
Old Peculier; Younger
No. 3** Ⓗ
Historic 1820s railway station
converted to an inn-
restaurant. Next to the branch
line. ♨ ▭ ❀ ◖▮ ⇌ P

High Conscliffe

Duke of Wellington

☎ (0325) 374283
11–3, 6–11
Camerons Strongarm Ⓗ
Traditional, one-roomed
village local opposite a
popular riverside beauty spot.
Quoits played. ♨ ❀ ◖ ♣ P

High Shincliffe

Avenue

1 Avenue Street (just off A177,
3 miles from centre)
☎ (091) 386 5954

11–11
**Vaux Samson; Wards
Sheffield Best Bitter** Ⓗ
Comfortable one-room pub
with an L-shaped bar; popular
with all ages since the
introduction of meals. A
village local off a main
highway. Q ❀ ⍢ ◖▮ ♣

Try also: Seven Stars,
Shincliffe (Vaux)

Holmeside

Wardles Bridge

☎ (091) 371 0926
7–11
**McEwan 70/-, 80/-; S&N
Theakston XB; Younger
No. 3** Ⓗ
Village pub with a large
friendly bar and a smaller
lounge. Thai meals available
by reservation.
♨ Q ▭ ❀ ◖▮ ⇦ ♣ ♣ P

Try also: Charlaw Inn (S&N)

Kirk Merrington

Half Moon

Crowther Place
☎ (0388) 811598
11–11
**Butterknowle Conciliation
Ale; Whitbread Boddingtons
Bitter; guest beer** Ⓗ
A pub which goes a long way
to being all things to all men.
One split room divided into a
quiet side and a boisterous
side by a central bar. Guest
beers change regularly and the
range may vary. ♨ ◖▮ &

Low Spennymoor

Frog & Ferret

Coulson Street (½ mile from
A167) ☎ (0388) 818312
11–11
**Bateman XB; S&N Theakston
XB; Whitbread Boddingtons
Bitter; Younger No. 3; guest
beers** Ⓗ
Small, one-roomed, street-
corner local which serves the
best selection of beers for
miles, though guests can be
expensive. Quite difficult to
get to by public transport but
worth it. Perhaps the only
permanent outlet for Bateman
beer in the county.

Try also: Steam Mill (Vaux)

Middleton St George

Fighting Cocks

☎ (0325) 332327
11.30–3, 5.30–11
**Vaux Double Maxim, Extra
Special; Wards Sheffield Best
Bitter** Ⓗ
Friendly country pub: one
large room with a bar area and
an area set aside for eating (no

---

food Sun eve). On a disused
railway branch line.
❀ ◖▮ ♣ P

Neasham

Fox & Hounds

24 Teesway (A66, 2 miles S of
Darlington) ☎ (0325) 720350
11–3, 6.30–11
**Vaux Samson, Double
Maxim; Wards Sheffield Best
Bitter** Ⓗ
Classic example of a 17th-
century village pub extended
to cater for busy food and
family trades but retaining its
original atmosphere. Good
locals' bar with games; large
riverside beer garden with
children's play area; new
family conservatory. Good
value home-cooked food
daily.
Q ▭ ❀ ◖▮ ⇦ & ♣ P

No Place

Beamish Mary Inn

Off A693 ☎ (091) 370 0237
12–3, 6–11 (11–11 Fri & Sat)
**McEwan 80/-; S&N
Theakston Best Bitter, XB** Ⓗ;
guest beer
Very lively pub in an ex-
mining community with a
Victorian/Edwardian
character to the lounge/diner.
Regular folk club (weekly)
and blues nights in the
converted stables. Beer
festivals twice-yearly.
Welcoming landlord.
♨ Q ❀ ⍢ ◖▮ & ♣ ♣ P

Try also: Sun Inn, Beamish
Museum (S&N)

North Bitchburn

Red Lion

North Bitchburn Terrace (off
B6286 towards Howden-le-
Wear, near Crook)
☎ (0388) 763561
12–2.30, 7–11
**John Smith's Bitter,
Magnet** Ⓗ; **guest beer**
Village pub offering a warm,
welcoming atmosphere: a
comfortable bar with a games
room off and a large lounge
where a good choice of meals
is served. Previous winner of
Durham CAMRA *Best Pub*
award. ♨ ❀ ◖▮ ⇦ ♣ P

Pelaw Grange

Wheatsheaf

On old Great North Road
☎ (091) 388 3104
11–11
**Draught Bass; Stones Best
Bitter** Ⓗ
Old coaching inn with
facilities for all. Large garden;
popular, good value meals.
▭ ❀ ◖▮ ⇦ & ♣ P

Durham

Romaldkirk

Kirk Inn
☎ (0833) 50260
12–3, 6–11
Butterknowle Conciliation Ale; Whitbread Boddingtons Bitter, Castle Eden Ale H;
guest beers
Charming, single-roomed pub on the village green. Craftwork from the Dales on offer. 🏠 Q 🏡 🚲 🍴 🍺 P

St John's Chapel

Golden Lion
Market Place (A689)
☎ (0388) 537231
11–3, 7–11
Ruddles County; John Smith's Magnet H
Large village pub based on an unusual E-shaped floor plan. Genial host; excellent menu (separate dining room). Holiday flats to let.
🏠 Q 🏡 🚲 🍴 🍺 🅿 P

Try also: Blue Bell (Tetley)

Seaton

Seaton Lane Inn
Seaton Lane (B1404, just off A19, 1 1/2 miles from Seaham)
☎ (091) 581 2038
12–3, 7–11
Butterknowle Bitter; S&N Theakston Best Bitter H;
guest beers
Free house, for 45 years with the same family. A *Guide* regular, with a basic bar and a comfortable lounge. Smart beer garden; photographs in the bar depict local history.
Q 🏡 🚲 🍺 P

Sedgefield

Dun Cow Inn
Front Street ☎ (0740) 20894
11–3, 5.30–11
S&N Theakston Best Bitter, XB H; **guest beers**
Busy, pleasant pub in the middle of the village. Popular with locals and visitors (close to the historic parish church). Friendly bar staff. Mon night quiz. 🚲 🍴 P

Golden Lion
1 East End ☎ (0740) 20371
11–11 (12–2, 7–10.30 Sun)
S&N Theakston XB, Old Peculier H
Unspoilt, traditional village pub offering lively local banter and very friendly service – the bonniest boozer in Sedgefield. Count the old pennies and halfpennies behind the bar.
🏠 Q 🍴 🍺 P

Try also: Black Lion (Tetley); Hardwick Arms (S&N)

Shield Row

Board Inn
On A6076 ☎ (0207) 233169
11–3 (not Tue), 4–11 (11–11 Fri & Sat)
Whitbread Castle Eden Ale H
A lively bar and a quiet lounge – except Sun (boisterous quiz night). A main road pub much valued by the numerous regulars.
Q 🚲 🏡 🚲 🍺 P

Try also: Ball Alley (Bass)

Shildon

King William
Cheapside (near market place)
☎ (0388) 777901
11–11
Camerons Strongarm H
Old main-street local with a large lounge and a serious drinking bar with darts and doms. Whippet fanciers welcome. 🏡 🚲 🚲 🍺

Try also: Timothy Hackworth (Camerons)

South Church

Red Alligator
☎ (0388) 605644
11–3 (4 Sat), 7–11
Wards Sheffield Best Bitter H
Popular village pub on the outskirts of Bishop Auckland with a friendly welcome for all. Named after the Grand National winner trained nearby. Subdued lighting adds to the comfortable and cosy atmosphere in this beamed hostelry. 🏠 Q 🏡 🏡 🍴 🍺 P

Try also: Coach & Horses (Free)

Spennymoor

Ash Tree
Carr Lane (1/4 mile from centre in Greenways estate)
☎ (0388) 814410
12–2.30 (4 Sat, not Thu), 7–11
Vaux Samson; Wards Sheffield Best Bitter H
Typical estate pub where the one room has been divided into a separate bar and lounge by a central partition. Games and TV in the bar; jukebox in the lounge. Designed to appeal to all ages and types. Enclosed garden. 🏡 🍴 🍺 P

Misty Blue Inn
Rock Road, Middlestone Moor (between Middlestone Moor and Kirk Merrington)
☎ (0388) 815351
7–11 (12–3, 7–11 Sat)
Camerons Strongarm H
Former farmhouse, then country club, a pub which has now taken on a more traditional guise. Several rooms, including a separate

dining room. Live music some nights; disco Sat nights. A bit off the main road but worth finding.
Q 🚲 🏡 🍴 🚲 🍺 P

Try also: Kingfisher (Whitbread)

Stanhope

Bonney Moorhen Hotel
25 Front Street (facing market place) ☎ (0388) 528214
11–4, 7–11
S&N Theakston Best Bitter; Whitbread Castle Eden Ale, Flowers Original H
Formerly the Phoenix: a large friendly bar, with a small pool room at one end, and a separate lounge.
🏠 Q 🏡 🚲 🍴 ⭐ (summer Suns only) 🍺

Try also: Pack Horse (Whitbread); Queens Head (Camerons)

Stanley

Blue Boar Tavern
Front Street (A693, 100 yds from bus station)
☎ (0207) 231167
11–3, 7–11 (11–11 Thu–Sat)
Butterknowle Conciliation Ale; Ind Coope Burton Ale; Stones Best Bitter; Tetley Bitter H; **guest beers**
Olde-worlde former coaching inn; a very popular pub with a varied clientele. Traditional and blues music feature regularly. Two guest beers from small independents. Recently restored fireplace.
🏠 Q 🚲 🏡 🍴 🚲 P

Stanley (Crook)

Earl Derby
5 Wilson Street (B6299)
☎ (0388) 767385
7–11 (12–3, 7–10.30 Sat)
Tetley Bitter H
Friendly, two-roomed village local with a separate dining room at the rear (no lunches Sat/Sun, no eve meals Mon).
🏠 🏡 🍴 🚲 🍺

Summerhouse

Raby Hunt
☎ (032 574) 604
11.30–3, 6.30–11
Marston's Burton Best Bitter, Pedigree H; **guest beers** (occasionally)
Neat, welcoming, old stone free house in a pretty whitewashed hamlet: a homely lounge and a bustling locals' bar. Magnificent Raby Castle can be visited five miles up the road. Good home-cooked lunches (not served Sun). 🏠 Q 🏡 🍴 🏡 🚲 🍺 P

Durham

Try also: Walworth Castle, Walworth (Ruddles)

Tantobie

Highlander Inn
White-le-Head (B6311)
☎ (0207) 232416
12–2.30 (summer only), 7–11
Belhaven 80/-; Marston's Pedigree H; guest beers
Popular village local: a very lively bar and a secluded lounge with a small dining room. Q ❄ ✤ ◑ ▶ ❦ ♣ P ✂

Toronto

Toronto Lodge
☎ (0388) 602833
11–11 (11–5, 7–11 Sat)
Draught Bass; Butterknowle Bitter, Conciliation Ale H; guest beers
Welcoming family pub given character by wooden beams and the use of natural stone in the decor. Well deserved reputation for meals; regular rotation of guest ales.
🏮 ❄ ✤ 🛏 ◑ ▶ ▣ ❦ ♣ P

Tudhoe Village

Green Tree
The Green ☎ (0388) 815679
11.30–2, 6.30–11
Wards Sheffield Best Bitter H
Quiet local with a separate bar and lounge. The hub of this upmarket village but always warm and welcoming. Enclosed garden.
🏮 Q ✤ ◑ ▶ ▣ ♣ P

West Cornforth

Square & Compass
The Green ☎ (0740) 654606
12–4, 7–11
Draught Bass; Federation Special; Stones Best Bitter H
Pub with a warm and welcoming atmosphere. Note the history – going back to the first landlord – on the plaque by the bar. Probably the cheapest pint for miles.
Q ❄ ✤ ◑ ▶ ▣ ❦ ♣ P

Wham

Malt Shovel
500 yds from B6282, E of Butterknowle ☎ (0388) 710033
5–11 (12–3, 5–11 Sat)
Butterknowle Bitter, Conciliation Ale, Black Diamond, High Force H
Pub long famous for food, now famous for beer! Large bar with open fire; separate dining/function room. Isolated but popular, with a warm welcome. Butterknowle Festival Stout and Ebeneezer served when available. The quizzes and karaoke nights are renowned.
🏮 ✤ ◑ ▶ ♣ P

Try also: Royal Oak (Camerons)

Witton Gilbert

Glendenning Arms
Front Street (A691)
☎ (091) 371 0316
11–4, 7–11
Vaux Samson H
17 years in the *Guide*, this popular local has two rooms adorned with pictures and memorabilia associated with horse racing and country sports. Basic but comfortable.
🏮 Q P

Travellers Rest
Front Street (A691)
☎ (091) 371 0458
11–3, 6–11
McEwan 80/-; S&N Theakston Best Bitter, XB, Old Peculier; Younger Scotch, No. 3 H
Very smart village pub with a wide variety of meals. Split-level no-smoking area; large conservatory, ideal for children. Traditional-style decor. Boules played in summer.
🏮 Q ❄ ✤ ◑ ♣ P ✂

Try also: Centurion, Langley Park (Vaux)

Woodhouses

Bay Horse
☎ (0388) 603422
11–3, 7–11
John Smith's Bitter, Magnet H
Open-plan bar and eating area, popular with locals. Many pictures of old Auckland. Sun lunch served.
🏮 Q ❦ ♣

"ANY OF THE REGULARS WANT A DRINK BEFORE I SERVE THIS BLOKE?"

From Good Beer Guide 1987

KenPyne

101

Essex

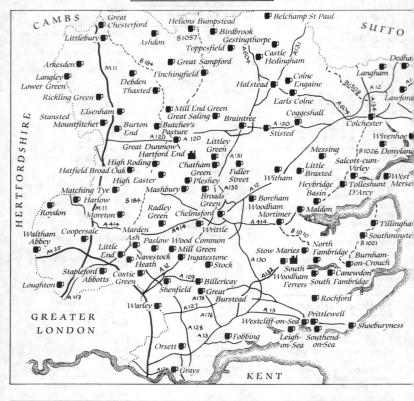

 Crouch Vale, South Woodham Ferrers; **Ridleys**,
Hartford End

Ardleigh

Wooden Fender Inn
Harwich Road (A137)
☎ (0206) 230466
11–3, 6–11
**Adnams Bitter; Greene King
IPA** Ⓗ**; guest beers**
Smart roadside pub
frequented by witchfinder
Matthew Hopkins in the
1640s, serving a fine range of
meals. A comfortably
furnished, open-plan bar.
🏘 Q ⊛ ◖▶ & ♣ P

Arkesden

Axe & Compasses
1½ miles N of B1038
OS483344 ☎ (0799) 550272
11–2.30, 6–11 (12–2.30, 7–10.30 Sun)
**Greene King IPA, Rayments
Special, Abbot** Ⓗ
Superb, welcoming 17th-
century local in a picturesque
village. Restaurant and bar
meals (no food Mon eve).
🏘 Q ⊛ ◖▶ ⊞ ♣ P

Ashdon

Bonnet
Steventon End OS598428
☎ (0799) 84513
12–3, 6–11
Greene King IPA, Abbot Ⓗ**;
Mauldons Squires** Ⓖ
Comfortable, oak-beamed old
pub, featured in *Reuben's
Corner* by Spike Mays. Well-
appointed upstairs restaurant
(no food Tue eve).
Q ⊛ ◖▶ ▲ ♣ P

Belchamp St Paul

Cherry Tree Inn
Knowl Green OS784413
☎ (0787) 237263
12–3, 7–11 (closed winter Tue; 12–11
Sat)
**Adnams Bitter, Broadside;
Greene King IPA** Ⓗ
Comfortable and isolated
16th-century pub with a good
play area for children. Good
value beer. No food Tue.
🏘 Q ⊛ ◖▶ ▲ ♣ P

Billericay

Chequers
High Street ☎ (0277) 651804
10.30–11
**Greene King IPA; Ind Coope
Benskins Best Bitter, Burton
Ale; Tetley Bitter** Ⓗ
Gentle decor and pleasant
clients and staff, in a bar of
two halves (the younger set
congregates near the
dartboard). A listed 16th-
century English pub of
character. Weekday meals.
◖⇌ ♣ P

Coach & Horses
36 Chapel Street (off High St)
☎ (0277) 622873
10–4, 5.30–11 (10–11 Fri, Sat & other
days if busy)
**Greene King IPA, Rayments
Special, Abbot** Ⓗ
Friendly regulars' pub where
new faces are made welcome.
A good atmosphere; wide age
range. Dozens of jugs hang
from the ceiling in this 1930s

L K

Bradfield   *Harwich*
Ardleigh   A 120

A 133

rightlingsea   *Walton-on-the-Naze*

Great Clacton

St Osyth

0   5   10 miles

0   5   10   15 km

Essex

building, retaining its pre-war character. On the site of an 18th-century tap house (note the photo on the wall).
🏚 ❀ ◖❚ ⇌ ♣ P

Birdbrook

Plough

The Street ☎ (044 085) 336
11–2.30, 6–11
Adnams Bitter; Greene King IPA, Abbot G; guest beer
Traditional village local with an interesting fireplace in the saloon bar; separate games room. Barbecues in summer. Book for Sun lunch.
🏚 Q ❀ ◖❚ ⊟ ♣ P

Boreham

Queen's Head

Church Street ☎ (0245) 467298
10.30–2.30 (3 Fri & Sat), 6–11
Greene King IPA, Abbot H
Friendly 16th-century local, which has been with the same family for the last 50 years. No food Sun. Q ❀ ◖❚ ⊟ ♣ P

Bradfield

Strangers Home Inn

The Street ☎ (0255) 870304
12–3 (later if busy), 7–11

Ind Coope Burton Ale; Tetley Bitter H
Derelict in 1980, now a fine local with a wood-burning open fire and a stove. A 200-year-old punt gun hangs in the bar. Good food, camping, and a garden with farm animals. On the Essex Way, so used by hikers. Pool table, but no jukebox.
🏚 Q ♣ ◖❚ ◖ ♠ ♣ P

Braintree

King William IV

114 London Road (A131, 1 mile S of town)
☎ (0376) 330088
11–11 (may close afternoons)
Ridleys IPA G
Small two-bar local enjoying a friendly atmosphere. The present licensee has been with the brewery for more than 30 years. Snacks served.
🏚 Q ❀ ⊟ ♣ P

Wagon & Horses

53 South Street (opp. Warners Mill) ☎ (0376) 553356
11–3, 5.30 (6 Sat)–11
Greene King XX Mild, IPA, Abbot H
300 years-old but recently renovated: a large, low-ceilinged lounge bar, a raised dining area, a cosy snug and an unusual well, covered with glass plate, set in the floor.
Q ⚲ ❀ ◖❚ ⊟ ⇌ P

Brightlingsea

Railway Tavern

Station Road ☎ (0206) 302581
11–3 (not Mon–Fri), 5.30–11
Bateman XXXB; Mauldons Bitter; guest beers
Basic pub – like a railway waiting room. The big public bar with its dartboard and piano attracts a mainly local trade. Railway memorabilia is a feature. 🏚 ⚲ ❀ ⊟ ♠ ♣

Broads Green

Walnut Tree

½ mile from old A130 at Great Waltham OS694125
☎ (0245) 360222
11.30 (11 Sat)–2.30, 6.30 (6 summer)–11
Ridleys IPA H
Clean, pleasant, three-bar country pub: a well-furnished lounge and a basic public bar with a real fire and a trophy cabinet. Entrance to both is through a cosy middle snug. Hot and cold lunchtime snacks. 🏚 Q ❀ ⊟ ♣ P

Burnham-on-Crouch

New Welcome Sailor

Station Road ☎ (0621) 784778

11–3, 6–11 (11–11 Sat)
Greene King IPA, Abbot H, Winter Ale G
Basic town pub, with a somewhat masculine ambience, but welcoming to all. Games played. ⇌ ♠ P

Olde White Harte

The Quay
☎ (0621) 782106
11–3, 6–11
Adnams Bitter; Tolly Cobbold Bitter H
Old riverside pub loved by the yachting fraternity; can be crowded and noisy in summer. Sit on the jetty and watch the sun set over the river. 🏚 Q ❀ ⊨ ◖❚ P

Burton End

Ash

OS532237
☎ (0279) 814841
11.30–3, 5.30–11
Greene King Rayments Special, Abbot H
15th-century thatched cottage pub of character. Despite the proximity of Stansted airport, noise is not a problem. Good simple food at reasonable prices (no meals Tue eve). Wheelchair access to lounge only. 🏚 Q ❀ ◖❚ ⊟ ♿ ♣ P

Butcher's Pasture

Stag

Duck Street (1 mile W of B184)
OS608241 ☎ (0371) 870214
11–2.30, 6–11 (11–11 if busy)
Ridleys IPA H
Friendly village pub with plain wooden benches and tables in the public bar but a refurbished and extended saloon bar. Fine views over the Chelmer valley from the garden. 🏚 ❀ ◖❚ ⊟ ♣ ♣ P

Canewdon

Chequers Inn

High Street
☎ (0702) 258251
11.30–3 (may extend summer), 7–11
Greene King IPA, Rayments Special, Abbot H; guest beers
Splendid pub serving the local community. Its extensive *à la carte* menu and Sun roasts are well recommended but booking is advisable (no meals Sun eve or Mon). The pub is mainly 18th-century, saved by local action, with CAMRA support, from demolition.
Q ⚲ ❀ ◖❚ ♿ ♣ P

Castle Hedingham

Bell Inn

10 St James Street
☎ (0787) 60350
11.30–3, 6–11
Greene King IPA, Abbot G

Excellent, genuine-timbered pub near the castle. No food Mon eve.
♛ Q ♘ ❀ ◖◗ ⊟ ▲ ♣ P

Chatham Green

Windmill

200 yds from A131 OS716151
11–3, 6–11
Ridleys IPA Ⓖ
Quiet and cosy country local with the base of an old windmill in the garden.
♛ Q ❀ ♣ P

Chelmsford

Endeavour

351 Springfield Road (A1113, old main road)
☎ (0245) 257717
11–11 (12–2, 7–10.30 Sun)
Greene King IPA, Rayments Special, Abbot Ⓗ
Traditional, friendly, cosy, three-roomed pub. No meals Sun. A mile from the town centre. ♛ Q ◖◗ ⊟ ♣

Partners

30 Lower Anchor Street
☎ (0245) 265181
11–3, 5–11 (11–11 Sat)
Adnams Bitter; Greene King IPA; Wadworth 6X Ⓗ**; guest beers**
Friendly, renovated and extended, street-corner local. A games room doubles (triples?) as a family/meeting room, and is separate from the bar. The patio is a summer suntrap. Near the cricket ground. No food Sun.
Q ♘ ❀ 🛏 ◖ ⇌ ♣ P

Red Lion

147 New London Road
☎ (0245) 354092
10.30–11
Adnams Extra; Ridleys IPA Ⓗ
Popular, traditional street-corner pub with a comfortable lounge and a basic public. New extension and garden to be completed soon. ❀ ◖ ⊟ ♣

White Horse

25 Townfield Street
☎ (0245) 269556
11–3, 5.30 (7 Sat)–11 (11–11 Dec weekdays)
Mauldons Black Adder; S&N Theakston Best Bitter; Whitbread Boddingtons Bitter, Flowers IPA Ⓗ**; guest beers**
Grand Victorian building (ex-Charrington) now demeaned and cowed by the surrounding architecture and several years of wine bar pretensions. A roomy, friendly one-bar pub with a good range of games, but no pool table or jukebox. Over 300 guest beers in its first year. Weekday lunches. ◖ ⇌ ♣

Coggeshall

Fleece

West Street ☎ (0376) 561412
11–11
Greene King IPA, Abbot Ⓗ
Handsome, timber-framed and pargetted pub built in 1503 next to Paycocke's House (NT) in a charming country town. Children welcome; the garden has a safe play area. Camping by prior arrangement. No food Tue eves.
♛ ❀ ◖◗ ♿ ▲ ♣ P

Colchester

British Grenadier

67 Military Road
☎ (0206) 579654
11–3, 6–11 (11–11 Sat)
Adnams Mild (summer), **Bitter, Old** Ⓗ
Workingman's pub with traditional games: a pool table in the back bar; darts in the front. Happy hour 6–7; snacks available. A popular local with friendly licensees.
Q ⊟ ⇌ (Town) ♣

Dragoon

82 Butt Road ☎ (0206) 573464
11–3, 5.30–11 (11–11 Fri & Sat)
Adnams Mild, Bitter, Old Ⓗ**; guest beers**
Friendly, two-bar pub close to the town centre. A basic public bar with a pool table and a comfortable, quiet saloon. At least three guest beers. Food Mon–Sat.
❀ ◖ ⊟ ⇌ (Town)

Goat & Boot

70 East Hill ☎ (0206) 867466
11–3, 6–11
Greene King XX Mild, IPA, Abbot Ⓗ
Popular, historic town pub, 100 yards downhill from the old Colchester Eagle brewery, now converted to flats. It has a basic public bar and a small pool room off the lounge bar. No food Sun.
♛ Q ❀ ◖ ⊟ ♣ P

Odd One Out

28 Mersea Road (B1025)
☎ (0206) 578140
11–2.30 (not Mon–Thu), 5.30 (6 Sat)–11
Archers Best Bitter; Mauldons Bitter; Ridleys Bitter Ⓗ**; guest beers**
The basic beer-drinkers' pub of Colchester where the cosy, friendly atmosphere attracts all sorts. Four guest beers: one always a mild. No-smoking bar Fri and Sat.
♛ ⇌ (Town) ⌓ ⊬

Stockwell Arms

West Stockwell Street
10.30–11 (10.30–3.30, 6.30–11 Sat)
Courage Directors; Nethergate Bitter; Ruddles Best Bitter, County; Webster's Yorkshire Bitter Ⓗ
Over 600 years-old, this pub stands in the town's acclaimed Dutch quarter. Popular with white collar workers weekday lunchtimes, otherwise quiet. Parking difficult. No food Sun eve. ❀ ◖◗ ⇌ (North) ♣

Tap & Spile

Crouch Street (opp. county hospital) ☎ (0206) 573572
11–2.30, 5.30–11
Adnams Bitter; Crouch Vale SAS; Mauldons Bitter; Nethergate Bitter; Whitbread Boddingtons Bitter Ⓗ**; guest beers**
Formerly the 'Hospital Arms', this pub has strong rugby and cricket connections: autographed players' pictures adorn the walls. Very good value (and good portions) food (not served Sun). Usually four guest beers. ❀ ◖ ⌓

Colne Engaine

Five Bells

7 Mill Lane (off Earls Colne road) OS851303
☎ (0787) 224166
11–3, 6–11 (11–11 Sat)
Greene King IPA; Mauldons Squires, Blackadder Ⓗ
Large, friendly local, often crowded. It has an upstairs restaurant and a children's/function room.
♛ ♘ 🛏 ◖◗ ♿ ♣ P

Coopersale

Theydon Oak

Stonards Hill (1 mile E of Epping) OS474018
☎ (0378) 72618
10.30–3, 5.30–11
Adnams Bitter; Draught Bass; Charrington IPA; Wadworth 6X Ⓗ**; guest beers**
Wood-clad outside walls, a small bar and two beer gardens; this pub gets very busy. Two guest beers are changed every four–six weeks.
♛ Q ❀ ◖◗ P

Coxtie Green

White Horse

173 Coxtie Green Road
OS564959 ☎ (0277) 372410
11.30–3, 5.30–11
Adnams Bitter; Courage Best Bitter, Directors; S&N Theakston Best Bitter, XB; Wadworth 6X Ⓗ
Ex-Allied pub, now a free house: a small, cosy and friendly country inn with a playground in the large garden. Popular with families in summer. The beer range may vary; occasional beer festivals held. No food Sun.
Q ❀ ◖◗ ⊟ P

Debden

Plough

High Street ☎ (0799) 40396
12–3, 6–11 (12–11 Sat)
Greene King IPA, Rayments Special, Abbot Ⓗ
Cosy 17th-century local with a superb garden for children. Summer barbecues.
🏚 Q ✿ ◑ ◐ ▲ ♣ P

Dedham

Lamb Inn

Birchwood Road (1 mile E of A12) OS045315
☎ (0206) 322216
11–3, 6.30–11
Tetley Bitter; Tolly Cobbold Bitter, Old Strong Ⓗ
Charming, 14th-century, Grade I listed, thatched and timber-framed pub with a stone-flagged bar. Busy food trade (no food Sun eve or Mon). The beer range is likely to change.
🏚 Q ⚲ ✿ ◑ ◐ ♣ P

Donyland

Walnut Tree

Fingringhoe Road (off Hythe Road) OS021216
☎ (0206) 728149
12–2.30 (not Mon-Thu), 6–11 (12–11 Sat; may vary winter)
Felinfoel Double Dragon; Wadworth 6X Ⓗ**; guest beers**
Cosy, comfortable pub on the outskirts of Rowhedge, a few miles from Colchester. A popular pub with a rock jukebox; can get busy. Excellent food includes vegetarian dishes. ✿ ◑ ◐ ♣ P

Earls Colne

Bird in Hand

Coggeshall Road (B1024)
☎ (0787) 222557
12–2.30 (later if busy), 7–11 (12–2.30, 7–10.30 Sun)
Ridleys IPA Ⓔ
Pleasant old pub with separate bars and warm coal fires. Pool table, darts and shove-ha'penny in the bar. During the war it was flat roofed, because it was in line with a runway of a nearby US air base (pics in lounge). A family pub (but no under 14s).
🏚 Q ✿ ◑ ◐ ♣ P

Castle

High Street
☎ (0787) 222694
11–3, 5–11 (11–11 Fri & Sat)
Greene King XX Mild, IPA, Abbot Ⓗ
12th-century pub with a small public bar.
🏚 ⚲ ✿ ⛴ ◑ ◐ ♣ P

Elsenham

Crown

High Street ☎ (0279) 812827
11–2.30, 6–11 (12–2.30, 7–10.30 Sun)
Adnams Broadside; Ind Coope Benskins Best Bitter Ⓗ
Deservedly popular village pub with a reputation for food (not served Mon eve or Sun). Friendly atmosphere. Fine pargetted exterior.
🏚 Q ✿ ◑ ◐ ⛴ ⇌ ♣ P

Finchingfield

Red Lion

Church Hill ☎ (0371) 810400
11–3, 6–11 (11–11 summer)
Adnams Extra; Ridleys IPA Ⓗ
500-year-old pub opposite the church in a picturesque village. Games room; occasional live music; good food. 🏚 Q ⚲ ✿ ◑ ◐ ▲ ♣ P

Fobbing

White Lion

Lion Hill (near church)
OS716839 ☎ (0375) 673281
11–2.30 (4 Sat), 5 (6.30 Sat)–11
Ind Coope Burton Ale; Tetley Bitter; Young's Bitter Ⓗ
300-year-old pub with a plaque on the wall commemorating the Peasants' Revolt which started in the village. Eve meals only if booked; no lunches Sun.
🏚 Q ✿ ◑ ⛴ ♣ P

Fuller Street

Square & Compasses

Between Terling and Great Leighs (1½ miles off A131) OS748161 ☎ (0245) 361477
11–3 (4 Sat), 6–11
Ridleys IPA Ⓖ
Traditional, welcoming country pub with good food. First Fri of each month is folk night and there is an annual folk weekend in summer. Note the unusual pitch-penny stool in the public bar. No food Thu or Sun eves.
🏚 Q ◑ ◐ ⛴ ▲ ♣ P

Gestingthorpe

Pheasant

Audley End OS813376
☎ (0787) 61196
11–3, 6–11
Greene King Abbot; Nethergate Old Growler Ⓖ**; Tolly Cobbold Original; Wadworth 6X** Ⓗ**; guest beer**
Multi-roomed pub, the focal point of the village. Good food includes an extensive vegetarian menu (book weekends). Occasional live jazz and rock music.
🏚 ⚲ ✿ ◑ ◐ ▲ ♣ P

Grays

Wharf

Wharf Road (off A126)
☎ (0375) 372418
11–3 (longer summer Sat), 6–11
Ind Coope Burton Ale; Tetley Bitter; Young's Bitter Ⓗ
Old listed pub beside the Grays sea wall, now surrounded by a housing estate. Popular with youngsters, but, despite a jukebox and machines, the bars still retain character. Bar meals lunchtimes, Mon to Sat. Own astroturf bowling green. May offer guest beers in summer. ✿ ◑ ⛴ ⇌ ♣ P

Great Burstead

Duke of York

Southend Road (A129)
☎ (0277) 651403
10–2.30, 6–11 (10–11 Sat)
Greene King IPA, Rayments Special, Abbot Ⓗ
Two early 19th-century cottages converted to a pub before 1837; a Gray & Sons house since 1868. Subdued lighting in cosy surroundings. Pleasant clientele; friendly service. Excellent restaurant and bar meals (no food Sat eve or Sun). 🏚 Q ✿ ◑ ◐ ⚇ P

Great Chesterford

Plough

High Street (near B1383 and M11 jct 9) ☎ (0799) 30283
11–2.30 (3 Sat), 6 (5.30 Fri)–11
Greene King IPA Ⓖ**; Rayments Special** Ⓗ**; Abbot** Ⓖ
Superb 18th-century village local, recently modernised but retaining its inglenooks. Seafood is a speciality.
🏚 Q ✿ ◑ ◐ ⚇ ⇌ ♣ P

Great Clacton

Robin Hood

211 London Road (A133)
☎ (0255) 421519
11–11
Adnams Bitter; Draught Bass; Welsh Brewers Worthington BB Ⓗ
Spacious, low-ceilinged, mellow and comfortable pub with good food. 🏚 Q ✿ ◑ ▲ ♣ P

Great Dunmow

Cricketers

22 Beaumont Hill (B184)
☎ (0371) 873359
11–3, 6–11 (11–11 Fri & Sat)
Ridleys IPA Ⓗ
Friendly local opposite the duck pond on the village green. Had a beer-only licence until 1976 when it was extended into the bakery next door. No food Mon or Wed.
✿ ◑ ⛴ ▲ ♣ P

Essex

Great Saling

White Hart
The Street (2 miles N of A120)
OS701254 ☎ (0371) 850341
11–3, 6–11
Adnams Extra; Ridleys IPA H
Superb Tudor pub with a
timbered gallery in the saloon
bar. The remains of the world's
largest smooth-leaved elm tree
stand opposite. The bar food
speciality is the Essex Huffer (a
very large bap); there is also a
large, comfortable restaurant.
🏨 ✿ ◑ ▶ 🍴 ♣ P

Great Sampford

Red Lion Inn
Finchingfield Road (B1053)
☎ (079 986) 325
12–3, 5.30–11
Adnams Extra; Ridleys IPA H
Pleasant, friendly local,
offering a varied menu in the
bar and restaurant.
🏨 ✿ 🚗 ◑ ▶ ♣ P

Halstead

Dog Inn
35 Hedingham Road (A604)
☎ (0787) 477774
12–3, 6–11
**Adnams Bitter; Nethergate
Bitter, Old Growler** H
Friendly local with original
beams in the open-plan bars.
Reasonably-priced
accommodation. Book for Sun
lunch. 🏨 Q 🚗 ✿ 🚗 ◑ ▶ P

Harlow

Willow Beauty
Hodings Road
☎ (0279) 437328
11–3 (4 Sat), 6–11
**Greene King XX Mild, IPA,
Rayments Special, Abbot** H
Despite its unassuming
exterior, this pub can get very
crowded at weekends.
✿ ◑ ▶ 🚗 & ♣ ♣ P

Harwich

Hanover Inn
65 Church Street
☎ (0255) 502927
10.30–3 (later if busy Sat), 6.30–11
**Tolly Cobbold Mild, Bitter,
Old Strong; Whitbread
Boddingtons Bitter** H
Cosy, timbered pub opposite
the oldest house in Harwich.
Admiralty charts in the front
bar; the fire burns coal trawled
from the sea. Still the favourite
of the local trawlermen at
lunchtime, so the mild has to
be just right. 🏨 🚗 🍴 ♣

Hatfield Broad Oak

Cock
High Street ☎ (0279) 718306
12–11

**Adnams Bitter, Broadside;
Greene King Abbot** H
Friendly village local featuring
bare floorboards, a large
collection of pictures, and
ancient oak beams. Hand-
painted, 16th-century walls in
the 'boardroom' and a large
restaurant. 🏨 ◑ ▶ ♣ P

Helions Bumpstead

Three Horseshoes
Water Lane OS650414
☎ (0440) 730298
11.45–2.30, 7–11 (12–2, 7–10.30 Sun)
Greene King IPA, Abbot H
Fine, friendly, old pub in a
remote setting, offering good
value food (not served
Mon/Tue eves or Sun).
Award-winning gardens.
🏨 Q ✿ ◑ ▶ 🚗 Å ♣ P

Heybridge Basin

Jolly Sailor
The Basin ☎ (0621) 854210
11–3, 6–11 (11–11 summer)
**Adnams Bitter; Tetley
Bitter** H
Traditional old riverside pub
close to the sea wall, with a
strong nautical flavour. Eve
meals in summer only.
Q 🚗 ✿ ◑ ▶ 🚗 ♣ P

High Easter

Cock & Bell Inn
The Street ☎ (0245) 31296
12–2.30, 7–11 (supper licence)
**Crouch Vale Woodham IPA;
Gibbs Mew Bishop's Tipple;
S&N Theakston XB; Younger
Scotch** H
14th-century, Grade II listed
building, steeped in history.
Noted for its food and good
value beer – the range is
constantly changing. Children
are most welcome.
🏨 Q ✿ ◑ ▶ P

High Roding

Black Lion
High Street ☎ (0279) 872847
11–3, 6.30–11
Adnams Extra; Ridleys IPA H
Classic, unspoilt 15th-century
inn. Very friendly; famous for
its home cooking.
🏨 Q ✿ ◑ ▶ 🚗 ♣ P

Ingatestone

Star
High Street ☎ (0277) 353618
11–2.30, 6–11
Greene King IPA, Abbot G
17th-century, cosy local with
large open fire, a hat collection
and a mynah bird. Reputedly
haunted by the dog whose
head hangs over the bar.
🏨 🚗 ✿ ⇌ P

Langham

Shepherd & Dog
Moor Road (1½ miles W of
A12) OS019318
☎ (0206) 272711
11–3, 5.30–11
**Courage Best Bitter; Greene
King IPA, Abbot; Nethergate
Bitter; John Smith's Bitter** H
Friendly country free house
and small restaurant, offering
home-cooked food. Paperback
library. 🏨 ✿ ◑ ▶ P

Langley Lower Green

Bull
OS437345 ☎ (0279) 777307
12–2.30, 6–11
**Adnams Bitter, Broadside;
Greene King IPA** H; **guest
beer** (occasionally)
Friendly, and well worth
finding. A pitch-penny game
is concealed under a bench
seat in the saloon bar. Doubles
as a doctor's surgery on Wed
afternoons. 🏨 Q ✿ 🚗 ♣ P

Lawford

Station Buffet
Manningtree Station (off
A137) ☎ (0206) 391114
11–11 (closed Sun eve)
**Adnams Bitter; Marston's
Pedigree; Mitchell's ESB;
Nethergate Old Growler;
Wadworth 6X** H; **guest beers**
Small station bar, recently
redecorated. Frequented by
locals and commuters alike,
and can get busy in commuter
hours and at Sun lunch. A rail
buff's dream and an Essex
institution. Q ✿ ◑ ▶ ⇌ P

Leigh-on-Sea

Crooked Billet
51 High Street (old town)
☎ (0702) 714854
11.30–3, 6–11
**Adnams Bitter; Ind Coope
Burton Ale; Taylor Walker
Best Bitter; Tetley Bitter** H
16th-century timber-framed
pub with two splendid and
characterful bars. Note the
huge fireplace in the public.
Panoramic views of the
estuary across Billet Wharf
and the famous cockle sheds.
Occasional mini beer festivals.
SE Essex CAMRA *Pub of the
Year 1992.* 🏨 Q ✿ ◑ 🚗 ⇌

Little Braxted

Green Man
Kelvedon Road (1½ miles SE
of village) OS849130
☎ (0621) 891659
11–3, 6–11
Ridleys IPA H
Traditional country pub in a

splendid village, with a delightful beer garden at the rear. Good value food.
🏠 Q ❀ ◑ 🍴 ♣ P

Littlebury

Queen's Head Inn

High Street ☎ (0799) 22251
12–11 (12–10.30 Mon & Tue in winter)
Bateman XXXB; Marston's Pedigree; Nethergate Bitter H; **guest beers**
600-year-old village local with many traditional features. ETB three crown accommodation.
🏠 Q 🛏 ❀ 🏡 ◑ 🍴 ♣ P

Little End (Stanford Rivers)

White Bear

London Road ☎ (0277) 362185
11–3 (4 Sat), 7–11
Adnams Bitter; Ind Coope Benskins Best Bitter, Burton Ale H; **guest beers** (occasionally)
Fine, traditional old pub with a lovely basic public bar which stages lots of events, particularly in summer e.g. car and motorcycle meets. The restaurant is open Sun only; no bar meals Mon eve.
🏠 Q ❀ ◑ 🍴 🍴 A ♣ P

Littley Green

Compasses

OS699172 ☎ (0245) 362308
11–3 (4 Sat), 6–11
Ridleys Mild, IPA G
A renovated country pub (voted CAMRA East Anglian *Pub of the Year* 1990) in a quiet hamlet near the Ridleys brewery. No meals, but Huffers (baps) for snacks. A monument to the hardwork of the retiring tenants.
🏠 Q ❀ ♣ P

Loughton

Wheatsheaf

15 York Hill ☎ (081) 508 9656
10–2.30 (3 Sat), 5.30 (6 Sat)–11
Adnams Bitter; Draught Bass; Charrington IPA; Fuller's London Pride, ESB (winter); **Welsh Brewers Worthington BB** H
Popular local with a friendly atmosphere. 🏠 ❀ ◑ P

Maldon

Blue Boar Hotel

Silver Street ☎ (0621) 852681
11–3, 6–11
Adnams Bitter G
14th-century, restful, coaching inn with Georgian features.
🏠 ❀ 🏡 🍴 ♣ P

White Horse

High Street ☎ (0621) 851708
10.30–3, 5.30–11

Adnams Extra; Courage Best Bitter, Directors; Crouch Vale Millennium Ale; Wadworth 6X H
16th-century coach house attracting a young clientele. Video games, etc. ◑ ♣

Marden Ash

Stag

Brentwood Road ☎ (0277) 362598
11–2.30 (3 Fri & Sat), 5.30 (6 Sat)–11
McMullen AK, Country, Stronghart H
Friendly local with a large garden. 🏠 Q ❀ ◑ 🍴 P

Mashbury

Fox

Fox Road OS650127 ☎ (0245) 31573
Adnams Extra; Ridleys IPA G
Very cosy, friendly country pub which has survived by turning the saloon bar into a restaurant. Casks are stillaged behind the bar. A 'fox' theme is in evidence. 🏠 ❀ ♣ P

Matching Tye

Fox Inn

On Matching Green road, 2 miles from Old Harlow OS516113 ☎ (0279) 731203
12–3, 6–11
Ind Coope Friary Meux Best Bitter, Burton Ale; Ridleys IPA H
Quaint and cosy village pub with three bars, containing many foxy artefacts. Petanque is played in the garden some Suns. Book Sun lunch; no food Sun eve. 🏠 ❀ ◑ 🍴 🍴 ♣ P

Messing

Old Crown

Lodge Road (1 mile N of B1022) OS898190 ☎ (0621) 815575
11–3, 6–11
Adnams Extra; Ridleys IPA H
Charming, beamed, typical rural Essex village local: pews, benches, refectory tables and cosy corners. The restaurant is popular for business lunches. Children welcome.
🏠 Q ◑ 🍴 ♣ P

Mill End Green (Great Easton)

Green Man

E of B184 OS619260 ☎ (0371) 870286
11.30–3, 6–11
Adnams Bitter, Broadside; Greene King IPA; Ridleys IPA H
Very pleasant, 15th-century country pub with oak studwork. Excellent gardens and a separate outdoor

drinking area for families. No meals Sun eve.
🏠 Q ❀ 🏡 ◑ A ♣ P

Mill Green

Viper

Mill Green Road (2 miles NW of Ingatestone; follow Highwood/Writtle signs) OS641019 ☎ (0277) 352010
10–2.30 (3 Sat), 6–11
Adnams Bitter; Ruddles Best Bitter, County H
Newly-freed Truman pub with an excellent country atmosphere. In a picturesque woodland setting, its gardens are a feature. Beers may vary.
🏠 Q ❀ 🍴 ♣ P

Moreton

White Hart Inn

Bridge Road (off B184 from Fyfield) OS533073 ☎ (0277) 890228
11–3, 5.30–11
Adnams Bitter; Courage Best Bitter; Wadworth 6X H; **guest beer** G
Excellent example of a typical old village community pub, cosy and welcoming. Good home-cooked food (not served Sun eve). Courage Best is sold as 'Webster's Wonderful Wallop'.
🏠 Q ❀ 🏡 ◑ 🍴 ♣ P

Navestock Heath

Plough

Off Sabines Road OS538970 ☎ (0277) 372296
11–3.30, 6–11
Adnams Bitter; Draught Bass; Brains Dark; Fuller's Mr Harry; Greene King Abbot; Mitchell's ESB H; **guest beers**
A superb free house, comfortable and friendly, usually with ten real ales, often including Exmoor, Gibbs Mew and Nethergate. Quiz nights and live C&W music. Hard to find but worth the effort. Local CAMRA *Pub of the Year* 1991.
🏠 🛏 ❀ ◑ 🍴 🍴 ♣ P

North Fambridge

Ferryboat Inn

Ferry Road ☎ (0621) 740208
11–3, 6–11
Adnams Bitter; Ind Coope Burton Ale; Tetley Bitter H
Very cosy pub at the end of the village near the river. popular with locals; small restaurant. 🏠 Q 🛏 ◑ 🍴 P

Orsett

Foxhound

18 High Road (near hospital) ☎ (0375) 891295
11–3.30 (4 Sat), 6–11
Courage Best Bitter, Directors; Crouch Vale Woodham IPA H

Essex

Village pub, popular with farmers and pharmacists alike, with contrasting public and saloon bars. The latter echoes the pub's name with pictures of foxhounds around the walls and in the carpet pattern; there's even a real one behind the bar. ♨ ✿ ◖ ⊟ ♣ P

Paslow Wood Common

Black Horse
Stondon Road (off A414, towards Stondon Massey) OS588017 ☎ (0277) 821915
12–3, 6–11
Adnams Bitter; Bateman XB; Fuller's ESB; Hook Norton Old Hooky; Thwaites Bitter Ⓗ
A popular pub offering a continually-changing list of beers – up to eight (usually including a mild). 1991 local CAMRA *Pub of the Year*. Barbecues in summer.
✿ ◖ ▶ ♣ ⌂ P

Pleshey

White Horse
The Street ☎ (0245) 37281
11–3, 7–11
Morland Old Speckled Hen; Nethergate Bitter; Whitbread Boddingtons Bitter Ⓗ
Pleasant old timber-framed building which makes attractive and interesting use of its interior space. Children welcome in most of the pub, except the bar.
♨ Q ✿ ◖ ▶ ♣ P

Prittlewell

Spread Eagle
267 Victoria Avenue (A127) ☎ (0702) 348383
11–2.30 (5 Sat), 5 (7 Sat)–11
Adnams Bitter; Charrington IPA; Welsh Brewers Worthington BB Ⓗ; **guest beers**
An excellent, traditional welcome in a Victorian-style lounge with local history pictures. Fri music club and quiz/party nights. Its listed frontage stands opposite an ancient church. Closes early Sat (3pm) when there's local league football.
✿ ⊟ ⇌ ♣ P

Radley Green

Thatchers Arms
500 yds from A414 OS622054 ☎ (0245) 248356
11–2.30, 6–11
Adnams Extra; Ridleys IPA Ⓗ
Secluded, friendly country local with a large beer garden which is safe for children. Snacks only Sun lunchtime.
♨ Q ✿ ◖ ♠ ♣ P

Rickling Green

Cricketers' Arms
¹/₂ mile W of B1383 OS511298 ☎ (079 988) 322/595
11–3, 6–11
Tolly Cobbold Mild, Original Ⓖ; **guest beer**
Enlarged pub in an idyllic situation overlooking the village cricket green. Excellent food; specialities include mussels and offal. Note the unusual gravity dispense through barrel ends mounted in the wall.
♨ ⚞ ✿ ⌂ ◖ ▶ ⊟ P

Rochford

Golden Lion
North Street ☎ (0702) 545487
12–11 (closed 3–5 if quiet)
Crouch Vale Best Bitter; Fuller's London Pride; Greene King Abbot Ⓗ; **guest beers**
17th-century free house in a former tailor's shop which became an ale house. A traditional building with a well-ventilated gents! 'Lions Den' is a house beer from Crouch Vale. Home-cooked lunches (not served Sun). 260 guest ales in 1992; usually four available, including a mild.
✿ ◖ ♠ ⇌ ♣

Old Ship
North Street ☎ (0702) 544210
11–3, 5 (6 Sat)–11
Ind Coope Burton Ale; Tetley Bitter; Young's Bitter Ⓗ
One of only two coaching inns in Rochford, a listed building with a cobbled courtyard. Former separate bars are discernible from the leaded windows. Eve meals finish at 8.30. ✿ ◖ ▶ ⇌ ♣ P

Roydon

White Hart
High Street ☎ (027 979) 2118
11–2.30, 6–11
Adnams Bitter; Greene King Abbot; Tetley Bitter; Wadworth 6X Ⓗ; **guest beers** (occasionally)
Pub popular at lunchtime: excellent value meals.
◖ ▶ ♠ ⇌ P

St Osyth

White Hart
Mill Street ☎ (0255) 820318
11–3, 7–11
Adnams Bitter; Courage Directors; John Smith's Bitter Ⓗ; **guest beer** (occasionally)
Friendly village pub featuring photos of old Essex life and strange nick-nacks in every corner. Gents – don't miss out on the ancient ceramic loos.
♨ ✿ ◖ ▶ ♣ P

Salcott-cum-Virley

Sun
The Street ☎ (0621) 860461
11–3, 6–11
Adnams Bitter Ⓗ; **Greene King Abbot** Ⓖ; **Tolly Cobbold Bitter** Ⓗ
Wonderfully basic, friendly, no-frills village local. Near the Essex marshes and bird sanctuary. New improved (a matter of opinion) inside toilets. ♨ Q ⊟ ♣ P

Shenfield

Old Green Dragon
112 Shenfield Road (A1023/A129 jct) ☎ (0277) 210086
11–2.30, 6–11 (11–11 Sat)
Adnams Bitter; Tetley Bitter; Wadworth 6X Ⓗ; **guest beers**
Restored 14th-century coaching inn, busy but welcoming. Popular with local sports clubs but attracts a good cross-section of the community. No-smoking family room.
⚞ ◖ ▶ ♿ ⇌ ♣ P ✗

Shoeburyness

Parsons' Barn
Frobisher Way, North Shoebury (by Asda store) ☎ (0702) 297373
12–2.30, 6–11 (12–11 Sat)
Greene King IPA, Abbot Ⓖ; **Ruddles County; Webster's Yorkshire Bitter** Ⓗ
Restored 18th-century barn, traditional in character with farm implements and a trap high up on the walls. Draws a mixed clientele, including the younger set. Pool table and darts. Cubicles offer privacy. Eve meals Thu–Sat. Beer range may vary.
♨ ⚞ ◖ ▶ ♿ ⇌ ♣ P

Southend-on-Sea

Cork & Cheese
363 Chartwell Square, Victoria Circus ☎ (0702) 616914
11–11
Greene King Abbot; Marston's Pedigree Ⓗ; **guest beers**
Modern, spacious town-style pub with a restaurant upstairs. Draws a varied clientele but a video jukebox dominates the bar. Convenient for shops and night clubs; disco nights at weekends. A worthwhile visit in the town centre.
✿ ⇌ (Victoria)

Liberty Belle
Marine Parade ☎ (0702) 466936
10–11
Courage Best Bitter, Directors Ⓗ; **guest beers**

Large seafront pub sporting nautical decor. A welcome retreat from the area's disco pubs. Pool played.
🐎 ❀ 🛏 ◐ ⇌ (Central) ♣

Railway Hotel

Clifftown Road
☎ (0702) 343194
11–11
Adnams Bitter; Draught Bass *or* Charrington IPA; Fuller's London Pride Ⓗ
Built as a hotel in 1870, this imposing three-storey building has a welcoming interior with comfortable furnishings and steam locomotive pictures. Pool table, fruit machines and a TV in the bars.
◐ ⊞ ♿ ⇌ (Central) ♣

South Fambridge

Anchor Hotel

Fambridge Road (4 miles N of Rochford) ☎ (0702) 203535
11–3, 6–11 (11–11 Sat)
Crouch Vale Best Bitter; Greene King Abbot; Tetley Bitter Ⓗ**; guest beers**
Victorian hotel built on the site of original inns and still serving the local community. The garden has a children's play area and holds summer barbecues. Varied menu. 92 guest ales in 1992 (guests often include a mild).
Q ❀ 🛏 ◐ ◑ ♣ P

Southminster

Rose Inn

Burnham Road (B1021, 3/4 mile S of town) ☎ (0621) 772915
11.30–2.30, 6–11
Greene King IPA, Abbot, Winter Ale; Ridleys Mild (occasionally) Ⓖ
Friendly, two-roomed roadside inn: a real public bar where darts and dominoes are played and a smaller bar where high quality, good value food is served (not Sun or Wed eve).
🔥 Q ❀ ◐ ◑ ⊞ ♣ ⌓ P

Station Arms

Station Road ☎ (0621) 772225
12–3, 6–11 (11–11 Sat)
Crouch Vale Best Bitter Ⓗ**; guest beers**
Weatherboarded high street pub (no pub sign). Admire the mirror over the fireplace. Three constantly-changing guest beers – over 100 in its first nine months as a free house. A ferocious domino game is often in progress.
🔥 Q 🐎 ❀ ⇌ ♣

South Woodham Ferrers

Curlew

80 Gandalf's Ride
☎ (0245) 321371
12–2.30, 6–11 (12–11 Sat)
Shepherd Neame Master Brew Bitter, Spitfire, Bishops Finger (occasionally) Ⓗ**; guest beers**
Modern estate pub with a friendly atmosphere.
◐ ◑ ♿ ♣ P

Stansted Mountfitchet

Dog & Duck

Lower Street (off B1351)
OS516251 ☎ (0279) 812047
10–2.30, 5.30 (6 Sat)–11
Greene King IPA, Rayments Special, Abbot Ⓗ
Excellent, weatherboarded, village local with a lovely pub sign. Watch out for the low beam in the lounge. Good lunchtime snacks (not Sun).
Q ❀ ⊞ ⇌ ♣ P

Stapleford Abbotts

Rabbits

Stapleford Road (B175, near Passingford Bridge)
☎ (040 28) 203
11–2.30, 6–11
Adnams Bitter; Ind Coope Benskins Best Bitter, Burton Ale Ⓗ
Friendly country pub with a children's play area in its large, attractive beer garden. Meals include vegetarian choices. 🔥 Q ❀ ◐ ◑ ♣ P

Stisted

Dolphin

Coggeshall Road (A120)
☎ (0376) 21143
10.30–3, 6–11
Adnams Extra; Ridleys IPA Ⓖ
Attractive, unspoilt, many-beamed pub featuring roaring log fires in winter, casks on stillage behind the bar and swings and an aviary in the garden. No eve meals Tue or Sun. 🔥 Q ❀ ◐ ◑ ⊞ ♣ P

Onley Arms

The Street (1 mile N off A120)
☎ (0376) 325204
11–3 (later if busy), 7–11
Ridleys IPA Ⓗ
Pleasant, gabled rural village pub built in 1853 for the Onley estate workers. Petanque league Sun morning and summer Wed eve. Sun roast lunch; dining room open Wed–Fri; meals in the bar at other times. 🔥 Q ❀ ◐ ◑ ♣ P

Stock

Bear

The Square ☎ (0277) 840232
11.30–3, 6–11
Adnams Bitter; Tetley Bitter; Wadworth 6X Ⓗ
Extensively yet sympathetically refurbished pub with three drinking areas.
Q 🐎 ❀ ◐ ◑ ⊞ ♿ ⛺ P

Hoop

High Street ☎ (0277) 841137
10–11
Adnams Mild, Bitter; Crouch Vale Best Bitter; Mitchell's ESB; Nethergate Bitter; Wadworth 6X Ⓗ**; guest beers**
Cosy one-bar pub, renowned for its real ales, with normally eight–ten available. Outdoor games on summer eves in the large garden. Dogs are welcome. Extensive range of home-cooked food served all day. Q ❀ ◐ ◑ ♣ ⌓

Stow Maries

Prince of Wales

Woodham Road (old B1012, 2 miles E of South Woodham Ferrers) OS830993
☎ (0621) 828971
11–11
Crouch Vale Woodham IPA; Hull Mild; Malton Pale Ale; Marston Moor Brewers Pride; Ringwood Old Thumper Ⓗ
Fine weatherboarded free house, CAMRA's Essex *Pub of the Year* 1991 and winner of the council's *Conservation Award*. Specialises in rare ales and Belgian beers (at least one mild available); stages beer festivals. No carpets or fruit machines – a traditional gem.
🔥 Q 🐎 ❀ ◐ ◑ ⛺ ♣ ⌓ P

Thaxted

Rose & Crown

Mill End ☎ (0371) 831152
11 (12 winter)–3, 5 (6 winter)–11
Adnams Broadside; Ridleys IPA Ⓗ**; guest beer**
Friendly local in an historic town with a magnificent Guildhall, church and working windmill. The pub is believed to have been built on the site of a monks' hostelry. Good value home-cooked food. ❀ ◐ ◑ ⊞ ⛺ ♣ P

Try also: Swan Hotel (Free)

Tillingham

Cap & Feathers

South Street ☎ (0621) 779212
11–11
Crouch Vale Best Mild, Woodham IPA, Best Bitter, Millennium Ale, SAS, Porter, Willie Warmer Ⓖ **&** Ⓗ
Unspoilt 15th-century village inn, now Crouch Vale brewery's only tied house. Good value food (try the home-smoked meat and fish). CAMRA *National Pub of the Year* 1989 and still maintaining that standard.
🔥 Q 🐎 ❀ 🛏 ◐ ◑ ♣ ⌓ P

Essex

Tolleshunt D'Arcy

Red Lion
South Street
☎ (0621) 860238
11–3, 6–11 (11–11 Fri & Sat)
**Adnams Bitter; Crouch Vale
Best Bitter; Ridleys IPA;
Webster's Yorkshire
Bitter** Ⓗ
Lovely, cosy, part-beamed
pub selling excellent value
beers and a wide range of
wines. Separate restaurant.
Watch out for the one-eyed
tom cat!
🏚 ✳ ◖ ⬥ ♣ P

Toppesfield

Green Man
Church Lane
☎ (0787) 237418
11–2.30, 7–11
Greene King IPA, Abbot Ⓗ
Excellent, welcoming and
roomy pub in a remote village.
Huffers (rolls) only on
weekdays; the restaurant is
open at weekends.
🏚 Q ✳ ◖ ▶ ⬥ ▲ ♣ P

Waltham Abbey

Green Dragon
Market Square
☎ (0992) 711205
11–3, 5.30–11
**Adnams Bitter; Ansells Mild;
Ind Coope Burton Ale; Tetley
Bitter; Wadworth 6X; Young's
Special** Ⓗ**; guest beers**
Comfortable two-bar pub,
recently converted to real ale.
🏚 Q ⏵ ✳ ◖ ▶ ⬥ ♣ P

Old English Gentleman
85 Highbridge Street
☎ (0992) 712714
11–11 (11–4, 7–11 Sat)
**Greene King Abbot;
McMullen AK, Country** Ⓗ
Old pub with gardens backing
down to the River Lea.
Q ✳ ⬥ P

Walton-on-the-Naze

Royal Marine
3 Old Pier Street
☎ (0255) 674000
10–3, 6–11 (10–11 summer)
**Adnams Bitter; Marston's
Pedigree; Whitbread
Boddingtons Bitter, Castle
Eden Ale** Ⓗ
Popular three-bar pub serving
a mixed collection of locals.
Newspapers available. A real
pub, with huge leaded
windows and a turn-of-the-
century atmosphere.
🏚 Q ◖ ▶ ⬥ ▲ ⇌ ♣

Warley

Alexandra
114 Warley Hill (B186)
☎ (0277) 210456
11–2.30 (3 Fri & Sat), 6–11 (12–2.30,
7–10.30 Sun)
**Greene King XX Mild, IPA,
Rayments Special, Abbot** Ⓗ**,
Winter Ale** Ⓖ
Classic, mid Victorian, two-
bar pub with traditional decor
and atmosphere. How many
pubs have a licensee, nearing
retirement, who started
working in the same pub as a
cellar-boy at 12 years-old?
⬥ ⇌ (Brentwood) ♣ P

Westcliff-on-Sea

Cricketers Inn
228 London Road (A13)
☎ (0702) 343168
10.30–11
**Greene King IPA, Rayments
Special, Abbot** Ⓗ
Three-bar, Tudor-style pub,
popular for darts. Pool table in
what is probably the last
public bar in the area. No food
Sun. ◖ ⬥ ⚄ ⇌ ♣ P

Palace Theatre Centre
430 London Road (A13)
☎ (0702) 347816
12–2.30, 6–11
**Crouch Vale Willie Warmer;
Greene King IPA, Abbot;
King & Barnes Festive** Ⓗ
Convenient, comfortable foyer
bar with a courtyard patio and
a restaurant. Live music Sun
lunch (piano), eve (rock).
Children tolerated until 7pm.
Beware thespians on show
nights! On a bus route;
parking difficult. Q ✳ ⚄ ⇌

Try also: **Melrose**, Hamlet
Court Rd (Grand Met)

West Mersea

Fountain
Queens Corner
☎ (0206) 382080
11–3 (4 Sat), 6 (7 Sat)–11
**Greene King IPA; Mauldons
Black Adder; Whitbread
Wethered Bitter, Boddingtons
Bitter** Ⓗ**; guest beer**
Comfortable island pub in a
popular area for watersports.
The guest beer is changed
regularly. Function room. The
menu caters for vegetarians.
⏵ ✳ 🏚 ◖ ▶ ⬥ ⚄ ▲ ♣ P

Witham

George
Newland Street
☎ (0376) 511098
10–2.30, 5.30–11 (10–11 Fri & Sat)
**Adnams Extra; Ridleys Mild,
IPA** Ⓗ

Good value, welcoming town-
centre pub with a public bar
and a quiet, 16th-century,
timber-framed saloon. The
function room doubles as a
children's room.
Q ⏵ ◖ ▶ ⇌ ♣ P

Victoria
Faulkbourne Road, Powers
Hall End OS807152
☎ (0376) 511809
11–2.30 (3.30 Sat), 6 (7 Sat)–11
Ridleys IPA Ⓗ **&** Ⓖ
Spacious, tastefully renovated
old country house on the edge
of town: a large public bar and
a comfortable lounge. Eve
meals Thu–Sat; no food Sun.
🏚 ⏵ ✳ ◖ ▶ ⬥ ♣ P

Wivenhoe

Black Buoy
Black Buoy Hill (off main
road) ☎ (0206) 822425
11–2.30 (3 Sat), 6–11
**Courage Directors; John
Smith's Bitter; Tolly Cobbold
Bitter, Old Strong** Ⓗ
Nautical pub with a good
atmosphere in the old part of
town. Reasonably-priced good
food. 🏚 Q ⏵ ◖ ▶ ⇌ P

Horse & Groom
55 The Cross (B1028)
☎ (0206) 824928
10.30–3, 5.30 (6 Sat)–11
**Adnams Mild, Bitter, Old
(winter)** Ⓗ**; guest beers**
Excellent local serving food
from 10am. Q ✳ ◖ ▶ ⚄ ♣ P

Station
Station Road ☎ (0206) 822991
10.30 (11 Sat)–11
**John Smith's Bitter; Tolly
Cobbold Bitter, Original, Old
Strong** Ⓗ
No-frills, basic pub with a
friendly atmosphere. Its single
bar is popular with old and
young. 🏚 ✳ ⚄ ⇌ ♣ P

Woodham Mortimer

Hurdlemakers Arms
Post Office Road
☎ (024 522) 5169
11–3, 6–11
Greene King IPA, Abbot Ⓗ
Lovely old country pub with a
fine garden and a stone-
flagged saloon bar.
🏚 Q ✳ ◖ ⬥ ♣ P

Writtle

Wheatsheaf
The Green ☎ (0245) 420695
11–2.30 (3 Fri, 4 Sat), 5.30–11
**Greene King IPA, Rayments
Special, Abbot** Ⓗ
Small, unspoilt village local.
Q ⬥ ♣

110

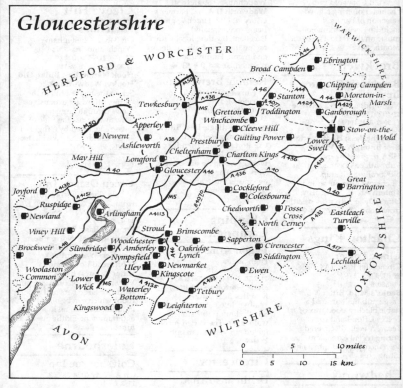

Gloucestershire

Map showing locations including: Ebrington, Broad Campden, Chipping Campden, Moreton-in-Marsh, Stanton, Toddington, Ganborough, Gretton, Winchcombe, Cleeve Hill, Stow-on-the-Wold, Lower Swell, Guiting Power, Tewkesbury, Apperley, Newent, Ashleworth, Prestbury, Charlton Kings, May Hill, Longford, Cheltenham, Gloucester, Great Barrington, Joyford, Ruspidge, Newland, Cockleford, Colesbourne, Chedworth, Fosse Cross, North Cerney, Eastleach Turville, Viney Hill, Arlingham, Stroud, Brimscombe, Sapperton, Cirencester, Lechlade, Brockweir, Slimbridge, Woodchester, Amberley, Oakridge Lynch, Siddington, Nympsfield, Newmarket, Ewen, Woolaston Common, Uley, Kingscote, Lower Wick, Waterley Bottom, Tetbury, Kingswood, Leighterton

HEREFORD & WORCESTER, WARWICKSHIRE, OXFORDSHIRE, WILTSHIRE, AVON

0 5 10 miles
0 5 10 15 km

 Donnington, *Stow-on-the-Wold*; **Uley**, *Uley*

Amberley

Black Horse
N of the village OS849016
☎ (0453) 872556
11.30–2.30, 6–11
Fuller's London Pride; Hook Norton Best Bitter; Tetley Bitter H; guest beers
Lively pub on the edge of Minchinhampton Common. Worth finding. ⚲ Q ❀ ◑ ◗

Apperley

Coal House Inn
Gabb Lane OS854283
☎ (0452) 780211
11–3, 7–11
Hook Norton Best Bitter; Smiles Best Bitter; Wadworth 6X H
Traditional pub on the Severn; liable to flooding in winter. Mooring points provided.
⚲ Q ❀ ◑ ◗ & ⏚ ♣ P

Farmers Arms
Ledbury Road (B4213)
☎ (0452) 780307
11–3, 6–11

Draught Bass; Hook Norton Best Bitter; Wadworth 6X H
Extended farmhouse-style inn and restaurant. Plans are afoot to open a small brewery and museum in the grounds.
⚲ ❀ ◑ ◗ & ⏚ P

Arlingham

Red Lion
High Street ☎ (0452) 740269
11.30–3, 6.30 (6 summer)–11
Draught Bass; Hook Norton Best Bitter; Smiles Best Bitter; Uley Bitter H; guest beers
Simple, two-bar pub in the village centre. Piano in the lounge. House beer available.
❀ ◑ ◗ ⏚ ♣ P

Ashleworth

Boat Inn
The Quay OS819251
☎ (0452) 700272
11–2.30, 6–11 (11–11 summer)
Arkell's 3B; Smiles Best Bitter, Exhibition G
Intimate riverside pub in the same family ownership for

over 400 years. Interior little changed in this century.
Q ❀ ⏚ ♣ ◠ P

Try also: Arkle (Free)

Brimscombe

Kings Arms
Bourne Lane (N of A419, 4 miles E of Stroud) OS874023
☎ (0453) 882552
11.30–2.30, 6.30–11
Ind Coope Burton Ale; S&N Theakston Best Bitter; Tetley Bitter; Wadworth 6X H
Small, split-level pub on the hillside overlooking the Frome valley. The lower public bar has a jukebox; comfortable upper lounge bar. No lunches Sun or eve meals Mon–Wed.
Q ❀ ◑ ◗ ⏚ ♣ ◠

Broad Campden

Bakers Arms
☎ (0386) 840515
11.30–3, 5.30 (6 winter)–11
Donnington BB; Younger IPA, No. 3 H

Fine old Cotswold pub of character offering a good selection of bar food, including vegetarian. Folk music on the third Tue of the month. ♨ Q ✤ ◑ ▶ ♣ P

Brockweir

Brockweir Country Inn

Near bridge over River Wye
☎ (0291) 689548
11.30–3, 6–11 (11.30–11 Thu–Sat summer)
Draught Bass; Hook Norton Best Bitter; Wye Valley HPA Ⓗ**; guest beers**
Pub with oak beams from an old locally-built ship. Chepstow racecourse and Tintern Abbey are nearby; Offa's Dyke path runs past the front door. ♨ Q ☜ ✤ ⌑ ▶ ⊟ ♣ ⌂ P

Charlton Kings

Clock Tower

Cirencester Road (A435)
☎ (0242) 571794
11–2.30, 5–11
Banks's Mild, Bitter Ⓔ
Large pub built around a stable block: a good mix of *art nouveau*, floral and rural decor. A well, discovered during recent extensions, has been incorporated into a new eating area. ✤ ◑ ▶ P

Chedworth

Seven Tuns

☎ (0285) 720242
12–2.30 (not Mon), 6.30–11 (11.30–3, 6–11 summer)
Adnams Bitter; Courage Best Bitter, Directors; John Smith's Bitter Ⓗ
Welcoming, picturesque pub in an attractive Cotswold village, within walking distance of a Roman villa. The garden has a stream and a waterwheel. A mummers' play is performed outside on Boxing Day.
♨ Q ☜ ✤ ◑ ▶ ▲ ♣ P

Cheltenham

Bayshill Inn

85 St Georges Place
☎ (0242) 524388
11–3 (4 Sat), 5 (6 Sat)–11
Draught Bass; Hall & Woodhouse Tanglefoot; Wadworth IPA, 6X, Old Timer Ⓖ
Very popular town-centre pub without frills. Good value lunches served. Pinball and cribbage. ✤ ✤ ◑ ⇌ ♣

Beaufort Arms

184 London Road (A40)
☎ (0242) 526038
11–2.30, 6–11
Draught Bass; Hall &

Woodhouse Tanglefoot;
Wadworth IPA, 6X, Farmer's Glory Ⓗ**, Old Timer** Ⓖ**; guest beers** (occasionally)
Excellent, bustling local with a racing theme in both the decor and menu. Family room planned. ✤ ✤ ◑ ▶ ⊟ ♣ P

Kemble Brewery Inn

27 Fairview Street (off Fairview Rd)
☎ (0242) 243446
11.30–2.30 (3 Sat), 6–11
Archers Village, Best Bitter, Golden Ⓗ**; guest beers**
Comfortable and friendly back-street local offering weekly-changing guest beers. Very popular for Sun lunch; eve meals finish at 8 (not served weekends).
✤ ◑ ▶ ♣ ⌂

Chipping Campden

Lygon Arms

High Street
☎ (0386) 840318
11–2.30, 6–11 (11–11 Sat & summer)
Hook Norton Best Bitter; Ruddles Best Bitter; Wadworth 6X Ⓗ**; guest beer**
Small, comfortable stone-walled bar. The varied menu includes a vegetarian option.
☜ ✤ ◑ ▶ P

Cirencester

Drillmans Arms

34 Gloucester Road (A417)
☎ (0285) 653892
11–3, 6–11 (11–11 Sat)
Archers Best Bitter; Wadworth 6X; Whitbread Flowers Original Ⓗ**; guest beers**
Two-bar pub dating from the 18th century; Archers' first tied house, but now free.
♨ ✤ ◑ ▶ ⊟ ▲ ♣ P

Golden Cross

20 Blackjack Street (near Corinium Museum)
☎ (0285) 652137
11–3, 6–11
Arkell's 2B, 3B, Mash Tun Mild, Noel Ale Ⓗ
A real pub without gimmicks, appealing to all age groups.
✤ ✤ ◑ ▲ ♣

Oddfellows Arms

10–14 Chester Street
☎ (0285) 641540
11–2.30, 5–11 (11.30–3, 7–11 Sat)
Courage Best Bitter, Wadworth 6X Ⓗ**; guest beers**
Recently renovated pub in a quiet back street. Note the original Victorian fireplace in the bar. Frequently-changed guest beers, but at upmarket prices. ♨ Q ✤ ◑ ▶

Try also: **Talbot**, Victoria Rd (Arkell's)

Cleeve Hill

High Roost

On B4632, Cheltenham–Winchcombe road
☎ (0242) 672010
11.30–2.30 (3 Sat), 7–11
Hook Norton Best Bitter, Old Hooky; Wadworth 6X Ⓗ
Set on the highest hill in the county affording expansive views through large bay windows across the Vale of Severn. Reached by a flight of steps. Children allowed in for meals. ✤ ◑ ♣ P

Cockleford

Green Dragon Inn

½ mile along Elkstone turn from A435 OS969142
☎ (024 287) 271
11–2.30, 6–11
Draught Bass; Butcombe Bitter Ⓖ**; Hook Norton Best Bitter** Ⓗ**; S&N Theakston Old Peculier; Wadworth 6X; Whitbread Boddingtons Bitter** Ⓖ**; guest beers**
Very popular, picturesque pub with two large bars and a side room which can be used by families. Occasional live entertainment. Skittle alley for functions. ♨ ✤ ◑ ▶ ⊟ ⌂ P

Colesbourne

Colesbourne Inn

On A435 ☎ (024 287) 376
11–3, 6–11
Wadworth IPA (summer), **6X, Farmer's Glory, Old Timer** Ⓗ
Traditional, 200-year-old Cotswold inn in a picturesque village with sedate and comfortable, panelled bars. The emphasis is on food in the main bar. The old stables, with rare windows, have been converted into bedrooms.
♨ ✤ ✤ ◑ ▶ ⊟ ♣ P

Eastleach Turville

Victoria Inn

OS198052 ☎ (036 785) 277
10.30–2.30, 7–11
Arkell's 3B, Kingsdown Ⓗ
18th-century village pub overlooking a charming Cotswold village. The L-shaped bar has a restaurant opening off the rear of its lounge section. Good food.
♨ Q ✤ ◑ ▶ ⊟ ♣ ⌂ P

Ebrington

Ebrington Arms

Just off B4035 ☎ (0386) 78223
11–2.30, 6–11
Donnington SBA; Hook Norton Best Bitter Ⓗ**; guest beer** (summer)
Friendly, old village-centre pub with a superbly preserved open fireplace in the dining

area. A wide selection of hot meals are listed on a beam (not served Sun eve).
🏚 🍴 ❀ 🛏 ◑▶ ♣ ⌂ P

Ewen

Wild Duck Inn

Drakes Island ☎ (0285) 770310
11–11
Draught Bass; S&N Theakston XB (summer), **Old Peculier** (winter); **Wadworth 6X** H
Superb country hotel built in 1563 and retaining a slightly rustic feel, with settles, old paintings and an imposing fireplace. Serious food. 'Duck Pond Bitter', the house beer, is Archers Village. Cider in summer.
🏚 Q ❀ 🛏 ◑▶ 🗡 ♣ ⌂ P

Fosse Cross

Hare & Hounds

On A429, Northleach–Cirencester road OS068095
☎ (0285) 720288
11–3 (2.30 Sat), 6–11
Hook Norton Best Bitter; S&N Theakston Best Bitter, Old Peculier; Wadworth 6X H
300-year-old Cotswold stone pub on the Fosse Way. An extensive range of food includes vegetarian and children's menus.
🏚 🍴 ❀ ◑▶ 🗡 🗡 ♣ P

Ganborough

Coach & Horses

On A424, 3 miles N of Stow OS172292 ☎ (0451) 30208
11–2.30, 6.30–11
Donnington XXX, BB, SBA H
A pleasant country pub on the main road, popular for its beer and food. The nearest pub to the brewery and one of few to keep mild all year round. Pub games include bottle walking (not for the faint-hearted). No eve meals Sun.
🏚 ❀ ◑▶ 🗡 ♣ ⌂ P

Gloucester

Linden Tree

73-75 Bristol Road (A38, 1½ miles S of centre)
☎ (0452) 527869
11–2.30 (3 Sat), 5.30–11
Draught Bass; Hall & Woodhouse Tanglefoot; Hook Norton Best Bitter; Wadworth 6X H, **Farmer's Glory** G; guest beers
Excellent pub in a Grade II listed building offering fine accommodation and a comprehensive menu of traditional fare (except Sun eve). 🏚 ❀ 🛏 ◑▶

Old Crown

81-83 Westgate Street (by Shire Hall) ☎ (0452) 310517

11–11
Samuel Smith OBB, Museum H
Highly commended for its refurbishment in CAMRA's *Pub Design* competition, this building was re-born as a pub in 1990. A traditional public bar downstairs and a comfortable lounge upstairs. One of few Sam Smith's outlets in the county.
Q ◑▶ 🗡 🗡 🗡 ♣

Waterfront

Merchants Road
☎ (0452) 308326
12–3, 5.30–11 (12–11 Thu–Sat)
Marston's Pedigree; Whitbread WCPA; guest beers G
An imaginative development of two floors of a former pillar house in the city docks. A permanent festival of 12 real ales with the ten guest ales constantly changing. With free peanuts by the sackful and various challenges, it's gimmicky but popular.
❀ ◑▶ ♣ P

Whitesmiths Arms

81 Southgate Street
☎ (0452) 414770
11–2.30 (may extend), 6–11
Arkell's 2B, 3B, Kingsdown H; guest beers (seasonal)
Named after maritime metal-workers, a former Whitbread pub opposite the historic docks and National Waterways Museum. Fitting maritime decor. 🏚 ◑▶ 🗡 ♣

Try also: **Crown & Thistle**, Barton St (Free); **Fountain**, Westgate St (Whitbread)

Great Barrington

Fox Inn

1 mile from the Barringtons turn off A40 OS204131
☎ (045 14) 385
11.30–2.30, 6.30–11 (12–2, 7–10.30 Sun)
Donnington XXX (occasionally), **BB, SBA** H
Excellent stone pub in a beautiful position by the River Windrush. Has been in every edition of the *Guide*. Cider in summer. No food Sun.
🏚 Q ❀ 🛏 ◑▶ ♣ ⌂ P

Gretton

Royal Oak

E end of village
☎ (0242) 602477
11–2.30, 6–11
Courage Best Bitter, Directors; Eldridge Pope Hardy Country; John Smith's Bitter; Wadworth 6X H
Well-established free house with one rambling bar. A recently-added dining area offers a wide range of meals.
🏚 ❀ ◑▶ ♣ P

Guiting Power

Olde Inn

On Winchcombe road N of village ☎ (0451) 850392
11.30–2.30, 5.30–11
Hook Norton Best Bitter; S&N Theakston Best Bitter H; guest beers
Friendly and warm Cotswold free house, popular with locals and tourists alike. The wide range of food includes Danish dishes. 🏚 Q ❀ ◑▶ 🗡 ♣

Try also: **Farmers Arms** (Donnington)

Joyford

Dog & Muffler

Off B4228 English Bicknor–Berry Hill road OS579132 ☎ (0594) 832444
11–3, 6 (7 winter)–11
Ruddles County; Samuel Smith OBB H
Out-of-the-way pub, well worth finding. An old cider press is a feature in the garden. New restaurant; car park available in summer only. 🏚 ❀ ◑▶ 🗡 🗡 🗡 ♣ P

Kingscote

Hunters Hall

On A4135, 5 miles W of Tetbury ☎ (0453) 860393
11–3, 6.30–11
Draught Bass; Hook Norton Best Bitter; Wadworth 6X; Uley Old Spot H
16th-century coaching inn with several small bars, stone-flagged floors and open fires. Welcoming for children.
🏚 Q 🍴 ❀ 🛏 ◑▶ ♣ P

Kingswood

Dinneywicks Inn

High Street ☎ (0453) 840828
10.30–3, 6 (7 Mon–Wed, Jan–Feb)–11
Draught Bass; Hall & Woodhouse Tanglefoot; Wadworth IPA, 6X, Farmer's Glory, Old Timer H
Lively local on the south side of the village. Its name derives from a local hill which was a burial ground for horses.
🏚 🍴 ❀ ◑▶ ♣ P

Lechlade

Crown Inn

High Street ☎ (0367) 52198
11.30–2.30, 6.30–11 (11.30–11 Sat)
Hook Norton Best Bitter; Morland Old Speckled Hen; Wadworth 6X H; guest beers (summer)
Friendly, comfortable front-of-house bar; the former rear bar is now used as a restaurant. Live music Sun eves. ❀ ◑▶ ♣

Gloucestershire

Leighterton

Royal Oak Inn
The Street
☎ (0666) 890250
12–2.30, 7–11
Butcombe Bitter; Eldridge Pope Royal Oak; Hook Norton Best Bitter; S&N Theakston Old Peculier Ⓗ
300-year-old free house, much modernised inside, offering a thoughtful range of beers; cider in summer. Worth finding.
Ⓜ Q ✿ ◑ ♣ ⏢ P

Longford

Queens Head
84 Tewkesbury Road (A38)
☎ (0452) 301883
11–2.30 (3 Sat), 6–11
Marston's Pedigree; Wadworth 6X; Whitbread WCPA, Boddingtons Bitter, Flowers Original Ⓗ; **guest beers**
18th-century inn with original beams inside. Recent refurbishment has retained the public bar, though not totally separate. Flower baskets are a blaze of colour in summer. Excellent snacks and meals from a changing menu.
◑ P

Lower Swell

Golden Ball
☎ (0451) 30247
11–2.30, 6–11
Donnington BB, SBA Ⓗ
Excellent but unspoilt village local. Good food and cider.
Ⓜ ✿ 🛏 ◑ ♣ ⏢ P

Lower Wick

Pickwick Inn
Off A38 OS712958
☎ (0453) 810259
11–2.30, 6–11
Draught Bass; Butcombe Bitter; S&N Theakston Best Bitter Ⓗ
Food-oriented, renovated country pub in the shadow of the M5. Well worth a two-mile detour from junction 14.
Ⓜ Q ✿ ◑ ♣ P

May Hill

Glasshouse Inn
Off A40, W of Huntley
OS709213 ☎ (0452) 830529
11–2.30, 6–11 (12–2, 7–10.30 Sun)
Butcombe Bitter; Whitbread WCPA Ⓖ; **guest beer**
Unspoilt old country pub with an original brick-tiled floor. Always one guest beer from a small independent brewer available. Well worth finding. No meals Sun eve.
Ⓜ ✿ ◑ ♣ P

Moreton-in-Marsh

Black Bear
High Street (A429)
☎ (0608) 50705
11–3 (10.30–4 Tue), 6–11
Donnington XXX, BB, SBA Ⓗ
Busy, two-bar town-centre pub, parts of which date back 300 years; home to a poltergeist called Fred. Paved courtyard for outside drinking.
Q ✿ 🛏 ◑ ♪ ⌸ ♣ ⇌ ♣ P

Try also: Wellington (Hook Norton)

Newent

George Hotel
Church Street ☎ (0531) 820203
11–11
Draught Bass; Wadworth 6X; Welsh Brewers Worthington BB Ⓗ
Mid 17th-century 'commercial and posting house' with a large bar resulting from the removal of internal walls. Its warm and pleasant atmosphere is enlivened at times by the local rugby team. Limited parking in the courtyard drinking area.
✿ 🛏 ◑ ♣ P

Newland

Ostrich
On B4231 ☎ (0594) 833260
12–2.30, 6–11
Marston's Pedigree; Shepherd Neame Spitfire; Whitbread Boddingtons Bitter Ⓗ; **guest beers**
Charming and unspoilt, with friendly staff and owners; a traditional English pub. Good food. Ⓜ ✿ 🛏 ◑ ♪ Ⓐ

Newmarket

George Inn
OS841997 ☎ (0453) 832530
11–3, 6–11
Archers Best Bitter; Draught Bass; Hook Norton Best Bitter Ⓗ; **guest beers**
Friendly, well-run local offering views over the valley. Bar skittles played.
Q ✿ ◑ ♪ Ⓐ ♣ P

North Cerney

Bathurst Arms
On A435 ☎ (0285) 831281
11–2.30, 6–11
Archers Best Bitter; Courage Best Bitter; Hook Norton Best Bitter; Whitbread Flowers Original Ⓗ; **guest beers**
Attractive 17th-century village pub with flagstone floors, settles and a stove in the inglenook. All one would expect from a Cotswold pub; even the tiny River Churn

runs through the garden. The family room is pleasant.
Ⓜ Q ✿ ✿ 🛏 ◑ ♪ ♣ Ⓐ P

Nympsfield

Rose & Crown Inn
Off B4066 ☎ (0453) 860240
11.30–2.30, 6–11
S&N Theakston Best Bitter; Uley Bitter, Old Spot; Wadworth 6X; Whitbread Boddingtons Bitter Ⓗ
Large village local with a good range of beer and food. Originally a coaching inn on the Gloucester to Bath road.
Ⓜ ✿ ✿ 🛏 ◑ ♪ ♣ P

Oakridge Lynch

Butchers Arms
On N edge of village
OS915038 ☎ (028 576) 371
12–3, 6–11
Archers Best Bitter; Ind Coope Burton Ale; Ruddles Best Bitter, County; S&N Theakston Best Bitter; Tetley Bitter Ⓗ
Superb, popular village pub, well worth seeking out. The fine 18th-century building was formerly a slaughterhouse and butcher's shop; now three sensitively modernised bars and a restaurant. Glos. CAMRA *Pub of the Year* 1991. Eve meals Wed–Sat.
Ⓜ Q ✿ ◑ ♪ Ⓐ ♣ P

Prestbury

Plough Inn
Mill Street ☎ (0242) 244175
11–2.30, 6–11
Whitbread WCPA, Flowers IPA, Original Ⓖ
Half-timbered, thatched pub with an attractive garden. The panelled lounge contrasts with the stone-flagged public bar. A good range of lunchtime snacks includes a substantial ploughman's with home-made bread. Ⓜ Q ✿ ✿ ◑ ✿ ♣

Ruspidge

New Inn
On B4227 ☎ (0594) 824508
12–3.30 (not Mon-Fri), 7–11
Archers Village, Golden Ⓗ
Fairly basic village pub where the games room boasts an interesting selection of games.
Ⓜ ✿ ♣ P

Sapperton

Daneway Inn
N of A419, 4 miles W of
Cirencester OS939034
☎ (0285) 760297
11–2.30 (3 Sat), 6.30–11
Archers Best Bitter Ⓔ / Ⓗ; **Hall & Woodhouse Badger Best Bitter** Ⓗ; **Wadworth 6X** Ⓖ; **guest beer**
Excellent pub built in 1784 for

canal workers, near the now-defunct Sapperton tunnel. The comfortable lounge is dominated by a magnificent fireplace with Dutch carving. A house beer, Daneway Bitter, is reputedly from Archers; Blands cider in summer. ♨ Q
🍴 ⊗ ◖ ▶ ⊕ ⇦ ⌂ P ⚿

Siddington

Greyhound
Ashton Road OS034994
☎ (0285) 653573
11.30–3, 7 (6.30 Mon, Tue & Sat)–11
Hall & Woodhouse Tanglefoot; Wadworth IPA, 6X Ⓗ
First-rate, 17th-century inn nestling between the canal and the railway line, both long disused. Two roaring fires and interesting furniture and artefacts. Small, quiet public bar; lounge tables can be booked eves for food.
♨ Q ⊗ ◖ ▶ ⊕ Å ♣ P

Slimbridge

Tudor Arms
Shepherds Patch
☎ (0453) 890306
11–2.30, 6 (7 winter)–11
Draught Bass; Hook Norton Best Bitter; Uley Bitter; Wadworth 6X Ⓗ
Well-run, large country pub on the road to the Wildfowl Trust. It has a restaurant and a no-smoking family room.
🍴 ⊗ ⇔ ◖ ▶ ⊕ Å ♣ P ⚿

Stanton

Mount Inn
Old Snowshill Road
☎ (0386) 73316
11–11 (11–3, 6–11 winter)
Donnington BB, SBA Ⓗ
Beautifully positioned inn on a hill above the village, affording splendid views. A delightful spot for summer eves and a good stopping place for hikers. Weston's cider. ♨ Q ⊗ ◖ ▶ ♣ ⌂ P

Stow-on-the-Wold

Queens Head
The Square ☎ (0451) 30563
11–2.30, 6–11
Donnington BB, SBA Ⓗ
Fine old Cotswold pub, popular with tourists and locals alike. Occasional live music. Weston's cider.
⊗ ◖ ▶ ♣ ⌂

Stroud

Clothiers Arms
1 Bath Road (A46)
☎ (0453) 763801
11–2.30, 4.30–11 (11–11 Sat)
Ind Coope Burton Ale; Ruddles Best Bitter; Tetley

Bitter; Wadworth 6X Ⓗ; guest beers
Friendly town free house with a three-quarter circular bar and a separate games alcove. Note the Stroud Brewery memorabilia. Terraced garden above the car park.
⊗ ◖ ▶ ⇌ ⇔ P

Duke of York
22 Nelson Street
☎ (0453) 758715
12–3, 7–11
Butcombe Bitter; Greene King Abbot; Wells Eagle Ⓗ; guest beers
Comfortable, one-bar stone town pub, very much a local to its regulars. ◖ ⇌

Try also: Pelican, Union St (Courage)

Tetbury

Trouble House Inn
On A433, 1 mile NE of town
☎ (0666) 502206
11–2.30, 6–11
Wadworth IPA, 6X Ⓗ
Cosy roadside pub with a long and colourful history.
♨ Q ⊗ ◖ ▶ ⊕ Å ♣ P

Tewkesbury

Berkeley Arms
Church Street ☎ (0684) 293034
10.30–2.30 (3 Sat), 6.30–11 (12–2, 7–10.30 Sun)
Wadworth 6X, Farmer's Glory, Old Timer Ⓗ
Popular and ancient pub of character. Access to the lounge is through an unusual alleyway. Good value lunches. The most northerly outpost of the Wadworth tied estate.
Q ⊗ ◖ ▶ ♣

Toddington

Pheasant Inn
At B4632/B4077 jct
☎ (0242) 621271
12–2, 6 (7 Sat)–11 (11–2.30, 7–10.30 Sun)
Hook Norton Best Bitter; Ind Coope Burton Ale Ⓗ
Two-bar pub adjacent to the HQ of the Gloucestershire and Warwickshire Railway. Beers may vary. ⊗ ◖ ▶ ⊕ Å P

Viney Hill

New Inn
OS657067 ☎ (0594) 510208
11–3, 6–11 (11–11 Sat)
Draught Bass; Courage Best Bitter; Hook Norton Best Bitter; John Smith's Bitter; Smiles Exhibition Ⓗ; guest beers
Old building with a modern-ised interior, offering a good range of beers. Notable penny-in-the-slot machine on the bar; occasional very loud music Sat. ♨ ⊗ ◖ ▶ ♣ P

Waterley Bottom

New Inn
E of N Nibley along 1½ miles of narrow lanes OS758964
☎ (0453) 543659
12–2.30, 7–11
Cotleigh Tawny; Greene King Abbot Ⓗ; S&N Theakston Old Peculier Ⓖ; Smiles Best Bitter Ⓗ, Exhibition Ⓖ
Large, friendly free house in a beautiful setting, surrounded by steep hills. A house beer, WB, is brewed by Cotleigh to the landlady's recipe. A detailed map is required for first-time visitors.
♨ ⊗ ⇔ ◖ ▶ ⊕ Å ♣ ⌂ P

Winchcombe

Corner Cupboard
Gloucester Street (B4632)
☎ (0242) 602303
11–2.30, 5.30–11 (12–2.30, 7–10.30 Sun)
Marston's Pedigree; Uley Bitter; Whitbread Boddingtons Bitter, Best Bitter, Castle Eden Ale, Flowers Original Ⓗ
Ancient stone pub with the traditional contrast in decor and company between public and lounge bars. Reputedly haunted.
♨ Q ⊗ ◖ ⊕ ♣ ⌂ P

Try also: Plaisterers Arms (Ansells)

Woodchester

Ram Inn
Station Road
☎ (0453) 873329
11–3, 6–11
Archers Village; Hook Norton Old Hooky; Tetley Bitter; Uley Bitter, Old Spot; Whitbread Boddingtons Bitter Ⓗ
Large, bustling pub, popular with younger drinkers. The outdoor drinking area has views across the valley.
♨ ⊗ ◖ ▶ P

Try also: Royal Oak (Free)

Woolaston Common

Rising Sun
1 mile off A48, through Netherend village OS590009
☎ (0594) 529282
12–2.30 (not Wed), 6.30–11
Hook Norton Best Bitter; S&N Theakston Best Bitter; Thwaites Bitter Ⓗ; guest beers
Lovely country pub with excellent views and a friendly landlord.
⊗ ◖ ▶ Å ♣ P

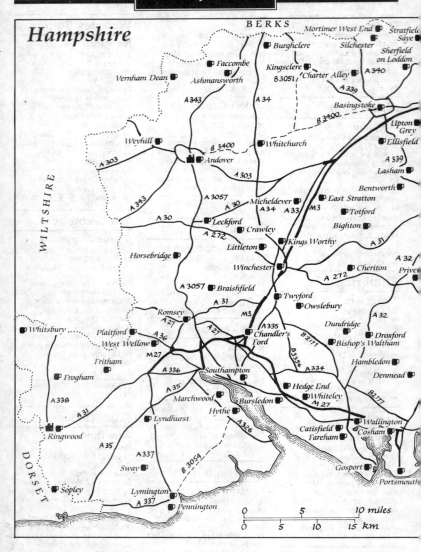

Hampshire

 Gale's, Horndean; **Hampshire,** Andover; **Ringwood,** Ringwood; **Worldham,** East Worldham

Aldershot

Garden Gate
4 Church Lane East
12–2.30 (3 Sat), 6–11
**Greene King XX Mild, IPA,
Rayments Special, Abbot** Ⓗ,
Winter Ale Ⓖ
Basic, friendly and intimate
pub with a highly popular
mild. Q ☸ ⇛ ♣ P

Red Lion
Ash Road ☎ (0252) 23050
11–11
**Courage Best Bitter,
Directors; Wadworth 6X** Ⓗ
Prominent 1930s pub with two
very contrasting bars. The
original Red Lion dates from
before the military moved in
to Aldershot.
Q ❀ ⌂ ◖ ⊟ P

Royal Staff
37a Mount Pleasant Road
☎ (0252) 22932
12–3, 5–11 (12–11 Sat)
**Fuller's Chiswick, London
Pride, Mr Harry, ESB** Ⓗ
Lively, single-bar, refurbished
community local with a strong
darts following. No food Sun.
❀ ◖ ⅊ ⇛ ♣

Alton

Barley Mow

72 Normandy Street
☎ (0420) 82081
11–11
Ruddles County; Webster's Yorkshire Bitter; Worldham Old Dray Ⓗ
300-year-old pub with an attractive, tile-hung exterior and a warm, open-fired interior. No food weekends.
♨ ◐ ⇌ ♣ P

Eight Bells

33 Church Street
☎ (0420) 82417
11–3, 6–11 (11–11 Fri & Sat)
Fuller's London Pride; Ringwood Best Bitter; Wadworth 6X; Worldham Old Dray Ⓗ
Alton's only free house, with beams a-plenty. A village atmosphere in a town pub.
Q ◐ ◑ ⇌

Andover

Globe

High Street
☎ (0264) 323415
10.30–2.30, 5–11
Marston's Burton Best Bitter, Pedigree Ⓗ
Well-renovated coaching inn dating from 1742, retaining a town pub atmosphere. Flagstone floors and carpeted areas suit all tastes. Dining area upstairs. Note the unusual coaching light window. Market outside Thu and Sat. ◐

Lamb

Winchester Street (opp. police station)
☎ (0264) 323961
11–2.30, 6 (5 Fri)–11
Adnams Bitter; Draught Bass; Wadworth 6X, Old Timer Ⓗ
A former Heath brewery house, this traditional pub has three rooms (one always quiet). The beamed lounge has a homely cottage atmosphere and a special cosiness.
♨ Q ❀ ◐ ⊟ ♣

Town Mills

Town Mill Road (off Bridge St)
☎ (0264) 332540
11–2.30, 7–11
Adnams Broadside; Draught Bass; Hall & Woodhouse Tanglefoot; Wadworth 6X, Farmer's Glory, Old Timer Ⓗ
Pub converted from the old town mill over the River Anton and incorporating a working water wheel. Two floors with several quiet corners. Families very welcome lunchtimes. Much improved since the break from Whitbread products. Can be lively at night. Wheelchair WC. ❀ ◐ ♿ P

Ashmansworth

Plough

Off A343, S of Highclere
☎ (0635) 253047
12–2.30 (not Mon or Tue New Year–Easter), 6–11
Archers Village, Best Bitter, Golden; guest beers Ⓖ
200-year-old pub in Hampshire's highest village; one of the county's finest rural locals, now opened out into a single bar but still retaining atmosphere. Beer is served direct from casks (cooled in summer). ❀ ◐ P

Basingstoke

Chineham Arms

Hanmoor Road, Chineham (W of A33) ☎ (0256) 56404
11.30–3, 5–11 (11.30–11 Fri & Sat)
Fuller's Chiswick, London Pride, ESB Ⓗ
Well-designed, modern pub with a much better atmosphere than the usual estate pub. Situated on the north-eastern outskirts of the Basingstoke sprawl.
☕ ❀ ◐ ◑ ♿ ♣ P

Bentley

Star

London Road (A31)
☎ (0420) 23184
11–3, 6–11
Courage Best Bitter, Directors; Wadworth 6X Ⓗ
Pub noted for quality food (no meals Sun/Mon eves). The car park is opposite across a very busy A-road; a mile from Bentley BR station. ❀ ◐ ◑ ♿ P

Bentworth

Sun

Sun Hill (off A339)
☎ (0420) 62338
11.30–3, 6–11 (12–2, 7–10.30 Sun)
Draught Bass; Bunces Best Bitter; Gale's HSB; Wadworth 6X Ⓗ**; guest beers**
Excellent country pub dating from the 17th century. Low beams, bare floors and two wood-burning stoves create a homely atmosphere complemented by old prints and farming memorabilia. Good value food.
♨ Q ❀ ◐ ◑ ♣ P

Bighton

Three Horseshoes

Off A31/B3047
☎ (0962) 732859
11–2.30, 6–11 (12–2, 7–10.30 Sun)
Gale's XXXD, BBB, Best Bitter (summer)**, 5X, HSB** Ⓗ
Delightful, rural local, well off the beaten track. Country crafts collection in the locals' bar; relaxing atmosphere in the quiet lounge. The sea angling club welcomes visitors. Handy for Mid-Hants Steam Railway (Ropley station two miles). In 19 editions of this Guide. No food Mon.
♨ Q ❀ ◐ ⊟ ♿ ♣ P

Bishop's Waltham

Bunch of Grapes

St Peter's Street
☎ (0489) 892935
10–2 (2.30 Sat), 6–11 (12–2, 7–10.30 Sun)
Courage Best Bitter Ⓖ**; Ushers Best Bitter, Founders** Ⓗ

Hampshire

Very traditional and remarkably unspoilt village local in a medieval street. 18th year in the *Guide*. Recently acquired by Ushers, though Courage beer will continue to be available for some time. An active community local (the harvest festival is a highlight).
Q ✿ ♣

Braishfield

Newport Inn
Newport Lane
☎ (0794) 68225
10–2.30, 6–11 (12–2.30, 7–10.30 Sun)
Gale's BBB, Best Bitter, 5X, HSB Ⓗ
Unspoilt, 19th-century village local, in the same family for 50 years. Piano accompanied sing-alongs Sun eve. Well-filled sandwiches served.
🏠 ✿ ⊟ ♿ ♣ P

Burghclere

Carpenters
Harts Lane (½mile E of A34)
☎ (0635) 27251
11–2.30, 6–11
Archers Best Bitter; Fuller's London Pride; Morland Bitter, Old Speckled Hen Ⓗ
Small, cosily furnished pub/restaurant with magnificent downland views. Next to the Sandham Memorial Chapel (NT) with its anti-war murals by WWI combatant Stanley Spencer. Occasional variation in beer range. Pub piano. No pub food Sun/Mon.
🏠 Q ⛵ ✿ 🏠 ◖ P ⌣

Queen
Harts Lane (1 mile E of A34, N of village) ☎ (0635) 27350
11–3, 6–11 (12–2.30 Sun)
Adnams Bitter, Broadside; Arkell's 3B Ⓗ
Out of the way hostelry with a strong local following. A difficult pub to leave once you have joined in the conversation. Great atmosphere. No food Sun.
✿ ◖ ♣ P

Buriton

Five Bells
High Street ☎ (0730) 63584
11–2.30 (3 Fri & Sat), 5.30 (6 Sat)–11 (11–11 summer)
Ballard's Best Bitter; Ind Coope Friary Meux Best Bitter, Burton Ale; Ringwood XXXX Porter, Old Thumper; Tetley Bitter Ⓗ
400-year-old pub built from local stone in a village at the start of the South Downs Way. A pleasant atmosphere attracts locals and visitors alike. A busy free house with a varied menu of bar and restaurant meals. Live music

most Weds (folk/jazz).
🏠 ✿ ◖ Ð ⊟ ♣ P

Bursledon

Linden Tree
School Road, Lowford (off A27/A3025)
☎ (0703) 402356
11–2.30 (3 Sat), 6 (5 Fri)–11
Draught Bass; Wadworth IPA, 6X, Farmer's Glory (summer), Old Timer Ⓗ
Excellent, comfortable one-bar pub with no obtrusive gaming machines. A children's play area makes it ideal in summer. High quality, home-cooked food (not served Sun).
🏠 ✿ ♣ P

Vine Inn
High Street, Old Bursledon (½ mile SW of station)
☎ (0703) 403836
11.30–3, 6–11 (11.30–11 Sat)
Marston's Burton Best Bitter, Merrie Monk, Pedigree Ⓗ
Smart, comfortable local on a narrow lane in *Howard's Way* country. Quiz night Tue; darts Wed; meat draw Sun. Roadside parking 100 yards towards the station.
✿ ◖ Ð ▲ ⇌ ♣

Catisfield

Limes at Catisfield
34 Catisfield Lane
☎ (0329) 42926
11–2.30, 6 (7 Sat)–11
Gale's HSB; Gibbs Mew Salisbury, Bishop's Tipple Ⓗ
Victorian building converted to a pub: a small, quiet lounge, a busier public bar and a function room. Petanque terrain in the garden.
✿ ◖ Ð ⊟ ♣ P

Chandler's Ford

Cleveland Bay
1 Pilgrims Close, Valley Park (off Knightwood Rd)
☎ (0703) 269814
11–11
Hall & Woodhouse Tanglefoot; Wadworth IPA, 6X, Farmer's Glory, Old Timer Ⓗ**; guest beers**
Nineties estate pub featuring modern-traditional decor and flashing light machines. Probably the best beer in Eastleigh borough, including genuine guests.
🏠 ⛵ ✿ ◖ Ð ♿ P

Charter Alley

White Hart
White Hart Lane (½ mile E of Ramsdell) ☎ (0256) 850048
12–2.30, 7–11
Fuller's London Pride; Hook Norton Best Bitter; Ringwood Best Bitter, Fortyniner; guest beers Ⓗ

Friendly, welcoming pub with a small, old front bar and a very large back bar with a popular skittle alley and a games area. Live music every Thu eve. Excellent selection of guest ales, changing weekly. Cider in summer only.
🏠 Q ◖ Ð ⊟ ♿ ♣ ⌂ P

Cheriton

Flower Pots Inn
Between B3046 & A272
☎ (0962) 771318
11.30–2.30, 6–11
Archers Village; Hop Back Summer Lightning; Smiles Best Bitter Ⓖ**; guest beers**
Excellent, multi-roomed country pub. Recent extensions ensure more space for drinkers in the public bar/games area which has a well. Large garden; cosy lounge; friendly atmosphere; home-cooked snacks. 19th year in the *Guide*!
🏠 Q ⛵ ✿ 🏠 ◖ Ð ♿ ▲ ♣ P

Cosham

Red Lion Hotel
Spur Road ☎ (0705) 382041
11–3, 5.30–11
Ind Coope Burton Ale; King & Barnes Sussex; Tetley Bitter Ⓗ
Enterprising inn with an interesting history. Lounge can be busy evenings. Good value food. No smoking area in the restaurant.
✿ 🏠 ◖ Ð ♿ ▲ ⇌ ♣ P

Cove

Plough & Horses
Fleet Road ☎ (0252) 545199
11–11
Ind Coope Friary Meux Best Bitter, Burton Ale; Tetley Bitter; Young's Special Ⓗ
Designated a 'Hampshire Treasure' by the County Council, this well-furnished pub has a fascinating collection of local Victoriana. The landlord is among the top Burton *Master Cellarmen*. A well-run, busy pub offering good value for the area (no food Sun). ✿ ◖ ♣ P

Crawley

Rack & Manger
Stockbridge Road (A272)
☎ (0962) 72281
11–2.30 (3 Sat), 6–11
Banks's Mild; Marston's Burton Best Bitter, Merrie Monk, Pedigree, Owd Rodger Ⓗ
Roadhouse with a quiet lounge and a lively public bar featuring a circular pool table. Live music Thu and 60s disco Sun. 🏠 ✿ ◖ Ð ⊟ ▲ ♣ P

Hampshire

Crondall

Castle
Croft Lane ☎ (0252) 850892
12–2.30 (3 Sat), 6–11
Fuller's London Pride, ESB H
Good, homely pub next to the
village hall, offering excellent
food (Dorchester Hotel-
trained chef). Plenty of wood
and atmosphere. Well worth a
visit. ✿ ◖ ▮ ₺ ♣

Crookham Village

Black Horse
The Street ☎ (0252) 616434
11–2.30 (3 Fri & Sat), 5.30–11
**Courage Best Bitter,
Directors; Wadworth 6X** H
First-rate, welcoming,
beamed, village hostelry
serving good value food (no
meals Sun); very popular,
hosted by an ebullient
landlord. Near the
Basingstoke Canal and good
for walks. The garden, with an
aviary, is excellent for
children. Q ✿ ◖ P

Denmead

Forest of Bere
Hambledon Road (B2150)
☎ (0705) 263145
10.30–2.30, 5–11
**Ind Coope Friary Meux Best
Bitter, Burton Ale; Ringwood
Best Bitter** H; guest beer
(occasionally)
Village pub with a boisterous
bar and a plusher lounge. No
food Sun. ♨ Q ✿ ◖ ▮ ♣ P

Droxford

White Horse
South Hill ☎ (0489) 877490
11–2.30, 6–11
**Draught Bass; Gale's HSB;
King & Barnes Sussex;
Morland Old Speckled Hen;
Wadworth 6X** H
16th-century coaching inn
with contrasting bars: a quiet
lounge and a noisier public.
The lounge has low ceilings
and uneven floors. There is a
well in the gents! No food Sun
eve in winter.
♨ Q ⌂ ✿ ⇔ ◖ ▮ ⊟ ♣ P

Dundridge

Hampshire Bowman
Dundridge Lane (1 mile off
B3035) OS579185
☎ (0489) 892940
11–2.30, 6–11
**Archers Village; King &
Barnes Sussex, Old,
Festive** G; guest beer
A classic country pub down a
classic country lane: a friendly
single bar with a brick floor
and wooden panels which
was once an abattoir. Well
regarded food available,

except Mon eve (quiz night),
and Sun eve.
♨ Q ✿ ◖ ▮ ▲ ♣ P

East Stratton

Plough
Off A33 ☎ (0962) 89241
11–2.30 (not Mon), 6–11
**Gale's BBB, HSB; Ringwood
Fortyniner** H
Basic old pub near the village
green. Friendly atmosphere;
children welcome; chip-free
bar menu! Skittle alley. ♨ Q
⌂ ✿ ⇔ ◖ ▮ ₺ ♣ P

East Worldham

Three Horseshoes
Cakers Lane (B3004)
☎ (0420) 83211
11–2.30, 6–11
**Gale's BBB, Best Bitter,
HSB** H
Pleasant roadside pub set in a
lovely village. Cheap Sun
roasts; no food Sun/Mon eves.
Q ✿ ◖ ▮ ♣ P

Ellisfield

Fox
Green Lane (off A339)
☎ (0256) 381210
11.30–2.30 (3 Sat), 6.30–11
**Bunces Best Bitter; Fuller's
London Pride; Gale's HSB;
Hall & Woodhouse
Tanglefoot; Marston's
Pedigree; Wadworth 6X** H
Country retreat with a good
selection of beers, just south of
modern Basingstoke. Excellent
menu. Darts, crib and
dominoes played. Worth a
visit, though hard to find.
♨ Q ✿ ◖ ▮ ⊟ ♣ P

Emsworth

Milkmans Arms
North Street ☎ (0243) 373356
10–3, 6–11 (11–11 Sat)
Gale's XXXL, BBB, HSB, 5X H
Small, one-bar locals' pub
with a room for bar billiards
and cribbage. The large
garden features swings and
slides, barbecue and a goat.
Children's entertainment in
summer. The epitome of a
local pub. ✿ ♣ ♣

Faccombe

Jack Russell
Off A343 ☎ (0264) 87315
12–2.30, 7–11
**Ringwood Best Bitter,
Fortyniner; guest beer** H
Pleasant, friendly pub set in
unspoilt countryside. The
good range of food caters for
all. Children over five allowed
in the conservatory. Genuine
wheelchair facilities.
♨ Q ✿ ⇔ ◖ ▮ ₺ ♣ P

Fareham

Buccaneer
The Avenue ☎ (0329) 230800
11–11 (11–3, 5–11 Sat)
**Draught Bass; Courage Best
Bitter** H
Pleasant 'Harvester' inn
catering for the discerning
drinker. Food is available
throughout the bar, which is
large and comfortable. Smart
dress is required weekend
eves. ✿ ◖ ₺ ⇌ ♣ P

Golden Lion
High Street ☎ (0329) 234061
11–11 (12–2.30, 7–10.30 Sun)
**Gale's BBB, Best Bitter, 5X,
HSB** H
Single-bar pub in a Georgian
street, close to the shopping
centre, offering a civilised,
restful drinking atmosphere.
Monthly quiz nights. No food
weekends. ♨ ✿ ◖ ♣ P

Farnborough

Imperial Arms
12 Farnborough Street
☎ (0252) 542573
11.30–2.30, 5–11 (11.30–11 Fri & Sat)
**Courage Best Bitter; John
Smith's Bitter; Wadworth
6X** H; guest beer
Three distinct bars: a pool
room, a sports room and a
saloon cater for all. Next to the
station, it was once a
distribution point for Courage
beers railed down from
Reading. Ever changing guest
beer. ✿ ◖ ⊟ ⇌ (North) ♣ P

Prince of Wales
184 Rectory Road (off A325)
☎ (0252) 545578
11.30–2.30, 6 (5.30 Fri)–11
**Brakspear Bitter; Eldridge
Pope Royal Oak; Fuller's
London Pride; Hall &
Woodhouse Badger Best
Bitter, Tanglefoot; Wadworth
6X** H; guest beers
The best free house for miles,
with a wide range of guest
beers: a convivial, traditional
hostelry which is invariably
busy. Occasional small
brewery promotions,
including mild. Warm,
friendly staff and excellent
lunches (not served Sun).
Q ✿ ◖ ⇌ (North) ♣ P

Fritham

Royal Oak
2 miles off B3078 OS232141
☎ (0703) 812606
11–3, 6–11
**Ringwood Fortyniner;
Whitbread Strong Country,
Flowers Original** G
Unspoilt, rustic thatched pub
deep in the New Forest. The
large open hearth is still used
for smoking hams. The last of

119

Hampshire

its kind in the area; in 19 editions of the *Guide*!
🏚 Q ❀ ♣

Frogham

Foresters Arms
Abbotswell Road OS173129
☎ (0425) 652294
11–3, 6–11 (11–11 Sat in summer)
**Hook Norton Best Bitter;
Ringwood XXXX Porter;
Taylor Landlord** (summer) Ⓗ;
guest beers
On the fringe of the New
Forest, this friendly, busy pub
offers a range of beers rarely
seen in this area. Mini beer
festival August Bank Holiday
weekend. 160 guest beers in
1991. Fresh fish specials at the
weekend. Booking advised for
Sun lunch. 🏚 ❀ ◖▶ ▲ ♣ P

Froyle

Prince of Wales
Lower Froyle (off A31)
OS759443
☎ (0420) 23102
11–2.30, 6–11
**Fuller's London Pride, Mr
Harry, ESB; S&N Theakston
Old Peculier; Wadworth 6X** Ⓗ
Splendid free house in a quiet
village. Welcomes all, from
evening diners to Sunday
footballers. No food Sun eve.
🏚 Q ❀ ◖▶ P

Gosport

Park Hotel
Park Road, Alverstoke
☎ (0705) 583074
11–2.30, 6–11 (11–11 Fri & Sat)
**Gale's HSB; Whitbread
Boddingtons Bitter** Ⓗ; guest
beer
Large, single-bar pub with a
separate area for pool.
Frequently changed guest
beer. ❧ ❀

Queens Hotel
Queens Road
☎ (0705) 525518
11.30–2.30 (3.30 Fri), 7-11 (11-11 Sat)
**Archers Village; Fuller's
London Pride; Greene King
Abbot** Ⓗ; guest beers
Pub with normally five ales on
offer (four guest beers per
week). Interesting collection of
carry kegs and bottle labels
around the bar. Quiz night
Thu. 🏚

White Swan
36 Forton Road (A32, ³/₄ mile
from ferry) ☎ (0705) 584138
11.30–3 (11–4 Sat), 5.30 (6.30 Sat)–11
**Courage Best Bitter,
Directors; John Smith's
Bitter; Ushers Best Bitter** Ⓗ
Basic locals' pub with several
darts teams and an eye-
catching pool table. A
Courage house recently sold
to Ushers (additional Ushers

beers should be available
soon). No food Sun. ◖ ♣

Hambledon

New Inn
West Street (off B2150)
☎ (0705) 632466
12–2.30, 7–11
**Ballard's Trotton; Eldridge
Pope Hardy Country;
Ringwood Fortyniner, Old
Thumper** Ⓗ
Pleasant, two-bar village pub
with no frills, just good old-
fashioned drinking and
socialising. No food.
🏚 ❧ ❀ ◖ ◿ A ♣ P

Vine Inn
West Street (off B2150 from
Waterlooville)
☎ (0705) 632419
11.30–3, 6–11
**Gale's BBB, HSB; Morland
Old Speckled Hen; Shepherd
Neame Master Brew Bitter** Ⓗ
Welcoming, two-bar village
pub dating from the 16th
century: a basic public bar and
an intimate lounge with
various small drinking areas.
Note the well in the lounge.
Food Thu–Sat only.
🏚 Q ❀ ◿ ◖ A

Hawkley

Hawkley Inn
Pococks Lane (2 miles off
A325 at West Liss) OS747291
☎ (0730) 84205
12–2.30 (3 Sat), 6–11
**Ballard's Trotton, Best Bitter;
Fuller's London Pride;
Ringwood Fortyniner** Ⓗ
The only pub in a small
village: a comfortable and
sometimes very busy free
house in a quiet location.
Home-cooked food in the bar
or restaurant. The no-smoking
area has bar billiards. Parking
can be difficult. Walkers
welcomed. Live music most
Sats. 🏚 ❀ ◖▶ ♣ ✄

Hawley

New Inn
Hawley Road ☎ (0276) 32012
11–11
**Morland Bitter, Old Masters,
Old Speckled Hen** Ⓗ
Large, single-bar
pub/restaurant which has
been refurbished in rural style.
Building a reputation for its
food (restaurant is open all
day Sun). ❀ ◖▶ ⅙ P

Hayling Island

Maypole
Havant Road ☎ (0705) 463670
11–11
**Gale's XXXD, BBB, Best
Bitter, HSB** Ⓗ & Ⓖ
Main road pub with a
welcoming atmosphere and a

good traditional feel.
Organises coach trips to local
beer festivals; darts team; clay
pigeon shooting club. The only
real mild on Hayling Island.
🏚 Q ❀ ◖▶ ◿ A ♣ P

Hedge End

Barleycorn
2 Lower Northam Road
☎ (0489) 784171
11–2.30 (3 Sat), 5.30 (5 Fri)–11 (11–2,
7–10.30 Sun)
**Banks's Mild; Marston's
Burton Best Bitter,
Pedigree** Ⓗ
Located in the original village
centre, this busy, good value
pub has one drinking area
divided into several sections,
plus an attractive garden. No
food Sun. ❀ ◖ ♣ ♣ P

Horndean

Ship & Bell Hotel
London Road (A3, look for
brewery tower)
☎ (0705) 592107
11–3, 5.30–11
**Gale's XXXD, BBB, Best
Bitter, HSB** Ⓗ
Picturesque, 17th-century
former coaching inn and site
of the original brewery; now
the Gale's brewery tap. A
popular lively pub with a
good range of games. Two
darts teams and a crib team.
Q ❧ ◿ ◖▶ ♣ P

Horsebridge

John O'Gaunt
¹/₂ mile E of A3057, 5 miles N
of Romsey OS346304
☎ (0794) 388394
11.30–2.30 (3 Sat), 6–11
**Adnams Bitter; Palmers IPA;
Ringwood Fortyniner** Ⓗ
Well worth-finding village
free house with a shove-
ha'penny board on the bar.
The good value range of beer
is liable to occasional changes.
Popular with walkers. No
food Tue eve. 🏚 ❀ ◖▶ ♣

Hythe

Lord Nelson
High Street ☎ (0703) 842169
11–11 (11–3, 6–11 Mon & Wed)
**Wadworth 6X; Whitbread
Strong Country, Flowers
Original** Ⓗ; guest beers
Small, waterfront pub with
quaint bars. Its gardens
overlook Southampton Water
and yacht marina. Good value
lunches. Convenient for the
Southampton ferry.
Q ❀ ◖ ▣ ♿ ♣ ㇔

Kingsclere

Swan
Swan Street ☎ (0635) 298314
11–2.30, 6–11

S&N Theakston XB; Tetley
Bitter; guest beers Ⓗ
Building dating back to 1459
in part, and restored to
include a minstrel's gallery.
Usually at least four beers;
separate restaurant.
🛏 🚲 ◑ ▶ P

Kings Worthy

Cart & Horses

London Road (A33/A3090 jct,
near M3 jct 9) ☎ (0962) 882360
11–3, 6–11 (11–11 bank hols)
Marston's Burton Best Bitter,
Pedigree, Owd Rodger Ⓗ
Large, smart, upmarket and
busy roadhouse with a good
selection of food at all times.
Restaurant, children's
playground and a large
garden; a converted 300-year-
old barn acts as a skittle
alley/family room. The bar is
a quiet drinker's retreat with
bar billiards.
🛏 🛏 ✿ ◑ ▶ 🍴 & ♣ ⊂ P ✕

Lasham

Royal Oak

Off A339 ☎ (0256) 381213
11–2.30, 6–11
Bunces Best Bitter; Fuller's
London Pride; guest beers Ⓗ
Pub in the centre of a rural
conservation area, beside the
parish church and close to the
UK's premier gliding location.
🛏 ✿ 🚲 ◑ ▶ 🍴 & P

Leckford

Leckford Hutt

On A30 ☎ (0264) 810738
11–2.30, 6.30–11
Marston's Burton Best Bitter,
Pedigree Ⓗ
Friendly, traditional local with
a 200-ft well, a blow-billiards
table and a collection of jerry
pots. Occasional music eves
and whippet racing. An 18th-
century beer engine is used to
dispense beer.
🛏 Q ✿ ◑ ▶ & ▲ ♣ P

Liss Forest

Temple

82 Forest Road
☎ (0730) 892134
11–3 (4 Wed & Sat), 6–11
Gale's BBB, Best Bitter,
HSB Ⓗ
Friendly, locals' pub a mile
north of Liss village. Built
c.1870 by Solomon Hounsome,
hence its name. Monthly
barbecues in summer.
Petanque terrain in the garden.
No meals Sun eve. ✿ ◑ ▶ P

Littleton

Running Horse

Main Road ☎ (0962) 880218
11–2.30 (3 Sat), 6–11
Gibbs Mew Local Line,

Salisbury Ⓗ, Bishop's
Tipple Ⓖ
Small village pub converted
into one bar but still with
'public' and 'lounge' ends.
The large garden has birds
and animals and play
equipment. 🛏 ✿ ◑ ▶ ♣ P

Long Sutton

Four Horseshoes

The Street ☎ (0256) 862488
11.30–2.30, 6–11
Gale's XXXL (summer),
XXXD, BBB, Best Bitter, 5X,
HSB Ⓗ
Compact, isolated local,
superbly situated a mile from
the village. Attracts foodies
who travel miles for the
award-winning fare; friendly,
relaxed atmosphere. An
attractive conservatory is open
all year. Good value Sun
roasts. 🛏 Q ✿ ◑ ▶ ▲ ♣ P

Lymington

Red Lion

High Street ☎ (0590) 672276
11–11
Marston's Pedigree;
Ringwood Best Bitter;
Wadworth 6X Ⓗ
Lively two-bar pub, popular
with locals and shoppers.
Large rear garden. Evening
meals in summer only.
🛏 ✿ 🚲 ◑ ▶ ➤ ♣ P

Tollhouse Inn

167 Southampton Road,
Buckland (A337, edge of
town) ☎ (0590) 672142
11–3, 6–11
Wadworth 6X Ⓗ; guest beers
Busy, prominent roadside pub
with contrasting bars and an
extensive menu. Over 300
years-old and full of historic
and antique items. A
Buckland heritage museum
(Roman encampment) is in the
garden. Book Sun lunch. At
least four guest ales.
🛏 Q ✿ ◑ ▶ 🍴 ⊂ P

Lyndhurst

Mailmans Arms

High Street ☎ (0703) 284196
11–2.30, 6–11
Marston's Burton Best Bitter,
Pedigree Ⓗ
Friendly and comfortable pub
in a popular New Forest town.
Occasional live entertainment;
barbecues in summer. Good
value lunches; extensive
evening pizza menus.
Landlord talks to his beer – as
featured on TV! Large free car
park nearby. 🛏 Q ✿ ◑ ♣

Marchwood

Pilgrim Inn

Hythe Road (S end of village)
☎ (0703) 867752

11–2.30 (3 Sat), 6–11
Draught Bass; Courage Best
Bitter, Directors Ⓗ
Beautiful thatched inn with
immaculate gardens; hanging
baskets are a speciality. Home
cooking with a vegetarian
option and a children's menu.
Eve meals in the adjacent
restaurant. 🛏 Q ✿ ◑ & P

Micheldever

Dever Arms

Winchester Road (just off A33)
☎ (0962) 89339
11.30–3, 6–11
Hall & Woodhouse Badger
Best Bitter; Hook Norton
Mild, Best Bitter Ⓗ; guest
beers
Friendly pub in a very pretty
village with many thatched
roofs. Always a choice of good
guest beers. Lots of original
wooden beams. Good food.
🛏 Q ✿ ◑ ▶ P

Mortimer West End

Turners Arms

West End Road (Aldermaston
road from church)
☎ (0734) 332961
11–3, 6–11
Brakspear Bitter, Special, Old
(winter) Ⓗ
Small quiet pub with friendly
locals. Plenty of character,
overlooking open fields. An
ideal stop-off on country
walks. Excellent pub food –
extensive, good value menu.
🛏 Q ✿ ◑ ▶ P

Oakhanger

Red Lion

The Street ☎ (0420) 472232
11–3, 6–11
Courage Best Bitter, Directors;
Worldham Old Dray Ⓗ
A real country local: a superb
public bar and a refined, food-
based saloon. Likely to be
crowded for all the right
reasons.
🛏 Q ✿ ◑ ▶ 🍴 & ♣ P

Owslebury

Ship Inn

Off B2177 ☎ (0962) 777358
11–2.30, 6–11
Banks's Mild; Marston's
Burton Best Bitter,
Pedigree Ⓗ
Cosy, one-bar country inn
with low beams (reputed to be
ships' timbers) in a sleepy
hamlet. The wide range of
home-made food includes a
vegetarian option. A proper
village pub with friendly staff
and locals, ideal for a quiet
drink. Popular with walkers
and near Marwell Zoo.
🛏 🛏 ✿ ◑ ▶ ♣ P

Hampshire

Pennington

Musketeer

North Street ☎ (0590) 676527
12 (11.30 Sat)–3, 5.30–11
**Bateman XXXB; Brakspear
Bitter; Felinfoel Cambrian;
Fuller's London Pride;
Ringwood Best Bitter** Ⓗ;
guest beers (occasionally)
A traditional, friendly, one-bar
local in the village centre. The
pub sign is based on an
original sculpture. No food
Sun. 15th year in the *Guide*.
🏠 Q 🏵 ◖▶ ♣ P

Plaitford

Shoe Inn

Salisbury Road (A36)
☎ (0794) 22397
11–3, 7–11
**Courage Best Bitter; Fuller's
London Pride; Wadworth
6X** Ⓗ; guest beer
Large, comfortable one-bar
pub on a busy main road.
Horse brasses adorn the
beams and walls, and fairy
lights line up the ceiling.
Large games area with pool
and darts, where children are
welcome. The car park is
opposite. 🏠 🏵 ◖▶ ♣ P

Portsmouth

Alexandra

Wingfield Street, Landport
☎ (0705) 823876
11–2.30, 6–11
Draught Bass Ⓗ
One of the city's few Bass
houses: a friendly,
comfortable, single-lounge,
estate pub, convenient for the
shops and the continental
ferry port. 🏵

Artillery Arms

1 Hester Road, Milton
☎ (0705) 733610
11–3, 6–11
**Gale's XXXD, Best Bitter,
HSB; Ind Coope Burton
Ale** Ⓗ; guest beer
Unchanging corner local
hidden away down a small
back street. Formerly a Gale's
house, now free, with two
separate bar areas: a lively
public bar with pool and darts
and a quieter lounge, with a
family room/overspill area
off. Probably the best value
pub in the city. 🌛 🍺 ♣ P

Connaught Arms

119 Guildford Road, Fratton
☎ (0705) 825873
11.30–2.30 (3.30 Fri), 6–11 (11–11 Sat;
12-3, 7.30-10.30 Sun)
**Marston's Pedigree;
Wadworth 6X; Whitbread
Best Bitter** Ⓗ; guest beer
Large and friendly, single-bar
local tucked away in the back
streets. Well-attended quiz

every other Mon; constantly
changing guest ale. Good food
lunchtime (not served Sun).
🏵 ◖ 🚃 (Fratton) ♣

Electric Arms

190–192 Fratton Road, Fratton
☎ (0705) 823293
11–3, 6–11 (11–11 Sat)
Ind Coope Burton Ale Ⓗ
Town-centre local with a
ready welcome for all. Many
sports teams share this centre
of the community and a
science fiction group meets on
alternate Tue eves. Reputed to
be haunted by the ghost of a
former landlady.
◖ 🍺 🚃 (Fratton) ♣

Fifth Hants Volunteer Arms

74 Albert Road, Southsea (E of
Kings Theatre)
☎ (0705) 827161
12 (11 Sat)–11
**Gale's BBB, Best Bitter, 5X,
HSB** Ⓗ
Small street-corner local with
two bars: the public bar is
decorated with naval cap
tallies and baseball caps.
Battalion history painting in
the lounge bar. Birthplace of
the local CAMRA branch.
Q ◖ 🍺 ♣

Florist

324 Fratton Road, Fratton
☎ (0705) 820289
11–3, 6–11 (11–11 Sat)
Wadworth IPA, 6X Ⓗ
Small two-bar pub, recently
taken over by Wadworth. The
front public bar has pool and
darts; small lounge at the rear.
The exterior has half
timbering and a 'witch's hat'
tower. Q 🍺 ♿ 🚃 (Fratton)

Mermaid

222 New Road, Copnor
☎ (0705) 824397
12–3, 6–11 (12–11 Sat)
**Draught Bass; Bunces Old
Smokey; Greene King Abbot;
Holden's Mild; Wadworth
6X** Ⓗ
Unblemished Victorian local
with a rare heated footrail and
wrought ironwork. The beer
selection is unusually varied
and full of surprises, with a
mild often available. All that a
good pub should be. 🏵 🍺 ♣

Red White & Blue

150 Fawcett Road, Southsea
☎ (0705) 814470
11–11
Gale's BBB, 5X, HSB Ⓗ
Pub decorated inside with
colours appropriate to its
patriotic name – although
there is also a hint of Canada
about it. Compact and often
crowded. Unfortunately the
handpumps on the customers'
side of the bar only serve fresh
air. Lunches served Sat.
🚃 (Fratton) ♣

Scotts Bar

37 Eldon Street, Southsea (off
Middle St, S of Churchill Ave)
☎ (0705) 826018
11–11
**Courage Best Bitter,
Directors; King & Barnes
Mild; Marston's Pedigree;
Ringwood Fortyniner** Ⓗ
Street-corner, two-bar popular
pub featuring an eight-
handpump beer engine c.1839.
Originally the Elm Tavern.
Popular live music attracts
younger customers without
driving out the locals.
◖▶ 🍺 🚃 ♣

Ship & Castle

90 Rudmore Road, Rudmore
☎ (0705) 660391
10.30–3, 6–11
Gale's BBB, HSB Ⓗ
Well-hidden, friendly locals'
pub, by the continental ferry
port, but originally on the
waterfront, overlooking Whale
Island. Small garden. 🏵 ◖ P

Tap

17 London Road, North End
☎ (0705) 699943
10.30–11
**Banks & Taylor SOD;
Felinfoel Cambrian; Fuller's
London Pride; Hall &
Woodhouse Tanglefoot;
Mitchell's Mild, Best Bitter** Ⓗ
Enterprising and successful
free house offering a regularly
changing range of eight real
ales. Situated in the North End
shopping area, this is a rare
outlet for real mild. Belgian
fruit beers; excellent range of
good value food. 🏵 ◖▶ ♿

Travellers Joy

253 Milton Road, Southsea
☎ (0705) 788006
11–3, 6–11
**Ind Coope Friary Meux Best
Bitter, Burton Ale** Ⓗ; guest
beer
Large two-room pub on the
main road. Handy for Fratton
Park football ground. Quiz
eve Mon. ♣ ♣ P

Wig & Pen

1 Landport Terrace, Southsea
☎ (0705) 820696
11.30–3.30, 7–11
Ringwood Best Bitter Ⓗ;
guest beers
Whitbread pub due to be sold
off, hopefully to the present
tenant. Four guest beers from
independent brewers, and
always one mild, are available
in the single bar with its two
separate areas. Busy
lunchtime trade (good value
meals; no food Sun). Parking
can be difficult weekdays.
Local CAMRA *Pub of the Year*
1990. ◖ 🚃 ♣

Wine Vaults

Albert Road, Southsea (opp.
Kings Theatre) ☎ (0705) 864712

11.30–3, 5.30–11 (11–11 Sat)
**Draught Bass; Felinfoel
Double Dragon; Fuller's
London Pride; Hop Back
Summer Lightning; Otter
Bitter; Ringwood Old
Thumper** H
Thriving, popular free house
with over ten ever-changing
real ales available (seasonal
beer festivals). Good value
meals prepared with
wholefood ingredients when
possible. Mon eve special offer
on one selected beer. ◖ ▶ ᕦ

Priors Dean

White Horse
(Pub With No Name)
OS714290 ☎ (042 058) 387
11–2.30 (3 Sat), 6–11
**Ballard's Best Bitter; Draught
Bass; Courage Directors;
Eldridge Pope Royal Oak;
Ringwood Fortyniner; S&N
Theakston Old Peculier** H
Famous old pub situated in a
field with no real pub sign.
Consequently hard to find, but
people manage and it can get
very busy in summer. The two
comfortable and quiet bars
have a variety of furnishings
and decorations. No lunches
Sun. Caravans allowed.
🏘 Q ❀ ◖ ▶ P

Privett

Olde Pig & Whistle
Gosport Road (A32)
☎ (0730) 88421
11–11
**Cotleigh Tawny; Ringwood
Old Thumper** H**; guest beers**
Large and spacious, friendly
free house. The single bar has
a games area at one end. Food
is available all day. Of the five
beers on offer, three are
guests. 🏘 ❀ 🚐 ◖ ▶ ♣ P

Ringwood

Inn on the Furlong
12 Meeting House Lane
☎ (0425) 475139
11 (10.30 Wed)–11
**Ringwood Best Bitter, XXXX
Porter, Fortyniner, Old
Thumper** H**; guest beers**
Superb thriving local in the
centre of a market town. A
central bar serves a multi-
roomed pub with flagstones
and traditional wooden
furnishings. Pleasant
conservatory/dining area.
Blues night Tue.
🏘 ⛌ ❀ ◖ ▶ ⏥ ⌣ ⍽

Romsey

Tudor Rose
3 The Cornmarket
☎ (0794) 512126
10–11

Courage Best Bitter,
Directors H
Listed 15th-century ale house
with a single small bar. Tables
in the cobbled courtyard in
summer. 20th year in the
Guide! 🏘 Q ❀ ◖ ♣

Sherfield on Loddon

White Hart
Reading Road (off A33)
☎ (0256) 882280
11–2.30, 5.30–11 (12–2.30, 7–10.30
Sun)
**Courage Best Bitter,
Directors; Fuller's London
Pride** H
Old coaching inn dating from
1642, now a one-bar pub with
a separate eating area. Large
lawn with a children's area.
🏘 Q ❀ ◖ ▶ ᕦ P

Silchester

Calleva Arms
☎ (0734) 700305
11–2.30 (5 Sat), 4.30 (6 Sat)–11
**Gale's XXXD, BBB, Best
Bitter, 5X, HSB** H
Old pub with Roman
connections and simple public
and lounge bars. Family
conservatory at lunchtime
only. Large, very well
maintained garden. Eve meals
in the restaurant.
Q ⛌ ❀ ◖ ⏥ ♣ P

Sopley

Woolpack
Ringwood Road (B3347, W
side of one-way system)
☎ (0425) 72252
11–11
**Marston's Pedigree;
Ringwood Best Bitter;
Wadworth 6X** H
Attractive thatched pub in the
village centre. The patio and
conservatory overlook a
stream and paddock with
ducks and geese; children's
playground. Good range of
meals at a fair price.
🏘 ❀ ◖ ▶ P

Southampton

Freemantle Arms
33 Albany Road, Freemantle
(off Firgrove Rd, near A3057)
☎ (0703) 772092
10.30–3, 6 (7 Sat)–11
**Banks's Mild; Marston's
Burton Best Bitter, Pedigree** H
Friendly local in a quiet cul-
de-sac. A lively public bar and
a quieter lounge with plenty
of plant and aquatic life.
Popular, colourful garden
with a large patio. Good value
beers. ❀ ⏥ ♣

Gate
138–140 Burgess Road, Bassett
(A35 close to university)
☎ (0703) 678250
11–3, 7–11
**Eldridge Pope Hardy
Country, Blackdown Porter,
Royal Oak** H
Large, open-plan pub, popular
with locals and students.
Children's room and good
garden with play equipment.
Eve meals by arrangement
only. ⛌ ❀ ◖ ♣ P

Guide Dog
38 Earls Road, Bevois Town
(1½ miles NE of centre)
☎ (0703) 220188
11.30–2.30, 6–11
Wadworth IPA, 6X H**; guest
beer**
Small locals' pub named after
charity fund-raising; however
non-guide dogs are not
allowed. Excellent value
pizzas. Note the large
collection of dolls. The guest
beer is usually Adnams
Broadside. ◖ ▶ ♣ ♣

Junction Inn
21 Priory Road, St Denys
☎ (0703) 584486
11.30–3, 5 (7 Sat)–11
**Banks's Mild; Marston's
Burton Best Bitter,
Pedigree** H**; Owd Rodger**
(winter) G
Splendid Victorian hostelry,
popular with all ages.
National winner of CAMRA's
Best Restored Pub 1990. Art
gallery of paintings and
photographs in the lounge
bar; collection of mugs in the
public bar. No food Sun. Q ❀
◖ ⏥ ᕦ ⇌ (St Denys) ♣ ⌣

Marsh
42 Canute Road (under A3025
Itchen bridge) ☎ (0703) 635540
11–11 (11–5, 7–11 Sat)
**Banks's Mild; Marston's
Burton Best Bitter,
Pedigree** H
Genuine, friendly and
unspoilt docklands pub which
was once a lighthouse, hence
the semi-circular bars. Prints
of the old town centre adorn
the public bar; separate pool
room. Brisk lunchtime office
trade. ❀ ⏥ ᕦ ♣

New Inn
16 Bevois Valley Road
☎ (0703) 228437
11.45–3, 6.45–11
Gale's XXXD (summer)**, BBB,
Best Bitter, 5X, HSB** H
Unpretentious, rather austere
local drawing much of its
latent charm from an ambience
which mixes erudition with
affability. A large malt whisky
collection and Belgian bottled
beers are added attractions.
Draught Prize Old Ale
available at Christmas. ◖ ♣

Hampshire

Park Inn
37 Carlisle Road, Shirley (off
A3057, Romsey road)
☎ (0703) 787835
11–3 (3.30 Sat), 5 (6 Sat)–11
**Hall & Woodhouse
Tanglefoot; Wadworth IPA,
6X, Farmer's Glory, Old
Timer** H
Popular, friendly side-street
local close to the shopping
centre. Maintains a two-bar
feel and some interesting
mirrors. Slightly more
upmarket than most local
pubs. ✿ ♣

Platform Tavern
Town Quay (near Royal Pier)
☎ (0703) 212036
11.30–3, 5–11 (11.30–11 Fri & Sat)
**Banks's Mild; Marston's
Burton Best Bitter, Merrie
Monk, Pedigree** H
Welcoming docklands pub
opposite the old Harbour
Board offices. The old town
walls are part of the pub's
structure. Busy lunchtime
trade. Near Ocean Village and
ferries. Q ◖ ᕼ ♣

Richmond Inn
108 Portswood Road,
Portswood
☎ (0703) 554523
11-11
**Banks's Mild; Marston's
Burton Best Bitter,
Pedigree** H
True locals' pub in a busy
shopping centre: a plain
public bar and a comfortable
lounge with ocean liner prints.
Good whisky selection and a
beautiful old LSD cash
register. Function room.
✿ ᕼ ᕤ (St Denys) ♣

Waterloo Arms
101 Waterloo Road,
Freemantle
☎ (0703) 220022
12–2.30, 4–11 (12–11 Fri & Sat)
**Hop Back GFB, Special,
Entire Stout, Summer
Lightning** H
Busy, one-bar pub completely
transformed by new owners.
Good value and never a dull
moment. Fancy dress nights.
Visitors miss at their peril;
worth the 15 mins' walk from
Central station. No food Sun.
✿ ◖ ᕤ (Millbrook) ♣

Wellington Arms
56 Park Road, Freemantle
☎ (0703) 227356
11.30–2.30, 6 (7 Sat)–11 (12–2.30,
8–10.30 Sun)
**Courage Directors; Fuller's
London Pride; Morland Old
Speckled Hen; Palmers IPA;
Ringwood Best Bitter,
Fortyniner, Old Thumper;
Wadworth 6X** H; **guest beers**
Busy, comfortable back-street
free house with two lounges.
A veritable shrine to the Iron

Duke – get there early for a
good look around. No food
Sun. ✿ ◖ ᕼ (Central)

South Warnborough

Poacher
Alton Road
☎ (0256) 862218
11.30–2.30, 6–11
**S&N Theakston Old Peculier;
Wadworth 6X; Worldham
Old Dray** H
Roomy single bar with a
varied clientele. Large
children's play area with a
wendy house and swings. The
beer range may vary.
ᕼ ✿ ᕼ P

Stratfield Saye

Four Horseshoes
West End Green OS668616
☎ (0734) 332320
12–2.30 (11–3 Sat), 5–11
**Morland Bitter, Old
Masters** H
Small, basic country pub, with
darts, dominoes and bar
billiards often played. Log
fires in both bars during
winter. Evening meals
available in summer only,
Tue–Sun. Situated right out in
the countryside, with a good
view from the beer garden
across open fields.
ᕼ ✿ ◖ ▶ ᕼ ♣ P

New Inn
Bramley Road
☎ (0734) 332255
11–11
**Hall & Woodhouse Badger
Best Bitter, Hard Tackle,
Tanglefoot; Wadworth 6X;
guest beer** H
Well-decorated country pub
with several areas. Friendly
service: children and dogs
especially welcome. Free use
of board games. Pleasant
garden. ᕼ ᕽ ✿ ◖ ▶ ♣ P

Sway

Hare & Hounds
Durnstown (on B3055 New
Milton–Brockenhurst road)
☎ (0590) 682404
11–11
Wadworth 6X H; **guest beers**
17th-century coaching inn
with hand-painted murals.
The varied menu includes
vegetarian dishes and daily
specials. Crafts night Mon;
skittles Tue; fish, chips and
folk Thu. At least three guest
beers from independent
breweries.
ᕼ Q ᕽ ✿ ◖ ▶ ▲ ♣ ⌂ P ✂

Totford

Woolpack
On B3046 ☎ (0962) 732101

11.30–2.30, 6–11
**Eldridge Pope Dorchester,
Hardy Country, Blackdown
Porter; Gale's HSB; Palmers
IPA** H
16th-century flint-stone
building with a large, open-
plan stone-floored interior.
Situated in Hampshire's
smallest hamlet, on Wayfarers
Walk near The Grange (NT).
ᕼ Q ✿ ᕼ ◖ ▶ ♿ ▲ ♣ P

Twyford

Dolphin Inn
Hazeley Road
☎ (0962) 712204
11.30–2.30, 6–11
**Marston's Burton Best Bitter,
Pedigree** H
Two-bar pub on a crossroads
at the centre of the village: a
comfortable lounge and a
basic public bar. Disused
garages attached to the pub
are to be converted to a skittle
alley. ᕼ ✿ ◖ ▶ ᕼ ♣ P

Upton Grey

Hoddington Arms
Bidden Road (off A339)
☎ (0256) 862371
11 (11.30 Sat)–2.30, 6 (7 Sat)–11
(12–2.30, 7–10.30 Sun)
**Morland Old Masters, Old
Speckled Hen** H; **guest beers**
18th-century listed building in
a pretty village encircled by
farmland; popular both with
locals and travellers attracted
by the extensive, interesting
menus. Well-presented guest
ales. ᕼ ᕽ ✿ ◖ ▶ ♣ P

Vernham Dean

George
Off A343 at Hurstbourne
Tarrant
☎ (0264) 87279
11–2.30 (3 Sat), 6–11
**Marston's Burton Best Bitter,
Pedigree** H
16th-century, brick and timber
building with low beams and
an inglenook. The focal point
of village life.
ᕼ Q ✿ ◖ ▶ ♣ P

Wallington

White Horse
44 North Wallington (off
A27/M27 jct 11)
☎ (0329) 235197
11–3, 5–11
**Draught Bass; Felinfoel
Bitter; Hoskins Premium;
Larkins Best Bitter** G
Pleasantly located by the River
Wallington, this agreeable
village local may be reached
by footbridge from Fareham
High Street. A varied range of
beers satisfies an increasing
demand. Dining room open
Thu/Fri eves. Q ✿ ◖ ᕼ ♿ ♣

West Wellow

Rockingham Arms

Canada Road (A36, 1 mile from centre) ☎ (0794) 22473
11.30–2.30, 6–11
Beer range varies Ⓗ
Constantly-changing selection of up to six real ales from a range of over 100 from all over the country in a smartly furnished pub with a games bar and a restaurant. Very friendly atmosphere for locals and visitors alike. A genuine free house.
Q ❀ ◖▮ ⌂ ♣ P

Weyhill

Weyhill Fair

On A342 just N of A303
☎ (0264) 773631
11.30–2.30, 6 (7 Sat)–11 (12–2.30, 7–10.30 Sun)
Morrells Bitter, Varsity, Graduate Ⓗ**; guest beers**
Over 100 different guest beers a year are served here and a real mild is always available. The single bar is unspoilt by obtrusive games or music and families are made very welcome. A mural upstairs relives the Weyhill Fair, an ancient Michaelmas sheep fair. No food Sun eve.
🚲 ❀ ◖▮ ⌂ P ✗

Whitchurch

Bell

Bell Street
☎ (0256) 893120
10.30–11
Courage Best Bitter; Gale's BBB, Best Bitter, HSB Ⓗ
Timber-framed building in a small country town with a silk mill. Some good local ales and fine food. A popular inn with the locals.
⧖ ❀ 🚲 ◖▮ ▮ ♣ P

Old Brewery

Bell Street ☎ (0256) 892145
11–3, 5 (6 Sat)–11
Archers Best Bitter; Gale's HSB Ⓗ**; guest beers**
Former tap room of the old Whitchurch brewery, recently refurbished into a pleasant one-bar pub. Much interesting pub and farming memorabilia. Most attentive licensees.
❀ ◖▮ ▮ ⇌

Prince Regent

London Street (B3400)
☎ (0256) 892179
11–11
Archers Best Bitter; Hop Back GFB Ⓗ**, Summer Lightning** Ⓖ**; guest beers** (occasionally)
Unpretentious local boozer with excellent value beer and food. Deservedly popular with locals and looked after by a keen landlord. Meat draw on

Sun. A good traditional pub, well worth a visit. ❀ ◖▮ ♣ P

Whiteley

Parsons Collar

Solent Business Park (N of M27 jct 9) ☎ (0489) 880035
11–2.30, 5 (6.30 Sat)–11
Thwaites Bitter, Craftsman Ⓗ
New pub in the grounds of a hotel: a plain brick exterior but a more welcoming interior, with a flagstone floor, wood beams and plenty of pictures. A large single bar is divided into separate drinking areas (food at one end). Monthly quiz and theme nights.
🚲 ❀ ◖▮ ▮ P

Whitsbury

Cartwheel

3 miles NNW of Fordingbridge OS129188
☎ (072 53) 362
11–2.30, 6–11
Adnams Broadside; S&N Theakston Old Peculier; Wadworth 6X Ⓗ
Comfortable free house in a remote village just outside the New Forest. Previous incarnations were a barn, a bakery and a wheelwright's – hence the name. Regularly-changed beer range and an imaginative menu (no eve meals Tue).
🚲 ❀ ◖▮ ♣ P

Winchester

County Arms

85 Romsey Road (A3090, next to hospital) ☎ (0962) 851950
11–11
Banks's Mild; Marston's Burton Best Bitter, Pedigree Ⓗ
Two smallish bars with a traditional local feel. Customers include students, prison officers, nursing staff and expectant fathers (close to the maternity ward). Several sports teams. Limited parking. The lounge is quiet.
🚲 Q ❀ ◖▮ ♣ P

Exchange

9 Southgate Street
☎ (0962) 854718
10–11
Courage Best Bitter, Directors; John Smith's Bitter Ⓗ
U-shaped, one-bar pub with quality furnishings, celebrating its bicentenary this year. The public bar area has darts carefully hidden in a corner. Good value food all day. Patio at the rear.
❀ ◖▮ ♣

Foresters Arms

71 North Walls (near station)
☎ (0962) 861539

11–2.30 (4.30 Sat), 5.30 (6 Sat)–11
Marston's Burton Best Bitter, Pedigree Ⓗ
One quiet lounge bar with regular quiz and cribbage games. Comfortable, unpretentious and friendly.
❀ ◖▮ ♣

Fulflood Arms

28 Cheriton Road (300 yds off A272) ☎ (0962) 865356
5–11 (12–2.30, 6–11 Fri; 11–3, 6–11 Sat)
Marston's Burton Best Bitter, Pedigree Ⓗ
Traditional, quiet, two-bar local tucked away behind the railway station. Its tiled sign still proclaims 'Winchester Brewery'. ❀ ▮ ⇌ ♣

Hyde Tavern

Hyde Street ☎ (0962) 862592
11–2.30 (3 Sat), 5.30 (6 Sat)–11
Marston's Burton Best Bitter, Pedigree Ⓗ
Interesting double gable-fronted, two-bar pub below street level. The oldest pub in town (15th century). Very homely, comfortable interior featuring a mantlepiece of brass ornaments, low ceilings and painful door frames for people over six-feet tall.
Q ▮ ⇌ ♣

King Alfred

11 Saxon Road, Hyde (off Hyde Street) ☎ (0962) 854370
11–3, 5.30–11 (11–11 Sat)
Banks's Mild; Marston's Burton Best Bitter, Pedigree Ⓗ
Good, basic two-bar pub: a spacious public with pool and darts in an area at the rear, and a small, cosy lounge. Large beer garden (barbecues in summer). Good value.
❀ ◖▮ ♣

Yateley

Anchor

Vigo Lane ☎ (0252) 872248
11–2.30, 5.30–11 (11–11 Fri & Sat)
Courage Best Bitter, Directors; Ushers Best Bitter, Founders Ⓗ
Aged building mentioned in the *Domesday Book*, which has played many roles, including a shop, a horse taxi rank, an abattoir and a chapel of rest! Large garden with aviary and summer barbecues. Families welcome. Beams and brasses in the saloon; more basic 'Sports' bar. ❀ ◖▮ ♣ P

Join CAMRA —
see page 508

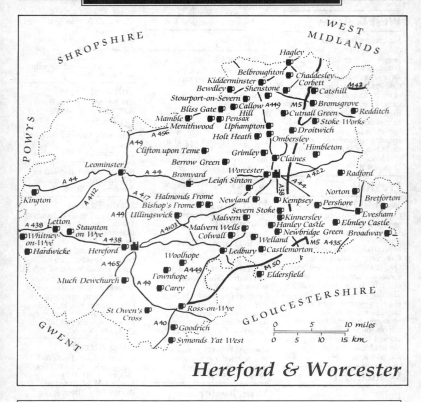

Hereford & Worcester

🏭 *Jolly Roger, Worcester; Wye Valley, Hereford*

Belbroughton

Holly Bush
Stourbridge Road (A491)
11–3, 6–11 (11–11 summer)
Ansells Mild; HP&D Bitter, Entire, Deakin's Downfall; Tetley Bitter Ⓗ
Three rooms divide this cosy pub. A room mainly for dining adjoins the welcoming main bar area. Next to this is a simple lounge where Ron plays the piano. No meals Sun eve. 🍴 Q ◖▮ P

Olde Horseshoe
High Street ☎ (0562) 730233
11–3 (4.30 Sat), 5.30 (6 or 7 Sat)–11
S&N Theakston Best Bitter, XB, Old Peculier; Younger No. 3 Ⓗ
Comfortable pub in the centre of a pretty village: a pleasant bar and a small lounge which can get very crowded as the home-cooked food is very popular (not served Mon eve). Barbecues in summer. The beer range may vary.
🕸 ◖▮ 🛋 ♣ ⌂ P

Berrow Green

Admiral Rodney
On B4197 ☎ (0886) 21375
11–3, 6–11
Banks's Mild, Bitter; Ruddles County; Webster's Yorkshire Bitter Ⓗ**; guest beer**
Welcoming and easy-going, large country free house, with a strong nautical feel. Separate restaurant and skittle alley. Convenient for walkers on the Worcestershire Way.
🍴 🏚 Q 🍴 🕸 ◖▮ 🛋 🅰 ♣ P

Bewdley

Black Boy
50 Wyre Hill (B4194 at Welch Gate)
12–3, 7–11
Banks's Mild, Bitter Ⓔ
After a steep climb from the town, a pint or two is most welcome at this friendly locals' pub. Q 🍴 🕸 🛋 ♣

Cock & Magpie
Severnside North
11–3, 6–11 (11–11 Sat & summer)
Banks's Mild, Bitter Ⓔ
Popular two-bar riverside local on the former Coles Quay near Bewdley Bridge.
Q 🛋 🚋 (SVR) ♣

Hop Pole Inn
Cleobury Road
☎ (0299) 402127
11–2.30, 6–11
Marston's Burton Best Bitter, Pedigree Ⓗ
Pleasant, two-roomed hostelry a mile's drive from the river. Meals served Tue–Sat.
Q 🕸 ◖▮ 🛋 ♣ P

Little Pack Horse
High Street ☎ (0299) 403762
11–3 (12–4 Sat), 6–11
Ind Coope Burton Ale; Lumphammer Ⓗ
The first of 'Mad O'Rourke's' somewhat eccentric chain of 'Little Pubs', retaining its traditional atmosphere and appearance. Good meals, including the famous Desperate Dan Pie. Lumphammer is brewed by Allied.
🍴 🛋 ◖▮ 🚋 (SVR) ♣

Bishop's Frome

Chase Inn
On B4214 ☎ (0885) 490234
12–3.30, 6–11 (11–11 Fri & Sat)
Hook Norton Best Bitter; Wye Valley Hereford Bitter, Hereford Supreme Ⓗ
Well-run free house in an area that has a reputation for fine pubs. The landlord will read your tarot cards. Imaginative, sensibly-priced menu.
🏚 ✿ 🛏 ◖◗ 🍴 ♣ P

Bliss Gate

Bliss Gate
Off A456, 2½ miles W of Bewdley ☎ (0299) 266321
12–2.30, 6–11 (12–2.30, 7–10.30 Sun)
Marston's Burton Best Bitter, Pedigree Ⓗ
Quiet, friendly local with a good selection of whiskies.
🏚 Q ✿ 🍴 ♣ P

Bretforton

Fleece
The Cross (50 yds S of B4035)
☎ (0386) 851173
11 (10 Sat)–2.30, 6–11 (12–2.30, 7–10.30 Sun)
Hook Norton Best Bitter; M&B Brew XI; Uley Pig's Ear; Wells Eagle Ⓗ
Famous old inn, owned by the NT. The interior, untouched for many years, features an inglenook, antiques and a famous pewter collection. Beer festival mid-July. No-smoking family room. Q ✿ ✿ ◖◗ ◗ 🍴 ▲ ♣ ☺ ⌁

Broadway

Crown & Trumpet
Church Street ☎ (0386) 853202
11–2.30 (3 Sat), 5.30–11 (11–11 July & Aug)
Whitbread Boddingtons Mild, Bitter, Flowers IPA, Original Ⓗ
17th-century Cotswold stone inn in a picturesque village, boasting a classic interior. Traditional and seasonal local food dishes; summer teas. Food for walking parties.
🏚 Q 🛏 ◖◗ ▲ ♣ ☺ P

Bromsgrove

Red Lion
High Street ☎ (0527) 35387
10.30–11
Banks's Mild, Bitter Ⓔ
A one-roomer, popular with locals studying racing form. Convenient for the shopping centre. The car park is very small. No food Sun. ◖ ♣ P

Bromyard

Crown & Sceptre
7 Sherford Street
☎ (0885) 482441
12–3, 6.30–11 (11–11 Fri & Sat in summer)
Hook Norton Best Bitter; M&B Brew XI; Wadworth 6X Ⓗ; **guest beers**
Bromyard's free house – always a friendly welcome in a rejuvenated ex-Whitbread house offering good food. Pleasing decor includes old maps and adverts. Usually two guest beers.
🏚 ✿ 🛏 ◖◗ ♣ P

Callow Hill

Royal Foresters
On A456 ☎ (0299) 266286
11–3, 5.30–11
Greene King Abbot; John Smith's Bitter Ⓗ
Pleasant, popular main road inn. Families welcome. A house mild is also sold.
🏚 Q ✿ ♣ P

Carey

Cottage of Content
1½ miles NE of Hoarwithy OS563310 ☎ (0432) 840242
12–2.30 (3 summer Sat; closed Tue & Thu winter), 7 (6 summer Sat)–11 (12–2.30 (3 summer), 7–10.30 Sun)
Draught Bass; Hook Norton Best Bitter, Old Hooky Ⓗ
Aptly-named pub in an idyllic setting. 500 years-old, it has a warren of oak-beamed rooms and simple but comfortable furnishings. Tremendous character; excellent food.
🏚 Q ✿ 🛏 ◖◗ 🍴 ♣ ☺ P

Castlemorton

Plume of Feathers
Gloucester Road (B4208)
☎ (0684) 81554
11–3, 7–11
Marston's Burton Best Bitter, Pedigree; Tetley Bitter; Whitbread Boddingtons Bitter, Castle Eden Ale Ⓗ
Friendly country pub on the edge of Castlemorton Common. One room is set out for eating: generous portions of food. ✿ ◖◗ ▲ P

Catshill

Plough & Harrow
On A19 Stourbridge road
☎ (0527) 77355
12–2.30 (3 Sat), 7–11
Ansells Bitter; Ind Coope Burton Ale Ⓗ
Two-roomed pub with a restaurant off the small lounge: a good roadside inn offering a range of food (not Sun eve or Mon). Live piano weekends. ✿ ◖◗ 🍴 ♣ P

Royal Oak
Barley Mow Lane (off A38/M42 jct 1)
☎ (0527) 70141
11–11

Banks's Mild, Bitter Ⓔ
Proper, unspoilt pub, its smallness not limiting its appeal: a lounge, a traditional snug bar, a pool room, a restaurant with its own lounge and a garden. Extensive menu. No meals Sun eve or Mon.
Q ✿ 🛏 ◖ ⚅ ♣ P

Chaddesley Corbett

Talbot
The Village ☎ (0562) 777388
11–3, 6–11
Banks's Mild, Bitter Ⓔ
Large, centuries-old, half-timbered inn with unusual double porches. One lounge has wood panelling. Restaurant. 🏚 🛏 ✿ ◖◗ 🍴 ♣ P

Claines

Mug House
Claines Lane (off A449)
☎ (0905) 56649
11–2.30 (3 Sat), 5–11 (11–11 summer)
Banks's Mild Ⓔ, **Bitter** Ⓗ & Ⓔ
Ancient, unspoilt country pub in the village churchyard. Parking limited. No food Sun.
🏚 Q 🐕 ✿ 🛏 ◗ ▲ ♣

Clifton upon Teme

Lion Inn
1 The Village ☎ (088 65) 617
12–3, 7 (6 Fri & Sat) –11
Banks's Mild, Bitter Ⓗ & Ⓔ
Homely, traditional, half-timbered village inn with a comfortable lounge and a restaurant. No food Mon.
🏚 Q 🛏 ◖◗ ⚅ ♣ P

Colwall

Chase Inn
Chase Road, Upper Colwall (200 yds off B4218, Wyche Rd, signed British Camp)
☎ (0684) 40276
12–2.30 (not Tue), 6–11 (12–2, 7–10.30 Sun)
Donnington BB, SBA; Wye Valley HPA, Hereford Supreme Ⓗ
Straightforward free house, tucked away in a backwater of the Malvern Hills. Limited, but wholesome, menu till 8.30pm (no food Sun eve). No children; no fruit machines.
Q ✿ ◖ ◗ ⚅ ♣

Cutnall Green

New Inn
On A442 ☎ (029 923) 202
12–2.30, 5.30 (6 Sat)–11
Marston's Burton Best Bitter, Pedigree Ⓗ
Small, friendly pub where the restaurant area offers reasonably-priced main meals and snacks. 🏚 ✿ 🛏 ◖ ◗ P

Hereford & Worcester

Droitwich

Railway Inn
Kidderminster Road
☎ (0905) 770056
12–3, 5.30–11 (11.30–11 Sat)
Marston's Burton Best Bitter, Merrie Monk, Pedigree Ⓗ
Canalside pub, close to the restored basin and Vines Park. Good atmosphere; railway memorabilia. Lunches served Thu–Sat. Weston's cider in summer. ❀ ⇔ ◐ ▶ ⇌ ⇔ P

Rifleman's Arms
Station Street ☎ (0905) 770327
11–3, 5–11 (11–11 Sat)
Banks's Mild, Bitter Ⓔ
Locals' pub which attracts customers of all ages. A 'Pint & Platter' pub, but no meals Sun. ❀ ◐ ▶ ⊟ ⇌ ♣

Eldersfield

Greyhound
Lime Street (off B4211)
OS814305 ☎ (0452) 840381
11–3, 6–11
Butcombe Bitter Ⓖ
Real, unspoilt village pub: wood panelling, bentwood bench seats and stone flags. Seats outside in summer (watch out for free range chickens!). Lunchtime snacks.
🏚 Q ❀ ⊟ ♣ P

Elmley Castle

Queen Elizabeth
Main Street
☎ (0386) 710209
11–3, 7–11
Marston's Burton Best Bitter Ⓗ
16th-century, black and white inn in a picturesque village. A traditional bar with games and an inglenook leads to a homely lounge with ancient tables and settles. Unchanged under the present landlord for 30 years. 🏚 Q ❀ ⊟ ♣

Evesham

Trumpet Inn
Merstow Green
☎ (0386) 446227
11–2.30, 5–11
Draught Bass; Stones Best Bitter Ⓗ; **guest beer** (occasionally)
Pleasant town pub just off the High Street, near the Almonry Museum: a single bar, though not cavernous. No meals winter Sun. No-smoking tables at lunchtime only.
❀ ◐ ⇌ ♣ P ⊬

Fownhope

Green Man Inn
On B4224 ☎ (0432) 860243
11–2.30, 6–11 (12–2.30, 7–10.30 Sun)
Hook Norton Best Bitter;

Marston's Pedigree; Samuel Smith OBB Ⓗ
500-year-old coaching inn with much character. Popular with out-of-town diners and drinkers alike. Fishing rights on the Wye for residents. The longest-standing Herefordshire pub in this *Guide*. Good value.
🏚 Q ❀ ⇔ ◐ ▶ ♣ ⇔ P

Goodrich

Hostelrie
Off B4229 ☎ (0600) 890241
11.30–2.30, 7–11 (12–2, 7–10.30 Sun)
Draught Bass Ⓗ
Two-star hotel near the 13th-century Goodrich Castle. A no children and no fruit machine policy operates in two discrete and pleasant bars. Restaurant closed Mon/Tue.
Q ❀ ⇔ ◐ ▶ P

Grimley

Camp House Inn
Camp Lane (1½ miles off A443) OS836607
☎ (0905) 640288
11–3, 6–11
Whitbread Flowers IPA, Original Ⓗ; **guest beers**
Pleasant, family-run pub in a scenic spot on the banks of the River Severn. Unspoilt, relaxed atmosphere; original quarry tiled floors. Birds in the grounds (peacocks, ducks, etc.). Guest beers from Whitbread. Eve food finishes at 8pm. No wheelchair access to the ladies' WC.
🏚 ❀ ◐ ▶ ♿ ⚓ ♣ ⇔ P

Hagley

Station Inn
Worcester Road (off A456)
☎ (0562) 882549
11–11
Banks's Mild, Bitter Ⓔ
Large one-room hostelry with various alcoves and drinking areas. Situated in a busy but tidy village. No food Sun.
❀ ◐ ⇌ P

Halmonds Frome

Majors Arms
1 mile down lane off A4103 at Fromes Hill OS675481
☎ (0531) 640371
12–2.30 (weekends and summer only), 6–11
Brakspear Bitter; Marston's Pedigree Ⓖ; **guest beer** (summer)
Isolated and friendly free house boasting spectacular views across the Frome valley. The rural tranquillity is only ever disturbed by weekend music soirées. Closed winter weekday lunchtimes, but it's worth phoning ahead for parties. 🏚 Q ❀ ♣ ⇔ P

Hanley Castle

Three Kings
Off B4211 ☎ (0684) 592686
11–3, 7–11
Butcombe Bitter; Thwaites Bitter Ⓗ; **guest beers**
Traditional, unspoilt, multi-roomed pub next to the village church. A real gem – full of character. CAMRA *Regional Pub of the Year* 1990. Live music Sun eve; folk music Thu eve. No food Sun eve.
🏚 Q ⊛ ❀ ⇔ ◐ ▶ ⊟ ♣ ⇔

Hardwicke

Royal Oak
On B4348, 1 mile from B4352 jct ☎ (049 73) 248
11–3 (not Wed/Thu in winter), 6–11
Marston's Burton Best Bitter, Pedigree Ⓗ; **guest beer**
Isolated 16th-century pub, very much alive with good local and food trade. Extensive menu, but beware the fat pub cat! Ideal for visitors to the Hay-on-Wye bookshops.
🏚 ❀ ◐ ▶ ⊟ ♣ ⇔ P

Hereford

Barrels
69 St Owens Street
11–2.30 (4 Wed & Thu), 5–11 (11–11 Fri & Sat)
Wye Valley Hereford Bitter, HPA, Hereford Supreme, Brew 69 Ⓗ; **guest beer**
Brash, lively and popular pub, home of the Wye Valley brewery and offering the best value pint in the county. Beer fest Aug Bank Holiday. Loud music at weekends, but often local banter. ❀ ⊟ ⇌ ♣ ⇔

Lancaster
1 St Martins Street
☎ (0432) 275480
11–3.30 (4.30 Sat), 6–11 (11–11 summer)
Beer range varies Ⓗ
Popular free house on the banks of the Wye, previously the Saracen's Head. The lounge has a down-to-earth local feel to it. Three varying beers available. ◐ ▶ ⊟ ♣ ⇔

Treacle Mine
83–85 St Martins Street (S of river) ☎ (0432) 266022
11 (12 Mon)–3, 6–11 (11–11 Thu–Sat)
Banks's Mild, Bitter Ⓔ; **Greene King Abbot** Ⓗ; **guest beer**
A traditional Herefordshire bar accommodating an unusual mix of old beams and satellite TV. ❀

Himbleton

Galton Arms
OS943586 ☎ (090 569) 672
12–2.30, 6.30–11
Banks's Mild, Bitter Ⓔ

Very friendly local with an attractive garden in the heart of the country. Beers may vary. 🏠 Q ⊛ ◑ ▌ ⊟ ♣ ⌐ P

Holt Heath

Red Lion
At A443/B4196 jct
☎ (0905) 620236
11.30–2.30, 6–11
Ansells Mild, Bitter; Ind Coope Burton Ale H; guest beer
Traditional village two-roomer. The comfortable lounge has a blazing log fire; the bar has a games area. Excellent menu.
🏠 Q ⊛ ◑ ▌ ⊟ A ♣ ⌐ P

Kempsey

Huntsman Inn
Green Street village (1½ miles off A38) ☎ (0905) 820336
12–2.30, 7–11
Banks's Mild, Bitter E; guest beer H
Welcoming village pub offering a wide range of good value food: a traditional bar and a cosy lounge with country furniture in alcoves. The guest beer is in the lounge. Children's play area and a skittle alley.
🏠 ⅍ ⊛ ◑ ▌ ⊟ P

Kidderminster

Castle
Park Way ☎ (0562) 69406
10–11
Marston's Pedigree; John Smith's Bitter H
Small two-roomed local with beer prices to match the local Banks's outlets. House mild also sold. Q ⊛ ⊟ ♣

Grand Turk
207 Sutton Road (opp. hospital) ☎ (0562) 66254
11–3, 5.30–11 (11–11 Fri & Sat)
Banks's Mild, Bitter H
Friendly three-roomed local where children are welcome and food is available all day.
Q ⊛ ◑ ▌ ⊟ ♣ ⌐ P

Station Inn
Farfield (off A448, Comberton Hill) ☎ (0562) 822764
12–3, 6–11 (12–11 Fri & Sat)
Greenalls Davenports Bitter; Tetley Bitter H
Comfortable, welcoming local, a few minutes' walk from the BR and SVR stations. Good lunches and snacks. The garden is safe for children.
Q ⊛ ◑ ⊟ ⇌ ♣ ⌐ P

Kington

Olde Tavern
22 Victoria Road
11.30–3 (Sat only), 7.30–11 (12–2.30, 7.30–10.30 Sun)

Ansells Bitter H
A true Victorian relic: a warren of wood-panelled rooms. The main bar is full of curios. Possibly the only concession to modern times is the electric light! Ten bottled ciders. Q ♣ ♠

Queens Head
Bridge Street
☎ (0544) 230680
11–11
S&N Theakston Best Bitter, XB, Old Peculier; Whitbread Flowers Original; Younger Scotch H
Very friendly locals' pub serving a wide range of good value pub fare at all times.
🏠 ⊛ ⅍ ◑ ▌ ⊟ ♣ ⌐ P

Royal Oak Hotel
Church Street
☎ (0544) 230484
11–3, 5–11 (11–11 summer)
Marston's Burton Best Bitter, Pedigree H
Straightforward and friendly, Kington's 'first and last' pub in England has a plain public bar and an intimate lounge at the rear. Restaurant open in summer. No lunches in winter; eve meals finish at 8.30. 🏠 ⊛ ⅍ ◑ ▌ ⊟ ♣ P

Kinnersley

Royal Oak
Off A38, S of Severn Stoke
OS871437 ☎ (0905) 371482
11–11 (midnight supper licence)
Banks's Bitter; Hook Norton Best Bitter H; guest beers
Village pub with a number of areas on different levels: an open-plan 'Oak Bar' at the front and a separate restaurant. 🏠 ⊛ ◑ ▌ ♣ P

Ledbury

Brewery Inn
Bye Street ☎ (0531) 4272
11–3, 7–11 (12–2.30, 7–10.30 Sun)
Banks's Mild; Marston's Burton Best Bitter, Pedigree H
Sympathetically improved local that has kept its original character. The splendid snug is possibly the smallest bar in the county. Sun lunch by arrangement only.
🏠 Q ⅍ ⊛ ◑ ▌ ⊟ & ⇌ ♣ ⌐

Olde Talbot Hotel
New Street ☎ (0531) 2963
11.30–3, 5.30–11
Ansells Bitter; Ind Coope Burton Ale; Wye Valley HPA H
AA two-star hotel that caters well for visiting drinkers and has a good local following. A number of different rooms offer plenty of atmosphere. Eve meals in the restaurant.
🏠 Q ⅍ ◑ ▌ ⇌ ♣

Leigh Sinton

Royal Oak
On B4503 ☎ (0886) 32664
11–3, 6–11
Marston's Burton Best Bitter, Pedigree H
Very friendly and attractive two-roomed village local boasting a wealth of unusual artefacts and exposed beams.
🏠 Q ⊛ ◑ ▌ ⊟ ♣ P

Leominster

Black Horse
South Street ☎ (0568) 611946
11–2.30, 6–11 (11–11 Sat)
Dunn Plowman Black Horse Bitter; Wadworth 6X H; guest beers
Outstanding free house that accommodates the Dunn Plowman brewery on the premises. A plain, friendly and lively pub, with occasional live music and good value restaurant (not open Sun eve).
⊛ ◑ ▌ ⊟ & ⇌ ♣ P

Grapes Vaults
Broad Street ☎ (0568) 612901
11–3, 5 (6 Sat)–11
Banks's Mild; Marston's Burton Best Bitter, Merrie Monk, Pedigree H
Behind a plain facade is concealed a well-run, superbly restored town pub. Wholesome menu available until 9pm. The Marston's range may vary. 🏠 Q ◑ ▌ ⇌

Letton

Swan Inn
On A438 ☎ (0544) 327304
11–11 (11–3, 6–11 Mon & Tue)
Beer range varies H
Rejuvenated, friendly roadside pub in the heart of the Wye Valley with at least two unusual beers always available. Meals and take-away food at all times. 🏠 Q ⊛ ◑ ▌ ⊟ ♣ P

Malvern

Star Inn
59 Cowleigh Road (B4219)
12–2 (3 Sat), 6–11
Draught Bass; M&B Mild, Brew XI H
Friendly and homely three-roomer: a dull exterior hides some magnificent Victorian furniture. Regular live folk music. 🏠 ⊟ ♣ ⌐

Malvern Wells

Malvern Hills Hotel
Wynds Point (A449) OS764404
☎ (0684) 40237
10.30–2.30, 6–11
Draught Bass; Hook Norton Best Bitter (summer); S&N Theakston Old Peculier; Wood Parish H

Hereford & Worcester

Comfortable lounge bar in an upmarket weekend retreat on the ridge of the Malvern Hills, close to the British Camp hill fort. Walkers welcomed but requested to remove muddy boots. ♨ Q ⌘ ❀ ⇄ ◑ ▶ P

Mamble

Dog & Duck
Clows Top (off A456 signed Mamble) ☎ (0299) 832291
12–2.30, 7–11 (closed Mon; 12–2.30 only Sun)
Hook Norton Best Bitter Ⓗ
Country inn and restaurant, specialising in brasserie-style food as well as traditional lunches. ♨ ◑ ▶ P

Menithwood

Cross Keys Inn
Between A443 and B4202 OS709690 ☎ (058 470) 425
10.30–3, 6–11
Marston's Burton Best Bitter, Pedigree Ⓗ**; guest beer**
Roadside pub in quiet countryside, very popular with the local community. Weston's cider in summer.
Q ⌘ ❀ ♣ ◠ P

Much Dewchurch

Black Swan
On B4348 ☎ (0981) 540295
11.30–2.30 (not Tue in winter), 6.30–11
Crown Buckley Best Bitter Ⓗ**; guest beers**
Arguably the oldest pub in the county: a quiet, traditional lounge and a more lively, renovated public bar. Always two guest beers. No meals Sun eve.
♨ Q ◑ ▶ ❀ ⅙ ▲ ♣ ◠ P

Newbridge Green

Drum & Monkey
On B4211 ☎ (068 46) 2238
11.30–2.30, 5–11
Banks's Mild, Bitter; Donnington BB; S&N Theakston Best Bitter Ⓗ**; guest beers**
Busy black and white country pub with lots of character. One large bar area is divided into cosy sections. Restaurant in the barn. ❀ ◑ ▶ ♣ ◠ P

Newland

Swan Inn
On A449 ☎ (0886) 832224
11.30–3, 6 (7 winter)–11
Butcombe Bitter; Hook Norton Best Bitter; Wadworth 6X Ⓗ**; guest beers**
Large, open bar with rather minimal seating; separate restaurant. On the edge of common land. The beer range varies (above average prices).
♨ ❀ ❀ ◑ ▲ P

Norton

Norton Grange Hotel
Evesham Road (A435/B439 jct) ☎ (0386) 870215
11.30–2.30, 7–11
Marston's Burton Best Bitter, Pedigree Ⓗ
Family-run hotel on the main road. The restaurant caters for children and curry-lovers. Children also welcome in the skittle alley/function room.
♨ Q ❀ ❀ ◑ ▶ ▲ ♣ P

Ombersley

Cross Keys
Kidderminster Road (N of roundabout)
☎ (0905) 620588
11–3, 6–11
Draught Bass; Batham Best Bitter; Marston's Burton Best Bitter, Pedigree Ⓗ
Village local whose car park is before the pub sign and easy to miss; the reverse of the sign depicts a pig and parrot! Small pool room. ♨ ❀ ◑ ▶ ♣ P

Pensax

Bell Inn
On B4202
☎ (0299) 896677
12–2.30, 6.30–11
Hook Norton Best Bitter; Moorhouse's Pendle Witches Brew; Wood Special Ⓗ**; guest beers**
Traditional snug and bar. The dining room serves home-cooked meals. ♨ ❀ ◑ ▶ P

Pershore

Millers Arms
Bridge Street
☎ (0386) 553864
11.30–2.30, 7–11
Hall & Woodhouse Badger Best Bitter; Wadworth 6X, Farmer's Glory, Old Timer Ⓗ**; guest beers**
Comfortable, olde-worlde market town pub, lively and popular with young people. Constantly changing guest beers. Eve meals in summer only. ❀ ◑ ▶ ♣

Radford

Wheelbarrow Castle
Alcester Road (off A422, take road to Flyford Flavell) OS012548
☎ (0386) 792207
11–3, 6–11
Banks's Mild, Bitter; Home Bitter; Hook Norton Best Bitter; S&N Theakston Best Bitter, XB Ⓗ
Friendly, two-roomed pub, popular with all age groups. Good value meals and Sun carvery (booking essential). ❀ ◑ ▶ ❀ ▲ ♣ P

Redditch

Gate Hangs Well
Evesham Road, Headless Cross (off A441)
12–3, 5.30–11 (12–11 Sat)
Ansells Mild, Bitter; Draught Bass Ⓗ
Small, one-roomed traditional pub. Often crowded – drink the mild and you'll know why. Good value food (not served Sun). ♨ ❀ ◑ ♣

Seven Stars
75 Birchfield Road, Headless Cross (off A441)
12–11
Ruddles Best Bitter, County; Webster's Yorkshire Bitter Ⓗ
Fine, proper pub in an area saturated by mediocrity: a bar area, a lounge and a games room. ❀ ♣ ◠

Ross-on-Wye

King Charles II
Broad Street
☎ (0989) 62039
11–11
Marston's Burton Best Bitter, Pedigree Ⓗ
Unusual pub in a town with many indifferent hostelries. The front locals' bar is a pub within a pub and contrasts with the neat lounge and eatery at the rear. No eve meals Sun. ♨ ◑ ▶ ⅙ ♣

St Owen's Cross

New Inn
At A4137/B4521 jct
☎ (0989) 87274
12–3, 6–11
Draught Bass; Courage Directors; Smiles Best Bitter Ⓗ**; guest beer**
16th-century pub on a remote crossroads. A number of bars with settles, benches and grand fireplaces offer a healthy balance of good food and locals' banter. Unusual pewter beer engines.
♨ ❀ ❀ ◑ ▶ ▲ P

Severn Stoke

Rose & Crown
On A38 ☎ (0905) 371249
11.30–2.30 (may extend summer), 6–11
Ansells Mild, Bitter; Ruddles Best Bitter Ⓗ
Attractive black and white pub on the village green, near the river (note flood levels). A huge log fire helps a cosy atmosphere in winter. Large garden. ♨ ⌘ ❀ ◑ ▶ ♣ P ✗

Shenstone

Plough
Off A450/A448 OS865735
11–3, 6.30–11

Batham Best Bitter, XXX H
A classic country pub. Since opening around 1840, there have been only eight licensees from four families. A large public bar, a small snug and a simple lounge. 🏚 Q ◑ ♣ P

Staunton on Wye

New Inn
Off A438 ☎ (098 17) 346
12–2 (not Mon in winter; 3 Sat), 7–11
S&N Theakston Best Bitter, XB (summer) H
Pleasing village pub that has come to life. A public bar having been reinstated, it now caters for all tastes. A good place for ramblers, with the Wye Valley hills and churches nearby. 🏚 ✿ ◑ ▮ ⌘ ♣ P

Stoke Works

Bowling Green
Shaw Lane (near M5 jct 5)
☎ (0527) 861291
11–11
Banks's Mild, Bitter E
Friendly three-roomer with plenty of conversation from the locals. A cosy snug with a wood-burning stove and TV adjoins the tiny public bar; an unfussy lounge. Bowling green. No food Mon eve or Sun. 🏚 ✿ ◑ ▮ ▲ ♣ P

Stourport-on-Severn

Hollybush Inn
54 Mitton Street
☎ (0299) 822569
12–3.30, 5.30–11 (11–11 Fri & Sat)
S&N Theakston Mild, XB, Old Peculier H
Friendly local recently refurbished. One main bar is split into three. Eve meals finish at 8pm. ⌘ ✿ ◑ ♣

Rising Sun
50 Lombard Street
☎ (0299) 822530
10.30–11
Banks's Mild, Bitter E
Small, friendly pub: an alcoved lounge and a small bar, plus a pleasant outside drinking area overlooking the canal. Meals Tue–Sat lunchtime and early eve. 🏚 ✿ ◑ ▮ ♣

Symonds Yat West

Olde Ferrie Inne
On River Wye at end of B4164
☎ (0600) 890232
11–3, 6–11 (11–11 Sat & summer)
Draught Bass; John Smith's Bitter H; guest beer
Riverside pub, popular with summer tourists, but always lively: a large bar with a basic games room, plus a restaurant. 🏚 ✿ 🛥 ◑ ▮ ♣ P

Ullingswick

Three Crowns
1½ miles from A417 (½ mile E of village) OS605497
☎ (0432) 820279
12–3 (4 Sat, not Tue), 7–11
Ansells Bitter; Ind Coope Burton Ale; Tetley Bitter H
Relaxing and friendly, isolated free house. The candlelit bar has many original features and divides into two distinct drinking areas. Good food (no meals Tue). 🏚 Q ✿ ◑ ▲ P

Uphampton

Fruiterers Arms
Uphampton Lane (off A449 at the Reindeer) OS839649
☎ (0905) 620305
12–2.30 (3 Sat), 7–11
Donnington BB; John Smith's Bitter; guest beer H
Rural pub just north of Ombersley. No meals Sun. 🏚 ✿ ◑ ▲ ♣ ⌂ P

Welland

Pheasant Inn
At A4104/B4208 jct
☎ (0684) 310400
Ansells Bitter; Ind Coope Burton Ale; Tetley Bitter H; guest beer
Roadside country pub with a spacious bar and a screened no-smoking eating area. The varied menu offers a wide range of daily specials; the large garden has an enclosed children's play area and a barbecue. 🏚 ✿ ◑ ▮ A P ✂

Whitney-on-Wye

Rhydspence Inn
On A438, 1½ miles W of village
☎ (0497) 831262
11–2.30, 7–11
Draught Bass; Marston's Pedigree; Robinson's Best Bitter H
Former drovers' inn lying across the Welsh border. With its many splendid original features, this pub successfully marries the 14th and 20th centuries. Genteel atmosphere; extensive wine selection and good food. Quoits. 🏚 Q ✿ 🛏 ◑ ▮ ⌘ ♣ ⌂ P

Woolhope

Crown Inn
☎ (0432) 860468
12–2.30, 7 (6.30 Fri, Sat & summer)–11 (12–2.30, 7–10.30 Sun)
Draught Bass; Hook Norton Best Bitter; Smiles Best Bitter H

Food-oriented country inn, but still with an area for drinkers. Typical of many Herefordshire rural inns: comfortable and relaxing. 🏚 ✿ ◑ ▮ ⌘ ⌂ P

Worcester

Brewery Tap
50 Lowesmoor
☎ (0905) 21540
11.30–11
Jolly Roger Quaff Ale, Severn Bore Special, Old Lowesmoor H; guest beers
Brew pub/brewery tap for Worcester's only brewery: a lively city-centre pub with a varied clientele. Frequent live music. Special occasion brews available. No food Sun. ◑ ⇌ (Foregate St/Shrub Hill) ⌂

Cardinals Hat
Friar Street
☎ (0905) 21890
11–11
Jolly Roger Ale, Shipwrecked H; guest beers
A comfortable, Jolly Roger brewery, multi-roomed pub – the oldest in Worcester (1518). Exposed beams and lots of oak panelling. Adjoins a jug and bottle shop and brewery. Food 12–6 (Mon–Sat) and 12–3 Sun (roast). 🏚 ◑ ▮ ⌘ ⇌ (Foregate St) ⌂

Crown & Anchor
233 Hylton Road
☎ (0905) 421481
12–2.30 (11.30–4.30 Sat), 7–11
Marston's Burton Best Bitter, Merrie Monk, Pedigree H
Unpretentious, friendly, roadside pub on the west bank of the Severn. Popular with students in the lounge, locals in the bar. The function room has its own bar and skittle alley. ✿ ◑ ⌘ ♣ ⌂

Lamb & Flag
The Tything
☎ (0905) 26894
10.30 (11 Sat)–2.30, 5.30 (6 Sat)–11
Marston's Burton Best Bitter, Pedigree H
Unspoilt, traditional, two-roomed, city-centre pub selling much draught Guinness. Friendly but smoky. ✿ ⌘ ⇌ (Foregate St) ♣

Virgin Tavern
Tolladine Road
☎ (0905) 23988
11–3, 5.30–11
Marston's Burton Best Bitter, Merrie Monk, Pedigree H
Friendly pub, a mile from the city centre, where the recent refurbishment is better than some. Good selection of food available. ◑ ▮ ♣ P

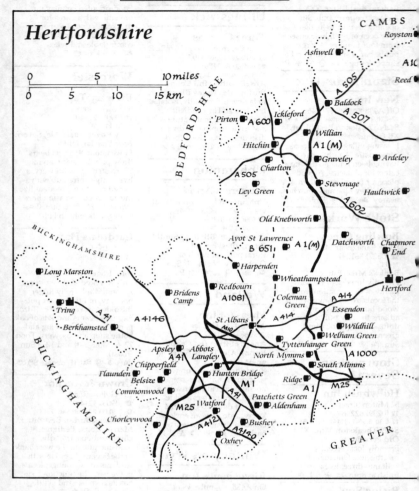

Hertfordshire

CAMBS

Royston

Ashwell

A10

Reed

Baldock

A 507

Ickleford

A 600

Pirton

Willian

A 1 (M)

Hitchin

Graveley

Ardeley

Charlton

A 505

Stevenage

Haultwick

Ley Green

A 602

Old Knebworth

Ayot St Lawrence

B 651

A 1 (M)

Datchworth

Chapmore End

Harpenden

Wheathampstead

Long Marston

Bridens Camp

Redbourn

A1081

Coleman Green

A 414

Hertford

Tring

A 41

A 4146

St Albans

M10

A 414

Essendon

Berkhamsted

Wildhill

Apsley

Abbots Langley

A 41

North Mymms

Welham Green

Tyttenhanger Green

A 1000

Chipperfield

Flaunden

Belsize

Commonwood

Hunton Bridge

South Mimms

M 1

Ridge

A 1

M 25

Patchetts Green

Chorleywood

M 25

Watford

A 41

Aldenham

A 412

Bushey

A 41 0

Oxhey

GREATER

BEDFORDSHIRE

BUCKINGHAMSHIRE

BUCKINGHAMSHIRE

Scale: 0 — 5 — 10 miles / 0 — 5 — 10 — 15 km

🏰 **McMullen**, Hertford; **Tring**, Tring

Abbots Langley

Compasses
95 Tibbs Hill Road
☎ (0923) 262870
11–11
**Courage Best Bitter,
Directors** Ⓗ; **guest beers**
Good range of guest beers in a
popular and comfortable pub.
A large malt whisky selection
too. Q ❀ ◑ ▶ & P

Aldenham

Roundbush
Near B462 ☎ (0923) 857165
11–3 (4 Sat), 5.30–11
**Ind Coope Benskins Best
Bitter, Burton Ale** Ⓗ

Genuine country pub circa
1800 with two distinctly
different bar areas catering for
all. Shove-ha'penny played.
🏚 ❀ ◑ ♣ P

Apsley

Albion
Durrants Hill Road
☎ (0442) 235116
11.30–3.30 (2.30 Tue–Thu), 5–11
**Adnams Bitter; Tetley
Bitter** Ⓗ
Split-level pub with a
comfortable but small saloon
and a public bar at street level.
Below, at canal level, is a small
bar, open May–Sept. A
traditional pub which has
escaped brewery

'improvements'. No food
winter weekends. Tiny car
park. ❀ ◑ ❶ ≥ P

Ardeley

Jolly Waggoner
(Off B1037, ½ mile from
village) OS310272
☎ (043 886) 350
11.30–3, 6–11
Greene King IPA, Abbot Ⓖ
Picturesque, 16th-century,
pink-washed former cottages
in a charming village setting.
Two small intimate bars; note
the impressive row of barrels
behind the counter.
Recommended food.
🏚 Q ❀ ◑ ▶ ❶ ♣ P

14th-century building housing a charming pub with a huge inglenook, excellent restaurant (no meals Sun or Mon eves) and enormous garden. Convenient for GB Shaw's house. 🏨 Q ❀ 🛏 ◖ ▶ 🚻 🅿 ♣ 🍺 P

Baldock

White Hart
21 Hitchin Street
☎ (0462) 893247
11–2.30 (3.30 Fri, 4 Sat), 5.30 (7 Sat)–11
Greene King XX Mild, IPA, Rayments Special, Abbot Ⓗ
Pleasant, one-bar pub with photographs of old Baldock around the walls. Concessions for OAPs on all real ales weekday lunchtime. A meeting place for the local church campanologists (without their bells). The darts area does not impose on the bar. A true drinkers' pub.
⇌ ♣ P

Barley

Chequers
London Road (B1368)
☎ (0763) 848378
12–2.30, 6–11
Greene King IPA, Abbot Ⓗ
Comfortable, one-bar, country pub with wood panelling, good food, a large garden and a petanque court.
🏨 ❀ ◖ ▶ ♣ P

Belsize

Plough
OS035009 ☎ (0923) 262800
11–3, 5.30–11
Greene King IPA; Ind Coope Benskins Best Bitter Ⓗ
Out-of-the-way pub, worth the effort to find. A locals' pub which is popular with horse riders and ramblers.
🏨 ❀ ◖ ♣ P

Berkhamsted

Boat
Gravel Path, Ravens Lane (off A41 by canal bridge)
☎ (0442) 877152
11–3, 5.30–11
Fuller's Chiswick, London Pride, Mr Harry, ESB Ⓗ
Large, modern canalside pub which is usually busy. Regular events held, from barbecues to live music. The pleasant patio has well-tended plants.
❀ ◖ ▶ ⇌ ♣ P

Rising Sun
George Street (canalside, by Lock 55) ☎ (0442) 864913
11–3, 6–11
Ind Coope Benskins Best Bitter Ⓗ
Friendly local facing the

Grand Union Canal. Families are welcome in the rear room, except when darts matches are played. Happy hour on weekdays and free draw Sun lunchtime. ❀ ◖ ▶ ⇌ ♣

Bishop's Stortford

Robin Hood
24 Hadham Road
☎ (027 965) 3271
11–3 (4 Sat), 5.30 (6 Sat)–11
Adnams Old; Ruddles Best Bitter, County Ⓗ**; guest beers**
A refurbished pub which has managed to maintain a cosy atmosphere. Popular children's room – one of the few in the area.
🧒 ❀ ◖ ▶ ⇌ P

Wheatsheaf
28 Northgate End
☎ (027 965) 6254
10.30–2.30 (3.30 Sat), 5.30–11
Greene King IPA, Rayments Special, Abbot Ⓗ
Pub whose landlord has a devoted following. Extensive wine and champagne selection; crisps and nuts are not for sale but free on the bar. Good value food. 🏨 ❀ ◖ ▶ P

Bridens Camp

Crown & Sceptre
Off A4146 at Water End
☎ (0442) 253250
11.30–3, 5.30 (6 Sat)–11
Greene King IPA, Rayments Special, Abbot Ⓗ
Fine old country pub with many low beams and horse brasses. The back room has a locals' public bar feel, while diners mingle with drinkers in the comfortable front bar. Don't trip over the sandwiches!
🏨 Q ❀ ◖ ▶ ♣ P

Buntingford

Crown
High Street ☎ (0763) 271422
12–3, 5.30–11
Banks & Taylor Shefford Bitter; Mauldons Squires; Ruddles Best Bitter, County Ⓗ**; guest beers**
Popular, small town pub with a function room. 🏨 🧒 ❀ ◖ ▶

Bushey

Swan
25 Park Road (off A411)
☎ (081) 950 2256
11–11
Ind Coope Benskins Best Bitter, Burton Ale Ⓗ
Small, convivial public bar in a Victorian terrace, unchanged and unspoilt, retaining a traditional atmosphere. 🏨 ♣

Ashwell

Rose & Crown
High Street
☎ (046 274) 2420
10.30–2.30, 6–11 (12–2, 7–10.30 Sun)
Greene King IPA, Abbot Ⓗ
Unspoilt, late 15th-century, timber-framed, village pub. Its excellent variety of wholesome home-made meals includes children's dishes.
🏨 Q ❀ ◖ ▶ ♣ P

Ayot St Lawrence

Brocket Arms
Shaws Corner OS196168
☎ (0438) 820250
11–2.30, 7–11
Adnams Extra; Greene King IPA, Abbot; Marston's Pedigree; Wadworth 6X Ⓗ**; guest beer**

Hertfordshire

Chapmore End

Woodman
30 Chapmore End (off B158)
OS328163 ☎ (092 046) 3143
12–3, 6–11
Greene King IPA, Abbot G
Unchanging drinking house in
a tiny village. Gardens at the
front and rear offer plenty for
children. Always a special
welcome from the landlord!
Note the magnificent pair of
antique bookends in the
public bar. 🏰 Q ❀ ◑ ♣ P

Charlton

Windmill
Charlton Road (1/2 mile from
A602 Hitchin bypass)
☎ (0462) 432096
10.30–2.30, 5.30–11
Adnams Broadside H;
Mansfield Riding Mild G;
Wells Eagle H
Refurbished pub with ducks
by the river and a resident
peacock. Has appeared in the
Guide 18 times, and has twice
been local CAMRA Pub of the
Year. ❀ ◑ ♣ P

Chipperfield

Royal Oak
1 The Street
12–2.30, 6 (6.30 Sat)–11 (12–2.30,
7–10.30 Sun)
**Adnams Bitter; Hook Norton
Best Bitter; Ind Coope Burton
Ale; Young's Special** H
Smart, tidy pub with a warm
welcome. Highly polished
wood abounds and there is an
ever-growing collection of
(empty!) matchboxes on one
side of the bar. Shut the Box
played. No food Sun.
🏰 Q ❀ ◑ ♣ ♠ P

Chorleywood

Black Horse
Dog Kennel Lane (off A404 W
of M25 jct 18) OS035961
☎ (0923) 287252
11–3, 5.30–11 (11–11 Thu–Sat
summer)
**Adnams Bitter; Ansells Mild;
Ind Coope Benskins Best
Bitter, Burton Ale** H
Pleasant pub in a fine location
on the edge of a common. One
bar is divided into several
drinking areas. Lunchtime
specials are often home-made;
buffets for groups can be
provided. NB: the sign looks
like a white horse! No food
Sun. 🏰 ❀ ◑ ▶ P

Old Shepherd
Chorleywood Bottom
☎ (0923) 282740
11–3, 5.30–11
**Ind Coope Benskins Best
Bitter; Tetley Bitter;
Wadworth 6X** H

Friendly pub with pleasant
views to the common. Good
food, including lunchtime
specials (no meals Wed eve).
🐌 ❀ ◑ ▶ ⇌ ⊖ ♣ P

Coleman Green

John Bunyan
Coleman Green Lane (1 mile
off B651) OS189128
☎ (058 283) 2037
11–2.30 (3 Sat), 6–11
McMullen AK, Country H
Isolated pub in a hamlet
where John Bunyan stayed
after his release from Bedford
Jail. Hundreds of jugs on
display. Good reasonably-
priced fast food (not served
Sun eve). Large garden with
plenty of room for children.
🏰 Q ❀ ◑ ▶ ⅙ ♣ P

Commonwood

Cart & Horses
Quickmoor Lane OS047005
☎ (092 77) 63763
11–3, 5.30–11
**Adnams Bitter; Ind Coope
Benskins Best Bitter** H; **guest
beer**
Difficult to find, near Sarratt,
this comfortable, friendly pub
is popular for its good value
food. The large garden can be
full in summer. 🏰 ❀ ◑ ▶ P

Datchworth

Plough
Datchworth Green (off A602, 2
miles from Watton) OS269182
☎ (0438) 813000
11.30–2.30 (3 Sat), 6–11
**Greene King XX Mild, IPA,
Abbot** H
Small village local with one
cosy bar. In this Guide 17
times. 🏰 Q ◑ P

Tilbury (Inn On The
Green)
Datchworth Green (off A602, 2
miles from Watton) OS269182
☎ (0438) 812496
11–3, 5 (6 Sat)–11
**Draught Bass; Fuller's
London Pride, ESB; Taylor
Best Bitter, Landlord** H; **guest
beers**
Friendly two-roomed pub
with a separate dining area.
The varied range of three–four
guest beers always includes a
mild. ❀ ◑ ▶ ⊟ ♣ P

Essendon

Candlestick
West End Lane (off B158)
OS262083 ☎ (0707) 261322
11–2.30, 5.30–11 (12–2.30, 7–10.30
Sun)
**Greene King Abbot;
McMullen AK, Country** H
Genuine, welcoming two-bar
pub, off the beaten track. The
landlord is a McMullen

Cellarman finalist and the food
is good as well (no lunches
Sun; book Tue–Fri eves). Over
200 candlesticks in the lounge
bar. 🏰 Q ❀ ◑ ▶ ⊟ ♣ P

Flaunden

Bricklayers Arms
Hogpits Bottom OS017013
☎ (0442) 833322
11–2.30, 6 (5.30
summer)–11
**Adnams Bitter; Brakspear
Bitter, Special; Fuller's
London Pride** H; **guest beers**
Much extended, often busy,
country pub which retains a
good pub atmosphere, despite
the many diners. The
restaurant area caters for all
ages (no meals Sun eve).
Always two guest beers.
🏰 Q ❀ ◑ ▶ P

Try also: Green Dragon (Free)

Graveley

George & Dragon
19 High Street (B197)
☎ (0438) 351362
11–3, 5–11 (11–11 Fri & Sat in
summer)
Greene King IPA, Abbot H
A Georgian façade on a one-
bar pub, known locally as
'Mad Mick's'. Cockney nights
Sat and live music Thu. Active
golf and clay pigeon clubs
(own shooting field). No food
Sun eve. Ask for the shove-
ha'penny; petanque also
played. ❀ ◑ ▶ ♣ P

Harpenden

Carpenters Arms
14 Cravells Road (off A1081)
11–3, 5.30–11
**Ruddles Best Bitter, County;
Webster's Yorkshire Bitter** H;
guest beer
Cosy, welcoming pub with a
fine collection of celebration
ales. Excellent menu (no meals
Sun or Mon eves).
🏰 Q ❀ ◑ ▶ ♣ P

Gibraltar Castle
70 Lower Luton Road
☎ (0582) 460005
11–3, 5.30–11 (11–11 Sat)
**Fuller's Chiswick, London
Pride, ESB** H
Sympathetically extended and
refurbished roadside inn.
Meals are always available
(including a vegetarian
choice). 🏰 ❀ ◑ ▶ ♣ P

Haultwick

Rest & Welcome
3 miles off A10, via Gt
Munden ☎ (0920) 438323
12–2, 6.30–11
McMullen AK, Country H
Not easy to find, a small, one-
bar pub with a friendly
welcome. 🏰 ❀ ◑ P

Hertford

Great Eastern Tavern
29 Railway Place
☎ (0992) 583570
11.30–2.30 (later summer), 6 (7 Sat)–11 (12–2.30, 7–10.30 Sun)
McMullen AK, Country Ⓗ
Welcoming local with many railway photos and prize-winning floral displays. Boasts a magnificent run of entries in this *Guide*. ◖ ⊟ ⇌ (East) ♣

Millstream
88 Port Vale
☎ (0992) 582755
11–3.30 (5 Sat), 5.30 (7 Sat)–11
Courage Directors; McMullen AK, Country Ⓗ
Laugh-a-minute local in the back streets of Hertford. The multi-named landlord has a wicked sense of humour. Ask him to sing his hit record! ❀ ⇌ (North) ♣ P

White Horse
33 Castle Street
☎ (0992) 550127
12–2.30, 5.30 (7 Sat)–11 (12–2.30, 7–10.30 Sun)
Greene King IPA; Marston's Border Exhibition, Pedigree Ⓗ**; guest beers**
A beer-drinkers' paradise, now catering for a wider market. Many guest beers on both gravity and handpumps, and various ciders.
🏚 Q ⊟ ⇌ (North) ↺

High Wych

Rising Sun
1 mile W of A1184, near Sawbridgeworth
☎ (0279) 724099
12–3, 5.30 (5 Fri & Sat)–11
Courage Best Bitter, Directors; guest beers (occasionally) Ⓖ
Unspoilt, no-frills local which fully deserves its *Guide* listing since 1975. In the same family for decades. A rare example of exclusively gravity dispense.
🏚 Q ⌕ ❀ ♣ ↺ P

Hitchin

Victoria
1 Ickleford Road
☎ (0462) 432682
12–3, 5.30–11
Greene King IPA, Rayments Special, Abbot Ⓗ
Friendly pub, recently tastefully refurbished. A haven for pub games teams. No food Sun. ❀ ◖▸ ⇌ ♣ P

Hoddesdon

Golden Lion
High Street ☎ (099 246) 3146
11–4, 5.30–11
Ind Coope Benskins Best Bitter; Tetley Bitter Ⓗ**; guest beers**

Old coaching inn with a genuine parlour bar. Meals Mon–Fri. 🏚 Q ❀ ◖⊟ ⅏ P

Hunton Bridge

Kings Head
Bridge Road (off A41 S of M25 jct 20) ☎ (0923) 262307
11–3, 5.30–11
Ind Coope Benskins Best Bitter, Burton Ale; Tetley Bitter Ⓗ**; guest beer**
Popular old pub whose large garden backs on to the canal. The old canal stables now house a skittle alley-cum-darts room-cum-children's area. A guest beer from the Allied range is normally available. No food Sun eve.
🏚 ⌕ ❀ ◖▸ ♣ P

Ickleford

Cricketers
107 Arlesey Road (off A600) OS185320 ☎ (0462) 432629
11–3, 5.30–11 (11–11 Sat & July–Dec)
Adnams Bitter; Taylor Landlord; Tetley Bitter; Wadworth 6X Ⓗ**; guest beers**
Lively, village ale house drawing custom from near and far. Specialises in beers from all over Britain, often as many as ten at one time; some gravity-dispensed but most on handpumps. Over 170 different beers during 1991. No food Sun. ❀ 🏚 ◖ ♣ ↺ P

Old George
Arlesey Road (off A600)
☎ (0462) 432269
11–3, 5.30–11 (11–11 Sat)
Greene King XX Mild, IPA, Rayments Special, Abbot Ⓗ
Very old country pub next to the village church. A warm and friendly lounge and a basic bar with very good food.
🏚 Q ❀ ◖⊟ ♣ P

Ley Green

Plough
Plough Lane (off A505, 2 miles S of Gt Offley) OS162243
☎ (0438) 871394
11.30–4, 6–11 (11–11 Fri & Sat)
Greene King IPA, Abbot Ⓗ
Friendly pub with wildlife prints on the wall. No food Sun. 🏚 Q ❀ ◖⊟ P

Long Marston

Boot
Station Road
☎ (0296) 662587
11–2.30, 5–11 (11–11 Sat)
Adnams Broadside; Hook Norton Best Bitter Ⓗ**; guest beers**
Pub totally rebuilt in the late 1940s after suffering severe bombing in WWII. As a result, the building is out of style with the surrounding area.

Two guest beers available. No-smoking restaurant.
🏚 ❀ ◖▸ ▲ ♣

Queens Head
Tring Road ☎ (0296) 668368
12–3, 5.30–11 (11–11 Sat)
Fuller's Chiswick, London Pride, Mr Harry, ESB Ⓗ
Thriving village pub which attracts locals and visitors alike. A newssheet, published monthly, features pub events and local news. Speciality curries offered every Thu night (no food Sun).
🏚 ⌕ ❀ ◖▸ ▲ ♣ P

Much Hadham

Bull Inn
High Street (2 miles S of A120)
☎ (027 984) 2668
11–3, 5.30–11 (11–11 Sat & summer)
Greene King IPA; Ind Coope Burton Ale; Tetley Bitter Ⓗ
Large, friendly old village pub with home-cooked meals always available (including vegetarian). Set in reputedly the most handsome village in Hertfordshire.
🏚 Q ❀ ◖▸ ⊟ ▲ ♣ P

North Mymms

Old Maypole
43 Warrengate Road, Water End (off B197) ☎ (0707) 42119
11–2.30, 5.30–11
Greene King IPA, Abbot Ⓗ
16th-century, split-level pub – mind your head. The family room doubles as the no-smoking area.
🏚 Q ⌕ ❀ ◖▸ P ⌀

Woodman
Warrengate Road, Water End (off B197) ☎ (0707) 50502
11–3, 5.30–11
Courage Directors; Marston's Pedigree; Wadworth 6X Ⓗ**; guest beers** (occasionally)
Old free house, popular with students from the local veterinary college. The house beer, Woodman's Best, is Courage. Q ❀ ◖ P

Old Knebworth

Lytton Arms
Park Lane (off B197)
☎ (0438) 812312
11–3, 5–11 (11–11 Fri & Sat)
Adnams Bitter; Banks & Taylor SOS; Draught Bass; S&N Theakston Best Bitter Ⓗ**; guest beers**
Very popular, large country pub near Knebworth Park. The varying range of up to eight guest beers always includes one mild; guest ciders and foreign bottled beers also available. Hitching post for horses in the car park. The three-legged cat is not Manx! 🏚 ❀ ◖▸ ↺ P

Hertfordshire

Oxhey

Villiers Arms
108 Villiers Road
☎ (0923) 221556
12–3.30, 5.30 (7 Sat)–11
Fuller's London Pride; Ind Coope Benskins Best Bitter Ⓗ
One-bar, street-corner local in a good drinking area. The landlord is into sport in a big way. Changes are likely under the new ownership. No food Sun. ❀ ◖ ⟁ (Bushey)

Patchetts Green

Three Compasses
Hillfield Lane (½ mile off B462 near B462/A41 jct)
☎ (0923) 856197
11–3, 5.30–11 (11 Fri & Sat)
Greene King IPA; Ind Coope Benskins Best Bitter, Burton Ale; Tetley Bitter Ⓗ**; guest beers**
Deceptively large pub in rural surroundings where the conservatory doubles as an eating area (no food Sun eve). Excellent children's facilities. Note the display of carpenter's tools. ➷ ❀ ◖ ▮ P

Pirton

Cat & Fiddle
7 Great Green (off main road)
OS146316 ☎ (0462) 712245
11.30–2.30, 5.30–11
Adnams Broadside; Wells Eagle Ⓗ
Beamed village pub on the green. The drinking area is divided by ornate wrought ironwork. Always a friendly welcome. ▦ ❀ ◖ ▮

Redbourn

Cricketers
East Common ☎ (0582) 792410
11–2.30, 5.30–11
Draught Bass; Charrington IPA; Welsh Brewers Worthington BB Ⓗ
Recently converted to a free house, this friendly pub has a parrot-in-residence in the lounge bar, and a spacious public bar. Food available (including vegetarian) all week, except Sun lunch.
Q ◖ ▮ ❦ ⬥ ✦ P

Reed

Cabinet
High Street (off A10 opp. transport café, first right, first left) OS364361
☎ (0763) 848366
11–3, 6–11
Adnams Bitter, Old; Banks & Taylor Shefford Mild, Shefford Bitter; Bateman XXXB; Greene King IPA Ⓗ
Cosy, weatherboarded village pub with a large garden;

difficult to find. The beer range can vary.
▦ ❀ ◖ ▮ ✦ P

Ridge

Old Guinea
Crossoaks Lane OS215004
☎ (0707) 42126
11–3, 6–11 (11–11 Sat)
Ind Coope Benskins Best Bitter, Burton Ale Ⓗ**; guest beers**
Restaurant/pub in rural surroundings; the garden overlooks green belt farmland. Regular guest beers.
▦ Q ❀ ◖ ▮ ❦ ⌂ P

Royston

Coach & Horses
Kneesworth Street
☎ (0763) 242299
11.25–2.30, 5.30 (7 Sat)–11
Ind Coope Benskins Best Bitter, Burton Ale; Tetley Bitter; Young's Special Ⓗ
Very hospitable and popular, 17th-century, town-centre inn at the crossing of the Roman roads Ermine Street and Icknield Way. The landlord is a Burton *Master Cellarman*.
❀ ◖ ⟁

St Albans

Blue Anchor
145 Fishpool Street
☎ (0727) 55038
11–3, 5.30 (6 Sat)–11 (11–11 summer)
McMullen AK, Country Ⓗ
Friendly two-bar pub, handy for Verulamium Park, the Roman Museum and the watermill. The cheapest pub in St Albans. No food Sun eve.
▦ Q ❀ ◖ ▮ ▯ ✦ P

Camp
Camp Road ☎ (0727) 51062
11–3, 6–11
McMullen AK, Country Ⓗ
Large, friendly, revamped estate pub serving an area of the city known as the 'Camp'. Landlord is a three-times winner of McMullen's *Master Cellarman* award. ❀ ◖ ▯

Farriers Arms
Lower Dagnall Street (off A5183) ☎ (0727) 51025
11–2.30, 5.30–11
Courage Directors; McMullen AK, Country Ⓗ
Perennial entry in the *Guide*: a thriving local, basically unchanged for years. Good for games; no food Sun. Q ◖ ✦

Garibaldi
61 Albert Street (off Holywell Hill) ☎ (0727) 55046
11–3, 5–11 (11–11 Fri & Sat)
Fuller's Chiswick, London Pride, ESB Ⓗ
Popular pub in a quiet side street: a central bar and

separate food servery, offering good value snacks and meals (not served Sat or Sun eves). ❀ ◖ ▮ ⟁ (Abbey) ✦ ✁

Lower Red Lion
34–36 Fishpool Street
☎ (0727) 55669
11–2.30 (3 Fri & Sat), 5.30–11
Adnams Bitter; Fuller's London Pride; Greene King IPA, Abbot Ⓗ**; guest beer**
Two comfortable bars in a 17th-century pub – a welcome refuge from the noise and traffic of modern St Albans and one of 72 listed buildings in the street. No food Sun.
▦ Q ❀ ⌖ ◖ P

Sawbridgeworth

King William IV
7 Vantorts Road
☎ (027 972) 2322
11–11
Courage Best Bitter, Directors Ⓗ
17th-century coaching inn set back off the main street.
▦ Q ❀ ◖ ▮ ⟁

Try also: **Gate** (Whitbread)

South Mimms

Black Horse
65 Blackhorse Lane (just off B556) ☎ (0707) 42174
11–3, 5.30–11
Greene King IPA, Abbot Ⓗ
Classic public bar with a thriving darts team; cosy saloon with a horsey theme. No food weekends. ▦ ❀ ◖ P

Stevenage

Two Diamonds
19 High Street, Old Town
☎ (0438) 354527
11–2.30 (3 Fri & Sat), 6 (5.30 Fri, 7 Sat)–11
McMullen AK, Country, Stronghart Ⓗ
Pub taking its name from the original owners. Recently modernised to a very high standard, but not distracting from the original building which still upholds all the traditional requirements of a good boozer. Q ❀ ◖ ✦

Try also: **Marquis of Lorne**, High St (Greene King)

Tring

Kings Arms
King Street (near Natural History Museum)
☎ (044 282) 3318
11.30–2.30, 7–11
Brakspear Special; Fuller's ESB; Wadworth 6X; Wells Eagle Ⓗ**; guest beer**
Hard to find, but impossible to miss, this excellent back-street local offers an ever-changing range of ales. Home-

made food always available.
No-smoking room at
lunchtime only.
🔥 Q ❀ ◖ ♣ ✄

Tyttenhanger Green

Plough
Off A414, via Highfield Lane
OS182059 ☎ (0727) 57777
11.30–2.30 (3 Sat), 6–11 (12–2.30,
7–10.30 Sun)
**Fuller's London Pride;
Greene King Abbot; Hook
Norton Best Bitter; Marston's
Pedigree; S&N Theakston
Best Bitter; Wadworth 6X** Ⓗ
Popular free house in a small
hamlet offering ten real ales.
The landlord is a keen
marathon runner and beer
bottle collector – 1200 on
display. Good value lunches
(not served Sun). Local
CAMRA *Pub of the Year* 1991.
🔥 ❀ ◖ ♣

Ware

New Rose & Crown
35 Watton Road
☎ (0920) 462572
11.30–2.30, 5.30–11 (11–11 Fri & Sat)
**Greene King XX Mild, IPA,
Rayments Special, Abbot** Ⓗ
Pub with an attractive exterior
but an unsympathetically
modernised, 'over-pined'
interior. Nevertheless, great
efforts have been made to
maintain a cosy atmosphere.
The only pub locally to serve
all four Greene King cask ales.
◖ ⇌ ♣

Wareside

Chequers
On B1004, Ware–Much
Hadham road ☎ (0920) 467010
12–2.30, 6–11
**Adnams Bitter; Bateman XB;
Nethergate Old Growler;
Wadworth 6X; Whitbread
Flowers Original; Young's
Special** Ⓗ**; guest beer**

Cottage pub with a friendly,
village atmosphere. Excellent
home-cooked food (not served
Sun eve). The strong guest
beer varies. Local CAMRA
Pub of the Year 1992.
🔥 Q ⇆ ◖ ⊞ ⚠ ♣ P

Try also: White Horse
(Greene King)

Watford

Nascot Arms
11 Stamford Road (400 yds
from station) ☎ (0923) 231336
11–3, 5.30–11 (11–11 Sat)
**Greene King XX Mild, IPA,
Rayments Special, Abbot** Ⓗ**,
Winter Ale** Ⓖ
Two-bar, street-corner pub
which can get crowded. No
jukebox; piped music varies
from night to night. A covered
area is usually available for
children (a bit chilly in
winter). Chess played. Voted
local CAMRA *Pub of the Year*
1992. No meals Sun.
❀ ◖ ⇌ (Junction)

White Lion
79 St Albans Road (A412)
☎ (0923) 223442
11–3, 5 (7 Sat)–11
**Courage Best Bitter,
Directors; Wadworth 6X** Ⓗ
Busy two-bar pub with a basic
public and a comfortable
saloon. Pub games are
popular. No food Sun.
❀ ◖ ⊞ ⇌ (Junction) ♣

Welham Green

Hope & Anchor
Station Road ☎ (0707) 262935
11–2.30 (3 Sat), 5.30 (6 Sat)–11
**Courage Best Bitter,
Directors; John Smith's
Bitter** Ⓗ
Genuine two-bar pub dating
back to the 19th century. Note
the display of scissored ties in
the saloon bar. The large
award-winning garden has a
children's play area. No food
Sun. Q ❀ ◖ ⊞ ⚲ ⇌ ♣ P

Wheathampstead

Nelson
Marford Road
☎ (0582) 832196
11–3, 5 (6 Sat)–11
**Draught Bass; Brakspear
Special; Fuller's London
Pride, ESB; S&N Theakston
Best Bitter, Old Peculier;
Whitbread Boddingtons
Bitter; Young's Special; guest
beers** Ⓗ
Single-bar pub broken up by a
central open fire. There is a 50-
ft illuminated well behind the
bar. Reasonably priced, home-
cooked meals served, except
Sun. Ten handpumps.
🔥 Q ❀ ⇆ ◖ ◗ P

Wildhill

Woodman
45 Wildhill Lane (between
B158 and B1000) OS263068
☎ (0707) 42618
11.30–2.30, 5.30–11 (12–2, 7–10.30
Sun)
**Greene King IPA, Abbot;
McMullen AK** Ⓗ
Genuine classless local. The
cost of a round is well below
the Hertfordshire average.
Check that Spurs and Barnet
have not lost before talking to
the landlord about football.
Chip-free meals (not served
Sun). Q ❀ ◖ ♣ P

Willian

Three Horseshoes
Baldock Lane (opp. church, up
tiny side lane) OS224307
☎ (0462) 685713
11–11
**Greene King IPA, Rayments
Special, Abbot** Ⓗ
Cosy, one-roomed country
pub attracting a wide cross-
section of clientele – contract
bridge players wanted! Home-
cooked lunches (not served
Sun). Park carefully in the
lane. Same landlord for 22
years. 🔥 Q ◖ ♣

The Symbols

🔥   real fire

Q   quiet pub (at least one bar)

⮝   indoor room for children

❀   garden or other outdoor
    drinking area

⇆   accommodation

◖   lunchtime meals

◗   evening meals

⊞   public bar

 ♿ easy wheelchair access

⚠   camping facilities at the pub
    or nearby

⇌   near British Rail station

⊖   near underground station

♣   pub games

⟠   real cider

P   pub car park

✄   no-smoking room or area

Humberside

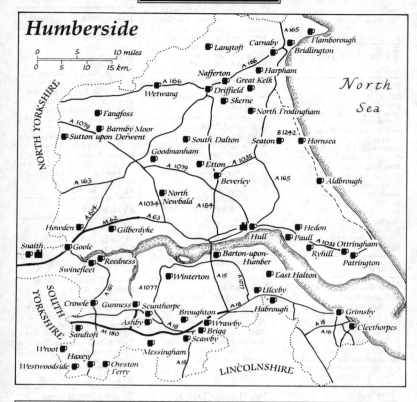

Aldbrough

George & Dragon
1 High Street (B1242)
☎ (0964) 527230
12–3, 7–11 (12–11 Sat)
S&N Theakston Best Bitter, XB; Younger Scotch Ⓗ
Welcoming renovated inn, nearly 500 years-old. Popular with visitors for its good quality food in both bar and restaurant. Accommodation available in adjoining cottages.
🏨 ❀ 🏠 ◑ ▶ 🍴 ⌂ ▲ P

Ashby

Crown Hotel
209 Ashby High Street
☎ (0724) 840889
11–11
Mansfield Riding Bitter, Old Baily Ⓗ
Former basic John Smith's pub, refurbished since its take-over by Mansfield, but retaining a drinkers' atmosphere. Large lounge and a separate public bar. Quiz nights and live music are popular, but beware karaoke Fri and Sun eves! ◑ 🍴 ♣ P

Try also: Open Hearth, Warley Rd (Samuel Smith)

Barmby Moor

Boot & Slipper
St Helens Square
☎ (0759) 303328
12–4, 7–11 (12–11 Sat)
S&N Theakston Best Bitter, XB, Old Peculier; Younger Scotch Ⓗ
Friendly village pub which started life as a cobbler's shop. The lounge bar leads to a games room with a pool table. The menu is unique – bread made in the shape of a boot with a choice of fillings (meals Thu–Sun). Hosts an annual feast and fair in mid July.
❀ ◑ ▶ P

Barton-upon-Humber

Volunteer Arms
13 Whitecross Street (off A1077) ☎ (0652) 32309
11–3, 6.45–11
Burtonwood Mild, Bitter Ⓗ
Pleasant two-roomed pub. On-street parking across the road. 🏨 Q ◑ 🍴 ⇌

Wheatsheaf
Holydyke ☎ (0652) 33175
11–3, 6.45–11
Wards Mild, Sheffield Best Bitter Ⓗ
Fine old pub with a lounge bar and separate snug. Weekday lunches. Q ❀ ◑ ⇌ P

Beverley

Queens Head
Wednesday Market
☎ (0482) 867363
11–3, 7–11 (11–11 Fri & Sat)
Wards Thorne Best Bitter Ⓗ; **guest beer**
Old refurbished pub with an extended rear room. The front bar retains a degree of character. Attractive Tudor-style frontage with a bow window overlooking Beverley's smaller market place. ❀ ◑ ▶ 🍴 ⇌

Rose & Crown
North Bar Without
☎ (0482) 862532
11–3, 6–11
Wards Mild, Thorne Best Bitter, Sheffield Best Bitter, Kirby H; **guest beers**
Prominently situated next to the North Bar – the nearest pub to Beverley Racecourse. Also handy for Beverley Westwood, a large area of common land. Comfortable, friendly atmosphere and good food. ❀ ◖ ▶ ♣ P

Royal Standard
30 North Bar Within
☎ (0482) 882434
11.30–2.30 (not Mon; 11–4 Fri & Sat), 7–11
Wards Mild, Thorne Best Bitter H
Small two-roomed town local next to Beverley's historic North Bar. The front bar is a traditional gem with a sports-oriented atmosphere. Handy for the racecourse and popular with rugby club members.
Q ❀ ◖

White Horse Inn (Nellie's)
22 Hengate ☎ (0482) 861973
11–11
Samuel Smith OBB, Museum H
Traditional pub with many gas-lit rooms, stone-flagged floors, Victorian pictures, huge mirrors, iron ranges and an ancient gas cooker. Folk and jazz music nights held upstairs. A must for visitors; usually very busy.
🚲 Q ❀ ◖ ◘ ♣ P

Woolpack Inn
37 Westwood Road (near Westwood Hospital)
☎ (0482) 867095
11.30–2.30, 7–11
Burtonwood Mild, Bitter H
Small, traditional local tucked away in a residential area close to Beverley Westwood. Collection of photographs and details of previous landlords and owners in the small snug area. ❀ ◖

Bridlington

Hilderthorpe Hotel
Hilderthorpe Road
☎ (0262) 672205
11–11
Bass Mild XXXX, Draught Bass; Stones Best Bitter H
Basic local, popular with fishermen; a dominoes pub. Straightforward but good meals in summer.
🚲 ❀ ◖ ◘ ◘ ♣

Kings Arms
King Street ☎ (0262) 673391
11–2.30, 6.30–11 (11–11 Fri & Sat)
Tetley Mild, Bitter H
Traditional drinkers' pub with

a classic corridor layout and a family room upstairs.
❀ ◖ ♣

Old Ship Inn
90 St John's Street
☎ (0262) 670466
11–4, 7–11
Hull Mild; Wards Thorne Best Bitter H
Thriving local by the old town with a good traditional atmosphere. Facilities for children include a covered outdoor play area. Dominoes a speciality. 🚲 ◖ ❀ ◖ ♣

Brigg

Queens Arms Hotel
Wrawby Street (A15/A18)
☎ (0652) 653174
11–3, 6.30–11 (11–11 Sat)
Bass Mild XXXX, Draught Bass; Welsh Brewers Worthington BB H; **guest beers**
Pleasant, open-plan lounge bar, where quizzes alternate with jazz on Tue eve. Good value meals (not served Sun/Mon eves). Children welcome in the dining area.
🍴 ◖ ▶ ♣

Try also: Brocklesby Ox (Burtonwood)

Broughton

Red Lion
High Street (B1207)
☎ (0652) 652560
11–3, 6–11 (11–11 Fri & Sat)
Mansfield Riding Mild, Riding Bitter, Old Baily H
Smart, unaltered pub with a small bar, medium-sized lounge/dining room and a large games room. Specialises in good value home-cooked meals (book Sun lunch). No food Sun eve or Mon. Own bowling green.
Q ❀ ◖ ◘ ◘ ♣ P

Carnaby

Ferns Farm Hotel
☎ (0262) 678951
11–3, 6–11
S&N Matthew Brown Mild, Theakston Old Peculier; John Smith's Bitter; Younger Scotch, No. 3 H
Popular hotel complex, often very busy with diners and travellers relaxing from the A166.
🚲 ❀ 🍴 ◖ ▶ ▲ ⇌ ♣ P

Cleethorpes

Crows Nest
Balmoral Road
☎ (0472) 698867
11.30–3.30 (4 Sat), 6.30 (7 Sat)–11
Samuel Smith OBB H
Pleasant, three-roomed estate pub with good value bed and

breakfast available. Bar snacks or full lunches on request.
Q ⇌ ❀ 🍴 ◖ ♣ P

Willys
17 High Cliff Road
☎ (0472) 602145
11–11
Bateman Mild, XB; Willys Original H; **guest beers**
Deservedly popular brew pub, attracting a cosmopolitan clientele; very busy at weekends. Three guest beers, although one may be replaced by a beer from the Willys range. The brewery may be viewed. ◖

Try also: Smugglers, High Cliff (Free)

Crowle

White Hart Hotel
96 High Street
☎ (0724) 710333
11.30–3, 7–11
Courage Directors; John Smith's Bitter H
Reputed to be the oldest pub on the Isle of Axholme: a wealth of beams and panelling. Excellent good value food. ❀ ◖ ▶ P

Try also: River Don, Eastoft (Free)

Driffield

Old Falcon
57 Market Place
☎ (0377) 241021
11–3, 7–11 (11–11 Thu–Sat)
Hull Mild; Ind Coope Burton Ale; Tetley Bitter H
Old coaching house retaining some character. Cosy seating area and a small bar. Quiet atmosphere; popular with locals. ◖ ⇌ ♣ P

East Halton

Black Bull
Townside ☎ (0469) 540207
11.30–3, 5–11 (11–11 Fri & Sat)
Bass Mild XXXX, Draught Bass; Stones Best Bitter H
Very popular village local: a good-sized bar and a comfortable lounge. Above average, good value meals.
Q ❀ ◖ ▶ ◘ ♣ P

Etton

Light Dragoon
Main Street (½ mile off B1248)
☎ (0430) 810282
12–2.30 (3 Fri & Sat), 7–11
Younger IPA, No. 3 H
18th-century pub in a fine estate village serving mainly food and passing trades. The public bar (not always open) retains a local pub feel. A folk club (first Tue of each month) features top acts.
🚲 ❀ ◖ ▶ ◘ ♣ P

Humberside

Fangfoss

Carpenters Arms
Wilberfoss (main
Pocklington–Full Sutton road)
☎ (075 96) 222
11.30–3.30, 6–11
John Smith's Bitter Ⓗ
Busy, comfortable and
welcoming country pub. Eve
meals Tue–Sat; half portions
for children.
🏠 Q ✿ ◑ ▶ A P

Flamborough

Royal Dog & Duck
Dog & Duck Square
☎ (0262) 850206
11–4, 6.30–11 (11–11 Fri)
**Bass Mild XXXX, Draught
Bass; Stones Best Bitter** Ⓗ
Old, village-centre pub with
beams, bric-a-brac and a
comfortable atmosphere.
Good meals (including local
specialities) are served.
Separate dining room.
🏠 ⚘ ✿ ◑ ▶ 🕮 A ♣ P

Try also: Rose & Crown
(Camerons)

Gilberdyke

Rose & Crown
Hull Road, Eastrington (B1230
at Slipper Bridge, 1 mile W of
Gilberdyke) ☎ (0430) 440048
11–11
**S&N Theakston XB; John
Smith's Bitter; Younger
Scotch, IPA** Ⓗ
Black and white, mock Tudor
building set back off the
former main Selby to Hull
road. Recently refurbished to a
high quality with a carvery
and restaurant (book Sun
lunch). Friendly and
welcoming. 🏠 Q ◑ ▶ 🕭 ♣ P

Goodmanham

Goodmanham Arms
Main Street ☎ (0430) 872379
12–3 (Sat & summer Fri only), 7–11
**Old Mill Bitter; S&N
Theakston Best Bitter** Ⓗ
Unspoilt village local opposite
a Norman church on the
Wolds Way long distance
footpath. The front room is
used by locals; families
welcomed. Fresh sandwiches
to order. 🏠 Q ✿ ▣ ♣ P

Goole

Woodlands
Rutland Road ☎ (0405) 762738
11–11
John Smith's Bitter Ⓗ
Three-roomed pub on a
housing estate. The snug is
quiet. 🏠 Q ◑ ▶ ▣ ♣ P

Try also: Vikings, Western Rd
(Bass)

Great Kelk

Chestnut Horse
Main Street (between
A165/B1249/A166) OS105583
☎ (026 288) 263
11–3, 6–11 (12–2.30, 7–11 winter)
**Draught Bass; John Smith's
Bitter; Stones Best Bitter** Ⓗ
Homely former coaching inn,
dating from 1793, in a small
village. Excellent value meals
every day. Children catered
for by arrangement.
🏠 Q ✿ ◑ ▶ ▣ ♣ P

Grimsby

Angel
175 Freeman Street
☎ (0472) 342402
11–11
**S&N Matthew Brown Mild;
Younger Scotch, IPA, No. 3** Ⓗ
Busy corner pub with a quiet
back room.
Q ▣ ⇌ (Docks) ♣ P

Corporation
88 Freeman Street
☎ (0472) 356651
11–11
**Bass Mild XXXX, Draught
Bass** Ⓗ
Busy three-roomed pub
offering darts and dominoes
in the bar; also a comfortable
snug and lounge. Note the
board giving details of a local
murder uncovered during a
recent refurbishment. ◑ ▣
⇌ (Docks) ♣

Hainton Inn
Weelsby Road
☎ (0472) 341767
11–3, 6–11 (11–11 Sat)
Bass Mild XXXX Ⓔ; **Draught
Bass** Ⓗ; **Stones Best Bitter** Ⓔ
Large estate pub on a busy
main road; restaurant
attached. Live music most
weekends. Q ✿ ◑ ▣ ♣ P

Hope & Anchor
148 Victoria Street
☎ (0472) 342565
11–11
**Ind Coope Burton Ale; Tetley
Mild, Bitter** Ⓗ; **guest beers**
Early 19th-century pub, close
to the town centre and
attracting a varied clientele.
Recent refurbishment has
retained much of its character.
Noted for its friendly
atmosphere and good value
meals (not served Sun). Four
guest beers normally
available.
✿ ◑ ▣ ⇌ (Town) ♣

Palace Buffet
Victoria Street
☎ (0472) 342837
**Bass Mild XXXX, Draught
Bass; Stones Best Bitter** Ⓗ;
guest beers
Built in 1904 in typical
Edwardian style, as the bar for
the now-demolished Palace
Theatre. Tiling on the car park
wall marks the site. The
modern interior retains some
character. Close to the
National Fishing Heritage
Centre. ✿ ◑ ▣ ♣ P

Swigs
21 Osborne Street
☎ (0472) 354773
11–11 (closed Sun lunch)
**Bateman XB; Willys
Original** Ⓗ; **guest beers**
Narrow town-centre bar in the
style of a continental café. The
emphasis is on food at
lunchtime, switching towards
a younger clientele in the
evening. Can be extremely
busy at weekends (no food
Sun). The second permanent
outlet for Willys' Cleethorpes-
brewed ales. ◑ ⇌ (Town) ⌂

Try also: White Knight,
Freeman Way (Tetley)

Gunness

Jolly Sailor
Station Road (A18)
☎ (0724) 782423
11–3, 5–11 (11–11 Sat)
**Ind Coope Burton Ale; Tetley
Bitter** Ⓗ; **guest beer**
1930s pub, renovated whilst
retaining the original style.
Friendly licensees and
reasonably priced guest beers.
Games in the public bar.
Function room.
🏠 ▣ ⇌ (Althorpe) ♣ P

Habrough

Horse & Hounds
Station Road (B1210)
☎ (0469) 576940
11–11 (may close 3–7)
**S&N Theakston Mild, XB,
Old Peculier; Younger IPA,
No. 3** Ⓗ
Tastefully converted former
farmhouse/rectory adjoining
the Habrough Hotel. Beer at
reasonable prices and
excellent pub food. Popular
quiz night Tue. The hotel is
renowned for its restaurant.
Good local trade.
🏠 ✿ ◑ ▶ ▣ 🕭 ⇌ P

Harpham

St Quintin Arms
☎ (026 289) 329
11.30–2.30, 6–11
**Courage Directors; John
Smith's Bitter** Ⓗ
Community pub at the heart
of a small village just off the
A166. One bar serves several
rooms. No food Mon.
🏠 ✿ ◑ ▶ P

Haxey

Loco
Church Street ☎ (0427) 752879

7–11
John Smith's Bitter, Magnet Ⓗ
Former village Co-op and fish shop, with a prominent railway theme. Memorabilia includes an engine smokebox – a museum within a pub.
🏠 ⛵ ♣

Hedon

Shakespeare Inn

9 Baxtergate ☎ (0482) 898371
11–11
Vaux Samson; Wards Mild, Thorne Best Bitter, Sheffield Best Bitter, Kirby Ⓗ
Popular and cosy, friendly one-roomer featuring a collection of breweriana and artefacts, plus Hedon memorabilia. Over 3000 beer mats adorn the ceiling. Real freshly squeezed orange juice from a Dutch fruit press available. 🏠 ❀ ◐ ♣ P

Hornsea

Alexandra

Railway Street
☎ (0964) 532710
11.30–3 (4 Fri), 6–11 (11–11 Sat)
Hull Mild; John Smith's Bitter, Magnet Ⓗ
Former station hotel which has lost its top floor over the years. Popular with locals and visitors, with many different rooms and areas, including a bar, lounge, and pool room.
◐ ⊞

Howden

Wheatsheaf

83 Hailgate ☎ (0430) 430772
11–11
Ruddles Best Bitter; John Smith's Bitter Ⓗ
Traditional one-roomed public house close to the centre of Howden. Welcoming atmosphere; popular with locals. Gaming facilities and an area for families. Book for eve meals. ❀ ◗ ♣

Try also: Minster View (Free)

Hull

Bay Horse

113 Wincolmlee (400 yds N of North Bridge, W side of river)
☎ (0482) 29227
11–11
Bateman Mild, XB, XXXB, Victory Ⓗ
Bateman's only tied house north of the Humber. The splendid lounge extension has lots of headroom while the bar is small and friendly with a good mix of customers. Special WC for wheelchairs. Hull CAMRA *Pub of the Year* 1992. Book for Sun lunch.
🏠 ◐ ◗ ⊞ ♿ ♣ P

Duke of Wellington

104 Peel Street (N of Spring Bank to NW of centre)
☎ (0482) 29603
12–3, 6–11 (11–11 Sat)
Hull Mild; Taylor Landlord; Tetley Bitter Ⓗ**; guest beers**
Back-street, re-styled Victorian corner local, popular with locals and students and often crowded. Three, usually strong, guest beers. ❀ ♿ ♣ P

East Riding

37 Cannon Street (left at end of Norfolk St)
☎ (0482) 29134
12–4.30, 6.30–11
Tetley Mild, Bitter Ⓗ
Small, street-corner, two-roomed industrial pub. The no-nonsense bar features rugby league memorabilia, whilst the cosy lounge is wood-panelled. Hull CAMRA *Pub of the Year* 1990. ⊞ ♣

George Hotel

Land of Green Ginger
☎ (0482) 226373
11–11 (11–3.30, 7–11 Sat)
Bass Mild XXXX, Draught Bass Ⓗ
Historic former coaching inn with wood-panelled walls and bare flooring providing a convivial, warm atmosphere. Note the smallest window in Hull at the side of the archway, dating from coaching days. Upstairs restaurant (closed Sun). ◐

Grapes Inn

Sykes Street
☎ (0482) 24424
12–3, 7–11
Ind Coope Burton Ale; Tetley Mild, Bitter Ⓗ
Friendly local just off the northern section of the central orbital road, near the Registry Office. Live music. Very popular with darts players.
🏠 ◐ ♣

Oberon Hotel

Queen Street
☎ (0482) 24886
11–3, 5.30–11
Bass Mild XXXX, Draught Bass Ⓗ
Traditional, basic, two-roomed pub close to the pier and marina. Decorated with nautical memorabilia and frequented by Humber pilots.
Q ⊞ ♣

Old Blue Bell

Market Place, Old Town
☎ (0482) 24382
11–3, 7–11
Samuel Smith OBB, Museum Ⓗ
Famous pub in the old town, with the original layout of snug, corridor and long narrow bar; pool room upstairs. A recently extended paved area at the back connects to the indoor market. Large collection of bells – count them if you can.
⛵ ❀ ◐ ⊞ ♣

Old English Gentleman

Mason Street ☎ (0482) 24659
11.30–3, 5–11
Mansfield Riding Mild, Bitter Ⓗ
Refurbished Georgian pub closely connected to Hull's largest theatre a few yards away. Dark wood panels, signed photos of artistes, and a huge collection of whiskies adorn this likeable pub.
Q ❀ ◐ ◗ ⇌ ♣

Olde White Harte

25 Silver Street, Old Town
☎ (0482) 26363
11–11
S&N Theakston XB, Old Peculier; Younger IPA, No. 3 Ⓗ
Superb courtyard pub with lots of dark timber, stained-glass, and two sit-in fireplaces. A central staircase leads to the restaurant in the Plotters Parlour, scene of the Civil War meeting which refused King Charles entry to the city. Varied lunch menu.
🏠 Q ❀ ◐ ♣

Plimsoll's Ship Hotel

103 Witham
☎ (0482) 25995
11–3, 7–11
Hull Mild, Bitter; Tetley Bitter Ⓗ
Old pub with one small, long room traditionally decorated in wood and brick with lots of bric-a-brac. On the outskirts of the city centre, just across North Bridge, it can be very crowded on Fri and Sat nights.
◐ ♣

Sailmakers Arms

Chandlers Court, High Street, Old Town ☎ (0482) 227437
11–3, 6–11 (11–11 summer)
Hull Mild; Taylor Landlord Ⓗ
Converted from a former ship's chandler's, this one-roomed pub has a friendly atmosphere and comfortable furnishings. The courtyard effectively doubles the pub's capacity in summer. ❀ ◐ ♣

Station Inn

202 Beverley Road (A1079, 3/4 mile from centre)
☎ (0482) 41482
11–11
Tetley Mild, Bitter Ⓗ
Unspoilt, mock Tudor-style, two-roomed pub next to a former railway crossing on the Hull–Hornsea and Withernsea line. A busy bar, alive with dominoes, darts and conversation is balanced by a quieter, comfortable lounge.
🏠 ◐ ⊞ ♣

Humberside

Whalebone Inn

165 Wincolmlee (between
Scott St and Sculcoates
Bridges, W of river)
☎ (0482) 27980
11–3, 6–11 (11–11 Fri & Sat)
Tetley Mild, Bitter Ⓗ
Popular, no-frills, friendly
local in an industrial area
deriving its name from the
city's former whaling
industry. ♣

Langtoft

Ship Inn

Front Street ☎ (0377) 87243
12–3, 7–11 (midnight supper licence)
Camerons Bitter Ⓗ
Cosy, friendly village local
with a reputation for good
food. Children welcome in the
pool room and restaurant.
🏚 ❀ ④ ◗ 🍴 ♣ P

Messingham

Bird in the Barley

Northfield Road
☎ (0724) 762994
11–3 (not Mon), 5–11
**Ruddles Best Bitter, County;
John Smith's Bitter;
Webster's Yorkshire Bitter** Ⓗ;
guest beer
Smart, one-roomed pub on the
Messingham–Scunthorpe road,
with a large bar and friendly
staff. The good value lunches
are very popular. 🏚 ④ P

Try also: Green Tree (Bass)

Nafferton

Cross Keys

2 North Street (200 yds off
A166) ☎ (0377) 44261
12–3 (not Mon), 7–11
**Old Mill Bitter; John Smith's
Bitter; Younger Scotch** Ⓗ
Very friendly and spacious
village inn with a good
reputation for food (no
lunches Mon). Two rooms and
a restaurant. 🍴 ④ ◗ 🍴 ⇌ ♣

North Frodingham

Star

Main Street (B1249)
☎ (0262) 488365
7–11 (12–2, 7–10.30 Sun)
**John Smith's Bitter; Younger
Scotch** Ⓗ
Relaxed and friendly pub with
good food from an
imaginative menu (not served
Thu). The games area is in a
new extension. An old BP sign
instructs customers to 'Buy
from the pump'. Note the
display of aircraft pictures.
Closed lunchtime except Sun.
🏚 ◗ ♣ P

North Newbald

Gnu

The Green

12–3 (not weekdays), 8–11
**Courage Directors; Hull
Mild; Tetley Bitter** Ⓗ
Pub just off the Green, with
working stables at the rear.
The cosy snug and bigger
lounge are both comfortable.
Country and Western concerts
Sun eves. On the Wolds Way
walking route. Please do not
park on the Green. Note
closed lunchtime, except
weekends. 🏚 ❀ 🍴 ♣ P

Ottringham

Watts Arms

Main Street (100 yds off
A1033, on Sunk Island road)
☎ (0964) 622034
12–3 (not Mon & Tue), 7–11
**Camerons Bitter; Tetley
Bitter** Ⓗ
Traditional local in the centre
of a village just off the Hull to
Withernsea road. Cosy
friendly atmosphere in three
rooms, including a dining area
(eve meals Thu–Sat). Piano on
Sat nights. Previously owned
by Darleys and the original
Hull Brewery. ④ ◗ ♣ P

Owston Ferry

Crooked Billet

Silver Street
☎ (0427) 72264
11–3 (not Mon), 7–11
Wards Thorne Best Bitter Ⓗ
Trent-side village pub where
games include boxing!
🏚 ⛄ ❀ ④ ◗ ♣ P

Patrington

Station Hotel

Station Road (A1033)
☎ (0964) 630262
11–3, 5–11
Younger IPA, No. 3 Ⓗ
Deceptively large, three-
roomed inn which served as
the station hotel until
Beeching closed the railway in
1963. Built by the Hull &
Withernsea railway company
in 1854. Separate restaurant/
grill room. ❀ ④ ◗ ♣ P

Paull

Humber Tavern

Main Street
☎ (0482) 899347
11–3, 7–11 (11–11 Fri, Sat & summer)
**John Smith's Magnet; Stones
Best Bitter; Tetley Bitter;
Wilson's Mild, Webster's
Yorkshire Bitter** Ⓗ
Victorian building backing
onto the Humber, with fine
views from a newly
constructed conservatory.
Excellent for outdoor drinking
on warm summer nights.
Three other large, well-
decorated rooms.
🏚 Q ⛄ ❀ ④ ♣

Reedness

Half Moon

Main Street
☎ (0405) 704484
12–3, 7–12 (12–3, 7–11 Sun)
**Marston's Pedigree;
Whitbread Trophy, Castle
Eden Ale** Ⓗ
200-year-old village local close
to Blacktoft Sands RSPB
Reserve. Family-run, with
good food always available.
🏚 ❀ ④ ▲ P

**Try also: Cross Keys,
Adlingfleet** (Free)

Ryhill

Crooked Billet

Pitt Lane (400 yds off A1033, E
of Thorngumbald)
☎ (0964) 622303
11–3 (not Tue or Thu), 7.30–11
**Burtonwood Mild, Bitter,
Forshaw's** Ⓗ
Traditional, old-style pub,
down a narrow lane with a
picturesque frontage, formerly
a smugglers' haunt. Wood-
panelled bar and split-level
lounge with stone paving. A
former Tetley tied house.
🏚 ④ ◗ 🍴 ♣ P

Sandtoft

Reindeer Inn

Off M180/A614/A18 jct
towards Belton OS743082
☎ (0724) 710774
12–3 (Fri, Sat & bank hols only), 7–11
(12–2.30, 7–10.30 Sun)
Tetley Bitter Ⓗ
Popular drinking spot near
Sandtoft Trolleybus Museum.
Comfortable and welcoming.
🏚 ④ ◗ ♣ P

Scawby

Sutton Arms

West Street (B1207)
☎ (0652) 652430
12–2.30 (not Mon), 6–11
Tetley Bitter Ⓗ; **guest beers**
Old free house, modernised
and extended. Children's play
area in the garden.
🏚 ❀ 🍴 ♣ P

Scunthorpe

Honest Lawyer

70 Oswald Road
☎ (0724) 849906
11–11
**Ind Coope Burton Ale; S&N
Theakston Old Peculier;
Tetley Bitter; Whitbread
Boddingtons Bitter** Ⓗ; **guest
beers**
Former restaurant converted
to an unusual two-floor pub
on the fringe of the town
centre. Basic wooden interior
decorated with authentic legal
memorabilia. Popular at

weekends. Bar snacks till 7pm. Up to four guest ales always available. ◑ ≢

Riveter

50 Henderson Avenue
☎ (0724) 862701
11–3 (4 Sat), 5.30–11
Old Mill Mild, Bitter, Bullion Ⓗ
Pub converted from a workingmen's club, noisy and crowded in the evening. Generally has an 'anything goes' atmosphere. Large games area for pool and darts. Limited parking. ◑ ♣ P

Try also: Clamart, Shelford St (Free)

Seaton

Swan Inn

On B1244 ☎ (0964) 533582
11–3, 7–11
John Smith's Bitter Ⓗ
Friendly village local with a very cosy lounge. The bar has a pool table. Good outdoor area for children. Handy for Hornsea Mere. ♨ ❀ ⊟ P

Skerne

Eagle Inn

Wandsford Road
☎ (0377) 42178
11–3, 7–11
Camerons Bitter Ⓗ
Very welcoming quiet pub with two unspoilt rooms and no bar! Drinks are brought to your table from a Victorian cash register beer engine situated in the small cellar off the entrance hall. Licensee was *Barmaid of the Year* 1991 in a local newspaper competition.
♨ Q ❀ ♣ P

Snaith

Brewer's Arms

10 Pontefract Road (A645, 200 yds from centre)
☎ (0405) 862404
11–2.30, 6 (6.30 Sat)–11 (12–2.30, 7–10.30 Sun)
Old Mill Bitter, Bullion Ⓗ
Grade II listed building, converted to an upmarket public house in 1988: a single large room with alcoves, plushly furnished, with original ceiling beams and a deep, illuminated well. Popular sing-along nights Sun (no food Sun eve). ❀ ⌂ ◑
≢ (limited service) P

Try also: Black Lion (Tetley)

South Dalton

Pipe & Glass

West End ☎ (0430) 810246
11.30–2.30, 7–11 (closed Mon)
Ruddles Best Bitter; Whitbread Castle Eden Ale Ⓗ

Historic inn in a superb location on the edge of the village, overlooking Dalton Park. Huge log fires in the comfortable bar and cocktail bar. Deservedly popular restaurant in a conservatory.
♨ ❀ ◑ ▶ P

Sutton upon Derwent

St Vincent Arms

Main Street
☎ (0904) 608349
11–3, 6–11
Courage Directors; S&N Theakston XB, Old Peculier; John Smith's Bitter; Taylor Landlord; Tetley Bitter Ⓗ
Picturesque village inn: cosy bars with real fires. Popular with locals and passing trade. Good value food (separate restaurant). Children welcome. ♨ Q ❀ ◑ ▶ ★ P

Swinefleet

Kings Head

10 High Street
☎ (0405) 704427
12–4, 7–11
Wards Thorne Best Bitter Ⓗ
Friendly local at the western end of the village. Well respected by real ale drinkers in the area; winner of brewery quality awards. No food Wed lunch or Sun eve.
♨ ❀ ◑ ▶ ⊟ ❤ ★ ♣ P

Ulceby

Fox Inn

Front Street
☎ (0469) 588161
11–11 (may close afternoons)
Ind Coope Burton Ale; Tetley Mild, Bitter Ⓗ
Traditional, cosy village local.
Q ⌂ ❀ ◑ ▶ ⊟ ♣ P

Westwoodside, Isle of Axholme

Park Drain Hotel

400 yds off B1396 OS726988
☎ (0427) 752255
11–11
Mansfield Riding Bitter; John Smith's Bitter Ⓗ; **guest beers**
Unusual, remote, Victorian pub. Built for the proposed mining community. The large bar, comfortable lounge and excellent restaurant are warmed by straw-fired central heating. Note the wells in the car park. ♨ ❀ ◑ ▶ ⊟ ★ ♣ P

Wetwang

Victoria Inn

Main Street ☎ (0377) 86677
11–2.30, 6–11
Courage Directors; John Smith's Bitter; Younger Scotch Ⓗ

Fronting onto the A166, this inn and restaurant is popular with locals and travellers alike. Pleasant, subdued interior with a separate pool area. ♨ ❀ ◑ ▶ ★ ♣

Winterton

Cross Keys

5 King Street
☎ (0724) 732215
11–3 (4 Sat), 5 (7 Sat)–11
Bass Special, Draught Bass Ⓗ
Former coaching inn, now a basic three-roomed locals' pub. Family room in the former lounge bar/dining room. ♨ ⌂ ❀ ⊟ ♣ P

Wrawby

Jollies

Brigg Road (A15/A18)
☎ (0652) 655658
11–3 (may extend in summer), 7 (6 summer)–11
Draught Bass Ⓗ
Small, modernised pub. The single lounge bar has a 'snug' created by partitions. Popular for meals (not served Wed) and can be very busy. Children's play area in the garden. ❀ ◑ ▶ P

Wroot, Isle of Axholme

Cross Keys

High Street (3½ miles off B1396) OS715032
☎ (0302) 770231
12–3 (not Tue–Thu), 7–11
S&N Theakston Best Bitter, XB Ⓗ
Focal point of this remote village community, catering for all ages and tastes. Separate games room and restaurant. No lunches Tue–Thu. ◑ ▶ ♣ P

Join CAMRA —
see page 508

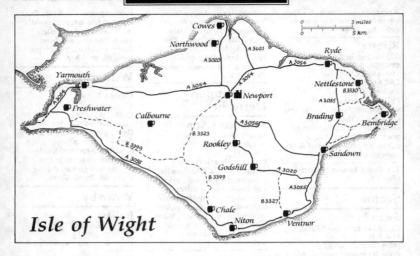

Isle of Wight

Isle of Wight

 Island, *Newport*

Bembridge

Rowbarge Inn
Station Road (near harbour)
☎ (0983) 872874
12–3, 6–11 (11–11 summer)
**Ind Coope Burton Ale; S&N
Theakston Old Peculier Ⓗ;
guest beers**
Large, one-bar pub with an
extensive menu (pizzas are
popular). A brewery is being
established next door.
🚾 ⅗ ❀ ◖◗

Try also: **Village Inn**
(Whitbread)

Brading

Anglers
Yarbridge (off A3055, E at
traffic lights) ☎ (0983) 406212
10.30–3 (2 winter), 6–11
Gale's XXXD (summer), **Best
Bitter, HSB** Ⓗ
Unusual, one-bar pub in a
rural setting. Derives its name
from the adjacent fishery. A
Whitbread pub leased to
Gale's. ❀ ◖◗ ⇌ P

Try also: **Bugle** (Whitbread)

Calbourne

Sun Inn
☎ (0983) 78231
11–11 (11–3, 6–11 winter)
**Courage Best Bitter,
Directors** Ⓗ
Traditional country pub, 100
years-old in 1992. Popular,
sometimes noisy, public bar;
quieter lounge bar and a
dining room (no-smoking).
Families welcomed.
Q ⅗ ❀ ◖◗ 🖽 ⅗ ▲ ✦ P

Chale

Wight Mouse
On B3399, 100 yds from A3055
☎ (0983) 730431
11–11 (12 restaurant)
**Fuller's Chiswick; Marston's
Pedigree; Wadworth 6X;
Whitbread Boddingtons
Bitter, Strong Country** Ⓗ
Very busy, old stone pub next
to an hotel. Large collections
of whiskies (365) and musical
instruments. The accent is on
food and families, with
children welcomed (garden
with play area). Near
Blackgang Chine theme park.
🚾 ⅗ ❀ 🖽 ◖◗ ▲ P

Cowes

Anchor
1 High Street
☎ (0983) 292823
11–11
**Whitbread Strong Country,
Flowers Original** Ⓗ; **guest
beers**
Ancient town-centre inn with
former stables converted to a
bar for events. Home-made
food (beef and ale pies a
speciality); Thatcher's cider.
Families welcome.
🚾 ❀ ◖◗ ✦ ⥀

Try also: **Portland Arms**,
Gurnard (Free); **Three Crowns**
(Free)

Freshwater

Vine Inn
School Green Road
☎ (0983) 752959

11–3, 6–11 (11–11 Sat & summer)
Gale's XXXD (summer), **BBB,
5X, HSB** Ⓗ
Friendly, two-bar, town-centre
pub, close to shops and main
car parks. Refurbishment
planned to provide a no-
smoking bar/dining area.
Separate restaurant with a
changing menu. Opens at 7am
for breakfasts from Easter.
🚾 Q ⅗ ❀ ◖◗ 🖽 ⅗ ✦ P

Godshill

Taverners
High Street
☎ (0983) 840707
11–11
**Courage Directors; Ind Coope
Burton Ale; Island Newport
Best Bitter; Ruddles County;
Whitbread Flowers
Original** Ⓗ; **guest beer**
Village pub in a tourist area,
including a restaurant with a
varied menu. Regular
entertainment to suit most
tastes.
🚾 ⅗ ❀ ◖◗ ⅗ ✦

Nettlestone

Roadside Inn
☎ (0983) 612381
11–11
Gale's BBB (summer), **Best
Bitter, HSB** Ⓗ
Friendly village pub formerly
a Whitbread tied house now
leased to Gale's. Two large
bars and a children's room.
Caravans allowed at the
campsites.
⅗ ❀ 🖽 ◖◗ 🖽 ▲ ✦ P

Try also: **Wishing Well**,
Pondwell (Free)

Newport

Railway Medina
1 Sea Street (200 yds from High St, at the bottom of Holyrood St) ☎ (0983) 528303
10.30–3, 6–11 (11–11 summer)
Gale's BBB, HSB Ⓗ
Splendid, cosy town pub with a railway theme, the lounge furnished with memorabilia and pictures from old island railways. Good, basic public bar in this street-corner, ex-Whitbread pub.
🏠 Q ⊛ ♣

Try also: Prince of Wales (Whitbread)

Niton

Buddle Inn
St Catherine's Road (follow signs to St Catherine's Point) ☎ (0983) 730243
11–3, 6–11 (11–11 Fri, Sat & summer)
Whitbread Boddingtons Bitter, Fremlins Bitter, Flowers IPA, Strong Country, Flowers Original Ⓗ**; guest beers**
Ancient, stone-built pub with strong smuggling connections. Not all beers are on at once. Home cooking. Family room in summer only.
🏠 ⋟ ⊛ ◑ ▶ ▲ ♣ P

Northwood

Travellers Joy
85 Pallance Road (off B3325) ☎ (0983) 298024
11–2.30, 5–11 (11–11 summer)
Draught Bass; Gibbs Mew Bishop's Tipple; Island Nipper; Ringwood Old Thumper; Ruddles County; S&N Theakston Old Peculier Ⓗ**; guest beers**
Excellent beer exhibition pub, unique to the island and well worth seeking out. Good

value food; Thatcher's cider. Petanque and pet rabbits in the back garden.
⋟ ⊛ ◑ ▶ ▲ ♣ ⌂ P

Try also: Horseshoe (Gale's)

Rookley

Chequers
Off A3020 (turn right at the start of the village) ☎ (0983) 840314
11–3, 6–11
Courage Best Bitter, Directors; John Smith's Bitter Ⓗ
Ex-Whitbread pub, sold into the free trade and extensively refurbished at some expense to character. Very popular and food oriented, yet still retaining a flagstoned-floored public.
🏠 Q ⋟ ⊛ ◑ ▶ ⊟ ▲ ♣ P

Ryde

Castle
164 High Street (10 mins' walk from ferry) ☎ (0983) 811138
10.30–11
Gale's XXXL (summer), **BBB, 5X, HSB** Ⓗ
Old town-centre pub with a split-level interior, retaining the original etched-glass and fireplace. Comfortable and unpretentious: a real pub. Bulmers cider. 🏠 ⌂

Hotel Ryde Castle
Esplanade ☎ (0983) 63755
11–11
Draught Bass; Gibbs Mew Bishop's Tipple; Island Newport Best Bitter Ⓗ**; guest beers**
Hotel bar in a Tudor-style building, decorated with arms and armour and boasting a small museum. No-smoking eating area at lunchtime.
Q ⋟ ⊛ 🛏 ◑ ▶ & ⇌ P

Sandown

Commercial
15 St Johns Road ☎ (0983) 403848
11–11
Gale's BBB, Best Bitter, 5X, HSB Ⓗ
Smart, two-bar, town-centre pub retaining all of its original features. Very popular with locals and holidaymakers. Good family room. Frequent, varied live music all year.
🏠 Q ⋟ ⊛ ◑ ▶ ⊟ & ♣

Ventnor

Spyglass Inn
Esplanade (W end) ☎ (0983) 855338
11–3, 7–11 (10–11 summer)
Gibbs Mew Wiltshire; Ind Coope Burton Ale Ⓗ**; guest beers** (winter)
Superb rambling pub which welcomes families. Regular live music. Wiltshire Bitter is sold as Kingrock Ale. Outside bar in summer. Seafood a speciality. Accommodation in one four-person flat.
⋟ ⊛ 🛏 ◑ ▶ & ▲ P ⚲

Yarmouth

Wheatsheaf Inn
Bridge Road ☎ (0983) 760456
11–3, 6–11
Gale's HSB; Thwaites Bitter; Whitbread Boddingtons Bitter Ⓗ**; guest beers** (summer)
Very popular local in a small harbour town. Excellent and varied food and a new extension provides superb family facilities. The public bar (can be noisy) has a pool table in winter. Usually busy summer weekends.
🏠 Q ⋟ ⊛ ◑ ▶ ⊟ & ♣

Try also: Bugle (Whitbread)

🛏

Accommodation

Where a pub offers accommodation, we add the bed symbol to the entry, but we make no assessment of the quality or price of the rooms available.

For more detailed information about real ale pubs which offer good value bed and breakfast, consult Roger Protz's **Beer, Bed & Breakfast**, now in its fourth edition, published by Robson Books at £7.99 and available from all good book shops or direct from CAMRA, 34 Alma Road, St Albans, Herts, AL1 3BW (post free).

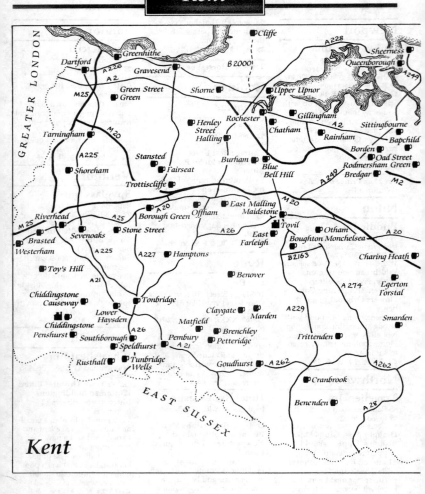

Kent

Kent

 Goacher's, Tovil; **Larkins,** Chiddingstone;
Shepherd Neame, Faversham

Ashford

Beaver Road Off-Licence

36 Beaver Road (A2070)
☎ (0233) 622904
11 (3 Wed)–10.15 (12–3, 7–10.15 Sun)
Beer range varies Ⓖ
Friendly off-licence with a
choice of at least two beers
during the week; four at
weekends. Fine ales, beers and
porters from around the
country. On average 20–25%
cheaper than pub prices. You
are welcome to taste the beers
before you buy. ⇌

Hare & Hounds

Maidstone Road, Potters
Corner (A20 2 miles from
centre) ☎ (0233) 621760
11–2.30, 6–11
**Draught Bass; Courage Best
Bitter; John Smith's Bitter** Ⓗ
Friendly and busy pub just
out of town. Function room.
No eve meals Sun or Tue.
⊛ ◑ P

Bapchild

Fox & Goose

The Street ☎ (0795) 472095
12–3, 7–11
Courage Best Bitter Ⓗ
Busy village pub; HQ of many
sporting societies. The large

garden has an aviary.
🛇 ⊛ ◑ ♣ P

Benenden

King William IV

The Street (B2086)
☎ (0580) 240636
11–3, 6–11 (11–11 Sat)
**Shepherd Neame Master
Brew Bitter, Best Bitter** or
Spitfire Ⓗ
Excellent village local with
two contrasting bars: the
public for those who prefer
the jukebox and bandit, the
saloon for those who like
convivial conversation.
Eve meals Wed–Sat;
no food Sun.
🏚 Q 🛇 ⊛ ◑ ⊟ ♣ P

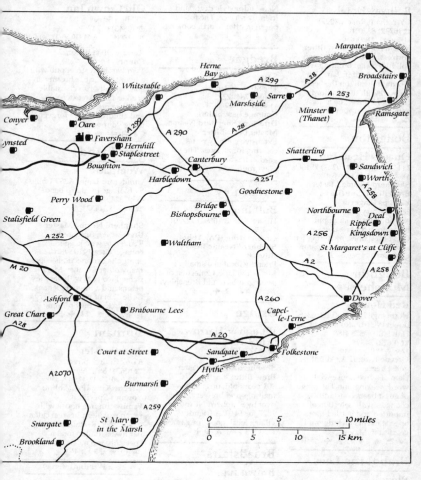

Benover

Woolpack Inn
Benover Road (B2162, 1 mile S
of Yalding) ☎ (089 273) 356
11–2.30 (3 Sat), 6–11
**Shepherd Neame Master
Brew Bitter, Bishops Finger** Ⓗ
Popular country local with
exposed beams and a warm
welcome from Shepherd
Neame's *Landlord of the Year*.
Beer-making memorabilia
displayed. Generous portions
of excellent food (specials
blackboard daily; no meals
Sun). ⚌ ☎ ❀ ◑ ♣ P

Bishopsbourne

Mermaid
400 yds off A2
☎ (0227) 830581
11–2.30, 6–11
**Shepherd Neame Master
Brew Bitter** Ⓗ

Attractive, friendly little pub
in a typically Kentish village,
the former home of author
Joseph Conrad. Unusual,
labour-saving electronic heads
and tails tosser by the
dartboard. Lunchtime snacks.
⚌ ❀ ◑ ♣

Blue Bell Hill

Robin Hood
364 Common Road (1 mile W
of village and A229) OS734628
☎ (0634) 861500
11–2.30, 6–11
**Courage Best Bitter,
Directors** Ⓗ
17th-century pub (with
additions) in an isolated rural
position. Three bars, one with
an inglenook. Modernised
(1975) and suits all tastes. Live
music and summer barbecues.
No food Sun. Warm and
friendly.
⚌ Q ☎ ❀ ◑ ▣ ▲ ♣ P

Try also: **Lower Bell**
(Courage)

Borden

Maypole
Borden Lane ☎ (0795) 424253
11–3, 7–11
**Courage Best Bitter,
Directors** Ⓗ
Pub opposite the church in a
pleasant village setting. Good
atmosphere. ◑ ▣ ♣ P

Borough Green

Fox & Hounds
Maidstone Road (A25)
☎ (0732) 882334
11–3, 6–11
Harveys BB Ⓗ
Friendly pub; the building is
deceptively old. Many
pictures and prints of bold
Reynard are displayed. Large
garden. ❀ ◑ ⇌ P

Kent

Railway Hotel
4 Wrotham Road (A227)
☎ (0732) 882016
11–3, 6–11 (11–11 Sat)
Mitchell's Mild, Best Bitter, Fortress, ESB Ⓗ; guest beers
Solid Victorian building which has kept its public bar. The 'northern head' on the beers fits well with the landlord's choice of brewer; he is an enthusiastic supporter of mild.
Q ◖◗ ⇌ ♣ P

Boughton

Queens Head Inn
111 The Street ☎ (0227) 751369
11–3, 6–11 (11–11 Fri & Sat)
Shepherd Neame Master Brew Bitter, Spitfire Ⓗ, Bishops Finger Ⓖ
16th-century pub, recently extended into a large public bar, saloon and restaurant. Good for games, including bat and trap and shove-ha'penny.
Q 🏾 ≠ ◖◗ ⊞ ♨ ▲ ♣ P

Boughton Monchelsea

Red House
Hermitage Lane (off B2163, S down Weirton Road and East Hall Hill) OS783488
☎ (0622) 743986
12–3, 7–11 (12–11 Sat)
Greene King IPA, Abbot Ⓗ; guest beers
Gem of a free house well worth seeking out. The range of guest beers constantly changes; wide selection of imported and bottled beers. Special events include mini beerfest in May.
🏾 🚲 🏾 ◖◗ ⊞ ▲ ♣ ⌂ P

Brabourne Lees

Plough
Lees Road OS080405
☎ (0303) 812169
12–2.30 (3 Sat), 7–11
Shepherd Neame Master Brew Bitter, Spitfire Ⓗ
Relatively unspoilt, 16th-century country pub. The saloon bar has an inglenook and oak beams. Two Bat and Trap teams. Annual Aunt Sally matches with a rival Oxfordshire pub. Occasional draught Best, Bishops Finger and Xmas Ale. No meals Wed eve. 🏾 🏾 ◖◗ ♣ P

Brasted

Bull
High Street (A25)
☎ (0959) 562551
10.30–2.30, 5.30–11 (10.30–11 Sat)
Shepherd Neame Master Brew Bitter, Spitfire, Bishops Finger Ⓗ
Busy main road pub catering for local and passing trades.

Neo-Tudor style decor and friendly service. The food is popular, often worth booking.
🏾 ◖◗ ♿ ♣ P

Bredgar

Sun
The Street (B2163)
☎ (062 784) 221
11–3, 7 (6 Fri & Sat)–11
Courage Best Bitter, Directors; Shepherd Neame Master Brew Bitter Ⓗ
Extensive country pub catering for all ages. The garden has an adventure playground. 🏾 🏾 ◖◗ P

Brenchley

Bull Inn
High Street ☎ (0892) 722701
11–3, 5–11
Greene King IPA, Abbot; Shepherd Neame Best Bitter Ⓗ
Friendly local in a small Kentish village. Collection of photographs of old Brenchley.
🏾 🏾 🏾 ◖◗ ♣ ⌂ P

Bridge

Plough & Harrow
86 High Street
☎ (0227) 830455
11–3, 6–11
Shepherd Neame Master Brew Bitter Ⓗ
301 years-old, originally a maltings and brewery, taken over by Shepherd Neame in 1877 for £410. A friendly village local, good for games.
🏾 Q ◖◗ ⊞ ▲ ♣ P

Broadstairs

Brown Jug
204 Ramsgate Road (A255)
☎ (0843) 62788
11–3 (4 Sat), 6–11
Fuller's Chiswick; Whitbread Fremlins Bitter Ⓗ; guest beers
In an area lacking decent real ale, a flint walled pub of quiet character run by two sisters. Special sports nights; crib, darts, dominoes, chess et al. Simply excellent! White Shield served. 🏾 Q 🏾 ⊞
≠ (Dumpton Park) ♣ P

Neptune's Hall
1–5 Harbour Street
☎ (0843) 61400
10–4, 6–11
Shepherd Neame Master Brew Bitter, Bishops Finger Ⓗ
Busy, three-bar Victorian pub, a short puff from the picturesque harbour below. A regular entry in this guide, it is always worth a visit. Often packed but still has an unspoilt feel. Private bar available. 🏾 🏾 ◖◗ ⊞ ♣

Old Crown Inn
23 High Street
☎ (0843) 61747
10.30–3 (4 Fri), 6–11 (10.30–11 Sat & summer)
Ruddles Best Bitter, County Ⓗ
Two-bar, high street pub with a lively public bar hosting an energetically-run charitable winkle club. An extensive menu caters for vegetarians and children. Don't forget to bring your winkle!
◖◗ ⊞ ⇌ ♣

Brookland

Woolpack
Guildeford Lane (A259 1 mile S of village by sharp bends) OS978245
☎ (0679) 344321
11–3, 7–11
Shepherd Neame Master Brew Bitter, Spitfire Ⓗ
Remote beacon keeper's cottage, circa 1410 with smuggling connections – like many other Romney Marsh pubs. Two bars with very low beams and a huge inglenook. Collection of water jugs. Try your luck on the Spinning Jenny. 🏾 🏾 ◖◗ ♣ P

Burham

Toastmaster
65–67 Church Street
☎ (0634) 861299
12–3, 5.30–11 (11–11 Fri & Sat)
Greene King IPA, Abbot; Young's Special Ⓗ
Family-run free house with seven real ales plus real cider in summer. Restaurant and bar meals; Italian food a speciality (no meals Sun eve).
🏾 Q 🏾 ◖◗ ⌂ P

Try also: Windmill (Free)

Burmarsh

Shepherd & Crook
Shear Way, Thorndyke Road
☎ (0303) 872336
11.30–3.30, 7–11
Adnams Bitter; Bateman XXXB; Tetley Bitter; Young's Special Ⓗ
Friendly two-bar village pub; the saloon is liberally adorned with china, copperware and firearms. Ring the Bull played. No meals Sun eve.
🏾 🏾 ◖◗ ♣ P

Canterbury

Canterbury Tales
12 The Friars (opp. Marlowe Theatre) ☎ (0227) 768594
11.30–2.30, 5.30–11 (11.30–11 Sat)
Goacher's Light; Shepherd Neame Master Brew Bitter Ⓗ; guest beers
Lively pub decorated in 1920s pastels and theatrical

memorabilia. Live music Mon.
Frequent theme nights.
◑ ▶ ≈ (East/West) ♣

New Inn

19 Havelock Street (just off
ring road, E side of town)
☎ (0227) 464584
11–3, 6–11
Beer range varies Ⓗ
Usually five beers on in this
tiny, friendly, free house.
Popular with students and
staff from nearby colleges.
Lunchtime snacks.
❀ ≈ (East)

Olive Branch

39 Burgate, The Buttermarket
☎ (0227) 462170
11–11
**Ind Coope Friary Meux Best
Bitter, Burton Ale; Young's
Special** Ⓗ
Pub opposite the medieval
Christ Church Gate of the
cathedral; ideal for visitors
and shoppers. Seating outside
in the Buttermarket. Good
value home-made lunches.
❀ ◑ ♿ ≈ (East/West)

Phoenix

67 Old Dover Road
☎ (0227) 464220
11–3, 5.30 (6.30 Sat)–11
**Courage Directors; Fuller's
London Pride; Shepherd
Neame Master Brew Bitter;
Young's Bitter** Ⓗ**; guest beers**
Pub close to the county cricket
ground and full of cricketing
memorabilia. Comfortable bar.
❀ ◑ ≈ (East) P ✄

**Try also: Canterbury Beer
Shop,** Northgate

Capel-le-Ferne

Royal Oak

Dover Road (A20 E of village)
☎ (0303) 44787
11.30–3 (4 Sat), 6 (7 Sat)–11
**Bateman XXXB; Wadworth
6X; Whitbread Strong
Country** Ⓗ
Split-level, two-bar pub near
panoramic views across the
Channel. The jukebox,
amusement machines and
pool table are kept well away
from the cosy main bar area.
Adjacent camping and
caravan park. ⚲ ◑ ♿ ▲ ♣ P

Charing Heath

Red Lion

Tile Lodge Road
☎ (023 371) 2418
11–2.30, 6.30–11
**Shepherd Neame Master
Brew Bitter** Ⓗ
Two-bar pub enjoying a
friendly local trade. The outside
drinking area is the village
green. First registered in 1709
as an ale house and became the
Red Lion in 1762. No food Tue
eve or Sun/Mon. ⚲ Q ◑ ▶ P

Chatham

Alexandra Hotel

43 Railway Street
☎ (0634) 843959
11–3 (4 Sat), 5 (7 Sat)–11
**Shepherd Neame Master
Brew Bitter, Spitfire** Ⓗ
Friendly one-bar pub very
near the station. Pleasant
garden. Additionally
alternates Shepherd Neame
Best Bitter, Stock Ale and
Bishops Finger. Meals
Mon–Fri. ❀ ◑ ≈ ♣

Ropemakers Arms

70 New Road (near station)
☎ (0634) 402121
12–3, 7–11
**Goacher's Light; Greene King
Abbot; S&N Theakston XB,
Old Peculier** Ⓗ
Friendly free house with long-
standing connections with the
former naval dockyard.
Weekday lunches. ◑ ≈ ♣

Chiddingstone

Castle Inn

(S off B2027, Leigh–Four Elms
Road) OS502452
☎ (0892) 870247
11–3, 6–11
**Harveys BB; Shepherd
Neame Master Brew Bitter** Ⓗ**;
guest beers**
Situated in a picturesque NT
village, this unspoilt pub
(dating from 1420) has a
traditional public bar, separate
restaurant and a large patio.
Limited parking. Larkins
Brewery is nearby.
⚲ Q ❀ ◑ ▶ ♿ ▲

Chiddingstone Causeway

Little Brown Jug

On B2027, opp. Penshurst
station ☎ (0892) 870318
11.30–3, 6–11
**Fuller's Chiswick; Harveys
BB; Whitbread Boddingtons
Bitter** Ⓗ**; guest beers**
Warm, family-run, traditional
inn with recently introduced
B&B and an extended
restaurant. Some foreign
bottled beers available. ❀
⇔ ◑ ▶ ♿ ≈ ♣ ⌂ P

Claygate

White Hart

On B2162, Collier
St–Horsmonden Road
OS714445 ☎ (0892) 730313
11–3, 6–11
**Goacher's Light; Shepherd
Neame Master Brew Bitter;
Wadworth 6X** Ⓗ
Friendly local; a comfortable
two-bar house set in open
countryside of orchards and
hop gardens. Bank note
collection above the bars.

Separate restaurant.
Biddenden cider. ⚲ Q ❀ ♣
◑ ▶ ♿ ▲ ♣ ⌂ P

Cliffe

Black Bull

Church Street ☎ (0634) 220893
12–3, 7–11
**Adnams Bitter; Charrington
IPA; Fuller's London Pride;
Goacher's Light** Ⓗ**; guest
beers**
Enterprising free house where
the cellar restaurant features a
sparkling water well and
specialises in SE Asian food
(national Guinness award for
pub food).

Try also: Victoria (Shepherd
Neame)

Conyer

Brunswick Arms

The Street ☎ (0795) 521569
12–2 (3 Sat), 7–11
**Courage Best Bitter;
Shepherd Neame Spitfire** Ⓗ
Small, welcoming local with
an L-shaped bar, a separate
eating area, skittle alley and a
rare example of a Kentish
dartboard. Excellent value
meals with generous
discounts before 1.30pm and
before 8.30pm eves.
⚲ ◑ ♣ P

Ship Inn & Smugglers Restaurant

Conyer Quay, Teynham
☎ (0795) 521404
11–3, 6–11
Beer range varies Ⓗ
This creekside pub is now in
its second year as a free house,
providing an ever-changing
range of five guest beers, as
well as Biddenden cider.
Happy hour until 7pm every
night. Noted for its food;
stocks over 150 malt whiskies.
❀ ◑ ▶ ♣ ⌂

Court at Street

Welcome Stranger

On B2067, 1 mile W of Port
Lympne Wildlife park
OS090354 ☎ (0233) 720400
12–2 (3 Sat), 6–11
**Shepherd Neame Master
Brew Bitter** Ⓗ**; guest beers**
Friendly one-bar pub, popular
with locals, where strangers
are made to feel welcome.
Occasional cider but no
draught lager. One of a dying
breed of pubs. Q ❀ ⌂ P

Cranbrook

Prince of Wales

High Street ☎ (0580) 713058
11.30 (11 Sat)–2.30, 6.30–11
Harveys BB Ⓗ**; guest beers**

Infamous, lively town-centre free house. Both bars can get very busy and chaotic – not for those with a delicate disposition! Occasional mini beer festivals.
🏨 ॐ ❀ ◖◗ 🍴 ♣

Dartford

Foresters
16 Great Queen Street (off A226, East Hill)
☎ (0322) 223087
11–11
Courage Best Bitter, Directors Ⓗ
Comfortable locals' pub with a lively public bar and a small, secluded lounge. Quizzes and barbecues. ❀ 🍴 ⇌ ♣ P

Fulwich
150 St Vincents Road (off A226 E of centre)
☎ (0322) 223683
11–2.30, 6.30–11 (11–11 Fri & Sat; 12–2.30, 7–10.30 Sun)
Ind Coope Burton Ale; Tetley Bitter Ⓗ
Thriving locals' pub with a large public bar (beer 2p cheaper). ◖◗ 🍴 ⇌ ♣

Two Brewers
33 Lowfield Street
☎ (0322) 223305
11–11
Ind Coope Burton Ale; Tetley Bitter Ⓗ
Town-centre pub, recently refurbished. Hot food always available. ❀ ◖◗ ⇌ P

Deal

Admiral Keppel
Manor Road, Upper Deal (off A258) ☎ (0304) 374024
10–11
Draught Bass; Charrington IPA Ⓗ
Former multi-bar pub, tastefully opened up whilst still preserving a cosy atmosphere. ❀ ◖ ♣ P

Ship Inn
141 Middle Street (parallel to seafront) ☎ (0304) 372222
11–11
Draught Bass; Fuller's ESB; Greene King Abbot; Shepherd Neame Master Brew Bitter; Welsh Brewers Worthington BB Ⓗ
Cosy pub with a nautical theme in an historic area near the seafront. Live piano music Sun. Vegetarian menu (no food Sun). 🏨 ❀ ◖◗ ⇌

Dover

Blakes
52 Castle Street (near market sq) ☎ (0304) 202194
11–3, 7–11 (closed Sun)
Charrington IPA Ⓗ; **guest beers**

Wine bar noted for its beer and food. Two bars attract a smart clientele. Popular at lunchtimes with office staff. Usually two guests.
Q ❀ ◖◗ ⇌ (Priory)

Boars Head
46–48 Eaton Road
☎ (0304) 204490
11–3, 6–11 (11–11 Sat)
Greene King IPA, Abbot Ⓗ; **guest beers**
Busy local, friendly and welcoming. The pub sign is a relic from its tied house days. Occasional mini beer festivals. New skittle alley.
🏨 ❀ ◖ ⇌ (Priory) ♣

Crown & Sceptre
25 Elms Vale Road (100 yds from A20 jct)
☎ (0304) 201971
11.30–3 (4 Sat), 7–11 (11.30–11 Fri)
Shepherd Neame Master Brew Bitter, Spitfire Ⓗ
Bought from Charrington in 1991, a two-bar local in a residential area. Impressive collection of ferry prints.
❀ ⇌ (Priory) ♣

Eagle Hotel
London Road ☎ (0304) 201543
10–11
Courage Best Bitter, Directors; John Smith's Bitter Ⓗ; **guest beer**
Impressive, two-bar corner pub surmounted by a golden eagle. Separate games room.
◖ ⇌ (Priory) ♣

Royal Oak
36 Lower Road, River (off A256) ☎ (0304) 822073
Hours vary
Shepherd Neame Master Brew Bitter, Spitfire Ⓗ
Open-plan local created by enlarging the original flint-built pub into a cottage next door. Situated in an attractive residential area near Crabble Mill. ◖ ⇌ (Kearsney) ♣ P

East Farleigh

Victory
Farleigh Bridge
☎ (0622) 726591
11–11
Goacher's Mild, Light; Ind Coope Burton Ale (summer) Ⓗ
Small, friendly, one-roomed village local serving an excellent example of a local brew. Q ॐ ❀ ◖◗ ⇌ ♣

Walnut Tree
Forge Lane (50 yds W of Dean St jct) OS743530
☎ (0622) 726368
12–3, 6–11
Shepherd Neame Master Brew Bitter, Spitfire Ⓗ
Low-beamed country pub with interesting memorabilia and a skittles table. The large

beer garden can get quite busy. Home-cooked food.
🏨 Q ❀ 🛏 ◖◗ ⇌ ♣ P

East Malling

Rising Sun
125 Mill Street
☎ (0732) 843284
11–11
Goacher's Light; Harveys BB; Shepherd Neame Master Brew Bitter Ⓗ; **guest beer**
Now a family-run free house situated in a row of terraced houses. Cheerful and welcoming with good wholesome food and sensible prices. Unusual guest beer for the area. ❀ ◖◗ 🍴 ⇌ ♣

Egerton Forstal

Queens Arms
Forstal Road (SW out of Egerton, right at T jct, then 1st left) OS893464
☎ (0233) 76386
11–3, 6–11
Adnams Bitter; Ind Coope Burton Ale; King & Barnes Sussex; Young's Bitter Ⓗ; **guest beers** (occasionally)
Two-bar country pub with timber beams and hops. Genuine chapel door inside the back entrance. Barbecues in summer; jazz every Sun lunch. No food Tue.
🏨 Q ◖◗ ♣ P

Fairseat

Vigo
Gravesend Road (A227, 1 mile N of Wrotham)
☎ (0732) 822547
12–2.30 (3 Sat; not Mon) 6–11
Harveys XX Mild, BB; Young's Bitter, Special Ⓗ; **guest beers**
Ancient drovers' inn; the basic structure is a medieval barn. Named after a landlord who was at the famous battle. Two quiet bars – an ale drinker's paradise. Try the Dadlums table (a form of Kentish skittles). A mild oasis. Goacher's house beer.
🏨 Q ♣ P

Farningham

Chequers
High Street ☎ (0322) 865222
11–11
Fuller's London Pride, ESB; Morland Old Speckled Hen Ⓗ; **guest beers**
Enterprising free house in a pleasant village just off A20. Constantly changing range of six guest beers. ❀ 🛏 ◖

Faversham

Mechanics Arms
44 West Street ☎ (0795) 532693
10.30–3, 7–11

Shepherd Neame Master Brew Bitter Ⓗ
Ten successive years in this guide underline the quality of this traditional, friendly, welcoming and unspoilt local. Beware the keg mild, despite handpumps in the public bar.
Q ⊛ ⓭ ♣

Try also: Swan & Harlequin, Quay Lane (Free)

Folkestone

Clifton Hotel
Clifton Gardens (opp. Leas Cliff Hall) ☎ (0303) 851231
10.30–2.30, 6–11
Draught Bass Ⓗ; **guest beers**
Relaxing and comfortable bar in a three-star hotel overlooking the sea.
Q ⇜ ◖ ▶ ⇌ (Central)

Frittenden

Knoxbridge Inn
Cranbrook Road (A229)
☎ (0580) 891298
12–11 (closed Mon lunch)
Fuller's London Pride; Harveys BB; Hook Norton Best Bitter Ⓗ; **guest beers**
Enterprising road house. One long bar in a U-shaped drinking area; one end is like a public bar, the other a saloon. Occasional live music.
⋈ ⛺ ⊛ ◖ ▶ ⚔ ♣ P

Gillingham

King George V
1 Prospect Row, Brompton (near old Chatham dockyard) ☎ (0634) 842418
11–3 (4 Sat), 6–11
Draught Bass Ⓗ; **guest beers**
A warm, cosy atmosphere in a pub with naval and military connections. Regular guest ales and a varied collection of malt whiskies. No food Sun.
⋈ ⛺ ⊛

Roseneath
79 Arden Street (200 yds off High St) ☎ (0634) 852553
11–11
Beer range varies Ⓗ
Enterprising back-street pub offering a selection of good value, home-made meals. Watch out for Golly the Snakehound! Snakehound Ale is brewed by Goacher's. Occasional beer festivals held in a marquee in the garden.
⊛ ◖ ▶ ⇌ ♣

Try also: Cricketers, Layfield Rd (Free)

Goodnestone

Fitzwalter Arms
The Street OS255546
☎ (0304) 840303
11–11

Shepherd Neame Master Brew Bitter, Spitfire, Bishops Finger Ⓗ
Former gate lodge of the Fitzwalter Estate, now an unspoilt house pub. Friendly and welcoming. Occasional live music and theme nights; bar billiards.
⋈ ⛺ ⊛ ◖ ▶ ⓭ ♣

Goudhurst

Green Cross Inn
Station Road (A262, 1 mile W of village) ☎ (0580) 211200
11–2.30, 6.30–11
Exmoor Ale; Harveys BB Ⓗ; **guest beers**
Country pub with a large uncluttered bar and a restaurant at the rear. Warmed by a wood-burning stove. Good quality food but no Sun lunches. Cider in summer.
⋈ ⊛ ⇜ ◖ ▶ ⌁ P

Gravesend

Darnley Arms
9 Trafalgar Road (off A227)
☎ (0474) 334051
11–3, 5.30–11
Beer range varies Ⓗ
Normally two real ales available in this typical urban local, with a modern interior. Worth a visit for the warm welcome. ⇌ ♣

Jolly Drayman
1 Love Lane (off A226)
☎ (0474) 352355
11–2.30, 5.30–11 (12–3, 7–11 Sat)
Draught Bass; Charrington IPA Ⓗ; **guest beers**
Low-ceilinged pub in the offices of a former brewery. Handy for shops and offices. Good friendly atmosphere. Occasional cider.
⊛ ◖ ⚓ ⇌ ♣ ⌁ P

New Inn
1 Milton Road (A226, one-way system) ☎ (0474) 566651
10–11
Marston's Pedigree; Whitbread Fremlins Bitter Ⓗ
Real locals' pub in the town centre. Pubs like this are hard to find now and should be preserved. Note the Rigden's brewery windows.
⋈ ⛺ ⓭ ⚓ ⇌ ♣

Somerset Arms
10 Darnley Road (one-way system near station)
☎ (0474) 533837
11–3.30, 5–11 (supper licence to 12 Thu–Sat, 11.30 Sun)
Beer range varies Ⓗ
Whitbread tied house with an adventurous attitude to guest beers. A town-centre pub with a dimly lit interior, due to be expanded into the shop next door with increased facilities.
⇜ ◖ ▶ ⇌ ♣

Windmill Tavern
45 Shrubbery Road, Windmill Hill (off Parrock St)
☎ (0474) 352242
11–11
Courage Directors; Ruddles Best Bitter; Webster's Yorkshire Bitter Ⓗ; **guest beers**
A country pub in town. Summer barbecues in the prize-winning garden; bookings taken for the attached public bowling greens and tennis courts. No-smoking area lunchtime only.
⊛ ◖ ▶ ⚓ ⚔ ⇌ ♣ P ✗

Try also: Kent & Essex, Old Road West (Grand Met); **Six Bells,** Northfleet (Courage)

Great Chart

Hooden Horse
The Street (old A28, 2 miles SW of Ashford) OS982421
☎ (0233) 625583
11–2.30, 6–11
Goacher's Light; Hook Norton Old Hooky; Hopback Summer Lightning Ⓗ; **guest beers**
Welcoming and friendly pub with tiled and timber floors, scattered tables and chairs, some with crib scorers. At least three guest premium beers at premium prices but well worth a visit. Formerly the Black Dog. ⊛ ◖ ▶

Greenhithe

Pier Hotel
High Street ☎ (0322) 382291
11–11
Charrington IPA Ⓗ
Old pub with a lot of history, in the old village centre. A listed building with views across the river from the large garden (moorings available). Very friendly atmosphere; numerous games played. The pub ghost haunts the cellar. Weekday lunches.
⛺ ⊛ ◖ ⓭ ⚓ ⇌ ♣ P

Green Street Green

Ship
Green Street Green Road (B260, 4 miles from Dartford)
☎ (0474) 702279
11 (12 Sat)–2.30, 6–11
Courage Best Bitter; Wadworth 6X; Young's Bitter Ⓗ
Popular 17th-century roadhouse where the landlord is always ready to discuss the merits – or otherwise – of Kent County Cricket Club. Excellent value lunches, especially the bacon doorsteps. Regular gourmet nights. Families welcome in summer only, in the converted stable. ⋈ ⛺ ⊛ ◖ ⚔ ▲ ♣ P

Kent

Halling

Homeward Bound
72 High Street (A228)
☎ (0634) 240743
12–3, 7–11
Shepherd Neame Master Brew Bitter Ⓗ
Friendly one-bar pub with pool and darts. Weekday lunches. ♨ ⑧ ◖ ⇌ ♣ P

Try also: Plough (Courage)

Hamptons

Artichoke Inn
Park Road (2nd right off Carpenters Lane)
☎ (0732) 810763
11.30–2.30, 6.30–11
Fuller's London Pride; Greene King Abbot; Young's Special Ⓗ**; guest beers**
15th-century, low-beamed pub with much brass and silver bric-a-brac. Warm, welcoming atmosphere in two bars, plus a restaurant. No machines or jukebox. 1992 *Clean Kitchen* award-holder.
♨ Q ⛄ ⑧ ◖ ♿ ♠ P

Harbledown

Old Coach & Horses
Church Hill (just off A2)
☎ (0227) 761330
11.30–2.30, 6–11 (11.30–3, 7–11 Sat)
Adnams Bitter; Fuller's Chiswick; Mitchell's Best Bitter Ⓗ
Pub near Black Prince's Well and opposite Canterbury's former leper hospital. Precipitous garden with views over orchards. Beers can change. ♨ ⑧ ◖ ▶ P

Henley Street

Cock Inn
1 mile from Sole St station
OS664672 ☎ (0474) 814208
12 (7 Mon)–11
Chiltern Ale; Ind Coope Burton Ale; Mauldons Special Ⓗ**; Suffolk Punch** Ⓖ**, Black Adder** Ⓗ**, Suffolk Comfort** Ⓖ
Isolated free house dating from the early 18th century. Up to 14 real ales and ciders available in a welcoming, congenial atmosphere. Bargain beers on Mon nights. A shining example of how a pub should be run.
♨ Q ⑧ ⊟ ♣ ♿ P

Herne Bay

Heron
Station Road ☎ (0227) 372990
11–2.30 (4 Fri), 5.30–11 (11–11 Sat)
Shepherd Neame Master Brew Bitter Ⓗ
Modern pub with a comfortable, lively interior.
⑧ ◖ ⊟ ⇌ ♣ P

Prince of Wales
173 Mortimer Street
☎ (0227) 374205
10–3, 6–11
Shepherd Neame Master Brew Bitter Ⓗ
Pub with a high-ceilinged Victorian interior with good glass and woodwork. Set between High Street and the seafront. Q ⊟ ⅙ ♣

Rose Inn
111 Mortimer Street
☎ (0227) 375081
10–11
Shepherd Neame Master Brew Bitter Ⓗ**; guest beers**
Smart, comfortable pub in a pedestrianised area. At least two guest beers offered. Good value food. ◖ ⊟

Hernhill

Red Lion
Follow signs to Hernhill from A299, Thanet Way
☎ (0227) 751207
11–3, 6–11
Fuller's London Pride; Greene King Abbot; Shepherd Neame Master Brew Bitter Ⓗ**; guest beer**
Enterprising pub set in an historic village. Originally a 14th-century hall house. A guest beer is usually available as is Theobolds cider in summer.
♨ ⑧ ◖ ▶ ⅙ ♿ ♠ P

Hythe

Kings Head
117 High Street
☎ (0303) 266283
10.30–2.30, 6.30–11
Shepherd Neame Master Brew Bitter Ⓗ
16th-century, town-centre pub. A separate room, with a hatch to the main bar, is used mainly as a restaurant: children welcome if dining (no meals Sun). ◖

Try also: Globe, Red Lion Sq

Kingsdown

Kings Head
Upper Street
☎ (0304) 373915
11–2.30, 7–11 (12–2.30, 7–10.30 Sun)
Draught Bass; Charrington IPA; Welsh Brewers Worthington BB Ⓗ
Popular two-bar local on a narrow street through the village. Parking can be difficult. ◖ ▶ ⊟ ♣

Lower Haysden

Royal Oak
W off A26 at Shell roundabout. Follow signs to village OS569457
☎ (0732) 350208

11–3.30, 5.30–11 (11–11 Sat)
Adnams Bitter; Fuller's London Pride Ⓗ**; guest beers**
Friendly, well-frequented pub with a helpful beer tasting guide on a blackboard. One beer is always on special offer. Weekly live music; annual beer festival in a field opposite. Eve meals Fri/Sat only. ♨ Q ⑧ ◖ ▶ ⊟ P

Lynsted

Black Lion
☎ (0795) 521229
11–3, 6–11
Courage Best Bitter, Directors Ⓗ
Thriving, community-spirited local in a quiet village.
Q ⑧ ◖ ▶ ⊟ ♠ P

Maidstone

Dog & Gun
213 Boxley Road
☎ (0622) 758478
11–2.30, 5.30–11 (11–11 Fri & Sat)
Shepherd Neame Master Brew Bitter Ⓗ
Popular, friendly, two-bar local. Landlord played in Chicory Tip pop group (gold discs on the walls). Good barbecues in summer.
⑧ ◖ ⊟ ⇌ (East) ♣

Fishers Arms
22 Scott Street (off A229, N of centre)
☎ (0622) 753632
11–3, 6–11 (usually 11–11 Sat)
Courage Best Bitter; Goacher's Mild (winter), **Light** (summer); **Wadworth 6X** Ⓗ**; guest beers**
Large, single-bar pub on a street corner; upstairs function room. Regular guest beers include Goacher's and others from the Courage approved list. ⑧ ◖ ⇌ (East) ♣

Greyhound
77 Wheeler Street
☎ (0622) 754032
10.45–3.30, 6–11
Shepherd Neame Master Brew Bitter, Stock Ale Ⓗ
Very friendly local. Also known, in certain circles, as the Fat Ox – ask landlord to reveal all! Home-cooked lunches Tue–Sat.
⑧ ◖ ⊟ ⇌ (East) ♣ P

Hare & Hounds
45–47 Lower Boxley Road
☎ (0622) 678388
11–3 (3.30 Fri, 4 Sat), 5.30 (7 Sat)–11
Marston's Pedigree; Whitbread Flowers IPA Ⓗ
Comfortable, welcoming town pub opposite the prison. An additional cask beer is to be introduced. Eve meals finish at 7.30. Occasional barbecues.
⑧ ◖ ▶ ⅙ ⇌ (East) ♣

152

Pilot

23–25 Upper Stone Street
(A229 one-way system
southbound) ☎ (0622) 691162
11–3, 6 (7 Sat)–11
**Harveys XX Mild, BB, XXXX
Old, Armada** H
Good, honest town pub with a
friendly welcome. The only
Harveys Mild for miles.
Petanque played, also Kentish
Doubles darts. Real value for
money home-made food (no
meals Sun lunch). 🏚 ⊛ ◑ ≠ ♣

Royal Paper Mill

39 Tovil Hill, Tovil (B2010, 1
mile from centre)
☎ (0622) 752095
11–3, 7–11
Goacher's Mild, Dark, Old H
Small, comfortable, one-bar
local with a very friendly
atmosphere. 🏚 ⊛ ๕ ♣

Try also: Dragoon, Sandling
Rd (Shepherd Neame)

Marden

West End Tavern

West End ☎ (0622) 831956
11–3 (4 Sat), 6–11
**Fuller's London Pride;
Harveys BB; Marston's
Pedigree; Whitbread
Fremlins Bitter** H; guest beers
Cosy free house in a village
with a market town feel. Good
tandoori nearby. No pub food
Sun lunch.
🏚 ⊛ ◑ ๕ ≠ ♣ P

Margate

Orb

243 Ramsgate Road (A254)
☎ (0843) 220663
11–11
**Shepherd Neame Master
Brew Bitter, Spitfire** H
Pub which has deservedly
appeared in this guide every
year since 1976; a two-bar
local with a loyal following.
Special garden events such as
barbecues and Greek nights.
Live music regularly played
by the landlord.
🏚 ⊛ ◑ ♣ P

Princess of Wales

20 Tivoli Road
☎ (0843) 223944
11–3, 6–11 (11–11 Sat)
**Shepherd Neame Master
Brew Bitter** H
Popular and friendly, typical
Victorian, two-bar corner
local. An unspoilt pub. Bar
snacks. ๖ ⊛ ⊟ ♣

Spread Eagle

25 Victoria Road, Charlotte
Square ☎ (0843) 293396
11.30–3, 5.30–11 (11.30–11 Sat)
**Adnams Bitter; Courage
Directors; Fuller's London

Pride; Greene King IPA;
Hook Norton Old Hooky;
Mitchell's Fortress, ESB** H;
guest beers
Excellent, comfortable,
Victorian corner pub with a
good selection of independent
ales. Well worth the walk to
the top of the high street.
Basketball played. No food
Sun. ๖ ⊛ ⊛ ◑ ♣

Marshside

Gate Inn

Boyden Gate (Chislet turn off
A28 in Upstreet)
☎ (0227) 86498
11–3, 6–11
**Shepherd Neame Master
Brew Bitter, Stock Ale** G
Splendid country pub with
ducks, apple trees, quizzes
and rugby and cricket teams.
Regular pub pianist and jazz.
No keg lager during Lent. Pub
beer festival in August.
Imaginative doorstep
sandwiches.
🏚 Q ๖ ⊛ ◑ ๕ ▲ ♣ P

Matfield

Walnut Tree

Brenchley Road (off B2160 at
Matfield, past fire station)
☎ (089 272) 3477
11.30–3, 6–11
**Cotleigh Tawny, Old
Buzzard; Harveys Pale Ale;
Marston's Border Bitter** H
Cosy and friendly one-bar
pub. Live music Fri. No food
Sun. Cider in summer.
🏚 ⊛ ◑ ♣ ♣ P

Minster (Thanet)

Saddler's

7 Monkton Road (B2047)
☎ (0843) 821331
11–2.30, 6–11 (11–11 Sat)
**Shepherd Neame Master
Brew Bitter** H
Excellent, friendly and
popular, two-bar local at the
village centre. Good value
meals lunch and eve (not
served Sun). Bat and Trap
played. ⊛ ◑ ๖ ⊟ ≠ ♣

Northbourne

Hare & Hounds

The Street ☎ (0304) 365429
10.30–3, 6–11
**Draught Bass; Shepherd
Neame Master Brew Bitter** H;
guest beers
Busy country pub in a rural
village. Justifiably popular for
food. Playground in the
garden. ⊛ ◑ ◑ P

Oad Street

Plough & Harrow

Opp. Oad Street craft centre
☎ (0795) 843351
11–11

**Adnams Bitter; Greene King
IPA; Shepherd Neame Master
Brew Bitter; Whitbread
Boddingtons Bitter** H; guest
beers
Thriving and popular real ale
oasis offering a range of eight
beers and a friendly
welcome from an energetic
landlord. Theobalds cider in
summer.
🏚 ๖ ⊛ ◑ ⊟ ♣ ⊂ P

Oare

Three Mariners

2 Church Road
☎ (0795) 533633
10–3 (5 Sat), 6 (7 winter)–11
**Shepherd Neame Master
Brew Bitter, Spitfire** H
Rambling village pub which
probably dates back 400 years,
with ships' timbers used in the
construction. Food available at
all times but book Sun lunch.
Children's playhouse and
swings in the garden. Bat and
Trap played.
🏚 Q ๖ ⊛ ◑ ♣ P

Offham

Kings Arms

The Green (¾ mile from A20)
☎ (0732) 845208
11–3, 6–11 (11–11 Fri & Sat)
**Courage Best Bitter;
Wadworth 6X** H
Cosy village local, close to the
green. A warm welcome is
guaranteed. The good value
lunchtime menu includes
sausages from the village
butcher.
🏚 ⊛ ◑ P

Otham

White Horse

White Horse Lane
☎ (0622) 861304
11–3, 6.30–11 (11–11 Fri & Sat)
**Courage Best Bitter,
Directors; Wadworth 6X;
Young's Special** H
Open-plan village pub near
Maidstone, with a reputation
for good food.
⊛ ◑ ๕ ♣ P

Pembury

Black Horse

12 High Street
☎ (0892) 822141
11–11
**Harveys BB, Old; Ruddles
Best Bitter; Young's
Special** H; guest beers
Cosy, friendly pub with a bar
in the centre, creating several
drinking areas. Caters for the
business trade at lunchtime;
more local in the evening.
House beer.
🏚 Q ⊛ ◑ ๕ ♣

Kent

Penshurst

Bottle House Inn
Smarts Hill (^{1}/$_2$ mile W of Smarts Hill on Coldharbour Lane) OS516421
☎ (0892) 870306
11–2.30, 6–11
Ind Coope Burton Ale; Larkins Bitter; Wadworth 6X Ⓗ
Popular, remotely situated, large pub, dating back to the 15th century, though extensively modernised. Good food in a separate restaurant (no meals Sun eve). Landlord is a *Burton Master Cellarman*. Immaculate toilets.
♨ ❀ ◖❋ ⬥ & P

Perry Wood

Rose & Crown
OS042552 ☎ (0227) 752214
12–2.30 (3 Sat), 7–11 (closed Mon)
Brakspear Special; Shepherd Neame Master Brew Bitter; Wadworth 6X; Whitbread Boddingtons Bitter Ⓗ**; guest beers**
15th-century inn set in pleasant woodland with a Bat and Trap pitch. Booking advisable for the restaurant. Families welcomed.
♨ Q ❀ ◖❋ ⬥ P

Petteridge

Hopbine
Petteridge Lane (off A21, ^{1}/$_2$ mile S of Brenchley) OS668412
☎ (0892) 722561
12 (11 Sat)–2.30, 6–11
King & Barnes Mild, Sussex, Broadwood, Old, Festive Ⓗ
Small, cosy, friendly pub which attracts local trade plus walkers and cyclists. Good for sightseeing. The only King & Barnes house in Kent. Good value food (not served Wed).
♨ Q ❀ ◖❋ & P

Queenborough

Old House at Home
High Street ☎ (0795) 662783
12–11
Greene King IPA, Abbot Ⓗ
Local pub with RNLA and nautical themes. Overlooks the Swale estuary. Generous portions of good food.
♨ ◖❋ ⬚ ⬥

Rainham

Green Lion
104 High Street (A2)
☎ (0634) 231938
11–11
Courage Best Bitter; John Smith's Bitter Ⓗ**; guest beer**
Originally built in 1346, a one-time coaching inn known simply as the Lion until this century. Pets corner and play area in the garden. Beware: the Scrumpy Jack is not real cider. Families welcome in the function room. ⬚ ❀ ◖❋ ⬥ P

Ramsgate

Churchill Tavern
The Paragon (overlooking Royal Harbour)
☎ (0843) 587862
11–11 (11–3, 6–11 Sat)
Adnams Broadside; Felinfoel Double Dragon; Fuller's ESB; Ringwood Old Thumper; Taylor Landlord Ⓗ**; guest beers**
Lately known as the Van Gogh or Steptoe's, a pub rebuilt a couple of years ago using much old wood, stained-glass panels and other fittings. Popular with students. Jazz Wed; folk Sun. Printed real ale handouts on the bar. ♨ ◖ ⬥ ✂

Ripple

Plough
Church Lane (off A258 at Ringwould) OS346499
☎ (0304) 360209
11–3, 6–11 (may vary)
Ind Coope Burton Ale; Shepherd Neame Master Brew Bitter Ⓗ**; guest beers**
Popular 16th-century rural local with a restaurant upstairs. Four guest beers usually available; occasional beer festivals.
♨ ⬚ ❀ ◖❋ ⬥ P

Riverhead

Beehive
28 Chipstead Lane (150 yds from A25/A2028 jct)
☎ (0732) 742601
12–3, 6–11
Adnams Bitter; Morland Old Speckled Hen; Thwaites Bitter; Young's Special Ⓗ
Small, low-ceilinged, cosy pub with a relaxed atmosphere; built in 1640. An occasionally used back room contains an old bread oven. A play area in the garden includes a wendy house. Situated on a narrow one-way lane.
♨ ❀ ⬚ ◖❋ ⬥

Rochester

Britannia
376 High Street
☎ (0634) 401514
11–11
Fuller's London Pride; Goacher's Light; Greene King IPA, Abbot Ⓗ**; guest beer**
Friendly town lounge with live music Thu nights. A free house between Rochester and Chatham stations. No food Sun. ◖ ✂

Granville Arms
83 Maidstone Road (B2097)
☎ (0634) 845243
11–3, 7–11
Greene King IPA, Abbot Ⓗ
Comfortable, friendly pub with a pleasant atmosphere. No food Sun. ❀ ◖ ✂ ⬥ P

Greyhound
68 Rochester Avenue
☎ (0634) 844120
10–3, 6–11 (10–11 Sat)
Shepherd Neame Master Brew Bitter Ⓗ
Late-Victorian terraced local. The public is rather basic but the saloon has a range and four chaises-longues. Warm and cosy with a relaxing atmosphere. Entrance to the enclosed garden is through the pub. No meals Sun.
♨ ❀ ◖❋ ✂

Ship Inn
347 High Street
☎ (0634) 844264
11–11
Courage Best Bitter; Wadworth 6X Ⓗ**; guest beer**
Lively two-bar pub displaying a collection of playbills and other theatre memorabilia. Live entertainment nightly in the theatre lounge. Live modern jazz Sun lunch. No food Sun. King & Barnes mild is an occasional guest beer.
❀ ◖ ✂

White Hart
15 High Street
☎ (0634) 848182
11–3, 7–11 (11–11 Fri & Sat)
Ind Coope Burton Ale; Whitbread Fremlins Bitter Ⓗ
Friendly city-centre pub near the cathedral and castle. Occasional live music. Popular with summer tourists.
✂ (Rochester/Strood) ⬥

Who'd Ha' Tho't It
9 Baker Street (50 yds off Maidstone Rd, B2097)
☎ (0634) 841131
11–11
Beer range varies Ⓗ
Down to earth drinker's den. One roomy bar with bare boards and low lights. A rear bar is used as a games or quiz room, or for meetings. 300-plus real ales were served in 1991 (seven, mainly from independents, always available). Woodham's XXX is a house beer brewed by Goacher's. No weekend food.
♨ ❀ ◖ ⬚

Try also: Norman Conquest, High St (Free)

Rodmersham Green

Fruiterers Arms
☎ (0795) 424198
11–3, 6–11

Courage Best Bitter, Directors H
Pleasant village inn set among acres of orchards.
🏚 🕯 ◖ ▶ 🍴 ⬥ P

Rusthall

The Brahms
1 Common View
☎ (0892) 526796
11–3 (not Wed), 6–11 (11–11 Sat)
Marston's Pedigree; Whitbread Fremlins Bitter H
Single U-shaped bar with a friendly atmosphere and a local clientele. A good basic drinker's pub; a third beer is expected soon. 🏚 Q 🕯 ⬥ P

St Margaret's at Cliffe

Hope Inn
High Street ☎ (0304) 852444
10.30–11
Shepherd Neame Master Brew Bitter H
Built in 1815 and tastefully refurbished. A friendly local which also caters for summer holiday trade.
🏚 🕯 ◖ ▶ 🍴 ⬥ P

St Mary in the Marsh

Star Inn
Pickney Bush Lane OS065279
☎ (0679) 62139
11–3, 7–11
Shepherd Neame Master Brew Bitter; Wadworth 6X H
Friendly, well-frequented country local built in 1476. Single L-shaped bar with an inglenook and different character in each part. A real pub. Good food with vegetables from the pub's garden. 🏚 🍴 🕯 🏚 ◖ ▶ ⬥ P

Sandgate

Ship Inn
65 High Street
☎ (0303) 248525
11–3, 6–11
Ind Coope Friary Meux Best Bitter H, **Burton Ale** G; **S&N Theakston Old Peculier** H
Busy two-bar pub which claims to sell more Burton Ale per square foot of bar space than any other pub in the world! HQ of Sandgate Clog Morris. Pavement tables. Excellent home-cooked food.
🕯 ◖ ▶ 🍴

Sandwich

Crispin
2 High Street ☎ (0304) 617365
11–11
Draught Bass; Charrington IPA H
Large corner pub whose

layout gives the impression of separate bars. Beamed ceiling. Cosy and friendly.
🏚 🕯 ▶ 🚲 ⬥

Greyhound
10 New Street ☎ (0304) 612675
10–4, 7–11 (may vary)
Courage Best Bitter H
One large, wood-panelled bar created from smaller bars. Spacious separate games area.
🚲 ⬥

Sarre

Crown Inn
Ramsgate Road (A28/A253 jct) ☎ (0843) 47808
11–11
Shepherd Neame Master Brew Bitter, Spitfire, Bishops Finger H
Old staging post known locally as the 'Cherry Brandy House'. Recently refurbished, with a sympathetically-built hotel annexe, low beams, cosy rooms, a restaurant and its own famous cherry brandy, by ancient charter.
Q 🕯 🏚 ◖ ▶ 🍴 ⬥ P

Sevenoaks

Royal Oak Tap
2 High Street (A225)
☎ (0732) 458783
11–3, 6–11
Webster's Yorkshire Bitter; Whitbread Fremlins Bitter H; guest beers
Old pub in the oldest part of town, near Knole Park entrance. Usually two guest beers, changed regularly. Often busy. Be careful to use the Tap's car park and not the hotel's (they clamp!).
🏚 🐂 🕯 ◖ ⬥ P

Try also: Anchor, London Rd (Bass)

Shatterling

Green Man
Pedding Hill (A257, Wingham–Ash road)
☎ (0304) 812525
11.15–2.30 (3 Sat), 6.30–11
Shepherd Neame Master Brew Bitter; Young's Bitter, Special H
Isolated roadhouse in an attractive rural setting. Caters for local, passing and touring trade. Good value meals. Bat and Trap played.
🕯 🏚 ◖ ⬥ P

Sheerness

Red Lion
High Street, Bluetown
☎ (0795) 663165
12–3, 6 (8 Sat)–11 (12–3, 8–11 Sun)
Greene King Abbot H; guest beers
Unpretentious and unspoilt

beer drinkers' haven offering one of the best ranges in the area, including a Greene King house beer. Jovial and gregarious landlord.
Q 🏚 🚲 ⬥

Shoreham

Royal Oak
2 The High Street
☎ (095 92) 2319
10.30–3, 6–11
Adnams Bitter; Brakspear Bitter, Special; Eldridge Pope Royal Oak H; guest beers
Popular and welcoming pub, now a free house. The Sephams Farm cider is made less than a mile away. Specialises in unusual pub games. 🏚 🕯 ◖ ▶ 🏚 🚲 ⬥ 🍏

Shorne

Rose & Crown
32 The Street (off A226)
☎ (047 482) 2373
11–2.30, 6–11
Adnams Bitter; Ruddles County; Webster's Yorkshire Bitter H
Attractive old pub in quiet surroundings. Good value food. 🕯 ◖ ▶ 🍴 P

Sittingbourne

Barge
17 Crown Quay Lane
☎ (0795) 423291
11–3, 5 (7 Sat)–11
Courage Best Bitter H; guest beers
Busy two-bar pub away from the centre, near the sailing barge museum. Good value food. Separate pool and darts area. Beware the keg Scrumpy Jack cider on fake handpump.
🕯 ◖ ▶ 🏚 🚲 ⬥ P

Long Hop
80 Key Street (A2, 1 mile W of centre) ☎ (0795) 425957
11–11 (11–2.30, 6–11 Tue)
Courage Best Bitter; Ruddles County H
Comfortable, rustically refurbished house, opposite Gore Court cricket ground. No food Sun. Menu and garden cater for children. Tiny car park. 🏚 🕯 ◖ ▶ ⬥ P

Ship Inn
22 East Street ☎ (0795) 425087
11–3 (4 Fri & Sat), 6.30–11
Courage Best Bitter H; guest beer
Friendly town local retaining two bars. Darts, pool, football and quiz teams. The guest beer is priced the same as the Courage Best but beware the keg Scrumpy Jack cider on fake handpump. No food Sun. Families welcome in the function room.
🐂 ◖ ▶ 🏚 🚲 ⬥ P

Kent

Smarden

Bell
Bell Lane OS870430
☎ (023 377) 283
11.30–2.30, 6–11
**Fuller's London Pride;
Goacher's Light; Harveys
Pale Ale; Ringwood Old
Thumper; Shepherd Neame
Master Brew Bitter;
Whitbread Fremlins Bitter** H
Large country inn dating from
the 13th century, situated
about one mile outside the
village. Justifiably popular, so
parking can be difficult.
Biddenden cider. ♨ Q ❀ ❀
🍴 🍺 🛏 ♿ & ♣ ⌂ P ⊬

Snargate

Red Lion
On B2080, Brenzett–
Appledore road OS990286
☎ (0679) 344648
11–3, 7–11
**Adnams Bitter; Bateman
Mild, XB** G; **guest beers**
Known as 'Doris's', a
wonderfully unspoilt,
unpretentious, small rural pub
featuring stone and timber
floors, a marble counter top, a
piano and Toad in the Hole.
Large garden. Unspoilt by
modern conveniences. A
must. ♨ Q ❀ ♣ ⌂ P

Southborough

Bat & Ball
141 London Road
☎ (0892) 528448
11–3, 6–11
**Fuller's London Pride;
Whitbread Fremlins Bitter** H;
guest beers
Bow-fronted old town pub
with a single low bar. Three
guest beers which vary and a
winter special. ♨ ❀ 🍺 P

Beehive
Modest Corner (take Victoria
Rd off main road, right at
sign) ☎ (0892) 529151
11–3, 6–11 (11–11 Sat)
Beer range varies G & H
Isolated old pub on the
common with seating outside.
Anything from six to nine
beers changed weekly. Worth
finding. ♨ Q ❀ 🍺 & ♣

Speldhurst

Northfield House
Penshurst Road
☎ (0892) 863727
2–3 (not Mon), 6–11
**King & Barnes Sussex;
Larkins Bitter; Wells
Bombardier** H
True village community pub
with one bar. A hat for every
occasion behind the bar!
Watch out for the dog's party
tricks. ♨ ♣

Stalisfield Green

Plough
Stalisfield Road (2 miles N of
Charing) OS954529
☎ (0795) 890256
11–3, 6–11 (closed Mon)
**Adnams Extra; Harveys BB;
Ind Coope Burton Ale;
Shepherd Neame Master
Brew Bitter** H
Old, welcoming pub of
character, set in impressive
countryside. Shut the Box and
shove-ha'penny played.
Families welcome in the new
conservatory; booking advised
for the new restaurant. No
meals Sun eve.
♨ Q ❧ ❀ 🍴 🍺 🛏 & ♣ P

Stansted

Black Horse
Tumblefield Road (1 mile
from A20 at top of Wrotham
Hill) ☎ (0732) 822355
11–2.30, 6 (7 winter)–11
Whitbread Fremlins Bitter H;
guest beers
Not just a fine pub but also the
local post office. Situated in
good walking country.
Always two guest beers –
changing every two months.
Theobolds Barn cider.
♨ ❧ ❀ 🍴 🍺 🛏 ♣ ⌂ P

Staplestreet

Three Horseshoes
Signed from Boughton
☎ (0227) 750842
11–3 (4.30 Sat), 6–11 (11–11 Thu &
Fri)
**Shepherd Neame Master
Brew Bitter** G
Typically Kentish building
with a list of landlords going
back to 1690, a collection of
stone bottles and many table-
top games.
♨ Q ❀ 🍴 🍺 🛏 ♣ P

Stone Street

Padwell Arms
1 mile S of A25, between Seal
and Ightham OS569551
☎ (0732) 61532
12–3, 6–11
**Hall & Woodhouse Badger
Best Bitter; Harveys BB;
Hook Norton Old Hooky;
Young's Bitter; guest beers** H
Old pub set in the heart of the
Garden of England, enjoying
pleasant views across the
orchards. Ideal for summer
evenings. Meals finish at 8.30.
♨ ❀ 🍴 ♣ P

Tonbridge

Chequers Inn
High Street ☎ (0732) 358957
11–3, 7–11
**Courage Best Bitter,
Directors; Harveys BB;**

Wadworth 6X H
Built in 1367, with several later
additions. Now only one
drinking area. Note the
collection of brasses.
🍴 🍺 🛏 ♣ P

Priory Wine Cellars
64 Priory Street
☎ (0732) 359784
11 (10 Sat)–2, 4–9 (9.30 Fri & Sat;
12–2, 7–9 Sun; 5–9 Mon)
**Adnams Broadside; Bateman
XXXB; Exmoor Gold; Harveys
BB; Hook Norton Old
Hooky** H
Off-licence which serves up to
four ales through handpumps
and others direct from casks in
the cellar. Beers quoted are the
most popular but a wide
range is available.

Toy's Hill

Fox & Hounds
S off A25 in Brasted OS471520
☎ (0732) 750328
11–2.30, 6–11
Greene King IPA, Abbot H
Traditional country pub on
the edge of woods decimated
by the 1987 hurricane: a single
bar furnished with domestic
furniture and a selection of
magazines. Close to
Chartwell. Lunchtime snacks.
♨ Q ❧ ❀ ♣ P

Trottiscliffe

Plough
Taylors Lane (1 mile N of A20
at Wrotham Heath)
☎ (0732) 822233
11.30–3, 6–11
**Whitbread Boddingtons
Bitter, Fremlins Bitter,
Flowers Original; Younger
No. 3** H; **guest beers**
Cosy two-bar pub in a quiet
village. No eve meals Sun.
♨ ❀ 🍴 🍺 & ♣ P

Tunbridge Wells

Bitter End
107 Camden Road
☎ (0892) 522918
11–2, 4–10 (11–2 Sat; 12–2, 7–9 Sun)
Beer range varies
Small off-licence with a very
good selection of bottled beers
from around the world and a
draught house beer. Others
change weekly. Weston's
cider. 🍺 ⌂

Grapevine
8 Chapel Place
☎ (0892) 534205
11.30–11
**Harveys BB; Young's
Special** H; **guest beers**
Set in the oldest part of town,
this wine bar is small with
simple decor, including bare
floorboards. Intimate basement
restaurant. Occasional jazz
evenings. ♨ Q ❀ 🍴 🍺

Sir Alf Ramsey

Surrey Close, Showfields
Estate (off Eridge Rd)
☎ (0892) 530996
11.30–3.30 (11–4 Sat), 6–11 (12–2.30,
7–10.30 Sun)
**Cotleigh Tawny; Harveys BB;
Shepherd Neame Spitfire;
Whitbread Fremlins Bitter** H **;
guest beers**
Friendly local pub. Guest
beers vary from week to week.
♣ P

Upper Upnor

Tudor Rose

29 High Street
☎ (0634) 715305
12–3, 7–11
**Young's Bitter, Special,
Winter Warmer** H **; guest
beers**
Friendly pub with two quiet
rooms. Near the castle and
river. Eve meals Tue–Sat.
🏚 🛏 🏮 🛈 ♣ ♠

Try also: Kings Arms
(Courage)

Waltham

Lord Nelson

☎ (0227) 700628
12–3, 7–11 (closed Tue)
**Adnams Bitter; Goacher's
Light; Harveys BB; Ind Coope
Burton Ale; Wells Eagle** H **;
guest beers**
Gracious Georgian main bar

and a small public bar.
Collection of blacksmith's
implements. Play area in the
enormous garden; Bat and
Trap pitch. Excellent food.
Biddenden cider.
🏚 🏮 🛈 🍴 🛏 🛈 ♣ ⌂ P

Try also: Compasses,
Crundale (Free)

Westerham

General Wolfe

High Street (A25)
☎ (0959) 562104
11–3, 6–11
**Greene King IPA, Rayments
Special, Abbot** H
Low-ceilinged, weather-
boarded house of much
character; the safest bet in this
popular tourist town and once
the Westerham Brewery tap.
Small outside sitting area. No
food at weekends.
🏚 Q 🏮 ♣ P

Whitstable

Coach & Horses

37 Oxford Street (A290)
☎ (0227) 264732
11–3 (3.30 Sat), 6.30–11
**Shepherd Neame Master
Brew Bitter, Stock Ale** H
Popular, lively high street
local with seasonal barbecues
and a separate restaurant.
Theme nights about twice a
month. 🏮 🛈 🍴 🛏 🛈 🅰 🛒 ♣

Noah's Ark

83 Canterbury Road (A290)
☎ (0227) 272332
11–3, 6–11
**Shepherd Neame Master
Brew Bitter** H
Basic, friendly local with the
same landlord for 29 years.
Euchre sessions Fri eve and
Sun lunchtime.
🏮 🛏 🅰 🛒 ♣ P

Smack Inn

Middle Wall (near beach)
☎ (0227) 273056
10.30–3, 6.30–11
**Shepherd Neame Master
Brew Bitter** H
Lively wood-panelled pub
named after the oyster smacks
whose crews used to drink
here. No weekday meals.
🏮 🛈 🛏 🅰 ♣ ♠

Worth

St Crispin

The Street (off A258 between
Deal and Sandwich)
☎ (0304) 612081
11–3, 6–11
**Gale's HSB; Marston's
Merrie Monk, Pedigree;
Shepherd Neame Master
Brew Bitter** H **; guest beers** G
Old village pub sympath-
etically refurbished and
extended. Popular locally for
meals. Chalet accommodation.
🏚 Q 🏮 🛌 🛈 🅰 ♣ P

DRAUGHT BEERS IN A CAN

All canned beers are keg: pasteurised and artificially gassed.
In recent years, brewers have launched so-called 'draught
beers in cans'. They are certainly less gassy than the old canned
beers, and therefore not quite so unpleasant in taste. But they are
still keg.

The brewers, in promoting the new cans, imply that they contain
real ale. Perhaps the most outrageous claim has come from Bass,
whose advertising shows real Draught Bass being hand-pulled
into a can. Of course Draught Bass and Bass-in-a-can are
different beers: one is real and the other isn't.

Independent taste tests of the canned 'draught' beers show that
they do not compare with the real thing. Claims that they do are
a con.

The Advertising Standards Authority, despite being fully briefed
by CAMRA, has refused to condemn misleading advertising.
Trading Standards Departments have also refused to act. Will we
have to wait for the supermarkets to produce 'fresh peas in a can'
before they wake up?

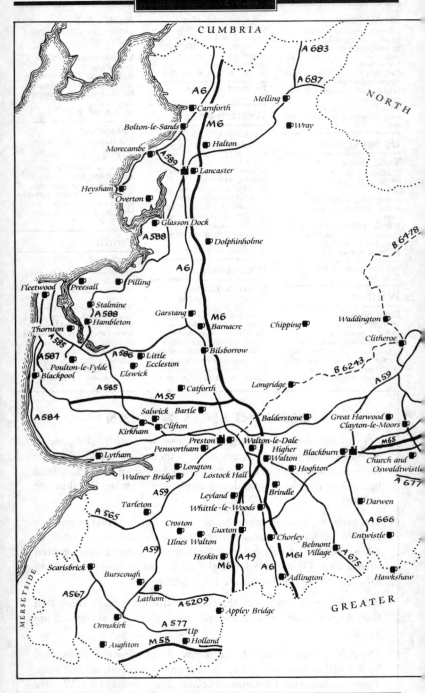

Lancashire

Lion's, Burnley; **Mitchell's**, Lancaster; **Moorhouse's**, Burnley; **Preston**, Preston; **Thwaites**, Blackburn

Y O R K S H I R E

0   5 miles
0   5   10 km

Bolton-by-Bowland A56
A 59
A 682
Black Lane Ends
Colne
Newchurch in Pendle A6068 Fence-in-Pendle
Brierfield
Padiham M65
A678 A679 Burnley
Huncoat Mereclough
Accrington A646
Rawtenstall Waterfoot Bacup
Haslingden
Cowpe

W E S T   Y O R K S H I R E

M A N C H E S T E R

Lancashire

Accrington

Abbey
Bank Street ☎ (0254) 235727

11.30–3.30, 7–11 (11.30–11 Fri)
John Smith's Bitter H
Small, two-roomed local in a
quiet corner of town, offering
good value lunches.
Q ✿ ⑧ ⊄ ◱ ≈ ♣

Great Eastern
Arnold Street
☎ (0254) 234483
12–5, 7–11 (12–11 Sat)
Thwaites Mild, Bitter H
Recently renovated pub, but
retaining its character; very
much a friendly local.
⊄ ≈ ♣

Nags Head
78 Blackburn Road
☎ (0254) 233965
11.30–11
Thwaites Best Mild, Bitter H
Three-roomed, street-corner
local. ≈ ♣

Adlington

White Bear
5a Market Street
☎ (0257) 482357
11–11
**S&N Matthew Brown Mild,
Theakston Best Bitter, XB,
Old Peculier; Younger No.3** H
Excellent three-roomed, stone
town pub on the main road.
Good atmosphere and good
value food. Open all day Sun
for food; no meals Mon eve.
♨ ⛄ ⑧ ◱ ⊄ ≈ ♣

Appley Bridge

Wheatsheaf
287 Miles Lane (B5375, 1 mile
from M6 jct 27)
☎ (0257) 252302
12–3.30, 5.30–11 (12–11 Fri & Sat)
Greenalls Mild, Bitter H
Immensely popular,
comfortable pub in a semi-
rural area. A wonderful
collection of mugs and water
jugs fills every inch of hanging
space. Excellent value food.
⑧ ◱ ≈ ♣ P

Aughton

Dog & Gun
233 Long Lane (³/₄ mile E of
A59) ☎ (0695) 423303
5–11 (12–3, 5–11 Sat)
**Burtonwood Mild, Bitter,
Forshaw's** H
Excellent, friendly village local
on the edge of town. Recently
redecorated but unspoilt.
Claims to sell the best pint of
mild in the district. Enjoy
good conversation without
piped music. Bowling green at
the rear. ♨ Q ✿ ⬥
≈ (Aughton Pk) ♣ P

Stanley Arms
St Michaels Road (off A59)
☎ (0695) 423241
11.30–3, 5.30–11

**Cains Bitter; Ind Coope
Burton Ale; Walker Mild,
Bitter** H
Comfortable, old village pub
opposite the church: a local
meeting place and popular at
all times. Very good value
food (eve meals until 7.30).
The children's play area with
climbing frame is well
patronised on summer eves.
Family room till 8pm. Crown
green bowling. ♨ ✿ ⑧ ◱
⬥ ≈ (Town Green) P

Bacup

New Inn
Rochdale Road
☎ (0706) 873130
11–11
Thwaites Best Mild, Bitter H
Comfortable, four-roomed
local with a central bar,
traditional wood-panelled
ceilings and interesting 19th-
century murals. ♨ ⛄ ♣

Try also: British Queen,
Union St (Banks's)

Balderstone

Myerscough
Whalley Road (A59)
☎ (0254) 812222
11.30–3, 5.30–11
**Robinson's Best Mild, Best
Bitter, Old Tom** H
Pleasant country pub with a
large, wood-panelled lounge
and a separate room with a
coal fire. Note the preserved
Canberra and Lightning
aircraft opposite at the BAe
factory. No meals Sun eve.
♨ Q ⛄ ✿ ◱ P

Barnacre

Kenlis Arms
Ray Lane (by former Garstang
& Catterall station) OS510439
☎ (0995) 603307
12–3 (not Mon), 6.30–11 (11–11 Sat)
**Burtonwood Bitter;
Whitbread Boddingtons
Bitter** H
Built in 1871 as a shooting
lodge, later a station hotel.
Now has more locals than its
isolated position would
suggest. Also runs discos
(quite separate from the bar).
⛄ ✿ ⌂ ◱ ♣ P

Bartle

Sitting Goose
Sidegreaves Lane (A5085)
☎ (0772) 690344
11.30–3, 6–11 (11–11 Fri & Sat)
Thwaites Best Mild, Bitter E
Comfortable, popular pub in
Fylde countryside. Cosy
atmosphere and a restaurant.
The large garden is good for
children. ⛄ ✿ ◱ ♣ P

159

Lancashire

Belmont Village

Black Dog
2 Church Street OS674163
☎ (020 481) 218
12–4, 6.30–11
Holt Mild, Bitter Ⓗ
Popular moorland village pub
on the old Bolton–Preston
road. The landlord whistles
the classics and invites
occasional live orchestras; no
jukebox. No food Mon. The
only Holt pub in Lancashire.
🏾 Q ⏰ ❀ ⇋ ◑ ♣ P

Bilsborrow

White Bull
Garstang Road ☎ (0995) 40324
12–3 (not Mon), 7–11 (may vary
summer)
**S&N Matthew Brown Mild,
Theakston Best Bitter** Ⓗ
Canalside pub on the main
A6; friendly and unspoilt.
🏾 Q ❀ ♣ P

Blackburn

Imperial Hotel
25 Devonport Road
☎ (0254) 54460
11–11
Thwaites Mild, Bitter Ⓗ
Very small corner pub which
feels crowded when only a
dozen people are in. Enjoys a
healthy passing trade, is rarely
empty and often boisterous
and full of building workers.
Q ⇋

Moorgate Arms
Liversey Branch Road
☎ (0254) 51408
11–11
Thwaites Mild, Bitter Ⓗ
Local which caters for all ages,
including families.
Q ⇋ (Mill Hill)

Try also: **Bank Hotel,** Hope St
(Lion's)

Black Lane Ends

Hare & Hounds
Skipton Old Road (3 miles
from centre) OS928433
☎ (0282) 863070
12–3 (not Tue or Thu), 6.30–11
**Taylor Dark Mild, Best
Bitter** Ⓗ
Friendly pub set high in a
Pennine landscape. Good
value, home-cooked food
available until 9pm. Live
music (country and jazz) Wed
and weekends.
🏾 ◑ ⇋ ♣ P

Blackpool

Bispham Hotel
Red Bank Road, Bispham (off
A584) ☎ (0253) 51752
11–3 (4 Sat), 6 (7 Sat)–11
Samuel Smith OBB Ⓗ

Well-managed, friendly pub,
popular with locals and
holidaymakers. ◑ ⇋ ♣

Clarence Hotel
88 Preston New Road (A583)
☎ (0253) 61064
12–3, 6 (7 Sat)–11
Thwaites Best Mild, Bitter Ⓗ
1950s open-plan, two-level
pub with a large, basic public
bar, well known for good
value local fare (eve meals
6–7.30). Children are allowed
into a restricted area
weekdays. Has won awards
for charity fundraising.
❀ ◑ ⇋ ♣ P

Empress Hotel
59 Exchange Street
☎ (0253) 20413
11–11 (11am–1am Fri & Sat in
summer)
Thwaites Best Mild, Bitter Ⓗ
Almost 200 years-old, this
centrally situated pub has
great character, its ceilings
embellished by Venetian
craftsmen. An old-fashioned
pub offering overnight
accommodation in large,
comfortable rooms. Other
attractions include: snooker,
darts, quiz nights, a late bar in
season, a dance floor and a
Wurlitzer organ.
⏰ ⇋ ⇋ (North) ♣

Mount Pleasant Inn
103 High Street
☎ (0253) 293335
11–11
**S&N Matthew Brown Mild,
Theakston Best Bitter, XB,
Old Peculier** Ⓗ
Small, friendly, basic local, full
of character. Close to all
amenities; Sky TV and
snooker available.
⇋ ⇋ (North) ♣ ⏪

Raikes Hall Hotel
Liverpool Road
☎ (0253) 294372
11–11
**Draught Bass; Stones Best
Bitter; Welsh Brewers
Worthington BB** Ⓗ
Built in 1750 as a family home,
then a Catholic convent; the
first house in Blackpool to be
carpeted! Offers crown green
bowls and shortmat bowls –
home of the Talbot Trophy.
Good food (eve meals on
request). ❀ ⇋ ◑ ♣ P

Ramsden Arms Hotel
204 Talbot Road (100 yds from
bus and rail stations)
☎ (0253) 23215
10.30–11
**Cains Bitter; Hydes' Anvil
Bitter; Ind Coope Burton Ale;
Jennings Bitter; Robinson's
Best Bitter; Tetley Walker
Bitter** Ⓗ**; guest beers**
Refurbished but retaining its
traditional atmosphere, this
award-winning, large, friendly

pub has collections of
tankards and stuffed deer
heads. Karaoke Tue nights.
🏾 ◑ ⇋ ⇋ (North) ♣ P ⚹

Welcome Inn
Vicarage Lane, Marton (off
A583, near Normid
hypermarket) ☎ (0253) 65372
11–11
**Burtonwood Mild, Bitter,
Forshaw's** Ⓗ
Large modern pub on the
outskirts of town. It has a
warm, friendly atmosphere in
its cosy, intimate lounge and
large vaults with a snooker
table. Good value food in its
restaurant. Children's safe
play area in the award-
winning garden. A former
local CAMRA *Pub of the Year.*
⏰ ❀ ◑ ⇋ & ♣ P

Wheatsheaf Hotel
192 Talbot Road (200 yds from
station) ☎ (0253) 25062
11–11
**S&N Matthew Brown Mild,
Theakston Best Bitter, XB,
Old Peculier** Ⓗ
Modernised, down-to-earth
local near the town centre. Full
of character and a popular
Guide entry. Pool played.
Q ⇋ & ⇋ (North) ♣

Bolton-by-Bowland

Copy Nook Hotel
2 miles off A59, ½ mile before
village OS778494
☎ (020 07) 205
11–3, 6–11
**S&N Theakston Best Bitter,
XB; Taylor Landlord** Ⓗ
Comfortable hotel in rural
surroundings, popular with
locals and visitors. Extensive
menu at all times and good
accommodation. 🏾 Q ⏰ ❀
⇋ ◑ & ♣ P ⚹

Bolton-le-Sands

Blue Anchor
Main Road ☎ (0524) 823421
11–11
**Mitchell's Mild, Best Bitter,
ESB** Ⓗ
Robust, friendly local at the
heart of a large village. It has a
games room, a restaurant and
a snug. Parking for residents
only, otherwise difficult.
🏾 ❀ ⇋ ◑ ♣

Brierfield

Waggon & Horses
Colne Road (near M65 jct 12)
☎ (0282) 613962
11.30–3, 5–11 (11.30–11 Fri & Sat)
Thwaites Best Mild, Bitter Ⓗ
A former CAMRA *Best
Refurbished Pub* winner: a
popular, multi-roomed
roadside house which hosts a
wide variety of meetings. One

Lancashire

room is still gas-lit. Resident ghost. 🏠 ✤ ◗ 🛱 ♣ P

Brindle

Cavendish Arms
Sandy Lane (B5256, Leyland–Blackburn road)
☎ (0254) 852912
11–3, 5.30–11 (11–11 Sat)
Burtonwood Mild, Bitter Ⓗ
Outstanding, traditional village pub with lots of stained-glass and wood carving. Originally named the Gerrard Arms after the family from nearby Hoghton Towers. Children welcome at mealtimes.
🏠 Q 🐦 ✤ ◗ ▷ 🛱 ♣ P

Burnley

General Scarlett
243–245 Accrington Road (A679, 400 yds from M65 jct 10) ☎ (0282) 831054
12–4, 7–11
Moorhouse's Black Cat Mild, Premier, Pendle Witches Brew; John Smith's Bitter Ⓗ
Lively two-roomed local opposite the brewery.
🛱 (Rose Grove) ♣ P

Lanehead
Hillingdon Road, Kibblebank Estate ☎ (0282) 59491
11–3, 7–11 (11–11 Fri & Sat)
Thwaites Bitter Ⓗ
Large, cosy estate pub with a friendly, very busy tap room. Excellent cheap lunches.
✤ ◗ 🛱 ♣ P

Manor Barn
Padiham Road (A671, off Lakeland Way)
☎ (0282) 56744
11–3, 6–11 (all day Sun for meals)
Burtonwood Bitter Ⓗ
Deservedly popular, split-level pub, with a restaurant in a converted farm building offering genuine Italian cuisine. Q ✤ ◗ ▶ ♿ 🛱 (Rose Grove) P

Burscough

Martin Inn
Martin Lane (off A570/B5242)
OS414127 ☎ (0704) 892302
11.30–3, 5.30–11
Courage Directors; Ruddles County; John Smith's Bitter; Tetley Walker Dark Mild Ⓗ
Remote but welcoming inn near Martin Mere Wildfowl Trust. Stone-floored in part; separate cottage grill restaurant. Local CAMRA *Summer Pub of the Year 1991.*
🏠 ✤ 🛏 ◗ ♣ P

Carnforth

Cross Keys
Kellet Road ☎ (0524) 732749
12–3, 7–11
Mitchell's Best Bitter Ⓗ

Cheerful, bustling local away from the town centre with two contrasting bars. ✤ ◗ ♣ P

Catforth

Running Pump
Catforth Road (off B5269)
☎ (0772) 690265
11.30–3 (not Mon), 6–11
Robinson's Best Mild, Best Bitter Ⓗ, **Old Tom** (winter) Ⓖ
Low-beamed country pub with coal fires in two rooms. Good value, home-cooked lunches available. Look out for the original village pump at the front. 🏠 Q 🐦 ◗ ▲ ♣ P

Chipping

Sun Inn
Windy Street ☎ (0995) 61206
11–4, 6–11 (11–11 Sat)
Whitbread Boddingtons Mild, Bitter Ⓗ
Deservedly popular, stone pub in a prize-winning picturesque village. Beware of the steep staircase at the front. Reputedly haunted.
Q 🐦 ▲ ♣ P

Chorley

Albion
29 Bolton Street
☎ (0257) 275225
12–11
Tetley Walker Mild, Bitter Ⓗ
Two-roomed, town-centre pub of character with a basic bar and a comfortable lounge.
✤ ◗ ▶ 🛱 🛱 ♣

Malt 'n' Hops
Friday Street ☎ (0257) 260967
12–2.30, 5–11 (12–11 Fri & Sat)
Moorhouse's Pendle Witches Brew; Taylor Landlord; Whitbread Boddingtons Bitter; Wilson's Mild, Webster's Yorkshire Bitter Ⓗ; **guest beers**
Small, comfortable free house, converted from a shop, just north of the town centre. Ideal for train spotters; large public car park opposite. A local CAMRA award winner. Four weekly guest beers. 🛱

Queens Tavern
Preston Road ☎ (0257) 275902
11.30–3, 6.30–11 (11.30–11 Fri & Sat)
Whitbread Chester's Mild, Boddingtons Bitter, Trophy, Castle Eden Ale Ⓗ
Large, main road local with an imposing frontage. Parking is difficult. ◗ ▶ 🛱 ♣

Shepherds Arms
Eaves Lane ☎ (0257) 275659
12–11 (11–11 Sat)
S&N Matthew Brown Mild, Bitter, Theakston Best Bitter Ⓗ
Friendly local on the north side of town comprising an opened-out lounge bar, a front

room and a cosy, part-enclosed snug; vault at the rear. A plaque on the wall lists only 11 licensees since 1902. Near Leeds–Liverpool Canal bridge 66. Licensed betting shop at the rear of the premises. 🛱 ♣

Spinners Arms
Cowling Road (SE of town on Rivington road)
☎ (0257) 265144
11.30–3, 5–11 (11–11 Fri & Sat)
S&N Matthew Brown Mild, Bitter, Theakston Best Bitter, XB Ⓗ
Pub with an L-shaped bar and side rooms for food and games, close to the Leeds–Liverpool Canal. Children welcome at mealtimes. 🐦 ✤ ◗ ♣ P

Church and Oswaldtwistle

Royal Oak Inn
334 Union Road, Oswaldtwistle
☎ (0254) 236367
12–4 (4.30 Sat), 7–11
Thwaites Mild, Bitter Ⓗ
Open-plan pub with a small games area, in the centre of Oswaldtwistle. 🛱 ♣

Thorn Inn
St James Road, Church
☎ (0254) 237827
12–3 (4 Fri), 7–11 (11–11 Sat)
Thwaites Mild, Bitter Ⓗ
Multi-roomed local, slightly opened-up, with three bar areas. ◗ 🛱 P

Try also: Black Dog (Thwaites); **Bridge Inn** (Bass)

Clayton-le-Moors

Wellington Hotel
Barnes Square
☎ (0254) 235762
1.30–11 (12–5, 7–11 Sat)
Thwaites Mild, Bitter Ⓗ
Large, multi-roomed local: semi-open-plan but retaining a separate tap room. Table football played. 🛱 ♣

Try also: Old England For Ever (Burtonwood)

Clifton

Windmill Tavern
Station Road (off A583)
☎ (0772) 687203
11–3, 6.30–11 (11–11 summer Sat)
Mitchell's Best Bitter, ESB Ⓗ
Based on one of rural Fylde's many old windmills, dating from 1700. The large lounge was once the grain store; the games room is part of the original windmill and has a pool table. Good value food. Children's farm; boules played. 🏠 🐦 ✤ ◗ ▶ ♿ 🛱 (Salwick) ♣ P

Lancashire

Clitheroe

Cross Keys
49 Lowergate ☎ (0200) 28877
4–11 (11–11 Thu–Sat)
Vaux Extra Special; Wards Sheffield Best Bitter H
Town-centre pub with a strong blues affiliation – take your ear plugs.
❀ ▲ ≷ (summer weekends only) ♣ ↻

Station
King Street ☎ (0200) 23604
11–11
Thwaites Mild, Bitter H
Large, multi-roomed pub near the town centre. A friendly, busy local with pool tables and darts. The comfortable lounge is used as a family room during the day. Eve meals in summer only.
♨ Q ❀ ⇌ ◖ ▶ ▲ ≷ (summer weekends only) ♣ P

Colne

Admiral Lord Rodney
Waterside Road, South Valley
☎ (0282) 864079
12–2, 7–11 (11–11 Sat)
Goose Eye Bitter; S&N Theakston Best Bitter, XB, Old Peculier H; guest beers
Historic pub, once home of the Chartist movement. Traditional English home-cooked food and regular guest beers and ciders available. Classic 60s, 70s, etc. jukebox.
❀ ◖ & ≷ ♣ ↻ P ⅃

Red Lion
31 Market Street
☎ (0282) 863473
11–11
Taylor Dark Mild, Best Bitter H
Popular, three-roomed watering-hole fielding a very keen pool team. Satellite TV caters for sports fanatics. Situated opposite the market hall. No food Sun. ◖ ♣ P

Cowpe

Buck
Cowpe Road, Waterfoot (1/2 mile off A681 at Waterfoot)
☎ (0706) 213612
12–2 (not Mon–Thu, 4 Sat), 7–11
John Smith's Bitter; Thwaites Best Mild, Bitter; Whitbread Boddingtons Bitter H
Comfortable, two-roomed local in a quiet village, offering good value lunches, Fri–Sun. ♨ ❀ ◖ ♣ P

Croston

Black Horse
Westhead Road
☎ (0772) 600338
11–11 (12 in restaurant)
Banks's Mild, Bitter; Draught Bass; Burton Bridge Bridge Bitter; Mitchell's Best Bitter H; guest beers
Excellent, large village pub with a restaurant and a family room. Bowling green at the rear. An example to all free houses: 250 different beers available each year. A local CAMRA award-winner and regional *Pub of the Year* 1990. Regular beer festivals.
♨ ⇖ ❀ ◖ ▶ ⊟ ≷ ♣ P

Crown Hotel
Station Road ☎ (0772) 600380
11.30–3 (2.30 Mon & Tue), 5.30 (6 Sat)–11
Tetley Walker Mild, Thwaites Mild, Bitter H; guest beer
Friendly, comfortable pub catering for locals and visitors. Two separate drinking areas are served by a central bar. Weekly guest beer. No food Sun. ♨ ⇖ ❀ ◖ ⊟ ≷ ♣ P

Darwen

Entwistle Arms
15 Entwistle Street
☎ (0254) 703575
12.30–3, 6.15–11 (12–11 Sat)
Thwaites Best Mild, Bitter H
Comfortable local, just off the town centre, behind St Peter's Church. The emphasis is on pub games. ≷ ♣

Golden Cup
610 Blackburn Road (A666)
☎ (0254) 702337
12–3, 5.30 (5 Fri, 7 Sat)–11
Thwaites Mild, Bitter H
The oldest pub in Darwen, dating back to 1807: three small rooms, with low ceilings, add to its cosy feel. Attractive cobbled forecourt for summer drinking. Q ❀ ◖ P

Greenfield Inn
Lower Barn Street
☎ (0254) 703945
12–3, 5.30–11 (12–11 Fri & Sat)
Lion's Bitter; Taylor Landlord; Whitbread Chester's Mild, Boddingtons Bitter H; guest beers
Small, one-roomed pub off the beaten track next to the Blackburn–Bolton railway. ❀ ◖

Sunnyhurst Hotel
Tockholes Road
☎ (0254) 873035
7–11 (12–3, 7–11 Fri; 12–11 Sat)
Thwaites Mild, Bitter H
Small, tidy, two-roomed pub with a games room at the back. Homely atmosphere. Situated close to the Darwen Moors and tower. Q ❀ ♣

Dolphinholme

Fleece Inn
On crossroads 1/2 mile W of village OS509532
☎ (0524) 791233
12–3, 6–11
Mitchell's Mild, Best Bitter, ESB H
Former farmhouse on a lonely crossroads with a cosy, oak-beamed lounge. The old tap room is now a games/family room; there is also a dining room. Good quality food (not served Sun eve or Mon).
♨ Q ❀ ◖ ▶ ♣ P

Elswick

Boot & Shoe
Beech Road (off B5269)
☎ (0995) 70206
12–3, 6–11 (11–11 Sat)
Thwaites Best Mild, Bitter H
Large, attractive, modern village local offering a friendly welcome and a good selection of food. A large family room is complemented by a spacious outdoor play area. Barbecues every Fri eve in summer. ♨ Q ⇖ ❀ ⇌ ◖ ▶ & ▲ ♣ P

Entwistle

Strawbury Duck
Overshaws Road OS727178
☎ (0204) 852013
12–3, 7–11 (12–11 Sat)
Marston's Pedigree; Robinson's Hartleys XB; Taylor Best Bitter, Landlord; Whitbread Boddingtons Bitter H; guest beers
Old, isolated but busy country pub, next to the station. A good base for walks in hill country, woods and around reservoirs. Authentic Indian cuisine. Children welcome until 8.30pm. Three guest beers a week.
♨ ⇖ ❀ ⇌ ◖ ▶ ⊟ ≷ ♣ P

Euxton

Euxton Mills
Wigan Road (A49/A581 jct)
☎ (025 72) 64002
11.30–3, 5.30–11
Burtonwood Mild, Bitter E, **Forshaw's** H
Very cosy, comfortable pub with excellent meals: a split-level, two-bar lounge and a small front vault. Children allowed in the rear room for meals. Q ◖ ▶ ⊟ ♣ P

Fence-in-Pendle

Harpers Inn
Harpers Lane (300 yds from A6068/B6248 jct) OS829377
☎ (0282) 616249
11.30–3, 6.30–11 (12–10.30 Sun)
S&N Theakston Best Bitter, Old Peculier (winter); **Thwaites Mild, Bitter** H
Attractive, open-plan pub with a split-level layout. The upper level restaurant offers good value food and also caters for families. ❀ ◖ ▶ P

Try also: **White Swan,**
Wheatley Lane Rd (Free)

Fleetwood

North Euston Hotel
The Esplanade
☎ (0253) 876525
11–3.30, 6–11 (11–11 summer Sat)
**Draught Bass; Ruddles
County; Wilson's Mild,
Bitter, Webster's Yorkshire
Bitter; guest beers** Ⓗ
Large, imposing, stone-fronted
Victorian building overlooking
the River Wyre estuary.
Impressive views on a clear
day of Morecambe Bay and the
Lakeland Hills. Close to the
pier, tram and bus terminus
and Knott End ferry. Large,
elegantly-appointed public
rooms, two restaurants and a
family room. ♿ ⇔ ◖▶ ᵫ P

Queens
Poulton Road (Beach Road jct)
☎ (0253) 876740
11–11
Thwaites Best Mild, Bitter Ⓗ
Busy pub in a residential area
at the junction of two major
roads. A central bar serves
several alcoves and areas for
snooker and pool. On a bus
route. ❋ ◖ P

Wyre Lounge Bar
Marine Hall, The Esplanade
☎ (0253) 771141
11–3.30, 7–11
**Moorhouse's Premier, Pendle
Witches Brew; Oak Best
Bitter** Ⓗ**; guest beers**
Part of the Marine Hall
complex, extremely popular
with CAMRA members and a
previous winner of the local
Pub of the Year award. A
comfortable lounge bar offers
an excellent choice of
regularly-changed guest beers.
Q ❋ ◖ ᵫ P

Garstang

Royal Oak
Market Place ☎ (099 52) 3318
11–3.30, 7–11 (11–11 Thu–Sat)
**Robinson's Best Mild,
Hartleys XB, Best Bitter, Old
Tom** Ⓗ
Former coaching inn with an
old-fashioned atmosphere.
Alterations are in hand and a
restaurant is expected.
Drinking area outside on the
old market square.
❋ ⇔ ◖ ᵫ P

Try also: **Kenlis Arms** (Free)

Glasson Dock

Victoria
Victoria Terrace
☎ (0524) 751423
11–3.30, 6–11 (11–11 summer)
**Mitchell's Mild, Best Bitter,
Fortress** Ⓗ

A 1991 renovation: a large
main bar with bays and
nautical-style decor; also a
games room and a dining
room. ♿ ❋ ⇔ ◖ ᵫ P

Great Harwood

Royal Hotel
Station Road ☎ (0254) 883541
12–1.30 (not Tue, 3 Sat) 7–11
Thwaites Bitter Ⓗ
Cosy pub with a separate bar,
lounge and restaurant within
an open-plan layout. Food
always available, and two or
more guest beers from
independent breweries.
Q ❋ ⇔ ◖▶ ᵫ ♣

Halton

White Lion
Church Brow
☎ (0524) 811210
11–3, 6–11
Mitchell's Mild, Best Bitter Ⓗ
17th-century local with a
restful country ambience: a
single bar and a games room.
♿ ❋ ◖▶ ♣ P

Hambleton

Wardleys Riverside Pub
Wardleys Creek, Kiln Lane
(off A588, at the Shovels pub)
OS365429 ☎ (0253) 700203
12–3, 6–11 (12–11 summer)
**Courage Directors; Ruddles
Best Bitter; John Smith's
Bitter; Tetley Bitter** Ⓗ
18th-century pub from the
days when the creek was a
centre for boat building and
the cotton trade: an open-plan
lounge around a central bar,
and a restaurant. The garden
and play area afford views
across the Wyre to the ICI's
Hillhouse plant. ❋ ◖▶ ᵫ ♠ P

Try also: **Shard Bridge Inn**
(Free)

Haslingden

Foresters Arms
12 Pleasant Street
☎ (0706) 216079
12–3, 7–11 (11–11 Sat)
**S&N Theakston XB; Wilson's
Mild, Bitter, Webster's
Yorkshire Bitter** Ⓗ
Popular, unspoilt, compact
local, close to the town centre.
♿ ♣ P

Hawkshaw

Red Lion
91 Ramsbottom Road (A676
Bolton road) ☎ (0204) 852539
12–3 (varies), 6.30–11 (12–11 Fri &
Sat)
**Taylor Golden Best, Best
Bitter, Landlord** Ⓗ**; guest
beers**
Set in a picturesque area, the

pub is just in Lancashire, with
its car park in Greater
Manchester. Completely
rebuilt in 1990 with a single,
very comfortable bar area (no
expense spared on
furnishings), and a restaurant.
Well worth a visit. ⇔ P

Heskin

Farmers Arms
Wood Lane (B5250) OS532154
☎ (0257) 451276
11–3, 5–11 (11–11 Fri & Sat)
**Whitbread Chester's Mild,
Chester's Best Bitter,
Boddingtons Bitter, Castle
Eden Ale** Ⓗ**; guest beers**
Comfortable and attractive
country pub with a split-level
lounge and a separate public
bar, plus a large garden for
children. Eve meals finish at
8pm. Open all day Sun for
meals. ❋ ◖▶ ᵫ ♣ P

Heysham

Royal
Main Street ☎ (0524) 859928
11–11, 6–11 Mon & Tue)
Mitchell's Mild, Best Bitter Ⓗ
Old, rambling, low-beamed
building near St Patrick's
chapel. Enjoys a good local
trade but is also packed with
holidaymakers in the season.
Children are admitted to the
games room. ♿ ❋ ◖▶ ᵫ ♣ P

Higher Walton

Mill Tavern
15 Cann Bridge Street (A675)
☎ (0772) 38462
11–3, 5.30–11
Burtonwood Bitter Ⓗ
Village pub at the foot of two
hills, with a pleasant, open-
plan lounge and a small
games area. The landlord
sponsors a motorcycle racing
team and a deteriorating
Jensen is still awaiting
restoration in the yard. No
food weekends. Bus stop
outside. ◖ ♣ P

Hoghton

Black Horse
Gregson Lane (off Preston–
Blackburn old road)
☎ (025 485) 2541
11.30–11
**S&N Matthew Brown Mild,
Bitter, Theakston Best Bitter,
XB** Ⓗ
Large friendly, open-plan
village pub with plush seating
and a separate games area.
❋ ◖ ♣ P

Huncoat

Railway Hotel
Station Road ☎ (0254) 234287
12–3 (5 Sat), 5 (7 Sat)–11
John Smith's Bitter Ⓗ

Lancashire

Open-plan local with one side room, next to the station.
≈ ♣

Kirkham

Queens Arms
7 Poulton Street (A585)
☎ (0772) 686705
11–11
S&N Theakston Best Bitter, XB, Old Peculier; Younger No. 3 Ⓗ
Excellent, well-run, lively town-centre local; always busy and full of character. The friendly landlord offers an excellent range of pizzas in the eve, hot roast beef sandwiches every Thu eve and barbecues in the summer. Children are welcome in the designated area and the excellent garden. Pool room; wheelchair WC.
❀ ◖ ▷ ㅿ ᴀ ≈ ♣

Lancaster

Brown Cow
Penny Street ☎ (0524) 66474
11–3 (4.30 Sat), 7–11 (11–11 Fri)
Thwaites Best Mild, Bitter Ⓗ
Cosy, narrow, oak-beamed pub, popular with students. Two rooms: the back one is used for food in the daytime (not served Sun). ◖ ≈ ♣

Fat Scot
2 Gage Street (near Dalton Sq)
☎ (0524) 63438
11–11
Mitchell's Best Bitter Ⓗ
Small, dark pub with heavy metal on the jukebox and leather on many of the customers. Devilishly interesting decor, with many abstract and original murals.
≈

Golden Lion
Moor Lane ☎ (0524) 39447
12–3, 7–11 (closed Sun lunch)
S&N Theakston Best Bitter, XB, Old Peculier Ⓗ
A pub since at least 1612; an L-shaped bar leads into a games room (bar billiards and skittles). The no-smoking 'Heritage' room off the bar displays Lancaster memorabilia. Caters for all.
≈ ♣ ⸱⸱

John O'Gaunt
55 Market Street
☎ (0524) 32011
11.30–3 (11–5 Sat), 7–11 (11.30–11 Fri)
Ind Coope Burton Ale; Jennings Bitter; Tetley Walker Bitter; Whitbread Boddingtons Bitter Ⓗ
Pub with a handsome original frontage: usually busy and popular with both students and older customers. Frequent live music; newspapers provided. Varied menu of home-cooked food (not served

Sat eve or Sun; eve meals finish early). Nearly 50 single malts on sale. ◖ ▷ ≈

Moorlands
Quarry Road
12–3 (not Mon), 7–11
Mitchell's Mild, Best Bitter Ⓗ
Lively turn-of-the-century local. The decor of its many rooms makes some concession to the 1990s but retains the original stained-glass. ⊞ ♣

Priory
Cable Street ☎ (0524) 32606
11–3, 6–11 (11–11 Fri & Sat; closed Sun lunch)
Holden's XB; Mitchell's Mild, Best Bitter, ESB, Winter Warmer Ⓗ**; guest beers**
Now established as the premier guest beer emporium of North Lancs – up to two always available. An over-large lounge bar has pictures of knights and Tudors, but alterations are mooted. Adjacent to the bus station.
≈ ♣ ◠

Lathom

Railway Tavern
Station Road, Hoscar Moss (³⁄₄ mile N of A5209) OS469116
☎ (0704) 892369
11–3, 5.30–11
Jennings Bitter; Tetley Walker Mild, Bitter Ⓗ
Comfortable, unpretentious and unspoilt pub, by a rural railway station. Work of a local artist is on display. Try the home-made hotpot. ♙ Q
❀ ◖ ▷ ⊞ ≈ (Hoscar) ♣ P

Ship Inn
Wheat Lane (off A5209, over canal swing bridge) OS452115
☎ (0704) 893117
12–3, 5.30–11 (12–3, 7-11 Sat)
S&N Theakston Best Bitter, XB; Taylor Landlord Ⓗ**; guest beers**
Locally known as the 'Blood Tub' and idyllically located on a canal bank in a picturesque conservation area. Recently extended in keeping with its character. A deservedly popular, excellent free house with seven handpumps and five guest beers always available. Regular beer festivals. No food Sun.
Q ⛨ ❀ ◖ ㅿ ᴀ ♣ P

Leyland

Crofters Arms
373 Leyland Lane
☎ (0772) 422420
11–3, 6–11
S&N Matthew Brown Mild, Bitter, Theakston Best Bitter Ⓗ
A town local with a lounge and a separate games area.
❀ ◖ ⊞ ♣ P

Dunkirk Hall
Dunkirk Lane (B5248/B5253 jct) ☎ (0772) 422102
11–3, 5–11 (11–11 Fri & Sat)
Courage Directors; John Smith's Bitter; Whitbread Boddingtons Bitter Ⓗ
17th-century converted farmhouse, now a listed building boasting flag floors, wood-panelled walls and oak beams. Children are allowed in for meals (vegetarian and children's meals on request).
❀ ◖ ▷ ♣ P

Original Ship
Towngate ☎ (0772) 456674
11–11
S&N Matthew Brown Mild, Bitter, Theakston Best Bitter, XB Ⓗ
Comfortable pine-panelled town pub with a split-level lounge and a large games area, served by one large bar. No food Sun. ❀ ◖ ≈ ♣ P

Little Eccleston

Cartford Country Inn & Hotel
Cartford Lane (½ mile off A586 by toll bridge)
☎ (0995) 70166
11.30–3, 6.30–11
Dent Bitter; Marston's Pedigree; Moorhouse's Pendle Witches Brew; North Yorkshire Best Bitter; Trough Wild Boar; Whitbread Boddingtons Bitter Ⓗ
Delightfully situated free house by the River Wyre offering an extensive bar menu with daily specials and children's meals. It has an outdoor play area and fishing rights. Ever-changing beers. Local CAMRA *Pub of the Year* 1992. See George the ghost, an 1820s sheep rustler.
♙ Q ⛨ ❀ ⌂ ◖ ▷ ㅿ ♣ P

Longridge

Alston Arms
Inglewhite Road
☎ (0772) 783331
10.30–11
S&N Matthew Brown Mild, Bitter, Theakston Best Bitter Ⓗ
Comfortable, friendly pub on the outskirts of town. A panoramic side window gives good views of the surrounding hills. The large garden (children's play area) has animals, a double decker bus and a tractor. Small games room for adults.
♙ ❀ ◖ ▷ ♣ P

Old Oak
111 Preston Road (B6243)
☎ (0772) 783648
5–11 (11–11 Sat)
S&N Matthew Brown Mild, Bitter, Theakston Best Bitter,

XB, Old Peculier H
Stone-built pub at a road
junction: a small bar and a
separate games room. Oak
settles around the fire.
🏚 🍴 ♣ P

Towneley Arms
Berry Lane ☎ (0772) 782219
11–3.30, 6–11
Tetley Walker Mild, Bitter H
Town-centre pub next to a
closed railway station. Wood
panelled rooms with a large
roaring fire. 🏚 Q 🍴 P

Longton

Dolphin (Flying Fish)
Marsh Lane OS459254
☎ (0772) 612032
12–3 (not Mon–Fri), 7–11
Thwaites Best Mild, Bitter H
Remote farmhouse on the
edge of Longton Marsh.
Haunt of wildfowlers and clay
pigeon shooters. It has a small
old-fashioned tap room and a
lounge in a modern extension.
Visitors arriving by boat on
the River Douglas please sign
the visitors' book. Q
🏚 Q ❀ 🍴 ♣ P

Lostock Hall

Victoria
Watkin Lane ☎ (0772) 35338
11–3, 6–11 (11–11 Sat)
**Ruddles Best Bitter; John
Smith's Bitter; Whitbread
Boddingtons Bitter** H
Popular pub with a large vault
where a friendly welcome is
assured. Home of the local
pigeon club. Bus stop outside.
❀ 🍴 ⧚ ♣ P

Lytham

Hole in One
Forest Drive (off B5261)
☎ (0253) 739968
11–3, 6–11 (11–11 Fri & Sat)
Thwaites Bitter H
Busy local, a pleasant modern
pub on a new housing
development, close to
Fairhaven Golf Course, and
full of golfing memorabilia.
Large games room; popular
quiz nights every Wed. Good,
home-made daily specials. Q
❀ 🍴 & ⧚ (Ansdell) ♣ P

Queens
Central Beach ☎ (0253) 737316
11–11 (11–3.30, 5–11 winter)
**S&N Theakston Best Bitter,
XB, Old Peculier; Younger
No. 3** (summer) H
Old, established Victorian
pub, full of character, opposite
the windmill and lifeboat
house. Enjoys a good
reputation for food. A busy
pub overlooking the green
and the Ribble estuary.
Satellite TV.
🏚 ❀ 🍴 🍴 🍴 ⧚ ♣

Melling

Melling Hall
☎ (052 42) 21298
12–2.30 (not winter Wed), 6–11
**Robinson's Hartleys XB;
Taylor Landlord; Whitbread
Boddingtons Bitter** H
17th-century manor house,
converted in the 1940s to a
well-appointed hotel. The
friendly locals' bar is entered
via the left-hand door. Garden
play area.
🏚 ❀ 🍴 🍴 🍴 & ♣ P

Try also: **Castle**, Hornby
(Mitchell's)

Mereclough

Kettledrum
302 Red Lees Road
☎ (0282) 24591
11–3, 5.30–11
**Courage Directors; S&N
Theakston Best Bitter, XB,
Old Peculier; John Smith's
Bitter** H; guest beers
Attractive roadside inn on the
outskirts of Burnley. A gaslit
restaurant serves a wide
variety of meals (booking
advisable). 🏚 Q 🍴 ▶ ♣ P

Morecambe

Joiners Arms
Queen Street ☎ (0524) 418105
11–11
Thwaites Best Mild, Bitter H
Lively and unpretentious
local, attracting a varied
clientele. Children admitted to
the back (games) room.
Sandwiches at all times. ♣

Newchurch in Pendle

Lamb Inn
☎ (0282) 698812
12–3, 7–11
**Lion's Bitter; Moorhouse's
Premier** H
Traditional village pub set in
Lancashire 'witch country'.
This family-owned inn offers
bed and breakfast, and
camping in the car park. 🏚 Q
🍴 ❀ 🍴 🍴 ▶ & ♣ P

Ormskirk

Greyhound
100 Aughton Street
☎ (0695) 576701
11–11
**Walker Mild, Bitter, Winter
Warmer** H; guest beers
(occasionally)
Characteristic market town
local, slightly opened-out but
retaining separate rooms,
including a well-patronised
public bar without TV or
piped music. Next to a public
car park. 🏚 Q ❀ 🍴 ⧚ ♣ P

Horse Shoe
24 Southport Road
☎ (0695) 572956
11–11
Tetley Walker Mild, Bitter H
Friendly alehouse in a terrace,
opposite the Civic Hall and
the famous tower-and-steeple
parish church. 'Henry' the pub
dog has been known to take
locals for a walk! 🏚 🍴 ⧚ ♣

Prince Albert
109 Wigan Road, Westhead,
Lathom (2 miles from centre,
down A577) ☎ (0695) 573656
12–3 (5 Sat), 5 (7 Sat)–11
**Ind Coope Burton Ale;
Jennings Bitter; Tetley
Walker Dark Mild, Bitter** H;
guest beers
Comfortable, friendly village
pub with staunch local
support. Note the beer bottle
collection. Quiz Thu; live
music Sat. Always two guest
beers available. Children
welcome Mon–Sat lunchtimes.
🏚 🍴 ❀ 🍴 ▲ ♣ P ✗

Yew Tree
Grimshaw Lane (towards
Southport, 1st right after
A59/A570 jct) ☎ (0695) 572261
12–3.30, 5–11.30
Cains Bitter H
Large, modern town pub,
away from the centre. The
landlord's previous pubs have
also been in the *Guide*. Popular
with locals of all ages.
Q ❀ 🍴 & ⧚ ♣ P

Overton

Globe
Main Street ☎ (0524) 858228
11–4, 7–11
Mitchell's Mild, Best Bitter H
Renovated in 1990 with all
modern amenities, including a
large conservatory (reinstating
an original feature). Child-
friendly (play garden, nappy-
changing, children's menu).
Often full of diners; no eve
meals Mon–Thu in winter.
🍴 ❀ 🍴 🍴 & ♣ P

Ship
Main Street ☎ (0524) 858231
11.30–3 (later summer, 4 Fri & Sat),
7–11
Thwaites Best Mild, Bitter H
A genuine, unspoilt late-
Victorian village inn. Features
include stuffed birds and birds'
eggs. Thick sandwiches always
available (no meals Tue). Own
bowling green; a haven of
quiet in small rooms (children
admitted). 🏚 ❀ 🍴 ♣ P

Padiham

Hand & Shuttle
Eccleshill Street (off main
road) ☎ (0282) 71795
11–3, 6–11
Thwaites Bitter H

165

Lancashire

Small town-centre pub with a quiet lounge and separate games room. Q ◖ ♣ P

New Black Bull
Mill Street
☎ (0282) 79946
11–3, 6–11
Jennings Bitter; Tetley Walker Bitter Ⓗ
Lively, town-centre, open-plan pub, busy in the evenings with regular live entertainment throughout the week. ❀ ♣

Penwortham

St Teresa's Parish Centre
Queensway (off A59, Liverpool road)
☎ (0772) 743523
12–4 (not Mon–Fri), 7–11
Burtonwood Mild, Bitter, Forshaw's; Ind Coope Burton Ale; Tetley Walker Mild, Bitter Ⓗ**; guest beers**
Thriving, three-bar Catholic club in a residential area: a comfortable lounge, and games and concert rooms, offering regular live entertainment and two monthly guest beers. Children admitted weekend lunchtime. CAMRA *Club of the Year* 1990. Entry restrictions: club and CAMRA members anytime; non-members six times a year (25p). ⛄ ⊟ ♣ P

Pilling

Golden Ball
School Lane (off A588)
OS403488
☎ (0253) 790212
6–11 (11–11 Sat & summer)
Thwaites Best Mild, Bitter Ⓗ
18th consecutive entry in the *Guide* for this village pub, dating from 1904, where the decor is as consistent as the beer. Quiet in winter but summer sees an invasion of caravanners and crown green bowlers (two greens). Pictures of old Pilling adorn the walls of the lounge.
🏰 ⛄ ❀ ◖ ▶ ⊟ ♿ ▲ ♣ P

Poulton-le-Fylde

Old Town Hall
Church Street (off Ball St)
☎ (0253) 892257
11–11
Courage Directors; Ruddles County; Webster's Yorkshire Bitter Ⓗ
Town-centre pub, previously council offices and before that the Bay Horse pub. Accessible from all parts of the Fylde and next to a shopping centre and large car park. Regular quiz and karaoke nights.
◖ ♿ ⇌ ♣

Preesall

Saracens Head
Park Lane
☎ (0253) 810346
12–3, 5.30–11
Thwaites Best Mild, Bitter Ⓗ
Busy 19th-century pub nicknamed the 'Big Head', after the stone effigy of a Saracen's head, once mounted above the front door and now guarding the car park. The lounge is often packed with diners. The public bar, upgraded in 1991, caters for drinkers. Fri eve piano sessions. ❀ ◖ ▶ ⊟ ▲ ♣ P

Preston

Black Horse
Friargate ☎ (0772) 52093
10.30–11 (10.30–4, 7–11 Sat; closed Sun lunch)
Robinson's Best Mild, Bitter, Hartleys XB, Best Bitter, Old Tom Ⓗ
Superb, town-centre pub in a busy shopping area. This Grade II listed building has side rooms, an upstairs 1920s-style bar, an unusual tiled curved bar, wood-panelled walls, stained-glass screens and a mosaic floor. A thriving meeting place, full of character. Q ◖ ⇌

Fox & Grapes
Fox Street ☎ (0772) 52448
10.30–11
S&N Matthew Brown Mild, Theakston Best Bitter, Old Peculier; Younger Scotch, IPA, No. 3 Ⓗ
Small, one-bar town-centre pub tastefully refurbished in 1920s town style, with wooden floors, etc. Popular and often crowded. ◖ ⇌

Gastons
30 Avenham Street
☎ (0772) 51380
12–4, 6–11 (12–11 Fri & Sat)
Cains Bitter, Formidable Ale; Dent Bitter, Ramsbottom; Lloyds Derby Bitter Ⓗ**; guest beers**
Multi-level, two-bar town-centre free house, comfortably furnished with a separate pool room. Two cockatiels reside in the downstairs bar. Own brewery. Large number of weekly guest beers. Local CAMRA award-winner.
◖ ⇌ ♣ ⌂

Lamb & Packet
Friargate
☎ (0772) 51857
11.30–11 (11.30–3.30, 6.30–11 Sat)
Thwaites Best Mild, Bitter, Craftsman Ⓗ
Small, well-run, one-bar pub near the Polytechnic, with a raised drinking area. Good value eve meals available

4.30–6.30 weekdays. Often crowded during term time.
◖ ▶ ⇌

New Britannia
6 Heatley Street
☎ (0772) 53424
11–3 (4 Fri & Sat), 6–11 (closed Sun lunch)
Marston's Pedigree, Robinson's Hartleys XB; Whitbread Trophy, Castle Eden Ale Ⓗ
Small one-bar pub near Lancashire Polytechnic. Popular with the heavy metal creed, but all are made welcome. Often crowded at weekends. No food Sat.
◖ ⇌ ⌂

New Inn
Queen Street
☎ (0772) 51602
12–11
Thwaites Best Mild, Bitter Ⓗ
Comfortable, two-bar urban pub on the edge of the town centre. ⊟ P

Old Black Bull
Friargate ☎ (0772) 54402
10.30–11
Whitbread Boddingtons Bitter Ⓗ**; guest beers**
A busy town-centre pub, this Grade II listed building has an attractive tiled frontage. A large main room, with a tiny vault at the front which gets very busy. Public car park at the rear. ❀ ◖ ⊟ ♣ ♣

Old Blue Bell
Church Street ☎ (0772) 51280
11–3 (4 Sat), 5 (7 Sat)–11
Samuel Smith OBB Ⓗ
Very old, comfortable town-centre pub: one large lounge with two small snugs. No food Sun. ◖ ⇌ P

Real Ale Shop
Lovat Road
☎ (0772) 201591
11–2, 5–10 (12–2, 7–10 Sun)
Moorhouse's Premier, Pendle Witches Brew; Taylor Landlord Ⓗ**; guest beers**
Busy real ale off-licence selling an ever-changing range of guest beers, exotic imported beers and fruit wines. ⌂

Unicorn
378 North Road (A6)
☎ (0772) 57870
12–3, 6–11 (11–11 Sat)
S&N Matthew Brown Mild, Theakston Best Bitter, XB, Old Peculier; Younger No. 3 Ⓗ
An attractive listed building, north of the town centre. A recently modernised, one-room layout with a separate pool area. Folk club Mon; live music Wed; quiz night Thu. Access to the outside drinking area is through the pub.
❀ ◖ ♣

Windsor Castle

Egan Street ☎ (0772) 53387
11–11

Thwaites Best Mild, Bitter Ⓗ
Homely, medium-sized local
on the edge of the town centre;
always friendly. Q 🏠 ◖ ♣

Rawtenstall

Rams Head

2 Newchurch Road
☎ (0706) 213687
11–11

**Bass Mild XXXX, Special,
Draught Bass** Ⓗ
Comfortable local next to the
market, with a spacious
outdoor drinking area at the
rear. Large through-lounge
and a separate dining room.
❀ 🍴 ◖ ♣

Try also: **Crown** (Webster's);
Sun Inn, Bank St (Thwaites)

Salwick

Hand & Dagger

Treales Road (off A583, signed
to Clifton past BNFL works)
☎ (0772) 690306
11.30–3, 7–11 (12–10.30 Sun)

**Greenalls Mild, Bitter,
Thomas Greenall's Bitter** Ⓗ
200-year-old country pub with
a unique name, on the
Lancaster Canal, popular with
local factory workers. Large
beer garden and very good,
home-cooked food; rabbit pie
is a speciality. 🏚 Q 🏠 ❀ ◖
◖ 🍴 ⚲ ♿ ≈ ♣ P

Scarisbrick

Heatons Bridge Inn

2 Heatons Bridge Road
(B5242) ☎ (0704) 840549
11.30–11

**Tetley Walker Mild, Walker
Best Bitter** Ⓗ
Cosy canalside pub, recently
extended. Well furnished,
with an abundance of bric-a-
brac; often crowded.
🏚 Q ❀ ♣ P

Stalmine

Seven Stars

Hallgate Lane (A588)
☎ (0253) 700207
11.30–3, 6.30 (7 Mon–Wed in
winter)–11

**Greenalls Thomas Greenall's
Bitter; Stones Best Bitter** Ⓗ
16th-century, family-run local
in an over Wyre village. The
lounge has a roaring fire,
brasses, jugs and hunting
scenes. Locals and families
mix in the games room.
Excellent value B&B and bar
meals (not served Tue) add to
the welcoming atmosphere.
Sells Worthington White
Shield. 🏚 ❀ 🍴 ◖ ◖ ♿ ♣ P

Tarleton

Cock & Bottle

70 Church Road (just off A59)
☎ (0772) 812258
11–3, 6–11 (11–11 Fri & Sat)

Thwaites Mild, Bitter Ⓗ
Popular, large, modernised
village pub with extensive
catering in the plush lounge.
The public bar acts as a games
room. Booking advisable for
Sun lunch. ❀ ◖ ◖ ◨ ♣ P

Thornton

Burn Naze

1 Gamble Road (off A585)
☎ (0253) 852954
11–11 (11–3.30, 7–11 Wed)

**Tetley Walker Dark Mild,
Bitter** Ⓗ**; guest beer**
Late Victorian pub of much
character, popular with locals.
Lively and friendly, it has one
of the few remaining public
bars in the area. Stands next to
the giant ICI complex.
🏚 🍴 ◖ ◖ ◨ ⭢ P

Ulnes Walton

Rose & Crown

120 Southport Road (A581)
☎ (0257) 451302
11.30–3, 5.30–11 (11.30–11 Sat)

**Burtonwood Mild, Bitter,
Forshaw's** Ⓗ
Attractive country pub with a
comfortable lounge and a
separate public bar. The large
garden for children has an
aviary of parrots and exotic
birds. Barbecues summer Sat
eves. 🏚 ❀ ◖ ◖ ◨ ♣ P

Up Holland

White Lion

10 Church Street (off A577)
☎ (0695) 622727
12–3, 7–11

**Ind Coope Burton Ale;
Jennings Bitter; Tetley
Walker Bitter** Ⓗ
Picturesque village pub
opposite the parish church.
🏚 ❀ ◖ ◖ P

Waddington

Lower Buck Inn

Church Road ☎ (0200) 28705
11–3, 6–11 (11–11 Thu–Sat)

**Taylor Best Bitter; Tetley
Walker Bitter; Robinson's
Best Bitter** Ⓗ
Unaltered, Dickensian pub in
a Grade I listed building: a
good village local with piano
sing-alongs at weekends.
🏚 Q 🏠 🍴 ◖ ◖ ◨ ♿ ♣

Walmer Bridge

Longton Arms

2 Liverpool Old Road
☎ (0772) 612335

2 (1 Fri, 12 Sat)–11

Greenalls Mild, Bitter Ⓔ
Small village local with a tiny
public bar at the front and a
lounge to the side and rear.
🏚 ◨ ♣ P

Walton-le-Dale

Victoria

97 Higher Walton Road
☎ (0772) 204420
11–3, 6–11

**Whitbread Boddingtons
Bitter** Ⓔ
Modernised late Victorian
local with a separate vault.
❀ ◖ ◨ ♣ P

White Bull

109 Victoria Road
☎ (0772) 54138
12 (2 Tue & Thu)–11

**Whitbread Boddingtons
Bitter** Ⓗ
Friendly local with a split-
level interior and a separate
games room. ❀ ♣ P

Waterfoot

Duke of Buccleugh

Bacup Road ☎ (0706) 215363
11–11 (11–3, 7–11 Wed)

**Courage Directors; John
Smith's Bitter; Whitbread
Boddingtons Bitter** Ⓗ
Large, open-plan lounge with
two games rooms and a TV in
the lounge. Named after the
Lord of the Manor. ◖ ♣

Jolly Sailor

Booth Road, Booth Place
☎ (0706) 214863
11–3, 7–11

**S&N Matthew Brown Mild,
Theakston Best Bitter;
Whitbread Boddingtons
Bitter** Ⓗ
Popular pub with an open-
plan lounge and a small pool
room. ♣

Whittle-le-Woods

Royal Oak

216 Chorley Old Road
☎ (0254) 76485
2.30–11

**S&N Matthew Brown Mild,
Bitter, Theakston Best
Bitter** Ⓗ
Small, terraced local, full of
atmosphere. A meeting place
for mature motorcyclists.
🏚 Q ◖ ♣

Try also: **Old Dog** (Thwaites)

Wray

George & Dragon

Main Street ☎ (052 42) 21403
11.30–3, 6.30–11

Mitchell's Best Bitter Ⓗ
Pub with a single, country-
style bar, a games area and a
restaurant. 🏚 ❀ 🍴 ◖ ◖ ♣

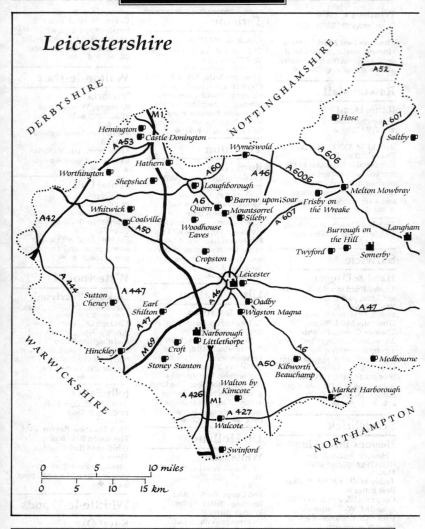

Leicestershire

 Everards, Narborough: **Featherstone, Hoskins, Hoskins & Oldfield,** Leicester; **Parish,** Somerby; **Ruddles,** Langham

Barrow upon Soar

Navigation Inn
Mill Lane ☎ (0509) 412842
11–2.30, 6–11
Draught Bass; Bateman Mild; Greenalls Shipstone's Mild, Shipstone's Bitter; Marston's Pedigree Ⓗ
Traditional canalside pub with a bar top consisting of old English coins. Skittles played. Weekday lunches. ✿ Ⓓ ♣

Riverside

14 Bridge Street
☎ (0509) 412260
11–3, 6–11
Courage Directors; Ruddles County; John Smith's Bitter Ⓗ
Pub fronting onto the River Soar, with an outside drinking area and moorings. Separate restaurant area and two lounge bars.
🎯 ✿ Ⓓ ▶ ♿ ▲ P

Burrough on the Hill

Stag & Hounds
Main Street ☎ (066 477) 375
12–2 (not Mon or winter weekdays, 3 Sat), 7–11
Lloyds Derby Bitter Ⓗ; **guest beers**
Honest free house in rural Leicestershire, the former home of the Parish brewery.

knowledgeable landlord is more than willing to talk beer. No food Sun. 🏠 ❀ ◑ ♣ P

Clipsham

Olive Branch

Main Street ☎ (0780) 410355
11–2.30, 6.30–11
S&N Theakston XB, Old Peculier Ⓗ**; guest beers** Ⓖ
Attractive old stone building; beware the obscure entrance to the car park. One bar serves both the public bar and restaurant. Cosy atmosphere. Three or four regular guest beers.
🏠 Q ⏰ ❀ ◑ ♦ ⊟ ♣ P

Coalville

Bulls Head

Warren Hills Road (B587, 2½ miles NE of centre)
☎ (0530) 810511
11–2.30, 6.30–11
Ansells Bitter; Ind Coope Burton Ale; Marston's Pedigree; Tetley Bitter Ⓗ
Busy roadside pub on the edge of Charnwood Forest. The lounge is pleasantly divided into several drinking areas. Large beer garden with plenty of seating; excellent for summer eves. No food Sun.
🏠 ❀ ◑ ▲ P

Try also: Gate Inn, Hugglescote (Bass)

Croft

Heathcote Arms

Hill Street ☎ (0455) 282439
11–2.30, 5.30–11 (11–11 Sat)
Adnams Bitter; Everards Mild, Beacon, Tiger, Old Original Ⓗ**; guest beers**
Unspoilt village pub on a hilltop overlooking the river. Relaxed and friendly atmosphere. Home-cooked food; table and alley skittles.
🏠 Q ◑ ♦ ⊟ ♣ P

Cropston

Bradgate Arms

Station Road ☎ (0533) 340336
11.30–2.30, 6–11
Bateman Mild; Hoskins Beaumanor Bitter, Penn's Ale, Premium Ⓗ
Recently extended and refurbished country pub, popular with visitors to Bradgate Park and the Great Central Railway's Rothley station. Skittles played. No eve meals Sun.
Q ⏰ ❀ ◑ ♦ ⊟ ♣ P

Earl Shilton

Red Lion

High Street (A47)
☎ (0455) 840829

11–2.30 (3 Sat), 5.30 (6 Sat)–11
Draught Bass; M&B Mild Ⓗ
Basic beer-drinkers' pub on the main through road. Still has three separate rooms and one central bar. No food at all.
❀ ⊟ P

Exton

Fox & Hounds

The Green ☎ (0572) 812403
11–2.30, 6.30–11
Marston's Pedigree; Samuel Smith OBB Ⓗ
Ivy-covered, 17th-century former coaching inn overlooking a village green. A traditional bar and a separate lounge with a dining area. 🏠
Q ❀ ❀ ◑ ♦ ⊟ ♣ ▲ ♣ P

Frisby on the Wreake

Bell Inn

2 Main Street ☎ (0664) 434237
12–2.30, 6–11 (12–2.30, 7–10.30 Sun)
Ansells Bitter; Bateman Mild, XXXB; Marston's Pedigree; Tetley Bitter Ⓗ**; guest beers**
Large rustic pub in a small village. Popular for its food and turnover of regular guest beers. Weston's cider sold.
🏠 ⏰ ❀ ◑ ♦ ⌁ P

Hathern

Dew Drop

Loughborough Road
☎ (0509) 842438
12–2.30, 7–11
Hardys & Hansons Best Mild, Best Bitter Ⓗ
Small, traditional pub with a tiny lounge. Large selection of malt whiskies (many not on display). Popular with locals. Car park for three cars only.
🏠 Q ⊟ ♣ P

Three Crowns

50 Wide Lane ☎ (0509) 842233
12–2.30, 5.30–11 (11–11 Sat)
Draught Bass; M&B Mild; Stones Best Bitter Ⓗ
Quiet local with three separate drinking areas. Shows an increased commitment to real ale. Skittle alley to the rear.
🏠 ❀ ⊟ ♣ P

Hemington

Jolly Sailor

Main Street ☎ (0332) 810448
11–11 (11–3, 5.30–11 Tue)
Draught Bass; M&B Mild; Marston's Pedigree Ⓗ**; guest beers**
Popular two-roomed local in a quiet village near East Midlands airport. Two guest beers always available. Table skittles played.
🏠 ❀ ⊟ ♣ ▲ ♣ P

Normally has five guest beers, predominantly from small breweries. Home-cooked food. Live music Thu eves. A Lloyds house beer, Stag (1038), is brewed exclusively for this pub. Weston's Old Rosie cider.
🏠 ⏰ ❀ ◑ ♦ ▲ ♣ ⌁ P

Castle Donington

Cross Keys

Bondgate ☎ (0332) 812214
11–3, 5.30–11
Draught Bass; Vaux Samson; Wards Sheffield Best Bitter Ⓗ**; guest beer**
Tastefully refurbished pub near the village centre. Three connecting rooms serve a friendly clientele from all walks of life. The

Leicestershire

Hinckley

Greyhound Inn
New Buildings
☎ (0455) 615235
11–2.30, 5 (5.30 Sat)–11 (12–2.30, 7–10.30 Sun)
Marston's Mercian Mild, Burton Best Bitter, Pedigree Ⓗ
Lively, traditional four-room pub with live jazz on Wed and Thu. Room set aside for families Sat lunchtimes.
Q ✿ ◖ ⌖ ♣

Hose

Rose & Crown
Bolton Lane ☎ (0949) 60424
12–3, 7–11
Beer range varies Ⓗ
Comfortable country inn with a large bar, cosy lounge and separate restaurant. Constantly changing range of real ales; usually six brews on tap. ♨ Q ✿ ◖▶ ⌖ ▲ P

Try also: Black Horse (Free)

Kibworth Beauchamp

Coach & Horses
2 Leicester Road
☎ (0533) 792247
11.30–3, 5–11 (11–11 Sat)
Ansells Mild, Bitter; Draught Bass; Tetley Bitter Ⓗ
Friendly old coaching inn popular with locals and passing trade. Home-cooked food. ♨ ◖▶ ♣ ⌣ P

Leicester

Black Swan
169 Belgrave Gate
☎ (0533) 513240
11–3, 5.30 (7 Sat)–11
Hoskins Beaumanor Bitter, Penn's Ale, Premium, Old Nigel Ⓗ; **guest beers**
Basic, one-roomed beer drinkers' pub with sawdust on the floor. Occasional live music. Regular, varied guest beers. Note the old picture of Nellie Hoskins. ◖ & ♣

Rainbow & Dove
185 Charles Street
☎ (0533) 555916
11.30–3, 5.30 (7 Sat)–11
Bateman Mild; Hoskins Beaumanor Bitter, Penn's Ale, Premium, Old Nigel Ⓗ; **guest beers**
One-roomed, town-centre beer drinkers' pub: a regular CAMRA meeting place. A map of England made from old shive holders adorns the end wall. Live music Wed nights. ◖ ⌖ ♣

Sir Charles Napier
Glenfield Road
☎ (0533) 621022

11–3, 4.30 (6.30 Sat)–11 (11–11 Fri)
Courage Directors; John Smith's Magnet Ⓗ
Deceptively spacious 1930s pub at the end of a row of terraced houses. Retains the original three-room layout (including a smoke room). The lounge doubles as a dance floor. No food Sun. Q ◖ ⌖ ♣

Tom Hoskins
131 Beaumanor Road (off A6, Abbey Lane) ☎ (0533) 611008
11.30–3, 5.30 (6 Sat)–11
Hoskins Beaumanor Bitter, Penn's Ale, Premium, Old Nigel Ⓗ; **guest beers**
Brewery tap, a lively, friendly bar and a comfortable lounge. Brewery trips can be arranged – ask for details. Handy for the Leicester end of the Great Central Steam Railway.
Q ✿ ◖ ⌖ ♣ P

Tudor
100 Tudor Road
☎ (0533) 620087
11–2.30 (3 Sat), 6–11 (12–2.30, 7–10.30 Sun)
Everards Mild, Beacon, Tiger, Old Original Ⓗ; **guest beers**
Popular Victorian corner pub in a terraced residential area: a cosy lounge, a lively bar and a games room. ⍟ ✿ ◖ ⌖ ♣

Victoria Jubilee
112 Leire Street (off A46, Melton road) ☎ (0533) 663599
11–2.30 (3.30 Sat), 6–11
Marston's Burton Best Bitter, Pedigree Ⓗ
Friendly locals' pub amidst terraced housing. Yard for outdoor drinking. ✿ ⌖

Wilkies
29 Market Street
☎ (0533) 556877
11–11 (closed Sun)
Marston's Pedigree; Whitbread Boddingtons Bitter, Flowers Original Ⓗ; **guest beer**
Lively German-styled bar, popular with younger drinkers. Weekly guest beer and a large selection of imported bottled beers from around the world. Continental-style food lunchtimes. Happy hour Mon–Fri 5–7. ◖

Littlethorpe

Plough Inn
Station Road ☎ (0533) 862383
11–2.30 (3 Sat), 6–11
Adnams Bitter; Everards Beacon, Tiger, Old Original Ⓗ; **guest beers**
Comfortable, well-maintained, thatched local dating back to the 16th century. Food served in the lounge or separate dining area. Long alley skittles. Friendly atmosphere.
✿ ◖▶ ⌖ ⇌ (Narborough) ♣ P

Loughborough

Greyhound Inn
69 Nottingham Road
☎ (0509) 216080
11.30–2, 5.30–11 (11–11 Fri & Sat)
Marston's Border Mild, Pedigree Ⓗ
Former coaching inn, now a lively pub, popular at night for pool and darts. The function room was formerly a pavilion for one of the largest sports grounds in Europe.
✿ ◖ ⇌ ♣ P

Pack Horse Inn
4 Woodgate ☎ (0509) 214590
12–2 (3.30 Sat), 4 (7.30 Sat)–11 (12–11 Fri)
Hardys & Hansons Best Mild, Best Bitter, Kimberley Classic Ⓗ
Old coaching inn which has a true 'locals' feel despite being near the town centre. Active quiz, darts and dominoes teams. Regular Fri night folk venue upstairs. Good value food. Limited parking.
♨ ✿ ◖▶ ♣ P

Peacock Inn
26 Factory Street
☎ (0509) 214215
11–2.30 (3 Sat), 7–11
Draught Bass; M&B Mild Ⓗ
Recently purchased from Bass, a three-roomed back-street pub now offering bed and breakfast. A traditional, friendly local.
♨ ✿ ⌂ ⌖ ♣ P

Royal Oak
70 Leicester Road
☎ (0509) 265860
11–3, 7–11
Burtonwood Mild, Bitter, Forshaw's Ⓗ
Large two-roomed pub on the main road through Loughborough. Collection of naval artefacts in the lounge. Basic bar. ♨ ✿ ◖ ⌖ ♣ P

Swan in the Rushes
21 The Rushes
☎ (0509) 217014
11–2.30 (3.30 Sat), 5 (6.30 Sat)–11 (11–11 Fri)
Bateman XXXB; Marston's Pedigree; S&N Theakston Old Peculier; Tetley Bitter Ⓗ; **guest beers**
Welcoming two-roomed pub which provides good food (including vegetarian). Large stock of bottled beers, and always a mild among the many guest beers. Real cider sometimes available. Eve meals Mon–Thu till 8pm.
♨ Q ⍟ ⌂ ◖▶ ⌖ & P

Try also: Black Lion, The Rushes (Hoskins); **Blacksmith's Arms,** Wards End (Home); **Windmill,** Sparrow Hill (Marston's)

170

Market Harborough

Red Cow
58–59 High Street
☎ (0858) 463637
11–3 (4 Fri & Sat), 6–11
Marston's Burton Best Bitter, Pedigree Ⓗ
Traditional, one-bar local with an emphasis on beer and conversation. Limited food. Q

Medbourne

Nevill Arms
12 Waterfall Way
☎ (085 883) 288
12–2.30, 6–11
Adnams Bitter; Marston's Pedigree; Ruddles Best Bitter, County Ⓗ
Built in 1876, a former coaching inn on the village green next to a pretty stream. A popular weekend venue for families, as the ducks and doves on the bank are very friendly. Pub games provided for organised parties on request.
🏠 Q 🍺 🏵 🚰 🅰 ◑ ♣ P

Melton Mowbray

Boat Inn
57 Burton Street
☎ (0664) 60518
11–2.30, 7–11
Burtonwood Bitter, Forshaw's Ⓗ
Small, single-roomed, cosy locals' pub, very close to the station. The pub dog, Saxon, rules the bar and vets all clientele. Note the collection of photographs of Old Melton. The jukebox has a good selection of true classics.
🏠 🏵 🚰 ♣

White Hart Inn
66 Sherrard Street
☎ (0664) 62721
11–3.30, 6–11
Marston's Pedigree Ⓗ
Friendly locals' pub, near the town centre. Live music at weekends, when it is very busy but friendly. Families always welcome. Long alley skittles. 🏵 🚉 ♣

Mountsorrel

Swan Inn
10 Loughborough Road
☎ (0533) 302340
11.30–3, 5.30–11 (11.30–11 Sat)
S&N Theakston Best Bitter, XB, Old Peculier Ⓗ; **guest beers**
17th-century coaching inn on the banks of the River Soar. Emphasis on quality food lunchtime and evening. Difficult car park access.
🏠 🏵 🏰 ◑ ◗ 🍺 P

Oadby

Cow & Plough
Stoughton Farm Park, Gartree Road (signed from A6)
☎ (0533) 720852
12–3, 5–7 (12–7 summer; closed Sun eve)
Hoskins & Oldfield Mild, Bitter Ⓗ; **guest beers**
Old converted barn with an elegant Victorian bar decorated with breweriana and old advertising signs. Good atmosphere. Limited opening, but hours can be arranged for party visits. Outdoor drinking in the farmyard. Q 🍺 🏵 🚰 ♣ ◔ P

Oakham

Wheatsheaf
2–4 Northgate
☎ (0572) 723458
11.30–2.30 (3 Sat), 6–11
Adnams Bitter; Everards Beacon, Tiger Ⓗ; **guest beer**
17th-century, two-roomed pub. Popular with locals and has a friendly atmosphere. No food Sun. 🏠 Q 🏵 ◑ 🍺 🚆

Try also: White Lion (Free)

Quorn

Royal Oak
2 High Street
☎ (0509) 413502
11.30–2.30 (3 Sat), 6.30–11 (12–2.30, 7–10.30 Sun)
Draught Bass; M&B Mild Ⓗ
Popular local with a good, friendly atmosphere. Darts and domino teams based here. The threat of a rent increase may cause a change of tenant.
🍺

White Horse
2 Leicester Road
☎ (0509) 620140
12–2, 6–11 (11–11 Sat)
Adnams Bitter; Everards Tiger, Old Original Ⓗ; **guest beers** (occasionally)
Large, friendly pub in the village centre. Quiz night Tue and live pianist Sat eve. No eve meals weekends.
🏠 🍺 🏵 ◑ ◗ 🍺 ♣ P

Saltby

Nags Head
1 Back Street
☎ (0476) 860491
12–3, 7–11
Greene King Abbot; Ruddles Best Bitter Ⓗ
Medium-sized village pub, popular with locals and visitors alike. The games area includes table skittles and bar billiards. Note the stone lintel over the front door. No eve meals Tue. 🏠 🏰 ◑ ◗ ♣ P

Shepshed

Crown
Brook Street
☎ (0509) 502665
12–2, 5–11 (11–11 Sat)
Everards Tiger, Old Original Ⓗ; **guest beers**
Formerly an 18th-century coaching inn, this lively local has four interconnecting rooms, each with its own distinctive character. Easy parking on the market place.
🏠 🏵 ◑ ♣

Try also: Pied Bull, Belton St (Marston's)

Sileby

Free Trade Inn
27 Cossington Road
☎ (0509) 814494
11.30–2 (2.30 Fri, 3 Sat), 5.30 (6.30 Sat)–11
Everards Mild, Beacon, Tiger, Old Original Ⓗ
Pleasant thatched pub in a Soar Valley village, between Loughborough and Leicester. Beware of low oak beams. Popular with locals. 🏵 ◑ ♣ P

South Luffenham

Halfway House
Stamford Road
☎ (0780) 720166
11–3, 5–11 (11–11 Fri & Sat)
Marston's Pedigree; John Smith's Bitter, Magnet; Whitbread Boddingtons Bitter Ⓗ
Friendly 19th-century pub consisting of an L-shaped lounge, with a games area at one end, and a separate dining room. 🏵 🏰 ◑ ♣ P

Sproxton

Crown Inn
Coston Road ☎ (0476) 860035
12–3, 6.30–11
Everards Mild, Tiger; Marston's Pedigree Ⓗ; **guest beers**
100-year-old, stone-built pub in a conservation village. The tables are old Singer sewing machine tables. Cosy atmosphere and excellent food. 🏠 🏵 ◑ ◗ 🚰 ♣ P

Stoney Stanton

Francis Arms
Huncote Road
☎ (0455) 272034
11–2, 5.30–11
Marston's Mercian Mild, Burton Best Bitter, Pedigree Ⓗ
Basic village beer drinkers' pub with a collection of rifles on the ceiling. Two separate rooms. Table skittles played.
🏠 🍺 ♣ P

Leicestershire

Sutton Cheney

Hercules
Main Street ☎ (0455) 291292
12–3, 7–11 (closed Mon, except bank hols)
Beer range varies Ⓗ
16th-century coaching inn, close to Bosworth Battlefield (the pub opens all day during events). Up to four beers, including two house beers. Food available in the bar or restaurant which is closed Mon–Wed. Happy hour 7–8pm. ⚄ ✿ ◑ ▲ ♣ P

Swinford

Cave Arms
North Street ☎ (0788) 860464
12–3 (may extend), 7–11
Adnams Bitter Ⓗ; **guest beers**
Cosy, thatched village local offering two or more guest beers. Caravan camping is available at nearby Stanford Hall. Table skittles and function room upstairs.
⚄ ✿ ◑ ▲ ♣

Twyford

Saddle Inn
10 Main Street
☎ (0664) 840237
12–2.30 (3 Sat), 5 (6 Sat)–11
Mansfield Riding Bitter, Old Baily; Parish Special Ⓗ; **guest beers**
Village country pub with a cosy, friendly atmosphere. Birthplace in 1991 of Featherstone brewery. Opens all day if busy or by prior arrangement. Petanque played. ⚄ ✿ ◑ ♣ P

Walcote

Black Horse
Main Street ☎ (0455) 552684
12–2.30 (not Mon), 6.30 (5.30 Fri)–11 (12–2, 7–10.30 Sun)
Hook Norton Best Bitter, Old Hooky; Taylor Landlord Ⓗ; **guest beers**
Roadside pub famous for its Thai food. Regular guest beers, continental bottled beers, country wines and Weston's Old Rosie cider all add to this popular pub's appeal. ⚄ ◑ ▷ ⌂ P

Walton by Kimcote

Dog & Gun
Main Street ☎ (0455) 552808
12–3 (4 Sat), 5 (7 Sat)–11
Banks's Mild, Bitter Ⓔ
Small, traditional village pub dating back to 1846. Used to be a butcher's shop: meat-hanging beams survive in the bar alongside other memorabilia. Hot food only for skittle evenings. ⚄ Q ⌓ ♣ P

Whitwell

Noel Arms
Main Road
☎ (078 086) 334
11–3, 6–11
Ind Coope Burton Ale; Ruddles County; Tetley Bitter Ⓗ
Listed two-roomed pub with a separate restaurant. Close to Rutland Water – ideal for fishing, cycling and windsurfing. Whitwell is twinned with Paris – see the plaque on the wall of the gents! ⚄ Q ✿ ⚓ ◑ ▷ ⌓ ♣ P

Whitwick

Kings Arms
22 Silver Street
☎ (0530) 832117
11–2.30, 5.30–11 (12–2, 7–10.30 Sun)
Marston's Pedigree Ⓗ
Welcoming village-centre pub, a meeting place for many local clubs, including brass bands who practise in the clubroom. Ornaments in the lounge include a collection of ducks.
⌓ ♣ P

Three Horseshoes
11 Leicester Road
☎ (0530) 837311
11–3, 6.30–11 (12–2, 7–10.30 Sun)
Draught Bass; M&B Mild Ⓗ
Attractive red brick locals' pub on the eastern edge of the village. Small, quiet lounge with a serving hatch; the bar is much larger and boisterous. Opposite is a monument to local mine and quarry workers. Free public car park adjacent. ⚄ Q ⌓ ♣

Wigston Magna

Meadowbank
Kelmarsh Avenue (200 yds from A50)
☎ (0533) 811926
11.30–2.30, 6–11 (11–11 Sat)
Banks's Mild, Bitter Ⓔ
Typical, large-roomed estate pub. Friendly and comfortable. TV in the bar. Eve meals on request.
✿ ◑ ⌓ ♣ P

Woodhouse Eaves

Curzon Arms
44 Maplewell Road (off Main Street)
☎ (0509) 890377
11–3, 6–11
Courage Directors; John Smith's Bitter Ⓗ
Lively locals' pub with a comfortable lounge and a red tiled-floor bar. Food is standard pub fare, plus a vegetarian dish.
✿ ◑ ▷ ⌓ ♣ P

Worthington

Malt Shovel
29 Main Street
☎ (0530) 222343
12–2 (not Mon, 2.30 Sat), 7–11
Marston's Pedigree Ⓗ
Lovely village pub with a welcoming atmosphere. The garden has a variety of animals and play equipment for children. Excellent home-cooked food (not served Mon). ⚄ ⚲ ✿ ◑ ▷ ⌓ ▲ ♣ P

Wymeswold

White Horse
22 Far Street (A6006)
☎ (0509) 880490
11.30–2 (not Mon), 6 (7 Mon)–11
Home Mild, Bitter; S&N Theakston XB Ⓗ
Thriving village local with a comfortable lounge and a bustling bar decorated with many trophies. Skittles played. Separate restaurant (eve meals Tue–Sat).
⚄ ⚲ ✿ ◑ ▷ ⌓ ♣ P

Try also: **Hammer & Pincers** (Free)

♣
Traditional Pub Games

The clubs symbol is added to entries for pubs where traditional games can be played. These include darts, dominoes, skittles, shove-ha'penny, card games and more unusual survivors like Ring the Bull and Aunt Sally. Not all the games may be on display: you may have to ask for them.

Lincolnshire

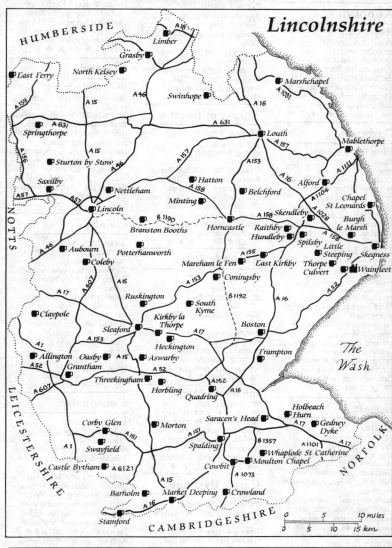

Lincolnshire

HUMBERSIDE · A18 · Limber · Grasby · North Kelsey · Swinhope · Marshchapel · A1031 · A16 · Louth · Mablethorpe · East Ferry · A159 · A631 · Springthorpe · A15 · A46 · A631 · A156 · Sturton by Stow · A15 · A57 · Saxilby · A157 · A153 · Alford · A1111 · A16 · Chapel St Leonards · NOTTS · A57 · Nettleham · Hatton · A158 · Belchford · A1104 · A1028 · Skendleby · Burgh le Marsh · Lincoln · Minting · A158 · Horncastle · Raithby · Hundleby · Spilsby · A158 · Little Steeping · Skegness · Branston Booths · B1190 · A46 · Aubourn · Potterhanworth · Mareham le Fen · A155 · East Kirkby · Thorpe Culvert · Wainfleet · Coleby · A607 · A15 · Ruskington · South Kyme · B1192 · A16 · A52 · The Wash · Claypole · Kirkby la Thorpe · Boston · A1 · Sleaford · A153 · A17 · Heckington · Frampton · Allington · Oasby · A15 · Aswarby · A52 · Grantham · A52 · Threekingham · Horbling · A152 · Quadring · A16 · Holbeach Hurn · A607 · Corby Glen · Morton · Saracen's Head · A17 · Gedney Dyke · A151 · A151 · B1357 · A1101 · A17 · Swayfield · Spalding · Whaplode St Catherine · Moulton Chapel · NORFOLK · Castle Bytham · A6121 · Cowbit · A1073 · A15 · Barholm · Market Deeping · Crowland · A16 · Stamford · CAMBRIDGESHIRE · 0 5 10 miles · 0 5 10 15 km

---

  Bateman, *Wainfleet*

Alford

Half Moon
West Street ☎ (0507) 463477
10.30–3.30, 6–11 (1am Fri & Sat
supper licence)
**Draught Bass; Bateman XB;
Vaux Samson; Welsh Brewers
Worthington BB** Ⓗ; guest beer
Popular and welcoming
market town pub with a cosmopolitan clientele. Expanded
into two neighbouring houses
to include a comfortable
lounge and restaurant. Host to
many clubs and societies.
❀ ⊛ ◑ ▸ ⊟ ♣ P

Allington

Welby Arms
The Green ☎ (0400) 81361
12–3, 5.30 (6.30 Sat)–11
**Courage Directors; John
Smith's Bitter** Ⓗ
Situated on the village green, a
three-roomed watering hole
worth seeking out. No eve
meals Sun. ♨ ⊛ ◑ ▸ ⊟ ▲ P

Aswarby

Tally Ho Inn
Main Road
☎ (0529) 5205
12–3, 6–11
**Bateman XB; Greene King
IPA** Ⓗ; guest beers
Attractive stone roadside inn,
formerly part of the local
estate. Welcoming
atmosphere; a long-standing
entry in this guide.
♨ ⊛ ⇔ ◑ ▸ P

173

Lincolnshire

Aubourn

Royal Oak
Royal Oak Lane
☎ (0522) 788291
12–2.30, 7–11 (12–2.30, 7–10.30 Sun)
Bateman XB, XXXB; Samuel Smith OBB Ⓗ; guest beers
Comfortable village local with a friendly welcome. Extensive collection of horse brasses in the lounge. ♔ ❀ ◐ ◑ ⊟ ♣ P

Barholm

Five Horseshoes
Main Street
☎ (0778) 36238
12–2.30 (not Mon–Fri), 7 (5 Fri)–11
Adnams Bitter; Bateman XXXB Ⓗ; guest beers
Fine stone pub in a tranquil village setting; relaxed atmosphere. Up to five guest beers each week. ♔ ⛵ ❀ P

Belchford

Blue Bell
Main Street
☎ (0507) 533602
11–2.30 (not Mon), 7–11
Ind Coope Burton Ale Ⓗ; guest beers
Situated in the heart of the unspoilt Wolds, a pub featuring an amazing array of old farm implements. Always two guest beers. Worthy member of the Ind Coope *Cellarmanship* Guild.
♔ Q ❀ 🛏 ◐ ◑ ♣ P

Boston

Eagle
144 West Street
☎ (0205) 361116
11–3, 6 (5 Thu & Fri)–11 (11–11 Sat)
Adnams Mild, Bitter, Broadside; Marston's Pedigree; Taylor Landlord Ⓗ; guest beers
Busy town pub. Local groups, including a folk club, meet here. Live music often at weekends. ♔ ❀ ◐ ⊟ ⇌ ♣

Magnet
South Square
☎ (0205) 369186
11–3, 6–11 (11–11 Sat)
Draught Bass; Stones Best Bitter; Taylor Landlord Ⓗ; guest beers
Riverside pub adjoining the music centre, close to the Guildhall and Arts Centre.
♔ 🛏 ◐ ◑ ⊟ ⇌ ♣

Mill
Spilsby Road (near Pilgrim Hospital) ☎ (0205) 352784
11–3, 7–11
Draught Bass; Bateman Mild, XB, XXXB Ⓗ
Smart and popular pub with an emphasis on food (separate restaurant). ❀ ◐ ◑ ♿ ▲ P

New Castle
Fydell Street ☎ (0205) 361144
11–4, 7–11 (11–11 Fri)
Draught Bass; Bateman Mild, XB Ⓗ
Large pub just out of the town centre, near the Sluice Bridge. Moorings for boats nearby on the River Witham. Games-oriented, including bar skittles. ❀ ⇌ ♣ P

Branston Booths

Green Tree
Bardney Road
☎ (0522) 791208
11–4, 7–11
Draught Bass; Stones Best Bitter; Wards Mild, Sheffield Best Bitter Ⓗ; guest beer
Cosy, welcoming village local. Drive carefully along the straight or you may miss it. The restaurant caters for children and vegetarians.
♔ Q ❀ ◐ ◑ ⊟ ♿ ▲ ♣ ⌓ P

Burgh le Marsh

Fleece
Market Place
☎ (0754) 810215
10.30–3, 6–11
Hardys & Hansons Best Bitter Ⓔ
Former coaching inn, about 400 years-old, in the village market place. Nowadays a thriving local, catering for regulars and travellers to 'Skeggy'. 🛏 ◐ ◑ ♣

Inn on the Marsh
☎ (0754) 810582
11–4 (3 Tue & Thu), 6–11
Draught Bass; Bateman XB Ⓗ
Toast your toes by the open kitchen range in winter; in summer just sit back and admire the large collection of bric-a-brac. ♔ Q ❀ ♣

Castle Bytham

Fox & Hounds
High Street ☎ (0780) 410336
12–2.30 (not Tue), 6–11
Draught Bass; Bateman XB; Greene King Abbot; Ind Coope Burton Ale; S&N Theakston Best Bitter; Wards Thorne Best Bitter Ⓗ
Delightful 300-year-old country inn with a low, beamed ceiling. Excellent decor. ♔ ◐ ◑ ♿ ▲ ♣

Try also: Castle Inn (S&N); **Willoughby Arms** (Free)

Chapel St Leonards

Ship
Sea Lane ☎ (0754) 72975
11–3, 7–11
Bateman Mild, XB, XXXB Ⓗ
Busy, cheerful and friendly pub, popular with locals and holidaymakers. Keen support for *Guide Dogs for the Blind*. Large garden and children's play area. Coarse fishing available. Meals in summer only. ♔ ❀ ◐ ◑ ▲ ♣ P

Claypole

Five Bells Inn
Main Street ☎ (0636) 626561
12–2.30, 6.30 (7 winter)–11
Bateman XB; Wards Sheffield Best Bitter Ⓗ; guest beers
Refurbished village pub with a comfortable, friendly atmosphere and an hospitable landlord. Value for money home-cooked food and excellent accommodation. Garden play area for children.
♔ Q ❀ 🛏 ◐ ◑ ⊟ ♿ ▲ ♣ P

Coleby

Tempest Arms
Hill Rise ☎ (0522) 810287
11.30–2.30, 6.30–11
Bateman XB; Ruddles Best Bitter; Webster's Yorkshire Bitter Ⓗ
Popular village local on the cliff edge. Redecoration has not affected its character. Named after the Tempest family who were local landowners. Good food and conversation. Fine views of the Vale of Trent.
Q ❀ ◐ ◑ ♿ ♣ P

Try also: Bell Inn (Free)

Coningsby

Leagate Inn
Leagate Road ☎ (0526) 42370
11.30–2.30, 7–11
Marston's Pedigree; Taylor Landlord; Whitbread Castle Eden Ale Ⓗ; guest beers
Celebrating its 450th year, this former tollgate and 'fen guide house' has long provided a warm welcome, unless you were destined for the gibbet which once stood nearby! A Jaguar Car Club and a Koi Keepers' Society meet here.
♔ Q ❀ ◐ ◑ P

Corby Glen

Woodhouse Arms
2 Bourne Road
☎ (047 684) 361
12–2, 7–11
Draught Bass; Bateman XB, XXXB; Tetley Bitter Ⓗ; guest beer (occasionally)
Popular village local with a cosy open fire in the lounge. Good value home-cooked food in a friendly atmosphere. The village recently celebrated the 350th anniversary of its annual sheep fair. Not to be missed.
♔ Q ❀ ◐ ◑ ⊟ ♿ ♣ P

Lincolnshire

Cowbit

Dun Cow
Barrier Bank
☎ (0406) 380543
11–3, 6.30–11

Adnams Broadside; Bateman XXXB; Tetley Bitter Ⓗ
Fenland pub dating from 1660: a large restaurant and a separate bar area. Several pub teams. ♨ ❀ 🛏 ◑ ▶ ⅛ ♣ P

Crowland

George & Angel
North Street ☎ (0733) 210550
10.30–3, 6–11 (11–11 Sat)

Ansells Mild; Ruddles Best Bitter, County; Webster's Yorkshire Bitter Ⓗ
Grade II listed, built in 1714, with stone from Crowland Abbey. Opposite the Trinity Bridge. Comfortable lounge and a busy, friendly bar.
♨ Q ❀ ◑ ▶ 🍺 ♣ P

East Ferry

Emerald Arms
Riverside, High Street
☎ (042 782) 522
12–3 (not Mon–Fri), 7–11

Wards Sheffield Best Bitter, Kirby Ⓗ
Friendly village local with an Irish influence, next to the River Trent. Small bar, large lounge plus conservatory. Good value meals. Live music Fri and Sun. Families welcome – children's play area provided. ⛴ ❀ ◑ ▶ 🍺 P

East Kirkby

Red Lion
Main Road ☎ (079 03) 406
11–3, 7–11

Bateman XB; Wards Sheffield Best Bitter Ⓗ; **guest beer**
The nearby Lincolnshire Air Museum houses its Lancaster Bomber; this friendly village local houses a 'collectomaniac' with a passion for clocks and breweriana. Camping and caravanning in the pub grounds. ♨ ⛴ ◑ ▶ 🅰 P

Frampton

Moores Arms
Church End OS328392
☎ (0205) 722408
10.30–3, 6.30–11

Draught Bass; Bateman XB Ⓗ
Pub with a good garden and a newly extended restaurant. Worth the trouble to find.
❀ ◑ ▶ P

Gedney Dyke

Chequers
☎ (0406) 362666
11–3, 7–11

Adnams Mild, Bitter;
Draught Bass; Bateman XXXB; Greene King Abbot Ⓗ
Comfortable country pub well worth seeking out, especially if hungry as well as thirsty. Circa 1795. Bridge played – beginners welcome.
♨ ❀ ◑ ▶ ♣ ⅛ P

Grantham

Angel & Royal
High Street
☎ (0476) 65816
11.30–2.30 (3 Fri, 4 Sat), 6 (7 Sat)–11

Adnams Bitter; Draught Bass; Bateman XXXB Ⓗ; **guest beers**
Reputedly England's oldest coaching inn, established in the 13th century and commissioned by the Knights Templar. Note the huge inglenook and the stone sculpture in the window of the Angel Bar. Cosmopolitan clientele.
♨ Q ❀ 🛏 ◑ ▶ 🍺 ⇌ P ⅛

Beehive
10–11 Castlegate (off High St, via Finkin St, then 2nd right)
☎ (0476) 67794
11–3, 7–11 (11–11 Fri)

Adnams Bitter, Broadside Ⓗ; **guest beers**
The only pub in England with a living pub sign: an historic house with a friendly atmosphere, popular with young people. Excellent lunches served. Q ❀ ◑ ⇌

Chequers
Market Place
☎ (0476) 76383
12–3.30 (4 Sat), 7–11 (11–11 Fri)

Home Bitter; S&N Theakston Best Bitter, XB, Old Peculier; Younger IPA, No. 3 Ⓗ
Popular town-centre pub, with a wide range of real ales, which attracts a cross-section of people. Lunches served Wed–Sat; bar snacks other days. ◑ ⇌

Odd House
Fletcher Street
☎ (0476) 65293
11.30–3 (4 Sat), 7.30 (7 Sat)–11

Bateman Mild, XB, XXXB; John Smith's Bitter Ⓗ
Old, terraced back-street local comprising a snug, a lounge and a large bar; enclosed patio. Handy for the railway and bus stations.
♨ ❀ 🍺 ♣

Shirley Croft Hotel
Harrowby Road (off A52, Boston road)
☎ (0476) 63260
12–2.30, 6–11

Draught Bass; Bateman XB Ⓗ
Hotel set back from the road in its own gardens. One large drinking area with various nooks and crannies. Hosts regional chess matches.
❀ 🛏 ▶ P

White Lion
53 Bridge End Road
☎ (0476) 62084
11–11

Courage Directors; John Smith's Bitter Ⓗ
Fine town pub catering for drinkers from most walks of life. The bar has an emphasis on games and the pub fields two football teams. Meals are wholesome and excellent value. ❀ ◑ 🍺 ♣

Grasby

Cross Keys
Brigg Road (A1084)
☎ (065 262) 247
12–3 (4 Sat), 7–11

Ind Coope Burton Ale; Tetley Bitter Ⓗ
Pleasant, two-roomed pub on a hillside. Convenient for Viking Way walkers. Sun lunches are very popular (no meals Mon eve). The garden contains a children's play area.
♨ ❀ ◑ ▶ 🍺 ♣ P

Hatton

Midge Inn
Main Road
☎ (0507) 578348
11–3, 7–11

Draught Bass; Greene King Abbot; Stones Best Bitter Ⓗ
Pleasant roadside inn on the Lincoln–Skegness route. Recently reopened after being a café. Good food and beer in a pleasant atmosphere. No eve meals winter Mon.
♨ ❀ ◑ P

Heckington

Nags Head
High Street
☎ (0529) 60218
11–3, 7–11

Ruddles Best Bitter, County; Webster's Yorkshire Bitter Ⓗ; **guest beer**
17th-century coaching inn with a friendly welcome. The emphasis is on catering, with many home-made dishes. Shut the Box played.
Q ❀ 🛏 ◑ ▶ 🍺 ⇌ ♣ P

Try also: Royal Oak
(Camerons)

Holbeach Hurn

Rose & Crown
Marsh Road
☎ (0406) 26085
11–11

Elgood's Cambridge Bitter Ⓗ
Happy rural pub with a mixed clientele, set in six acres of land, ideal for picnics and barbecues (barbecues provided but bring your own food). Camping for tents and caravans. ♨ ❀ 🅰 ♣ P

175

Lincolnshire

Horbling

Plough
4 Spring Lane (off B1177)
☎ (0529) 240263
11–2, 7–11
**Greene King IPA, Abbot;
Wards Sheffield Best
Bitter** Ⓗ; **guest beer**
Small, village local: a tiny
snug; pool in the back bar;
quiet lounge. Good value food
and accommodation. One of
few pubs in Britain owned by
the parish (in the parish
council records since 1813). ∰
Q ⌖ ❀ ⇔ ◑ ▶ ⬥ & ♣ P

Try also: Fortescue Arms,
Billingborough (Ind Coope)

Horncastle

Kings Head
Bullring ☎ (0507) 523360
11–3 (4 Sat), 7–11
**Draught Bass; Bateman Mild,
XB, XXXB** Ⓗ
Sandwiched between taller
buildings, this cosy,
diminutive thatched pub
(known locally as 'the Thatch')
affords a warm welcome.
Once popular with petty
thieves during the town's fairs
and market days, due to the
ease of escape through the
back door. ∰ ◑ ♣

Red Lion
Bullring ☎ (0507) 523338
11–3, 7–11
**Greenalls Shipstone's Bitter;
Tetley Bitter** Ⓗ
Pleasant market town pub,
with a friendly welcome.
Supports a flourishing theatre
in the converted stables which
were regularly used during
the famous horse fairs of days
gone by.
∰ Q ⌖ ⇔ ◑ & ♣ P

Hundleby

Hundleby Arms
Main Road ☎ (0790) 52577
11–3, 6.30–11
Draught Bass; Bateman XB Ⓗ
Friendly, two-bar, wood-
panelled pub. Strong links
with *Guide Dogs for the Blind*;
money raised has bought 21
dogs so far. Is this a record?
Ideally situated for the
Franklin Way.
∰ ❀ ◑ ▶ ⬥ & ⯅ ♣ P

Kirkby la Thorpe

Queens Head
Church Street
☎ (0529) 305743
11.30–3, 6.30–11
Draught Bass Ⓗ
Large pub just off the Sleaford
bypass. Food oriented, with an
excellent cold carvery.
❀ ◑ ▶ P

Limber

New Inn
High Street ☎ (0469) 60257
11–2.30 (3 Sat), 7–11
**Bateman XXXB; McEwan 80/-;
Tetley Bitter** Ⓗ; **guest beer**
Pub owned by the Earl of
Yarborough, whose name is
used to describe a poor bridge
hand and adorns many pubs
in the area not owned by him.
A magnificent mausoleum can
be visited close by. No food at
weekends.
∰ Q ❀ ⇔ ◑ ⬥ ♣ P

Lincoln

Golden Eagle
High Street ☎ (0522) 521058
11–3, 5.30–11 (11–11 Fri & Sat)
**Bateman XB, XXXB; Exmoor
Gold; Fuller's London Pride;
Taylor Golden Best** Ⓗ; **guest
beers**
Friendly, traditional local with
old Lincoln prints and
memorabilia on the walls.
Wide range of guest beers and
Belgian bottled beers. Part of
the Small Beer wholesale and
pub chain. Family room
upstairs. No food Sun.
Q ⌖ ❀ ◑ ⬥ ♣ P

Jolly Brewer
Broadgate ☎ (0522) 528583
11–11
**Bass Special, Draught Bass;
Everards Tiger; S&N
Theakston XB; Younger
Scotch, No. 3** Ⓗ; **guest beers**
Popular city-centre pub which
has recently been extended
without losing any of its
character. Regular guest beers
contribute to the excellent
nature of a pub which is in its
11th year in this guide.
❀ ◑ ⬥ ⇌ ♣ ⌂ P

Peacock Inn
Wragby Road ☎ (0522) 524703
11.30–2.30, 5–11 (11–11 Sat)
**Hardys & Hansons Best Mild,
Best Bitter, Kimberley
Classic** Ⓗ; **guest beer**
Friendly local within easy
walking distance of the city
centre and tourist area. No
food Sun. ❀ ◑ ⬒ P

Portland Arms
50 Portland Street
☎ (0522) 513912
11–11
**Draught Bass; Courage Best
Bitter, Directors; John
Smith's Bitter, Magnet** Ⓗ;
guest beers
Simple, lively town tap room
with a pool table, darts and
dominoes. A cosy, quiet best
room offers occasional live
entertainment. Friendly
welcoming atmosphere. Two
guest beers always available.
Q ⬒ ⇌ ♣ P

Prince of Wales
77a Bailgate ☎ (0522) 528894
11–3, 7–11
**Courage Directors; John
Smith's Bitter, Magnet** Ⓗ
Friendly two-roomed pub in
the tourist area. Good value
lunches. Darts and dominoes
also very popular. The historic
cathedral is within two
minutes' walk. ❀ ◑ ⬒ ♣

Queen in the West
Moor Street (200 yds from
A57) ☎ (0522) 526169
11–3, 5.30–11
**Bateman XB; S&N Theakston
Best Bitter, XB; Taylor
Landlord; Younger Scotch,
No. 3** Ⓗ; **guest beers**
Pleasant pub on the western
edge of the city – well worth
the walk. Popular with local
workers at lunchtime and
residents in the evening. Two
contrasting rooms, and two
guest beers at all times. ◑ ⬒ ♣

Small Beer
(Off-Licence)
91 Newland Street West (200
yds from A57)
☎ (0522) 528628
10.30–10.30
**Bateman XXXB; Taylor
Landlord; Ward's Sheffield
Best Bitter** Ⓗ; **guest beers**
Back-street off-licence selling a
wide range of guest beers,
together with many unusual
bottled beers.

Strugglers Inn
Westgate ☎ (0522) 524702
11–3, 5.30–11 (11–11 Fri & Sat)
**Bass Mild XXXX, Draught
Bass** Ⓗ
Basic and bursting with
people: a veritable little gem
attracting customers from all
areas of Lincoln life. Reputed
to have an underground
passage to the castle next
door. Home of a successful
Sunday football team.
Q ❀ ⬒ ♣

Victoria
6 Union Road (behind castle)
☎ (0522) 536048
11–11
**Bateman XB; Everards Old
Original; S&N Theakston
Old Peculier; Taylor
Landlord** Ⓗ; **guest beers**
At least three guest beers at all
times here, including a mild.
Mini beer festivals June and
Xmas. Brewery feature nights
with music a speciality
(usually Wed). Almost worth
the visit for the landlord's
comments at closing time. East
Midlands CAMRA *Pub of the
Year* 1991. Q ❀ ◑ ⬒ ♣ ⌂

Little Steeping

Eaves
Main Street ☎ (0754) 86325

11–3, 6–11
**Ruddles Best Bitter; John
Smith's Bitter** H
Delightful pub in an unspoilt
rural location, offering an
exotic menu. ♨ ◖ ▶ P

Louth

Boars Head
Newmarket ☎ (0507) 603561
11–3 (4 Wed, Fri & Sat), 7–11
Bateman Mild, XB, Victory H
Traditional two-roomed pub
next to the cattle market.
🚶 Q ❀ 🛏 ◖ ▶ ♣ P

Olde Whyte Swanne
Eastgate ☎ (0507) 601312
11–3 (2 Wed & Fri), 7–11 (11–11 Sat)
**Bass Mild XXXX, Draught
Bass; Stones Best Bitter** H
Built in 1612; the oldest pub in
Louth. Magnificent public bar
at the front and a modern
lounge at the rear. Reputedly
haunted by a subterranean
ghost. Next to a public car
park (free in the evening).
🚶 ◖ 🍺 ♣

Wheatsheaf
Westgate ☎ (0507) 606262
11–3, 5–11
**Whitbread Boddingtons
Bitter, Bentley's Yorkshire
Bitter, Flowers Original** H
Situated in a quiet Georgian
terrace, this inn, dating from
1625, is equally attractive
inside and out. Weekday
lunches. 🚶 Q ◖ ♣ P

Woolpack
Riverhead Road
☎ (0507) 606568
11–3 (not Mon), 7–11
Bateman Mild, XB, XXXB H
Former 19th-century wool
merchant's house, now a
traditional, friendly inn with
three rooms to suit all tastes.
The short walk from the town
centre is well rewarded.
🚶 Q ❀ 🍺 ♣ P

Mablethorpe

Montalt Arms
George Street (off High St)
☎ (0507) 472794
11–3, 7–11
**Draught Bass; Bateman XB;
Stones Best Bitter** H; **guest
beers**
Comfortable, L-shaped lounge
bar with a well-appointed
restaurant. Named after a
local medieval knight who
was killed in a duel. Plenty of
woodwork and photos of
bygone Mablethorpe. Not a
typical seaside trippers' pub.
Limited parking. 🚶 ❀ ◖ ▶ P

Mareham le Fen

Royal Oak
Main Street ☎ (0507) 568357
11–3, 7–11

Bateman XB, XXXB
(summer) H; **guest beer**
Sir Richard Mint's 500-year-
old thatched smithy retains
many of its former customs.
The attractive garden houses
amusements and 'old original'
stocks for either children or
unruly customers! Excellent
home-made food includes
XXXB sausages.
🚶 Q ❀ ◖ ▶ 🍽 P

Market Deeping

Vine
19 Church Street
☎ (0778) 342387
11–2.30, 5–11
Wells Eagle, Bombardier H
Former 1870s prep school,
now a very friendly local: a
small lounge with a larger,
busy bar area. The many social
events include quiz nights and
barn dances. Active charity
fund-raisers. Eve meals finish
early (not served Sun).
🚶 ❀ ◖ ▶ 🍺 ♣ P

Try also: **Bull Hotel**
(Everards); **Goat**, Frognall
(Free)

Marshchapel

Greyhound
Seadyke Way (A1031)
☎ (047 286) 267
11–4, 7–11 (11–11 Sat)
**Bateman Mild, XB; Tetley
Bitter** H; **guest beer**
Typical, two-bar village pub
with a cosy, quiet atmosphere.
Popular with the locals.
🚶 Q ❀ ◖ ▶ 🍺 ♣ P

Minting

Sebastopol Inn
Church Lane
☎ (0507) 578688
12–2, 7–11
**Adnams Bitter, Broadside;
Bateman XB** H
Comfortable, 16th-century
village local offering good
food in pleasant surroundings
(no meals Tue eve).
🚶 Q 🛏 ❀ ◖ ▶ 🍺 ♣ P

Morton

Five Bells
2 Haconby Lane
☎ (0778) 570332
12–2 (not Mon or Thu, 2.30 Sat), 7–11
(12–2.30, 7–10.30 Sun)
**S&N Theakston Best Bitter;
Wards Mild, Thorne Best
Bitter, Sheffield Best Bitter** H;
guest beers (summer)
An increasing rarity: a
traditional village local, warm
and friendly, and a centre for
village life – darts teams,
support for the village football
team and other organisations.
Frequented by all ages.
🚶 ❀ ◖ ♣ P

Moulton Chapel

Wheatsheaf
Fengate ☎ (0406) 380525
11–2.30 (not Wed, 11.30–4 Sat), 7–11
**Draught Bass; Elgood's
Cambridge Bitter; Greene
King IPA** H; **guest beer**
Friendly two-room pub in an
out-of-the-way Fenland
village. Boasts a collection of
pottery pigs. Used to be
Bradford's brewery (closed
1928). Eve meals and camping
by prior arrangement.
🚶 ❀ ◖ 🍺 ♿ ♣ P

Nettleham

Black Horse
The Green
☎ (0522) 750702
11.30–2.30, 7.15–11
**Ansells Mild; Draught Bass;
Tetley Bitter; Whitbread
Boddingtons Bitter** H; **guest
beers**
Picturesque pub on the green
in a pleasant village. Recently
became a free house and is
popular for food.
🛏 ◖ ▶ 🍺 ♣ P

Plough
The Green ☎ (0522) 750275
11–2.30, 6–11
Bateman Mild, XB H
Friendly village pub where the
landlord is well known for his
rabbit pies (no food Sun).
Excellent facilities for
meetings or special occasions.
Outdoor drinking in the small
courtyard. 🛏 ❀ ◖ ♣

White Hart
High Street ☎ (0522) 751976
11–3.30, 7–11
**Draught Bass; Bateman Mild,
XB, XXXB, Victory** H
Large, pleasant pub in a
prominent village position.
Distinct drinking areas; games
played. Meals are filling and
popular. Suffered a fire in
March 1992. 🛏 ❀ ◖ ▶ 🍺 ♣ P

North Kelsey

Royal Oak
High Street ☎ (0652) 678544
12–3, 7–11
**Stones Best Bitter; Vaux
Samson; Wards Sheffield
Best Bitter** H
Fine, friendly village pub with
an open-plan bar, a separate
games room and a small snug.
Quiz nights Tue; music quiz
alternate Sat. Popular for
meals. 🚶 ❀ ◖ ▶ 🍺 ♣ P

Oasby

Houblon Arms
Main Street ☎ (052 95) 215
12–3, 7–11
**Ansells Bitter; Draught Bass;
Ind Coope Burton Ale** H

Lincolnshire

Built of local stone, this old village pub is a rural gem. The beamed interior provides a splendid environment for drinking, eating and generally enjoying oneself. Not to be missed. 🍴 Q ❀ 🛏 ◖▶ P

Potterhanworth

Chequers
Cross Street ☎ (0522) 790189
12–3 (not Mon–Thu), 7–11
Mansfield Riding Mild, Riding Bitter, Old Baily Ⓗ
Friendly village local with a popular host: a bar with a pool table and other games, plus a small room with an emphasis on food in the evenings. Beer garden to the rear. Restricted lunchtime opening (Fri–Sun only). Q ❀ ▶ 🛏 ♣ P

Quadring

White Hart
7 Town Drove (S off A152)
☎ (0775) 821135
11–3 (not Mon), 6.45–11
Bateman Mild, XB, XXXB Ⓗ
Busy village local which offers a welcoming atmosphere and caters for all ages. At one time the rear of the pub was a bakery. Wheelchair access from the car park.
🍴 ❀ ♿ ♣ P

Raithby

Red Lion
Main Road ☎ (0790) 53727
11–3 (not Mon–Fri), 7–11
Home Bitter; S&N Theakston XB Ⓗ
Attractive pub with an intimate restaurant in a picturesque Wolds village. An enterprising landlord with culinary skills has built a reputation for excellent home-made food; fresh pizzas available at the bar.
🍴 ❀ 🛏 ◖▶ P

Ruskington

Black Bull
Rectory Road ☎ (0526) 832270
11–2.30 (4 Sat), 6.30–11
Bateman XB, XXXB Ⓗ
One of the oldest buildings in a fast-expanding village; formerly a farmhouse with part of the bar once used as stables. A warm welcome in a comfortable interior, but leave your horse outside. Book for Sun lunch; no meals Sun eve.
🛏 ◖▶ ♿ ≠ P

Saracen's Head

Saracen's Head
Washway Road
☎ (0406) 22708
11–4, 6–11
Greene King Abbot Ⓖ; **Wards Sheffield Best Bitter** Ⓗ

Unspoilt, hospitable pub of rural character, situated on a sharp bend. Regular weekend sing-songs. Well frequented by locals. 🍴 Q ❀ 🛏 ♣ P

Saxilby

Ship
Bridge Street ☎ (0522) 702259
11–2.30 (3 Fri & Sat), 7–11
John Smith's Bitter Ⓗ
Simple village pub in a pleasant canalside village; popular with locals and boaters. Good plain food. Children's play area in the garden. Eve meals for parties only. ❀ ◖ ♿ ≠ ♣ P

Skegness

Vine
Vine Road (1 mile S of centre, off Drummond Rd)
☎ (0754) 610611
11–3, 6–11
Draught Bass; Bateman Mild, XB, XXXB Ⓗ
In its secluded wooded setting, a mile from the hurly burly of the resort, this hotel is an oasis of peace and calm. Leafy gardens in summer; roaring fires in winter. Possibly visited by Tennyson; reputedly haunted by a murdered excise man. No lunches Sun.
🍴 Q ❀ 🛏 ◖▶ ♿ ♣ P

Skendleby

Blacksmiths Arms
Main Road ☎ (075 485) 662
11–3, 6.30–12
Bateman XB, XXXB Ⓗ
Pub where a cosy bar has an open view of the cellar. The large restaurant houses a pear tree and an original well. Five-bedroomed converted barn for rent, overlooking the picturesque Wolds. Village sheepdog trials in August.
🍴 Q ❀ 🛏 ◖▶ ♣ P

Sleaford

Nags Head
Southgate ☎ (0529) 413916
11–3, 7–11 (11–11 Fri & Sat)
Draught Bass; Bateman XB, XXXB, Salem Porter Ⓗ
Friendly, no-frills town pub serving an excellent range of filled rolls. Live music Sun nights. 🍴 ❀ ◖▶ ≠ ♣ P

Rose & Crown
Watergate ☎ (0529) 303350
11–2.30, 7–11
Mansfield Riding Bitter, Old Baily Ⓗ
Popular, busy local in the town with strong pub games teams; the games area is on a different level to the bar. Large enclosed outdoor drinking area. Weekday lunches. Limited parking. ❀ ◖ ≠ ♣ P

Wagon & Horses
Eastgate ☎ (0529) 303388
10.30–3, 5–11 (11–11 Sat)
Bass Mild XXXX, Draught Bass; Stones Best Bitter Ⓗ
Large, comfortable pub just past the church. Can get very crowded some nights. Good range of bar meals. Accommodation planned.
❀ ◖▶ ≠ P

South Kyme

Hume Arms Hotel
High Street ☎ (0526) 861004
12–2.30, 7–11
Tetley Bitter; Wards Sheffield Best Bitter Ⓗ; **guest beers** (occasionally)
A regular meeting place for the Sleaford Navigation Society: a small, friendly bar and a comfortable, quiet lounge. Caravan parking facilities.
Q ❀ 🛏 ◖▶ 🛏 ♿ ♣ P

Spalding

Lincolnshire Poacher
11 Double Street
☎ (0775) 766490
11–3, 6.30 (7 Fri & Sat, 6 summer)–11
S&N Theakston Best Bitter, XB, Old Peculier Ⓗ; **guest beers**
Busy and lively pub which always serves at least four guest beers. The enterprising landlord has created a cosmopolitan atmosphere. Pleasant riverside frontage.
❀ ◖▶ ♿ ≠ ↻

Red Lion Hotel
Market Place ☎ (0775) 722869
10.30–3.30, 5–11
Adnams Bitter; Draught Bass; Taylor Landlord Ⓗ
Historic market town hotel, richly refurbished yet retaining a good atmosphere. A popular meeting place for locals. Eve meals in the restaurant. 🛏 ◖ ≠

Try also: **White Horse**, Churchgate (Samuel Smith)

Spilsby

White Hart
Cornhill Market Square
☎ (0790) 52244
11–11
Hardys & Hansons Best Bitter, Kimberley Classic Ⓗ
Comfortable coaching inn in the centre of a small market town with its own 150-year-old post box and a more recent taxi and minibus service. Snooker room available by prior booking.
🍴 Q 🛏 ◖▶ 🛏 ♣ P

Try also: **George Hotel**, Boston Rd (Home)

Springthorpe

New Inn

Hill Road ☎ (042 783) 254
12–2, 7–11 (12–2, 7–10.30 Sun)
**Bateman XXXB; Tetley
Bitter** Ⓗ
Small country pub on the
village green – very
picturesque. Fine food
available in the restaurant.
🏠 Q ❀ ◑ ⊟ ♣

Stamford

White Swan

Scotgate ☎ (0780) 52834
11–3, 6–11
**Bateman Mild, XB, XXXB,
Victory** Ⓗ
Former Manns pub, taken
over, refurbished and
reopened by Bateman in 1988.
Winner of the local CAMRA
Pub of the Month award. 🏠 ♣

Try also: Daniel Lambert, St
Leonard's St (Free)

Sturton by Stow

Plough

Tillbridge Lane (A1500)
☎ (0427) 788268
11.30–2.30, 7–11
**Bateman XB; Ind Coope ABC
Best Bitter; Marston's
Pedigree; Tetley Bitter** Ⓗ
Much-extended, friendly
village pub, serving an
excellent range of meals
(booking advised Fri and Sat
eve). Holder of local council
Health & Hygiene award.
Q ❀ ◑ ⊟ ♿ ♣ P

Swayfield

Royal Oak

High Street ☎ (047 684) 247

11–2.30, 6–11
**Draught Bass; Greene King
Abbot; Welsh Brewers
Worthington BB** Ⓗ
Well worth seeking out: an old
village pub with stone walls,
beamed ceilings and a
welcoming fire. The rugby-
playing owner of this free
house sets high standards,
extending to excellent home
cooking at very reasonable
prices. 🏠 ❀ ◑ ◐

Swinhope

Click'em Inn

On B1203, 3 miles from
Binbrook
☎ (047 283) 253
11–2.30 (not Mon, 3 Sat), 7–11
**Bateman XXXB; S&N
Theakston XB, Old
Peculier** Ⓗ; **guest beer**
Isolated but popular Wolds
pub; a genuine free house. Its
name derives from the click of
the gate to the field opposite
into which farmers drove
flocks whilst drinking at the
pub. 🏠 ❀ ◑ ♣ P

Thorpe Culvert

Three Tuns

Culvert Road OS471603
☎ (0754) 880495
11–2.30, 7–11
**Ind Coope Burton Ale; Tetley
Bitter** Ⓗ; **guest beers** (winter)
250-year-old riverside pub
with a large garden,
convenient for fishing.
Regularly lit with old-
fashioned gas lamps to
enhance the atmosphere. A
warm welcome is provided to
all by the small pub dog. 36oz
steaks and traditional Irish
dishes served.
🏠 Q ❀ ◑ ▲ ⇌ ♣ P

Threekingham

Three Kings Inn

Salters Way
☎ (0529) 240249
11–3, 7–11
**Draught Bass; Welsh Brewers
Worthington BB** Ⓗ
Welcoming 17th-century
coaching inn. Interesting
collection of handpumps,
including an original swan
neck pump.
🛏 ❀ 🏠 ◑ ◐ ⊟ ♣ P

Wainfleet

Red Lion

High Street ☎ (0754) 880301
11–3, 7–11
Bateman Mild, XB, XXXB Ⓗ
Large bar and a comfortable
lounge with a growing
waddle of ducks nesting
around the fireplace, guarded
by a bitter-drinking labrador.
The nearest Bateman pub to
the brewery. Camping in the
grounds; Bateman pilgrims
awake to the sight and aromas
of the brewery. Book for Sun
lunch. 🏠 Q ❀ 🏠 ◑ ◐ ⊟
▲ ⇌ ♣ P

Try also: Jolly Sailor, St Johns
St (Bateman)

Whaplode St
Catherine

Blue Bell

Cranesgate ☎ (0406) 34300
11–3 (not Mon-Thu), 7–11
**Bateman XB; Wards Sheffield
Best Bitter** Ⓗ
Friendly village local run by
the same couple for over 20
years. Built in approximately
1780. 🏠 Q 🛏 ❀ ⊟ ▲ ♣ P

From Good Beer Guide 1989

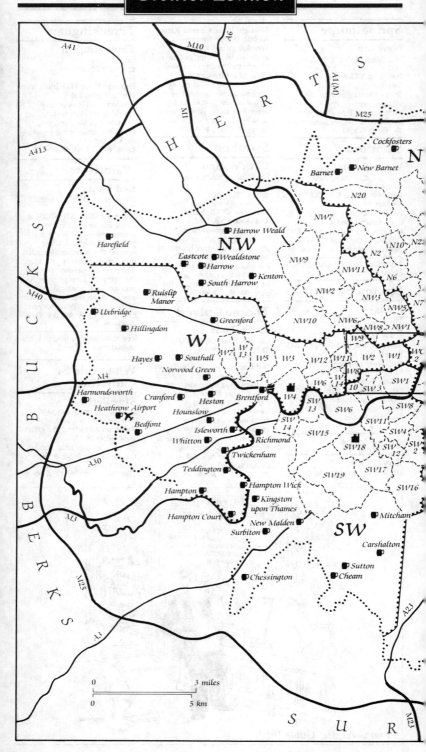

Greater London

- Numbered postal districts contain recommended pubs
- Inner London inset map
- London 'sector' boundaries

A10

E

S

S

E

X

M11

M25

A12

Enfield
Whitewebbs

Enfield
Town

Enfield
Lock

Noak Hill

N21

N9

E4

A12

Woodford Green

Barkingside

A127

Romford

E17

N16

E10

E11

A406

Chadwell Heath

Hornchurch

Cranham

N1

E5

E8

E9

E12

Ilford

E

E15

Barking

E2

A13

EC
4

2

E1

A13

SE1

SE17

SE8

SE
10

SE18

Upper
Belvedere

A13

SE14

SE3

SE15

SE
4

SE13

Bexleyheath

SE22

SE12

SE23

SE6

SE26

Sidcup

A2

SE19

Footscray

SE20

Chislehurst

SE25

Bromley

Thornton
Heath

Beckenham

Croydon

Bromley Common

Addiscombe

SE

Downe

M25

T

N

E

K

E

N

T

M20

M26

R

E

Y

A21

Greater London

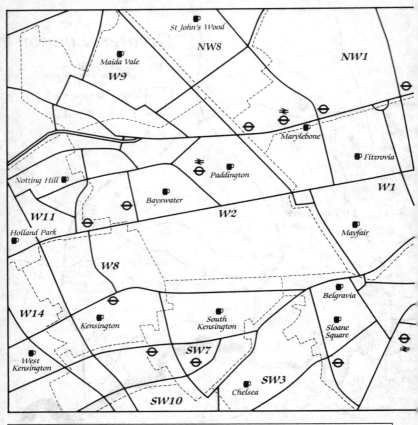

Fuller's, Chiswick; **Young's**, Wandsworth

Pubs within Greater London are divided into seven geographical sectors: Central, East, North, North-West, South-East, South-West and West, reflecting London postal boundaries (see Greater London map on previous pages). Look under Central London for postal districts EC1 to EC4, and WC1 and WC2. For each of the surrounding sectors, postal districts are listed in numerical order (E1, E2, etc.), followed in alphabetical order by the outlying areas which do not have London postal numbers (Barking, Chadwell Heath, etc.). The Inner London map, above, shows the area roughly covered by the Circle Line and outlines regions of London (Bloomsbury, Holborn, etc.) which have featured pubs. Some regions straddle more than one postal district.

Central London

EC2: City

Fleetwood
36 Wilson Street
☎ (071) 247 2242
11–9 (3 Sat; closed Sun)
Fuller's Chiswick, London Pride, ESB Ⓗ
Modern pub built within the Broadgate development. A busy city venue serving good cooked food and snacks lunchtimes and evenings.
❀ Ɑ ▶ ⇌ (Liverpool St)
↔ (Moorgate)

EC3: City

East India Arms
67 Fenchurch Street
☎ (071) 480 6562
11–9 (closed weekends)
Young's Bitter, Special, Winter Warmer Ⓗ
Always crowded, a small pub where Reg has been mine host, with a smile, for 18 years.
Q Ɑ ⇌ (Fenchurch St)

Lamb Tavern
10–12 Leadenhall Market
☎ (071) 626 2454
11–9 (closed weekends)
Young's Bitter, Special, Winter Warmer Ⓗ
Set in a Victorian covered market and established in 1780, a pub with superb marble panelling.
Q Ɑ ⇌ (Liverpool St) ↔ ⦧

Three Lords
27 Minories ☎ (071) 481 4249
11–11 (earlier if quiet; closed weekends)
Young's Bitter, Special, Winter Warmer Ⓗ
Quieter pub than those close by. Rebuilt in 1985 as an exact external copy of an earlier pub. Q Ɑ ⇌ (Fenchurch St)
↔ (Aldgate) ⦧

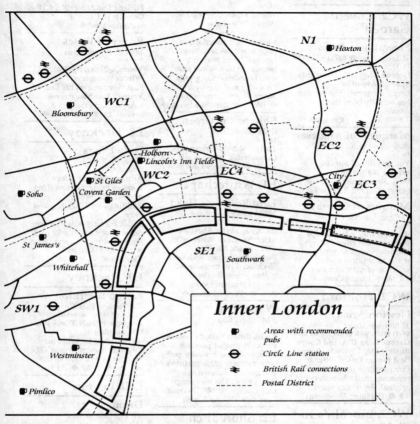

Inner London

- 🍺 Areas with recommended pubs
- ⊖ Circle Line station
- ⇌ British Rail connections
- ------- Postal District

EC4: City

City Retreat
Shoe Lane ☎ (071) 353 7904
11–9.30 (11 if busy; closed weekends)
**Young's Bitter, Special,
Winter Warmer** Ⓗ
Ground-floor office block pub,
previously a wine bar/yuppie
hostelry, now a Young's tied
house. ◖▮ ⇌ (Farringdon)
⊖ (St Paul's) ♠

WC1: Bloomsbury

Calthorpe Arms
252 Grays Inn Road
☎ (071) 278 4732
11–3, 5.30–11 (11–11 Thu–Sat)
**Young's Bitter, Special,
Winter Warmer** Ⓗ
Relaxed, welcoming local,
near the new ITN studios. The
upstairs dining room is open
at lunchtimes; eve meals on
request. Q ❀ ◖▮ ⇌ (King's
Cross) ⊖ (Russell Sq)

Lamb
94 Lamb's Conduit Street
☎ (071) 405 0713
11–11

**Young's Bitter, Special,
Winter Warmer** Ⓗ
An absolute gem, with original
Victorian etched-glass, snob
screens and old photographs
of music hall artistes. Clientele
span all walks of life, from
professors to porters from the
nearby hospital. Regular quiz
nights. Cold meals only eves.
Q ❀ ◖▮ ⇌ (Farringdon)
⊖ (Russell Sq) ♠ ✄

Rugby Tavern
19 Great James Street
☎ (071) 405 1384
11.30–11 (closed weekends)
**Fuller's Chiswick, London
Pride, ESB** Ⓗ
Comfortable pub, the only
Fuller's house in WC1.
Decorated with old pictures of
Rugby School. Children are
admitted to the function room.
❀ ◖▮ ⇌ (Farringdon)
⊖ (Russell Sq) ♠

WC1: Holborn

Cittie of Yorke
22 High Holborn
☎ (071) 242 7670

11.30–11 (11.30–3, 5.30–11 Sat;
closed Sun)
**Samuel Smith OBB,
Museum** Ⓗ
Very distinctive Gothic
building on the site of an
earlier inn and coffee house.
The magnificent baronial hall
at the rear boasts vats and
screened compartments. There
is also a comfortable front bar
and a maze of vaulted cellars.
♨ Q ◖▮ ৬ ⇌ (Farringdon)
⊖ (Chancery Lane) ♠

Three Cups
21–22 Sandland Street
☎ (071) 831 4302
11–11 (11–3 Sat; closed Sun)
**Young's Bitter, Special,
Winter Warmer** Ⓗ
Friendly, comfortable pub
with a mostly young clientele
including office workers. A
former Finch's house, much
improved since Young's took
it over. Rather whimsical,
concealed dartboard – see if
you can find it! Q ❀ ◖ ⇌
(Farringdon) ⊖ (Holborn/
Chancery Lane) ♠

Greater London

WC2: Covent Garden

Freemasons Arms
81 Long Acre ☎ (071) 836 3115
11–11
Greene King IPA, Rayments Special, Abbot H
Large, busy pub. The interior has recently been totally rebuilt.
◑ ▶ ≠ (Charing Cross) ⊖

Marquess of Anglesey
Bow Street ☎ (071) 240 3216
11–11
Young's Bitter, Special, Winter Warmer H
Busy corner pub handy for Covent Garden Piazza. ◑ ▶ ⊖

Marquis of Granby
51 Chandos Place
11–11
Adnams Bitter; Ind Coope Burton Ale; Tetley Bitter H
Narrow, wedge-shaped pub with many prints and a selection of malt whiskies.
◑ ▶ ≠ (Charing Cross) ⊖

WC2: Holborn

Newton Arms
31 Newton Street
11–11 (11–3, 5.30–11 Sat; closed Sun)
Greene King IPA; Ind Coope Burton Ale; Taylor Walker Best Bitter; Tetley Bitter H
Pub rebuilt in the 1950s, replacing the 18th-century original. Beers may vary.
◑ ▶ ⊖ (Holborn/Kingsway)

WC2: Lincoln's Inn Fields

Seven Stars
53 Carey Street (off Strand)
11–11 (closed weekends)
Courage Best Bitter, Directors H
17th-century pub, popular with the legal profession.
◑ ≠ (St Paul's) ⊖ (Temple)

WC2: St Giles

Angel
61 St Giles High Street
12–11 (12–3, 7–11 Sat; closed Sun)
Courage Best Bitter, Directors; John Smith's Bitter H
Historic pub, near Centrepoint; reputed to be the last place convicted felons could call for a drink on the way to Tyburn. Weekday lunches.
◑ ⊖ (Tottenham Ct Rd) ♣

East London

E1: Stepney

Hollands
Brayford Square

11–11
Young's Bitter, Special H, **Winter Warmer** G
A treasure house of Victoriana, breweriana, old photos and press cuttings. A Grade II listed building because of its original interior with boarded ceiling, pine panelling and glasswork.
🏠 ❀ ⊞ ⊖ (Limehouse) ⊖ (Whitechapel/Shadwell) ♣

Ship on the Green
60 Stepney Green
11–3, 6–11
Tolly Cobbold Original H
Comfortable, one-bar pub.
🏠 ❀ ⊖ (Stepney Green)

E1: Whitechapel

Lord Rodney's Head
285 Whitechapel Road
11–11
Banks & Taylor Shefford Mild, Shefford Bitter, SOS, SOD, Black Bat H
Busy pub adorned with over 50 clocks. Live music most nights. Pricey for the area. Only vegetarian food is served.
❀ ◑ ⊖ (Whitechapel) ♣

White Hart
1 Mile End Road
11–11
Cains Bitter; Fuller's London Pride; Young's Bitter H
Basic and clean boozers' pub with a superb glass partition and mirrors. Known as 'Murphy's'. The beer range may change. ⊞ ≠ (Bethnal Green) ⊖ (Whitechapel)

E2: Shoreditch

Owl & Pussycat
34 Redchurch Street
11–11 (11–3, 6–11 Sat)
Courage Best Bitter; Harveys BB, Old; Hook Norton Best Bitter, Old Hooky H
Good atmosphere in a slightly expensive pub with good service. A Grade II listed building. House beer.
❀ ◑ ♿ ≠ (Liverpool St) ⊖

E4: Chingford

Royal Oak
219 Kings Head Hill
11–3, 5.30 (5 Sat)–11 (11–11 Sat in public)
Courage Directors; Greene King Abbot; McMullen AK, Country, Stronghart H
Large brick-built suburban house. The public bar is a welcome haven for the games and/or serious ale enthusiast. The lounge is more decorous, with food. ❀ ◑ ▶ ⊞ ▲ ♣ P

E5: Clapton

Anchor & Hope
15 High Hill Ferry
11–3, 5.30 (6 Sat)–11

Fuller's London Pride, ESB H
One-bar pub on the waterfront. ❀ ♣

Prince of Wales
146 Lea Bridge Road
11–11
Young's Bitter, Special, Winter Warmer H
Superbly sited on the Lea, a Young's tied house now enjoying something of a revival. ⟿ ❀ ◑ ▶ ⊞ ▲ ♣ P

E8: Hackney

Lady Diana
95 Forest Road
11.30–3, 5–11
Adnams Bitter; Fuller's London Pride; Greene King Abbot; Whitbread Boddingtons Bitter H; **guest beer**
Small, friendly pub. The beer range may vary. Snacks at all times, and pizzas a speciality.
❀ ◑ ▶ ≠ (Dalston/Kingsland)

E9: Hackney

Falcon & Firkin
360 Victoria Park Road
11–3, 5–11 (11–11 summer)
Dogbolter; S&N Theakston Old Peculier H
As described by William Rushton: 'Designer grot'. The brewery is visible from the bar. ⟿ ❀ ◑ ≠ ⊖ P

E10: Leyton

Drum
557 Lea Bridge Road
11–11
Greene King IPA, Abbot; Marston's Pedigree; S&N Theakston XB; Younger Scotch H; **guest beers**
Always a busy pub with regular promotions. Decorated with drums. No meals Sun eve. Q ◑ ▶ ≠ (Walthamstow Central) ⊖

Holly Bush
32 Grange Road
11.30–3, 5–11
Greene King IPA, Abbot H
A welcome oasis in an area of poor pubs. Convenient and essential for those intent on watching Leyton FC.
❀ ≠ (Midland Rd) ⊖ ♣

E11: Leyton

Birkbeck Tavern
45 Langthorne Road
11–11
Draught Bass; Tetley Bitter H; **guest beer**
Friendly, two-bar back-street local with no frills. Q ❀ ◑ ⊞ ⊖ ♣ ⟳

Woodhouse Tavern
119 Harrow Road

11–3 (4 Sat), 5 (7 Sat)–11 (11–11 Fri)
Young's Bitter, Special Ⓗ;
guest beer
Tidy, two-bar local with a club
room. ♨ Q ⊛ ◑ ▮ ⬥ ♣ ♡

E12: Manor Park

Blakesley Arms
Station Road ☎ (081) 478 6023
11–11
**Charrington IPA; Fuller's
London Pride** Ⓗ
Large, friendly pub with old
prints and posters in an
unusual-shaped saloon bar.
⊛ ⬥ ⇌ ♣

E15: Stratford

Theatre Royal
Jerry Raffles Square
☎ (071) 534 7374
11–3, 5 (6 Sat)–11 (closed Sun except
variety night once monthly)
**Adnams Broadside;
Mansfield Riding Mild;
Wells Eagle, Bombardier** Ⓗ
The bar of the Theatre Royal,
Stratford, which is likely to
close around 7.30 if there's no
show. A great place to
stargaze – celebrities abound.
Food is very very good and
varied. The theatre is a gem.
Q ⛴ ⊛ ◑ ▮ ⇌ ⊖ P

E17: Walthamstow

Coppermill
205 Coppermill Lane
11–11
**Fuller's London Pride, ESB;
Greene King IPA; Marston's
Pedigree; Morland Bitter;
Tetley Bitter** Ⓗ
Small free house near the
waterworks and a disused
copper mill.
⊛ ⇌ (St James's St) ♣

Flower Pot
128 Wood Street
11–3, 5.30–11 (11–11 Sat)
Draught Bass Ⓗ
One of the best pints of Bass
you will find anywhere, in the
surroundings of a traditional-
style pub. Q ⇌ (Wood St)

Grove Tavern
Grove Road
☎ (081) 509 0230
11–11
**Ruddles Best Bitter; Tetley
Bitter; Welsh Brewers
Worthington BB** Ⓗ
Friendly local, built in 1868,
with darts and a function
room. ⊛ ◑ ▮ ⇌ ⊖ ♣ ♡

Village
Orford Road
☎ (081) 521 9982
11–11
**Draught Bass; Fuller's
London Pride; Greene King
IPA; Welsh Brewers
Worthington BB; Young's
Special** Ⓗ
Pub with a fascinating display

of cameras. No smoking
family room.
⛴ ⊛ ◑ ▮ ⬥ ⇌ ⊖ ✂

Barking

Britannia
1 Church Road
11–3, 5–11 (11–11 Sat)
**Young's Bitter, Special,
Winter Warmer** Ⓗ
Plush large saloon and a small
basic public; Young's only tied
house in Essex. Good value
lunches. Friendly atmosphere.
⊛ ◑ ⬥ ⇌ ⊖ ♣ P

Spotted Dog
15 Longbridge Road
☎ (081) 594 0228
11.30–3 (3.30 Sat), 5 (7 Sat)–11
**Courage Best Bitter,
Directors** Ⓗ
A 'Davy's Wine Lodge' with
lots of wood panelling and
sawdust on the floor. Food at
all times, except Sun. Good
atmosphere and excellent bar
service. Guest beers may be
introduced. The expensive
Directors is labelled as 'Davy's
Old Wallop'. Q ◑ ▮ ⬥ ⇌ ⊖

Barkingside

New Fairlop Oak
Fencepiece Road, Fulwell
Cross ☎ (081) 500 2217
11–11
**Greene King IPA, Abbot;
Marston's Pedigree; S&N
Theakston XB; Younger
Scotch** Ⓗ; **guest beers**
Recently totally refurbished in
typical Wetherspoon style.
Good value beer – particularly
the Scotch.
⊛ ◑ ▮ ⊖ (Fairlop) P

Chadwell Heath

White Horse
118 High Road (A118)
11–11
**Ind Coope Benskins Best
Bitter, Burton Ale; Tetley
Bitter; Young's Bitter** Ⓗ; **guest
beers**
A 'White Horse' has been on
this Roman road since the 16th
century. Refurbished in
comfortable, traditional style,
it has a large garden (no dogs
allowed). Special prices for
senior citizens Mon–Fri.
⊛ ◑ ⇌ ♣ ♡ P

Cranham

Thatched House
348 St Mary's Lane (B187)
☎ (0708) 228080
12–3 (3.30 Fri, 4 Sat), 5.30 (6 Sat)–11
**Draught Bass; Charrington
IPA; Fuller's London Pride;
Young's Special** Ⓗ; **guest
beers**
Friendly, popular local with a
restaurant. Four guest beers

are served from Fri – but get
in quick as they are usually
drunk dry by Sat eve!
Occasional beer festivals. An
example for other managers.
No food Mon. Q ⛴ ⊛ ◑ P

Hornchurch

Bull
High Street ☎ (0708) 442125
11–11 (11–3.30, 6–11 Fri & Sat)
**Ind Coope Burton Ale; Taylor
Walker Best Bitter; Tetley
Bitter** Ⓗ
Friendly town-centre pub
serving good value lunches. A
traditional pub with wide
stone cladding on the bar.
Watch for the lip on the edge
of the stone floor when
leaving the bar. No food Sun.
⊛ ◑ P

Chequers
North Street ☎ (0708) 442094
11–3 (4 Sat), 5.30 (6 Sat)–11
**Ind Coope Friary Meux Best
Bitter; Tetley Bitter** Ⓗ
Friendly town pub. The old
off-licence area is now a
games room. The cheapest
Allied beer for miles. Lunches
served Wed–Fri.
◑ ⇌ (Emerson Pk) ♣ P

Ilford

Rose & Crown
16 Ilford Hill (A118, near
A406) ☎ (081) 478 7104
11–11
**Adnams Bitter; Ind Coope
Friary Meux Best Bitter,
Burton Ale; Tetley Bitter** Ⓗ;
guest beers
Large, friendly one-bar pub,
an oasis in a beer desert. The
range of guest beers varies,
with Young's, Wadworth's
and Arkell's often available;
occasional beer festivals. ◑ ⇌

Noak Hill

Bear
Noak Hill Road, Harold Hill
11–3.30 (4 Fri & Sat), 5.30 (6 Sat)–11
**Draught Bass; Charrington
IPA; guest beer** Ⓗ
Popular pub in the traditional
style with a good menu. The
large beer garden has a play
area. No food Sun. Wheelchair
WC. ⛴ ⊛ ◑ ♿ P

Romford

Durham Arms
101 Brentwood Road
11–3.30, 5–11 (11–11 Sat)
**Tetley Bitter; Young's
Bitter** Ⓗ
Comfortable local just outside
the town centre. The garden is
safe for children. Stages quiz
and karaoke nights plus
summer barbecues. ⊛ ◑ ⇌

Greater London

Woodford Green

Cricketers
299–301 High Road
☎ (081) 504 2734
11–3 (4 Sat), 5.30–11
Courage Directors; McMullen AK, Country, Stronghart Ⓗ
Friendly, traditional local offering excellent value beer. London CAMRA's *Pub of the Year* 1991. Q ❀ ◖ ⊟ ⊖ ♣ P

Travellers Friend
496–498 High Road
11–11
Courage Best Bitter, Directors; Crouch Vale SAS; Ridleys IPA; Ruddles Best Bitter; Wadworth 6X Ⓗ
A gem of a free house: wood-panelled and with original snob screens. A friendly pub. Courage Best is sold as 'Webster's Wonderful Wallop'. Q ◖ ◗ ⊖ ᴆ ⊖ P

North London

N1: Barnsbury

Crown
116 Cloudesley Road
☎ (071) 837 7107
11–11
Fuller's Chiswick, London Pride, ESB Ⓗ
19th-century pub retaining some original etched-glass and tilework. It has a dining area at the rear and whole pigs are spit-roasted on the front patio on summer Suns. ⋈ ❀ ◖ ◗ ⊖ (Angel) ♣

N1: Canonbury

Compton Arms
4 Compton Avenue
☎ (071) 359 2645
11–11
Greene King XX Mild, IPA, Rayments Special, Abbot Ⓗ**, Winter Ale** Ⓖ
Small cottage-style building in a narrow side street off Highbury Corner. Busy early eves, but no fruit machines or music. TV for major sporting events only. A hidden oasis! No food Sun. Q ❀ ◖ ◗ ⊖ (Highbury & Islington)

Marquess Tavern
32 Canonbury Street
☎ (071) 354 2975
11–11
Young's Bitter, Special, Winter Warmer Ⓗ
Excellent pub, in a fine Georgian building, close to the New River Walk. The single bar, with distinct saloon and public areas, is traditional and comfortable. No music. No food Sun.
⋈ Q ❀ ◖ ◗ ⊖ (Essex Rd) ⊖ (Highbury & Islington) ♣

N1: Highbury

Earl of Radnor
106 Mildmay Grove
11–11
Fuller's London Pride, ESB Ⓗ
Lovingly restored Victorian pub enjoying a village atmosphere. ᴆ ⊖ (Dalton/Kingsland) ⊖ (Highbury) ♣

N1: Hoxton

George & Vulture
63 Pitfield Street
☎ (071) 253 3988
11–3 (4 Sat), 5 (7 Sat)–11
Fuller's Chiswick, London Pride, ESB Ⓗ
Large, family-run pub, hosted by a congenial landlord. Close to the other Hoxton pub.
Q ◖ ◗ ⊖ ᴆ ⊖ ⊖

Prince Arthur
49 Brunswick Place
11–11 (11–5, 8–11 Sat)
Shepherd Neame Master Brew Bitter, Bishops Finger Ⓗ
Small, lively, corner pub run by an ex-boxer, with a very strong local, 'sporting', clientele. Efficiently run; best to behave yourself.
Q ⊖ (Old St) ⊖

N1: Islington

Dog & Dumplings
113 Southgate Road
☎ (071) 359 6596
11–12
Ind Coope Friary Meux Best Bitter, Burton Ale Ⓗ
Well-run pub. Regular weekend music includes Cajun fortnightly and trad. jazz monthly. Used by Islington Folk Club and the North London Pigeon Federation. ❀ ◖ ◗ ᴆ ⊖ (Essex Rd/Dalston Jct) ♣

Mitre
181 Copenhagen Street
11–11
Draught Bass; Highgate Mild Ⓗ**; guest beers**
Side-street pub close to the notorious King's Cross district, with an enterprising landlord. Sometimes only Crouch Vale guest beers are available.
Q ⊟ ⊖ (King's Cross) ♣

N2: East Finchley

Old White Lion
121 Great North Road (A1000)
☎ (081) 444 0554
11–11
Draught Bass; Charrington IPA; Fuller's London Pride; Welsh Brewers Worthington BB Ⓗ**; guest beer**
Spacious and comfortable pub. Fine wood-panelling is a

feature of this 1930s Wenlock brewery house. No food Sun.
❀ ◖ ◗ ⊟ ᴆ ⊖ ♣ P

Welch's Ale House
130 High Road (A1000)
11–3, 5.30–11 (11–11 Sat)
Fuller's London Pride; Greene King Abbot; Ruddles County; Wadworth 6X Ⓗ**; guest beers**
Popular shop conversion, often crowded: a genuine free house offering an enterprising range of guest beers. Weekday lunches. ◖ ♣ ⌕

N6: Highgate

Red Lion & Sun
North Road
☎ (081) 340 1780
12–4, 6–11 (12–11 Fri & Sat)
Draught Bass; Charrington IPA; Fuller's London Pride Ⓗ
Old, panelled, traditional house in one of London's true villages. Most other pubs in the village also merit consideration. Q ❀ ᴆ ⊖ P

N7: Holloway

Admiral Mann
7 Hargrave Place
11–3 (4 Sat), 5.30 (7.30 Sat)–11
McMullen AK, Country, Stronghart Ⓗ
Small, two-bar pub, in a back street. Fairly quiet. ◖ ◗ ᴆ

N9: Lower Edmonton

Beehive
24 Little Bury Street
11–3, 5.30–11 (11–11 Sat)
Ind Coope Burton Ale; Tetley Bitter; Young's Bitter Ⓗ
Large, well-furnished, one-bar suburban pub. No food Sun.
Q ❀ ◖ ♣ P

N10: Muswell Hill

Spoons
89 Colney Hatch Lane
11–11
Greene King Abbot; Marston's Pedigree; Ruddles County; Wadworth 6X Ⓗ**; guest beers**
Small but lively one-bar pub which saw the birth of the Wetherspoon idea. ❀

N16: Stoke Newington

Steptoes
102 Stoke Newington Church Street ☎ (071) 254 2906
11–11
Adnams Broadside; Morland Old Speckled Hen; Wadworth 6X; Wells Eagle, Bombardier Ⓗ**; guest beers**
Formerly the 'Clarence Tavern', this corner house, in

Stoke Newington's trendiest street, houses a bizarre assortment of stuffed animals and ornaments. Outrageously expensive. Live music.
❀ ◖ ≈

Tanners Hall

145 Stoke Newington High Street ☎ (071) 249 6016
11–11
Greene King Abbot; Marston's Pedigree, Owd Rodger; S&N Theakston XB; Younger Scotch, IPA Ⓗ; guest beers
Large 'gin palace' interior, different from the general Wetherspoon style, with multi-mirrored walls and a glass-roofed rear area. Always well patronised. ❀ ◖ ▮ ◖ ♿

N20: Whetstone

Cavalier

67 Russell Lane (100 yds off A109) ☎ (081) 368 2708
11–3, 5.30–11 (11–11 Fri & Sat)
Courage Best Bitter, Directors; John Smith's Bitter Ⓗ
Large, well-appointed, two-bar 1930s estate pub in classic mock Tudor style with wood panelling. Excellent garden. Weekday lunches.
❀ ◖ ⊟ ≈ ♣ P

N21: Winchmore Hill

Green Dragon

889 Green Lanes
11–11
Courage Best Bitter, Directors Ⓗ; guest beer
An imposing frontage opens on to a fine public bar with a small adjacent pool room. The large, comfortable lounge gives access via the conservatory to the garden with children's play area.
Q ❀ ◖ ⊟ ≈ ♣ P

N22: Wood Green

Moon Under Water

423 Lordship Lane
☎ (081) 889 7397
11–11
Courage Best Bitter; Greene King IPA, Abbot; Marston's Pedigree; Whitbread Boddingtons Bitter, Flowers Original Ⓗ
Former corner furniture store acquired by Devenish from Wetherspoon but remaining under the same enthusiastic management. One beer is always sold at a bargain price. Superb food includes Sun roasts. ❀ ◖ ▮

Phoenix

Alexandra Palace
☎ (081) 365 2121
11–11

Ansells Mild; Courage Directors; Crouch Vale Woodham IPA; Ind Coope Burton Ale; John Smith's Bitter; Tetley Bitter Ⓗ
Superb 1920s Gatsby-style free house at the south-western end of the Alexandra Palace complex. Families are welcome in the palm court or 180-acre outdoor area which provides a panoramic view of North London.
🛏 ❀ ◖ ♿ ≈ (Alexandra Palace) ◔ ♣ ◇ P

Barnet

Albion

Union Street
☎ (081) 441 2841
11–3, 5.30 (7 Sat)–11 (12–2.30, 7–10.30 Sun)
Adnams Bitter; Ind Coope Benskins Best Bitter, Burton Ale Ⓗ
Small side-street pub of character with a loyal local patronage. Barnet's last surviving outside gents'. Weekday lunches. ❀ ◖ ♣ P

Olde Mitre Inn

High Street
☎ (081) 449 6582
11–11 (11–3, 6–11 Sat)
Ind Coope Benskins Best Bitter, Burton Ale; Tetley Bitter Ⓗ; guest beer
Traditional coaching inn, renovated with care. Quiet and tranquil in comparison with some of its neighbours. Weekday lunches. Q ◖
◔ (High Barnet) P

Cockfosters

Trent Tavern

20 Cockfosters Road (A111)
11–11
Courage Best Bitter, Directors; John Smith's Bitter Ⓗ
Typical 1950s roadhouse with two bars and lots of wood panelling; excellent gardens.
🛏 ❀ ◖ ⊟ ◔ ♣ P

Enfield Lock

Greyhound

425 Ordnance Road
11–2.30, 6.30–11
McMullen AK, Country Ⓗ
Fine, unspoilt canalside pub opposite the now defunct small arms factory. An oasis in the area. Weekday lunches.
🛏 Q ❀ ◖ ⊟ ≈ ♣ P

Enfield Town

Cricketers

17–19 Chase Side Place
☎ (081) 363 5218
11–3, 5.30–11 (11–11 Sat)
Courage Directors; McMullen AK, Country, Stronghart Ⓗ
Friendly locals in the large

public bar plus a more cosmopolitan saloon, part set aside for lunches and pre-booked eve meals. Fine collection of cricket ties. Can be difficult to find. Q ❀ ◖
▮ ⊟ ≈ (Enfield Chase) ♣ P

Enfield Whitewebbs

King & Tinker

Whitewebbs Lane
11–3, 5.30–11
Adnams Bitter; Ind Coope Burton Ale; Taylor Walker Best Bitter; Tetley Bitter Ⓗ
Rural gem nestling between the M25 and suburbia, with a high reputation for its food, floral displays and service. No food Sun. 🛏 ❀ ◖ ▮ ♣ ◇ P

New Barnet

Builders Arms

Albert Road
☎ (081) 441 1215
11–3, 5.30–11
Greene King IPA, Abbot; Rayments Special Ⓗ
Excellent two-bar local. No food Sun. Q ❀ ◖ ⊟ ≈ ♣

Railway Bell

13 East Barnet Road
☎ (081) 449 1369
11–11
Greene King IPA, Abbot; Marston's Pedigree; S&N Theakston XB; Shepherd Neame Spitfire; Younger Scotch Ⓗ; guest beer
Unusual, large one-bar pub near the railway viaduct. Local CAMRA *Pub of the Year* 1991. Weekend guest beer. No eve meals Sun. Q ❀ ◖ ≈ P

North-West London

NW1: Camden Town

Neptune

51 Werrington Street
11–11
Wells Eagle, Bombardier Ⓗ
Popular local, unfortunately no longer selling mild.
◔ (Mornington Cres)

Quinns

65 Kentish Town Road
☎ (071) 267 8240
11–11
Gale's HSB; Greene King IPA, Rayments Special, Abbot; Marston's Pedigree; Palmers BB Ⓗ
Run by a longstanding Irish family, this pub has recently undergone a magnificent refurbishment. Free of a tie.
Q ❀ ◖ ▮ ≈ (Camden Rd) ◔

Greater London

Spread Eagle

141 Albert Street
☎ (071) 267 1410
11–3, 5–11 (11–11 Fri & Sat)
Young's Bitter, Special ⎔
Busy town refuge, converted
from several Georgian houses.
The steady local trade
predominates over the trendy
Camden Lock crowd that
descends at weekends.
Q ◑ ▶ ⇌ (Camden Rd)

Square Tavern

26 Tolmers Square
☎ (071) 387 3959
11–11 (closed weekends)
**King & Barnes Mild; Young's
Bitter, Special** ⎔**; guest beers**
Modern pub tucked away in a
square very close to Euston
Station.
❀ ◑ ▶ ⇌ ⊖ (Euston Sq) ♣

NW1: Marylebone

Perseverance

11 Shroton Street
11–11 (may vary in winter)
**Draught Bass; Welsh Brewers
Worthington BB** ⎔
Friendly one-bar pub with a
large skylight. Meeting place
for a local sub-aqua club and
RU officials. ◑ ♿ ⇌ ⊖ ♣

NW2: Cricklewood

Beaten Docket

50–56 Cricklewood Broadway
☎ (081) 450 2972
11–11
**Greene King IPA, Abbot;
Marston's Pedigree; S&N
Theakston XB; Younger
Scotch; guest beer** ⎔
Rare oasis in an Irish district.
A large pub typical of the
Wetherspoon chain, but arrive
early eve to ensure a seat. A
bargain beer is always
available, plus weekend guest
beers.
Q ◑ ▶ ♿ ⇌ ⊖ (Kilburn)

NW3: Hampstead

Duke of Hamilton

New End ☎ (071) 794 0258
11–11
**Fuller's Chiswick, London
Pride, ESB** ⎔
Traditionally-run Victorian
pub, with a forecourt at the
front. One horseshoe-shaped
bar. ❀ ◑ ♣

Flask

Flask Walk ☎ (071) 435 4580
11–11
**Young's Bitter, Special,
Winter Warmer** ⎔
Late Victorian pub: a
comfortable saloon with a new
family conservatory. Basic
public bar. Q ⛄ ◑ ▶ ⊟ ⊖ ♣

Holly Bush

Holly Mount ☎ (071) 435 2892
11–3, 5.30 (6 Sat)–11

**Ind Coope Benskins Best
Bitter, Burton Ale; Tetley
Bitter; Young's Special** ⎔
Traditional pub featuring
snugs, alcoves, gas lighting
and a Benskins mirror. Live
music eves in the back room.
Children welcome in the side
room. Eve meals Tue–Sat.
❀ Q ⛄ ◑ ▶ ♣

Horse & Groom

Heath Street ☎ (071) 435 3140
11–11
**Young's Bitter, Special,
Winter Warmer** ⎔
Imposing Edwardian building
where real ale is served in the
downstairs bar only. A well
preserved pub. Q ◑ ⊖

Magdala Tavern

2a South Hill Park
11–11
**Draught Bass; Charrington
IPA** ⎔
U-shaped traditional pub
divided into a portrait-
adorned saloon and a plainer
Heath Bar. Quiz Thu.
🐾 ◑ ⊟ ⇌ (Heath)

Sir Richard Steel

97 Haverstock Hill
11–11
**Courage Directors; John
Smith's Bitter** ⎔
Eccentric clientele and decor;
it helps to be Irish, have a
sense of humour and no hang-
ups! ◑ ▶ ⊖ (Belsize Pk) ♣ P

Spaniards Inn

Spaniards Road
☎ (081) 455 3276
11–11
**Bass Highgate Mild;
Charrington IPA; Fuller's
London Pride; Greene King
IPA; Stones Best Bitter** ⎔
A classic intact old inn on the
heights of Hampstead Heath.
A must for walkers, with its
various panelled bars, large
garden and good food.
🐾 Q ⛄ ❀ ◑ ▶ ♿ P

NW5: Dartmouth Park

Lord Palmerston

33 Dartmouth Park Hill
11–11
**Courage Best Bitter, Directors;
Fuller's London Pride** ⎔
Well-managed, comfortable
pub with pleasing decor. No
food Sun.
❀ ◑ ⊖ (Tufnell Pk) ♣

NW5: Kentish Town

Pineapple

51 Leverton Street
12–11
**Brakspear Bitter; Marston's
Pedigree; Whitbread
Boddingtons Bitter** ⎔
A gem of a small pub tucked

---

away behind the station. Free
of a tie, although it might not
seem so. 🐾 Q ⇌ ⊖ ♣

NW6: Kilburn

Queens Arms

1 Kilburn High Road
11–11
**Young's Bitter, Special,
Winter Warmer** ⎔
1950s corner pub separated
into different areas. Wood-
panelled, featuring an
abundance of prints and an
unusual roof garden. No food
weekends.
🐾 Q ❀ ◑ ♿ ⇌ (High
Road) ⊖ (Kilburn Pk) ♣ P

NW7: Mill Hill

Rising Sun

Marsh Lane ☎ (081) 959 3755
12 (11 Sat)–3, 5.30 (6 Sat)–11
**Ind Coope Burton Ale; Taylor
Walker Best Bitter** ⎔
400-year-old, Grade II listed
pub of character in a rural
setting. Three separate
drinking areas, including a
cosy snug, plus a lounge. Still
has outside loos. Children are
welcome up to 8pm in three of
the rooms. Eve meals Tue–Sat.
Q ❀ ◑ ▶ P

NW8: St John's Wood

Blenheim

21 Loudoun Road
11–3, 5.30 (6.30 Sat)–11
Greene King IPA, Abbot ⎔
Pleasant local with attentive
service. Weekday lunches. Q
❀ ◑ ⇌ (S Hampstead) ⊖ P

Knight of St John

7 Queens Terrace (off Queens
Grove) ☎ (071) 586 5239
11–3, 5.30–11
**Mansfield Riding Mild;
Wells Eagle, Bombardier** ⎔
One of the few remaining
locals in the area. A separate
room at the back of the pub
has a dartboard, but no bar.
The landlord has won Wells
Best Kept Cellar award twice.
⇌ (S Hampstead) ⊖ ♣

Rossetti

23 Queens Grove
☎ (071) 722 7141
11–3, 5.30–11 (11–11 Sat)
Fuller's London Pride, ESB ⎔
Friendly, split-level pub, built
in 1968: very plush, with
marble-top tables and efficient
staff. Thai restaurant upstairs
(no food Sun). Q ❀ ◑ ▶ ⊖ P

NW9: The Hyde

Moon Under Water

10 Varley Parade (A5)
☎ (081) 200 7611
11–11
Greene King IPA, Abbot;

Marston's Pedigree; S&N
Theakston XB; Younger
Scotch Ⓗ; guest beers
Where FW Woolworth
retreats, JD Wetherspoon
boldly goes. A welcome
addition of choice and comfort
for the area. Q ◖ ▶

NW9: Kingsbury

Green Man
125 Slough Lane
11–11
Courage Directors; Ruddles
Best Bitter, County; Thwaites
Best Mild; Webster's
Yorkshire Bitter Ⓗ
Large 1930s pub in the
conservation area. One
horseshoe-shaped bar serves
three rooms. The tenant has
occupied the pub since 1936.
Restaurant open lunchtime.
❀ ◖ & ♣ P ⊬

JJ Moon's
553 Kingsbury Road
☎ (081) 204 9675
11–11
Greene King IPA, Abbot;
Marston's Pedigree; S&N
Theakston XB; Younger
Scotch Ⓗ; guest beers
Small Wetherspoon pub,
converted from a shop, with
one long, narrow bar. Popular
for its good value Sunday
roasts. Q ◖ ▶ ⊖

NW10: Harlesden

Grand Junction Arms
Acton Lane ☎ (081) 965 5670
11–11
Young's Bitter, Special,
Winter Warmer Ⓗ
Large, comfortable three-bar
pub with moorings on the
canal. The garden contains
play equipment and barbecues
are held in summer. Good
value food all day (not served
Sun). Q ❀ ◖ ▶ ⊞ & ⇌ ⊖ P

NW10: Neasden

Outside Inn
314 Neasden Lane
☎ (081) 452 3140
11–11
Greene King IPA, Abbot;
Marston's Pedigree; S&N
Theakston XB; Younger
Scotch Ⓗ; guest beers
Wood-panelled ex-
Woolworth's store. A
comfortable pub and a rare
outlet for the real elixir in the
area. No meals Sun eve. ◖ ▶ ⊖

NW11: Golders Green

White Swan
243 Golders Green Road
11–11
Ind Coope Burton Ale; Tetley
Bitter Ⓗ

Warm and welcoming local
with a lot of character. No
food Sat/Sun eves or Sun
lunch. ❀ ◖ ▶ & ♣ ⊖ P

Eastcote

Case is Altered
High Road ☎ (081) 866 0476
11–3, 5–11 (11–11 Fri & Sat)
Ind Coope Benskins Best
Bitter, Burton Ale; Tetley
Bitter; Young's Bitter Ⓗ
Grade I listed ex-farmhouse
with a stone-flagged floor; the
old stables are now part of the
bar. There is a new restaurant
in the old barn just behind.
Very popular. ⚏ Q ❀ ◖ ▶ P

Harefield

Plough
Hillend Road ☎ (0895) 822129
11–3, 5.30–11
Fuller's London Pride;
Marston's Pedigree; Ruddles
Best Bitter; S&N Theakston
Best Bitter, XB; Wadworth
6X Ⓗ; guest beers
Off the beaten track, a one-bar
free house, near the hospital.
Very busy in summer. Good
value food (not served Sun);
three guest beers. ❀ ◖ P

White Horse
Church Hill ☎ (0895) 822144
11–3, 6–11
Ansells Mild; Ind Coope
Benskins Best Bitter, Burton
Ale; Tetley Bitter Ⓗ; guest
beer
Excellent, lively, traditional
local on the south side of the
village: a Grade II listed
building dating back to the
17th century.
⚏ ❀ ◖ ▶ ⊞ ♣ P

Harrow

Castle
30 West Street, Harrow on the
Hill ☎ (081) 422 3155
11.30–11 (11–11 Fri & Sat)
Fuller's London Pride, Mr
Harry, ESB Ⓗ
Well-run, relaxing pub: its
comfortable lounge makes it
feel like home. Darts is played
in the small public bar. The
food is generally good.
Q ❀ ◖ ▶ ⇌ (Harrow on the
Hill) ⊖ (S Harrow) ♣

Moon on the Hill
373–375 Station Road
☎ (081) 863 3670
11–11
Greene King IPA, Abbot;
Marston's Pedigree; S&N
Theakston XB; Younger
Scotch Ⓗ; guest beer
Former chemist's shop next to
McDonald's, popular with
office staff and shoppers.
Meals until 10pm (3pm Sun).
Q ◖ ▶ & ⇌ ⊖ (Harrow on
the Hill)

Harrow Weald

Seven Balls
749 Kenton Lane
11.30–3, 5.30 (6 Sat)–11
Ansells Mild; Ind Coope
Benskins Best Bitter; Tetley
Bitter Ⓗ; guest beers
250-year-old pub with a
country feel: horse brasses on
the beams and walls. The mild
is very rare for the area. No
food Sun. Q ❀ ◖ ⊞ ♣ P

Kenton

New Moon
25–26 Kenton Park Parade,
Kenton Road ☎ (081) 909 1103
11–11
Greene King IPA, Abbot;
Marston's Pedigree; S&N
Theakston XB; Younger
Scotch Ⓗ; guest beers
Conversion of two shops in
typical Wetherspoon style,
drawing a varied clientele (no
dogs allowed). No food Sun
eve. Q ◖ ▶

South Harrow

JJ Moon's
Shaftsbury Parade, Shaftsbury
Circle ☎ (081) 423 5056
11–11
Greene King IPA, Abbot;
Marston's Pedigree; S&N
Theakston XB; Younger
Scotch Ⓗ
Former bakery in a small
parade looking onto a green
roundabout. Meals served all
day (12–2.30 Sun). Q ◖ ▶ ⏥

Wealdstone

Royal Oak
60 Peel Road ☎ (081) 427 3122
11–11
Ind Coope Benskins Best
Bitter, Burton Ale; Tetley
Bitter Ⓗ; guest beers
Imposing early 1930s pub
with a conservatory.
Collection of miniatures
behind the lounge bar.
❀ ◖ ▶ ⊞ ⇌ (Harrow &
Wealdstone) ⊖ P

South-East London

SE1: Bermondsey

Ship Aground
33 Wolseley Street
11–11
Courage Best Bitter,
Directors; John Smith's
Bitter Ⓗ
Next door to Dockhead, alias
Blackwall, fire station from
TV's *London's Burning*: a
family pub that is proud of its
home-cooked meals. ❀ ◖ &
⇌ (London Bridge) ⊖ ♣

189

Greater London

SE1: Southwark

Blue Eyed Maid
173 Borough High Street
11–11
Greene King Abbot; Ruddles Best Bitter; Webster's Yorkshire Bitter Ⓗ
Comfortable one-bar pub with an upstairs licensed function room. A guest beer may soon be added. ✿ ◖ ≉ (London Bridge) ⊖ (Borough) ♣

Founders Arms
52 Hopton Street (take footpath from Blackfriars Bridge) ☎ (071) 928 1899
11–11
Young's Bitter, Special, Winter Warmer Ⓗ
Well-planned modern pub and restaurant on the Thames by Bankside power station. Frequented by business people during the week; pleasant atmosphere. Excellent views across to St Paul's. Q ✿ ◖ ◗ & (Blackfriars) ⊖

Grapes
121 Borough High Street
☎ (071) 407 1856
11–11 (11–4, 7–11 Sat)
Courage Best Bitter; Wadworth 6X Ⓗ; **guest beers**
The front bar concentrates on meals at lunchtimes while the rear bar (access by a side alley) has a wider range of beers at very reasonable prices. Imperial Russian Stout is available. ◖ ◗ ≉ (London Bridge) ⊖ ♣

Kings Arms
25 Roupell Street (under platform A of Waterloo East)
☎ (071) 928 5745
11–3 (11–11 Fri; 11–3.30, 8–11 Sat; 12–2.30, 7–10.30 Sun)
Ind Coope Burton Ale; Taylor Walker Best Bitter; Tetley Bitter; Young's Special Ⓗ
One of the finest two-bar pubs of its kind in London. Extensive collection of miniatures. Q ✿ ◖ ◗ ⊞ ≉ (Waterloo) ⊖ ♣

Lord Clyde
27 Clennam Street
11–11 (11–4, 7–11 Sat)
Ruddles Best Bitter, County; Webster's Yorkshire Bitter Ⓗ
Very comfortable and traditional, two-roomed pub, in the same family for 35 years. Note the superb tiled exterior; typical Truman's house style. ◖ ≉ (London Bridge) ⊖ (Borough) ♣

Prince William Henry
217 Blackfriars Road
☎ (071) 928 2474
11–11 (11–3, 7–11 Sat)
Young's Bitter, Special, Winter Warmer Ⓗ

Modern pub named after King Henry IV, 'The Sailor King'. Busy lunchtimes and early eves, it is frequented late in the eves by musicians from the Festival Hall. Q ✿ ◖ ◗ ≉ (Waterloo/Blackfriars) ⊖

Ship
68 Borough High Street
☎ (071) 403 7059
11–11
Fuller's Chiswick, London Pride, Mr Harry, ESB Ⓗ
One comfortable bar; very busy weekday lunchtimes and early eves. ✿ ◖ ◗ ≉ (London Bridge) ⊖ (Borough) ♣

Wheatsheaf
6 Stoney Street
11–11 (11–5, 7–11 Sat; closed Sun)
Courage Best Bitter; King & Barnes Sussex; Wadworth 6X Ⓗ; **guest beer**
Classic market pub with a real public bar; always busy, with an imaginative tenant ensuring that a dark beer from an independent brewery is always available. ◖ ⊞ ≉ (London Bridge) ⊖ ♣ ◌

SE3: Blackheath

Bitter Experience
129 Lee Road
☎ (081) 852 8819
11–9.30 (10–2, 3–9.30 Sat; 12–2, 7–9 Sun)
Fuller's London Pride; Shepherd Neame Master Brew Bitter Ⓗ; **guest beers** Ⓖ
Off-licence with an excellent range of beers and ciders, plus British and foreign bottled beers. The beers above are usually stocked, plus four others at least. ≉ ◌

British Oak
109 Old Dover Road
11–3 (4 Sat), 5 (6.30 Sat)–11 (11–11 Fri)
Courage Best Bitter, Directors; John Smith's Bitter Ⓗ
Two-bar pub just off the main road. The saloon is panelled in standard Courage style; the other bar is more basic. Caters mainly for the local trade, with a very high turnover of cask beers.
Q ✿ ◖ ⊞ ♣

SE4: Brockley

Wickham Arms
69 Upper Brockley Road
11–11
Courage Best Bitter, Directors Ⓗ
Well-established, cosmopolitan pub, busy with students at lunchtime and locals eves. Open-plan but with distinct areas, including a large saloon. Q ✿ ◖ ≉

SE6: Catford

Catford Ram
9 Winslade Way
11–3, 5.30–11 (11–3.30, 6.30–10.30 Sat)
Young's Bitter, Special, Winter Warmer Ⓗ
The exterior (in a busy shopping precinct) belies the comfortable interior of this cosy, split-level pub. Q ◖ ≉

Tigers Head
350 Bromley Road (A21/A2218 jct)
☎ (081) 698 8645
11–11
Greene King IPA, Abbot; Marston's Pedigree; S&N Theakston XB; Younger Scotch Ⓗ; **guest beers**
Recent acquisition by Wetherspoon, offering competitively priced beers: a large roadside house. Boasts an unusual collection of wooden shoe inserts! Occasional beer festivals. No food Sun eve. Q ✿ ◖ ◗ & ≉ (Beckenham Hill)

SE8: Deptford

Dog & Bell
116 Prince Street
11–11
Fuller's London Pride, ESB Ⓗ; **guest beers**
Friendly back-street local which stocks a wide range of malt whiskies, and at least two guest beers from independent breweries. Q ✿ ◖ ◗ ≉ ♣

Royal George
Tanners Hill ☎ (081) 692 2594
11–3, 5.30–11 (11–11 Fri & Sat)
Samuel Smith OBB, Museum Ⓗ
Quiz nights Wed in this back-street local with a pool room upstairs. Eve meals finish early. ✿ ◖ ◗ ≉ ⊖ (New Cross) ♣

SE10: Greenwich

Admiral Hardy
7 College Approach
11–11
Draught Bass; Charrington IPA; Shepherd Neame Master Brew Bitter, Best Bitter Ⓗ; **guest beers**
One-bar pub whose central bar has wood-panelled walls and lots of pictures bearing (of course) a nautical theme. Meals served until 6pm (later summer) ✿ ◖ ◗ ≉

Ashburnham Arms
25 Ashburnham Grove
☎ (081) 692 2007
12–3, 6–11 (12–11 Sat)
Shepherd Neame Master Brew Bitter, Spitfire, Bishops Finger Ⓗ
Popular back-street pub in an

upmarket area. Vegetarian meals are a speciality. Works by local artists are for sale.
❀ ◖ ▶ ⇌ ♣

Cricketers
22 King William Walk
11–11 (11–4, 7.30–11 Sat)
Charrington IPA Ⓗ
Popular pub near the Cutty Sark. Can be very busy Sat when the market is in full flow. Parking difficult.
◖ ⇌ ♣

Pilot
68 River Way
☎ (081) 858 5910
11–3.30, 5–11 (11–11 summer)
Courage Best Bitter; Whitbread Boddingtons Bitter (summer); **Young's Special, Winter Warmer** Ⓗ
Recently extensively enlarged and comfortably furnished pub, well known to long-distance lorry drivers.
❀ ◖ ▶ ♿ ⇌ (Westcombe Pk)

Richard I
52 Royal Hill
☎ (081) 692 2996
11–3, 5.30–11 (11–11 Fri & Sat)
Young's Bitter, Special, Winter Warmer Ⓗ
Popular classic pub with two lively bars and half-moon bay windows. O'Hagan's famous sausages are served here. No food Sun. Q ❀ ◖ ⊟ ⇌ ♣

SE12: Lee

Crown
117 Burnt Ash Hill
11–11
Young's Bitter, Special Ⓗ; **Winter Warmer** Ⓖ
Large saloon bar and a smaller public bar providing a village-type atmosphere when not too busy. Alcove seating areas by the front windows. Q ❀ ◖ ⊟ ⇌ (Grove Pk/Lee) ♣ P

SE13: Lewisham

Joiners Arms
66 Lewisham High Street
11–11
Draught Bass; Fuller's London Pride Ⓗ
A pub only 20 feet wide. Ridiculous fake wooden beams and copper kettles on the ceiling, but a friendly landlord and staff. ⇌

SE14: New Cross

Rose Inn
272 New Cross Road
11–4, 5.30 (7 Sat)–11
Courage Best Bitter, Directors; Young's Special Ⓗ
Popular house. Can be very busy when Millwall are at home. ❀ ◖ ♿ ⇌ (New Cross Gate) ⊖ ♣

SE15: Peckham

Asylum Tavern
40 Asylum Road
Courage Best Bitter, Directors; Young's Special Ⓗ
Typical inner-city back-street local where the 'canned' music is impossible to avoid. ⇌ (Queen's Rd)

SE17: Walworth

Crown .
115–117 Brandon Street
11–3, 5.30–11 (11–11 Fri & Sat)
Draught Bass; Fuller's London Pride; Welsh Brewers Worthington BB; Young's Special Ⓗ
Traditional back-street local with old handpumps. Photos on the wall from its days as a Wenlock house. ❀ ⊟ ⇌ (Elephant & Castle) ⊖

SE18: Plumstead

Star Inn
158 Plumstead Common Road
☎ (081) 854 1524
11–11
Courage Best Bitter, Directors; Wadworth 6X Ⓗ; **guest beers**
Very comfortable three-bar local. An ex-Beasley's house which retains many features (partitioning, fireplace surrounds etc.) of the former brewery's house style. Regular guest beers of the landlord's choice. ❀ ◖ ▶ ⊟ ⇌ ♣

SE18: Shooters Hill

Bull
151 Shooters Hill
11–3, 5.15 (7 Sat)–11
Courage Best Bitter, Directors Ⓗ
Two-bar local, almost at the top of Shooters Hill – the opening setting of *A Tale of Two Cities*. Very pleasant with a rare outdoor gent's loo! No food Sun. Q ❀ ◖ ⊟ ♣

Red Lion
6 Red Lion Place
11–11
Courage Best Bitter, Directors Ⓗ
Formerly a Beasley's house; there's been a pub on this site for centuries. ❀ ♣ ⌂ P

SE19: Upper Norwood

Railway Bell
14 Cawnpore Street
11–3.30, 5–11 (11–11 Fri & Sat)
Young's Bitter, Special, Winter Warmer Ⓗ
Excellent, popular small pub, recently refurbished. ♨ ❀ ◖ ▶ ⚤ ⇌ (Gipsy Hill) ♣

SE20: Penge

Hop Exchange
149 Maple Road
11–11
Adnams Bitter; Everards Tiger; Ruddles County; Young's Bitter, Special Ⓗ
Popular free house. ❀ ◖ ▶ ♣

Maple Tree
52–54 Maple Road
11–11
Fuller's London Pride; Ruddles County; Shepherd Neame Master Brew Bitter; Wadworth 6X; Webster's Yorkshire Bitter Ⓗ
Friendly, side-street local.
◖ ⊟ ♣

SE22: East Dulwich

Clock House
196a Peckham Rye Common
☎ (081) 693 2901
11–11
Young's Bitter, Special, Winter Warmer Ⓗ
Former off-licence, overlooking the common and decorated in Victorian style, containing many clocks. ❀ ◖ ▶

Crystal Palace Tavern
193 Crystal Palace Road
12–11
Ind Coope Burton Ale; Taylor Walker Best Bitter; Tetley Bitter Ⓗ
Characterful back-street local with many surviving Victorian features. ❀ ⊟ ⇌

Uplands Tavern
90 Crystal Palace Road
12–11 (12–5.30, 7.30–11 Sat)
Courage Best Bitter, Directors; John Smith's Bitter; Young's Special Ⓗ
Ignore the fake beams: this large street-corner pub often gets the crowds in with its regular quizzes, discos and live music. ♨ ⇌

SE23: Forest Hill

Dartmouth Arms
7 Dartmouth Road
11–3 (4 Sat), 5.30 (7 Sat)–11
Courage Best Bitter, Directors Ⓗ
Typical local Edwardian pub with an Irish flavour: three separate rooms with a large rear bar. ❀ ⊟ ⇌ P

Railway Telegraph
112 Stanstead Road
11–3, 5.30–11 (11–11 Fri & Sat)
Shepherd Neame Master Brew Bitter, Best Bitter, Spitfire, Bishops Finger Ⓗ
Large, popular pub on the South Circular, noted for stocking the full range of Shep's beers. Railway memorabilia. ❀ ◖ ⊟ ⇌

191

Greater London

SE25: South Norwood

Albion
26 High Street (A213/A215 jct)
11–11
Courage Best Bitter, Directors; Ruddles County; Young's Special Ⓗ
Busy, friendly, crossroads pub offering good value beer. Live music Thu and Fri; chess played. No food weekends.
Ⓓ ⅆ ⚹ (Norwood Jct) ♣

Alliance
91 High Street (A213)
11–11
Courage Best Bitter, Directors; Wadworth 6X; Young's Special Ⓗ
Street-corner pub with an L-shaped bar; now refitted with the loss of its water-heated bar-front foot rail.
Ⓓ ⅆ ⚹ (Norwood Jct) ♣

Clifton Arms
21 Clifton Road (off A213)
11–4, 5.30–11 (11–11 Fri & Sat)
Fuller's London Pride; Ind Coope Burton Ale; Tetley Bitter Ⓗ**; guest beer**
Imposing three-storey, street-corner building housing a single bar. Can be busy on Crystal Palace match days when admission is restricted. Weekday lunches.
⚹ ⅆ ⚹ (Selhurst) ♣

SE26: Sydenham

Bricklayers Arms
189 Dartmouth Road
11–11
Young's Bitter, Special, Winter Warmer Ⓗ
Large, friendly pub, whose back room houses many interesting prints. Q ⚹ ⚹ ⚹

Dulwich Wood House
39 Sydenham Hill
11–3, 5.30–11 (11–11 Thu–Sat)
Young's Bitter, Special, Winter Warmer Ⓗ
Busy house with one main bar and a back room displaying rare pictures of the motor racing circuit in Crystal Palace Park. The large garden has petanque, children's area and barbecue, plus a garden bar.
♨ Q ⚹ ⅆ ⚹ ⚹ (Sydenham Hill) ♣ P

SE27: West Norwood

Hope
49 Norwood High Street
11–11
Young's Bitter, Special, Winter Warmer Ⓗ
Excellent local behind the station. Friendly, with a

typical Young's decor. Often very popular at weekends.
Q ⚹ ⚹ ♣ ♠

Addiscombe

Claret Wine Bar
5a Bingham Corner, Lower Addiscombe Road (A222)
11.30–11
Eldridge Pope Royal Oak; Palmers IPA Ⓗ**; guest beers**
Small, welcoming bar in a shopping parade, offering two guest beers despite its minute cellar. Good value lunches served Tue–Fri. ⚹ ⅆ ⚹

Beckenham

Coach & Horses
Burnhill Road
11–3, 5.30 (7 Sat)–11
Courage Best Bitter, Directors Ⓗ
Popular local just off the High Street, rather noisy at times. Weekday lunches served.
⚹ ⅆ ⚹ (Beckenham Jct)

Jolly Woodman
9 Chancery Lane
11–3, 5–11 (11–11 Fri & Sat)
Draught Bass; Charrington IPA Ⓗ
Pub with the feel of a village local, in deepest suburbia.
Q ⚹ ⅆ ⚹ (Beckenham Jct) ♣

Bexleyheath

Bitter Experience (Off-Licence)
Broadway ☎ (081) 304 2039
11 (10 Sat)–2, 3–9.30 (12–2, 7–9 Sun)
Beer range varies Ⓖ
One of two off-licences in Bexley Borough which are the only reliable outlets for independent real ales. ⚹ ⌕

Robin Hood & Little John
Lion Road ☎ (081) 303 1128
11–2.30, 6–11
Courage Bitter Ale, Best Bitter, Directors; John Smith's Bitter Ⓗ**; guest beer**
Small cosy local with a friendly atmosphere. No food Sun; eve meals on request.
Q ⚹ ⅆ ♣

Royal Oak (Polly Clean Stairs)
Mount Road (off A227)
11–3, 6–11
Courage Best Bitter; John Smith's Bitter; Wadworth 6X Ⓗ**; guest beers**
Historic, village-style local surviving in the midst of suburbia. A real gem. Q ⚹ P

Bromley

Arkwright's Wheel
10 Widmore Road
☎ (081) 460 4828
10.30–11

Taylor Walker Best Bitter; Tetley Bitter Ⓗ
Recently refurbished pub by the new shopping centre.
♨ ⅆ ▮ ⚹ (North)

Bitter End (Off-Licence)
139 Masons Hill (A21)
12–3, 5–10 (9 Mon); 11–10 Sat; 12–2, 7–9 Sun)
Bateman XXXB; Fuller's London Pride; Greene King Abbot Ⓖ
The beer festival continues: an ever-changing variety from a cool room in full view of the shop. Up to nine ales at weekends, plus a house beer.
Q ⚹ (South) ⌕

Bricklayers Arms
143 Masons Hill
11–2.30, 5.30–11
Shepherd Neame Master Brew Bitter, Spitfire Ⓗ
One-bar local, friendly and comfortable, adorned with racehorse pictures. Run by the same landlord for over 20 years. No food Sun.
ⅆ ⚹ (South) ♣

Freelands Tavern
31 Freelands Road (off A222)
☎ (081) 464 2296
11–3, 5.30 (6.30 Sat)–11
Courage Best Bitter, Directors Ⓗ
A suburban local whose landlord is an ex-West Ham footballer. Very friendly atmosphere and lots of charity work. ⚹ ⅆ ⚹ (North) ♣

Bromley Common

Bird in Hand
Gravel Road
☎ (081) 462 1083
11–2.30, 5.30–11 (11–2.30 Sun)
Courage Best Bitter, Directors; Ruddles Best Bitter Ⓗ
A gem of a pub retaining the best of the past, off the main road in a one-way street. Caters for local residents' needs and is friendly to visitors. The well-kept garden is a treat. Snacks if you ask!
♨ Q ⚹

Chislehurst

Ramblers Rest
Mill Place
☎ (081) 467 1734
11–3, 5.30–11
Courage Best Bitter, Directors; Wadworth 6X Ⓗ**; guest beers**
Split-level bar where the upper level is normally bustling. In a pleasant setting at the edge of the common; an ideal stop for commuters after the trek up the hill. No food Sun. Q ⚹ ⅆ ⚹ P

Croydon

Builders Arms

65 Leslie Park Road (off A222)
11.30–3, 5 (6.30 Sat)–11 (11.30–11 Fri)
Fuller's Chiswick, London Pride, Mr Harry, ESB Ⓗ
Popular back-street pub with two cosy saloon-standard bars. One is the former public bar and the other gives access to a rear garden. Eve meals weekdays only. Q ✪ ◖ ▶ ⇌ (E Croydon/Addiscombe)

Crown

90 Stanley Road (between A23 and A235) ☎ (081) 684 4952
11–11
Ruddles County; Webster's Yorkshire Bitter Ⓗ
Excellent street-corner local. Extensive range of pub games (ask). Modern jazz Tue; live music Sat. Eve meals finish at 7.30pm. ✪ ◖ ▶ ♣

Dog & Bull

24 Surrey Street (off High St, A235) ☎ (081) 688 3664
11–11
Young's Bitter, Special, Winter Warmer Ⓗ
Historic, atmospheric pub where office workers sup with market traders. Good food – home-cooked specials for two pounds or less. No food Sun. Q ✪ ◖ ⇌ (E/W Croydon)

Duke of Gloucester

258 Sydenham Road (off A222) ☎ (081) 684 3971
12–11
Courage Best Bitter, Directors Ⓗ
Traditional, friendly, corner one-bar local with a comfortable mock Tudor interior. Pizzas are a speciality. ♨ ◖ ▶ ♿ ♣ P

Golden Lion

144 Stanley Road (between A23 and A235)
11–11
Courage Best Bitter, Directors; King & Barnes Sussex Ⓗ
Warm, friendly street-corner local fielding ten darts teams. Regular fund-raising. ✪ ⒽBeer ♣

Nowhere Inn Particular

78 Sumner Road (A213)
11–11
Fuller's London Pride, ESB; King & Barnes Sussex; Wadworth 6X Ⓗ; **guest beers**
Former Allied pub, now an open-plan bar with friendly staff. Note the old advertising posters on the walls. No food Sun. ✪ ◖ ♿ ♣

Porter & Sorter

Station Road ☎ (081) 688 4296
11–11 (11–3, 7–11 Sat; closed Sun eve)
Courage Best Bitter, Directors Ⓗ
Welcome oasis in a desert of glass and concrete – the only old building in the area. Very popular with commuters and postal workers. Weekday lunches.
✪ ◖ ⇌ (E Croydon) P

Downe

Queens Head

High Street
☎ (0689) 852145
11–3, 6–11
Ind Coope Friary Meux Best Bitter, Burton Ale; Tetley Bitter Ⓗ
Pleasant two-bar local.
♨ ☙ ✪ ◖ ▶ ⒽBeer ♣ P

Footscray

Seven Stars

High Street
☎ (081) 300 2059
Draught Bass; Charrington IPA; Fuller's ESB (winter) Ⓗ
16th-century pub retaining many nooks and crannies. Good value for the area and popular. No food Sun. ✪ ◖ P

Sidcup

Bitter Experience (Off-Licence)

3 Elm Parade, Main Road
11 (10 Sat)–2, 3–9.30 (12–2, 7–9 Sun)
Beer range varies Ⓖ
Off-licence serving a range of ales and ciders. ⇌ ⌂

Charcoal Burner

Main Road
10.30–4, 5–11
Courage Best Bitter, Directors Ⓗ; **guest beers**
Comfortable modern pub.
✪ ◖ ⒽBeer P

Thornton Heath

Fountain Head

114 Parchmore Road (B273)
11–3.30, 5.30–11 (11–11 Fri & Sat)
Young's Bitter, Special, Winter Warmer Ⓗ
Large, detached building: a small public bar and a larger lounge. Enclosed garden at the side. No food Sun.
♨ Q ✪ ◖ ⒽBeer ♿ ⇌ ♣ P

Horseshoe

745 London Road (A23/A235 jct) ☎ (081) 684 1956
11–3, 5.30 (7 Sat)–11 (11–11 Fri)
Courage Best Bitter, Directors Ⓗ
Welcoming two-bar pub. The public bar can be loud; the saloon bar is comfortable and the seating area at the rear of the pub can be lively. Good value food weekdays. ✪ ◖ P

Upper Belvedere

Royal Standard

39 Nuxley Road
11–3, 5.30–11 (11–11 Mon, Fri & Sat)
Draught Bass; Charrington IPA Ⓗ; **guest beers**
Popular local with a maritime flavour. No food Sun.
☙ ✪ ◖ ▶ P

SW1: Belgravia

Grouse & Claret

14–15 Little Chester Street
☎ (071) 235 3438
11–11
Arkell's Kingsdown; Brakspear Bitter; Wards Sheffield Best Bitter; Whitbread Boddingtons Bitter Ⓗ; **guest beers**
Split-level, two-bar pub with a separate wine bar and a restaurant serving Thai food.
◖ ▶ ⇌ (Victoria) ⊖

Star Tavern

6 Belgrave Mews West (off West Halkin St)
☎ (071) 234 2806
11.30–3, 5.30 (6.30 Sat)–11 (11.30–11 Fri)
Fuller's Chiswick, London Pride, ESB Ⓗ
Unspoilt mews pub with two real fires. An original entry in this *Guide*, and still going strong. No food Sun.
♨ ◖ ▶ ⊖ (Hyde Pk Corner)

Turks Head

10 Motcomb Street
11–11
Draught Bass; Charrington IPA Ⓗ
Comfortable pub with a raised section at the rear. No food Sun. ◖ ▶ ⊖ (Hyde Pk Corner)

SW1: Pimlico

Rising Sun

44 Ebury Bridge Road
11–11
Young's Bitter, Special, Winter Warmer Ⓗ
Popular local near Victoria coach station.
Q ✪ ◖ ▶ ⇌ (Victoria) ⊖

SW1: St James's

Red Lion

23 Crown Passage
11–11 (11–3 Sat; closed Sun)
Ruddles County; Webster's Yorkshire Bitter; Young's Bitter Ⓗ
Small, unspoilt pub in an alley off Pall Mall. Said to hold the second oldest licence in the West End. Q ◖ ⊖ (Green Pk)

Greater London

SW1: Sloane Square

Fox & Hounds
29 Passmore Street
11–3, 5.30–11 (12–2 Sun, closed Sun eve)
Draught Bass; Charrington IPA H
Small, cosy, friendly pub just off Sloane Square. Holds probably the last remaining beer and wine licence. Q ⊖

SW1: Westminster

Barley Mow
104 Horseferry Road
☎ (071) 222 2330
11–11 (11–3, 7–11 Sat)
Ruddles Best Bitter, County; Webster's Yorkshire Bitter; Young's Bitter H
Large pub handy for horticultural halls. Grand piano in the bar. ◑ ➤ (Victoria) ⊖ (St James's Pk)

Buckingham Arms
62 Petty France
☎ (071) 222 3386
11–11
Young's Bitter, Special, Winter Warmer H
Popular pub near the passport office. Q ◑ ➤ (Victoria) ⊖ (St James's Pk)

Morpeth Arms
58 Millbank ☎ (071) 834 6442
11–11
Young's Bitter, Special, Winter Warmer H
Comfortable pub overlooking the Thames and handy for the Tate Gallery. ◑ ➤ (Vauxhall) ⊖ (Pimlico)

Paviours Arms
Page Street ☎ (071) 834 2150
11–11
Fuller's Chiswick, London Pride, ESB H
Large three-bar pub decorated in Art Deco style. Darts and pool played. ◑ ➤ ⊞ ♣

Royal Oak
2 Regency Street
11–11 (11–3, 8–11 Sat)
Young's Bitter, Special, Winter Warmer H
Wedge-shaped, one-bar pub near the horticultural halls. No food weekends. ◑ ➤ (Victoria) ⊖ (St James's Pk)

Westminster Arms
9 Storeys Gate
11.30–11 (closed Sun eve)
Brakspear Bitter; Marston's Pedigree; Whitbread Boddingtons Bitter H
Small pub near Parliament Square, with a wine bar downstairs. Up to six constantly-changed beers.
◑ ⊖ (St James's Pk)

SW1: Whitehall

Old Shades
37 Whitehall
11–11 (11–3, 7–11 Sat; closed Sun eve)
Draught Bass; Charrington IPA; Fuller's London Pride H
Long, wood-panelled bar with a lounge at the rear which obtains its licence from Buckingham Palace. No eve meals Sun.
🍴 ◑ ➤ (Charing Cross) ⊖

SW2: Brixton

Hope & Anchor
123 Acre Lane
☎ (071) 274 1787
11–11
Young's Bitter, Special H, **Winter Warmer** H or G
Local CAMRA award-winning pub which caters for the local community. The open fires in winter and large garden in summer are popular features. 🍴 Q ❀ ◑ ➤ ⊖

SW2: Streatham

JJ Moon's
2 Streatham Hill
11–11
Greene King IPA, Abbot; Marston's Pedigree; S&N Theakston XB; Younger Scotch H; **guest beer**
Typical Wetherspoon pub with no diversions from the art of conversation and drinking. Weekly guest beer; occasional beer festivals. Q ❀ ◑ ➤ (Streatham Hill) P

SW3: Chelsea

Coopers Arms
87 Flood Street
☎ (071) 376 3120
11–11
Young's Bitter, Special, Winter Warmer H
One of the new wave of Young's pubs, furnished in café-bar style. No meals Sun eve. Q ◑ ⊖ (Sloane Sq)

Princess of Wales
145 Dovehouse Street
11–11 (11–4, 8–11 Sat)
Courage Best Bitter, Directors H
Small one-bar pub behind the Royal Marsden Hospital.
Q ◑ ⊖ (S Kensington)

Rose
86 Fulham Road
☎ (071) 589 6672
11–3, 5.30 (7 Sat)–11 (11–11 Fri)
Fuller's Chiswick, London Pride, ESB H
Ornate pub with much wood and tilework. Theatre upstairs.
◑ ➤ ⊖ (S Kensington)

SW4: Clapham

Rose & Crown
2 The Polygon, Old Town
☎ (071) 720 8265
11–11
Courage Best Bitter H; **guest beers**
Cosy one-bar pub with many homely features. Jazz background music of quality. Meals till 8pm. ❀ ◑ ➤ ⊖ (Clapham Common) ♣

SW6: Fulham

Jolly Brewer
308–310 North End Road
11–11
Ruddles County; Webster's Yorkshire Bitter; Young's Bitter H
Popular street-market local.
⊖ (Broadway)

SW6: Parsons Green

Duke of Cumberland
235 New Kings Road
11–11
Young's Bitter, Special, Winter Warmer H
Originally called 'Ponds End Tavern', established in 1657 and rebuilt in 1893. Nicely furnished with some original tiling remaining. ◑ ⊞ ⊖

White Horse
1 Parsons Green
☎ (071) 736 2115
11.30 (11 Sat)–3, 5 (7 Sat)–11
Draught Bass; Charrington IPA; M&B Highgate Mild; Traquair House Ale (winter) H; **guest beers**
Large, extremely busy, upmarket pub facing the green, with a terrace for outside drinking. Hearty breakfasts at weekends. Hosts beer festivals. ❀ ◑ ➤ ⊖

SW7: South Kensington

Anglesea Arms
15 Selwood Terrace
☎ (071) 373 7960
11–3, 5.30 (7 Sat)–11
Adnams Bitter; Brakspear Special; Eldridge Pope Hardy Country; Fuller's London Pride; Whitbread Boddingtons Bitter; Young's Special H; **guest beer**
Popular beer-drinkers' free house; often very busy. No music machines. ❀ ◑ ➤ ⊖

SW8: Battersea

Plough Inn
518 Wandsworth Road (near B224 jct)
☎ (071) 622 2777
11–11

**Young's Bitter, Special,
Winter Warmer** H
One-bar pub, comfortably
furnished, which retains a
public bar end. Formerly the
tap of the Plough brewery. No
food Sun.
❀ ◖ ▶ ≋ (Wandsworth Rd)

SW8: South Lambeth

Surprise
16 Southville
☎ (071) 622 4623
11–3, 5–11 (11–11 summer)
**Young's Bitter, Special,
Winter Warmer** H
Pub situated at the side of
Larkhall Park; ideal for
children during the summer.
Pinball in the back room. ᵺ
Q ❀ ◖ ▶ ≋ (Wandsworth
Rd) ⊖ (Stockwell) ♣

SW8: Stockwell

Priory Arms
83 Landsdowne Way
11–11
**Fuller's London Pride;
Webster's Yorkshire Bitter;
Young's Bitter, Special;
guest beer**
Small, friendly pub, very
popular with students. Raised
section for darts. Special
afternoon prices for
pensioners. ❀ ◖ ▶ ⊖ ♣

SW10: West Brompton

Fox & Pheasant
1 Billing Road
11–3, 5.30–11
**Draught Bass; Charrington
IPA; Wadworth 6X** H
Tiny two-bar pub much used
by locals, near Chelsea
football ground. Billing Road
is private, so parking may be
difficult. Weekday lunches.
❀ ◖ ⊖ (Fulham Broadway)

SW10: West Chelsea

Chelsea Ram
22 Burnaby Street
11–3, 5.30–11 (11–11 Fri)
**Young's Bitter, Special,
Winter Warmer** H
Comfortable pub without a
jukebox or piped music. Q ◖

SW11: Battersea

Duke of Cambridge
228 Battersea Bridge Road
11–11
**Young's Bitter, Special H,
Winter Warmer** H & G
Despite recent renovations,
this remains essentially a
family pub. It is superbly
managed with plenty of

banter on both sides of the
bar! Eve meals in summer
only. Q ❀ ◖ ▶ ≋ ♣

Falcon
2 St John's Hill
11–11
**Draught Bass; Charrington
IPA; Fuller's London Pride** H;
guest beers
Large, busy crossroads pub
with bars all round. ◖ ≋

SW12: Balham

Nightingale
97 Nightingale Lane
☎ (081) 673 1637
11–3, 5.30–11 (11–11 Fri & Sat)
**Young's Bitter, Special,
Winter Warmer** H
Between Clapham and
Wandsworth Commons,
almost a country local in the
town, run by staff who care.
Good company; often busy.
CAMRA South-West London
Pub of the Year 1991. Q ⚲ ❀ ◖
▶ ≋ (Wandsworth Common)
⊖ (Clapham S) ♣

Prince of Wales
270 Cavendish Road
11–11
**Courage Best Bitter,
Directors; Hop Back GFB;
John Smith's Bitter** H
A basic and loud public bar of
character and a more relaxed
saloon make this a popular
pub especially at lunchtime.
Strong commitment to the
local community and to its
guest beer (GFB).
Q ❀ ◖ ⊞ ≋ ⊖

SW13: Barnes

Bull's Head
373 Lonsdale Road
☎ (081) 876 5241
11–11
**Young's Bitter, Special,
Winter Warmer** H
Impressive building with
comfortable bars. There has
been a pub on the site since at
least 1672. Internationally
renowned as a seven-day-a-
week jazz venue. The art of
good conversation lives on
here. Excellent restaurant.
❀ ◖ ▶ ≋ (Barnes Bridge) ♣

Coach & Horses
27 Barnes High Street (A3003)
☎ (081) 876 2695
11–11
**Young's Bitter, Special,
Winter Warmer** H
A village local in London: an
18th-century gem with a
bustling atmosphere. Small
but thriving, it once
comprised five rooms.
ᵺ ❀ ◖ ▶ ≋ (Barnes Bridge)

Red Lion
2 Castlenau (A306)
☎ (081) 748 2984

11–11
**Fuller's Chiswick, London
Pride, Mr Harry, ESB** H
Imposing main road pub near
playing fields. A friendly,
comfortable lounge and bar.
The ornate rear dining room
opens at 10am for breakfast
(weekdays). ❀ ◖ ▶ ≋

SW14: Mortlake

Railway Tavern
Sheen Lane
☎ (081) 878 7361
11–11
**Hall & Woodhouse Badger
Best Bitter, Hard Tackle,
Tanglefoot; Shepherd Neame
Bishops Finger; Wadworth
6X; Wells Eagle** H; **guest beer**
A large modern bar leads into
a smaller traditional front
room in a friendly, games-
oriented pub which has
regular quiz nights. Wide
range of meals and bar snacks.
❀ ◖ ▶ ≋ ♣

SW15: Putney

Jolly Gardeners
61 Lacy Road
☎ (081) 788 7508
11–11
**Fuller's Chiswick, London
Pride, ESB** H
Built in 1938 for Charrington,
a good example of the
architecture of the time;
comfortable and friendly. Live
jazz Sun lunch, when no meals
are served.
ᵺ Q ❀ ◖ ⊞ ≋ ♣

SW15: Putney Heath

Green Man
☎ (081) 788 8096
11–11
**Young's Bitter, Special,
Winter Warmer** H
Compact pub whose large
garden has a barbecue and
outdoor bar. The present
building can be traced back to
1700; it was once frequented
by Swinburne, the poet. No
eve meals except in summer.
Q ❀ ◖ ⊞ ♣

SW16: Streatham

Earl Ferrers
Ellora Road
☎ (081) 769 2181
11.30–11
**Courage Best Bitter; Fuller's
London Pride** H
A straightforward and
unpretentious back-street local,
behind Streatham ice rink. It
features original bar fittings
and an unusual fob watch
clock. ᵺ ≋ (Common) ♣

Pied Bull

498 Streatham High Road
☎ (081) 764 4003
11–3.30, 5.30–11 (11–11 Sat)
**Young's Bitter, Special,
Winter Warmer** Ⓗ
Two-bar pub with many areas
in the saloon. Very handy for
harassed shoppers. Food is
recommended, with cut price
offers certain days for
pensioners.
🏭 Q ⊛ ◑ 🍽 ⇌ ♣ P

SW17: Tooting

Castle

High Street
☎ (081) 672 7018
11–11
**Young's Bitter, Special,
Winter Warmer** Ⓗ
Pub due to be completely
restructured into one bar;
handy for the local market and
shops. Always a good bet in a
poor area for real beer. No
meals Sun eve. 🏭 Q ⊛ ◑
◑ & ⊖ (Broadway) ♣ P

JJ Moon's

56a Tooting High Street
☎ (081) 672 6547
11–11
**Greene King IPA, Abbot;
Marston's Pedigree; S&N
Theakston XB; Younger
Scotch** Ⓗ; **guest beers**
Ex-pizza parlour sensitively
redesigned into an intimate,
friendly, bustling pub. Handy
for public transport. Guest
beers Fri. No meals Sun eve.
Q ◑ ⊖ (Broadway)

SW18: Wandsworth

Grapes

39 Fairfield Street
☎ (081) 874 8681
11–11
**Young's Bitter, Special,
Winter Warmer** Ⓗ
Well-kept main road local
near the brewery, with a
welcoming atmosphere. It
features a wall seat down one
side, ironwork on top of the
bar and copper and brass
vases. ⊛ ◑ ⇌ (Town)

Old Sergeant

104 Garratt Lane
☎ (081) 874 4099
11–3, 5–11 (11–11 Mon, Fri & Sat)
**Young's Bitter, Special,
Winter Warmer** Ⓗ
Very friendly, two-bar local.
No food Sun. ◑ ♣

Spread Eagle

71 Wandsworth High Street
☎ (081) 874 1326
11–11
**Young's Bitter, Special,
Winter Warmer** Ⓗ
Magnificent glass screens in a
large saloon, and a smaller

back room mainly for diners
at lunchtime (no eve meals
Sat/Sun; till 7pm Mon–Fri).
Popular public bar.
Q ◑ ▶ ⌑ ⇌ (Town) ♣ P

SW19: Merton

Princess Royal

Abbey Road ☎ (081) 542 3273
11–3, 5 (6.30 winter Sat)–11
**Courage Best Bitter,
Directors; Hop Back GFB;
John Smith's Bitter;
Wadworth 6X** Ⓗ
Friendly locals' corner pub
comprising a small public bar
and a larger saloon. Used to be
part of the Hodgson's of
Kingston estate. No lunches
Sun.
⊛ ◑ ▶ ⌑ ⊖ (S Wimbledon) ♣

SW19: Wimbledon

Hand in Hand

6 Crooked Billet, Wimbledon
Common (off A281)
☎ (081) 946 5720
11–11
**Young's Bitter, Special,
Winter Warmer** Ⓗ
Large, often busy pub off
Wimbledon Common. The no-
smoking children's room is
also the evening darts area.
Good vegetarian selection, but
no crisps/nuts (common bye-
laws). No Sun eve meals.
🏭 Q 🐕 ⊛ ◑ ♣ ⊬

King of Denmark

83 Ridgway (off A219)
11.30–3, 5.30 (7 Sat)–11
**Courage Best Bitter,
Directors** Ⓗ
Friendly, award-winning pub
with several distinct areas
(including a quiet end) in a
large single bar. Plenty of
loyal local support for its
reasonably priced beer.
Weekday lunches. Q ⊛ ♣

Rose & Crown

55 High Street (A219)
11–11
**Young's Bitter, Special,
Winter Warmer** Ⓗ
Popular village pub on a site
which has had an inn since the
17th century. Families are
welcome in the glazed rear
corridor. Q 🐕 ⊛ ◑ P ⊬

Carshalton

Railway Tavern

47 North Street (off A232)
12–3, 5–11
**Fuller's London Pride, Mr
Harry, ESB** Ⓗ
Small, street-corner local with
ornate windows and mirrors.
A home for many teams from
marbles to morris dancing. No
food Sun. ◑ ⇌ ♣

Cheam

Red Lion

17 Park Road (off A217/A232)
11–3, 5.30–11
**Draught Bass; Charrington
IPA** Ⓗ; **guest beer**
Reputedly built in the 16th
century and now consisting of
a number of separate drinking
areas around a central bar;
some low ceilings and wood
panelling. No food Sun; no-
smoking room Mon–Thu.
🏭 Q ⊛ ◑ ⇌ ♣ ⊬

Chessington

North Star

271 Hook Road, Hook (A243)
12–11 (11–3, 5.30–11 Sat)
**Draught Bass; Charrington
IPA; M&B Highgate Mild** Ⓗ
Pub on the main road to
Chessington, recently
redecorated. The only regular
mild outlet in the Royal
Borough. May also have
Highgate Old in season and
another beer. Weekday
lunches. Q ⊛ ◑ ♣ P

Kingston upon Thames

Bricklayers Arms

53 Hawks Road (off A2043)
☎ (081) 546 0393
11–11
**Courage Best Bitter,
Directors; John Smith's
Bitter** Ⓗ
Comfortable one-bar pub just
off the Fairfield. Most of the
meals on the wide-ranging
menu (served till 8pm) are
prepared by the landlord
himself (generous portions).
No meals Sun. Q 🐕 ⊛ ◑ ♣

Cocoanut

16 Mill Street (off Fairfield
South) ☎ (081) 546 3978
11–3, 5.30–11 (11–11 Sat)
**Fuller's Chiswick, London
Pride, ESB** Ⓗ
One-bar pub offering a
community atmosphere and
good food. The pub dog gets
upset when people leave
before closing time! No food
Sun. ⊛ ◑ ♣

Newt & Ferret

46 Fairfield South
☎ (081) 546 3804
11–11
**Hall & Woodhouse Badger
Best Bitter, Hard Tackle,
Tanglefoot; Mauldons Black
Adder; Shepherd Neame
Bishops Finger; Wadworth
6X** Ⓗ
Busy and popular pub with a
quiz night (Wed). Occasional
beer festivals are held in the
garden. The beer range tends
to vary. ⊛ ◑ ♣ ⌂

Park Tavern
19 New Road
11–11
Brakspear Bitter; Young's Bitter, Special, Winter Warmer Ⓗ**; guest beers**
Small pub near the Kingston gate of Richmond Park. Parking difficult. ♨ Q ⚘ ♣

Wych Elm
Elm Road
☎ (081) 547 0321
11–3, 5–11 (11–11 Sat)
Fuller's Chiswick, London Pride, ESB Ⓗ
Welcoming pub with an ornately decorated lounge and a basic but comfortable public bar. Impressive floral displays. Off the beaten track. No food Sun. ⚘ ◗ ⊟

Mitcham

White Lion of Mortimer
223 London Road
☎ (081) 646 7332
11–11
Greene King IPA, Abbot; Marston's Pedigree; S&N Theakston XB; Younger Scotch Ⓗ**; guest beer**
Large, welcoming pub with a both interesting and informative decor. Regular mini-festivals. Formerly the 'Buck's Head'.
♨ Q ⚘ ◗ ◖ ♿ ♣ ◌

New Malden

Royal Oak
90 Coombe Road (B283)
☎ (081) 942 0837
11–11
Ind Coope Benskins Best Bitter, Burton Ale; Tetley Bitter; Young's Bitter Ⓗ**; guest beers**
Corner pub with a large garden. Occasional theatre or other entertainment in the function room. No meals Sun eve. ⛴ ⚘ ◗ ◖ ⊟ ⇌ ♣ P

Richmond

Mitre
20 St Mary's Grove (off A305)
11–4, 5–11 (11–11 Sat)
Young's Bitter, Special Ⓗ
Small, single-roomed pub in a quiet location off Sheen Road. Home-cooked lunches Mon–Fri. Note the fine stained-glass windows. ⚘ ◖ ♣

Princes Head
The Green
☎ (081) 940 1572
11–11
Fuller's Chiswick, London Pride, ESB Ⓗ
Attractive pub, established circa 1740. The lounge bar is in traditional style, enhanced with prints and photographs

of Richmond's bygone days. Good, home-cooked bar food. ⚘ ◖ ⇌ ♣

Red Cow
59 Sheen Road (A305)
☎ (081) 940 2511
11–11
Young's Bitter, Special, Winter Warmer Ⓗ
Fine local with many original Victorian features. The simply furnished, compact, but comfortable lounge creates a welcoming atmosphere. Good value, home-cooked food (not served Sun eve). Quiz eves.
♨ ◖ ⊟ ⇌ ⊖ ♣

White Cross Hotel
Water Lane
☎ (081) 940 6844
11–11
Young's Bitter, Special, Winter Warmer Ⓗ
Extremely popular Thames-side pub in a splendid picturesque setting. Excellent bar food and service complement the fine interior. The function room, up from the bar, provides extra space at busy times. Riverside terrace bar in summer.
♨ Q ⚘ ◖ ◗ ⇌ ⊖

Surbiton

Bun Shop
22–26 Berrylands Road (off A240) ☎ (081) 399 3124
11–11
Adnams Bitter; Greene King IPA, Abbot; Young's Bitter, Special Ⓗ
Pub off the main road with two bars, but no difference in price. Skittles may be played in the function room by arrangement. A genuine free house whose range of beers may change. Weekday lunches. Q ⛴ ◖ ⇌ ♣

Waggon & Horses
1 Surbiton Hill Road (A240)
11–2.30 (3 Fri & Sat), 5–11
Young's Bitter, Special, Winter Warmer Ⓗ **&** Ⓖ
Pub at the foot of Surbiton Hill, noted for its charity collections. The landlord celebrated his 25th anniversary in July 1992. The only Young's pub in the Royal Borough to retain a public bar. Weekday lunches.
Q ⚘ ◖ ⊟ ⇌ ♣

Sutton

Jenny Lind
53 Carshalton Road (A232)
12–11
Ind Coope Friary Meux Best Bitter, Burton Ale; Tetley Bitter Ⓗ
Corner-site pub with a galleried exterior. The single-bar interior is furnished in

wine red, with many prints and photos; games area at one end. Named after the opera-singing 'Swedish Nightingale' who visited the area in 1847. No food Sun. ⚘ ◖ ⇌ ♣

New Town
Lind Road
☎ (081) 642 0567
11–3, 5–11 (11–11 Sat)
Young's Bitter, Special Ⓗ**, Winter Warmer** Ⓖ
Recently refurbished, street-corner pub. The public bar has an adjoining games room and there is a contrasting, three-level saloon bar. Good food. Q ⚘ ◖ ◗ ⊟ ⇌ ♣

Robin Hood
West Street
☎ (081) 643 7584
11–3, 5–11
Young's Bitter, Special, Winter Warmer Ⓗ
Large one-bar pub, close to the new St Nicholas shopping centre; very popular with the locals. Small courtyard and pavement seating. No food Sat eve or Sun. ♨ ⚘ ◖ ◗ ⇌ ♣

W1: Fitzrovia

Bricklayers Arms
31 Gresse Street
11–11
Samuel Smith OBB, Museum Ⓗ
Small, wood-panelled pub with food service upstairs.
◖ ◗ ⊖ (Tottenham Ct Rd) ♣

George & Dragon
151 Cleveland Street
12–11 (12–3, 7–11 Sat)
Draught Bass; Charrington IPA; Fuller's London Pride; Wadworth 6X Ⓗ
Small corner pub with a mainly local clientele. Weekday lunches.
◖ ◗ ⊖ (Gt Portland St)

King & Queen
1 Foley Street
☎ (071) 636 5619
11–11
Fuller's London Pride; Ruddles Best Bitter, County Ⓗ
Impressive, red brick Gothic-style building with friendly service. Weekday lunches.
◖ ⊖ (Goodge St)

W1: Marylebone

Beehive
7 Homer Street
11–3, 5.30–11 (7–10.30 Sat; 11–11 Fri)
Whitbread Wethered Bitter, Boddingtons Bitter, Flowers Original Ⓗ
Small, neat side-street local.
⚘ ⇌ ⊖

197

Greater London

Dover Castle

43 Weymouth Mews
11–11 (11–3, 7–11 Sat)
Adnams Bitter; Marston's Pedigree; Ruddles County; Whitbread Boddingtons Bitter Ⓗ
Cosy, panelled pub in a mews; an old coaching inn dating from 1777. Note the mirrors under the beam to enable coachmen in the public bar to see when passengers in the saloon bar were ready to leave. Q Ⓓ ⊖ (Regents Pk)

Turners Arms

26 Crawford Street
11–11
Shepherd Neame Master Brew Bitter Ⓗ; **guest beers**
A welcome oasis in a sea of the big brewers. Ⓓ ▸ ⇌ ⊖

Windsor Castle

29 Crawford Place
11–11
Draught Bass; Charrington IPA Ⓗ
Comfortable pub with a British royalty theme. Decorated in the landlord's inimitable style.
Ⓓ ⊖ (Edgware Rd)

Worcester Arms

89 George Street
11–11 (11–3, 5.30–11 Sat)
Brakspear Bitter; Marston's Pedigree; Nethergate Bitter; Thwaites Bitter Ⓗ; **guest beers**
Busy free house with a nice Courage Alton mirror.
Ⓓ ⊖ (Baker St) ♣

W1: Mayfair

Guinea

30 Bruton Place
11–11 (11–3, 6.30–11 Sat; closed Sun)
Young's Bitter, Special Ⓗ
Small mews pub, originally known as the 'Old One Pound One'. There has been a pub here since 1423. High-class restaurant at the rear. Winner of 1991 *Steak and Kidney Pie* and *Pub Sandwich* competitions. No lunches Sat.
Q Ⓓ ▸

Windmill

6–8 Mill Street
11–11 (7 Sat; closed Sun)
Young's Bitter, Special, Winter Warmer Ⓗ
Split-level pub with a first-floor restaurant; opposite the Rolls Royce showroom.
Ⓓ ▸ ⊖ (Oxford Circus)

W1: Soho

Ship

116 Wardour Street
11–11 (11–3, 5.30–11 Sat; closed Sun)
Fuller's Chiswick, London Pride, ESB Ⓗ
Corner pub with nice

windows, frequented by film company staff.
Ⓓ ⊖ (Oxford Circus)

W2: Bayswater

Archery Tavern

4 Bathurst Street
11–11
Adnams Bitter; Draught Bass; Hall & Woodhouse Badger Best Bitter; Tetley Bitter; Wadworth 6X Ⓗ
Wood-fronted pub which probably dates from 1840, next to a mews with a working stables. Takes its name from a nearby archery ground.
Ⓓ ▸ ⇌ (Paddington)
⊖ (Lancaster Gate) ♣

Victoria

10a Strathearn Place
☎ (071) 262 5696
11–3, 5.30–11
Draught Bass; Charrington IPA; Fuller's London Pride; M&B Highgate Mild Ⓗ
Victorian pub with much woodwork. Queen Victoria is said to have visited here when opening Paddington station. Wine bar downstairs.
Ⓓ ▸ ⇌ (Paddington) ⊖

W2: Paddington

Marquis of Clanricarde

36 Southwick Street
11–11
Courage Best Bitter, Directors Ⓗ
Large pub offering live music at weekends. No food Sun.
Ⓓ ▸ ⇌ ⊖ ♣

Monkey Puzzle

30 Southwick Street
11–3, 5.30 (7 Sat)–11
Draught Bass; Brakspear Mild, Bitter; Marston's Merrie Monk; Thwaites Bitter; Wadworth 6X Ⓗ; **guest beers**
Pleasant, modern free house with a friendly local clientele and a friendly atmosphere. The beer range varies. Barbecues in summer.
❀ Ⓓ ▸ ⇌ ⊖

White Hart

31 Brook Mews North
12–11
Courage Best Bitter, Directors Ⓗ
Well-hidden, wood-panelled pub at the end of a mews. Separate room for food service. An ex-Reffel's of Bexley house. Ⓓ ⇌ ⊖

W3: Acton

Kings Head

High Street
☎ (081) 992 0282
11–11

Fuller's Chiswick, London Pride, ESB Ⓗ
Coaching inn displaying old photographs of Acton. Jasper the parrot is as sharp as ever. Alternative cabaret on Fri nights. ❀ Ⓓ ⊖ (Town) ♣

W4: Chiswick

Bell & Crown

72 Strand-on-the-Green
☎ (081) 994 4164
11–11
Fuller's Chiswick, London Pride, Mr Harry, ESB Ⓗ
Busy riverside pub with a conservatory. Handy for the Kew Bridge Engine Museum.
Q Ⓓ ▸ ⇌ (Kew Bridge)

Duke of York

107 Devonshire Road
11–3, 5.30–11 (11–11 Sat)
Fuller's London Pride, Mr Harry, ESB Ⓗ
Corner pub with a tiled facade and much interior woodwork; very much a local.
Ⓓ ⊖ (Turnham Green) ♣

George & Devonshire

8 Burlington Lane
☎ (081) 994 1859
11–11
Fuller's Chiswick, London Pride, Mr Harry, ESB Ⓗ
Large, comfortable pub near the notorious Hogarth roundabout. ❀ Ⓓ ▸ ⊟

Windmill

214 Chiswick High Road
11–11
Fuller's Chiswick, London Pride, ESB Ⓗ
Popular pub decorated in 'Swiss chalet'-style, very busy at times. No food Sun eve.
❀ Ⓓ ▸ ⊖ (Turnham Green) ♣

W5: Ealing

Castle

36 St Mary's Road
☎ (081) 567 3285
11–11
Fuller's London Pride, ESB Ⓗ
Friendly local frequented by all ages. The garden won *Ealing in Bloom* 1990. Weekday lunches. ❀ Ⓓ ⊟ ♣

Fox & Goose

Hanger Lane
☎ (081) 997 2441
11.30–11
Fuller's Chiswick, London Pride, ESB Ⓗ
Nearest pub to the world-famous Hanger Lane gyratory system. A cosy public, large saloon and pleasant garden set amidst office blocks. ❀ Ⓓ ▸ ⊟ ♿ ⊖ (Hanger Lane) P

Red Lion

13 St Mary's Road
11–3, 5.30–11 (11–11 Fri, Sat & summer)

Greater London

Fuller's Chiswick, London Pride, ESB H
Also known as 'Stage 6', due to its proximity to the Ealing film studios (now BBC). This gem of a pub has its walls lined with photographs of film and TV. Deservedly popular.
Q ❀ ◖ ≢ (Broadway) ⊖

Wheatsheaf
Haven Lane
☎ (081) 997 5240
11–11
Fuller's Chiswick, London Pride, ESB H
Very much a local, a single bar with defined drinking areas, retaining its character. Offers a welcome change of beer and atmosphere from its Chef & Brewer neighbour. Q ❀ ◖ ▶
≢ (Broadway) ⊖ ♣

W6: Hammersmith

Blue Anchor
Lower Mall
☎ (081) 748 5774
11.30–3.30, 5–11 (11–11 summer)
Courage Best Bitter, Directors H
Busy Thames-side pub with a pewter bar top and eight pewter-mounted handpulls. Eve meals in summer only.
◖ ▶ ⊖

Builders
81 King Street
11–11 (11–4, 6–11 Sat)
Young's Bitter, Special, Winter Warmer H
Two-bar pub in a busy shopping area. ❀ ◖ ⊖

Cross Keys
57 Black Lion Lane
11–11
Fuller's Chiswick, London Pride, ESB H
Popular pub, half-way between King Street and the River Thames.
❀ ◖ ⊖ (Stamford Brook) ♣

Dove
Upper Mall
☎ (081) 748 5405
11–11
Fuller's London Pride, ESB H
Historic riverside pub, originally called the 'Dove Coffee House' in 1796. In the *Guinness Book of Records* as having the smallest public bar (4'2" x 7'10"). *Rule Britannia* was composed upstairs.
◖ ▶ ◪ ⊖

Salutation
154 King Street
11–11
Fuller's Chiswick, London Pride, ESB H
Ex-coaching house with a tiled frontage. ❀ ◖ ♣

Thatched House
115 Dalling Road
11–11

Young's Bitter, Special, Winter Warmer H
Popular local with a great atmosphere. Barbecues in summer.
❀ ◖ ⊖ (Ravenscourt Pk)

W7: Hanwell

White Hart
324 Greenford Avenue
11–11
Fuller's London Pride, ESB H
Quality suburban local, featuring a large public, saloon, and a smaller public bar. Antique handpumps are mounted on the saloon wall.
🏘 Q ❀ ◪ ⊖ (Castle Bar Pk) ♣ P

W8: Kensington

Britannia
1 Allen Street
☎ (071) 957 1864
11–11 (may close Sat afternoon)
Young's Bitter, Special, Winter Warmer H
Busy, wood-panelled pub close to shops. The split-level lounge has two bars and a conservatory, which serves as a no-smoking area at lunchtime. No food Sun.
Q ❀ ◖ ◪ ⊖ (High St) ⚲

Windsor Castle
114 Campden Hill Road
☎ (071) 927 8491
11–11
Draught Bass; Charrington IPA H
Cosy three-bar pub, built in 1835. A garden bar is used in good weather. A real gem.
Q ◖ ▶ ⊖ (Notting Hill Gate)

W9: Maida Vale

Warrington
93 Warrington Crescent
11–11
Brakspear Special; Fuller's London Pride, ESB; Ruddles County; Young's Special H
Large Victorian gin palace with florid decoration and a semi-circular, marble-topped bar. The restaurant upstairs serves Thai food (eves).
◖ ▶ ◪ ⊖ (Warwick Ave)

W11: Holland Park

Prince of Wales
14 Princedale Road
☎ (071) 727 0045
11.30–11
Draught Bass; Charrington IPA H
Large Victorian pub built in 1845 with elegant etched windows. The pub fronts two streets and a public right of way exists through it. No food Sun eve. ❀ ◖ ▶ ⊖ ♣

W11: Notting Hill

Portobello Star
171 Portobello Road
11–11
Whitbread Castle Eden Ale, Flowers Original H
Tiny pub in the market area.
◖ ⊖ (Notting Hill Gate)

W12: Shepherds Bush

Crown & Sceptre
59 Melina Road
11–11
Fuller's Chiswick, London Pride, ESB H
Popular back-street local. Weekday lunches.
◖ ◪ ⊖ (Goldhawk Rd) ♣

Moon on the Green
172–174 Uxbridge Road
☎ (081) 749 5709
11–11
Greene King IPA, Abbot; Marston's Pedigree; S&N Theakston XB; Younger Scotch H; **guest beers**
New pub in typical Wetherspoon style; formerly an electrical shop. Q ◖ ▶ ♣

W13: West Ealing

Forester
2 Leighton Road (B452)
11–3 (4 Sat), 5.30 (7 Sat)–11
Courage Best Bitter, Directors H
Imposing Edwardian structure with many original features, in four separate drinking areas. The beer garden extends from the conservatory – children are welcome. Imperial Russian Stout may be available. ❀ ⚲ ≢ ⊖ (Northfields) ♣

Kent Hotel
Scotch Common (B455)
11–11
Fuller's London Pride, ESB H
Large neighbourhood pub with a public bar and a split-level saloon. The garden is popular in summer. ☼ ❀ ◖ ◪ ≢ (Castle Bar Pk) ♣ P

W14: West Kensington

Britannia Tap
150 Warwick Road
11–11 (11–3, 6–11 Sat)
Young's Bitter, Special, Winter Warmer H
Small, friendly local with lots of character, close to both Olympia and Earl's Court. Can get busy lunchtime and during exhibitions. Q ❀ ◖ ≢ (Olympia) ⊖ (Earl's Court)

Seven Stars

253 North End Road
11–11
Fuller's Chiswick, London Pride, ESB Ⓗ
Two-bar pub built in the 1930s in Art Deco style. ⚹ ◖ ⊞ ⊖

Warwick Arms

160 Warwick Road
☎ (071) 603 3560
11–3, 5.30–11 (11–11 Fri & Sat)
Fuller's Chiswick, London Pride, Mr Harry, ESB Ⓗ
Busy local dating from 1828; the rear section has exposed brick. Wedgwood handpumps. No eve meals Sun. ﷼ Q ⚹ ◖ ▶ ⇌
(Olympia) ⊖ (Earl's Court) ♣

Bedfont

Beehive

333 Staines Road
☎ (081) 890 8086
12–4, 5.30–11 (may vary)
Fuller's London Pride, ESB Ⓗ
Excellent pub with a friendly, lively atmosphere: an attractive lounge and a well-kept garden. Good value food (not served Sun); barbecues in summer. ⚹ ◖ ▶ P

Brentford

Brewery Tap

17 Catherine Wheel Road
11–11
Fuller's London Pride, ESB Ⓗ
Cosy pub in the heart of old dockland; modernised but retaining its original features. Trad. jazz Tue and Thu; charity quiz Mon. Weekday lunches. ⚹ ◖ ♣ ♠

Express Hotel

Kew Bridge Road
11–3, 5.30–11
Draught Bass; Young's Bitter, Special Ⓗ
Remarkable pub which, despite its busy location, retains a tranquil interior. Three separate drinking areas. Pleasant garden.
Q ⚹ ◖ ⊞ ⊖ (Kew Bridge)

Lord Nelson

Enfield Road
☎ (081) 568 1877
12–11
Fuller's London Pride, ESB Ⓗ
A strong Antipodean flavour is to be found in this friendly, sports-oriented local. Its wide range of food is often featured in the press. Eve meals finish at 8pm. ⚹ ◖ ▶ ⊞ ⇌ ♠

White Horse

Market Place
☎ (081) 560 0188
11–3, 5.30–11 (11–11 Fri)
Draught Bass; Charrington IPA; Stones Best Bitter Ⓗ
Historic roomy inn, tastefully modernised with an added conservatory and an attractive garden on the riverside. No food Sat; carvery other lunchtimes. ⚹ ◖ ⇌ ♠

Cranford

Queens Head

123 High Street (off Parkway)
☎ (081) 897 0722
11–11
Fuller's Chiswick, London Pride, Mr Harry, ESB Ⓗ
Tudor-style pub: one bar, but two distinct drinking areas. A lounge to one side is used for dining (home-cooked food; not served weekend eves). Award-winning garden.
﷼ ⌂ ⚹ ◖ ♠ P

Greenford

Bridge Hotel

Western Avenue (A40/A4127 jct) ☎ (081) 566 6246
11–3, 5.30–11
Young's Bitter, Special, Winter Warmer Ⓗ
Large 1930s roadhouse with an impressive tiled frontage. Re-opened with a three-star hotel attached in May 1990. The pub bar has retained its original character, with wood-panelling and cosy window alcoves.
Q ⚹ ⛟ ◖ ♿ ⇌ ♠ P

Hampton

White Hart

High Street ☎ (081) 979 5352
11–3, 5.30–11 (11–11 Fri & Sat)
Archers Best Bitter; Eldridge Pope Blackdown Porter; Moorhouse's Pendle Witches Brew; Whitbread Boddingtons Bitter, Flowers Original Ⓗ; **guest beers**
Comfortable, tasteful, mock Tudor pub. Eight handpumps serve a selection from 90 regularly-changed beers; a true free house. Good lunches.
﷼ Q ⚹ ◖ ♿ ⇌ ♠ P

Hampton Court

Kings Arms

Lion Gate
☎ (081) 977 1729
11–11
Hall & Woodhouse Badger Best Bitter, Hard Tackle, Tanglefoot; Mauldons Black Adder; Shepherd Neame Bishops Finger Ⓗ; **guest beers**
Imposing historic pub with a friendly atmosphere, beside the world-famous maze. Sawdust on the floor in the public bar; mosaic flooring in the saloon. Bar billiards.
⚹ ◖ ▶ ⊞ ⇌ ♠ P

Hampton Wick

White Hart

High Street
☎ (081) 977 1786
11–11
Fuller's Chiswick, London Pride, Mr Harry, ESB Ⓗ
Large pub with tasteful oak panelling, serving a wide range of food. ⚹ ◖ ⇌ ♠ P

Harmondsworth

Crown

High Street ☎ (081) 759 1007
11–3, 5–11 (11–11 Fri & Sat)
Brakspear Special or Old; Courage Best Bitter, Directors Ⓗ
One-bar pub with separate drinking areas and several secluded corners. A keenly-priced, extensive menu is offered, including sandwiches for those daunted by the portions of the main meals.
﷼ Q ⚹ ◖ ▶ ♠ P

Hayes

Blue Anchor

Printing House Lane
11–11 (11–3, 7–11 Sat)
Courage Directors; Fuller's London Pride; Ruddles County; Wadworth 6X; Webster's Yorkshire Bitter; Young's Special Ⓗ
Smart, one-bar pub with several drinking areas, situated on the towpath of the Grand Union Canal. The beer range may vary. ⚹ ◖ ⇌ ⌂ P

Heathrow Airport

Tap & Spile

Terminal One
☎ (081) 897 3696
11–11
Adnams Bitter; Marston's Pedigree; Tolly Cobbold Original Ⓗ; **guest beers**
Busy airport bar in the departure lounge. Friendly service and always a cheap guest beer amongst the eight-plus available. ♿ ⊖

Heston

Master Robert Hotel (Robert Inn)

366 Great West Road (A4/B358 jct)
☎ (081) 570 6261
11–3, 5–11 (11–11 Fri & Sat)
Fuller's Chiswick, London Pride, ESB Ⓗ
The public house part (entrance at the corner with Sutton Lane) offers real ale; the hotel's cocktail bar doesn't! ⛟ ◖ ♠ P

Greater London

Hillingdon

Turks Head
47 Harlington Road
11–11
**Courage Best Bitter,
Directors** H**; guest beer**
Ex-Harman's pub with one
guest beer always available,
plus real pork scratchings!
Very cosy and highly
recommended. Q ❀ ◖▶ P

Hounslow

Earl Russell
274 Hanworth Road (A314)
11–11
Fuller's London Pride, ESB H
Traditional Victorian local
with a friendly atmosphere,
serving good value weekday
lunches.
❀ ◖ ⊟ ⇌ ⊖ (Central) ♣ P

Jolly Farmer
177 Lampton Road (off A4)
11–11
**Courage Best Bitter,
Directors; Fuller's London
Pride; Ruddles Best Bitter** H
Popular, cosy local. Friendly
licensees offer very good
lunches and snacks (Mon–Fri).
❀ ◖ ⊟ ⅄ ⊖ (Central) P

Moon Under Water
84–86 Staines Road (A315)
☎ (081) 572 7506
11–11
**Greene King IPA, Abbot;
Marston's Pedigree; S&N
Theakston XB; Younger
Scotch** H**; guest beers**
Traditional-style mock
Victorian pub, converted from
a locksmith's shop, on a main
bus route. Very lively lunch
trade (including Sun roasts);
crowded eves, especially at
weekends. Two guest beers
change weekly. No food Sun
eve.
Q ❀ ◖▶ ⅄ ⇌ ⊖ (Central)

Isleworth

Castle
18 Upper Square, Old
Isleworth
☎ (081) 560 3615
11–11
Young's Bitter, Special H
Popular pub near the River
Thames, with a large
conservatory suitable for
families. ⋈ ❀ ◖ ♣ ♣ P

Coach & Horses
183 London Road
☎ (081) 560 1447
11–11
**Young's Bitter, Special,
Winter Warmer** H
Former coaching inn close to
Syon Park. Extensive
conference and banqueting
facilities. ⋈ ❀ ◖▶ ⇌ (Syon
Lane) ♣ P

Town Wharf
Swan Street (off A300)
☎ (081) 847 2287
11.30–3, 5.30–11 (11.30–11 summer)
**Samuel Smith OBB,
Museum** H
Smart riverside pub on the site
of a former wharf. The
sumptuous upstairs lounge
has an outside balcony. Quiz
night Mon. ❀ ◖▶ ♣ P

Norwood Green

Plough
Tentelow Lane (A4127)
11–11
**Fuller's Chiswick, London
Pride, ESB** H
Originating in the 14th
century, this is the oldest pub
in the area. Expensive beer.
Q ❀ ◖ ♣ P

Ruislip Manor

JJ Moon's
12 Victoria Road
☎ (0895) 622373
11–11
**Greene King IPA, Abbot;
Marston's Pedigree; S&N
Theakston XB; Younger
Scotch** H**; guest beer**
Traditional style, mock
Victorian ale house, converted
from an old Woolworth store.
Always very busy.
Q ❀ ◖▶ ⅄ ⊖ ⌂

Southall

Old Oak Tree
The Common (off A3005)
OS787120
☎ (081) 574 1714
11–11
**Courage Best Bitter,
Directors** H
Hard-to-find canalside local;
you can moor your narrow
boat alongside. ❀ ◖ ⊟ ♣ P

Scotsman
96 Scotts Road (800 yds off
A3005) ☎ (081) 574 1506
11–3, 5.15–11
Fuller's London Pride, ESB H
Another hard-to-find back-
street local, comprising two
very contrasting bars: a
boisterous public and a quiet,
relaxed saloon. ⋈ Q ◖ ⊟ ♣

Teddington

Queen Dowager
49 North Lane (S of Broad
Street) ☎ (081) 977 2583
11–3 (4 Sat), 5.30 (7 Sat)–11 (11–11
Fri)
**Young's Bitter, Special,
Winter Warmer** H
Small pub off the main street.
The landlord is justly proud of
the garden. Named after
Queen Adelaide, although the
sign bears a portrait of Queen
Mary. Q ❀ ◖ ⊟ ⇌ ♣

Twickenham

Albany
Station Yard
☎ (081) 892 1554
11–3, 5.30–11
**Draught Bass; Charrington
IPA; M&B Highgate Mild;
Stones Best Bitter; Wadworth
6X; Welsh Brewers
Worthington BB** H
Large, comfortable pub with a
friendly atmosphere. Serves
good food and offers a pool
room, bar billiards and table
football, plus two function
rooms. Within walking
distance of the town centre
and riverside. ⅃ ◖▶ ⇌ P

Eel Pie
9–11 Church Street (off A305)
☎ (081) 891 1717
11–11
**Hall & Woodhouse Badger
Best Bitter, Hard Tackle,
Tanglefoot; Shepherd Neame
Best Bitter; Wadworth 6X;
Wells Eagle** H**; guest beers**
Ex-wine bar in Twickenham's
oldest shopping street,
offering traditional and
continental lunches (not Sun).
A popular venue for rugby
fans. ◖ ⇌ ♣

Pope's Grotto
Cross Deep
☎ (081) 892 3050
11–3, 5.30–11 (11–11 Sat)
**Young's Bitter, Special,
Winter Warmer** H
Large, comfortable pub
overlooking Radnor Gardens
and the Thames. Popular with
all ages. Friendly staff serve
excellent, home-made food
from a varied menu (no meals
Sun eve). ❀ ◖▶ ⊟ ⇌
(Strawberry Hill) ♣ P

Uxbridge

Crown & Sceptre
High Street
☎ (0895) 236308
11–11
**Courage Best Bitter,
Directors; Wadworth 6X** H
Grade II listed building,
dating from 1759. Home-
cooked food is a speciality; the
award-winning steak and
kidney pie is a must (no food
Sun). ❀ ◖ ⊖ ♣

Whitton

Admiral Nelson
123 Nelson Road (B361)
11.30–11
**Fuller's Chiswick, London
Pride, ESB** H
Busy, high street pub, popular
with Harlequins RFC. Offers a
varied menu at all times,
Mon–Sat. Trad. jazz Tue eves.
⋈ ❀ ◖▶ ⇌

Greater Manchester

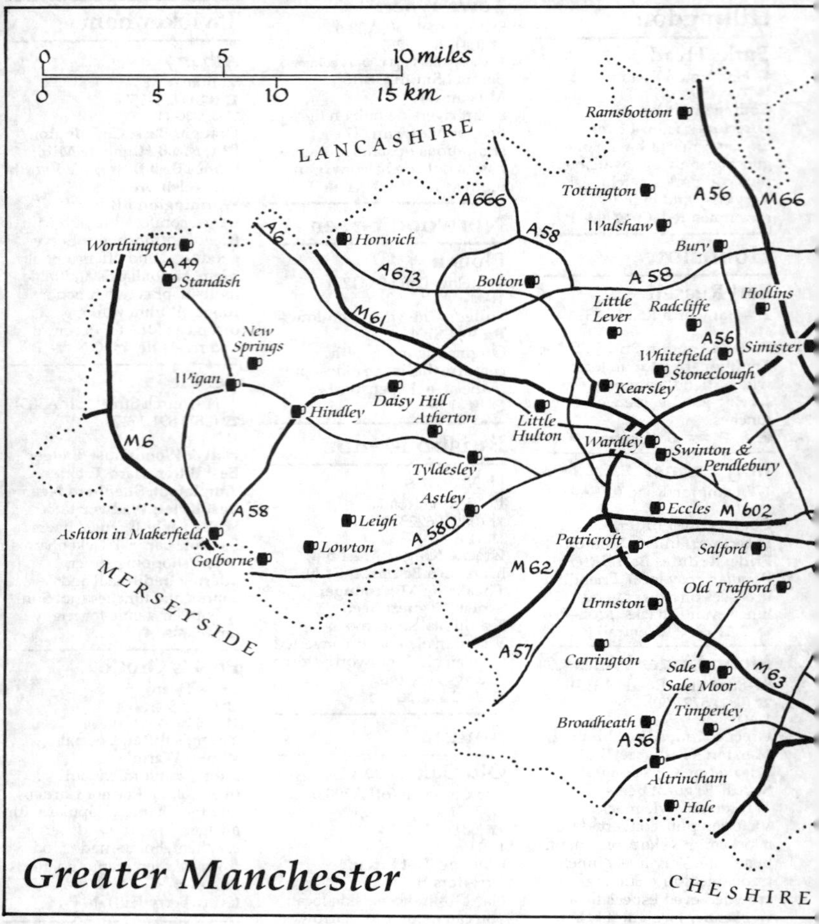

Hydes' Anvil, *Manchester;* **Holt,** *Cheetham;* **Lees,** *Middleton Junction;* **Thomas McGuinness,** *Rochdale;* **Oak,** *Heywood;* **Robinson's,** *Stockport;* **West Coast,** *Chorlton-on-Medlock*

Altrincham

Bakers Arms

Pownall Road ☎ (061) 928 1411
11.30–11
Hydes' Anvil Mild, Bitter Ⓔ
Modern pub next to Sainbury's: a large lively vault in the only Hydes' pub in Altrincham. ☾ ⊞ ⇌ ⊖ ♣ P

Malt Shovels

68 Stamford Street
☎ (061) 928 2053
12–3 (4 Sat), 5 (7 Sat)–11 (12–11 Fri)
Samuel Smith OBB, Museum Ⓗ
Friendly town pub with live jazz almost every night. Stands between the former sites of Altrincham's only brewery (Richardson & Goodall) and maltings. No food Sun. ☾ ♿ ⇌ ⊖ ♣

Orange Tree

Old Market Place (A56)
☎ (061) 928 2600
11–11
Courage Directors; Ruddles Best Bitter; Wilson's Bitter; guest beer Ⓗ
Once the smallest pub in Altrincham, where, in 1823, a man sold his wife for 1/6d. The present building dates from 1880. Note the old photos showing local pubs now gone. Independent guest beer policy. No eve meals Sun.
Q ♨ ☾ ◗ ⇌ ⊖ ♣ ⊬

Tatton Arms

3–5 Tipping Street (near Sainsbury's) ☎ (061) 941 2502
11–11
Whitbread Boddingtons Bitter Ⓗ
Thriving, refurbished two-room local. Pictures reflect the landlord's nautical background and interests.
❀ ☾ ⊞ ♿ ⇌ ⊖ ♣ P

Greater Manchester

pub close to Daisy Nook
Country Park. Tempting
menu. ⊠ ❀ ◖ P

Heroes of Waterloo
Mossley Road
☎ (061) 330 2181
11–3, 5–11
John Smith's Bitter Ⓗ**; guest
beers**
Pub standing alone, facing
open country and a wall of the
former Ladysmith barracks
(listed). Open-plan lounge
with army cartoons; popular
beer garden. Q ⊠ ❀ ◖ P

Oddfellows Arms
Kings Road, Hurst
☎ (061) 330 6356
12–11
**Robinson's Best Mild, Best
Bitter** Ⓗ
In the same family since 1914:
a cosy, many-roomed pub
with traditional features.
Holds a *Loo of the Year* award!
The walled water garden with
Koi carp hosts barbecue
nights. Q ❀ ◖ ⊞ ✚ ⅟

Witchwood
Old Street
☎ (061) 344 0321
11.30–3, 5.30–11 (11–11 Fri & Sat; late
licence Thu–Sat in concert room)
**Banks's Bitter; Holt Bitter;
Marston's Pedigree; Old Mill
Bullion; S&N Theakston XB;
Whitbread Boddingtons
Bitter** Ⓗ**; guest beers**
Popular pub in a quiet part of
town. Thriving concert room –
a premier suburban venue for
various bands. Good lunches.
◖ ⇌ P

Astley

Cart & Horses
221 Manchester Road
☎ (0942) 870751
12–11
Holt Mild, Bitter Ⓗ
Pub with a smart, large, open-
plan lounge, a standing area in
front of the bar, a separate tap
room and a raised no-smoking
area. Children welcome until
8pm. ⊠ ❀ ◖ ⊞ ✚ P ⅟

Atherton

Atherton Arms
6 Tyldesly Road
11–11
Holt Mild, Bitter Ⓗ
An immense, comfortable
lounge and a tap room
sporting a full-size snooker
table. A hall drinking area is
served by a small bar.
Function room. ⊞ ⅊ ⇌ ✚ P

Bay Horse
30 Bolton Old Road
11–11
**Tetley Walker Dark Mild,
Bitter** Ⓗ

Ancoats

Jolly Angler
47 Ducie Street (between A665
and A6) ☎ (061) 236 5307
11–4, 5.30–11 (11–11 Fri & Sat)
Hydes' Anvil Mild, Bitter Ⓗ
Excellent, welcoming, friendly
basic boozer; superb local
atmosphere. Live folk music
Mon and Thu.
♨ ⇌ (Piccadilly) ⊖ ✚

White House
122 Great Ancoats Street
☎ (061) 228 3231
**Coach House Coachman's
Best Bitter, Innkeeper's
Special Reserve; Holt
Bitter** Ⓗ**; guest beer**
(occasionally)
Comfortable, friendly pub
near Ashton and Rochdale
Canals, yet convenient for the
city centre. ❀ ◖ ⊞ ⅊
⇌ (Piccadilly) ⊖ ✚

Ashton in Makerfield

Eagle & Child
233 Heath Road (off A49)
☎ (0942) 726421
12–3.30, 7–11 (12–11 summer Sat)
**Greenalls Mild, Bitter,
Thomas Greenall's Bitter** Ⓗ
Friendly local just out of the
town centre, near Haydock
Park racecourse. Fine display
of plates. ❀ ▶ ⅊ ✚

Ashton-under-Lyne

Dog & Pheasant
528 Oldham Road
☎ (061) 330 4894
12–4.30, 7–11
**Marston's Mercian Mild,
Burton Best Bitter, Merrie
Monk, Pedigree** Ⓗ
Hospitable and comfortable

203

Greater Manchester

Large corner pub with a spacious, high-ceilinged lounge, a rear pool room and a tap room. 🏠 🍴 ⇌ ♣ P

Beswick

Britannia
2 Rowsley Street (off A662)
☎ (061) 223 1604
12–11
Lees GB Mild, Bitter Ⓗ
Welcoming, classic side-street local which continues to prosper despite a depressed local economy and a new threat from Manchester's dreams of Olympic glory. The vault has TV, darts, panelled seating and many trophies; a quieter lounge has a pool table. No food Sun. ❀ 🍴 🍴 ♣

Blackley

Pleasant
390 Chapel Lane (off A6104)
1 (12 Sat)–11
Robinson's Best Mild, Best Bitter Ⓗ, **Old Tom** (winter) Ⓖ
Small community pub with a vault, lounge and golf society club room. On the edge of 18th-century Crab village.
Q ❀ ♣

Bolton

Ainsworth Arms
606 Halliwell Road
(A6099/A58 jct)
☎ (0204) 40671
11.30–3, 5.30–11 (11–11 Sat)
Ind Coope Burton Ale; Walker Mild, Best Bitter, Winter Warmer Ⓗ
Warm, friendly pub attracting a range of customers. 🍴 ♣

Anchor Inn
14–16 Union Buildings
☎ (0204) 26467
11–11 (12–5, 7–11.30 Sat)
Draught Bass Ⓗ
Tastefully renovated (1987) with a ship theme. A locals' pub. 🍴 ⇌

Clifton Arms
94 Newport Street (opp. bus/rail interchange)
☎ (0204) 392738
11–11 (11–3, 7–11 Sat)
Jennings Bitter; Moorhouse's Premier; Tetley Walker Mild, Bitter, Walker Best Bitter Ⓗ
Comfortable, homely town-centre local which has kept its character despite refurbishment. Quiz night every Wed. No food Sun. Regular mini beer festivals. 🍴 ⇌ ♣

Doffcocker
780 Chorley Old Road (follow B6226 from centre, signed Horwich) ☎ (0204) 43656
12–3 (4 Sat), 7–11
Walker Mild, Best Bitter, Winter Warmer Ⓗ

Originally a Calender pub, now tastefully refurbished to consist of a games room and a lounge. Relaxed. ❀ 🍴 P

Dog & Partridge
Manor Street
☎ (0204) 388596
12–2.30 (11.30–4 Sat), 7–11 (closed Sun lunch)
Thwaites Bitter Ⓗ
Well-run, town-centre local, one of few not to have dress restrictions. 🍴 ⇌ ♣

Howcroft Inn
Pool Street
☎ (0204) 26814
12–4 (5 Sat), 5.30, (7 Sat & winter)–11
Walker Mild, Best Bitter Ⓗ
Excellent, old-fashioned, back-street local just outside the town centre: a vault, a snug and two other rooms. A former CAMRA award-winner for the *Best Refurbishment* of an urban pub. Bowling green. 🏠 ❀ ♣ P

Kings Head
52–54 Junction Road, Deane (off A58)
☎ (0204) 62609
12–3, 5.30–11 (may vary)
Walker Mild, Bitter, Best Bitter Ⓗ
Grade II listed building, mainly 18th century but refurbished in 1991. Known locally as the 'Strawberry Gardens'. Busy bowling green in summer. ❀ 🍴 ♣ P

Lodge Bank Tavern
264 Bridgeman Street
12–11
Lees GB Mild, Bitter Ⓗ
Large, Victorian, brick pub standing alone by Bobby Heywood's park. A cheerful locals' pub. ❀ ♿ ♣ P

Maxim's
28 Bradshawgate
☎ (0204) 23486
11.30–4, 7.30–11 (closed Sun)
Vaux Samson Ⓗ; **guest beers**
Large modernised, town-centre pub. An upstairs function room doubles as a disco. Children welcome lunchtimes; cellar visits available when quiet. Weekly-changed guest beers from small breweries. Smart dress at weekends, when it is crowded and noisy. 🍴 ♿ ⇌

Sweet Green Tavern
Crook Street
☎ (0204) 392258
11–3, 6.30–11 (11.30–11 Thu & Fri)
Hydes' Anvil Bitter; Tetley Walker Mild, Bitter Ⓗ
Excellent town-centre local near bus/rail stations. Multi-roomed layout; no dress restrictions. Very popular prior to BWFC home matches.
Q ❀ 🍴 ⇌ ♣ P

Bredbury

Arden Arms
Ashton Road
11.30–3 (4 if busy), 5.30–11 (11.30–11 Fri & Sat)
Robinson's Best Mild, Best Bitter Ⓔ
One of the few traditional Robinson's pubs left. Small individual rooms contribute to the comfortable and intimate atmosphere. In a semi-rural location. Q ❀ P

Rising Sun
57 Stockport Road
11.30–3, 5.30–11
Holt Bitter; Webster's Yorkshire Bitter, Wilson's Mild, Bitter Ⓗ
Thriving, end-of-terrace local with a good games room. Low ceilings hold in a cosy atmosphere. ❀ 🍴 ⇌

Broadheath

Railway Inn
153 Manchester Road (A56)
11–11 (11–3, 7–11 Sat)
Whitbread Boddingtons Bitter Ⓗ
Unspoilt, small terraced pub by a railway bridge. A corridor to the bar divides two rooms named after Manchester's mainline stations (Victoria and Piccadilly); there is also a room named Waterloo!
🍴 ⇌ (Navigation Rd) ⊖ ♣

Bury

Dusty Miller
87 Crostons Road (B6213/B6214 jct)
☎ (061) 764 1124
12–3, 7–11
Moorhouse's Black Cat Mild, Premier, Pendle Witches Brew, Owd Ale; John Smith's Bitter Ⓗ
Moorhouse's second tied pub, small but comfortable.
❀ 🍴 🍴 ♣

Old Blue Bell
Bell Lane
☎ (061) 761 3674
12–11 (12–4.30, 7–11 Sat)
Holt Mild, Bitter Ⓗ
Extensive, multi-roomed pub, acquired by Holt and tastefully refurbished. Live music Thu eves. A former Star brewery house. 🍴 ♣

Rose & Crown
36 Manchester Old Road
☎ (061) 764 6461
12–3, 7 (5 Fri)–11 (12–11 Sat)
Butterknowle Conciliation Ale; Moorhouse's Pendle Witches Brew; Thwaites Best Mild, Bitter; Whitbread Boddingtons Bitter Ⓗ; **guest beers**

A short walk from the town centre, an end-of-terrace pub featuring a range of beers unequalled in Bury. May become a Tap & Spile. Children welcome until 7pm.
🏚 ☧ ⊖ ✦ ♲

Carrington

Windmill Inn
Manchester Road (A6144)
☎ (061) 774 2251
11.30–3 (4 Sat), 5 (7 Sat)–11 (11.30–11 Fri)
Samuel Smith OBB Ⓗ
Former 18th-century coaching house with a low-ceilinged but now open-plan interior. Opposite an industrial complex. Lunches weekdays.
✿ ☖ ⊞ ₤ ♣ P

Chadderton

Horton Arms
19 Streetbridge
☎ (061) 624 7793
11–11
Lees GB Mild, Bitter Ⓗ
Smart roadside pub under a motorway bridge. Open-plan, but several distinct drinking areas create a varied and pleasant atmosphere. No food weekends. ✿ ☖ ₤ P

Rifle Range Inn
372 Burnley Lane
☎ (061) 624 0874
11.30–3 (4 Sat), 5 (7 Sat)–11
Lees GB Mild, Bitter Ⓗ
Popular, four-roomed detached local near Oldham Athletic football ground. Sporting and musical interests dominate. No food Sun. ☖ ◗ P

Cheadle

Printers Arms
220 Stockport Road (A560)
☎ (061) 491 1448
11–11 (11–3, 6.30–11 Sat)
Robinson's Best Mild, Best Bitter Ⓔ
An underway refurbishment should retain the character of this busy, family-run local. Weekday lunches.
✿ ☖ ⊞ ♣ P

Queens Arms
177 Stockport Road (A560)
☎ (061) 428 3081
11.45–11 (12–4, 6–11 Sat)
Robinson's Best Mild, Bitter Ⓗ
Traditional, multi-roomed pub, busy at lunchtimes with workers from nearby offices. The garden includes a children's play area (children welcome inside until 7.30). The only Stockport outlet for Robinson's rare ordinary bitter. No food weekends.
🏚 🏚 ✿ ☖ ♣ P

Cheadle Hulme

Cheadle Hulme
47 Station Road (A5149)
☎ (061) 485 4706
11–11 (11–3, 7–11 Sat)
Holt Mild, Bitter Ⓗ
Totally renovated in 1989, this is anything but a traditional Holt house. Despite the move upmarket, they maintained their low price policy. Restaurant open till 4pm Sun; pub lunches Mon–Fri.
✿ ☖ ≒ P

Church
90 Ravenoak Road (A5149)
☎ (061) 485 1897
11–3, 5–11 (11–11 Fri & Sat)
Robinson's Best Mild, Best Bitter Ⓗ
Attractive, cottage-style pub, with an unspoilt, multi-roomed interior and a lively atmosphere. Eve meals served 5–7.30.
🏚 Q ✿ ☖ ◗ ⊞ ≒ ♣ P

Cheetham

Queens Arms
4–6 Honey Street
☎ (061) 834 4239
Bateman Mild, XB, XXXB, Victory; Taylor Best Bitter, Landlord Ⓗ; guest beers
A rare example of an Empress brewery tiled facade. Belgian bottled beers available plus five guest ales. A large garden overlooks the Irk valley. 🏚 ✿ ☖ ≒ (Victoria) ⊖ ♣ ♲

Chorlton-on-Medlock

King's Arms
4a Helmshore Walk (off A6 at Ardwick Green; follow Cale St, Skerry Close)
☎ (061) 273 1053
11–11
West Coast Mild, Best Bitter, Porter, Yakima Grande PA, Ginger Beer, Extra Special Ⓗ; guest beers
Still showcasing the superb West Coast beers brewed on site (look for one-off brews), now also has a wide bottled range (mainly Belgian) and occasional guest beers. Music Mon (Irish), alternate Tue (R&B) and Thu (singers' night). An essential call. No food Sun.
☖ ≒ (Piccadilly) ⊖ ♣ ♲ P

Clayton

Strawberry Duck
74 Crabtree Lane (off A662)
☎ (061) 223 4415
11.30–11 (11.30–4.30, 7–11 Sat)
Holt Mild, Bitter; Whitbread Boddingtons Bitter Ⓗ; guest beers

Welcoming, well-run free house standing by lock 13 of the Ashton Canal. Recently refurbished and extended in a manner to put most brewery schemes to shame. Lunches weekdays. 🏚 ☖ ⊞ ♣ P

Compstall

Andrew Arms
George Street ☎ (061) 430 2806
11.30–11 (11.30–3, 5–11 Mon & Wed)
Robinson's Best Mild, Best Bitter Ⓗ
Pub which pleases all who visit. Open fire in the winter in a comfortable lounge and a separate vault for TV fans and card-players. Handy for visitors to Etherow Country Park. 🏚 ✿ ☖ ◗ ♣ P

Daisy Hill

Rose Hill Tavern
321 Leigh Road, West-houghton ☎ (0942) 815529
12–11 (12–4, 7–11 Sat)
Holt Mild, Bitter Ⓗ
Large, comfortable local, undergoing extension. Busy at weekends. ≒ P

Delph

Royal Oak Inn (Th' Heights)
Broad Lane, Heights (above Delph, 1 mile off Denshaw Rd) OS982090 ☎ (0457) 874460
7–11
Whitbread Chester's Mild, Boddingtons Bitter Ⓗ; guest beers
Isolated 250-year-old stone pub on an historic packhorse route overlooking the Tame valley. A cosy bar and three separate rooms. Good home-cooked food. 🏚 Q ✿ ◗ ♣ P

Denton

Dog & Partridge
148 Ashton Road
12.30–11
Robinson's Best Mild, Bitter, Best Bitter Ⓗ
Surprisingly large, multi-roomed, end-of-terrace, town pub with a friendly atmosphere. Unashamedly a locals' house. Q ⊞ ♣

Red Lion Hotel
1 Stockport Road, Crown Pt
☎ (061) 336 2066
11–11 (11–4, 7–11 Sat)
Hydes' Anvil Mild, Light, Bitter Ⓔ
Prominent, red-brick, Victorian-style, town-centre local. A spacious interior, divided into four open rooms, caters for all. Warm and friendly, but can be busy. Weekday lunches. Q ☖ ≒

Greater Manchester

Diggle

Diggle Hotel
Station Houses (off A670, via
Huddersfield Rd)
☎ (0457) 872741
12–3, 7–11 (12–11 Sat)
**Taylor Golden Best,
Landlord; Whitbread OB
Mild, Boddingtons Bitter, OB
Bitter** H
Family-run stone pub in a
pleasant hamlet, dating back
to the 18th century. A well-
kept bar area and two rooms,
often visited by morrismen in
summer. Accent on home-
cooked food (served all day
Sat). ☎ ✿ 🖼 ◑ 🍴 ♿ P

Dukinfield

Lamb Inn
103 Crescent Road
☎ (061) 330 4944
11–11
**Whitbread Boddingtons
Bitter** H
Well cared-for and popular
pub with a good vault and a
comfortable lounge. Hand-
some red brick exterior with
Dutch gables. ✿ ◑ ♣ P

Eccles

Crown & Volunteer
171 Church Street
11.30–5, 7–11
Holt Mild, Bitter H
Cosy two-roomed community
pub saved from demolition by
local CAMRA activists. The
interior takes you back to the
1930s. 🍴 ♣

Lamb Hotel
33 Regent Street
11–11 (11–5, 7–11 Sat)
Holt Mild, Bitter H
Recently redecorated but
unchanged, four-roomed
Edwardian pub of great
character. Superb curved
mahogany bar with etched-
glass. Full-size snooker table
in the billiard room. A good
starting point for a crawl of
the 12 Holt pubs of Eccles/
Patricroft. Q 🍴 🍴 ≠ ♣ P

Stanley Arms
295 Liverpool Road, Patricroft
(A57) ☎ (061) 788 8801
12–11 (11–11 Sat)
Holt Mild, Bitter H
Lively street-corner local with
a small front vault, a separate
piano room and a games room
at the back. Lunchtime snacks.
🎵 Q 🍴 ≠ ♣

Golborne

Horns Inn
Lowton Road ☎ (0942) 724760
12–4, 7–11 (11–11 Fri & Sat in
summer)
Greenalls Mild, Bitter; Stones

Best Bitter H
Roadside local with a
comfortable main lounge and
a second lounge away from
the bar. The tap room is a
recent addition. Children
welcome until 8pm.
🍴 ✿ 🖼 ◑ 🍴 ♣ P

Mill Stone Inn
Harvey Lane ☎ (0942) 728031
12–11
**Greenalls Mild, Bitter; Stones
Best Bitter** H
Locals' pub off the town
centre, close to Haydock Park.
Separate tap room and two
comfy lounges. Vast collection
of brass ornaments. Weekday
lunches; eve meals on request.
Children welcome until 8pm.
🍴 ◑ 🍴 ♣ P

Gorton

Waggon & Horses
736 Hyde Road (A57)
11–11
Holt Mild, Bitter H
Well-modernised main road
pub where the one-room
layout accommodates four
very distinct areas. Low prices
and high quality make it the
area's busiest pub. Visit in mid
Sept for the local morris side's
Rushcart Ceremony – a
bibulous day of dance and
music. ≠ (Ryder Brow) ♣ P

Hale

Railway
Ashley Road (opp. station)
☎ (061) 941 5367
11–11
**Robinson's Best Mild, Best
Bitter, Old Tom** (winter) H
Comfortable multi-roomed
pub. Families welcome in the
snug at lunch and early eve.
Q 🍴 ✿ 🍴 ≠ 🍴 P

Hazel Grove

Three Tunnes
194 London Road (A6)
☎ (061) 483 3563
11–11
**Robinson's Best Mild, Best
Bitter** H
Traditional, busy, former
Bell's house with six separate
drinking areas. Weekday
lunches. ✿ ◑ ≠ ♣ P

Heald Green

Griffin
124 Wilmslow Road (A34)
☎ (061) 437 1596
11–11
Holt Mild, Bitter E
Thriving large estate pub with
three rooms and an
enthusiastic local following.
The interior is plain but
comfortable; quiet snug. Prices
keen for suburban Stockport.
Weekday lunches. Q ◑ 🍴 P

Heaton Mersey

Griffin
552 Didsbury Road (A5145)
☎ (061) 432 2824
12–11
Holt Mild, Bitter H
Multi-roomed local with a
classic mahogany bar. Sells the
cheapest beer in the area so
not surprisingly is often very
busy. Currently being
extended. No food weekends.
Q ✿ ◑ ≠ (E Didsbury) P

Heaton Norris

Nursery
Green Lane (off A6)
☎ (061) 432 2044
11.30–3, 5.30–11 (11.30–11 Sat &
bank hols)
Hydes' Anvil Mild, Bitter E
Large, comfortable 1930s pub,
hidden away in a pleasant
suburban area. Traditional
layout: vault, smoke room,
lobby and lounge with fine
wood panelling. Immaculate
bowling green. Children
admitted Mon–Fri lunch, if
dining. Limited menu Sat; no
food Sun. Q ✿ ◑ 🍴 ♣ P

Heywood

Wishing Well
York Street ☎ (0706) 365673
11–11
Taylor Landlord H**; guest
beers**
Welcoming, many-roomed
free house with an interesting
tiled entrance hall. Heavy rock
Sun. Cheap accommodation
and lunches.
Q 🍴 ✿ 🖼 ◑ 🍴 ♣ P

Hindley

Edington Arms
186 Ladies Lane (1/2 mile N of
A58) ☎ (0942) 59229
12–11
**Holt Mild, Bitter; Tetley
Walker Dark Mild, Bitter** H**;
guest beers**
Recently refurbished pub that
has become immensely
popular with beer drinkers.
Several guest beers; the
brewer of the house beer is a
closely-guarded secret.
✿ ♿ ≠

Ellesmere Inn
32 Lancaster Road (100 yds S
of A58) ☎ (0942) 56922
11.30–4.30, 6.45–11
Burtonwood Mild, Bitter H
Friendly, two-roomed local
with a very good atmosphere.
Q 🍴 ≠ ♣

Hollins

Hollins Bush Inn
257 Hollins Lane
☎ (061) 766 6596

206

12–3, 6–11 (12–11 Fri & Sat)
Lees GB Mild, Bitter Ⓔ
Busy three-roomed pub; an
extremely friendly local.
🐦 ✿ ◖▮ P

Hollinwood

Bridgewater
197 Manchester Road
11.30–11 (11.30–3, 7–11 Sat)
Holt Mild, Bitter Ⓗ
Holt's 100th tied house, newly
built, tastefully decorated and
often very busy. Excellent
value for the area. Good social
feel, but can be smoky. Bar
snacks served. ✿ ▮ ᕀ ♣ P

Horwich

Toll Bar
2 Chorley New Road
(A673/B5238 jct)
12–3 (not Mon–Fri), 7–11
Thwaites Mild, Bitter Ⓗ
Home of the Horwich morris
men; also hosts a club
Mon. Handy for walks.
🚶 Q 🐦 ▮ ♣ P

Hyde

White Lion
Clarendon Place
12–3 (4 Sat), 6.30 (6 Sat)–11
**Robinson's Best Mild, Best
Bitter** Ⓔ, **Old Tom** Ⓗ
Former Kays' Atlas brewery
town-centre pub, much used
on market days. The main
room has been badly
'Robinsonised' and superb
tilework outside painted over.
The public bar, however, is
unspoilt and retains a fine,
long wooden bar.
▮ ⇌ (Central/Newton) ♣

Kearsley

Clock Face
65 Old Hall Street (off A5082)
11–3.30, 5 (7 Sat)–11
Tetley Walker Mild, Bitter Ⓗ
Excellent, unspoilt ale house
with a loyal clientele and long-
serving landlord.
▮ ⇌ (Farnworth) ♣

Leigh

Eagle & Hawk
78 Chapel Street
☎ (0942) 606600
11.30–3.30, 7–11
**Walker Mild, Bitter, Best
Bitter** Ⓗ
Huge, open-plan pub served
by a horseshoe-shaped bar.
Several drinking areas,
popular at weekends. Award-
winning landlord. ✿ ◖♣ P

Victoria
68–70 Kirkhall Lane
12–4, 7–11 (12–11 Sat)
**Tetley Walker Dark Mild,
Bitter** Ⓗ
Excellent, end-of-terrace town

local: a keen sporting pub. The
closest pub to Leigh RL
ground. 🚶 🐦 ▮ ▮ ♣

Levenshulme

Sidings
Broom Lane (B6178, off A6)
☎ (061) 257 2084
12–11
Holt Mild, Bitter Ⓗ
Highly commended as a new
pub in 1988: a large, two-part
lounge and a games-playing
vault. Busy, friendly and
cheap. ✿ ◖▮ ⇌ ♣ P

Littleborough

Queens
Church Street
☎ (0706) 379394
12–3.30, 6 (7 Sat)–11 (12–11 Fri)
Thwaites Best Mild, Bitter Ⓗ
Popular, friendly pub in the
centre of 'the village'. Eve
meals finish early.
✿ ◖▮ ⇌ ♣

Little Hulton

Dun Mare
277 Manchester Road West
(A6, 1/2 mile from centre)
12–4 (5 Sat), 7–11
Walker Mild, Best Bitter Ⓗ
Fine example of a refurbished
Walker outlet, very popular
with locals. Q ✿ ▮ ♣ P

Little Lever

Horse Shoe
Lever Street
☎ (0204) 72081
11–3, 7–11
Hydes' Anvil Mild, Bitter Ⓔ
Busy, friendly, unspoilt two-
roomed ale house. ▮ ♣

Lowton

Red Lion
324 Newton Road (A579, off
A580)
☎ (0942) 671429
11.30–3.30, 5.30–11 (11.30–11 Sat;
12–10.30 Sun food licence)
**Greenalls Mild, Bitter,
Thomas Greenall's Bitter;
Stones Best Bitter** Ⓗ
Large smart pub with a
restaurant and conservatory.
Bowling green open in
summer. ✿ 🛏 ◖▮ ▮ & ♣ P

Manchester City Centre

Beerhouse
6 Angel Street (off A664)
☎ (061) 839 7019
11.30–11
**Courage Directors; Taylor
Landlord; Thwaites Best
Bitter; West Coast Best Bitter,
Guiltless Stout, Extra
Special** Ⓗ
Over 15 handpumped and 150

bottled beers available. Basic
surroundings.
◖⇌ (Victoria) ⊖ ⌣

Castle Hotel
66 Oldham Street
11.30–5.30 (4.30 Sat), 7.30 (8 Sat)–11
(12–3, 7.30–10.30 Sun)
**Robinson's Best Mild, Bitter,
Best Bitter, Old Tom** Ⓗ
Untouched Victorian
beerhouse and Robinson's
only city-centre outlet.
Friendly locals' bar at the
front; quieter parlour behind.
Separate games room.
Q 🐦 ▮ ⇌ (Piccadilly)
⊖ (Piccadilly Gdns)

Circus
86 Portland Street
12–11 (may vary and close weekend
eves)
Tetley Walker Bitter Ⓗ
A remarkable pub: a tiny bar
and two small, simply-
furnished rooms. No frills, no
jukebox, no draught lager. A
totally unspoilt survivor.
Q ⇌ (Piccadilly) ⊖

City Arms
48 Kennedy Street
☎ (061) 236 4610
11–11 (closed Sun & bank hols)
**Ind Coope Burton Ale;
Jennings Bitter; Moorhouse's
Premier, Pendle Witches
Brew; Tetley Walker Bitter** Ⓗ
The 18th-century, former
meeting rooms for city
councillors, now frequented
by office workers.
◖▮ ⇌ (Oxford Rd) ⊖ (St
Peters Sq) ♣

Crown & Cushion
192 Corporation Street
☎ (061) 839 1844
11.30–11 (11.30–4, 7–11 Sat)
Holt Mild, Bitter Ⓗ
A transformation – formerly
owned by Whitbread and
often empty. Holt bought it in
1989, tastefully refurbished it
and the pub hasn't looked
back. ◖▮ ⇌ (Victoria) ⊖

Dutton Hotel
Park Street
☎ (061) 834 4508
11–11
Hydes' Anvil Mild, Bitter Ⓔ
Situated between Strangeways
brewery and Strangeways
prison. An unusually-shaped
pub, owing to an acute corner
location, but welcoming. Bar
snacks.
▮ & ⇌ (Victoria) ⊖ ♣

Grey Horse
80 Portland Street
11.30–5, 7 (7 Sat)–11 (closed Sun)
Hydes' Anvil Mild, Bitter Ⓔ
The second smallest pub in the
city, in the same hands for
many years. The beer is good
value. Handy for Chinatown.
⇌ (Piccadilly)
⊖ (Piccadilly/Moseley St)

Greater Manchester

Peveril of the Peak
127 Great Bridgwater Street
12–3 (not Sat), 5.30 (7 Sat)–11 (closed Sun)
Ruddles Best Bitter, County; Webster's Yorkshire Bitter, Wilson's Bitter H
Named after a famous stage coach: a classic pub, triangular in shape. Look for the exterior tiling, and the stained-glass interior. Ceilidh nights during the week. Popular with students. Opens Sat lunch if United are at home.
⚲ ⊟ ≥ (Oxford Rd) ⊖ (G Mex/St Peters Sq) ♣

Vine
38 Kennedy Street
☎ (061) 236 3943
11.30–11 (11.30–3, 7–11 Sat; closed Sun eve)
Courage Directors; John Smith's Bitter; Whitbread Boddingtons Bitter H
Busy pub with a listed original exterior. The basement makes a cosy eatery (meals Mon–Fri) and function room. ⊄ ≥ (Oxford Rd) ⊖ (St Peters Sq)

Marple

Bowling Green
Stockport Road
11.30–11
Holt Bitter; John Smith's Magnet; Webster's Yorkshire Bitter, Wilson's Mild H
Not a place for fainthearts or aesthetes: usually very busy and lively. Look out for the ladies' darts team and the inescapable karaoke.
⚶ ⊟ ≥ (Rose Hill) ♣

Crown Inn
Hawk Green Road (off Upper Hibbert Lane)
☎ (061) 427 2678
11–3, 5.30–11 (11–11 Sat & Sun)
Robinson's Best Mild, Best Bitter H
Originally a farmers' pub, now mostly a haunt of the young. Strong accent on food.
⚶ ⊄ ▶ & P

Hatters Arms
Church Lane
☎ (061) 427 1529
11–3, 5.30–11 (12–2, 7.30–10.30 Sun)
Robinson's Best Mild, Best Bitter H
A last refuge for traditional pub lovers: a tiny, terrace-end local with a legendary landlady, lovely bar panelling and separate rooms. Pity about the jukebox. ⊟ ♣

Romper
Ridge End (Marple–Disley road) ☎ (061) 427 1354
12–2 (2.30 Sat), 6.30–11 (12–2.30, 7–10.30 Sun)
S&N Theakston Old Peculier; Taylor Landlord; Wadworth 6X H; **guest beer**
Longtime haunt of the Cheshire set, now giving beer the same prominence as its well-known food. Tucked on a bend of the road with the Dark Peak on one side, its neon sign illuminates the Cheshire Plain on the other: a setting now threatened by a new road. ⚶ ⊄ ▶ P

Middleton

Brunswick
122 Oldham Road
12–3 (not Wed), 7–11 (12–11 Fri & Sat)
Ind Coope Burton Ale; Tetley Walker Bitter; West Coast Best Bitter H; **guest beers**
Boisterous, three-roomed corner local. Bikers and loud rock music predominate but all types are found within. ⚶

Crown Inn
52 Rochdale Road
11.30–11
Lees GB Mild, Bitter E
Incredibly busy end-terraced, two-roomed local. A large, comfortable brass-hung lounge complements the small snug-cum-darts room. Note the dispense system now seen in few Lees pubs. ♣ P

Tandle Hill Tavern
14 Thornham Lane, Slattocks
OS898091
☎ (0706) 345297
12–3 (not Mon–Fri in winter, and sometimes summer), 7 (7.30 winter)–11
Lees Bitter H, **Moonraker** E
Pub set among farm buildings down an unmetalled, unlit track, one mile from A671 or A664. A welcoming, cosy, two-roomed hostelry with a keen quiz room. The base for the annual CAMRA branch 10km run. Children welcome in the darts room. Snacks. ⚲

Milnrow

Waggon Inn
Butterworth Hall
11–11
Burtonwood Mild, Bitter H
Attractive, friendly, 18th-century local just off the main street. ⊠ ⚶ ≥ ♣ P

Mossley

Tollemache
415 Manchester Road
☎ (0457) 832354
11–3, 5–11
Robinson's Best Mild, Best Bitter H
Popular, cosy and friendly, this stone local stands close to countryside on the edge of Mossley. The garden overlooks the Huddersfield Narrow Canal. Small oak-panelled rooms; polished wood bar. ⚲ Q ⚶ ⊄ ▶ ♣ P

Moston

Dean Brook Inn
St Mary's Road (off Oldham road) ☎ (061) 682 4730
11.30–11 (11.30–4, 7–11 Sat)
Marston's Border Mild, Burton Best Bitter, Pedigree H
Friendly regulars' pub converted from six terraced cottages. A central bar and three drinking areas, plus a games room.
⚶ ⊄ ≥ (Dean Lane) ♣ P

Newhey

Bird in the Hand (Top Bird)
113 Huddersfield Road (A640)
11.30–3, 5–11 (11.30–11 Sat)
Samuel Smith OBB H
Small, friendly pub, one of the few traditional Sam's pubs in the area. Q ≥ ♣ P

New Springs

Colliers Arms
Wigan Road (B5238, near canal) ☎ (0942) 831171
12.30–5.30, 7.30–11
Burtonwood Mild, Bitter H
Superb 18th-century pub, stone-built, with later rendering in mock Tudor style. Note the beams. Warm welcome. ⚲ Q ⊟ ♣ P

Oldham

Beer Emporium
92 Union Street
12–3 (not Tue), 5 (7 Tue)–11 (12–11 Sat)
S&N Theakston XB, Old Peculier; Taylor Landlord; West Coast Best Bitter H; **guest beers**
Popular town-centre free house with the widest beer choice in Oldham: five ever-changing guest beers (normally including a mild). Foreign bottled beers and various ciders.
≥ (Mumps) ♣ ⌂

Bridge Inn
31 Moorhey Street (30 yds off A669) ☎ (061) 624 8626
11–11
Lees GB Mild, Bitter E
Street-corner local with a friendly welcome. Note the stained-glass sign behind the bar. ⚶ & ≥ (Mumps) ♣ P

Dog & Duck
25 St Domingo Street
11–11
Banks's Mild, Bitter E
Detached, red-brick, three-storey town-centre pub, tastefully refurbished, despite a mainly open-plan layout. Timber fireplace (gas fire); black and white photographs

on the walls. Irish music on the jukebox; live folk band weekends. Separate pool room.

⇌ (Werneth/Mumps) ♣

Dog & Partridge

376 Roundthorn Road, Roundthorn (off B6194)
7 (12 Sat)–11
Lees GB Mild, Bitter Ⓔ
Welcoming, half-timbered, three-roomed village local dating back to 1780. The interior has beams, brasses and leaded-glass over the bar. Timber ceiling in the 'Mayor's Parlour' (children welcome). Traditionally, the pub is used whenever the Mayor of Roundthorn is elected.
Q ⭫ ⊛ ♣ P

Gardeners Arms

Dunham Street/Waterhead
☎ (061) 624 0242
11.30–11 (11.30–5, 7–11 Sat)
Robinson's Best Mild, Best Bitter Ⓗ
Popular, detached, three-roomed local with a fine combination of brasses, leaded windows and tiles in the bar area. Live entertainment Sat. Weekday lunches.
⭫ ⊛ ◑ ♣ P

Old Trafford

Tollgate

Seymour Grove
☎ (061) 873 8213
11–11 (11–3, 7–11 Sat when United are at home)
Banks's Mild, Bitter Ⓔ
Built in 1986 on the site of the original Trafford toll bar, a comfortable pub with much incongruous Victoriana, including a stage coach and passenger in a bell tower! Convenient for MUFC and Lancashire CC. No food weekends.
◑ ⌖ & ⊖ (Trafford Bar) ♣ P

Openshaw

Concert

13 Fairfield Road, Higher Openshaw (off A635, Ashton old rd) ☎ (061) 371 8013
11–11
Whitbread Boddingtons Bitter Ⓗ
Pub where the recent renovation avoided earlier mistakes: still one of the few genuine and atmospheric pubs in the area. Attractive etched-glass. Lively locals.
⌖ ⇌ (Gorton) ♣

Patricroft

Grapes

439 Liverpool Road, Peel Green ☎ (061) 789 6971
11–11 (11–4.30, 7–11 Sat)
Holt Mild, Bitter Ⓗ

Classic Edwardian Holt pub with a vault. Bar parlour, smoke room and billiard room (now with pool tables).
⭫ ⌖ ⇌ ♣ P

Radcliffe

Masons Arms

Sion Street
☎ (061) 724 5836
12–3, 6–11 (12–11 Sat)
Thwaites Best Mild, Bitter Ⓗ
A new bypass gives this pub a rural feel, enhanced by the ancient Bull Ring game and a fine atmosphere. 🏳 ⊛ ◑ ♣ P

Ramsbottom

Royal Oak

Bridge Street ☎ (0706) 822786
12–5, 7–11 (12–11 Fri & Sat)
Thwaites Best Mild, Bitter Ⓗ
Friendly village-centre pub near the East Lancs railway. The lounge features brassware and paintings. Also a games room and a cosy snug. ⭫ ◑ ♣

Rochdale

Albert

62 Spotland Road (A608)
11–11
Burtonwood Mild, Bitter Ⓗ
Popular local with a good early evening atmosphere. Games, TV and quiet rooms, with an open-plan bar. Free 'oldies' jukebox. Q ♣

Healey Hotel

172 Shawclough Road
☎ (0706) 45453
12–3 (4 Sat), 5 (7 Sat)–11
Robinson's Best Mild, Best Bitter Ⓗ, **Old Tom** Ⓖ
Friendly pub with an outdoor boules area and a splendid tiled interior, opened out into a cosy lounge. Eve meals Tue–Thu. ⭫ ⊛ ◑ ♣

Merry Monk

234 College Road (30 yds from A6060/B6222 jct)
12–11
Marston's Border Mild, Burton Best Bitter, Pedigree Ⓗ; guest beers
Friendly, unpretentious back-street local with a Ring the Bull game. ♣ ⌣ P

Royal Hotel

452 Oldham Road (A671, near M62 flyover) ☎ (0706) 40374
12–11
Thwaites Best Mild, Bitter Ⓗ
Red-brick Victorian coaching house. Many original features include superb tilework and pine doors to the separate rooms. Food available by previous order. Q ⭫ ⊛ ♣

Spring Inn

Broad Lane (¹/₄ mile off A671 Oldham road) ☎ (0706) 33529

11–11
Lees GB Mild, Bitter Ⓔ
Traditional house with a friendly atmosphere and good facilities. Outdoor children's activity centre and menagerie. No-smoking restaurant.
⭫ ⊛ ◑ ♣ P

Tap & Spile

Hope Street (off Whitworth Road, A671)
☎ (0706) 47171
12–3, 7–11 (12–11 Sat; may vary)
Thwaites Bitter; Whitbread Boddingtons Bitter Ⓗ; guest beers
Spacious, lively pub offering a wide range of frequently changing guest beers. Rightly popular. Note the splendid war memorial plaque in the front room. Folk night Tue. Children welcome lunchtimes.
⭫ ◑ ♣ P ⤬

Romiley

Duke of York

Stockport Road
☎ (061) 430 2806
11.30–11
Courage Directors; John Smith's Bitter; Whitbread Boddingtons Bitter Ⓗ
Long, low, white building of harmonious proportions. Just as pleasing inside, with a beamed lounge and a big, active public bar.
Q ⭫ ⊛ ◑ ◗ ⌖ ♣ P

Royton

Dog & Partridge Inn

148 Middleton Road
☎ (061) 620 6403
11–11
Lees GB Mild, Bitter Ⓗ
Always busy. Very popular with football fans; good atmosphere. Wide range of whiskies. No food Sun.
⭫ ◑ ⌖

Greyhound

1 Elly Clough, Holden Fold (off A663) ☎ (061) 624 4504
11.30–3, 7–11
Lees GB Mild, Bitter Ⓔ
Popular, friendly pub, once in a rural area, but slowly being surrounded by housing. Weekday lunches.
Q ⊛ ◑ ♣ P

Rusholme

Osborne House

32 Victory Street (off B5177)
11.30–11 (11.30–4 – 3 when City are at home, 7–11 Sat)
Hydes' Anvil Mild, Bitter Ⓔ
Fine, friendly back-street local, now one room but retaining several areas. Handy for Maine Road and excellent curry houses. & ♣ P

Greater Manchester

Sale

Railway Inn
35 Chapel Road (behind town hall)
11.30–3 (4 Fri & Sat), 5.30–11
Robinson's Best Mild, Best Bitter E, **Old Tom** (winter) G
Rendered unimaginatively open-plan in the mid 70s, but comfortably furnished and still very much a local. Access to Bridgewater Canal across the road. Quiz night Tue; barbecues Wed eves in summer. No food Sun.
✿ ◑ ⊕ ⊖ ♣ P

Sale Moor

Legh Arms
178 Northenden Road (A6144/B5166 jct)
11.30–3, 5.30 (7 Sat)–11
Holt Mild, Bitter E
Large, multi-roomed local, acquired from Taylor's Eagle brewery in 1924. Many original features, including a revolving door. An island bar serves a large vault, lounge, snug, lobby and smoke room. Bowling green. Live music Fri–Sun nights. Q ✿ ⊕ ♣ P

Salford

Ashley Brook
517 Liverpool Street, Seedley (off A5186) ☎ (061) 737 0988
11–11
Holt Mild, Bitter H
Opened late 1990 but every bit the traditional community local. Licence first sought in the 1920s and granted 70 years later, thanks to the efforts of locals – led by a Methodist minister. Q ◑ ⊕ ♿ ♣ P

Crescent
20 The Crescent (A6)
☎ (061) 736 5600
12 (7.30 Sat)–11 (12–2.30, 7.30–10.30 Sun)
Beer range varies H
Friendly atmosphere; good home-cooking includes curries and local dishes. Haunt of staff and students from the nearby university. ♨ Q ✿ ◑ ♿ ⇌ (Crescent) ♣ ⌂ P

Eagle
19 Collier Street
12–11
Holt Mild, Bitter H
A long-time favourite: three rooms of genuine atmosphere. Until recently, the last beer house in Salford.
✿ ⊕ ⇌ (Victoria) ⊖ ♣

Kings Arms
11 Bloom Street (across A6 from Central station)
☎ (061) 839 4338
12–11
Cains Bitter; Holt Bitter; S&N Theakston Best Bitter; Taylor

Landlord** H
A successful venture by the Boddington Pub Co. into the free trade: a former Groves & Whitnall pub, built 1873, now Grade II listed. One large room and a small room off a corridor. Selection of Belgian and German bottled beers. ✿ ◑ (Central) ⊖ (Victoria) ♣ ⌂

Olde Nelson
285 Chapel Street (opp. cathedral) ☎ (061) 832 6189
11–3.30, 5.30 (7 Sat)–11
Whitbread Chester's Mild, Boddingtons Bitter, Trophy H
Classic, multi-roomed Victorian pub with strong community support. The etched-glass, screen and sliding door to the vault all add to the character. Sadly under threat from a road widening scheme.
Q ⊕ ⇌ (Central) ♣

Peel Park Inn
270 Chapel Street (A6 next to Salford Royal Hospital)
☎ (061) 832 2654
11–11
Courage Directors; John Smith's Bitter H
Smart, single-room pub with a tiny frontage.
🛏 ◑ ⇌ (Central) ♣

Star
Back Hope Street (off Gt Clowes St)
1–4, 7–11
Robinson's Best Mild, Best Bitter, Old Tom (winter) H
Characterful multi-room pub with just one tiny bar in the vault. Manchester's oldest folk club meets here every Wed. Run by the same family for decades. Indoor gents' and outside ladies'! Q ✿ ⊕ ♿ ♣

Union Tavern
105 Liverpool Street
11–11
Holt Mild, Bitter H
Honest, basic boozer in a desolate area, bordering on the enterprise zone.
Q ⊕ ⇌ (Crescent) ♣ P

Welcome Inn
Robert Hall Street (off A5066)
11.30–4, 7–11
Lees GB Mild, Bitter E
Smart, comfortable modern local near Salford quays. The 'handpumps' activate electric motors. ⊕ ♣ P

Simister

Farmers Arms
51 Simister Lane (signed off A665) ☎ (061) 773 4623
11.30–11 (11.30–4, 5.15–11 Tue)
Lees GB Mild, Bitter H
Built in the 17th century as a bakehouse and converted to a pub in the 1780s. Retains the atmosphere of a local.

Children welcome until 8.30pm. ✿ ◑ ⊕ ♿ ♣

Stalybridge

Station Buffet
Rassbottom Street (Platform One) ☎ (061) 338 2020
12–3 (not Sun, Mon & Tue), 5 (7 Sat)–11
Beer range varies H
Victorian station buffet bar with a unique atmosphere. Three guest beers, which change frequently, and a Burton Bridge house beer. Now safe from the threat of sale. CAMRA regional *Pub of the Year 1991*. ♨ ◑ ♦ ⇌ ⌂ P

White House
Market Street
11–11
S&N Matthew Brown Mild, Theakston Best Bitter, XB, Old Peculier H; guest beers
Comfortable, well-used local, modernised but still with separate rooms. A burgeoning centre for local folk music. Foreign bottled beers. ◑ ⇌ ♣

Standish

Horseshoe
Wigan Road ☎ (0257) 421240
2 (12 Sat)–11
Burtonwood Mild, Bitter H
Comfortable village local, its lounge resembling a mini-Labour club. ◑ ♦ ⊕ P

Stockport

Arden Arms
23 Millgate (near market place) ☎ (061) 480 2185
11.30–3, 5.30–11 (11.30–11 Fri & Sat)
Robinson's Best Mild, Best Bitter, Old Tom H
An unspoilt gem, oozing atmosphere. Recently extended, but totally in keeping with its character. Don't miss the snug. Collection of grandfather clocks. Limited parking. No food Sun. Q ◑ ♣ P

Blossoms
2 Buxton Road, Heaviley (A6/Bramall Lane jct)
☎ (061) 480 2246
11.30–4, 5.30–11
Robinson's Best Mild, Best Bitter, Old Tom H
An old Bell's pub on a busy road junction. Three separate rooms and a large bar area attract a variety of drinkers, including a local lacrosse team. Always a lively atmosphere – a deservedly popular traditional local. Weekday lunches.
Q ✿ ◑ ⇌ (Davenport) ♣ P

Grapes
1c Castle Street, Edgeley
11–11
Robinson's Best Mild, Best Bitter, Old Tom (winter) H

Lively, basic boozer, handy for County FC. ⊟ ≋ ♣

Olde Vic

1 Chatham Street, Edgeley
12–3, 5.30 (5 Thu)–11 (12–11 Fri & Sat and occasionally midweek in summer)
Marston's Pedigree; Taylor Landlord 🄷; guest beers
The first Stockport pub to offer guest beers (up to three available). Often crowded and can be smoky. Expensive for the area. Occasional cider. ❀ ≋ ◯̆

Olde Woolpack

70 Brinksway (A560)
☎ (061) 429 6621
11.30–3, 5.30 (7.45 Sat)–11 (11.30–11 Fri)
Marston's Pedigree; S&N Theakston Best Bitter; Tetley Walker Bitter 🄷; guest beers
Comfortable and traditional free house in the shadow of a giant blue pyramid. Always a guest bitter and mild. Sun lunch is a set meal. Parking difficult. ◖ ⊟ ≋ ♣ P

Red Bull

14 Middle Hillgate
☎ (061) 480 2087
11–3, 5 (7 Sat)–11 (11–11 Fri)
Robinson's Best Mild, Best Bitter 🄷
Only ten minutes from the town centre, but with the air of a country hostelry. A central bar with numerous drinking areas off, some with stone-flagged floors and wooden benches. A second bar supplies a lounge area. Imaginative weekday lunches. ♨ ◖ ≋ P

Stanley Arms

40 Newbridge Lane (200 yds from ring road, A626)
12–3 (not Mon–Thu in winter), 5–11 (11.30–11 Sat)
Ryburn Best Bitter, Bitter, Stabbers 🄷; guest beers
Split-level pub with a main bar area dominated by a large-screen TV. Separate pool room and a comfortable lounge area dedicated to Laurel & Hardy. Lively clientele of all ages. Features Ryburn-brewed Stanley's Mild and Ollie's Mild, plus many guests. Live music weekends. ❀ ♣ ◯̆ P

Stoneclough

Horseshoe

395 Folds Road, Ringley Road
☎ (0204) 71714
12–3, 7–11
Thwaites Best Mild, Bitter 🄷
Comfortable, friendly pub in an interesting location.
♨ ❀ ◖ ≋ (Kearsley) ♣

Strines

Sportsman Arms

105 Strines Road (B6101)
☎ (061) 427 2888
11–3 (4.30 Sat), 5.30–11
Ruddles Best Bitter; Webster's Yorkshire Bitter 🄷, Wilson's Bitter 🄴; guest beers 🄷
Enterprising pub in a rural location, enjoying excellent views from the garden. A spacious, pleasant lounge and a traditional vault. The guest beer is changed three times a week. Soon to be free of tie.
Q ❀ ◖ ◗ ⊟ ⛺ ≋ ♣ P

Swinton & Pendlebury

Buckley Arms

137 Partington Lane, Swinton (B5231 near A6 jct)
12–4, 5.30–11 (12–11 Fri & Sat)
Tetley Walker Mild, Bitter 🄷
Smart local with a strong community tradition. The lounge serves as a dining room weekday lunchtimes (no food weekends).
❀ ◖ ⊟ ≋ (Swinton) ♣ P

Lord Nelson

653 Bolton Road, Pendlebury (A666/B5231 jct)
12–11
Holt Mild, Bitter 🄴
Large, late 1960s-style pub; a big, basic vault and an enormous lounge with a stage. Always busy and can have a club-like atmosphere.
❀ ⊟ ≋ (Swinton) ♣ P

Park Inn

137 Worsley Road, Swinton (A572) ☎ (061) 794 4296
12–11 (12–4, 7–11 Sat)
Holt Mild, Bitter 🄷
Smart old local with a tiny snug at the rear and a triangular public bar. ⊟ ♣

Timperley

Quarrybank Inn

151 Bloomsbury Lane
☎ (061) 980 4345
11.30–3, 5.30–11 (11.30–11 Fri & Sat)
Hydes' Anvil Mild, Bitter 🄴
Thriving village local with a lively vault. Recently refurbished with an eating area; the menu caters for vegetarians and children (eve meals Sat only). Bowling green. 🐴 ❀ ◖ ◗ ⊟ ♣ P

Tottington

Dungeon Inn

Turton Road ☎ (0204) 883346
12–3 (4 Fri & Sat), 7–11
Thwaites Best Mild, Bitter 🄷
Recently altered but the tilework and a unique frieze of local scenes were retained. ♣

Tyldesley

Colliers Arms

105 Sale Lane (A577, 1 mile E of centre) ☎ (061) 790 2065
2 (1 Fri, 12 Sat)–11
Courage Directors; Holt Bitter; Wilson's Mild, Bitter 🄷
Pleasant roadside hostelry with a long, comfy lounge and a tap room. ❀ ⊟ ♣ P

Half Moon

115 Elliot Street
11–4 (4.30 Sat), 7–11
Holt Mild, Bitter 🄷; guest beers
Large lounge with a bar; separate pool room. Busy at weekends. The only free house in the area. ❀ ♣

Uppermill

Cross Keys

Running Hill Gate (off A670, up Church Rd)
☎ (0457) 874626
11–3, 6.30–11 (11–11 Sat & summer)
Lees GB Mild, Bitter 🄷
Attractive, 18th-century, stone building overlooking Saddleworth church. The public bar has a stone-flagged floor and a Yorkshire range. The hub of many activities, including mountain rescue!
♨ Q ❀ ◖ ⊟ ♿ ⛺ ♣ P

Urmston

Lord Nelson

Stretford Road
11–11
Holt Mild, Bitter 🄷
Built shortly after Nelson's death (1805), rebuilt and extended in 1877. Now transformed from an ale house to a comfortable, modern-style pub, retaining a multi-roomed layout. Popular with all ages.
⊟ ♿ ≋ ♣ P

Walshaw

White Horse Hotel

Hall Street
☎ (020 488) 3243
12–3, 7–11
Thwaites Mild, Bitter 🄷
Superior, friendly local in a pleasant village setting. Thriving games room. Lunches Mon–Fri. Q ◖ ⊟ ♣

Wardley

Morning Star

Manchester Road (A6)
☎ (061) 794 4927
12–11 (12–3 Sun)
Holt Mild, Bitter 🄷
Isolated, friendly outlet serving locals; a fine building. No food Sun.
❀ ◖ ⊟ ≋ (Moorside) ♣ P

West Gorton

Travellers Call

521–523 Hyde Road (A57/A6010 jct) ☎ (061) 223 1722
11–11
Hydes' Anvil Mild, Bitter 🄴

Greater Manchester

Visit this slice of old-style Manchester pub life while you can – it should last out this *Guide*, but road widening will soon sweep away this unspoilt gem. The heart of the pub is the narrow front vault, but don't miss the delightful back room, where families are welcome. ⊟ ⇌ (Belle Vue/ Ashburys) ♣

Whitefield

Coach & Horses

71 Bury Old Road (A665)
11.30–11 (11.30–5, 7–11 Sat)
Holt Mild, Bitter Ⓗ
Built in 1830 and virtually unchanged; once a staging post for the Burnley–Manchester mail coach and still used by postmen! One of a declining number of tenanted Holt pubs.
Q ⊟ ♿ ⇌ (Besses O' Th' Barn) ⊖ ♣ P

Eagle & Child

Higher Lane (A667)
☎ (061) 766 3024
12–11
Holt Mild, Bitter Ⓗ
Large 1930s pub with an imposing mock Tudor exterior and a genuine Holt interior. Comfortable and friendly, it boasts a magnificent bowling green. Cheap food.
Q ♨ ❀ ◖ ◗ ⊟ ♿ ♣ P

Wigan

Beer Engine

69 Poolstock Lane (B5238, off A49) ☎ (0942) 42497
11.30–11
Taylor Landlord; Tetley Walker Dark Mild, Bitter Ⓗ**; guest beers**
Multi-roomed pub with a comfortable lounge, separate vault and a large function room, providing the focus for a wide variety of live music. Annual 'Beer, Pie and Music' festival. At least four guest beers. Full-size snooker table in the vault; own bowling green. ❀ ◖ ◗ ⇌ (NW/ Wallgate) ♣ P

Bird I' Th' Hand (Th 'En 'Ole)

100–102 Gidlow Lane (off B5375)
☎ (0942) 41004
12–11
Ind Coope Burton Ale; S&N Theakston Best Bitter; Tetley Walker Dark Mild, Mild, Bitter Ⓗ
A rare pub – one actually improved by renovation! A fine two-roomed local with an impressive Walker's mosaic over the doorway.
❀ ◖ ◗ ⊟ ♿ ♣ P

Bold Hotel

161 Poolstock Lane (B5238, off A49) ☎ (0942) 41095
12–4.30 (5 Fri & Sat), 7–11
Burtonwood Mild, Bitter Ⓗ
Small, no-nonsense, two-roomed local. Q ❀ ⊟ ♣

Gems

15 Upper Dicconson Street
☎ (0942) 826588
11.30–11
Cains Bitter; Holt Bitter; Ind Coope Burton Ale; Tetley Walker Mild, Walker Best Bitter Ⓗ
Single-roomed bar, popular for business lunches. Often busy in the evening, with a good atmosphere. The TV is usually tuned to sport.
❀ ◖ ⇌ (NW/Wallgate)

Millstone

67 Wigan Lane (old A49, N of centre) ☎ (0942) 45999
12–3.30, 7.30–11
Thwaites Best Mild, Bitter Ⓗ
Comfortable pub with a warm welcome. Near the rugby ground and busy on match days. Good lunches. ❀ ◖

Orwell

Wigan Pier, Wallgate
☎ (0942) 323034
11–11
Cains Bitter; Greenalls Thomas Greenall's Bitter; Jennings Bitter; Tetley Walker Bitter; West Coast Best Bitter, Porter Ⓗ
Large, modern pub at the heart of the pier complex. During the day, it caters for the tourist trade; in the evenings, it is more lively and attracts the younger set. Happy hour 5–7pm.
◖ ⇌ (NW/Wallgate) P

Raven Hotel

5 Wallgate ☎ (0942) 43865
11–11
Walker Mild, Bitter, Winter Warmer Ⓗ
Ornate Victorian pub with many original features.
❀ ◖ ⇌ (NW/Wallgate)

Seven Stars

262 Wallgate ☎ (0942) 43126
12–4 (5 Sat), 7.30 (7 Sat)–11
Thwaites Mild, Bitter Ⓗ
Splendid red-brick ex-Magee's pub handy for the canal and Wigan Pier. Very friendly.
⊟ ⇌ (NW/Wallgate) ♣ P

Silverwell

Darlington Street (Hindley road) ☎ (0942) 41217
12–4, 7–11
Walker Mild, Best Bitter Ⓗ
Large, multi-roomed town pub, popular with locals but welcoming to visitors. Refurbishment has not spoilt the atmosphere.
♛ ⊟ ⇌ (NW/Wallgate) ♣

Springfield

47 Springfield Road (off B5375) ☎ (0942) 42072
11.30–3.30, 5.30–11
Walker Mild, Best Bitter, Winter Warmer Ⓗ
Imposing ex-Oldfield brewery house near the football ground. Popular with locals and football fans alike. Regular live music – big band jazz. ♛ ⊟ ♣ P

Swan & Railway

80 Wallgate ☎ (0942) 495032
11–3.30, 5.30 (6 Sat)–11 (12–2.30, 7–10.30 Sun)
Banks's Mild, Bitter; Bass Mild XXXX, Draught Bass; Courage Directors; John Smith's Bitter; Stones Best Bitter Ⓗ
Victorian pub offering the town centre's widest range of excellent value beers. Fine collection of clocks and railway memorabilia. No food Sun.
🛏 ◖ ⊟ ⇌ (NW/Wallgate)

Tudor House Hotel

New Market Street
☎ (0942) 42190
11–11
Bass Mild XXXX, Draught Bass Ⓗ**; guest beers**
Excellent family hotel where the atmosphere appeals to a wide range of clientele. Guest beers from independents change daily; various ciders. Breakfast and meals from 7am. ♛ ❀ 🛏 ◖ ◗ ♿
⇌ (NW/Wallgate) ⌓

Woodford

Davenport Arms (Thief's Neck)

550 Chester Road (A5102)
11–3.30, 5.15 (5.30 Sat)–11
Robinson's Best Mild, Best Bitter Ⓗ**, Old Tom** Ⓔ
Classic country pub, multi-roomed and unspoilt, on the edge of prosperous suburbs. In the same family for 60 years. Mild outsells all lagers put together.
♛ Q ❀ ◖ ⊟ ♣ P ⊬

Worthington

Crown

Platt Lane (between A5106 and A49, Bradley Lane at Standish) ☎ (0257) 421354
11–11
Marston's Pedigree; S&N Matthew Brown Mild, Theakston Best Bitter, XB; Samuel Smith OBB; Taylor Landlord Ⓗ**; guest beers**
Not to be missed: a country pub with antique furniture and a wide range of good value meals. The new restaurant has not interfered in any way. ♛ Q ◖ P

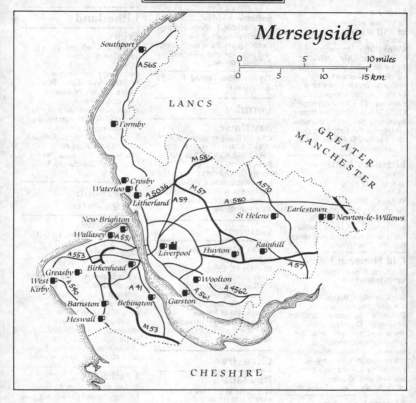

Merseyside

 Cains, Liverpool

Barnston

Fox & Hounds
107 Barnston Road (A551)
☎ (051) 648 7685
11.30–3.30, 5.30–11
**Courage Directors; Ruddles
Best Bitter, County; Webster's
Yorkshire Bitter, Wilson's
Mild** H
Converted 18th-century coach
house with a snug, bar and
lounge, popular with locals.
Food is good value (not
served Sun), but beer is pricey.
Impossible to use the
dartboard most evenings.
🏚 Q ❀ ◑ ⊞ & ♣ P

Bebington

Cleveland Arms
31 Bebington Road, New Ferry
☎ (051) 645 2847
11–11
Thwaites Best Mild, Bitter H
Always lively and busy, open-
plan pub in a pedestrian area.
A previous local CAMRA *Pub
of the Year* winner whose

standards remain high. Darts
played. ⇌ ♣

Great Eastern
New Ferry Road, New Ferry
☎ (051) 645 3282
11–11
Banks's Mild, Bitter E
Spacious, two-room pub with
a large garden catering for
younger clientele. The lounge
is quiet during the week;
country music alternate Fris.
Some doors, windows and
timbers originate from
Brunel's *Great Eastern* ship
which was broken up on a
nearby bank of the Mersey.
❀ ◑ ⊞ & ⇌ ♣ P

Rose & Crown
57 The Village, Lower
Bebington ☎ (051) 645 5024
11.30–3, 5.30–11
Thwaites Best Mild, Bitter H
Excellent, bustling, friendly
old local, popular with office
workers at lunchtime and
local residents at night. No
food Sun. Q ◑ ⊞ ⇌ ♣ P

Three Stags
Church Road
☎ (051) 334 3428
11.30–3, 5.30 (5 Fri)–11 (11.30–11 Sat)
**Cains Bitter; Tetley Walker
Mild, Bitter** H; guest beers
(occasionally)
Large pub with an adjoining
Porterhouse restaurant. The
huge lounge was recently split
into a smoke room (with
satellite TV), a comfortable
lounge and a family room.
🛏 ❀ ◑ ▶ & ⇌ P

Birkenhead

Argyle
Prince's Pavement
☎ (051) 647 5372
11–11
Cains Bitter H
Comfortable, modern, one-
roomed pub next to
Birkenhead market. The walls
are adorned with photos of
famous music hall stars that
once appeared at the Argyle
Theatre, which was close by.
◑ ⇌ (Central) ♣

Merseyside

Crown
128 Conway Street
☎ (051) 647 9108
11.30–11
Cains Bitter; Jennings Cumberland Ale, Sneck Lifter Ⓗ; **guest beers**
Revitalised town-centre alehouse serving nine cask beers. One bar serves three rooms and a varied clientele. Quiet at lunchtime but busier eves, especially at weekends. Handy for the shopping centre and market. ⊟ ✿ (Central) ⊖ (Hamilton Sq) ♣

Firemans Arms
36 Oliver Street
☎ (051) 647 8226
11–11
Wilson's Bitter Ⓗ
Hectic shoppers' pub by day and equally hectic pre-club pub by night. A comfortable one-roomer, served by a single bar. ⇌ (Central)

Old House at Home
30 Queen Street, Tranmere
☎ (051) 666 1578
11–11
Banks's Mild, Bitter Ⓔ
CAMRA Wirral branch 1992 *Pub of the Year*, serving drinkers of all ages. The bar and lounge are served from one area. The cosy, compact garden has swings. The landlord seldom misses a chance to speak to customers. Local pensioners are well looked after.
✿ ⊟ ♿ ⇌ (Green Lane) ♣

Shrewsbury Arms
38 Claughton Firs, Oxton
☎ (051) 652 1775
11.30–3, 5.30–11 (11.30–11 Fri & Sat)
Cains Bitter; Ind Coope Burton Ale; S&N Theakston Best Bitter Ⓗ
Traditional pub, with beamed ceilings. The rose garden has seating and tables. Very popular at weekends, attracting a mixed clientele. No food Sun. Q ✿ Ⓓ P

Crosby

Crow's Nest
61 Victoria Road
11.30–3, 5.30–11 (11.30–11 Fri & Sat)
Cains Bitter Ⓗ
Well-established local preserving its separate bar, snug and lounge. Regulars' spirited opposition prevented the intrusion of a jukebox and fruit machine, thus retaining the pub's lively conversational character. Deservedly popular. Q ⊟ ⇌ (Blundellsands/Crosby) P

Earlestown

Wellington
37–39 Earle Street
☎ (0925) 226267

11–11
Burtonwood Mild, Bitter Ⓗ
Comfortable, L-shaped lounge and a separate tap room, located just off the town centre and popular with all ages.
⚏ Ⓓ ⇌ ♠

Try also: Rams Head, Earle St (Greenalls)

Formby

Bay Horse
Church Road ☎ (0704) 874229
11.30–3, 5.30–11 (11.30–11 Fri & Sat)
Bass Mild XXXX, Draught Bass Ⓗ
Smart old pub adjoining a good restaurant. Genuine pub vaults; the warm and inviting lounge gets very crowded.
⚏ Q ✿ ⊟ ⇌ P

Garston

King Street Vaults
74 King Street
☎ (051) 427 5850
11–11
Walker Mild, Bitter Ⓗ
Old and interesting pub, close to the docks and parish church. Has a keen (champion) darts team and sporting trophies galore.
⊟ ♿ ♣

Greasby

Irby Mill
Mill Lane ☎ (051) 604 0194
11.30–3, 5–11 (11.30–11 Sat)
Cains Bitter; Ind Coope Burton Ale; S&N Theakston Best Bitter; Tetley Walker Bitter Ⓗ; **guest beers**
Two-roomed, traditional country pub. No background music or slot machines. Eve meals served Fri only.
⚏ Q ✿ Ⓓ ♦ ♣ P

Heswall

Black Horse
Village Road, Lower Heswall (off A540) ☎ (051) 342 2254
11.30–11
Bass Mild XXXX, Special, Draught Bass Ⓗ
Popular village pub; refurbished to provide a conservatory whilst retaining its lively bar and snug.
Q Ⓓ ⊟ ♣

Huyton

Rose & Crown
2 Archway Road
☎ (051) 489 1735
11–11
Walker Mild, Bitter Ⓗ
Large, three-roomed pub built in the 1930s on the site of the old Barker's brewery.
⚏ ✿ ⊟ ⇌ ♣ P

Litherland

Priory
64 Sefton Road (off A5036)
☎ (051) 928 1110
11.30–11
Ind Coope Burton Ale; Walker Mild, Bitter, Best Bitter, Winter Warmer Ⓗ
Large, multi-level, comfortable lounge and a fair-sized public bar, situated in the residential area of Litherland, where real ale is a rarity. Good food at lunchtime. ✿ Ⓓ ⊟ ♿ ⇌ (Seaforth/Litherland) ♣ P

Liverpool: *City Centre*

Bonapartes
21a Clarence Street, L3 (off Brownlow Hill)
☎ (051) 709 5089
11.30am–12.15am (7–12.15 Sat; 7–10.30 Sun)
Vaux Samson, Extra Special; Wards Mild, Sheffield Best Bitter Ⓗ
Bistro-style at lunchtime; candlelit tables in the evenings. Popular with students, especially late at night. Special offers available at lunchtime (pint plus food). ✿ Ⓓ ⇌ (Lime St) ⊖ (Central)

Cambridge
51 Mulberry Street, L7 (near University and Children's Hospital)
11.30–11
Burtonwood Mild, Bitter, Forshaw's Ⓗ
Split-level, two-room pub, popular with students and nurses. Sunday breakfasts are especially good value. Ⓓ

Carnarvon Castle
5 Tarleton Street, L1
☎ (051) 709 3153
11–11 (8 Mon & Tue; closed Sun)
Draught Bass; Cains Bitter Ⓗ
Friendly, cosy pub in the pedestrianised shopping area. Boasts an extensive Dinky toy collection. ⚏ Q ⇌ (Lime St) ⊖ (Central)

Cracke
13 Rice Street, L1 (near Philharmonic Hall)
☎ (051) 709 4171
12–11
Oak Best Bitter Ⓗ; **guest beers**
One of the best traditional pubs in Liverpool: small rooms and Bohemian customers give it a special atmosphere. Excellent, cheap lunches include vegetarian dishes; eve meals finish early. Three guest beers change weekly. ✿ Ⓓ ♦ ⊟ ⇌ (Lime St) ⊖ (Central) ♣

Merseyside

Everyman Bistro
Hope Street, L1
☎ (051) 708 9545
12–12 (closed Sun)
Brakspear Bitter; Fuller's Chiswick; Marston's Pedigree H**; guest beers**
Brasserie-style cellar bar below the Everyman Theatre, with a relaxed atmosphere. Busy after 10.30pm. Recommended for high quality, inexpensive food with a good range of vegetarian options. Q ⌂ ◑ ▶ ⇌ (Lime St) ⊖ (Central) ⌂

Grapes
60 Roscoe Street, L1
☎ (051) 709 8617
11–11
Cains Bitter H**; guest beers**
Smallish homely pub on the edge of Chinatown, and handy for the Anglican cathedral. Popular with Philharmonic musicians and locals alike. Cajun/Irish folk nights occasionally held. Well worth seeking out. Free food is laid out on the bar Sun lunchtimes. ⌂ ❀ ◑ ⇌ (Lime St) ⊖ (Central)

Poste House
23 Cumberland Street, L1
☎ (051) 236 4130
11–11
Cains Bitter H
Small, cosy pub, recently refurbished without loss of character or customers, who are a mix of blue and white collar. Sometimes still known by its nickname of the 'Muck Midden'. Lunches weekdays only. Q ◑ ⊞ ⇌ (Lime St) ⊖ (Moorfields)

Railway
18 Tithebarn Street, L2
☎ (051) 236 7210
11.30–11
Draught Bass; Cains Bitter, Formidable H
Former Mellor's pub opposite the now-closed Exchange station. Popular with office staff for its good value lunches; also serves breakfast from 9.15 (no food Sun). The pub sign shows an inappropriate choice of locomotive.
◑ ⊖ (Moorfields) ♣

Roscoe Head
24 Roscoe Street, L1
☎ (051) 709 4490
11–11
Ind Coope Burton Ale; Jennings Bitter; Tetley Walker Mild, Bitter H
Ever-present in this *Guide*. Customers come first in this small, unspoilt four-room pub, a former winner of the local CAMRA *Pub of the Year*. Collection of ties in the lounge. Quiz on Tue night. No food Sun. Q ◑ ⊞ ⇌ (Lime St) ⊖ (Central)

Ship & Mitre
133 Dale Street, L2 (near Birkenhead tunnel entrance)
☎ (051) 236 0859
11–8 (11–11 Thu & Fri, 8–11 Sat; closed Sun)
Cains Bitter; Oak Wobbly Bob H**; guest beers**
Gas-lit pub, popular with students from the local polytechnic. Good value weekday lunches. Features wooden beams made to look like a ship's deck. Live music Fri teatime. Upstairs function room available. ◑ ♿
⇌ (Lime St) ⊖ (Moorfields)

Swan
86 Wood Street, L1
☎ (051) 709 5281
11.30–11
Marston's Merrie Monk, Pedigree; Oak Wobbly Bob H
Old pub in a back street close to the shopping area and Chinatown. The downstairs bar has rock music on the jukebox; tapes of rock and roll on Mon nights in the upstairs lounge. Attracts bikers, Bohemians and a wide cross-section of visitors and locals. Good value meals include Sun breakfast (at lunchtime). ◑ ▶
⇌ (Lime St) ⊖ (Central) ⌂

White House
185 Duke Street, L1
☎ (051) 709 9894
11–11
Walker Mild, Bitter H
Two-roomed pub which offers occasional happy hours plus strippers on stage Sun lunchtime. ⊞ ⇌ (Lime St) ⊖ (Central)

Liverpool: *East*

Claremont
70 Lower Breck Road, L6
12–11
John Smith's Bitter; Tetley Walker Dark Mild, Mild, Bitter H
Basic two-roomed local in a quite handsome building. No food Sun. ◑ ⊞ ♣

Edinburgh
4 Sandown Lane, L15 (off Wavertree High St)
11–11
Cains Bitter; Walker Mild, Bitter H
Tiny locals' pub in a quiet side street. Usually very busy and very much a community pub. ⊞

Farnworth Arms
1 Farnworth Street, L6
☎ (051) 260 4190
11.30–11
Tetley Walker Dark Mild, Bitter H
Friendly Irish house with two rooms served from a central bar. A warm, lively community pub. ⊞ ♣

Prince Alfred
77 High Street, Wavertree, L15
☎ (051) 733 5991
11–11
Cains Bitter; Tetley Walker Bitter H
Comfortable pub with an inglenook, on a busy high street. The first pub on this side of the river to throw out Higsons Sheffield Bitter. ⚑ ◑

Rocket
2 Bowring Park Road, L14
☎ (051) 220 8829
11–11
Cains Bitter H
Excellent modern pub at the end of the M62. Beware of the artificial Higsons and high prices. No food at weekends. Named after the pioneer railway loco which is depicted in relief on the side of the pub.
❀ ◑ ♿ ⇌ (Broadgreen) P

Royal Hotel
213 Smithdown Road, L15 (A562, near Sefton General Hospital) ☎ (051) 733 6408
11–11
Tetley Walker Mild, Bitter H
Pub with a wonderfully ornate exterior (mosaics) and a gas-lit lounge with wood panelling and stuffed animals. ⊞ ♣

Royal Standard
Deysbrook Lane, West Derby, L12
11.30–11
Cains Bitter; Greenalls Mild, Bitter, Thomas Greenall's Bitter H
Tastefully revamped, one-room lounge bar with low lighting, low music, and various alcoves. ❀ P

Liverpool: *North*

Abbey
153 Walton Lane, L4
☎ (051) 207 0086
11–11
Walker Mild, Bitter H
Three-storey building with a pleasing blend of timber and maroon tilework. The compact interior houses bar and snug areas. Close to Everton FC. ⊞ ♣

Bull
2 Dublin Street, L3 (A565, upper dock road)
☎ (051) 207 1422
11–11
Tetley Walker Mild, Bitter H
Blue collars rub shoulders with suited clientele in this Irish-flavoured, one-bar, street-corner local. Always a friendly welcome in a truly classic Liverpool pub. Hearty lunchtime snacks available.

Clock
167 Walton Road, L4
☎ (051) 207 3594
11–11
Walker Mild, Bitter H

Merseyside

Small, two-roomed local with a bustling bar (TV and darts) and a cosy lounge. The licensee's vivacious personality adds to the attraction. Close to Everton FC. 🏠 🍺 ≠ (Kirkdale) ♣

Melrose Abbey
331 Westminster Road, L4
☎ (051) 922 3637
11.30–11
Tetley Walker Dark Mild, Mild, Bitter H
Three-roomed local: a busy bar with a TV, and a main lounge with a real fire. Popular with dart-players, off-duty railmen and well-behaved football fans of both local persuasions. 🎱 🍺 ≠ (Kirkdale) ♣

Prince Arthur
93 Rice Lane, L9 (A59)
☎ (051) 525 4508
11–11
Walker Mild, Bitter, Winter Warmer H
Former CAMRA Preservation Award-winning pub: a veritable feast of original woodwork, etched-glass, tiling and mosaic, sensitively restored outside and in. A narrow L-shaped bar, lots of standing space in the corridor and a cosy lounge: a fully appreciated pub, not just a showpiece. 🍺 ≠ (Rice Lane/Walton) ♣ P

Selwyn
106 Selwyn Street, L4
☎ (051) 525 0747
11–11
Tetley Walker Mild, Bitter H
Three rooms: the bar has darts and TV, the lounge offers pool and live music, and the snug peace and quiet. Q 🍺 ≠ (Kirkdale) ♣

Liverpool: *South*

Anglesea Arms
36 Beresford Road, L8 (opp. Toxteth market)
☎ (051) 727 4874
11–11
Tetley Walker Mild, Bitter H
Excellent, convivial pub close to a good shopping area. Well worth the short trip from town. 🍺

Poet's Corner
27–29 Park Hill Road, Dingle, L8 ☎ (051) 727 3249
11–11
Tetley Walker Mild, Bitter H
Medium-sized pub with a larger lounge than bar. The sign depicts Liverpool poets McGough, Patten and Henri. 🍺

New Brighton

Commercial
19 Hope Street
☎ (051) 639 2105
11.30–11

Walker Mild, Bitter, Best Bitter, Winter Warmer H
Traditional, two-roomed, street-corner local with a basic bar and a cosy lounge (table service). A peaceful haven for older people. Note the black and white pictures of Victorian New Brighton. Q 🍺 ≠ ♣

Newton-le-Willows

Old Crow Inn
248 Crow Lane East (A572, 1 mile from centre)
☎ (0925) 225337
12–3.30 (5 Fri & Sat), 7–11
Tetley Walker Mild, Bitter H
Welcoming local on the Newton–St Helens road. The large lounge is divided in two and there is a popular tap room. ❀ 🍸 🍺 ♣ P

Rainhill

Commercial
Station Road (A57)
☎ (051) 426 6446
12–11
Cains Bitter; S&N Theakston Best Bitter; Tetley Walker Bitter H
Large Victorian pub resplendent with Joseph Jones Knotty Ash Ales windows. Very much a characterful, busy local. ❀ 🍺 ≠ ♣

St Helens

Duke of Cambridge
27 Duke Street
☎ (0744) 613281
12–11
Vaux Lorimers Best Scotch, Samson, Double Maxim H; **guest beers**
Handy for the town centre. Guest beers are from the Vaux group. 🎱 🍺 ≠ (Central)

Hope & Anchor
174 City Road ☎ (0744) 24199
11.30–3.30 (5 Fri), 6.30–11 (11.30–11 Sat)
Tetley Walker Mild, Bitter H
Discos and other entertainment are provided on various nights in this pub opposite Victoria Park. 🍺 ♣

Royal Alfred
Shaw Street (opp. station)
11–11
Cains Bitter H
Large, comfortable pub close to the town centre. Make sure you ask for Cains. 🛏 🍸 🍺 (Central) ♣ P

Sportsmans
97 Duke Street ☎ (0744) 38848
12–11
Cains Bitter H
Pub standing opposite a local nightclub and so popular with the younger set. 🍺 ♣

Wheatsheaf
36 Westfield Street (A58)
☎ (0744) 37453
12–11
Tetley Walker Mild, Bitter H
One-bar town-centre local. ≠ (Central) ♣

Southport

Blundell Arms
34 Upper Aughton Road, Birkdale (off A5267)
☎ (0704) 28192
11.30–3, 5–11 (11.30–11 Fri & Sat)
Ind Coope Burton Ale; Walker Mild, Bitter H
Tastefully refurbished village local, comprising a large vault/games room and a medium-sized lounge. Home of the Southport Bothy Folk Club. 🍸 🍺 ≠ (Birkdale) ♣ P

Cheshire Lines
81 King Street ☎ (0704) 532178
11.30–11
Tetley Walker Dark Mild, Mild, Bitter H
Half-timbered-style hostelry in one of the resort's main guest house areas. It features old stone from the original Cheshire Lines railway station. ❀ ♣

Guest House
16 Union Street
☎ (0704) 537660
12–3.30, 6–11
Draught Bass H; **guest beer**
Popular town-centre pub with several rooms: one of Southport's few remaining traditional pubs. Pie and peas are a speciality at a reasonable price. Hosts charity quizzes. Q 🍺 ♣ ✗

Legendary Lancashire Heroes
101 Shakespeare Street
☎ (0704) 533668
12–10.30 (12–2.30, 7–10.30 Sun)
Moorhouse's Pendle Witches Brew; Oak Best Bitter; Taylor Landlord H; **guest beers**
Enterprising off-licence with an ever-changing range of real ales, plus a decent choice of bottled beers from around the world.

Upsteps
20 Upper Aughton Road, Birkdale (off A526, Eastbourne road) ☎ (0704) 69931
11.30–11
S&N Matthew Brown Mild, Bitter, Theakston Best Bitter, XB H
Cosy, traditional pub with a friendly licensee, a welcome addition to the Birkdale area. The name comes from the flight of stairs up to the door (its former name was Bankfield House but everyone called it the 'Upsteps'). 🍺 ≠ (Birkdale) ♣

Zetland Hotel
Zetland Street
11.30–11
Burtonwood Mild, Bitter, Forshaw's H
Large, greatly improved, Victorian pub with its own competition bowling green. Friendly welcome; weekend entertainment and regular quizzes. ♨ ❀ ⊟ ♣ P

Wallasey

Brighton
133 Brighton Street (A554, opp. Town Hall) ☎ (051) 638 1163
11.30–3, 5.30–11 (11.30–11 Fri & Sat)
Cains Bitter H
Very friendly pub, popular with locals, town councillors, wedding parties and local CAMRA members. Architecturally, one of the best buildings in the area, over 100 years-old. Has been selling beer since 1883. ⊟ ⅙ ♣

Cheshire Cheese
2 Wallasey Village
☎ (051) 638 3152
11–11
Cains Bitter H
Wallasey's oldest licensed premises, rebuilt in 1884. King William of Orange is said to have stayed in the original building in 1690. Very comfortable interior and a homely atmosphere. No muzak! Q ⊟ ⅙ ⇌ ♣

Farmers Arms
225 Wallasey Village
☎ (051) 638 2110
11–3, 5–11 (11–11 Fri & Sat)
Cains Bitter H**; guest beers**
Well-maintained local with a public bar, a lounge and a snug creating a warm, friendly atmosphere.
◖ ⊟ ⇌ (Grove Rd)

Ferry
48 Tobin Street
☎ (051) 639 1753
11–11
Cains Bitter H
Very popular pub, known locally as the 'Eggy', with a convivial atmosphere. Situated on the bank of the Mersey, it affords good views across the river. One of the area's oldest pubs, within walking distance of the ferries. No food Sun. ⌘ ❀ ◖ ◗ ♣ P

Try also: Primrose, Withens Lane, Liscard (Cains)

Waterloo

Volunteer Canteen
45 East Street ☎ (051) 928 6594
12–11
Cains Bitter H
Two-roomed local with a comfortable lounge (table service). This 170-year-old building is small and can get packed. Q ❀ ⊟ ⇌ ♣

West Kirby

Moby Dick
Village Road (off A540)
☎ (051) 625 5892
11.30–11
Bateman XXXB; Cains Bitter H
Spacious lounge featuring whaling memorabilia. Occasional live jazz music. The restaurant specialises in fish and grills.
Q ❀ ◖ ◗ P

Woolton

Cobden Vaults
85 Quarry Street
☎ (051) 428 2978
11–11
Courage Directors; John Smith's Bitter, Magnet H
Friendly, olde-worlde-style pub in a conservation-conscious village. A gem in an area where real ale is rare.

REAL ALE IN A BOTTLE

The great bottle-conditioned beer revival continues. Bottle-conditioned beers, like cask-conditioned beers, contain yeast and continue to ferment in the bottle. Like wine, they improve with age (up to a point!).

For years there were five classic bottle-conditioned beers: Guinness Original (though some of this is now filtered and pasteurised; Worthington White Shield, brewed by Bass; Courage Imperial Russian Stout; Gale's Prize Old Ale; and Thomas Hardy's Ale, brewed by Eldridge Pope. They are all fine beers.

Britain's newer breweries have risen to the challenge and produced their own bottle-conditioned beers. Ross produce no less than three real bottled beers. Burton Bridge produce a bottled porter, reviving this ancient beer style. For the vulgar there is Robinwood's Old Fart.

To promote bottle-conditioned beers, CAMRA commissioned Bateman to produce a special 21st Birthday Ale. This 1060 OG beer is brewed with only English malt, hops, water and yeast, and limited stocks may still be available from CAMRA.

There is growing interest in imported speciality beers, some of which are bottle-conditioned. Let us hope this also revives interest in our own bottled beers.

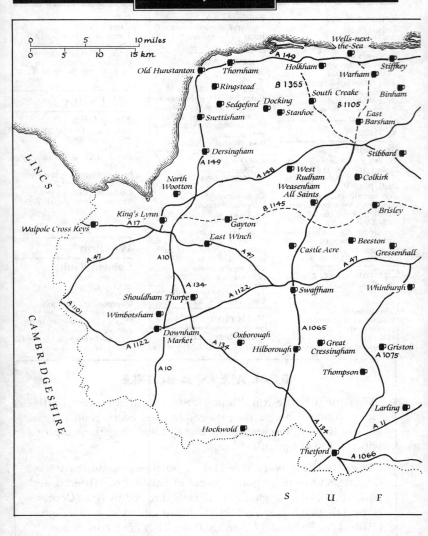

 ***Reepham**, Reepham; **Reindeer**, Norwich;
Woodforde's, Woodbastwick*

Acle

Reba's Riverside Inn
Old Road (A1064 off new Acle
bypass) ☎ (0493) 750310
11–3 (3.30 Sat), 7–11 (varies summer;
12–3, 8–10.30 Sun)
**Scotties Blues & Bloater;
Woodforde's Wherry** ⊞
Comfortable bar and an
adjoining restaurant area with
a friendly atmosphere. Handy
for River Bure boat moorings.
🏠 ◑ ▶ ≈ ♣ P

Attleborough

Griffin Hotel
Church Street ☎ (0953) 452149
10.30–2.30, 5.30–11
**Greene King Abbot;
Marston's Pedigree;
Whitbread Wethered
Bitter** ⊞; **guest beers**
A comfortable atmosphere in
a 16th-century coaching inn at
the centre of this market town.
Varied guest beers on offer,
with always a surprise in

store. A good menu includes
vegetarian dishes. 🏠 Q ❀
🏠 ◑ ▶ ⊞ ₺ ▲ ≈ ♣ ⌂ P

Beeston

Ploughshare
The Street (2 miles N of A47 W
of Dereham) ☎ (0328) 701845
11–2.30, 6–11
**Adnams Bitter, Old; Greene
King Abbot** ⊞; **guest beers**
16th-century village pub with
an *à la carte* restaurant and the

Norfolk

chef's own bar meals. Annual beer festival in July. Beeston Jem, the house beer, is brewed by Woodforde's.
🏚 ⛵ ❀ ◖❓ ♣ P

Binham

Chequers
Front Street
☎ (0328) 830297
11–11
Adnams Bitter; Draught Bass; Woodforde's Wherry Ⓗ
17th-century village inn with genuine beams and a cosy, comfortable atmosphere. An old inglenook is still in place, but a smaller brick fireplace is built into the wall.
🏚 Q ⛵ ❀ 🚌 ◖❓ ▲ ♣ P

Blickling

Buckinghamshire Arms
On B1354 ☎ (0263) 731133
11–2.30, 6–11 (12–2.30, 7–10.30 Sun)
Adnams Bitter, Broadside; Woodforde's Wherry Ⓗ**; guest beer**
Old, unspoilt pub with a snug, by Blickling Hall.
🏚 Q ❀ 🚌 ◖❓ P

Brisley

Bell
The Green (B1145)
☎ (0362) 668686
11–3, 6–11
Ind Coope Burton Ale; Tetley Bitter; Whitbread Boddingtons Bitter Ⓗ

17th-century, single-bar pub next to the largest common in Britain: a small, cosy bar with a largely bare-brick decor, rumoured to be haunted. The separate restaurant specialises in seafood. 🏚 ❀ 🚌 ◖❓ ♣ P

Briston

Green Man
Hall Street (S of B1354)
☎ (0263) 860993
11–11
Greene King IPA, Abbot; Woodforde's Wherry Ⓗ
200-year-old house with an original inglenook. A long-established, popular village pub serving reasonably-priced food. Pool room.
🏚 Q ⛵ ❀ ◖❓ ♣ P

Norfolk

(handwritten: COCKLEY CLEY 1990 TWENTY CHURCH WANDERS ✓)

Brooke

White Lion
The Street ☎ (0508) 50443
12–3, 5.30–11 (11–11 Sat)
Adnams Bitter; Webster's Yorkshire Bitter H
17th-century village pub off the main road, by the mere, in a picturesque village centre. Part of the pub is occupied by a restaurant. Other features include a range of pub games and a three-legged cat.
🍴 ❀ ◑ ♣ P

Brundall

Yare
Station Road ☎ ((0603) 713786
10.30–2.30 (3 Sat), 5.30–11
Courage Directors; John Smith's Bitter; Woodforde's Wherry H; **guest beers**
Adjacent to boatyards and the river, the interior of this popular pub contains many Broads photos and curios. It has a family/games room and children are also welcome in the dining area (good food).
🍴 ⛱ ❀ ◑ ▯ ⇌ P

Cantley

Cock Tavern
Manor Road (3 miles from A47 on Cantley road) ☎ (0493) 700895
11–3 (4 Sat), 6 (7 Sat)–11
Woodforde's Wherry H; **guest beers**
Popular brick and beam pub with one bar but several drinking areas. Good value food, and barbecues in summer; families welcome. Petanque played. Music can be turned off in one seating area on request. Four guest beers. 🍴 ⛱ ❀ ◑ ▯ ▲ ♣ P

Carleton St Peter

Beauchamp Arms
Buckenham Ferry (off A146, Loddon bypass) OS350044 ☎ (0508) 480247
11–3 (not Mon–Fri), 6–11 (11–11 summer)
Adnams Bitter; Draught Bass; Woodforde's Wherry, Nelson's Revenge H
Quiet country pub with bars, restaurant and extensive boat moorings on the south bank of the River Yare. Formerly a hotel, near the site of the old ferry. Pleasant walks are close by. Good family facilities and good food.
🍴 Q ⛱ ❀ ◑ ▯ ⊞ ▲ ♣ P

Castle Acre

Ostrich Inn
Stocks Green ☎ (0760) 755398
12–3, 7 (6 summer)–11
Greene King XX Mild, IPA,

Rayments Special, Abbot H
This attractive 16th-century coaching inn has built up a fine reputation over many years. It is close to the Peddars Way and the village boasts a castle and a ruined priory.
🍴 Q ❀ ⛱ ◑ ▯ ▲ ♣ P

Cley next the Sea

George & Dragon
High Street ☎ (0263) 740652
11–3, 6–11 (12–2, 7–10.30 Sun)
Greene King Abbot, IPA, Rayments Special H
Pub where interesting rooms display bird paintings and George & Dragon artefacts. Accommodation includes a four-poster. A new birdwatchers' hide in the attic has a telescope.
🍴 ⛱ ❀ ⛱ ◑ ▯ ⊞ ▲ ♣ P

Colkirk

Crown
Crown Road ☎ (0328) 862172
10.30–2.30, 6–11
Greene King XX Mild, IPA, Rayments Special, Abbot H; **guest beer**
Popular pub with two wood-panelled bars serving good food. 🍴 ❀ ◑ ▯ ▲ ♣ P

Coltishall

Red Lion
Church Street ☎ (0603) 737402
11–3, 5–11
Greene King Abbot; Marston's Pedigree; Whitbread Boddingtons Bitter, Flowers IPA H
16th-century pub on two levels near the River Bure. Broads paintings and sepia photos for sale. The house beer is brewed by Woodforde's. ❀ ◑ ▯ ▲ ♣ P

Cromer

Bath House
The Promenade ☎ (0263) 514260
11–11 (11–2.30, 6.30–11 winter; closed mid Jan–mid Mar)
Bateman XXXB; Samuel Smith OBB; Tolly Cobbold Original H; **guest beers**
Very pleasant, split-level bar on the lower promenade, by the pier. Outside seating on the prom. Friendly landlord.
Q ❀ ⛱ ◑ ▯ ▲ ⇌ ♣ P

Red Lion Hotel ✓
Brooke Street ☎ (0263) 514964
10–11
Adnams Bitter; Draught Bass; Greene King Abbot H
Updated Victorian hotel.
❀ ⛱ ◑ ▯ ♣ P

Deopham

Victoria
Church Road ☎ (0953) 850783
12–2.30 (not Mon–Tue), 7–11
Adnams Bitter; Draught Bass; Greene King Abbot; Woodforde's Wherry H; **guest beer**
Quiet, friendly village pub: a single bar and original wooden beams. Very good food including vegetarian and children's dishes. Fields quiz and petanque teams.
🍴 ◑ ▯ ▲ ▲ ♣ P

Dersingham

Feathers Hotel
Manor Road ☎ (0485) 540207
11–2.30, 5.30–11
Adnams Bitter; Draught Bass; Charrington IPA H
A fine Carrstone building with wood-panelled bars and an extensive garden. Games bar in the old stable block. Close to Sandringham House.
🍴 ❀ ⛱ ◑ ▯ ▲ ▲ ♣

Dickleburgh

Crown Inn
The Street ☎ (0379) 741475
12–2, 7–11 (11–11 summer)
Adnams Bitter H; **guest beers**
16th-century pub, extending way back beyond its small frontage. The real beams are complemented by the decor, furnishings and fireplace.
🍴 ⛱ ❀ ◑ ▯ ▲ ♣ P ⚲

Docking

Railway Inn
Station Road ☎ (0485) 518620
11.30–3 (not Thu), 7–11
Adnams Bitter H; **guest beers**
Two-bar village pub with strong local support. Guest beers often include a mild.
Q ❀ P

Downham Market

Crown Hotel
Bridge Street ☎ (0366) 382322
11–2.30, 6–11 (11–11 Fri & Sat)
Draught Bass; Bateman XB; Greene King Abbot; Woodforde's Wherry H; **guest beers**
Interesting bar in an old coaching inn. A large open fire makes it warm and welcoming, while exposed beams add character.
🍴 Q ⛱ ◑ ▯ ♣ P

East Barsham

White Horse
Fakenham Road (B1105 near hall) ☎ (0328) 820645
11–3, 7 (6 summer)–11
Greene King Abbot; Tolly Cobbold Original; Whitbread

220

(handwritten: ADNAMS TRY WELLINGTON 1990 NEW SIGNS)

Norfolk

Boddingtons Bitter; Woodforde's Wherry Ⓗ Comfortable, 17th-century inn which caters for the tourist trade as well as locals. Next to the Manor (10th century origins) where Henry VIII stayed before his pilgrimage to Walsingham.
🏚 Q ❀ 🏚 ◑ ▶ ♣ P

East Ruston

Butchers Arms
Oak Street (village signed from B1159) ☎ (0692) 650237
12–3, 7–11
Adnams Bitter, Broadside; Courage Directors; Woodforde's Wherry Ⓗ; guest beers
Comfortable, refurbished rural pub with ornate windows and a very friendly atmosphere. Superb food, unbelievable value; separate restaurant.
Q ☔ ❀ ◑ ▶ ♣ P

East Winch

Carpenters Arms
Lynn Road ☎ (0553) 841228
11–11
Greene King IPA, Abbot Ⓗ; guest beers
A much-needed roadside pub on a dry stretch of the A47. Good food and occasional country and western music.
☔ ❀ ◑ ▶ ♣ P

Eccles

Old Railway Tavern (Eccles Tap)
Station Road ☎ (095 387) 788
12–2.30 (1 Wed), 5.30–11
Adnams Bitter; Greene King IPA, Abbot Ⓗ; guest beer
Known locally as the 'Tap', this pub has a reputation for conversation. Low beams can prove a threat to the unwary. Occasional speciality evenings. No lunches Sun.
🏚 Q ❀ ◑ ▶ ⇌ (Eccles Rd) ♣ ♥ P

Edgefield

Three Pigs
On B1149, 3 miles S of Holt ☎ (0263) 87634
11–2.30, 6 (7 winter)–11
Adnams Bitter; Woodforde's Wherry Ⓗ
Unspoilt pub, over 200 years-old, with a single brick-fronted bar which is thought to have had smuggling connections. Small site for five caravans (CC approved); home-cooked food (not served Mon eve). Q ❀ ◑ ▶ ♣ P

Elsing

Mermaid Inn
Church Street ☎ (0362) 637640
11–3, 7–11

Adnams Bitter; Draught Bass; Woodforde's Wherry Ⓗ
17th-century inn situated at the heart of the village, opposite a beautiful 13th-century church. An open fire with gleaming brass adds to the friendly atmosphere. The cosy restaurant offers a good choice of food. Pool and darts are popular. 🏚 ❀ ◑ ▶ ♣ P

Erpingham

Spreadeagle
2 miles W of A140, Norwich–Cromer road ☎ (0263) 761591
11–2.30, 6.30–11
Woodforde's Wherry, Nelson's Revenge, Norfolk Nog, Baldric, Headcracker Ⓖ
Pub situated on the Weavers Way, formerly Woodforde's brewery tap – the old brewhouse stands alongside. Dining room; games room leading on to a garden. The house beer is Spreadeagle BB (Woodforde's).
🏚 ☔ ❀ ◑ ▶ ♿ ♣ ▲ P

Gayton

Crown
Lynn Road ☎ (0553) 636252
11–3, 6–11
Greene King XX Mild, IPA, Rayments Special, Abbot Ⓗ
A fine example of a Norfolk village pub. It may be the centre of village life, but the roaring fire and good food ensure a warm welcome for visitors too.
🏚 Q ☔ ❀ ◑ ▶ ♣ P

Gorleston

New Entertainer
80 Pier Plain ☎ (0493) 653218
11.30–4, 7–11 (11–11 Sat)
Adnams Extra, Broadside Ⓗ; guest beers
A former Lacon's house that has been tastefully refurbished. A good range of beers always available, with six guest ales. Q ♣ P

Short Blue
47 High Street ☎ (0493) 602192
11–11
Elgood's Cambridge Bitter; Scotties Blues & Bloater Ⓗ; guest beers
Small, cosy, wood-panelled single bar selling its own brewery beers and regular guests. 🏚 ❀ ◑ ▶

Great Cressingham

Windmill Inn
Water End ☎ (076 06) 232
11–2.30, 6.30–11 (12–2.30, 7–10.30 Sun)
Adnams Bitter, Broadside; Draught Bass; Greene King

IPA; Samuel Smith OBB; Stones Best Bitter Ⓗ; guest beers
A large oak-beamed pub in a small village between Watton and Swaffham. Many drinking areas, some suitable for families, and a games room.
🏚 Q ☔ ❀ ◑ ▶ ▲ ♣ P

Great Yarmouth

Clipper Schooner
Friars Lane ☎ (0493) 854926
11–11
Adnams Mild, Bitter, Broadside, Old Ⓗ; guest beers
Two-roomed 1930s pub close to the old town wall and docks, offering a warm welcome to both locals and visitors. Q ☔ ❀ ◑ ♿ ♣ P

Oliver Twist
62 North Market Road ☎ (0493) 855836
11–3, 7–11
Adnams Bitter; Draught Bass Ⓗ; guest beer
Two-bar local close to the market place; tastefully modernised, and offering a good selection of food at reasonable prices. Q ❀ ◑ ▶ ♿ ▲ ⇌ (Vauxhall) ♣ ♥

Red Herring
24–25 Havelock Road (along the quay, left at Nottingham Way, 3rd right off St Peter's Rd) ☎ (0493) 853384
11–3, 6–11
Adnams Mild, Bitter Ⓗ; guest beers
The only real ale free house in Great Yarmouth. Enjoys a relaxing atmosphere with pictures of the old fishing days, and sells books and records in aid of two local charities. Beer festivals held twice yearly; four guest beers served. ☔ ◑ ▶ ♣ ♡

Gressenhall

Swan
The Green ☎ (0362) 860340
11–3, 7–11 (11–11 summer)
Beer range varies Ⓗ
Single-bar village pub on the green. There is a small reference library at one end, ideal for a leisurely pint and crossword session.
🏚 ☔ ❀ ◑ ▶ ♿ ▲ ♣ P

Griston

Waggon & Horses
Church Road ☎ (0953) 883847
11–3, 6.30–11
Greene King IPA, Rayments Special, Abbot Ⓗ
Large, comfortable village pub divided into three distinct areas, including a games room. Good value food always available.
❀ ◑ ▶ ▲ ♣ P

221

Norfolk

Happisburgh

Hill House
Off B1159 ☎ (0692) 650004
11–2.30, 7–11
**Adnams Bitter; Greene King
Abbot; Woodforde's
Wherry** H**; guest beer**
16th-century pub with a
beamed ceiling. Popular with
locals and holidaymakers. The
good family room has plenty
of toys.
🏠 ⅃ ❀ 🍴 ◑ ▶ ▲ ♣ P

Harleston

Cherry Tree
London Road ☎ (0379) 852345
11–2.30, 6–11
**Adnams Mild, Bitter, Old,
Broadside** H
Wonderful village pub
unspoilt by modernisation or
refurbishment. The beer is
served from a bank of
handpumps behind the bars.
Petanque played.
🏠 Q ❀ & ♣ P

Hedenham

Mermaid
On B1332, 2 miles from
Bungay ☎ (050 844) 480
11–3, 5 (7 Sat)–11
**Adnams Bitter; Draught Bass;
Greene King IPA** G
Comfortable, recently
refurbished country pub,
which has retained much of its
old character. With two large
open fires offering a warm
welcome. 🏠 ❀ 🍴 ◑ ▲ ♣ P

Heydon

Earle Arms
Off B1149 ☎ (026 387) 376
11–3, 6.30–11
**Adnams Bitter, Broadside;
Greene King Abbot** G
Unspoilt pub in a picturesque
village. 🏠 ❀ ⅃ 🍴 ◑ 🚪 ♣ P

Hilborough

Swan
On A1065 ☎ (076 06) 380
11–2.30, 6–11
**Adnams Bitter; Greene King
IPA, Abbot** H**; guest beers**
Comfortable roadside free
house six miles south of
Swaffham.
🏠 Q ❀ 🍴 ◑ ▶ ♣ P

Hockwold

New Inn
Station Road ☎ (0842) 828668
11–3, 6–11 (11–11 Sat)
Greene King IPA, Abbot H
Long, part-flint-built pub
which was once a coaching
inn. Now a village local with a
warm welcome. No meals Sun
eve. 🏠 ❀ 🍴 ◑ ▶ ♣ P

Holkham

Victoria
Park Road (by A149)
☎ (0328) 710469
11–3, 7–11 (11–11 summer)
**Greene King IPA; Marston's
Pedigree** H
Children are welcome in this
c. 1820 pub on the edge of the
Holkham estate. The pub,
presumably, was built to serve
the estate staff, but now has a
fair amount of tourist trade.
Two small bars and a larger
lounge/eating area.
🏠 Q 🍴 ◑ ▶ ♣ P

Hunworth

Hunny Bell
The Green ☎ (0263) 712300
10.30–3, 5.30–11
**Adnams Bitter; Greene King
Abbot; Woodforde's
Wherry** H
Long-established, welcoming
free house on the green of a
picturesque village. Real log
fire and good food.
🏠 ⅃ ❀ 🍴 ◑ ▶ P

King's Lynn

Crossways
Valingers Road
☎ (0553) 771947
11–3, 7–11
**Greene King XX Mild, IPA,
Abbot** H
Friendly street-corner local in
the old part of town, off
London Road. Tastefully
refurbished without losing its
local character.
Q ❀ 🍴 ◑ ▶ ≠ ♣

Dukes Head Hotel
(Lynn Bar)
Tuesday Market Place
☎ (0553) 774996
11–2.30, 6–11
**Adnams Bitter; Draught Bass;
Greene King Rayments
Special, Abbot** H
Small bar to the left of the
entrance of an impressive THF
hotel on the Tuesday Market
Place. Don't be put off by the
grandeur of the building – this
is an island of calm in what
can be a loud and busy area.
Q 🍴 ◑ ▶ ≠

London Porterhouse
78 London Road
☎ (0553) 766842
11.30–2.30, 6–11
Greene King IPA, Abbot G
Small traditional bar, close to
the south gate. Full of lively
locals. Q ❀ 🍴 ≠ ♣

Tudor Rose
St Nicholas Street
☎ (0553) 762824
11–11
**Adnams Bitter, Broadside;
Draught Bass** H**; guest beers**

Historic, 15th-century
timbered hotel, just off the
Tuesday Market Place. One
quiet and one noisy bar.
Excellent food and a good
range of malt whiskies.
Q ❀ 🍴 ◑ ▶ ≠

White Horse
9 Wootton Road, Gaywood
☎ (0553) 763258
11–3 (3.30 Sat), 6–11
**Courage Directors; John
Smith's Bitter; Webster's
Yorkshire Bitter** H**; guest
beers**
Busy local close to the
Gaywood clock; always full of
activity. ♣ P

Larling

Angel
☎ (0953) 717963
11–11
**Adnams Bitter; Charrington
IPA; Courage Directors** H
Ignore the shabby exterior, for
inside is an excellent local. As
might be expected from its
situation on the A11, it is also
popular with travellers. Eve
meals Thu–Sat only. 🏠 ❀ 🍴
◑ ▶ ≠ (Harling Rd) ♣ P

Letheringsett

Kings Head
Holt Road (A148, 1 mile W of
Holt) ☎ (0263) 712691
10.30–3, 5.30–11
**Adnams Bitter; Greene King
IPA, Abbot** H**; guest beers**
Comfortable, old beamed pub
in a delightful garden setting,
adjoining old brewery
buildings. A quiet walk from
the watermill nearby, along
the River Glaven. Families
welcome.
🏠 Q ❀ 🍴 ◑ ▶ 🚪 ♣ P

Mundesley

Royal Hotel
30 Paston Road (B1159, coast
road) ☎ (0263) 720096
11–2.30 (longer in summer), 6–11
**Adnams Bitter; Greene King
IPA, Abbot** H**; guest beer**
Pub where the bar is dark,
comfortable, and well-
upholstered, with a better-lit
lounge; original parts are 16th
century. Nelson used to stay
here whilst attending school at
nearby Paston.
🏠 ⅃ ❀ 🍴 ◑ ▶ ▲ P

New Buckenham

Kings Head
Market Place ☎ (0953) 860487
11.30–2.30, 7–11
**Whitbread Boddingtons
Bitter** H**; guest beers**
Welcoming, two-roomed pub
on the village green, serving
good, home-made food.
🏠 Q ❀ 🍴 ◑ ▶ & ♣

Norfolk

North Walsham

Scarborough Hill House Hotel
Old Yarmouth Road
☎ (0692) 402151
11–3, 7–11
Bateman XB G**; guest beer** (occasionally)
Hotel with a bar and dining area, set in large grounds in rural surroundings on the outskirts of town.
🏄 Q ⍣ ✿ 🛏 ◖ ▶ ⚓ P

North Wootton

Red Cat Hotel
Station Road ☎ (0553) 631244
11–2.30, 6–11
Adnams Bitter; Draught Bass H
Retains its welcoming atmosphere despite a major refurbishment. The mummified cat is still present. The house beer is Woodforde's.
🏄 ⌣ ✿ 🛏 ◖ ▶ ⚓ P

Norwich

Angel Gardens
96 Angel Road (almost opp. Waterloo Park)
☎ (0603) 427490
11–2.30, 5.30–11 (11–11 Sat)
S&N Theakston Best Bitter; Whitbread Castle Eden Ale; Woodforde's Wherry; Younger Scotch H**; guest beers**
Recently released free house with post-war decor in its single bar; separate dining/function room. Often offers unusual guest beers; Kingfisher Farm cider.
⌣ ✿ ◖ ▶ ⚓ ⌂ P

Black Horse
50 Earlham Road
☎ (0603) 624682
11–2.30, 5.30–11 (11–11 Sat)
Adnams Extra; Marston's Pedigree; Whitbread Boddingtons Bitter, Flowers IPA; Woodforde's Wherry H
Busy, yet comfortable, two-bar pub with a friendly atmosphere and a carvery restaurant. Covered outdoor area. Close to the catholic cathedral. ⌣ ✿ ◖ ▶ ⚓ P

Bread & Cheese
111 Adelaide Street
☎ (0603) 615303
11–3, 5.30 (7 Sat)–11
Adnams Bitter; Draught Bass H**; guest beer**
Friendly corner local with notable original Bullards stained-glass windows.
✿ ◖ ⚓

Catherine Wheel
61 St Augustines (1½ miles from Anglia Sq)

☎ (0603) 627852
11–11
Adnams Bitter; Draught Bass; Ind Coope Burton Ale; Tetley Bitter H**; guest beers**
A warm welcome in a free house to suit most tastes (lively at the weekend). Distinctive red brick and beams (mind the well); imaginative bar menu and an upstairs restaurant. Four guest beers usually available: well worth a visit. 🏄 ✿ ◖ ▶ ⚓

Fat Cat
49 West End Street (100 yds from A47) ☎ (0603) 624364
10.30–3, 4.45–11 (11–11 Sat)
Adnams Bitter; Elgood's Cambridge Bitter; Wells Bombardier; Woodforde's Nelson's Revenge H**; guest beers**
Sympathetically refurbished, very popular, Victorian corner pub with a friendly atmosphere. Eleven beers always available, including a mild, plus Burnard's cider.
& ⚓ ⌂

Golden Star
Duke Street ☎ (0603) 632447
11–11
Greene King XX Mild, IPA, Rayments Special, Abbot H
Single bar with a separate dining area which also has a small bar. Good value food, even if the beer is rather highly priced. ◖ ⚓

Horse & Dray
137 Ber Street ☎ (0603) 624741
11–11
Adnams Mild, Bitter, Broadside; Robinson's Best Bitter; Wells Bombardier; Young's Bitter H
Busy, city-centre pub with a very friendly atmosphere.
🏄 ✿ ◖ ⚓

Jubilee
26 St Leonards Road, Thorpe Hamlet ☎ (0603) 618734
11–11
Fuller's London Pride; Marston's Pedigree; Whitbread Boddingtons Bitter H**; guest beers**
A wide choice of beers (including six guests) is always available at this popular free house. The house beer is Woodforde's. Keen sports teams.
🏄 ✿ ◖ ▶ ⊞ & ⇌ ⚓ ⌂

Micawbers
92 Pottergate ☎ (0603) 626627
11–3, 5–11 (11–11 Sat)
Adnams Bitter, Old; Draught Bass; Samuel Smith OBB; S&N Theakston XB; Wadworth 6X H
Comfortable corner pub with one long bar in a beamed interior. No food Sun. ◖

Mill Tavern
2 Miller's Lane, Angel Road
☎ (0603) 410268
11–2.30, 6-15–11 (12–2.30, 7–10.30 Sun)
Adnams Mild, Bitter, Old, Broadside H
This old favourite never varies. It just keeps on producing good beer with no frills. One long bar with plain, solid decor – a good reliable boozer. & ⚓ P

Pottergate Tavern
23 Pottergate ☎ (0603) 614589
10.30–11
Greene King XX Mild, IPA, Rayments Special, Abbot H**; guest beers**
Distinctive, corner city-centre pub on two levels, close to the market, attracting a varied clientele. 1930s-style decor creates a flavour of bygone days. Good value, home-cooked lunches. ◖ ⚓ ⌂

Reindeer
10 Dereham Road
☎ (0603) 666821
11–11
Bateman XXXB; Elgood's Cambridge Bitter H**; guest beers**
Very popular free house and brewery featuring six guest, and six house beers. Recently modified to one long bar but the bare boards, tiles and decor remain (as does the phone box). Good food includes wonderful garlic bread. Q ✿ ◖ ▶ ⚓ ⌂ P

Ribs of Beef
24 Wensum Street
☎ (0603) 619517
10.30–11
Adnams Bitter; Bateman Mild; Marston's Pedigree; Reepham Rapier; Woodforde's Wherry H**; guest beer**
River views help create a special atmosphere at this old, long pub, with a no-smoking/children's area in the cellar. This is one of Norwich's tourist attractions – not to be missed. Woodforde's house beer. Q ⌣ ◖ ⇌ ◖ ⌀

Rosary Tavern
95 Rosary Road
☎ (0603) 666287
11–3, 5.30–11
Adnams Bitter; Draught Bass; Bateman XXXB; Marston's Pedigree; Woodforde's Wherry H**; guest beers**
Small, friendly and popular pub near the yacht station and small hotels. About ten beers on handpump or gravity dispense. Keen CAMRA crib league supporters. House beer brewed by Woodforde's. Eve meals only by arrangement.
⌣ ✿ ◖ ⇌ ⚓ ⌂ P

223

Norfolk

St Andrew's Tavern

4 St Andrew's Street
☎ (0603) 614858
11–3, 5–11 (11–11 Fri & Sat; closed Sun)
Adnams Mild, Bitter, Old, Broadside; Wells Bombardier; Young's Special H
Good city pub popular with business people at lunchtime. The cosy cellar bar (open most sessions) contrasts with the airy conservatory to the rear. The wooden floorboards in the public bar area help give the feel of a real drinkers' haven. ⚗ ◑

Tap & Spile (White Lion)

73 Oak Street ☎ (0603) 620630
11–11
Bateman XXXB H**; guest beers**
Popular three-bar pub which concentrates on beer, offering a varying range of up to 11 ales, available in quantities from nips (1/3 pint) to jugs. Live music Mon and Wed. No food Sun. ⚗ ◑ ♣ ⌂ P

Wild Man

29 Bedford Street
☎ (0603) 627686
10.30–3, 5.30–11
Courage Directors; Tolly Cobbold Bitter, Original, Old Strong H
Pleasant pub, popular with city workers and shoppers at lunchtime, and a younger, mixed evening clientele. ◑

Old Buckenham

Ox & Plough

The Green (just off B1077)
☎ (0953) 860004
12–2.30, 5–11 (12–11 Sat)
Adnams Bitter; Greene King IPA H**; guest beer**
Friendly free house in a picturesque setting on the village green.
⚗ ⛵ ❀ ◑ ◗ ⊟ ⚸ ▲ ♣ P

Old Hunstanton

Ancient Mariner

Golf Course Road
☎ (0485) 534411
11–3, 6–11
Adnams Bitter, Broadside; Draught Bass; Charrington IPA H**; guest beer**
Despite being part of the Lestrange Arms Hotel, there is a pub-like atmosphere here. The large bar is well divided into intimate drinking areas for the adults, plus a room and a garden for children.
⚗ ⛵ ❀ ⌷ ◑ ◗ ♣ P

Lodge Hotel

Old Hunstanton Road (A149)
☎ (0485) 532896
11–11
Draught Bass; Greene King

IPA, Rayments Special, Abbot H
Friendly hotel on the coast road. ⚗ ⛵ ❀ ⌷ ◑ ◗ ♣ P

Ormesby St Margaret

Grange Hotel

On A149, Caister bypass
☎ (0493) 731877
12–11
Adnams Bitter; Bateman XXXB; Charrington IPA H**; guest beers**
Former 18th-century country house, catering for all the family. Two bars enjoy a relaxed atmosphere, and there is a pool room. Eve meals in summer only.
⚗ ⛵ ❀ ⌷ ◑ ▲ ♣ P

Oxborough

Bedingfeld Arms

☎ (036 621) 300
12–3, 5 (7 Sat)–11
Greene King IPA; Marston's Pedigree; Morrells Bitter H**; guest beers**
Popular with locals and visitors alike, not least because of the unusual guest beers. Close to the entrance of the superb Oxborough Hall.
⚗ ❀ ◑ ◗ ♣ P

Rackheath

Sole & Heel

2 Salhouse Road
☎ (0603) 720146
11.30–3 (5 Sat), 7–11
Webster's Yorkshire Bitter H**; guest beer**
Two-bar village local built in the 1930s and thought to have a unique name. Eve meals Fri–Sun; lunches Tue–Sun.
⚗ ❀ ◑ ◗ ♣ P

Reepham

Old Brewery House

Market Square
☎ (0603) 870881
11–3, 6–11 (flexible afternoon opening)
Adnams Bitter, Old; Greene King Abbot; Reepham Rapier; Whitbread Boddingtons Bitter H**; guest beers**
Fine old building overlooking the market square; genuine beams and wood-panelled rooms. The food is well recommended. Popular with locals and visitors.
Q ⛵ ❀ ⌷ ◑ ◗

Ringstead

Gin Trap Inn

High Street ☎ (048 525) 264
11.30–2.30, 7 (6 summer)–11
Adnams Bitter; Greene King IPA, Abbot; Woodforde's

Norfolk Nog H**; guest beers**
Fine country village pub featuring a collection of animal traps and associated memorabilia. The split-level bar and extensive garden make ideal venues for sampling the excellent food. Try a game of petanque. House beer from Woodforde's.
⚗ Q ❀ ◑ ◗ ♣ P

Rockland St Mary

New Inn

12 New Inn Hill (N of A146 at Yelverton) OS327046
☎ (050 88) 395
12 (11 summer)–3, 7.30 (6 summer)–11
Greene King Abbot; Tetley Bitter; Tolly Cobbold Mild; Whitbread Flowers IPA H**; guest beers**
Comfortable, friendly local on the edge of the village. Boat moorings opposite. Games include shove-ha'penny.
⚗ Q ⛵ ❀ ◑ ◗ ♣ P

Salhouse

Lodge

Vicarage Road
☎ (0603) 782828
10.30–3, 6–11
Draught Bass; Greene King IPA, Abbot; Woodforde's Wherry H**; guest beers**
Eighty malt whiskies are available in this converted Georgian vicarage with lovely gardens near the Broads.
⚗ ❀ ◑ ▲ ♣ P

Sedgeford

King William IV

Heacham Road
☎ (0485) 71765
11–3, 5.30 (7 winter)–11
Draught Bass; Charrington IPA; Greene King Abbot; Stones Best Bitter H**; guest beers**
Extremely popular pub which features excellent food, unusual guest ales and various ciders. Close to Peddars Way footpath.
⚗ ❀ ◑ ▲ ♣ ⌂ P

Shouldham Thorpe

Jolly Brewers

Shouldham Gap
☎ (036 64) 7896
10.30–2.30 (3 Sat), 5.30–11
Adnams Broadside; Draught Bass; Greene King IPA H**; guest beers**
Well-decorated, country-style roadside pub, whose main drinking area is dominated by a horseshoe-shaped bar. Good food. ⚗ ❀ ⌷ ◑ ◗ ⚸ ♣ P

Smallburgh

Crown

North Walsham Road (A149)
☎ (0692) 536314
11.30–2.30, 5.30–11 (12–4, 7–11 Sat).
**Greene King IPA; Ind Coope
Burton Ale; Tetley Bitter;
Tolly Cobbold Original** H;
guest beers
Thatched and beamed
building which dates from the
15th century. It features a
large open fire and tables and
chairs made from wooden
barrels and firkins. A friendly
local, offering good food in an
attractive dining room (no
food Sun eve).
🏠 Q ☎ ❀ 🛏 🌓 🍺 ♣ P

Snettisham

Grapes

33 Lynn Road ☎ (0485) 541350
11–3, 7–11
**Courage Directors;
Whitbread Flowers
Original** H; **guest beers**
Quiet pub in the centre of the
village. The food is excellent.
🏠 Q 🌓 🍺

South Creake

Ostrich Inn

Fakenham Road
☎ (0328) 823320
12–11
**Ruddles County;
Woodforde's Wherry** H
Whitewashed flint and brick
village pub containing a single
bar and a small eating area.
Used to be a pub in the
'proper' sense of the word, i.e.
a room in someone's house.
🏠 ☎ ❀ 🌓 ♣ P

South Walsham

Ship

The Street ☎ (060 549) 553
11–3, 6–11 (11–11 Sat & summer
hols)
**Ruddles Best Bitter;
Woodforde's Wherry** H
Attractive pub dating from the
17th century, popular with
cyclists and walkers, and close
to South Walsham Broad and
some interesting historical
sites. The garden is well used;
the family room is only open
in summer.
🏠 Q ☎ ❀ 🌓 🛏 ♣ P

Stanhoe

Crown

Burnham Market Road
☎ (048 58) 330
11–3, 6–11
**Elgood's Cambridge Bitter,
GSB** H
Single-bar pub in a quiet
village; the only Elgood's pub
for miles. Eve meals to order
only. 🏠 Q ❀ 🌓 🅰 ♣ P

Stibbard

Ordnance Arms

Guist Bottom (A1067, 1 mile
NW of Guist)
☎ (032 878) 471
11–2.30, 5.30–11
**Draught Bass; Greene King
IPA** H
A friendly landlord hosts this
two-bar pub. Snacks available
lunchtimes and a Thai
restaurant is open evenings.
🏠 ❀ 🌓 P

Stiffkey

Red Lion

44 Wells Road (A149, just E of
Wells) ☎ (0328) 830552
11–2.30 (3 Sat), 6–11
**Greene King IPA, Abbot;
Ruddles Best Bitter** H;
Woodforde's Wherry G; **guest
beers**
Superb pub, with separate
bars and open fires, in an
unspoilt village which attracts
ramblers on the coastal walks.
Re-opened in 1990 after 20
years as a private house – one
of three former pubs in the
village which were victims of
the Watney revolution.
Excellent food.
🏠 Q ☎ ❀ 🌓 🛏 🍺 🅰 P

Swaffham

Kings Arms Hotel

Lynn Street ☎ (0760) 721495
11–11
**Courage Directors;
Whitbread Flowers
Original** H
Old, unspoilt one-roomed pub
close to one of Norfolk's finest
Saturday markets.
🛏 🌓 ♣ P

Swanton Abbot

Weavers Arms

Aylsham Road (2 miles from
B1150 at Westwick)
☎ (069 269) 655
11–3 (5 Sat), 7–11
**Brakspear Bitter; Greene
King Abbot; Whitbread
Flowers Original** H
Quiet, unspoilt country pub
with beams and an open fire.
Old agricultural implements
adorn the walls.
🏠 Q ☎ ❀ 🌓 🍺 ♣ P

Swanton Morley

Darby's

Elsing Road
☎ (0362) 637647
11–2.30, 6–11
**Adnams Bitter, Broadside;
Woodforde's Wherry** H; **guest
beers**
Friendly village pub which
features four guest beers
(including a mild). The
general decor is bare brick and

beams. Families welcome.
Overnight accommodation is
in a nearby farm, with
camping facilities by the pub.
🏠 ☎ ❀ 🛏 🌓 🅰 P

Tasburgh

Countryman

Ipswich Road (A140)
☎ (0508) 470946
11–2.30, 6.30–11
**Adnams Bitter; Draught Bass;
S&N Theakston Best Bitter** H
Comfortable roadside free
house where food is a major
feature. ❀ 🌓 ♿ ♣ P

Thetford

Albion

Castle Street ☎ (0842) 752796
11–2.30, 6–11 (12–2, 7–10.30 Sun)
Greene King IPA, Abbot H
Small, but comfortable and
friendly, this traditional flint-
faced local is in the older part
of town, close to Castle Hill
ancient monument. Q ❀ ♣ P

Thompson

Chequers Inn

Griston Road OS923969
☎ (095 383) 360
11–3, 6–11
**Adnams Bitter; Draught Bass;
Greene King IPA; Welsh
Brewers Worthington BB** H;
guest beers
16th-century thatched pub
featuring very low ceilings.
Enjoys a well-deserved local
reputation for good food and
can get extremely busy.
Q ☎ ❀ 🌓 ♣ 🍴 P

Thornham

Lifeboat Inn

Ship Lane ☎ (048 526) 236
11–11
Adnams Bitter, Broadside H;
Greene King XX Mild G, **IPA,
Abbot** H; **guest beers**
The original 16th-century inn
still remains, lit by oil lamps,
but the pub has been greatly
extended which may dilute
the atmosphere but does
provide room for excellent
food and accommodation. The
mild is hidden from view.
🏠 Q ☎ ❀ 🛏 🌓 ♣ P

Thorpe St Andrew

Gordon

88 Gordon Avenue
☎ (0603) 34658
11–2.30 (4 Sat), 7–11
**Courage Directors; Greene
King Abbot; John Smith's
Bitter; Whitbread Flowers
IPA** H
Friendly local with a long,
curved single bar; pool table
and darts available. Large
garden. ❀ ♣ 🍴 P

Norfolk

Tibenham

Greyhound

The Street (2 miles E of B1113)
OS136895
☎ (0379) 77676
12–3 (not Mon–Fri), 7–11
Beer range varies Ⓖ *or* Ⓗ
Difficult to find but worth it:
two bars and a collection of
traditional pub games. 'K-9'
house beer from Woodforde's.
🏿 Q ⅏ ⚑ & ♠ P

Toft Monks

Toft Lion

Beccles Road (A143, just N of
Beccles)
☎ (050 277) 702
11.30–2.30, 6.30–11
Adnams Bitter, Old Ⓗ
Friendly local, modernised but
comfortable; a former
Morgan's house called the
'White Lion', renamed to
avoid confusion with a nearby
pub at Wheatacre. No food
Tue eve in winter.
🏿 Q ⅏ ❀ ◑ & ♠ P

Walcott

Lighthouse Inn

Coast Road (B1159)
☎ (0692) 650371
11–3, 6.30–11
**Adnams Bitter; Tetley
Bitter** Ⓗ**; guest beer**
Very popular roadside pub
with good value food and a
friendly landlord. Close to
Bacton gas terminal.
🏿 ⅏ ❀ ◑ & ♠ P

Walpole Cross Keys

Woolpack

Sutton Road
☎ (0553) 828327
12–3, 7–11
Adnams Bitter, Broadside Ⓗ**;
guest beer**
Friendly and welcoming pub
on the old A17, offering good
value food (no meals Mon or
Tue eves).
🏿 Q ⅏ ❀ ◑ ♠ P

Warham

Three Horseshoes

The Street
☎ (0328) 710547
11–2.30, 6–11 (12–2.30, 7–10.30 Sun)
Greene King IPA Ⓗ**, Abbot;
Woodforde's Wherry,
Nelson's Revenge** Ⓖ**; guest
beers**
Old, unspoilt, gas-lit pub with
a 1921 electric pianola and an
old gramophone. Good food
lunchtimes and Thu–Sat eves.
🏿 Q ⅏ ❀ ⌂ ◑ ♠ P

Weasenham All Saints

Ostrich Inn

On A1065 Swaffham–
Fakenham road
☎ (032 874) 221
11–3, 7–11
Adnams Bitter, Broadside Ⓗ
Friendly roadside pub with a
log fire in the inglenook. A
good old-fashioned village
local with an out-of-sight
children's room. Get your fruit
and veg here!
🏿 Q ⅏ ❀ ◑ ▲ ♠ P

Wells-next-the-Sea

Crown Hotel

The Buttlands ☎ (0328) 710209
11–2.30, 6–11 (12–2.30, 7–10.30 Sun)
**Adnams Bitter; Marston's
Pedigree; Tetley Bitter**
(summer) Ⓗ
A coaching inn since the 18th
century, this fine hotel, facing
a tree-lined green, is a Tudor
building with a Georgian
facade. 🏿 ⅏ ❀ ⌂ ◑ & P

Weston Longville

Parson Woodforde

Church Street ☎ (0603) 880106
11.30–3, 6–11
**Adnams Bitter; Draught Bass;
Whitbread Boddingtons
Bitter; Woodforde's
Wherry** Ⓗ**; guest beer**
One-bar pub with some bare
bricks and plenty of beams
(not original). Named after
James Woodforde, the country
parson and imbiber. No-
smoking eating area.
🏿 ❀ ◑ ♠ P

West Rudham

Dukes Head

Lynn Road (A148)
☎ (048 522) 540
11–3, 5.30–11
**Adnams Bitter, Broadside;
Woodforde's Nelson's
Revenge** Ⓗ
1663 flint and Carrstone pub
with a log fire in its small
inglenook. A cosy, friendly
pub, popular with locals and
visitors. 🏿 Q ❀ ◑ ♠ P

West Somerton

Lion

Martham Road (Yarmouth–
Cromer coast road, at B1152
jct) ☎ (0493) 393289
11–4, 6–11
**Greene King XX Mild, IPA,
Abbot** Ⓗ**; guest beers**
Friendly, two-bar village local
close to the river and well
used by tourists. Half portions
of food are served for
children. Three guest beers.
Q ⅏ ❀ ◑ P

Whinburgh

Mustard Pot

On B1135 ☎ (0362) 692179
11–3, 6.30–11
**Adnams Bitter; Draught
Bass** Ⓗ
17th-century building which
has only been a pub for 14
years, after a former life as a
row of cottages and a village
shop. The interior is long and
narrow, with a single bar.
🏿 ❀ ◑ ♠ P

Wimbotsham

Chequers

7 Church Road
☎ (0366) 387704
11.45–2.30, 6.30–11
**Greene King XX Mild, IPA,
Abbot** Ⓗ
Recently extended by the
addition of a function room,
this excellent village pub is
one of the few local outlets for
XX Mild. Q ❀ ◑ ♠ P

Winterton-on-Sea

Fisherman's Return

The Lane (off B1159)
☎ (0493) 393305
11–2.30, 6 (7 winter)–11
**Adnams Bitter; Webster's
Yorkshire Bitter** Ⓗ
Popular two-bar local, close to
the beach and much used by
visitors in summer. Good
selection of food.
🏿 Q ⅏ ❀ ◑ ⚑ ♠ ⌂ P

Wreningham

Bird in Hand

Church Road (B1133 from
Norwich) ☎ (0508) 41438
11–3, 5.30–11
**Adnams Bitter; Marston's
Pedigree; Whitbread Castle
Eden Ale, Flowers
Original** Ⓗ**; guest beers**
Well-tiled floor and wooden
rafters in a modern bar with a
pleasant, relaxed atmosphere.
Landscaped gardens include a
children's play area.
🏿 Q ⅏ ❀ ◑ & ♠ P

Wymondham

Feathers

Town Green ☎ (0953) 605675
11–2.30, 6 (7 Sat)–11
**Adnams Bitter; Draught Bass;
Greene King Abbot;
Marston's Pedigree;
Wadworth 6X** Ⓗ
17th-century free house which
also offers food and has a
good, friendly atmosphere.
House beer (Feathers Tickler)
is brewed by Woodforde's.
🏿 ❀ ◑ ♠ ≢

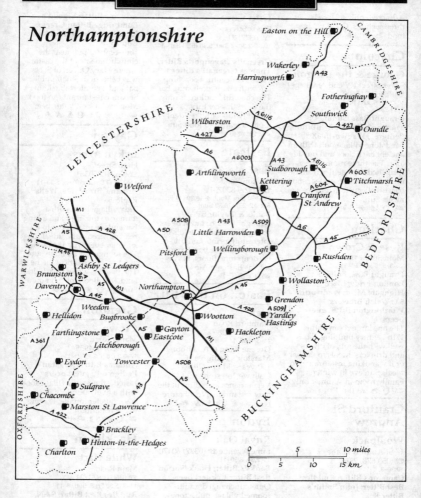

Northamptonshire

Easton on the Hill
Wakerley
Harringworth
Fotheringhay
Southwick
Wilbarston
Oundle
Arthlingworth
Sudborough
Kettering
Titchmarsh
Cranford St Andrew
Welford
Little Harrowden
Wellingborough
Pitsford
Rushden
Braunston
Ashby St Ledgers
Wollaston
Daventry
Northampton
Grendon
Hellidon
Weedon
Bugbrooke
Wootton
Yardley Hastings
Farthingstone
Gayton
Eastcote
Hackleton
Litchborough
Eydon
Towcester
Sulgrave
Chacombe
Marston St Lawrence
Brackley
Charlton
Hinton-in-the-Hedges

LEICESTERSHIRE · CAMBRIDGESHIRE · BEDFORDSHIRE · BUCKINGHAMSHIRE · OXFORDSHIRE · WARWICKSHIRE

0   5   10 miles
0 5 10 15 km

Arthlingworth

Bulls Head

Kelmarsh Road ☎ (0858) 86204
6–11 (11.30–2, 6–11 Sat; 12–2.30,
7–10.30 Sun)
**Bateman XB; Greene King
IPA, Abbot; Morland Old
Masters Ⓗ; guest beers**
(summer)
Converted in 1920 from a mid-
19th century farmhouse. Three
sections plus a restaurant.
Beer can be served in three-
pint jugs in the bar (50p
discount). ♨ Q ✿ ◑ ▶ P

Ashby St Ledgers

Old Coach House Inn

☎ (0788) 890349
12–2.30, 6–11 (12–2.30, 7–10.30 Sun)
**Everards Old Original;
Samuel Smith OBB; Thwaites
Bitter; Whitbread**

Boddingtons Bitter, Flowers
IPA, Original Ⓗ
Perfect example of a country
inn. Cosy in winter with a real
fire, an old range and wood
panelling throughout. Month-
long beer festivals.
♨ ➔ ✿ ◑ ◐ ▶ ♣ P

Brackley

Red Lion

Market Place ☎ (0280) 702228
11–3, 5.30–11 (11–11 Fri & Sat)
**Adnams Broadside; Wells
Eagle, Bombardier Ⓗ**
Stone-built pub tucked away
behind the town hall.
Formerly a Hopcraft & Norris
house: a public bar and a pool
lounge with a large inglenook.
Smoke-free room for children
if required. Live music most
Fris. Eve meals by
arrangement. ➔ ✿ ◑ ⊞ ♣

Braunston

Admiral Nelson

Dark Lane, Little Braunston
(off A45 via deadend lane)
☎ (0788) 890075
11.30–2.30, 7–11 (12–2.30, 7–10.30
Sun)
**Bateman XB; Ruddles County;
Webster's Yorkshire Bitter Ⓗ**
Difficult to find pub in an
attractive lock-side location.
The interior is split into eating,
drinking and games areas by
exposed brick which
complements the exposed
beams. Q ✿ ◑ ▶ ⅙ ♣ P

Bugbrooke

Five Bells

Church Lane ☎ (0604) 832483
12–2.30, 6–11
**Ruddles Best Bitter; Webster's
Yorkshire Bitter Ⓗ; guest beer**

227

Northamptonshire

Attractive pub: a large bar in three sections. Good value food. ❧ ⊛ ◑ ▷ ⓰ ♣ P ⚲

Chacombe

George & the Dragon
Silver Street (W end of village)
☎ (0295) 710602
12–2.30, 5.30–11 (11–11 Fri; 12–4, 7–11 Sat)
Draught Bass (summer); **Marston's Border Exhibition, Pedigree; Wadworth 6X** H
Sandstone village pub with an ancient back door and outside loos. The three rooms are furnished with settles from the unique, now dismantled, snug bar. Lively customers. No eve meals Sun.
♨ Q ❧ ⊛ ◑ ▷ ♣ P

Charlton

Rose & Crown
Main Street ☎ (0295) 811317
12–3, 5 (6.30 Sat)–11
Draught Bass; Fuller's London Pride; M&B Highgate Mild; Wadworth 6X; Welsh Brewers Worthington BB H; **guest beers**
The one large room of this 17th-century building copes well with the mix of diners and drinkers. Meals in the bar or no-smoking restaurant. No meals Sun eve in winter. Family room in summer only.
♨ Q ❧ ⊛ ◑ ▷ P

Cranford St Andrew

Woolpack
17 St Andrews Lane
☎ (053 678) 256
10.30–3, 6–11
Camerons Bitter; Ruddles Best Bitter; John Smith's Bitter H
Classic country pub; wooden beams, brass, and open fires in all rooms. Traditional games in a separate room. Ask for directions. A gem!
♨ Q ⊛ ⓰ ♣ P

Daventry

Coach & Horses
Warwick Street
☎ (0327) 76692
11–2.30, 5 (4.30 Fri)–11 (12–4, 7–11 Sat)
Ind Coope Burton Ale; Marston's Pedigree; Tetley Bitter H
Originally a coaching inn, rebuilt internally but retaining some style. One large public bar, but very civilised and friendly. Live jazz alternate Thu; pool, etc. in the rear bar area. Separate stable bar for music and functions. No food Sat/Sun. ♨ Q ⊛ ◑

Dun Cow
Brook Street
☎ (0327) 71545
10.30–2.30 (4 Sat), 5.30 (6.30 Sat)–11 (10.30–11 Fri)
Greenalls Davenports Bitter, Thomas Greenall's Bitter H
Early 17th-century coaching inn with an unspoilt snug bar. The cheerful landlord is only the third this century. Monthly folk club; resident football team. No food Sun.
♨ Q ⊛ ◑ ♣ P

Eastcote

Eastcote Arms
Gayton Road
☎ (0327) 830731
12–2.30 (not Mon), 6–10.30 (11 Fri & Sat; 12–2, 7–10.30 Sun)
Banks & Taylor SPA; Draught Bass H; **guest beers**
Stone-built local with lots of interesting prints and bric-a-brac around the bar. Large garden; stone floors. SPA is sold as Eastcote Ale.
♨ Q ⊛ ◑ P

Easton on the Hill

Oak
Stamford Road
☎ (0780) 52286
11–3, 6.30–11
Greene King IPA, Abbot; Marston's Pedigree H
150-year-old inn with a Collyweston stone roof. Vegetarians catered for in the new restaurant. Near nature reserve. ⊛ ◑ ▷ ⓰ ▲ ♣ P

Eydon

Royal Oak
Lime Avenue ☎ (0327) 60470
11–2.30, 6.30–11
Banks's Bitter; Hook Norton Best Bitter H; **guest beer**
Quiet, unchanged, multi-roomed village pub, stone-built with flagged floors and outside loos, but none of the beams/horsebrass cliché. Ask about the guest beer.
♨ Q ❧ ⊛ ◑ ♣ P

Farthingstone

Kings Arms
☎ (032 736) 604
11–3, 6–11
Home Bitter; Hook Norton Best Bitter; S&N Theakston XB; Wadworth 6X H
Attractive sandstone pub built in 1870 from stone left over from a church. A stone-flagged, L-shaped bar on several levels; separate skittle room. ♨ Q ❧ ⊛ ◑ ▷ ♣ P

Fotheringhay

Falcon
Main Street ☎ (083 26) 254
11.30 (10 public bar)–2.30, 7–11

Adnams Bitter; Elgood's Cambridge Bitter; Greene King IPA, Abbot; Ruddles County H
18th-century pub near the church and site of the castle where Mary Queen of Scots was beheaded. Small public bar and a comfortable lounge. Separate restaurant (no food Mon eve). Good value beer.
♨ Q ⊛ ◑ ▷ ⓰ ⓰ ▲ ♣ P

Gayton

Eykyn Arms
High Street
☎ (0604) 858361
11–2.30 (3 Sat, not Tue), 5.30–11
Adnams Broadside; Wells Eagle H
Tidy village local with a lounge to the front and a long bar and a games room to the rear; covered patio, ideal for summer eves with the family. The lounge has an interesting aviation and nautical theme. The piano is a must – ask the landlady. Book for food on Sun. ♨ Q ⊛ ◑ ⓰ ♣

Grendon

Crown
Manor Road
☎ (0933) 664955
12–2.30, 6 (6.30 Sat)–11
Adnams Bitter; Marston's Pedigree H; **guest beers**
Listed, stone-built village local with a lively public and a cosy, quieter lounge, leading to the restaurant.
♨ Q ⊛ ◑ ▷ ⓰ P

Hackleton

White Hart
Main Road
☎ (0604) 870721
11–3 (3.30 Fri & Sat), 6–11
Ruddles Best Bitter; S&N Theakston XB; Webster's Yorkshire Bitter H
Stone-built pub whose first landlord was back in 1739. A 40ft well is built into the lounge bar; the public bar has an inglenook and Northants skittles. Good food (no meals Sun). Q ⊛ ◑ ▷ ⓰ ♣ P

Harringworth

White Swan
Seaton Road
☎ (057 287) 543
11.30–2.30, 6.30–11
Greene King IPA, Abbot; S&N Theakston XB H
16th-century, stone-built coaching inn. The stairs up to the accommodation have a 'trip step' – an early form of burglar alarm. Walter de la Mare carved his name on the chimney breast.
Q ⇌ ◑ ♣ P

228

Hellidon

Red Lion
☎ (0327) 61200
12–2.30, 5.30–11
**Courage Best Bitter,
Directors; Hook Norton Best
Bitter** H
Substantial village pub with a
smart image; professionally
run but still genuine.
🏾 ✤ 🏠 ◖▶ 🍺 & ♣ P

Hinton-in-the-Hedges

Crewe Arms
☎ (0280) 703314
11–2.30, 6.30–11
**Hook Norton Best Bitter;
Marston's Pedigree; Morland
Old Speckled Hen; S&N
Theakston XB** H; guest beers
Stone-built pub tucked away
in the centre of a remote
village. Three bars, all with
their own character: open fires
and wood beams. Restaurant
and function room. Two guest
ales. 🏾 Q ✤ ◖▶ 🍺 & P

Kettering

Old Market Inn
Sheep Street (opp. church)
☎ (0536) 310311
11–2.30 (3 market days), 7–11
(12–2.30, 7–10.30 Sun)
**S&N Theakston Old Peculier;
Younger IPA** H; guest beers
Tastefully modernised single
lounge-bar pub with a
separate restaurant. The range
of beers changes, with four
guests. 🏠 ◖▶ ≷

Litchborough

Old Red Lion
Banbury Road
☎ (0327) 830250
11.30–2.30 (not Mon in winter, 11–3
Sat), 6.30–11
Banks's Bitter E
Stone-built village pub on the
Knightly Way footpath, with a
single small bar, large
inglenook, pool and skittle
rooms. No food Sun/Mon.
🏾 Q ✤ ◖▶ 🍺 & P

Little Harrowden

Lamb Inn
Orlingbury Road
☎ (0933) 673300
11–2.30 (3 Fri & Sat), 6–11
**Adnams Broadside; Wells
Eagle, Bombardier** H
Pleasant village pub with a
cosy, oak-beamed lounge and
a good games room
(Northants skittles). Very
popular for the varied menu
in the restaurant (book), as
well as good value bar meals.
Live jazz first Sat of summer
months. Trad. roast only Sun

lunch; no food Sun eve.
🏾 ✤ ◖▶ 🍺 & ♣ P

Marston St Lawrence

Marston Inn
☎ (0295) 711906
12–2.30 (3 Sat), 7–11
**Hook Norton Best Bitter, Old
Hooky** H
Small, friendly village pub
converted from a row of
cottages. Three small rooms,
one of which serves as a
dining room, with the
emphasis on fish and home
cooking (no eve meals
Sun/Mon). Folk nights last
Thu of the month.
🏾 Q ⌚ ✤ ◖▶ ▲ ♣ P

Northampton

Barn Owl
Olden Road, Rectory Farm (off
A4500 4 miles E of centre)
☎ (0604) 416483
11–3, 6–11
Greene King IPA, Abbot H
A great estate pub – the only
Greene King pub in
Northampton. Winner of
CAMRA's *Best New Pub*
award 1986: one large bar on
two levels. No food Sun.
◖▶ ♣ P

Garibaldi
19 Baliff Street (off Campbell
Sq) ☎ (0604) 30356
11.30–11
**Draught Bass; Welsh Brewers
Worthington BB** H
Easy-going local in a side
street near the police station.
Boxing gym upstairs. 🍺 ♣

King Billy
20 Commercial Street
☎ (0604) 21307
12–3, 5.30–11 (12–11 Fri & Sat)
**Bruce's Dogbolter; Samuel
Smith Museum; S&N
Theakston XB, Old Peculier;
Tetley Bitter; Younger IPA** H;
guest beers
Town-centre pub with a large,
open-plan, dimly-lit bar.
Entertainment of the heavier
nature: can get loud and
crowded at weekends. Special
price promotions. Dogbolter
comes from the Firkin brew
pubs. & ≷ ↺

Lamplighter
66 Overstone Road (400 yds E
of bus station)
☎ (0604) 31125
11–2.30, 6–11
**Courage Best Bitter,
Directors; Marston's
Pedigree** H
Comfortable, small, side-street
local done up as a high-class
London pub, with real wood
and leaded-glass screens. No
food Sat/Sun. ✤ ◖ &

Queen Adelaide
50 Manor Road, Kingsthorpe
(off A50) ☎ (0604) 714524
11–3, 5.30–11
**Banks's Bitter; Ruddles Best
Bitter; Webster's Yorkshire
Bitter** H
Popular pub in old
Kingsthorpe village. The
separate public bar retains
original ceiling panelling and
an area for Northants skittles.
Q ✤ ◖▶ ♣ P

Oundle

Ship
West Street ☎ (0832) 273918
11–3, 6–11 (11–11 Sat)
**Draught Bass; Greene King
IPA; Marston's Pedigree;
S&N Theakston XB** H; guest
beer
Large, three-room pub in an
attractive small town.
🏾 ⌚ ✤ 🏠 ◖▶ 🍺 & P

Pitsford

Griffin
High Street ☎ (0604) 880346
12–2.30 (3 Sat), 6–11
**S&N Theakston Best Bitter,
XB, Old Peculier** H
Listed, stone-built village
local. Friendly, pleasant and
relaxing. ✤ ◖ 🍺 ♣ P

Rushden

Feathers
High Street ☎ (0933) 50251
11.30–3, 6–11 (11–11 Sat)
**Adnams Broadside;
Mansfield Riding Mild;
Wells Eagle, Bombardier** H
Typical town-centre hostelry:
a comfortable lounge and a
recently redecorated wood-
panelled bar. Quiz night Sun;
no food Sun. ✤ ◖ 🍺 ♣ P

King Edward VII
158 Queen Street (N off ring
road) ☎ (0933) 53478
11–11
**Adnams Broadside; Wells
Eagle, Bombardier** H
Fine, traditional drinking pub
with a good atmosphere.
Home cooking. 🏾 ◖ 🍺 ♣

Southwick

Shuckburgh Arms
Main Street ☎ (0832) 247007
11–2.30, 6–11
**Adnams Bitter; Exmoor Ale,
Gold; Hook Norton Best
Bitter, Old Hooky; Taylor
Landlord** G; guest beer
Classic, unspoilt, 16th-century
village local: basic bar and a
cosy lounge with bar billiards
in the passage. Lunches by
arrangement.
🏾 Q ✤ 🍺 ♣ ↺ P

Northamptonshire

Sudborough

Vane Arms
Main Street ☎ (080 12) 3223
11.30–3 (not Mon), 5.30 (6 Sat)–11
Morland Old Speckled Hen; Moorhouse's Pendle Witches Brew Ⓗ**; guest beers**
Deservedly popular, old thatched village free house, with stonework and beams throughout the good, basic public and the plusher lounge. Small upstairs restaurant. Seven guest beers, plus Belgian cherry beer and German wheat beer. Ask for the sample tray. No food Sun eve or Mon.
🏚 ❀ ◑ ◖ 🍽 ➜ ⌂ P

Sulgrave

Star
Manor Road ☎ (0295) 760389
11–2.30, 6–11
Hook Norton Best Bitter, Old Hooky Ⓗ
Professionally-run, single-roomed village pub, with stone walls and floors. Quirky decorations include a skeleton in the fireplace and a hand reaching out of the wine rack. Small separate dining room. No food Sun eve.
🏚 Q ❀ 🍽 ◑ ◖ ♿ P

Titchmarsh

Dog & Partridge
High Street ☎ (080 12) 2546
12–3, 6 (6.30 Sat)–11
Adnams Broadside; Wells Eagle, Bombardier Ⓗ
18th-century village pub, much improved by the addition of a public bar. Two real fires to keep the local quiz fanatics warm. 🏚 ❀ 🍽 ♣ P

Towcester

Peacock
Watling Street ☎ (0327) 52615
11–3 (4 Sat), 6–11
Morrells Varsity; Tetley Bitter Ⓗ**; guest beers**
Popular at all sessions, a main road pub with a small lounge. Very sport-based. Many and varied beers. 🏚 ❀ 🍽

Plough
Watling Street ☎ (0327) 50738
11–11
Adnams Broadside; Wells Eagle Ⓗ
Great atmosphere in a main road pub where the landlord takes pride in the food he offers. A very popular lunchtime meeting place.
🏚 ◑ ♣

Sun
36 Watling Street East (A5)
☎ (0327) 50580
11–3, 5.30–11 (11–11 Fri & Sat)

Bateman XB; Greene King IPA; Hook Norton Old Hooky Ⓗ
Cosy, dimly-lit pub, with exposed brick and beams, and stone-flagged floors throughout. Parts date back 400 years. An L-shaped bar with a function/family room, plus a games room.
👥 🍽 ◑ ♣ 🚭 P

Wakerley

Exeter Arms
Main Street ☎ (057 287) 817
12–2.30 (not Mon), 6 (7 Sat)–11
Adnams Broadside; Bateman XB; Marston's Pedigree Ⓗ
Reputedly haunted, 300-year-old pub near Wakerley Woods: a public bar and a comfortable lounge with a wood-burning stove. No food Mon. 🏚 ❀ ◑ ◖ 🍽 ▲ ♣ P

Weedon

Globe Hotel
High Street ☎ (0327) 40336
11–11
Marston's Burton Best Bitter, Pedigree; Ruddles County Ⓗ
More a hotel than a pub, but with a large, friendly lounge bar open to all. Q 🍽 ◑ ◖ P

Wheatsheaf
High Street ☎ (0327) 40670
12 (11 summer)–3, 5–11 (11–11 Sat)
Banks's Mild, Bitter Ⓗ
Old village pub displaying photos of the area; a noisy young people's pub with taped pop music, pool, games machines, etc., yet still keeps mild on draught. 🏚 ❀ ◑ ◖ P

Welford

Shoulder of Mutton
High Street ☎ (0858) 575375
12–2.30, 7–11
Bateman XB; Ruddles Best Bitter Ⓗ
Welcoming 17th-century local, well renovated into a single bar split by arches. The large garden offers play equipment (family room in inclement weather). Good value food which caters for children's and vegetarians' tastes (no meals Thu). 🎮 👥 ❀ ◑ ◖ ♣ P

Wellingborough

Cannon
Cannon Street (A510)
☎ (0933) 279629
11–4, 5.30–11
Banks & Taylor SOS; Fuller's London Pride, ESB; Wells Eagle, Bombardier Ⓗ**; guest beers**
Town pub: two rooms in a central U-shaped bar, recently extended in a rather hackneyed, half-timbered style. 🏚 ❀ 🍽 ♿ P

Vivian Arms
Knox Road ☎ (0933) 223660
11–2.30 (3 Sat), 6 (7 Sat)–11
Adnams Broadside; Mansfield Riding Mild; Wells Eagle, Bombardier Ⓗ
Superb, friendly, back-street local: a cosy lounge with a real fire, a wood-panelled bar and a large games room.
🏚 Q ❀ 🍽 ♿ ➜ P

Try also: Horseshoe, Sheep St (Bass)

Wilbarston

Fox Inn
Church Street ☎ (0536) 771270
12–3, 6.30–11
Marston's Burton Best Bitter, Pedigree Ⓗ
Excellent village local, parts from the 14th century: a good, basic public and a large, split-level lounge. Good value food; separate restaurant (no meals Sun eve). ❀ 🍽 ◑ ◖ 🍽 ♣ P

Wollaston

Boot
High Street ☎ (0933) 664270
11.30–2.30 (3 Sat), 6–11
Tetley Bitter; Tolly Cobbold Original Ⓗ
Pub with a restful atmosphere. A whitewashed, thatched, listed building, ideal for the thinking drinker, but still a family pub.
🏚 Q ❀ ◑ 🍽 ♿ ♣ P

Wootton

Wootton Workingmen's Club
High Street ☎ (0604) 761863
12–2 (2.30 Fri & Sat), 7–11 (12–2.30, 7–10.30 Sun)
Greene King IPA; Mansfield Riding Mild; Wells Eagle Ⓗ**; guest beers**
Formerly the Red Lion, this club retains the atmosphere of a village local. A comfortable bar with a games room to the rear, original stone walls exposed in both rooms. Concert room with a raised level, doubling as a lounge. Five real ales. CIU entry restrictions. Q 👥 🍽 ♣ P

Yardley Hastings

Red Lion
High Street ☎ (060 129) 210
11–2.30 (3 Sat), 6–11
Adnams Broadside; Wells Eagle Ⓗ
Popular village local with a traditional public bar and a pleasant lounge with exposed stonework and brasses. Separate games room. No food Sun.
🏚 Q ❀ ◑ 🍽 ♿ ♣ P

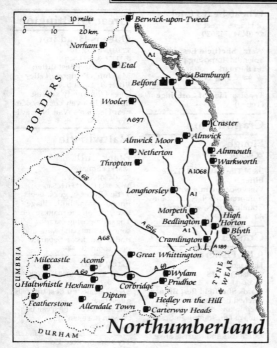

Longstone, Belford

Northumberland

Acomb

Miners Arms Inn
Main Street ☎ (0434) 603909
11–4, 5–11 (11–11 summer)
**Big Lamp Prince Bishop Ale;
Federation Best Bitter,
Buchanan's Original;
Morrells Varsity** [H]**; guest
beers**
Popular village pub offering
good food, including
vegetarian dishes. Shove-
ha'penny board.
🏠 Q ❀ ◑ ▶ ◁ ♣ ♠

Allendale Town

Golden Lion
Market Square (B6303)
☎ (0434) 683225
11–11
Beer range varies [H]
Pleasant, friendly town-centre
pub with good food at
affordable prices. 🏠 ❀ ◑ ▶ P

Alnmouth

Red Lion Inn
Northumberland Street
☎ (0665) 830584
12–2.30, 7–11 (may vary)
Tetley Bitter [H]
A good addition to this small

seaside town: a pub with
much oak and brass in
evidence and a warm
welcome assured. 🏠 Q ◑ ◁

Alnwick

Oddfellows Arms
Narrowgate ☎ (0665) 602695
11–11
**Vaux Samson; Wards
Sheffield Best Bitter** [H]
Friendly pub near Alnwick
Castle. Fishing memorabilia
and animal heads abound in
the bar. Note the old till still in
use. Q ◁ ◑ ▶

Queens Head Hotel
Market Street ☎ (0665) 602442
11–11
**Vaux Samson, Extra Special;
Wards Sheffield Best Bitter** [H]
Comfortable county town
hotel bar; can be busy in the
evening.
🛏 ❀ ◑ ▶ ◁ ♠ &

Tanners Arms
Hotspur Street
☎ (0665) 602553
12–3 (not Mon or Tue), 7–11
Belhaven 80/- [H]**; guest beers**
Slightly eccentric and
fascinating, long a CAMRA
favourite. 🏠

Alnwick Moor

Shepherds Rest
☎ (0665) 510809
11–11
**Hadrian Gladiator;
Wadworth 6X** [H]**; guest beers**
Welcoming, comfortable
country hostelry with a good
range of freshly-prepared food
available all day in the
attractive small restaurant
area. Families welcome.
Conservatory planned.
🏠 Q 🛏 ❀ ◑ ▶ ◁ ◠ P

Bamburgh

Castle Hotel
Front Street ☎ (066 84) 351
12–3, 6–11
**Vaux Lorimers Best Scotch,
Samson** [H]
Pub offering friendly and
comfortable family facilities
and a warm welcome. Handy
for Bamburgh Castle –
featured in the film *Prince of
Thieves* and many others.
🏠 ❀ 🛏 ◁ ♣ ♠

Victoria Hotel
The Grove ☎ (066 84) 431
11–11
**Longstone Bitter; Tetley
Bitter** [H]**; guest beers**
Welcoming retreat in the
public bar of an impressive
family-run hotel, near
magnificent Bamburgh Castle.
Good food and an outlet for
the county's only brewery.
🏠 Q 🛏 🛏 ◑ ▶ ◁ ♠

Bedlington

Northumberland Arms
Front Street East
☎ (0670) 822754
11–3, 6–11
Camerons Strongarm [H]**;
guest beers**
Town-centre local with a longstanding reputation for cask
ales. 🏠 ◁ ▶

Belford

Salmon
High Street ☎ (0668) 213245
11–3, 6–11 (11–11 Sat)
Vaux Lorimers Best Scotch [H]
Comfortable, cosy village local
with a warm welcome, nestling
just off the A1. 🔥 ♠ P

Berwick-upon-Tweed

Brown Bear
Hide Hill ☎ (0289) 306214
12–11
Vaux Lorimers Best Scotch [H]
Long, split-level one-roomer,
with a pool table and a mixed
clientele. ⇌

Northumberland

Free Trade
Castlegate ☎ (0289) 306498
12–3, 7–11 (varies in winter)
Vaux Lorimers Best Scotch Ⓗ
Still basic, still beautiful and
still keeping eccentric hours.
Catch it open for a rare treat.
🏠 ≠ ♣

Hen & Chickens
Sandgate ☎ (0289) 306314
11–3, 6–11
McEwan 70/-, 80/- Ⓗ
Pine-clad, characterful local
with a relaxed atmosphere. TV
in the bar. 🏚 Q ≠

Blyth

Flying Horse
Bridge Street ☎ (0670) 353314
11–3, 6–11
**Courage Directors; S&N
Theakston Best Bitter;
Whitbread Boddingtons
Bitter** Ⓗ; guest beers
Comfortable local in an old
industrial harbour town,
offering a good array of beers
for this area.

Oddfellows Arms
Bridge Street
☎ (0670) 356535
11–11 (11–3, 6–11 winter)
**Marston's Pedigree; Ruddles
County** Ⓗ; guest beers
Uncompromising bar of the
locally-renowned Legendary
Yorkshire Heroes free house
chain. Two rooms with a
pleasantly spartan interior.
🏠 ♣

Carterway Heads

Manor House Inn
On A68, near county
boundary ☎ (0207) 55268
11–3, 6–11
**Butterknowle Bitter; Fuller's
London Pride** Ⓗ; guest beers
Popular hostelry on a major
route, with fine views over the
Derwent valley.
🏚 Q ⊛ ◖ ▶ ⅋ P

Corbridge

Dyvels
Station Road ☎ (0434) 633566
7–11 (12–3, 7–11 Sat; may vary
winter)
**Draught Bass; Stones Best
Bitter** Ⓗ
Welcoming pub. Visit
Hadrian's Wall and stock up
with antiques at the pub's
own shop next door.
Thatcher's cider.
🏚 ⊛ 🏠 ⅋ ≠ ▭ P

Tynedale Hotel
Market Place
☎ (0434) 712149
12–3, 7–11
S&N Theakston XB Ⓗ; guest
beers
Popular local in an historic
town. 🏠 ◖

Wheatsheaf Hotel
St Helens Street
☎ (0434) 712020
11–11
Wards Sheffield Best Bitter Ⓗ
Splendid, imposing pub just
off the market square.
⊛ 🏠 ◖ ▶ 🏠 ⅋ P

Try also: Lion of Corbridge
(Tetley)

Cramlington

Plough
☎ (0670) 737633
11–3, 6–11
**S&N Theakston XB; Tetley
Bitter** Ⓗ
Village-centre pub with a
comfortable feel. Note: not in
Cramlington New Town.
🏚 ◖ ⅋ ≠

Craster

Jolly Fisherman
The Heugh
☎ (0665) 76218
11–3, 6–11
Wards Sheffield Best Bitter Ⓗ
Perched beside the sea and
overlooking the dramatic
ruins of Dunstanburgh Castle:
a friendly village pub, popular
with locals and tourists alike.
◖ P

Dipton

Dipton Mill Inn
On minor road off B6306 S of
Hexham
☎ (0434) 606577
12–3, 6–11
**Hadrian Gladiator; Malton
Double Chance; S&N
Theakston Best Bitter; Yates
Premium** Ⓗ; guest beers
Welcoming country inn in
pleasant surroundings. Good
food. 🏚 Q 🍴 ⊛ ◖

Etal

Black Bull
Off B6354
12–3, 6–11 (may vary winter)
Vaux Lorimers Best Scotch Ⓗ
As well as this picturesque
thatched pub, Etal also boasts
a castle and a water mill.
Q ◖ ▶ ⅋ ♣ P

Featherstone

Wallace Arms
On minor road off B689
OS683608 ☎ (0434) 321833
11–11
**Marston's Pedigree;
Whitbread Boddingtons
Bitter, Castle Eden Ale** Ⓗ;
guest beers
Popular, friendly hostelry in
beautiful countryside near
Featherstone Castle.
🏚 Q 🍴 ⊛ ◖ ▶ P

Great Whittington

Queens Head Inn
☎ (0434) 672267
6–11 (12–3, 6–11 Sat)
**Hook Norton Best Bitter;
Marston's Pedigree; Tetley
Bitter** Ⓗ; guest beers
One of the county's oldest
inns, set in lovely countryside
near Hadrian's Wall. No meals
Tue eve. 🏚 Q ⊛ ▶ ⅋ P

Haltwhistle

Black Bull
Market Square
☎ (0434) 320463
11–3, 6–11 (11–11 Fri & Sat)
Tetley Bitter Ⓗ; guest beers
Friendly stone-built village
local, just off the main street.
The unimposing exterior
conceals fine oak beams and
traditional decor. Separate
pool room. ⊛ ≠

Grey Bull
Main Street ☎ (0434) 320298
11–2.30, 7–11
S&N Theakston Best Bitter Ⓗ;
guest beers
Friendly local which can be
busy in the evening.
🏠 ◖ ▶ ≠ P

Try also: Spotted Cow
(Webster's)

Hedley on the Hill

Feathers Inn
On minor road, off B6309
OS078592 ☎ (0661) 843268
6–11 (12–3, 6–11 Sat)
**Ind Coope Burton Ale;
Ruddles Best Bitter** Ⓗ; guest
beers
Friendly pub in a small hilltop
village. Food available at
weekends only.
🏚 Q 🍴 ◖ ▶ 🏠

Hexham

Globe
Battle Hill ☎ (0434) 603742
11–11
S&N Theakston Best Bitter Ⓗ
Comfortable, basic local
oozing charm and a
traditional feel. An asset to
this historic market town.
🏚 ⅋ ≠

Tap & Spile
Battle Hill ☎ (0434) 602039
11–11
Hadrian Gladiator Ⓗ; guest
beers
Comfortable and relaxing
two-roomed pub where a
warm welcome is assured.
Q ◖ 🏠 ≠ ♣

High Horton

Three Horseshoes
Hathery Lane ☎ (0670) 822410

Northumberland

11–3, 6–11
Tetley Bitter Ⓗ; **guest beers**
Large and comfortable, a
former Northumberland
CAMRA *Pub of the Year*.
🏠 ❀ ⑴ P

Longhorsley

Linden Pub

Linden Hall Hotel
☎ (0670) 516611
12–3, 6–11
**Jennings Bitter; S&N
Theakston Best Bitter** Ⓗ;
guest beers
Comfortable converted
granary in the grounds of
Linden Hall Hotel. Good food.
🏠 ⛄ ❀ 🛏 ⑴ ♿ P

Milecastle

Milecastle Inn

Military Road (B6318)
☎ (0434) 320682
12–3, 7–11
**S&N Theakston Best Bitter,
XB; Webster's Yorkshire
Bitter** Ⓗ; **guest beers**
Small, cosy pub with a
restaurant renowned for its
game dishes. Set in a popular
rambling area (walkers are
requested to remove their
boots). 🏠 Q ❀ ⑴ P

Morpeth

Joiners Arms

Wansbeck Street
12 (11 Fri)–3 (11–4 Wed), 5.30–11
(11–11 Sat)
**Draught Bass; S&N
Theakston; Taylor
Landlord** Ⓗ; **guest beers**
Superb pub owned by a local
pub chain which was
successful long before pub
chains came into fashion. Two
comfortable bars. ❀ ⑴ ▶ 🍺 ⇌

Tap & Spile

Manchester Street
☎ (0670) 513894
11–11
**Camerons Strongarm;
Hadrian Gladiator** Ⓗ; **guest
beers**

Comfortable and cosy pub
with friendly service, situated
close to the bus station. The
cider is changed frequently.
Q ⑴ ♿ ⓪

White Swan

18 Newgate Street
☎ (0670) 513532
11–11
**Vaux Extra Special; Wards
Sheffield Best Bitter** Ⓗ; **guest
beers**
Well-refurbished town-centre
pub serving good food. ⑴ ▶

Netherton

Star Inn

On B634 ☎ (0669) 80238
11–2, 7–11 (may vary winter)
Whitbread Castle Eden Ale Ⓖ
Remote, unspoilt, marvellous
pub in beautiful countryside.
🏠 Q ❀ 🍺

Norham

Masons Arms

West Street (B6470)
☎ (0289) 82326
11–3, 6–11
Vaux Lorimers Best Scotch Ⓗ
Traditional bar in an historic
borders town. Q ⛄

Prudhoe

Halfway House

Edgewell (A695)
☎ (0661) 832688
11–3, 6–11 (11–11 Fri & Sat)
**Hadrian Gladiator; S&N
Theakston XB** Ⓗ; **guest beers**
Friendly two-roomed local.
Traditional games in the bar
most eves; popular quiz nights
in the lounge Mon and Thu.
Fine view across the valley.
⑴ 🍺 ♣ P

Thropton

Cross Keys

☎ (0669) 20362
11–11
Draught Bass Ⓗ
Comfortable, two-roomed pub
set in pleasant countryside. A

fine selection of traditional
pub food available.
🏠 Q ❀ ⑴ ▶ P

Warkworth

Masons Arms

Dial Place ☎ (0665) 711398
11–4, 6–11 (11–11 Sat)
**S&N Theakston Best Bitter;
Younger No. 3** Ⓗ
Cosy, welcoming village pub
serving good food.
❀ ⑴ ▶ 🍺 ⚡

Wooler

Anchor

2 Cheviot Street
☎ (0668) 81412
11–4.30, 6–11
**Vaux Lorimers Best Scotch,
Samson** Ⓗ
Cosy and unaffected local in
traditional style, on the road
to the Cheviot Hills.
🏠 Q 🛏 ⑴ 🍺

Ryecroft Hotel

Ryecroft Way ☎ (0668) 81459
11–11
**Marston's Pedigree; Tetley
Bitter; Yates Bitter** Ⓗ; **guest
beers**
Popular, well-run family hotel
with a reputation for good
food. The lounge has a
conservatory extension.
🏠 Q ❀ 🛏 ⑴ ▶ ♿ ⚡ ♣ P

Wylam

Boathouse Inn

Wylam Station
☎ (0661) 853431
12–3 (not Mon), 6–11 (11–11 all week
summer)
**Draught Bass; Belhaven 80/-;
Butterknowle Conciliation
Ale; Ind Coope Burton Ale;
S&N Theakston XB; Taylor
Landlord** Ⓗ; **guest beers**
Pub with a warm welcome
and a fine collection of malts
(27 presently). An old bar
billiard table and a resident
ghost add to the charm.
🏠 ⛄ ❀ ⑴ ⇌ ♣ P

The Symbols

🏠 real fire

Q quiet pub (at least one bar)

⛄ indoor room for children

❀ garden or other outdoor
drinking area

🛏 accommodation

⑴ lunchtime meals

▶ evening meals

🍺 public bar

♿ easy wheelchair access

🅰 camping facilities at the pub
or nearby

⇌ near British Rail station

⊖ near underground station

♣ pub games

⚲ real cider

P pub car park

⚡ no-smoking room or area

233

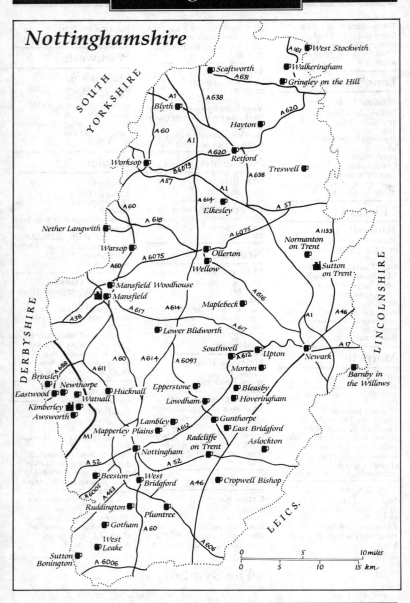

Nottinghamshire

(map of Nottinghamshire showing towns including West Stockwith, Walkeringham, Gringley on the Hill, Scaftworth, Blyth, Hayton, Worksop, Retford, Treswell, Elkesley, Nether Langwith, Warsop, Ollerton, Normanton on Trent, Sutton on Trent, Wellow, Mansfield Woodhouse, Mansfield, Maplebeck, Lower Blidworth, Southwell, Upton, Newark, Morton, Barnby in the Willows, Brinsley, Newthorpe, Eastwood, Hucknall, Epperstone, Bleasby, Hoveringham, Kimberley, Awsworth, Watnall, Lowdham, Gunthorpe, East Bridgford, Lambley, Mapperley Plains, Radcliffe on Trent, Aslockton, Nottingham, Beeston, West Bridgford, Cropwell Bishop, Ruddington, Plumtree, Gotham, West Leake, Sutton Bonington; neighbouring counties SOUTH YORKSHIRE, DERBYSHIRE, LINCOLNSHIRE, LEICS.)

 Hardys & Hansons, *Kimberley;* **Mansfield,** *Mansfield;* **Springhead,** *Sutton on Trent*

Aslockton

Cranmer Arms
Main Street ☎ (0949) 50362
11–3, 5.30–11 (11–11 Sat)
Home Mild, Bitter Ⓗ
Friendly local with a children's play area in the large garden. Named after Thomas Cranmer, a native of the village. No lunches Mon–Wed. Long alley skittles.
🏚 Q ✤ ◖ ⊟ 🅐 ⇌ ♣ P

Old Greyhound
Main Street
☎ (0949) 50957
11–3, 6–11 (11–11 Sat)
Home Bitter; S&N Theakston XB Ⓗ
Convivial pub with a single bar serving various small drinking areas. A large indoor skittles alley doubles as a family room.
🐚 ✤ 🅐 ⇌ ♣ P

Nottinghamshire

Awsworth

Gate Inn
Main Street ☎ (0602) 329821
10.30–2.30, 6–11
Hardys & Hansons Best Bitter Ⓔ
Old traditional local of distinction near the site of the once-famous Forty Bridges (see photos in passage). Pool room upstairs.
Q ✿ ◖ 🍺 ♣ P

Barnby in the Willows

Willow Tree Inn
Front Street ☎ (0636) 626613
11.30–3, 7–11
Wards Sheffield Best Bitter Ⓗ; **guest beers**
Late 17th-century, heavily-beamed village inn, in a conservation area. James Hole, a former local brewer, bought this as his first pub in 1874. The centre of village activities.
Q ❧ ✿ 🏠 ◖ 🌙 ♿ ♣ P

Beeston

Commercial Inn
Wollaton Road
☎ (0602) 254480
11 (12 Sat)–2.30, 5.30–11 (11–11 Fri)
Hardys & Hansons Best Mild, Best Bitter, Kimberley Classic Ⓗ
Comfortable and friendly local just off the town centre.
✿ ◖ 🍺 ⇌ ♣ P

Jolly Anglers
Meadow Road ☎ (0602) 256497
11.30–3 (4 Sat), 6–11
Home Bitter Ⓔ
Three-roomed locals' pub close to a nature reserve, canal and river. The beer range is due to be extended to include a mild and a premium ale.
❧ ✿ ◖ 🍺 ⇌ ♣ P

Bleasby

Waggon & Horses
Gypsy Lane ☎ (0636) 830283
12–3, 6.30–11
Home Mild, Bitter; S&N Theakston XB Ⓗ
Comfortable, olde-worlde village pub with a wood-panelled interior. In the shadow of the village church.
🏠 Q ✿ 🍺 ♿ ♣ P

Blyth

Angel
Bawtry Road ☎ (0909) 591213
11–3, 6–11
Hardys & Hansons Best Bitter Ⓔ
Longstanding *Guide* entry. Large garden for summer and huge fires in winter.
🏠 Q ❧ ✿ 🏠 ◖ 🌙 🍺 ♣ P

Brinsley

Robin Hood
Hall Lane ☎ (0773) 713604
12–3, 6 (7 winter)–11
Hardys & Hansons Best Mild, Best Bitter Ⓔ
Village pub of character in DH Lawrence country. Rumoured to be haunted upstairs by a former licensee. Display of colliery plates. Disco Fri; guest singers Sat. Two skittle alleys.
Q ✿ ◖ 🍺 ♣ P

Cropwell Bishop

Wheatsheaf
Nottingham Road
☎ (0602) 892247
12–3 (11–4 Sat), 6–11
Home Bitter; S&N Theakston XB Ⓗ
Friendly village local with a cosy lounge and a down-to-earth bar, featuring a collection of early village photographs. Pool room at the rear. Excellent locally-made Stilton usually on sale.
🏠 ❧ ✿ 🍺 ♿ ♣ P

East Bridgford

Reindeer
Kneeton Road ☎ (0949) 20227
12–3, 5.30–11 (12–11 Sat)
Courage Directors; Jennings Cumberland Ale; John Smith's Bitter Ⓗ; **guest beers**
Pleasing white-painted local on the edge of the village. A small restaurant at the rear overflows into the lounge when busy (no food Sun eve or Mon). The bar has interesting old photos of village life. 🏠 ✿ ◖ ♿ ♣ P

Eastwood

Greasley Castle
1 Castle Street, Hilltop (off B6010) ☎ (0773) 761080
11–4, 6–11 (11–11 Fri & Sat)
Hardys & Hansons Best Mild, Best Bitter Ⓔ
Street-corner Victorian local on a one-way street. Split-level interior; friendly and comfortable. Extremely busy at weekends with live local artistes. ✿ 🍺 ♣

Lord Raglan
Newthorpe Common (SW off B6010) ☎ (0773) 712683
11.30–3, 5.30 (6.30 Sat)–11
Hardys & Hansons Best Mild, Best Bitter Ⓔ, **Kimberley Classic** Ⓗ
Pub serving the local estates. Spacious games-oriented bar; weekend sing-along in the olde-worlde lounge. Wed night quiz. Good quality food. Beer garden and swings for children. Friendly hosts.
🏠 ✿ ◖ 🍺 ♣ P

Elkesley

Robin Hood
High Street ☎ (077 783) 259
11–3.30, 6–11
Whitbread Boddingtons Bitter, Flowers Original Ⓗ
Popular village local also attracting passing trade from the A1. Possibly selling some of the finest pub food along the Great North Road.
🏠 ✿ ◖ 🌙 🍺 ♿ ♣ P

Epperstone

Cross Keys
Main Street
☎ (0602) 663033
11.45–2.30 (not Mon; may vary), 6–11 (12–2.30, 7–10.30 Sun)
Hardys & Hansons Best Mild, Best Bitter Ⓔ, **Kimberley Classic** Ⓗ
Friendly and attractive old village pub drawing a loyal clientele from a wide area. Impromptu folk sessions and occasional morris dancing. Reduced food menu weekday lunchtimes; no meals Sun eve.
🏠 Q ❧ ✿ ◖ 🍺 ♿ ♣ P

Gotham

Sun Inn
The Square
☎ (0602) 830484
12–2.30, 6–11 (12–2.30, 7–10.30 Sun)
Everards Mild, Beacon, Tiger, Old Original Ⓗ; **guest beers**
Comfortable, friendly local in a small village. Food is served in the lounge, with the bar reserved for conversation and games. ✿ ◖ 🌙 ♣ P

Gringley on the Hill

Blue Bell Inn
High Street
☎ (0777) 817406
11–3 (Fri, Sat & Xmas only), 6.30–11
Draught Bass; Stones Best Bitter Ⓗ; **guest beers**
Lively village local with a safe garden. 🏠 ❧ ✿ ♣

Gunthorpe

Unicorn Hotel
Gunthorpe Bridge
☎ (0602) 663612
11–11
Mansfield Riding Bitter, Old Baily Ⓗ
Pub extensively redeveloped from a much smaller public house, now with a white floodlit frontage and mooring facilities for rivercraft. Spacious interior in modern country inn style with large sofas and small tables with stools. Children welcome in the conservatory. Wheelchair access at the rear. ◖ 🌙 ♿ ♣ P

235

Nottinghamshire

Hayton

Boat Inn
Main Street ☎ (0777) 700158
11–3, 6–11
**Draught Bass; Stones Best
Bitter; Whitbread Castle Eden
Ale** H
Busy country pub catering for
drinkers and diners alike.
Children's garden play area.
On the bank of the
Chesterfield Canal with its
own moorings.
🏠 ❀ 🛏 ◑ ▲ P

Hoveringham

Reindeer Inn
Main Street ☎ (0602) 663629
12–3, 5 (5.30 Mon & Sat)–11
**Marston's Burton Best Bitter,
Pedigree** H**; guest beer**
Beautifully-beamed old place
with a bar full of curios and a
separate restaurant. Guest ale
from a wide-ranging and
regularly-changed list.
🏠 Q ❀ ◑ 🍺 ⅙ ⇌ ♣ P

Hucknall

Red Lion
High Street
10.30–2.30, 6–11
Home Mild, Bitter E
Traditional town local with a
through passage and four
interconnecting rooms. Can be
crowded weekends. 🍺 ♣ P

Yew Tree
2 Nottingham Road
☎ (0602) 630173
11–3, 7–11
**Courage Directors; John
Smith's Bitter** H**; guest beers**
Friendly pub on the edge of
town with pool and various
fruit/game machines, but
always three guest beers. Mini
beer festival held end of
March. Lunches Fri–Sun only.
◑ ♣

Kimberley

Cricketers Rest
Chapel Street (off Main Street)
☎ (0602) 380894
11–3.30 (4 Sat), 6.30–11
**Hardys & Hansons Best Mild,
Best Bitter** H
Comfortable, well-appointed,
open-plan pub with a discreet
dartboard area. Reputedly
haunted by a former landlady.
Attracts young people. Mon
night disco; Thu night quiz.
❀ ◑ ♣

Nelson & Railway
Station Road (off Main Street)
☎ (0602) 382177
10.30–3, 5–11 (10.30–11 Fri, Sat &
bank hols)
**Hardys & Hansons Best
Mild** E **&** H**, Kimberley
Classic** H

Homely, pleasantly located
pub, a long-time favourite of
ale drinkers: a wood-panelled
bar and an attractively
restored, beamed lounge with
an adjoining dining area.
Budget B&B; cheap beer 5–7
Mon–Fri. Growing reputation
for good food (no meals Sun
eve). ❀ 🛏 ◑ ▶ 🍺 ♣ P

Queens Head
Main Street ☎ (0602) 382117
10.30–4, 6–11
**Hardys & Hansons Best Mild,
Best Bitter** H
Prominent street-corner local
of quality. Busy with young
people at weekends, but has a
small, quieter snug in the top
corner, with a fine collection
of photos of old Kimberley.
The upstairs lounge features
live music from local artistes.
❀ ◑ ♣

Lambley

Nags Head
Main Street ☎ (0602) 312546
11–3, 5.30–11
Home Mild, Bitter E**; S&N
Theakston XB** H
Spacious village inn, popular
with families (safe play area
and separate games room).
The raised patio fronting the
road is very pleasant in fine
weather. 🍃 ❀ ◑ ▶ 🍺 ⅙ ♣ P

Robin Hood
Main Street ☎ (0602) 312531
11–3 (3.30 Sat), 6–11
**Home Bitter; S&N Theakston
XB** H
Over 100 years-old, a former
WH Hutchinson & Sons pub,
well known for beer and
skittles parties. A collection of
whisky water jugs hangs over
the bar. Q 🍺 ♣ P

Lowdham

Old Ship Inn
Main Street ☎ (0602) 663049
11.30–2.30, 5.30–11 (11.30–11
summer Sat)
**Courage Best Bitter, Directors;
Mansfield Riding Bitter** H
Warm and friendly
atmosphere in a lively pub.
Originally a coaching house
which has been well
renovated and has an eating
area at the end of the lounge
(waitress service). Pool table
in the bar.
🍃 ❀ ◑ ▶ 🍺 ▲ ⇌ ♣ P

Lower Blidworth

Fox & Hounds
Calverton Road OS590548
☎ (0623) 792383
11–3.30, 6–11
**Hardys & Hansons Best Mild,
Best Bitter, Kimberley
Classic** H
Welcoming, multi-roomed

country inn. Tropical fish in
the lounge; stray dogs in the
bar. No food Wed eve.
🏠 Q 🍃 ❀ ◑ ▶ 🍺 ♣ P

Mansfield

Kings Arms
Ratcliffe Gate (A617, just out
of centre) ☎ (0623) 24077
11–11
**Ind Coope Burton Ale; Tetley
Bitter** H
Small, one-roomed street-
corner local with a separate
pool area. Quiz nights and
free beer draw Fri. Ales may
vary according to Brent
Walker supply deals. ◑ ♣

William IV
Stockwell Gate (opp. Victoria
Hospital) ☎ (0623) 21283
11–11
**Mansfield Riding Mild,
Riding Bitter, Old Baily** H
Comfortable and well-
furnished pub: a large tap
room with two pool tables and
a spacious family room. Small
garden with play facilities. A
deservedly popular pub.
🍃 ❀ ◑ 🍺 ♣ P

Yew Tree Inn
Woodhouse Road
☎ (0623) 23729
11–11
**Courage Directors; Ind Coope
Burton Ale; Tetley Bitter** H
Popular pub just off the town
centre, handy for the cinema
and theatre. One room with a
separate pool area. Regular
quiz nights and karaoke Sat
eve. Eve meals to order only.
❀ ◑ ⅙ ♣ P

Mansfield Woodhouse

Portland Arms
High Street ☎ (0623) 422903
11.30–3, 7–11
**Vaux Samson; Wards Thorne
Best Bitter** H
Popular meeting place for local
hockey teams. The landlord
plays the organ for a sing-
along Sun night. ◑ 🍺 ♣ P

Star Inn
Warsop Road ☎ (0623) 24145
11.30–3, 7–11 (may vary in summer)
**Wards Thorne Best Bitter,
Sheffield Best Bitter, Kirby** H
One of the oldest buildings in
the area, a low-beamed, three-
roomed pub. Excellent play
facilities for children in the
garden. Good food; eve meals
to order only. ❀ ◑ P

Maplebeck

Beehive
OS710608 ☎ (063 686) 306
12–2.30 (3 Sat), 7–11
**Mansfield Riding Bitter, Old
Baily** H

The smallest pub in Nottinghamshire, in an idyllic country village setting. Very welcoming landlord.
🏕 Q ❀ 🍺 P

Mapperley Plains

Travellers Rest

On B684 ☎ (0602) 264412
11–11
Home Bitter; S&N Theakston XB; Younger IPA Ⓗ
Country pub on the edge of Nottingham with a friendly atmosphere. Separate children's facilities in the 'Pop Inn' family room. Hot and cold food (including vegetarian) available until 8pm.
🏕 🍴 ☕ ◖ ♪ & ▲ ❀ P ✉

Morton

Full Moon

Main Street ☎ (0636) 830251
11–3, 6–11
S&N Theakston Best Bitter, XB, Old Peculier Ⓗ
Traditional, oak-beamed village local, popular with all ages. Note the rhyme above the entrance. The excellent food means it can get crowded with diners. Handy for Southwell Racecourse (1¼ miles).
🏕 ❀ ◖ ♪ ≢ (Fiskerton) P

Try also: Bromley Arms, Fiskerton (Hardys & Hansons)

Nether Langwith

Jug & Glass

Queens Walk ☎ (0623) 742283
11.30–3.30, 7–11
Hardys & Hansons Best Mild, Best Bitter Ⓔ**, Kimberley Classic** Ⓗ
Stone pub in the old part of the village. Popular in summer for its pleasant setting by the River Poulter.
🏕 ❀ 🍺 & ♣

Newark

Castle & Falcon

London Road ☎ (0636) 703513
11–3, 7–11
Courage Directors; John Smith's Bitter, Magnet Ⓗ
Three-roomed, 18th-century pub, popular with the locals. A lot of darts, pool and long alley skittles played. No food Sun.
Q ❀ ◖ ♪ & ≢ (Castle) ♣ P

Mail Coach

13 London Road, Beaumond Cross ☎ (0636) 605164
11–3, 5.30–11
Ansells Mild; Ind Coope Benskins Best Bitter, Burton Ale; Tetley Bitter Ⓗ**; guest beers**
Very pleasant, busy town pub, a mainly Georgian building, but some parts are older. The

cellar reputedly contains part of the old town wall. Charity 'frog' racing in summer; infuriating Ball-Round-a-Maze game. 🏕 ❀ 🏠 ◖ & ≢ (Castle) ♣ P

Old Malt Shovel

Northgate ☎ (0636) 702036
11.30–2.30, 7 (5 Fri)–11
Adnams Broadside; Lloyds Country Bitter; Taylor Landlord; Wards Sheffield Best Bitter Ⓗ
A pub for all ages; office workers predominate at lunchtimes. A cheerful place where the emphasis is on convivial conversation. Dates from the 16th century and was originally a bakery. 🏕 ❀ ◖ ≢ (Castle/Northgate)

Newthorpe

Ram Inn

Beauvale (N off B600 via Dovecote Rd) ☎ (0773) 713312
11–4, 6–11 (11–11 Sat)
Hardys & Hansons Best Mild, Best Bitter Ⓔ**, Kimberley Classic** Ⓗ
Lively roadside local with a friendly welcome for all. Excellent value food.
❀ ◖ ▶ 🍺 ♣ P

Normanton on Trent

Square & Compass

East Gate ☎ (0636) 821439
12–3, 6–11
Adnams Broadside; Stones Best Bitter; Wards Sheffield Best Bitter Ⓗ**; guest beers**
Popular, low-beamed pub on the edge of the village. A small restaurant (the Gun Room) specialises in game. Note the unique way of calling time.
🏕 ❀ 🏠 ◖ ♪ & ▲ ❀ P

Nottingham

Boat Inn

Priory Street, Old Lenton (2¼ miles W of centre)
☎ (0602) 786482
11–2.30 (3 Sat), 6 (6.30 Sat)–11 (12–2.30, 7–10.30 Sun)
Home Mild, Bitter Ⓔ**; S&N Theakston XB; Younger Scotch** Ⓗ
One-roomed local with a friendly atmosphere. Attractive wood panelling with inlaid mirrors. Near Queen's Medical Centre and the ring road. ◖ ♣

Canal Tavern

2 Canal Street (S of centre, 200 yds from Broad Marsh)
☎ (0602) 240235
12–2.30, 6.30 (5 Fri)–11 (closed Sun lunch)
Ind Coope Burton Ale; S&N Theakston Old Peculier; Tetley Bitter Ⓗ**; guest beers**

Opened in June 1991 as a simple one-roomed pub with bare wood floors. The emphasis is on traditional beer, with guests always available. Sky TV can sometimes be obtrusive. Usually quiet midweek but very popular at weekends. Special price promotions. ◖ ≢ ♣

Castle

202 Lower Parliament Street (next to ice stadium)
☎ (0602) 504601
11.30–2.30, 6–11 (12–2.30, 7–10.30 Sun)
Ansells Bitter; Ind Coope ABC Best Bitter, Burton Ale; Tetley Bitter Ⓗ
One large room with alcoves and split-level areas. Features a summerhouse, built half-in and half-out of the pub. Unusual floral light fittings; lots of pine and open brickwork. Opens at 5pm on Sat eves when the ice hockey team is playing. ❀ ♣

Coopers Arms

3 Porchester Road, Thorneywood (1½ miles from centre, near Carlton Rd jct)
☎ (0602) 502433
11–2.30 (3.30 Mon & Fri), 6 (5.30 Fri)–11 (11.30–4.30, 6.30–11 Sat)
Home Mild, Bitter Ⓔ
1890s pub with four rooms, including a pool room and a skittle alley. Q 🍴 🍺 ♣ P

Fox at Sneinton

17 Dale Street, Sneinton
☎ (0602) 504736
11–3, 6–11
Ind Coope ABC Best Bitter, Burton Ale; Taylor Landlord; Tetley Bitter Ⓗ
18th-century hostelry in the shadow of a restored working windmill. A drinkers' pub with a boisterous public bar and a quiet, uncomplicated lounge. Games room upstairs.
Q ❀ 🍺 ♣

Grove

273 Castle Boulevard (1¼ miles W of centre)
☎ (0602) 410637
11.30–3, 5.30 (6 Sat)–11
Home Bitter; S&N Theakston XB, Old Peculier; Younger IPA, No. 3 Ⓗ**; guest beer**
Prominent Victorian pub. One multi-level room, refurbished with bare floorboards and bric-a-brac. Popular with students. Eve meals 5.30–7.
◖ ♪ & P

Limelight Bar

Nottingham Playhouse, Wellington Circus
☎ (0602) 418467
10.30–11
Adnams Bitter; Bateman XB; Marston's Pedigree; S&N Theakston XB, Old Peculier Ⓗ**; guest beers**

Nottinghamshire

Part of an early 1960s theatre complex but with an individual character. The wide range of ever-changing guest beers includes a mild. Usually quite busy. Q ✤ ⬧ ◑ ▶ ⬥

Lincolnshire Poacher

161 Mansfield Road (400 yds from Victoria Centre)
☎ (0602) 411584
11–3, 5 (6 Sat)–11
Bateman Mild, XB, XXXB, Salem Porter, Victory; Marston's Pedigree Ⓗ**; guest beers**
Not to be missed – a drinking house with a wide variety of excellent hand-pulled ales. Guest ales change frequently. Twinned with a bar in Amsterdam. Collection of pub memorabilia. Q ✤ ◑ ▶ ⬥ ✦

Magpies

Meadow Lane (500 yds from Notts County FC)
☎ (0602) 863851
11–3, 5–11 (11–11 Fri)
Home Mild, Bitter Ⓔ
Pub on the eastern edge of the city, handy for Trent Bridge cricket, Nottingham Racecourse and both football clubs. Pool table in the bar. Eve meals finish at 7.30.
✤ ◑ ▶ ⬧ ✦ P

March Hare

248 Carlton Road, Sneinton
☎ (0602) 504328
11.30–2.30, 6–11 (12–2.30, 7–10.30 Sun)
Courage Directors; John Smith's Bitter Ⓗ
Pub where a post-war brick exterior leads to a welcoming interior: a functional bar and a comfortable lounge.
◑ ⬧ ⬥ ✦ P

New Market Inn

38 Lower Parliament Street
☎ (0602) 411532
11–4, 5.30 (7 Sat)–11 (12–2.30, 7–10.30 Sun)
Home Mild, Bitter; S&N Theakston XB; Younger Scotch, IPA Ⓗ**; guest beers**
Cheap beer in three quiet and comfortable lounge areas and a bar filled with railway items. Quiz, table skittles, darts and domino teams. Eve meals to order only. Q ⬧ ◑ ⬧ ✦ P

Norfolk Arms

66 London Road (400 yds from Trent Bridge) ☎ (0602) 863003
12–11 (may close Sat afternoon in football season; 12–2.30, 7–10.30 Sun)
Home Mild, Bitter Ⓔ**; S&N Theakston XB** Ⓗ
Victorian local with a lively bar where games include skittles. A passage drinking area contrasts with a quiet lounge. A survivor from the days when the locality was known for good pubs.
Q ◑ ▶ ⬧ ✦ P

Plainsman

149 Woodthorpe Drive, Mapperley (2¹⁄₂ miles NW of centre, off B684)
☎ (0602) 622020
10.30–2.30, 6–11
Hardys & Hansons Best Mild, Best Bitter Ⓔ**, Kimberley Classic** Ⓗ
Pub consisting of two houses knocked together: a lounge and a bar on different levels with distinct characters – both equally welcoming and unpretentious. A popular quiz venue. ⬧ ✦ P

Portland Arms

24 Portland Road (off A610)
☎ (0602) 782429
11.30–3, 7–11
Hardys & Hansons Best Bitter, Kimberley Classic Ⓗ
Relaxed, friendly local, just out of the city centre; open-plan but with defined drinking areas. Good value cob rolls. ✤ ⬧ ✦

Queens Hotel

Arkwright Street (opp. station)
☎ (0602) 864685
11–2.30, 5.30–11 (11–11 Fri)
Greenalls Shipstone's Mild, Bitter; Stones Best Bitter; Tetley Bitter Ⓗ
Traditional town pub with a Victorian-style bar and a comfortable lounge.
✤ ⬧ ◑ ▶ ⬧ ✦ P

Trip to Jerusalem

1 Brewhouse Yard, Castle Road ☎ (0602) 473171
11–3 (4 Sat), 5.30 (6 Sat)–11 (11–11 summer Sat)
Hardys & Hansons Best Mild, Best Bitter, Kimberley Classic; Marston's Pedigree Ⓗ
Claims to be the oldest inn in England (AD 1189): a unique pub hewn out of the castle rock. The upstairs bar has a famous 60-ft chimney. Stone-flagged floors and a collection of foreign bank notes adorn the bar area. Busy at peak times but an absolute must.
🍴 Q ✤ ◑ ⬧ ✦

Ollerton

White Hart

Station Road ☎ (0623) 822410
11.30–4, 7–11
Samuel Smith OBB Ⓗ
Tucked-away in the centre of the old village, a pub popular with locals and tourists from nearby Sherwood Forest.
⬧ ✤ ◑ ▶ ⬧ ✦ P

Plumtree

Griffin Inn

Main Street ☎ (0602) 335743
11–3, 5.30–11 (12–2, 7–10.30 Sun)
Hardys & Hansons Best Mild, Best Bitter Ⓔ**, Kimberley Classic** Ⓗ

150-year-old country pub, tastefully refurbished. A central oblong bar serves a main lounge area, plus a darts and dominoes area, and a conservatory to the rear. Weekly folk club. The local cricket club plays at the rear of the pub. ⬧ ✤ ◑ ▶ ✦ P

Radcliffe on Trent

Black Lion

Main Road
☎ (0602) 332138
11–2.30 (3 summer), 6–11
Home Mild, Bitter Ⓔ
Large pub in the centre of the village, with a friendly bar and comfortable lounge. Charity steam fair held first Sat in October. No meals weekends. Large garden with play area. ✤ ◑ ⬧ ⬧ ✤ ✦ P

Retford

Market Hotel

West Carr Road, Ordsall
☎ (0777) 703278
11–3, 6–11 (11–11 Sat)
Adnams Broadside; Draught Bass; Marston's Pedigree; Taylor Landlord; Tetley Bitter; Whitbread Boddingtons Bitter Ⓗ**; guest beers**
Large pub with a separate restaurant. Usually about 14 beers available.
Q ✤ ◑ ▶ ⬧ ✤ P

Turks Head

Grove Street
☎ (0777) 702742
11–3, 7–11
Wards Sheffield Best Bitter Ⓗ
Popular and friendly pub close to the town centre: an impressive exterior and a panelled interior. Busy lunchtime food trade.
🍴 🍴 ✦ P

Ruddington

Red Lion

1 Easthorpe Street
☎ (0602) 844654
11–2.30 (3 Fri), 5.30–11 (11–11 Sat)
Home Mild, Bitter; S&N Theakston XB; guest beers Ⓗ
Popular, two-roomed village local. The mock-beamed lounge has rough plastered walls adorned with brassware. Usually about three guest beers per week.
Q ✤ ✤ ⬧ ⬥ ✦ P

Scaftworth

King William

Off A631 ☎ (0302) 710292
12–2.30 (not Mon–Wed), 7–11 (12–4.30, 7–10.30 Sun)
Marston's Pedigree; Tetley Bitter; Whitbread Boddingtons Bitter, Castle Eden Ale Ⓗ

Unspoilt, multi-roomed
village pub with a large
garden and play area.
Renowned for its food (not
served Mon eve, except bank
hols). 🍴 Q ⛄ ❀ ◑ ◗ P

Southwell

Bramley Apple

51 Church Street
☎ (0636) 813675
11–3, 6–11
**Bateman XB; Marston's
Pedigree** H; **guest beers**
Pleasant, single-roomed pub
with a strong emphasis on
food (no eve meals Sun/Mon).
Southwell Minster, just up the
road, is well worth a visit. The
eponymous apple originated
in a nearby cottage garden in
the same year as Trafalgar –
1805. ❀ 🍴 ◑ ◗ ♿ ⚓ ♣

Saracens Head

Market Place
☎ (0636) 812701
11–3, 6–11 (11–11 summer)
**Draught Bass; John Smith's
Bitter** H
Historic 12th-century coaching
inn, originally the Kings
Arms. Much visited by royalty
over the years; Charles I spent
his last night of freedom here;
Byron was also a regular
visitor. Collection of old prints
and photographs. No lunches
Sun. 🍴 Q ❀ 🍴 ◑ ◗ ♿ ⚓ P

Sutton Bonington

Anchor Inn

16 Bollards Lane (off Main
Street) ☎ (0509) 673648
12–3 (Fri only), 7–11 (12–11 Sat)
**Marston's Merrie Monk,
Pedigree** H
Family-run pub catering for
drinkers rather than the food
trade: a single room with a
separate pool area. Reputed to
be haunted by an earlier
landlord. 🍴 ❀ ♣ P

Treswell

Red Lion

Town Street ☎ (0777) 248599
12–2.30, 7–11
**Adnams Bitter, Broadside;
Tetley Mild, Bitter** H
Large, friendly village pub
with an extensive, well-priced
menu served in the bar or
small restaurant.
🍴 ❀ 🍴 ◑ ◗ ♿ ♣ P

Upton

Cross Keys

Main Street
☎ (0636) 813269
11.30–2.30, 6–11 (12–2.30, 7–10.30
Sun)
**Bateman XXXB; Brakspear
Bitter; Marston's Pedigree;
Whitbread Boddingtons
Bitter** H; **guest beers**

Friendly old pub in a
conservation area. The
upstairs restaurant is open
Fri–Sat eves and Sun lunch;
bar meals at all times. Live
music Sun eves. Guest ales are
changed two or three times
per week. The tap room seats
are pews from a local church.
🍴 ⛄ ❀ ◑ ◗ ♿ ♣ P

Walkeringham

Three Horseshoes

High Street
☎ (0427) 890959
11.30–2, 7–11
**Draught Bass; Stones Best
Bitter** H; **guest beers**
Comfortable village pub with
a large lounge and a
restaurant offering home-
cooked food.
🍴 ❀ ◑ ◗ ♿ ♣ P

Warsop

Hare & Hounds

Church Street
☎ (0623) 842440
11–3, 6–11 (11–11 Fri & Sat)
**Hardys & Hansons Best Mild,
Best Bitter, Kimberley
Classic** H
Traditional, lively, mock
Tudor pub in the centre of
town. Busy tap room.
🍴 Q ⛄ ❀ ◑ ◗ ♿ ♣ P

Try also: Gate, Mansfield Rd
(Courage)

Watnall

Queens Head

Main Road (B600)
☎ (0602) 383148
11–3, 5.30–11
**Home Mild, Bitter; S&N
Theakston XB, Old
Peculier** H
Old village local, recently
altered but retaining its fine
character. Friendly
atmosphere, with a small
intimate snug. The rear
garden has a children's play
area. Recommended, good
value lunches. Q ❀ ◑ ♣ P

Wellow

Red Lion

☎ (0623) 860001
11–3, 5.30–11
**Ruddles Best Bitter, County;
Whitbread Boddingtons
Bitter** H
Old country pub consisting of
several cosy rooms. Good food
served lunch and eves at
moderate prices. Q ❀ ◑ ◗ P

West Bridgford

Bridgford Wines
(Off-Licence)

116 Melton Road
☎ (0602) 816181
5–11 (11–11 Thu–Sat)

Beer range varies
Off-licence with an ever-
changing range of ales;
usually four–six available.
Polypins and firkins provided
for parties. Wide range of
British, Belgian and German
bottled beers – usually 100-
plus in stock. ⌂ P

West Leake

Star Inn

Melton Lane, West Leake ($2^1/2$
miles from M1 jct 24)
OS523261
☎ (0509) 852233
12–2.30, 6–11 (12–2, 7–10.30 Sun)
**Adnams Bitter; Draught
Bass** H
A real gem of an olde-worlde
pub run by a cat lover. Good
value and excellent quality
weekday lunchtime cold table
(no meals Sat/Sun). Known
locally as the 'Pit House'.
🍴 Q ❀ ◑ ♿ ⚓ P

West Stockwith

Waterfront Inn

☎ (0427) 891223
12–3, 6–11
**Adnams Broadside; S&N
Theakston XB; Taylor
Landlord** H; **guest beers**
Historic pub overlooking a
marina on the River Trent.
Popular with the boating
fraternity and busy in
summer.
Q ⛄ ❀ ◑ ◗ ♿ ⚓ ♣ P

Worksop

Manor Lodge

Mansfield Road (off A60)
☎ (0909) 474177
11–3, 5.30–11
**Adnams Broadside; S&N
Theakston Old Peculier;
Taylor Landlord** H; **guest
beers**
Unusual, five-storey
Elizabethan manor house,
built in 1593 for the Earl of
Shrewsbury. Many original
features are still intact.
Children's play area in the
extensive grounds.
🍴 Q ❀ 🍴 ◑ ◗ ♿ ⚓ ➤ P ✗

Newcastle Arms

Carlton Road
☎ (0909) 485384
11–3, 5.30–11
**Marston's Pedigree;
Webster's Yorkshire Bitter;
Whitbread Boddingtons
Bitter, Flowers Original** H;
guest beers
Popular free house catering
for all ages. Comfortable and
friendly atmosphere; busy at
weekends. Varied guest beers.
⛄ ❀ ◑ ◗ ♿ ⚓ ➤ ♣

Try also: Lion Hotel, Bridge
St (Stocks)

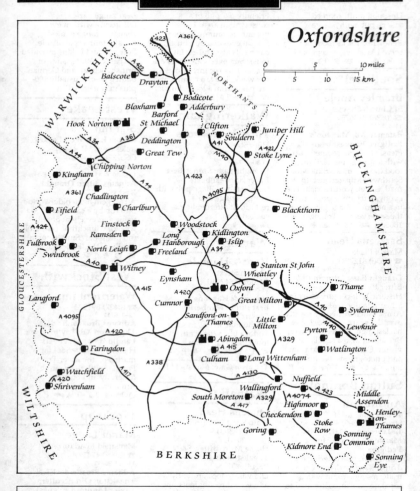

Oxfordshire

Map of Oxfordshire showing towns including Balscote, Drayton, Bodicote, Adderbury, Bloxham, Barford St Michael, Hook Norton, Clifton, Souldern, Juniper Hill, Deddington, Great Tew, Stoke Lyne, Chipping Norton, Kingham, Chadlington, Charlbury, Blackthorn, Fifield, Finstock, Ramsden, Woodstock, Kidlington, Islip, Fulbrook, Swinbrook, North Leigh, Long Hanborough, Freeland, Stanton St John, Wheatley, Witney, Eynsham, Oxford, Thame, Langford, Cunnor, Great Milton, Sydenham, Sandford-on-Thames, Little Milton, Pyrton, Lewknor, Faringdon, Abingdon, Watlington, Watchfield, Culham, Long Wittenham, Shrivenham, Nuffield, Middle Assendon, Wallingford, Henley-on-Thames, South Moreton, Highmoor, Checkendon, Stoke Row, Sonning Common, Goring, Kidmore End, Sonning Eye

---

Brakspear, Henley-on-Thames; **Hook Norton,** Hook Norton; **Morland,** Abingdon; **Morrells,** Oxford; **Wychwood,** Witney

---

Abingdon

College Oak

Peachcroft Road (next to shops) ☎ (0235) 554937
12 (11 Sat)–3, 5.30 (6 Sat)–11
Draught Bass; Welsh Brewers Worthington BB H
Unusual estate pub; one large bar with many artefacts on the walls. ◑ ▮ & P

Adderbury

White Hart

Tanners Lane, West Adderbury ☎ (0295) 810406
11–3, 5–11
Marston's Pedigree;
Whitbread Boddingtons Bitter H**; guest beers**
Tastefully refurbished, 17th-century village inn. Quiet and friendly. ♨ Q ✿ ⇌ ◑ ▮ P

Balscote

Butchers Arms

Shutford Road (off A422)
11–2.30, 6–11
Hook Norton Best Bitter H
Classic one-roomed village pub. No food but plenty of conversation. ♨ Q ✿ ♣ P

Barford St Michael

George Inn

Lower Street ☎ (0869) 38226
12–2.30, 6–11
Adnams Bitter; Hall & Woodhouse Tanglefoot; Wadworth 6X, Old Timer; guest beers H
300-year-old stone and thatch pub with beams and open fires. Set in the Swere valley. Games/function room; blues bands Mon eve. Large garden. A multi-purpose pub! Children welcome in the rear room. ♨ ✿ ◑ ▮ ▮ ▲ ♣ P

Blackthorn

Rose & Crown

12–2.30, 7–11
Morrells Bitter H
Splendid Victorian pub with a convivial atmosphere. Wholesome bar snacks. ♨ ✿ ♣ P

Bloxham

Red Lion
High Street ☎ (0295) 720352
11–2.30, 7–11
Adnams Bitter; Wadworth 6X H; guest beers
Pleasant, friendly country pub: two bars.
🏺 Q ❀ ◖▶ 🛏 & ♣ P

Bodicote

Plough
High Street ☎ (0295) 262327
11–2.30, 5–11 (12–2.30, 7–10.30 Sun)
Bodicote Bitter, No. 9, Porter, Triple X H
Lively home-brew pub. Good food. 🏺 Q ❀ ◖▶ 🛏 ♣

Chadlington

Tite Inn
Mill End ☎ (060 876) 475
12–2.30, 6.30 (7 winter)–11 (closed Mon, except bank hols)
Adnams Bitter; Wadworth 6X; Young's Special; guest beers H
16th-century free house and restaurant, overlooking rolling countryside. No jukebox, slot machines or games. Children welcome.
🏺 Q ❀ 🛏 ◖▶ & P

Charlbury

Rose & Crown
Market Street
☎ (0608) 810103
12–3, 5.30–11
Fuller's London Pride; Greene King Abbot; Hook Norton Best Bitter; Wychwood Best; Young's Special H; guest beers
Popular and friendly local.
🏺 ❀ 🛏 ◖▶ 🚲 ♣

Checkendon

Black Horse
Between Stoke Row and Checkendon, up a narrow track OS667841
11–2.30, 6.30–11
Brakspear Bitter G
No food, no music, no indoor loos! An unspoilt gem of a basic pub off the beaten track. The landlady has run it for 60 years. CAMRA regional *Pub of the Year* 1991.
🏺 Q 🛏 ❀ ▲ ♣ P

Chipping Norton

Chequers
Goddards Lane
11–2.30, 5.30–11
Fuller's Chiswick, London Pride, Mr Harry, ESB H
Recent Fuller's acquisition; so subtly renovated you can hardly tell. Now once again a real local. Eve meals till 8.30.
🏺 ❀ ◖▶ & ♣

Clifton

Duke of Cumberland's Head
On B4031 ☎ (0869) 38534
12–2.30, 6.30–11
Adnams Bitter; Felinfoel Cambrian; Hook Norton Best Bitter; Jennings Bitter; Wadworth 6X H
Thatched, 17th-century, stone building with beams, an inglenook and a restaurant. Vibrant atmosphere. No food Sun eve in winter.
🏺 Q ❀ 🛏 ◖▶ & P

Culham

Lion
High Street ☎ (0235) 520327
11–2.30 (3 Sat & summer), 7 (6.30 Sat & summer)–11
Morrells Bitter, Mild H
Village local from 1906. Mind your head on the bed leg!
🏺 Q 🚲 ◖▶ 🛏 & P

Cumnor

Bear & Ragged Staff
Appleton Road
11–11
Felinfoel Double Dragon; Morrells Bitter, Varsity, College; Whitbread Strong Country or Morrells Mild H
16th-century, olde-worlde inn; previously a farmhouse. One main bar with open fires at each end. 🏺 ❀ ◖▶ ♣ P ✗

Deddington

Crown & Tuns
New Street/Oxford Road
11–4, 6–11
Hook Norton Mild, Best Bitter, Old Hooky H
Fine Georgian coaching inn, now a friendly one-bar local. Conversation and dominoes rule. 🏺 Q ❀ 🛏 ♣

Drayton

Roebuck
Stratford Road
☎ (0295) 730542
11–2.30, 6–11
Bateman XXXB; Hook Norton Best Bitter; Marston's Pedigree; Ruddles County H
17th-century picturesque village inn with a split-level bar. 🏺 Q ❀ 🛏 ◖▶ 🛏 ♣ P

Eynsham

Queens Head
Queen Street ☎ (0865) 881229
12–2.30, 6.30–11
Courage Best Bitter, Directors; Ruddles County H; guest beer
18th-century, basic village pub. The public bar has a darts area. 🏺 ❀ 🛏 & ♣

Faringdon

Bell Hotel
Market Place
☎ (0367) 240534
11–11
Hall & Woodhouse Tanglefoot (summer); Wadworth 6X, Farmer's Glory, Old Timer H
16th-century inn where the bar still retains original features. Pleasant courtyard.
🏺 Q 🚲 ❀ 🛏 ◖▶ ♣ P ✗

Fifield

Merrymouth Inn
Stow Road ☎ (0993) 831652
11–2.30, 6–11 (12–2.30, 7–10.30 Sun)
Donnington BB, SBA H
13th-century inn with a beamed bar and a stone floor. Cooking on an open log grill.
🏺 Q 🚲 ❀ 🛏 ◖▶ ▲ ♣ P

Finstock

Plough Inn
The Bottom (off B4022)
12–2.30, 6–11 (12–11 Sat)
Adnams Broadside; Draught Bass; Hook Norton Best Bitter; Ringwood Old Thumper H; guest beers
Traditional, thatched pub, built in 1772, offering fine food. Weekly guest beers. Cider in summer.
🏺 Q ❀ 🛏 ◖▶ 🛏 & ♣ (limited service) ♣ ➷ P

Freeland

Oxfordshire Yeoman
Wroslyn Road
☎ (0993) 882051
11–2.30, 6–11
Morrells Bitter, Mild H
Cotswold stone pub with a low ceiling and beams. The stone-floored area used to be a cattle shed. No food Mon; eve meals till 8 (not Sun).
🏺 ❀ ◖▶ ♣

Fulbrook

Masons Arms
Shipton Road
☎ (0993) 822354
12 (11.30 Sat)–3 (not Mon), 6.30–11
Hook Norton Best Bitter; Wadworth 6X H
200-year-old, friendly Cotswold stone pub with original beams. Home-made food. 🏺 Q ❀ ◖▶ ♣ ➷

Goring

John Barleycorn
Manor Road ☎ (0491) 872509
10–2.30, 6–11
Brakspear Bitter, Special H
16th-century, low-beamed inn with a cosy saloon and good food. Q ❀ 🛏 ◖▶ 🛏 🚲 ♣

Oxfordshire

Great Milton

Bell Inn
The Green ☎ (0844) 279270
12–2, 7–11 (12–2, 7–10.30 Sun)
Brakspear Bitter; Uley UB40, Old Spot Ⓗ; **guest beers**
Welcoming, 17th-century country pub with good home-made food. Beer festivals.
🍴 Q ✿ ◑ ▮ 💺 & ♣

Great Tew

Falkland Arms
Off B4022 ☎ (0608) 83653
11.30–2.30 (not Mon), 6–11 (12–2, 7–10.30 Sun)
Donnington BB; Hall & Woodhouse Tanglefoot; Hook Norton Best Bitter; Wadworth 6X Ⓗ; **guest beers** Ⓗ & Ⓖ
Outstanding, 16th-century, thatched pub: oak panels, settles and flagstoned floors; malts, fruit wines, snuff, oil lamps, clay pipes and walking sticks. A gem! No food Sun or Mon. 🍴 Q ✿ 🛏 ◑ ▲ ♣ ⌂

Henley-on-Thames

Saracen's Head
129 Greys Road (up hill)
11–2.30 (3 Sat), 5.30–11
Brakspear Mild, Bitter, Special Ⓗ
Friendly welcome in a busy local which has an emphasis on pub games. The range of food is limited (especially Sun). 🍴 ✿ 🛏 ◑ ▮ ▲ 💺 (not winter Sun) ♣ P

Highmoor

Dog & Duck
On B481 ☎ (0491) 641261
12–3, 6–11
Brakspear Bitter, Special, Old Ⓗ
Cosy, two-bar pub in Chiltern woodland. No-smoking dining room. Large garden with barbecues on summer weekends. Good food (no meals Mon).
🍴 Q ✿ ◑ ▮ ♣ P

Hook Norton

Pear Tree
Scotland End
☎ (0608) 737482
12–2.30 (3 Sat), 6–11
Hook Norton Mild, Best Bitter, Old Hooky Ⓗ
Brewery tap refurbished into one room. Eve meals till 8.
🍴 Q ✿ 🛏 ◑ ▮ ▲ ♣ P

Islip

Swan
Lower Street ☎ (086 75) 2590
10.30–3, 6.30–11
Draught Bass; Morrells Bitter, Graduate Ⓗ

Quiet, comfortable, one-bar pub. Q 💺 ✿ ◑ ▮ 💺 P

Juniper Hill

Fox Inn
Off A43 ☎ (0869) 810616
11–2.30, 7–11
Hook Norton Best Bitter, Old Hooky Ⓗ
Friendly pub in the centre of a hamlet, described in *Lark Rise to Candleford*. 🍴 Q ✿ ♣ P

Kidlington

Wise Alderman
Station Approach, Banbury Road (A423)
☎ (086 75) 2281
11–2.30, 5.30–11
Hook Norton Best Bitter; Tetley Bitter; Wadworth 6X Ⓗ
Comfortable, friendly canal-side pub. 💺 ✿ ◑ ▮ & ♣ P

Kidmore End

New Inn
Chalkhouse Green Road
11–2.30, 6–11
Brakspear Bitter, Special Ⓗ, **Old** Ⓖ
Comfortable, two-bar pub with beams, wood panelling and a large garden. Near the village pond. Good cooking.
💺 ✿ ◑ ▮ P ↯

Kingham

Plough
Main Street ☎ (0608) 658327
10.30–3.30, 6–11
Draught Bass; Wychwood Shires, Best Ⓗ
Lively local opposite the green. 🍴 ✿ ▲ 💺 ♣ ⌂ P

Langford

Bell
Off A361 through Filkins, bear right, then first right
11–2.30, 6.30–11
Archers Village; Morland Bitter; Wadworth 6X Ⓗ
Quiet, 17th-century village local. Unpretentious but home-cooked food (no meals Sun lunch or Mon eve).
🍴 Q ✿ ◑ ▮ 🖸 ♣ P

Lewknor

Olde Leathern Bottel
High Street ☎ (0844) 51482
11–2.30, 6–11
Brakspear Bitter, Special, Old Ⓗ
Comfortable family-run village pub. Food is good.
🍴 💺 ✿ ◑ ▮ 🖸 & ♣ P

Little Milton

Plough
Thame Road ☎ (0844) 278180
11–11

Morrells Bitter, Varsity, Graduate Ⓗ; **guest beers**
17th-century, stone-walled and timber-beamed pub with a village atmosphere. Good value food. Large garden.
🍴 Q 💺 ✿ ◑ ▮ ▲ ♣ P

Long Hanborough

Bell
Main Road ☎ (0993) 881324
10.30–3, 6.30–11
Morrells Bitter, Varsity Ⓗ
18th-century pub revived. Good food and atmosphere.
💺 ✿ ◑ ▮ 🖸 💺 ♣ P

Long Wittenham

Machine Man Inn
Fieldside ☎ (086 730) 7835
11–3, 6–11
Eldridge Pope Hardy Country, Royal Oak; Exmoor Gold; Hook Norton Best Bitter; guest beers Ⓗ
Genuine village local, which used to belong to the machine mender. No food Sun eve.
🍴 💺 ✿ 🛏 ◑ ▮ & ♣ ⌂ P

Middle Assendon

Rainbow
On B481 ☎ (0491) 574879
11–2.30, 6–11 (12–2.30, 7–10.30 Sun)
Brakspear Bitter, Special Ⓔ, **Old** Ⓖ
Friendly, old, low-beamed local in a beautiful dry valley. No meals Sun lunch (bar snacks available). The handpulls operate electric pumps. ✿ ◑ ▮ 🖸 ♣ P

North Leigh

Woodman
New Yatt Road (off A4095)
12–3, 6 (7 Sat)–11
Hook Norton Best Bitter; Wadworth 6X Ⓗ; **Wychwood Shires; guest beers**
Small village pub with a large garden, and a well in the bar. Home-made food. Twice-yearly beer festivals. Jazz music. Cider in summer. 🍴 Q ✿ 🛏 ◑ ▮ & ♣ ⌂ P ↯

Nuffield

Crown
On A423 ☎ (0491) 641335
11–2.30, 6–11
Brakspear Bitter, Special, Old Ⓗ
17th-century, beamed waggoners' inn. Excellent home-made food. Children allowed in the dining area at lunch. 🍴 Q ✿ ◑ ▮ ▲ ♣ P

Oxford

Anchor Inn
2 Hayfield Road, Walton Manor ☎ (0865) 510282

11.30–2.30, 6–11 (11.30–11 Sat & summer)
Adnams Broadside; Draught Bass; Wadworth 6X, Farmer's Glory H; **guest beers**
Large, popular pub with a dining room; recently refurbished in 1930s style. Quality food with some exotic dishes (no meals Sun eve)..
🏠 Q ❀ ◖ ▶ ♣ P ⊁

Bookbinders Arms
17–18 Victor Street, Jericho
10.30–3, 6–11 (10.30–11 Sat)
Morrells Bitter, Mild H
Large, friendly, single-bar pub. No food Sun. ◖ ♣

Butchers Arms
5 Wilberforce Street, Headington (past the Shark, first left, first right)
11.30–2.30 (not Tue), 6–11 (11.30–11 Fri; 11–3.30, 5.30–11 Sat)
Fuller's London Pride, Mr Harry, ESB H
Local with a warm atmosphere. Good pub grub. Families welcome lunch and early eve. 🏠 ❀ ◖ ♣

Eagle & Child
49 St Giles ☎ (0865) 58085
11–3, 5.30–11 (12–2.30, 7–10.30 Sun)
Ind Coope Burton Ale; Tetley Bitter; Wadworth 6X H
Well-restored, multi-alcoved pub. Once frequented by CS Lewis and Tolkien. Q ❀ ◖ ▶

Fir Tree Tavern
163 Iffley Road (A4158)
12–3, 5.30–11
Morrells Bitter, Varsity, Graduate H
Small, split-level pub. Quiet lunchtimes; popular with locals and students in the eve. Pizzas a speciality. ❀ ◖ ▶

Gardeners Arms
39 Plantation Road (off A4144)
11–2.30, 6–11 (11–11 Fri & Sat)
Morrells Bitter, Graduate H
Comfortable, one-bar pub between Woodstock Rd and Walton St. Popular with town and university folk. Home-cooked meals. ☞ ❀ ◖ ▶

Gloucester Arms
Friars Entry ☎ (0865) 241177
11–11
Ind Coope Burton Ale; Tetley Bitter; Wadworth 6X; Wychwood Best, Dr Thirsty's Draught H
Traditional pub with a lively weekend atmosphere. Close to the Oxford Playhouse. The decor is unfussy but it retains original snob screens. ◖ ⇛

Marlborough House
60 Western Road, Grandpont
11–3, 6–11 (11.30–11 Sat)
Ind Coope ABC Best Bitter, Burton Ale; Tetley Bitter H; **guest beers**
Back-street local, on the site of the city's first station. Popular

with students. Pool room. Guest milds. ☞ 🏠 ◖ ⇛ ♣

Old Tom
St Aldates ☎ (0865) 243034
10.30–3, 5 (5.30 Fri & Sat)–11
Morrells Bitter, Mild, Varsity H
Lively pub built around 1600. Popular with office workers, students and the clergy. Takes its name from the bell at Christ Church college. No-smoking area lunchtime. Eve meals finish early. Q ❀ ◖ ▶ ⇛ ⊁

Osney Arms
45 Botley Road, Osney
11–2.30, 6–11
Greene King IPA, Abbot H
Local with an established pool-playing, cricketing and quizzing clientele. Friendly but can be smokey. ⊟ ⇛

Prince of Wales
73 Church Way, Iffley
11.30–2.30, 6–11
Adnams Bitter, Broadside; Wadworth 6X, Farmer's Glory H; **guest beers**
Welcoming pub in an old riverside village; popular for its Sun lunches. Once a bakery in part. 🏠 ❀ ◖ ▶ P

Quarry Gate
19 Wharton Road, Headington
11–3, 6–11 (11–11 Fri)
Courage Best Bitter, Directors; Gale's HSB; John Smith's Bitter H; **guest beers**
Friendly suburban local with a lounge/family room and a busy public bar. Over 160 beers in 12 months. Good pub grub. Q ☞ ❀ ◖ ▶ ⊟ ♣ ⊔ P

Temple Bar
21 Temple Street (off B480)
12–2.30, 7–11
Hall & Woodhouse Tanglefoot; Wadworth IPA, 6X, Farmer's Glory (summer), **Old Timer** H
The basic public bar has a games area; the small, comfortable lounge hosts a folk session every Sun eve. Wheelchair access and car park in Stockmore St.
❀ ⊟ ◖ P

Victoria
90 Walton Street, Jericho
11.30–3, 6–11 (11.30–11 Sat & summer)
Banks's Bitter E
Lively main bar; panelled snug; function room. Lunches weekends. 🏠 Q ❀ ◖ ♣

Victoria Arms
Mill Lane, Old Marston
11.30–2.30, 6–11
Draught Bass; Hall & Wood-house Tanglefoot; Wadworth 6X, Farmer's Glory, Old Timer H; **guest beers**
Large riverside pub in extensive grounds, including a

play area. Popular with punters. Antique furniture; old paintings. Wheelchair access is good. Wide range of food. 🏠 ❀ ◖ ▶ ♿ P

Pyrton

Plough
Off B4009 ☎ (0491) 612003
11.30–2.30, 7 (6 Fri & Sat)–11 (closed Mon eve)
Adnams Bitter; Brakspear Bitter; Fuller's ESB H
Attractive, 17th-century, thatched pub. Popular for its home-made food, in the bar and restaurant. Families welcome in the restaurant at lunch. 🏠 ❀ ◖ ▶ ⚓ ♣ P

Ramsden

Royal Oak
High Street ☎ (0993) 868213
11.30–2.30, 6.30–11
Banks's Bitter; Hook Norton Best Bitter, Old Hooky H; **guest beers**
Friendly, 17th-century inn: one room but a separate restaurant. 🏠 Q ❀ 🏠 ◖ ▶ ♿ P

Sandford-on-Thames

Fox
29 Henley Road (off A423)
11–2.30, 6–11
Morrells Bitter G
Lovely, basic old pub, selling the cheapest Morrells for miles around. 🏠 Q ❀ ⊟ ♿ P

Shrivenham

Prince of Wales
High Street ☎ (0793) 782268
11–3, 6–11
Hall & Woodhouse Tanglefoot; Wadworth IPA, 6X H, **Old Timer** H
Cosy, stone-built country pub; a 17th-century coaching inn. Good food (no meals Sun eve). 🏠 Q ❀ ◖ ▶ ♣ P

Sonning Common

Bird in Hand
Reading Road (B481)
11–2.30, 6–11
Courage Best Bitter; Ruddles County; Wadworth 6X H
Low-beamed, 16th-century pub with a large inglenook and traditional pub furnishings. Very popular restaurant (standard pub menu). No meals Sun eve. Enclosed garden. Q ❀ ◖ ▶ P

Sonning Eye

Flowing Spring
Henley Road ☎ (0734) 693207
12–2.30 (3 Fri & Sat), 5.30 (6 Sat)–11
Fuller's Chiswick, London Pride, Mr Harry, ESB H

Comfortable, roadside pub. A wrought iron staircase leads up from the huge garden. Events include the national Mamod/Meccano steam rally (April) and a steam engine rally (July). No food Sun or eve meals Mon/Tue.
🏠 ✤ ◖❱ ♣ P

Souldern

Fox
Off B4100
☎ (0869) 245284
11.30–3, 5 (6 Sat)–11
Draught Bass; Fuller's London Pride; Hook Norton Best Bitter Ⓗ**; guest beers**
Friendly, Cotswold stone pub. Exceedingly good food.
🏠 Q ✤ 🛏 ◖❱ ♣ P

South Moreton

Crown Inn
High Street
☎ (0235) 812262
11–3, 5.30–11
Adnams Bitter; Hall & Woodhouse Tanglefoot; Wadworth IPA Ⓗ**, 6X** Ⓖ**; guest beer**
Popular village local with a spacious single bar, floorboards, rugs and deep red walls. Good, home-cooked food. 🏠 Q ⛴ ✤ ◖❱ ▲ ♣ P

Stanton St John

Star Inn
11–2.30, 6.30–11 (12–2.30, 7–10.30 Sun)
Hall & Woodhouse Tanglefoot; Wadworth IPA, 6X, Farmer's Glory, Old Timer Ⓗ
17th-century inn retaining some interesting features. Home-cooked food. Children may bring well behaved parents to the family room (no-smoking), and beer garden.
🏠 Q ⛴ ✤ ◖❱ 🍴 ♣ P ⟋

Stoke Lyne

Peyton Arms
Off B4100
☎ (0869) 345285
10.30–2.30 (not Mon), 6–11 (12–2, 7–10.30 Sun)
Hook Norton Mild, Best Bitter, Old Hooky (winter) Ⓖ
Small, basic village local unchanged by time – a real rural gem. 🏠 Q ✤ 🍴 ♣ ⌂

Stoke Row

Cherry Tree
10–2.30, 6–11
Brakspear Mild, Bitter, Special, Old Ⓖ
Picturesque, low-beamed local. Families are welcome in the games room. No food Mon. 🏠 ⛴ ✤ ◖❱ 🍴 ♣ P

Swinbrook

Swan
11.30–2.30, 6–11
Morland Bitter; Wadworth 6X Ⓗ
Characterful, 16th-century, riverside country inn, a former watermill. Good home-cooked food. Darts, cards and shove-ha'penny in the flagstoned tap room. 🏠 Q ◖❱ ♣ P

Sydenham

Crown Inn
Sydenham Road (off B4445)
☎ (0844) 51634
12–2.30, 6–11
Morrells Bitter, Varsity Ⓗ
Low-beamed, single bar village pub. Busy meal trade at weekends (booking essential). 🏠 ✤ ◖❱ ♣

Thame

Rising Sun
High Street ☎ (084 421) 4206
11–2.30, 6–11
Hook Norton Best Bitter; Marston's Pedigree; Wadworth 6X Ⓗ**; guest beer**
Attractive, 16th-century, oak-beamed building with an overhanging first floor and low ceilings. Excellent menu. Board games. 🏠 ✤ ◖❱ ♣

Swan Hotel
9 Upper High Street
☎ (0844) 261211
11–11
Brakspear Bitter; Hook Norton Best Bitter; Whitbread Flowers Original Ⓗ**; guest beers**
Popular town-centre inn, with many unusual fittings. Uncommon guest beers, although prices are on the high side. Excellent meals.
🏠 Q ⛴ ✤ 🛏 ◖❱ 🍴 P

Wallingford

Cross Keys
High Street ☎ (0491) 37173
11–3, 6–11
Brakspear Mild, Bitter, Special, Old Ⓗ
Unspoilt, three-roomed, 17th-century town pub. Small, comfortable lounge; public bar with darts room. Eve meals till 8.30; no food Sun.
Q ✤ ◖❱ 🍺 ♣ P

Watchfield

Royal Oak
Oak Road ☎ (0793) 782668
11.30–2.30 (3.30 Sat), 6.30–11 (may vary)
Ushers Best Bitter, Founders Ⓗ
Friendly local, ivy-covered and dating back to the 18th century. No food Tue eve.
✤ ◖❱ ♣ P

Watlington

Fox & Hounds
Shirburn Street (B4009)
11–3, 6–11
Brakspear Mild, Bitter Ⓗ
15th- or 16th-century, locals' inn: the bar is where the coaches pulled in, and the butcher's shop next door used to be part of the pub. No food Sun. 🏠 ✤ ◖ ▲ ♣ P

Wheatley

Railway
Station Road ☎ (086 77) 4810
11–3, 5.30–11 (11–11 Sat)
Fuller's Chiswick, London Pride, Mr Harry, ESB Ⓗ
Friendly, one-room local with railway memorabilia. Entertainment in the function room every Sat eve. Families welcome lunch and early eve. No food Sun. ✤ ◖ ♣ P

Witney

Carpenters Arms
132 Newland ☎ (0993) 702206
10.30–2.30, 6–11
Morrells Bitter; Whitbread Strong Country Ⓗ
Comfortable, one-bar pub with a small games room. Ideal for a quiet drink. ✤ P

Court Inn
Bridge Street ☎ (0993) 703228
10.30–3, 6–11
Courage Best Bitter; John Smith's Bitter Ⓗ
17th-century coaching inn with a large, comfortable lounge and small bar/games room. The landlord is fanatical about his beer. 🛏 ◖❱ 🍺 ♣ P

House of Windsor
West End ☎ (0993) 704277
12–3.30 (not Mon), 6 (7 Sat)–11
Hook Norton Best Bitter; Marston's Pedigree; Wadworth 6X Ⓗ**; guest beers**
Popular local featuring aeronautical memorabilia. Three guest beers vary. No food Mon eve. 🏠 ✤ ◖❱ ♣

Woodstock

Black Prince
Manor Road ☎ (0993) 811530
12–2.30, 6.30–11
Archers Village; S&N Theakston XB, Old Peculier Ⓗ**; guest beer**
16th-century pub of character with a suit of armour in the bar. Good food. 🏠 ✤ ◖❱ P

Rose & Crown
Manor Road ☎ (0993) 812009
11–3, 6.30–11
Morrells Bitter, Mild Ⓗ
Friendly, basic, 18th-century pub. Good food.
✤ ◖❱ 🍺 ♣ P

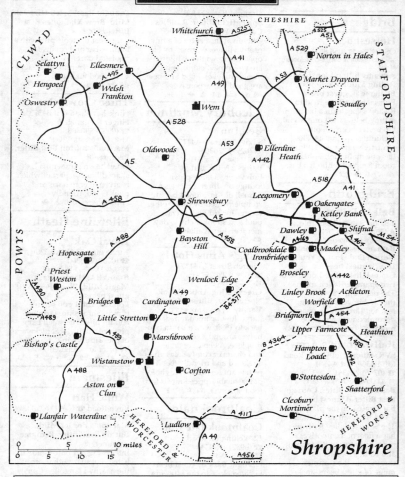

Ackleton

Folley Inn
On B4176, 6 miles S of Telford
☎ (074 65) 225
12–2.30 (3.30 Sat), 6.30–11
Banks's Mild, Bitter Ⓔ
Large open-plan, single-bar
pub, with a small games room.
Brass and copper adorn the
feature fireplace. Barbecues in
summer. No dogs allowed.
Q ❀ ♣ P

Aston on Clun

Kangaroo Inn
Near Craven Arms, Clun
Road (B4368)
☎ (058 87) 263
12–3, 7–11
**Draught Bass; M&B Highgate
Mild; Welsh Brewers
Worthington BB** Ⓗ

Welcoming and roomy pub
with a large public bar and a
separate lounge. Big well-kept
garden with a children's play
area; caravans and campers
welcome. The village is
famous for its arbor tree,
decorated each May 29th for
the ancient custom of tree
dressing. The beer range may
change. ◑ ▶ ▲ ♣ P

Try also: Engine & Tender,
Broome (Free)

Bayston Hill

Compasses
Hereford Road (A49)
☎ (0743) 722921
12–2, 5–11 (12–11 Fri & Sat)
**Draught Bass; M&B Highgate
Mild, Brew XI** Ⓗ**; guest beers**
Friendly local on the main
road, with a snug and a

separate public bar featuring a
nautical décor. Note the
collection of carved wooden
elephants.
🏨 ❀ ◑ ◐ ♣ P

Bishop's Castle

Castle Hotel
Market Square
☎ (0588) 638403
12–3, 6.30–11
**Marston's Pedigree;
Whitbread Boddingtons
Bitter, Flowers Original** Ⓗ
Truly at the top of the town,
this hotel's bowling green is at
the highest point. A small
attractive bar at the front
boasts fine woodwork and
there is a larger room with
different areas off to the side.
🏨 Q ❀ ◑ ◐ ◵ ♣ P

Try also: Three Tuns (Free)

Shropshire

Bridges

Horseshoes
OS394964 ☎ (058 861) 260
12–2.30 (extends Sat), 6–11 (closed Mon)

Adnams Bitter; Mansfield Riding Mild; Marston's Pedigree H**; guest beers**
Pub set just off the road to Bishop's Castle, in a beautiful setting below the Long Mynd. Up to five beers on offer, including two guests. The attractive, rendered building has one main room, plus a room for pool without a bar.
🏶 Q ◑ ♣ ⌣

Bridgnorth

Bell & Talbot
2 Salop Street (B4364, old A458) ☎ (0746) 763233
11.30–3, 6 (7 winter)–11

Batham Best Bitter; Hook Norton Old Hooky; Younger IPA H**; guest beer**
Grade II listed free house with two character-laden rooms. The rear courtyard contains the old brewery building, reached through a passage decorated with a real ale mural. 🏶 ❀ ◑ 🍴 ≋ (SVR)

Railwayman's Arms
SVR station, Hollybush Road (off B4364, old A458)
☎ (0746) 764361
11–11 (11–2.30, 7–11 winter)

Batham Best Bitter; Courage Best Bitter H**; guest beers**
Bar located on the platform of a Victorian railway station. The Severn Valley Railway has a fleet of locomotives running between Bridgnorth and Kidderminster throughout the summer. Good range of guest beers stocked.
🏶 Q ≋ (SVR) ♣ ⌣ P

Broseley

Cumberland Hotel
Jackson Avenue (off B4375)
☎ (0952) 882301
11–11

Ruddles Best Bitter; Webster's Yorkshire Bitter H
Elegant country house dating from 1715. The landlord's family has made clay tobacco pipes in the town since 1823; lots of 'pipe' mementoes are displayed. Home-made bar meals available in a quiet, well-furnished lounge and a lively bar, while the no-smoking restaurant serves *à la carte* meals. 🏶 ❀ ◑ ▶ 🍴 ≋ P

Cardington

Royal Oak Inn
Off B4371 at Longville
OS506953 ☎ (069 43) 266
12–2.30, 7–11 (closed winter Mon)

Draught Bass; M&B Springfield Bitter; Ruddles County; Wadworth 6X H
Old inn at the centre of a tiny, pretty village, warmed by big open fire in winter. Children are welcome if eating (no meals Sun eve). Food and beer are good but expensive.
🏶 Q ≋ ◑ ▶ ▲ 🍴 P ⊬

Cleobury Mortimer

Bell Inn
8 Lower Street (A4117)
☎ (0299) 270305
11–3, 7 (6 Fri & Sat)–11

Banks's Mild, Bitter H
Pub where a large plush lounge on different levels and a small old-fashioned bar are complemented by many other rooms, including a private pool and snooker club – day membership available.
🏶 🍴 ♣ ⌣

King's Arms Hotel
Church Street (A4117)
☎ (0299) 270252
11–11

Greene King Abbot; Hook Norton Best Bitter; Morrells Varsity H**; guest beers**
Large, low-beamed inn, dating back to 1530, with a bar in two halves around a central fireplace. A choice of tables and chairs or comfy sofas gives a relaxed and friendly feel. The restaurant serves a wide choice of reasonably-priced meals (no food Sun eve). 🏶 🍴 ◑ ▶

Coalbrookdale

Coalbrookdale Inn
12 Wellington Road
☎ (0952) 433953
12–2.30, 5.30–11

Draught Bass H**; guest beers**
Located close to the Museum of Iron, this pub offers a good range of guest beers. Eve meals finish early.
🏶 ❀ 🍴 ◑ ▶ ♣ P

Corfton

Sun Inn
On B4368 ☎ (058 473) 239
11–2.30, 6–11

Draught Bass H**; guest beers**
Family-run inn dating back to the 17th century, featuring a coal fire in the bar, a dining area in the lounge and exposed beams, tastefully decorated throughout. Ducks and chickens inhabit the garden play area. Always two–three guest beers; guest cider in summer.
🏶 Q ❀ 🍴 ◑ ▶ ▲ ♣ ⌣ P

Dawley

Crown Inn
High Street ☎ (0952) 505015
11–4, 7–11

Draught Bass; M&B Highgate Mild, Brew XI; Stones Best Bitter H **&** E
Large, comfortable pub with a lounge, bar and rooms for pool and darts. A good, friendly town pub for all ages. Very good jukebox.
🏶 ⅍ ❀ ◑ 🍴 ♣

Three Crowns Inn
Hinkshay Road (off B4373 at Finger Rd garage)
☎ (0952) 590868
11–3 (4 Fri & Sat), 6.30–11

Marston's Burton Best Bitter, Pedigree H
Small, town pub with a U-shaped lounge, part of which is given over to darts and pool. Good, friendly atmosphere. ❀ ◑ ▲ ♣ P

Ellerdine Heath

Royal Oak
1 mile off A53 OS603226
☎ (0939) 250300
11–3, 5–11 (11–11 Fri & Sat)

Brains SA; Hanby Black Magic Mild; Wood Parish H**; guest beers**
Popular, rural pub set in a typical Shropshire farming community. The small bar gives rise to its local nickname of the 'Tiddlywink'. Camping by prior arrangement.
🏶 ⅍ ❀ ◑ ▶ ▲ ♣ ⌣ P

Ellesmere

White Hart
Birch Road ☎ (0691) 622333
12 (varies summer)–3, 7–11

Marston's Border Mild, Burton Best Bitter, Pedigree (summer) H
Interesting old pub, Grade II listed. Popular with users of the nearby Llangollen Canal, at the centre of Shropshire's 'Lake District'. ❀ ◑ ▲ ♣

Try also: Black Lion (Marston's); **Ellesmere Hotel** (Free)

Hampton Loade

Lion Inn
1 mile off A442 S of Quatt
OS748862 ☎ (0746) 780263
12–2.30 (not Mon or winter), 7 (7.30 winter)–11

Hook Norton Old Hooky; Whitbread Boddingtons Bitter H**; guest beers** (summer)
Totally unspoilt, multi-roomed free house, close to the River Severn. Built in the 17th century as a cider house, it now offers a large selection of country wines and guest beers in summer, plus a house beer (not brewed here). Accessible by chain ferry from the SVR station. 🏶 Q ❀ ◑ ▶ 🍴 ▲ ≋ (SVR) P

Heathton

Old Gate Inn

1 mile NW of Halfpenny
Green airfield, off B4176
OS813924 ☎ (074 66) 431
12–3, 7–11
**HP&D Bitter, Entire; Taylor
Landlord** Ⓗ
16th-century country inn well
off the beaten track, but worth
discovering. Its relaxing,
pleasant atmosphere is
complemented by good food
(vegetarian choice). A sandpit
and barbecue in the garden,
plus a drinking area on the
new patio. The only HP&D
pub in Shropshire.
🏮 ❀ ◖ ▮ ▲ P

Hengoed

Last Inn

3 miles N of Oswestry, off
B4579 ☎ (0691) 659747
7–11 (12–3, 7–10.30 Sun)
**Draught Bass; Cains Bitter;
Wood Special** Ⓗ**; guest beers**
Country pub with separate
games and family rooms. No
meals Tue; Sun lunch
served. Weston's Old Rosie
cider available.
🏮 Q ▷ ◖ ◀ ⅋ ⌓ P

Hopesgate

Stables Inn

Off A488 OS343019
☎ (0743) 891344
11.30–2.30, 7–11 (closed Mon)
**Ind Coope Benskins Best
Bitter; Marston's Pedigree;
Wood Special** Ⓗ
Small remote pub on the high
ground between the Hope and
Rea valleys. It foregoes the
distractions of jukebox, pool
and fruit machine in favour of
quoits. A massive log fire in
winter warms the U-shaped
bar which leads into a small
dining room.
🏮 Q ❀ ◖ ▮ ⅋ P

Ironbridge

Crown

10 Hodge Bower
☎ (0952) 433128
12–3, 7–11
Banks's Mild, Bitter Ⓔ
Tucked away from the tourist
area, a locals' pub supporting
an enthusiastic dominoes
team. Excellent views across
the Severn Gorge. No eve
meals Sun. Q ❀ ◖ ▮ ▲ ⅋ P

Ketley Bank

Lord Hill Inn

Main Road ☎ (0952) 613070
11–2.30 (3 Sat), 7 (5 Thu & Fri)–11
(12–2.30, 7–10.30 Sun)
**Hook Norton Best Bitter;
M&B Highgate Mild; Stones
Best Bitter** Ⓗ**; guest beers**

A truly cosmopolitan, friendly
local where everyone feels
comfortable. Not surprisingly
it has won the local CAMRA
Pub of the Year award three
times. At least two guest beers
available. 🏮 ▷ ❀ ◀ ⅋ P

Leegomery

Malt Shovel

Hadley Park Road (A442)
☎ (0952) 242963
11.30–2.30, 5–11 (12–2.30, 7–11 Sun)
**Marston's Burton Best Bitter,
Pedigree** Ⓗ
Friendly local with a compact
bar and a pleasant lounge
featuring brass decorations,
with open fires in both.
Lunchtime bar meals Mon–Fri.
🏮 Q ◖ ◀ ⅋ P

Linley Brook

Pheasant Inn

Off B4373 ☎ (0746) 762260
12–2.30, 6.30 (7 winter)–11
Hook Norton Mild Ⓗ**; guest
beers**
Two-roomed pub between
Brosley and Bridgnorth, well
worth finding. Two guest
beers always available, also
excellent food. Children are
only allowed in the garden.
🏮 Q ❀ ◖ ▮ ⅋ ⌓ P

Little Stretton

Green Dragon

On B4370 ☎ (0694) 722925
11–3, 6–11 (11–11 Sat)
**Marston's Pedigree; Ruddles
Best Bitter; Wood Parish** Ⓗ
Well-appointed pub set in
idyllic surroundings at the
start of Ashes Hollow – a
valley which leads up on to the
Long Mynd, one of the many
walks in the area. Nearby
campsite. 🏮 Q ❀ ◖ ▮ ▲ P

Llanfair Waterdine

Red Lion

☎ (0547) 528214
12–2 (not Tue), 7–11
**Marston's Pedigree; Tetley
Bitter** Ⓗ
Archetypal village inn run on
traditional lines: a long black
and white building on the
bank of the River Teme.
Q ❀ 🛏 ◖ ▮ ◀ P

Ludlow

Church Inn

Buttercross ☎ (0584) 872174
11–11
**Ruddles County; Webster's
Yorkshire Bitter** Ⓗ**; guest
beers** (summer)
Tucked away in the heart of
Ludlow, behind Buttercross
and away from the traffic, on
one of the town's most ancient
sites; an upmarket inn close to
the parish church of St

Laurence, the largest and most
majestic in Shropshire. A
house beer – Bellringer – is
also available. Q 🛏 ◖ ▮ ≠

Wheatsheaf

Lower Broad Street
☎ (0584) 872980
12–2.30, 6.30–11
**Whitbread WCPA,
Boddingtons Bitter, Castle
Eden Ale** Ⓗ
Pub nestling under the historic
Broadgate, the last of seven
town gates built in the 13th
century (the town walls
dominate at this point). A
through-lounge bar and a
restaurant. The choice of beers
may vary. 🏮 Q 🛏 ◖ ▮ ▲ ≠

Try also: Bull (Marston's);
Bull Ring Tavern (Allied)

Madeley

All Nations

Coalport Road (near Blists Hill
Open Air Museum)
☎ (0952) 585747
12–3 (3.30 Sat), 7–11
All Nations Pale Ale Ⓗ
Famous home-brew pub with
a dedicated band of followers
and full of local character(s).
Its one bar can get packed on
darts/doms eves; the outdoor
drinking area is a sun trap.
Probably serves the cheapest
beer in Shropshire. One of the
few home-brew pubs left in
the early 1970s. ❀ ⅋ P

Market Drayton

Kings Arms

Shropshire Street
☎ (0630) 652417
11–3, 7–11 (11–11 Wed, Fri & Sat)
**Marston's Mercian Mild,
Burton Best Bitter,
Pedigree** Ⓗ
Ancient former coaching inn,
built in 1674. A friendly, two-
roomed local with an L-
shaped bar and a small snug,
catering for all ages. Good
selection of malt and Irish
whiskies. A former CAMRA
Potteries *Pub of the Year.*
Q ❀ ◖ ⅋ P

Marshbrook

Wayside Inn

On B4370 ☎ (0694) 781208
11.30–2.30, 5.30–11
**Ansells Bitter; Banks's Bitter;
Draught Bass** Ⓗ
Off the A49 and just over the
level crossing, a friendly, one-
roomed local with a long bar.
The Shropshire Vintage Motor
Cycle Club meets here once a
month, while the collection of
cups bears witness to the
prowess of the Pentre tug-of-
war team (Welsh national
champions).
🏮 ❀ 🛏 ◖ ▮ ▲ ⅋ P

Shropshire

Norton in Hales

Hinds Head
Main Road (1$\frac{1}{2}$ miles W of
B5415, Woore–Market
Drayton road) OS703387
☎ (0630) 43014
12–3, 5–11 (11–11 Sat)
**Draught Bass; M&B
Springfield Bitter; Stones
Best Bitter; Welsh Brewers
Worthington BB** H
Remote country inn, well
worth the trip: a large,
comfortable lounge, a small
bar and a restaurant. An
etched window with a hind's
head logo advertises Joule's
Stone Ales. Stocks over 30
malt whiskies.
🏨 ✿ ◖ ▶ ⊟ & ♣ ♠ P

Oakengates

Rose & Crown
Holyhead Road
☎ (0952) 614348
12–2.30, 7–11
**Ansells Mild, Bitter; Ind
Coope Burton Ale; Tetley
Bitter** H
Two-roomed, friendly, old-
fashioned local with a cosy
lounge full of brass and
mirrors. The L-shaped bar has
a jukebox (not loud). Excellent
lunches served, but don't be
late. ✿ ◖ ⊟ ♠ P

Oldwoods

Romping Cat
☎ (0939) 290273
12–3 (2 Tue, Wed; not Fri), 7–11
**Whitbread Castle Eden Ale;
Wood Parish** H; **guest beer**
Neat and welcoming country
pub, well-known locally for its
charitable functions.
Q ✿ ♠ P

Try also: **Railway,** Yorton
(Free)

Oswestry

Black Gate
Salop Road ☎ (0691) 653168
10–3, 6–11
**Banks's Bitter; Fuller's
ESB** H; **guest beers**
Black and white, timber
building dating from 1621 and
named after the south
entrance to the town. Two
guest beers always available.
Q ◖ ◗

Sun Inn
Church Street
☎ (0691) 653433
12–2.30 (3 Sat; not Tue–Fri), 7–11
Beer range varies
Street-corner pub sympathetically renovated as a genuine
free house. The dining area
serves home-cooked food. The
house brew, Clog Iron Bitter,
is available alongside at least

two guest beers. Note the
original Walkers windows.
Q ◖ ⊟ ♠ P

Try also: **Golden Lion,** Upper
Church St (Marston's)

Priest Weston

Miners Arms
OS293973 ☎ (093 872) 352
11–3, 6–11
**Draught Bass; Welsh Brewers
Worthington BB** H
Classic country pub whose
name reflects the history of the
area. The historic remains and
nearby stone circle more than
justify a diversion to this
remote pub which stages its
own folk festival.
🏨 Q ✿ ◖ ♣ ⌂ P

Selattyn

Cross Keys
Ceiriog Road (B4579)
☎ (0691) 650247
11.30–closing varies (not Wed; 11–4
Sat), 6–11
Banks's Mild, Bitter H
17th-century gem of a village
pub which incorporates the
village shop. Just off Offa's
Dyke. 🏨 Q ✿ & ♠ P

Shatterford

Red Lion
Bridgnorth Road (A442)
☎ (029 97) 221
11.30–2.30, 6.30–11
Banks's Mild, Bitter E;
Batham Best Bitter H; **guest
beers**
Busy roadside free house with
a large restaurant serving food
of excellent quality, including
home-produced lamb and
beef. Special entertainment
eves are a feature. Choice of
car parks – one in Shropshire,
one in Worcs. Two guest ales
always available.
🏨 ✿ ◖ ◗ ▲ ♠ P

Shifnal

Anvil Inn
Aston Street (300 yds off
B4379 alongside railway line)
☎ (0952) 461124
12–3, 7–11
Banks's Mild, Bitter E
This small pub is a good
example of a 'locals'' Banks's
house, but visitors are made
equally welcome. A long
tradition of well-kept ale
means both the main bar and
back room can be busy. Live
pianist on Sat eve.
🏨 Q ✿ ⇌ P

Plough Inn
26 Broadway (B4379)
☎ (0952) 460678
7 (12 Fri & Sat)–11
**Draught Bass; S&N
Theakston XB** H; **guest beers**

Long bar with subdued
lighting, serving ever-
changing guest beers
alongside its regular brews.
The hi-fi system is controlled
by staff so as not to be
excessive. Quieter garden
behind the snug bar. Live
bands Tue. ✿ ⊟ ⇌

Shrewsbury

Boat House
Port Hill ☎ (0743) 362965
11–11
**Marston's Pedigree;
Whitbread Boddingtons
Bitter, Flowers IPA, Castle
Eden Ale, Flowers Original** H
Set outside the loop of the
River Severn, which almost
surrounds the town centre,
with an extensive garden
running along the riverbank.
This fine 15th-century
building can be reached by
road or foot from the town
centre (across Quarry Park
and over the footbridge).
✿ ◖ ⊟ ♠ P

Castle Vaults
Castle Gates ☎ (0743) 358807
11–3, 6–11 (closed Sun eve)
**Hanby Treacleminer;
Marston's Border Mild,
Pedigree; Tetley Bitter** H;
guest beers (occasionally)
Free house in the shadow of
the castle; the landlord
exercises discretion over the
customers he admits. Mexican
food is a speciality in the
smoke-free dining area (no
food Sun). Unusual roof
garden. 🏨 Q ✿ ⇔ ◖ ⇌

Dog & Pheasant
Severn Street, Castlefields
☎ (0743) 352835
12–3 (5 Fri), 7–11 (12–11 Sat)
**Burtonwood Mild, Bitter,
Forshaw's** H
Pub with a lively bar at the
front and a quieter lounge
displaying wartime RAF
memorabilia. The outside
seating faces the world's first
iron-framed houses.
Q ✿ ⊟ ⇌ ♠

Dolphin
St Michaels Street
☎ (0743) 350419
12–3, 5.30–11 (12–11 Sat)
Beer range varies
Late Georgian pub with a
porticoed entrance. No keg
beers or lager, but a choice of
up to six guest beers from a
constantly changing range. No
under-21s admitted.
Q ⊟ ⇌ ♠

Golden Cross Hotel
Princess Street
☎ (0743) 362507
11–3 (4 Tue, Fri & Sat), 7.30–11 (12–2,
7.30–10.30 Sun)
Banks's Mild, Bitter H
One of the country's oldest

inns, dating back to 1428. Its ancient history is connected with the local church. Popular with office workers at lunchtime and with locals in the eve. The split-level smoke room and lounge both enjoy an intimate atmosphere.
🏚 ◖ ▶

Loggerheads
Church Street
☎ (0743) 355457
10.30–11
Draught Bass; M&B Mild Ⓔ
Cosy side-street pub with four rooms, one with a shove-ha'penny board and strong sporting links. Don't miss the room on the left, with its scrubbed-top tables and high-backed settles.
Q ◖ ▶ ⌼ ⇌ ♣

Nags Head
Wyle Cop
☎ (0743) 362455
Ansells Bitter; Ind Coope Burton Ale; Tetley Bitter Ⓗ; **guest beers**
Historic house with considerable architectural interest (lots of wood mouldings) and a jetty at the rear. Reputed to be haunted.
❀ ⇌ ♣

Station Hotel
Castle Foregate
☎ (0743) 344716
11–3 (3.30 Mon, 4 Fri & Sat), 7–11
Draught Bass; M&B Highgate Mild, Brew XI Ⓔ
Large, traditional bar with a small lounge and pool room at the rear. A corridor links all three rooms and the streets to the front and rear.
⌼ ⇌ ♣

Swan
Frankwell
☎ (0743) 364923
11–3 (not Tue), 7–11
Ansells Bitter; Ind Coope Burton Ale; Wadworth 6X; Wood Wonderful Ⓗ; **guest beers**
Neat, comfortable free house with cosy corners. Live jazz piano Fri eves, plus occasional folk music. Q ❀ 🏚 ◖ ▶

Soudley

Wheatsheaf Inn
Off A41, 1½ miles N of Newport; follow signs for Cheswardine OS725288
☎ (063 086) 311
12–3 (summer only), 7.30–11
Marston's Border Mild, Burton Best Bitter, Pedigree Ⓗ, **Owd Rodger** (winter) Ⓖ
Friendly, but remote village pub near the Staffs border, dating back to 1784. Visitors include users of the Shropshire Union Canal, one

mile to the south. Bar skittles and other games played. Good range of home-cooked meals until 10pm, but not Tue lunchtimes.
🏚 Q ❀ ◖ ▶ ⌼ ▲ ♣ P

Stottesdon

Fox & Hounds
High Street (off B4363 at Billingsley) ☎ (074 632) 222
12–3 (not Mon-Fri), 7–11
Woody Woodward's Wust, Bostin
Small home-brew pub in the heart of the Shropshire countryside. A skittle alley at the rear can be hired; camping is also possible. Two new beers have replaced the previous brews (the landlord is now doing the brewing). Winter ale Nov–Dec.
🏚 Q ❀ ◖ ▲ ♣ P

Upper Farmcote

Red Lion O'Morfe
Off A458, 3 miles from Bridgnorth OS770919
☎ (074 66) 678
11.30–2.30 (3.30 Sat), 7–11
Banks's Mild, Bitter Ⓔ; **Wood Special** Ⓗ
Country pub with a lounge, small bar, pool room and a no-smoking conservatory for families. Very popular, serving excellent food (eve meals Mon–Thu until 9pm).
🏚 Q ⇌ ❀ ◖ ▶ ⌼ ▲ ♣ P ✕

Welsh Frankton

Narrowboat Inn
Ellesmere Road (A495)
☎ (0691) 661051
11–3, 7–11
Wadworth 6X Ⓗ; **guest beers**
Modern pub at the side of the Shropshire Union (Llangollen) Canal. Generally has three other handpumped beers.
❀ ◖ ▶ ♣ P

Wenlock Edge

Wenlock Edge Inn
Hilltop, Much Wenlock (B4371) OS570963
☎ (074 636) 403
11.30–2.30 (3 Sat), 6–11 (closed Mon)
Robinson's Bitter; Ruddles Best Bitter; Webster's Yorkshire Bitter Ⓗ
Good atmosphere in a welcoming, family-run pub on top of the beautiful Wenlock Edge. Children welcome if eating. 🏚 Q ❀ 🏚 ◖ ▶ ⌼ P

Whitchurch

Horse & Jockey
Church Street ☎ (0948) 4902
12–11
Vaux Samson; Wards Kirby Ⓗ

Tidy pub right by the church, a recent 'convert' from John Smith's to Vaux. A curved bar in one room contains a wealth of gleaming brassware. There is a servery to a neat second room and eating area off the hall. Do the nearby graveyard and Roman burial ground have anything to do with the pub's ghost?
❀ ◖ ▶ ⇌ ♣ P

Try also: Old Town Hall Vaults, St Mary's St (Marston's)

Wistanstow

Plough
Off A489, W of A49
☎ (0588) 672523
12–2.30, 7–11
Wood Parish, Special, Wonderful Ⓗ
As this is ostensibly the Wood brewery tap, all its beers (when brewed) are available. The high, vaulted lounge boasts a large bottle collection; the lower public bar stands in the original part of the building. Locally-produced food served.
🏚 ❀ ◖ ▶ ⌼ ♣ P

Worfield

Davenport Arms (Dog)
Main Street
☎ (074 64) 320
12–3 (Sat only), 7–11 (12–2.30, 7–10.30 Sun)
Banks's Mild, Bitter; Draught Bass; Marston's Pedigree; Wood Special Ⓗ
Locals' pub with a low ceiling and much timber, set in a gem of a village with very little traffic. Folk eve every other Thu. Well worth hunting out.
🏚 Q ⌼ ♣

Somerset

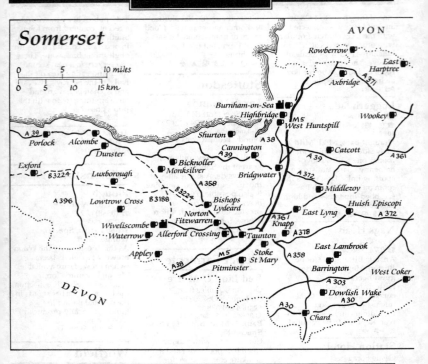

Somerset

AVON
Rowberrow
East Harptree
Axbridge A371
Wookey
Burnham-on-Sea
Highbridge M5
West Huntspill
Shurton A38
Cannington A39
Catcott A361
Porlock A39
Alcombe
Dunster
Bicknoller
Monksilver
Exford B3224
Luxborough
Bridgwater A372
Middlezoy
Lowtrow Cross B3188
Bishops Lydeard
B3224 A358
Huish Episcopi
A396
Norton Fitzwarren
East Lyng A372
Wiveliscombe
Knapp A361
Waterrow
Allerford Crossing
Taunton A318
Appley
A38
Stoke St Mary
East Lambrook
Pitminster M5
Barrington A358
West Coker
DEVON
Dowlish Wake A303
A30 A30
Chard

Ash Vine, *Trudoxhill*; **Berrow**, *Burnham-on-Sea*;
Cotleigh, Exmoor, *Wiveliscombe*; **Oakhill**,
Oakhill

Alcombe

Britannia Inn
1 Manor Road (signed from
A39) ☎ (0643) 702384
11.30–3, 7 (6.30 summer)–11 (11–11
summer Sat)
**Eldridge Pope Hardy
Country; Ushers Best Bitter;
Webster's Yorkshire Bitter** Ⓗ
Good family local fielding
numerous pub teams. Lively
atmosphere especially Mon
(folk night). An annual folk
festival is held at the end of
May. Good value pub food
(not served Mon) and Taunton
cider.
🏫 ⬚ 🛏 ⊛ 🐕 ◑ ➍ 🍴 ➕ ◔

Try also: York Inn, The
Avenue, Minehead (Free)

Allerford Crossing

Victory Inn
On Taunton–Wellington road
☎ (0823) 461282
11–2.30 (3 Sat), 6–11
**Cotleigh Tawny; Exmoor Ale;
Fuller's London Pride; Hall &
Woodhouse Tanglefoot;
Wadworth 6X; Whitbread**

Boddingtons Bitter Ⓗ**; guest
beer** (occasionally)
Large, multi-area pub with a
good reputation for food.
Eleven regular beers, plus the
odd guest. Excellent children's
facilities include a play area
and animals. Recently
renovated in good taste,
maintaining its original
character.
🏫 Q ⬚ 🛏 ⊛ ◑ 🍴 ➕ P

Appley

Globe Inn
Off A38, through Greenham
☎ (0823) 672327
11–2.30, 6.30–11
**Cotleigh Tawny; Whitbread
Boddingtons Bitter** Ⓗ
Country pub with a
traditional corridor serving
area and a variety of rooms
off. Food available in the bar
or dining room.
🏫 Q ⊛ ◑ 🍴 P

Axbridge

Lamb Inn
The Square ☎ (0934) 732253
11–2.30 (3 Sat), 6.30–11
Draught Bass; Butcombe

Bitter; Wadworth 6X Ⓗ**; guest
beers**
Rambling pub opposite King
John's hunting lodge and now
owned by Butcombe. Large,
terraced garden; unusual bar
made of bottles. No food
winter Sun or Mon eves.
Q ⊛ 🛏 ◑ 🍴 🐕 🍴 ▲ ➕ ◔ 🍴

Barrington

Royal Oak
1/2 mile off B3168 at Westport
☎ (0460) 53455
12–2.30, 6.30–11
Berrow 4Bs Ⓗ**; guest beers**
Old, stone pub in a pretty
village near the A303, serving
good beer and good food.
Always at least four guest
beers available from a large
range. Upstairs function room
and skittle alley. The landlord is a
continental beer enthusiast and
offers a range of bottled beers.
🏫 Q ⊛ ◑ 🍴 🐕 🍴 ➕ ◔ P

Bicknoller

Bicknoller Inn
Church Lane ☎ (0984) 56234
11–2.30, 5.30 (6 Sat)–11 (12–2.30,
7–10.30 Sun)

Somerset

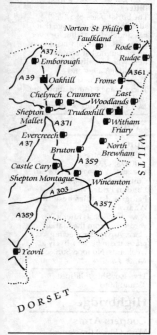

Draught Bass; Charrington
IPA Ⓗ
Late 14th-century, traditional
thatched country inn nestling
on the south side of the
Quantock Hills. Ideally sited
for walkers, riders and
holidaymakers. Skittle alley
and a games room.
🏘 Q 🌣 ⬧ ◑ ▮ & ♣ P

Bishops Lydeard

Bell Inn

6 West Street (off A358)
☎ (0823) 432968
11.30–2.30, 6–11
Exmoor Ale; Wadworth 6X;
Webster's Yorkshire Bitter Ⓗ;
guest beers
Village pub with a large
public bar and an adjoining
games area/children's room;
lounge bar with a dining area
offering a wide choice of food.
Close to West Somerset
Railway station.
🏘 Q 🌣 ⬧ ◑ ▮ & ▲ ♣ P

Bridgwater

Fountain Inn

1 West Quay (by town bridge)
☎ (0278) 424115
11.30–2.30, 6–11
Butcombe Bitter; Wadworth
IPA, 6X, Farmer's Glory Ⓗ;
guest beers
Enlarged town pub by the
river. One long bar with

enamel signs on the walls
attracts a mixture of clientele.
Taken over by Wadworth in
1991. Darts and table skittles
and an obtrusive jukebox.
Cheap and cheerful meals.
⬧ & ▮ ♣

Try also: **Commercial**,
Redgate St; **White Lion**, High
Street (Courage)

Bruton

Blue Ball

2 Coombe Street (A359)
☎ (0749) 812315
11.30–3, 5.30–11
Tetley Bitter; Wadworth 6X Ⓗ
A basic public bar with
character, and a quiet,
comfortable lounge. John
Steinbeck reputedly wrote *The
Grapes of Wrath* in the
traditional 'Forge Bar'.
Occasional ciders.
🏘 🛏 ⬧ ◑ ▮ ♣ ⬠

Burnham-on-Sea

Royal Clarence Hotel

The Esplanade ☎ (0278) 783138
11–11
Butcombe Bitter; Clarence
Pride, Regent; Wadworth
6X Ⓗ; guest beers
Large seafront hotel with its
own brewery, a bar and a
lounge. Winner of Somerset
CAMRA *Pub of the Year*. A
large range of guest beers.
Hosts the largest annual beer
festival in Somerset.
Q 🛏 🛏 ⬧ ◑ ▮ & ▲ P ✗

Cannington

Malt Shovel

Blackmoor Lane (off A39)
☎ (0278) 653432
11.30–3, 7 (6.30 summer)–11
Butcombe Bitter; Wadworth
6X Ⓗ; guest beer
Thatched country pub on a
secluded road at the back of
the village. Warm, friendly
atmosphere, free of machines
and music. 🏘 Q 🌣 🛏 🛏
◑ ▮ ▮ & ♣ ⬠ P

Castle Cary

Countryman

South Street (B3152)
☎ (0963) 50782
11.30–3 (11–3.30 Sat), 6–11
Fuller's London Pride Ⓗ;
guest beers
Family-run pub with a relaxed
atmosphere in a listed
building. At least two regular
guest beers.
🏘 Q 🌣 🛏 ⬧ ◑ ▲ ♣ P

Catcott

King William

Off A39 ☎ (0278) 722374
11.30–2.30, 6–11

Eldridge Pope Dorchester,
Hardy Country, Royal Oak;
Palmers IPA Ⓗ
Village pub with a restaurant
area. The small public bar has
darts; the traditional lounge
bar boasts an old well in the
food area. The skittles alley
and the garden can be used by
children.
Q 🌣 ⬧ ◑ ▮ & ♣ ⬠ P

Try also: **Red Tile**, Cossington
(Free)

Chard

Old Ship

94 Furnham Road (A358)
☎ (0460) 65485
11.30–3, 5.30–11
Cotleigh Old Buzzard;
Exmoor Ale; S&N Theakston
XB Ⓗ; guest beers
One-bar pub with a good local
trade. The games area has a
pool table.
🏘 🌣 🛏 ◑ ▮ & ▲ ♣ P

Try also: **Green Dragon**,
Combe St Nicholas

Chelynch

Poachers Pocket

1/2 mile N of A361 at Doulting
OS648438 ☎ (0749) 88220
11.30–3, 6.15–11
Oakhill Bitter; Wadworth
6X Ⓗ
Part 14th-century pub in a
small village some way from
the A361. Mostly given over to
food. 🏘 🌣 ◑ ▮ P

Cranmore

Strode Arms

Off A361, follow signs to East
Somerset Railway
☎ (0749) 88450
11.30–2.30, 6.30–11
Bunces Best Bitter; Wadworth
IPA, 6X Ⓗ; guest beer
Substantial, upmarket 14th-
century inn overlooking the
village duck pond. Strong
emphasis on food. Wilkins
cider; no eve meals Sun,
Oct–Feb. 🏘 🌣 ◑ ▮ ⬠ P

Dowlish Wake

New Inn

☎ (0460) 52413
11–3, 6–11
Butcombe Bitter; Wadworth
6X Ⓗ; guest beer
Traditional village pub with a
locals' bar and a comfortable
lounge. Near Perrys Cider
Farm. Home-cooked fare and
a good range of bar games
available. 🏘 Q 🌣 🛏 ◑ ▮
& ♣ P

Try also: **Rose & Crown**,
Dinnington (Free)

251

Somerset

Dunster

Luttrell Arms
☎ (0643) 821255
11–11
Draught Bass; Whitbread Flowers IPA H
Originally a 15th-century guest house for the monks of Cleeve Abbey, this hotel remains, at present, totally individual, with excellent food. The hoped-for return of local ales will improve an atmospheric public and lounge bar. Taunton Cider.
🏨 Q ✿ ◑ ◗ ⚖

Try also: **Castle Hotel** (Exmoor)

East Harptree

Castle of Comfort
On B3134, ½ mile N of B3135 jct ☎ (0761) 221321
12–2.30, 7–11
Draught Bass; Butcombe Bitter; Welsh Brewers Worthington BB H**; guest beers**
Stone-built coaching inn on the former Roman road. Ask the landlord about the real ale ghost. Live music Fri; good food. Noted for its guest beers which often sell out over a weekend. Q ✿ ◑ ◗ ♿ ♣ P

East Lambrook

Rose & Crown
Silver Street (off A303, follow South Petherton signs for East Lambrook)
☎ (0460) 40433
11.30–2.30 (3 Sat), 7.30–11
Berrow 4Bs; Hook Norton Mild; Ind Coope Burton Ale; Otter Bitter H**; guest beers**
Cosy oak-beamed, two-bar pub, one of the few outlets in the South-West with a regular mild available. Smoking restrictions apply at lunchtime only.
🏨 Q ✿ ◑ ◗ ♿ ⚖ ♣ ⌂ P ✗

East Lyng

Rose & Crown
On A361, Taunton–Glastonbury road
☎ (0823) 698235
11–2.30, 6.30–11
Butcombe Bitter; Eldridge Pope Hardy Country, Royal Oak H
Comfortable, civilised old pub with an unhurried feel to it. The one bar has exposed beams and antique furniture; a small restaurant leads off. A fairly large garden gives pleasant views across the Somerset Levels.
🏨 Q ✿ ✿ 🛏 ◑ ◗ ♿ ♣ P

East Woodlands

Horse & Groom
1 Mile E of A361/B3092 jct OS792445 ☎ (0373) 462802
12–2.30 (not Mon), 6–11
Butcombe Bitter; Hook Norton Best Bitter; Wadworth 6X G**; guest beers**
17th-century inn on the western edge of the Longleat estate: a cosy bar with an open fireplace and a flagstone floor, plus a small dining room. Twelve single malts always available. Three guest beers. No food Sun eve or Mon.
🏨 Q ✿ ✿ ◑ ◗ ♿ ⚖ ♣ P ✗

Emborough

Old Down Inn
At A37/B3139 jct
☎ (0761) 232398
11.30–3, 7–11
Draught Bass H
Atmospheric coaching inn circa 1640, with a diversity of rooms and antique furniture. Burnt down in 1886, but fortunately rebuilt. No lunch Sun. ⚖ 🛏 ◑ ⚖ ♿ P

Evercreech

Bell Inn
Bruton Road (B3081)
☎ (0749) 830287
12–3, 6–11 (11–11 Sat)
Butcombe Bitter; Courage Best Bitter, Directors; Hall & Woodhouse Badger Best Bitter, Hard Tackle, Tanglefoot H**; guest beers**
17th-century inn with roaring fires; one large bar with a restaurant area and a separate games room. Popular with the locals. Good range of food (not served Mon eve).
🏨 Q ◑ ◗ ♿ ♣ ⌂ P

Exford

Exmoor White Horse Inn
☎ (0643) 83229
11–11
Cotleigh Tawny; Exmoor Ale, Gold, Stag; Whitbread Flowers Original H**; guest beers**
Family-run centuries-old inn on the River Exe in a picturesque village. Whilst the pub forms the hub of village life, the well-appointed hotel is an excellent base for touring Exmoor. Families welcome, and coach parties catered for.
🏨 Q ✿ ✿ 🛏 ◑ ◗ ♿ ♿ ♣ ⌂ P ✗

Faulkland

Tucker's Grave Inn
On A366 ☎ (0373) 834230
11–2.30, 6–11

Draught Bass; Butcombe Bitter G
The burial place of a 1752 suicide; a former cottage that has doubled as an inn for over 200 years. Three old-fashioned rooms but no bar counter. Renowned locally for its cider (Cheddar Valley and Thatcher's). The story of Tucker can be found above the parlour fire.
🏨 Q ✿ ✿ ◑ ♿ ♣ ⌂ P

Frome

Sun
6 Catherine Street
☎ (0373) 473123
11–2.30, 5–11 (11–11 Mon, Fri & Sat)
Courage Directors; Fuller's London Pride; Marston's Pedigree; Ruddles Best Bitter; Wadworth 6X H
A welcome oasis after a 200-yard walk from the Market Place. A popular meeting place, it can be very lively at weekends. No food Sun.
🏨 ✿ 🛏 ◑ ♣ ⌂

Try also: **Ship**, Oldford (Grand Met)

Highbridge

Coopers Arms
Market Street (by station)
☎ (0278) 783562
11–3, 5.30–11
Berrow Topsy Turvy; Greene King Abbot; Palmers IPA; guest beers E
Modernised pub comprising two lounge bars and a public/skittle alley/darts bar. Large blackboards display beers in stock. Sometimes a mystery beer is available to try your tasting skills.
Q ✿ ✿ ⇆ ⇋ ♣ P

Huish Episcopi

Rose & Crown ('Eli's')
☎ (0458) 250494
11.30–2.30, 5.30–11 (11.30–11 Fri & Sat; 12–2.30, 7–10.30 Sun)
Draught Bass; Butcombe Bitter; Whitbread Boddingtons Bitter H**; guest beer**
Old thatched cottage inn with lots of rooms and no bar. The serving area has to be seen. A thriving local with a guest beer and ciders; well worth a visit. Snacks available.
Q ✿ ♣ ♣ ⌂ P

Knapp

Rising Sun
Off A361 OS301254
☎ (0823) 490436
11–2.30, 6.30–11
Draught Bass; Exmoor Ale; Whitbread Boddingtons Bitter H
Country food pub with a

252

plush bar and a separate dining area. Close to walking routes on the Somerset Levels. A meeting/children's room is to the side of the bar area.
🏧 Q ☎ 🏮 ◑ 🅿

Lowtrow Cross

Lowtrow Cross Inn
OS006292 ☎ (039 87) 220
11–4 (12–3, not Tue in winter), 6–11
Draught Bass; Cotleigh Tawny H
Old stone pub, convenient for the Brendon Hills and Wimbleball Reservoir. It has a wood fire and exposed beams. A caravan and camping site adjoins the pub. Paul McCartney's deer sanctuary is nearby. Children welcome in the games room.
🏧 Q ◑ ▶ ♿ ♣ 🅿

Luxborough

Royal Oak of Luxborough
OS304257 ☎ (0984) 40319
11–2.30, 6 (7 winter)–11
Cotleigh Tawny; Eldridge Pope Royal Oak; Exmoor Gold; Whitbread Flowers IPA G; **guest beers** (summer)
Old, unspoilt, flagstoned pub in a remote valley in the Brendon Hills. Known locally as the Blazing Stump. Folk club Fri. 🏧 Q ☎ 🏮 🛏 🍴
🏮 ♿ 🅿

Middlezoy

George
Main Street (just off A372)
☎ (0823) 69215
12–3, 7–11
Cotleigh Harrier, Tawny H; **guest beers**
Traditional village pub with flagstone floors. Four constantly-changing guest beers; beer festivals at regular intervals. Skittle alley and a pool room, children welcome. CAMRA's SW *Pub of the Year* 1991.
🏧 Q 🏮 ◑ ▶ ♣ ♿ 🅿

Monksilver

Notley Arms
On B3288 ☎ (0984) 56217
11–3, 6–11
Ruddles Best Bitter; S&N Theakston Best Bitter; Ushers Best Bitter H
Historic village local offering good food and good family facilities; also a large garden.
🏧 Q ☎ 🏮 ◑ ▶ ♣ 🅿

North Brewham

Old Red Lion
On Maiden Bradley–Bruton road OS722368 ☎ (0749) 85287
6–11 (12–2.30, 6–11 Sat)

Butcombe Bitter H; **guest beers**
Stone-built, former farmhouse, with flagged floors. The bar is in the former dairy. Two regular guests and a selection of foreign bottled beers always available, plus Gale's Prize Old Ale. Lunch is served weekends only; limited menu in winter. Isolated, rural setting.
🏧 Q ☎ 🏮 ◑ ▶ ♣ ♿ 🅿

Norton Fitzwarren

Ring of Bells
☎ (0823) 275995
11–2.30, 6–11 (11–11 Sat)
Cotleigh Tawny H; **guest beers**
Popular pub at the village centre. Traditional decor in the two lounge-type bars, the games room and the skittle alley. Normally three guest beers available.
🏧 ☎ 🏮 ◑ ♣ 🅿

Norton St Philip

Fleur de Lys
High Street (B3110)
☎ (0373) 834333
11–2.30, 6–11
Draught Bass; Charrington IPA; Oakhill Bitter; Wadworth 6X H
Ancient stone building, dating perhaps from the 13th century, which has been undergoing major alterations. A former central passageway (now blocked) was used as access to the gallows by Judge Jeffries.
🏧 Q ☎ 🏮 ◑ ▶ 🏮 ♣ 🅿

Pitminster

Queens Arms
Off B3170 at Corfe
☎ (0823) 42529
11–11
Draught Bass; Cotleigh Tawny; Eldridge Pope Blackdown Porter; Exmoor Ale H; **guest beers**
Village free house with eight beers normally on. Parts reputedly date back to the *Domesday Book*. Wheelchair access to the Mill bar only (food served here, but not Sun eve).
🏧 Q ☎ 🏮 🛏 ◑ ▶ ♿ 🅿

Try also: White Hart, Corfe (Whitbread)

Porlock

Ship Inn
High Street ☎ (0643) 862507
10.30–3, 5.30–11
Draught Bass; Cotleigh Old Buzzard; Welsh Brewers Worthington BB H

Historic coaching inn which featured in *Lorna Doone*, at the bottom of the notorious Porlock Hill. Superb public bar with a lounge for families. A restaurant behind the pub does a good range of reasonably-priced meals.
🏧 ☎ 🏮 ◑ ▶ 🏮 ♿ ▲
♣ ♿ 🅿

Rode

Cross Keys
20 High Street (off A361)
☎ (0373) 830354
11–2.30, 6–11
Draught Bass; Welsh Brewers Worthington BB H
Traditional, two-bar village pub, formerly the brewery tap for Fussells. Extensive range of single malt scotch whiskies on sale. 🏮 ♣

Rowberrow

Swan Inn
From Churchill on A38, fork left after ½ mile OS451583
☎ (0934) 852371
12–2.30, 6–11
Draught Bass; Butcombe Bitter; Wadworth 6X H; **guest beers**
A former cider house converted from three stone cottages. Two bars with fake beams and a big fireplace. No food Sun. 🏧 Q 🏮 ◑ ▶ 🅿

Rudge

Full Moon
1 mile N of A36 at Standerwick OS829518
☎ (0373) 830936
12–3 (not Mon), 6–11
Draught Bass; Butcombe Bitter; Wadworth 6X H
Splendid 300-year-old inn, greatly extended in 1991, but still retaining most of its original features, including the stone floors. The emphasis is on the food trade (no meals Sun eve/Mon lunch). 🏧 Q
☎ 🏮 ◑ ▶ 🏮 ▲ ♣ ♿ 🅿

Shepton Mallet

Horseshoe Inn
Bowlish (A371)
☎ (0749) 342209
12–2.30 (11.30–3.30 Sat), 6–11
Draught Bass; Brains SA; Wiltshire Stonehenge Bitter H; **guest beers**
An excellent pub on the outskirts of town with a roomy public bar and a comfortable lounge. Wide range of guest beers.
🏧 Q 🏮 🏮

Try also: Kings Arms, Leg Sq (Ansells)

Somerset

Shepton Montague

Montague Inn
Off A359 S of Bruton
OS675316 ☎ (0749) 813213
5.30–11 (12–3, 5.30–11 Sat)
Marston's Pedigree G**; guest beers**
Remote but convivial country pub. Normally at least two or three guest beers and Bridge Farm cider available.
🏾 Q ⇘ ✿ ⬨ ◖ ⬭ ⬡ P

Shurton

Shurton Inn
Follow signs to Hinckley Point power station
☎ (0278) 732695
11–3, 6–11
Exmoor Ale; Hall & Woodhouse Badger Best Bitter H**; guest beer**
Lively village local offering a good range of meals in the bar or restaurant. Regular music and theme nights.
🏾 Q ⇘ ✿ 🛏 ◖ ◗ ✚ ⬡ P

Stoke St Mary

Half Moon
Off A358 at Henlade
☎ (0823) 442271
11–2.30, 6–11
Marston's Pedigree; Whitbread Boddingtons Bitter, Flowers IPA H
Popular, renovated country pub with a stone-flagged bar and areas for diners and children.
Q ⇘ ✿ ◖ ◗ ⬥ ▲ P

Taunton

Black Horse
Bridge Street
☎ (0823) 272151
11–3, 7–11
Draught Bass; Exmoor Ale; Whitbread Boddingtons Bitter H
Lively, modernised one-bar pub with interconnecting areas which extend a surprisingly long way back. Popular with all ages. The landlord is fiercely independent of the brewery owners. ✿ ◖ ◗ ⬥ ✚

Masons Arms
Magdalene Street
☎ (0823) 288916
11–2.30, 5 (6 Sat)–11
Draught Bass; Exmoor Ale H**; guest beers**
Comfortable one-bar pub in a back street in the town centre.
Q 🛏 ◖ ◗ ⇶

Try also: Denmark Inn (Ushers); **Hangmans Bar**, The Parade (Free); **Wood Street Inn** (Courage)

Trudoxhill

White Hart
1/2 mile S of A361 at Nunney Catch OS749438
☎ (0373) 836324
12–2.30, 7–11
Ash Vine Trudoxhill, Bitter, Challenger, Tanker, Hop & Glory H
Comfortable, open-plan village pub with exposed beams and a large fireplace. Ash Vine brewery is at the rear of the pub.
🏾 ✿ ◖ ◗ ◖ P

Waterrow

Rock
On B3227 ☎ (0984) 23293
11–2.30, 6–11
Cotleigh Tawny; Courage Directors; Exmoor Gold H
Old pub set against a rock face in a small valley. One bar with a public area at one end and a lounge area at the other, leading to the restaurant.
🏾 Q ✿ ◖ ◗ ▲ ✚ ◖ P

West Coker

Royal George
11 High Street (A30)
☎ (093 586) 2334
11–2.30, 6–11
Draught Bass; Welsh Brewers Worthington BB H**; guest beer**
Traditional pub with oak-beamed ceilings. The games room/skittle alley/function room extension is in keeping with the rest of the pub.
🏾 Q ✿ ◖ ◗ ⬥ ▲ ◖ P

West Huntspill

Royal Artillery
On A38 ☎ (0278) 783553
11–2.30, 7 (5.30 summer)–11
John Smith's Bitter; Ushers Best Bitter, Founders H
Cosy locals' one-bar pub with a dartboard in the bar area and a small lounge area. Recently taken over by Ushers. No food Sun lunch.
✿ ◖ ◗ ▲ ✚ P

Try also: Crossways (Free)

Wincanton

Bear Inn
Market Place ☎ (0963) 32581
11–2.30, 5.30–11 (11–11 Sat)
Draught Bass; Fuller's London Pride; Marston's Pedigree H**; guest beer**
Large former coaching inn with several drinking areas, including a substantial games/function room. Weekly archery takes place in the skittle alley. Large screen TV.
🏾 Q 🛏 ◖ ◗ ⬥ ▲ ✚ P

Dolphin Hotel
High Street ☎ (0963) 32215
11–3, 6–11
Oakhill Bitter; Whitbread Boddingtons Bitter, Flowers Original H
18th-century former coaching inn with a lively, convivial public bar and a quieter lounge bar to the rear.
🏾 ⇘ ✿ 🛏 ◖ ◗ ⬡ ✚ P

Try also: Red Lion (Free)

Witham Friary

Seymour Arms
Minor road off B3092, by old railway station OS745410
☎ (074 985) 742
11–3, 6–11
Ushers Best Bitter H
Old village local, unspoilt by progress, with a central serving hatch and a fine garden. Cider is on gravity dispense.
🏾 Q ✿ ⬡ ▲ ✚ ◖ P

Wiveliscombe

Courtyard Hotel
10–12 High Street
☎ (0984) 23737
11.30–3, 7–11 (11–11 Sat)
Exmoor Ale, Gold H**; guest beers**
Small bar area with the feel of a locals' lounge bar; a quiet pub but the downstairs cellar bar is used for music nights twice a month. Two guest beers minimum. Q 🛏 ▲

Wookey

Burcott Inn
On B3139, 2 miles W of Wells
☎ (0749) 673874
11–2.30 (3 Sat), 6–11
Butcombe Bitter H**; guest beers**
Deservedly popular, roadside pub with a friendly atmosphere. Over 40 different guest beers per year and always two available (mid and high gravity). An L-shaped bar with a copper serving top, and a small games room. The good-sized garden boasts an old cider press. No eve meals Sun/Mon. 🏾 Q ✿ ◖ ◗ ✚ P

Yeovil

Armoury
1 The Park ☎ (0935) 71047
11–3, 6–11
Adnams Broadside; Butcombe Bitter; Wadworth 6X, Farmer's Glory, Old Timer H
Lively, simply furnished town pub, converted from an old armoury. Q ✿ ◖ ⬥ ✚ P

Try also: Somerset (Courage)

BEER FESTIVAL CALENDAR 1993

DESPITE THE ADVENT of the guest beer law, it's not always easy to sample beers brewed outside your own locality, unless, of course, they are national brands. CAMRA beer festivals provide excellent opportunities for beer enthusiasts to acquaint themselves with beers from all over the country, and sometimes from overseas too. This is a calendar of proposed festivals for 1993; precise dates and venues can be obtained closer to the time from CAMRA head office, on (0727) 867201.

JANUARY
Atherton
Bradford
Exeter
York

FEBRUARY
Basingstoke
Battersea
Durham
Hove
Truro
Wrekin

MARCH
Acton
Bristol
Darlington
Eastleigh
Fleetwood
Furness
London Drinker
Oldham
Rugby
Wigan

APRIL
Darlaston
Ealing
Farnham
Greenmount Fair
   (N Ireland)
Newcastle
Swansea

MAY
Alloa
Barnsley
Camden (Cider and
   Perry Exhibition)
Cleethorpes
Dudley
Grays
Great North-Western
Halifax
Lincoln

Maidstone
Merseyside
Northampton
Wolverhampton
Yapton

JUNE
Cambridge
Chester
Chippenham
Dorking
Greenwich
Kirklees
Salisbury
Surrey

JULY
Ashton Canals
Canterbury
Chelmsford
Colchester
Cotswolds
Derby
Exeter
Furness
Fleetwood
Sussex
Wirral
Woodcote (Reading)

AUGUST
Great British Beer
   Festival
Cornwall
Dengie Hundred
Hereford
Peterborough
Portsmouth

SEPTEMBER
Burton upon Trent
Chappel & Wakes Colne
Heart of England
Ipswich
Letchworth
Maidstone

Sheffield
Shrewsbury
Strathspey

OCTOBER
Bath
Bedford
Blackburn
Cardiff
Darlington
Durham
Eastleigh
Edinburgh
Furness
Hull
Holmfirth
Keighley
Lancaster
Leeds
Llandudno
Loughborough
Middlesbrough
Northampton
Norwich
Nottingham
Overton
Peckham
Stoke-on-Trent
Wrekin

NOVEMBER
Aberdeen
Dorchester
Dudley
Eastleigh
Jersey
Mid Wales
Pig's Ear (London)
Rochford
Taunton

DECEMBER
Bury
Holmfirth
Kirklees

Staffordshire

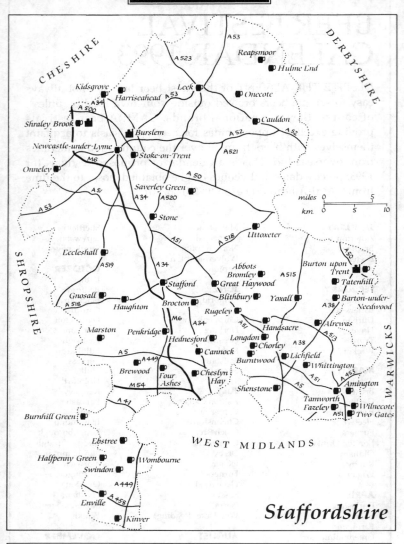

Staffordshire

 Burton Bridge, Heritage, Marston's, *Burton upon Trent;* **Rising Sun,** *Shraley Brook;* **Titanic,** *Burslem*

Abbots Bromley

Bagot Arms
Bagot Street ☎ (0283) 840371
11–2.30, 5.30–11
Marston's Pedigree Ⓗ
18th-century coaching inn serving bar food six days a week (not Sun). ♨ ✸ ◑ ▶ P

Alrewas

George & Dragon
Main Street ☎ (0283) 790202

11–2.30 (3 Sat), 5.30–11 (12–2.30, 7–10.30 Sun)
Marston's Pedigree Ⓗ
Popular and friendly inn.
♨ ⛱ ✸ ◑ ▶ ♣ P

Amington

Pretty Pigs
Shuttington Road (B790)
☎ (0827) 63129
11–3.30, 4.30–11 (11–11 Fri & Sat)
Draught Bass; M&B Mild, Brew XI Ⓗ
Large, busy, family pub,

geared up for bar meals in the lounge. Welcome return of handpumps in the lounge and bar. Large open-plan rooms with beamed ceilings. ♨ ⛱
✸ ⋈ ◑ ▶ 🅿 ⅋ ♿ ♣ ⌂ P

Barton-under-Needwood

Top Bell
Barton Gate ☎ (0283) 712510
12–3, 6–11
Burtonwood Bitter,

Staffordshire

Forshaw's H
Typical country pub with oak
beams. Encourages live music
(Wed, Fri and Sun) and raises
money for charity.
🏠 ⛟ ✿ ◑ 🍴 🎱 ♣ P

Blithbury

Bull & Spectacles
Uttoxeter Road
☎ (088 922) 201
12–3, 6–11
**Ind Coope Burton Ale;
Marston's Pedigree** H
16th-century country pub near
Blithfield Reservoir. Popular
for food. 🏠 Q ✿ ◑ 🍴 ♣ P

Brewood

Admiral Rodney
21 Dean Street (Coven road)
☎ (0902) 850853
11–3, 5.30–11
HP&D Bitter, Entire H
Black country-style pub
adapted to a rural
Staffordshire setting, boasting
a collection of Staffordshire
dogs. No meals Sun eve;
booking advised.
🏠 ✿ ◑ 🍴 ♣ P

Brocton

Chetwynd Arms
Cannock Road
☎ (0785) 661089
11.30–3, 5.45–11 (11–11 Sat)
Banks's Mild, Bitter E
Bustling main road pub at the
north-western boundary of
Cannock Chase.
✿ ◑ 🍴 🎱 ♣ P

Burnhill Green

Dartmouth Arms
Snowden Road
☎ (074 65) 268
12–2.30, 7–11 (12–2.30, 7–10.30 Sun)
**Ansells Mild, Bitter; Ind
Coope Burton Ale** H; guest
beer
Popular village pub,
renowned for its home-made
bar meals. Children's meals
served in the garden only (no
food Sun eve/Mon lunch).
Allied 'guest' beer.
🏠 Q ✿ ◑ 🍴 P

Burntwood

Trident
166 Chase Road (off B5190)
12–3 (4 Sat), 7–11
Marston's Pedigree H
Popular local: a lounge full of
pictures and models, many
with an aviation theme, and a
large bar. Q 🎱 ♣ P

Burton upon Trent

Anglesey Arms
104 Bearwood Hill Road,
Winshill (off A5047)
10.30–2.30 (3.30 Sat), 5.30–11
(12–2.30, 7–10.30 Sun)
**Marston's Burton Best Bitter,
Merrie Monk, Pedigree, Owd
Rodger** H
Popular urban local with a
lounge and conservatory/
family room, and the oldest
bowling green in Burton. Quiz
most Tues. ⛟ ✿ 🎱 ♣ P

Beacon Hotel
277 Tutbury Road (off A50)
☎ (0283) 68968
11–3, 6–11
**Draught Bass; Ruddles
County** H
Comfortable, spacious, three-
roomed hostelry, run by an
entrepreneurial landlord.
Excellent bar meals; purpose-
built family room.
Q ⛟ ✿ 🎱 ◑ 🍴 ♣ P

Burton Bridge Inn
24 Bridge Street (A50)
☎ (0283) 36596
11.30–3, 5.30–11
**Burton Bridge BST Summer
Ale, XL, Bridge Bitter, Porter,
Top Dog Stout, Festival, Old
Expensive** H; guest beer
Small but lively brewery tap
offering at least four of the
range regularly and a guest
beer every Sun. 🏠 Q ◑ 🎱 ♣

Roebuck
Station Street
☎ (0283) 68660
11–11 (11–3, 6–11 Sat)
**Ansells Mild, Bitter; Ind
Coope ABC Best Bitter,
Burton Ale; Tetley Bitter** H;
guest beer
Lively one-roomer just across
the road from the Ind Coope
brewery. 🏠 ◑ ≡ ♣ ☺

Swan Hotel
Trent Bridge (A50)
☎ (0283) 63552
11–2.30, 5.30–11 (12–2.30, 7–10.30
Sun)
**Hardys & Hansons
Kimberley Classic** H
Good local in a prominent
position. Darts and dominoes.
⛟ ✿ 🏠 ◑ 🎱 ♣ P

Thomas Sykes
Heritage Brewery Museum,
Anglesey Road ☎ (0283) 63563
11–2.30, 5.30–11 (11–11 Fri; 12–2.30
Sun)
Draught Bass G; **Burton
Bridge Bridge Bitter; Heritage
Bitter** H, **Thomas Sykes
Ale** G; **Ind Coope Burton Ale;
Marston's Pedigree** H
Former stable block and
wagon shed of the old Thomas
Sykes brewery. Stone-cobbled
floors, wooden benches and
breweriana in the bar and
side-room (known as 'Helen's
Parlour'). The only outlet for
Heritage beers in town. Bar
snacks include home-made
cow pies. Q ✿ 🎱 P

Cannock

Shoal Hill Tavern
Sandy Lane (B5012, Penkridge
road) ☎ (0543) 503302
12–2.30 (3 Sat), 7 (6 Sat)–11
**Home Mild, Bitter; S&N
Theakston Best Bitter, XB,
Old Peculier; Younger
No. 3** H
Established pub with a large
lounge extension added on to
the original building; on the
edge of a good walking area.
The landlord is keen on music
events. Q ✿ ◑ 🎱 🔥 A P

Cauldon

Yew Tree
Off A52/A523
☎ (0538) 308348
11–3, 6–11
**Draught Bass; Burton Bridge
XL; M&B Mild** H
One of the finest pubs in the
country, dating back to the
17th century. Its superb
collection of antiques includes
working polyphonia, a
pianola, grandfather clocks,
and sundry Victoriana. Note
the old yew tree in the car
park. Q ⛟ ✿ 🔥 A ♣ P

Cheslyn Hay

Mary Rose
Moons Lane (one-way system)
☎ (0922) 415114
12–2.30, 6.30–11 (12–2.30, 7–10.30
Sun)
**Ansells Bitter; HP&D Entire;
Ind Coope Burton Ale; Tetley
Bitter** H
Converted farmhouse
displaying *Mary Rose*
memorabilia and serving
excellent food. 🏠 ✿ ◑ 🔥 P

Chorley

Malt Shovel
Ford Lane (1 mile N of B5190;
Lichfield–Cannock road)
12–2.30, 7–11 (12–2.30, 7–10.30 Sun)
**Ansells Mild, Bitter; Ind
Coope Burton Ale; Tetley
Bitter** H
Village green pub close to
Cannock Chase, with a cosy
lounge and sing-alongs in the
bar. 🏠 Q ✿ 🎱 ♣ P

Ebstree

Holly Bush
Ebstree Road OS854959
☎ (0902) 895587
12.30–2.30 (11.30–3 Sat), 6–11
(12–2.30, 7–10.30 Sun)
**Ansells Mild, Bitter; Ind
Coope Burton Ale; Tetley
Bitter** H
Pleasant country pub, half a
mile west of the Staffs and
Worcs Canal. Beware of the
spider! 🏠 ✿ ◑ 🍴 ♣ P

Staffordshire

Eccleshall

Royal Oak
High Street
☎ (0785) 850230
11.30–3, 6.30–11
**Burtonwood Bitter,
Forshaw's** H
Large, town-centre free house
and restaurant with a
comfortable lounge and a
small, cosy snug. Imposing
mock Tudor, arched frontage.
ॐ ✿ ◑ ▶ ▲ ♣ P

St George Hotel
Castle Street
☎ (0785) 850300
11–11
**Ind Coope Burton Ale; Tetley
Bitter; Whitbread
Boddingtons Bitter** H**; guest
beer**
Enterprising hotel offering
restaurant and conference
facilities. The site has been
occupied at various times by a
coaching inn, a draper's shop
and an undertaker's – one area
is still referred to as the
'Coffin Room'.
ﬞ ॐ ✿ ﬞ ◑ ▲ ♣ P

Enville

Cat
Bridgnorth Road (A458)
☎ (0384) 872209
11–3, 6.30–11 (closed Sun)
**Holden's Special; Marston's
Pedigree; S&N Theakston
Mild, XB, Old Peculier;
Whitbread Boddingtons
Bitter** H
Part-16th-century country inn
with a games room and
upstairs restaurant. Boules
played. The beer range varies.
ﬞ Q ✿ ◑ ▶ ♿ ♣ P

Fazeley

Three Horseshoes
New Street
☎ (0827) 289754
12–3, 7–11
**Draught Bass; Ruddles
County** H
Small, cosy traditional pub
with a strong local following:
an old coaching inn situated
near the junction of the
Birmingham and Fazeley and
Coventry Canals and Drayton
Manor Park.
ॐ ✿ ⇌ (Wilnecote) ♣

Four Ashes

Four Ashes
Station Drive (A449, Stafford
road) ☎ (0902) 790229
11–3, 5–11 (11–11 Sat)
Banks's Mild, Bitter E
Comfortable, large roadside
pub enjoying a rural vista,
apart from the chemical
works! No food Sun.
ﬞ ✿ ◑ ♿ P

Gnosall

Boat
Wharf Road
☎ (0785) 822208
11 (11.30 winter)–11
**Marston's Burton Best Bitter,
Pedigree** H
Popular pub adjacent to
bridge 34 on the Shropshire
Union Canal. Meals served
Easter–end Sept.
ﬞ ✿ ◑ ▶ ♣ P

Royal Oak
Newport Road (A518)
☎ (0785) 822362
12–3, 6–11
**Ansells Bitter; Ind Coope
Burton Ale; Tetley Bitter** H
Hospitable, two-roomed
village local with a narrow
basic bar and a comfortable
lounge. ﬞ ✿ ◑ ▶ ♿ ♣ P

Great Haywood

Fox & Hounds
Main Road ☎ (0889) 881252
12–11
**Ansells Bitter; Marston's
Pedigree; Tetley Bitter** H**;
guest beer**
Extended open-plan pub near
the Trent and Mersey Canal.
ﬞ ✿ ◑ ▶ ▲ ♣ P

Halfpenny Green

Royal Oak
OS825920 ☎ (0384) 88318
11.30–2.30 (3 Sat), 6–11
Banks's Mild, Bitter E
Popular old country local on
the crossroads near the
aerodrome.
ﬞ ✿ ◑ ▶ ♿ ♣ ⌂ P

Handsacre

Crown
The Green ☎ (0543) 490239
11–3, 6–11
**Draught Bass; M&B Highgate
Mild; Marston's Pedigree** H
Picturesque and friendly
canalside pub.
Q ॐ ✿ ◑ ♿ ♣ P

Harriseahead

Royal Oak
High Street ☎ (0782) 513362
12–3 (Sat only), 7–11 (12–2.30,
7–10.30 Sun)
**Ind Coope Burton Ale;
Marston's Burton Best Bitter;
John Smith's Bitter** H**; guest
beers**
Two-roomed local with a
smallish bar and a larger
lounge. Busy at most times
with people of all ages. Two
guest beers almost always
available, providing the
widest choice of ales in the
area. Handy for refreshment
after a walk up Mow Cop!
✿ ♿ ♣ P

Haughton

Bell
Newport Road (A518)
☎ (0785) 780301
11–3, 6–11
**Banks's Mild; Courage Best
Bitter, Directors** H
One-roomed village pub
displaying a vast collection of
book matches. ﬞ ✿ ◑ ▶ ♣ P

Hednesford

Queens Arms
Hill Street ☎ (0543) 878437
12–3, 6.30–11
**Draught Bass; M&B Highgate
Mild, Springfield Bitter;
Welsh Brewers Worthington
BB** E
Excellent, traditional local,
friendly and comfortable.
Q ✿ ♿ ♿ ⇌ ♣ P

Hulme End

Manifold Hotel
On B5054 ☎ (028 84) 537
11–3, 7–11
**Wards Mild, Thorne Best
Bitter, Sheffield Best Bitter** H**;
guest beers** (summer)
Formerly the 'Light Railway',
an impressive stone hotel in
open countryside by the River
Manifold, offering a friendly
welcome. Occasional live folk
or jazz music.
ﬞ Q ✿ ⇌ ◑ ▶ ♿ ▲ ♣ P

Kidsgrove

Clough Hall Hotel
Clough Hall Road
☎ (0782) 777131
12–3, 5.30–11 (11–11 Sat)
Banks's Mild, Bitter E**;
Marston's Pedigree** H
Recently refurbished; open-
plan, but with four distinct
drinking areas; a 1930s building
with a garden leading down to
a 19th-century ornamental lake.
Attracts a wide age-range of
locals, although mostly early
20s Fri/Sat. ✿ ◑ ▶ ♣ P

Kinver

Cross
Church Hill ☎ (0384) 872435
12–5, 6–11 (varies in winter)
**Banks's Hanson's Mild,
Bitter** H
Popular local with a smart
lounge, next to a restored
Tudor house and near the
Staffs and Worcs Canal.
ﬞ Q ♿ ♣ ⌂ P

Plough & Harrow
High Street ☎ (0384) 872659
12–3 (5 summer), 7–11
Batham Mild, Best Bitter H
Three-roomed pub known
locally as the 'Steps', handy
for the Canal. No meals Sun
eve. ﬞ ॐ ✿ ◑ ▶ ♿ ♣ P

258

Staffordshire

Whittington Inn
On A449 ☎ (0384) 872110
11–2.30, 5.30–11
Courage Directors; Marston's Owd Rodger (winter); **Whitbread Flowers IPA, Original** Ⓗ
Historic 14th-century inn with priest holes, old furniture and the remains of a Tudor walled garden. No meals Sun.
🏠 ✾ ◑ ▶ P

Leek

Abbey Inn
Abbey Green Road (1 mile from Leek on Macclesfield road) ☎ (0538) 382865
11–3, 7–11
Draught Bass Ⓗ**; guest beers**
Delightful, three-storey stone pub, close to the former site of Dieulacres Abbey. A central bar serves all rooms. Good food at lunchtime and early eve. 🏠 Q ✾ 🛏 ◑ ▶ P

Sea Lion
36–38 Russell Street
11–3, 7–11
Banks's Mild, Bitter Ⓗ
Popular street-corner local, refurbished but retaining a lively atmosphere. ⊞ ♣

Swan
St Edwards Street
☎ (0538) 382081
11–3, 7–11
Draught Bass Ⓗ**; guest beers**
The oldest pub in Leek which has seen inaugural meetings of many local societies. Two main rooms. A lively bar and comfortable lounge.
🏠 ✾ ◑ ⊞ ♣ P

Wellington
104 Strangman Street
11–3, 7–11
Marston's Border Mild, Burton Best Bitter, Pedigree Ⓗ
Popular, good old-fashioned street-corner local with two rooms. All beer is served from the lounge. Note the unusual pump sleeves. Q ⊞ ♣

Lichfield

George IV
Bore Street ☎ (0543) 263032
11–3 (4 Fri & Sat), 7–11
Draught Bass; M&B Highgate Mild Ⓗ
Large, busy inn in an historic part of the city. Popular with shoppers. Two bars and a communal room.
⊞ ≠ (City) ♣ P

Greyhound Inn
121 St John Street
☎ (0543) 262303
11.45–3, 5–11 (11.30–11 Fri & Sat)
Ansells Bitter Ⓗ**; guest beers**
Friendly, traditional pub providing ever-changing

guest beers. No meals Sun.
🏠 ✾ ◑ ▶ ⊞ ≠ (City) ♣ P

Horse & Jockey
Sandford Street
11–3, 5.30–11 (11–11 Sat)
Banks's Mild, Bitter Ⓔ
Basic drinking house close to Asian restaurants.
⊞ ≠ (City) ♣ P

Queens Head
Queen Street ☎ (0543) 262529
11–3 (4 Sat), 7–11
Marston's Pedigree Ⓗ
No-frills traditional pub.
⊞ ♿ ≠ (City) ♣ P

Longdon

Swan with Two Necks
Brook End ☎ (0543) 490251
12–2.30, 7–11 (12–2, 7–10.30 Sun)
Ansells Mild, Bitter; Ind Coope Burton Ale; Lloyds Derby Bitter Ⓗ
400-year-old village pub with low ceiling beams; an unusual fireplace divides the bar. No food Sun. 🏠 Q ✾ ◑ ▶ P

Marston

Fox
1 mile NW of Wheaton Aston
OS935140 ☎ (0785) 240729
12–3, 7–11
Lloyds Classic, Derby Bitter; Mansfield Old Baily; Marston's Pedigree; Wadworth 6X; Wood Special Ⓗ**; guest beers**
Somewhat isolated rural free house, especially popular with cyclists. Snacks available.
🏠 Q ✾ ⊞ ▲ ♣ ⌂ P

Newcastle-under-Lyme

Crossways
Nelson Place ☎ (0782) 616953
11–11 (11–4, 7–11 Sat)
Vaux Samson, Extra Special; Wards Sheffield Best Bitter Ⓗ**; guest beers**
Large corner pub opposite the Queen's Gardens. A substantial lounge and a smaller games room-cum-bar.
🛏 ◑ ▶ ⊞ ♣

Old Brown Jug
Bridge Street (off Liverpool Rd) ☎ (0782) 616767
11.30–2.30 (4 Sat), 6 (7 Sat)–11
Marston's Merrie Monk, Pedigree, Owd Rodger Ⓗ
Local-style pub just out of the town centre, retaining much of its original character. One bar counter serves both the wooden-floored bar area and the plusher lounge. Lunches served Fri. ♣ P

Victoria
62 King Street (A53, Hanley road) ☎ (0782) 615569
11–3 (4.30 Sat), 5 (7 Sat)–11

Draught Bass; Whitbread Boddingtons Bitter Ⓗ
Two-roomed corner pub, handy for the New Victoria Theatre. Strong games and quiz following. Q ✾ ◑ ⊞ ♣

Onecote

Jervis Arms
On B5054
☎ (0538) 304206
12–3, 7–11
Draught Bass; Ruddles County; S&N Theakston XB, Old Peculier; Webster's Yorkshire Bitter Ⓗ
Popular country inn, noted for its hospitality. With its large garden and excellent food it is good for families. Takes its name from Nelson's second lieutenant, Admiral Jervis.
Q 🏠 ✾ ◑ ▶ ⊞ ♿ ▲ ♣ P

Onneley

Wheatsheaf Inn
Bar Hill Road (A525)
☎ (0782) 751589
11.30–2.30, 6–11 (11.30–11 Sat & summer)
Coach House Coachman's Best Bitter; Fuller's Chiswick; Marston's Pedigree; Wadworth 6X; Whitbread Boddingtons Bitter Ⓗ
18th-century country inn with an emphasis on food but drinkers are most welcome in the lounge and bar, which stocks a wide range of malt whiskies. The restaurant specialises in Spanish cuisine. Beer prices above average. No-smoking family room.
🛏 ✾ ◑ ▶ ⊞ ♿ ▲ ♣ P ✗

Penkridge

Cross Keys
Filance Lane (by bridge 86 of Staffs and Worcs Canal)
OS925134
☎ (0785) 712826
11–3 (4 Sat), 6.30 (5 Fri)–11
Draught Bass Ⓗ**; M&B Highgate Mild, Springfield Bitter; Welsh Brewers Worthington BB** Ⓔ
Modernised pub, attracting much canal trade. Barbecues in the garden (no food Sun eve). 🛏 ✾ ◑ ▶ ♣ P

Reapsmoor

Butchers Arms
8 miles E of Leek on Longnor road
☎ (029 88) 4477
12–3, 7–11
Marston's Pedigree Ⓗ**; guest beers**
Welcoming rural pub, popular with the locals. Can be isolated in winter. 🏠 Q ▲ P

Staffordshire

Rugeley

Prince of Wales
Church Street ☎ (0889) 586421
12–3, 6–11
Draught Bass; M&B Mild Ⓗ
Friendly local with pleasant
company. ⊛ ◖ ⊟ ♣ P

Saverley Green

Hunter
Sandon Road ☎ (0782) 392067
12–3, 7–11
**Burtonwood Bitter,
Forshaw's; Tetley Bitter** Ⓗ;
guest beers
Cosy country pub offering
great hospitality and
occasional beer festivals.
🏨 🕭 ⊛ ⊟ ▲ ♣ P

Shenstone

Railway
Main Street ☎ (0543) 480503
11–2.30, 5.30–11 (11.30–11 Sat)
**Marston's Merrie Monk,
Pedigree** Ⓗ
Popular village pub
comprising a locals' bar and a
split-level lounge. No food
Sun. ⊛ ◖ ▶ ⊟ ♣ P

Shraley Brook

Rising Sun
Knowle Bank Road (signed
from B5500, 1¹⁄₂ miles W of
Audley) ☎ (0782) 720600
12–3 (may vary), 7–11 (11–11 Sat)
**Rising Sun Rising, Setting,
Sunstroke** Ⓗ; **guest beers**
Free house with its own
brewery, in the shadow of the
M6. Sunlight, Total Eclipse
and Solar Flare are
occasionally available, plus a
wide range of foreign beers,
ciders and malt whiskies (120).
🏨 ⊛ ◖ ▶ ⊟ ▲ ♣ ⌣

Stafford

Bird In Hand
Victoria Square, Mill Street
☎ (0785) 52198
11–11 (11–4, 7–11 Sat)
**Courage Best Bitter,
Directors; John Smith's
Bitter** Ⓗ; **guest beer**
Popular and enterprising
town-centre pub with a bar,
snug, lounge and games room.
⊛ ◖ ⊟ ♣

Coach & Horses
Mill Bank ☎ (0785) 223376
11.30–4, 7 (6 Fri)–11
Draught Bass; Tetley Bitter Ⓗ
Straightforward pub near the
main post office. ⊟ ⇌ ♣

Cottage By The Brook
Peel Terrace (just off B5066,
Sandon road) ☎ (0785) 223563
12–3, 7–11 (12–11 Fri, Sat & summer)
**Ind Coope ABC Best Bitter,
Burton Ale; Marston's**

Pedigree; Tetley Bitter Ⓗ
Large, lively, four-roomed
pub warmed by real fires in
the lounge and club room,
where children are welcome.
Bar snacks available. Regular
folk jam sessions.
🏨 🕭 ⊛ ⊟ ♣

Eagle
Newport Road
☎ (0785) 223833
12–3, 7–11
Draught Bass Ⓔ; **Wood
Special** Ⓗ
Homely wood-panelled pub
built at the time of Stafford's
first railway station.
🏨 ◖ ⊟ ⇌ ♣ P

Luck Penny
62 Crab Lane (off A5013, ¹⁄₂
mile from M6 jct 14)
☎ (0785) 58622
11–3, 6–11
**Courage Directors; John
Smith's Bitter** Ⓗ
Mature estate pub.
⊛ ◖ ▶ ⊟ ▲ ♣ P

New Victoria
43 Browning Street (off A34)
☎ (0785) 211008
11–2.30 (5 Sat), 5.30–11
Beer range varies Ⓗ
Modern, refurbished and
extended lounge bar serving
four or five guest beers. No
food Sun. 🏨 ⊞ ◖ ▶ ♣

Railway
23 Castle Street, Castletown
☎ (0785) 42890
12–2 (not Sat), 5.30 (7 Sat)–11 (closed
Sun lunch)
**Ansells Bitter; Ind Coope
Burton Ale** Ⓗ; **guest beer**
Victorian street-corner local
boasting a large array of
whiskies. 🏨 Q ◖ ▶ ⇌ ♣

Rifleman
Common Road
☎ (0785) 40515
12–3, 5–11
**Ansells Bitter; Ind Coope
Burton Ale; Marston's
Pedigree** Ⓗ
Comfortable one-roomer next
to Stafford Common. Firearms
are featured in the decor. Live
music. 🏨 ◖ ▶ P

Stafford Arms
Railway Street ☎ (0785) 53313
12–2 (not Sat), 5 (7.30 Sat)–11
(7.30–10.30 Sun, closed Sun lunch)
Beer range varies Ⓗ
Fine one-roomed pub with at
least five beers. ⇌ P

Sun
7 Lichfield Road (near Apollo
cinema) ☎ (0785) 42208
11.30–2.30, 6–11
Draught Bass Ⓗ; **guest beer**
Pleasant, multi-roomed town-
centre pub and olde-worlde
restaurant. Reference library
for crosswords and quizzes.
🕭 ⊛ ◖ ▶ ⊟ ⇌ ♣ P

Stoke-on-Trent:
Burslem

Duke William
2 St John Square
☎ (0782) 810023
11–6, 8 (7 Mon, Fri & Sat)–11
Draught Bass Ⓔ
Large Victorian black and
white building in a prominent
position; a basic bar and
comfortable lounge divided
into two areas, featuring much
good quality, original
woodwork. Occasional music
in the upstairs room. ◖ ⊟ ♣

Fenton

Malt 'n' Hops
295 King Street (A50,
Stoke–Longton road)
12–3, 7–11
**Burtonwood Mild, Bitter;
guest beers** Ⓗ
Very popular, this pub always
has four guest beers on
handpump, with the range
changing daily. The newly
extended lounge area gives
more elbow room. Attracts all
ages, all classes. ⇌ (Longton)

Hanley

Coachmakers Arms
65 Lichfield Street
12–3.30, 7–11
Draught Bass; M&B Mild Ⓗ
Classic, small mid terrace
traditional pub: three rooms
and a drinking corridor, with
a tiny public bar. A very
friendly local. 🏨 Q ⊟ ♣

Golden Cup
65 Old Town Road
☎ (0782) 212405
11–5, 7.30–11
Draught Bass Ⓗ
Convivial small local with
splendid bar fittings. Its ornate
Edwardian exterior proudly
proclaims 'Bass only'; the L-
shaped interior is divided into
a bar and snug. 🏨 ⊛ ◖ ♣

Smithfield
Lower Bethesda Street
☎ (0782) 215606
11.30–3, 5–11
Marston's Pedigree Ⓗ
Two-roomed street-corner pub
with a comfortable split-level
lounge and a bar with a pool
table. Food (served till 8pm) is
particularly good value (no
meals Sun). Karaoke Fri/Sun.
🕭 ⊛ ◖ ▶ ⊟ ♣

Hartshill

Jolly Potters
296 Hartshill Road
11–3, 6–11
Draught Bass; M&B Mild Ⓗ
Old pub of immense character
in the conservation area next
to the church. Four small

rooms suit most tastes, with a central drinking corridor. A classic cosmopolitan town pub. Q ❀ ⊞ ♣

Penkhull

Terrace
Penkhull New Road (off B5041)
☎ (0782) 47631
11–3.30 (4.30 Fri, 4 Sat), 6–11
Draught Bass H
Modern pub on a steep hill. Strong emphasis on pub games in the bar; comfortable lounge. Only 15 minutes' walk from the centre of Stoke. Wheelchair WC.
Q ❀ ◐ ⊞ ♿ ♣ P

Stoke

Black's Head
16 North Street (just off A500)
☎ (0782) 415594
12–3 (4 Sat), 5.30 (7 Sat)–11
Beer range varies H
Back-street pub recently extended and updated. Six beers are always available. The landlord has introduced his own brew 'Roache's Best Ale'. The atmosphere is always buzzing, particularly on the occasional karaoke nights. ◐ ⊞ ⇌ ♣

Glebe
Glebe Street
☎ (0782) 44600
11–11
Banks's Mild, Bitter E
Large two-roomed listed building, now surrounded by the new civic offices. The bar is basic and the larger lounge is popular with students at night. ◐ ⊞ ⇌ ♣

Staff of Life
13 Hill Street (off Campbell Place)
☎ (0782) 48680
11–3 (4 Fri & Sat), 7–11
Draught Bass E
Old, unchanged, popular street-corner town pub: three rooms off a central drinking corridor. Note the fine locally-made tiled floor in the back room. Bags of character.
Q ⊞ ⇌ ♣

Tunstall

White Hart
43 Roundwell Street
☎ (0782) 835817
11–5, 7–11 (11–11 Fri & Sat)
Marston's Border Bitter, Pedigree H
Friendly, well-kept street-corner drinkers' pub on the edge of the town centre: the only Marston's pub in town. Pianist Sun nights. Lunches weekdays. No wheelchair access to gents'. Q ❀ ◐ ♿ ♣

Stone

Pheasant
Old Road ☎ (0785) 814603
11.30–3, 6–11
Draught Bass; Welsh Brewers Worthington BB H
Friendly local, immaculately maintained. ❀ ◐ ⊞ ⇌ ♣

Swindon

Green Man
High Street ☎ (0384) 400532
11–11
Banks's Mild, Bitter E
Popular local with a friendly atmosphere, near the Staffs and Worcs Canal. Boxing memorabilia. Live music Tue, Fri and Sat. No food Sun eve.
◐ ◑ ⊞ ♣ P

Tamworth

Albert Hotel
Albert Road ☎ (0827) 64694
11–2.30, 7–11
Bateman Dark Mild; Hoskins Beaumanor Bitter, Penn's Ale, Premium H
The short walk from the town centre is well worth the effort. The long-established landlady maintains a friendly, unhurried atmosphere in this unspoilt pub where the Hoskins beers make a pleasant change. Local CAMRA *Pub of the Year*. 🛏 ◑ ⊞ ⇌ P

Boot Inn
Lichfield Street
☎ (0827) 68024
11–3, 6–11
Marston's Border Mild, Pedigree H
Lively town-centre pub drawing business people at lunchtime and locals eves; packed at weekends. Strong sporting following. Freshly cooked food. ◐ ⊞ ♿ ⇌ ♣ P

Hamlets Wine Bar
13–15 Lower Gungate
☎ (0827) 52277
10.30–2.30, 7 (6.30 Fri)–11 (10.30–11 Sat)
Marston's Pedigree; Samuel Smith OBB H**; guest beers**
Don't be fooled: this is no ordinary wine bar! At least one, often more, guest beer complements the regulars. A quiet place to have lunch, becoming loud and lively but still friendly in the eve. ◐ ⇌

Tatenhill

Horseshoe Inn
Main Street ☎ (0283) 64913
11–3, 5.30–11
Marston's Pedigree H
18th-century village pub internally altered to provide drinking and dining areas, but retaining simple, beamed features. Highly regarded food (not served Mon eve).
Q ❀ ◐ ◑ ♿ P

Two Gates

Bull's Head
Watling Street (A5/A51 jct)
☎ (0827) 287820
11.30–2.30, 7–11
Marston's Border Mild, Pedigree H
Small and friendly pub, popular with the locals: a cosy lounge and a traditional public bar with darts, etc. Q
❀ ◐ ⊞ ⇌ (Wilnecote) ♣ P

Uttoxeter

Black Swan
Market Street
☎ (0889) 564657
11–3.30, 5.30–11 (11–11 (Wed, Fri & Sat)
Draught Bass H
17th-century listed building of great character. ⊞ ⇌ ♣ P

Whittington

Swan Inn
Burton Road ☎ (0543) 432264
12–3, 5–11 (12–11 Sat)
Ansells Mild, Bitter; Ind Coope Burton Ale; Marston's Pedigree H**; guest beer**
Deservedly popular local with an ever-changing guest beer. The large canalside garden has a treehouse. Can be noisy.
♔ ❀ ◐ ◑ ♣ P

Wilnecote

Globe Inn
Watling Street
12–3, 7–11
Marston's Border Mild, Pedigree H
This brick building stands alone, just a few feet from the busy A5, but is easily passed. Basic but unspoilt inside, the small front bar and larger lounge host darts and dominoes matches. ❀ ⊞ ♣

Wombourne

Old Bush
High Street ☎ (0902) 893509
11.30–3, 6–11 (12–2.30, 7–10.30 Sun)
Banks's Mild, Bitter E
Two-roomed 1930s pub, noted for its family atmosphere and its lunches (not served Sun).
Q ◐ ⊞ ♿ ♣ P

Yoxall

Crown Inn
Main Street ☎ (0543) 472551
11.30–3, 5.30–11
Marston's Pedigree H
Large stone pub in an attractive village. The bar contains a snug; eating area in the lounge. ♨ ◐ ◑ ⊞ ♣ P

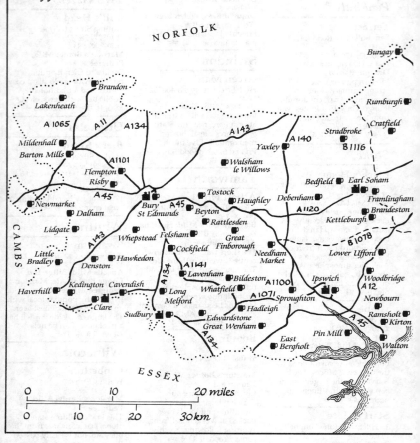

Suffolk

NORFOLK

Bungay
Lakenheath · Brandon
Rumburgh
Cratfield
A 1065 A 11 A 134 A 143 A 140 Stradbroke
Mildenhall Yaxley B 1116
Barton Mills A 1101 Walsham Bedfield Earl Soham
Flempton le Willows Debenham Framlingham
Risby A 45 Tostock Brandeston
Newmarket Bury Haughley A 1120 Kettleburgh
Dalham St Edmunds Beyton
Lidgate A 143 Whepstead Felsham Rattlesden Lower Ufford
Little Cockfield Great Needham Woodbridge
Bradley Denston Hawkedon Finborough Market Ipswich A 12
Haverhill Kedington Cavendish A 1141 Lavenham Bildeston A 1100 Newbourn
Clare Long Whatfield A 1071 Sproughton Ramsholt
Sudbury Melford Hadleigh Kirton
Edwardstone Pin Mill Walton
Great Wenham
East
Bergholt A 134

CAMBS

ESSEX

0	10		20 miles
0	10	20	30 km

Aldeburgh

Railway
Leiston Road ☎ (0728) 453864
11–3, 6–11
Adnams Mild, Bitter Ⓗ
Locals' pub on the outskirts of
town: an ideal place to escape
from the summer crowds on
the seafront. Keen darts
players; old parlour quoits
game. ✿ ⇔ ◑ ▶ ♣ ♠

White Hart
High Street ☎ (0728) 453205
11–11 (may vary)

**Adnams Bitter, Old,
Broadside** Ⓗ
Despite its prominent seaside
position, this pub remains a
true drinkers' haunt,
successfully integrating local
and holiday trade. Bank hols
and summer weekends often
see the compact, wood-
panelled bar bursting at the
seams. ⚌ ✿ ◑ ▲ ♣

Barton Mills

Bull Inn
☎ (0638) 713230
11–11

**Adnams Bitter; Draught Bass;
Greene King IPA** Ⓗ
Fine old coaching inn with a
traditional U-shape and an
inner courtyard. Family-run,
offering full hotel facilities.
✿ ⇔ ◑ ▶ P

Bedfield

Crown
Church Lane (leave A1120 in
Earl Soham) ☎ (072 876) 431
11–11 (may close 3–6 if quiet)
Greene King IPA Ⓗ**; guest
beer**

Village local with a warm and friendly welcome, offering a good selection of pub games and usually a guest beer.
🏨 🚲 🏵 ◑ ▶ ▲ ♣ P

Beyton

White Horse
The Green (off A45)
☎ (0359) 70324
11.30–3, 6.30–11
Greene King XX Mild, IPA, Abbot Ⓗ
A fine pub catering for all ages. It has exposed red brick walls in the bar, a formal eating area in the lounge and an illuminated well in the entrance passage. TV and video games in the bar. No meals Sun eve.
🏨🏨 🏵 ◑ ▶ 🍺 ▲ ♣ P

Bildeston

Kings Head
High Street ☎ (0449) 741434
12–2.30 (11–3.30 summer), 5–11
Fuller's London Pride; Greene King IPA Ⓗ**; guest beers**
Large, 15th-century timbered inn with a separate games room and a restaurant. Also offers an adventure playground in the garden, regular live music and an annual beer festival.
🏨 🚲 🏵 🛏 ◑ ▶ ▲ ♣ ⌂ P

Blaxhall

Ship
☎ (072 888) 316
11–3, 7–11
Adnams Bitter; Tolly Cobbold Mild Ⓗ
Thoroughly traditional pub whose regulars include local folk artists. Excellent value pub meals (not served Mon lunch). 🏵 🛏 ◑ ▶ ▲ ♣ P

Bramfield

Bell
The Street (beside A144)
11–2.30, 6.30–11
Adnams Mild, Bitter Ⓖ
Good, basic two-bar pub with a Ring the Bull game in the public bar. Q 🏵 🍺 ▲ ♣ P

Brampton

Dog Inn
London Road ☎ (050 279) 645
11–3, 6–11
Adnams Mild, Bitter, Old, Broadside Ⓗ
Unpretentious rural local. Beware the deep pond in the garden if you have small children. 🏨🏨 🏵 ◑ ▶ 🍺 ▲ ♣

Brandeston

Queens Head
The Street ☎ (072 882) 307
11.30–2.30, 5.30 (6 Mon)–11
Adnams Mild, Bitter, Old, Broadside Ⓗ
Excellent country pub with a large children's play area and good value, home-made food. The back bar is quiet.
🏨🏨 🚲 🏵 🛏 ◑ ▶ 🍺 ▲ P

Brandon

Five Bells
Market Hill ☎ (0842) 813472
11–2.30, 5–11 (11–11 Fri & Sat)
Greene King XX Mild, IPA, Abbot Ⓗ
Busy pub on the market square. The patio drinking area gives a good view of the market activities. Eve meals in summer only.
Q 🏵 ◑ ▶ 🍺 🚲 ♣ P

Bungay

Chequers
Bridge Street ☎ (0986) 893579
12–3, 5.30–11 (12–11 Sat)
Adnams Bitter; Greene King IPA, Abbot Ⓗ**; guest beers**
17th-century drinkers' pub with a covered patio area. Four ever-changing guest beers from independent breweries. 🏵 ◑ ▲ ♣

Green Dragon
Broad Street ☎ (0986) 892681
11–11 (may close 3–5 midweek)
Adnams Bitter; Green Dragon Chaucer, Bridge St Bitter, Dragon Ale; Greene King IPA Ⓗ**; guest beer**
Formerly the Horse and Groom, reopened as a free house in 1991 and now named after the residence of the owner, which was a former pub. Brews its own beer.
🏨🏨 🏵 ◑ 🍺 ▲ ♣ P

Bury St Edmunds

Black Boy
69 Guildhall Street
☎ (0284) 752723
11–2.30, 5–11
Greene King XX Mild, IPA, Rayments Special, Abbot Ⓗ
Building dating back to the 15th century, and a brewery site until 1890. Just off the town centre. ◑ ▶ 🍺 ♿ P

Elephant & Castle
2 Hospital Road (A134/A143 jct) ☎ (0284) 755570
11–2.30, 5–11
Greene King XX Mild, IPA, Abbot Ⓗ
Homely, two-bar family pub. The garden has petanque and a good playing area for children. 🏵 ◑ ▶ ♣ P

Flying Fortress
Cherry Tree Farm, Thurston Road (WWII airfield)
OS648883 ☎ (028 487) 665
12–2.30, 5–11
Adnams Bitter; Draught Bass; Greene King IPA; Marston's Pedigree; Whitbread Flowers IPA, Original Ⓔ
Pub with displays and artefacts connected with the former local WWII airfield. The large garden is safe for children. 🏵 ♣ P

Ipswich Arms
Tayfen Road ☎ (0284) 703623
12–2.30 (3 Fri, Sat & summer), 6–11
Greene King IPA, Abbot Ⓗ
19th-century, white brick pub on a busy corner. The early photograph (1871) in the lounge was taken from the nearby church spire – the highest in Suffolk.
🏵 ◑ ▶ 🚲 P

Suffolk

Butley

Oyster
The Street ☎ (0394) 450790
11–3, 5–11
Adnams Mild, Bitter, Old, Broadside (summer)**, Tally Ho; Tetley Bitter** Ⓗ
Dating from the 12th century, the Oyster has regained its former traditional atmosphere through tasteful alterations. Note the sketches of some of the older locals above the public bar fire; the people featured can tell tales of Suffolk past. All food is home-cooked (not served Sun eve or Mon/Tue eve in winter).
🏚 Q ❀ ⑪ ▮ ▲ ♣ P

Cavendish

Bull
High Street ☎ (0787) 280245
11–3, 6–11 (11–11 summer)
Adnams Mild, Bitter, Old, Broadside Ⓗ
Building dating from 1530, with original beams and fireplaces: a single bar with a dining area, where children are welcome. An Adnams oasis in Greene King country!
🏚 ❀ ⇔ ⑪ ▮ ♣ P

Clare

Bell Hotel
Market Hill ☎ (0787) 277741
11–11
Greene King IPA, Abbot; Nethergate Bitter, Old Growler Ⓗ
Fine, timber-framed, 16th-century hotel of character. Family-run, it offers a cosy bar area, excellent bar food and a restaurant. ❀ ⇔ ⑪ ▮ P

Cockfield

Three Horseshoes
On A1141, Lavenham road
☎ (0284) 828177
12–3, 6–11
Greene King XX Mild, IPA, Abbot Ⓗ
Thatched, 14th-century former Hall House and court. The striking lounge bar boasts an exposed crown post and tie beam circa 1350; games-oriented public bar. The excellent selection of home-made food includes traditional puddings. Greene King *Pub Caterers of the Year* 1991–92. No meals Tue eve.
🏚 Q ⇔ ❀ ⑪ ▮ ♣ P

Cratfield

Poacher
Bell Green OS313752
☎ (0986) 798206
11–11 (may vary in winter)
Adnams Bitter; Greene King IPA, Abbot Ⓗ

Remote rural pub – well worth taking the trouble to find. The outside walls are covered with murals while the interior features many stuffed animals.
🏚 ⇔ ❀ ⑪ ▮ ▲ ♣ P

Dalham

Affleck Arms
Brookside
☎ (0638) 500306
11–2.30, 6.30–11
Greene King XX Mild, IPA, Abbot Ⓗ
Elizabethan thatched pub with a friendly atmosphere.
🏚 Q ❀ ⑪ ▮ ▤ P

Debenham

Woolpack
High Street
☎ (0728) 860516
11–3, 5.30–11 (11–11 Fri & Sat)
Tetley Bitter; Tolly Cobbold Bitter, Original; Whitbread Wethered Bitter, Flowers Original Ⓗ**; guest beers** (occasionally)
Traditional village ale house with a crazy dog and an appropriate motto – *ergo bibamus*. Serves as the regimental pub for the Sealed Knot and the English Civil War Society. 🏚 ❀ ♣

Denston

Plumbers Arms
Wickham Street
☎ (0440) 820350
11–2.30, 5–11
Greene King XX Mild, IPA, Abbot Ⓗ
Large country pub dating back to 1700, an original stopping-point for horse traffic. Book for eve meals.
🏚 Q ❀ ⑪ ▮ ▤ ♣ P

Dunwich

Ship
St James Street
☎ (072 873) 219
11–3, 6–11 (11–11 summer)
Adnams Bitter, Old; Greene King Abbot Ⓗ
Nautical-flavoured inn on the one remaining street of the once great port of Dunwich. The handpumps are on the back of the timbered bar.
🏚 Q ⇔ ❀ ⇔ ⑪ ▮ ▲ ♣ P

Earl Soham

Victoria
On A1120 ☎ (0728) 685758
11–2.30, 5.30–11
Earl Soham Gannet Mild, Victoria, Albert Ale, Jolabrugg
A fine old country pub serving beer and food which are both made on the premises. Very popular and can get crowded, especially

when local musicians arrive to entertain. Note the old wooden beams and the large see-right-through fireplace.
🏚 Q ❀ ⑪ ▮ ♣ ⇔ P

East Bergholt

Royal Oak (Dickey)
East End Lane OS099353
11.30–3, 6–11
Greene King IPA, Abbot Ⓗ
Basic public bar on the outskirts of the village. A friendly welcome to all is guaranteed. 🏚 Q ❀ ▲ ♣ P

Eastbridge

Eel's Foot
☎ (0728) 830154
11–3, 6–11 (11–11 Sat)
Adnams Mild Ⓖ**, Bitter** Ⓗ**, Old** Ⓖ
Very pleasant public house with a name only shared by one other. Tales of satanic fish and exorcism by local clergy, coupled with a collection of footwear fixed to the outside wall, make this an unusual venue. The nearest pub to the RSPB's Minsmere reserve.
🏚 ⇔ ❀ ⑪ ▮ ▲ ♣ P

Edwardstone

White Horse
Mill Green ☎ (0787) 211211
11.30–2, 6.30–11
Greene King XX Mild, IPA Ⓗ**, Abbot** Ⓖ
Traditional Suffolk pub with a basic public bar and a comfortable lounge. Good value food available all week – full meals Thu–Sun (book Sun lunch).
🏚 Q ⑪ ▮ ▤ ♣ ⇔ P

Felsham

Six Bells
5–11 (11–3, 5–11 Fri; 12–3, 7–11 Sat)
Greene King XX Mild, IPA, Abbot Ⓗ
Basic but comfortable village local in an interesting building which dates back to the 16th century. Still displays the rules for the Felsham Jolly Boys Society, circa 1930.
🏚 Q ❀ ▤ ♣ P

Flempton

Greyhound
The Green (off A1101, behind church) ☎ (0284) 728400
11–2.30, 5–11
Greene King XX Mild, IPA, Abbot Ⓗ
Very traditional village pub, the centre of village activities. The popular public bar has a tiled floor; the lounge is smart. A large garden and play area overlook the village green.
🏚 ⇔ ⑪ ▮ ▤ ♣ P

Framlingham

Railway Inn

Station Road ☎ (0728) 723693
11–3, 5.30–11
Adnams Bitter, Extra, Old Ⓗ
Pub where the plush lounge bar boasts a Victorian fireplace and fine decor; the friendly public bar has basic wood tables, settles, and a beer barrel seat. A fine country pub with good prices, quality and atmosphere.
🏚 Q ⚙ ◑ ⬚ ▲ ♣ P

Great Finborough

Chestnut Horse

High Road ☎ (0449) 612298
11–3, 6–11
Greene King XX Mild, IPA, Rayments Special, Abbot Ⓗ
Good, friendly village local attracting a varied clientele. It features working sewing machine table bases, and an open brick fireplace. Try the 'Huffers'. No food Tue or Sun eve. 🏚 Q ⚙ ◑ ⬚ ▲ ♣ P

Great Wenham

Queens Head

The Row (Capel St Mary road) ☎ (0473) 310590
12–2.30, 6 (6.30 Sat)–11
Adnams Bitter; Greene King IPA, Abbot Ⓗ**; guest beers**
Victorian, cottage-style, one-bar house with exposed beams. 🏚 ⚙ ◑ ▲ ♣ P

Hadleigh

George

High Street ☎ (0473) 822151
11–2.30, 5.30–11
Greene King IPA, Abbot Ⓗ
Large, traditional public bar and a comfortable lounge.
⚙ ◑ ♣ P

Halesworth

White Hart

The Thoroughfare ☎ (0986) 873386
11–3, 6–11
Adnams Bitter; Draught Bass; Tetley Bitter Ⓗ**; guest beers**
A former keg Whitbread house which has been dramatically improved by the new owner. Open-plan but with many alcove seating areas. Q ⚙ ◑ ⬚ ⇌ ♣

Haughley

Railway Tavern

Station Road ☎ (0449) 673577
11–2.30, 5.30 (6.30 Sat)–11
Greene King XX Mild, IPA, Abbot Ⓗ**; guest beer**
Friendly local, a 19th-century tavern near the closed station on the main London–Ipswich–

Norwich line. The landlord breeds champion labradors. No food Mon eve.
🏚 ⚘ ⚙ ◑ ⬚ ♣ P

Haverhill

Queens Head

9 Queens Street ☎ (0440) 702026
11–2.30, 5–11 (11–11 Fri & Sat)
Courage Best Bitter, Directors; Nethergate Bitter; S&N Theakston Old Peculier Ⓗ
Interesting building, probably the oldest in a mainly new town. Retains a superb etched window from the long-defunct Wards brewery.
◑ ⬚ ♣ P

Hawkedon

Queens Head

☎ (028 489) 218
12–2.30, 6.30–11 (closed Mon)
Greene King IPA; Nethergate Bitter Ⓗ
Classic village bar near the church, with an unusual, quality menu. Low, moulded black beams, a large inglenook with a log burner, and comfy chairs complete the picture.
🏚 Q ⚙ ◑ P

Ipswich

County Hotel

29 St Helens Street ☎ (0473) 255153
11–3, 4–11
Adnams Mild, Bitter, Old, Extra, Broadside, Tally Ho; guest beer Ⓗ
Large, imposing building near the town centre, with a contrasting boisterous bar and quieter lounge/dining area. One of the few pubs in town to serve evening meals. The only Adnams pub to offer the complete brewery range.
◑ ⬚ ♣

Lord Nelson

Fore Street ☎ (0473) 254072
11–11
Adnams Mild (summer), **Bitter, Old, Broadside** Ⓗ
Lively bar, but the lounge is much more subdued, the ideal place for a quiet chat. It dates back to 1663 but it is a vibrant dockside local. ⚘ ♣

Plough

2 Dogs Head Street ☎ (0473) 288005
11–2.30, 5–11 (closed Sun)
Courage Directors; Greene King IPA; Tolly Cobbold Mild, Bitter, Original, Old Strong Ⓗ
Recently reopened by its two ale-loving landlords after a long spell as an horrendous 'fun pub'. It has reverted to its original name and a much

more traditional atmosphere. No lager. Q ◑ ⇌ ♣

Water Lily

166 St Helens Street ☎ (0473) 257035
11.30–2.30, 7.30–11
Tolly Cobbold Mild, Bitter, Old Strong; guest beer Ⓖ
The only Ipswich pub with gravity-dispensed beer, as unchanging as ever, with its basic but comfortable bar and tiny snug. Families welcome in the large garden. No food Sun. 🏚 ⚘ ⚙ ◑ ♣ ♠

Woolpack

1 Tuddenham Road ☎ (0473) 253054
11.30–2.30, 5.30–11
Courage Directors; Tolly Cobbold Mild, Bitter, Original, Old Strong Ⓗ
16th-century building housing a comfortable, medium-sized lounge, a small bar and a smoke room, plus a games room. A country pub in town. 🏚 Q ⚙ ◑ ⬚ ♣ P

Kedington

White Horse

Sturmer Road ☎ (0440) 63564
11–11
Greene King XX Mild, IPA, Abbot Ⓗ
Very popular village pub near a Saxon church. The large garden hosts summer barbecues while the excellent bar food includes vegetarian dishes. Q ⚙ ⚘ ◑ ⬚ ⬚ ♣ P

Kettleburgh

Chequers

Easton Road ☎ (0728) 723760
11–3, 6–11
Marston's Pedigree; Tolly Cobbold Mild, Bitter Ⓗ
Pub erected in 1912 after the previous one was destroyed by fire. In the last century, the Deben brewery stood adjacent. Now a good all-round venue, with grounds extending down to the River Deben. 🏚 ⚙ ◑ ◑ P

Kirton

White Horse

Bucklesham Road ☎ (039 48) 615
12–4, 7–11 Thu–Sat)
Tolly Cobbold Mild, Bitter Ⓗ
Comfortable but basic pub with a lively local clientele. A wide range of food is available (not Sun). ⚙ ◑ ▲ ♣ P

Lakenheath

Plough

Mill Road ☎ (0842) 860285
11–2.30, 6–11
Greene King XX Mild, IPA Ⓗ

Suffolk

Popular pub in the centre of a busy village. A fine flint exterior, typical of the locality, conceals a spacious bar area and a pool room. ❀ 🍺 ♣ P

Lavenham

Angel

Market Place ☎ (0787) 247388
11–3, 6–11
Nethergate Bitter, Old Growler (winter); **Ruddles County; Webster's Yorkshire Bitter** Ⓗ
Impressive, 14th-century coaching inn overlooking the Market Cross and Guildhall. Pick a quiet time and ask to see the medieval vaulted cellars. Very relaxed atmosphere. Large garden.
🏚 Q ❀ 🏠 ◖▶ ♣ P

Lidgate

Star

The Street ☎ (0638) 500275
11–2.30, 7–11
Greene King IPA, Abbot Ⓗ
The centre of activity in an almost unchanged village. Spit-roast beef is a speciality; barbecues held every summer weekend. Note the unusual handpumps. 🏚 ❀ ◖▶ ♣ P

Little Bradley

Royal Oak

☎ (044 083) 229
11–3, 6–11
Adnams Bitter; Greene King IPA; Nethergate Bitter Ⓗ
Welcoming, main road pub which is very busy at weekends. 🏚 ◖▶ P

Long Melford

George & Dragon

Hall Street ☎ (0787) 71285
11–11
Greene King XX Mild, IPA, Rayments Special, Abbot Ⓗ
Coaching inn, recently refurbished to provide a large lounge-style bar and a restaurant. 🏚 Q ❀ 🏠 ◖▶
🍺 ♿ ▲ ♣ P ⌀

Lower Ufford

White Lion

☎ (0394) 460770
11.30–2.30, 6.30–11
Tetley Bitter; Tolly Cobbold Mild, Bitter, Old Strong Ⓖ
Excellent, traditional rural pub with a roaring fire in winter and gravity-dispensed beer from behind the bar. The setting is nearly as idyllic. Good food includes daily specials (not served Sun eve or Mon). 🏚 Q ❀ ◖▶ P

Lowestoft

Prince Albert

Park Road ☎ (0502) 573424
11–3.30, 5–11 (may vary)
Adnams Mild, Bitter, Old, Broadside Ⓗ
Back-street pub catering for those who want a quiet drink and a natter in a friendly atmosphere. The food is home-made (not served Sun).
❀ ◖ 🍺 ♣ P

Mildenhall

Queens Arms

Queensway ☎ (0638) 713657
11–2.30, 7–11
Greene King XX Mild, IPA, Rayments Special Ⓗ
Homely pub on the outskirts of this small town, attracting local trade of all ages. Limited range of food, but all home-made. Q ❀ 🏠 ◖▶ ♣ P

Needham Market

Swan

High Street ☎ (0449) 720280
11–11
Greene King XX Mild, IPA, Rayments Special, Abbot Ⓗ
Fine, beamed, 500-year-old pub with a welcoming atmosphere. Food is available in the bar, as well as in the no-smoking restaurant (no meals Sun eve). ❀ 🏠 ◖▶ ⇌ P

Newbourn

Fox Inn

The Street ☎ (0473) 36307
11–3, 7–11 (11–11 Fri, Sat & summer)
Tolly Cobbold Mild, Bitter, Old Strong Ⓖ; **guest beers** (occasionally)
Busy, 15th-century inn, taken over by the current landlord last year. Now providing a wide range of home-cooked food. 🏚 🍺 ❀ ◖▶ ▲ ♣ P

Newmarket

Five Bells

16 St Marys Square
☎ (0638) 664961
11–3 (4 Sat), 6–11
Greene King XX Mild, IPA, Abbot Ⓗ
One-bar, traditional pub with a very friendly atmosphere. Fields a strong band of local teams. 🏚 Q ❀ ◖▶ ♿ ♣ P

Orford

Jolly Sailor

Quay Street ☎ (0394) 450243
11–2.30, 6–11 (12–2.30, 7–10.30 Sun)
Adnams Bitter Ⓗ
Quayside inn in a medieval port, now cut off from the sea. A tiny public bar is hidden behind the open fireplace which dominates the front bar

and dining area.
🏚 🍺 ❀ 🏠 ◖▶ 🍺 ♣ P

Pin Mill

Butt & Oyster

☎ (0473) 780764
11–3, 7–11 (11–11 summer)
Tolly Cobbold Mild Ⓗ, **Bitter** Ⓗ & Ⓖ, **Original, Old Strong** Ⓗ
Internationally-known, unchanging riverside inn with a family room and restaurant. Busy in summer, but much more laid-back in the winter months, when the landlord operates a clocking-in scheme (the reward for a number of hours in the pub is a free pint).
🏚 Q 🍺 ❀ 🏠 ◖▶ ▲ ♣ P

Ramsholt

Ramsholt Arms

Dock Road OS307416
☎ (0394) 411229
11–2.30 (3 Sat), 7–11 (11–11 July & Aug)
Adnams Bitter, Old, Broadside Ⓗ
Large, comfortable pub with a country house atmosphere. A nautical theme dominates the bar, which has fine views of the River Deben. Despite its obscure location, down narrow winding lanes, a busy food trade throughout the summer helps nourish the sailing fraternity.
🏚 Q 🍺 ❀ 🏠 ◖▶ P

Rattlesden

Five Bells

High Street ☎ (0449) 737373
11–2.30, 5.30–11 (11–11 Sat)
Adnams Bitter, Broadside, Old; Wadworth 6X Ⓗ
Small pub next to the church on the high road overlooking the village. Good local drinking trade and a warm welcome. 🏚 ❀ ♣ P

Risby

Crown & Castle

☎ (0284) 810393
11–2.30, 7 (6.30 Sat)–11
Greene King IPA, Rayments Special, Abbot Ⓗ
Pub featuring a deep well in the entrance, a lounge with an adjoining formal eating area and a public bar. The frontage bears local flint work. 🍺 ♣ P

Rumburgh

Buck

Mill Road ☎ (098 685) 257
11–2, 5.30–11
Adnams Bitter, Old; Greene King IPA, Rayments Special; Webster's Yorkshire Bitter Ⓗ; **guest beers** (occasionally)
Originally thought to have been the guest house for the priory, this historic inn has

been tastefully refurbished and extended to give lots of small, interlinked areas, including for dining and games. 🏚 ❀ ◖◗ ⊞ ♣ P

Sibton

White Horse

Halesworth Road (off A1120 by garage in Peasenhall) ☎ (072 879) 337
11.30–2.30 (not Mon, except bank hols), 7–11

Adnams Bitter H; guest beer
16th-century free house with a very pleasant dining room. Well-behaved children are welcomed. No food Sun eve.
🏚 Q ⅏ ❀ ◖◗ ▲ ♣ P

Southwold

Lord Nelson

East Street ☎ (0502) 722079
10.30–11 (closed Wed afternoon)

Adnams Mild, Bitter, Old, Broadside, Tally Ho H
Lively bar in a 17th-century coaching inn near the coastal cliff. A collection of 250 soda syphons is on display in the snug; lovely sun-trap patio.
🏚 Q ⅏ ❀ ◖▶

Sproughton

Beagle

Old Hadleigh Road ☎ (047 386) 455
11–2.30, 5–11

Adnams Mild, Bitter, Broadside; Greene King IPA, Abbot; Mauldons Bitter; S&N Theakston Best Bitter H; guest beers
A converted row of cottages, forming a large, comfortable lounge and a friendly bar. Good selection of meals available (not served Sun).
🏚 Q ❀ ⊞ ♣ P

Stradbroke

Queens Head

On B1118 ☎ (0379) 384384
11–3, 6.30–11

Adnams Bitter; Greene King IPA, Abbot H
Friendly village pub frequented by many interesting characters. The interior is divided by the huge brick fireplace. The garden has a DIY barbecue.
🏚 ❀ ⊨ ◖◗ ▲ ♣

Sudbury

Waggon & Horses

Acton Square, Church Walk ☎ (0787) 312147
11–3, 6.30–11 (11–11 Sat)

Greene King XX Mild, IPA, Abbot H
Revitalised back-street pub with a public bar, a games room, a restaurant and a snug. The architecture incorporates several different styles and

ages. Next to the site of the old Phoenix brewery. No food Sun eve. 🏚 Q ◖◗ ⊞ ⇌ ♣ P

Tostock

Gardeners Arms

Church Road ☎ (0359) 70460
11–2.30, 7–11

Greene King IPA, Rayments Special, Abbot H
Original-beamed building, next to the village green. The restaurant offers a varied menu (including vegetarian fare). A basic public bar, but a comfortable lounge with an open fire. No meals Sun lunch or Mon/Tue eves.
🏚 ❀ ◖◗ ⊞ ♣ P

Walberswick

Bell

Ferry Road ☎ (0502) 723109
11–4, 6–11

Adnams Bitter, Old, Extra, Broadside H
600-year-old inn close to the beach and River Blyth estuary. Worn flagstone floors and exposed brickwork and timber, together with high-backed wooden settles, make this a real step back in time. Eve meals are served in the dining area (not Sun eve). 🏚 Q ⅏ ❀ ⊨ ◖◗ ⊞ ▲ ♣ P

Walsham le Willows

Six Bells

High Street ☎ (0359) 259726
11.30–2.30, 5.30 (6.30 Sat)–11

Greene King XX Mild, IPA, Abbot H
Large, old, beamed pub in the centre of a pleasant village. Maintains a traditional public bar with a good, comfortable lounge (no food at weekends).
🏚 ❀ ⊨ ◖◗ ⊞ ♣ P

Walton

Tap & Spile (Half Moon)

High Road ☎ (0394) 282130
11–4, 5.30–11 (11–11 Fri & Sat)

Adnams Bitter; guest beers H
Pub in traditional ale house-style, still featured on local bus timetables under its former name, 'Half Moon'. Up to eight different beers are available. 🏚 Q ❀ ◖◗ ♣ P

Whatfield

Four Horseshoes

The Street ☎ (0473) 827971
11.30–3, 6.30–11

Adnams Bitter, Broadside; Greene King IPA H; guest beers
Homely, traditional two-bar local with a caravan for hire.
🏚 Q ❀ ◖▶ ⊞ ▲ ♣ P

Whepstead

White Horse

Rede Road (use B1066 off A143, 1 mile N of church) ☎ (0284) 735542
11.30–3, 6.30–11

Greene King IPA, Rayments Special, Abbot H
Two very separate bars: the tap room remains traditional while the lounge/restaurant offers home-cooked specials with an oriental theme. Difficult to find, but worthwhile.
🏚 Q ❀ ◖◗ ⊞ ♣ P

Woodbridge

Olde Bell & Steelyard

New Street ☎ (0394) 382933
11–2.30, 6–11

Greene King IPA, Rayments Special, Abbot H
Traditional, Grade I listed building, with an unusual weighbridge over the road. A generally smoke-free atmosphere, with a no-smoking family room. Boasts a vast range of pub games. Pizzas only served (not Wed).
🏚 Q ⅏ ❀ ◖◗ ⇌ ♣ ✂

Seckford Arms

Seckford Street ☎ (0394) 384446
11–11

Adnams Bitter, Broadside; Draught Bass; Greene King IPA H; guest beers
Genuine, family-run free house featuring superb Mayan wood carvings throughout. Exposed beams in the lounge; heated foot-rail in the bar. Caters for families in a no-smoking extension. ⅏ ⊨ ◖◗ ⊞ ♣ ✂

Tap & Spile

New Street ☎ (0394) 382679
11.30–2.30, 5.30–11 (11–11 Sat)

Adnams Bitter; Wells Eagle, Bombardier H; guest beers
Formerly the Mariners Arms, now decorated in the Tap & Spile style with a traditional interior and real beams. On the site of the original Castle brewery. Six real ales midweek, eight at the weekend.
🏚 Q ❀ ⊞ ⇌ ♣ ⌂ P

Yaxley

Bull

Ipswich Road ☎ (0379) 783604
11–3, 5.30–11 (11–11 Fri, Sat & bank hols)

Adnams Bitter, Broadside; Woodforde's Wherry H; guest beers
Genuine 16th-century free house with a high, beamed roof and a country garden with a children's play area. A relaxed and friendly pub on the main road near the Thornham estate.
Q ❀ ⊨ ◖◗ ▲ ♣ P

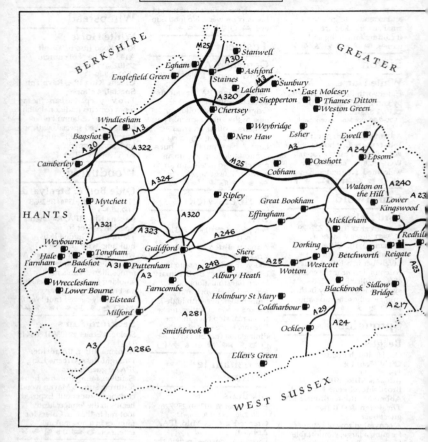

 Pilgrim, Reigate

Albury Heath

William IV

Dark Lane, Little London ($\frac{1}{2}$ mile S of Shere village)
OS066467 ☎ (048 641) 2685
11–3, 5.30–11
Courage Best Bitter; Greene King IPA, Abbot; Tetley Bitter; Young's Special, Winter Warmer H
Characterful 400-year-old free house featuring beams, flagstone floor, large open fireplace and a garden. Separate eating area. Crowded early evening but quieter later. Rather expensive and difficult to find, but worth the effort.
🏄 Q ❀ ◖◗ ♣ P

Ashford

Ash Tree

Convent Road (B378)
☎ (0784) 252362
11–11
Fuller's London Pride, ESB H
Friendly two-bar pub outside the town centre. ❀ ◖ ⊕ ♣ P

Badshot Lea

Crown Inn

Pine View Close
☎ (0252) 20453
11–2.30 (3 Fri & Sat), 6.30–11
Fuller's Chiswick, London Pride, ESB H
Cosy local with diverse clientele, close to a large garden centre. Good value food, including Sun roasts (but no meals Sun eve). Lots for children in the garden.
❀ ◖◗ ♣ P

Bagshot

Foresters Arms

173 London Road (A30)
☎ (0276) 72038
11–3, 5.30–11 (11–11 Fri & Sat)
Courage Best Bitter, Directors; John Smith's Bitter H; **guest beer**
Comfortable and deceptively roomy locals' pub with a skittle alley and a convivial atmosphere. The garden has a children's play area. Interesting guest beer, regularly changed. No food Sun. Q ❀ ◖ ♣ P

Try also: Three Mariners, High St (Courage)

Betchworth

Dolphin

The Street
☎ (0737) 842388
11–3, 5.30–11
Young's Bitter, Special, Winter Warmer H
Attractive 17th-century village inn with a well-worn stone-flagged floor, a large

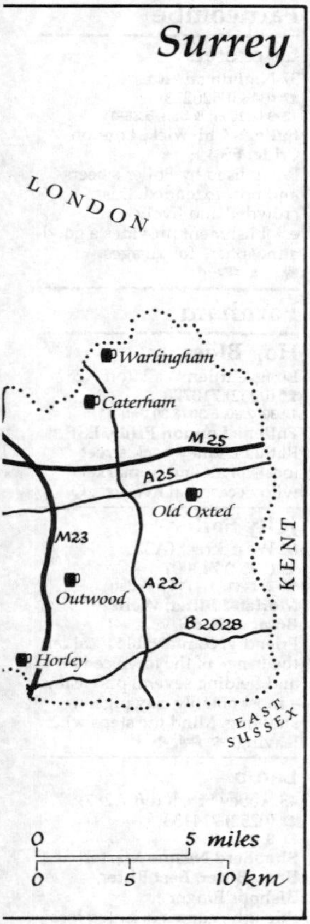

inglenook and solid wood tables. One bar but three distinct drinking areas.
⛼ Q ❀ ◖◗ ♣ P

Blackbrook

Plough at Blackbrook

Blackbrook Road (off A24) OS181466
☎ (0306) 886603
11–2.30, 6–11 (12–2.30, 7–10.30 Sun)
King & Barnes Sussex, Broadwood, Old, Festive Ⓗ
Nineteenth consecutive year in the *Good Beer Guide*. An excellent menu offers a variety of home-cooked specials and vegetarian options (no food Mon eve). The Blackbrook Bar features a collection of saws and 600 ties. ❀ ◖◗ ⊞ P ⚟

Camberley

Bridgers

299 London Road (A30)
☎ (0276) 21534
11.30–3, 5–11 (11.30–11 Sat)
Gibbs Mew Local Line, Salisbury, Bishop's Tipple Ⓗ
Completely restored, traditionally furnished town pub. Comfortable, with a brisk business trade which gives way to the younger crowd mid-evening. Named after one of the founders of Gibbs Mew Brewery. No food Sun eve.
❀ ◖◗ ♿ ♣ P

Try also: Ancient Foresters, Park St (Charrington)

Caterham

Clifton Arms

110 Chaldon Road (B2031, Coulsdon Rd jct)
☎ (0883) 343525
11–2.30 (3 Sat), 5 (6 Sat)–11
Draught Bass; Charrington IPA; Pilgrim Progress; Welsh Brewers Worthington BB Ⓗ
Pub where the main bar has a large number of photos of local historical interest. The fenced garden, popular in summer, has ducks, rabbits and goats. Live music once a month; a pianola is used to raise money for charity. No food Sat/Sun. ❀ ◖ P

Try also: King & Queen (Free)

Chertsey

Golden Grove

St Anns Hill Road (off A320/B388 roundabout)
☎ (0932) 562132
11.30–3.30, 5.30–11 (11–3, 6–11 Sat)
Ind Coope Burton Ale; Tetley Bitter; Young's Special Ⓗ
A 16th-century, former coaching inn which still has stabling attached. Low beamed ceiling and an attractive garden. Handy for St Anns Hill Park. Eve meals Tue–Fri, no food Sun.
Q ❀ ◖◗ ♣ P

Vine

5 Bridge Road
☎ (0932) 563010
11–3, 5–11 (11–11 Sat in summer)
Brakspear Bitter; Courage Best Bitter, Directors Ⓗ
Dating back 400 years, this well-run pub is deservedly popular. Regular quiz night, and, among other attractions, a collection of cameras. Good reputation for bar meals.
❀ ◖◗ ♿ ▲ ♣ P

Cobham

Silvermere Tavern

Silvermere Golf Club, Redhill Road (B366)
☎ (0932) 864988
11–11
Tetley Bitter; Wadworth 6X; Young's Bitter Ⓗ
Bar of a golf club and leisure complex, open to all and overlooking a man-made ornamental lake. Next door is a bus museum, housed in the only surviving part of a local aircraft factory famed for the Wellington Bomber. Barbecues in summer. Only two beers at any one time. ❀ ◖◗ ♿ P

Coldharbour

Plough Inn

Coldharbour Lane OS152441
☎ (0306) 711793
11.30–3, 6 (7 winter)–11
Adnams Broadside; Gibbs Mew Bishop's Tipple; Hall & Woodhouse Badger Best Bitter; Ringwood Old Thumper; S&N Theakston Old Peculier Ⓗ**; guest beers**
350 years-old, the highest pub in the South-East, on the slopes of Leith Hill in good walking country. Normally another three beers in addition to the above, including a winter brew. Children welcome lunchtime.
⛼ ⛟ ❀ ◖◗ ⊞ ♿ ♣ ⬭

Dorking

Bush

10–11 Horsham Road (A2003, 400 yds S of one-way system)
☎ (0306) 889830
11–2.30 (3 Sat), 6 (5.30 Fri)–11
Brakspear Bitter; Fuller's London Pride; Harveys BB Ⓗ**; guest beers**
Friendly local with a sensible range of beers (one or two guests always available). A covered patio area, used by families, leads to a marbles ring and a sloping, grassy garden. Barbecues in summer. No food Mon eve, or Sun.
❀ ◖◗ ♣

Cricketers

81 South Street (A25 one-way system) ☎ (0306) 889938
11–3, 5.30 (6 Sat)–11
Fuller's Chiswick, London Pride, Mr Harry, ESB Ⓗ
Busy one-bar pub with a small, pleasant patio garden. Games include chess and backgammon. Weekday lunches. ❀ ◖ ♣

Old House at Home

24 West Street (A25 one-way system)
☎ (0306) 889664
11–3, 5.30 (6 Sat)–11
Young's Bitter, Special Ⓗ
Pub dating from the 15th-century, decorated with brasses and other artefacts. Sometimes sells Winter Warmer from a pin on the bar. Eve meals finish at 8.30.
⛼ Q ❀ ◖◗ ⥂ (West)

Try also: Star, West St (Greene King); **Queens Head,** Horsham Rd (Fuller's)

Surrey

East Molesey

Europa
171 Walton Road (B369)
☎ (081) 979 8838
11–2.30, 5–11 (11–11 Sat)
**Courage Best Bitter,
Directors; John Smith's
Bitter; Wadworth 6X** H
Three distinctive bars
including a no-nonsense
public with a pool table and
darts. Happy hour 5–7
weekdays, 7–8 Sun. ❀ ◖ ⊞ ♣

Try also: New Inn and **Prince
of Wales** (both Courage)

Effingham

Plough
Orestan Lane (off A246 via
The Street) ☎ (0372) 458121
11–2.45 (3 Sat), 6–11
Young's Bitter, Special H
Good beer does travel – from
Wandsworth into the
stockbroker belt. An oasis of
quality. This also applies to
the food which quickly gives
way to drinking in the
evening. Q ❀ ◖ ▶ ♣ P

Egham

Crown
38 High Street (off A30)
☎ (0784) 432608
11–3, 5.30–11
**Courage Best Bitter,
Directors; John Smith's
Bitter** H
Very popular town-centre
pub. An inn has stood on this
site since the 17th century. The
current pub was built in 1934
and hasn't changed much
since. Arrive early for the
popular weekday lunches.
❀ ◖ ⊞ & ⇌

Ellen's Green

Wheatsheaf Inn
Off A281, signed Hooks Green
(near Bucks Green)
☎ (0403) 822155
11–3, 6–11
**King & Barnes Mild, Sussex,
Broadwood, Old, Festive**
(summer) H
Traditional, low-beamed 17th-
century country pub.
Children's garden with lots of
play equipment and even their
own toilets. ⋈ Q ❀ ◖ ▶ ♣ P

Elstead

Golden Fleece
Farnham Road (B3001)
☎ (0252) 702349
11–3, 6–11
**Courage Best Bitter,
Directors** H; **guest beer**
Spacious, smart but not formal,
sturdy single-bar pub. Live
music Sun eve (when no meals
are served). Q ❀ ◖ ▶ & P

Try also: Star (Courage);
Woolpack (Friary Meux)

Englefield Green

Beehive
34 Middle Hill (off A30)
☎ (0784) 431621
12–3, 5.30–11
Gale's XXXD (summer), **Best
Bitter, 5X, HSB** H; **guest beers**
Popular small pub, offering a
wide range of good beers. One
of only two pubs in North
Surrey to sell real mild. Eve
meals 7–9pm. ❀ ◖ ♣ P

Epsom

Barley Mow
12 Pikes Hill (off Upper High
Street, A2022) ☎ (0372) 721044
11–3, 5.30 (5 Fri)–11
**Fuller's Chiswick, London
Pride, ESB** H
Back-street local with an
unusual layout and a
conservatory at the rear. Not
overly large, so, in summer,
the pleasant garden is a bonus.
Parking is difficult but there is
a large public car park nearby.
Eve meals to order. ❀ ◖ ♣

Kings Arms
144 East Street (A24)
☎ (0372) 723892
11–3, 5.30–11 (11–11 Sat)
**Young's Bitter, Special,
Winter Warmer** H
Large roadside inn which
retains a lively public bar, a
pleasantly decorated saloon
bar and a landscaped garden.
Barbecues summer weekends.
❀ ◖ ⊞ ♣ P

Esher

Claremont Arms
2 Church Street (A244
westbound) ☎ (0372) 464083
10.30–11
**Courage Best Bitter,
Directors** H; **guest beers**
Small side-street local divided
into two distinct drinking
areas. Guest beers are rotated
– see blackboards for details.
Racing pictures adorn the
walls. Good value meals (not
served Sun). ◖ ♣

Ewell

King William IV
17 High Street (off A24)
☎ (081) 393 2063
11–11
**Ind Coope Friary Meux Best
Bitter, Burton Ale; Tetley
Bitter** H
Friendly, 19th-century local
with original etched windows.
Occasional live jazz. Pool table
in the large public bar. Eve
meals until 7pm.
❀ ◖ ▶ ⇌ (West/East) ♣ P

Farncombe

Cricketers
37 Nightingale Road
☎ (0483) 420273
12–3 (3.30 Fri & Sat), 5.30–11
**Fuller's Chiswick, London
Pride, ESB** H
Revitalised by Fuller's beers
and now extended, this
crowded and lively
establishment provides a good
atmosphere for all ages.
❀ ◖ ▶ ⇌ ♣

Farnham

Hop Blossom
Long Garden Walk (off A287)
☎ (0252) 710770
12.30–2.30, 5.30 (6.30 Sat)–11
**Fuller's Chiswick, London
Pride, ESB** H
Rather cliquey back-street
local, small and upmarket
with occasional live jazz. Q

Jolly Sailor
64 West Street (A325)
☎ (0252) 713001
12–3, 7–11 (11–11 Fri & Sat)
**Morland Bitter; Wells
Bombardier** H
Friendly, comfortable local on
the fringe of the town centre
and fielding several pub teams
– most notably clay pigeon
shooting. Mind the steps when
leaving! ❀ ⋈ ♣ P

Lamb
43 Abbey Street (off A287)
☎ (0252) 714133
11–3, 6–11
**Shepherd Neame Master
Brew Bitter, Best Bitter,
Bishops Finger** H
Friendly, games-oriented local
with a roaring log fire, two big
dogs and excellent value food
(not served Sun). Park in the
town centre. Highly
recommended and close to
The Maltings, where the
highly successful local beer
festival is held in April.
⋈ ❀ ◖ ⇌ ♣

Queens Head
9 The Borough (A287/A325
one-way system)
☎ (0252) 726524
11–11
**Gale's BBB, Best Bitter, 5X,
HSB** H
Bustling, traditional two-bar
pub in the town centre. Part of
the Gale's estate for over 100
years. No food Sun.
⋈ ◖ ⊞ ⇌ ♣

Try also: Blue Boy (Courage)

Great Bookham

Anchor
161 Lower Road (off A246 via
Eastwick Rd) ☎ (0372) 452429
11–3, 5.30–11
**Courage Best Bitter,
Directors** H; **guest beer**

500 years-old local,
traditionally decorated with
exposed brickwork and oak
beams; large inglenook. A
different guest beer each
month. No food Sun.
🏚 ❀ & ♣ P

Guildford

Kings Head
27 Kings Road ☎ (0483) 68957
11–2.30, 5.30 (6 Sat)–11
Fuller's London Pride, ESB H
A welcome addition to the
town's beer range in a slightly
off-centre location. Small
drinking areas with a friendly
local atmosphere. Close to
Stoke Park and college. Eve
meals finish at 8. ❀ ◖ ▶ ⧄ ≷

Sanford Arms
58 Epsom Road (A246)
☎ (0483) 572551
11–3, 5.30–11 (11.30–3.30, 6–11 Sat)
**Courage Best Bitter,
Directors** H; **guest beer**
Friendly, wood-panelled,
locals' pub with well
separated bars. The garden
has an aviary and a small
conservatory. The guest beer
from independent breweries is
changed regularly. Q ❀ ◖ ⧄
≷ (London Rd) ♣

Spread Eagle
46 Chertsey Street (A320)
☎ (0483) 35018
10.30–2.30 (3 Fri, 3.30 Sat), 5–11
**Courage Best Bitter,
Directors; John Smith's
Bitter; Young's Special** H;
guest beers
Close to the town centre; a
popular pub offering good
value lunches (no food Sun).
An adventurous guest beer
policy guarantees an
interesting choice. Over 100
different guests in two years.
Very busy weekend evenings.
Family room in adjacent
stables. ⏚ ❀ ◖ ≷ ♣ P

Try also: **Prince Albert**
(Courage)

Hale

Prince Alfred
9 Bishops Road (off A3016
opp. B3005) ☎ (0252) 712546
11–2.30 (3 Thu–Sat), 6–11
**Draught Bass; Charrington
IPA** H
Warm, friendly pub with a
genuine welcome from the
ebullient landlady and her
dedicated regulars.
Q ❀ ◖ ▶ ⧄ & ♣ P

Holmbury St Mary

Kings Head
Pitland Street (off B2126)
☎ (0306) 730282
12–2.30 (not Mon), 6–11 (11–11 Sat)

**Fuller's London Pride;
Ringwood Best Bitter, Old
Thumper; Young's Bitter** H;
guest beer
Compact, basic local with a
separate games area. Good
range of food. The guest beer
changes monthly.
🏚 ❀ ◖ ♣ P

Horley

Farmhouse
Ladbroke Road (off A23 opp.
Chequers) ☎ (0293) 782146
11–2.30 (3 Fri & Sat), 6–11 (12–2.30,
7–10.30 Sun)
**Courage Best Bitter,
Directors; John Smith's
Bitter** H
As its name suggests, this was
once a farmhouse, and still has
original timbers and
inglenooks. King Edward
VIII's abdication papers were
signed here. Beware of the
ghost and the pot holes in the
car park! No-smoking area at
lunchtime only.
🏚 ❀ ◖ ▶ P ⌿

Try also: **Tracks**, by station
(Free)

Laleham

Turks Head
Broadway (B377)
☎ (0784) 469078
11–3, 4.30–11 (11–11 Sat)
**Courage Best Bitter,
Directors; Wadworth 6X** or
Ind Coope Burton Ale H
Village pub in a pleasant
location near the river. Good
range of meals – see the
chalkboard (eve meals
Tue–Fri). ◖ ▶ & ⚓

Lower Bourne

Spotted Cow
3 Bourne Grove (signed off
Tilford–Farnham road)
☎ (0252) 726541
11.30–2.30, 6–11
**Courage Best Bitter,
Directors** H; **guest beer**
Popular old pub of character
set in its own, extensive
grounds. Drinkers and diners
vie for elbow room. Children's
equipment in the garden. The
guest beer changes every two
or three months. Eve meals
Tue–Sat. Q ❀ ◖ ♣ ♠ P

Try also: **Fox** (Morland)

Lower Kingswood

Fox Hotel
Brighton Road (A217
southbound) ☎ (0737) 832638
11–11
**Ind Coope Friary Meux Best
Bitter, Burton Ale; Tetley
Bitter** H; **guest beer**
This roadside inn is a useful
stop on the way to Gatwick

airport. One large bar with a
games area to one end. The
guest ale is changed every
couple of days. No eve meals
Tue. ❀ 🏚 ◖ ♣ P

Mickleham

King William IV
Byttom Hill (off A24
southbound)OS174538
☎ (0372) 372590
11–3, 6–11
**Adnams Bitter; Hall &
Woodhouse Badger Best
Bitter; Whitbread
Boddingtons Bitter** H; **guest
beers**
Charming pub perched on a
rocky hillside. The main bar
houses a large grandfather
clock; the small lounge bar
doubles as a family room and
the splendid garden can be a
real suntrap. Vegetarian food
a speciality (no meals Mon
eve). Winter price promotions
for the guest beers.
🏚 Q ⏚ ❀ ◖ ▶

Milford

Red Lion
Old Portsmouth Road (A3100)
☎ (0483) 424342
11–3, 5–11 (11–11 Sat)
**Gale's XXXL, BBB, Best
Bitter, 5X, HSB** H
Pub where a quiet and roomy
saloon bar contrasts with a
smaller boisterous public bar.
Separate restaurant; large
garden.
❀ 🏚 ◖ ▶ ⧄ & ♣ P

Mytchett

Miners Arms
2 Mytchett Road (A321)
☎ (0252) 544603
12–11
**Courage Best Bitter;
Wadworth 6X** H
A 'village' pub with a good
local atmosphere: a spacious
saloon of split-level design
with much polished wood.
Quiz night Thu. B&B in an
adjacent guest house. No food
Tue eve.
🏚 ❀ 🏚 ◖ ▶ ⧄ ♣ P

New Haw

White Hart
New Haw Road (A318)
☎ (0932) 842927
11.30 (11 Sat)–3, 5.30 (6 Sat)–11
**Courage Best Bitter,
Directors; John Smith's
Bitter** H; **guest beers**
(summer)
Pleasant pub, dating from the
1850s, built on the banks of the
Wey Navigation with an
attractive canalside garden.
Q ❀ ◖ ≷ (Byfleet/New
Haw) ♣ P

Surrey

Ockley

Cricketers Arms
Stane Street (A29)
☎ (0306) 79205
11–3, 6–11
Fuller's London Pride; Hall & Woodhouse Badger Best Bitter; Ringwood Best Bitter H
One of the cheapest pubs in the area, also serving good value food. The building dates from the 16th century and has a large inglenook and Horsham flagstones. Patio with tables at the front; side garden with a fishpond.
🏚 ❀ ◖ ♣ P

Try also: **King's Arms**, Stane St (Free)

Old Oxted

Crown
53 High Street (just off A25)
☎ (0883) 717583
12–2.30, 6–11 (12–2.30, 7–10.30 Sun)
Adnams Bitter; Fuller's London Pride; Pilgrim Talisman H; guest beer
Pub so-called because it used to be on the crown of the hill. Bars on two levels, the upper one has a restaurant, fine Victorian pine panelling and *Play School* windows. On the third storey is a children's room. Floodlit petanque in the safe garden. ☎ ❀ ◖ ▶ ≠ ♣

Try also: **George** (Free)

Outwood

Dog & Duck
Prince of Wales Road
OS313460 ☎ (034 284) 2964
11–11
Hall & Woodhouse Badger Best Bitter, Hard Tackle, Tanglefoot, Gribble Reg's Tipple; Shepherd Neame Bishops Finger; Wadworth 6X H; guest beers
Friendly rural pub serving good food in the bar and restaurant. Traditional games include Ring the Bull. Quiz night Sun. 🏚 ❀ ◖ ▶ ♣ P

Oxshott

Bear
Leatherhead Road (A244)
☎ (0372) 842747
11–3, 5.30–11
Young's Bitter, Special, Winter Warmer H
Open-plan pub with a large conservatory, where children are allowed. Comfortably appointed, with a friendly atmosphere. The extensive menu of home-cooked food changes daily (no meals Sun eve). 🏚 Q ☎ ❀ ◖ ▶ ♿ P

Puttenham

Good Intent
62 The Street (off B3000)
☎ (0483) 810387
11–3, 6–11 (11–11 Sat)
Courage Best Bitter; Wadworth 6X; guest beer
The guest beer changes every two months at this village local which dates from the 16th century. The saloon is beamed and features a huge fireplace. Handy for the North Downs Way. 🏚 Q ❀ ◖ ▶ ♣ P

Redhill

Hatch
44 Hatchlands Road (A25)
☎ (0737) 764593
11 (12 Sat)–3, 5.30 (6.30 Sat)–11
Greene King IPA, Rayments Special, Abbot H; guest beers
Former 17th-century forge, renovated to expose original beams. The Edwardian theme is more tasteful than most. Over a hundred guest beers in the first year (four always available), plus Belgian bottled beers and a house beer brewed by British Oak (ABV 6.5%). No lunches weekends. ❀ ◖ ♣

White Lion
40 Linkfield Street (off A25)
☎ (0737) 764045
11–3, 5 (6 Sat)–11
Greene King IPA, Rayments Special, Abbot H
Traditional back-street local which has several rooms on different levels. Sympathetic renovation makes one aware of the age of the building – the oldest in town. Notice the windows. Weekday lunches.
❀ ◖ P

Try also: **Home Cottage**, on A25 (Young's)

Reigate

Yew Tree
99 Reigate Hill (A217)
☎ (0737) 244944
11–11
Courage Best Bitter, Directors; John Smith's Bitter; Wadworth 6X H
Wood-panelled pub halfway up Reigate Hill. Popular with business people working late at the office. Oversized glasses used. Food all day. ❀ ◖ ▶ P

Try also: **Black Horse**, West St (Allied)

Ripley

Seven Stars
Newark Lane (B367, 1/2 mile W of Ripley) ☎ (0483) 225128
11–3, 5.30–11
Ind Coope Benskins Best Bitter, Burton Ale; Tetley Bitter H; guest beers

FOOD OK

Imposing 30s-style building in a rural setting close to the Wey Navigation. Handy for a drink, meal and river walk. The licensee is keen on automobile matters. Q ❀ ◖ ▶ P

Shepperton

Barley Mow
67 Watersplash Road (off B376) ☎ (0932) 225580
11–11
Courage Best Bitter; Wadworth 6X; Webster's Yorkshire Bitter H; guest beer
Bustling open-plan pub which retains a traditional local atmosphere through its several distinct areas. Frequently-changed guest beer. 🏚 ❀ ⬥ ◖ ♣ P

Three Horseshoes
131 High Street (B376)
☎ (0932) 225726
11–11
Courage Best Bitter, Directors H; guest beer
Small pub with a big welcome and an interesting display of old advertising posters. The guest beer changes weekly.
🏚 ❀ ◖ ≠ ♣ P

Shere

Prince of Wales
Shere Lane ☎ (048 641) 2313
11–2.30, 6–11
Young's Bitter, Special, Winter Warmer H
Raised pub on the edge of a delightful village apparently fixed in a 1950s time warp. Ideal for a local stroll or as a stop-off for the more serious walker. The small public bar is dominated by a pool table and the saloon is more geared to eating (eve meals Wed–Sat). Excellent children's room.
🏚 Q ☎ ❀ ◖ ▶ ⬥ ♣ P

Sidlow Bridge

Three Horseshoes
Irons Bottom Road (off A217)
OS249463 ☎ (0293) 862315
12–2.30 (3 Sat), 7–11
Fuller's London Pride, ESB; Greene King IPA H; guest beer
Small rural ale house, dating from the 17th century when it was a coaching stop on the London to Brighton run. Helicopters very welcome, but not motorcyclists. The London Pride quality is a local legend.
Q ❀ ◖ ♣ P

Smithbrook

Leathern Bottle
On A281 ☎ (0483) 274117
11–2.30 (3 Sat), 6–11
King & Barnes Sussex, Broadwood, Old, Festive H

272

Surrey

Large 18th-century, roadside pub with a modern but pleasant interior. Doubles as the local tourist information point. ♨ Q ❀ ◑ ▣ & ◡ P

Staines

Blue Anchor
13–15 High Street
☎ (0784) 452622
11–11
Ruddles Best Bitter; Wadworth 6X; Webster's Yorkshire Bitter Ⓗ
Deservedly popular town-centre pub, a listed building which retains its window-tax frontage. Music most eves, pleasing a wide variety of tastes. ♨ ❀ ◄ ◑ ▣ & ⇌ P

Wheatsheaf & Pigeon
Wheatsheaf Lane (off B376)
☎ (0784) 452922
11–3, 5–11 (11–11 Sat)
Courage Best Bitter, Directors Ⓗ**; guest beers**
Pleasant pub near the riverside to the south of the town. The floral display in summer is remarkable. Excellent food – Sun lunch a speciality. Q ❀ ◑ ▶ &

Stanwell

Wheatsheaf
Town Lane (B378)
☎ (0784) 253372
11–11 (11–4, 7–11 Sat)
Brakspear Special; Courage Best Bitter, Directors Ⓗ
Good basic, traditional pub, popular with locals.
❀ ◑ ▣ ♣ P

Sunbury

Flower Pot
Thames Street ☎ (0932) 780741
11–11
Draught Bass; Brakspear Mild, Special; Greene King IPA; Tetley Bitter; Young's Special Ⓗ
Quiet, friendly village local overlooking the Thames. A rare outlet for real mild.
Q ◄ ◑ ▶ & ♣ P

Thames Ditton

Crown
Summer Road (off A309)
☎ (081) 398 2376
11–11
Ruddles County; John Smith's Bitter; Webster's Yorkshire Bitter Ⓗ**; guest beer**
Although the building only dates from 1925, there has been a pub here since 1700. Note the two impressive fireplaces. The guest beer is changed about every fortnight. Beware the keg Courage Best. Eve meals till 7pm (not Sun).
♨ ◑ ▶ ⇌ ♣ P

Red Lion
85 High Street
☎ (081) 398 8862
11–3, 5.30–11
Courage Best Bitter; Fuller's London Pride; Webster's Yorkshire Bitter Ⓗ**; guest beer**
A friendly one-bar pub and restaurant near the river and church. No meals Sun eve. May sometimes have a different guest instead of Fuller's. Q ❀ ◑ ▶ ⇌ ♣ P

Tongham

White Hart
76 The Street ☎ (025 18) 2419
11–3, 5.30–11 (11–11 Fri & Sat)
Courage Best Bitter; Fuller's London Pride; John Smith's Bitter; Young's Special Ⓗ
Attractive, rambling local, busy and convivial. Mixed clientele with many local clubs and societies using its distinct bars. ❀ ◑ ▣ ♣ P

Walton on the Hill

Chequers
Chequers Lane (B2220)
☎ (0737) 812364
11–3, 5.30–11 (11–11 Fri & Sat)
Young's Bitter, Special, Winter Warmer Ⓗ
First licensed in 1815, one of the two original inns in the village. Once contained a brewhouse and bakehouse. A large, friendly pub with one bar, but four areas, including a large public bar area. Barbecues Easter to October. Boules pitch in a garden with slide and swings.
♨ Q ❀ ◑ & ♣ P

Try also: Bell (Charrington)

Warlingham

White Lion
3 Farleigh Road (B269 jct)
☎ (0883) 624106
11–3, 5.30 (6 Sat)–11
Draught Bass; Charrington IPA; Young's Special Ⓗ
A pub for 300 years although the building dates from 1476. The attractive feature is a network of interconnected drinking areas with low beams, cosy corners and much wood panelling. The enclosed garden provides a pleasant alternative. ♨ Q ❀ ◑ ♣ P

Westcott

Cricketers
Guildford Road (A25)
☎ (0306) 883520
11–3, 5.30–11
Adnams Bitter; Fuller's London Pride; Hall & Woodhouse Badger Best Bitter, Tanglefoot; Pilgrim SPA Ⓗ

Single, three-level bar with a small top area mainly for food, the middle having darts and most of the seating, while the bottom houses a pool table. Mixture of locals, passing trade and regulars from further afield. Competitively priced for the area. No eve meals Mon or Wed. ❀ ◑ ♣

Try also: Crown, Guildford Rd (Friary Meux)

Weston Green

Alma Arms
Alma Road (off A309)
☎ (081) 398 4444
11–2.30 (3 Fri & Sat), 6–11
Courage Best Bitter, Directors Ⓗ
Former hunting lodge with an oak-beamed interior. Overlooks a picturesque green and pond, and features mementoes of a Crimean war battle, from which the pub takes its name. Tenth year in this *Guide*.
Q ❀ ◑ ⇌ (Esher) ♣ P

Weybourne

Running Stream
66 Weybourne Road (B3007)
☎ (0252) 23750
11–3, 6–11
Morland Bitter, Old Masters, Old Speckled Hen Ⓗ
Single-bar, roadside pub with a friendly local atmosphere, presided over by a licensee of long standing. No food Sun.
Q ❀ ◑ P

Weybridge

Old Crown
83 Thames Street (off A317)
☎ (0932) 842844
10.30–2.45 (3.30 Sat), 5–11
Courage Best Bitter, Directors; Young's Special Ⓗ
16th-century riverside pub with a weatherboarded facade. The interior is divided into several rooms with different atmospheres. Food at all times – fresh fish a speciality. Q ❀ ◑ ▶ ♣ P

Prince of Wales
11 Cross Road, Oatlands (off A3050) ☎ (0932) 852082
11–11
Adnams Bitter; Fuller's London Pride; Tetley Bitter; Wadworth 6X; Whitbread Boddingtons Bitter Ⓗ
Popular, cosy pub with traditional decor. No fruit machines or other noisy games to spoil the atmosphere. The restaurant is used for bar meals at lunchtime and full menus in the evening (not Sun eve). Good value food. Q ❀ ◑ ▶ P

Surrey

Windlesham

Bee Inn
School Road (B386, 50 yds from A30) ☎ (0276) 73359
11–11
Courage Best Bitter, Directors; Everards Tiger; Gale's HSB H
Pleasant pub with a strong local following and a good reputation for food. The only 'Bee' in the country. Punch & Judy shows in summer.
Q ❀ ◑ ▲ ♣ P

Wotton

Wotton Hatch
Guildford Road (A25)
☎ (0306) 885665
11–2.30, 5.30–11 (11–11 Sat)
Fuller's Chiswick, London Pride, Mr Harry, ESB H
One of few pubs in this area with a separate public bar offering lower prices. Food only in the saloon which is mainly for dining and has a conservatory. Large, safe garden with children's play area. ❀ ❀ ◑ ◘ ♣ P

Wrecclesham

Bat & Ball
Bat & Ball Lane, Boundstone OS833445 ☎ (025 125) 2108
12–11
Fuller's London Pride; Hook Norton Best Bitter; Whitbread Boddingtons Bitter; Young's Bitter, Special H
Out of the way free house with good family facilities. Excellent meals all week. The range of beers may vary. Worth finding. ❀ ❀ ◑ ♣ P

Sandrock
Sandrock Hill Road (off B3384) ☎ (0252) 715865
11–2.30, 5.30–11 (11–11 Sat)
Batham Mild, Best Bitter; Brakspear Bitter; Holden's Bitter; Whitbread Boddingtons Bitter; Worldham Old Dray H
Unsurpassed for quality and selection, a veritable beer festival. Provides all the essential elements for the serious beer drinker; a functional but comfortable, no-frills pub with bar billiards and a good selection of Black Country beers. Usually eight beers available at any one time. No food Sun.
❀ Q ❀ ♣ P

CAMRA GOES INTERNATIONAL

As Roger Protz declares elsewhere in this book, good beer is more than just a British concept. On a whole range of issues affecting pubs and the brewing industry decisions are now being taken by the powers-that-be in Europe, rather than in Britain.

Take, for instance, the EC proposal to tax cider as wine, which would have closed down the UK cider industry. CAMRA successfully opposed this crazy suggestion.

CAMRA is a founder member of the European Beer Consumers Union, which brings together independent, voluntary, beer consumer groups from across Europe. The other members of EBCU are OBP (Belgium), PINT (the Netherlands), and SO (Sweden). The EBCU has already put proposals to the European Commission on matters such as labelling and a sliding scale of excise duty to help smaller brewers.

CAMRA has also been active in the wake of the dramatic changes in Eastern Europe. We were alarmed by news that the world famous Budweiser Budvar brewery in Czechoslovakia might fall into the hands of Anheuser-Busch (brewers of American Budweiser and the largest brewery in the world). A world classic beer (albeit a lager) was under threat.

The future of Budvar remains uncertain, but CAMRA's campaign across the Continent has at least raised the issues of brewery independence, at a time when the international combines are poised to pounce.

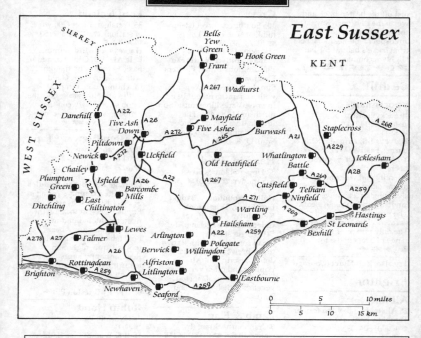

East Sussex

SURREY

Bells
Yew
Green
Hook Green

KENT

Frant

Wadhurst

WEST SUSSEX

Danehill
A22
Mayfield
Five Ash
Down
A26
A272
Five Ashes
Burwash
A21
Staplecross
A268
Piltdown
A265
A229
Icklesham
A28
Newick
A272
Uckfield
Whatlington
Battle
A259
Chailey
Old Heathfield
Plumpton
Green
A275
Isfield
A26
A267
Catsfield
A269
Telham
Ditchling
East
Chiltington
Barcombe
Mills
A271
Ninfield
Wartling
Hastings
St Leonards
Lewes
Hailsham
A269
Falmer
A273
A27
Arlington
A22
A259
Bexhill
Berwick
Willingdon
A26
Alfriston
Rottingdean
A259
Litlington
A259
Eastbourne
Brighton
Newhaven
Seaford

0   5   10 miles
0   5   10   15 km

 Harveys, Lewes

Alfriston

Market Cross/Smugglers
Waterloo Square
☎ (0323) 870241
11–3 (may extend summer), 6.30–11
Courage Best Bitter, Directors Ⓗ**; guest beer**
Attractive 12th-century village pub with two ghosts and two names. Lots of drinking areas create a warm intimate atmosphere. Attractive conservatory and a small garden area. Note the large collection of early kitchen implements and watch out for the 'Devil's Step'. Q ⊛ ◑ ▶ ▲

Arlington

Old Oak Inn
Cane Heath (½ mile off Hailsham–Upper Dicker road)
☎ (0323) 482072
11–3, 6–11
Hall & Woodhouse Badger Best Bitter; Harveys BB; guest beers Ⓖ
Oak beams, an inglenook and log fires: a cosy pub with a separate restaurant. Handy for Abbots Wood and Michelham Priory. Sells Xmas trees in season. Good reputation for food (not served Sun/Mon eves). ⋈ Q ⊛ ◑ ▶ ⅃ P

Barcombe Mills

Anglers Rest
1 mile W of A26, N of Lewes
OS428150 ☎ (0273) 400270
Hours vary
Harveys BB, Old; Wadworth 6X Ⓗ**; guest beers**
Single-bar pub in a rural location near the River Ouse. Popular and extensive menu. Children's games in the garden. ⋈ ◑ ▶ ▲ ♣ P

Battle

Chequers
Lower Lake (A2100 S of town)
☎ (042 46) 2088
11–3, 6–11 (11–11 Sat)
Marston's Pedigree; Whitbread Boddingtons Bitter, Fremlins Bitter, Flowers Original Ⓗ
Smart and well-kept pub on the site of the Battle of Hastings. A 15th-century building with oak beams and a copper bar top. Caters for locals and tourists – handy for the Abbey. Family atmosphere.
⋈ ⊛ ⋈ ◑ ▶ ▲ ⇌ P

1066
High Street (A2100)
☎ (042 46) 3224
10–3, 5–11 (10–11 Fri, Sat & summer)
Wadworth 6X; Whitbread Fremlins Bitter, Flowers Original Ⓗ
Busy and lively, split-level pub near the Abbey. Very well-attended folk club, often featuring big names. Function room and restaurant upstairs. The only pub in Britain with a year as its name?
⋈ Q ⊛ ⋈ ◑ ▶ & ▲ ⇌ ♣ ✳

Try also: **Kings Head** (Courage)

Bells Yew Green

Brecknock Arms
☎ (0892) 750237
11.30–2.30, 6 (7 winter)–11
Harveys XX Mild, Pale Ale, BB, Old Ⓗ
Village pub near Tunbridge Wells, run by an active CAMRA member. Hop memorabilia and a bottle collection in the public bar; mini handpumps in the saloon. ⋈ Q ⊛ ◑ ⅞ & ⇌ (Frant) ♣ P

Berwick

Cricketers Arms
On A27, 300 yds W of Drusillas roundabout
☎ (0323) 870469
11–3, 6–11
Harveys BB, Old Ⓖ

East Sussex

Just off the beaten track and worth the finding, a low, cottage pub oozing atmosphere. Stone floors; beer from barrels behind the bar. Highly recommended.
🏚 Q 🏵 ◖▶ 🍴 ♨ ▲ ➹ ♠ P

Bexhill

Sportsman
15 Sackville Road
☎ (0424) 214214
10.30–11
Harveys BB, Armada; King & Barnes Festive; Webster's Yorkshire Bitter ⊞; guest beers
Friendly and welcoming town-centre pub in a busy shopping street. Outgoing landlady and sociable locals. The sunny and secluded garden is ideal for sunbathing. The only pub offering a decent range of beers in the town.
🏵 ◖▶ ➹ ♣ ♠

Try also: Bell Hotel (Courage)

Brighton

Albion
28 Albion Hill (behind former Tamplins brewery)
☎ (0273) 604439
10.30–11
Gale's XXXD; Whitbread Boddingtons Bitter, Strong Country, Flowers Original ⊞
Friendly, two-bar, split-level local, popular with people from all walks of life. Strongly games oriented, with two bar billiards tables. Gale's XXXD is a permanent guest beer and is the pub's biggest seller.
🏵 ♣ ♠ ⌣

Basketmakers Arms
12 Gloucester Road
☎ (0273) 689006
11–3, 5.30–11 (11–11 Fri & Sat)
Gale's XXXD, BBB, 5X, HSB ⊞
Tucked away in the back streets, a lively local worth seeking out. The interior is adorned with tins and other ephemera. Live music Sun lunch. A *Good Beer Guide* regular. ◖▶ ➹ ♣ ♠

Evening Star
55 Surrey Street (200 yds from station)
☎ (0273) 28931
11–11
Beer range varies ⊞
One-bar free house featuring bare floorboards and plain wood seating. The pictures on the walls follow a transport theme, based on the last BR steam engine built at Swindon. Pub specialities: good company, good conversation and good blues music. A continually changing range of nine beers always includes a mild. 🏵 ◖▶ ➹ ⌣

Greys
105 Southover Street (steep hill E of 'The Level')
☎ (0273) 680734
11–3, 5.30–11 (11–11 Sat)
Adnams Bitter; Whitbread Boddingtons Bitter, Flowers Original ⊞
Simple, single-bar, corner pub with a characterful but basic interior. Varied live music Sun lunch and Mon eve. The imaginative menu includes vegetarian meals (no food Sun). Q 🏵 ◖▶ ♠

Hand in Hand
33 Upper St James Street, Kemptown ☎ (0273) 602521
11–11
Hall & Woodhouse Badger Best Bitter, Tanglefoot; Kemptown Mild, Bitter, Celebrated Staggering Ale, SID ⊞; guest beers
Small corner pub with its own tower brewery. The decor defies description! Always popular and often very busy. Home-made meals include vegetarian dishes (no food Sun). ◖

Lamb & Flag
9 Cranbourne Street (by Churchill Sq) ☎ (0273) 26415
10.30–11 (closed Sun)
Fuller's London Pride; Welsh Brewers Worthington BB ⊞
Town local, busy at lunchtime. Its proximity to the main shopping centre leads to a good passing trade. The popular and friendly landlord's future is under threat. ➹

Lion & Lobster
24 Sillwood Street (100 yds S of Norfolk Sq)
☎ (0273) 776961
11–3, 6–11 (11–11 Sat)
Draught Bass; Exmoor Beast; Greene King Abbot; Harveys BB; Thwaites Bitter ⊞
Large, street-corner, single-bar pub with enterprising management and a good mix of customers. Regular events throughout the week; live music most weekends. The restaurant has original Victorian tiles and specialises in Thai and Malaysian dishes. The beer range changes regularly. ◖▶ ♠

Lion & Unicorn
26 Sussex Street
☎ (0273) 625555
12–2, 5–11 (11–11 Sat)
Ind Coope Burton Ale; Tetley Bitter ⊞; guest beers
One-bar enterprising local; a much improved musical pub with a panoramic view of Brighton. Growing breweriana collection. Good bar snacks.
▶ P

Lord Nelson
36 Trafalgar Street (200 yds E of station) ☎ (0273) 682150
10.30–3, 5.30–11
Harveys XX Mild (summer), Pale Ale, BB, Old, Armada ⊞
Basic two-bar pub thankfully without a jukebox. Good lunchtime food. Original settles and fireplaces; note the 'snob screen' between the drinking areas. Town-centre prices! Q ◖▶ ➹ ♠

Preston Brewery Tap
197 Preston Road (A27, outskirts of centre)
☎ (0273) 508700
11–11
Courage Best Bitter; Ruddles Best Bitter, County; Young's Special ⊞; guest beers
Popular one-bar local on the main Brighton–London road. Three regular guest beers. Pool table, darts and table football; quiz night Sun. Regular happy hours featuring real ales; occasional live music and pub events. No meals Sun eve.
🏵 ◖▶ ➹ (Preston Pk) ♠

Robin Hood
2–3 Norfolk Place
10.30–11
Hall & Woodhouse Badger Best Bitter; Harveys BB ⊞; guest beers
Popular local off Western Road, with a wide selection of guest beers. Bar billiards and darts. Quiet drinking area away from the main bar. The decor is based on Sherwood Forest. ◖ ♠

Royal Oak
46 St James's Street
☎ (0273) 699248
10.30–11
Courage Best Bitter, Directors; Young's Special ⊞
Proper local in the town centre. Two bars, both wood-panelled: pool dominates the public; the saloon is more comfortable and quiet, except on Fri and Sun eves when folk/country music takes over. Reasonable prices. No meals Fri eve. Q 🏵 ◖▶ ♠

Sir Charles Napier
50 Southover Street
☎ (0273) 601413
11–3, 6–11
Gale's XXXD, BBB, 5X, HSB ⊞
Busy, deceptively spacious corner local, with a collection of bottles, including many from defunct Brighton breweries. The full range of Gale's country wines is available. 🥃 🏵 ◖▶ ♠ ⌣

Sussex Yeoman
7 Guildford Road (150 yds W of station) ☎ (0273) 27985
10.30–11

Harveys BB; Mitchell's Best Bitter; Thwaites Bitter H**; guest beers**
Recently renovated, but not destroyed, single-bar pub with a constantly varied range of beers. Large speciality sausage menu. The landlord ran the nearby Royal Standard until recently. ◖ ⌀ ⇌

Try also: George Beard, Gloucester Rd (Beards); **Pig in Paradise**, Queens Rd (Free)

Burwash

Bell
High Street (A265)
☎ (0435) 882304
11–2.30, 6–11
Harveys BB, Old H**; guest beers**
Superb 17th-century house with plenty of history. Unusual collection of barometers and mulling irons. 1991 *East Sussex Pub of the Year* – very well deserved.
🏨 Q ☎ ❀ ⋈ ◖ ▶ ◔ P

Catsfield

White Hart
On A261 ☎ (0424) 892650
10–3, 6–11
Draught Bass; Charrington IPA; Harveys BB H
Busy village local with a warm welcome. An ideal centre for walking and rambling in beautiful and historic countryside (1066 and all that!). Big fireplace for wet winter nights. Snacks only Sun. 🏨 ☎ ❀ ◖ ▶ ▲ ♣ P

Chailey

Horns Lodge
South Street (A275)
☎ (0273) 400422
Hours vary
Greene King IPA; Harveys BB H**; guest beers**
Family-run pub with a restaurant, children's area and a large garden. Winner of pub games trophies.
🏨 ☎ ❀ ◖ ▶ ♣ P

Try also: Kings Head (Beards)

Danehill

Coach & Horses
School Lane (³/₄ mile NE of village, off A22) OS412286
☎ (0825) 740369
11–2.30, 6–11 (12–2, 7–10.30 Sat)
Greene King IPA, Abbot; Harveys BB H**; guest beers**
Sympathetically restored, bustling local in a picturesque setting. Separate restaurant; garden overlooking the valley. Cider in summer.
🏨 Q ❀ ◖ ◭ ♣ ◔ P

Ditchling

North Star
19 North End (B2112)
☎ (0273) 843402
11–2.30, 6–11 (11–11 Sat)
Draught Bass; Fuller's London Pride; Harveys BB; S&N Theakston Best Bitter; Wells Bombardier; Young's Special H
Popular free house with normally seven real ales available in two contrasting sized bars, one very small. For current ranges of beer and food see the blackboards near the bar. No food Sun.

White Horse Inn
16 West Street (20 yds W of B2116/B2112 jct)
☎ (0273) 842006
11–3, 5.30–11 (11–11 Fri & Sat)
Harveys BB H**; guest beers**
Single-bar village pub which is striving to be *the* local: a free house recently acquired from Whitbread, reputedly haunted and close to Anne of Cleves's house. The landlord also runs the Watermill at Burgess Hill.
🏨 ❀ ◖ ▶

Eastbourne

Arlington Arms
360 Seaside (A259, 2¹/₂ miles E of centre)
11–11
Harveys BB, Old H
Local with a newly added restaurant. Large garden with children's play area; quiet saloon and traditional public bar. Heavily pool and darts-oriented, with a separate snooker room – rare for this area. Bar snacks always available. Q ☎ ❀ ❀ ◭ ♣ P

Hurst Arms
76 Willingdon Road (A22, 1¹/₂ miles N of centre)
☎ (0323) 21762
11–3, 6–11
Harveys XX Mild (summer), **BB, Old, Armada** H
Traditional, red-brick Victorian local named after a former windmill. Always busy public bar and quieter saloon: a continuous *Good Beer Guide* entry since 1978, offering the best quality Harveys for miles and the best value filled rolls in town. Also sells Harveys' commemorative brews when available. ❀ ◭ ♣

Lamb Inn
High Street (A259, 1 mile N of centre) ☎ (0323) 20545
10.30–3, 5.30–11
Harveys XX Mild (summer), **BB, Old, Armada** H
Harveys' showpiece in the oldest part of town, featuring a half-timbered exterior. Full

of antique furniture. A secret passageway connected the pub's 12th-century crypt with a nearby church. Handy for the art gallery, museum and Gildredge Park. Popular with locals and students. Tiny car park. Q ☎ ◖ ▶ ◭ P

Maxims
53 South Street (near town hall) ☎ (0323) 21713
11–11
S&N Theakston Best Bitter; Young's Bitter, Special H
Smart, sophisticated town-centre café-bar, a million miles from your typical back-street local and not beloved of traditionalists: a basement tapas bar, ground-floor bar and first-floor restaurant. Food is highly recommended and good value. Unusual beers for the area. ◖ ⇌

Try also: **Porthole**, Cornfield Tce (Free)

East Chiltington

Jolly Sportsman
Chapel Lane (off B2116)
OS372153
☎ (0273) 890400
11.30–2.30, 6 (7 winter)–11 (closed Mon all year and Tue lunch in winter)
Harveys BB; Shepherd Neame Master Brew Bitter H**; guest beers** (summer)
A true centre of village life: a pub well off the beaten track, with good views of the South Downs and Sussex Weald. Popular with ramblers. Separate areas for dining and pool. Meals served Wed–Sat.
❀ ◖ ▶ ♣ P

Falmer

Swan
Middle Street, North Falmer
☎ (0273) 681842
11–2.30, 6–11
Palmers BB, Tally Ho!; Shepherd Neame Master Brew Bitter, Bishops Finger H
Friendly, traditional village local: L-shaped saloon bar and a cosy village bar. Good spread of real ales. No food Sun. 🏨 ❀ ◖ ▶ ⇌ ♣

Five Ash Down

Firemans Arms
On old A26 N of A272 cross-roads OS477237
☎ (082 581) 2191
11–3, 6–11 (may vary – phone first)
Harveys BB; S&N Theakston Best Bitter; Younger IPA H**; guest beers**
Two-bar pub run by a steam railway enthusiast and attracting good local trade. Traction engine meet on New Year's Day.
🏨 ☎ ❀ ◖ ▶ ◭ ◔ P

East Sussex

Five Ashes

Five Ashes Inn
On A267, near Mayfield
☎ (082 585) 485
11–3, 6–11
**Greene King IPA, Abbot;
Harveys BB; Young's
Bitter** H; guest beers
Small roadside inn with an
inglenook and oak beams.
Small saloon and a tiny public
bar. Not for the
claustrophobic.
🏰 Q ⌒ ❀ ◑ ▮ ⬚ ♣

Frant

Abergavenny Arms
Frant Road (A267)
☎ (0892) 750233
11–2.30, 6–11
**Bunces Pigswill; Cotleigh
Rebellion; Fuller's ESB;
Gale's HSB; Harveys BB;
King & Barnes Broadwood** H
Sprawling country pub with
lots of beams and a warm,
friendly atmosphere. Unusual
and constantly changing range
of beers. An ale house has
been on this site since 1450
and the lounge was used as a
parish courtroom in the 18th
century, with cells in the
cellar. Haunted.
Q ❀ ◑ ▮ ♣ P

Hailsham

Grenadier
High Street ☎ (0323) 842152
11–3, 6–11
Harveys XX Mild, BB, Old H
Popular two-bar town pub.
Tastefully renovated interior:
a genuine public bar and a
popular saloon. In the same
family for over 40 years.
❀ ◑ ▮ ⬚ ♣

Hastings

First In, Last Out
14–15 High Street, Old Town
(off the Bourne)
☎ (0424) 425079
12–3, 7–11
**Adnams Broadside; Fuller's
London Pride; St Clements
Crofters, Cardinal** H
Small, friendly brew pub; a
window in the bar overlooks
the full mash brewery,
producing the cheapest beers
in the area. Alcove seating;
impressive open central
fireplace. Not to be missed.
🏰 Q ◑ ▲

Old Pump House ✓
64 George Street, Old Town
(off A259) ☎ (0424) 422016
11–3, 7–11
**Brakspear Bitter; Marston's
Pedigree; S&N Theakston
Old Peculier; Whitbread
Boddingtons Bitter** H
Originally a water pump
house, this attractive timbered
building dates from the 15th
century. Situated in a
pedestrianised street, busy
with tourists. The bar is
upstairs and busy and
popular, especially with
young people. Eve meals until
8.30pm. ➳ ❀ ◑ ▮

Royal Standard
East Beach Street, Old Town
(A259) ☎ (0424) 420163
10 (12 winter)–3, 7–11
**Shepherd Neame Master
Brew Bitter, Spitfire
(summer), Bishops Finger
(summer)** H
Compact, old two-bar pub on
the seafront, handy for tourist
attractions. Naval and military
theme inside, but watch out
for the door-operated spider
on the bar. Regular folk
evenings. 🏰 ❀ ◑ ▲ ♣

Stag Inn
14 All Saints Street, Old Town
(off the Bourne)
☎ (0424) 425734
11 (12 Mon)–3, 6 (7 Mon)–11 (11–11
Sat)
**Beer Engine Rail Ale;
Whitbread Fremlins Bitter** H;
guest beers
Ancient smugglers' pub in the
town's most picturesque
street. Boasts a smugglers'
tunnel, the unique game of
'Loggits', a small collection of
mummified cats and beermat-
catching dogs. Unusual guest
beers at reasonable prices. A
friendly welcome guaranteed.
Features a malt whisky of the
week.
🏰 Q ➳ ❀ ➦ ◑ ▮ ⬚ ▲ ♣

Hook Green

Elephants Head
On B2169 ☎ (0892) 890279
11–3, 6–11
**Harveys XX Mild, Pale Ale,
BB, Old, Armada** H
Country pub astride the
county boundary; overlooks
hop fields. Lots of nooks,
crannies and olde-worlde
charm. Thoroughly
recommended.
🏰 Q ❀ ◑ ▮ ♣ P

Icklesham

Queens Head
Parsonage Lane (off A259, just
past Oast House)
☎ (0424) 814552
11–3, 6–11 (11–11 Sat)
**Fuller's London Pride;
Greene King Abbot; Harveys
Pale Ale; Hop Back Special** H
Tile-hung country pub with a
magnificent, long mahogany
public bar and walls hung
with old farm tools. A warm
friendly atmosphere is
guaranteed. Superb views
from the quiet, rural garden.

Boules pitch outside. The beer
range often changes.
🏰 Q ❀ ◑ ▮ ⬚ ⬚ ♣ ⌂ P

Isfield

Laughing Fish
Isfield Station (off A26)
☎ (082 575) 349
11–3, 6–11
Harveys Pale Ale, BB, Old H
Village inn next to a station
converted to the Lavender
Line, near Bentley Motor
Museum and Wildfowl Park.
No food Mon eve.
🏰 ➳ ❀ ◑ ▮ ♣ P

Lewes

Black Horse Inn
Western Road (old A27)
☎ (0273) 473653
11–2.30, 6–11
**Brakspear Special; Fuller's
London Pride; Harveys BB,
Old** H; guest beers
Two-bar local, a former
coaching inn, with a secluded
lounge at the rear. Old photos
of Lewes pubs in the public
bar. Wheelchair access to
public bar only. Toad in the
Hole played. ❀ ➦ ◑ ▮ ⬚ ♣

Gardeners Arms
46 Cliffe High Street
☎ (0273) 474808
11–2.30, 5.30–11 (11–11 Sat)
Beer range varies H
Comfortable, friendly free
house, offering an ever-
changing range of eight beers.
Church-style seating;
occasional live music. A must
for real ale drinkers. Close to
Harveys brewery.
◑ ▮ ⇌ ♣ ⌂

Royal Oak
8 Station Street
☎ (0273) 474803
11–2.30, 5 (6 Sat)–11
**Adnams Broadside; Harveys
BB, Old; Wadworth 6X** H;
guest beers
Thriving, single-bar pub,
emerging from a renovated,
quiet local. Particularly busy
at weekends. Many reminders
of historic Lewes adorn the
walls. ❀ ◑ ▮ ⇌

Litlington

Plough & Harrow
On Exceat–Alfriston road
☎ (0323) 870632
11–2.30, 6.30–11
**Hall & Woodhouse Badger
Best Bitter, Tanglefoot;
Harveys BB** H; guest beers
Always an additional three
beers on, which often change,
in this smart, busy village pub
with a huge food trade. The
railway theme includes model
trains in the bar. Children's
servery and an aviary.
🏰 Q ❀ ⬚ ◑ ▮ P

East Sussex

Mayfield

Middle House Hotel
High Street
☎ (0435) 872146
11–11
Adnams Bitter; Greene King Abbot; Harveys Pale Ale; Morland Old Speckled Hen Ⓗ
Grade I listed building: a fine example of Elizabethan architecture, built in 1575 for the founder of the London Stock Exchange. Convivial atmosphere. Large inglenook which provides a weekly spit roast. Live music Sun nights.
🏠 Q ❀ 🍴 ◁ ▷ ♣ P

Rose & Crown
Fletching Street (¼ mile E of village) ☎ (0435) 872200
11–3, 5–11
Adnams Bitter; Everards Tiger; Greene King Abbot; Harveys BB Ⓗ**; guest beers**
Superb atmospheric pub still unspoilt: varied rooms at different levels and a large inglenook. Rare guest beers and good food combine to make this an excellent village local well worth seeking out.
🏠 Q ❀ 🍴 ◁ ▷ 🍴 ♣ P

Try also: Railway (Free)

Newhaven

Bridge Inn
Bridge Street
☎ (0273) 514059
11–11
Whitbread Boddingtons Bitter, Best Bitter, Flowers Original Ⓗ
Old pub which used to be Tipper's brewery (commissioned by the Prince of Wales to supply the Royal Pavilion in Brighton; his crest is still displayed above the front door). Upstairs restaurant open weekends.
🍴 ◁ ▷ ≠ (Town) ♣

Engineer
76 Railway Road, East Side (off A259) ☎ (0273) 514460
11–11
Draught Bass; Harveys BB Ⓗ
Cheerful pub used by workmen and dockers. Special evenings, eg barbecues. Animals in the garden – a pony, a lamb and rabbits. Tiny car park. Snacks available (not Sun). 🏠 ❀ 🍴 ≠ (Town/Harbour) ♣

Try also: Ark (Grand Met); Hope (Whitbread)

Newick

Royal Oak
Church Road (off A272)
☎ (082 572) 2506
Hours vary – phone first

Harveys BB; Whitbread Boddingtons Bitter, Strong Country, Flowers Original Ⓗ
Traditional, oak-beamed public bar in what used to be the manor house. Wattle and daub panel exposed in the wall between bars. Used by the cricket club. Very small garden. 🏠 ❀ ◁ ▷ 🍴 ♣ P

Try also: Crown (Beards)

Ninfield

United Friends Inn
The Green (A271)
☎ (0424) 892462
11.30–3 (not Mon), 5–11
Fuller's London Pride; Harveys BB; Ind Coope Burton Ale; Tetley Bitter Ⓗ**; guest beers**
Genuine free house: eight beers always available, including one porter or stout, and a wide range from regional and micro-breweries. Good facilities, keen prices and a warm welcome. 🏠 Q 🍴 ❀ 🍴 ◁ ▷ 🍴 ♣ P

Old Heathfield

Star Inn
Church Street (off B2096)
☎ (0435) 863570
11–3, 6–11
Gale's HSB; Harveys Pale Ale Ⓗ**; guest beers**
14th-century village local actually in the churchyard. Comfortable saloon, dining room upstairs and a cosy public bar. Resident cider-drinking ghost and award-winning garden with superb views. Folk music on Sun eve. 🏠 Q ❀ ◁ ▷ 🍴 ♣ P

Piltdown

Peacock
Shortbridge (B2102, off A272)
☎ (0825) 762463
Hours vary
Harveys BB; Larkins Bitter; Whitbread Flowers Original Ⓗ
Picturesque, upmarket oak-beamed pub with an inglenook; separate restaurant. Pleasant garden front and back. Near the site of the Piltdown Man hoax.
🏠 ❀ ◁ ▷ P

Plumpton Green

Fountain
Station Road
☎ (0273) 890294
10.30–2.30, 6–11 (may vary)
Young's Bitter, Special, Winter Warmer Ⓗ
Young's most southerly tied house; has appeared in every *Good Beer Guide*. The landlord is a well-known local

---

character who has received many awards and prizes for his pub. Large inglenook. No food Sun.
🏠 ◁ ≠ (Plumpton) ♣ P

Polegate

Dinkum
54 High Street
☎ (0323) 482029
10.30–11
Harveys BB, Old, Armada Ⓗ
Well-kept traditional pub with entirely separate public and saloon bars; adjacent games/family room. The name comes from Aussies stationed nearby in WWI – a fair dinkum boozer today too!
Q 🍴 ❀ ◁ ▷ ≠ ♣ P

Rottingdean

Black Horse
65 High Street
☎ (0273) 302581
10.30–2.30, 6–11
Harveys BB Ⓗ**; guest beers**
Three-bar, Tudor-style village local: a basic public, a large saloon and a cosy snug. Good selection of guest beers in a friendly village atmosphere. No food Sun. 🏠 Q ◁ 🍴 ♣

St Leonards

Horse & Groom
Mercatoria (off A259)
☎ (0424) 420612
11–3, 5.30–11
Courage Directors; Harveys Pale Ale, BB, Old Ⓗ
Smart, comfortable pub, decorated with sporting prints, tucked away in the heart of St Leonards. Popular and frequently busy, with a pleasant atmosphere. Q 🍴 ◁ 🍴 ≠ (Warrior Sq) ♣

Try also: Nags Head (Free)

Seaford

Beachcomber
Marine Parade
☎ (0323) 892719
11–11
Draught Bass; Charrington IPA; Hall & Woodhouse Tanglefoot; Harveys BB Ⓗ
Spacious seafront pub recently damaged by fire but now redecorated in a quiet 1940s style with little ornamentation. Live music Thu eves; disco Sun eves. No eve meals Sun/Mon in winter.
🍴 ❀ ◁ ▷ 🍴 ≠ ♣ P

Wellington Hotel
Steyne Road
☎ (0323) 890032
11–2.30 (3 Sat), 5.30–11
Harveys BB, Old; Wadworth 6X Ⓗ

279

East Sussex

Saloon decorated with old pictures, ceramics and brass. Separate games/public bar and a large function room. Hosts events such as wine tastings, curry evenings and folk nights. No electronic intrusions at lunchtimes by popular demand. No food Sun. Old Wellie house beer (ABV 4.5%, not brewed here).
🔥 Q ◐ ⊞ ♣ P

White Lion Hotel
74 Claremont Road (A259 jct)
☎ (0323) 892473
11–2.30 (3 Sat), 6–11
Harveys BB, Old; Shepherd Neame Bishops Finger Ⓗ; guest beers
Comfortable, modern bars; the games bar is off the saloon. Very food-oriented: extensive and exotic menu, plus a children's menu in the restaurant. No food Sun eve.
❀ 🛏 ◐ ▲ ⇌ ♣ P

Try also: Seven Sisters (Whitbread)

Staplecross

Cross Inn
On B2165, N of Cripps Cnr (A229) ☎ (0580) 830217
11–2.30, 6–11
Fuller's London Pride; Harveys BB; Ruddles Best Bitter Ⓗ; guest beers
15th-century local full of beams, an inglenook and a ghost! Good beer choice for the area. 🔥 Q ⊃ ❀ ♣ P

Telham

Black Horse
Hastings Road (A2100)
☎ (042 46) 3109
11–3, 6–11
Marston's Pedigree; Whitbread Fremlins Bitter, Flowers Original Ⓗ; guest beers

Attractive, weatherboarded and beamed pub with a welcoming atmosphere. An unusual feature is the skittle alley on the second floor. Also a first-floor games room and boules in summer. Always two guest beers – a deserved Guide entry for many years.
🔥 Q ❀ ◐ ▶ & ♣ P

Uckfield

Alma Arms
Framfield Road (B2102, E of town) ☎ (0825) 762232
11–2.30, 6–11
Harveys XX Mild, Pale Ale, BB, Old Ⓗ
Traditional town pub in the same family for generations: an original public bar, an enlarged saloon and a children's room. A rare opportunity to sample mild in an otherwise poor town for drinking. Weekday lunches.
Q ⊃ ◐ ⊞ & ⇌ ♣ P

Wadhurst

Greyhound
St James Square (B2099)
☎ (0892) 783224
11–3, 6–11 (11–11 Sat)
Draught Bass; Charrington IPA; Fuller's London Pride; Harveys BB Ⓗ
An inn since 1502 and the haunt of the locally famous Hawkhurst Gang in the 18th century. Cosy, welcoming atmosphere; impressive inglenook and separate restaurant. Large garden with play area.
🔥 Q ❀ ◐ ▶ & ♣ P

Wartling

Lamb in Wartling
On minor road N of roundabout E of Pevensey village ☎ (0323) 832116

11–2.30, 7–11 (11–3, 6.30–11 Sat & summer)
King & Barnes Sussex, Broadwood, Old Ⓗ
Pub next door to the church in the centre of a small village. Cosy bars with log fires in winter; separate snooker room. Always a warm welcome.
🔥 Q ⊃ ❀ ♣ P

Whatlington

Royal Oak
On A21
☎ (0424) 870492
11–3, 6–11 (closed Tue)
Harveys Pale Ale; Marston's Pedigree; Ruddles Best Bitter; Young's Special Ⓗ
Attractive country inn dating from 1490. Beams and hop festoons give a welcoming atmosphere and unusual features include an 80ft well in the bar and a list of landlords since 1509. High quality food – the landlord is also a butcher.
🔥 Q ❀ ◐ ▶ ♣ P

Willingdon

Red Lion
99 Wish Hill (just off A22)
☎ (0323) 502062
11–2.30, 5.30–11 (12–2.30, 7–10.30 Sun)
King & Barnes Sussex, Broadwood, Old, Festive Ⓗ
Pleasant local in a small village at the foot of the downs. Much improved since escaping the clutches of Watneys. Friendly atmosphere. The model for the pub in Animal Farm, written by Orwell whilst staying in the village. No food Sun.
❀ ◐ ▶ ♣ P

Try also: Wheatsheaf (Courage)

STAPLEFIELD
JOLLY TANNERS 94 (GOOD FOOD)

The Symbols

🔥 real fire

Q quiet pub (at least one bar)

⊃ indoor room for children

❀ garden or other outdoor drinking area

🛏 accommodation

◐ lunchtime meals

▶ evening meals

⊞ public bar

& easy wheelchair access

▲ camping facilities at the pub or nearby

⇌ near British Rail station

⊖ near underground station

♣ pub games

⇌ real cider

P pub car park

⊁ no-smoking room or area

West Sussex

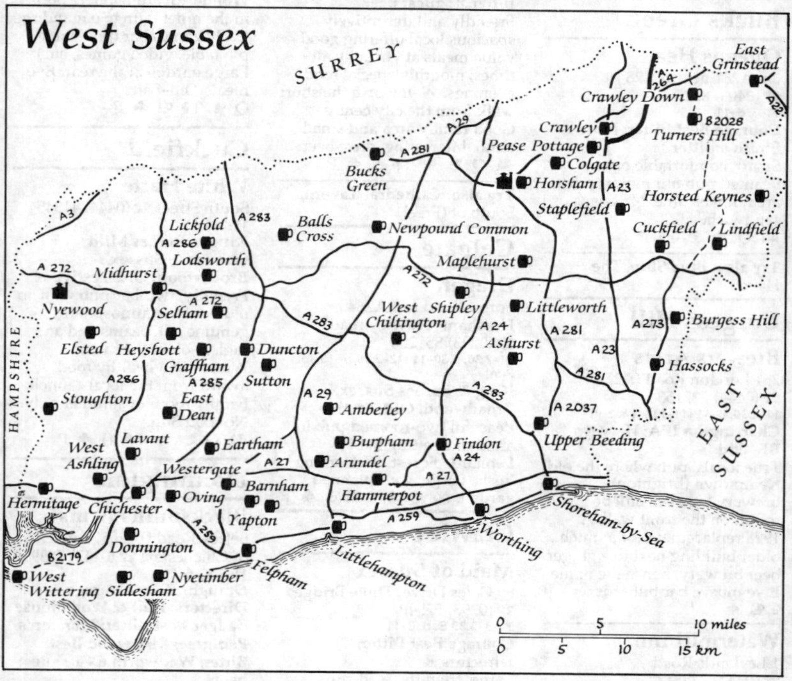

Ballard's, Nyewood; **King & Barnes**, Horsham

Amberley

Black Horse

High Street (off B2139)
☎ (0798) 831552
11–3, 6–11
Ind Coope Friary Meux Best Bitter, Burton Ale [H]
Fine example of an unspoilt, two-bar village local, near the Industrial Museum and South Downs Way.
♨ Q ⛐ ❀ ◑ ◐ ⊟ ♿ ♣

Arundel

Eagle

41 Tarrant Street
☎ (0903) 882304
11–3, 5.30–11 (11–11 Sat)
Fuller's London Pride; Young's Special [H]**; guest beers**
Welcoming half-panelled local in a side street below the cathedral and castle. The beer range changes regularly. Downstairs bistro/restaurant open in summer (eve pub meals Christmas–Easter).
♨ ◑ ◐ ⇌ ♣

Swan Hotel

High Street ☎ (0903) 882314
11–11
Courage Directors; Hall & Woodhouse Badger Best Bitter, Tanglefoot [H]**; guest beers**
Pleasant one-bar hotel in the historic town centre. Three guest beers always available; occasional live music at weekends. ⛼ ◑ ◐ ♿ ⇌

White Hart

High Street ☎ (0903) 882374
11–3, 5.30–11 (11–11 Sat)
King & Barnes Sussex, Festive [H]**; guest beers**
Popular pub whose small frontage belies a roomier interior. Extensive range of guest ales (usually three on). Upstairs rooms are used for shows by the Drip Action Theatre Co. ♨ ❀ ◑ ◐ ⇌ ♣

Ashurst

Fountain

On B2135, S of Partridge Green ☎ (0403) 710219
11–2.30, 6–11
King & Barnes Broadwood, Old; Whitbread Fremlins Bitter, Strong Country [H]**, Flowers Original; guest beers** [G]
16th-century village pub with an inglenook, oak beams, stone floor and adjacent duck pond. Good food (vegetarian and children's menu). Up to four guest beers.
♨ Q ⛐ ❀ ◑ ◐ ⊟ ▲ ♣ P

Balls Cross

Stag

Off A283 near Kirdford
OS987263 ☎ (0403) 77241
11–3, 6–11
King & Barnes Mild (occasionally), Sussex, Broadwood, Old, Festive [H]
Welcoming village local with a stone floor, low ceilings and an inglenook. Also serves as a polling station. No eve meals Sun; Sun lunch in summer only. ♨ Q ⛐ ❀ ◑ ◐ ⊟ ♿ P

Barnham

Murrell Arms

Yapton Road (by station)
☎ (0243) 553320
11–2.30, 6–11 (11–11 Sat)
Gale's BBB, Best Bitter [G]**, HSB** [H]
Three-bar local laden with drinking memorabilia. Antique auctions are held alternate Wed. Live music every Thu night and the penultimate Sun of the month. Ring the Bull played. SE CAMRA *Pub of the Year* 1990.
♨ Q ❀ ◑ ◐ ⊟ ▲ ⇌ ♣ P

West Sussex

Bucks Green

Queens Head
On A281 near B2128 jct
☎ (0403) 82202
11–3, 6–11
Courage Best Bitter; John Smith's Bitter H
Smart, comfortable oak-beamed pub but motorcyclists are not welcome. No crisps or sandwiches.
🎱 Q 🍽 🏵 ◐ ▶ P

Try also: Blue Ship, The Haven

Burgess Hill

Brewers Arms
251 London Road (A273)
☎ (0444) 232153
11–2.30, 6–11 (11–11 Fri & Sat)
Charrington IPA; Harveys BB, Old H
True locals' pub where the old Kemptown (Brighton) brewery logo can still be found on the front wall. A 1928 replacement for a much older building next to a ginger beer brewery, hence the name. Live music; bar billiards.
◐ 🍺 ♣

Watermill Inn
1 Leylands Road
☎ (0444) 235517
11–11
Courage Best Bitter; Webster's Yorkshire Bitter H; **guest beers**
Comfortable pub in the World's End area of town. Although converted to a single bar some years ago, there is still a very much local, public bar area at one end. Two guest beers. The landlord also runs the White Horse, Ditchling (Free). 🎱 🏵 ◐ ▶ ⇌ (Wivelsfield) 👃 P

Burpham

George & Dragon
Off A27, 2 miles NE of Arundel OS039089
☎ (0903) 883131
11–2.30, 6–11 (closed Sun eve in winter)
Courage Directors; Harveys BB; Ruddles County H; **guest beers**
Popular free house in a pleasant village. Regular changes to the menu and beer range. Good base for walks on the downs or in the Arun valley. No eve meals Sun.
🏵 ◐ ▶ P

Chichester

Rainbow
56 St Pauls Road (B2178)
☎ (0243) 785867
10–11
Ind Coope Friary Meux Best Bitter, Burton Ale; Tetley

Bitter H; **guest beer**
Friendly and deceptively spacious local offering good value meals at virtually all times; monthly special food evenings. Well worth the short walk from the city centre. Good family area and small patio. Interesting guest beers.
🎱 Q 🍽 🏵 ◐ ▶ 👃 P

Try also: Cathedral Tavern, South St (Free)

Colgate

Dragon
Forest Road (off A264, Horsham–Crawley road)
☎ (0293) 851206
11–2.30, 5.30–11 (12–2.30, 7–10.30 Sun)
King & Barnes Sussex, Broadwood, Old, Festive H
Peaceful two-roomed pub in an idyllic setting in St Leonards Forest. Welcoming hosts. Large, well-planned garden. 🎱 Q 🏵 ◐ 🍺 👃 ♣ P

Crawley

Maid of Sussex
89 Gales Drive, Three Bridges
☎ (0293) 525404
11–3 (3.30 Sat), 6–11
Courage Best Bitter, Directors H
Large, friendly, well-run estate pub offering simple food Mon–Sat. Imperial Russian Stout stocked. Has been in this guide for over ten years. 🍽 🏵 ◐ ▶ 🍺 ⇌ (Three Bridges) ♣ P

Plough
Ifield Street, Ifield
☎ (0293) 524292
11–3 (4 Sat), 6–11
King & Barnes Sussex, Broadwood, Old, Festive H
Traditional village local now on the edge of town, next to the old church and Ifield Barn Theatre. Food is basic but very good value (not served Sun lunch).
Q 🏵 ◐ ▶ 🍺 ⇌ (Ifield) ♣

White Hart
High Street ☎ (0293) 520033
11–11
Harveys Pale Ale, BB, Old H
Friendly, two-bar town-centre pub which can be quite busy. Good value weekday lunches.
🏵 ◐ 🍺 ⇌ ♣ P

Crawley Down

Royal Oak
Grange Road (off B2028)
☎ (0342) 713170
11–3, 5.30–11 (11–11 Thu–Sat)
King & Barnes Sussex; Ind Coope Friary Meux Best Bitter, Burton Ale; Tetley Bitter H
Quaint, traditional village local in a quiet, remote village.

Wonderful atmosphere both in the quiet lounge bar and the lively games bar (pool table, pin table, video games, etc.). Large garden at the rear. Eve meals Thu–Sat.
Q 🏵 ◐ ▶ 🍺 ♣ P

Cuckfield

White Harte
South Street ☎ (0444) 413454
11–3, 6–11
King & Barnes Mild (summer), Sussex, Broadwood, Old, Festive H
Friendly, two-bar pub with an olde-worlde atmosphere; genuine oak beams and an inglenook in the saloon. Winner of a healthy food award from the local council. Family room in summer only. No food Sun.
🎱 Q 🍽 🏵 ◐ ▶ 🍺 ♣ P

Donnington

Blacksmiths Arms
Selsey Road (B2201, 2 miles S of Chichester) ☎ (0243) 783999
11–2.30, 6–11
Draught Bass; Courage Directors; Hall & Woodhouse Badger Best Bitter; Marston's Pedigree; Ringwood Best Bitter; Wadworth 6X H; **guest beers**
An intriguing collection of antique bric-a-brac festoons the interior of this rural free house, noted for its food (not served Sun eve). Nice garden with play equipment. Ringwood Best is sold as 'Blacksmiths Bitter'.
🎱 🏵 ◐ ▶ ♣ P

Duncton

Cricketers
On A285 ☎ (0798) 42473
11–3, 6–11 (11–11 Sat in summer)
Ind Coope Friary Meux Best Bitter, Burton Ale H; **guest beers**
Pleasant downland village local, a Grade II listed pub with cricketing memorabilia and a pianola in the bar. Children welcome in the restaurant; weekend barbecue lunches in summer. No eve meals Sun/Mon in winter.
🎱 🏵 ◐ ▶ 👃 ♣ P

Eartham

George Inn
OS938094 ☎ (0243) 65340
11–3, 6–11
Courage Directors; S&N Theakston Best Bitter, Old Peculier H; **guest beer**
Downland pub with a restaurant; families welcomed. House bitter Eartham Ale (not brewed here).
🎱 Q 🏵 ◐ ▶ 🍺 ♣ P

East Dean

Hurdlemakers

$1^1/_2$ miles E of A286 at
Singleton ☎ (024 363) 318
11–2.30 (3 Sat), 6–11
**Adnams Bitter; Ballard's
Wassail; Courage Directors;
King & Barnes Festive;
Ruddles Best Bitter;
Webster's Yorkshire Bitter** ⒽA;
guest beers
Friendly, well-run free house
in the centre of this South
Downs village; walkers
welcome. Excellent garden
with covered patio. Good
range of food and good access
to Goodwood Racecourse and
country park. Mind the duck
crossing nearby. Wheelchair
access is via the garden.
🏾 Q ⛟ ❀ ⓓ ⓛ ⬧

East Grinstead

Dunnings Mill

Dunnings Road
☎ (0342) 326341
11.30–2.30, 5–11 (11–11 Sat)
**Draught Bass; Harveys BB;
Welsh Brewers Worthington
BB** Ⓗ
Very low-ceilinged pub on the
outskirts of town. Split-level
bars; the more established
clientele can be found in the
top bar. Watch out for the
legendary pig pen! Very
popular in summer: a well-
known and loved old house.
🏾 ⛟ ❀ ⓓ ⓔ P

Try also: **Ship**, Ship St (Free)

Elsted

Elsted Inn

Elsted Marsh (SW of
Midhurst off A272) OS834207
☎ (0730) 813662
11–3, 5.30–11
**Ballard's Trotton, Best Bitter,
Wassail; Marston's Pedigree;
Mitchell's Fortress** Ⓗ; guest
beers
Welcoming Victorian pub
which has been extensively
and tastefully refurbished.
Excellent home-made food
with imaginative dishes as
well as traditional Sussex fare.
Highly recommended.
🏾 Q ❀ ⓓ ⓛ ⬧ P

Felpham

Old Barn

Felpham Road (off A259)
☎ (0243) 821564
11–11
**Greene King Abbot;
Kemptown SID; Mitchell's
Mild, ESB** Ⓗ; guest beers
Thatched, one-bar pub at the
southern end of the main road
through the village. Close to
the sea and Butlins. Good

range of guest beers.
🏾 ❀ ⓓ ⓛ ⬧ P

Try also: **George**

Findon

Village House

Old Horsham Road
☎ (0903) 873350
10.30–11
**Hall & Woodhouse Badger
Best Bitter; Harveys BB; King
& Barnes Sussex; Ruddles
County** Ⓗ; guest beers
16th-century village local
where the bar is decorated
with racing silks from local
stables. Three guest ales.
🏾 Q ⛟ ❀ 🛏 ⓓ ⓘ P

Graffham

White Horse

OS926176 ☎ (079 86) 331
11–3, 6–11
**Bateman XXXB; Eldridge
Pope Dorchester, Hardy
Country, Blackdown Porter;
Palmers IPA** Ⓗ; guest beers
Popular family and walker's
pub situated at the foot of the
South Downs. Very popular
for Sun lunches (book). Jazz
every third Tue eve of the
month.
🏾 Q ⛟ ❀ ⓓ ⓛ ⓐ ⬧ P

Hammerpot

Woodmans Arms

On A27, Arundel–Worthing
road ☎ (090 674) 240
11–3, 6–11
**Gale's BBB, Best Bitter,
HSB** Ⓗ
Family-run 16th-century,
roadside pub with low beams,
a stone floor and a real fire.
Good food.
🏾 Q ❀ ⓓ ⓘ ⓛ ⬧ ⬦ P

Hassocks

Hassocks Hotel

Station Approach, East
Hassocks ☎ (0273) 842113
11–11
**Marston's Pedigree;
Whitbread Best Bitter,
Flowers Original** Ⓗ
Large, single-bar pub with a
hall at the rear. Very popular
with the young. Live band in
the bar Thu eve. Tea and
coffee all day; lunches 12–2.
❀ ⓓ ⇌ ⬧ P

Hermitage

Sussex Brewery

Main Road (A259)
☎ (0243) 371533
11–11
**Eldridge Pope Hardy
Country; Hall & Woodhouse
Badger Best Bitter, Hard
Tackle, Tanglefoot; Marston's
Pedigree** Ⓗ; guest beers

Friendly local – like all pubs
used to be! A small pub with
plenty of atmosphere.
Sausage, mash and beans are
popular. 🏾 Q ❀ ⓓ ⓘ
⇌ (Emsworth) ⬧ P

Try also: **Barleycorn,
Nutbourne** (Allied)

Heyshott

Unicorn Inn

$1^1/_4$ miles E of A286 OS898180
☎ (0730) 813486
11–2.30 (3.30 summer), 7 (6.30
summer)–11
**Ballard's Best Bitter;
Marston's Burton Best Bitter,
Pedigree** Ⓗ; guest beers
(summer)
Beautifully-situated country
pub overlooking the village
green. Popular with walkers,
being close to the South
Downs Way. Good choice of
bar meals, including
vegetarian (no meals Mon
eve). Dog-owner friendly!
🏾 Q ❀ ⓓ ⓘ ⬧ P

Horsham

Bedford

Station Road ☎ (0403) 253128
11–11, (11–4, 6–11 Sat)
**Fuller's London Pride;
Whitbread Strong Country,
Flowers Original** Ⓗ; guest
beers
Large and welcoming, street-
corner pub with two
contrasting bars. Lunchtime
snacks. 🏾 ⛟ ❀ ⓔ ⇌ ⬧ P

Boars Head Tavern

Worthing Road (B2237, 1 mile
S of centre) ☎ (0403) 254353
11–2.30, 6–11
**Eldridge Pope Dorchester,
Hardy Country, Royal Oak;
Palmers IPA; Wadworth
6X** Ⓗ; guest beers
(occasionally)
Popular, comfortable pub on
the south side of town. A good
selection of home-cooking is
always available. Dorchester
Bitter is sold as 'Boars Head
Bitter'. ❀ ⓓ ⓘ P

Dog & Bacon

North Parade (B2237, old A24)
☎ (0403) 252176
11–2.30, 6–11
**King & Barnes Mild, Sussex,
Broadwood, Old** Ⓗ
Popular pub on the north side
of town. Pub games promoted
with regular Sat quiz nights.
One dark beer always
available.
🏾 Q ⛟ ❀ ⓓ ⓔ ⓛ ⬧ P

Stout House

29 Carfax ☎ (0403) 267777
10–4 (3 Tue & Wed), 7.30–11 (closed
Tue eve)
King & Barnes Mild
(summer), **Sussex,
Broadwood, Old, Festive** Ⓗ

West Sussex

Small, friendly, traditional town-centre pub, one of King & Barnes's best. Lunchtime snacks. Can get smokey.
Q 🍴 ➤ ♣

Tanners Arms
78 Brighton Road
☎ (0403) 250527
11–3, 6–11
King & Barnes Mild, Sussex, Old Ⓗ
Popular locals' pub on the southern edge of town. Tiny lounge bar but a more extensive public bar, providing a range of traditional games. No pub sign outside – could easily be missed! Q 🏡 ➤ ♣

Try also: **Bax Castle**, near Christ's Hospital (Free)

Horsted Keynes

Green Man
The Green ☎ (0825) 790656
11–2.30 (3 Sat), 6–11
Harveys BB Ⓗ**; guest beers**
Railway-oriented pub on the village green: a rambling, traditional building incorporating two separate bars. A mile from the Bluebell Steam Railway.
🏚 🏡 ◑ ▶ ➤ ♣ P

Lavant

Earl of March
Lavant Road (A286, 2 miles N of Chichester) ☎ (0243) 774751
10.30–2.30, 6–11
Ballard's Best Bitter; Bateman XB; King & Barnes Festive; Ringwood Fortyniner, Old Thumper; Ruddles County Ⓗ
Roomy roadside pub with an oak-panelled interior and a splendid view of the downs from the garden. Game is prominent amongst the home-cooking; quiet dining area. Consistently the best value pub in the area. Dogs welcome. Q 🏡 ◑ ▶ ➤ ♣ ➪ P

Try also: **Royal Oak** (Gale's)

Lickfold

Lickfold Inn
2 miles N of Lodsworth, off A272 ☎ (079 85) 285
11–2.30, 6.30–10.30 (11 Fri & Sat; closed Mon eve)
Adnams Bitter; Ballard's Best Bitter; Fuller's London Pride; ESB; Hall & Woodhouse Badger Best Bitter, Tanglefoot
Fairly isolated country pub; a 15th-century building, recently renovated. A single large bar with a separate restaurant; huge inglenook.
🏚 Q 🏡 ◑ ▶ P

Try also: **Noah's Ark** Lurgashall (Greene King)

Lindfield

Linden Tree
47 High Street
☎ (0444) 482995
11–3, 6–11
Harveys BB, Old; Hook Norton Old Hooky; Greene King Rayments Special; Marston's Pedigree; Ringwood Old Thumper; Wadworth 6X Ⓗ
Small, upmarket free house with subdued lighting and shop-like bay windows, sited in a picturesque village. Friendly, though it can get very busy and rather smokey in winter. The beer range may vary. No food Sun. 🏚 ◑

Try also: **Snowdrop**, Snowdrop Lane (King & Barnes)

Littlehampton

Dew Drop
96 Wick Street, Wick (E side of A284, 400 yds S of A259)
☎ (0903) 716459
10.30–3, 5.30 (6.30 Sat)–11
Gale's XXXD, BBB, HSB Ⓗ
Ex-Henty & Constable pub built in the mid-19th century when the railways came. Fairly busy lunchtime trade. Local clubs meet in the lounge bar (including the Arun Mountaineering Club).
Q 🏡 ◑ 🍴 ♣

New Inn
5 Norfolk Road (off B2140)
☎ (0903) 713112
11–2.30, 5–11 (11–11 Sat)
Brakspear Bitter; Fuller's ESB; guest beers
Large, long coaching inn from the 1760s, once part of the Norfolk Estate. Two bars plus a games room at the rear. Eight guest beers; over 150 different beers in 15 months. Food always available.
🏚 🏡 ◑ ▶ ♣

Try also: **Foresters Arms**, Horsham Rd (Ind Coope)

Littleworth

Windmill
Littleworth Lane OS193205
☎ (0403) 710308
11–3, 5.30 (6 Sat)–11
King & Barnes Mild, Sussex, Old, Festive Ⓗ
Friendly local with a strong agricultural theme.
🏚 Q 🏡 ◑ ▶ 🍴 ♣ P

Lodsworth

Hollist Arms
☎ (079 85) 310
11–3, 6–11
Ballard's Trotton, Best Bitter; King & Barnes Sussex, Festive Ⓗ

Small village pub with a narrow bar but a more extensive restaurant. Popular with diners.
🏚 ➤ 🏡 ◑ ▶ ♣ ➤ P

Maplehurst

White Horse
Park Lane (between A281 and A272 S of Nuthurst)
☎ (0403) 891208
12 (11 Sat)–2.30, 6–11
Adnams Broadside; Brakspear Bitter, Special; King & Barnes Sussex Ⓗ**; guest beers**
Popular pub with the widest bar in Sussex in the public. Pleasant garden with a fine outlook. Conservatory reserved for non-smokers and families at lunchtime. 🏚 Q
➤ 🏡 ◑ ▶ ➤ ➪ P ✗

Midhurst

Crown
Edinburgh Square
☎ (0730) 813462
11–11
Fuller's Chiswick Ⓖ**, London Pride** Ⓗ**, ESB** Ⓖ**; S&N Theakston Old Peculier** Ⓗ**; Shepherd Neame Master Brew Bitter; Taylor Landlord** Ⓖ
Popular, traditional old pub offering an occasional spit-roast in the large fireplace. Separate restaurant and function hall. 🏚 🏡 🍴 ◑ ▶ ♣

Royal Oak
Chichester Road (1 mile S of town) ☎ (0730) 814611
11–11
Ballard's Best Bitter; Ringwood Old Thumper; Wadworth 6X; Whitbread Boddingtons Bitter, Flowers IPA, Original Ⓗ
Spacious single-bar pub with low partitions forming individual areas. Large car park; long, sloping, lawned garden with plenty of benches and tables. Look out for Dwile Flonking days in July.
🏚 🏡 ◑ ▶ P

Swan
Red Lion Street, Market Square ☎ (0730) 812853
10–11 (supper licence; 12–10.30 Sun for food)
Harveys Pale Ale, Sussex, Old, Armada Ⓗ
15th-century, split-level local with a restaurant where children are welcome. Food is available all day, except 4–5 Mon–Sat; vegetarian options. Opens at 8 for breakfasts. See the mural in the upper bar.
🏚 Q 🏡 🍴 ◑ ▶ ♣

Wheatsheaf
Rumbolds Hill (A272)
☎ (0730) 813450
11–11

King & Barnes Sussex, Broadwood, Old, Festive H
Smart, large-roomed pub with an oak-beamed interior. In a narrow road, so best approached on foot (municipal car park 200 yds north). 🏠 🎠 ❀ ◖◗

Newpound Common

Bat & Ball
Set back off B2133 OS006269
☎ (0403) 700313
11–2.30 (3 Sat), 6–11
King & Barnes Sussex, Broadwood (summer), **Old, Festive** H
Part-14th-century country pub with a flagstoned floor. Children are welcome in the large lounge area away from the bar. Friendly landlord. Good choice of food. Large pond in the garden.
🏠 Q 🍴 ❀ ◖◗ ▲ ♣ P

Nyetimber

Lion Hotel & Country Club
Nyetimber Lane
☎ (0243) 262149
11–3, 5–11 (11–11 Fri & Sat)
Courage Best Bitter, Directors; John Smith's Bitter; Ringwood Best Bitter, Old Thumper H
15th-century inn with beams a-plenty. Popular and comfortable; food is good value. Forty malt whiskies.
Q ❀ 🚷 ◖◗ ♣ P

Oving

Gribble Inn
Gribble Lane OS900050
☎ (0243) 786893
11–2.30, 6–11
Hall & Woodhouse Badger Best Bitter, Tanglefoot; Gribble Harvest Pale, Gribble Ale, Reg's Tipple H
Impressive village inn, housed in a 16th-century thatched building. Home-brewed ales are produced in a tiny brewhouse adjoining the skittle alley. Fine garden. Good bar food (not served Sun eve).
🏠 Q 🍴 ❀ ◖◗ ♿ ♣ ⏱ P ⌀

Pease Pottage

James King
Horsham Road
☎ (0293) 612261
11–2.30, 6–11
King & Barnes Sussex, Broadwood, Old, Festive H
Comfortable, one-roomed pub with adjoining restaurant areas. Close to M23.
❀ ◖◗ ♿ P

Selham

Three Moles Inn
Follow sign for Selham off A272, Petworth–Midhurst road OS935206
☎ (079 85) 303
11–2.30, 5.30–11
King & Barnes Mild, Sussex, Broadwood, Old H
Traditional country pub that is hard to find but well worth the effort. Ploughman's and sandwiches always available. Sing-song eves first Sat, and folk nights second Fri, monthly. Beware of trains suddenly appearing on the nearby disused line after long visits! 🏠 Q ❀ ♣ ▲ P

Shipley

Countryman
1½ miles SW of A24/A272 jct OS136214
☎ (0403) 741383
10–3, 5.30–11 (10–11 Tue–Sat)
Draught Bass; Young's Special H; **guest beers**
This pub's recent conversion to the free trade has done nothing to change the following which its regularly-changing menu and pleasant country setting had already gained. Good area for summer walks. 🏠 ❀ ◖◗ 🍴 ♣ P

Shoreham-by-Sea

Crabtree
6 Buckingham Road
☎ (0273) 463508
10.30–3, 5–11 (10.30–11 Sat)
Gale's BBB, Best Bitter, HSB, Prize Old Ale H
Friendly, well-run local with a beer garden and children's play area at the rear.
Q 🍴 🚷 🚲 🍴 ♣ P

Marlipins
High Street (A259)
☎ (0273) 455369
10–4.30, 5.30–11
Draught Bass; Charrington IPA; Harveys BB H
Small town pub with very low beams, 300 years-old and next to the town museum. Good food at all times (take-away pizzas). Small garden.
Q ❀ ◖◗ 🚲

Royal Sovereign
Middle Street
☎ (0273) 453518
11–11
Marston's Pedigree; Whitbread Strong Country, Pompey Royal H; **guest beers**
Original green tiles from the old United Brewery still adorn this pub which is small inside but always busy, well run and friendly. Plenty of hanging baskets. Next to a council car park. Q ❀ ◖◗ 🚲

Sidlesham

Crab & Lobster
Mill Lane (off B2145)
OS862937 ☎ (0243) 641233
11–2.30, 6–11
Gale's BBB, Best Bitter, HSB H
Splendidly positioned pub on the edge of Pagham Harbour and ideal for ornithologists. Interesting and reasonably priced menu. No piped music or machines. Book for the campsite. 🏠 Q ❀ ◖◗ ▲ P

Staplefield

Jolly Tanners
Handcross Road
☎ (0444) 400335
11–3, 5.30–11 (11–11 some summer Sats)
Fuller's London Pride; Thwaites Best Mild; Wadworth 6X H; **guest beers**
Welcoming, recently refurbished village pub with a small inglenook and a separate dining room. Overlooks the village green. Unusual choice of mild for the area. 🏠 ❀ ◖◗ 🍴 ♣ P

Try also: Victory (Free)

Stoughton

Hare & Hounds
Off B2146, through Walderton OS791107 ☎ (0705) 631433
11–3, 6–11 (11–11 Fri & Sat in summer)
Ballard's Wassail; Fuller's London Pride; Gibbs Mew Salisbury; King & Barnes Festive; Whitbread Boddingtons Bitter H; **guest beers**
Fine Sussex flint building: a welcoming, remote pub, nestling in the South Downs. Humorous posters advertise the guest beers. Local seafood features prominently on a menu which also caters for children. 18th year in the *Guide*. 🏠 Q ❀ ◖◗ 🍴 ♣ P

Sutton

White Horse
5 miles SW of Petworth, off A285 OS979152 ☎ (079 87) 221
11–3, 6–11
Bateman XB; Courage Best Bitter, Directors; Young's Bitter H; **guest beers** (occasionally)
Characterful Georgian village inn: comfortably furnished saloon but bare boards in the welcoming village bar. Popular in summer with walkers and visitors to the nearby Roman villa at Bignor. Regularly changing menu.
🏠 Q 🚷 ◖◗ 🍴 ♣ P

Turners Hill

Red Lion

Lion Lane ☎ (0342) 715416
11–3, 6–11
Harveys Pale Ale, BB, Old Ⓗ
Compact village local which
has been in this guide for
many years. Occasional live
music in the upstairs club
room but access to it can be
hair raising! Fine collection of
bottled beers in cabinets in the
upper lounge. A gem!
🏠 Q ❀ ◑ ▲ ♣

**Try also: Cowdray Arms,
Balcombe**

Upper Beeding

Bridge

High Street ☎ (0903) 812773
11–2.30 (3 Sat), 5.30–11
King & Barnes Mild
(summer), **Sussex, Old,
Festive** Ⓗ
Pub which was a friendly two-
roomed local, now three
rooms following internal
modifications. On the bank of
the River Adur; parking can
be difficult. ❀ ◑ 🍺 ♣

West Ashling

Richmond Arms

Mill Lane (400 yds W of
B2146) OS807074
☎ (0243) 575730
11–3, 5.30–11 (11–11 Sat in summer)
**Brakspear Bitter; Fuller's
Chiswick; Greene King
Abbot; Marston's Pedigree;
Whitbread Boddingtons
Bitter, Castle Eden Ale** Ⓗ;
guest beers
Convivial ten-pump, small
village free house, catering for
locals and visitors from afar.
Four guest beers and good
food. Bar billiards; skittle
alley. Near the village duck
pond. Children welcome until
9pm. Cider in summer.
🏠 Q 🛏 ❀ ◑ ▲ ♣ ⌂ P

West Chiltington

Five Bells

Smock Alley OS091172
☎ (0798) 812143
11–3, 6–11

King & Barnes Sussex Ⓗ;
guest beers
Spacious one-bar pub near the
village, with an imaginative
selection of guest ales. A rare
outlet in this area for real mild
and cider. Trad. jazz first Sun
eve of the month.
🏠 Q ❀ ◑ ▶ ⌂ P

Queens Head

The Hollows (2 miles SW of
B2139/B2133 jct) OS090185
☎ (0798) 813143
11–3, 6–11
**Wadworth 6X; Whitbread
Boddingtons Bitter, Flowers
Original** Ⓗ; **guest beers**
400-year-old two-bar pub at
the village centre, now run by
a former King & Barnes
brewhouse manager.
Collections of coins, banknotes
and bottles everywhere. Clog
and morris dancing are
specialities. ❀ ◑ ▶ 🍺 ♣ P

Westergate

Labour in Vain

Nyton Road ☎ (0243) 543173
11–2.30 (5 Fri & Sat), 6–11
**Ballard's Wassail; Bateman
XB; Greene King Abbot;
Young's Bitter, Special** Ⓗ
Friendly village pub offering a
wide range of good value bar
meals, including curries and a
vegetarian option. Thai food
eves. Popular games room.
Handy for Fontwell
Racecourse.
🏠 Q ❀ ◑ ▶ & ♣ P

West Wittering

Lamb Inn

Chichester Road (B2179, 1
mile N of centre)
☎ (0243) 511105
11–2.30, 6–11
Ballard's Best Bitter Ⓗ,
Wassail Ⓖ; **Bunces Benchmark, Best Bitter; Harveys
Old; Ringwood Fortyniner** Ⓗ;
guest beers
Old roadside inn with a
welcoming atmosphere.
Diners delight in the extensive
menu of good value, home-
made food, yet adequate
elbow room remains for the
drinkers. No meals Sun eve in
winter.
🏠 Q ❀ ◑ ▶ & ▲ P ⌀

Worthing

Old House at Home

77 Broadwater Street East
☎ (0903) 232661
10.30–2.30, 5.30 (6.30 Sat)–11
**Draught Bass; Charrington
IPA; Fuller's London Pride** Ⓗ
Genuine Sussex flint-faced
pub in Broadwater village: a
warm, comfortable saloon and
a lively public bar with a real
fire and games. No food Sun.
🏠 Q ❀ ◑ 🍺 ♣ P

Pawn & Castle

21 Rowlands Road
☎ (0903) 236232
11–2.30, 6–11 (11–11 Sat)
**Courage Directors; Harveys
BB; Whitbread Flowers
Original; Young's Special** Ⓗ;
guest beers
Small, welcoming free house
with two bars; near the town
centre and popular with
shoppers. Good selection of
guest beers. Can be noisy at
weekends. Best value lunches
in town. ◑ 🍺 ♣

Vine

High Street, Tarring
☎ (0903) 202891
11–2.30 (3 Sat), 6–11
**Bateman XB; Hall &
Woodhouse Badger Best
Bitter, Hard Tackle; Harveys
BB; Hop Back Summer
Lightning** Ⓗ; **guest beers**
Popular local in a well-
preserved village street, the
former Parsons brewery
stands at the rear. Occasional
live music. No food Sun.
Q ❀ ◑ & ⇌ (West) P

Yapton

Maypole Inn

Maypole Lane (off B2312)
OS977042 ☎ (0243) 551417
11–2.30, 5.30–11 (11–11 Sat)
**Bateman XB; Mansfield
Riding Mild; Ringwood Best
Bitter; Whitbread Flowers
Original; Younger IPA** Ⓗ;
guest beers
Excellent, welcoming pub,
worth finding. Regular mini
beer festivals. Meals are
exceptionally good value (not
served Sun or Tue eves).
🏠 Q ❀ ◑ 🍺 & ♣ P

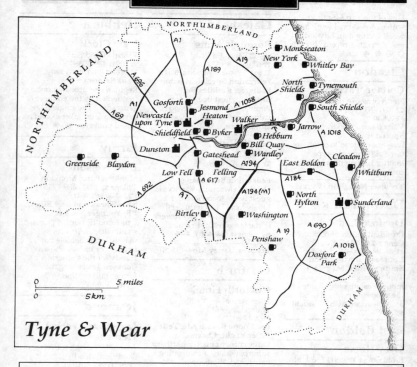

Tyne & Wear

 Big Lamp, *Newcastle upon Tyne*; **Federation**, *Dunston*; **Hadrian**, *Walker*; **Vaux**, *Sunderland*

Bill Quay

Albion Inn
Reay Street ☎ (091) 469 2418
11.30–3 (may extend), 7–11
McEwan 80/-; S&N
Theakston Best Bitter, XB;
Younger No. 3 Ⓗ
Now a one-roomer with a central bar, but distinct bar and lounge areas. Beams and lots of nick-nacks, including a mangle and a piano. Good views across the River Tyne. 🏛 ❀ ◖ ♣

Birtley

Board Inn
Portobello ☎ (091) 410 2311
11.30–3, 6–11 (11.30–11 Fri & Sat)
Big Lamp Bitter Ⓗ
Two-room pub with a bar and a split-level, food-oriented lounge. Near the Washington-Birtley service station on A1(M). ◖ ◗ 🍴 ♣ P

Blaydon

Black Bull
Bridge Street ☎ (091) 414 2846
11.30–3, 6–11
Camerons Bitter,
Strongarm Ⓗ**; guest beers**

Friendly local, convenient for bus and rail stations.
🏛 Q ❀ 🚲 ♣

Byker

Cumberland Arms
Byker Buildings, Stephen Street ☎ (091) 265 6151
11–11
Beer range varies
Basic, two-roomed boozer with an upstairs music venue/function room. Attracts a mixed clientele. Very small car park and outdoor drinking area. ❀ P

Free Trade Inn
St Lawrence Road (off A186, near Glasshouse Bridge)
☎ (091) 265 5764
11–11
McEwan 80/-; S&N
Theakston Best Bitter, XB;
Younger No. 3 Ⓗ
No frills, just good beer in a basic, split-level, single room pub. Regular live music from local bands and performers. Can get very full, but has friendly bar staff and regulars. Excellent view up the river to the bridges. 🏛 ❀

Glendale
Potts Street ☎ (091) 265 5174
11–11 (11–3, 6–11 Wed & Thu)
Draught Bass; Stones Best
Bitter Ⓗ
Two-roomed local with a friendly bar and a comfortable lounge. A former local CAMRA *Pub of the Year.*
◖ 🍴 ⊖ ♣

Ship Inn
Stepney Bank (under Byker Bridge next to City Farm)
☎ (091) 232 4030
11–11
Whitbread Boddingtons
Bitter, Castle Eden Ale,
Flowers Original Ⓗ
Small, friendly local, popular with artists and musicians from the nearby arts workshops. Unspoiled and comfortable, it hosts regular live folk music sessions. Very loyal local following.
❀ 🍴 ⊖ (Manors) ♣ P

Tap & Spile
33 Shields Road
☎ (091) 276 1440
11–11
Bateman XXXB; Marston's
Pedigree Ⓗ**; guest beers**

287

Tyne & Wear

First of the Tap & Spile chain, with exposed brickwork and wood giving it an Edwardian feel. Attracts a mixed clientele.
Q ᛘ ⊖ ♣ ○

Cleadon

Cottage Tavern
North Street (A1018)
☎ (091) 536 7883
11–3, 5.30–11
Vaux Samson, Extra Special ⒣
Busy roadside village inn. Its tasteful farmhouse-type interior is open plan but compact. ❀ ♣

Try also: **New Ship** (Vaux)

Doxford Park

Doxford Lad
President Carter Shopping Centre ☎ (091) 528 0119
11–3, 5.30–11 (11–11 Fri & Sat)
Courage Directors; John Smith's Bitter, Magnet ⒣
Typical, large, one-roomed, modern estate pub, situated in the shopping centre named after the former US president.
❀ ♣

East Boldon

Grey Horse
Front Street ☎ (091) 536 4186
11–11
Vaux Samson ⒣; **guest beer**
Large village pub, a former coaching inn, with a mock Tudor exterior. The large lounge has a welcoming atmosphere. Recent awards for its floral decor.
Q ❀ ◖ ᛘ ♣ P

Try also: **Black Horse** (Whitbread)

Felling

Old Fox
Carlisle Street
☎ (091) 438 0073
12–4, 6–11 (12–11 Fri & Sat)
Courage Directors; Ruddles County; Webster's Yorkshire Bitter ⒣; **guest beers**
Comfortable local which stages numerous events eves and weekends (quiz, discos, live music, etc). Excellent value bed and breakfast.
🚲 🛏 ◖ ⊖ ♣

Wheatsheaf
26 Carlisle Street
☎ (091) 438 6633
12–3, 7–11 (12–11 Fri & Sat)
Big Lamp Bitter, Prince Bishop Ale, Summerhill Stout ⒣; **guest beers**
One-bar traditional local, two minutes' walk from Felling Metro. The brewery's only pub. Folk night Tue.
🚲 ᛘ ⊖ ♣

Gateshead

Borough Arms
80–82 Bensham Road
☎ (091) 478 1323
11.30 (11 Sat)–3 (4 Fri & Sat), 6–11
Federation Special; Marston's Pedigree; Ruddles Best Bitter ⒣; **guest beers**
Popular pub offering good value lunches and a relaxed atmosphere. ◖ ⊖ P

North Run
Hawks Road
☎ (091) 478 6496
11–11
Federation Buchanan's Original; Morrells Varsity ⒣; **guest beers** (occasionally)
Lively local in an industrial area. Plans to set up a brewery in the large cellar. Eve meals by request. 🚲 🛏 ◖ ▶ ♣

Try also: **Barley Mow** (S&N)

Gosforth

Gosforth Hotel
High Street
☎ (091) 285 6617
11–3, 5.30–11
Ind Coope Burton Ale; Tetley Bitter ⒣; **guest beers**
Large corner pub in a northern suburb, with two contrasting bars each with its own friendly atmosphere. A former Camerons house, now Allied Tetley. ◖ ᛘ

Try also: **Earl Grey** (Vaux)

Greenside

White Swan
Main Street (B6315)
☎ (091) 413 4255
11–3, 6–11
S&N Theakston Best Bitter ⒣; **guest beers**
A warm welcome is assured at this many-roomed pub with a country feel. Toasted sandwiches available at lunchtime.
🚲 Q 🛥 ❀ ᛘ P ⊁

Heaton

Chillingham Hotel
Chillingham Road
☎ (091) 265 5915
11–11
Draught Bass; S&N Theakston Best Bitter, XB; Taylor Landlord; Tetley Bitter ⒣; **guest beers**
Two very well-furnished large rooms with decor including fittings and mirrors from a former ocean liner. Lots of good quality woodwork helps make this an above average pub refurbishment.
◖ ᛘ ⊖ (Chillingham Rd)

Hebburn

New Clock
Victoria Road East
☎ (091) 489 3556
11–3, 6–11 (11–11 Fri & Sat)
Vaux Samson ⒣
Regularly refurbished pub frequented by the younger generation. The single large bar has a loud jukebox and a raised pool area. ❀ ♣ P

Jarrow

Lord Nelson
Monkton Lane, Monkton Village ☎ (091) 489 1758
11–3 (3.30 Sat), 6–11
S&N Theakston Best Bitter, XB; Younger No. 3 ⒣
Large, multi-roomed pub in a small village. Attracts a mainly local clientele but is famous for its leek show. Handy for the Catherine Cookson Trail along the former railway line.
Q ❀ ᛘ ♣ P

Jesmond

Legendary Yorkshire Heroes
Archbold Terrace (off Sandyford Road)
☎ (091) 281 3010
11–11
Federation Buchanan's Original; McEwan 70/-; S&N Theakston Best Bitter ⒣; **guest beers**
Mellowing happily since being purchased from S&N. Twelve handpumps and an atmosphere for all tastes.
🛥 ᛘ ⊖ ⊁

Lonsdale
Lonsdale Terrace, West Jesmond (opp. Metro station)
☎ (091) 281 0039
11–11
McEwan 80/-; S&N Theakston Best Bitter, XB ⒣
A separate bar and lounge for an extremely varied clientele, plus an upstairs function room.
◖ ▶ ᛘ ⊖ (W Jesmond) ♣

Low Fell

Aletaster
706 Durham Road
☎ (091) 487 0770
11–3, 6–11 (11–11 Sat)
Bateman XXXB; McEwan 80/-; S&N Theakston Best Bitter, XB; Younger No. 3; Whitbread Boddingtons Bitter ⒣; **guest beers**
L-shaped bar in traditional style with ten handpumps. Bar skittles played. A dining area may be added. ❀ ᛘ ♿ ♣ P

Monkseaton

Shieling

Hepscott Drive, Beaumont
Park ☎ (091) 251 3408
11–3, 5–11
**S&N Theakston Best Bitter;
Tetley Bitter** H**; guest beers**
Well-decorated two-roomer
around a central bar.
⓭ ▶ ⊟ ♿ ⌂

Newcastle upon Tyne

Bacchus

High Bridge ☎ (091) 232 6451
11.30–11 (11.30–4, 7–11 Sat; closed
Sun lunch)
**McEwan 80/-; S&N
Theakston XB; Stones Best
Bitter; Tetley Bitter** H**; guest
beers**
Large, comfortable two-
roomed pub with a varied
clientele. Holds occasional
beer festivals and gets very
crowded Fri/Sat nights.
Q ⓭ ⊖ (Monument)

Bridge Hotel

Castle Garth (opp. Castle
Keep) ☎ (091) 232 7780
11.30 (11 Fri & Sat)–3, 5.30 (5 Fri, 6
Sat)–11 (12–2.40, 7–10.30 Sun)
**Draught Bass; S&N
Theakston Best Bitter** H**;
guest beers**
Imposing pub between Henry
II's castle and Stephenson's
High Level bridge. The garden
overlooks the river and city
walls. Downstairs is a live
music venue.
Q ✲ ⊟ ⇌ (Central) ⊖ ♣

Broken Doll

Blenheim Street
☎ (091) 232 1047
11–11
**S&N Theakston Best Bitter,
XB, Old Peculier** H
Still under threat from a
ludicrous road scheme and
still combining the finest in
local live music with good
beer in a unique atmosphere
of leather-clad conviviality.
✲ ⇌ (Central) ⊖

Cooperage

32 The Close, Quayside
☎ (091) 232 8286
11–11
**Ind Coope Burton Ale; Tetley
Bitter** H**; guest beers**
Medieval building with some
14th-century beams
remaining. Restaurant and a
disco on the upper floors.
Busy evenings and at
weekends. An economiser is
in use on the handpumps.
⓭ ⇌ (Central) ⊖ ♣ ⌂

Crown Posada

The Side ☎ (091) 232 1269
11–3 (4 Sat), 5.30 (7 Sat)–11 (11–11
Fri)
Butterknowle Conciliation

Ale; Hadrian Gladiator; S&N
Theakston Best Bitter; Stones
Best Bitter** H**; guest beers**
Presently CAMRA Tyneside
Pub of the Year, it boasts some
beautiful stained-glass
windows and a traditional
atmosphere. The scene of a
spiritual experience for *Beer
Hunter* Michael Jackson.
Q ♿ ⇌ (Central) ⊖

Duke of Wellington

High Bridge
☎ (091) 261 8852
11–11
**Ind Coope Burton Ale; Tetley
Bitter** H**; guest beers**
Situated in a busy
thoroughfare on the city's
fashion boutique street. Mixed
clientele; very busy evenings
and weekends. ⓭ ⇌ (Central)
⊖ (Monument)

Forth Hotel

Pink Lane
☎ (091) 232 6478
11–3, 5–11
**Ind Coope Burton Ale; Tetley
Bitter** H**; guest beers**
Popular and welcoming, L-
shaped pub with a recent
split-level extension, situated
in a lane opposite Central
Station. ⇌ (Central) ⊖

Newcastle Arms

57 St Andrews Street
☎ (091) 232 3567
11 (12 Sat)–11
**Ind Coope Burton Ale; Taylor
Landlord; Tetley Bitter** H
Refurbished, L-shaped pub
with a separate snug; friendly
atmosphere. Live music on
Thu. Please note: not to be
confused with the quayside
pub of the same name.
⓭ ⊖ (Monument)

Old George Inn

Old George Yard (off Cloth
Market) ☎ (091) 232 3956
11–11
**Draught Bass; Stones Best
Bitter** H
Newcastle's oldest inn,
attracting a varied clientele.
Two rooms on the ground
floor, including a recent split-
level extension. A three-tier
price list is in operation.
⓭ ⊖ (Monument)

Rose & Crown

164–166 City Road (opp. Tyne-
Tees TV studio)
☎ (091) 232 4724
11–11 (11–4, 6.30–11 Sat; 12–2,
7–10.30 Sun)
**Draught Bass; Butterknowle
Conciliation Ale; S&N
Theakston XB** H**; guest beer**
Excellent, friendly, two-
roomed pub. Very popular,
except with the developers
who plan to demolish it soon.
A no-frills bar and a
comfortable lounge
overlooking the river.

Interesting mirror and jug
collection. ⊟ ⊖ (Manors) ♣

Villa Victoria

144 Westmorland Road
☎ (091) 232 2460
12–3, 6–11
**Draught Bass; Stones Best
Bitter** H
Unspoilt, Victorian corner
local with an occasional
smattering of students from
the Newcastle College
opposite. An oasis in the West
Newcastle beer desert.
Q ⇌ (Central) ⊖ ♣

**Try also: Quayside, Quayside
(Vaux)**

New York

Shiremoor House Farm

Middle Engine Lane
☎ (091) 257 6302
11–11
**S&N Theakston Best Bitter,
Old Peculier; Stones Best
Bitter; Taylor Landlord** H**;
guest beers**
CAMRA award-winning
conversion of old farm
buildings into a welcoming
pub and restaurant.
Q ✲ ⓭ ▶ ♿ P

North Hylton

Shipwrights

Ferryboat Lane (off A1231,
under A19 Wear Bridge)
☎ (091) 549 5139
11–3, 7–11
**Vaux Samson; Wards
Sheffield Best Bitter** H
Pleasant riverside pub, with a
first-floor restaurant serving *à
la carte*, vegetarian and
children's meals. Twelve
consecutive years in the *Guide*.
🛏 ✲ ⓭ ▶ ♣ P

North Shields

Chainlocker

50 Duke Street, New Quay
(opp. North Shields ferry
landing) ☎ (091) 258 0147
11.30–3.30, 6–11 (11–11 Fri & Sat)
**Taylor Landlord; Tetley
Bitter** H**; guest beers**
Small and popular, with a
reputation for good food. Folk
music on Fri. 🛏 ⓭

Magnesia Bank

1 Camden Street
☎ (091) 257 4831
11–11
**Butterknowle Conciliation
Ale; Ind Coope Burton Ale;
Taylor Landlord; Tetley
Bitter** H**; guest beers**
Former workingmen's club,
now an established favourite
with local CAMRA members.
Superb function room.
🛏 ✲ ⓭ ▶ ⊖ P

Tyne & Wear

Tap & Spile
184 Tynemouth Road
☎ (091) 257 2523
11.30–3, 5.30–11 (11–11 Fri & Sat)
Ruddles County Ⓗ; guest beers
Twice winner of local CAMRA *Pub of the Year* award. The enthusiastic landlord maintains excellent standards. Weston's cider.
Ⓠ ⚬

Wolsington House
Burdon Main Row
☎ (091) 257 8487
11–11
Ruddles Best Bitter, County Ⓗ
Unspoilt Edwardian two-roomer which hosts live music Tue, Fri and Sat. Eve meals finish at 7.30pm.
♨ Q ⚬ ⚬ ◗ ⊟

Try also: **Wooden Doll** (Tetley)

Penshaw

Grey Horse
Village Green, Old Penshaw (on Penshaw Lane, off A183)
☎ (091) 584 4882
11–3 (4 Sat), 6 (5.30 Sat)–11
Tetley Bitter Ⓗ
Busy, welcoming, traditional village pub, ten years in the *Guide*. Excellent bar meals. Packed at weekends. Situated near a local landmark and folly, 'Penshaw Monument'. No food Sun. ⛫ ◗

Shieldfield

Globe Inn
2 Barker Street
☎ (091) 232 0901
11–11
Draught Bass; Stones Best Bitter Ⓗ
Two rooms frequented by a mixed group of drinkers. Very friendly; popular with students and locals alike. Comfortable but basic, housing an ever-changing art display in the lounge.
Q ⛫ ⊟ ⊖ (Manors) ♣ P

Queens Arms
1 Simpson Terrace (near Manors multi-screen cinema)
☎ (091) 232 4101
12–3, 5 (5.30 Sat)–11 (12–11 Fri)
McEwan 80/-; S&N Theakston Best Bitter, XB, Old Peculier; Younger No. 3 Ⓗ
Warm, welcoming single-room pub which displays the work of a local artist. Friendly staff and regulars create a happy atmosphere, making it popular with a wide clientele. Can get very full but is always comfortable. Not flashy, not trendy, just serving good beer. No food Sun.
♨ ⛫ ◗ & ⊖ (Manors)

South Shields

Bamburgh
175 Bamburgh Avenue (A183, coast road) ☎ (091) 454 8199
11–11
Marston's Pedigree; Whitbread Boddingtons Bitter, Trophy, Castle Eden Ale, Flowers Original Ⓗ; guest beers (occasionally)
Large coastal pub at the finish of the Great North Run route. Split-level interior and panoramic views of the coast. Hosts an annual beer festival. Occasional guest beers from Whitbread. Sun lunches summer only. ⛫ ◗ & ▲ ♣ P

Chichester Arms
Laygate (A194/B1298 jct)
☎ (091) 456 1711
11–3, 5–11 (11–11 Sat)
Ind Coope Burton Ale; Tetley Bitter Ⓗ; guest beers
Comfortable, airy pub near the shops and public transport interchange. Popular with locals; always two guest ales.
Q ◗ ⊖ (Chichester) ♣

Dolly Peel
137 Commercial Road (B1301/B1302 jct)
☎ (091) 427 1441
11–11
Bateman XXXB; S&N Theakston XB; Taylor Landlord; Younger No. 3 Ⓗ; guest beers
CAMRA award-winning pub with an excellent atmosphere. Two guest ales and an extensive whisky selection. Charismatic landlord.
Q ◗ ⊖ (Chichester) ♣

Holborn Rose & Crown
East Holborn (opp. middle dock gate) ☎ (091) 455 2379
11–11
Draught Bass; McEwan 80/-; S&N Theakston XB; Younger No. 3 Ⓗ
Open-plan, riverside pub, retaining a dockside atmosphere. Weekly live music. Off the beaten track, but worth finding. ⛫ ⊖ ♣

West Park
138 Stanhope Road (B1298, 400 yds from metro)
☎ (091) 456 3311
11–11 (11–3, 6–11 lounge)
S&N Theakston Best Bitter, XB; Younger No. 3 Ⓗ
Large roadside pub in a residential area, tastefully refurbished in a traditional manner. The excellent menu caters for children and vegetarians. Always a warm welcome. ♨ Q ◗ ◗ ⊟ ⊖ (Chichester) P

Try also: **Alum House** (Free); **Scotia** (S&N)

Sunderland: *North*

Howard Arms
183 Roker Avenue, Roker
☎ (091) 510 2559
11–11
Vaux Samson, Double Maxim; Wards Sheffield Best Bitter Ⓗ
Recent Vaux refurbishment of a former run-down Tetley house. Close to Roker Park, hence very busy on matchdays. Friendly atmosphere and enthusiastic staff. ♣

St Hilda's Parish Centre
Beaumont Street, Southwick (opp. library)
☎ (091) 549 4999
11–3 (Sat only), 7–10.30 (closed Tue)
McEwan 70/-, 80/-; S&N Theakston Best Bitter, XB, Old Peculier; Younger No. 3 Ⓗ; guest beer (occasionally)
Multi-roomed clubhouse for the local community but all are welcome. Local CAMRA branch *Club of the Year* 1991–92. Excellent value beer; regular bingo nights, quizzes, etc. Occasional guest ales; the other beers are available two at a time, in rotation.
Q ⚬ ⊟ & ♣ ⚬

Sunderland: *South*

Brewery Tap
Dunning Street
☎ (091) 567 7472
11–11
Vaux Samson, Double Maxim, Extra Special Ⓗ
Compact pub on the brewery doorstep, once an S&N house! Naturally popular with brewery staff. The walls are adorned with photographs of old Sunderland.
◗ ⊟ ≩ ♣ P

Coopers Tavern
Deptford Road, Millfield (off Hylton Rd)
☎ (091) 567 1886
11–11
Vaux Lorimers Best Scotch, Samson, Double Maxim, Extra Special Ⓗ
Pleasantly refurbished, a cask-only traditional alehouse used by the brewery as its licensee training centre. Situated just out of the city centre, serving a local community. Q ♣

Greensleeves
12 Green Terrace
☎ (091) 567 0853
12–3, 6–11 (closed Sun lunch)
Draught Bass; S&N Theakston Best Bitter, XB, Old Peculier Ⓗ; guest beers
City-centre free house in a

listed building behind the leisure centre, close to the Empire Theatre and University. Massive refurbishment planned.
❀ ◖ ≉

Saltgrass
Hanover Place, Ayres Quay, Deptford (E of Queen Alexandra Bridge on Riverside Rd)
☎ (091) 565 7229
11.45–3, 5.30–11 (11.30–11 Fri & Sat)
Vaux Samson, Double Maxim, Extra Special; Wards Sheffield Best Bitter Ⓗ
Ten years in the *Guide* and CAMRA local *Pub of the Year* 1992–93; a classic pub in a dramatic industrial setting. Warm and friendly atmosphere; cheap drinks Tue night. ∰ ❀ ◖ ⊟

Tap & Spile
Salem Street, Hendon
☎ (091) 514 2810
12–3, 6–11 (11–11 Thu–Sat)
Camerons Bitter; Hadrian Gladiator; Stocks Old Horizontal Ⓗ**; guest beers**
Successful Tap & Spile conversion of a former Camerons pub on the city outskirts, across Mowbray Park. Popular with students. Bare floorboards, exposed brickwork and up to ten ales make this a traditional alehouse worth seeking. Annual pub beer festival.
∰ ⊟ ≉ ♣

Try also: Chesters, Chester Rd (Vaux)

Tynemouth
Turks Head
Front Street ☎ (091) 257 6547
11–11
Jennings Bitter, Cumberland Ale; S&N Theakston Best Bitter, XB; Younger No. 3 Ⓗ**; guest beers**
Busy at weekends, this pub features a stuffed dog with a strange story attached! ⊖

Tynemouth Lodge Hotel
Correction House Bank, Tynemouth Road
☎ (091) 258 5758
11–11
Draught Bass; Belhaven 80/-; Ruddles County; S&N Theakston Best Bitter Ⓗ**; guest beers**
Established in 1779, a cosy one-roomed pub with copper-topped Victorian tables. The popular landlord was a founder member of the Tyneside branch of CAMRA; full measures and a warm welcome assured.
∰ Q ❀ ⊖ ⌂ P

Wardley
Green
Whitemare Pool
☎ (091) 495 0171
11.30–3, 5.30–11 (11–11 Sat)
Draught Bass; Ruddles County; S&N Theakston Best Bitter Ⓗ**; guest beers**
Pub on the edge of Heworth golf course. A large comfortable lounge connects to a popular restaurant.
❀ ◖ ▷ ⊟ & P

Washington
Three Horse Shoes
Washington Road, Usworth Village
☎ (091) 536 4183
12–3, 5.30–11 (12–11 Fri & Sat)
Vaux Samson, Extra Special; Wards Sheffield Best Bitter Ⓗ
Large, isolated pub with multiple rooms catering for all tastes. Specialises in good quality bar food. Handy for the Sunderland Aircraft Museum and Nissan car plant.
❀ ◖ ▷ ⊟ ♣ P

Whitburn
Jolly Sailor
1 East Street (A183)
☎ (091) 529 3221
11–11
Bass Light, Draught Bass Ⓗ
Traditional, bustling, village pub with multiple rooms. Well known for its good value pub lunches. ∰ Q ❀ ◖ ⊟ ♣

Whitley Bay
Briardene
The Links
☎ (091) 252 0926
11–11
S&N Theakston Best Bitter, XB, Old Peculier; Stones Best Bitter Ⓗ**; guest beers**
Large seafront pub, refurbished to a high standard. The lounge has a children's area (until 9pm) while the bar maintains its traditional feel.
Q ⋟ ❀ ◖ ▷ ⊟ & ▲ ♣ P

WHO OWNS WHOM?

There are still many drinkers who believe that when they drink Theakston, Ruddles or Boddingtons beers, they are supporting a small, family-owned brewery.

In fact, Theakston has been owned by Scottish & Newcastle since 1987, though you would never know it from the advertising. Ruddles, far from being the archetypal, independent real ale brewery, has been pushed from pillar to post between international breweries. Grand Metropolitan sold it to Courage and Courage have now passed it on to Dutch giants Grolsch. And then there is Boddingtons, the 'Cream of Manchester', top of the Whitbread beer list. But does it say so on the pump clip?

Isn't it strange how giant brewers, masters at closing down independent breweries, think small is beautiful when it suits them?

 Judge's, *Rugby*

Ardens Grafton

Golden Cross
Wixford Road, Bidford-on-Avon OS104538
☎ (0789) 772420
11–2.30, 6–11
Ansells Mild; Ind Coope Burton Ale; Tetley Bitter Ⓗ
Food-oriented stone pub commanding fine views. Boasts a collection of antique dolls and toys. ♨ Q ➤ ◑ ▸ P

Atherstone

Hat & Beaver
Long Street
☎ (0827) 715604
12–3, 7–11

Courage Directors; Marston's Pedigree; John Smith's Bitter Ⓗ; guest beers
Small, friendly pub, popular with the locals.
Q ◑ ▸ ⊟ & ⇌ ♣ P

Baxterley

Rose Inn
Main Road
☎ (0827) 713939
11–2.30, 7–11 (12–2.30, 7–10.30 Sun)
Draught Bass; M&B Highgate Mild, Brew XI Ⓗ
Pub set in a quiet, picturesque location near the now derelict Baddesley Ensor coal mine. Derives its name from the family who had the pub for 115 years. ➤ ❀ ◑ ▸ ⊟ ♣ P

Bedworth

Newdigate Arms
Newdigate Road
☎ (0203) 314867
11.30–2.30 (3 Fri, 3.30 Sat), 5–11
Ansells Mild, Bitter; Ind Coope Burton Ale; Tetley Bitter Ⓗ
Pleasantly decorated, modern estate pub. A newly-built children's room leads off the bar and on to the garden.
Q ➤ ❀ ◑ ▸ ⊟ ♣ P

Prince of Wales
Bulkington Road
12–2.30 (5 Sat), 7–11
Mansfield Riding Mild; Wells Eagle, Bombardier Ⓗ

Small, lively locals' pub acquired from M&B. ⊟ ⇌ P

White Swan
All Saints Square
☎ (0203) 312164
11.45–3 (4 Sat), 7–11
Wells Eagle, Bombardier Ⓗ
Friendly ex-M&B pub in the town centre, near the open-air market. ◐ ⊟

Brailes

Gate Inn
Upper Brailes (B4035)
☎ (0608) 85212
12–3, 7 (6 Fri)–11
Hook Norton Mild, Bitter, Old Hooky Ⓗ
Friendly, old village local where children are always welcome. Next to the site of the former Brailes brewery. Aunt Sally. No food Sun.
♔ ❀ ◐ ◑ ⊟ ▲ ♣ P

Brinklow

Raven
Broad Street ☎ (0788) 832655
11–2.30, 7–11
Marston's Mercian Mild, Burton Best Bitter, Pedigree Ⓗ
Two-roomed village pub with four fires and a ghost. The lounge has a very woody feel, but the bar is more basic. Stands beneath an old castle.
♔ Q ♿ ❀ ◐ ◑ ⊟ ♣ P

White Lion
Broad Street ☎ (0788) 832579
11–3, 7–11
Banks's Mild, Bitter
Large, imposing village local in Tudor style: a large beamed bar with pool and darts, plus a small lounge used for food at lunchtimes (not Sun); interesting windows. Folk music Fri. ♿ ❀ 🛏 ◐ ⊟ ♣ P

Bubbenhall

Malt Shovel
Lower End ☎ (0203) 301141
11.30–2.30, 6–11 (12–2.30, 7–10.30 Sun)
Ansells Mild, Bitter; Draught Bass; Tetley Bitter Ⓗ
Deservedly popular village pub with a welcoming atmosphere. The Italian landlord is justly proud of his Italian food (not served Sun). Own bowling green. ♔ Q ❀ ◐ ◑ ⊟ ♣ P

Bulkington

Weavers Arms
Long Street ☎ (0203) 314415
11–3, 6–11
Draught Bass; M&B Mild Ⓗ
Friendly village pub tucked up a quiet dead-end road. Ex-M&B free house which may soon have a wider beer range; the Bass is superb. ❀ ◐ ⊟ ▲

Caldecote

Royal Red Gate
Watling Street (A5/A444 jct)
11–3, 6–11
Marston's Burton Best Bitter, Pedigree Ⓗ
Two-roomed pub with bar billiards. Richard III passed here on his way to Bosworth Field. Q ❀ ◐ ⊟ ♣ P

Ettington

BANOFFIE PIE ✓

Chequers
Main Road (A422, off Fosse Way) ☎ (0789) 740387
10.30–2.30, 6–11
Adnams Bitter; Everards Tiger, Old Original Ⓗ
Popular village pub with a good reputation for food. Registered as a brewhouse in 1823 and originally used by drovers. Two bars.
Q ❀ ◐ ◑ ⊟ ▲ ♣ P

Five Ways

Case is Altered
Case Lane (near A4177/A41 jct) OS225701 ☎ (0926) 484206
11.30–2.30, 6–11 (12–2, 7–10.30 Sun)
Ansells Mild, Bitter; Ind Coope Burton Ale Ⓖ**; Samuel Smith OBB** Ⓗ**; Whitbread Flowers Original** Ⓖ
Unspoilt old farmers' pub with unusual cask pumps on the beer. The bar billiards takes old 6d pieces.
♔ Q ♿ ❀ ⊟ ♣ P

Haseley

Falcon Inn
Birmingham Road (A4177, old A41) ☎ (0926) 484281
11.30–2.30 (3 Sat), 6–11
Ind Coope Burton Ale; M&B Brew XI Ⓗ
Large half-timbered pub, partly dating back 400 years. An alcove separates the irregularly-shaped public bar from the comfortable lounge. Beware low doorways. Good value food. ❀ ◐ ◑ ⊟ P

Henley-in-Arden

Golden Cross
High Street
☎ (0564) 793769
11–2.30, 5.30–11 (11–11 Wed & Sat)
Ansells Mild, Bitter Ⓗ
Three-roomed pub including a lounge with darts and a separate games room with two pool tables. Eve meals until 8pm. ♔ 🛏 ◐ ◑ ⇌ ♣ P

Hunningham

Red Lion
Main Street (off B4453 after Weston) ☎ (0926) 632715
12–3, 6.30–11 (12–2.30, 7–10.30 Sun)
Draught Bass; M&B Brew XI; S&N Theakston XB Ⓗ**; guest beer**
Friendly period riverside pub with fishing and camping facilities. The large garden has a barbecue and swings. Two games rooms and an unusual corridor room behind the bar.
♔ ♿ ❀ ◐ ◑ ⊟ ▲ ♣ P

Kenilworth

Clarendon Arms
Castle Hill ☎ (0926) 52017
11–3, 5.30–11
Courage Directors; John Smith's Bitter; Tetley Bitter Ⓗ
Pleasingly restored old pub which is very food oriented but still welcomes drinkers. Small restaurant. Q ♿ ❀ ◐ ◑

Clarendon House Hotel
High Street
☎ (0926) 57668
11.30–2.30 (3 Fri & Sat), 6–11
Hook Norton Best Bitter, Old Hooky; Whitbread Flowers IPA, Original Ⓗ
Plush hotel with a welcoming atmosphere and a separate restaurant. Q 🛏 ◐ P

Earl Clarendon
Warwick Road
☎ (0926) 54643
11–2.30, 7–11
Marston's Burton Best Bitter, Pedigree Ⓗ
Yes, another Clarendon, but this one is a locals' pub where some lively debates take place. No food Sun; eve meals Thu–Sat. ◐ ◑ ⊟

Lapworth

✓ 93

Navigation
HIGHGATE MILD
Old Warwick Road (B4439)
☎ (0564) 78337
11–2.30 (3 Sat), 5.30 (6 Sat)–11
Draught Bass; M&B Mild, Brew XI Ⓗ**; guest beer**
Comfortable, friendly pub with a popular garden overlooking the Grand Union Canal. The only tenant this side of Birmingham to take a genuine guest beer from smaller breweries. A brave man . . . don't miss!
♔ Q ❀ ◐ ◑ ⊟ ⇌ P

Leamington Spa

Black Horse
Princes Street
☎ (0926) 425169
11–2.30 (3 Mon), 5.30–11 (11–11 Fri; 10.30–11 Sat)
Hook Norton Mild, Best Bitter Ⓗ
Recently improved locals' pub, tucked away in the back streets near Campion Hills. Large bar popular for games; small lounge. ⊟ ♣ ⌓ P

Warwickshire

George
High Street ☎ (0926) 451975
11–11
Adnams Broadside; Mansfield Riding Mild (occasionally); **Wells Eagle, Bombardier** [H]
Fine, friendly beer drinker's pub in the old south end of town. A plain public bar is complemented by a comfortable, wood-panelled lounge. A popular venue for card players. ♨ ⊟ ≋ ♣

Red House
Radford Road ☎ (0926) 881725
11.30–3, 5.30–11 (11–11 Fri & Sat)
Draught Bass; M&B Mild, Springfield Bitter [H]
Good, roadside town pub that has a relaxed atmosphere and a diverse mix of customers – feels more like a country pub. The only outlet for cask Springfield Bitter for miles. St Patrick's Day is celebrated with enthusiasm! Q ❀

Somerville Arms
Campion Terrace
11–2.30 (3 Fri & Sat), 5.30 (6 Sat)–11
Ansells Mild, Bitter; Ind Coope Burton Ale; Marston's Pedigree; Tetley Bitter [H]
Excellent, friendly pub with a small, cosy lounge at the rear and a large, busy front bar. Well worth the walk from the town centre. Q ⊟ ♣

Leek Wootton

Anchor Inn
Warwick Road ☎ (0926) 53355
11–3, 6–11
Draught Bass; M&B Brew XI [H]
Popular village local which retains a traditional bar and a smarter lounge. No food Sun. ♨ Q ❀ ◐ ⊟ ♿ ♣ ⌓ P

Long Itchington

Harvester
Church Road ☎ (0926) 812698
11–3, 6–11
Hook Norton Best Bitter, Old Hooky [H]; **guest beers**
Superb, welcoming pub at the village centre: the only Hook Norton pub in the area. Guest beers change weekly. Customers come a long way for what must be the cheapest beer around. ♘ ◐ ◗ ⊟ P

Long Lawford

Sheaf & Sickle
Coventry Road (A428, Rugby road) ☎ (0788) 544622
12–3, 6 (7 Mon–Fri in winter)–11 (12–11 Sat)
Ansells Mild, Bitter; Marston's Pedigree; Tetley Bitter [H]; **guest beers**
Roadside pub with a cosy lounge and comfortable bar leading into a games/family room. Contains the smallest room in the area, with just four seats. The garden has playthings and a cricket pitch. ♘ ❀ ◐ ♿ ▲ ♣ P

Monks Kirby

Denbigh Arms
Main Street ☎ (0788) 832303
12–2.30, 7–11
Draught Bass; M&B Highgate Mild, Brew XI; S&N Theakston XB [H]
Old village pub opposite a 13th-century church. Formerly a farmhouse-cum-inn, part of the Earl of Denbigh's estate. Welcoming to locals and outsiders, offering games and a folk club. Book weekend meals (no food Mon lunch). ❀ ◐ ◗ ⊟ ♿ ♣ P ⊬

Moreton Morrell

Black Horse
2 miles from M40
☎ (0926) 651231
11–2.30 (3 Sat & Sun), 6.30–11
Everards Old Original; Hook Norton Best Bitter [H]
Traditional village pub, friendly and unpretentious. Popular with students from the local agricultural college. The pleasant, peaceful garden boasts good views. ❀ ◐ ◗ ▲

Nether Whitacre

Dog Inn
Dog Lane (off B4098)
☎ (0675) 81318
12–3, 6 (5 Sat)–11 (12–2.30, 7–10.30 Sun)
Draught Bass; M&B Mild, Brew XI [H]
Friendly, country pub, popular in summer, when children can use the garden. Q ❀ ◐ ⊟ P

No Man's Heath

Four Counties Inn
On B5493 (old A453) near M42 jct 11 ☎ (0827) 830243
11–2.30, 6.30–11
Ansells Mild; Ind Coope Burton Ale [H]; **guest beers**
Popular roadside inn close to the point where Warks, Staffs, Leics and Derbys meet. Warm, cosy atmosphere with three real fires and good value food. Recently purchased from Ansells by the existing tenant. Regular guest beers, eg Burton Bridge, Everards, Bass. ♨ ❀ ◐ ◗ ♣ P ⊬

Nuneaton

Fox Inn
11a The Square, Attleborough Green ☎ (0203) 383290
11–3.30, 6.30–11 (12–2.30, 7–10.30 Sun)
Draught Bass; M&B Mild, Brew XI [H]
Basic local, ex-M&B and now a free house. The beer range may change after refurbishment. Very low prices for the area. ⊟ ♣

Punchbowl Inn
Tuttle Hill ☎ (0203) 383809
11.30–3, 7–11 (12–2.30, 7–10.30 Sun)
Mansfield Riding Mild; Wells Eagle [H]
Three-room, roadside, ex-M&B pub. A handy stop on the A47, but a limited menu (more choice in summer). ❀ ◐ ⊟ ♣ P

Priors Marston

Holly Bush
Holly Bush Lane
☎ (0327) 60934
12–3 (4 Fri), 5.30–11 (12–11 Sat)
Hook Norton Best Bitter; Marston's Pedigree; S&N Theakston Old Peculier; Wadworth 6X; Whitbread Flowers IPA [H]
Old stone pub with many individual areas (including a restaurant), once separate rooms. The main room is dominated by a large inglenook. Appealing atmosphere. ♨ ♘ ❀ ◐ ◗ ♿ ♣ P

Rugby

Engine Inn
1 Bridget Street (off Lawford Rd) ☎ (0788) 579658
11–11
M&B Mild [E], **Brew XI; Marston's Pedigree** [H]
Traditional, Victorian corner local now in the middle of a new housing development. A Grade II listed building with two lounges, a corner bar and a small snug. Q ❀ ⊟ ♿ ♣

Half Moon
28–30 Lawford Road
11–2.30, 5.30–11 (11–11 Fri; 10–11 Sat)
Ansells Mild, Bitter; Ind Coope Burton Ale [H]; **guest beers**
Small, friendly, terraced pub close to Rugby town centre. The L-shaped bar displays photos of old Rugby pubs. ♣

London House
Chapel Street
☎ (0788) 575981
11–3 (4 Sat), 7–11
Marston's Border Mild, Burton Best Bitter, Pedigree, Owd Roger (winter) [H]
Recently refurbished, single-room, town-centre pub with drinking areas on two levels served by one U-shaped bar. The facade is listed. Very busy at weekends, catering for a wide variety of people. Not to be missed on a town crawl. ♣

Peacock

Newbold Road
☎ (0788) 567923
12–3, 7–11
Hoskins Beaumanor Bitter, Penn's Ale, Premium, Old Nigel H**; guest beers**
Large Victorian corner pub near the police station. The small snug (separate from the friendly lounge) can be used as a family room. Large games room. ◐ ▶ ≠ ♣

Victoria

1 Lower Hillmorton Road
☎ (0788) 544374
12–2.30, 6–11 (11–4, 7–11 Sat)
Draught Bass; M&B Highgate Mild, Brew XI; Stones Best Bitter H**; guest beer**
Victorian corner pub with original fittings, near the town centre. The bar is dominated by pool and darts; friendly lounge. Trad. jazz Mon eves. No weekend food. ◐ ⊞ ≠ ♣

Ryton-on-Dunsmore

Blacksmiths Arms

High Street ☎ (0203) 301818
12–3, 6–11
Draught Bass; M&B Brew XI H
Quaint village pub with a vast array of brass ornaments. A very popular eating house (children welcome if eating).
Q ♫ ❀ ◐ ▶ ᳘ P

Shipston-on-Stour

Black Horse

Station Road
☎ (0608) 661617
12–2 (2.30 Sat), 7–11
Home Bitter; Ruddles Best Bitter; S&N Theakston XB; Webster's Yorkshire Bitter H**; guest beer**
Pub dating back to the 12th century, originally a row of cottages for Cotswold sheep farmers. Illegally brewed its own ale until a full licence was granted in 1862. Interesting interior and family room leading to the garden. No eve meals Sun or Mon.
▲ Q ♫ ❀ ◐ ▶ ⊞ ᳘ ♣ P

Shustoke

Plough Inn

The Green (B4114, 2 miles from Coleshill, off M6 jct 4)
☎ (0675) 81557
12–2.30, 7 (6.30 Thu–Sat)–11 (12–2.30, 7–10.30 Sun)
Draught Bass; M&B Mild, Brew XI H
Excellent, traditional village pub offering friendly service: popular with locals. Separate games room. No food Sun; eve meals until 8.30 Thu–Sat.
▲ Q ❀ ◐ ▶ ♣ P

Southam

Old Mint

Coventry Street
☎ (0926) 812339
11–3, 6.30 (6 Fri)–11 (11–11 Sat)
Draught Bass; Hook Norton Best Bitter; Taylor Landlord; Wadworth 6X; Whitbread Boddingtons Bitter, Flowers Original H**; guest beers**
15th-century stone building, a mint in the Civil War. Bars are adorned with copper, brassware and weaponry. Reputedly haunted, but friendly. A very busy pub offering two guest beers, one a mild. ▲ ♫ ❀ ◐ ▶ P

Stockton

Crown

High Street ☎ (0926) 812255
12–3, 7–11 (11–11 Fri & Sat in summer)
Ansells Mild, Bitter; Ind Coope ABC Best Bitter H**; guest beers**
Welcoming, popular village pub and restaurant with jug and brass collections. Converted barn for functions; international petanque piste in hand. Up to four guest beers.
▲ ❀ ◐ ▶ ⊞ ♣ P

Stratford-upon-Avon

Queens Head

Ely Street ☎ (0789) 204914
11–11 (12–2.30, 7–10.30 Sun)
Draught Bass; M&B Highgate Mild, Brew XI H**; guest beer**
Popular, old town-centre pub with an L-shaped bar. Unpretentious, with a friendly atmosphere. ▲ ❀ ◐ ▶ ≠

Shakespeare Hotel

Chapel Street
☎ (0789) 294771
11–2, 6–11
Draught Bass; Donnington SBA; Hook Norton Best Bitter, Old Hooky H
Real ale is found in the Froth & Elbow section of this beautiful, half-timbered Tudor building. A small bar but a large spacious lounge.
▲ Q ❀ ◐ ▶ ≠ P

Stretton-on-Dunsmore

Shoulder of Mutton

Village Green
☎ (0203) 542601
12–2.30 (not Wed), 7.30–11 (12–2.30, 7–10.30 Sun)
M&B Mild, Brew XI H
Superbly unspoilt, welcoming 19th-century village local with an added 1940s lounge, a small, wood-panelled snug and a tiled bar with bentwood furniture. Lunchtime snacks;

keen beer prices. Gramophone and grand piano.
▲ Q ♫ ❀ ⊞ ᳘ ▲ ♣ P

Studley

Shakespeare

Redditch Road ☎ (0527) 852137
11–11
Banks's Mild, Bitter E
Friendly village local with mock Victorian decor and a Shakespearian theme. Plenty of atmosphere. ◐ ▶ ♣ P

Warwick

Kings Head

39 Saltisford (A425)
☎ (0926) 493096
11–2.30, 6–11
Ansells Mild, Bitter; Marston's Pedigree; Tetley Bitter H
Traditional two roomer: bar on the left, lounge on the right. One of Warwick's many fine Georgian buildings. A good, old-style town pub – well worth finding. ▲ ◐ ⊞ P

New Bowling Green

13 St Nicholas Church Street
12–2.30, 5–11 (11–11 Fri & Sat)
Wells Eagle, Bombardier H
Excellent, old timbered pub complete with low ceilings and exposed beams: two small bars and a games room. The passage through the pub leads to a large walled garden.
Q ❀ ◐ ≠ ♣

Old Fourpenny Shop Hotel

27 Crompton Street (linking A429 and A4189)
12–2.30 (11.30–3 Sat), 6–11
Draught Bass; M&B Brew XI H**; guest beers**
Popular pub well known for its varied guest beers. Split-level interior. Pleasant walled garden at the rear. Near the racecourse. ❀ ᳘ ♣ P

Whichford

Norman Knight

12–2.30 (3 Fri & Sat), 7–11
Hook Norton Best Bitter; Whitbread Flowers Original H
Undeveloped little village local. ▲ Q ❀ ⊞ ▲ ♣ P

Wilmcote

Swan House Hotel

The Green ☎ (0789) 267030
11–11
Hook Norton Best Bitter; S&N Theakston XB H
Listed building, dating back to the 18th century, with a natural well and beamed ceilings. Very close to Mary Arden's House. Friendly atmosphere. Excellent food.
▲ ❀ ᳘ ◐ ▶ ▲ ≠ P

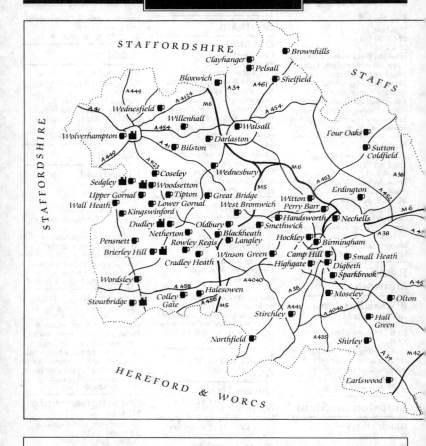

 Banks's, Wolverhampton; **Batham**, Brierley Hill;
British Oak, Dudley; **Holden's**, Woodsetton;
Sarah Hughes, Sedgley; **Pitfield**, Stourbridge

Barston

Bulls Head
Barston Lane ☎ (067 544) 2830
11–2.30, 5.30 (6 Sat)–11
**Draught Bass; M&B Brew
XI** Ⓗ
Pub partly dating back to
1490; oak beams and log fires
feature in both rooms. A
traditional country pub, and
the centre of village life. No
meals Wed or Sun eves.
🏚 Q ❀ ◑ ▶ ﴾ P

Bilston

Spread Eagle
Lichfield Street
☎ (0902) 403801
12–3, 7–11
British Oak Castle Ruin,

Eve'ill Bitter, Pickering's
Porter, Dungeon Draught Ⓗ
Three-roomed urban pub,
British Oak brewery's second
outlet. ◑ ▶ ⊞ ♣ P

Trumpet
High Street ☎ (0902) 493723
12–3 (4 Sat), 8–11 (12–3, 8–10.30 Sun)
**Holden's Mild, Bitter,
Special** Ⓗ
Popular one-roomed jazz
centre featuring live groups
nightly and Sun lunchtime (no
food Sun). ◑ P

White Rose
20 Lichfield Street (A41)
☎ (0902) 492497
12 (11 Sat)–3, 7–11
M&B Highgate Mild Ⓔ,
Springfield Bitter Ⓖ
Two–roomed high street pub.
⊞ ♣

Birmingham:
Camp Hill

Brewer & Baker
Old Camp Hill
☎ (021) 772 8185
11–11
Banks's Mild, Bitter Ⓔ
Welcoming pub catering for
all ages. 🏚 ❀ ◑ ⊞ ♣ P

City Centre

Atkinsons Bar
(Midland Hotel)
Stephenson Street
☎ (021) 643 2601
11–3, 5 (5.30 Sat)–11 (closed Sun)
**Draught Bass; Holden's
Bitter; Marston's Pedigree;
Ruddles County; S&N
Theakston Old Peculier;**

West Midlands

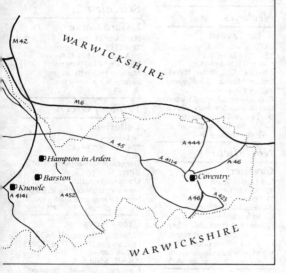

WARWICKSHIRE

M 42

M 6

A 45

A 444

P Hampton in Arden

A 414

A 46

P Barston

Coventry

Knowle

A 452

A 46

A 423

A 414

WARWICKSHIRE

**Whitbread Boddingtons
Bitter; guest beer** Ⓗ & Ⓖ
Cosy hotel bar. The price
explosion in other pubs has
made its prices competitive.
Memorabilia of the old
Atkinsons brewery.
Q ⛩ ◖ ≉ (New St)

Gough Arms
52 Upper Gough Street
11–3, 5 (7 Sat)–11 (11–11 Thu & Fri;
12–2, 7–10.30 Sun)
**Courage Best Bitter,
Directors** Ⓗ; **M&B Mild** Ⓔ
Friendly street-corner local,
very popular with workers
from the nearby post office.
🍺 ≉ (New St) ♣

Prince of Wales
84 Cambridge Street
☎ (021) 643 9460
11.30–3, 5 (7 Sat)–11
**Ansells Mild, Bitter; Ind
Coope Burton Ale; Marston's
Pedigree; Tetley Bitter** Ⓗ
A new bar extension and
redecoration complete this
pub which fits snugly behind
the convention centre and
indoor arena.
◖ 🍺 ≉ (New St) ♣

Shakespeare
Lower Temple Street
☎ (021) 643 4202
11–10.30 (11–11 Thu–Sat)
**Draught Bass; M&B Brew
XI** Ⓗ
Part of a Victorian terrace; the
interior has been knocked into
one room but it is smart and
retains the original half-tiling.
A refuge from the town-centre
disco pubs. ◖ ≉ (New St)

Digbeth

Adam & Eve
Bradford Street
☎ (021) 772 8390
11–11
**HP&D Mild, Entire;
Marston's Pedigree;
Wadworth 6X** Ⓗ; **guest beers**
Friendly corner pub with an
upstairs function room staging
regular live music. ◖ ▶ 🍺 ♣

Market Tavern
Moseley Street
☎ (021) 622 5560
11–11 (closed Sun)
**Ansells Mild, Bitter;
Marston's Pedigree** Ⓗ

Listed building with original
old tiles, behind the markets
area. Live entertainment and
quizzes. ◖ 🍺 ◖ ♣

Spotted Dog
104 Warwick Street
7–11 (12–3, 7–10 Sun)
Ansells Mild, Bitter Ⓗ
Homely, friendly Irish pub
which runs occasional rugby
and netball teams. A small bar
and an L-shaped lounge;
stained-glass windows.
≉ (New St)

Erdington

Beer Shop
(Off-Licence)
55 New Street (off A38)
☎ (021) 384 3636
5.30–10 (12–2, 7–10 Sun)
Beer range varies
Traditional jug and bottle
offering an ever-changing
variety of guest beers from all
over the country, plus an
extensive range of imported
bottled beers. ≉

Lad in the Lane
Bromford Lane
☎ (021) 377 7184
11–11
**Ansells Mild, Bitter; Ind
Coope Burton Ale** Ⓗ
Old pub, well-restored with
character. ❀ ◖ 🍺 ◖ ≉ ♣ P

Hall Green

Bulls Head
1320 Stratford Road
☎ (021) 778 5107
11–3, 5–11
M&B Mild, Brew XI Ⓗ
Georgian-style building, built
about 1850, refurbished with a
pleasant, large lounge and a
bar. ❀ ◖ 🍺 ≉

Handsworth

Woodman
375 Holyhead Road
☎ (021) 525 3532
11–3, 5 (6 Sat)–11 (12–2.30, 7–10.30
Sun)
**M&B Highgate Mild, Brew
XI; Stones Best Bitter** Ⓗ
Tiny bar at the side and a
large modern lounge in this
pub opposite West Bromwich
FC. The door is locked on
football Sats when only
regulars gain access. ◖ 🍺

Highgate

British Oak
77 Gooch Street North
☎ (021) 692 1253
11–11
**Ansells Mild, Bitter;
Marston's Pedigree; Ruddles
County** Ⓗ

West Midlands

Turn-of-the-century traditional local with a roomy bar and a small backroom. The beer range varies.
◑ ⇌ (New St)

Fountain Inn
Wrentham Street
☎ (021) 622 1452
12–3, 6 (7 Sat)–11
Ansells Bitter; Ind Coope Burton Ale; Marston's Pedigree Ⓗ
Busy, traditional-style pub with two rooms plus a quiet snug bar. The pleasant mixed crowd often includes theatre-goers. Q ❀ ⇄ ◑

Lamp Tavern
157 Barford Street
☎ (021) 622 2599
12–3, 5.30–11
Fuller's ESB; Hook Norton Best Bitter, Old Hooky; Jennings Bitter; Marston's Pedigree; Wadworth 6X Ⓗ; guest beers
Friendly pub where live bands perform in the lounge on weekday nights. The beer range varies.
◑ ⊞ & ⇌ (New St)

Queens Arms
Macdonald Street
11–3, 5.30–11
Banks's Mild; M&B Mild, Springfield Bitter Ⓗ
Friendly, basic corner pub attracting a mixed clientele.
Q ⊞ ⇌ (New St) ♣

White Swan
Bradford Street
11–3, 6–11
Ansells Mild; Tetley Bitter Ⓗ
A gem of a pub unspoilt by progress. The mild is superb.
⊞ ⇌ (New St) ♣

Hockley

Black Eagle
16 Factory Road (400 yds from A41/B4144 jct)
☎ (021) 523 4008
11–3 (4 Sat), 5.30 (7 Sat)–11 (11–11 Fri)
Ansells Mild, Bitter; Marston's Pedigree Ⓗ
Century-old, four-roomed pub and restaurant situated on the site of an old brewery. Good wholesome food at very reasonable prices (no meals Sun eve). Popular with everybody; warm welcome. A little gem. Q ❀ ◑ ▶ ⊞

Church Inn
2 Great Hampton Street
☎ (021) 515 1851
12 (7 Sat)–11
Ansells Mild, Bitter; Batham Best Bitter; Ind Coope Burton Ale Ⓗ
U-shaped lounge and a small bar. The landlord is famous for his generous portions of food. Q ◑ ▶ ⊞ ♣

Moseley

Prince of Wales
118 Alcester Road
☎ (021) 449 4198
11–3 (3.30 Sat), 5.30 (6 Sat)–11
Ansells Mild; Ind Coope Burton Ale Ⓗ
The recent face-lift is an improvement; a pub with a large, pleasant bar and two back rooms, served by a hatch. Suspected to have the largest throughput of Burton in the country. Q ❀ ⊞ &

Nechells

Villa Tavern
307 Nechells Park Road
☎ (021) 328 9831
11–3, 5.30 (6.30 Sat)–11
Ansells Mild, Bitter; HP&D Entire; Marston's Pedigree; Tetley Bitter Ⓗ
Recently refurbished Victorian tavern with two bars, plus a pool room. Popular with locals and draymen.
◑ ⊞ ⇌ (Aston) ♣ P

Northfield

Cavalier
214 Fairfax Road
☎ (021) 475 4083
11–11 (11–3, 6–11 Sat)
Ansells Mild, Bitter Ⓗ
Quiet lounge which can be crowded at weekends when the local folk band appears; basic bar with a pool table and wooden handpumps which depict cavaliers. ❀ ⇌ ♣ P

Perry Barr

Wellhead Tavern
Franchise Street
☎ (021) 331 4554
12–3, 5 (7 college hols)–11 (12–2.30, 7–10.30 Sun)
Ansells Mild; Aston Manor Dolly's Mild, JCB; Ind Coope Burton Ale; Tetley Bitter Ⓗ
Local CAMRA *Pub of the Year* three times; a well-liked and well-known pub with a good atmosphere. Popular with all ages. Q ❀ ◑ ⊞ ⇌ ♣ ◠

Small Heath

Black Horse
61 Green Lane (200 yds from A45) ☎ (021) 773 7271
11–11 (11–3, 7.30–11 Sat)
M&B Mild, Brew XI; Stones Best Bitter Ⓔ
Small two-roomer a stone's throw away from the beautiful disused Victorian terracotta swimming baths building.
⊞ ♣

White Lion
152 Muntz Street (B4145)
11–11 (11–3, 7–11 Sat)
M&B Mild, Brew XI Ⓔ

Much-altered, late Victorian pub, that still manages a traditional atmosphere. ⊞ ♣

Sparkbrook

Rose Tavern
47 Henley Street
☎ (021) 771 0600
11–11
Ansells Mild, Bitter; Tetley Bitter Ⓗ
Basic bar attracting a mixed clientele; pleasant and friendly. ◑ ⊞ ♣

Stirchley

Lifford Curve
Fordhouse Lane
☎ (021) 451 1634
11–3, 5.30–11 (11.30–11 Sat)
Banks's Mild, Bitter Ⓔ
Modern pub with a quiet lounge but a lively bar.
❀ ◑ ⊞ & P

Winson Green

Bellefield
36 Winson Street
☎ (021) 558 0647
12–3, 6–11
Greenalls Davenports Mild, Bitter Ⓗ
Unspoilt, beautifully tiled pub with a notable ceiling in the bar. The lounge has tile-framed pictures. ❀ ◑ ▶ ⊞ P

Cross Keys
81 Steward Street (off A457, Dudley road) ☎ (021) 454 3058
12–2.30, 5.30–11
Ansells Mild Ⓗ
L-shaped pub which must be the smallest in Brum. A strong domino theme in one room with black and white timbers.
◑ ♣

Witton

Safe Harbour
Moor Lane (between A4040 and A453) ☎ (021) 356 4257
11–2.30 (3 Fri & Sat), 5 (6 Sat)–11
Ansells Mild, Bitter; Tetley Bitter Ⓗ
Pub locally known as the 'Diggers', opposite the main gate of the cemetery. A basic bar and comfortable lounge cater for local factory workers and residents. Friendly and efficient staff. Weekday lunches. ❀ ◑ ⊞ ♣ P

Blackheath

Bell & Bear
71 Gorsty Hill Road (A4099)
☎ (021) 561 2196
11–11 (11–3, 6–11 Sat; 12–2.30, 7–10.30 Sun)
HP&D Mild, Bitter, Entire; Ind Coope Burton Ale; Marston's Pedigree; Taylor Landlord Ⓗ
Many features of the 400-year-

old former farmhouse have been retained in this refurbished, rambling one-room pub. Look out for the life-sized stuffed bear in the entrance hall. A restaurant has been opened and the range of beers extended. No meals Sun. ✿ ◑ ▶ P

Waterfall

Waterfall Lane
☎ (021) 561 3499
12–2.30, 6–11
Batham Best Bitter; Everards Old Original; Hook Norton Old Hooky; Marston's Pedigree; guest beers Ⓗ
Well worth the half-mile walk from station or town to sample seven or eight real ales. A varied, inexpensive menu caters for the 'inner man'. Quizzes Mon eve in the function room. The garden features a waterfall.
✿ ◑ ▶ ⊟ ⇌ (Old Hill) P

Bloxwich

Knave of Hearts

Lichfield Road
☎ (0922) 405576
12–2.30 (3 Fri & Sat), 5 (6.30 Sat)–11
HP&D Mild, Bitter, Entire; Tetley Bitter Ⓗ
Main road establishment once again refurbished, this time in the colours of HP&D. Nice to see it still has a separate bar.
✿ ◑ ▶ ⊟ ♣ P

Romping Cat

97 Elmore Green Road
12–11
Banks's Mild, Bitter Ⓔ
Small, lively, three-roomed pub with a round-cornered bar and a tiny smoke room. Occasional sing-songs around the piano. ✿ ⊟ ⇌ ♣

Saddlers Arms

Fishley Lane, Lower Farm Estate ☎ (0922) 405839
11.30–3, 6–11 (11–11 Sat)
Banks's Mild, Bitter Ⓔ
Modern estate pub with a comfortable lounge and atmosphere. Sat lunches served. ♨ ➷ ✿ ⊟ ♣ P

Brierley Hill

Black Horse

Delph Road ☎ (0384) 79142
11.30–3, 5.30–11 (11.30–11 Sat; 12–2.30, 7–11 Sun)
Banks's Mild; Courage Directors Ⓗ
Popular, bustling hostelry on the famous Delph crawl.
♨ ✿ ◑ ▶ ♿ ♣ P

Vine (Bull & Bladder)

Delph Road (³/₄ mile off A461)
☎ (0384) 78293
12–4, 6–11 (12–11 Fri & Sat)
Batham Mild, Best Bitter, XXX Ⓗ
Boisterous Black Country

brewery tap; its brightly-painted frontage features a quotation from *Two Gentlemen of Verona*. Live jazz Mon.
➷ ✿ ◑ ⊟ ♣ P

Brownhills

White Horse

White Horse Road (off A5)
☎ (0543) 374053
11.30–11 (12–3, 5.30–11 Wed)
Banks's Mild, Bitter Ⓔ
Friendly local with two lounges, handy for Chasewater. ✿ ◑ ▶ ⊟ ♣ P

Clayhanger

George & Dragon

Church Street (off A4124)
12–3 (not Mon–Thu), 7.30–11
Ansells Mild, Bitter Ⓗ
Pleasant village local enjoying a good community atmosphere; popular games room. Limited parking.
➷ ⊟ ♣ P

Colley Gate

Little Chop House

Windmill Hill (A458, 1¹/₂ miles from centre)
☎ (0384) 635089
11–3, 6–11
Lumphammer; Tetley Bitter Ⓗ**; guest beer** (occasionally)
Ancient pub, fronting a steep street, subjected in the mid 1980s to Mad O'Rourke's unique sense of humour. More recently refurbished in a less cluttered style. ◑ ▶ ♿ P

Coseley

White House

Daisy Street, Daisy Bank (B4163) ☎ (0902) 402703
11–3, 6–11
HP&D Mild, Bitter, Entire Ⓗ**; guest beers**
Friendly, popular, two-roomed pub dominating the crossroads and featuring a cat collection in the lounge. No food Sun.
♨ ✿ ◑ ▶ ⊟ ⇌ ♣ P

Coventry

Adam & Eve

Eden Street, Paradise
11–3, 6–11
Wells Eagle, Bombardier Ⓗ
Excellent renovation of a run-down inner city pub, designed for the mature customer.
✿ ♿ P

Albany

24 Albany Road, Earlsdon
☎ (0203) 715227
11–2.30 (3 Fri), 6–11 (11–11 Sat)
Marston's Burton Best Bitter, Pedigree, Owd Rodger Ⓗ
Popular pub with a smart lounge, used mainly by a

younger clientele, and a friendly bar. Upstairs the games room has three pool tables. ✿ ◑ ⊟ ♣

Biggin Hall Hotel

214 Binley Road, Copsewood
☎ (0203) 451046
11–11 (11–3.30, 6–11 Sat)
Marston's Border Mild, Burton Best Bitter, Pedigree, Owd Rodger Ⓗ
Not a hotel but a smart bar and a plush lounge with a large central table. The decor has been recently re-done but still looks little changed since it opened in 1923, according to long-established locals. A rarity: a 'gem' that you can take your mother to. No food Sun. Children welcome in the games room. Q ✿ ◑ ⊟ ♣ P

Black Horse

Spon End ☎ (0203) 677360
10–3, 4.30–11
Draught Bass; M&B Mild, Brew XI Ⓗ
Old, very popular pub, threatened with conversion to a dual carriageway.
♨ Q ⊟ ♣ P

Boat Inn

Black Horse Road, Exhall
☎ (0203) 361438
11–3 (may be earlier), 6–11
Ansells Mild, Bitter; Ind Coope Burton Ale; Marston's Pedigree; Tetley Bitter Ⓗ
Heritage inn: one room with three distinct areas. The wood-panelled 'snug' is the old bar area; the newest area is the smartest. Very handy for the canal (Sutton Stop).
♨ ➷ ✿ ◑ P

Elastic Inn

214 Lower Ford Street
☎ (0203) 227039
11–3, 5.30 (6.30 Sat)–11 (12–3, 7–11 Sun)
Ansells Mild, Bitter; Tetley Bitter Ⓗ
Small corner pub upholding traditional values. Near the bus station. ◑ ♣

Elephant & Castle

Aldermans Green Road, Aldermans Green
☎ (0203) 364606
12–3, 7–11
Mansfield Riding Mild; Wells Eagle Ⓗ
Canalside pub with a small cosy lounge, pool room and a large garden with a playground. The life of the pub revolves around its comfortable bar with piano. Live music Sat. ♨ ✿ ⊟ ♣ P

Greyhound

118 Much Park Street
☎ (0203) 221274
11–3, 7–11 (11–11 Mon & Fri in summer)
Mansfield Riding Mild; Wells Eagle, Bombardier Ⓗ

West Midlands

Recently renovated city-centre pub, opposite the Toy Museum, with a rame enclosed patio. Q ❀ ◑ ♣ ⇌

Greyhound Inn

Sutton Stop, Black Horse Road, Longford
☎ (0203) 363046
11–2.30, 6–11
Banks's Bitter; Draught Bass; M&B Highgate Mild H; guest beer
Popular pub at Hawkesbury canal junction. An old, three-roomed place full of bric-a-brac and a large toby collection. The outdoor drinking area is on the canal bank. High quality food (no meals Sun lunch). ❀ ❀ ◑ ▶ P

Malt Shovel

Spon End
☎ (0203) 220204
11–2.30 (3 Sat), 7–11
Ansells Mild, Bitter; Tetley Bitter; guest beers H
Small, cosy, deservedly popular one-roomer with many nooks and crannies; the original Heritage pub (opposite M&B's Coventry depot). Everyone should have a 'local' like this.
🏺 Q ❀ ◑ ▶ P

Nursery Tavern

Lord Street, Chapelfields
☎ (0203) 674530
12–2.30 (3 Sat), 7–11
Ansells Mild; Ruddles Best Bitter, County; Webster's Yorkshire Bitter H; guest beer
Small local in a former watchmaking area – one of the first suburbs of Coventry and now a conservation area (with plenty of pubs). Jennings Bitter is a regular guest. Children are welcome in the games room. Weekday lunches. ❀ ◑ ♣ ⌂

Old Ball

62 Walsgrave Road, Ball Hill
☎ (0203) 459016
11–11 (12 Fri & Sat)
Marston's Burton Best Bitter E, **Pedigree** H
Popular games pub – if they haven't got your game they will get it! The public bar has a board floor with sawdust.
🏺 Q ⮜ 🍴 ◑ ▶ ❀ 🛇 ♣ P

Old Windmill

Spon Street
☎ (0203) 252183
11–2.30, 5.30 (6 Mon & Fri, 7 Sat)–11 (12–2, 7–10.30 Sun)
Ansells Mild; Ruddles Best Bitter, County; John Smith's Bitter; Webster's Yorkshire Bitter H
The oldest licensed building in Coventry. The yard has recently become the bar, the old brewery a drinking area and the old bar a 'Donkey Box'. 🏺 Q ◑ ⇌ ♣ P

Peacock

Gosford Street
10.30–11
Ansells Mild, Bitter; S&N Theakston Old Peculier; Tetley Bitter H
Traditional inner city pub just outside the ring road, alongside the old Morris motor works. ❀ ◑ ♣ ⌂

Prince William Henry

252 Foleshill Road (A444)
☎ (0203) 687776
11.30–11
Banks's Mild; Draught Bass H; **M&B Brew XI** E
Lively pub beside the Coventry Canal. Always busy, due to its deservedly good reputation for Indian food (no meals Sun). Q ❀ ◑ ▶ 🛇 ♣ P

Town Wall Tavern

Bond Street
☎ (0203) 220963
11–3, 5–11
Draught Bass; M&B Mild, Brew XI; Stones Best Bitter H
Old pub in the city centre, behind the Belgrade Theatre; a comfortable lounge, busy bar and a small snug.
🏺 Q ❀ ◑ ▶ ⬛ ♣

Cradley Heath

Cradley Sausage Works

78 St Anne's Road (off A4100)
☎ (0384) 635494
11.30–3, 6 (6.30 Sat)–11
Ind Coope Burton Ale; Lumphammer H
One of the Little Pub Co. chain, a single-room pub decorated with a sausage-making theme. Scrubbed tables. ❀ ◑ ▶ ⇌

Swan (Jasper's)

Providence Street
☎ (0384) 61206
11–11 (11–4, 7–11 Sat)
Holden's Mild, Bitter, Special E
Lively local with two rooms plus a comfortable family room. Barbecues in summer. Handy for the speedway.
⮜ ❀ ◑ ⇌ ♣

Waggon & Horses

100 Reddal Hill Road (A4100)
☎ (0384) 636035
11.15–3, 7–11
Banks's Mild, Bitter E
Boisterous Black Country local. The bar features photos of Staffordshire bull terriers.
❀ ⬛ ⇌ ♣ P

Darlaston

Fallings Heath Tavern

Walsall Road (A4038)
12–2.30 (3 Sat & if busy), 7–11
Ansells Mild, Bitter; Tetley Bitter H

Two-roomed main road local with a pig collection above the bar. ⮜ ❀ ⬛ ♣ P

Dudley

Lamp Tavern

High Street ☎ (0384) 254129
11–11
Batham Mild, Best Bitter, XXX H
Welcoming local with a plain bar, a comfortable lounge and an adjacent eating area (lunchtimes). The former Queen's Cross brewery at the rear is undergoing conversion.
🏺 Q ❀ ◑ ♣ P

Malt Shovel

Tower Street
☎ (0384) 252735
11–3, 5.30–11 (11–11 Sat)
Banks's Mild, Bitter E
Cosy one-roomed pub near the market place, overshadowed by the castle and zoo. No eve meals Wed or Sun. Q ❀ 🍴 ◑ ▶ P

Earlswood

Bulls Head

Lime Kiln Lane
☎ (021) 728 2335
12–2.30, 6–11
Ansells Mild, Bitter; Ind Coope Burton Ale; Tetley Bitter H
Pub with a red-tiled bar with a separate dart throw and a rambling lounge with an unusually high bar. Two outside drinking areas: one has a children's play area. The bar is popular with Sunday cyclists. Eve meals till 8pm.
🏺 Q ❀ ◑ ▶ ⬛ ♣ P

Four Oaks

Crown

Walsall Road
☎ (021) 308 1258
11–11
Ansells Mild, Bitter; Ind Coope Burton Ale; Marston's Pedigree; Tetley Bitter H
Very large, comfortable suburban pub boasting leather Chesterfields for seating! The tasteful decor complements the architecture. Noted for its varied food and a popular haunt for all ages, supporting local soccer teams and charity.
◑ ▶ 🛇 ⬛ ⇌ (Butler's Lane) P

New Inns

444 Lichfield Road (B5127)
☎ (021) 308 0765
11.30–2.30, 5.30–11 (11.30–11 Sat)
Ansells Mild, Bitter; Ind Coope Burton Ale H
Traditional pub, popular with business people lunchtime and early eve. Regulars enjoy darts, dominoes, cribbage, crown green bowls, football and charity events. Try the

home-cooked daily specials
(no meals Sun eve). ❀ ◖ ♿
≠ (Butler's Lane) ♣ P

Great Bridge

Port 'n Ale

178 Horseley Heath (A461)
☎ (021) 557 7249
12–3, 6.30 (6 summer)–11
**Batham Best Bitter; Everards
Tiger, Old Original; Hook
Norton Bitter, Old Hooky;
Marston's Pedigree** ⊞
Recently renovated two-
roomed pub with a
welcoming atmosphere. Q ❀
◖ ▮ ⊟ ≠ (Dudley Port) P

Halesowen

Fairfield

Fairfield Road, Hurst Green
11–3, 5.30–11 (11–11 Sat)
**Banks's Hanson's Mild, Mild,
Bitter** Ⓔ
Popular two-roomed local: a
traditional bar with pub
games and a large, smart
lounge. ❀ ◖ ▮ ≠ (Rowley
Regis) ♣ P

Hare & Hounds

Hagley Road, Hasbury
(B4183) ☎ (021) 550 1264
12–2.30, 6–11
**Greenalls Davenports
Bitter** ⊞
Large, cheerful one-roomed
hostelry offering excellent
value meals; bookings advised
for early eve (no meals Sun
eve). ◖ ▮ P

Loyal Lodge

15 Furnace Hill (off A459)
☎ (021) 585 5863
11–2.30, 5 (6 Sat)–11 (12–2.30,
7–10.30 Sun)
**HP&D Mild, Bitter, Entire;
Tetley Bitter** ⊞
Very old pub, recently
converted from Ansells to a
smart but traditional hostelry
in the HP&D estate. No food
Sun eve. ❀ ◖ ▮ ♿ P

Rose & Crown

Hagley Road, Hasbury
(B4183) ☎ (021) 550 2757
12–2.30 (3 Sat), 6–11
HP&D Mild, Bitter, Entire ⊞
Ever-popular pub catering for
the local scene and passing
trade alike. Many unusual
artefacts in the various
drinking areas which are
served from a central bar.
Excellent lunches (not served
Sun). ⨝ ◖ ♣ P

Hampton in Arden

White Lion

High Street
☎ (0675) 442833
12–2.30, 5.30 (6 Sat)–11
**Draught Bass; M&B Highgate
Mild, Brew XI** ⊞
Homely, welcoming pub with

a basic bar that has remained
unchanged for 50 years.
⨝ Q ⨯ ◖ ▮ ⊟ ≠ P

Kingswinford

Swan Hotel

Stream Road
☎ (0384) 287232
11.30–2.30, 6–11 (11–11 Sat)
Banks's Mild, Bitter Ⓔ
Comfortable old hotel of
character, lying back off the
main road. ❀ ⨯ ◖ ▮ P

Knowle

Vaults

St George Close, High Street
☎ (0564) 773656
12–2.30, 5 (6 Sat)–11
**Ansells Mild; HP&D Bitter;
Ind Coope Burton Ale; Tetley
Bitter** ⊞
Multi-level basement pub
where the arrangement of
seating offers some privacy.
Home-made soup is a
speciality (no food Sat eve).
◖ ▮ ♣

Langley

Crosswells

High Street (off B4182)
11.30–2.30 (3 Fri & Sat), 6 (7 Sat)–11
HP&D Mild, Bitter, Entire ⊞
Cosy two-roomed pub near
the HP&D brewery.
⨝ ≠ (Langley Green) ♣

New Navigation

Titford Road (off A4123)
☎ (021) 552 2525
11.30–3 (3.30 Sat), 6 (7 Sat)–11
**HP&D Mild, Bitter, Entire;
Tetley Bitter** ⊞
Friendly, welcoming pub on
the Titford Canal. Eve meals
till 8pm; no lunches Sun.
⨝ ❀ ◖ ▮ ♣ P

Lower Gornal

Red Cow

84 Grosvenor Road (off B4176)
12–4.30, 6.30 (7 Sat)–11
**Banks's Hanson's Mild,
Bitter** Ⓔ
Old Black Country local of
character; a pub since 1835
and a traditional oasis in an
area of redevelopment.
Comfortable, snug lounge.
❀ ⊟ ♿ ♣ P

Netherton

White Swan
(Tommy Turner's)

45 Baptist End Road (off A459)
☎ (0384) 256101
12–3.30, 7–11
**Banks's Mild; HP&D Entire,
Deakin's Downfall; Ind
Coope Burton Ale; Marston's
Pedigree; Tetley Bitter** ⊞
Welcoming 18th-century
former home-brew house
(Roe's), known in more recent

times as 'Tommy Turner's',
with a contrasting bar and
lounge. Good value food.
⨝ ❀ ◖ ▮ P

Oldbury

Waggon & Horses

Church Street (off A4034)
☎ (021) 552 5467
12–2.30 (3 Fri), 5 (6 Sat)–11 (12–2.30,
6–10.30 Sun)
**Draught Bass; Batham Best
Bitter; Everards Old Original;
Marston's Pedigree;
Wadworth 6X; Whitbread
Boddingtons Bitter** ⊞**; guest
beers**
Pub with tiled walls, copper
ceiling and original Holts
brewery windows. A varying
menu of excellent home-
cooked food (including
vegetarian) is served in the
pub or in the upstairs function
room (weekday lunches);
book for Sun lunch. ⨝ ❀ ◖
≠ (Sandwell & Dudley)

Olton

Lyndon

Barn Lane (between A41 and
A45) ☎ (021) 743 2179
12–2.30, 6 (6.30 Sat)–11 (12–2.30,
7–10.30 Sun)
**Ansells Mild, Bitter; Tetley
Bitter** ⊞
Large, comfortable pub, with a
children's adventure
playground. ❀ ▮ ⊟ ♣ P

Pelsall

Royal Oak

Norton Road
☎ (0922) 691811
11.30–3, 5.30–11
**Ansells Mild, Bitter; Ind
Coope Burton Ale; Marston's
Pedigree** ⊞
Pleasant canalside pub serving
good food. ◖ ▮ ⊟ ♣ P

Pensnett

Holly Bush

Bell Street (off A4101)
1–3.30, 7–11
**Batham Mild, Best Bitter,
XXX** ⊞
Bright and welcoming,
modern estate pub.
⛘ ❀ ⊟ ♣ P

Rowley Regis

Sir Robert Peel

1 Rowley Village (B4171)
☎ (021) 559 2835
12–4, 7–11
Ansells Mild, Bitter ⊞**; guest
beers**
The oldest building in Rowley
Village: a truly traditional
three-roomed pub where a
warm welcome is assured.
Separate servery in the
entrance passageway.
⨝ Q ❀ ⊟ ♣ ⛾

West Midlands

Sedgley

Beacon Hotel
129 Bilston Street (A463)
☎ (0902) 883380
12–2.30, 5.30–10.45 (11 Fri; 11.30–3, 6–11 Sat; 12–2.30, 7–10.30 Sun)
Sarah Hughes Sedgley Surprise, Ruby Mild; M&B Mild, Springfield Bitter Ⓗ**; guest beers**
The recently completed brewery reception area does not detract from the charm of the pub's carefully restored Victorian interior. Weekly brewery open days (phone for details) enable visitors to see how the Sarah Hughes beer is made. Q ♞ ❀ ◐ ⊞ ♣ P

Bull's Head
Bilston Street (A463)
☎ (0902) 679606
12–3 (4 Sat), 6–11
Holden's Mild, Bitter Ⓔ**, Special** Ⓗ
Locals' pub with a strong darts following. The lively bar has an interesting photo collection; quiet, comfortable lounge. Q ❀ ◐ ⊞ ♣ ⌓

Shelfield

Four Crosses Inn
Green Lane
☎ (0922) 682518
12–4, 7–11
Banks's Mild, Bitter Ⓔ
Recently refurbished, popular local. ⊞ ♣ P

Shirley

Bernie's Real Ale Off-Licence
266 Cranmore Boulevard (off A34)
☎ (021) 744 2827
12–2 (not Mon), 5.30–10
Butterknowle Conciliation Ale; Fuller's London Pride; Hook Norton Best Bitter; Jennings Sneck Lifter; Marston's Pedigree; Titanic Premium Ⓗ
Titillate your tastebuds at this real ale haven. Over 200 different beers a year, mostly from small breweries, pass over the counter; five always available. Try before you buy system. Q ♿ ⌓

Smethwick

Ivy Bush
St Pauls Road (B4169)
☎ (021) 565 0929
11–3, 6–11 (11–11 Fri & Sat)
Holden's Stout, Mild, Bitter, Special Ⓗ
Recently renovated pub with a friendly atmosphere. No food Sun. Q 🛏 ◐ ⊞ ⇌ (West) ♣

Stourbridge

Gladstone Arms
High Street, Audnam (A461)
☎ (0384) 442703
11–3, 6–11 (12–3, 7–11 Sun)
HP&D Mild, Bitter, Entire; Tetley Bitter Ⓗ
One-roomer with a lively and friendly atmosphere, several alcoves and many artefacts. *A la carte* meals served until 9.30 Mon–Sat eves. ◐ ◗ P

Longlands Tavern
Western Road ☎ (0384) 392073
11–3, 6.30–11 (11–11 Sat)
Banks's Mild, Bitter Ⓔ
Smart back-street pub where the local CAMRA branch was formed. Still as popular as ever.
Q ♞ ❀ ⊞ ⇌ (Junction) P

Moorings Tavern
80 High Street, Amblecote
☎ (0384) 374124
12–2.30 (3 Sat), 5 (6 Sat)–11
Draught Bass; Pitfield Mild, Bitter Ⓗ
Lively one-roomer, just off the ring road, near the Grade II listed Stourbridge bonded warehouse and canal basin. The pub sports a canal-influenced decor and serves good food (except Sun eve) and a wide selection of ales.
♛ ❀ 🛏 ◐ ◗ ⇌ (Town) P

Red Lion
Lion Street ☎ (0384) 397563
11.30 (12 Mon)–3, 7–11
Draught Bass; M&B Highgate Mild Ⓗ
Popular, two-roomed pub with an additional parlour for functions or meals. Good value, award-winning food includes vegetarian and Indian dishes.
♛ Q ❀ ◐ ◗ ⊞ ⇌ (Town) ♣

Robin Hood
196 Collis Street, Amblecote (off A461) ☎ (0384) 440286
12–3, 6–11
Banks's Mild; Batham Best Bitter; Everards Tiger, Old Original; Hook Norton Old Hooky Ⓗ**; guest beers**
Established, popular free house which offers varied vegetarian and *à la carte* meals. Watch out for the backwards clock. ♛ Q ❀ 🛏 ◐ ◗

Royal Exchange
Enville Street ☎ (0384) 396726
12–11
Batham Mild, Best Bitter Ⓗ
Traditional, unspoilt local with a smart upstairs restaurant.
Q ❀ ◐ ◗ ⊞ ⇌ (Town) ♣

Seven Stars
Brook Road, Oldswinford
☎ (0384) 394483
11–11
S&N Theakston Best Bitter, XB, Old Peculier Ⓗ**; guest beers**
Free house, full of character: look out for the ornate tiling and the beautiful carved-wood back bar fitting. Two large rooms plus a restaurant area.
❀ ◐ ◗ ⊞ ⇌ (Junction) P

Shrubbery Cottage
28 Heath Lane, Oldswinford
☎ (0384) 377598
12–2.30, 6–11 (12–2.30, 7–10.30 Sun)
Holden's Mild, Bitter, Special, XL Ⓗ
Ever-popular local, near the college, with a recent smart extension. Many charity events organised. The small garden is popular in summer.
❀ ◐ ⇌ (Junction) P

Sutton Coldfield

Anvil Inn
Springfield Road (off B4148)
☎ (021) 378 0128
12–3.30, 5.30–11
Ansells Mild, Bitter Ⓗ
Comfortable, modernised pub on the outskirts of town.
❀ ◐ ⊞ ♿ ♣ P

Duke Inn
Duke Street ☎ (021) 355 1767
11.30–3, 5.30–11
Ansells Mild, Bitter; Ind Coope Burton Ale; Tetley Bitter Ⓗ
Traditional side-street local, boasting splendid Victorian back bar fittings and a very friendly atmosphere: a gem.
Q ❀ ⊞ ⇌ ♣ P

Laurel Wines (Off-Licence)
63 Westwood Road (off A452)
☎ (021) 353 0399
12–2, 5.30 (5 Sat)–10.30 (12–2 Sun)
Batham Best Bitter; Burton Bridge Festival; Marston's Pedigree Ⓖ
Friendly and popular off-licence which sells a wide range of real ales.

Three Tuns
High Street ☎ (021) 355 2996
11.30–2.30, 5–11 (11.30–11 Sat)
Ansells Mild, Bitter; Ind Coope Burton Ale; Marston's Pedigree; Tetley Bitter Ⓗ
Historic pub with a friendly atmosphere and very distinct bars: kids to the left, old 'uns to the right!
♛ ❀ ◐ ⊞ ♿ ⇌ ⌓ P

Tipton

Fountain
Owen Street (off A457)
☎ (021) 520 8777
11.30–2.30, 6–11 (11.30–11 Sat)
HP&D Mild, Bitter, Entire; Tetley Bitter Ⓗ
One of the original six HP&D outlets; a cosy, two-roomed local, inextricably associated

with the 'Tipton Slasher', a former world champion prizefighter. ♨ ◖ ▮ ⬥ ⬌ ♣

Upper Gornal

Crown
Holloway Street, Ruiton (off A459) ☎ (0902) 884035
12–3.30, 7–11
Banks's Hanson's Mild, Bitter Ⓔ
Popular, friendly old local at the top of the 'Bonk'. Its windows indicate it was once a home-brew house.
♨ ⏳ ⬥ ⬥ ♣ ⌂ P

Old Mill
Windmill Street (off A459) ☎ (0902) 887707
12–2.30 (4 Sat), 6.30–11
Holden's Stout, Mild, Bitter, XB, Special, XL Ⓔ; guest beers (occasionally)
Comfortable and welcoming, two-roomed hostelry serving good food in the bars and restaurant. XB is sold as 'Old Mill'.
♨ ⏳ ⬥ ◖ ▮ ⬥ ♣ ⌂ P

Wall Heath

Wall Heath Tavern
High Street ☎ (0384) 278319
11–3, 6–11
HP&D Mild, Bitter, Entire; Tetley Bitter Ⓗ
Popular, recently refurbished, roadside pub with a welcoming atmosphere in its public bar. ❀ ◖ ▮ ⬥ ⬥ ♣ P

Walsall

Butts Tavern
Butts Street ☎ (0922) 29332
12–3, 6.30–11 (12–11 Sat)
Ansells Bitter; Banks's Mild Ⓗ
Large pre-war pub with a very friendly bar and a quiet lounge. ♨ Q ❀ ◖ ▮ ♣

Duke of Wellington
Birmingham Street (off A34) ☎ (0922) 25604
12–11
M&B Highgate Mild, Springfield Bitter, Brew XI Ⓔ
Victorian pub with some original features in its bright, busy bar and comfortable lounge. Near the market and parish church. Weekday lunches. Q ◖ ⬥ ♣

Duke of York
Lumley Road ☎ (0922) 27593
12–3, 6–11
Draught Bass; M&B Highgate Mild, Brew XI, Highgate Old Ⓗ
Large, comfortable bar offering a selection of board games and table skittles, and a plush lounge. Other beers from the Bass range are occasionally available.
❀ ⬥ ♣ P

Hamemaker's Arms
87 Blue Lane West (A454) ☎ (0922) 28083
11.30–3, 6–11 (11–11 Sat)
Banks's Mild, Bitter Ⓔ
Pleasantly modernised 1930s pub with a well laid-out bar and a fading but comfortable, farmhouse-style lounge. Handy for town. No meals Sun. Q ❀ ◖ ▮ ⬥ ♣ P

New Fullbrook
West Bromwich Road (A4031/A4148 jct) ☎ (0922) 21761
11.30–11
Banks's Mild; M&B Highgate Mild, Springfield Bitter, Brew XI, Highgate Old Ⓔ
Large 1930s roadhouse, the biggest seller of Highgate Mild and real Springfield. It has a games room and a lounge reserved for diners until 9.30pm (no food Sun).
❀ ◖ ▮ ⬌ (Bescot Stadium) ♣ P

New Inns
John Street ☎ (0922) 27660
12–3, 5.30 (7 Sat)–11 (12–3, 8–10.30 Sun)
Ansells Mild, Bitter; Ind Coope Burton Ale Ⓗ
Traditional, small-roomed, Victorian back-street local with a cosy lounge and a passageway drinking area. A rare haven from jukeboxes and fruit machines. Beautifully-cooked, interesting food (not served Mon eve or Sun). ♨ Q ❀ ◖ ▮ ♣

Oak
336 Green Lane ☎ (0922) 645758
12–2.30 (11.30–3 Sat), 7–11 (closed Sun lunch)
Pitfield Mild, Bitter; Wiltshire Stonehenge Bitter Ⓗ; guest beers
Increasingly popular one-roomed pub with an unusual island bar, stocking up to six real ales. No meals Sat eve or Sun. ◖ ▮ ⬥ ♣ P

White Lion
Sandwell Street ☎ (0922) 28542
12–3, 7–11
Ansells Mild, Bitter; HP&D Entire; Ind Coope Burton Ale; S&N Theakston Old Peculier Ⓗ
Very popular, three-roomed pub: the large bar has a sloping floor; smaller lounge and a pool room. ❀ ◖ ⬥ ♣

Wednesbury

Cottage Spring
106 Franchise Street (off B4200) ☎ (021) 526 6354
12–2.30 (5 Sat), 5 (7 Sat)–11 (12–11 Fri)
Holden's Mild, Bitter Ⓔ, **Special, XL** Ⓗ
Small, friendly sports-oriented local, serving good value meals and snacks. ◖ ▮ ⬥ ♣ P

Woodman
74 Wood Green Road (500 yds from M6 jct 9) ☎ (0922) 405872
11.30–11 (11.30–4, 6–11 Sat)
Banks's Mild; Courage Best Bitter Ⓔ, **Directors; Ruddles County** Ⓗ
Large pub on a busy crossroads, under threat of demolition for road improvement: a large bar and a smaller, more comfortable smoke room. Children are welcome in the basic games room at the rear. Very good prices for the area.
⏳ ⬥ ⬌ (Bescot Stadium) P

Wednesfield

Broadway
Lichfield Road (A4124) ☎ (0922) 405872
11.30–2.30, 5–11 (12–3, 6–11 Sat)
Ansells Mild, Bitter; HP&D Entire; Ind Coope Burton Ale; Tetley Bitter Ⓗ
Pleasant, multi-roomed pub with wood panelling in the lounge. The back lounge features ornate plaster coving, stained-glass partitions and wooden-framed mirrors. No lunches Sun. Ramp entrance for wheelchairs. ❀ ◖ ⬥ ⬥ P

Cross Guns
43 Lichfield Road ☎ (0902) 726025
11–3, 6–11
HP&D Mild, Bitter, Entire Ⓗ; guest beer
Large(ish) open-plan pub on the main road. Weekday lunches. ❀ ◖ ♣ P

Dog & Partridge
High Street ☎ (0902) 723490
11–11
Banks's Mild, Bitter Ⓔ
Old beamed pub with a modern conservatory over-looking a large garden. ◖ P

Pyle Cock
Rookery Street
10.30–4, 6–11
Banks's Mild, Bitter Ⓔ
Excellent locals' boozer with lovely etched windows depicting a pyle cock. P

Spread Eagle
Broad Lane South (off A4124) ☎ (0902) 606890
11.30–2.30, 5–11 (11–11 Fri & Sat)
Banks's Mild, Bitter Ⓔ
Large, post-war estate pub: three spacious rooms, all usually lively. ◖ ⬥ P

West Bromwich

Churchfield Tavern
18 Little Lane
11–11
Banks's Hanson's Mild, Bitter Ⓗ
Deceptively large pub where

West Midlands

the excellent garden features livestock and play equipment. 🏃 ⛄ 🏛 ◗ ⬟ 🚻 ♣ P

Old Hop Pole
High Street, Carter's Green (off A41)
☎ (021) 525 6648
11.30–3, 5.30–11 (11–11 Sat & summer Fri)
HP&D Mild, Bitter, Entire, Deakin's Downfall; Tetley Bitter Ⓗ
19th-century local in Victorian style, with a warm atmosphere. 🏃 🏛 ◗ ♣

Wheatsheaf
High Street, Carter's Green (off A41)
11–2.45 (3.15 Sat), 5 (6 Sat)–11 (11–11 Fri)
Holden's Mild Ⓔ, **Bitter** Ⓗ **&** Ⓔ, **Special, XL** Ⓗ
Friendly, two-roomed local where blow-football is played. Eve meals Sat only.
🏛 ◗ ⬟ ♣ ◗

Willenhall

Brewers Droop
44 Wolverhampton Street
☎ (0902) 607827
12–3 (4 Sat), 6–11
Batham Best Bitter; Everards Old Original; Hook Norton Old Hooky Ⓗ**; guest beers**
Comfortable, two-roomed former coaching house staging folk music every Thu in an upstairs room, and a monthly quiz night. At least two guest beers. Eve meals Fri and Sat only. 🏛 ◗ ▶ ♣

Falcon
Gomer Street West (near Brewers Droop)
☎ (0902) 633378
12–11
Banks's Mild, Bitter; Ruddles Best Bitter, County Ⓗ**; guest beers**
Two-roomed local with a strong darts following.
🏛 ⬟ ♣ ⌣

Robin Hood
54 The Crescent, Shepwell Green
☎ (0902) 608006
12–3, 7 (5.30 Fri)–11 (12–2.30, 7–10.30 Sun)
Ansells Mild; Ind Coope Burton Ale; Tetley Bitter Ⓗ**; guest beers**
A regular in the *Guide* and local CAMRA *Pub of the Year* for the last three years. An excellent example of a friendly pub. 🏃 🏛 ⬟ P

Three Tuns
Walsall Road
☎ (0902) 631652
11–11
M&B Highgate Mild Ⓔ
Small, traditional Black Country boozer. If you're not a mild drinker when you go

in, you probably will be by the time you leave. Q ⬟ ♣

Wolverhampton

Brewery Tap
Dudley Road
☎ (0902) 351417
11.30–10.30
HP&D Mild, Bitter, Entire Ⓗ
Spacious comfortable house with a viewing gallery for the HP&D brewery. ◗ P

Clarendon
Chapel Ash
☎ (0902) 20587
11–11
Banks's Mild, Bitter Ⓔ
Brewery tap with an extensive, split-level lounge. A cosy snug has been retained following its 1991 refurbishment, which sadly removed the unusual corridor bar. Regular folk club. No food Sun. Car park only available after 6pm. ◗ P

Combermere Arms
90 Chapel Ash (A41)
11–2.30 (3 Fri, 3.30 Sat), 5–11
Draught Bass; Stones Best Bitter Ⓗ
Cunningly disguised as a terraced house, this pub boasts a tree growing in the gents'. ♣ ♣

Exchange
Exchange Street
10.30 (11 Sat)–11
Banks's Mild, Bitter Ⓔ
Busy town-centre pub, crowded at lunchtimes with office workers. ◗ ⬟ ⇌

Feathers
Molineux Street
12–3, 5–11 (12–11 Fri; 11–11 Sat)
Banks's Mild, Bitter Ⓔ
Basic pub next to Molineux, popular with students. ◗

Great Western
Sun Street (off A4124)
☎ (0902) 351090
11–11 (11–2.30, 5.15–11 Sat; 12–2.30, 7–10.30 Sun)
Batham Best Bitter; Holden's Stout, Mild, Bitter, Special, XL Ⓗ
Revitalised pub, next to an old low-level station, displaying railway memorabilia. Excellent value Black Country food (eve meals for parties with advance notice). Cobbled patio and a small garden.
🏃 🏛 ◗ ⇌ P

Homestead
Lodge Road, Oxley
☎ (0902) 787357
11–2.30, 6–11
Ansells Mild, Bitter; Ind Coope Burton Ale; Marston's Pedigree Ⓗ
Suburban pub with a children's playground.
🏛 ◗ ♣ P

Lewisham Arms
Prosser Street, Park Village (off A460)
☎ (0902) 453505
11.30–3, 6–11 (11–11 Sat; 12.30–3, 7–10.30 Sun)
Banks's Mild, Bitter Ⓔ
Unspoilt Victorian ale house. ♣

Newhampton Inn
Riches Street, Whitmore Reans
☎ (0902) 745773
11–11
Ansells Mild; Courage Best Bitter, Directors; Ruddles County; John Smith's Bitter Ⓗ**; guest beer**
Busy street-corner local attracting a cosmopolitan crowd to its three, distinctly different rooms. The large beer garden stands next to a bowling green; the smoke room is quiet. The guest beer changes daily. 🏛 Q 🏛 ⬟

Posada
Lichfield Street (opp. art gallery)
☎ (0902) 710738
11–2.30, 5–10.30 (11–10.30 Fri & Sat)
HP&D Mild, Bitter, Entire Ⓗ
Town-centre, Victorian pub with a tiled frontage. Lively and popular with students, but usually closes when Wolves are at home. Weekday lunches served. ◗ ⇌

Stamford Arms
Lime Street
☎ (0902) 24172
12–3, 6–11 (12–11 Sat)
Banks's Mild, Bitter Ⓔ
Victorian, multi-roomed street-corner pub. 🏛 ⬟

Woodsetton

Park Inn
George Street (off A457/A4123) ☎ (0902) 882843
12–3, 6–11 (11–11 Fri & Sat)
Holden's Mild, Bitter, Special, XL Ⓗ
Friendly, comfortable brewery tap which holds regular summer barbecues. No food Sun. A house beer (XB) is stocked occasionally.
🏃 🏛 ◗ 🚻 ⇌ (Tipton) ♣ P

Wordsley

Samson & Lion
140 Brierley Hill Road (B4180)
☎ (0384) 77796
11 (10 summer)–11
Banks's Mild Ⓔ**; Batham Best Bitter; Vaux Samson** Ⓗ**; guest beers**
Sympathetically restored hostelry, adjacent to lock 4 on the Stourbridge Canal. Still undergoing development, but has facilities for boaters and a skittle alley. No food Sun. 🏃 Q ⛄ 🏛 🚐 ◗ ▶ ⬟ 🚻 ♣ P

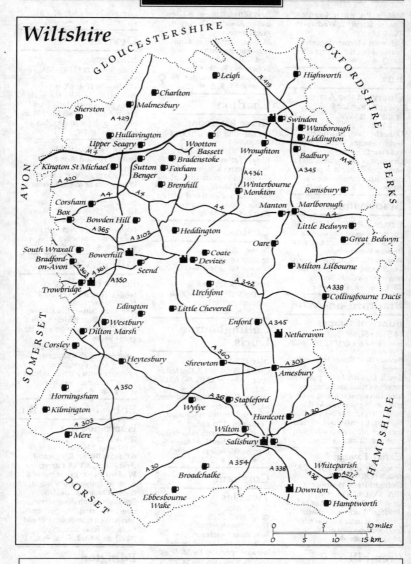

Wiltshire

Archers, Arkell's, Swindon; Bunces, Netheravon; Gibbs Mew, Salisbury; Hop Back, Downton/Salisbury; Mole's, Bowerhill; Ushers, Trowbridge; Wadworth, Devizes

Amesbury

Antrobus Arms Hotel
Church Street ☎ (0980) 623163
10.30–2.30, 6–11
Draught Bass; Wadworth IPA (summer), 6X, Old Timer Ⓗ
Georgian hotel with displays of coaching memorabilia.

Pretty garden with cedars and fountains. 🏮 Q ✿ ⇔ ◑ ▶ P

Badbury

Bakers Arms
Off A345, near M4 jct 15
☎ (0793) 740313
11–3, 6.30–11

Arkell's 2B, 3B Ⓗ
Small, neat pub tucked away in a lane. 🏮 Q ✿ ◑ ♣ P

Bowden Hill

Rising Sun
1 mile E of Lacock
☎ (024 973) 363
12–2.30 (not Mon), 7–11

Wiltshire

Mole's IPA, Bitter, Landlord's Choice, Brew 97; Wadworth 6X Ⓗ
Pub with a terraced garden overlooking the Avon valley.
🏾 Q ⊛ ◑ ✦ P

Box

Quarrymans Arms
Box Hill OS834693
☎ (0225) 743569
11–3, 7–11
Draught Bass; Butcombe Bitter; Smiles Brewery Bitter; Wadworth 6X Ⓗ
Open-plan lounge area and a small public bar in a popular pub with extensive views.
🏾 ⊛ 🚐 ◑ ▣ Å ✦ P

Bradenstoke

Cross Keys
Off B4069 ☎ (0249) 890279
12–2.30 (not Mon–Thu, 3 Sat), 7–11
Bunces Benchmark; Wadworth 6X Ⓗ; guest beers
Traditional 200-year-old local in a pretty village setting.
🏾 Q ⊛ ◑ ▣ & ✦ P

Bradford-on-Avon

Bunch of Grapes
14 Silver Street (200 yds from town bridge) ☎ (022 16) 3877
11–2.30, 6.30–11
Smiles Best Bitter Ⓗ; guest beers
Small, friendly town pub with excellent food and always at least three guest beers. A cosy front lounge overlooks the street; larger, livelier public at the rear. Occasional live trad. jazz Sun nights (no food Sun eve). ◑ ▣ ⇄ ✦ ⌂

Canal Tavern
Frome Road ☎ (022 16) 5232
12–2.30 (3.30 Wed & Sat), 6–11
Draught Bass; Wadworth IPA, 6X, Old Timer Ⓗ
Busy canalside pub, just below Bradford Lock and wharf. Large restaurant at the rear (no food Sun eve or Wed).
🏾 ◑ ▣ ⇄ ✦

Bremhill

Dumb Post
Dumb Post Hill (Calne road) OS975272 ☎ (0249) 813192
11.30–2.30, 7–11
Archers Best Bitter; Hall & Woodhouse Tanglefoot; Wadworth 6X, Old Timer Ⓗ
Excellent value free house in a rural setting high above Calne.
🏾 ⊛ ◑ ▣ ✦ P

Broadchalke

Queens Head
Off A354 via Coombe Bissett
☎ (0722) 780344
11–3, 7–11
Draught Bass; Hook Norton

Best Bitter; Ringwood Best Bitter; Ruddles County Ⓗ; guest beers
15th-century pub in a quiet rural setting with exposed flint walls and a large inglenook. Formerly a bakehouse and stables. 🏾 Q 🍴 ⊛ 🚐 ◑ Å ✦ ⌂ P

Charlton

Horse & Groom
On B4040 ☎ (0666) 823904
12–2.30, 7–11
Archers Village; Mole's Bitter; Tetley Bitter; Wadworth 6X Ⓗ; guest beers
Country inn in traditional Cotswold stone, set back from the road: a saloon and a large public. Good restaurant.
🏾 Q ⊛ ◑ ▣ P

Coate

New Inn
☎ (0380) 860644
12–2 (not Tue or Thu), 5–11 (11–3.30, 6.30–11 Sat)
Wadworth IPA, 6X Ⓖ
Proper village local with a genuine public bar.
🏾 🍴 ⊛ ▣ & ✦ P

Collingbourne Ducis

Shears Inn
Cadley Road (off A338; left at Spar, ¹⁄₂ mile) ☎ (0264) 850304
11–11
Ushers Best Bitter; Wadworth 6X; guest beers Ⓗ
Busy pub with a restaurant. Refurbished to a high standard but with reasonable prices. The landlord takes beer from small independents.
Q ⊛ 🚐 ◑ ▣ & P

Corsham

Two Pigs
38 Pickwick
☎ (0249) 712515
12–2.30 (not Mon–Thu), 7–11
Beer range varies Ⓗ
Pub with two house beers, brewed specially by Mole's and Bunces. Always at least two other guest beers. Wooden clad walls, stone floor, friendly atmosphere. Over 21s only. Local CAMRA Pub of the Year 1991. 🏾 ⊛ ⌂

Corsley

Cross Keys
Lye's Green (¹⁄₂ mile N of A362 at Royal Oak)
☎ (0373) 832406
12–3 (not Mon, Tue, Thu or Fri), 6.30 (7 Sat & Mon)–11
Draught Bass; Butcombe Bitter; Mole's Bitter Ⓗ
Welcoming free house of character: a popular, spacious pub. Grand open log fire.

Lunches Wed and Sat only.
🏾 ⊛ ◑ ▣ Å ✦

Devizes

Elm Tree
Long Street ☎ (0380) 723834
11.30–2.30, 7–11
Wadworth IPA, 6X Ⓗ
Popular (especially for food) town pub which dates back beyond the English Civil War. Smoking discouraged. No food Sun. ⊛ 🚐 ◑ ▶ P

Hare & Hounds
Hare & Hound Street
☎ (0380) 723231
10.30–2.30, 6.30 (7 Sat)–11
Wadworth IPA, 6X, Farmer's Glory Ⓗ
Building dating back to at least the 17th century. Many renovations later, it is a popular back-street pub used mainly by locals. No food Sun.
🏾 ⊛ ◑ ✦ P

Dilton Marsh

Prince of Wales
High Street ☎ (0373) 865487
11–2.30 (3 Sat), 6.30–11
Ash Vine Bitter; Ind Coope Benskins Best Bitter; Smiles Best Bitter; Wadworth 6X Ⓗ; guest beers
Simple, well-run locals' pub, open plan with a separate dining area. Pub games-oriented, with a lively skittles team. No meals Sun eve.
⊛ ◑ ▶ ⇄ ✦ P

Ebbesbourne Wake

Horseshoe Inn
Off A30 ☎ (0722) 780474
11 (12 Mon)–2.30, 6.30 (7 Mon)–11
Adnams Bitter; Ringwood Best Bitter, XXXX Porter; Wadworth 6X; guest beers Ⓖ
Remote, 18th-century inn at the foot of an old ox drove. Formerly hatch door service, now converted into two small bars with a fine display of old tools. No food Mon eve.
🏾 Q ⊛ 🚐 ◑ ▣ Å ✦ ⌂ P

Edington

Lamb
Westbury Road (B3098)
☎ (0380) 830263
11–2.30 (3 Sat), 5.30 (6 Sat)–11
Gibbs Mew Local Line, Premium Ⓗ
Attractive village pub with low beamed ceilings and stone fireplaces. Function room upstairs. No food Tue eve.
🏾 Q ⊛ ◑ ▣ Å ✦ P

Enford

Swan
Longstreet ☎ (0980) 70338
11.30 (12 winter)–2.30, 6.30 (7 winter)–11 (11–6, 7–11 Sat)

Wiltshire

Hop Back Special; Wadworth
6X Ⓗ; guest beers
Cosy, unspoilt thatched free
house with an unusual gantry
sign straddling the road.
Children welcome in the small
bar at lunchtime. Good value
for money. ⚒ ❀ ◖ ▶ ♣ P

Foxham

Foxham Inn
Off A429 ☎ (0249) 74665
11.30–2.30 (not Tue), 6–11 (12–11 Sat)
Mole's Bitter; Wadworth
6X Ⓗ
Small village local off the
beaten track. Very cosy.
Home-made meals.
⚒ Q ❀ ◖ ▶ ♣ ↺ P ⅙

Great Bedwyn

Cross Keys
High Street ☎ (0672) 870678
11–2.30 (3 Sat), 6–11
Draught Bass; Wiltshire
Stonehenge Bitter, Old
Grumble Ⓗ; guest beers
Large, busy L-shaped pub
with a pool table in the main
bar. Bar meals are good value
for money. Guest beers
include small independents'
brews. ☎ ❀ ◖ ▶ ♣ ♣

Hamptworth

Cuckoo Inn
Hamptworth Road (off B3079)
OS243197 ☎ (0794) 390302
11.30–2.30, 6–11 (11–11 Sat)
Adnams Broadside; Draught
Bass; Bunces Best Bitter; Hall
& Woodhouse Badger Best
Bitter, Tanglefoot; Wadworth
6X Ⓖ; guest beers
Popular, basic but cosy pub in
a quiet rural setting on the
edge of the New Forest: three
small interlinked rooms of a
public bar standard; good
garden for children.
⚒ Q ☎ ❀ ⊞ & ▲ ♣ ↺ P

Heddington

Ivy
Off A3102 ☎ (0380) 850276
11–3, 6.30–11
Wadworth IPA, 6X Ⓖ
Traditional thatched village
pub. ⚒ Q ☎ ❀ ▲ ♣ ↺ P

Heytesbury

Angel Inn
High Street ☎ (0985) 40330
11–3, 6–11
Ash Vine Challenger;
Marston's Border Bitter,
Pedigree; Ringwood Best
Bitter Ⓗ
17th-century coaching inn
with a highly regarded
restaurant. The bar area is
mostly original, enjoying a
strong local trade from a
friendly village now bypassed.
⚒ Q ❀ ☎ ◖ ▶ P

Highworth

Plough
Lechlade Road (A361)
☎ (0793) 762224
11–2.30, 6–11
Arkell's 2B, 3B Ⓗ
Friendly locals' pub with one
cosy bar. Separate games
room with pool. ⚒ ☎ ❀ ♣

Horningsham

Bath Arms Hotel
Longleat (off B3092) OS809416
☎ (0985) 844308
11–11 (12–2.30, 7–10.30 Sun)
Draught Bass; Eldridge Pope
Dorchester, Hardy Country;
Wadworth 6X Ⓗ
Fine country hotel in an idyllic
setting on the edge of Longleat
Park. Wide choice of whiskies.
⚒ Q ❀ ⊨ ◖ ▶ ⊞ ♣ P

Hullavington

Queens Head
The Street (off A429)
☎ (0666) 837221
11.30–2 (3 Sat, not Mon), 7–11
Archers Village, Best Bitter;
Wadworth 6X Ⓗ
Homely, village local where
the open fires and recent
refurbishment generate a
warm atmosphere. Small
function room and skittle
alley. No food Sun.
⚒ Q ❀ ⊨ ◖ ♣ P

Hurdcott

Black Horse
Black Horse Lane (off A338)
☎ (0980) 611565
11–2.30, 6–11
Gibbs Mew Wiltshire,
Salisbury Ⓗ
Old building at the end of a
country lane; formerly three
cottages and a forge. Wattle
and daub upstairs; beamed
bar below. Good company.
⚒ ◖ ▲ ♣ P

Kilmington

Red Lion
On B3092 ☎ (0985) 844263
11–3.30, 6.30–11
Draught Bass; Butcombe
Bitter Ⓗ; guest beer
Unspoilt National Trust-
owned pub near Stourhead
Gardens. A single bar, partly
curtained-off. Good choice of
meals (no food Fri–Sun eves).
⚒ Q ☎ ❀ ⊨ ◖ ▶ ⊞ ♣ ↺
P

Kington St Michael

Jolly Huntsman
☎ (0249) 75305
11.30–2.30, 6.30–11
Ind Coope Burton Ale; Tetley
Bitter; Wadworth 6X Ⓗ; guest
beers

Roomy village pub with a
separate dining area (children
permitted). Extensive range of
whiskies. ⚒ Q ◖ ▶ & ▲ P

Leigh

Foresters Arms
Malmesbury Road (B4040)
☎ (0793) 750901
7–11 (12–2.30, 7–11 Sat; 12–2.30,
7–10.30 Sun)
Hall & Woodhouse
Tanglefoot; Hook Norton
Best Bitter; Wadworth 6X Ⓖ;
guest beer
Intimate bar with a tiled floor.
⚒ ❀ ◖ ▲ ♣ P

Liddington

Village Inn
Ham Road ☎ (0793) 790314
12–2.30, 6–11
Draught Bass; Fuller's ESB;
Marston's Pedigree;
Wadworth 6X; Whitbread
Flowers IPA, Original Ⓗ;
guest beer
Cosy, carpeted split-level
lounge bar with red brick
facings. ⚒ Q ❀ ⊨ ◖ ▶ P

Little Bedwyn

Harrow Inn
Off A4 ☎ (0672) 870871
11.30–2.30, 6–11 (12–2.30, 7–10.30
Sun)
Hook Norton Best Bitter;
guest beers Ⓗ
Pub recently bought and
carefully refurbished by
villagers who did not want to
lose their pub. Regular guests
include local independents'
brews. No food Sun/Mon
eves. ⚒ Q ❀ ⊨ ◖ ▶ & ▲ ♣

Little Cheverell

Owl
Low Road ☎ (0380) 812263
12–2.30 (not Mon), 6.30 (7 winter)–11
Wadworth IPA, 6X Ⓗ; guest
beer
One-bar local with a separate
dining area (no food Mon).
Pleasant, steep-sloping
garden. ⚒ Q ☎ ❀ ◖ ▶ ↺ P

Malmesbury

Red Bull
Sherston Road (B4040, W of
centre) ☎ (0666) 822108
11–2.30 (not Tue, 3.30 Sat), 7 (6
summer)–11
Draught Bass; Whitbread
WCPA, Boddingtons Bitter Ⓗ;
guest beers
Popular family pub with a
skittle alley.
⚒ Q ☎ ❀ ◖ & ♣ P

Manton

Up the Garden Path
High Street ☎ (0672) 512677
11–2.30, 6.30–11

Archers Best Bitter; Hook Norton Best Bitter; Wadsworth 6X Ⓗ
Pub at the top of a steep path, with cosy corners in a carpeted bar. No meals Mon eve. 🍴 ❀ ◖▶ ♣ P

Marlborough

Lamb Inn
The Parade ☎ (0672) 512668
11–3, 6–11 (11–11 Fri & Sat)
Adnams Broadside; Hall & Woodhouse Tanglefoot; Wadworth IPA, 6X Ⓖ
Popular local just down from the town hall. ❀ 🍴 ♞ ◖▶ ◖ ♣

Mere

Butt of Sherry
Castle Street (B3095)
☎ (0747) 860352
11.30–2.30 (3 Sat), 5 (6 Sat)–11
Gibbs Mew Premium, Bishop's Tipple; Ind Coope Burton Ale Ⓗ
Traditional, lively local. Collection of photographic equipment in the lounge. No food Sun eve in winter.
🍴 ❀ 🍴 ◖▶ ◖ ♣

Milton Lilbourne

Three Horseshoes
On B3087 ☎ (0672) 62323
11–2.30, 6.30–11
Adnams Bitter; Wadworth 6X Ⓗ; guest beer
Smart open-plan bar featuring a 30ft-deep well. No-smoking restaurant (no food Mon).
🍴 ♞ ❀ ◖▶ ▲ ♣ P

Oare

White Hart
On A345 ☎ (0672) 62273
11–2.30, 6.30–11
Wadworth IPA, 6X Ⓗ
Genuine, unspoilt, village roadside local. No food Mon lunch or Sun eve.
🍴 ❀ 🍴 ◖▶ ♣ P

Ramsbury

Bell Inn
The Square ☎ (0672) 20230
11.30–3, 6–11
Eldridge Pope Royal Oak; Fuller's London Pride; Wadworth IPA, 6X Ⓗ; guest beers
Large pub popular for meals. The painting on the wall in the bar is a listed feature. Guests include many local independents' brews.
🍴 Q ♞ ❀ ◖▶ ◖ ♣ P

Salisbury

Haunch of Venison
Minister Street (opp. Poultry Cross) ☎ (0722) 322024
11–11

Courage Best Bitter, Directors; Ringwood Best Bitter Ⓗ
Old-English chop house (c.1320), now a busy city-centre pub with many historic and unusual features, including a mummified hand, a pewter-topped bar and rows of taps. No meals Sun eve.
🍴 Q ◖▶ ⇒

Queens Arms
Ivy Street (by Brown St car park) ☎ (0722) 334144
11–2.30, 5.30–11 (11–11 Sat)
Ushers Best Bitter; Webster's Yorkshire Bitter Ⓗ; guest beers (occasionally)
Grade II listed building. One split-level bar, lively at weekends. Good food.
🍴 🍴 ◖ ⇐

Red Lion Hotel
Milford Street
11–2.30, 6–11
Draught Bass; Ushers Best Bitter; Wadworth 6X Ⓗ; guest beers
Coaching inn dating in part from the 13th century. Its clocks are famous; the case of the skeleton/organ clock was reputedly carved by prisoners from the Spanish Armada.
🍴 Q ♞ ❀ 🍴 ◖▶ ⇒ P

Tollgate Inn
Tollgate Road (200 yds from college) ☎ (0722) 327621
11–2.30 (3 Sat), 6 (6.30 Sat)–11
Hall & Woodhouse Badger Best Bitter; Wells Eagle Ⓗ
Friendly, part-18th-century pub near the city's former eastern tollgate. Some internal walls have been removed to give a long, low bar, very narrow at one end. Snacks at lunchtime. Accommodation in summer. ♣ P

Village
Wilton Road (off St Paul's roundabout) ☎ (0722) 329707
11–11 (11–3.30, 5.30–11 Mon–Wed in winter)
Oakhill Bitter, Yeoman; St Austell XXXX Mild, HSD; Taylor Landlord Ⓗ; guest beers
Convivial pub with a cosy cellar bar (occasional live music). Popular with railway enthusiasts: Class 33 loco horns in use! Guest beers are chosen by customers. High prices. ⇒ ♣

Wyndham Arms
Estcourt Road (off Churchill Way E ring road)
☎ (0722) 331026
4.30 (4 Fri, 12 Sat)–11
Hop Back GFB, Special, Entire Stout, Summer Lightning Ⓗ
Wiltshire's only pub-brewery, a pleasantly refurbished Victorian corner local.

Excellent value; good atmosphere. Q ♣

Seend

Bell
Bell Hill ☎ (0380) 828338
11–3, 6–11 (11–11 Sat)
Wadworth IPA, 6X Ⓗ
Cosy lounge and larger public bar. An attractive, well-run old inn, deservedly popular for its home-cooked lunches –come early. Imposing former brewery at the rear. Sweeping views from the garden. No food Sun. Family room doubles as a function room.
🍴 Q ♞ ❀ ◖▶ ▲ ♣ P

Sherston

Rattlebone Inn
Church Street ☎ (0666) 840871
12–2.30, 5.30–11 (12–11 Sat)
Moorhouse's Pendle Witches Brew; Wadworth 6X; Wickwar Brand Oak Ⓗ; guest beer
Friendly free house in the centre of a charming village. Good value bar and restaurant meals.
🍴 Q ❀ ◖▶ ◖ ♣ ⌂ P

Shrewton

George Inn
London Road (B3086, N end of village) ☎ (0980) 620341
11.30–3 (not Wed), 6–11
Ushers Best Bitter; Wadworth 6X Ⓗ; guest beer
Part-15th-century, chalk, flint and stone-built inn which once housed its own brewery. A friendly, corner village local with good home-cooked food. Weekly guest beer. 🍴 ♞ ❀ 🍴 ◖▶ ◖ ▲ ♣ ⌂ P

South Wraxall

Longs Arms
Upper South Wraxall (off B3109) ☎ (022 16) 4450
12–2.30, 5.30–11 (11–3, 7–11 Sat)
Wadworth IPA, 6X Ⓗ
Relaxed, friendly village pub with a spacious, comfortable lounge and a snug, locals' public bar. Good food (no meals Sun/Mon eves).
🍴 Q ❀ ◖▶ ◖ ♣ P

Stapleford

Pelican Inn
Warminster Road (A36)
☎ (0722) 790241
11–3, 5.30–11 (11–11 Sat)
Otter Bitter; Ringwood Best Bitter, Fortyniner Ⓗ; guest beers
250-year-old, flint and stone inn, once part-stables and mortuary. Good food in generous helpings. Pitchers of ale offered – any four pints for £4.40. 🍴 ❀ ◖▶ ▲ ♣ ⌂ P

Sutton Benger

Wellesley Arms
High Street ☎ (0249) 720251
11–3, 6.30–11
Wadworth IPA, 6X Ⓗ
Popular, well-run village pub.
🏚 Q ☀ ◗ ▯ & ♣ P

Swindon

Beehive
Prospect Hill ☎ (0793) 523187
12–11
Morrells Mild, Varsity Ⓗ;
guest beer
Unusual, lively pub with a bar
on five levels. 🏚 ◗ ⇌ ♣

Glue Pot
Emlyn Square
☎ (0793) 523935
11–11
**Archers Village, Best Bitter,
Golden** Ⓗ; guest beer
Imposing, listed, stone
building in Brunel's Railway
Village. One busy bar. No
food Sun. ◗ ⇌ ♣

Wheatsheaf
Newport Street, Old Town
☎ (0793) 523188
11–2.30, 5.30 (6 Sat)–11
**Wadworth IPA, 6X, Farmer's
Glory, Old Timer** Ⓗ; guest
beer
Pub with a good, plain front
bar with bare floorboards,
mercifully sound-insulated
from the decibel-loaded
lounge. Q ☀ 🛏 ◗ ▯ ▯ & ♣

Trowbridge

Lamb Inn
Mortimer Street
☎ (0225) 755497
11.30–2.30 (3 Sat), 7–11
**Wadworth IPA, 6X, Old
Timer** Ⓗ
Popular pub with an award-
winning beer garden.
🏚 Q ☀ 🛏 ◗ ⇌ ♣ P ✂

Rose & Crown
36 Stallard Street (opp. station)
☎ (0225) 752862
12–3 (4 Fri, 5 Sat), 7–11
**Morland Old Speckled Hen,
John Smith's Bitter; Ushers
Best Bitter** Ⓗ
Small pub with a main bar
decorated with old sporting
memorabilia.
🏚 ◗ ▯ ▯ ⇌ ♣ ◠

Upper Seagry

New Inn
☎ (0249) 721083
11.30–2.30, 6.30–11 (12–2.30, 7–10.30
Sun)
**Ansells Bitter; Draught Bass;
Wadworth 6X** Ⓗ
Tastefully decorated village
pub, well equipped with
dining tables.
🏚 Q ☀ ◗ ▯ & ♣ P

Urchfont

Lamb
The Green ☎ (0380) 840361
12–2.30, 6–11
**Wadworth IPA, 6X, Old
Timer** Ⓗ
Cosy, welcoming ale-drinkers'
local. 🏚 Q ☀ ◗ ▯ ♣ P

Wanborough

Black Horse
Bishopstone Road (old B4507)
☎ (0793) 790305
11–3, 5.30–11 (11–11 Sat)
**Arkell's 2B, 3B, Mash Tun
Mild** Ⓗ, **Kingsdown
(winter)** Ⓖ, **Noel Ale** Ⓗ
Small, friendly local that is
slightly offbeat: brass £sd till,
three-legged dog, garden with
animals, games and a fine
view. No food Sun.
☀ ◗ ▯ ▲ ♣ P

Plough
High Street ☎ (0793) 790523
12–2.30, 6–11 (11–11 Fri & Sat)
**Archers Village; Draught
Bass; Wadworth 6X;
Whitbread Boddingtons
Bitter, Flowers Original** Ⓗ
Handsome thatched pub with
long, heavily timbered bars.
One could almost be on a ship
of Nelson's time. No food
Sat/Sun.
🏚 Q ☀ ◗ ▯ ♣ ◠ P

Westbury

Oak Inn
Warminster Road (A350)
☎ (0373) 823169
11–2.30, 6–11
**Draught Bass; Hardington
Best Bitter; Ringwood Best
Bitter, Fortyniner** Ⓗ; guest
beers
A mock Tudor exterior
conceals a 16th-century,
purpose-built inn with more
recent additions. Beer range
may change. 🏚 ☀ ◗ ▯ ♣ P

Whiteparish

Kings Head
The Street ☎ (0794) 884278
11–2.30, 6–11
Ringwood Best Bitter Ⓗ & Ⓖ
Part-14th-century inn with
stables at the rear. Features a
preserved window. A good,
friendly village local. No
lunches Mon.
🏚 Q ☀ ◗ ▯ ▯ ▲ ♣ ◠ P

Wilton

Bear
West Street ☎ (0722) 742398
11–2.30, 5.30–11
**Hall & Woodhouse Badger
Best Bitter** Ⓗ
Small, 16th-century pub with
one public bar. 🏚 ☀ ◗ ▯ ♣

Winterbourne Monkton

New Inn
Off A4361 ☎ (067 23) 240
11–3, 6–11
**Adnams Bitter; Wadworth
6X** Ⓗ; guest beer
Small, friendly local near
Avebury Stone Circle.
🏚 ☀ 🛏 ◗ ▯ & ♣ P

Wootton Bassett

Old Nick
Station Road ☎ (0793) 848102
11–2.30, 6–11 (11–11 Fri & Sat)
**Gibbs Mew Wiltshire,
Bishop's Tipple; Tetley
Bitter; Wadworth 6X** Ⓗ; guest
beers
Formerly the police station,
now an extensive bar. The
adjoining courthouse is a
disco bar. Regular beerexes.
🏚 ☀ ◗ ▯ & ♣ P

Wroughton

Carters Rest
High Street ☎ (0793) 812288
11.30–2.30, 5.30–11 (11–11 Sat)
**Archers Village, Best Bitter,
Golden; Marston's Owd
Rodger; Morland Old
Speckled Hen** Ⓗ
Built in 1904, a former
Courage house with two busy
bars. Usually ten beers
available, including a draught
kriek. 🏚 Q ☀ ◗ ▯ ♣ P

Fox & Hounds
Markham Road
☎ (0793) 812217
11–3, 5.30–11
Arkell's 2B, 3B, Kingsdown Ⓗ
Neat, single-bar motel.
🏚 ☀ 🛏 ◗ ▯ & ♣ P

Wylye

Bell
High Street ☎ (098 56) 338
11 (11.30 winter)–2.30, 6–11
**Gibbs Mew Local Line; Hall
& Woodhouse Badger Best
Bitter; Wadworth 6X** Ⓗ; guest
beers
14th-century inn in a quiet
setting, with beamed bars
featuring exposed stone and
an inglenook.
🏚 Q ☀ 🛏 ◗ ▯ ▲ ♣ P

Join CAMRA —
see page 508

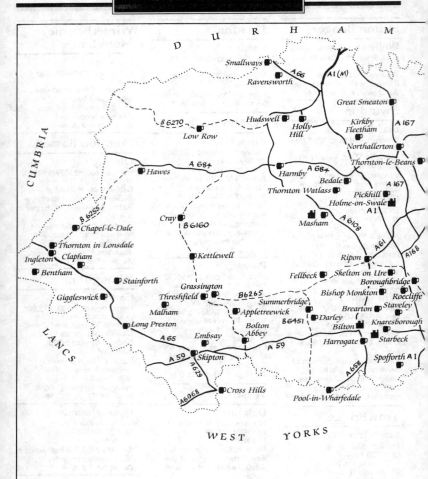

North Yorkshire

 Black Sheep, Masham; **Cropton**, Cropton; **Daleside**,
Starbeck; **Franklin's**, Bilton; **Hambleton**, Holme-on-Swale;
Keystone, Sherburn in Elmet; **Malton**, Malton; **Marston
Moor**, Kirk Hammerton; **Rudgate**, Tockwith; **Selby**, Selby;
Samuel Smith, Tadcaster; **Whitby's**, Whitby

Acaster Malbis

Ship Inn
Moor End ☎ (0904) 705609
11.30–3, 6.30–11 (11–11 summer)
**Taylor Landlord; Tetley Mild,
Bitter** Ⓗ
17th-century coaching house
beside the River Ouse. Once
an inn for bargees who plied
their trade on the river, now
popular with boaters and
campers.
🏠 ❀ 🍴 ◑ ▶ ▲ ♣ P

Ampleforth

White Horse
West End ☎ (043 93) 378
11–2.30, 6–11
Tetley Bitter Ⓗ
Deservedly popular, cosy
village pub. Comfortable oak
beamed interior with settles.
One main bar and a separate
dining room.
🏠 ❀ 🍴 ◑ ♣ P

Appletreewick

New Inn
Main Street (back road
between Barden Tower and
Burnsall) ☎ (0756) 720252
11.30–3 (not Mon), 7–11

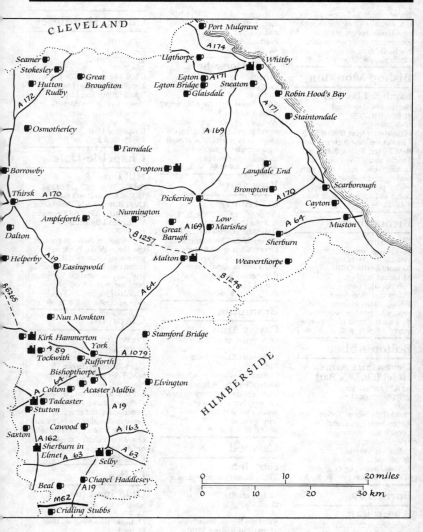

John Smith's Bitter; Younger
Scotch, No. 3 Ⓗ
Welcoming, friendly pub
where the emphasis is on
drink rather than food. The
bar is in an L-shaped room
with another room across the
hall. Gated beer garden across
the road. Large range of
foreign bottled beers;
Liefmans Kriek on tap. No. 3
may give way to a guest.
🏚 Q ♿ ⊛ 🛏 ◖◗ 🅰 ♣ ⌂ P

Beal

Kings Head
Main Street ☎ (0977) 673487
7–11 (12–4, 7–11 Sat)
Ruddles Best Bitter; Tetley
Bitter Ⓗ
With its time-warp bar and
numerous rooms, this pub
really is the hub of village life in
the evening. Known locally as
'Fred's', it has been in the same
family for 48 years. 🏚 ⊕ ♣ P

Bedale

Waggon & Horses
Market Place ☎ (0677) 422747
11–11
Tetley Bitter Ⓗ
Originally two rooms, now
partly opened out into a
bar/lounge with a large open
fire. Friendly atmosphere.
Quiz night Tue; dominoes Sun
(visitors welcome to play).
🏚 ⊛ 🛏 ♣

Try also: Green Dragon,
Market Pl (Free)

Bentham

Coach House
Main Street, High Bentham
☎ (052 42) 62305
Robinson's Hartleys XB, Best
Bitter Ⓗ
A fine 17th-century exterior
overlooks a small cobbled
square with seats. The 1985
interior has a single large bar
and a restaurant to the rear.
🏚 ⊛ 🛏 ◖◗ ⇌ ♣ P

Punch Bowl
Low Bentham (B6480, Wray
road) ☎ (052 42) 61344
11.30–2.30, 6–11
Mitchell's Best Bitter Ⓗ

18th-century, old-time village inn, extended in 1986, though small, neat rooms remain. Restaurant open weekends. No food Mon. Angling available. 🏚 Q 🛏 🍴 ◑ ♣ P

Bishop Monkton

Lamb & Flag Inn

Boroughbridge Road
☎ (0765) 677322
12–3, 5.30–11
Hambleton Best Bitter; S&N Theakston Best Bitter; Stones Best Bitter; Tetley Bitter H
Traditional village local: a comfortable lounge with pew seating and a separate bar with a pool table. Lunches finish at 1.45, eve meals at 8.45. 🏚 🌸 ◑ ▶ P

Bishopthorpe

Ebor Inn

Main Street ☎ (0904) 706190
11–3, 5.30–11 (11–11 Sat)
Samuel Smith OBB, Museum H
Pub popular with locals, diners and race-goers. Friendly atmosphere; good food; plenty of ornate brass. Beware the lurid tiling in the gents! 🏚 🌸 ◑ ▶ 🍴 ◑ 🐕 ♣ P

Bolton Abbey

Devonshire Arms Hotel (Duke's Bar)

At A59/B6160 jct
☎ (0756) 710441
11–11
Franklin's Bitter; Tetley Bitter; Younger Scotch H; **guest beers** (summer)
Friendly bar, pleasantly done out as a tribute to Percy Braithwaite, sportsman extraordinaire. Quiz night Sun. 🏚 🌸 🍴 ◑ 🐕 ♣ P

Borrowby

Wheatsheaf

Main Street ☎ (0845) 537274
12–2 (Tue–Fri in summer only), 6.30–11 (12–3, 6.30–11 Sat)
S&N Theakston XB; Tetley Bitter; Younger Scotch H
Friendly, relatively unspoilt, 17th-century village local. Retains a welcome emphasis on beer, rather than food. Children welcome in the lounge. 🏚 Q 🌸 ◑ ▶ 🍴 P

Boroughbridge

Black Bull Inn

St James Square
☎ (0423) 322413
11–3, 6.30–11 (11–11 Fri)
S&N Theakston Best Bitter; John Smith's Bitter; H; **guest beers** (occasionally)
Attractive 13th-century inn: three separate drinking areas – a lounge, a snug and a small

restaurant. A friendly pub, busy with locals and visitors and popular for its good food. Fortnightly quizzes. 🏚 🍴 ◑ ▶ 🍴

Three Horseshoes Hotel

Bridge Street ☎ (0423) 322314
11–3, 5–11
S&N Theakston Best Bitter H; **Vaux Samson** E
Welcoming 1930s pub with wood panelling and stained-glass. Very friendly landlord; a good pub for meals and sociable conversation. 🏚 Q 🛏 🍴 ◑ 🐕 ▶ 🍴 P

Brearton

Malt Shovel

Off B6165 ☎ (0423) 862929
12–3 (not Mon), 6.45–11
Daleside Bitter; Old Mill Bitter; S&N Theakston Best Bitter, XB; Tetley Bitter H
16th-century pub with stone walls and original beams. Reputation for good food (not served Mon). 🏚 Q 🌸 ◑ ▶ ♣ P

Brompton

Cayley Arms

Main Street ☎ (0723) 859372
11–11
Camerons Bitter; Tetley Bitter H
Prominent wayside pub in an ancient village. A functional lounge is complemented by a hallway bar serving other areas. Pleasant but basic family room. 🏚 🛏 🌸 ◑ ▶ 🍴 ♣ P

Cawood

Ferry Inn

2 King Street (narrow lane on upstream side of swing bridge, off B1222)
☎ (0757) 268515
12–11
Adnams Bitter, Broadside; Mansfield Riding Mild, Riding Bitter, Old Baily; Tetley Bitter H
Original 16th-century pub with low ceilings and a large open hearth; quiet and friendly. Menu for children and vegetarians. Garden overlooks the river. 🏚 Q 🛏 🌸 🍴 ◑ ▶ 🍴 ♣ P

Cayton

Blacksmiths Arms

Main Street ☎ (0723) 582272
11–2.30, 6–11
Camerons Bitter H
Village-centre pub with various rooms, including a basic but popular bar, with a separate pool area, a snug/lounge and carvery. 🏚 🌸 ◑ ▶ ♣

Chapel Haddlesey

Jug Inn

First Road (100 yds from A19)
☎ (0757) 270307
12–4, 7–11
S&N Theakston XB; Taylor Landlord; H; **guest beer**
Small village local by the River Aire. Keen darts team and a friendly ghost. The small restaurant serves Desperate Dan Cow Pies. 🏚 Q 🌸 ◑ ▶ 🍴 ♣ P

Chapel-le-Dale

Hill Inn

On B6255 ☎ (052 42) 41256
11.30–3, 6.30–11 (11–11 Sat)
Dent Bitter; S&N Theakston Best Bitter, XB, Old Peculier; Whitbread Boddingtons Bitter H
Well-known, isolated pub on the Three Peaks Walk in potholing country. Utility furnishings: varnished boards and bare stonework. Separate pool room and food bar (children welcome). Folk every Sat. 🏚 🌸 ◑ ▶ 🍴 ♣ P

Clapham

New Inn

☎ (052 42) 51203
11.30–3, 7–11 (supper licence)
Dent Bitter; McEwan 70/-, 80/-; Tetley Bitter; Younger No. 3 H
Large coaching inn, dated 1776. One bar has leather bench seats and stucco-decorated walls; the other has oak panelling (1990 vintage). Occasional Dent Ramsbottom or Moorhouse's Premier. 🏚 🌸 🍴 ◑ ▶ 🍴 ♣ P

Colton

Olde Sun Inne

Main Street ☎ (0904) 84261
11.30–3, 7–11
Draught Bass; Stones Best Bitter H
Busy, popular pub (17th century) in a lovely village off the A64. Three rooms with a central bar, resident ghost, gardens and a landlady who signs for hearing-impaired customers. Q 🌸 ◑ ▶ 🍴 ♣ P

Cray

White Lion

On B6160, 1½ miles N of Buckden ☎ (0756) 760262
11–11
Moorhouse's Premier, Pendle Witches Brew; S&N Theakston Best Bitter H; **guest beers** (summer)
Five-bedroom rural inn amid fine scenery. Two small, stone-flagged public rooms: a main bar with log fire and Ring the

Bull, and a family/no-smoking/dining room. Garden with play area. Open daily 8.30am–11pm for food and non-alcoholic drinks. ▲

Cridling Stubbs

Ancient Shepherd
Off A1/M62 (jct 33/34)
☎ (0977) 673316
12–3 (not Sat), 7–11
Marston's Pedigree; Whitbread Trophy Ⓗ
A daunting exterior belies a welcoming Victorian interior. Restaurant (no meals Sat lunch). ❀ ◑ ▶ ⊟ ♣ P

Cropton

New Inn
Rosedale turn off A170 at Wrelton OS755890
☎ (075 15) 330
11–3, 5.30–11 (12–2.30, 7–11 winter)
Cropton Two Pints, Special Strong Ⓗ
Free house which set up its own brewery in 1984, now well established. Situated in an attractive village near Cropton Forest and Rosedale, so is popular with walkers and tourists as well as being the focal point of the village. Tetley beers usually available. ▲ ➤ ❀ ⊨ ◑ ▶ ⊟ ▲ ♣ P

Cross Hills

Old White Bear
Keighley Road ☎ (0535) 632115
11.30–3, 5–11 (11–11 Sat)
Goose Eye Bitter; Whitbread Boddingtons Mild, Bitter, Trophy Ⓗ**; guest beers**
Old inn (built 1735) undergoing sensitive refurbishment to retain separate rooms and drinking areas. Leased by the owners of Goose Eye Brewery. Families welcome at lunchtime. ▲ ❀ ◑ ▲ ♣ P

Dalton

Jolly Farmers of Olden Times
Between A19 and A1, just S of A168 near Thirsk OS431762
☎ (0845) 577359
12–2 (not Mon–Thu), 7.30–11
Courage Directors; John Smith's Bitter Ⓗ**; guest beers**
200-year-old, beamed village pub, modernised with a comfortable lounge area, a quiet bar/games room and a small dining room. ▲ ❀ ◑ ▶ ▲ ♣ P

Darley

Wellington Inn
Darley Head (B6451, 5 miles S of Pateley Bridge, off B6165)
☎ (0423) 780362
11–11

Ind Coope Burton Ale; Taylor Best Bitter; Tetley Mild, Bitter Ⓗ
Rebuilt pub in a delightful Dales setting.
▲ ➤ ❀ ◑ ▶ ⊟ ♣ P

Easingwold

Station Hotel
Knott Lane (off Raskelf Rd, 400 yds from A19)
☎ (0347) 22635
11–11
Hambleton Best Bitter; Tetley Bitter Ⓗ**; guest beers**
Historic Victorian relic of Britain's shortest standard gauge railway. Always two guest beers and one cider. The comprehensive beer list includes Belgian cherry beer on draught. Freshly cooked bar meals and a restaurant.
▲ ❀ ◑ ▶ ♣ ○

Egton

Horseshoe Inn
☎ (0947) 85274
12–3, 6 (6.30 winter)–11
S&N Theakston Best Bitter, XB, Old Peculier; Tetley Bitter Ⓗ
Grade II listed building, with a low, oak-beamed ceiling and church settles. Old rural pub atmosphere with an equestrian theme. Do not confuse with the Horseshoe at Egton Bridge.
▲ Q ➤ ❀ ⊨ ◑ ▶ ⊟ ♣ P

Egton Bridge

Postgate Inn
☎ (0947) 85241
11–11
Camerons Bitter, Strongarm Ⓗ
Attractive hotel overlooking a rustic railway station. Quoits played; children welcome. Children's and vegetarian menu offered. ▲ Q ➤ ❀ ⊨ ◑ ▶ ⊟ ⇌ ♣ P

Elvington

Grey Horse
Main Street ☎ (0904) 608335
12–2.30, 5.30–11 (12–3, 7–11 Sat)
Courage Directors; John Smith's Bitter Ⓗ**; guest beers**
Traditional village pub overlooking the green. Excellent tap room with log fires. Good value pub food and regularly-changed guest beers. Notable collection of wirelesses and clocks in the lounge.
▲ ❀ ◑ ▶ ⊟ ▲ ♣ ○ P

Embsay

Elm Tree
Elm Tree Square
☎ (0756) 790717
11.30–3, 5.30–11 (11–11 summer)

Trough Wild Boar; Whitbread Boddingtons Bitter, Trophy, Castle Eden Ale Ⓗ**; guest beers**
Large Whitbread pub with an enterprising licensee. Split into two main areas, one largely given over to games. Handy for the privately-owned Embsay Steam Railway. Whitbread guest beers. Food served all day in summer.
❀ ⊨ ◑ ▶ ⊟ ▲ ⇌ ♣ P

Farndale

Feversham Arms
Church Houses OS669974
☎ (0751) 33206
11–2.30, 7 (6.30 Sat)–11 (closed Mon eve)
Tetley Bitter Ⓗ
Remote inn set in a tiny hamlet deep in the N Yorks moors, popular with walkers. The bar has a stone-flagged floor, a cast iron range, and ceiling hooks, once used for curing hams, now used for a dangling jug collection.
▲ Q ➤ ❀ ⊨ ◑ ▶ ⊟ ♣ P

Fellbeck

Half Moon
On B6265, 3 miles E of Pateley Bridge
☎ (0423) 711560
12–3, 6.30–11
S&N Theakston Best Bitter; Taylor Landlord; Younger Scotch Ⓗ
Pleasant roadside inn close to the local beauty spot, Brimham Rocks: a traditional bar and a large sunny lounge. Accommodation in self-catering cottages.
▲ Q ➤ ❀ ⊨ ◑ ▶ ⊟ ▲ P

Giggleswick

Black Horse
Church Street
☎ (0729) 822506
12–3, 6.30–11
Taylor Best Bitter; Tetley Bitter; Younger Scotch Ⓗ**; guest beers** (summer)
17th-century village pub in a traditional position next to the church and market cross. Superb mullion-windowed exterior and a pleasant though modern, wood-panelled interior, with a semi-divided lounge and a separate dining room. ▲ ❀ ⊨ ◑ ▶ ▲ ♣ P

Glaisdale

Anglers Rest
Off A171 OS779053
☎ (0947) 87261
11–3 (varies Sat), 6–11 (11–2.30, 7–11 winter)
Camerons Strongarm; S&N Theakston Best Bitter; Tetley Bitter Ⓗ

North Yorkshire

Very popular, old hilltop pub formerly called the Three Blast Furnaces and known locally as the Middle House. Popular with walkers and campers. Home-cooked food includes vegetarian options; gourmet eves Fri and Sat. Children welcome. ♨ Q ☙ ⚑ P

Grassington

Black Horse

Garrs Lane (off the square)
☎ (0756) 752770
11–3, 6.30–11 (11–11 Fri, Sat & summer)
Ruddles Best Bitter; S&N Theakston Best Bitter, XB, Old Peculier; Tetley Mild, Bitter Ⓗ
Comfortable and welcoming, L-shaped hotel bar and separate dining room.
♨ Q ☙ ☙ ⚑ ◑ ▲ ♣

Great Barugh

Golden Lion

☎ (0653) 86242
12–3, 7–11
Malton Double Chance; Tetley Bitter Ⓗ**; guest beer** (summer)
Cosy country pub dating back to 1630 with Royalist connections. Welcoming and friendly, it comprises two rooms, one used as a diner in summer and for pool in winter. No meals Sun eves.
♨ Q ☙ ◑ ▲ P

Great Broughton

Wainstones Hotel

High Street ☎ (0642) 712268
11–3, 6.30–11
Ind Coope Burton Ale; Tetley Bitter Ⓗ
Originally a farmhouse, converted and extended in the mid 1960s to create the only hotel in the village. The bar has a Flemish vaulted ceiling. Strong local patronage.
♨ Q ☙ ⚑ ◑ ▲ ♣ P

Great Smeaton

Bay Horse

On A167 ☎ (060 981) 466
12–3 (not Mon/Tue), 6.30–11
Ruddles County; John Smith's Bitter Ⓗ**; guest beers**
Small free house in the middle of a row of roadside cottages. Two linked rooms: a functional bar and a soft-furnished lounge. ♨ ☙ ◑ ▮ ⚑ ♣ P

Harmby

Pheasant Inn

On A684, 1 mile E of Leyburn
☎ (0969) 22223
12–2.30 (3 summer), 7–11
Tetley Bitter Ⓗ
Small, friendly rural inn with

an original stone cellar. Caravan site to the rear.
♨ Q ☙ ⚑ ▲ P

Harrogate

Coach & Horses ✓

16 West Park (A61)
☎ (0423) 568371
11–11 .
John Smith's Bitter; Tetley Bitter Ⓗ
Welcoming pub within easy reach of the town centre, boasting a commanding view over the Stray. Split-lounge and a public bar. Q ◑ ⚑ ♣

Dragon

Skipton Road (A59, 1½ miles from centre) ☎ (0423) 503405
11–11
John Smith's Bitter, Magnet; Younger No. 3 Ⓗ
Popular, large corner local with a roomy lounge, a conservatory and a small wood-panelled snug.
Q ☙ ☙ ◑ ⚑ ♣ P

Hales Bar ✓

Crescent Road ☎ (0423) 569861
11–11
Draught Bass; Stones Best Bitter Ⓗ
One of the few pubs left in Harrogate that retain any character: a gas-lit lounge with unusual gas cigar lighters on the bar; old barrels and stuffed birds add to the atmosphere. The smaller bar is a haven for locals. ◑ ⚑

Muckles

11 West Park (A61)
☎ (0423) 504463
11–11
Tetley Bitter Ⓗ
Recently refurbished, single U-shaped bar. ◑ ♣ P

Tap & Spile

31 Tower Street (400 yds from West Park Stray)
☎ (0423) 526785
11.30–3, 5–11 (11.30–11 Sat)
Beer range varies Ⓗ
Three rooms with exposed brickwork, and no carpets or curtains. Serves a mixed clientele, offering a range of up to ten constantly changing beers – none permanent. No wheelchair access to ladies' WC. ◑ ⚑ ♿ ≈ ♣

Woodlands

Wetherby Road (A59)
11.30–3, 5.30–11
Ruddles Best Bitter; Webster's Yorkshire Bitter Ⓗ
Spacious open-plan bar and conservatory, next to the Yorkshire showground.
Q ☙ ◑ ⚑ ♿ P

Hawes

Crown Hotel

Main Street ☎ (0969) 667212

11–11
S&N Theakston Mild (summer), **Best Bitter, XB, Old Peculier** Ⓗ
Early 19th-century pub in Ashlar. Two comfortable rooms – a simple wood-furnished bar and a modernised lounge.
♨ ☙ ☙ ◑ ▮ ⚑ ▲ ♣

Helperby

Golden Lion

Main Street ☎ (0423) 360870
12–3 (not Mon), 6–11
Taylor Best Bitter; Tetley Bitter Ⓗ**; guest beers**
Friendly and inviting village local, formerly a coaching inn. Offers an ever-changing selection of guest beers.
♨ Q ◑ ▮ ♣

Holly Hill

Holly Hill Inn

Take Leyburn road out of Richmond over River Swale
☎ (0748) 825171
11–2.30, 4.30–11
Fuller's London Pride; S&N Theakston Best Bitter, XB, Old Peculier; Younger 80/- Ⓗ**; guest beers**
Traditional ale-drinking house of local repute. Pool, darts and dominoes played. ☙ ⚑ ♣ P

Hudswell

George & Dragon

2 miles SW of Richmond
☎ (0748) 823082
12–3 (not Mon except bank hols), 6.30–11
Ruddles County; S&N Theakston XB; Webster's Yorkshire Bitter Ⓗ
Well worth seeking out: locals' bar on the right; small second room on the left; fine views to the rear. No meals Sun eve.
♨ Q ☙ ☙ ◑ ▮ ⚑ ♣ P

Hutton Rudby

King's Head

36 Northside ☎ (0642) 700342
6.30–11 (12–3, 6.30–11 Sat)
Camerons Bitter, Strongarm Ⓗ
Extremely popular local with strong regular patronage. Welcoming traditional bar with a low, beamed ceiling; small bistro in the old snug (eve meals Thu–Sat, plus Sun lunch). ♨ Q ☙ ☙ ▮ ♣

Ingleton

Masons Arms

New Road (A65)
☎ (052 42) 41158
12–11
Thwaites Bitter Ⓗ
Recently renovated pub, but still consisting of one small room. ♨ ⚑ ◑ ▮ ▲ ♣ P

Kettlewell

Kings Head

On Leyburn road, 1/4 mile from
B6160 ☎ (0756) 760242
11–3 (may extend in summer), 6–11
**Ind Coope Burton Ale; Taylor
Landlord; Tetley Mild**
(summer), **Bitter** Ⓗ
Three-storey building tucked
well away from the main road
and attracting a good mix of
visitors and locals. The
opened-out bar retains an
inglenook. An excellent base
for walking, caving, touring,
etc. ♨ Q ⛱ ✿ ♠ ◖ ▶ ▲ ♣

Kirkby Fleetham

Black Horse

3 miles from A1
☎ (0609) 748279
11–2.30, 6.30–11
**Courage Directors; John
Smith's Bitter, Magnet** Ⓗ;
guest beers
Pleasant village pub
frequented by young locals.
Tasteful lounge where talk of
hunting and shooting is the
order of the day; dining room.
♨ Q ✿ ◖ ▶ ♠ ♣ P

Kirk Hammerton

Crown Inn

Station Road ☎ (0423) 330341
7.30–11 (12–3, 7.30–10.30 Sun)
Marston Moor Cromwell Ⓗ
Straightforward village pub
better known as the home of
Marston Moor brewery.
Operates Sun extensions for
fishermen (Jun–Nov
8am–10am and 4pm–7.30pm);
oilskins and sou'westers not
essential! One other Marston
Moor beer is also always
available. ♨ ♠ ▲ ≹ P

Knaresborough

Blind Jack's

Market Place ☎ (0423) 869148
11.30–3, 6–11 (11.30–11 Wed–Sat)
Beer range varies Ⓗ
Intimate gem created in 1991
in a Georgian listed building
and named after a local hero.
Retains many original
features; a single bar and a
small snug with upstairs
dining rooms. Six ever-
changing beers, always
including a mild. Q ◖ ▶ ≹

Groves

Market Place ☎ (0423) 863022
11–11 (12–3, 7.30–10.30 Sun)
**S&N Theakston Best Bitter;
Younger Scotch, No. 3** Ⓗ
Increasingly popular pub in
the corner of an historic
market place. Q ◖ ♠ ≹ ♣

Marquis of Granby

31 York Place (A59 York road)
☎ (0423) 862207

11–3, 6–11 (12–3, 7.30–10.30 Sun)
Samuel Smith OBB Ⓗ
Pub with a Victorian-styled
interior, close to the town
centre. Next to a large car
park. ♨ Q ♠ ▲

Langdale End

Moorcock Inn

OS938913 ☎ (0723) 882268
11–2.30 (2 Sat; not Mon–Thu in
winter), 8 (7 Fri & Sat)–11
Beer range varies Ⓗ
Rural gem recently rescued
from oblivion with a very
sympathetic renovation. Out
of the way and either quiet or
packed, this recent convert to
real ale is well worth seeking
out. ♨ Q ✿ ♠ ◖ ▲ ♣

Long Preston

Maypole Inn

On A65, next to the green.
☎ (0729) 840219
11–3, 6–11
**Taylor Best Bitter; Whitbread
Boddingtons Mild, Bitter,
Castle Eden Ale** Ⓗ
Village local comprising
comfortable lounge and public
bars. A separate dining room
offers a vegetarian option.
Children welcome.
♨ ✿ ♠ ◖ ▶ ♠ ≹ ♣ P

Low Marishes

School House Inn

3 miles N of A64/A169 jct
☎ (0653) 86247
11–3 (may extend), 6.30–11 (supper
licence)
**Malton Double Chance;
Marston's Pedigree; Tetley
Bitter** Ⓗ; **guest beers**
Tidy pub with good food and
excellent facilities for all the
family both inside and out.
Ukers, a violent form of ludo,
is a local favourite.
♨ ✿ ◖ ▶ ♠ ♣ P

Low Row

Punch Bowl Inn

E end of Low Row on N side
of B6270 ☎ (0748) 86233
11–11
**S&N Theakston Mild, Best
Bitter, XB, Old Peculier;
Younger No. 3; guest beers** Ⓗ
Village inn built in 1638,
offering warm hospitality.
Folk music festival last
weekend in June and
traditional music all year. Beer
festivals Easter and August
Bank Holiday. 100 different
single malt whiskies.
Mountain bikes for hire. ♨ Q
✿ ♠ ◖ ♠ ▲ ♣ P

Malham

Listers Arms

☎ (0729) 830330
12–3 (not Tue, may vary winter), 7–11

**Ind Coope Burton Ale;
Younger Scotch** Ⓗ; **guest
beers**
Large, stone-built pub just over
the bridge on the Goredale
Scar road. Three separate
drinking areas and a sizeable
dining room. Two guest beers
in winter, more in summer,
plus cider. Hikers welcome.
No eve meals winter Mon.
♨ ✿ ▶ ◖ ▲ ♣ ♣ P

Malton

Crown Hotel
(Suddaby's)

Wheelgate ☎ (0653) 692038
11–3 (4 Sat), 5.30–11 (11–11 Fri)
**Malton Pale Ale, Double
Chance, Pickwick's Porter,
Owd Bob** Ⓗ; **guest beers**
Neat hotel offering a full
range of local beers. The
functional bar is
complemented by a
conservatory-style extension
where children are welcome.
The menu includes three
vegetarian options.
♨ Q ✿ ♠ ◖ ≹ ♣ P

Golden Lion

Market Place ☎ (0653) 692364
11–3, 5.30–11 (11–11 Fri)
Tetley Bitter Ⓗ
Small locals' pub with a gem
of a front bar overlooking the
market place. ✿ ♠ ≹ ♣

Masham

White Bear

Brewery Yard ☎ (0765) 689319
11–11
**S&N Theakston Mild, Best
Bitter, XB, Old Peculier** Ⓗ
Theakston's brewery tap, now
neighbour to the Black Sheep
brewery – a true Theakston
enterprise. An atmospheric
pub crammed with unusual
curios. Regular live music.
♨ ✿ ◖ ▶ ♠ ♣ P

Muston

Ship Inn

☎ (0723) 512722
11–2.30, 6–11
**Camerons Bitter; Courage
Directors; Everards Old
Original; Tolly Cobbold
Bitter, Original** Ⓗ
Village pub with one spacious
room serving a good range of
beers and wholesome food.
✿ ◖ ▶ ▲ ♣ P

Northallerton

County Arms

219a High Street
☎ (0609) 770610
11–11
**Draught Bass; Tetley Bitter;
John Smith's Bitter** Ⓗ; **guest
beers**
Pub recently refurbished to a
high standard. ◖ ♠ ≹ ♣

North Yorkshire

Nun Monkton

Alice Hawthorn
2 miles NE of A59: (at jct opp. Happy Eater)
☎ (0423) 330303
12–2, 7–11
Camerons Bitter, Strongarm; Tetley Bitter Ⓗ
Warm and welcoming pub overlooking a picturesque village scene, complete with duck pond and maypole. A little off the beaten track but worth the search.
🏨 🛏 ❀ ◑ ▶ ⊞ ▲ P

Nunnington

Royal Oak
11.45–2.30, 6.30–10.30 (11 Fri & Sat); 12–2, 7–10.30 Sun; closed Mon)
S&N Theakston Best Bitter, Old Peculier Ⓗ
Caters almost exclusively for diners, but also serves a good pint. Note the large collection of old keys and agricultural tools. ◑ ▶ P

Osmotherley

Golden Lion
West End
☎ (060 983) 526
11–3, 6–11
Courage Directors; John Smith's Bitter, Magnet Ⓗ
Attractive old pub in the village centre. Tables with fresh flowers and candles underline the emphasis on food. Children welcome at lunchtime. The original starting point for the Lyke Wake long-distance walk.
🏨 ❀ ◑ ▶ ▲ ✦

Pickering

Black Swan
Birdgate
☎ (0751) 72286
10.30–3, 6–11 (10.30–11 Mon & summer)
Courage Directors; John Smith's Bitter, Magnet Ⓗ
Former coaching inn, still popular with travellers as well as enjoying a lively local trade.
🏨 🖾 ◑ ▶ ✦ P

Pickhill

Nag's Head
Signed from A1 (1½ miles)
☎ (0845) 567391
11–11
Hambleton Best Bitter; S&N Theakston Best Bitter; Younger Scotch Ⓗ
Country inn and restaurant whose atmosphere and quality reflect the owners' 20-plus years of experience. Still retains a tap room for the serious drinker.
🏨 Q ❀ 🖾 ◑ ▶ ⊞ ✦ P

Pool-in-Wharfedale

Hunters Inn
Riffa (A658) ☎ (0532) 841090
11–11
Daleside Dalesman; Ind Coope Burton Ale; S&N Theakston Best Bitter; Taylor Landlord; Tetley Bitter Ⓗ; guest beers
Formerly the Red House café, now completely refurbished – no fake beams here!
🏨 ❀ ◑ ▱ ✦ P

Port Mulgrave

Ship Inn
20 Rosedale Lane (off A174, Staithes–Hinderwell road)
OS793188 ☎ (0947) 840303
11–11
John Smith's Bitter; Tetley Bitter; Younger No. 3 Ⓗ
Friendly old terraced pub near the high cliffs on the Cleveland Way. Caters for children.
🏨 Q 🛏 🖾 ◑ ▶ ▲ ✦

Ravensworth

Bay Horse
☎ (0325) 718328
12–3, 6.30–11
Ind Coope Burton Ale; John Smith's Bitter; Tetley Bitter Ⓗ
Stone-built village local facing the expansive green and ancient castle ruins beyond. A front, beamed bar and a separate restaurant (no meals Mon lunch). 🏨 ❀ ◑ ▶ ✦ P

Ripon

Golden Lion
Allhallowgate
☎ (0765) 602598
11–3, 7–11 (varies in summer)
Marston Moor Cromwell; S&N Theakston Best Bitter; John Smith's Bitter Ⓗ; guest beers
Friendly, welcoming 16th-century town pub and restaurant, modernised to an extent, but not unpleasantly; very comfortable. Eve meals finish at 8.30. 🛏 ❀ 🖾 ◑ ▶ ✦

One Eyed Rat
Allhallowgate ☎ (0765) 607704
6–11 (12–3, 6–11 Fri & Sat)
Marston's Pedigree; Taylor Landlord Ⓗ; guest beers
Very popular terraced pub. Bar billiards played. Three guest beers, and a range of bottle-conditioned beers.
🏨 Q ❀ ✦

Station
North Road ☎ (0765) 602140
11–3, 11–11 Sat & summer)
Tetley Mild, Bitter Ⓗ
Large three-roomed pub with traditional decor and a friendly atmosphere. Separate pool room.
Q ❀ ◑ ▶ ⊞ ▲ ✦ P

Wheatsheaf
Harrogate Road (A61, S of city) ☎ (0765) 602410
11–3, 6–11 (12–11 Thu, 11–11 Fri & Sat)
Vaux Lorimers Best Scotch, Samson; Wards Sheffield Best Bitter Ⓗ
Old inn with intricate carving. Small separate dining room. Sunken garden with peacocks.
🏨 Q ❀ ◑ ▶ P

Robin Hood's Bay

Laurel Inn
☎ (0947) 880400
12–3 (may vary summer), 6–11
Malton Double Chance; S&N Theakston XB; John Smith's Bitter Ⓗ; guest beers (winter)
Small, friendly local in a picturesque cliffside village. Self-catering cottage and flat available. 🏨 Q 🛏 ❀ 🖾 ✦

Victoria Hotel
Station Road ☎ (0947) 880205
11–3, 6.30–11
Camerons Bitter, Strongarm Ⓗ; guest beers
Large hotel, built in 1897, with imposing garden views over the bay and village. Modern family room with pool table.
🏨 🛏 ❀ 🖾 ◑ ▶ ⊞ ▲ ✦ P

Roecliffe

Crown Inn
☎ (0423) 322578
11.30–3, 6.30–11 (supper licence till 12)
Bass Special; Tetley Bitter Ⓗ; guest beers (occasionally)
Rather spartan tap room contrasting well with a plush lounge. The tap bar is more of a hatch, with the beer pumps on the lounge bar. Children welcome.
🏨 Q ❀ 🖾 ◑ ▶ ⊞ ▲ ✦ P

Rufforth

Tankard Inn
Wetherby Road (B1224)
☎ (0904) 83621
11–3, 6–11 (11–11 Sat)
Samuel Smith OBB Ⓗ
Neat and tidy, two-roomed village pub, featuring old prints of the village. Large children's play area to the rear. No meals Mon lunch or Sun eve. Q ❀ 🖾 ◑ ▶ ⊞ P

Saxton

Greyhound
Main Street ☎ (0937) 557202
11–3, 6–11 (11–11 Sat)
Samuel Smith OBB, Museum (summer) Ⓗ
Small village pub: three rooms served by a single bar. Low

ceilings and lots of character. One room is used by families, but not exclusively.
♨ Q ☺ ❀ ♣ P

Scarborough

Cask
Cambridge Terrace
☎ (0723) 500570
11.45–2.30 (3 Fri), 6–11 (11–11 Sat)
McEwan 80/-; Tetley Bitter; Younger Scotch, No. 3 ⊞; guest beers
Popular, especially with the young, but welcoming to all. Attractions include guest beers, a children's room and child-friendly self-catering flats (baby-listening service). Eve meals finish early.
☺ ❀ ⌸ ◖ ◗ ≢

Highlander
Stresa Hotel, 15 The Esplanade
☎ (0723) 365627
11–11
Wm Clark's Mild, EXB, No. 68, Bitter; Tetley Bitter; Younger IPA ⊞; guest beers
Large hotel with a public bar overlooking the South Bay. Serves its own beers. The distinctive Scottish flavour is enhanced by a huge whisky collection. ♨ Q ❀ ⌸ ≢

Hole in the Wall
Vernon Road ☎ (0723) 373746
11.30–2.30 (3 Sat), 7–11
Malton Double Chance; S&N Theakston Best Bitter, XB, Old Peculier ⊞; guest beers
Thriving ale house just off the town centre. Vegetarian menu option (no food Sun).
Q ◖ ⊟ ≢ ♣

New Tavern
131 Falsgrave Road
☎ (0723) 366965
12–3 (4 Sat), 7–11 (12–11 Fri)
Camerons Bitter, Strongarm; Tolly Cobbold Mild ⊞
Popular two-roomer just away from the town, with a straightforward bar and a smaller, cosy lounge. ❀ ♣

North Riding Hotel
163 North Marine Road
☎ (0723) 362386
11–2.30, 6–11 (11–11 Fri & Sat)
Camerons Bitter; Tetley Bitter; Tolly Cobbold Mild ⊞
Busy local, close to the cricket ground: a popular bar dominated by a pool table and a quieter lounge. Note the pictures of North Bay and of the stars of the late lamented Floral Hall. ☺ ⌸ ◖ ⊟ ♣

Spa Hotel
Victoria Road ☎ (0723) 372907
11–3 (4 Fri & Sat), 5.30 (5 Fri, 6 Sat)–11
Tetley Mild, Bitter ⊞
Town-style pub fielding various highly successful games teams. ❀ ◖ ≢ ♣

Trafalgar Hotel
Trafalgar Street, West Scarborough
☎ (0723) 372054
11–11
Camerons Bitter, Strongarm ⊞
Smart, busy, games-oriented local, attracting a varied clientele, especially at weekends. Note the large picture of the famous battle hanging in the lounge.
⊟ ≢ ♣

Seamer (Stokesley)

King's Head
Hilton Road
☎ (0642) 710397
7–11 (12–3, 7–11 Sat)
McEwan 80/-; S&N Theakston XB; Younger Scotch ⊞
Four cosy rooms built around a central bar area. Polished brass and firelight make this a marvellous haven on cold evenings. ♨ ☺ ⊟ P

Selby

Abbey Vaults
James Street ☎ (0757) 702857
11–11 (11–3, 6.30–11 Wed)
Mansfield Riding Bitter, Old Baily ⊞
Busy pub, especially on market day (Mon). Traditionally modernised decor; separate games and function rooms. The outside wall is the original 13th-century abbey tithe barn.
Q ❀ ◖ ⊟ ≢ ♣ P

New Inn
Gowthorpe ☎ (0757) 703429
11–11
Tetley Mild, Bitter ⊞
Distinctive pre-war design pub: a separate front smoke room and three main linked rooms. Disco/night club in the yard at the rear. ❀ ⊟ ≢ ♣

Sherburn

Pigeon Pie
Malton Road ☎ (0944) 70383
11–2.30, 6–11
Younger Scotch ⊞
Low-fronted pub on the busy A64. A small lounge at the front and a larger, more functional bar.
♨ ☺ ❀ ⌸ ◖ ◗ ⊟ ▲ ♣ P

Skelton on Ure

Black Lion
☎ (0423) 322516
12–3 (not winter weekdays), 7–11
John Smith's Bitter; S&N Theakston Best Bitter; Tetley Bitter ⊞; guest beers
Welcoming local in a village close to lovely Newby Hall (open to the public), and three miles outside Ripon.
Modernised into two rooms – a worthy stopping-off point.
♨ ❀ ⌸ ◖ ◗ ⊟ ▲ ♣ P

Skipton

Craven Hotel
Craven Street (over canal footbridge from bus station)
☎ (0756) 792595
11.30–3 (or 4), 7–11
Thwaites Best Mild, Bitter ⊞
Large, 19th-century hotel situated between the bus station and railway line: a spacious, high-ceilinged bar with a separate room for darts and entertainment, plus a small pool room. The only Thwaites tied house in the area. ❀ ♿ ≢ ♣ P

Royal Shepherd
Canal Street (via alley off High St) ☎ (0756) 793178
11–4, 5–11 (11–11 Fri & Sat)
Marston's Pedigree; Robinson's Hartleys XB; Whitbread Boddingtons Bitter, Trophy, Castle Eden Ale ⊞
Popular pub in a quiet back street, immediately opposite the canal. Photos of old Skipton abound; a stained-glass window features a canal theme. The small garden to the side wins awards.
Q ❀ ◖ ⊟ ≢ ♣

Smallways

Smallways
Off A66 behind A66 Motel
☎ (0833) 27225
12–3, 6.30–11
John Smith's Bitter, Magnet ⊞; guest beers
Comfortable, modernised country free house. Quoits played. ❀ ◖ ◗ ♣ P

Sneaton

Wilsons Arms
Beacon Way (B1416, 2 miles from Ruswarp)
☎ (0947) 602552
12–3 (varies in summer), 7–11
S&N Theakston Best Bitter, XB, Old Peculier ⊞
Grade II listed, a large extended pub catering for families. Traditional Sun lunch served and eve meals (except Mon).
♨ Q ☺ ❀ ⌸ ◗ ▲ ♣ P

Spofforth

Railway Inn
High Street ☎ (0937) 590257
11.30–3, 5.30–11
Samuel Smith OBB ⊞
Typical Victorian village pub – sited near a long-gone railway station. Warm and friendly; hosts a good local evening trade. No eve meals in winter.
♨ Q ❀ ◖ ◗ ⊟ ▲ ♣ P

North Yorkshire

Stainforth

Craven Heifer
☎ (0729) 822599
12 (11 summer)–3, 7 (6 summer, 6.30 Sat)–11
Thwaites Best Mild, Bitter H
Traditional, multi-roomed village pub alongside a beck. Real fires in the lounge and tap room; no smoking in the family/pool room and possibly in the snug. ﹘ ﹘ ﹘ ﹘ ﹘ ﹘ ﹘ ﹘ ﹘ ﹘

Staintondale

Shepherds Arms
OS993981
☎ (0723) 870257
11.30–2.30, 7–11
Camerons Bitter H
Pub at the roadside with superb views down to Flamborough Head, 25 miles away: a country two-roomer serving a scattered local community and discerning regulars. Good food.
﹘ Q ﹘ ﹘ ﹘ ﹘ ﹘ ﹘ P

Stamford Bridge

Three Cups Inn
York Road (A166)
☎ (0759) 71396
11.30–2.30, 6.30–11
Draught Bass; Tetley Bitter H
Charming country inn of olde-worlde character with open log fires, exposed beams and an ancient well (visible through portholes in the bar). Separate restaurant (book weekends). Large garden with children's playground; occasional barbecues.
﹘ ﹘ ﹘ ﹘ A P

Staveley

Royal Oak
Main Street
☎ (0423) 340267
11.30–3, 5.30–11
Ind Coope Burton Ale; Tetley Bitter H
Pretty setting for an old, white-rendered pub. The main bar has a cosy feel and is much frequented by locals. Woe betide anyone who does not give up Jack's stool at the bar when he arrives. Children welcome. No eve meals Sun or Mon. ﹘ Q ﹘ ﹘ ﹘ ﹘ P

Stokesley

Station
1 mile along Kirby road
OS532075
☎ (0642) 710436
12–4, 7–11
S&N Theakston Best Bitter, XB, Old Peculier H
Pub built in 1861 to serve a now-defunct railway: a light and airy front bar, a small

snug, plus a large bar/function room at the rear. Live blues night Thu. No food Sun; eve meals by arrangement. ﹘ Q ﹘ ﹘ ﹘ ﹘ ﹘ P

White Swan
West End ☎ (0642) 710263
11.30 (11 Sat)–3, 5.30 (7 Sun)–11
Younger No. 3 H; guest beers
Five real ales and traditional scrumpy or cider always available in a cosy, old-style pub with oak panelling and agricultural memorabilia on the walls. The only food served is fresh pizzas.
﹘ Q ﹘ ﹘ ﹘ ﹘

Stutton

Hare & Hounds
Manor Road (1 mile W of A162) OS481414
☎ (0937) 833164
11.30–3, 6.45 (6.30 Fri & Sat)–11
Samuel Smith OBB H
Busy country pub with a popular restaurant. One large bar with low ceilings.
﹘ Q ﹘ ﹘ ﹘ ﹘ P

Summerbridge

Flying Dutchman
Hartwith Bank
☎ (0423) 780321
11.30–3, 6–11 (11–11 Sat)
Samuel Smith OBB H
Stone-built, modernised country inn with views over the Nidd. Named after a racehorse which won the Derby and St Leger in 1849.
﹘ ﹘ ﹘ ﹘ ﹘ ﹘ P

Tadcaster

Angel & White Horse
Bridge Street (A659)
☎ (0937) 835470
11–2.30, 5 (7 Sat)–11
Samuel Smith OBB, Museum H
Large town pub next to Sam Smith's brewery, with brewery photos displayed in the wood-panelled bar. The brewery's shire horses are stabled in the coachyard which also serves as an outdoor drinking area.
﹘ Q ﹘ ﹘ ﹘

Thirsk

Olde Three Tuns
Finkle Street ☎ (0845) 523291
11–11
Tetley Bitter H; guest beers
16th-century town pub, lively and popular. ﹘ ﹘ ﹘ ﹘ ﹘ P

Thornton in Lonsdale

Marton Arms
Off A65/A687 jct
☎ (052 42) 41281

11–11
Dent Bitter; S&N Theakston Best Bitter; Thwaites Bitter; Younger Scotch H; guest beers
Pre-turnpike coaching inn, dated 1679 but reputedly older. A large, comfortable oak-beamed lounge and a restaurant. Good home cooking. Eleven beers.
﹘ ﹘ ﹘ ﹘ ﹘ ﹘ P

Thornton-le-Beans

Crosby
Main Street (off A168, 3 miles S of Northallerton)
☎ (0609) 772776
12–3 (not Mon), 7–11
Ruddles Best Bitter; John Smith's Bitter; Webster's Yorkshire Bitter H
Large, well-appointed village pub with a restaurant. The horseshoe-shaped partitions were installed by a former jockey owner.
﹘ Q ﹘ ﹘ ﹘ A ﹘ P

Thornton Watlass

Buck Inn
On B6268, SW out of Bedale, turn right after 2 miles
☎ (0677) 422461
11–2.30, 6–11
S&N Theakston Best Bitter, XB; Tetley Bitter H; guest beers
Pub situated next to the village green (cricket played in summer): a cosy lounge and a large function room. Live music Sat/Sun. Locally brewed Hambleton beer is a regular guest.
﹘ Q ﹘ ﹘ ﹘ A ﹘ P

Threshfield

Long Ashes Inn
Signed through chalet/caravan park off B6160
☎ (0756) 752434
11–3, 6.30–11 (may be all day summer)
Moorhouse's Pendle Witches Brew; S&N Theakston Best Bitter, XB; Tetley Bitter ; guest beers H
Ex-lodge of nearby Netherside Hall which served for many years as tea rooms. Now an unusual three-level drinking area. A resident female ghost is known to be mischievous. Adjacent to chalet/caravan park and leisure centre.
﹘ ﹘ ﹘ ﹘ ﹘ A ﹘ P

Old Hall
On B6265
☎ (0756) 752441
11–3, 5.30–11
S&N Theakston Best Bitter; Taylor Best Bitter, Landlord; Younger Scotch; guest beer H
Opened-out pub with an attractive L-shaped room, a

conservatory and a games room attached. Splendid Yorkshire range. Ever-changing menu of good quality, upmarket food. Wheelchair access via garden.
🏃 ⛺ ❀ ◐ ▶ ♿ ▲ ♣ P

Tockwith

Spotted Ox
Westfield Road
☎ (0423) 358387
11–3, 6–11 (11–11 Sat)
McEwan 80/-; John Smith's Bitter; Tetley Bitter; Younger Scotch Ⓗ; guest beers (occasionally)
Quite large village pub, somewhat opened-up, but still appearing like separate drinking areas. No meals Sun eve. 🏃 Q ❀ ◐ ▶ P

Ugthorpe

Black Bull
Off A171, 6 miles W of Whitby
☎ (0947) 840286
11–3, 7–11 (may vary in summer)
Camerons Strongarm; S&N Theakston Best Bitter, XB, Old Peculier; Tetley Bitter Ⓗ; guest beers (occasionally)
Excellent village pub set in a row of 19th-century cottages. Children welcome in the pool room; quoits played. Children's and vegetarian menu.
🏃 ⛺ ❀ ◐ ▶ ◐ ♣ P

Weaverthorpe

Star Inn
☎ (094 43) 273
12–3 (not Mon–Fri), 7–11
Taylor Landlord; Tetley Bitter; Webster's Yorkshire Bitter Ⓗ
Country inn with a bar for everyone. The front lounge is comfortable and popular with diners, while the more functional bar is used by the locals. Separate pool area.
🏃 ⛺ ❀ ◐ ▶ ◐ ▲ ♣ P

Whitby

Buck Inn
11 St Annes Staithe (quayside)
☎ (0947) 601378
10.30–11
John Smith's Bitter, Magnet Ⓗ
Pub dating back to the mid 18th century, but rebuilt in the 1930s after a fire. Good family atmosphere with a quiz night, pool and a darts team. Karaoke four nights a week. Excellent food, especially freshly-caught Whitby cod (eve meals summer only). Popular with many local fishermen. ⛺ 🏃 ◐ ▶ 🚉 ♣

Jolly Sailors
St Annes Staithe
☎ (0947) 605999
11.30–4, 6.30–11 (varies in summer)
Samuel Smith OBB Ⓗ
Busy local, recently refurbished, with a 'brewers Tudor' exterior: a bar plus a lounge/dining room. Live music during Folk Week.
❀ ◐ 🚉 ♣

Metropole Hotel (Henry's Bar)
Argyle Road, West Cliff
☎ (0947) 820652
11–3, 7–11 (11–11 summer)
Malton Double Chance; Tetley Bitter Ⓗ
Large Victorian hotel, prominently situated on the West Cliff. Henry's Bar (real ale) is in the left side of the hotel, offering spectacular sea views. 🏃 ❀ 🏠 ◐ ▶ ◐ P

York

Fox Inn
Holgate Road (A59/B1224 jct)
☎ (0904) 798341
11–11 (may close winter afternoons)
Tetley Bitter Ⓗ
Delightful, multi-roomed *Good Beer Guide* stalwart near (and popular at lunchtime with) the carriage works. A pub renovation that's worked! A great local and a popular prelude to a York night out. If you think you can eat, come here for Sunday lunch (no meals at other times). ❀ ◐ P

Golden Ball
2 Cromwell Road, Bishophill (off Micklegate)
☎ (0904) 652211
11.45–3, 7–11
Courage Directors; Malton Double Chance; John Smith's Bitter, Magnet Ⓗ; guest beer
Busy three-roomed, unspoilt, traditional pub away from tourist haunts. A fine, friendly local. True guest beer.
Q ❀ ◐ ♿ ♣ ⏱

Golden Slipper
20 Goodramgate
☎ (0904) 651235
11–11
Courage Directors; John Smith's Bitter, Magnet; Tetley Bitter Ⓗ
Good food (including vegetarian meals) and friendly atmosphere. Paperback book library for locals and a collection of photos of old York. ◐ ▶ ♣

John Bull
Layerthorpe
☎ (0904) 621593
11–3, 6–11 (11–11 Fri & Sat)
Franklin's Bitter; Taylor Golden Best, Landlord Ⓗ; guest beers
Thriving free house, always

offering several guest beers. Large collection of old photos and enamel signs; splendid Russells brewery mirror over the fireplace.
🏃 Q ❀ ◐ ♿ ⏱

Minster Inn
24 Marygate, Bootham
☎ (0904) 624499
11.30–3, 6–11
Draught Bass; Old Mill Bitter; Stones Best Bitter Ⓗ; guest beer
Traditional, terraced multi-roomed pub. Spot the deliberate spelling mistake on the old pub sign hanging in the passage. Q ◐ ▶ ◐ ✂

Other Tap & Spile
North Street
☎ (0904) 656097
11.30–3, 5–11 (11.30–11 Fri & Sat)
Butterknowle Conciliation Ale; Daleside Bitter Ⓗ; guest beers
Multi-roomed and often busy city-centre pub offering seven ever-changing guest beers.
Q 🏃 ❀ ◐ ▶ ◐ 🚉 ♣ ✂

Spread Eagle
Walmgate ☎ (0904) 635868
11–11
Taylor Best Bitter, Landlord Ⓗ; guest beers
Beers from independents as well as S&N ales. Good snacks. ❀ ◐ ▶ ⏱

Tap & Spile
Monkgate
☎ (0904) 656158
11–11
Hadrian Gladiator; Old Mill Bitter Ⓗ; guest beers
Large, single-roomed pub with a raised games area to the rear. Often packed with students. Up to eight, regularly changed beers.
Q ❀ 🏠 ◐ ▶ P

York Arms
26 High Petergate
☎ (0904) 624508
11–11
Samuel Smith OBB, Museum Ⓗ
Polished gem near York Minster in an end-of-terrace building: a small front bar and a comfortable lounge. A second salubrious lounge is next door. 🏠 ◐ ◐ ♣

York Beer Shop
28 Sandringham Street (off A19/Fishergate)
☎ (0904) 647136
11 (10 Sat, 4.30 Mon)–10 (12–2, 7–10 Sun)
Bateman XXXB; Malton Owd Bob; Old Mill Bitter; Taylor Landlord Ⓗ; guest beers
Superb off-licence, with friendly and knowledgeable staff. Draught beer, plus a large range of bottled beers and imported lager. ▲ ⏱

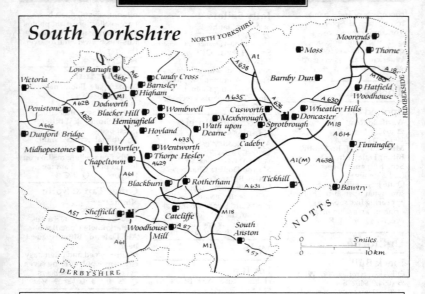

South Yorkshire

Kelham Island, Sheffield; **Stocks,** Doncaster; **Wards,** Sheffield; **Wortley,** Wortley

Barnby Dun

White Hart
Top Road ☎ (0302) 882959
10.30–3.30, 6–11
John Smith's Bitter, Magnet Ⓗ; guest beer
Modernised village pub which has retained much of its character. Popular with locals and those who visit for the excellent meals. Fascinating collection of old clocks. 🏧 ◑ ▶

Barnsley

Brownes Bar
Grahams Orchard
☎ (0226) 282594
12–3, 7–11
John Smith's Bitter, Magnet Ⓗ
Small one-room pub with a modern interior. Popular with office workers at lunchtime. Very busy weekend eves. ◑ ≥

Manx Arms
32 Sheffield Road (A61, near Alhambra Centre)
☎ (0226) 293766
11.30–3.30, 7–11
Ind Coope Burton Ale; Taylor Landlord; S&N Theakston Old Peculier; Tetley Bitter; guest beers Ⓗ
One of the oldest pubs in town but modified internally and extended. Live bands on Wed and Sun can be very loud. Up to four guest beers. ≥

Old White Bear
150 Pontefract Road, Hoyle Mill (A628, ½ mile from centre)
☎ (0226) 284947
12–3 (4 Sat), 6.30–11
Courage Directors; Ruddles Best Bitter, County; John Smith's Magnet; Taylor Landlord; Tetley Bitter; guest beers Ⓗ
Popular pub (twice a local CAMRA award-winner) with a friendly landlord. Handy for the football ground. Up to six guest beers. Eve meals till 8. Quiz nights. ❀ 🛏 ◑ ▶ ♣ P

Bawtry

Turnpike
High Street
☎ (0302) 711960
11–3, 6–11
Stocks Best Bitter, Select, Old Horizontal Ⓗ; guest beers
Converted from a wine bar to cater for all tastes. The interior is of wood, glass and brick with a part-concrete floor – mind the step! Good value, varied menu (eve meals Mon–Thu). Weekly guest beers. 🏧 ❀ ◑ ▶

Blackburn

Crown
88 Blackburn Road (near M1 jct 34 N) ☎ (0709) 560498
11–3, 6–11
Tetley Bitter Ⓗ

Solid stone pub, a real haven despite its proximity to the motorway. The garden is a delight for families. ❀ ◑ ≥ (Meadowhall) ♣ P

Blacker Hill

Royal Albert
Wentworth Road (800 yds off B6096)
☎ (0226) 742193
11–3, 7–11
Wards Sheffield Best Bitter Ⓔ
Attractive pub on a bend in the road; the hub of village life. Splendid wood-panelled snug; larger games-oriented bar; pool room upstairs.
Q ❀ 🛏 ♣ P

Cadeby

Cadeby Inn
Main Street
☎ (0226) 864009
11–3, 5–11 (may extend summer; 11–11 Sat)
Courage Directors; Ind Coope Burton Ale; John Smith's Bitter, Magnet; Samuel Smith OBB; Tetley Bitter Ⓗ
Converted farmhouse in a rural village which has retained its atmosphere and character. Large lounge and cosy public bar. Good bar meals and traditional Sun lunch. Pleasant garden, popular with families.
🏧 Q ❀ ◑ ▶ 🛏 P ⅍

Catcliffe

Waverley

Brinsworth Road (B6067)
☎ (0709) 360906
12–4, 6–11
Ruddles County; Taylor Landlord; Webster's Yorkshire Bitter Ⓗ; **guest beers**
Pub with an entrepreneurial landlord. An extensive family room doubles as a concert room with regular entertainment for children and adults. Many playthings in the garden and family room.
Q ⅏ ⊛ ◑ ⊕ ♣ P

Chapeltown

Norfolk Arms

White Lane (A6135/Warren Lane jct, near M1 jct 35A)
☎ (0742) 468414
12–3, 7–11 (12–2.30, 7–10.30 Sun)
Wards Sheffield Best Bitter Ⓔ
Very old pub with newer extensions. Active football and angling clubs. Children welcome in the family/ function room. Separate pool room. ⅏ ⊛ ◑ ⇌ P

Prince of Wales

80 Burncross Road (1 mile from M1 jct 35)
☎ (0742) 467725
11–3 (4 Sat), 5.30 (6.30 Sat)–11 (11–11 Fri; 12–2, 7–10.30 Sun)
Wards Sheffield Best Bitter Ⓗ
Traditional tap room with a wood-panelled lounge.
Q ⊛ ◑ ⇌ ♣ P

Cundy Cross

Mill of the Black Monks

Grange Lane (A633)
☎ (0226) 242244
12–3, 7–11
S&N Theakston Best Bitter, XB, Old Peculier; Younger No. 3 Ⓗ
Winner of CAMRA's 1991 *Special Conservation Award*: a fine Grade II listed building, a former 12th-century monastic watermill, converted with great sensitivity. Superb garden. Ruins of Monk Bretton Priory nearby.
⅏ ⊛ ◑ ◗ P

Cusworth

Mallard

Cusworth Lane (off Gt North Rd) ☎ (0302) 784396
4–11 (11–11 Fri & Sat)
S&N Theakston Best Bitter; John Smith's Magnet Ⓗ
Typical 1960s estate pub with a comfortable, uncluttered lounge and a popular public bar. Happy hour 6–7 Mon–Sat. Close to historic Cusworth Hall museum. ⊛ ⊕ ♣ P

Dodworth

Travellers Inn

Green Road ☎ (0226) 284173
11–4.15, 7–11
Wards Thorne Best Bitter Ⓗ
Built in 1782, a Grade II listed roadside pub. The original front is now at the back, where there is also a secluded garden (many awards for flower displays). Basic tap room and comfortable lounge. Friendly.
⅏ Q ⊛ ◑ ⊕ ⅋ ⇌ ♣ P

Doncaster

Corner Pin

St Sepulchre Gate West
☎ (0302) 323142
11.30–3.30, 4.45 (6 Sat)–11
John Smith's Bitter, Magnet; Stones Best Bitter Ⓗ
Street-corner local just away from the town centre. Wide variety of good value, home-cooked meals (finish early eves). ◑ ◗ ⇌ ♣

Hallcross

Hallgate ☎ (0302) 328213
11–3, 6–11
Stocks Best Bitter, Select, Old Horizontal Ⓗ
Brewery tap which serves the full Stocks range. Situated on the edge of the town centre.
⊛ ◑

Masons Arms

Market Place ☎ (0302) 364391
11.30–4, 7.30–11
Tetley Bitter Ⓗ
200-year-old Tetley Heritage inn. Many photos of old 'Donny' and a history of the pub on display. Q ⊛ ⊕ ⇌

Railway

West Street ☎ (0302) 349700
11–11
S&N Theakston XB; John Smith's Bitter, Magnet Ⓗ
Bustling town pub with an enormous bar and a tiny lounge. Popular with postal and railway workers.
◑ ⊕ ⅋ ⇌ ♣

White Swan

Frenchgate ☎ (0302) 366573
11–11
Wards Thorne Best Bitter Ⓗ, **Sheffield Best Bitter** Ⓗ & Ⓔ
Popular, friendly town-centre pub. A tiled passageway leads to a large comfortable lounge; the front tap room boasts the highest bar in Britain (5ft 3ins). Live entertainment Wed eves; quiz night Sun. Good value lunches (not served Sun). ◑ ⊕ ⇌ ♣

Dunford Bridge

Stanhope Arms

Windle Edge Lane (off A628)
☎ (0226) 763104
11–3, 7–11

Tetley Mild, Bitter Ⓗ
Originally built as a shooting lodge, now several rooms interlink with a small bar: games room, tiny snug, large lounge and dining room. The quintessential village pub. Excellent home-cooked meals. Children welcome in the snug until 8pm. ⅏ Q ⅏ ⊛ ⊨ ◑ ◗ ⊕ ⅋ ⚲ ♣ P

Finningley

Harvey Arms

Old Bawtry Road (just off A614) ☎ (0302) 770200
11–3, 7–11 (11–11 Sat)
Draught Bass Ⓗ
Village pub near the green and duckpond, close to an RAF base famous for its air display. The busy, traditional bar has a collection of Robert Taylor aircraft prints; the large lounge boasts leaded windows. Good lunchtime carvery; eve meals Sat only.
⅏ ⊛ ◑ ⊕ ⚲ ♣ P

Hatfield Woodhouse

Green Tree

Bearswood Green (1 mile from M18 jct 5 at A18/A614 jct)
☎ (0302) 840305
11–3, 6–11
Vaux Samson; Wards Thorne Best Bitter Ⓗ
Very welcoming and comfortable 17th-century posting house. Good, reasonably-priced bar food; also separate restaurant and B&B. Children allowed in the eating area of the bar.
⅏ ⊛ ⊨ ◑ ◗ ⊕ P

Robin Hood & Little John

Main Street ☎ (0302) 840213
10.30–4, 6–11
Draught Bass; Stones Best Bitter Ⓗ
Friendly village local, very busy at weekends. The large garden attracts families.
⊛ ◑ ⊕ ♣ P

Hemingfield

Lundhill Tavern

Beech House Road (off A633, 1/2 mile along Lundhill Road)
☎ (0226) 752283
12–4, 7–11
John Smith's Bitter, Magnet; Taylor Landlord; Vaux Samson; Wards Sheffield Best Bitter Ⓗ; **guest beers**
Off the beaten track and steeped in local coal mining history. Unusual brass blow lamps hang from the wooden beams. Meals served in the bar (except Mon) or restaurant. Competitively priced guest beers. ⊛ ◑ ◗ ♣ P

South Yorkshire

Higham

Engineers Arms
Higham Common Lane
(A635) ☎ (0226) 384204
11.30–3, 7–11
Samuel Smith OBB H
Village pub with a superb,
unspoilt tap room and a plush
lounge. Lawned beer garden
with swings. Q ❀ ⇔ P

Hoyland

Furnace Inn
Milton Road (500 yds from
centre, off B6097)
☎ (0226) 742000
11.30–3, 6–11
Vaux Samson H; **Thorne Best
Bitter, Sheffield Best Bitter** E;
Kirby H
Welcoming stone-built inn by
an old forge pond. Good value
lunchtime snacks. Award-
winning flower displays. 1991
winner of Kimberley-Clarke
Superloo Award. Q ❀ ♣ P

Low Barugh

Millers Inn
Dearne Hall Road (B6428)
☎ (0226) 382888
11.30–2.30, 5.30–11 (11–11 Sat)
**Burtonwood Bitter; John
Smith's Bitter; Taylor
Landlord; Tetley Bitter** H;
guest beers
Free house on the site of a
former water mill, by River
Dearne. ❀ ◖ ▶ P

Mexborough

Concertina Band Club
9a Dolcliffe Road
☎ (0709) 580841
12–4, 7–11 (12–2, 7–10.30 Sun)
**John Smith's Bitter; Samuel
Smith OBB; Tetley Bitter;
Wards Sheffield Best
Bitter** H; guest beers
Small, friendly private club,
steeped in history. Visitors
welcome. ⇔ ♣

Falcon
Main Street
☎ (0709) 571170
11.30–4, 7–11
**Old Mill Mild, Bitter,
Bullion** H
Large lounge with raised
drinking areas. Traditional
games and pool in the tap
room; fish tank in the
entrance. Wheelchair access
via the outside passage.
❀ ◖ ⌂ ♿ ♣

George & Dragon
81 Church Street (off A6023)
☎ (0709) 584375
12–3.30, 7–11 (11.30–4, 6.30–11
summer; 12–3.30, 7–10.30 Sun)
**Vaux Samson; Wards
Sheffield Best Bitter** H
Cosy and attractive, one-

roomed pub with a central
bar. Many prints of old
Mexborough. Children's
playground. ❀ ⇔ P

Midhopestones

Club Inn
Off A616 (Bradfield sign),
between Stocksbridge and
Langsett ☎ (0226) 762305
11.30–3, 7–11 (12–2, 7–10.30 Sun)
Wards Sheffield Best Bitter H
Old-fashioned village local –
no frills. One bar serves three
different rooms.
🏚 Q ❀ ♣ P

Moorends

Moorends Hotel
156 Marshland Road
☎ (0405) 812170
11–3.30, 6.30–11
Wards Thorne Best Bitter H
Imposing edifice built in 1927
to serve a mining community.
The pits are long gone but the
pub thrives. Known locally as
'Uncle Arthur's' after a key
figure in the (1936) miners'
strike. Live entertainment
weekends. New no-smoking
area. 🏚 ❀ ◖ ⌂ ♣ P ✗

Moss

Star
Moss Road (½ mile W of
village) OS589143
☎ (0302) 700497
12–3, 6.30–11 (12–2.30, 7–10.30 Sun)
**John Smith's Bitter,
Magnet** H; guest beers
Great for ramblers and rail
buffs: a snug but isolated pub
on a web of footpaths next to
the London–Edinburgh rail
line. Swings and slides in the
garden. 🏚 ❀ ◖ ⚑ P

Penistone

Cubley Hall
Mortimer Road, Cubley
☎ (0226) 766086
11–3, 6–11
**Ind Coope Burton Ale; Tetley
Bitter** H
Former country house with a
plush, multi-room interior.
Fine plasterwork and mosaic
tiled floors. Regular foreign
beer festivals and live
entertainment in the large
function suite. Excellent
home-cooked meals. Extensive
children's accommodation.
Q ⚲ ❀ ◖ ▶ P ✗

Rose & Crown
Shrewsbury Road
☎ (0226) 763609
11–3, 7–11
**Hardys & Hansons
Kimberley Classic** H
Imposing brick pub in the
centre of town. An open
interior with high ceilings is
partitioned into smaller areas;

also a games room.
❀ ⇔ ⇔ ♣ P

Rotherham

Bridge Inn
Greasbrough Road (opp.
station) ☎ (0709) 363683
10.30–3, 5.30–11
**Draught Bass; John Smith's
Bitter** H; **Stones Best Bitter** E
Many-roomed pub next to the
Chapel-on-the-Bridge, its
meetings rooms used by
various local groups. Popular
with all ages.
◖ ⌂ ♿ ⇔ (Central) ♣

Effingham Arms
Effingham Street (opp. bus
station) ☎ (0709) 363353
11–11
Stones Best Bitter H
Typical town-centre pub with
four separate rooms. Stained-
glass windows depict the
voyage of Sir Francis Drake,
whose round the world trip
was sponsored by the local
Duke of Effingham. ⌂ ⇔ ♣

Kingfisher
Centenary Way
☎ (0709) 838422
11–11
**Old Mill Mild, Bitter,
Bullion** H
First licensed in 1882, a pub
carefully renovated when
taken over by Old Mill in
1991. Various species of
kingfisher are depicted in
paintings by a local artist.
❀ ⇔ ◖ ♿ ⇔ ♣ P

Limes
Broom Lane ☎ (0709) 363431
10.30–11
**S&N Theakston Best Bitter;
Younger Scotch, IPA, No. 3** H
Well-appointed hotel with a
comfortable lounge bar. The
emphasis is on a range of
meals, served all day until
early eve. Q ❀ ⇔ ◖ ▶ P

Turners Arms
Psalters Lane, Holmes
☎ (0709) 558937
12–3, 7–11
Wards Sheffield Best Bitter E
Smart, compact pub
modernised in 1992 but
retaining three separate areas
with lots of pub memorabilia.
Known locally as the 'Green
Bricks' because of its
distinctive external tiling.
❀ ◖ ♣ P

Woodman
Midland Road, Masbrough
☎ (0709) 561486
12–3, 7–11
Stones Best Bitter H
Solid stone-built ex-Bentley's
pub. Pool table and dartboard
in the games room, with a
snooker table upstairs; quieter
lounge. Q ❀ ⌂ ♣

Sheffield: *Central*

Bath Hotel
66 Victoria Street (off Glossop Rd) ☎ (0742) 729017
12–3, 5.30 (7.30 Sat)–11 (12–2, 7.30–10.30 Sun)
Ind Coope Burton Ale, Tetley Bitter; Wards Sheffield Best Bitter H
Tetley Heritage pub converted from Victorian cottages to form a small, friendly, two-roomed local. The original ground lease prohibited the use of the site as an alehouse or for other noxious activities!
◖ ⌂ ♣

Boulogne
Waingate
☎ (0742) 726270
12–3, 7–11 (closed Sun lunch)
Beer range varies H
Large street-corner, ex-Gilmour's pub. Sheffield's embryonic 'Tap & Spile', offering up to seven beers.
Ġ ⧲ ♣

Fagans
Broad Lane
☎ (0742) 728430
11.30–3, 5.30–11 (11.30–11 Fri & Sat)
Ind Coope Burton Ale; Tetley Bitter H
Lively, popular pub with a small snug. Frequent impromptu folk music sessions. Q ❀ ◖ ♣

Fat Cat
23 Alma Street (near Kelham Island Industrial Museum)
☎ (0742) 728195
12–3, 5.30–11
Kelham Island Bitter; Marston's Pedigree, Owd Rodger; S&N Theakston Old Peculier; Taylor Landlord H
Sheffield's first real ale free house, opened in 1981. Two comfortable rooms, a corridor drinking area and an upstairs function room for an overspill (children at lunchtime). Kelham Island brewery operates from the grounds. Quiz Mon. ♨ Q ❀ ◖ ⌂ ✁

Howard
53 Howard Street (opp. station) ☎ (0742) 780183
11–11 (11–3, 5.30–11 Sat; closed Sun lunch)
Mansfield Riding Mild, Riding Bitter, Old Baily H
Large, open-plan lounge bar on two levels, with a separate pool area. Popular with students from the nearby polytechnic – can be very busy. ◖ ⧲ (Midland) ♣

Lord Nelson
166 Arundel Street
☎ (0742) 722650
11–3, 5.30–11
Hardys & Hansons Best Bitter H

Welcoming, basic street-corner local in an area of small workshops near the edge of the city centre. ⧲ ♣

Moseley's Arms
West Bar (A61)
☎ (0742) 721591
11–11 (11–3.30, 7–11 Sat)
Draught Bass; Stones Best Bitter H
Superbly renovated pub just off the city centre: three comfortably furnished rooms, with a friendly, homely atmosphere. A function room upstairs houses a full-sized snooker table.
◖ ⌂ Ġ ⧲ (Midland) ♣

Norfolk Arms
Suffolk Road
☎ (0742) 727598
11–11
Courage Directors; John Smith's Bitter, Magnet H
Triangular-shaped pub, popular with workers and students. Busy tap room with a pool table; comfortable lounge. ⌂ ⧲ (Midland) ♣

Red Deer
18 Pitt Street (off West St)
☎ (0742) 722890
11.30–3, 5–11 Fri; 12–3, 7–10.30 Sat; closed Sun lunch)
Ind Coope Burton Ale; Tetley Mild, Bitter; Wards Sheffield Best Bitter H
Busy, friendly one-roomed local with an active folk club. Popular with students and professionals. Excellent home-cooked meals (eves by arrangement). Children allowed in the function room for meals. Quiz Sun. Q ❀ ◖

Red House
Solly Street ☎ (0742) 727926
11.30–3, 5–11
Taylor Landlord; Wards Sheffield Best Bitter H
Comfortably furnished local with three separate drinking areas around a central bar. Friendly atmosphere; popular with all ages. Live music Sun; quiz Thu. ❀ ◖ ▶ ♣

Royal Standard
156–158 St Mary's Road (inner ring road, near Bramall Lane football ground)
☎ (0742) 722883
11.30–3, 5–11
Taylor Landlord; Wards Mild, Sheffield Best Bitter, Kirby H
Busy pub with tap room, a snug and a large lounge. Fine wood-panelled bar. ❀ ◖ ⌂ ⧲ (Midland) ♣ P

Rutland Arms
Brown Street
☎ (0742) 729003
11–3, 5.30 (7 Sat)–11 (closed lunch Sat matchdays)
Ind Coope Burton Ale; Tetley Bitter; Younger No. 3 H

City-centre gem in a resurgent cultural corner of the city. Behind the distinctive Gilmour's frontage lies a comfortable lounge.
Q ❀ ⌂ ◖ ⧲

Sheffield: *East*

Alma Inn
76 South Street, Mosborough (behind Eckington Hall)
☎ (0742) 484781
11.30–3.30, 6.30–11
Wards Thorne Best Bitter H; **Sheffield Best Bitter** H & E
Two-roomed local, split by a central bar. Off the beaten track, hosted by a jovial and friendly landlord. Children's playground in the garden.
Q ❀ ⌂ ♣ P

Carlton
563 Attercliffe Road
☎ (0742) 443287
11.45–3 (3.45 Sat), 5 (7.30 Sat)–11 (11.45–11 Fri)
Mansfield Riding Bitter; Webster's Yorkshire Bitter H; **guest beers**
Warm and friendly watering hole, attracting custom from many parts of the city. Like the Tardis, the interior appears larger than the outside would imply. Separate games room to the rear of the bar. ♨ ⧲ (Attercliffe Rd) ♣

Cocked Hat
Worksop Road
☎ (0742) 448332
11–11 (11–3, 7–11 Sat)
Marston's Burton Best Bitter, Pedigree H
In the Attercliffe Environmental Corridor, an excellent, welcoming Victorian pub next to the Don Valley Stadium. Display of bottled beers from around the world. Good lunches. ♨ Q ❀ ◖ ♣

Cross Keys
400 Handsworth Road (A57)
☎ (0742) 694413
11–11
Stones Best Bitter H
Popular three-roomed local next to Handsworth parish church. Boasts a very long history; an outstanding example of an unspoilt, friendly watering hole. ⌂ ♣

Milestone
12 Peaks Mount, Mosborough (Crystal Peaks Shopping Centre) ☎ (0742) 471614
11–11
Banks's Mild, Bitter E
Frequented by shoppers at lunchtimes and young cinema-goers in the eves: a large lounge and a conservatory with a pool table. Note the viewing glass to the cellar in the tap room.
♨ ❀ ◖ ⌂ Ġ ♣ P

South Yorkshire

Sheffield: *North*

Foundry Arms
111 Barrow Road, Wincobank
☎ (0742) 426498
12–3.30, 7–11
Stones Best Bitter; Tetley Bitter Ⓗ
One-bar pub with a lounge, a tap room and a raised area for pool. Scenes of old Sheffield adorn the walls. Close to Meadowhall shopping complex. ❀ ⓓ ⅍ ⇌ (Meadowhall) ♣ P

Mill Tavern
2–4 Earsham Street, Burngreave ☎ (0742) 756461
11–4, 7–11 (11–11 Fri & Sat)
Old Mill Mild, Bitter, Bullion Ⓗ
A mock Tudor frontage leads into a single bar serving all areas of the pub which is a big charity fund-raiser. Regular live entertainment; bar billiards. ⓓ ♣

Pitsmoor
448 Pitsmoor Road
☎ (0742) 723962
11.30–4.30 (5 Fri & Sat), 6.30 (7 Sat)–11
Stones Best Bitter; Tetley Bitter Ⓗ
Open-plan pub with a horseshoe-shaped lounge around a central bar: a community pub with a friendly atmosphere. Live entertainment Wed.
❀ ⓓ ⅍ ♣ P

Robin Hood
Greaves Lane, Little Matlock, Stannington (right turn after Pinegrove Country Club)
☎ (0742) 344565
11.30–3, 7–11
Stones Best Bitter Ⓔ
Country pub dating from 1800, on the site of a failed spa. Friendly atmosphere with a pianist at weekends. Large children's play area. Eve meals Tue–Sat. Q ❀ ⓓ ▶ ⅍ ♣ P

Sheffield: *South*

Abbey
944 Chesterfield Road, Woodseats ☎ (0742) 745374
11–11
Tetley Bitter Ⓗ
Large main road pub in a prominent corner location. The small, cosy bar contrasts with a large, comfortable lounge. The emphasis is on food at lunchtime and early eve, but a mixed crowd of drinkers is attracted later on. Own bowling green at the rear. ❀ ⓓ ▶ ⅍ P ⅏

Earl of Arundel & Surrey
528 Queens Road (1 mile S of centre) ☎ (0742) 551006

11–11
Taylor Landlord; Wards Sheffield Best Bitter Ⓗ; **guest beers**
Architecturally-unusual corner pub in an area where many buildings have been demolished. A single bar, but several distinct drinking areas. Own folk club. The last remaining Pound House in Sheffield. Eve meals Fri and Sat only. ⓓ ⅍

Fleur de Lys
Totley Hall Lane, Totley
☎ (0742) 361476
11–11
Draught Bass; Stones Best Bitter; Welsh Brewers Worthington BB Ⓗ
Large, country-style pub on the very edge of the city. Spacious, plain lounge bar at the rear with video games, TV and a dining area. Smaller cosy bar at the front with a more relaxed, warmer atmosphere. Eve meals for booked groups. ❀ ⓓ ⅏ P

Mount Pleasant
291 Derbyshire Lane (left off main Chesterfield road)
11–3, 6–11
Banks's Bitter; Tetley Bitter Ⓗ
Extremely cosy local with more patrons than space. Two bars reflect the varied clientele: the public bar is basically furnished and friendly; the lounge is plusher with quieter music and a large water jug collection. ⓓ ⅏ ⅍ P

Old Mother Redcap
Prospect Road, Bradway
☎ (0742) 360179
11–3, 5.30–11 (11–11 Sat)
Samuel Smith OBB Ⓗ
Modern pub in an estate on the southern edge of the city. Single L-shaped lounge bar; each end offers a discernibly different drinking atmosphere. Mainly local clientele, but all made welcome. Eve meals Thu and Fri. ❀ ⓓ ▶ ♣ P

Small Beer Off-Licence
57 Archer Road
☎ (0742) 551356
12 (10.30 Sat)–10.30 (12–2, 7–10.30 Sun)
Bateman XXXB; Taylor Landlord; Wards Sheffield Best Bitter Ⓗ; **guest beers**
Small but well stocked, back-street off-licence with a wide range of foreign bottled beers. Guest beers vary. ⅍ ⌂

Sheffield: *West*

Banner Cross
971 Ecclesall Road (A625)
☎ (0742) 661479
11.30–11

Ind Coope Burton Ale; Tetley Bitter Ⓗ
Busy suburban local with wood panelling in the lounge and large, well decorated tap room. An upstairs games room has snooker and pool.
❀ ⓓ ⅏ ♣

Devonshire Arms
118 Ecclesall Road
☎ (0742) 722202
11–11
Wards Thorne Best Bitter Ⓗ, **Sheffield Best Bitter** Ⓔ, **Kirby** Ⓗ
Popular local with one main bar and a conservatory off. Several separate areas furnished with breweriana and old prints. Opposite Wards brewery. Eve meals finish at 7.30 (not served Sun eve). Q ❀ ⓓ ▶ ♣ P

Fox & Duck
223–227 Fulwood Road, Broomhill (A57)
☎ (0742) 663422
11–11
Courage Directors; John Smith's Bitter, Magnet Ⓗ
Busy pub in the middle of Broomhill shopping centre. A large bar serves several distinct areas, all traditionally furnished. ❀ ⓓ ▶ ♣

Norfolk Arms
Hollow Meadows, Manchester Road (A57, opp. Rivelin Dams)
☎ (0742) 309253
11.30–3.30, 7–11 (11–11 Sat)
Vaux Samson Ⓗ; **Wards Thorne Best Bitter, Sheffield Best Bitter** Ⓔ
Roadside inn with an aquarium in the bar. Large plush lounge with a grand piano. Jazz on Thu; folk Fri nights. ♫ Q ⇟ ❀ ⓓ ▶ ▲ P

Old Grindstone
3 Crookes
☎ (0742) 660322
11–11
Taylor Landlord Ⓗ; **Wards Sheffield Best Bitter, Kirby** Ⓗ & Ⓔ
Spacious, Victorian-style lounge with a conservatory; oak-panelled games room modelled on a gentleman's club and offering snooker, pool and darts. Quiet until 7.30 when the last food orders are taken. Q ❀ ⓓ ▶ ⅏

Old Heavygate
114 Matlock Road
☎ (0742) 340003
12–3.30, 7–11
Hardys & Hansons Best Bitter, Kimberley Classic Ⓗ
Dating from 1696, with some original beams in the oak room; the lounge has high bar stools and lovingly cared for potted plants. ❀ ⅏ ♣ P

Pomona

255 Ecclesall Road
☎ (0742) 665922
11–11
S&N Theakston XB, Old Peculier; Younger Scotch, No. 3 H
Large, modern suburban local served by a long bar, with four comfortable drinking areas and a conservatory. Live jazz Wed; quizzes Mon and Thu. Busy at all times with first class meals all day. Snooker table. ⚲ ❀ ◖ ▶ ♣ P

South Anston

Loyal Trooper

34 Sheffield Road (off A57)
☎ (0909) 562203
12–3, 6–11 (12–11 Sat)
Tetley Bitter H
Very old village pub with two cosy rooms at the front. The larger back room has a pool table and a darts area.
Q ❀ ◖ ♣ P

Sprotbrough

Boat Inn

Nursery Lane, Lower Sprotbrough
☎ (0302) 857188
11–3, 6–11 (11–11 summer Sat)
Courage Directors; John Smith's Bitter, Magnet H
17th-century former coaching house where Sir Walter Scott wrote *Ivanhoe*. Refurbished in 1985: exposed beams, stone floor, wooden furniture and ornamental china give a farmhouse feel. Set in a deep gorge by the River Don (beware twisty roads). Bar meals (not Sat/Sun eves) and separate restaurant.
❀ ◖ ▶ ♿ P

Thorne

Green Dragon

Silver Street
☎ (0405) 812797
11–5, 6.30–11
Wards Thorne Best Bitter H
Town-centre pub near the former Darley brewery. Extensively and sympathetically refurbished in 1991. No food Mon.
◖ ▶ ⊟ ♣ P

Thorpe Hesley

Horse & Tiger

Brook Hill (B6086)
☎ (0742) 468072
11–3, 6–11 (11–11 Sat)
Stones Best Bitter; Tetley Bitter H
Restored to its former glory, a pub on the site of an earlier one. Its history and plans are displayed near the bar.
❀ ♣ P

Tickhill

Scarbrough Arms

Sunderland Street
☎ (0302) 742977
11–3, 6–11
Courage Directors; Ruddles County; John Smith's Bitter, Magnet H; **guest beer**
Deservedly popular local with three separate rooms of differing character. Barrel furniture and a real fire make the middle room the archetypal village bar. Different guest beer every week. Extensive garden. No food Sun. Smoking restriction applies lunchtime only.
🏚 Q ❀ ◖ ⊟ ♣ P ⊬

Three Crowns

Northgate
☎ (0302) 745191
11 (12 winter)–3, 7–11
Tetley Mild, Bitter H; **guest beers**
Formerly the Buttercross, a Whitbread house, this comfortable old pub has reverted to its original name. Same keen landlord; new beers with a varied guest ale. The garden has won prizes. A new family room is planned.
🏚 Q ❀ ❀ ▲ ♣

Victoria

Victoria Inn

Hepworth (A616)
☎ (0484) 682785
12–2, 7–11 (12–2, 7–10.30 Sun)
Tetley Bitter; Younger IPA H
1950s time capsule; old-fashioned and unspoilt, with a snug and a lobby bar, also a lounge only open in summer. Toasted sandwiches available from an antique grill behind the bar. P

Wath upon Dearne

New Inn

West Street
☎ (0709) 872347
11–11 (11–3, 7–11 Sat)
John Smith's Bitter, Magnet H
Lively two-roomed local, once Whitworth's brewery tap and popular with a wide cross-section of the community. Good food in the bar and upstairs restaurant. ❀ ◖ ⊟ ♣

Sandygate

On A633, near A6023 jct
☎ (0709) 877827
11–3, 5 (7 Sat)–11
S&N Theakston Best Bitter, Old Peculier; Younger IPA, No. 3 H
Large, imposing former hospital, overlooking the Dearne valley. Decorated and furnished to a high standard.
🏚 ❀ 🚗 ◖ ▶ ⊟ ♣ P

Wentworth

George & Dragon

Main Street ☎ (0226) 742440
12–3, 7–11
Ind Coope Burton Ale; Oak Double Dagger; Taylor Best Bitter, Landlord; Tetley Bitter H; **guest beers**
Traditional village local full of character and characters. A typical English country pub with stone-flagged floors and rural artefacts. Speciality bottled beers available. On the Rotherham–Barnsley bus route. 🏚 Q ❀ ◖ ▲ P

Wheatley Hills

Wheatley Hotel

Thorne Road ☎ (0302) 364092
10.30–11
Courage Directors; John Smith's Bitter, Magnet H
Large, well-appointed hotel. The lounge is divided by impressive sliding doors. Popular with coach parties on summer eves. Well-equipped play area for children outside.
Q ⚲ ❀ 🚗 ◖ ▶ ⊟ ♿ ♣ P

Wombwell

Wat Tyler

Station Road (B6035 towards Darfield) ☎ (0226) 340307
11.30–3, 7–11
John Smith's Magnet; Stones Best Bitter; Whitbread Boddingtons Bitter H; **guest beers**
Named after the original Poll Tax protester; a roadside pub with a pleasant lawned garden (barbecues in summer). Regular beer festivals. Difficult access to car park. 🏚 ❀ ◖ ▶ ♣ P

Woodhouse Mill

Princess Royal

680 Retford Road (A57)
☎ (0742) 692615
11–3, 7–11
Ind Coope Burton Ale; Stones Best Bitter; Tetley Bitter H
Large rambling pub of several rooms. Live jazz in the concert room Tue eves. No food Sun.
⚲ ❀ ◖ ▶ ⇌ ♣ P

Wortley

Wortley Arms Hotel

Halifax Road (A629)
☎ (0742) 882245
11–11
Wortley Bitter, Earls Ale H; **guest beers**
Old coaching house with a Grade II listing and an attractive roadside facade. Retains a tap room and a large lounge dominated by its fireplace. Micro-brewery in the pub cellar. Excellent food.
🏚 ❀ 🚗 ◖ ▶ ⊟ ♣ P

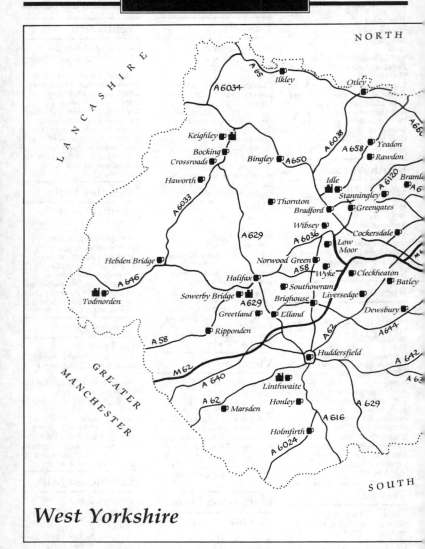

West Yorkshire

 Clark's, Wakefield; **Commercial, Goose Eye**, Keighley; **Linfit**, Linthwaite; **Robinwood**, Todmorden; **Ryburn**, Sowerby Bridge; **Taylor**, Keighley; **Trough**, Idle

Aberford

Arabian Horse
Main Street ☎ (0532) 813312
11–2.30, 5–11 (11–11 Sat)
S&N Theakston Best Bitter; Younger Scotch, No. 3 Ⓗ
18th-century inn on the green of one of Leeds's most attractive villages. Friendly, with a warm welcome.
♨ Q ✿ ◗ ⊟ ♣ P

Armley

Nelson Inn
212 Armley Road (A647, 2 miles from Leeds)
☎ (0532) 638505
11.45 (11 Thu–Sat)–3, 5.30–11
S&N Theakston XB; Younger Scotch, No. 3 Ⓗ
Two-roomed pub near the Industrial Museum. The last home-brew pub in Leeds – it ceased brewing on the death of the owner in 1952. Home-cooked food, good value.
◗ ♿ ♣

Barwick in Elmet

New Inn
Main Street ☎ (0532) 812289
11.30–3, 5.30–11 (11–4, 6–11 Sat)
John Smith's Bitter; Webster's Green Label Ⓗ

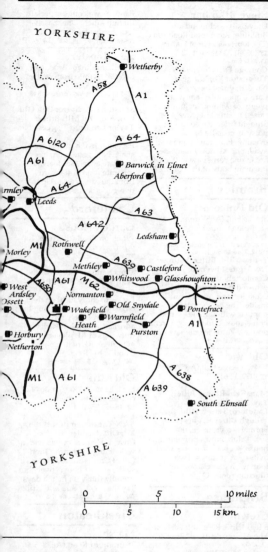

YORKSHIRE

Wetherby

A58

A1

A6120

A61

A64

Barwick in Elmet

Aberford

rnley

Leeds

A642

A63

Ledsham

Morley

Rothwell

M1

Methley

A639

Castleford

West Ardsley

A61

Whitwood

Glasshoughton

Ossett

M62

Normanton

Old Snydale

Pontefract

Wakefield

Warmfield

Heath

A1

Horbury

Purston

Netherton

A638

M1

A61

A639

South Elmsall

YORKSHIRE

0 ... 5 ... 10 miles
0 ... 5 ... 10 ... 15 km

Bocking

New Inn
Halifax Road (A629, 500 yds
from A6033 jct)
☎ (0535) 643191
11 (2 winter)–11
Mansfield Riding Bitter ⒣;
Taylor Golden Best ⒠; **guest
beers**
Popular, two-room local with
a constantly changing range of
guest beers. Recently
renovated and comfortably
refurbished using stained-
wood and Yorkshire stone.
Traditional pub games teams.
❀ ⅋ ♣ P

Bradford

Bedford Arms
2 Wakefield Road (100 yds up
hill from the Interchange,
A650) ☎ (0274) 733837
11–11
Tetley Bitter ⒣
Good, honest workingman's
pub with separate rooms.
Darts and pool played;
popular with the Irish.
Friendly staff.
⊞ ⇌ (Interchange) ♣

Brown Cow
880–886 Little Horton Lane
☎ (0274) 574040
12–3, 7–11
Samuel Smith OBB ⒣
Thriving basic tap room;
comfortable lounge. Live
music Thu, Fri and Sun eves. ⊞

Corn Dolly
110 Bolton Road (400 yds from
Forster Sq) ☎ (0274) 720219
11.30–11
**Moorhouse's Premier; S&N
Theakston Best Bitter, XB;
Stones Best Bitter** ⒣; **guest
beers**
Family-run pub on the edge of
the city centre. Huge
sandwiches prove popular
with office workers and all
meats are home-cooked, as is
the chilli. Two quiz, pool and
doms teams. Country and
Western nights Wed and Sun.
At least four varied guest
beers. ⅏ ❀ ⅋ ⇌ (Forster
Sq) ♣ P

Jacobs Well
14 Kent Street (near
Interchange, Hall Ings/A641
jct) ☎ (0274) 390654
11–11 (11–3.30, 6.30–11 Sat)
Tetley Bitter ⒣
Village-type pub with a
friendly atmosphere.
Originally a waterhouse, and
was one of the last pubs in
Bradford to gain a spirits
licence. Popular with a wide
cross-section of people.
Recently refurbished.
❀ ⅋ ⅅ ⇌ (Interchange) ♣

Friendly, roadside village inn:
a real locals' pub with service
from a tiny bar and hatchway.
Q ⅅ ♣

Batley

Wilton Arms
4 Commercial Street (off A652)
☎ (0924) 479996
11–11 (11–3, 5–11 Tue & Thu)
**Bass Light, Mild XXXX,
Draught Bass; Stones Best
Bitter** ⒣; **guest beer**
Busy, three-roomed, basic
town-centre pub between the
bus and rail stations, close to the
listed 1869 'Shoddy Temple'.
Mild pump in the tap room,

wrought ironwork in the front
room, people in every room. No
food Sun. ⋈ ⅅ ⊞ ⅋ ⇌ ♣ P

Bingley

Ferrands Arms
Queen Street (off main street)
☎ (0274) 563949
11.30–11
**Taylor Golden Best, Best
Bitter, Landlord** ⒣
Thriving local next to an arts
centre. Nearby building
society workers enjoy the
large range of pub lunches.
Reinstatement of some
partitions has improved the
interior. Large function room
upstairs. ⅅ ⅋ ⇌ ♣ P

West Yorkshire

New Beehive
171 Westgate (200 yds from John St market)
☎ (0274) 721784
12–11 ✓
Old Mill Bitter; Taylor Golden Best, Landlord; Tetley Bitter Ⓗ**; guest beers**
Genuine Edwardian pub, catering for a wide clientele. Massive selection of malt whiskies; trad. jazz every Fri, Irish music Sun lunch. Good food: try the chilli. Up to six guest beers. Collection of toby jugs. ⚏ ❀ ⌑ ◑ ⬥ ⏼
⇌ (Forster Sq)

Prospect of Bradford
527 Bolton Road
☎ (0274) 727018
1–4, 7–11
Bass Light; Stones Best Bitter; Taylor Golden Best Ⓗ**; guest beer** (occasionally)
Pub with a spacious drinking area and panoramic views over Bradford (watch City play free). Excellent function room. Organist sing-along Fri, Sat and Sun. ⚏ ♣ P

Red Lion
881 Manchester Road, Bankfoot
☎ (0274) 304360
11–11
Tetley Mild, Bitter Ⓗ
Popular local, handy for Odsal Stadium. ❀ ◑ ⊟ ♣ P

Red Lion
589 Thornton Road (B6145, 2 miles from centre)
☎ (0274) 496684
11–3, 5.30–11 (11–11 Fri & Sat)
Samuel Smith OBB Ⓗ
Straightforward old main road pub with a popular games room. Buses stop right outside. ❀ ◑ ⊟ ♣ P

Royal
738 Gt. Horton Road (A647 Halifax road, 2 miles from centre) ☎ (0274) 572335
12–3 (Mon–Wed, not winter), 5–11 (11–11 Thu–Sat all year)
S&N Theakston Best Bitter; John Smith's Bitter; Webster's Green Label, Yorkshire Bitter Ⓗ
Small local, with pool, darts and doms. Disco Thu nights; folk music summer Suns.
Q ⊟ ♣ P

Shoulder of Mutton
Kirkgate
☎ (0274) 726038
11–11 (12–2, 7–10.30 Sun) ✓
Samuel Smith OBB, Museum Ⓗ
Small, multi-roomed pub, rebuilt in 1825. Its surprisingly large and high-walled beer garden is a quiet suntrap. High quality and good value lunches.
Q ❀ ◑ ⊟ ⇌ (Interchange/ Forster Sq) ♣

Steve Biko Bar
University Richmond Building, Richmond Road (on 'D' Floor, near Great Hall)
☎ (0274) 733466 ext 3257
11.30–11 (7 Sat)–11
Courage Directors; S&N Theakston XB; Younger No. 3 Ⓗ**; guest beers**
Large, open-plan bar with plenty of seating, including a raised no-smoking area. Student oriented, so can be noisy, especially in the evening. Hot snacks often available. All noisy machines are in one corner away from the main body of the bar. ⌑ ⊬

Bramley

Old Unicorn
Stocks Hill (A657, opp. shopping centre)
☎ (0532) 564465
11.30–3 (4 Fri & Sat), 5.30 (7 Sat)–11 (12–2, 7–10.30 Sun)
Tetley Mild, Bitter; Younger No. 3; guest beers Ⓗ
Comfortable, popular, 200-year-old free house, much extended and opened out inside. The beer garden is very popular with families. Good home-cooked food (vegetarian option). Value for money meals. ❀ ◑ ♣ P

Old Vic
17 Whitecote Hill (A657)
☎ (0532) 561207
11–3, 7–11
Mansfield Riding Bitter; Taylor Golden Best, Landlord; Tetley Mild, Bitter; Trough Bitter Ⓗ**; guest beers**
Formerly a vicarage, then a social club, now a popular free house, set back from the road in its own grounds. Two lounges, a games room and a function room. Q ⊟ ♣ P

Brighouse

Crown
6 Lightcliffe Road (off A644 at The Albion) ☎ (0484) 715436
11.30–11
Tetley Mild, Bitter Ⓗ
Genuine locals' pub in a residential area just outside the town centre. Feels as if it has more than three rooms. Perhaps part of a terrace once, it now stands alone behind modern old people's bungalows. Q ❀ ❀ ♣ P

Forte Crest Hotel
Coal Pit Lane, Clifton Village (between Clifton and M62 jct 25, 1 mile from Brighouse centre) ☎ (0484) 400400
11–11 (24 hrs residents)
Taylor Landlord Ⓗ
Newish, purpose-built, four-star hotel. Prices match the status of the establishment but bar snacks are reasonable.

Families welcome, especially for Sun lunch. One massive lounge area leads into the restaurant. Q ❀ ⌑ ◑ ⬥ P

Red Rooster
123 Elland Road, Brookfoot (A6025, ½ mile from centre)
☎ (0484) 713737
12–2 (3 Sat, not Mon or Tue), 5 (6 Sat)–11
Marston's Pedigree; Oak Old Oak Ale; Old Mill Bitter; Taylor Landlord Ⓗ**; guest beers**
Excellent free house on a sharp bend; one room has separate areas that feel like separate rooms. 400 yards from the canal locks. Up to five guest beers. ⚏ ♣ ⌑ P

Castleford

Garden House
Wheldon Road (off A656, 100 yds from river bridge)
☎ (0977) 552934
11–11
Vaux Samson (occasionally)**; Wards Thorne Best Bitter, Kirby** Ⓗ
Large, friendly local on the edge of town, overlooking the River Aire. Lively tap room adorned with a local artist's drawings of RL players. Can get full on RL match days. Good value food.
⚏ Q ❀ ◑ ⊟ ⇌ ♣ P

Old Mill
Lock Lane (A656 ½ mile N of centre, next to canal)
☎ (0977) 557034
11–11
S&N Theakston Best Bitter, XB, Old Peculier Ⓗ
Cosy, L-shaped lounge with a welcoming open fire. Often full of Castleford RL players so the atmosphere is lively but friendly (busy on match days). Try the good value Mill Grills.
⚏ ❀ ◑ ⊟ ⇌ ♣ P

Cleckheaton

Marsh
28 Bradford Road (A638, 500 yds S of bus station)
☎ (0274) 872104
11–3, 7–11
Old Mill Mild, Bitter, Bullion Ⓗ
Typical Old Mill colour-co-ordinated refurbishment of a triangular pub, complete with ubiquitous old wrinkly brick fireplace wall and discreet dais! Quiet but not sedate atmosphere. ❀ ◑ ♣ P

Try also: **Wheatsheaf**, Gomersal (Tetley)

Cockersdale

Valley
68 Whitehall Road (A58)
☎ (0532) 852483

11.30–3 (4.30 Sat), 5.30 (7 Sat)–11
Samuel Smith OBB Ⓗ
An ideal place to start the
Leeds Country Way walk,
with fine views over Leeds.
Ever-growing menu with
limited children's option.
❀ ◖▶ ♣ P

Crossroads

Quarry House Inn

Bingley Road (1 mile from
A629, Halifax–Keighley road)
☎ (0535) 642239
12–3, 7–11 (11.30 if dining)
**Ind Coope Burton Ale; Taylor
Landlord; Tetley Bitter** Ⓗ
Family-run converted
farmhouse in open
countryside. The bar, a former
church pulpit, is set in a small
cosy area. Good quality home-
made food (especially soups
and the mixed grill on Wed
night). Fresh fish menu Fri
night. ♨ Q ⌚ ❀ ◖▶ ⅄ Å P

Dewsbury

John F Kennedy

2 Webster Hill (A644, near bus
and rail stations)
☎ (0924) 455828
1–4 (Sat only), 7–11
**Taylor Landlord; Tetley
Bitter** Ⓗ**; guest beers**
(weekends)
Not the way the big brewers
would design a pub but the
long-established licensee has
successfully blended a
younger clientele with more
staid customers and still
retains the enterprising
jukebox and atmosphere.
⅄ ⇌ ♣

Market House

Church Street (near bus
station)
☎ (0924) 457310
11–11
Tetley Mild, Bitter Ⓗ
Two-level, basic town-centre
hostelry noted for its
protected exterior. Usually has
more customers in the
corridor area than in the two
rooms! Famed for its bank of
five pulls, it has now added
satellite TV to its charms.
Wheelchair access at the rear.
♨ Q ◖🍴 ⅄ ⇌ ♣

Elland

Colliers Arms

66 Park Road (A6025)
☎ (0422) 372007
11.30–3, 5.30 (5 Fri)–11 (11.30–11 Sat)
**Samuel Smith OBB,
Museum** Ⓗ
Smart, cottage pub with two
low-ceilinged rooms and a
conservatory to the rear. Own
moorings on the canal. Eve
meals Fri/Sat only (till 8pm).
♨ Q ⌚ ❀ ◖▶ P

Oddfellows Arms

12 Elland Lane (off A629,
behind Howarth Timber)
☎ (0422) 373605
12–11 (may close Wed afternoon)
**Hambleton Best Bitter; Tetley
Bitter** Ⓗ**; guest beers**
Small back-street boozer with
a comfortable lounge and a
small tap room. Strong RL
following. ❀ ◖▶ ⅄ ♣ P

Glasshoughton

Rock Inn

Rock Hill (off Front Street,
B6136 to Ferrybridge)
☎ (0977) 552985
11–11
**Wards Mild, Thorne Best
Bitter, Kirby** Ⓗ
Popular, friendly, locals' pub,
comprising a lounge, a snug
and a traditional tap room, all
with open fires. Runner-up in
the national *Pub of the Year*
1990. Upstairs pool room.
Parking is a pain.
♨ Q ❀ ◖▶ ⅄ ♣ P

Greengates

Hogshead

25 Haigh Hall Road (off New
Line)
☎ (0274) 612670
12–11 (11–3, 6.30–11 Sat)
Trough Bitter, Wild Boar Ⓗ**;
guest beers** (occasionally)
Former Conservative club
with a lounge area and a
games room (ten pin bowling)
separated by a large bar.
Function room upstairs.
& ♣ P

Greetland

Branch Road Inn

Saddleworth Road (A6025)
☎ (0422) 372746
12–3 (4 Fri & Sat), 7–11 (12 supper
licence Fri & Sat)
**Bass Mild XXXX, Draught
Bass; Stones Best Bitter** Ⓗ
Small tap room and a large
lounge on two levels. No eve
meals Mon or Wed.
♨ ❀ ◖▶ ⅄ ♣ P

Star Inn

1 Lindwell (off B6113)
☎ (0422) 373164
12–4 (not Tue), 7–11
**Wards Thorne Best Bitter,
Sheffield Best Bitter** Ⓗ
Small locals' pub with a single
bar serving distinct games and
lounge areas. ❀ ♣

Halifax

Brown Cow

569 Gibbet Street, Highroad
Well (1¹⁄₂ miles from centre)
☎ (0422) 361640
11.30–3, 5–11 (11–11 Fri & Sat)
**Whitbread Trophy, Castle
Eden Ale** Ⓗ

Unpretentious local with
sporting connections. No food
weekends. ◖& ♣

Clarence Hotel

Lister Lane
☎ (0422) 363266
11.30–11
**Old Mill Bitter; Stones Best
Bitter; Taylor Landlord;
Tetley Bitter** Ⓗ**; guest beer**
(occasionally)
Busy, street-corner local on the
fringe of the town centre, in
four-room, open-plan style
with an upstairs dining/
function room. Active sports
following. Happy hour daily.
❀ ◖& ⇌ ♣ P

Duke of York

West Street, Stone Chair Shelf
(A644 near A6036 jct; 3¹⁄₂
miles from centre)
☎ (0422) 202056
11.30–11
**Taylor Best Bitter; Whitbread
Castle Eden Ale** Ⓗ
Ancient inn with a remarkable
roof-scape. Refurbished
within but still cosy and
comfortable. Very popular for
food (including vegetarian) till
9pm. Quiz night Wed.
❀ 🛏 ◖▶ ♣ P

Shears Inn

Paris Gates, Boys Lane
(behind flats, between mills,
down into mill yard)
☎ (0422) 362936
11.45–4, 7–11 (11.30–11 Sat)
**Taylor Golden Best, Best
Bitter, Landlord; Younger
Scotch, No. 3** Ⓗ**; guest beer**
Pub enjoying a sublime
location in a wooded valley
bottom, dominated by
towering mills. Though
difficult to find, this tiny,
popular house is a rendezvous
for numerous sporting groups.
No food weekends.
♨ ❀ ◖⇌ ♣ P

Sportsman

Bradford Old Road,
Ploughcroft (¹⁄₄ mile E of
A647, 1 mile N of town)
☎ (0422) 367000
12–3, 6–11 (12–11 Sat)
**Old Mill Bitter; Ruddles
County; S&N Theakston Old
Peculier; Taylor Landlord;
Tetley Bitter** Ⓗ**; guest beer**
Popular hill-top free house
with expansive views. Squash,
solarium and sauna are all
available; all-weather ski slope
attached. Folk club Thu; quiz
nights Mon–Wed. No food
Mon or Tue.
♨ ⌚ ❀ ◖▶ ♣ P

Sportsman Hotel

48–50 Crown Street
☎ (0422) 355704
11–11
Tetley Bitter Ⓗ**; guest beer**

West Yorkshire

18th-century inn with an Edwardian frontage. A central bar serves four drinking areas, including a separate room. Wide range of drinkers: rock music fans are attracted by the jukebox. Can get lively and noisy weekends, but a friendly atmosphere prevails. ⮌

Haworth

Fleece Inn
Main Street ☎ (0535) 642172
11–11
Taylor Dark Mild (summer), **Golden Best, Best Bitter, Landlord, Porter** or **Ram Tam** Ⓗ
Ancient coaching inn, popular with 'spirits': a village local which welcomes visitors. Stone flagged bar area and a quiet room with a spoof Brontë museum and displays by local artists. Two family rooms. Food every day (Sun lunches). Live music, quiz and games nights. ♨ Q ⬥ ◑ ▲ ⮌ (KWVLR) ♣

Haworth Old Hall
Sun Street (bottom of Main St) ☎ (0535) 624709
11–11
Bass Mild XXXX; Draught Bass; Stones Best Bitter; Tetley Mild, Bitter Ⓗ
Three-room, 17th-century, Tudor-style building with open stonework, oak beams and mullioned windows. Friendly atmosphere; large beer garden (children welcome). Sun lunch a speciality; à la carte restaurant. Accommodation includes a family room.
Q ⬥ ❀ 🛏 ◑ ⬛ ▲ ⮌ (KWVLR) P

King's Arms
2 Church Street ☎ (0535) 643146
11–11
Ind Coope Burton Ale; S&N Theakston Best Bitter; Tetley Bitter Ⓗ
Attractive old pub very close to the church. Secluded beer garden; opened-up interior. Quiz Sun nights.
❀ ◑ ⮌ (KWVLR)

Heath

King's Arms
$^1/_2$ mile off A655, 2 miles SE of Wakefield ☎ (0924) 377527
11.30–3, 6–11
Clark's Bitter; Taylor Landlord; Tetley Bitter Ⓗ; guest beer
Historic country inn in an attractive conserved village: a lounge and three small rooms featuring wood panelling, gas lighting, stone-flagged floors and coal fires, linked by passageways. Very warm,

cosy and atmospheric on cold eves. The restaurant also has cask ale. No children after 8.30. No eve meals Sun.
♨ Q ⬥ ❀ ◑ � ⬛ P

Hebden Bridge

Cross Inn
46 Towngate, Heptonstall ☎ (0422) 843833
11.30–4, 7–11
Taylor Golden Best, Best Bitter, Landlord Ⓗ
Pub perched on the roadside in the ancient village of Heptonstall, approached from the cobbled main street. Parking difficult. ❀ ◑ ◐ ▲ ♣

Fox & Goose
9 Heptonstall Road (A646 jct) ☎ (0422) 842649
11.30–3, 7.30–11
Ruddles Best Bitter; guest beers Ⓗ
Arched ground-floor cellars form this cosy local which has a comprehensive guest beer policy – three on sale, all from small independents.
❀ ◑ ◐ ⮌ ♣

Nutclough House Hotel
Keighley Road (A6033) ☎ (0422) 844361
12–3, 6–11 (11–11 Sat)
S&N Theakston Best Bitter; Taylor Landlord; Thwaites Bitter Ⓗ; guest beers
Roomy, comfortable family pub with many activities, including live music. Menu with vegetarian specialities. The crispaholic feline is a pub feature. Up to three guest beers. ♨ ❀ ◑ ◐ ⮌ ♣ P

Shoulder of Mutton
38 New Road, Mytholmroyd (B6138) ☎ (0422) 883165
11.30–3, 7–11
Whitbread Boddingtons Bitter, Flowers IPA, Trophy, Castle Eden Ale Ⓗ; guest beers
Popular roadside local with a display of toby jugs and china. Eve meals 7–8.30 (not Tue).
♨ ◑ ◐ ▲ ⮌ (Mytholmroyd) ♣ P

Holmfirth

Farmers Arms
Liphill Bank Road, Burnlee (off A635) ☎ (0484) 683713
11–3 (not Mon; may vary winter), 6–11
Taylor Best Bitter; Tetley Mild, Bitter Ⓗ; guest beers
Pub on a narrow lane (parking often difficult) with an open-plan set of enclosed spaces! No food Mon lunch. ♨ ◑ ◐

Rose & Crown (Nook)
7 Victoria Square (behind Barclays Bank, down alley off Hollowgate) ☎ (0484) 683960
11.30–11

Samuel Smith OBB; Stones Best Bitter; Taylor Best Bitter, Landlord; Ram Tam; Younger No. 3 Ⓗ; guest beers
Down-to-earth, no-frills, basic boozer in the heart of the *Summer Wine* tourist area. A drinkers' pub, a must for the seasoned tippler. Occasional folk music. ♨ ❀ ▲ ♣

Honley

Railway
1 Huddersfield Road (at A616/A6024 jct) ☎ (0484) 661309
11–3, 5–11 (11–11 Fri & Sat)
Ind Coope Burton Ale; Marston's Pedigree; Taylor Landlord; Tetley Mild, Bitter Ⓗ
Recently extended free house proudly displaying its merited brewery cellarmanship awards. Popular with locals and visitors to the Holme Valley. Q ❀ ▲ ⮌ P

Try also: Jacobs Well (Free)

Horbury

Calder Vale Hotel
Millfield Road, Horbury Junction (Horbury Junction signs from bypass, A642) ☎ (0924) 275351
11–3.30, 6.15–11
John Smith's Bitter Ⓗ
Built in 1884 as a 12-bedroom hotel by Fernandes Brewery when Charles Roberts railway wagon works was in its heyday. Still retains its two separate rooms, with the bar in a central corridor.
Q ❀ ♣ P

Shepherds Arms
Cluntergate (off B6128, 200 yds from centre) ☎ (0924) 274877
11–11
S&N Theakston XB, Old Peculier; Younger Scotch, No. 3 Ⓗ
Historic, oak-beamed Tudor inn with a friendly and comfortable atmosphere. Large open-plan lounge with a raised dining area; tidy tap room and a large beer garden with children's play facilities.
♨ ❀ ◑ ◐ ⬛ ♣ P

Huddersfield

Albert Hotel
38 Victoria Lane (near town hall) ☎ (0484) 421065
11–11
Bass Light, Draught Bass; Stones Best Bitter; Taylor Landlord; Welsh Brewers Worthington BB Ⓗ; guest beers
Superb etched Victorian glass in a genuine mahogany bar, now protected as one of the

last in the area. Two busy function rooms. Typical town centre mix of drinkers, though a haunt of councillors as well. Q ◁ ⟐ ⟲

Ale Shoppe

205 Lockwood Road, Lockwood (A616, 1 mile S of centre) ☎ (0484) 432479
10–9 (6 Sat; closed Sun)
Samuel Smith OBB H; **guest beers**
Off-licence with up to four draught beers: Oak or Taylor beers always available. Over 200 bottled beers from Germany, Belgium, Britain and the rest of the world. Home-brew supplies. Budding Michael Jacksons start here! ⟐ (Lockwood) ○

Berry Brow Liberal Club

Parkgate, Berry Brow (A616, 2¹/₂ miles S of centre)
☎ (0484) 662549
12–2, 7.30–11 (11.30–2.30, 8–11 Sat; 12–2.30, 8–10.30 Sun)
Old Mill Mild, Bitter; Tetley Bitter H; **guest beers**
Small club with a homely atmosphere, housed in a former Co-op building. CIU affiliated. Show this guide or CAMRA membership at the bar to be signed in. Snooker table. & ⟐ (Berry Brow) ○

ICI Recreation Club

Leeds Road (A62)
☎ (0484) 514367
12–11
Taylor Best Bitter; Tetley Mild, Bitter H; **guest beer**
Large club with three lounges, two bars, eight snooker tables, bowls, tennis, hockey, etc. CAMRA *Club of the Year* 1991. Function suite for hire. Weekday lunches. Show this guide or a CAMRA membership card to the doorman to be signed in. ✿ ◁ ○ P

Rat & Ratchet

40 Chapel Hill (A616, just off ring road) ☎ (0484) 516734
12–11 (11.30–11 Fri & Sat)
Bateman Mild; Mansfield Old Baily; Marston's Pedigree; Taylor Best Bitter, Landlord; Thwaites Best Mild H; **guest beers**
No-frills ale house with an amiable atmosphere, usually boasting 12 different real ales. Happy hour 4–7. Loud and lively in the evening. ✿ ◁ ⟐ ○ P

Shoulder of Mutton

11 Neale Road, Lockwood (off B6108 near A616 jct)
☎ (0484) 424835
7 (3 Sat)–11
Taylor Best Bitter, Landlord; Tetley Mild, Bitter; Thwaites Bitter H; **guest beers**

Walnut panelled pub tucked way up a cobbled street and filled with old-fashioned charm. Traditional tap room. Games downstairs and a pool room upstairs. ✿ ⟐ (Lockwood) ○

Slip Inn

156a Longwood Gate, Longwood (3 miles W of centre) ☎ (0484) 654423
11.30–3 (not Mon), 7–11 (11–11 Fri; 11–4, 7–11 Sat)
Burtonwood Mild, Forshaw's H
Close to textile mills, hugging the valley side, a pub awarded a beer medal by the brewery. Snooker table. ✿ ○ P

Slubbers Arms

1 Halifax Old Road, Hillhouse (just off A641, ³/₄ mile from centre) ☎ (0484) 429032
11.30–3.30, 6.30 (7 Sat)–11
Marston's Pedigree; Old Mill Mild; Taylor Best Bitter H; **guest beers**
Wedge-shaped pub boasting a dog with a limp! The unique name derives from the woollen textiles industry and is reflected in wall displays. The traditional Yorkshire range warms you after a Dickensian visit to the toilets! ⚌ ◁ ⟐ ○

Woolpack

19 Westgate, Almondbury (2 miles SE of centre)
☎ (0484) 435702
12–2, 5–11 (12–11 Sat)
Courage Directors; John Smith's Bitter, Magnet H
Open-plan village local, still retaining character. Next to Wormald Hall (1631) and opposite a perpendicular church with a 1522 cornice. Close to Castle Hill Iron Age fort (fine views). No food Sun/Mon. ✿ ◁ ○ P

Try also: Dusty Miller, Longwood (Free)

Idle

Brewery Arms

Louisa Street (off High Street)
☎ (0274) 610546
12–11
Trough Bitter, Wild Boar, Festival Ale H
Former Liberal Club and restaurant next to the brewery, refurbished following a fire. A large lounge with a separate area for pool. Regular disco nights. ✿ ◁ ○ P

Brewery Tap

51 Albion Road
☎ (0274) 613936
11.30–3 (4 Sat), 6.30 (7 Sat)–11
Trough Bitter, Wild Boar H; **guest beer**
Local converted from a baker's shop: a mixture of

stone and wood-panelled walls with a large central bar area. Regulars have formed a golfing society. Live rock music Tue and Sat nights. ✿ & ○

Ilkley

Midland

Station Road ☎ (0943) 607433
11–11
Courage Directors; John Smith's Bitter, Magnet; Tetley Bitter H
Victorian pub refurbished a few years ago. Very comfortable and usually quiet lounge; thriving tap room. ◁ ⟐ ○ P

Keighley

Albert Hotel

Bridge Street (Oakworth and Halifax Roads jct)
☎ (0535) 602306
11–5, 7–11 (11–11 Fri & Sat)
Taylor Golden Best, Best Bitter, Ram Tam (winter) H
Large, Victorian town-centre hotel: a popular meeting place, with a mainly local clientele. Long thin front room and a large pool room with an interesting mural. Small car park. ⟐ ○ P

Boltmakers Arms

117 East Parade (150 yds S of station) ☎ (0535) 661936
11.30–11 (11–4.30, 7–11 Sat)
Taylor Golden Best, Best Bitter, Landlord H
Very popular, well-known town pub. Small, so liable to be crowded at weekends. Very close to BR and Worth Valley Railway. Unusual 'crown' above the door. Good range of malt whiskies. ⟐ ○

Friendly Inn

2 Aireworth Street (off South St beyond Albert)
☎ (0535) 605031
12–4, 7–11
Taylor Golden Best, Best Bitter E
Small, two-roomed locals' pub that lives up to its name. & ○

Globe

2 Parkwood Street (follow signs to Harden from centre, beyond Cricketers)
☎ (0535) 600435
11–11
Taylor Golden Best, Best Bitter E, **Landlord; Tetley Bitter** H
Large, multi-roomed pub which used to be an Aaron King house. Interesting tropical fish. An organist entertains at weekends. The upstairs function room overlooks the Worth Valley Railway. ⟰ ✿ ⟐ ○ P

West Yorkshire

Grinning Rat/Rat Trap
2 Church Street
☎ (0535) 609747
11–11 (longer in Rat Trap)
**Butterknowle Black
Diamond; Old Mill Bitter;
Taylor Landlord; guest
beers** H
Very popular, centrally-placed
pub with several distinct
drinking areas. Guest beers
(four–six) are regularly
changed to give the widest
range for miles. Always a mild
available plus a cider
(sometimes perry). Frequent
live music. The Rat Trap is a
separate room with two bars.
♿ ⇌ ○

Red Pig
Church Green ☎ (0535) 605383
12–3, 7–11 (11–11 Sat)
**Commercial Worth Bitter;
Taylor Golden Best,
Landlord** H**; guest beers**
Basic but comfortable town-
centre pub frequented by
cavers, artists (some of whose
works adorn the walls) and a
good mix of other types. At
least three guest beers and a
good range of Belgian bottles
and malt whiskies. No food
Sun. ⚲ ◖ ⇌ ♣

Vine
Greengate Road (off South St
near Worth Way jct)
☎ (0535) 607066
11–11
**Taylor Golden Best, Best
Bitter** E
Comfortable local with a
friendly welcome. Informal
folk sessions on Tue. See the
incredible invulnerable
goldfish! ♣ ♣

Volunteer Arms
Lawkholme Lane (behind
Cavendish pub in Cavendish
St) ☎ (0535) 600173
11–11
**Taylor Golden Best, Best
Bitter** H
Smartly decorated pub in the
town centre with a largely
local clientele. Two rooms, the
smaller mainly for pub games;
function room for meetings.
⊞ ⇌ ♣

Keighley to Oxenhope and Back

Keighley and Worth Valley Railway Buffet Car ✓
Stations at Keighley, Ingrow
West, Damens, Oakworth,
Haworth and Oxenhope
☎ (0535) 645214/643629
(talking timetable)
Sat/Sun only Mar–Oct; Sun only
Oct–Dec, check timetable
Beer range varies
Railway buffet car giving

changing views of the Worth
Valley. Usually one or two
beers from metal containers,
refilled a few times a day.
Available for hire with beer to
your own requirements. Q
⚲ (Oxenhope) ⇌ (Keighley)
P (Keighley/Ingrow/
Oxenhope) ✁

Ledsham

Chequers
Claypit Lane ☎ (0977) 683135
11–3, 5.30–11 (11–11 Sat; closed Sun)
**John Smith's Bitter; S&N
Theakston Best Bitter;
Younger Scotch, No. 3** H
Delightful, ivy-covered village
inn with several rooms around
a tiny central bar. Unique six-
day licence. Excellent
restaurant upstairs.
⚲ Q ⛄ ⊛ ◖ ♣ P

Leeds

Adelphi
1 Hunslet Road (A61, towards
centre, left at Tetley brewery)
☎ (0532) 456377
11.30–3, 5 (7.30 Sat)–11 (11–11 Fri;
12–3, 7–11 Sun)
Tetley Bitter, Mild H
Listed Edwardian building,
built from granite: a Tetley
Heritage pub and the brewery
tap. Multi-roomed with fine
tiles, etched-glass and wooden
panelling. Function rooms
upstairs. No food Sun.
◖ ⊞ ⇌ (City) ♣

Ale House
79 Raglan Road (near main
entrance of University
campus) ☎ (0532) 455447
12 (4 Mon, 10 Sat)–10.30 (12–3, 7–10
Sun)
**Hyde Park Best, Monster
Mash, XB, No. 9, White Rose
Ale, Housewarmer** H**; guest
beers**
Off-licence which started
brewing in 1987, following
Reinheitsgebot rules. Up to four
guest beers as well as four real
ciders, Belgian and German
bottled beers, and unusual
wines, including one from
Zimbabwe! ○

Brick
Tong Road, Wortley
☎ (0532) 630567
11.30–11
**Tetley Mild, Bitter; Trough
Wild Boar** H
Friendly local with a popular
quiz on Wed and a loud disco
on Sun nights. ⊞ ♣ P

Chemic Tavern
9 Johnston Street, Woodhouse
☎ (0532) 440092
11–3, 5.30–11 (11–11 Sat)
**Ind Coope Burton Ale; Tetley
Bitter** H
Attractive stone-fronted house
which gives way to two
relaxing, low-ceilinged, wood-

panelled bars. No jukebox or
taped muzak, just lively
conversation. Q ⊞ ♣ P

City of Mabgate
45 Mabgate (near West
Yorkshire Playhouse)
☎ (0532) 457789
11.30–11
**Whitbread Boddingtons
Bitter, Trophy, Castle Eden
Ale, Flowers Original** H**;
guest beers**
Popular, award-winning pub
with a green-tiled exterior; a
well-used traditional tap room
and a superb lounge with
many photos of old Leeds.
Cast iron, wood-burning
stove; many guest ales plus
cider and organic wines;
Mabgate Old Ale brewed by
Burton Bridge. Mini festival in
Sept. No food Sat or Sun.
⚲ Q ⊛ ◖ ♣ ○

Duck & Drake
Kirkgate ☎ (0532) 465806
11–11
**Old Mill Bitter; S&N
Theakston Best Bitter, XB,
Old Peculier; Taylor
Landlord; Younger No. 3** H**;
guest beers**
Leeds's premier ale house,
popular with all walks of life
and winner of many CAMRA
awards, including *Pub of the
Year*. At least ten beers; live
music Tue, Thu and Sun. No
food at weekends.
⚲ ◖ ⊞ ⇌ ♣ ○

Eagle Tavern
North Street, Sheepscar (A61
at Sheepscar interchange)
☎ (0532) 457146
11.30–3, 5.30–11
**Taylor Golden Best, Dark
Mild, Best Bitter, Landlord,
Ram Tam** H**; guest beers**
White Georgian building with
a large tap room (regular live
music) and a smaller, comfy
lounge. Two guest beers –
over 500 different ales in three
years. ⊛ ⚲ ◖ ○ P

Garden Gate
37 Waterloo Road, Hunslet
☎ (0532) 700379
11–11
Tetley Mild, Bitter H
Victorian Tetley Heritage Inn
with separate rooms, frosted-
glass partitions and loads of
wood panelling. Organist on
Sat. ⚲ ⛄ ◖ ⊞ ♣

Grove Inn
Backrow, Holbeck (between
M1 & Hilton) ☎ (0532) 439254
11.30–11 (12–3, 7–11 Sun)
**Courage Best Bitter,
Directors; John Smith's Bitter,
Magnet; Taylor Landlord** H
Typical 'Yorkshire corridor'
pub, home of acoustic music
in Leeds (celebrates 31 years
this year): music most nights.
Recently threatened by an

Asda development but saved by campaigning and the property market trend.
🏚 ❀ ◖ ⊟ ≷ (City) ♣ P

Mulberry

Hunslet Road ☎ (0532) 457621
11.30–3, 6.30–11 (11.30–11 Fri & Sat)
S&N Theakston Best Bitter, XB; Younger Scotch Ⓗ
Roadside pub with very limited parking. Popular with factory workers at lunchtime. Quiz Sun and Thu. ◖ ♣

Mustard Pot

20 Stainbeck Lane, Chapel Allerton (off A61)
☎ (0532) 696284
11–11
Mansfield Riding Mild, Riding Bitter, Old Baily Ⓗ
Listed 18th-century house with low settees and comfy chairs. The garden is busy in nice weather (children's slides and swings). Always ask for a top-up! No food Sun. ❀ ◖ P

Nags Head

Town Street, Chapel Allerton (one-way street at side of police station) ☎ (0532) 624938
11–3.30, 5.30–11 (11–11 Fri & Sat)
Samuel Smith OBB Ⓗ
Old coaching inn at the hub of Chapel Allerton village. No-smoking area off from the large lounge and busy tap room. No food weekends.
Q ❀ ◖ ⊟ ♣ P ✄

New Roscoe

Bristol Street, Sheepscar (10 mins from bus station along Regent St) ☎ (0532) 460778
11–11
Moorhouse's Premier; Robinwood Best Bitter; Tetley Mild, Bitter Ⓗ**; guest beers**
Large pub, formerly a workingman's club, with three rooms: a spacious games room with three pool tables; a large music lounge, which has mementoes from the old Roscoe, and a small, quiet lounge. ◖ ⊟ ⅃ ♣ P

Prince of Wales

Mill Hill ☎ (0532) 452434
11–11 (11–4, 7–11 Sat)
Courage Directors; Ruddles County; John Smith's Bitter, Magnet Ⓗ**; guest beer** (occasionally)
Bustling city-centre 'local', popular with workers from the nearby station and bus depot. ≷ ♣

Prospect

Moor Road, Hunslet
☎ (0532) 705175
11.30–3 (4 Fri & Sat), 6–11
John Smith's Bitter Ⓗ
Cosy, two-roomed locals' pub with rugby league photos in the tap room. Friendly lounge.
🏚 ◖ ⊟ ♣ P

Victoria Family & Commercial

Great George Street (rear of Town Hall) ☎ (0532) 451386
11–11
Tetley Mild, Bitter Ⓗ
19th-century hotel originally built for visiting judges and lawyers. Splendid, large, genuine Victorian lounge and three smaller, comfy rooms, popular with Town Hall staff and students. Buoyant atmosphere. No food Sun.
Q ◖ ⅃ ≷ (City)

West Yorkshire Playhouse

Quarry Mount ☎ (0532) 442141
12–3.30, 5.30–11 (may vary; closed Sun)
Ind Coope Burton Ale; Tetley Bitter Ⓗ
New theatre and bar built on the former Quarry Hill flats complex; The Huntsman bar serves a large lounge. Live jazz bands eves; families welcome; good atmosphere. Theatre buff clientele. Bazaars all day Sat. Food all day except Sun.
Q ⅃ ◖ ▶ ⅃ ≷ (City) P

Whitelocks

Turks Head Yard, Briggate (alley at side of Marks & Spencer) ☎ (0532) 453950
11–11
Younger Scotch, IPA, No. 3 Ⓗ
Nothing changes in this long, narrow Edwardian pub which has two bars and was called the Turks Head in 1715. The cellars are 20 yards away! Children allowed in the restaurant.
🏚 Q ❀ ◖ ▶ ≷ (City)

Wrens

61a New Briggate
☎ (0532) 458888
11–3, 5–11 (11–11 Sat)
Ansells Mild; Ind Coope Benskins Best Bitter, Burton Ale; Tetley Mild, Bitter Ⓗ
Three bars and the 'Charity Corridor' make up this pleasant pub. Proper public bar; no-smoking room. Popular with theatre-goers and close to restaurants. Winner of *Leeds in Bloom* contests for its imaginative floral displays. ◖ ⊟ ≷ ✄

Linthwaite

Bulls Head

Blackmoorfoot (opp. reservoir) OS097132
☎ (0484) 842715
11–11 (11–4.30, 6.30–11 Sat)
Stones Best Bitter; Whitbread Boddingtons Mild, Bitter Ⓗ
Converted from a house and barn in 1853, this recently extended but not spoilt, cosy and friendly pub is very popular. The Lamb, as it was originally known, is larger than it looks. Specialises in

food: the Mon eve Steak and Bake is recommended.
🏚 ❀ ◖ ▶ ⅃ P

Liversedge

Black Bull

37 Halifax Road, Millbridge (A649, 400 yds from A62 jct)
11.30–3.30, 5.30–11
Old Mill Bitter; Stones Best Bitter; Tetley Bitter; Trough Wild Boar Ⓗ**; guest beers**
One of the earliest free trade real ale pubs in the valley: a utilitarian drinking man's hostelry with no pretentions or frills. Small front room bar but opened-out main room. Sporting conversation. Three guest beers. ❀ ♣

Low Moor

Drop Kick

Huddersfield Road
☎ (0274) 670207
11.30–3, 7–11
Thwaites Mild, Bitter Ⓗ
Modern pub (1980) near Odsal RL ground, hence the name. Three pool tables in the large tap room. Home-cooked lunches in the open-plan lounge (famous for steak pie).
❀ ◖ ⊟ ♣ P

Try also: British Queen (Tetley)

Marsden

Railway

34 Station Road (opp. Huddersfield Narrow Canal)
☎ (0484) 844417
12–3.30, 5–11 (11–11 Fri & Sat)
Burtonwood Mild, Bitter, Forshaw's Ⓗ
Homely pub catering for all ages, festooned with canal and railway memorabilia. The old coaching stables remain intact. Weekend breakfast for walkers till 11am in summer. Try Sue's free supper on the first Sat every month!
🏚 ⅃ ❀ ⊟ ≷ ♣

Methley

New Bay Horse

Main Street ☎ (0977) 553557
12–5, 7–11 (maybe 11–11 summer)
Tetley Bitter Ⓗ**; guest beers**
A real locals' local, the focus of village life. The owner, Brian Lockwood, is an ex Gt Britain RL captain and cares more for people than profit. Big brewers take note: a very busy, friendly pub. ⅃ ❀ ◖ ⊟ ⅃ ♣ P

Morley

Gardeners Arms

Wide Lane ☎ (0532) 534261
12–3, 7 (6.30 summer)–11 (12–4, 6.45–11 Sat)
Tetley Mild, Bitter Ⓗ

West Yorkshire

Past winner of Tetley's *Master of Mild* competition, a smart pub with pictures of old Morley and a collection of brewery artefacts. No food weekends. ✿ ◖ ⊟ P

Netherton

Star Inn
211 Netherton Lane (B6117, 1 mile from A642)
☎ (0924) 274496
11–4, 6.30–11
Samuel Smith OBB Ⓔ
Friendly and well-kept village local with a lively tap room, a small lounge and a large function room. Spacious beer garden overlooking open countryside. The same family have been tenants for several generations. No food Sun.
Q ✿ ◖ ⊟ ♣ P

Normanton

Junction Inn
Market Place ☎ (0924) 893021
11–4.30, 7–11 (12–2.30, 7–10.30 Sun)
Wards Thorne Best Bitter Ⓗ
Victorian-style lounge, popular with a younger clientele at weekends; traditional tap room. Extensive range of good value lunches. Landlord is trying other Vaux/Wards beers.
✿ ◖ ⊟ ▲ ⇌ ♣ P

Norwood Green

Old White Beare
Village street (1/2 mile NW of A58/A641) ☎ (0274) 676645
11.30–4 (2.30 Mon, 3 Thu & Sat), 6–11
Whitbread Trophy, Castle Eden Ale Ⓗ
16th-century inn named after an English ship which sailed against the Spanish Armada. Modernised and extended, but retaining many of its oldest features. No meals Sun. May add a Taylor beer.
☎ ✿ ◖ ♣ P

Try also: Pear Tree (Tetley)

Old Snydale

Cross Keys
New Road (1 mile SW of Black Swan lights, Normanton)
☎ (0924) 892238
12–3, 7–11
S&N Theakston XB; Younger Scotch Ⓗ
Old village local that has been opened up both inside and out to accommodate car trade. Extensive beer gardens. Resident ghost. Q ✿ ◖ ♣ P

Ossett

Coopers Arms
Intake Lane (behind police station) ☎ (0924) 275916
11–4, 6.30–11

Thwaites Bitter Ⓗ
Friendly town-centre local that is compact but still boasts a public bar, a darts room and a separate pool room. ⊟ ♣ P

Horse & Jockey Inn
18 Dale Street (near Town Hall) ☎ (0924) 274061
11–4, 7–11 (12–4, 7.30–11 Wed & Thu; 12–3, 7.30–10.30 Sun)
Samuel Smith OBB Ⓗ
Listed building with two bars on a split level and nice windows. Very popular at weekends. The bottom room has a display of shop advertising posters from old Ossett. ◖ ♣ P

Little Bull
99 Teall Street (1/4 mile from Queens Drive)
☎ (0924) 273569
12–3 (4 Sat), 7–11
Thwaites Best Mild, Bitter, Craftsman Ⓗ
Friendly local with a cheerful, L-shaped lounge and a small, lively tap room. Originally belonged to Springwell Brewery of Heckmondwike.
⚌ ✿ ⊟ ♣ P

Masons Arms
2 The Green (1/2 mile from Town Hall via Bank St and Queen St)
☎ (0924) 275219
11–3, 7–11
John Smith's Bitter, Magnet Ⓗ
Two-roomed pub with low, wood-beamed ceilings. The main room has a large display of copperware and paintings. A popular pub with locals.
⊟ ♣ P

Otley

Junction Inn
Bondgate
☎ (0943) 463233
11–3, 5.30–11 (11–11 Fri & Sat)
S&N Theakston XB, Old Peculier; Taylor Best Bitter, Landlord; Tetley Bitter Ⓗ
Very busy, one-roomed, stone corner pub with oak beams, a tiled floor and wood panelling. Old photos of Otley and bric-a-brac adorn the walls and ceiling. Popular with younger people. A Tetley 'free house'. ⚌ ◖ ♣

Red Lion
Kirkgate
☎ (0943) 462226
11–11
Courage Directors; John Smith's Bitter, Magnet Ⓗ
Very well-kept pub near the market place. Quite small, with three separate drinking areas served by a single bar. Huge whisky collection in one room. The menu includes a vegetarian option (no food Sun). Q ✿ ◖

Pontefract

Tap & Spile
28 Horsefair (opp. bus station)
☎ (0977) 793468
12–3, 5–11 (11–11 Fri & Sat)
Beer range varies Ⓗ
Typical conversion to a Victorian-style alehouse, with bare floorboards and nice woodwork. Three separate drinking areas (one in lounge-style) off a long bar. Approx. 11 beers make it a mecca for fans of independents' ales. No food Sun. ✿ ◖ ⊟ ⇌ (Baghill & Monkhill) ♣ P

White Rose
Cobblers Lane (off Knottingley Road, A645)
☎ (0977) 702254
11.30–3, 5–11
Mansfield Riding Bitter, Old Baily Ⓗ
Large, comfortable, modern pub on the outskirts of town. Extensive restaurant with a good choice of food.
Q ✿ ◖ ▶ ὒ ♣ P

Purston

White House
Pontefract Road (A645)
☎ (0977) 791878
11–4, 7–11
Samuel Smith OBB Ⓗ
Imposing village meeting place: comfortable surroundings for a pint and a chat. Popular with the après-sports centre crowd and a women's football team.
✿ ◖ ♣ P

Rawdon

Emmott Arms
Town Street ☎ (0532) 506036
11–3, 5.30–11 (11–11 Sat)
Samuel Smith OBB Ⓗ
Busy, low-ceilinged pub with a separate restaurant. Bare stonework and panelled beams give a cosy atmosphere. Mixed clientele in both bars. Eves and Sun restaurant meals only. Q ◖ ⊟ ♣ P

Ripponden

Alma Inn
Cottonstones, Millbank (1 1/4 miles off A58 at Triangle pub) OS028215 ☎ (0422) 823334
12–3, 6 (5 Fri)–11 (12–11 Sat)
Taylor Golden Best; Tetley Bitter Ⓗ**; guest beer**
Welcoming hillside inn in a Pennine village. Large, varied food menu: pizzas a speciality.
⚌ ☎ ✿ ◖ ▶ ♣ P

Blue Ball Inn
Blue Ball Lane, Soyland (signed off A58) OS011192
☎ (0422) 823603
12–2 (not Tue), 7–11

**Bass Special, Draught Bass;
S&N Theakston Old Peculier;
Stones Best Bitter; Taylor
Dark Mild, Golden Best,
Landlord** H
Welcoming moorland inn
dating from 1672. Wonderful
views of the surrounding
moors; near a reservoir. Folk
music and sing-alongs feature.
🛏 ✿ ❀ ◁ ▶ ♿ P

Old Bridge Inn
Priest Lane ☎ (0422) 822595
11.30–3.30, 5.30–11 (11–11 Sat)
**Samuel Smith OBB; Taylor
Golden Best, Best Bitter;
Thwaites Bitter** H
Ancient hostelry with a
splendid timbered structure;
full of interesting ornaments.
Most beer pumps are
unlabelled. HQ of Pork Pie
Eaters' club. No food Sat eve
or Sun. ♨ Q ✿ ◁ ▶ P

Rothwell

Rosebud
Westfield Road (off Leadwell
Lane, Carlton)
☎ (0532) 822236
12–3 (4 Sat), 5.30 (7 Sat)–11
**Ruddles County; Stones Best
Bitter; Webster's Yorkshire
Bitter** H; **guest beers**
Pleasant, village locals' pub. A
well decorated lounge has a
Delft rack, with jugs and bric-
a-brac; the traditional tap
room has a real fire. Cosy and
welcoming with a friendly
clientele. Occasional live
music. No food Sun.
♨ Q ✿ ◁ ▶ ♿ ♣ P

South Elmsall

Chequers Inn
Barnsley Road (opp. station
approach and bus station)
☎ (0977) 645805
11–4, 7–11 (11–11 Fri & Sat)
Mansfield Riding Mild
(occasionally), **Riding Bitter,
Old Baily** (occasionally) H
Large, mock-Tudor pub in the
centre of a mining community.
Large lounge; games room
with pool and snooker;
function room. Disco Fri, Sat,
Sun. ✿ ◁ ▶ ♿ ➤ ♣ P

Southowram

Malt Shovel Inn
Church Lane ☎ (0422) 369604
11–11 (12.30 supper licence)
**Moorhouse's Pendle Witches
Brew; Taylor Best Bitter,
Landlord; Tetley Bitter** H;
guest beer
Stone-built, friendly family
free house on the rural edge of
a hilltop village, where Bull
Ring can still be played. At
least one guest beer which
changes regularly. Beware keg
Addlestones cider on
handpump. ♨ ✿ ◁ ▶ ♿ ♣ P

Sowerby Bridge

Puzzle Hall
21 Hollins Mill Lane (off A58
by Lloyds bank)
☎ (0422) 835547
12–11
**Wards Thorne Best Bitter,
Sheffield Best Bitter** H; **Vaux
guest beers**
Interesting old pub, nestling
between the canal and the
river, which is at the bottom of
the car park. A tower used to
house a brewery – the plans
are on display inside. A log
burning stove provides
warmth in winter. Guest
ciders. ♨ Q ✿ ◁ ➤ ♠ ⌂ P

William IV
80 Wharf Street (A58)
☎ (0422) 833584
11.30–11
**Ind Coope Burton Ale; Old
Mill Bitter; Ryburn Mild,
Best Bitter; S&N Theakston
Best Bitter; Tetley Bitter** H;
guest beer (occasionally)
Comfortable, relaxed free
house with the emphasis on
beer. The only local outlet for
the town's brewery.
✿ ◁ ▶ ➤ ♠ P

Stanningley

Old Fleece
116 Town Street (A647)
☎ (0532) 577832
12–11
**S&N Theakston Best Bitter,
XB, Old Peculier; Tetley
Bitter** H; **guest beer**
(occasionally)
Old, white-painted roadside
pub with a lounge and a
separate public bar. Now
extended into the barber's
shop next door. 🖛 ◁ ▶ ♣

Thornton

Blue Boar
354 Thornton Road
☎ (0274) 833298
12–3, 5.30–11 (11–11 Fri & Sat)
**Taylor Best Bitter, Landlord;
Trough Bitter** H
Single-bar locals' pub on the
main road through the village.
Separate pool room at the
back. ♣

Duke of York
Dean Lane Head (take
Allerton Road to end from
B6145: 4 miles) OS095345
☎ (0274) 832462
11.30–3, 5.30–11
**Courage Directors; John
Smith's Bitter** H; **guest beer**
(occasionally)
Very quiet pub with an older
clientele. Spotless brassware.
Spectacular views from its
rural location. No food Sun.
✿ ◁ ♿ P

White Horse Inn
Well Heads (take James Street
in Thornton from B6145: 2
miles) OS084331
☎ (0274) 832044
12–11 (supper licence)
**Ruddles Best Bitter, County;
S&N Theakston Best Bitter;
Webster's Yorkshire Bitter** H
Old pub with a long history
and a semi-rural location with
spectacular views. Very
pleasant surroundings; lovely
food – superb value for
money. Occasional barbecues
in summer. ♨ ✿ ◁ ▶ P

Todmorden

Masons Arms
1 Bacup Road, Gauxholme
(A6033/A681 jct)
☎ (0706) 812180
7–11 (12.30–3, 7.30–11 Sat; 12–3,
7.30–10.30 Sun)
**John Smith's Bitter, Magnet;
Thwaites Bitter** H
Cosy pub nestling under a
railway bridge. The unusual
snug boasts sycamore-topped
tables, reputedly once used for
post mortems. Easy access
from the canal.
♨ ✿ ♿ ➤ ≠ (Walsden)

Woodpecker
224 Rochdale Road, Shade
(A6033)
☎ (0706) 816088
12–2.30, 5–11 (11.30–11 Sat)
Lees GB Mild, Bitter H
Busy locals' pub on the main
road: a single L-shaped room
accommodates both lounge
and games areas. Still the only
Lees pub in Yorkshire.
✿ ◁ ♿ ♣

Try also: Staff of Life (Free)

Wakefield

Albion
94 Stanley Road (take Peterson
Road from Kirkgate
roundabout: ¹/₄ mile)
☎ (0924) 376206
11–3 (4 Fri), 6–11 (11–11 Sat)
Samuel Smith OBB H
Impressive 1920s estate pub
on the edge of the town: home to
two football teams. Very
popular at lunchtimes due to
landlady's daily-changing
menu of home-cooked food.
Unusual collection of coloured
glassware in the lounge. Lively
and friendly local
clientele. ✿ ◁ ▤
≠ (Kirkgate) ♣ P

Beer Engine
77 Westgate End (A642/A638,
¹/₂ mile W of centre)
☎ (0924) 375887
12–11
**Goose Eye Bitter; Marston
Moor Brewers Pride; Taylor
Landlord** H; **guest beers**

West Yorkshire

Atmospheric, traditional alehouse with three separate rooms, featuring stone flagging and gas lighting. Good range of continental beers. Good tapes played. Wakefield's only true free house. Quiz night Mon.
🏠 ❀ ◑ ≢ (Westgate) ♣ ♥

College
138 Northgate (¼ mile N of centre on A61)
☎ (0924) 384972
11–11
Mansfield Riding Mild, Bitter, Old Mild
Pub with a Brewers Tudor exterior and a long, pleasant lounge with several drinking areas. A welcome change from the national brewers' pubs which dominate the town. No food Sat/Sun.
❀ ◑ ≢ (Westgate) P

Elephant & Castle
109 Westgate (opp. station)
☎ (0924) 376610
11–11
Courage Directors; John Smith's Bitter, Magnet Ⓗ
A beautiful old Warwick's Boroughbridge Ales tiled frontage leads into a traditional town pub, only partially opened out and retaining a tap room at the rear. Reasonably-priced food and accommodation – a good place to stay when visiting the town. 🏠 ❀ ◑ ▶ ⌂
≢ (Westgate) ♣

Inns of Court
22 King Street (behind Town Hall) ☎ (0924) 375560
11–11 (11–4, 7–11 Sat)
John Smith's Magnet Ⓗ
Imposing three-storey town-centre hotel tucked away among narrow streets housing solicitors' practices, offices and law courts. The long, open-plan lounge bar is divided into small drinking areas. Popular with members of the legal profession, their clients and students.
❀ ◑ & ≢ (Westgate)

Warmfield

Plough Inn
45 Warmfield Lane (400 yds from A655) ☎ (0924) 892007
11.30–2.30, 7–11 (11.30–11 summer)
S&N Theakston Mild, Best Bitter, XB, Old Peculier; Younger IPA Ⓗ
Unspoilt, 18th-century country inn overlooking the lower Calder Valley, acquired from Bass by a former tenant. Low, beamed ceilings and a small corner bar. Lively piano sing-alongs Sat eve. Good bar meals (try Old Peculier pie). Summer barbecues. ❀ ◑ ▶ P

West Ardsley

British Oak
407 Westerton Road (off A653)
☎ (0532) 534792
12–3, 6–11
Whitbread Boddingtons Bitter, Trophy, Castle Eden Ale, Flowers Original Ⓗ; **guest beer**
Leeds CAMRA *Pub of the Season* winter 91/92 proves the dedication of the landlord, who will hopefully keep his guest beer policy (and his sense of humour) when he finalises his agreement with Whitbread. We hope that you will find this pub unchanged – i.e. a gem! No food Sun.
❀ ◑ & ♣ P

Wetherby

George & Dragon
High Street ☎ (0937) 582888
11–4 (5 Sat), 6 (7 Sat)–11
John Smith's Bitter, Magnet Ⓗ; **guest beers**
Stone-built former coaching inn at the side of the River Wharfe: a three-roomed interior in traditional decor. Quiet lounge; superb garden with views of the riverside. Annual charity event in Feb. Popular with cycle clubs, and a mature clientele. Eve meals 6–8, Mon–Thu.
Q ❀ ◑ ▶ & ▲ ♣ P

Royal Oak
60 North Street
☎ (0937) 580508
11–11 (11–3, 5–11 Sat; may vary in summer)
McEwan 80/-; S&N Theakston Best Bitter; John Smith's Bitter; Tetley Bitter Ⓗ; **guest beers**
White-painted pub on the main road with an opened out L-shaped interior. A stone bar with a pantiled roof and a large tree trunk feature in the lounge area. Busy on market day (Thu). Quizzes Sun eve; trad. jazz band Tue. Buoyant atmosphere; sensible clientele. No eve meals Sun.
❀ ◑ ▶ & ▲ ♣ P

Whitwood

Bridge Inn
Altofts Lane (½ mile from A655, at Rising Sun)
☎ (0977) 550498
11–11 (11–3.30, 7–11 Sat)
S&N Theakston Mild, Best Bitter, XB, Old Peculier; John Smith's Bitter, Magnet; Tetley Bitter; Younger No. 3 Ⓗ
Large, modern pub/hotel built in attractive, old-style red brick with pantile roofs.

The interior features reclaimed timber beams, exposed brickwork and stone-flagged floors. Several drinking areas around a long bar. Food and business-oriented. No food Sun eve. 🏠 ◑ ▶ & P ⌀

Wibsey

Gaping Goose
5–6 Slack Bottom Road
☎ (0274) 601701
12–3, 7–11
Marston's Pedigree; S&N Theakston Old Peculier; Taylor Landlord; Tetley Bitter; Whitbread Trophy Ⓗ
Friendly and intimate, two-roomed local opposite the location of TV's *Silver Lady*.
❀ ⊟ & P

Wyke

Junction
459 Huddersfield Road
☎ (0274) 679809
12–11
Thwaites Mild, Bitter Ⓗ
Two-roomed pub with a split lounge and a separate pool room. Good friendly atmosphere. Eve meals Fri/Sat only (early). ◑ ▶ ♣

Yeadon

New Inn
Cemetery Road
☎ (0532) 503220
11.30–3, 5.30–11 (11.30–11 Sat)
John Smith's Bitter, Magnet Ⓗ; **guest beer**
Pub with an 18th-century exterior, but extensively altered inside: a public bar and a pleasant, rustic-style lounge with a real log-fire. Near Yeadon Tarn. Good value bar meals (vegetarian option). No lunches Sat; pie and peas Mon–Sat eves.
🏠 ❀ ◑ ▶ ⊟ ♣ P

Join CAMRA —
see page 508

OF TUNS AND COPPERS
How your beer is brewed

The brewing process – in a nutshell – involves the mashing of malt (partially germinated, baked barley) with hot water to produce a thick, sugary liquid called wort. This is boiled with hops to add bitterness and, when cooled, yeast is added and it ferments. Most of the yeast is removed and there follows a period of conditioning during which the beer matures.

KEG BEERS

Keg beers are then usually pasteurised, chilled and filtered, removing all the remaining yeast. They are packed into sealed, pressurised containers (kegs) and are ready to serve on arrival at the pub. To propel the beer to the bar, canisters of carbon dioxide are used, which makes the beer even more gassy. Keg beers are mostly chilled like lagers.

REAL ALES

Cask-conditioned beers (real ales) are living products. They are not filtered or pasteurised. Yeast remains in the cask and continues to work on sugars in the beer, creating a natural effervescence, which is moderated by venting the cask.

Because of their yeast content, real ales need time to settle in the pub cellar before serving. A substance called finings is added at the brewery to drag the yeast to the bottom of the cask and help keep the beer clear. The beer is not chilled but kept at a cool 55° F/13° C and pulled to the bar by the traditional handpump, a simple electric pump or – in Scotland – an air pump. Real ale can also be served by pouring it straight from the cask.

BOTTLED BEERS

Bottled beers are generally treated like keg beers, though some are not pasteurised and are allowed to keep some yeast for extra conditioning in the bottle. These are known as bottle-conditioned beers and are mentioned in The Breweries at the back of the book.

LAGERS

Lager brewing is much the same in principle, but there are some key variations in technique. The most important concern the type of yeast used, the temperature of fermentation and the amount of time allowed at the brewery for the beer to mature. Whereas an ale yeast sits on the top of the fermenting wort, a lager yeast sinks to the bottom of the fermenting vessel. At temperatures around freezing point, the lager is allowed to condition for at least three weeks. In the case of genuine continental Pilsners, this 'lagering' period may extend to thirteen weeks; British versions are generally on sale within a month.

Furthermore, most British lagers are pasteurised, packed into kegs and gassed to the bar like keg beers. They are convenience beers of little character, quite unlike their European namesakes.

Each brew, whether ale or lager, is clearly different. The choice and proportions of malts, hops, water and yeast – not to mention additives like sugar and other cereals – dictate the final flavour. The strength of the beer depends on how sugary the wort is and how long it is allowed to ferment.

Breweries also differ. Their equipment and their methods impart an individual character to their beers. Some are high-tech; others like Caledonian (illustrated opposite) are very traditional and idiosyncratic. The brewing industry is thankfully more colourful and interesting as a result.

The Caledonian Brewing Process

The MILL crushes the malt to grist. Malt is selected from choicest pale ale, crystal, amber and black malts to provide the flavour and colour.

Grist goes through the MASHING MACHINE mixed with hot water into one of the few remaining traditional deep bed infusion MASH TUNS in Britain.

Malt infusion is run off from the MASH TUN through the UNDERBACK to the OPEN COPPERS - which are fired by direct flame. These coppers are the last of their type still in use in Britain.

Fuggles and Golding hop flowers are added and the mixture is boiled.

Spent hops are filtered through the HOP BACK. The liquid then passes through the COOLER.

From the COOLER the liquid passes into the FERMENTING VESSEL where yeast is added and fermentation takes place for 7 days, and up to 10 days for strong ale.

The beer is racked into casks and allowed to condition for a further 7 days. Finings are then added prior to despatch to trade. The finings clarify the beer and ensure the clarity and polish for which Caledonian Beers are renowned.

Cold storage for keg and bottled beers.

Clwyd

Clwyd

[Map of Clwyd region showing towns including Rhos-on-Sea, Upper Colwyn Bay, Colwyn Bay, Mochdre, Old Colwyn, Llanelian-yn-Rhos, Llysfaen, Rhyl, Towyn, Glan yr Afon, Abergele, Rhuddlan, Llanddulas, Llandonewydd, Llanfair Talhaiarn, St Asaph, Bontnewydd, Dyserth, Whitford, Holywell, Ffynnongroew, Halkyn, Denbigh, Hendrerwydd, Cadole, Llanynys, Llanferres, Maeshafn, Cyffylliog, Llanfwrog, Ruthin, Graigfechan, Connah's Quay, Pen-y-Mynydd, Cymau, Rossett, Brymbo, Moss, Gresford, Wrexham, Bersham, Acrefair, Eyton, Carrog, Rhewl, Llangollen, Cynwyd, Llandegwyn, Hanmer. Neighbouring regions: CHESHIRE, SHROPSHIRE, POWYS, GWYNEDD]

🏰 **Plassey**, Eyton

Abergele

Pen-y-Bont
Bridge Street
11–11
S&N Matthew Brown Mild, Theakston Best Bitter, XB, Old Peculier Ⓗ
Refurbished, single bar; a comfortable, locals' pub. 🏨
🛏 ⊛ 🚪 ◑ & ▲ ⇌ ✦ P

Try also: **George & Dragon** (Allied)

Acrefair

Hampden Arms
Llangollen Road (A483)
☎ (0978) 821734
11.30–4, 7–11 (11–11 Sat)
Banks's Mild, Bitter Ⓔ
Large public house situated on the main road near a large housing estate and leisure centre (Plas Madoc): a small cheerful lounge and a spacious no-frills bar with a TV for racing fans. ⊟ ✦ P

Bersham

Black Lion
Bersham Road (off B5099)
☎ (0978) 365588
11.30–3.30 (11–5 Sat), 6.45 (6.30 Sat)–11
Hydes' Anvil Mild, Bitter Ⓔ
Friendly three-roomed local in a hollow by a stream. Handy for Bersham Heritage Centre.
🏨 ⊛ ⊟ & ✦ P

Bontnewydd

Dolben Arms
Via minor roads W of Trefnant
OS015705
☎ (0745) 582207
12–3 (not winter), 7–12
S&N Theakston XB Ⓗ
16th-century country inn in a picturesque river valley, accessible only by scenic country lanes. One long room is separated into restaurant, lounge and games areas.
Q ⊛ ◑ ▲ ✦ P

Brymbo

Black Lion
Railway Road ☎ (0978) 758307
12–4 (not Mon), 7–11
Burtonwood Mild, Bitter Ⓗ
Pub full of beams and brasses, overshadowed by the steelworks (now closed).
🏨 ⊟ & ✦ P

Cadole

Colomendy Arms
Gwernaffield Road (off A494(T), 3 miles W of Mold)
OS204627 ☎ (0352) 85217
12–3 (not winter), 7–11 (11–11 Sat)
Burtonwood Bitter Ⓗ
Straightforward village local which welcomes children in the lounge. A footpath leads from the car park to the Loggerheads Country Park. A caving society visiting the Parris lead mines are regulars. One of the new breed of free houses, bought from Burtonwood three years ago.
🏨 ⊛ ✦ P

Carrog

Grouse
On B5437 ☎ (049 083) 272
12–4, 7–11 (may vary)
Lees GB Mild, Bitter Ⓗ
Homely pub in the Dee valley, affording delightful views across the river. Old photos adorn the walls of the three separate drinking areas. Llangollen Steam Railway is due to reach the village. Children are welcome if dining. ⚶ Q ❀ ⇔ ◖▶ ♣ P

Colwyn Bay

Park Hotel
128 Abergele Road
☎ (0492) 530661
11–11
Draught Bass; M&B Mild; Stones Best Bitter; Welsh Brewers Worthington BB Ⓗ
Large single room bar with a TV and pool table; games and quizzes are held. ⇶ ♣

Platform 3
Colwyn Bay Station, Princes Drive ☎ (0492) 533161
11–11
Tetley Bitter Ⓗ
Old renovated part of a BR station, in an elevated position overlooking the bay. It features a railway carriage restaurant, a lounge bar, a function room, enclosed gardens and a covered mall. House bitter. ◖▶ ⇶

Toad Hall
West Promenade
☎ (0492) 532726
11.30–3, 6–11
Marston's Border Mild, Burton Best Bitter, Pedigree Ⓗ
Seafront first-floor bar and restaurant. Note the large collection of old bottles around the bar area.
Q ⌕ ❀ ◖▶ ⇶ ♣ P

Try also: **Café Royal** (Bass); **Central** (Bass); **Lloyds** (Ansells)

Connah's Quay

Sir Gawain & the Green Knight
Golftyn Lane (200 yds from A548) ☎ (0244) 812623
11.30–3, 5.30–11 (11.30–11 Fri & Sat)
Samuel Smith OBB Ⓗ
Converted former farmhouse on the outskirts of town, popular with college students at lunchtimes. No meals weekends. ⚶ ❀ ◖ ♣ P

Cyffylliog

Red Lion
Off B5105 at Llanfwrog
☎ (082 46) 664
12–3, 6.30–11
Lees Bitter Ⓗ
Attractive, unspoilt rural village inn offering good value food and accommodation, with a public bar, pool room and lounge bar. Ask for cask bitter.
⚶ Q ❀ ⇔ ◖▶ ⊟ ▲ ♣ P

Cymau

Olde Talbot Inne
Cymau Road (off A541)
OS297562 ☎ (0978) 761410
12–3, 7–11
Hydes' Anvil Mild, Bitter Ⓔ
Busy village local off the beaten track, housing a large, active public bar and a smaller, quiet lounge. Fine views from the village.
Q ◖▶ ⊟ ♿ ♣ P

Cynwyd

Blue Lion
On B4401 ☎ (0490) 2106
12–3 (may vary winter), 6–11
Marston's Mercian Mild, Border Exhibition Ⓗ
Friendly, bustling village pub with a town-centre feel, but a peaceful lounge at the rear. Situated in the idyllic Dee valley. Locals may burst into song. ⚶ Q ❀ ⇔ ◖▶ ⊟ ♣ P

Prince of Wales
On B4401 ☎ (0490) 2450
12–2 (4 Sat; not winter), 6–11
Burtonwood Mild Ⓗ
Unspoilt village local where Welsh is the main language. Note the old clock and chair from Corwen station. Pub games have a boisterous following. ⚶ ⊟ ♣ P

Denbigh

Golden Lion
Back Row ☎ (0745) 812227
11–11
Marston's Mercian Mild, Burton Best Bitter, Pedigree Ⓗ
Town-centre pub where the friendly locals are committed to promoting real ale.
❀ ♿ ▲ ♣

Masons Arms
Rhyl Road
☎ (0745) 812463
11.30–3, 5.30–11 (12–11 Sat)
Vaux Lorimers Best Scotch; Wards Mild, Sheffield Best Bitter, Kirby Ⓗ
Small, friendly town pub: one room separated by a modernised bar; well worth a visit. Serves simple pub fare and is one of the growing number of good pubs in the area with a large range of beer.
⚶ ⇔ ◖▶ ▲ ♣ P

Try also: **Vaults** (Free)

Dyserth

Red Lion
Waterfall Road
☎ (0745) 570404
11–3, 5.30–11
Banks's Mild, Bitter; Stones Best Bitter Ⓗ
Tidy, quiet pub whose decor needs to be seen to be believed; recently redeveloped. Food available until 8.30pm. It stands opposite the waterfall.
⚶ Q ❀ ⇔ ◖▶ ▲ P

Try also: **New Inn**, Waterfall Rd (Marston's)

Ffynnongroew

Railway Tavern
Main Road ☎ (0745) 560447
11.30–3, 6.30–11
Vaux Lorimers Best Scotch, Double Maxim; Wards Mild Ⓗ
Sporty village pub, with the local football team in attendance at weekends. This local offers the best beer range along the coastal strip.
⚶ ❀ ▲ ♣ P

Try also: **Garth Mill**, Garth Lane (Free)

Glan yr Afon

White Lion
2 miles off A548 at Ffynnongroew, through Penyffordd ☎ (0745) 570280
11.30–3 (not Mon), 6–11
Ruddles Best Bitter, County Ⓗ**; guest beers**
Old-fashioned pub enjoying a lively local trade. Somewhat isolated but well worth the visit. Watch out for the low entrance. ⚶ Q ❀ ▶ ⊟ ♣ P

Graigfechan

Three Pigeons
On B5429 ☎ (082 42) 3178
12–3 (not winter), 6.30–11
Draught Bass Ⓖ**; guest beers**
Tastefully extended 17th-century pub affording fine views over the Vale of Clwyd. Good food, with children well catered for. Beer is served from the jug; ask for a $3^1/_2$-pint jug for your table. Classical music on request! Caravan site attached.
⚶ ⌕ ❀ ⊟ ▲ ♣ P

Gresford

Griffin
The Green ☎ (097 883) 2231
1–3.30 (12–4 Sat), 7–11
Greenalls Mild, Bitter Ⓗ
Excellent village local which has mercifully escaped the attentions of brewery planners. Close to the impressive parish church. Q ❀ ♣ P

Clwyd

Halkyn

Britannia
Pentre Road (just off A55)
OS211711
☎ (0352) 780272
11.30–3, 6–11
Lees GB Mild, Bitter Ⓗ,
Moonraker Ⓔ
500-year-old stone pub with
four rooms, popular with the
local community. A restaurant
in the conservatory overlooks
the Dee estuary; it is worth a
visit just for the view.
🏚 Q ❀ 🛏 ◁ ▶ 🍴 ▲ ♣ P

Hanmer

Hanmer Arms
6 miles W of Whitchurch, off
A539 ☎ (094 874) 532
11–11
**Ind Coope Burton Ale; Tetley
Bitter** Ⓗ
Family-run hotel in a pretty
mereside village, set in a
peaceful rolling landscape.
Local produce features on the
menu (vegetarian options).
Own bowling green. 🏚 Q ⚲
❀ 🛏 ◁ ▶ 🍴 ♣

Hendrerwydd

White Horse
1/2 mile from B5429 OS122634
☎ (082 44) 218
12–3.30, 6.30–11
**Thwaites Bitter; Whitbread
Boddingtons Bitter** Ⓗ**; guest
beers**
Delightful, two-roomed
country inn in a rural location.
The restaurant has a no-
smoking area.
🏚 Q ❀ ▶ 🍴 ♣ P

Holywell

Feathers Hotel
Whitford Street
☎ (0352) 714792
11.30–11
**Stones Best Bitter; Welsh
Brewers Worthington BB** Ⓗ
Town-centre pub with regular
entertainment. Friendly locals
of all ages. 🏚 ◁ ▶ 🍴 ♣

Glan yr Afon
Milwr (300 yds from old A55
by Hill Crest garage)
☎ (0352) 710052
11.30–3, 6.30–11
**Ruddles Best Bitter;
Webster's Yorkshire Bitter** Ⓗ
17th-century inn with a deer
antler collection in the public
bar. 🏚 Q ⚲ ❀ ◁ ▶ 🍴 P

Llanddulas

Dulas Arms Hotel
Abergele Road
☎ (0492) 515747
11–4, 6–11 (12–3, 7–11 winter)
**Lees GB Mild, Bitter,
Moonraker** Ⓗ

Large lounge, an adjoining
bar, a snug, a large family
room and a spacious garden.
Beer festival August Bank
Holiday. The restaurant has a
no-smoking area.
Q ⚲ ❀ 🛏 ◁ ▶ 🍴 ▲ ♣ P

Llanelian-yn-Rhos

White Lion Inn
1 1/4 miles up minor road from
Erias Park OS863764
☎ (0492) 515807
11–3, 6–11
**Ruddles Best Bitter; John
Smith's Magnet; Wilson's
Mild** Ⓗ
Unspoilt, traditional village
pub with a lounge/restaurant,
snug, and a games room. Well
worth making the effort to
find. 🏚 Q ❀ 🛏 ◁ ▶ 🍴 ♿ ▲
♣ P

Llanfair Talhaiarn

Swan
Swan Square
☎ (0745) 84233
11–3, 5.30–11 (11–11 Sat)
**Marston's Mercian Mild,
Burton Best Bitter,
Pedigree** Ⓗ
Traditional village pub with a
small, cosy lounge at the front.
🏚 Q ⚲ ❀ ◁ ▶ 🍴 ♣

*Try also: Black Lion
(Robinson's)*

Llanferres

Druid Inn
On A494
☎ (035 285) 225
11.30–3, 5.30–11
Burtonwood Bitter Ⓗ
Pleasant main road pub
offering good views. Real ale
is only available in the top bar,
which may be closed some
winter lunchtimes. Old photos
of the village adorn the walls,
complementing the feature
fireplace. Children welcome if
eating. 🏚 ❀ 🛏 ◁ ▶ P

Llanfwrog

Olde Cross Keys
On B5105, 1 mile from Ruthin
☎ (082 42) 5281
11.30–3 (not Mon–Wed in winter),
6.30–11
Banks's Mild, Bitter Ⓗ
Cosy village pub with an
interesting dark, wood-
panelled bar serving two
small lounge areas plus a large
dining room.
🏚 ⚲ ❀ 🛏 ◁ ▶ ♣

Llangedwyn

Green Inn
At the Llansilin turn off the
B4396 ☎ (0691) 828234
11–3, 6–11

**Whitbread Boddingtons
Bitter** Ⓗ
Welcoming travellers' pub,
outside the village, set in the
Tanat valley against a
backdrop of hills. A cluster of
old farm buildings stands
behind the pub which has
restaurant, public and lounge
bars. 🏚 ❀ ◁ ▶ 🍴 P

Llangollen

Cambrian Hotel
Berwyn Street (A5)
☎ (0978) 860686
12–3 (may extend), 7–11
Younger Scotch Ⓗ
Simply the best in Llangollen:
a plain and friendly, old-
fashioned hotel with a small
locals' bar and a peaceful front
lounge. Q 🛏 🍴 ▲ P

*Try also: Wynstay Arms,
Bridge St (Allied)*

Llanynys

Cerigllwydion Arms
2 miles off A525 between
Ruthin and Denbigh OS102627
☎ (074 578) 247
11.30–3, 7–11
**Crown Buckley Best Bitter;
Felinfoel Bitter** Ⓗ**; guest beers**
Out-of-the-way, food-oriented
house boasting a large
collection of teapots and jugs.
Pretty garden on the other
side of the road. Splendid
views. 🏚 Q ❀ P

*Try also: Y Cymro, same road
(Free)*

Llysfaen

Semaphore Inn
Ffordd y Llan OS892775
☎ (0492) 517411
12–3, 6.30 (7 winter)–11
Webster's Yorkshire Bitter Ⓗ
Pub with a comfortable lounge
and family room, popular
with tourists. The traditional
public bar enjoys a good local
atmosphere. The superb sea
views give the pub its name.
🏚 ⚲ ❀ ◁ ▶ 🍴 ▲ ♣ P

Maeshafn

Miners Arms
☎ (0352) 85464
12–3 (not always in winter), 5.30–11
S&N Theakston Best Bitter Ⓗ
Friendly village local with an
impressive log fire. Popular
with walkers. Separate dining
room. 🏚 ❀ ◁ ▶ ♿ P

Mochdre

Mountain View
7 Old Conwy Road
☎ (0492) 44724
11–11
**Burtonwood Mild, Bitter,
Forshaw's** Ⓗ

Village pub with a large, friendly lounge serving excellent meals, plus a good locals' bar with a pool table.
🌺 ◖▶ 🍷 🚷 🅰 ♣ P ⚲

Moss

Bird in Hand

Down track off B5433
OS303538 ☎ (0978) 755809
12–3 (not Mon–Fri), 7–11
Hydes' Anvil Bitter E
Distinctive pub, hard to find but worth the effort. It has an unusual layout, good views and is handy for Moss Valley Country Park. Three-quarter size snooker table. No eve meals Mon. Q 🌺 ◖▶ P

Try also: Cross Foxes, Pentre Broughton (Burtonwood)

Old Colwyn

Marine Hotel

Abergele Road
☎ (0492) 515484
11.30–11
Draught Bass; M&B Mild H
Large public house comprising three bars, a pool room and a restaurant.
Q 🚢 ◖▶ P

Try also: Plough, Abergele Rd (Greenalls)

Pen-y-Mynydd

White Lion Inn

On A5104
12–3, 7–11 (12–2, 7–10.30 Sun)
Marston's Border Bitter H
Well cared for and virtually untouched by the passage of time: three rooms displaying mementoes of the past. The welcome from behind the bar is as genuine as the home-made pickled eggs!
🚢 Q 🛥 🍷 ♣ P

Rhewl

Sun Inn

2 miles off B5103 OS178448
☎ (0978) 861043
12–3, 6 (7 winter)–11
Felinfoel Double Dragon H
Old drovers' inn set in the beautiful Dee valley. A 14th-century house with low-beamed ceilings and stone floors; a great attraction to hikers and hillwalkers. A portacabin in the garden has children's games.
🛥 🌺 ◖▶ 🅰 ♣ P

Rhos-on-Sea

Rhos Abbey Hotel

111 The Promenade
☎ (0492) 546601
11–3, 5–11 (11–11 Sat)
Courage Directors; John Smith's Bitter H

Large seafront hotel with a bar open to the public in summer. Popular for meals.
Q 🌺 🚢 ◖▶ 🍷 P

Try also: Boathouse Club (Free); **Cayley Arms** (Bass)

Rhuddlan

New Inn

High Street ☎ (0745) 591305
12–3, 6–11
S&N Theakston Best Bitter, XB, Old Peculier H
Recently refurbished town pub and restaurant, near the castle, offering the best beer range in town. Popular with all ages. 🌺 🚢 ◖▶ ♣ P

Rhyl

Caskeys

Vale Road ☎ (0745) 338308
12–3, 6–11
Draught Bass; M&B Mild H
Popular town pub with a good-sized bar, a lounge and a restaurant. Popular with local football and rugby clubs, and always busy at weekends.
◖▶ 🍷 🚷 🅰 🚆 ♣ P

Rossett

Butchers Arms

Chester Road
☎ (0244) 570233
11.30–11
Burtonwood Bitter H
Welcoming roadside hostelry in a busy village. The small public bar is popular with locals and the plush lounge serves good value meals.
🌺 ◖▶ 🍷 ♣ P

Ruthin

Wine Vaults

St Peters Square
☎ (082 42) 2867
12–3, 5–11 (11–2 Thu–Sat)
Robinson's Best Bitter H
Unchanging local of the main square. 🌺 🚢 🅰 ♣ P

St Asaph

Swan

The Roe ☎ (0745) 582284
1–3, 7–11
Marston's Mercian Mild, Burton Best Bitter, Pedigree H
Small, basically furnished pub with a fish tank and a good-sized bar. Hosted by long-serving tenants.
Q 🌺 🚷 🅰 ♣ P

Towyn

Morton Arms

Sandbank Road (200 yds from A548) ☎ (0745) 330211
11–11
M&B Mild; Whitbread Boddingtons Bitter H

Modern, seaside pub and restaurant, with pleasant decor; a recent convert to real ale but already planning to extend its range. The only pub in this seaside village with the real thing. Regular entertainment can be noisy.
🌺 ◖▶ 🅰 ♣ P

Upper Colwyn Bay

Taylor's

Pen-y-Bryn Road (B5113)
OS842783 ☎ (0492) 533360
11–3, 5.30–11
Courage Directors; Marston's Pedigree; John Smith's Bitter H
Large lounge, very nicely furnished, together with a restaurant area and a downstairs bar. Built about 15 years ago, on the site of an old golf course, it offers magnificent views of Rhos-on-Sea from the lounge. Please dress smartly!
Q 🛥 🌺 ◖▶ 🍷 🚷 P

Whitford

Huntsman Inn

Whitford Road (W of Holywell on unmarked road)
☎ (0745) 360232
11.30–3, 7–11
Draught Bass; S&N Theakston Best Bitter H
Good village pub, not spoilt by progress, with a lively public bar. Good value meals.
🚢 🌺 ◖▶ 🍷 ♣ P

Wrexham

Golden Lion

High Street
☎ (0978) 364964
12–11 (12–4, 7–11 Sat)
Draught Bass; Stones Best Bitter; Welsh Brewers Worthington BB H
Old pub with a newly decorated lounge/dining area. Can be crowded at weekends.
◖ 🚆 (Central)

Oak Tree Tavern

Ruabon Road (A5152)
☎ (0978) 261450
12–3, 6.30–11 (11–11 Sat)
Marston's Border Bitter, Burton Best Bitter, Pedigree H
Traditional two-bar local with a friendly atmosphere, on the edge of town.
◖ 🍷 🚆 (Central) ♣ P

Turf

Mold Road (A541)
☎ (0978) 261484
11.30–11
Marston's Border Exhibition, Pedigree H
Busy two-bar pub built into the side of Wrexham football ground. 🌺 🚢 ◖▶ 🍷
🚆 (Central) ♣ P

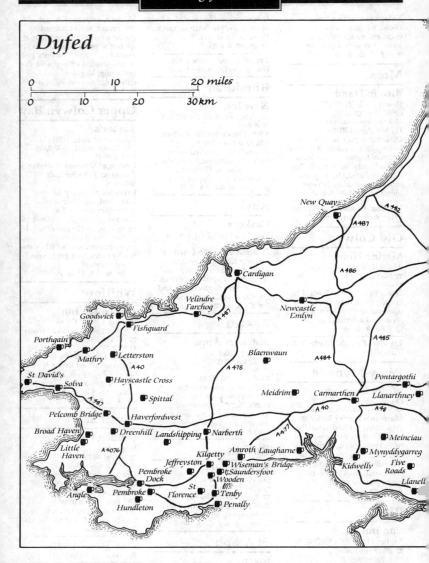

Dyfed

```
0        10        20 miles
0   10   20   30 km
```

New Quay

Cardigan

Velindre
Farchog

Newcastle
Emlyn

Goodwick
Fishguard
Porthgain
Mathry   Letterston
St David's   A 40
Solva   Hayscastle Cross   Blaenwaun
Spittal   Meidrim   Carmarthen
Pelcomb Bridge   Haverfordwest
Broad Haven   Dreenhill   Landshipping   Narberth
Little   Laugharne
Haven   A 4076   Amroth
Pembroke   Kilgetty   Wiseman's Bridge
Angle   Dock   Jeffreyston   Saundersfoot   Kidwelly
Pembroke   St   Wooden
Hundleton   Florence   Tenby
Penally

Pontargothi
Llanarthney
Meinciau
Mynyddygarreg
Five
Roads
Llanell

A 482, A 487, A 486, A 485, A 484, A 476, A 48, A 477

Crown Buckley, Felinfoel, Llanelli

Aberystwyth

Castle
South Road ☎ (0970) 612188
12–3, 5.30–11 (12–11 Sat)
Draught Bass Ⓗ
Large, former Roberts' pub
built in imitation of a London
gin palace. Recently acquired
by the landlady from Bass. A
guest beer is probable in
summer. The closest pub to
South Marine beach and
harbour – hence many

seafaring connections.
⊠ ⇥ ◑ 🖿 ﭏ ⇌ ✦

Nag's Head
Bridge Street ☎ (0970) 624725
11–11
Banks's Mild, Bitter Ⓔ
Large public bar and a small,
tidy lounge in the old part of
town, with much evidence of
its darts teams' illustrious
past. Please use the back
entrance (High Street) for the
small family room.
ᘐ ❁ ◑ ▶ ﭏ ⇌ ✦

Pier Hotel
Pier Street
☎ (0970) 615126
11–4, 5.30–11
Banks's Mild, Bitter Ⓔ
Almost on the promenade,
and directly opposite the pier;
a large public bar fronts the
street while the tiny lounge
has its own side entrance up
the alley. 🖿 ﭏ ⇌ ✦

Try also: Mill (Free); **Weston
Vaults**, Thespian St (Banks's)

344

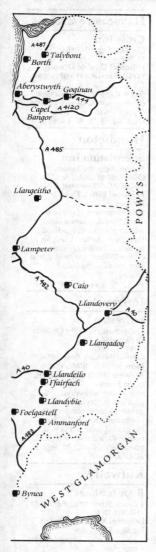

set in its own grounds. The guest beers are changed weekly.
🍴 Q 🍺 ⊛ 🛏 🍴 ◗ 🍴 ᗢ P

Amroth

New Inn
☎ (0834) 812368
11–3 (may extend), 5.30–11
Ind Coope Burton Ale; Tetley Bitter Ⓗ**; guest beers**
400-year-old inn of great character with a Flemish inglenook fireplace, an enclosed garden and a restaurant upstairs. It enjoys a superb location, just yards from the beach, but can get very crowded in summer. Meals April–October.
🍴 Q 🍺 ⊛ 🛏 🍴 ◗ ᗢ P

Angle

Hibernia Inn
Main Street ☎ (0646) 641517
11–3, 6.30–11
Welsh Brewers Worthington BB Ⓗ
A friendly welcome in a village pub with strong nautical connections.
🍴 Q 🍺 ⊛ 🍴 ◗ ◗ ᗢ P

Blaenwaun

Lamb Inn
☎ (0994) 448440
Hours vary
Beer range varies Ⓗ
Tiny, basic free house in an isolated hilltop hamlet. Usually two interesting beers available. ⊛ ♣ P

Borth

Friendship
High Street ☎ (0970) 871213
12 (11 summer)–3, 6.30 (6 summer)–11
Tetley Bitter; guest beer Ⓗ
Welcoming, cottage-style free house, below road level in the main street of this resort village. The same family has held the licence for more than 70 years. Horses are served in the public bar on Xmas Day (please book). The corridor and lounge serve as an art gallery. Lunchtime snacks.
🍴 Q ⊛ 🛏 ᗢ ◗ ♣

Broad Haven

Royal
200 yds from coast road
☎ (0437) 781249
11–11
Draught Bass; Ind Coope Burton Ale; Marston's Pedigree; Wadworth 6X; Welsh Brewers Worthington BB Ⓗ
Completely renovated old pub on the coastal path, close to a sandy beach in a sheltered,

sunny location. Specialises in menus at affordable prices.
Q 🍺 ⊛ 🛏 🍴 ◗ 🍴 ᗢ ♣ P

Bynea

New Plough
76 Cwmfelin Road
☎ (0554) 777187
11.30–3.30, 6.30–11
Crown Buckley Dark, Best Bitter, Reverend James Ⓗ**; guest beer**
Cosy pub, tastefully modernised. The restaurant has a supper licence until midnight. Play area in the garden. ⊛ ◗ ♣ P

Caio

Brunant Arms
1 mile NE of A482
☎ (055 85) 483
11–11
Adnams Broadside; Hook Norton Old Hooky; Welsh Brewers Worthington BB Ⓗ**; guest beers** (weekends)
Caio is a compact, attractive village in the middle of the UK's largest parish and close to the Dolicothi Roman gold mines. The pub is friendly and full of character with a vast number of pub games. Join in the Sunday evening debates.
🍴 ⊛ 🛏 ◗ ᗢ ♣ P

Capel Bangor

Tynllidiart Arms
On A44 ☎ (0970) 84248
11–2.30, 6–11 (closed winter Sun eve)
Brains SA (summer)**; Whitbread Boddingtons Bitter, Flowers Original** Ⓗ
303-year-old cottage inn, formerly connected with the mailcoach trade. Two small bars both have open fires. A rare outlet for real cider. The beer range is likely to vary.
🍴 Q ◗ 🍴 ᗢ ♣ ᗢ

Cardigan

Red Lion
Pwll-hai (off A484, behind Finch Sq) ☎ (0239) 612782
11–11 (closed Sun eve)
Crown Buckley Best Bitter, Reverend James Ⓗ
Ancient back-street pub where the large front bar has various drinking areas. Pool room at the rear. 🍺 ⊛ ◗ ◗ ♣

Carmarthen

Drovers
Lammas Street
☎ (0267) 231800
11–3, 6–11 (may vary)
Felinfoel Cambrian, Double Dragon Ⓗ
Town pub, offering good value meals. Q ◗ 🚃

Ammanford

Perrivale
Pontamman Road (A474)
☎ (0269) 593785
11–3.30, 5.30–11
Wadworth 6X; Welsh Brewers Worthington BB Ⓗ
Pleasant main road pub.
Q 🛏 ◗ ◗ P

Wernoleu Hotel
Off Pontamman Road (A474)
☎ (0269) 592598
11–11
Beer range varies Ⓗ
Cosy lounge bar in an imposing Victorian mansion

Dyfed

Dreenhill

Denant Mill
Left at Masons Arms, then ³/₄ mile along Dale Road
☎ (0437) 766569
11–3, 6–11
Beer range varies H
Very old converted mill set in seven acres of bird-protected woodland. Unspoilt decor highlights an internal mill wheel. The beer range changes often with up to five brews on sale; also Belgian bottled beers, and cider in summer. ♨ Q ♨ ♨ ❂ ◑ ◗ ♨ ✦ ⌂ P

Masons Arms
1 mile from Haverfordwest on Dale Road ☎ (0437) 760815
11–11
Draught Bass; Welsh Brewers Worthington BB H
Country pub with a newly-added extension, offering good beer and chat.
♨ ♨ ❂ ◑ ◗ ♨ ▲ P

Ffairfach

Torbay
Heol Cennen (A483)
☎ (0558) 822029
11–3, 5.30–11
Draught Bass; Crown Buckley Best Bitter H
Popular, comfortable house specialising in home-cooked food from its extensive, good value menu. ♨ Q ❂ ◑ ◗ ♨ ♨ ▲ ♨ (not winter Sun) ✦ P

Fishguard

Old Coach House
High Street ☎ (0348) 873883
11–11
Crown Buckley Best Bitter, Reverend James; Welsh Brewers Worthington BB H
Modern but tastefully furnished: predominantly wood beams and exposed timbers. Clean, light and airy, it has a cosy family nook, an open-plan pool room, a patio and an outside children's play area. Cider and eve meals in summer only. ❂ ◑ ◗ ⌂

Ship Inn
Newport Road, Lower Town (A40) ☎ (0348) 874033
11–3, 7–11 (12–2, 7–10.30 Sun)
Welsh Brewers Worthington Dark, BB H
Marine nick-nacks dominate this low-ceilinged, beamed pub, famous for hosting film crews from *Moby Dick* and *Under Milk Wood*. A haven for sailors, locals and tourists. Set near the beautiful Lower Town and harbour. A delightful experience. See your bounced cheque pinned to the ceiling! ♨ ✦

Five Roads

Waun-Wyllt
Horeb (off B4309)
12–3, 7 (6 Fri, 5.30 Sat)–11
Felinfoel Double Dragon; S&N Theakston Best Bitter H; guest beers
Splendidly isolated free house, offering excellent cuisine.
Q ❂ ◑ ◗ ♨ P

Foelgastell

Smiths Arms
Signed on A48
☎ (0269) 842213
11.30–3.30, 6.30–11 (11–11 summer)
Crown Buckley Dark, Best Bitter H; guest beer
Attractive, cosy pub in a quiet village near a busy main road.
♨ ◑ ◗ ♨ P

Goginan

Druid Inn
On A44 ☎ (0970) 84650
11–3, 5.30–11
Banks's Mild, Bitter; Thwaites Bitter H
Pub set into a hillside of the Melindwr valley, in a former lead-mining village. The beer range varies; it also sells Romanian vodkas, bottled Czech lager and duck eggs (in season). ◑ ◗ ♨ ✦ P

Goodwick

Glendower Club & Hotel
The Square ☎ (0348) 872873
11–11
Crown Buckley Dark, Best Bitter H
Two bars, a games room and a dining/meeting room, which doubles as a family room. Note the rogues' gallery (portraits of regulars by a local artist). Q ♨ ♨ ♨ ◑ ♨ ♨ ✦

Haverfordwest

Castle Hotel
Castle Square ☎ (0437) 769322
11–11
Wadworth 6X; Welsh Brewers Worthington BB H
Busy town-centre hotel attracting a broad spectrum of clientele to its recently refurbished bar and restaurant. ♨ ◑ ◗ ♨

Pembroke Yeoman
Hill Street ☎ (0437) 762500
11–11
Ansells Bitter H; **Draught Bass; Felinfoel Double Dragon; Ind Coope Burton Ale; Marston's Pedigree;** guest beers G
Well-used establishment offering good ales, food and chat. ♨ ❂ ◑ ◗

Hayscastle Cross

Cross Inn
On B4330 ☎ (0348) 840216
11.30–3, 6–11
Felinfoel Double Dragon; Welsh Brewers Worthington BB H
Stone-flagged floor in a typical country pub with an excellent reputation for fun and good food. ♨ Q ♨ ❂ ◑ ◗ ♨ ▲ P

Hundleton

Speculation Inn
Follow signs for Texaco
OS947997 ☎ (0646) 661306
12–2.30 (11.30–3 summer), 6–11
Felinfoel Bitter, Double Dragon H
Pub where one of the two small bars displays a letter warning a former landlord of the sins of the locality. The leisure activities are now coarse fishing, sea fishing and surfing, all to be found nearby.
♨ Q ❂ ◑ ♨ ♨ ▲ ✦ P

Jeffreyston

Jeffreston Inn
Sharp turn off B4586 OS088065
☎ (0646) 651394
11–11
Crown Buckley Best Bitter; John Smith's Bitter; Welsh Brewers Worthington BB H; guest beers
Something for everyone: a goat and a playhouse in the garden; a large comfortable restaurant area; and a 'head-banger express' to get you home. Varied selection of guest beers. ♨ Q ♨ ❂ ◑ ◗ ♨ ♨ ▲ ✦ ⌂ P

Kidwelly

Boot & Shoe
2 Castle Street ☎ (0554) 891341
11–3.30, 6.30–11
Felinfoel Bitter, Cambrian, Double Dragon H
Small pub with a very friendly atmosphere. ◑ ◗ ✦

Kilgetty

Kilgetty Arms
Carmarthen Road
☎ (0834) 813219
11–11
Felinfoel Bitter H
A friendly welcome assured in a pub full of strong local character. Very near the station and handy for the auction rooms, it has a lively public bar and a quiet lounge, which doubles as a children's room at lunchtime. ♨ Q ❂ ♨ ◑ ◗ ♨ ♨ ▲ ♨ ✦ P

Try also: White Horse (Felinfoel)

Lampeter

Kings Head

14 Bridge Street (A482/A485)
☎ (0570) 422598
11–3.30 (may extend), 5.30–11 (12.30 supper licence)
Crown Buckley Best Bitter Ⓗ
Pleasant little university town local. The recently revamped public bar displays the publican's sense of humour. Comfortable rear lounge with an aviary in the garden beyond. The menu caters for children and vegetarians.
🛏 Q ❀ ◖ ▶ ❷ ⅄ ♿ ♣ P

Landshipping

Stanley Arms

OS013117 ☎ (0834) 891227
12–3, 6–11 (may be 12–11 in summer)
Crown Buckley SBB; Welsh Brewers Worthington BB Ⓗ
Well-worth-finding, rambling, stone-flagged pub set in a large garden, a stone's throw from the Cleddau river, where there is mooring for customers. No meals Mon eve.
🛏 Q ⅀ ❀ ⋈ ◖ ▶ ❷ ⅄ ♣ P

Laugharne

New Three Mariners

Victoria Street (A4066)
11–3, 5.30–11 (11–11 summer)
Crown Buckley Best Bitter Ⓗ
Former home-brew pub, built about 1703 with two small, friendly locals' bars and a large, comfortable pool room where children are admitted.
🛏 ⅀ ⋈ ❷ ⅄ ♣

Letterston

Harp Inn

31 Haverfordwest Road (A40)
☎ (0348) 840061
11–3, 5.30–11
Ansells Bitter; Ind Coope Burton Ale; Tetley Bitter Ⓗ
An excellent pub for both locals and tourists of discerning taste; beautifully furnished and decorated. Food in the restaurant and bars is excellent and reasonably priced. 🛏 Q ❀ ◖ ▶ ❷ ⅄ ♿ P

Little Haven

Swan Inn

Off B4341 ☎ (0437) 781256
11–3, 6.30–11
Felinfoel Double Dragon; Welsh Brewers Worthington BB Ⓗ
Delightful old coastal pub in a rocky cove approached by a footpath. Wide range of home-cooked food specials and locally-caught seafood. The restaurant is open Wed–Sat eves (book). 🛏 Q ❀ ◖ ⅄

Llanarthney

Paxton Inn

On B4300 ☎ (0558) 668705
4–11
Ind Coope Burton Ale; Wadworth 6X; Welsh Brewers Worthington BB Ⓗ; guest beers
250 years-old, this traditional pub is one of the most unusual in Wales. Free live music four nights a week – bring own instrument! A real ale and rock festival is held each summer. Full of character. Occasional draught cider.
⋈ ◖ ▶ ♿ ⅃ P

Llandeilo

Three Tuns

1 Market Street (off A483)
2 (12 Sat)–11 (closed Sun)
Ansells Mild; Ind Coope Friary Meux Best Bitter, Benskins Best Bitter, Burton Ale; Tetley Bitter Ⓗ; guest beers
Back-street, 17th-century town local, traditional and friendly, but with well-attested evidence of supernatural phenomena. ⋈ ❷ ⅄
⇌ (not winter Sun) ♣

White Horse

125 Rhosmaen Street (through archway from main A483)
☎ (0558) 822424
11.45–3, 5.30–11 (12–2.30, 7–10.30 Sun)
Brains Dark; Wadworth 6X; Welsh Brewers Worthington BB Ⓗ; guest beers
17th-century coaching inn with a courtyard, and railway photographs in the snug. Two guest beers always available – 150 in two years. A regulars' pub with a warm welcome for all; a regular *Guide* entry. No food Sun; eve meals by arrangement. 🛏 Q ❀ ◖ ⅄ ❷ ⅃
⇌ (not winter Sun) ⅃ P

Llandovery

Red Lion

Market Square ☎ (0550) 20813
11–3 (not Wed), 5.30–11 (often closes earlier; closed Sun)
Crown Buckley Dark, Best Bitter Ⓖ
Ancient, eccentric, friendly and welcoming pub with erratic opening times. One spartan drinking room without a counter – beer is drawn from casks out the back. With no visible sign, it is hard to find, but worth the effort for a step back in time. In the same family for more than a century.
🛏 Q ⇌ (not winter Sun)

White Swan

High Street ☎ (0550) 20816
12–3.30, 5.30–11

Llandybie

Hook Norton Best Bitter; Wadworth 6X Ⓗ
200-year-old pub, formerly a coaching inn. The garden affords superb views. 🛏 Q ❀ ◖ ▶ ⅄ ⇌ (not winter Sun) ♣

Red Lion

The Square ☎ (0269) 851202
11.30–3, 6–11 (closed Sun eve)
Marston's Pedigree; Whitbread Boddingtons Bitter, Flowers Original Ⓗ
A listed building opposite an historic church. CAMRA regional *Pub of the Year* 1990. Always worth a visit, it boasts two family rooms and a garden play area. No food Sun eve. Q ⅀ ❀ ⋈ ◖ ▶ ❷ ⇌ P

Llanelli

Halfway Hotel

Swansea Road
☎ (0554) 773571
12–3, 6–11
Draught Bass; Welsh Brewers Worthington BB Ⓗ
A magnificent, original oak bar, immaculately kept; spacious and comfortable.
Q ⅀ ❀ ◖ ❷ P

Masons

28 Thomas Street
12–11
Felinfoel Bitter; Fuller's London Pride Ⓗ
Small, locals' bar with a large, refurbished lounge. 🛏 ❷

Queen Victoria

Murray Street
☎ (0554) 772444
12–11
Draught Bass; Welsh Brewers Worthington BB Ⓗ
Comfortable local. ♣

Stradey Arms

Furnace ☎ (0554) 757968
12–3, 6–11 (12–11 Fri & Sat)
Crown Buckley Dark, Best Bitter Ⓗ
Well-appointed pub close to Buckley's brewery. ❀ ◖ ❷ P

Try also: Thomas Arms (Crown Buckley)

Llangadog

Castle Hotel

Queen's Square
☎ (0550) 777377
11–2, 6–11 (11–11 Sat)
Wadworth 6X Ⓗ; guest beers
Listed building dating from the 15th-century with many original features. Friendly welcome; the car park is for hotel guests only. Locally-caught fish is a speciality on a menu also catering for children and vegetarians.
🛏 ⋈ ◖ ▶ ❷ ⅄ ⅃ ⇌ (not winter Sun) ♣ P

Dyfed

Llangeitho

Three Horseshoe
The Square ☎ (097 423) 244
12–3, 5.30–11 (closed Sun eve)
Tetley Bitter ⓗ; **guest beer**
(summer)
Traditional local in a quiet
village, which doubles as a
fish and chip shop on Fri
nights. Full meals six days a
week, but no food Sun. The
beer range varies.
🛏 Q ❀ ◑ 🅭 ♿ ♣ P

Mathry

Farmers Arms
Off A487 ☎ (0348) 831284
11–11
**Draught Bass; Welsh Brewers
Worthington BB** ⓗ
Pub with an old, timbered
interior displaying 96
Guinness cartoons, plus rural
bric-a-brac, set atop an ancient
hill-fort settlement. Local
artists' paintings are also on
show. Families welcome. This
ancient (1291) building is a
former monks' brewhouse.
❀ 🛌 ♿ ♣ P

Meidrim

Maenllwyd Inn
³/₄ mile W of village OS278212
6–11 (closed Sun)
Crown Buckley Best Bitter ⓖ
Rare example of an utterly
traditional country local with
a whitewashed parlour and a
cottage-style sitting room.
Beer is served from the jug; no
keg at all. 🛏 Q 🅭 ♿ ♣ P

Meinciau

Black Horse
On B4309
11–3, 5.30–11 (may vary)
**Felinfoel Bitter, Double
Dragon** ⓖ
Country pub with a friendly
atmosphere. 🛏 ❀ ◑ 🅭 P

Mynyddygarreg

Prince of Wales
Meinciau Road
☎ (0554) 890522
12–11
Beer range varies ⓗ
Interesting pub where every
nook and cranny is filled with
bric-a-brac, changed weekly. Meals served
all day. 🛏 ❀ ◑ ♣ P

Narberth

Kirkland Arms
St James's Street
☎ (0834) 860423
**Felinfoel Cambrian, Double
Dragon** ⓗ
Pub where a lively
participation in local events is

---

reflected in the photographs
and other memorabilia lining
the walls. Its proximity to the
rugby ground makes it ideal
for celebrating wins or
drowning sorrows.
🛏 Q ❀ ◑ 🅭 ♿ ♠ ⇌ ♣ P

Newcastle Emlyn

Bunch of Grapes
Bridge Street (A475)
☎ (0239) 711185
11.30–11
**Courage Best Bitter,
Directors** ⓗ; **guest beers**
17th-century building now
opened out, its pine floors and
furniture giving it a café-bar
atmosphere. 🛏 ❀ ♠ ♣

Coopers Arms
Station Road (A484/B4333 jct)
☎ (0239) 710323
11.30–3 (may extend), 5.30–11
**Draught Bass; Welsh Brewers
Worthington BB** ⓗ
Small pub on the main road,
featuring an attractive bar area
with stone walls and brick
arches, a games area and a no-
smoking lounge.
❀ 🅭 ♠ ♣ P ⚤

Red Cow
Adpar (B4333/B4571 jct)
11–11 (may close 3–5.30; closed Sun
eve)
Draught Bass ⓖ
Noted traditional pub just
across the Teifi from the town
centre. The single room is
basic at one end and furnished
as a lounge, full of character,
at the other. Q ♣ P

New Quay

Dolau Inn
Church Street ☎ (0545) 560881
11–4, 5.30–11 (11–11 Fri, Sat &
summer)
**Welsh Brewers Hancock's
HB** ⓗ
Extended, early 19th-century
cottage inn, one of the oldest
buildings in the town, with
traditional settle seating
amongst shipping mementoes.
❀ 🅭 ♠ ♣

Seahorse
Margaret Street
☎ (0545) 560736
11–11
**Crown Buckley Dark, Best
Bitter, Reverend James** ⓗ
Welcoming, Victorian one-bar
pub in the town centre, high
above the fishing harbour.
Fine reputation for beer and
accommodation. 🛌 ♿ ♠ ♣

Pelcomb Bridge

Rising Sun Inn
On A487 ☎ (0437) 765171
11.30–3, 7 (6 summer)–11
**Ind Coope Burton Ale; Tetley
Bitter** ⓗ

Old country inn tastefully
rebuilt and retaining its
original character; a family
business offering a warm
welcome and a friendly
atmosphere. Popular for its
good value meals.
Q ❀ 🛌 ◑ 🅭 ♿ ♣ P

Pembroke

Old Cross Saws
Main Street ☎ (0646) 682475
11–11
Crown Buckley Best Bitter ⓗ
Centrally-placed for the
station, Norman castle, mill-
pond and antique shops, this
pub is larger than it looks
from outside. Popular with
rugby-followers. The annual
fair (second week in Oct) has
rides practically on the
doorstep. Hillside garden.
❀ 🛌 ◑ ♠ ⇌ ♣ P

Pembroke Dock

Charlton Hotel
Bush Street ☎ (0646) 682285
11–11
**Draught Bass; Welsh Brewers
Worthington Dark, BB** ⓗ
A wonderful bank of six
handpumps feature in this
turn-of-the-century local
where red brick and dark
wood predominate. Large
games room; keen
participation in local events,
and much interest in sport.
Lunchtime snacks. 🛏 ⇌ ♣

White Hart
Pembroke Street (near ferry)
☎ (0646) 682586
11–5, 7–11
**Brains Bitter; Draught Bass;
Welsh Brewers Worthington
BB** ⓗ; **guest beers**
Excellent, friendly small pub/
hotel. The side room is used as
a children's room when not
needed for pigeon-fanciers'
meetings. Lunchtime snacks.
Q ❀ 🛌 ⇌

Penally

Cross Inn
☎ (0834) 844665
12–3, 7–11 (12–11 Sat & summer)
**Welsh Brewers Worthington
BB** ⓗ; **guest beers** ⓖ
A warm welcome is assured in
this slate-floored pub, with
scrubbed-wood furniture. It
enjoys a good local
atmosphere and wholehearted
participation in local events.
Marvellous view across to
Caldey Island.
Q ◑ ♿ ⇌ ♣

Pontargothi

Cresselly Arms
Carmarthen Road (A40)
☎ (0267) 290221
11.30–3, 5–11

348

...owers

...y pub on the
...th a restaurant
...he river.
◁ ▷ ◁ P

...ain

...nn

☎ (0348) 831449
...-11 (11.30–11 Fri & Sat)
...el Bitter, Double
...n H; guest beers
...mer)
...characterful seafarers'
..., established in 1743 in an
...toric harbour village on the
...oastal Path in the National
Park. A popular eating house
for bar snacks and full meals,
including locally-caught
seafood. ⚲ ❀ ◁ ▷ ♣ P

St David's

Farmers Arms

Goat Street ☎ (0437) 720328
11–11
**Whitbread Boddingtons
Bitter, Flowers Original** H
19th-century stone pub with
beams, flagstone floor and an
original fireplace. Popular
with local fishermen, farmers
and lifeboatmen, it serves
excellent, home-cooked meals.
A spacious terrace at the rear
affords a view of the hills and
the cathedral.
⚲ Q ප ❀ ◁ ▷ ◁ ♣

St Florence

New Inn

High Street ☎ (0834) 871315
11–3, 5.30–11
Brains Bitter H (summer), G
(winter)
The pub and the garden have
both been extended without
losing their essential character.
Centrally situated in a
renowned floral village, where
a peaceful pint may be
enjoyed only a few miles from
the holidaymakers' beaten
track.
⚲ Q ❀ ◁ ▷ ◁ ප ⓗ A ♣ P

Saundersfoot

Old Chemist Inn

The Strand ☎ (0834) 813982
11–11
**Draught Bass; Welsh Brewers
Hancock's HB** H; guest beers
(summer)
A pub with a real boon for
harassed parents – a beer-
garden which leads directly
onto the beach! Loyal local
following.
⚲ ප ❀ ◁ ▷ ◁ A ♣

Solva

Cambrian Inn

Main Street ☎ (0437) 721210
11–3, 7–11

**Ind Coope Burton Ale; Tetley
Bitter** H
18th-century village pub with
a beamed bar and an attractive
restaurant, near the bridge
over the Solva river and the
Coastal Path. Daily specials in
the bar, plus an *à la carte* menu
Mon–Sat eves and a roast Sun
lunch, make this a popular
eating house. ⚲ ◁ ▷ ◁ P

Ship Inn

Main Street ☎ (0437) 721247
11–11

**Draught Bass; Brains SA;
Felinfoel Double Dragon;
Wadworth 6X; Welsh Brewers
Worthington BB** H; guest
beers (summer)
300-year-old pub in a fishing
and sailing village. The
restaurant offers a home-
cooked, full menu with daily
specials. ⚲ Q ❀ A ♣

Spittal

Pump on the Green

☎ (043 787) 339
12 (11 Wed–Fri)–3, 5.30–11
**Draught Bass; Felinfoel
Double Dragon; Welsh
Brewers Worthington BB** H
Traditional village pub with a
most pleasant atmosphere.
Cosy corners and relaxing
dining room.
⚲ Q ප ❀ ◁ ▷ ◁ ⓗ ♣ P

Talybont

White Lion

The Square ☎ (0970) 832245
11–4, 5.30–11 (11–11 Sat)
Banks's Mild, Bitter E
Large, warm, slate-flagged
bar, providing everything
from cribbage to bus
timetables. Tidy lounge at the
rear and a small dining room
at the side. Renowned for its
accommodation and meals. ⚲
Q ප ❀ ◁ ▷ ◁ ◁ A ♣ P

Tenby

Coach & Horses

Upper Frog Street
☎ (0834) 842704
11–11
**Marston's Pedigree;
Whitbread Flowers IPA** H;
guest beers
Snug, welcoming pub which is
usually packed with young
people late eve, but is good for
a quiet drink or meal earlier
on. Tigger the tail-less cat
presides over this old pub
which offers good food.
⚲ ප ❀ ◁ ▷ ◁ ⓗ ≉ ♣

Normandie Hotel

Upper Frog Street
☎ (0834) 842227
11–3 (often extends in summer), 7–11
**Ruddles County; Welsh
Brewers Worthington BB** H;
guest beers (occasionally)

Old coaching inn set in the
town walls, with a nook for
everyone.
Q ප ⓗ ◁ ▷ ◁ ⓗ ≉ ♣

Tenby & District Ex-Servicemen's Club

Ruabon House, South Parade
11–3, 6–11 (12–2, 7–10.30 Sun)
**Welsh Brewers Worthington
Dark** E, **BB** H
Large, friendly club which
welcomes temporary
members. The upstairs
function room has bingo,
dancing, sing-alongs and
country music, while
downstairs there are two
snooker tables. Children
welcome at lunchtime.
Q ප ≉ ♣

Try also: **Evergreen Inn**
(Welsh Brewers); **Hope &
Anchor** (Free); **Three
Mariners**, St Georges St
(Welsh Brewers)

Velindre Farchog

Salutation Inn

On A487 ☎ (0239) 820564
11–3 (12–2 winter), 5.30–11
Ind Coope Burton Ale G
Pub catering well for families.
Separate restaurant.
Q ප ❀ ⓗ ◁ ▷ ◁ ⓗ ⓓ P

Wiseman's Bridge

Wiseman's Bridge Inn

☎ (0834) 813236
11–3, 7–11 (11–11 summer)
**Draught Bass; Welsh Brewers
Hancock's HB, Worthington
BB** H; guest beers (summer)
Delightful pub opening on to
the beach. Popular both
summer and winter, it offers
an excellent range of food and
accommodation for
holidaymakers, as well as
enjoying a strong local
clientele. Wheelchair access is
via the kitchen. ⚲ Q ප ❀
ⓗ ◁ ▷ ◁ ⓗ A ♣ P

Wooden

Woodridge Inn

On A478 ☎ (0834) 812259
11–11
**Ind Coope Burton Ale; Tetley
Bitter** H
Large roadside pub offering
sports and health club
facilities, plus music nightly in
summer. Spacious and
comfortable, it appeals to all
ages and tastes. Good
playground.
ප ❀ ◁ ▷ ◁ ⓓ A ♣ P

Join CAMRA —
see page 508

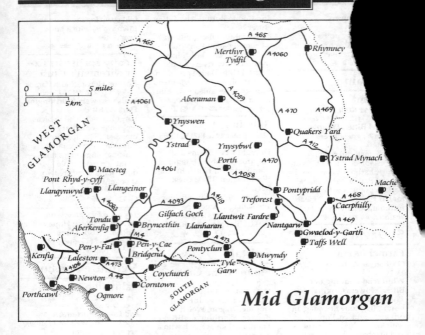

Mid Glamorgan

Mid Glamorgan

Aberaman

Temple Bar

Cardiff Road (B4275)
12–4, 7–11 (may vary)
**Brains SA; Felinfoel Double
Dragon** H**; guest beers**
Homely local kept by the
same family for 105 years: a
bar full of bric-a-brac and a
library; separate games room.
🏚 Q 🍺 ♣ P

Aberkenfig

Swan

128 Bridgend Road
☎ (0656) 725612
11–3.30 (4 Sat), 6–11 (12–2.30,
7–10.30 Sun)
**Brains Dark, Bitter, SA;
Whitbread Flowers
Original** H
Pleasant, comfortable village
pub. Good meals (no food
Mon eve or Sun).
◖ ▶ ᵹ ⇌ (Sarn Hill) P

Bridgend

Famous Pen-y-Bont
Inn

Derwen Road ☎ (0656) 652266
11.30–3, 5.30–11 (11–11 Sat)
**Brains Dark, SA; Marston's
Pedigree; Whitbread
WCPA** H**; guest beers**
Recently renovated town pub
with a railway theme and a
warm atmosphere. Beware of
the fake handpump for cider.
◖ ▶ ⇌

Oldcastle Inn

90 Nolton Street
12–4, 6–11 (12–11 Fri & Sat)
**Draught Bass; Brains SA;
Welsh Brewers Worthington
BB** H
Cosy, friendly town pub
without an inn sign.
🏚 Q 🍺 ◖ ⇌ ♣

Two Brewers

Brackla (200 yds from B4181)
☎ (0656) 661788
12–3, 5.30–11 (12–11 Fri & Sat)
Brains Dark, Bitter, SA H
Large, modern estate pub with
a plush lounge. No meals Sun;
eve meals only if booked.
ᵹ ⏰ ◖ ᵹ ♣ P

Bryncethin

Masons Arms

Bridgend Road
☎ (0656) 720253
11–11
**Draught Bass; Brains Dark,
SA; Welsh Brewers
Worthington BB** H
Unspoilt bar and plush
lounge. Live entertainment in
the high-class restaurant Wed.
◖ ▶ ᵹ P

Caerphilly

Moathouse

30 Lon y Llyn (between
Martins Farm and the Miners
Hospital) ☎ (0222) 882850
12–4.30, 6–11 (11.30–11 Sat)
**Welsh Brewers Hancock's
HB** H

Lively estate pub with a basic
bar and a large, comfortable
lounge. ◖ ⏰ ⇌ (Caerphilly/
Aber) ♣ P

Corntown

Golden Mile Inn

¹⁄₂ mile from A48/B4524 jct
☎ (0656) 654884
11.30–3.30, 5–11
**Draught Bass; Welsh Brewers
Hancock's HB, Worthington
BB** H**; guest beers**
Old converted farmhouse,
with a stone fireplace and
exposed beams. Warm
atmosphere. Boules played.
🏚 ⏰ ◖ ♣ P

Coychurch

White Horse

Main Road ☎ (0656) 652583
11.30–4, 5.30–11 (11.30–11 Fri & Sat)
Brains Dark, Bitter, SA H
Comfortable village pub.
Landlord is Brains's *Cellarman
of the Year*. Q ⏰ ◖ ▶ ♣ P

Gilfach Goch

Griffin

Hendreforgan (600 yds S of
A4093)
12–11 (may close afternoons)
Brains SA H
Exceptional, traditional local
remotely situated in a small
valley bottom. Old bric-a-brac
and furniture; cosy and
friendly. Q ⏰ ◖ P

Gwaelod-y-Garth

Gwaelod-y-Garth Inn

600 yds off Taffs Well–
Pentyrch road ☎ (0222) 810408
12–11 (12–3, 5–11 winter)
**Draught Bass; Welsh Brewers
Hancock's HB** Ⓗ; guest beers
Recently refurbished, friendly
village local. Patio with valley
views; live music; restaurant
planned. No food Sun, or
Mon/Tue eves. ❀ Ⓓ ♣ P

Kenfig

Prince of Wales

Ton Kenfig (off B4283)
☎ (0656) 740356
11.30–4, 6–11
**Draught Bass; Felinfoel
Double Dragon; Marston's
Pedigree; Wadworth 6X** Ⓖ;
**Welsh Brewers Worthington
BB** Ⓗ
Old pub with exposed stone
walls: a large main bar and
two smaller rooms. Linked
with historic Kenfig which lies
buried under sand dunes. Beer
range varies; good cooking.
🏛 Q ❀ Ⓓ ♿ ♠ ▲ ♣ P

Laleston

Laleston Inn

Wind Street (off A473)
☎ (0656) 652946
12–3, 7–11 (may extend)
Draught Bass Ⓖ; **Wadworth
6X; Welsh Brewers
Worthington BB** Ⓗ; **guest
beers**
15th-century free house with
exposed stone walls, beams
and nautical items. Good food.
🏛 Ⓓ ▷ P

Llangeinor

Llangeinor Arms

Off A4093 OS924879
☎ (0656) 870268
12–4, 7–11 (12–11 Sat)
**Draught Bass; Welsh Brewers
Hancock's HB, Worthington
BB** Ⓗ
Isolated hilltop (700 ft) pub
with superb views. Separate
quality restaurant.
🏛 Q 🍴 ❀ Ⓓ ♿ 🅿️ ♠ P

Llangynwyd

Yr Hen Dy
(Old House)

Off A4063 on hilltop OS857887
☎ (0656) 733310
11–11 (11–4, 6.30–11 winter)
**Brains SA; Tetley Bitter;
Whitbread Flowers
Original** Ⓗ
Very old inn dating back to
1147, connected with the Cefn
Ydfa legend. Thatched roof,
beams, inglenook and bags of
atmosphere – a real gem.
🏛 Q ❀ Ⓓ ♿ 🅿️ P

Llanharan

High Corner House

The Square ☎ (0443) 238056
11–11
**Brains SA; Whitbread
Boddingtons Bitter, Castle
Eden Ale, Flowers Original** Ⓗ
Large, plush village pub,
given the Whitbread 'Brewers'
Fayre' refurbishment. ❀ Ⓓ ▷ P

Llantwit Fardre

Crown

Main Road ☎ (0443) 208531
12–2.30, 5–11 (12–11 Fri & Sat)
Brains Bitter, SA Ⓗ
Large village local; plush and
comfortably furnished, but
lacking in character.
Ⓓ ▷ 🅿️ ♠ P

Machen

White Hart

Nant y Ceisiad (100 yds N of
A468) ☎ (0633) 441005
11–4, 6–11
Brains SA Ⓗ; **guest beers**
Rambling pub with extensive
wood panelling, some
salvaged from a luxury liner.
The small restaurant
resembles a ship's cabin.
Enterprising guest list – one or
two mini-festivals every year.
🏛 Q ❀ Ⓓ P

Try also: **Royal Oak** (Welsh
Brewers)

Maesteg

Beethoven's

81 Castle Street
☎ (0656) 738484
11.30–4.30, 6.30–11
**Crown Buckley Best Bitter,
SBB** Ⓗ
Plush and deceptively
spacious local, popular with a
youngish clientele.
Q 🍴 Ⓓ ♿ ♣ ♠

Sawyers Arms

4 Commercial Street
☎ (0656) 734606
11–4, 7–11 (11–11 Fri & Sat)
Brains Dark, Bitter, SA Ⓗ
Town pub with a Victorian
exterior and a comfortable
interior. Sometimes loud live
music on Thu. Ⓓ 🅿️ ♠ 🚬 ♣

Merthyr Tydfil

Tregenna Hotel

Park Terrace (next to
Penydarren Park)
☎ (0685) 723627
12–2.15, 6–11.30
Brains Bitter, SA Ⓗ
Two-star hotel: a small lounge
bar abuts a dining area and
offers good bar meals. Well
situated for the Brecon
Beacons. Q 🛏 Ⓓ ▷ 🚬 P

Mwyndy

Barn

100 yds E of A4119
☎ (0443) 222333
11.30–2.30, 5.30–11
**Felinfoel Double Dragon;
Welsh Brewers Hancock's
HB; Wadworth 6X** Ⓗ; **guest
beers**
Conversion of an old barn,
with two contrasting bars and
an upstairs restaurant. Beams,
stone walls and agricultural
artefacts. No bar meals Sun.
🏛 Q 🍴 ❀ Ⓓ P

Castell Mynach

Llantrisant Road (A4119, 800
yds N of M4 jct 34)
☎ (0443) 222298
11–11
**Draught Bass; Welsh Brewers
Hancock's HB, Worthington
BB** Ⓗ
Ever-popular meeting, eating
and drinking house. Eve
meals Wed–Sat 5.30–8; no
food Sun. Q ❀ Ⓓ P

Nantgarw

Cross Keys

Cardiff Road ☎ (0443) 843262
11–11
Brains Bitter Ⓗ; **guest beer**
Comfortable, open-plan house
with a small dining area.
Serves both as a lunchtime
business retreat and an
evening local. ❀ Ⓓ ♣ P

Newton

Globe

Bridgend Road
☎ (0656) 783535
11–11 (11.30–3.30, 5.30–11 Mon–Thu
in winter)
**Draught Bass; Welsh Brewers
Worthington BB** Ⓗ
Welcoming local with
excellent provision for
families. No catering Thu.
🏛 🍴 ❀ Ⓓ 🅿️ ▲ ♣ P

Jolly Sailor

Church Street (off A4106)
☎ (0656) 782403
11.30–11
Brains Dark, Bitter, SA Ⓗ
Village green pub full of
character. The bar has a
nautical flavour; comfortable
lounge. 🏛 ❀ 🅿️ ♣

Ogmore

Pelican

Ewenny Road (B4524, opp.
castle) ☎ (0656) 880049
11.30–4, 6.30–11 (11.30–11 Fri & Sat;
12–3, 7.30–10.30 Sun)
**Brains SA; Courage Best
Bitter; John Smith's Bitter;
Wadworth 6X** Ⓗ
Smart, comfortable country
pub with a restaurant.
❀ Ⓓ ♿ ▲ ♣ P

Mid Glamorgan

Pen-y-Cae

Ty'r Isha
Off A4061, Bridgend side of
M4 services OS903827
11.30–4, 6–11 (11–11 Sat)
**Draught Bass; Welsh Brewers
Hancock's HB** H
Popular, converted 15th-
century farmhouse, previously
a courthouse. ♨ ❀ ◖ ♦ ⅃
≠ (Sarn Hill) ♣ P

Pen-y-Fai

Pheasant
Heol-yr-Eglwys (off A4063)
11.30–4, 6–11 (11–11 Fri & Sat)
**Brains Dark; Courage Best
Bitter; Ruddles Best Bitter,
County; S&N Theakston Best
Bitter** H
Large village pub with a
luxurious lounge. Eve meals
Thu–Sat. Beer range may vary.
Q ▨ ❀ ◖ ◗ ♦ P

Pont-Rhyd-y-cyff

Railway Inn
Station Road
☎ (0656) 732188
11.30–4, 6.30–11 (12–2, 7–10.30 Sun)
**Brains SA; Courage Best
Bitter** H
Unspoilt, traditional valleys
village pub. Q ▨ ❀ ⅃ ♦

Pontyclun

Bute Arms
Llantrisant Road
12–3.30, 6.30–11
**Brains Bitter; Ind Coope
Burton Ale; Tetley Bitter** H
Corner pub, popular with a
young clientele. ◖ ≠ ♣

Pontypridd

Bunch of Grapes
Ynysangharad Road (off
A4054) ☎ (0443) 402934
11–11
**Brains Bitter, SA; Welsh
Brewers Hancock's HB** H;
guest beer
Comfortable pub with a suntrap patio and a restaurant
dominated by the famous
vine. ▨ ❀ ◖ ♦ P

Globe
High Street, Graig (400 yds
uphill from the station)
Brains Bitter H; guest beers
Free house with a warm
musical welcome! ⅃ ≠

Llanover Arms
Bridge Street (at A470
Ynysybwl jct)
☎ (0443) 403215
11–11
**Brains Dark, Bitter, SA;
Wadworth 6X** H
Bustling town pub with three
small bars. ❀ ◖ ≠ ♣ P

Porth

Lodge
Eirw Road ☎ (0443) 685393
11–11
Brains Bitter, SA ; guest beer
Comfortable roadside house
convenient for Rhondda
Heritage Centre. ❀ ◖ ⅃ ♦ P

Porthcawl

Lorelei Hotel
Esplanade Avenue
☎ (0656) 782683
12–3, 6–11
Beer range varies G
Traditionally-built Victorian
hotel near the seafront. Smart,
comfortable lounge bar,
separate restaurant and
function room. ♨ ◖ ♦ ⚲

Rock Hotel
98 John Street (opp. police
station) ☎ (0656) 782340
11–11
**Draught Bass; Welsh Brewers
Worthington BB** H
Town pub with a basic bar
and a comfortable lounge.
Meals of generous proportions
(book for Sun lunch). No
meals Sun eve.
♨ ❀ ◖ ◗ ⅃ ◗ ♣

Quakers Yard

Glan Taff Inn
Cardiff Road
☎ (0443) 410822
11–11
**Courage Best Bitter,
Directors; John Smith's
Bitter** H; guest beer
Comfortable, popular inn. The
beer range may change. Book
for Sun lunch. ❀ ◖ ◗ ≠ P

Rhymney

Farmers Arms
Off B4257 ☎ (0685) 840257
12–5, 7–11 (12–11 Fri & Sat)
Brains Bitter H
Basic local; no food Sun.
❀ ◖ ⅃ ≠ ♣ P

Taffs Well

Taffs Well Inn
Cardiff Road ☎ (0222) 810324
11–11
**Ind Coope Burton Ale; Tetley
Bitter** H
Open-plan pub with quiet
corners. Uncommon cigarette
card collections. No food Sun.
Q ❀ ◖ ◗ ≠ P

Tondu

Llynfi Arms
Maesteg Road
☎ (0656) 720010
12–4, 6.30–11
**Brains Dark, Bitter; Welsh
Brewers Worthington BB** H

Roadside pub with
comfortable lounge and lively
public bars. Lunch Sat only;
eve meals Thu–Sat. ◗ ⅃ ♣

Treforest

Otley Arms
Forest Road ☎ (0443) 402033
11–11
**Brains Dark, SA; Crown
Buckley SBB; Welsh Brewers
Hancock's HB** H; guest beer
Bustling suburban pub,
popular with students and
locals. ◖ ◗ ⅃ ♣ P

Tyle Garw

Boars Head
Coed Cae Lane (½ mile off
A473) ☎ (0443) 225400
11.30–4, 6–11
Draught Bass H; guest beer
Small, simply furnished,
unspoilt local. Forest walks
opposite. Q ❀ ⅃ ♣

Ynyswen

Crown Hotel
Ynyswen Road (A4061)
11–11 (may close afternoons)
**Draught Bass; Brains SA;
Courage Best Bitter** H;
Felinfoel Double Dragon G;
**Whitbread Flowers Original;
Welsh Brewers Worthington
BB** H
Compact but comfortable pub.
Bar features a red telephone
box. ♨ ⅃ ≠ ♣

Ynysybwl

Roberttown Hotel
Robert Street
☎ (0443) 791574
12–4, 6–11 (12–11 Fri & Sat)
Brains Bitter, SA H
Valley local with a cavernous
bar and a comfortable lounge.
Lunch Sun only. ⅃ ♣ P

Ystrad

Greenfield
William Street
☎ (0443) 435953
12–5, 7–11
**Draught Bass; Welsh Brewers
Hancock's HB** H
Comfortable pub, extended
into a neighbouring terraced
house. Q ▨ ❀ ◖ ◗ ⅃
≠ (Ystrad Rhondda)

Ystrad Mynach

Olde Royal Oak
Commercial Street
11–11
**Draught Bass; Welsh Brewers
Hancock's HB** H
Unmistakable 'Brewers Tudor'
pub. Popular food (not served
Sun). Q ◖ ◗ ⅃ ≠ P

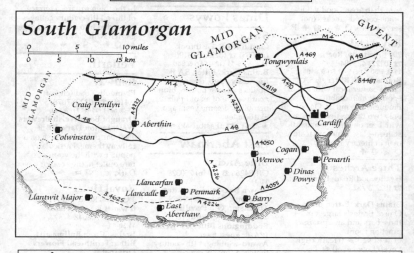

South Glamorgan

MID GLAMORGAN · GWENT

Tongwynlais · Craig Penllyn · *Aberthin* · Colwinston · Cardiff · Cogan · Wenvoe · Penarth · Dinas Powys · Llancarfan · Llancadle · Penmark · Llantwit Major · Barry · East Aberthaw

---

 Brains, Bullmastiff, *Cardiff*

Aberthin

Hare & Hounds
On A4222 ☎ (0446) 774892
11.30–11
Draught Bass G**; Welsh Brewers Hancock's HB** H**, Worthington BB** G
Excellent, traditional village local of character. Limited parking. Q ♿ ❀ ◑ ☕ ♣ P

Barry

Bindles
The Knap ☎ (0446) 734371
11–11
Brains SA; Bullmastiff Best Bitter; Welsh Brewers Hancock's HB H**; guest beers** (summer)
Superbly sited at the quieter end of Barry's shoreline, a lounge bar created from the gutted remains of a noted ballroom. Families welcome until 5.30. ♿ ❀ ◑ ⇌ P

Glenbrook Inn
Dobbins Road, Cadoxton (off A4231) ☎ (0446) 747808
11.30–3.30, 6–11 (11.30–11 Fri & Sat)
Brains Dark, Bitter, SA H**; guest beers**
Large, comfortable suburban pub about ten years old. Climb into the giant's chair in the lounge. Large selection of malt whiskies. ❀ ◑ ☕ ♣ P

Cardiff

Black Lion
High Street, Llandaff
11–3, 5–11 (11–11 Fri & Sat; 12–2.40, 7–10.30 Sun)
Brains Dark, Bitter, SA H

Typical Brains town pub: a large, comfortable lounge and a traditional bar. Very popular with locals. Children welcome in the lounge at lunchtime. No lunches Sun or eve meals Tue.
Q ◑ ◗ ☕ ♣

Fox & Hounds
Chapel Row, St Mellons (off B4487) ☎ (0222) 777046
11–11
Brains Dark, Bitter, SA H
Pub where part of the large lounge converts into a dining room to serve award-winning lunches. Q ❀ ◑ ☕ ♣ P

Golden Cross
283 Hayes Bridge Road (opp. ice rink) ☎ (0222) 394556
12–3, 5–11 (11–11 Sat; closed Sun lunch)
Brains Dark, Bitter, SA H
Wonderfully preserved, but easily overlooked pub tucked behind the Holiday Inn. Beautiful tiled pictures of old Cardiff in the bar and entrance. Q ◑ ⇌ (Central) ♣

Kiwis
Wyndham Arcade, St Mary Street ☎ (0222) 229876
12–2am (closed Sun lunch)
Beer range varies H
Pub accessed via an arcade (admission charge after 10pm Thu–Sat). Three cask ales and some 60 bottled beers from around the globe.
◑ ⇌ (Central)

Millers Mate
Thornhill Road, Thornhill (A469) ☎ (0222) 626794
11–3, 5.30–11 (11–11 Sat)
Banks's Mild, Bitter H
Old farmhouse converted to a

pub, surrounded by a new housing estate. ❀ ◑ ☕ ♣ P

Old Arcade
Church Street ☎ (0222) 231740
11–11 (closed Sun lunch; 7–10.30 alternate Sun eves)
Brains Dark, Bitter, SA H
Famous watering hole located in a pedestrian precinct next to the central market. Basic bar; the lounge is open Fri and Sat nights only and is used for weekday lunches. ◑ ☕ ⇌ (Queen St/Central) ♣

Old Cottage
Cherry Orchard Road, Lisvane ☎ (0222) 747582
11.30–3, 5.30–11 (11.30–11 Wed–Sat)
Ansells Bitter; Ind Coope Burton Ale; Tetley Bitter H
Converted 200-year-old farmhouse in a semi-rural area. Good food (not served Sun eve). ❀ ◑ ❀ ⇌ (Lisvane & Thornhill) P

Park Vaults
Park Lane (off Queen St) ☎ (0222) 383471
11–11
Brains Dark; Courage Best Bitter, Directors H**; guest beers**
Popular spit-and-sawdust bar reached by a side entrance to a four-star hotel. Imaginative guest beers. Eve meals 5.30–7. 🛏 ◑ ◗ ♿ ⇌ (Queen St)

Quarry House
St Fagans Rise, Fairwater ☎ (0222) 565577
11–3, 6–11 (11–11 Sat; 12–2, 7–10.30 Sun)
Courage Best Bitter, Directors H
Converted manor house in a

353

South Glamorgan

suburban area. Good value home-cooked lunches (not served Sun). Q ✿ ⬤ ⬤ ♣ P

Royal Oak
200 Broadway, Roath
☎ (0222) 473984
11–3, 5.30–11 (11–11 Fri & Sat)
Brains Dark, Bitter Ⓗ**, SA** Ⓖ
Large corner local with lots of sporting memorabilia. Frequent live music. One of only two Brains tied houses with beer on gravity. Splendid stained-glass windows feature men of literary renown.
Q ✿ ⬤ ♣

Three Arches
Heathwood Road, Llanishen
☎ (0222) 752395
11–11
Brains Dark, Bitter, SA Ⓗ
One of Brains's largest pubs: three bars and an upstairs function room.
Q ✿ ⬤ ⬤ ⇌ (Heath High Level/Low Level) ♣ P

Try also: Maltsters Arms, Llandaff; **Rompney Castle,** Wentloog Rd; **Wharf,** Schooner Way (all Brains)

Cogan

Cogan
Pill Street ☎ (0222) 704280
12–11
Crown Buckley Best Bitter; Welsh Brewers Hancock's HB Ⓗ
Classic suburban local, the public bar is inhabited by a loud parrot! Separate lounge.
✿ ⬤ ⬤ ⇌ ♣

Colwinston

Sycamore Tree
Off A48 ☎ (0656) 652827
11–3, 5.30–11 (may vary)
Beer range varies Ⓗ
Welcoming village pub offering three guest beers (five in summer). Good home-cooked meals (not served Sun eve). Opening hours (and meal times) are longer in season. Live music (folk based) on Fri.
🏠 Q ⛵ ✿ ⬤ ▶ ⚓ ♣ P

Craig Penllyn

Barley Mow
Off A48 OS978773
☎ (0446) 772558
12–3.30 (not Mon), 6.30–11
Draught Bass; Welsh Brewers Hancock's HB, Worthington BB Ⓗ**; guest beers**
Regular guest beers and excellent value food make this friendly pub well worth finding. Three cosy rooms and a restaurant, served from a central bar. A popular family destination. No eve meals Sun.
🏠 Q ⛵ ✿ ⬤ ▶ ♣ P

Dinas Powys

Swan
Cardiff Road, Eastbrook (A4055) ☎ (0222) 513106
12–3.30, 6–11 (12–11 Fri & Sat)
Brains Dark, Bitter, SA Ⓗ
Impressive pub, one of Brains's newest houses, built near the site of an old pub demolished some years ago. Skittle alley.
✿ ⬤ ⬤ ⇌ (Eastbrook) ♣ P

East Aberthaw

Blue Anchor
Off B4265 ☎ (0446) 750329
11–11
Crown Buckley Best Bitter; Marston's Pedigree; S&N Theakston Old Peculier; Wadworth 6X; Whitbread Boddingtons Bitter, Flowers IPA Ⓗ**; guest beer**
Award-winning, 14th-century thatched inn: six inter-connecting rooms around a central bar. Beware low oak beams and narrow gangways. Excellent pub food; separate restaurant.
🏠 Q ⛵ ✿ ⬤ ▶ ⚓ ♣ P

Llancadle

Green Dragon
Off B4265 ☎ (0446) 750367
11–11
Bullmastiff Ebony Dark, Best Bitter, Son of a Bitch; Welsh Brewers Hancock's HB Ⓗ**; guest beer**
Thatched village pub, popular with locals and visitors. Three rooms, two without a bar; children welcome in the back lounge. No food Mon. Bullmastiff beers, including a house beer (a dry hopped version of bitter), on rotation. Happy hour 4–6. One of few regular Bullmastiff outlets.
🏠 Q ✿ ⬤ ▶ P

Llancarfan

Fox & Hounds
3 miles off A48 at Bonvilston OS052703 ☎ (0446) 781297
11–3.30, 6.30–11 (11–11 Sat)
Brains Bitter; Ruddles Best Bitter; Wye Valley Hereford Supreme Ⓗ**; guest beers**
1991 S Glamorgan CAMRA *Pub of the Year*: a 16th-century village inn, popular at all times, serving good food. High quality restaurant. No food Sun eve.
🏠 Q ⛵ ✿ ⬤ ▶ P

Llantwit Major

Old White Hart
Wine Street ☎ (0446) 793549
11.30–11
Draught Bass; Welsh Brewers Worthington BB Ⓗ

In the town square, a terrace of three 14th-century cottages converted into two bars. Large garden with play area.
🏠 Q ✿ ⬤ ⚓ ♣

Penarth

Railway
Plymouth Road (end of A4160) ☎ (0222) 707873
11–3, 5–11 (11–11 Fri & Sat)
Draught Bass; Welsh Brewers Worthington Dark, BB Ⓗ
Two-bar pub very much on a railway theme. Particularly popular with the young. A rare outlet in the area for Dark. ✿ ⬤ ⬤ ⇌ ♣

Royal Hotel
1 Queens Road (off A4160 towards Penarth Head)
☎ (0222) 708048
11.30–11
Brains Bitter; Bullmastiff Bitter; Whitbread Flowers Original Ⓗ
Pub boasting the cheapest beers in the area. Newly-opened upstairs restaurant and accommodation. Bar/basket meals available until 10.30. Occasional noisy disco.
🛏 ⬤ ▶ ⇌ (Dingle Rd) ♣ ⟳

Try also: Golden Lion, Glebe St (Welsh Brewers)

Penmark

Six Bells
☎ (0446) 710229
12–11
Welsh Brewers Hancock's HB Ⓗ
Friendly, traditional country pub: a public bar with an adjoining darts area and a separate lounge. Much Hancock's memorabilia in the bar. The 1966–69 publican wrote a book featuring the pub. 🏠 Q ✿ ⬤ ▶ ⚓ ♣ P

Tongwynlais

Lewis Arms
Mill Road ☎ (0222) 810330
11–3.30, 5.30–11
Brains Dark, Bitter, SA Ⓗ
Friendly locals' pub named after Col. Henry Lewis whose picture hangs in the lounge. Near Castell Coch. No food Sun. Q ⬤ ⬤ ♣ P

Wenvoe

Wenvoe Arms
Old Port Road (off A4050)
☎ (0222) 591129
11.30–3.30, 5.30–11 (11–11 Fri & Sat)
Brains Dark, Bitter, SA Ⓗ
Comfortable village pub. The upstairs lounge has been converted to a restaurant. No food Sun lunch. Families welcome in summer.
🏠 Q ⛵ ✿ ⬤ ▶ ⬤ ⚓ ♣ P

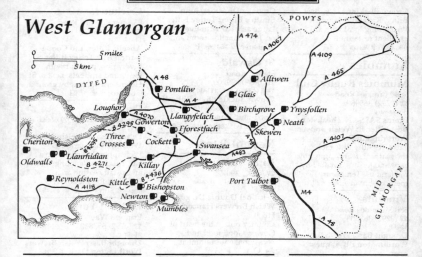

West Glamorgan

POWYS

DYFED

MID GLAMORGAN

Alltwen

Butchers Arms
Alltwen Mill ☎ (0792) 863100
12–3, 6.30–11
**Courage Directors; Everards
Old Original; John Smith's
Bitter; Wadworth 6X** Ⓗ**; guest
beer**
Comfortable free house with
excellent bar meals. The
restaurant overlooks the
Swansea valley. Selection of
whiskies. ♨ Q ❀ ◖ ▶ P

Try also: Pen-yr-allt (Free)

Birchgrove

Bowens Arms
Birchgrove Road (200 yds
from M4 jct 44)
☎ (0792) 812321
12–3, 6–11 (11–11 Fri & Sat)
**Courage Best Bitter,
Directors; Wadworth 6X** Ⓗ
Locals' pub. Good selection of
food. ♨ ❀ ◖ ▣ P

Bishopston

Joiners Arms
50 Bishopston Road (off
B4436) ☎ (044 128) 2658
11–11
**Courage Best Bitter; John
Smith's Bitter** Ⓗ**; guest beers**
Attractive, popular village
pub. ❀ ◖ ♣ P

Cheriton

Britannia
Llanmadoc Road OS450930
12–3.30, 7–11
**Marston's Pedigree; Welsh
Brewers Hancock's HB** Ⓗ**;
guest beers** (summer)
A necessary halfway watering
hole on the annual Round
Gower Bike Ride. Q ❀ P

Cockett

Cockett Inn
Waunarlwydd Road
11.30–3.30, 5.30–10.30 (11–11
Thu–Sat)
**Crown Buckley Dark, Best
Bitter** Ⓗ
Large locals' bar and a com-
fortable lounge. ❀ ◖ ▣ ♣ P

Fforestfach

Star Inn
1070 Carmarthen Road
11.30–3.30, 5.30–11
**Crown Buckley Dark, Best
Bitter** Ⓔ
Popular local serving a nearby
industrial estate. Lunchtime
bar snacks. ▣ ♣ P

Glais

Old Glais
On B4291 ☎ (0792) 843316
12–4, 6–11
**Ruddles Best Bitter, County;
Webster's Yorkshire Bitter** Ⓗ
Friendly village pub near
Mond works. ♨ Q ❀ ◖ ▣ P

Gowerton

Berthlwydd
☎ (0792) 873454
12–3.30, 6–11
**Courage Directors; Felinfoel
Double Dragon** Ⓗ**; guest
beers**
Renovated, extended free
house overlooking the
Loughor Estuary. Excellent
meals. ❀ ◖ ▶ P

Welcome to Gower
Mount Street ☎ (0792) 872611
11.30–3.30, 5.30–11 (11.30–11
summer)
**Crown Buckley Dark, Best
Bitter, Reverend James** Ⓗ
Comfortable pub. ◖ ⇌ P

Killay

Railway Inn
Gower Road ☎ (0792) 203946
11.30–3.30, 5.30–11
**Draught Bass; Welsh Brewers
Worthington Dark,
Hancock's HB** Ⓗ**; guest beer**
Pub near an old railway,
convenient for Clyne Valley
Walk. ❀ ◖ ▣ ♣ P

Kittle

Beaufort Arms
18 Pennard Road
12–4, 6.30–11 (may vary)
**Crown Buckley Dark, Best
Bitter, Reverend James** Ⓗ
Pleasant country pub offering
good food and occasional live
entertainment. ❀ ◖ ▶ ▣ ♣ P

Llangyfelach

Plough & Harrow
Llangyfelach Road
11.30–4, 6–11
**Courage Best Bitter,
Directors; John Smith's
Bitter** Ⓗ
Large, comfortable pub
overlooking Penllergaer
Woods. ♨ ❀ ◖ ▶ ♣ P

Llanrhidian

Welcome to Town
Off B4295 ☎ (0792) 390015
12–3, 6–11
Younger IPA Ⓗ
Pleasant pub opposite the
village green, overlooking the
estuary. Q ❀ ◖ ▶

Loughor

Reverend James
180 Borough Road (just off
A484) ☎ (0792) 892943
11.30–11

West Glamorgan

Crown Buckley Dark, Best
Bitter, Reverend James Ⓗ
Welcoming local with an
excellent restaurant.
🏠 ❀ ◑ ▶ ⊞ & P

Mumbles

Mumbles Rugby Club
588 Mumbles Road
☎ (0792) 368989
Hours vary
Brains SA; S&N Theakston
Best Bitter Ⓗ; Welsh Brewers
Worthington Dark Ⓔ
Cosy, friendly little club on
the seafront, featuring rugby
caps and jerseys donated by
the famous. Temporary
membership available.

Vincents
580 Mumbles Road
☎ (0792) 368308
12–11
Draught Bass; Welsh Brewers
Worthington BB Ⓗ; guest
beer
Based loosely on a Spanish
bar. The guest ale comes from
the Felinfoel range – some 35
beers from other regional
independents. ◑

Neath

Greyhound
Water Street ☎ (0639) 637793
11–11
Ruddles County Ⓗ
Comfortable pub serving good
food. ◑ ⇌

Newton

Newton Inn
Newton Road
☎ (0792) 368329
12–4, 6–11 (12–11 Fri & Sat)
Draught Bass; Welsh Brewers
Worthington BB Ⓗ
Comfortable inn. Q ❀ ◑

Oldwalls

Greyhound
On Llanrhidian–Llangennith
road ☎ (0792) 390146
11–11
Draught Bass; Welsh Brewers
Hancock's HB Ⓗ; guest beers
Large popular pub on the
quieter north side of Gower.
Excellent food (seafood).
🏠 Q ☙ ❀ ◑ ▶ ⊞ P

Pontlliw

Castle Inn
On A48 ☎ (0792) 882961
11–4, 6–11
Felinfoel Bitter Ⓗ
Pleasant, rural pub. Q ⊞

Port Talbot

Accolade
Green Park Ind. Est.
☎ (0639) 891467
12–3, 6–11 (12 Thu; 11–11 Fri & Sat)

Courage Directors; John
Smith's Bitter; Tetley Bitter Ⓗ
Large airy bar with live music
on Thu. Function room and
pool area. ◑ ⇌ ♣ P

St Oswalds
Station Road
☎ (0639) 899200
11–3 (4 Thu), 5–11 (11–11 Fri & Sat)
Crown Buckley Best Bitter Ⓗ
Comfortable bar with
restaurant. Lunches and
evening basket meals. ◑ ⇌

Reynoldston

King Arthur Hotel
☎ (0792) 390775
12–3, 6–11 (12–11 Fri & Sat; may
vary)
Felinfoel Double Dragon;
Welsh Brewers Hancock's
HB Ⓗ
Country pub in the heart of
Gower. Good food and
occasional entertainment.
🏠 Q ❀ ◑ ▶ ⊞ P

Skewen

Crown Hotel
216 New Road
11.30–4, 6–11 (may vary)
Brains Dark, MA, SA Ⓗ
Regulars' bar and comfortable
lounge. The only outlet for
MA – a brewery mix of dark
and bitter. Snooker table. ⊞ ♣

Swansea

Adam & Eve
High Street ☎ (0792) 655913
11–4, 5.30–11 (11–11 Fri & Sat)
Brains Dark, Bitter, SA Ⓗ
Traditional three-room pub
with plenty of atmosphere. In
every edition of this guide.
◑ ⊞ ⇌ ♣

Bryn-y-mor Hotel
Bryn-y-mor Road
☎ (0792) 466650
11–3.30, 5.30–11 (11–11 Thu–Sat)
Ansells Mild, Bitter; Ind
Coope Burton Ale; Tetley
Bitter Ⓗ
Side-street public bar with a
games area; comfortable
lounge with live music most
Sun nights. ❀ ◑ ⊞ ♣

Builders
Oxford Street
☎ (0792) 476189
11–3.30, 7–11 (closed Sun)
Crown Buckley Dark, Best
Bitter, Reverend James Ⓗ
Split-level bar offering good
food (book for eve meals). ◑ ▶

Cardiff Arms
The Strand ☎ (0792) 456092
12–11
Ruddles Best Bitter; Welsh
Brewers Worthington Dark Ⓗ
Pulsating all week to live
music, not for the faint
hearted. Excellent blues
session Sat, 2–6 pm. ❀ ⇌

Cricketers
83 King Edward Road
☎ (0792) 466524
11–11
Ansells Bitter; Ind Coope
Burton Ale; Tetley Bitter Ⓗ
Lively pub, popular with
locals and students, next to St
Helens cricket/rugby ground.
Good food. ❀ ◑ ⊞

Duke
Wind Street ☎ (0792) 460604
11–11
Draught Bass; Welsh Brewers
Worthington Dark, BB Ⓗ
Well appointed pub with a
bar, comfortable lounge and
an upstairs eating area.
Excellent food (book), not
served Sun. 🏠 ◑ ⊞ ⇌

Duke of York
Princess Way
☎ (0792) 653830
11–11
Draught Bass; Welsh Brewers
Worthington Dark, BB Ⓗ
Home of 'Ellingtons'
blues/jazz venue: live acts
Tue–Fri. ◑ ⊞ ⇌ ♣

Queens
Gloucester Place
11–11
S&N Theakston Best Bitter,
Old Peculier Ⓗ;
Wadworth 6X Ⓔ
Refurbished single-bar pub on
the edge of the marina. Old
photographs with a nautical
flavour. Live entertainment
Thu. Quiz nights. ❀ 🛏 ◑ ⇌

Rhyddings
Brynmill ☎ (0792) 648885
11–11
Ansells Bitter; Ind Coope
Burton Ale; Tetley Bitter Ⓗ
Spacious bar and lounge near
Singleton Park. ❀ ◑ ⊞

Vivian Arms
Sketty Cross ☎ (0792) 203015
12–11
Brains Dark, Bitter, SA Ⓗ
Solidly comfortable, suburban
mecca with good food. Large
lounge; unusual bar with
wood panelling. ❀ ◑ ⊞

Three Crosses

Joiners Arms
Joiners Road ☎ (0792) 873479
12–4, 6–11 (12–11 Fri & Sat)
Ruddles Best Bitter, County;
Webster's Yorkshire Bitter Ⓗ
Popular village local. ◑ ⊞ ♣

Ynysgollen

Rock & Fountain Inn
On A465 ☎ (0639) 642681
12–3, 6–11 (may vary)
Crown Buckley Best Bitter;
Wadworth 6X Ⓗ; guest beers
Welcoming free house on the
Heads of the Valleys road.
Excellent menu. At least four
real ales. Q ◑ ▶ P

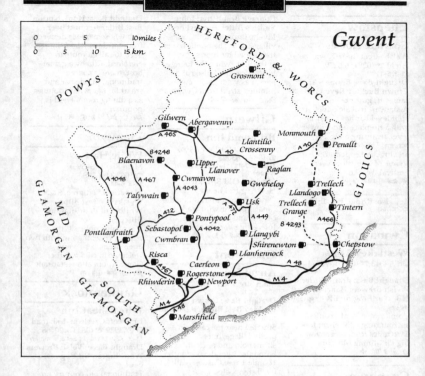

Gwent

Abergavenny

Great Western Hotel

Station Road (off Monmouth Rd, follow signs to BR station)
☎ (0873) 853593
11.30–3, 7–11
Draught Bass; Ruddles Best Bitter H**; guest beer**
A handy refuge for rail travellers: a friendly family-run pub with a bar decorated with pictures of the steam age and railway items. Stylish lounge and separate dining room. Good range of food.
🏥 ✿ 🍴 ◖ ▶ ⊞ ⇌ ♣ P

Hen & Chickens

Flannel Street (off High St)
☎ (0873) 853613
10.30–4, 7–11 (10–11 Tue; 10.30–11 Fri & Sat)
Draught Bass; Welsh Brewers Worthington BB H
Excellent example of an unspoilt town pub, run by a life-long Bass devotee. Cosy bar and snug with ochre coloured walls and wooden floorboards; dining room aptly named the 'Chick's Parlour'. Good food from a limited but well-balanced menu. Q ♣

Somerset Arms

Victoria Street (Merthyr Rd jct) ☎ (0873) 852158
12–3, 7–11

Draught Bass; Welsh Brewers Hancock's HB H**; guest beer**
Smart family-run pub a short stroll from the centre. Tastefully decorated public bar and lounge, the latter popular with diners who enjoy the well-presented food (not served Sun lunch). Also a separate dining/function room. 🏥 Q ✿ ◖ ▶ ⊞ ♣

Try also: Station, Brecon Rd (Free)

Blaenavon

Cambrian Inn

Cambrian Row
☎ (0495) 790327
6–11 (12–11 Sat)
Brains Bitter, SA H
Traditional, well-used local with a separate pool and darts room and a comfortable lounge. Quiz night Thu. ⊞ ♣

Try also: Riflemans Arms, Rifle St (Whitbread)

Caerleon

Hanbury Arms

Uskside ☎ (0633) 420361
12–11
Draught Bass; Brains SA; Welsh Brewers Hancock's HB H
Beautifully situated pub on

the bank of the River Usk. The large garden and play area make it ideal for children. Good range of meals served (no food Sun eve). Close to the site of the Roman remains.
🏥 ✿ 🍴 ◖ ▶ ⊞ ♣ P

Kings Arms

Belmont Hill ☎ (0633) 420329
11.30–2.30, 5.30–11
Draught Bass; Tetley Bitter; Welsh Brewers Worthington BB H
Popular 17th-century inn whose separate restaurant has an excellent reputation. The roaring fire lends to the cosy setting. A children's playground adjoins the large car park. No food Sun.
🏥 ✿ ◖ ▶ ⊞ ♣ P

Tabard Brasserie

9 High Street ☎ (0633) 422822
12–3, 7–11 (closed Sun lunch)
Beer range varies H
Increasingly popular bistro/restaurant with an ever-expanding beer range and a wide variety of high quality meals (not served Sun eve). Small, comfortable bar popular with students. Very committed to real ale and the range usually includes Felinfoel. Q ✿ ◖ ▶ P

Try also: Angel, Goldcroft Common (Welsh Brewers)

Gwent

Chepstow

Coach & Horses
Welsh Street (near Town Arch) ☎ (0291) 622626
11–3, 6–11
Draught Bass; Brains SA; Crown Buckley Reverend James Ⓗ**; guest beers**
A stalwart real ale outlet: its split-level bar has a cosy end with a fireplace and a lower level, featuring a big TV screen. The serving area has an attractive copper top. Venue of Chepstow Beer Festival. Weekday lunches.
❀ ⌷ ◖ ≠ ♣

Try also: **Bridge Inn**, Bridge St (Free)

Cwmavon

Westlakes Arms
On A4043 ☎ (0495) 772571
11–11
Draught Bass; Brains Bitter; Welsh Brewers Hancock's HB, Worthington BB Ⓗ**; guest beers**
Comfortable local in quiet surroundings. Excellent food. Two miles from Blaenavon's Big Pit Mining Museum.
Q ❀ ◖ ⌷ ♣

Cwmbran

Blinkin' Owl
The Oxtens, Henllys Way, Coed Eva ☎ (0633) 484749
11.30–3.30 (4.30 Sat), 5.30 (6.30 Sat)–11
Brains Dark, Bitter, SA Ⓗ
The best Brains for miles in a pub with an award-winning cellar. The large public bar is very friendly despite being a 'local' estate pub; comfortable lounge with a dining area. A long running *Guide* entry. The menu includes take-away meals. Q ❀ ◖ ◗ ♣ P

Bush Inn
Graig Road, Upper Cwmbran (off Upper Cwmbran Rd) ☎ (0633) 483764
11–3, 7 (6 Fri & Sat)–11
Courage Best Bitter Ⓗ**; guest beer**
Popular pub, especially at weekends, with the most comfortable seats in town. If the landlady's teapot collection doesn't amuse you, the over-friendly Rottweiler will! A 'fun' pub in the proper sense of the word. Weekly discos. Home-made curries a speciality. Food Mon–Thu (book). ⌷ ❀ ◖ ◗ ♣ P

Rose & Crown
Victoria Street ☎ (0633) 866700
11–11

Courage Best Bitter; John Smith's Bitter Ⓗ**; guest beer**
Lively, unpretentious locals' village pub. The public bar is frequented by sports enthusiasts while the lounge hosts occasional disco and karaoke evenings. A few minutes' stroll from Cwmbran Stadium. ❀ ⌷ ♣ P

Gilwern

Bridgend Inn
Main Road (just off A465) ☎ (0873) 830939
11.30–5, 7–11 (11–11 Fri & Sat in summer)
Morland Old Speckled Hen Ⓗ**; guest beers**
Olde-worlde pub right on the canal. Popular with walkers, cavers, and canal people. Interesting variety of guest beers. ❀ ⌷ ◖ ▲ ♣ ✦

Grosmont

Angel Inn
Main Street ☎ (0981) 240646
12–3, 7–11
Draught Bass; Crown Buckley Best Bitter, Reverend James Ⓗ
Situated near the castle in a pretty village, once a border stronghold and ancient borough. A good base for the 18-mile Three Castles Walk (well signposted).
⌷ ❀ ⌷ ◖ ◗ ♣

Gwehelog

Hall Inn
Old Raglan Road (3 miles off Usk–A449 road)
☎ (029 13) 2381
12–3 (not Mon), 6–11
Ansells Bitter; Tetley Bitter Ⓗ
Stone-built country inn which doubles as a polling station. Refurbished after a fire a few years ago. Pleasing to both the eye and tastebuds. Small public bar; lounge popular with diners, especially at weekends. Advisable to book meals. ⌷ ❀ ◖ ◗ ♣ P

Llandogo

Old Farmhouse Inn
Off A466 behind filling station ☎ (0594) 530095
12–2, 7–11 (11–11 Sat & summer)
Draught Bass; Hook Norton Best Bitter Ⓗ**; guest beer**
Situated in the heart of an outdoor pursuits area, this former motel is a fine old building which has become a comfortable inn. Boasts its own filling station. Extensive range of food.
⌷ ❀ ⌷ ◖ ◗ ♣ P

Sloop Inn
On A466 ☎ (0594) 530291
11–3, 5–11 (11–11 Fri & Sat)

Draught Bass; Hook Norton Best Bitter Ⓗ**; guest beer**
Pub whose name is derived from the days when sloops used to call en route to Hereford. Run by a genial host, there is a large traditional public bar and a smart lounge which doubles as a dining room. Food is popular.
⌷ ❀ ⌷ ⌷ ◖ ♣ P

Llangybi

White Hart
Main Road (B4596) ☎ (063 349) 258
11–3, 6–11
Marston's Pedigree; S&N Theakston Best Bitter; Whitbread Boddingtons Bitter Ⓗ
Hospitable pub: a 12th-century coaching inn with two open fireplaces – very welcome in cold weather. Games room and restaurant.
⌷ ❀ ⌷ ◖ ♣ P

Llanhennock

Wheatsheaf Inn
1 mile off Caerleon–Usk road OS353929 ☎ (0633) 420468
11–3, 5.30–11 (11–11 Sat & summer)
Draught Bass; Welsh Brewers Worthington BB Ⓗ**; guest beer**
Traditional old country inn with a pleasant beer garden where chickens and ducks provide entertainment. Cricket and French boules in summer. Try the doorstep sandwiches.
⌷ Q ❀ ◖ ♣ P

Llantilio Crossenny

Hostry Inn
On B4233 between Monmouth and Abergavenny ☎ (060 085) 278
12–3, 6.30–11
Wye Valley Hereford Bitter, Hereford Supreme Ⓗ**; guest beers**
Distinctive, 15th-century village pub with a large hall. Fortnightly folk music on Thu, and rock music alternate Fri. Good range of food, including vegetarian. Gwent CAMRA *Pub of the Year* 1991.
❀ ⌷ ◖ ◗ ⌷ ▲ ♣ P

Marshfield

Port O'Call
Marshfield Road (2 miles S of A48, by railway line)
☎ (0633) 680171
12–3, 5.30–11 (11–11 Sat)
Courage Best Bitter Ⓗ**; guest beer**
Country pub with a comfortable public bar and

lounge. The latter comprises three areas on different levels.
❀ ◖ ▶ ⊟ ♣ P

Try also: Masons Arms (Ansells)

Monmouth

Green Dragon Inn
St Thomas Square
☎ (0600) 712561
11–11
Draught Bass; Marston's Pedigree; Welsh Brewers Hancock's HB Ⓗ
Close to the town's fortified bridge, a traditional style pub with a distinctive front bearing a green dragon emblem, also featured in the windows. Comfortably furnished, attracting a good mix of clientele. Very good value lunches. ◖ ⊟ ♣

Punch House
Agincourt Square
☎ (0600) 713855
11–3, 5–11 (11–11 Fri & Sat)
Draught Bass; Wadworth 6X; Welsh Brewers Hancock's HB, Worthington BB Ⓗ
Famous inn with a large comfortable bar displaying naval and rural memorabilia, and an old bound set of *Punch* volumes. Beautiful hanging baskets adorn the outside in summer. Excellent home-produced fare. Q ❀ ◖ ▶

Newport

Black Horse
Somerton Road, Liswerry
☎ (0633) 273058
11.30–3, 7–11
Ansells Bitter; Crown Buckley Best Bitter; Tetley Bitter Ⓗ
Large, popular pub with two distinct drinking areas, two miles from the town centre. Beer garden with children's playthings. Good reputation for meals (no food Sun eve).
❀ ◖ ▶ ♣ P

Hornblower
126 Commercial Street
☎ (0633) 267575
11.30–11 (11–11 Sat)
Ansells Bitter; Ind Coope Burton Ale Ⓗ**; guest beer**
Classic example of a bikers' pub, loud and lively with a friendly atmosphere. Walls are covered with bike rally info and photographs. An American Union flag hangs from the rafters. Frequent live music, otherwise jukebox on constantly. ⊟ ≠

Ivy Bush
65 Clarence Place (near Cenotaph)
☎ (0633) 267571
11–11
John Smith's Bitter Ⓗ

Traditional locals' pub on the fringe of the town centre. The recently extended public bar, geared for darts and pool, boasts an impressive trophy collection. The lounge hosts regular live music. Convenient for Newport RFC and local restaurants. No food Sun.
❀ ⊟ ◖ ⊟ ≠ ♣

Lamb
6 Bridge Street
☎ (0633) 266801
11–11
Courage Best Bitter, Directors; John Smith's Bitter Ⓗ
Good town boozer, popular with all. Long solid bar with smart matching gantry. Pictures of local scenes hang on the walls. Handily placed for town centre amenities. ≠

Queens Hotel
Bridge Street
☎ (0633) 262992
11–11 (Tudor Bar); 12–2.30, 7–11 (Queens Bar)
Draught Bass Ⓗ**; Brains Dark, Bitter, SA** Ⓔ
Large, two-bar hotel in the town centre. The spacious Queens Bar is very popular with the younger element and can be extremely crowded at weekends. The comfortable Tudor Bar offers quieter surroundings. Separate restaurant. Firm commitment to real ale. ❀ ◖ ▶ ≠ ≠ ♣

St Julians
Caerleon Road
☎ (0633) 258663
11.30–11
Brains Dark; Courage Best Bitter; John Smith's Bitter; Ruddles Best Bitter; Wadworth 6X Ⓗ**; guest beer**
Welcoming hostelry on the main road from Newport to the Roman village of Caerleon, on the River Usk. (The balcony bar offers fine views of the river.) The wood panelling in the lounge was rescued from the ocean liner *Doric*. No food Sat eve or Sun.
⊟ ❀ ◖ ▶ ⊟ ♣ P

Penallt

Boat Inn
Lone Lane (off A466, access by footbridge from Redbrook)
☎ (0600) 712615
11–3, 6–11
Draught Bass; Greene King Abbot; Hook Norton Old Hooky; S&N Theakston Best Bitter, Old Peculier; Wadworth 6X Ⓖ**; guest beers**
Standing in the shadow of an old railway bridge, the banks of the River Wye provide a scenic backdrop for this superb little pub. Beers are served direct from the stillage visible from the bar. Regular

jazz and folk nights; tasty food. Cider in summer.
⊟ ⊱ ❀ ◖ ▶ ♣ ⊂ P

Pontllanfraith

Crown Inn
On roundabout linking A472 and A4049
☎ (0495) 223404
12–3, 5–11 (12–11 Fri & Sat)
Courage Best Bitter; Felinfoel Double Dragon; John Smith's Bitter Ⓗ
Situated on a large roundabout system, this popular pub often doubles as the 19th hole for local golfers. The lounge offers diners a wide range of dishes. Good outdoor playing facilities for children. ❀ ◖ ▶ ♣ P ⊬

Pontypool

Prince of Wales
Prince of Wales Terrace, Lower Cwmynyscoy
☎ (0495) 756737
11.30–4, 6–11
John Smith's Bitter Ⓗ**; guest beers**
Overlooking an old railway viaduct, a pleasant old pub noted for its warmth and hospitality. The cosy bar is a popular venue for rugby-goers to nearby Pontypool Park. Occasional live music; guest beers at weekends.
⊟ ❀ ◖ ▶ P

Raglan

Ship Inn
High Street
☎ (0291) 690635
11–3, 5.30–11 (11–11 Sat)
Draught Bass Ⓗ**; guest beer**
Old country town coaching inn with lots of character, a half-mile from Raglan Castle. Separate dining area.
⊟ Q ❀ ◖ ▶ ⊟ ♣

Rhiwderin

Rhiwderin Inn
Caerphilly Road
☎ (0633) 893234
12–3, 5.30 (5 Fri)–11 (12–11 Sat)
Draught Bass; Brains Dark; Welsh Brewers Hancock's HB Ⓗ
Smart roadside inn with a small public bar, a plushly furnished lounge and an adjacent conservatory. Good food. ❀ ◖ ▶ ⊟ ♣ P

Risca

Exchange Inn
52 St Mary Street
☎ (0633) 612706
12–5, 6.30–11
Crown Buckley Best Bitter, SBB, Reverend James Ⓗ

Gwent

Pleasant traditional local enjoying a new lease of life since becoming a free house. The front has been given a smart face-lift which gives way to a neat public bar and a comfortably furnished lounge. Reasonably priced lunches.
❀ ◖ 🍴 ♣ P

Rogerstone

Tredegar Arms
Cefn Road
☎ (0633) 893417
12–3, 6–11 (12–2, 7–10.30 Sun)
Brains Dark; Courage Best Bitter, Directors Ⓗ**; guest beer**
Traditional local with a pleasant public bar and an open-plan lounge, giving an impression of separate areas. The menu offers a number of adventurous dishes.
❀ ◖ 🍴 🍺 ♣ P

Sebastopol

Open Hearth
Wern Road (off B4244)
☎ (0495) 763752
11.30–3, 6–11
Draught Bass; Courage Best Bitter Ⓗ**; guest beers**
Very popular canalside pub complete with an adopted waddle of ducks. Tricky to find – ask any local. The large range of guest ales – competitively priced – usually includes Welsh independents. Good value and varied range of food. 🏚 ❀ ◖ 🍴 ♣ P

Shirenewton

Carpenters Arms
On B4235 Usk–Chepstow Road, N of village
☎ (029 17) 231
11–2.30, 7–11
Courage Best Bitter; Hook Norton Best Bitter; Marston's Pedigree, Owd Rodger; Ruddles County; Wadworth 6X Ⓗ**; guest beer**
Lovely country pub of deceptive size. Seven varied rooms feature items like a chamber pot collection and bellows from a smithy which became part of the pub. The

menu includes tasty, home-made local dishes.
🏚 Q ❀ ◖ 🍴 🍺 🅰 P

Talywain

Globe Inn
Commercial Road
(Abersychan–Varteg road)
☎ (0495) 772053
6–11 (11–11 Sat)
Brains Bitter; Crown Buckley Best Bitter Ⓗ**; guest beer**
Typical valley pub; friendly and busy. Separate pool room; Sun night quiz. 🏚 🍺 ♣

Tintern

Cherry Tree
Devauden Road (off A466)
☎ (0291) 689292
11–3, 6–11
Welsh Brewers Hancock's HB Ⓖ
A rare opportunity to sup beer brought up from the cellar in a small, friendly single-roomed pub. Old Hancock's Toastmaster sign outside.
🏚 Q ❀ ♣ ◠ P

Rose & Crown
On A466
☎ (0291) 689254
12–3, 7 (6.30 Fri & Sat)–11
Courage Best Bitter, Directors Ⓗ
Comfortable pub situated near the River Wye in the beautiful and historic village of Tintern. The beer range may change to Ushers. 🏚 ❀ ◖ 🍴 🍺 ♣

Try also: **Moon & Sixpence** (Free)

Trellech

Lion
On B4293
☎ (0600) 860322
12–3, 6–11
Banks's Mild; Draught Bass; Hook Norton Best Bitter Ⓗ**; guest beers**
Fine 17th-century inn with a comfortable and relaxed atmosphere. Excellent home-cooked food, using fresh produce from local farms.
🏚 Q ❀ 🛏 ◖ 🍴 🍺 🅰 ♣ P

Trellech Grange

Fountain Inn
Off B4293 OS503011
☎ (0291) 689303
12–3, 6–11
Wadworth 6X Ⓗ**; guest beers**
Spacious, friendly pub in a wooded valley, known for its industrial archaeology. Good variety of meals, including vegetarian, Sun lunch, children's portions and Fri eve fish and chip suppers. A stream runs beneath the pub.
🏚 ❀ 🛏 ◖ 🍴 ♣ P

Upper Llanover

Goose & Cuckoo
Off A4042 OS293073
☎ (0873) 880277
11.30–3, 7–11
Brains SA; Bullmastiff Best Bitter Ⓗ**; guest beer**
Very friendly and welcoming pub, hard to find but well worth the effort. Variety of vegetarian meals. Situated in good walking country.
🏚 Q ◖ 🍴 ♣ P

Usk

Kings Head
Old Market Street
☎ (029 13) 2963
11–11
Brains Bitter; Fuller's London Pride; Whitbread Flowers Original Ⓗ**; guest beers** (occasionally)
Smart, spacious pub with contrasting bars: a traditional public, a comfortable lounge with an impressive stone fireplace, and a separate restaurant.
🏚 Q 🛏 ◖ 🍴 🍺 ♣ P

Royal Hotel
New Market Street
☎ (029 13) 2931
11–3, 7–11
Draught Bass; Felinfoel Double Dragon; Welsh Brewers Hancock's HB Ⓗ
Splendid and very popular, traditional, Victorian-style local, full of character and memorabilia. Excellent food – especially noted for its Sun lunches. 🏚 ◖

Opening Hours

Permitted opening hours in England and Wales are 11-11, though not all pubs choose to take advantage of the full session and many close in the afternoons. Some pubs have special licences and there are sometimes local arrangements for market days and other events. Standard Sunday hours are 12-3, 7-10.30. Scottish licensing laws are more generous in terms of opening hours and pubs may stay open longer.

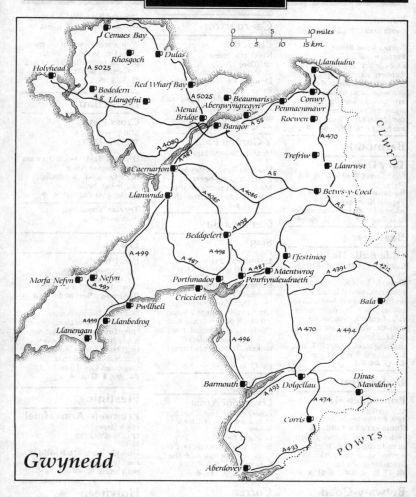

Gwynedd

Aberdovey

Penhelig Arms
On A493 ☎ (0654) 767215
11–3, 6–11
**Ind Coope Burton Ale;
Marston's Pedigree; Tetley
Walker Bitter** H
Small, 19th-century, seaside
town hotel with a restaurant.
Meals are also served in the
wood-panelled 'Fisherman's
Bar'. 🏨 ◗ ⊟ 🍴 ≷

Abergwyngregyn

Aber Falls Hotel
☎ (0248) 680579
11–11 (12 Thu–Sat)
Draught Bass; M&B Mild H;
guest beer
Friendly, warm local bar
beside the main road. Sells
German-brewed lager.
🏮 Q ❀ ⊛ 🏨 ◗ ♣ P ⌁

Bala

White Lion
High Street ☎ (0678) 520314
11–11
**Ind Coope Burton Ale; Tetley
Walker Bitter** H
Black and white Grade II
listed hotel reputedly one of
Wales's oldest coaching inns: a
'Poachers Bar', a pool room
and a beamed lounge. A
Welsh-speaking favourite
with hill-walkers.
🏮 ❀ 🏨 ◗ ▷ ⅄ ♿ ⚓ ♣ P

Bangor

Ffriddoedd Bar
Menai Avenue
☎ (0248) 364131
12–2, 6 (7 university hols)–11
**Ansells Mild; Ind Coope
Friary Meux Best Bitter;**

**Marston's Pedigree; Plassey
Cwrw Tudno; Ruddles
County; S&N Theakston Old
Peculier** H; **guest beers**
Bar on the university campus,
open to the public. Family
room and overnight
accommodation in summer.
Lunches during term-time.
Four pool tables; guest beers
change almost daily.
🌄 🏨 ◗ ⅄ ♿ ⚓ ≷ ♣ ⌣ P

Ship Launch
Garth Road ☎ (0248) 364067
11–11
Draught Bass H
Old terraced pub, now opened
out and refurbished, with
separate lounge and games
areas served by a central bar.
Note the large old
Worthington mirror over the
fireplace. The cheapest (and
best) Bass in the area. Near the
Victorian pier. ◗ ≷ ♣

Gwynedd

Union

Garth Road ☎ (0248) 362462
11–11
Burtonwood Bitter, Forshaw's Ⓗ
One bar serves a number of different rooms, all packed with a huge variety of china, brassware and nautical artefacts. Adjoins the local boatyard, with views across the Menai Strait from the garden. Q ❀ ⇔ ◑ ≒ ♣ P

Barmouth

Tal y Don

High Street ☎ (0341) 280508
11–11
Burtonwood Mild, Bitter Ⓗ
Typical town-centre pub adorned with brass from floor to ceiling. ⇔ ⊟ & ⅃ ≒ ♣

Beaumaris

Olde Bulls Head

Castle Street ☎ (0248) 810329
11–11
Draught Bass Ⓗ
Historic Grade II listed inn, in an interesting old town, on the Menai Strait. The main bar is full of antique weapons and armour, with a water clock and the town's original ducking stool. A small 'China' bar adjoins. No food Sun.
⇔ Q ◑ P

Beddgelert

Prince Llewelyn

☎ (076 686) 242
12–3, 6–11 (closed Sun)
Robinson's Best Bitter Ⓔ
Hotel bar with a stone floor, open to the public. Walkers are welcome. Car park only available in winter.
⇔ Q ⏃ ❀ ⇔ ◑ ⊟ ⅃ P

Betws-y-Coed

Pont-y-Pair Hotel

Holyhead Road
☎ (0690) 710407
11–11
Draught Bass; Ind Coope Burton Ale; Tetley Walker Bitter Ⓗ
Large granite building: a meeting place for walkers, and popular with the locals.
Q ⇔ ◑ ◐ ⊟ ⅃ ♣ P

Bodedern

Crown Hotel

☎ (0407) 740734
12–3.30, 6–11 (11–11 Sat & bank hols)
Burtonwood Bitter Ⓗ
Popular, friendly village pub, with a lounge, more spartan bar and a pool room that doubles as a children's room. An ideal spot to stay when exploring Anglesey.
⇔ ❀ ⇔ ◑ ◐ ⊟ ♣ P

Caernarfon

Black Boy

Northgate Street
☎ (0286) 673023
11–11 (10.45 Fri & Sat)
Draught Bass; Stones Best Bitter Ⓗ
Old-fashioned town pub and restaurant with a small bar and lounge.
⇔ Q ❀ ◑ ◐ ⊟ ⅃ ♣

Y Gordon Fach

Hole in the Wall Street
11–11
Draught Bass; Tetley Walker Bitter Ⓗ**; guest beers**
Modernised pub, recently extended. Not far from the castle. ◑ ◐ ⊟ & ⅃

Cemaes Bay

Stag

High Street
☎ (0407) 710281
11–3.30, 6 (7 winter)–11 (11–11 Sat & summer)
Burtonwood Bitter, Forshaw's Ⓗ
Friendly village pub, with a comfortable lounge, a larger bar and a pool room, where children are welcome. Popular with locals and holiday-makers. The most northerly pub in Wales.
⇔ Q ❀ ◑ ◐ ⊟ ♣

Conwy

Liverpool Arms

Lower Gate Street, The Quay
11.30–3, 6–11 (11–11 Fri, Sat & summer)
Draught Bass Ⓗ
Small, single-roomer on the quayside, popular with the fishermen.
⇔ ❀ ◑ & ⅃ ≒ ♣

Corris

Slater's Arms

Bridge Street
☎ (0654) 761324
11.30–11
Banks's Mild, Bitter Ⓔ
Old-fashioned, two-roomer in a former slating village.
⇔ Q ◑ ◐ ⊟ ⅃ ♣

Criccieth

Castle

Station Road
☎ (0766) 522624
11–11
Draught Bass Ⓗ
Small, terraced pub where the public bar is full of railway pictures. ⇔ ❀ ⊟ ⅃ ≒

Dinas Mawddwy

Red Lion

Off A470 ☎ (0650) 531247
11–3, 6–11 (11–11 summer)
Draught Bass; Welsh Brewers Worthington BB Ⓗ**; guest beers**
Well worth a visit to see the brass bar: a friendly local popular with hill-walkers and fishermen. ⇔ ⏃ ❀ ⇔ ◑ ◐

Dolgellau

Cross Keys

Mill Street
☎ (0341) 423342
11–11
Draught Bass; Welsh Brewers Worthington BB Ⓗ
Basic town pub; a popular, single-bar, back-street, workingman's local. ⅃ ♣

Try also: Royal Ship (Robinson's)

Dulas

Pilot Boat

On A5025 ☎ (024 888) 205
11 (11.30 winter)–3.30, 6 (7 winter)–11 (11–11 Sat & bank hols)
Robinson's Best Mild, Best Bitter Ⓔ
Old pub. The main bar features a low-beamed ceiling, stone fireplace, and a servery made from a clinker-built boat. Also a lounge and a games room (children welcome). Good food.
⇔ ❀ ◑ ◐ ⅃ ♣ P

Ffestiniog

Pengwern Arms Hotel

High Street
☎ (076 676) 2722
11–11
Draught Bass; M&B Mild Ⓗ
Family-run hotel, popular with locals. ❀ ⇔ ◑ ◐ ⊟ & P

Holyhead

Boston

London Road
☎ (0407) 762449
11–3.30, 6–11
Burtonwood Mild, Bitter Ⓗ
Long-time Ansells pub now acquired by Burtonwood. Largely open plan, with a central bar servery, separate areas for pool and darts, and a small lounge. ⊟ ≒ ♣

Llanbedrog

Ship Inn

Pig Street
☎ (0758) 740270
11–3.30, 5.30–11 (11–11 summer; closed Sun)
Burtonwood Mild, Bitter Ⓗ
Cosy, friendly pub popular with visitors, with an unusually-shaped family room. Seafood is a speciality.
⇔ Q ⏃ ❀ ◑ ◐ ⊟ & ⅃ ♣ P

Llandudno

Cottage Loaf
Market Street
☎ (0492) 870762
11–11
Courage Directors; Ruddles County; Webster's Yorkshire Bitter Ⓗ
Pub built from ships' timbers on top of an old bakehouse, with a stone and wood floor. Very popular for lunches; busier at night with drinkers.
🏤 Q ❀ ◐ ⇌ P

London
Mostyn Street
☎ (0492) 876740
11.30–4 (5 Sat), 7–11
Burtonwood Mild, Bitter, Forshaw's Ⓗ
Busy, town-centre pub with a London theme, featuring an old red phone box in the folk club. 🐴 ❀ 🛏 ◐ ⇌ ♣

Llanengan

Sun Inn
☎ (075 881) 2260
11–11 (closed Sun)
Ind Coope Burton Ale; Tetley Walker Bitter Ⓗ
Popular pub near Hell's Mouth beach. Excellent food.
🏤 ❀ ◐ ▶ 🛏 ♣ P

Llangefni

Railway
High Street ☎ (0248) 722166
11–3.30 (5 Sat), 6.30–11 (12–2, 7–11 Mon–Wed, Xmas–Easter)
Lees GB Mild, Bitter Ⓗ
Friendly town pub, now refurbished, but retaining its character, with separate drinking areas. Q ❀ ♣

Llanrwst

New Inn
1 Denbigh Street
11–11
Marston's Mercian Mild, Burton Best Bitter, Pedigree Ⓗ
Modernised but not spoiled; a popular local. Snacks lunchtime. 🏤 ❀ ▲ 🛏 ⇌ ♣

Llanwnda

Goat Hotel
11.30–3, 7–11
Draught Bass; Whitbread Boddingtons Bitter Ⓗ
Friendly roadside village pub enjoying a busy lunchtime trade (buffet). ❀ ◐ ▶ ▲ ♣

Maentwrog

Grapes Hotel
☎ (076 685) 208
11–11
Draught Bass; S&N Theakston XB Ⓗ

Family-run hotel built in the 13th century, overlooking the Vale of Ffestiniog.
🏤 ❀ 🛏 🛏 ◐ ▶ ♣ P

Menai Bridge

Liverpool Arms
St George's Pier (100 yds off A545) ☎ (0248) 712453
11–3.30, 5.30–11
Greenalls Bitter, Thomas Greenall's Bitter Ⓗ
Old pub near the Menai Strait, with two cosy bars full of old prints and nautical artefacts. Several other areas for eating/drinking where children are welcome, including a conservatory and a bistro. Q ❀ ◐ 🛏

Morfa Nefyn

Y Bryncynan
☎ (0758) 720879
11–3.30, 6.30–11 (closed Sun)
Ind Coope Burton Ale; Tetley Walker Bitter Ⓗ
Well modernised country pub and restaurant.
🏤 🐴 ❀ ◐ ▲ ♣ P

Nefyn

Sportsmans
Stryd Fawr
☎ (0758) 720205
11–11 (closed Sun)
Marston's Burton Best Bitter, Pedigree Ⓗ
Friendly pub, popular with locals and tourists. Snacks available. 🏤 Q ❀ 🛏 ▲ ♣

Penmaenmawr

Bron Eryri
Bangor Road
☎ (0492) 623978
12–11
Marston's Mercian Mild, Burton Best Bitter, Merrie Monk, Pedigree Ⓗ
Typical village local with a friendly atmosphere; visitors welcome. 🛏 ⇌ ♣

Penrhyndeudraeth

Royal Oak
High Street
☎ (0766) 770501
11–3, 6–11
Burtonwood Mild, Bitter Ⓗ
1930s pub with modern decor and sporty locals; dominoes played. 🏤 ◐ ▲ ⇌ ♣

Porthmadog

Ship
Lombard Street
☎ (0766) 512990
11–11 (closed Sun)
Ind Coope Burton Ale; Tetley Walker Dark Mild, Bitter Ⓗ; **guest beers**
Popular town pub overlook-

ing the local park and near the Ffestiniog Railway. Known for its oriental cuisine. 🏤 🐴 ❀ ◐
▶ 🛏 ▲ ⇌ ♣ P

Pwllheli

Whitehall
Gaol Street
☎ (0758) 613239
11–3.30, 5.30–11 (11–11 summer; closed Sun)
Ind Coope Benskins Best Bitter, Burton Ale Ⓗ
Popular with the under 25s. Unspoilt by recent modernisation.
🏤 🐴 ❀ ◐ ▲ ⇌ ♣

Red Wharf Bay

Ship
Off A5025
☎ (0248) 852568
11–11 (11.30–3.30, 7–11 winter)
Marston's Pedigree; Tetley Walker Dark Mild, Bitter Ⓗ; **guest beers**
Pub of real character – a long white building facing the sea, with low beamed ceilings, flagged floors, exposed stone walls and huge fireplaces. A regular pub food award winner. 🏤 Q 🐴 ❀ 🛏 ◐ ▶
🛏 ♣ P

Rhosgoch

Rhosgoch Hotel (Ring)
1 mile off B5111 OS409892
☎ (0407) 830720
12–3 (not Mon–Thu in winter), 6–11 (11–11 Fri & Sat)
Draught Bass; Stones Best Bitter Ⓗ
Friendly country pub, off the beaten track. It has a central servery for the snug, lounge and games areas. Extended and much improved in recent years, it features a new dining room, a garden, and an adjoining caravan/camping area. 🏤 ❀ ◐ ▲ ♣ P

Roewen

Ty Gwyn Hotel
12–11 (12–2, 5–11 winter)
Lees GB Mild, Bitter Ⓗ
Village pub in an idyllic setting, changed internally but keeping its atmosphere.
🏤 Q 🐴 ❀ ◐ 🛏 ▲ ♣ P

Trefriw

Princes Arms Country Hotel
☎ (0492) 640592
12 (11 summer)–3, 7 (6 summer)–11
S&N Theakston Best Bitter, XB, Old Peculier Ⓗ
Cheerful and welcoming country hotel and pub. 🏤 Q
🐴 ❀ 🛏 ◐ ▶ 🛏 ♣ P

Powys

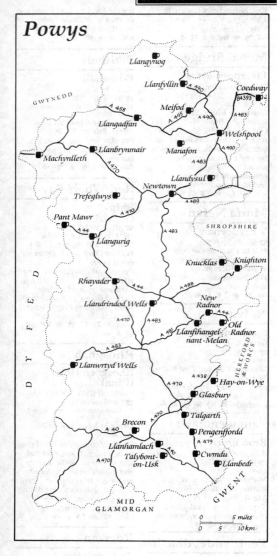

Coedway

Old Hand & Diamond

On B4393 ☎ (0743) 884379
11.30–11
**Draught Bass; M&B Mild;
Welsh Brewers Worthington
BB** Ⓗ**; guest beer**
(occasionally)
A plain exterior hides an
immaculate, comfortable
interior in this old pub of
character: four rooms,
including a restaurant, with
oak beams and an inglenook
in the bar. Children welcome.
🏾 Q ✿ ◑ ▯ ⑤ ♿ ▲ P

Cwmdu

Farmers Arms

On A479, 6 miles S of Talgarth
☎ (0874) 730464
11–3, 6–11
Draught Bass; Brains SA Ⓗ**;
guest beers**
Friendly country pub where
families are welcome (no
separate room). Plentiful,
wholesome meals are this
hostelry's forte.
🏾 Q ✿ 🛏 ◑ ▯ ⑤ ▲ P

Glasbury

Harp

Take Hay road out of
Glasbury ☎ (0497) 847373
11–3, 6–11
**Robinson's Best Bitter;
Whitbread Boddingtons
Bitter, Flowers IPA,
Original** Ⓗ
Welcoming riverside inn on
the Wye: a 17th-century cider
house welcoming children (no
special room).
🏾 Q ✿ 🛏 ◑ ▯ ⑤ ♣ P

Maesllwch Arms
Hotel

Off A438, N side of Wye
bridge ☎ (0497) 847226
11–3, 7–11
Draught Bass Ⓗ**; guest beers**
Informal hotel with a small,
cosy public bar, popular with
the locals. Ideally situated for
exploring the Upper Wye
valley and surrounding
countryside. 🏾 Q ✿ 🐾 🛏
◑ ▯ ⑤ ▲ ♣ P

Hay-on-Wye

Blue Boar

Castle Street ☎ (0497) 820884
11–3, 6–11 (11–11 Sat)
**Brains Dark, SA; Whitbread
Boddingtons Bitter, Flowers
IPA, Original** Ⓗ**; guest beers**
Traditional pub next to the
main gate of the castle, with
an inviting wood-panelled
public bar. A fine pub in
which to sit and read the
books you have unearthed in
the world famous local

Brecon

Bulls Head

The Struet ☎ (0874) 622044
12–3, 7–11
Brains SA; Tetley Bitter Ⓗ
Pub with a small bar and
lounge area, but very friendly
and comfortable. Tiny outdoor
area, overlooking the River
Honddu, offers a view of
Brecon Cathedral (100 yards).
Good quality, reasonably-
priced bar snacks are served
as well as meals (not Sun/
Mon eves). ✿ 🛏 ◑ ▯ ⑤ ♣

Gremlin Hotel

The Watton (B4601)
☎ (0874) 623829
12–3, 7–11
**Draught Bass; Brains
Bitter** Ⓗ**; guest beers**
(occasionally)
400-year-old pub, reputedly
haunted by a piano playing
ghost! A busy bar and a small
but very comfortable lounge
area, offering good quality
and reasonably-priced bar
snacks and meals (no food
Sun/Mon eves).
✿ 🛏 ◑ ▶ ♣ P

bookshops. Eve meals in summer only. 🏠 Q ◖ ▷ 🍴

Knighton

Central Wales Hotel
Station Road (A488)
☎ (0547) 520065
12–3, 5.30–11 (12–11 summer)
Ind Coope Burton Ale; Tetley Bitter Ⓗ
Small country town hotel slap bang on the English border and originally owned by the railway. Conveniently close to Offa's Dyke path. Recently reverted to its former name after a spell as the 'Kinsley': a lounge, a public bar and a games room.
🏠 Q 🏵 🍴 ◖ ▷ 🍴 🚃 ♣ ♠

Try also: Swan (Free)

Knucklas

Castle Inn
200 yds off B4355
☎ (0547) 528150
1–4 (may extend), 7–11
Tetley Bitter Ⓗ
Village pub in a large Victorian, baronial-style building. Walking holidays can be arranged. Bed and breakfast only by prior booking.
🏠 🏵 🍴 ▷ ♿ ▲ 🚃 ♠ P

Llanbedr

Red Lion
☎ (0873) 810754
12–2.30, 6–11
Felinfoel Double Dragon; Hook Norton Old Hooky; Morland Old Speckled Hen Ⓗ**; guest beers**
Friendly country pub next to a church, in the heart of the Black Mountains. Families welcome (no separate room).
🏠 Q 🏵 ◖ ▷ ▲ ♠ P

Try also: Bear, Crickhowell

Llanbrynmair

Wynnstay Arms Hotel
On A470 ☎ (065 03) 431
11–2.30, 6–11
Ansells Bitter; Whitbread Boddingtons Bitter, Flowers IPA Ⓗ
Well-kept, comfortable, two-bar, village hotel with a pool room and real fires in both bars. Food is served in the quiet lounge or restaurant. The beer range may vary.
🏠 Q 🍴 ◖ ▷ 🍴 ♠ P

Llandrindod Wells

Llanerch Inn
Llanerch Lane
☎ (0597) 822086
11.30–2.30 (3 Fri & Sat), 6–11
Draught Bass; Robinson's Best Bitter; Welsh Brewers

Hancock's HB Ⓗ**; guest beers** (occasionally)
Comfortable, 16th-century coaching inn with low-beamed ceilings and a large stone hearth. Its mini-beer festival forms part of the town's Victorian Week every August.
🍴 🏵 🍴 ◖ ▷ 🚃 🍴 ♠ P

Llandysul

Upper House
Off B4386
12–3 (not Wed), 6.30–11
Wood Special Ⓗ
Excellent, friendly, unspoilt village local where quoits are played. 🏠 Q 🍴 ♠

Llanfihangel-nant-Melan

Red Lion
On A44 ☎ (054 421) 220
11–3, 6–11
Hook Norton Best Bitter Ⓗ
Comfortable and peaceful watering hole on the main A44 road in Radnor Forest. Popular with hillwalkers.
🏠 Q 🏵 🍴 ◖ ▷ 🍴 ♠ P

Llanfyllin

Cain Valley Hotel
On A490 ☎ (069 184) 366
11–11
Ansells Bitter; Draught Bass Ⓗ
Historic coaching inn boasting an original Jacobean staircase and two attractive, wood-panelled lounge bars. The basic public bar has table football.
🏠 Q 🏵 🍴 ◖ ▷ 🍴 ♠ P

Try also: Old New Inn (Marston's)

Llangadfan

Cann Office Hotel
On A458 ☎ (093 888) 202
12–2.30 (may extend), 6–11
Marston's Burton Best Bitter, Pedigree (summer) Ⓗ
Attractive and extremely interesting old posting inn on the main road. Six rooms and a large garden mean that all tastes are catered for. Fishing rights on the River Banwy. 🏠 Q 🍴 🏵 🍴 ◖ ▷ 🍴 ▲ ♠ P

Llangurig

Blue Bell
On A44 ☎ (055 15) 254
11–2.30, 6–11
Whitbread Best Bitter, Flowers Original Ⓗ
16th-century hotel with a fine slate-floored bar and inglenook; also a pool room, two dining rooms and a family room. Book for Sun lunch.
🏠 🍴 🍴 ◖ ▷ 🍴 ♿ ▲ ♠ P

Llangynog

New Inn
On B4391 ☎ (069 174) 229
12–3 (not always winter weekdays), 6–11
Marston's Border Mild, Pedigree Ⓗ
Friendly pub offering good value beer in comfortable surroundings, which contrast with the bleak views outside. Dates back to the 17th century when this was a thriving mining area. Children are welcome in the residents' lounge or the bar when dining.
🏠 Q 🍴 🍴 ◖ ▷ ▲ ♠ P

Llanhamlach

Old Ford Inn
On A40, 3 miles E of Brecon
☎ (087 486) 220
11–3, 6–11 (11.30–2.30, 6.30–11 winter)
Marston's Pedigree; Whitbread Boddingtons Bitter Ⓗ
Roadside pub affording a magnificent view of the Brecon Beacons. A public house since the mid 19th century when it was a coaching inn. A small public bar and a spacious lounge displaying 150 different old bottled beers. A very friendly pub with a warm welcome.
🏵 🍴 ◖ ▷ 🍴 ♠ P

Llanwrtyd Wells

Neuadd Arms Hotel
The Square (A483)
☎ (059 13) 236
11.30–11 (may close afternoons)
Draught Bass; Felinfoel Double Dragon; Welsh Brewers Worthington Dark, Hancock's HB Ⓗ**; guest beers**
Imposing hotel in Britain's smallest town. The enterprising landlord organises events such as morris dancing, a folk festival, bog snorkelling, and of course the Mid Wales Beer Festival each November. This includes real ale rambles around the surrounding mountains and forests. 🏠 Q 🏵 🍴 ◖ ▷ 🍴 ▲ 🚃 ♠ P ⚇

Machynlleth

Dyfi Forester Inn
4 Doll Street (A487)
☎ (0654) 702004
11–3, 6–11 (11–11 Sat)
Marston's Burton Best Bitter, Pedigree, Owd Rodger Ⓗ
Very friendly town pub with an attractive fireplace and a small downstairs restaurant.
🏠 🍴 ◖ ▷ 🍴 ♠ P

Powys

Skinners Arms

Main Street (A487)
☎ (0654) 702354
11–11
**Burtonwood Bitter,
Forshaw's** Ⓗ
Wood-beamed, town-centre
pub with a comfortable lounge
and a friendly atmosphere.
🛏 ◖ ▶ 🍴 ♣

Manafon

Beehive

On B4390
☎ (068 687) 244
12–3, 7–11
Banks's Mild, Bitter Ⓗ
Pleasant, well-run,
comfortable pub with an
unusual fireplace in the public
bar. 🛏 ❀ ◖ ▶ ▲ ♣ P

Meifod

Kings Head Hotel

On A495
☎ (093 884) 256
11–3, 6–11
Burtonwood Bitter Ⓗ
Impressive, ivy-clad, stone-
built inn in the centre of the
village. Children are admitted
to the lounge for meals.
❀ ◖ ▶ 🍴 ♿ ▲ ♣ P

New Radnor

Eagle Hotel

Broad Street (on B4372, off
A44) ☎ (054 421) 208
12–2 (may extend in summer), 7–11
(11–11 Sat)
**Draught Bass; Welsh Brewers
Worthington BB** (summer) Ⓗ
Pub comprising a busy,
traditional bar, a bright,
comfortable lounge with a
piano, a games room, and a
restaurant and coffee shop.
Organises paragliding at
weekends in the nearby
Radnor Forest. Local
farmhouse perry is sometimes
available. 🛏 Q ❀ 🍴 ◖ ▶ 🍴
▲ ♣ ⌂ P

Newtown

Pheasant

Market Street
☎ (0686) 625966
11–11
Burtonwood Bitter Ⓗ
Friendly, timbered local with a
popular main bar, a quiet rear
room and a games room.
❀ 🍴 ◖ 🍴 ⇌ ♣

Queens Head

Kerry Road (A483)
☎ (0686) 626421
11–3, 5–11 (11–11 Sat)
Tetley Bitter Ⓗ
Friendly edge-of-town local
offering a warm welcome.
❀ 🍴 🍴 ⇌ ♣ P

Try also: Buck Inn, High St
(Free)

Old Radnor

Harp Inn

1 mile W of A44/B4362 jct
☎ (054 421) 655
12–2.30 (not Tue), 7–11
Wood Special Ⓗ**; guest beer**
15th-century inn, beautifully
restored by the Landmark
Trust, featuring a stone-
flagged floor, stone walls,
beamed ceiling, antique
furniture and bric-a-brac.
Outside, noisy geese and a
memorable view of the
Radnor Forest complete the
picture. Families are welcome.
🛏 Q ❀ 🍴 ◖ ▶ 🍴 ▲ ♣ P

Try also: Royal Oak,
Gladestry (Bass)

Pant Mawr

Glan Severn Arms Hotel

On A44, 4 miles W of
Llangurig ☎ (055 15) 240
11–2, 6.30–11 (closed Sun before
Christmas – New Year's Eve)
**Draught Bass; Welsh Brewers
Worthington Dark** Ⓗ
Two impeccable, quiet,
comfortable bars in a hotel
high up in the Wye Valley.
Restaurant meals only (book
eves and Sun lunch; no food
Sun eve). 🛏 Q 🍴 P

Pengenffordd

Castle Inn

☎ (0874) 711353
11–3, 6–11
**Wadworth 6X; Whitbread
Boddingtons Bitter** Ⓗ**; guest
beers**
Friendly country local,
popular with trekkers and
walkers, on the summit of the
mountain road between
Talgarth and Crickhowell. The
highest hill fort in England
and Wales, Castle Dinas,
stands above the pub. Families
welcome. Campsite in the
grounds.
🛏 ❀ 🍴 ◖ ▶ 🍴 ▲ ♣ ⌂ P

Rhayader

Cornhill Inn

West Street (B4518)
☎ (0597) 810869
11–3 (may extend), 6–11
**Hook Norton Best Bitter;
Marston's Pedigree; Wye
Valley Hereford Bitter** Ⓗ**;
guest beers**
Friendly, low-beamed, 400-
year-old pub, reputedly
haunted by a female
poltergeist.
🛏 🍴 ◖ ▶ ▲ ♣ ⌂

Triangle Inn

Cwmdauddwr (Off B4518)
☎ (0597) 810537
11–3, 6.30–11

**Draught Bass; Welsh Brewers
Hancock's HB** Ⓗ
Beautiful, little
weatherboarded gem,
overlooking the River Wye.
The ceilings are so low that
customers have to stand in a
hole in the floor to play darts!
Vegetarian meals served on
request. ❀ ◖ ▶ ▲ ♣

Talgarth

Tower Hotel

The Square ☎ (0874) 711253
11–3, 7–11
**Draught Bass; Whitbread
Boddingtons Bitter, Flowers
IPA, Original** Ⓗ**; guest beers**
Popular market town hotel
which takes its name from the
14th-century Norman tower
on the opposite side of the
square.
🛏 ⇝ ❀ 🍴 ◖ ▶ P

Talybont-on-Usk

Star Inn

On B4558, ¾ mile off A40
☎ (087 487) 635
11–3, 6–11 (11–11 Sat)
**Felinfoel Bitter, Double
Dragon; Hook Norton Best
Bitter; Marston's Pedigree;
Morland Old Speckled Hen;
Whitbread Boddingtons
Bitter** Ⓗ
Popular canalside pub dating
back to the 1770s. Up to 12
real ales available at any one
time; bar food includes
vegetarian and Indian menus.
Jazz every Thu night; quiz
nights most Mon. Coach
parties are welcome (advance
notice preferred). Large
garden.
🛏 ❀ 🍴 ◖ ▶ 🍴 ▲ ♣

Trefeglwys

Red Lion

On B4569 ☎ (055 16) 255
11.30–2.30, 6–11
Burtonwood Bitter Ⓗ
Traditional local with old
village photographs
displayed. Good reputation
for bar meals.
🛏 ◖ ▶ 🍴 ♣ P

Welshpool

Talbot

High Street (A458/A490)
☎ (0938) 553711
11–11 (may close afternoons)
Banks's Mild, Bitter Ⓔ
Little, two-bar, half-timbered
local of character. Handy for
the bus stops and shops; only
a few minutes' walk from the
Welshpool & Llanfair
Caereinion light railway.
Q ❀ ◖ ▶ 🍴 ⇌ ♣ P

Borders

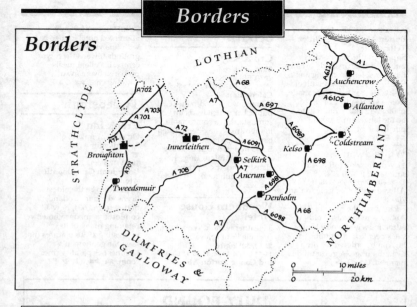

Borders

LOTHIAN

STRATHCLYDE

A702
A703
A701
A72
Broughton
A701
Tweedsmuir

A72
Innerleithen
A706
Selkirk
A7
Ancrum
Denholm

A68
A7
A697
A6091
A698
A6098

A6112
Auchencrow
A6105
Allanton
A689
Kelso
A698
Coldstream

A1

DUMFRIES & GALLOWAY

NORTHUMBERLAND

0   10 miles
0   20 km

 Broughton, Broughton; **Traquair House**, Innerleithen

Allanton

Allanton Inn
On B6437 ☎ (089 081) 260
12–2.30, 6–11 (12 Thu & Fri, 11.30
Sat; 12.30–2.30, 6.30–11.30 Sun;
closed Mon lunch in winter)
**Belhaven 80/-, St Andrew's
Ale** Ⓗ**; guest beer**
Friendly village inn with low
ceilings and a cosy real fire: a
lounge bar with ample
standing room and plenty of
seating at the rear. Fine
reputation for excellent food.
🏚 ◑ ▶ P

Ancrum

Cross Keys Inn
The Green (B6400, off A68, 4
miles N of Jedburgh)
☎ (083 53) 344
12–2.30, 5 (6 winter)–11 (12 Thu & Fri;
11–12 Sat; 12.30–11 Sun)
Alloa Arrol's 80/- Ⓗ**; guest
beers**
Wonderfully unspoilt, stand-
up village boozer with a
friendly welcome for locals
and first-time visitors alike.
Restaurant planned. Guest
beer (two in summer).
🏚 Q ❀ ⊟ ♣ P

Auchencrow

Craw Inn
On B6438 (off A1)
☎ (089 07) 61253
12–2.30, 6–11 (12.30–2.30, 6.30–11
Sun)
Broughton Greenmantle Ale,

Special (summer) Ⓗ
Isolated gem with a two-
roomed bar (reminiscent of an
English country pub) and a
comfortable lounge at the
back. Probably the only pub in
Scotland with its own putting
green. No meals Tue eve.
🏚 Q ❀ 🛏 ◑ ▶ ⊟ & ♣ P

Coldstream

Crown Hotel
Market Square (off A697)
☎ (0890) 2558
11–12 (11.30 Sat; 12.30–11 Sun)
**Caledonian 80/-; Tetley
Bitter** Ⓗ
Nestling in the peaceful
market square, a busy hotel
lounge bar with an incredible
display cabinet, stuffed with
drinking collectables. Mind
the step on entering – the
locals keep watch for tourists
crashing to the floor!
❀ 🛏 ◑ ▶ P

Denholm

Auld Cross Keys Inn
Main Street (A698, between
Hawick and Jedburgh)
☎ (045 087) 305
11–2.30, 5 (7 winter Mon)–11 (12 Thu,
1am Fri; 11–12 Sat; 12.30–11 Sun)
**Broughton Greenmantle
Ale** Ⓗ
Picturesque 17th-century pub
and restaurant in a planned
conservation village. The
restaurant has a good
reputation and it's worth

booking, especially at
weekends. 🏚 ◑ ▶ ⊟ ♣

Fox & Hounds
Main Street (A698)
☎ (045 087) 247
11–11 (12 Thu & Sat, 1am Fri;
12.30–11 Sun)
**Belhaven 80/-; Courage
Directors** Ⓗ**; guest beers**
Thriving village local with a
warm and welcoming
atmosphere, situated in the
border heartland of horse and
farming country. Good home-
cooked meals and two regular
guest beers. 🏚 Q 🐃 ❀ 🛏
◑ ▶ ⊟ & ♣ P

Innerleithen

Traquair Arms Hotel
Traquair Road (B709, off A72)
☎ (0896) 830229
11–12 (12.30–12 Sun)
**Broughton Greenmantle Ale,
Oatmeal Stout** (summer)**;
Traquair House Bear Ale** Ⓗ
Family-run, 18th-century hotel
with a plush lounge bar,
warmed by a welcoming log
fire. Good home-cooked food,
prepared from local produce.
Near Traquair House brewery,
Scotland's oldest inhabited
house. 🏚 Q ❀ 🛏 ◑ ▶ P

Kelso

Red Lion Inn
Crawford Street (off town
square) ☎ (0573) 224817
11–12 (1am Fri; 12.30–11 Sun)

Borders

Alloa Arrol's 80/-; Ind Coope Burton Ale; Jennings Bitter; Tetley Bitter Ⓗ
Superb traditional Borders pub with a surprisingly ornate interior: splendid ceiling and a fine bar-back, topped with old casks. The bar counter is made from a single piece of mahogany and is thought to be the longest in Scotland. A pub not to be missed. 🛏 🍺 ♣

White Swan
11 Woodmarket (off town square) ☎ (0573) 224348
11–12 (1am Fri; 12.30–11 Sun)
Alloa Arrol's 80/-; Caledonian 70/- Ⓗ
Facing onto the ruins of Kelso Abbey, a modernised old pub attracting a good local trade. Cask beer is in the public bar, but can be ordered for the distant lounge. A guest mild is planned. 🍺 🍷 🍺 ♣

Selkirk

Cross Keys Inn
Market Place
☎ (0750) 21283
11–11 (12 Thu–Sat; 12.30–11 Sun)
Caledonian 80/- Ⓗ
Vibrant, wee wood-panelled public bar which leads up some steps to a comfortable lounge area. The often packed bar causes congestion in the Boy's Room, which is, to say the least, an interesting, if claustrophobic experience. Excellent pub food. No food Sat eve. 🍷 🍷

Woodburn House Hotel
5 Heatherlie Park, Woodburn (1/2 mile W of centre)
☎ (0750) 20816
11–11 (12 Fri & Sat; 12.30–11 Sun)
Ind Coope Burton Ale Ⓗ

Small but comfortably appointed hotel lounge bar with fine views over the grounds toward the town centre. Excellent meals prepared by an award-winning chef. 🛏 🍷 🍷 P

Tweedsmuir

Crook Inn
On A701, 1 mile N of Tweedsmuir
☎ (089 97) 272
12–11 (12 Sat; 12.30–11 Sun)
Broughton Greenmantle Ale Ⓗ
Reputed to be the oldest licensed inn in Scotland, dating from 1604, now a comfortable modern hotel, yet retaining many of its interesting 1930s features (not least the gentlemen's facilities). Separate games room. 🛏 🛏 🍷 🍷 ♣ P

DUTY-BOUND

After the Irish, the British pay the highest beer taxes in the European Community.

The poor beer drinker coughs up 24p in excise duty and 20p in VAT on each pint of ordinary bitter. The Germans, by contrast, pay only a couple of pence duty a pint.

Small brewers are the most heavily taxed small businesses in the country. Seventy per cent of their turnover goes in excise duty, VAT, and the usual payroll taxes. Plus, they pay tax when the beer is brewed, but have to wait for pubs to pay them before they see a profit. The tax system hits them where it hurts, in the cashflow.

CAMRA has proposed a sliding scale of excise duty, a modest exemption in tax for smaller brewers. This would not only relieve the burden, but encourage growth amongst small brewers. We would expect more choice, and more competition.

The 1989 Monopolies and Mergers Commission report recommended such a system; the European Community has agreed that countries can implement it. Sliding scale is a long-established feature of the Belgian, Dutch and German brewing scene.

As yet though, there has been no enthusiasm from the UK Government. It looks like our small brewers will go into the Single Market to compete with foreign brewers at a significant disadvantage.

Central

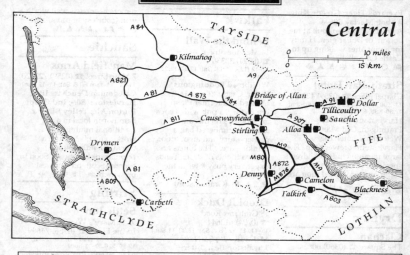

 Harviestoun, Dollar; **Maclay,** Alloa

Alloa

Crams Bar
8 Candleriggs ☎ (0259) 722019
11–11 (11–12 Sat; 11–11 Sun)
Maclay 80/- Ⓐ
Modernised workingman's
bar in a central location. Q

Thistle Bar
1 Junction Place
☎ (0259) 723933
11–12 (11–1am Fri–Sun)
Maclay 80/- Ⓐ
Town-centre pub: the brewery
tap for Maclay's brewery (next
door). Popular lounge and
sociable bar. ◑ 🍺

Blackness

Blackness Inn
18 The Square (B903, off A904)
☎ (0506) 834252
11–2.30, 6–11 (12 Fri & Sat; 12–11
Sun)
**Alloa Arrol's 80/-; Ind Coope
Burton Ale** Ⓔ; guest beers
Typical country inn, nicely
situated on the edge of the
River Forth, close to Blackness
Castle. A warm welcome is
assured with real fires in both
bars and award-winning,
home-cooked food.
🏰 ❀ 🛏 ◑ ▶ 🍺 ♣

Bridge of Allan

Queens Hotel
24 Henderson Street
☎ (0786) 833268
12–12 (12–1am Fri & Sat; 12–12 Sun)
Belhaven 80/-; Tetley Bitter Ⓗ;
Younger IPA Ⓐ
Built in the early 19th century,

this hotel has been serving real
ale for many years,
particularly the Younger IPA
(rare in these parts).
🛏 ❀ 🛏 ◑ ▶ 🍺 ♿ ⇌ P

Camelon

Rosebank
Main Street ☎ (0324) 611842
11–12 (1am Fri & Sat; 11–11.30 Sun)
Whitbread Castle Eden Ale Ⓗ
Opened in 1988 after a £1.5
million renovation of the
former Rosebank Distillery
bonded warehouse on the
Forth and Clyde Canal. If you
need cheering up look at the
customer's comments book in
the foyer. ❀ ◑ ▶ 🍺 P

Carbeth

Carbeth Inn
Stockiemuir Road (A809 near
Strathblane turn-off)
☎ (0360) 70002
12-11 (1am Fri & Sat; 12.30-12 Sun)
**Belhaven 80/-, St Andrew's
Ale** Ⓗ
Old established pub with a
wood-panelled public bar
overlooked by an ancient stag;
newly renovated lounge. Eve
meals till 8.30.
🍺 ❀ ◑ ▶ 🍺 ▲ P

Causewayhead

Birds & Bees
Easter Cornton Road (left off
A91, 1 mile out of Stirling)
☎ (0786) 73663
11–12 (11–1am Fri & Sat; 12.30–12
Sun)
**Caledonian 80/-; Harviestoun
Old Manor; Tetley Bitter** Ⓐ

Converted farm building at
the edge of a quiet residential
area. Relaxed atmosphere
with piped music. Fittings
include milk churns and
sheep! Beware occasional DJ
and karaoke. Wide range of
tasty food. Families
welcomed.
🍺 ❀ ◑ ▶ ♿ ▲ ♣ P

Denny

Royal Oak Hotel
169 Stirling Street
☎ (0324) 823768
11–2.30, 5–11 (11–2.30, 6.30–11 Sun)
Younger No. 3 Ⓐ
The only outlet for No. 3 in the
area. Built in 1794 as a
coaching inn and has been run
by the same family since 1925.
The comfortable, quiet bar
provides a pleasant
atmosphere. Q 🛏 P

Dollar

King's Seat
19 Bridge Street
☎ (0259) 42515
11–2.30, 5–11 (12 Thu–Sat; 12–2.30,
6.30–11 Sun)
**Caledonian 80/-; Ind Coope
Burton Ale; Jennings Bitter** Ⓗ
Comfortable, two-roomed pub
in the centre of the village. The
menu is a good read – not just
for meals (funny and
misinterpreted newspaper
headlines on the cover). ◑ ▶ ▲

Lorne Tavern
17 Argyle Street
☎ (0259) 43423
11–2.30 (not Tue), 5–11 (12 Mon;
11–12 Thu; 11–1am Fri & Sat;
12.30–11 Sun)

Central

Everards Tiger; Greene King Abbot; Maclay 80/- Ⓐ
Attractive, modern pub at the bottom of Dollar glen. Handy for a pint after walking up to Castle Campbell!
🏨 Q 🛏 🍺🍴 🍽 🍴 ♣ P

Strathallan Hotel

Chapel Place ☎ (0259) 42205
11-2.30, 5-12 (11-2.30, 5-1am Fri-Sat; 12.30-2.30, 6-12 Sun)
Harviestoun 70/-, 80/-, Ptarmigan, Old Manor Ⓗ
Welcoming hotel, the Harviestoun brewery tap. The large menu includes children's specials. A children's room and more accommodation are planned.
🌞 🛏 🍺🍴 🍴 ♣ P

Drymen

Clachan

The Square ☎ (0360) 60824
11-12 (12.30-11 Sun)
Belhaven 80/- Ⓐ
Friendly locals' bar dating from the 18th century, in a tourist village. Note the fine collection of historical photographs of Drymen. Food is served in the comfortable lounge. 🏨 🍺🍴 🍽 🍴

Winnock Hotel

The Square ☎ (0360) 60245
11-12 (1am Fri & Sat; 12-12 Sun)
Broughton Greenmantle Ale; Courage Directors; Ruddles County; Webster's Yorkshire Bitter Ⓗ
Low, whitewashed hotel with a long frontage on the village square, comprising a comfortable lounge to one side and a long, wood-beamed bar to the other. The big open fires boast ornamental griddles. Petanque played. 🏨 Q 🍻 🌞 🛏 🍺🍴 🍴 ♣ P

Falkirk

Behind the Wall

14 Melville Street
☎ (0324) 33338
11-12 (12.45 Fri & Sat; 12.30-11.30 Sun)
Whitbread Boddingtons Bitter, Castle Eden Ale Ⓗ
Housed in a former Playtex bra factory, a pub with a cops and robbers theme: an attractive timbered bar, a conservatory and an outdoor drinking area. The toilets are up two flights of stairs. Tends to get very busy later in the evening.
🌞 🍺🍴 🚃 (Grahamston)

Drookit Duck

18 Grahams Road
☎ (0324) 613644
11-11 (11-12 Fri & Sat; 12.30-11 Sun)
McEwan 80/-; S&N Theakston Best Bitter; Younger No. 3 Ⓗ
The Drookit Duck is the latest incarnation of a pub of long standing, with the duck theme represented quite tastefully. Very busy on Sat when Falkirk FC are playing at home.
🍺🍴 🍴 🚃 (Grahamston)

Kilmahog

Lade Inn

At A84/A821 jct
☎ (0877) 30152
12-11 (12-12 Fri & Sat; 12-11 Sun; closed Mon & Tue, Dec-Feb)
Ruddles County; Webster's Yorkshire Bitter Ⓗ
Owned and managed by Canadians, the Lade Inn has a wee touch of international flair. The owners' son runs a mini-brewery in Canada so good beer runs in the family. Perfect for hill walkers, a fairly remote beer oasis well worth a visit (courtesy bus available).
Q 🌞 🛏 🍺🍴 🍴 P

Sauchie

Mansfield Arms

7 Main Street ☎ (0259) 722020
11-12 (11-1am Fri & Sat; 11-12 Sun)
Caledonian Deuchars IPA; Harviestoun 80/-; Ind Coope Burton Ale; Tetley Bitter Ⓔ
Family-run local in a traditional mining area: a workingman's bar and a warm, friendly lounge, popular for bar meals. Soon to become Scotland's newest brew pub. 🌞 🍺🍴 🍽 🍴 ♣ P

Stirling

Settle Inn

91 St Mary's Wynd (top of Irvine Place) ☎ (0786) 74609
11-11 (11-1am Wed-Fri; 11-12 Sat; 12.30-5, 6.30-11 Sun)
Maclay 80/-, Porter Ⓐ**; guest beers**
Small, friendly house in a central residential area: a comfortable and unspoilt bar with an informal back room. The bar prices make it a must for the price-conscious ale drinker. 🍽 🍴 🚃

Tillicoultry

Wool Pack

Glassford Square (bottom of Tillicoultry glen; follow signs from main road)
☎ (0259) 50332
11-12 (11-1am Fri & Sat; 12.30-11 Sun)
Caledonian 80/-; Ind Coope Benskins Best Bitter Ⓗ
Welcoming bar, handy for walkers returning from a trek around the glen. Very good value bar lunches (Thu–Sun).
Q 🍺🍴 ♣ ♠

From Good Beer Guide 1985

"I was a convicted vandal, so you see, modernizing pubs for a brewery was the only job my probation officer could get me"

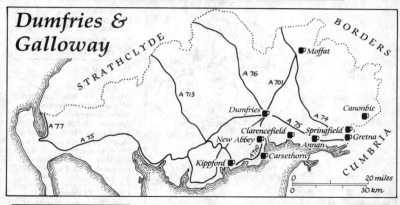

Dumfries & Galloway map showing Moffat, Dumfries, Clarencefield, New Abbey, Kippford, Carsethorn, Annan, Springfield, Gretna, Canonbie, with surrounding regions STRATHCLYDE, BORDERS, CUMBRIA. Roads A76, A701, A713, A75, A74, A77, A710. Scale 20 miles / 30 km.

Annan

Blue Bell

High Street ☎ (0461) 202385
11–11 (12 Thu–Sat; 12.30–11 Sun in summer)
McEwan 80/-; S&N Theakston Best Bitter Ⓗ
Excellent, traditional boozer with impressive wood-panelling. Q ❀ 🐾 🍴 ◖ 🍺 🛏 ⚓ ♣

Canonbie

Riverside Inn

☎ (038 73) 71512
11–11, 6.30–11 (12 Thu–Sat; closed Sun lunch)
Yates Bitter Ⓗ; **guest beer**
Charming country inn.
🏨 Q ❀ 🍴 ◖ ▶ P

Carsethorn

Steamboat Inn

Off A710 ☎ (038 788) 631
11–2.30, 5.30–11 (12 Fri & Sat; 12.30–11 Sun in summer; 12.30–2.30, 6.30–11 Sun in winter)
Belhaven 80/-, St Andrew's Ale Ⓗ
Small comfortable bar with a conservatory overlooking the Firth. 🏨 Q 🐾 ❀ ◖ 🍺 ♣ P

Clarencefield

Farmers Inn

Main Street ☎ (0387) 87675
11–2.30, 6–11 (12 Fri; 11–12 Sat; 12.30–11 Sun; 11–11 bank hols)
Draught Bass; Caledonian 70/-, 80/- Ⓗ; **guest beer**
Welcoming 18th-century inn – frequented by Burns.
🏨 ❀ ◖ ▶ 🍺 🛏 ♣ P

Dumfries

Douglas Arms

Friars Vennel ☎ (0387) 56002
11–11 (12 Fri & Sat)
Broughton Greenmantle Ale, Special, Oatmeal Stout, Old Jock Ⓗ; **guest beer**
Grand wee pub with a snug.
🍺 🛏 ♣

Globe Inn

High Street ☎ (0387) 52335
11–11 (11–11 Sun)
Belhaven 80/-; McEwan 80/- Ⓗ
17th-century howff in a narrow alley. Superb wood-panelled snug. Eve meals Thu–Sat in summer only.
◖ ▶ 🛏 ♣

Ship Inn

97 St Michael Street
11–2.30, 5–11 (12.30–2.30, 6.30–11 Sun)
McEwan 70/-, 80/- Ⓐ
Very traditional two-roomed pub with toby jugs and seafarers' items. Q 🐾 🍺 ♣

Station Hotel (Somewhere Else Bar)

Lovers Walk ☎ (0387) 54316
11–2.30, 5–11 (11.45 Fri & Sat; 11.30–2.30; 6.30–11 Sun)
Draught Bass Ⓗ
Pleasant, café-style, basement bar. Wheelchair access via hotel. ❀ 🍴 ◖ ▶ ♿ 🛏 P ⌀

Tam O'Shanter

117 Queensberry Street
11–2.30, 5–11 (closed Sun)
Caledonian 70/-, 80/-; McEwan 80/-;
Excellent, cosy bar with several rooms. Q 🍺 🛏 ♣

Troqueer Arms

Troqueer Road ☎ (0387) 54518
11–11 (11–12 Thu; 11–1am Fri & Sat; 12.30–12 Sun)
Belhaven 80/-; Caledonian 70/-, 80/- Ⓗ
Very friendly local; much better inside than the austere outside. ❀ 🍺 ♣ P

Gretna

Solway Lodge Hotel

Annan Road ☎ (0461) 38266
11–2.30, 5–11 (11–11 summer; 12–2.30, 6.30–11 Sun; 12–11 Sun in summer)
Broughton Special; Tetley Bitter Ⓗ
Comfortable, friendly hotel.
🐾 ❀ 🍴 ◖ ▶ ♿ 🛏 🛏 P

Kippford

Anchor Hotel

Off A710 ☎ (055 662) 205
10.30–12 (10.30–2.30, 6–11 winter)
McEwan 80/-; S&N Theakston Best Bitter, Old Peculier Ⓗ
Splendid wood-panelled bar with a seafaring flavour.
🏨 Q 🐾 ❀ ◖ 🍴 🍺 ♣ P

Moffat

Black Bull Hotel

Churchgate ☎ (0683) 20206
11–11 (11–12 Thu–Sat)
McEwan 80/- Ⓐ; **S&N Theakston Best Bitter, Old Peculier** (summer) Ⓗ
Attractive, 16th-century inn. 80/- only available in the bar.
🏨 🐾 ❀ 🍴 ◖ ▶ 🍺 ♿ ♣

Star Hotel

High Street ☎ (0683) 20156
11–11 (11–2.30, 5–11 winter; 11–12 Fri–Sun all year)
S&N Theakston Best Bitter Ⓗ
Welcoming family-run hotel. Real ale is in the bar, but can be ordered from the lounge. The narrowest detached hotel in Britain. High teas.
🍴 ◖ ▶ 🍺 ♣

New Abbey

Criffel Inn

On A710 ☎ (0387) 85305
11.30–2.30, 5.30–11
Broughton Special, Oatmeal Stout Ⓐ
Traditional public bar in a typical Scottish village hotel. Eve meals till 7pm.
🏨 Q 🐾 ❀ 🍴 ◖ ▶ 🍺 ♣ P

Springfield

Queens Head

Main Street ☎ (0461) 37173
12–2.30, 7–11
McEwan 70/-, 80/- Ⓗ
Friendly local. ❀ 🛏 ♣ P

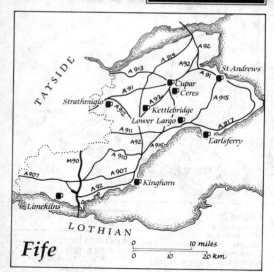

Fife

Ceres

Brands Inn

High Street ☎ (033 482) 325
11–3, 5.30–12 (1am Fri; 11–12 Sat;
12.30–11.30 Sun)
Caledonian 80/- Ⓗ
Low-ceilinged bar recently
restored to its former state of
(real) beams and stone walls.
Three fine mirrors include a
Ballingall's – a rarity.
🏠 🛏 ⊛ ◑ P

Cupar

Drookit Dug

43 Bonnygate (A91)
☎ (0334) 55862
11–12 (11–11 Sun)
Ind Coope Burton Ale Ⓗ;
guest beers
Town-centre meeting place
mainly for the young.
🏠 ◑ ⇌

Earlsferry

Golf Tavern

Links Road ☎ (0333) 330610
11–2.30, 5–11 (11–12 Sat; 12.30–11
Sun)
Caledonian 70/- Ⓗ
Traditional pub affording a
fine view over the golf links
and sporting a golfing theme
in the clubhouse bar and the
Bunker games room. Note
wooden gantry, two original
mirrors and the gas lighter on
the bar. Children welcome
until 8pm. Q 🛏 ◑ 🍴 ♣

Kettlebridge

Kettlebridge Inn

9 Cupar Road (A92)
☎ (0337) 30232
11–2.30, 5–11 (12 Thu; 11–12 Fri &
Sat; 12.30–11 Sun)
Belhaven 60/-, 80/- Ⓗ; **guest
beers**
Small, welcoming village local
boasting a collection of old
photographs of the area.
🏠 Q 🛏 ◑ ▸ 🍴

Kinghorn

Auld Hoose

8 Nethergate (off A92)
☎ (0592) 891074
12 (11 Fri, Sat & summer)–12
(12.30–12 Sun)
**Broughton Greenmantle Ale;
Caledonian 80/-** Ⓗ; **guest
beers**
Well-appointed public bar
with a pool table and a
comfortable lounge, adjacent
to the best chip shop in Fife.
Two guest beers range from
Orkney to Exmoor. 🍴 ⇌ ♣

Limekilns

Ship Inn

Halkett's Hall (off A985)
☎ (0383) 872247
11–2.30, 5–11 (12 Thu & Fri; 11–12
Sat; 12.30–12 Sun)
**Belhaven 80/-, St Andrew's
Ale; Courage Directors;
Marston's Pedigree** Ⓗ
Small but comfortably
appointed, one-room lounge
bar. Nautical bric-a-brac and
fine views over the Firth of
Forth. Warm and friendly.
◑ 🍴 ♣

Lower Largo

Railway Inn

Station Wynd ☎ (033 320) 239
11–12 (inc. Sun)
**Maclay 80/-; Marston's
Pedigree** Ⓗ
Friendly pub where beer and

atmosphere are of prime
importance. Skittles played in
summer. Q 🛏 ⊛ 🍴 ◑ 🍴 ▲ ♣

St Andrews

Bert's Bar

99 South Street
11–12 (11–11.45 Sat; 12.30–12 Sun)
**Alloa Arrol's 80/-; Caledonian
80/-; Ind Coope Burton Ale;
Tetley Bitter** Ⓗ; **guest beers**
Another splendid facsimile of
a traditional Scots bar, though
significantly changed: women
are welcome, tea is served and
snacks include hard-boiled
eggs and pickled jalopenos!
Try the pies. 🏠 ◑ ▲ ♣

Castle Tavern

Castle Street ☎ (0334) 74977
11–12 (11.30–2.30, 7–10.45 Sun)
**Broughton Greenmantle Ale;
Caledonian 80/-** Ⓗ
Modernised town-centre bar
retaining a George Younger
mirror.

Cellar Bar

Bell Street ☎ (0334) 77425
11–11.45 (4.30–11 Sun)
Belhaven 80/- Ⓗ; **guest beers**
Small, pleasant bar below
street level, popular with
students. A wide and varied
menu can be ordered in the
upstairs wine bar. Always two
guest beers available.

Jigger Bar
(Old Course Hotel)

☎ (0334) 74371
11–11 (12.30–11 Sun)
**Belhaven St Andrew's Ale;
Broughton Greenmantle
Ale** Ⓗ; **guest beer**
Decor reflects the strong
golfing connection in this
attractive stone and wood
hotel bar. Q ⊛ 🛏 ◑ 🍴 P

Playfair Lounge
(Ardgowan Hotel)

2 Playfair Terrace
☎ (0334) 72970
12–2.30, 5–11.30
**McEwan 80/-; Younger
No. 3** Ⓐ; **guest beers**
Modern basement lounge,
decorated with photographs
of Old Fife; very popular for
meals. No accommodation
from mid December to end
January. Guest beers during
university term time. 🛏 ◑ ▸

Strathmiglo

Strathmiglo Inn

High Street ☎ (033 76) 252
11–2.30, 6–11 (11–12 Fri & Sat;
12.30–7 Sun, closed Sun eve)
Maclay 80/- Ⓗ; **guest beers**
Small, friendly public bar with
a lounge to the rear. The beer
shown is fairly regular, but
may change.
🛏 ◑ ▸ 🍴 ▲ ♣ P

Grampian

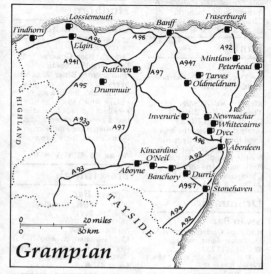

Grampian

Aberdeen

Ale Cellar
114 Rosemount Viaduct
☎ (0224) 624700
10–9 (closed Sun)
Beer range varies H
Off-licence stocking two regular draught beers plus a large range of British, German and especially Scottish bottled beers.

Atholl Hotel
Kingsgate ☎ (0224) 323505
11–2.30, 5–11 (11.30 Fri & Sat)
Draught Bass H; **McEwan 80/-** A
Very comfortable West End hotel. Q ⇔ ◖▶ & P

Betty Burkes
45 Langstane Place
☎ (0224) 210359
11–12 (6.30–11 Sun)
Caledonian 80/-; Ind Coope Burton Ale; Tetley Bitter H
Modern city-centre bar, very popular and attractively done up without going over the top like other wine bars. 'Drink the World' is an ongoing competition to drink beers from all over the world. Large selection of bottled beers. Opens at 10am for coffee.
◖▶ ⇌

Blue Lamp
Gallowgate ☎ (0224) 647472
11–12 (6.30–11 Sun)
McEwan 80/- A; **S&N Theakston Best Bitter** H; **guest beers**
Pub with a small, dark, but very comfortable bar and a large, stone-floored lounge. Free jukebox in both, with

some gems among the old 45s in the public bar. Two regular guest beers in the public bar.
🍺 & ⇌ ♣

Camerons Inn
6 Little Belmont Street
☎ (0224) 644487
11–11.45 (closed Sun)
Draught Bass; Ind Coope Burton Ale H; **Younger No. 3; guest beer** A
Old coaching inn whose tiny, listed snug remains unchanged, despite modern extensions at the back.
◖▶ 🍺 ⇌ ♣

Carriages
Brentwood Hotel, 101 Crown Street ☎ (0224) 595440
11–2.30, 5–11.30 (6–11.30 Sun, closed Sun lunch)
Whitbread Wethered Bitter, Boddingtons Bitter, Castle Eden Ale, Flowers Original; guest beer
Recently refurbished to a very high standard but still retaining a cosy pub atmosphere. Very popular with visitors as well as locals. The host recently won an award from the local branch of CAMRA. Liefmans Kriek is available on draught.
Q ⇔ ◖▶ ⇌ P

Churchills
Crown Street ☎ (0224) 586916
11–11
Draught Bass H; **guest beer**
Upmarket pub, nice and friendly, serving excellent, good value food. Two small enclosed areas are available for meetings. Nice prints on the walls. ◖▶ ⇌

Cutters Wharf
65 Regents Quay
☎ (0224) 580684
11–11
Guest beers H
Pub on the harbour, used mostly by office workers. A modern bar with old prints on walls. Choice of two varied guest beers. ◖ ⇌

Ferryhill House Hotel
169 Bon Accord Street
☎ (0224) 590867
11–11 (11.30 Thu–Sat; 12.30–5, 6.30–11 Sun)
Broughton Greenmantle Ale A; **Orkney Dark Island** H; **McEwan 80/-; S&N Theakston Best Bitter; Taylor Landlord; Younger No. 3** A
Quaint bar and a large, attractive lounge, popular in summer. Stocks the largest selection of malt whiskies in Aberdeen. Large seating area and play equipment outside.
Q ⛱ ❀ ◖▶ ⇌ P

Filthy McNasty's
37 Summer Street
☎ (0224) 625588
11–12 (6.30–11 Sun)
Draught Bass; Whitbread Flowers IPA H
Live bands on Tue, folk music on Sat in this family-run pub where the bar staff make you feel part of the family. T-shirt printing available. Four bottled Belgian beers and many others in stock. &

Globe
13 North Silver Street
☎ (0224) 624258
11–12 (12.30–11 Sun)
McEwan 80/- A; **S&N Theakston Best Bitter; Whitbread Boddingtons Bitter** H; **Younger No. 3** A
Small, attractive bar with a musical theme throughout, two minutes from the music hall. It must have the best decorated toilets in town. Opens at 9am for coffee; Sun breakfasts from 11.30am.
◖▶ ⇌

Malt Mill
82 Holburn Street
☎ (0224) 573830
11 (downstairs bar 7)–12 (12.30–11 Sun)
Draught Bass H
Old local bar upstairs; real ale only in the modern downstairs bar which is very well set out. If the nightly live bands are not for you, an alternative seating area is available. Q ◖ 🍺

Moorings
2 Trinity Quay
☎ (0224) 587602
11–12 (12.30–11 Sun)
Draught Bass; guest beers H

Grampian

Dark, narrow, city-centre pub with a host of electronic games. Weird and wonderful artwork on the walls is set against a decor of red and black. A pub for rock/heavy metal fans. Two regular guest beers. ♣

Prince of Wales
5 St Nicholas Lane
☎ (0224) 640597
11–10.45 (11.45 Thu–Sat; 12.30–10.45 Sun)
Draught Bass; Caledonian 80/-; S&N Theakston Old Peculier Ⓗ; Younger No. 3 Ⓐ; guest beers
Still largely unspoilt, a very popular pub for all ages. Possibly boasts the longest straight bar in Scotland. Large helpings of good lunches; two regular guest beers.
Q Ⓓ ♣ ♠

Tilted Wig
55 Castle Street (opp. court house) ☎ (0224) 583248
12–12 (7–11 Sun)
Alloa Arrol's 80/-; Caledonian 80/-; Ind Coope Burton Ale; Tetley Bitter Ⓗ
Busy, comfortable, students' city-centre pub whose walls are covered in pictures with a law theme and anecdotes.
Ⓓ ♣

Aboyne

Charleston Hotel
Charleston Road
☎ (033 98) 86475
11–2.30, 5–11 (12 Fri & Sat; 11–2.30, 5–11 Sun)
Ind Coope Burton Ale Ⓗ
Family-run hotel, popular all-year round but especially in summer for meals and refreshment stops. Good view from the lounge.
Q ❀ 🚗 Ⓓ ♿ Ⓐ P

Banchory

Scott Skinners
Station Road (A93 E side of town) ☎ (033 02) 4393
11–2.30, 5–12 (11–12 Sat; 12.30–11 Sun)
Draught Bass; Whitbread Boddingtons Bitter Ⓗ; guest beers
Comfortable local with a welcoming atmosphere. The garden has a play area. Camping for tents and caravans.
🚶 Q ❀ Ⓓ Ⓓ ♿ Ⓐ P

Tor-Na-Coille Hotel
Inchmarlo Road (A93 W side of town) ☎ (033 02) 2242
11.30–2.30, 5–11.30
S&N Theakston Best Bitter Ⓗ
Lovely, imposing hotel enjoying a very quiet, friendly atmosphere, on the verge of all Royal Deeside has to offer. Very welcoming staff; large

selection of malt whiskies. A former haunt of Charlie Chaplin. Croquet played. 🚶
Q 🛏 ❀ 🚗 Ⓓ Ⓓ ♿ Ⓐ ♣ P

Banff

Ship Inn
7–8 Deveronside (by harbour)
☎ (0261) 812620
11–12 (12.30–11 Sun)
McEwan 80/- Ⓐ; S&N Theakston Best Bitter Ⓗ
Established in 1710, an original bar where the movie *Local Hero* was partly made. Designed as a clinker-built boat. A friendly pub; note the Archibald Arrol mirror. Children welcome till 8pm.
🚶 🛏 Ⓓ Ⓓ ♿ ♣

Drummuir

Swan Bar
Rosebank Cottage (off B9104 Dufftown–Keith road)
☎ (054 281) 230
11–11 (11.45 Fri & Sat; 12.30–11 Sun)
Tetley Bitter Ⓗ
Friendly, but very basic, single-bar village local, run by an ex-Tetley employee.
Ⓓ Ⓓ ♿ ♣ P

Durris

Crofters Inn
Lochton of Durris (A957, Stonehaven–Crathes road)
☎ (033 044) 543
11.30–3, 5.30–12 (closed Tue in winter)
Ind Coope Burton Ale Ⓗ
Relaxed, comfy surroundings and a homely atmosphere in a peaceful pub, situated in the middle of the countryside. Very friendly host and locals.
Q 🛏 ❀ 🚗 Ⓓ Ⓓ ♿ P

Dyce

Greentrees
Victoria Street (off A947)
OS887135 ☎ (0224) 722283
11–11 (12 Thu–Sat; 12.30–11 Sun)
Beer range varies Ⓐ
Large, lively village local with a busy meal-time trade. The bar is decorated with football memorabilia and the lounge nicely appointed. Vegetarian food served.
Q Ⓓ Ⓓ Ⓓ ♿ Ⓐ ♣ ♣ P

Elgin

Thunderton House
Thunderton Place
☎ (0343) 548767
11–11 (11.45 Fri & Sat; 12.30–11 Sun)
Draught Bass; Courage Directors; Maclay 80/- Ⓗ; guest beer
Carefully restored historic building, reputed to be the site of Bonnie Prince Charlie's last fling before Culloden.
🚶 🛏 Ⓓ Ⓓ ♿ ♣

Findhorn

Crown & Anchor
☎ (0309) 690243
11–11 (12 Fri & Sat)
Draught Bass; Courage Directors; Whitbread Boddingtons Bitter Ⓗ; guest beers
Comfortable bar in a scenic village which stocks an excellent range of bottled beers. Food is served all day. The alternative Findhorn Foundation! Three guest beers.
🚶 🚗 Ⓓ Ⓓ ♿ Ⓐ ♣ P

Fraserburgh

Crown Bar
45 Broad Street (up alley)
☎ (0346) 24941
11–11.30
McEwan 80/- Ⓗ
Old-fashioned, cosy public bar overlooking the harbour. Note the unusual old Guinness fount. Ⓓ ♣

Inverurie

Thainstone House Hotel
Off A96, Aberdeen–Inverurie road, N of Kintore OS775187
☎ (0467) 21643
11–11 (12.30–11 Sun)
Beer choice varies Ⓗ
Imposing country house set back from the main road. A genteel atmosphere in a popular food-oriented establishment. Guest ale on rotation.
🚶 Q 🛏 ❀ 🚗 Ⓓ Ⓓ P

Kincardine O'Neil

Gordon Arms Hotel
☎ (033 98) 84236
11.30–11 (12 Thu–Sat)
S&N Theakston Best Bitter; Younger No. 3; guest beer Ⓗ
Typical public bar with no frills, but a very unusual lounge featuring superb decor in wood, with alcoves, piano and swords; its big wooden tables are uncommon. Very popular as a refreshment stop.
Q 🛏 Ⓓ Ⓓ ♿

Lossiemouth

Clifton
5 Clifton Road
☎ (0343) 812100
11–2.30, 5–11 (11–11.45 Fri & Sat)
McEwan 80/-; S&N Theakston Old Peculier Ⓔ; guest beer
Comfortable bar on the road to the harbour. The walls reflect the nautical and aeronautical connections of the bar and local community.
🚶 Ⓓ ♿ Ⓐ ♣ P

Mintlaw

Country Park Inn
Station Road (off A950, New Pitsligo road)
☎ (0771) 22622
11–11.30 (including Sun)
Courage Directors
Pleasant, well-appointed lounge with a summer outdoor area. An ideal lunchtime retreat (serving good vegetarian food) before or after visiting the adjacent Aden Country Park and Heritage Centre. Children welcome.

Newmachar

Beekies Neuk
Station Road (by A947)
OS885195
☎ (065 17) 2740
11–11 (1am Fri, 11.45 Sat; 12.30–11 Sun)
Draught Bass; Courage Directors **; guest beer**
Congenial snug bar with a bay window, real coal fire and an intimate, friendly atmosphere. Exceptional, large wood-panelled lounge bar, providing good food and entertainment. German bottle-conditioned beer available.

Oldmeldrum

Redgarth
Kirk Brae (off A947, Aberdeen–Banff road)
OS812273
☎ (065 12) 2353
11–2.30, 5–11 (11.45 Fri & Sat; 12.30–2.30, 5.30–11 Sun)
Draught Bass **; guest beers**
Very popular pleasant bar whose garden enjoys a magnificent panoramic view.

Good value, fresh home-cooked food including vegetarian. The attentive host is a previous national CAMRA *Pub of the Year* winner, settling in at a new location. Children welcome. House beer on sale.

Peterhead

Grange Inn
West Road (A950)
☎ (0779) 73472
11–2.30, 5–11 (12 Wed; 11–12 Thu & Sat; 11–1am Fri)
S&N Theakston Best Bitter
Comfortable open lounge and a small, plain public bar with barrel seats. Normally quiet but stages live entertainment once a month.

Palace Hotel
Prince Street
☎ (0779) 74821
11–11.45 (12.45 Thu & Fri; 12–11 Sun)
Tetley Bitter
Large city hotel with plenty of activities suited to the younger person; TV and bandits in evidence in the dark, comfy lounge.

Ruthven

Borve Brew House
Off A96, N of Huntly
☎ (046 687) 343
12.30–11 (11.45 Fri & Sat; 12.30–11 Sun)
Borve Ale, Bishop Elphinstone Ale, Tall Ships IPA, Cairm Porter
Happiness is handpulled at this one-bar, one-stove, full-mash brew pub in a rural converted school. It offers respectable and distinctive ales brewed by a master brewer. If deserted call next door!

Stonehaven

Ship Inn
Shorehead ☎ (0569) 62617
11–12 (12.30–12 Sun)
Caledonian 80/- **; McEwan 80/-** **; Orkney Dark Island**
Basic but comfortable bar with a nautical theme and a spacious lounge in green decor. Popular for food, and well worth a visit in summer for sitting outside and watching the activities in the harbour.

Tarves

Globe Inn
Millbank (by B999) OS865312
☎ (065 15) 623
11–2.30, 5–12 (1am Fri; 11–11.45 Sun)
Broughton Greenmantle Ale (winter)
Small, friendly village pub with a lively, compact bar and a multi-purpose meals/pool lounge adjacent. Note: real ale is available in winter only.

Whitecairns

Whitecairns Hotel
Off B999, Aberdeen–Tarves road OS922183
☎ (065 17) 2218
11–12 (1am Fri, 11.45 Sat; 12–11 Sun)
Broughton Greenmantle Ale
Straightforward roadside inn with a busy, friendly, earthy bar and a popular, relaxed lounge. Attentive staff and superb value, fresh home-cooked food from an extensive menu which includes vegetarian dishes. Live entertainment Fri eves. Note: the Orkney Dark Island was bright (filtered) at the time of survey.

"IT USED TO BE PACKED OUT UNTIL THEY GOT IN FRUIT MACHINES, A TV AND A JUKE BOX TO ATTRACT THE YOUNGSTERS"

From Good Beer Guide 1988

KenPyne

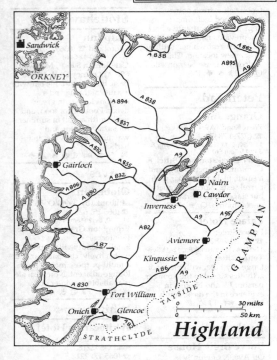

Orkney, Sandwick, Orkney

Aviemore

Winking Owl
Grampian Road
☎ (0479) 810841
11–11 (12 Fri, 11.45 Sat)
Alloa Arrol's 80/-; Caledonian 70/- Ⓐ**; Tetley Bitter** Ⓗ**; guest beers**
Bar popular with the après-ski crowd and tourists. Fine restaurant. ⬚ ◖◗ ▯ ⊟ Ⓐ P

Cawdor

Cawdor Tavern
The Lane ☎ (066 77) 316
11–2.30, 5–11 (1am Fri, 11.45 Sat)
McEwan 80/- Ⓗ
Old coaching inn, set in a picturesque village on a back road from Inverness to Nairn. Close to the Culloden battlefield and the magnificent Cawdor Castle.
🍺 ✿ ◖◗ ▯ ⊟ Ⓐ P

Fort William

Alexandra Hotel
The Parade ☎ (0397) 70 2241
11–11 (12–11 Sun)
Caledonian 80/- Ⓗ
The town's principal hotel: a listed building (1876), elegant and traditional, quiet and friendly. It has modern facilities but is furnished in restful and restrained style. Well lit, with comfortable seating and courteous service.
Q ✿ ⊯ ◖◗ Ⓖ ⅄ Ⓐ ⇌ P

Nevis Bank Hotel
Belford Road (A82, near turnoff for Glen Nevis)
☎ (0397) 705721
11–11 (1am Fri, 11.45 Sat; 12–11 Sun)
McEwan 80/-; Younger No. 3 Ⓐ
Modernised hotel that serves as a useful base for the mountains. A comfortable lounge at the front is complemented at the rear by the more basic Ceilidh Bar, used by locals, including a shinty team.
⬚ ⊯ ◖◗ ⊟ Ⓐ ⇌ ⊹ P

Gairloch

Old Inn
The Harbour ☎ (0445) 2006
11–12 (11.30 Sat; 12.30–11 Sun)
Draught Bass; Younger No. 3 Ⓗ **(occasionally)**
Old West Highland coaching inn, set by a footbridge in a quiet glen with views of loch and mountain. A warm and friendly, family-run, country inn. Food is served noon to 10pm.
⬚ ✿ ⊯ ◖◗ ▯ ⊟ Ⓐ ⊹ P

Glencoe

Clachaig Inn
Off A82, behind NT centre
☎ (085 52) 252
11–11 (12 Fri, 11.30 Sat; 12.30–11 Sun)
Alloa Arrol's 80/-; Ind Coope Burton Ale; Tetley Bitter; Younger No. 3; guest beers Ⓗ
One of the biggest sellers of real ale in the Highlands; an almost legendary pub with absolutely no local customers but known and frequented by climbers, walkers and many others from all over Britain and abroad.
🍺 Q ✿ ⊯ ⊟ Ⓖ ⅄ P

Inverness

Clachnaharry Inn
High Street ☎ (0463) 239806
11–11 (11.45 Thu–Sat)
McEwan 80/- Ⓐ
Traditional coaching inn beside the sea lock of the Caledonian Canal and the single track railway line. The lounge bar offers magnificent views across the Beauly Firth to the Black Isle. 🍺 ◖◗ ⊟ ⊹

Gellions Hotel
10 Bridge Street
☎ (0463) 233648
11–11 (1am Wed–Fri, 11.45 Sat; 12.30–11 Sun)
Caledonian 80/-; McEwan 80/-; S&N Theakston Best Bitter Ⓐ
Small town-centre hotel with a long-established bar trade. Pleasant surroundings. No real ale is served in the public bar. ◖◗ Ⓐ ⇌

Glenmhor Hotel
10 Ness Bank
☎ (0463) 234308
11–2.30, 5–11 (1am Thu & Fri, 11.45 Sat; 11–11 summer; 12.30–11 Sun)
Ind Coope Burton Ale Ⓗ
Busy riverside hotel with a magnificent view of the cathedral. The popular public bar (selling real ale) in the converted stables takes the name of 'Nicky Tam's'.
🍺 ✿ ⊯ ◖◗ ⊟ Ⓐ ⇌ P

Heathmount Hotel
Kingsmills Road (Crown area)
☎ (0463) 235877
11–11 (12.30 Thu & Fri, 11.30 Sat; 12.30–11 Sun)
McEwan 80/-; S&N Theakston Best Bitter Ⓗ**; guest beer**
Busy hotel lounge bar with distinctive decor and a friendly atmosphere. Excellent value, imaginative menu.
⊯ ◖◗ ⊟ ⇌ ⊹ P

Phoenix

108–110 Academy Street
☎ (0463) 233685
11–11 (12.30 Thu & Fri, 11.30 Sat)
Draught Bass; Belhaven St Andrew's Ale; Maclay 80/- H**; guest beers**
Lively, traditional horseshoe bar, complete with fresh sawdust and many interesting artefacts around the walls, including the pub's original beer engine (now in a glass case). ☎ ◑ ▶ ⊟ �

Kingussie

Royal Hotel

Main Street ☎ (0540) 661236

11–11 (12 Sat)
Alloa Arrol's 80/-; Ansells Mild, Bitter; Ind Coope Burton Ale; Tetley Mild, Bitter H
Large, extended hotel with friendly staff. Excellent accommodation and food – very good value. Pleasant lounge bar.
Q ☎ ⊨ ◑ ▶ ♿ ♠ P ⚥

Nairn

Invernairne Hotel

Thurlow Road ☎ (0667) 52039
11–2.30, 5–11 (12 Mon & Sat, 1am Fri)
McEwan 80/- A
Spacious lounge bar in a family-run hotel, a magnificent Victorian building right on the seashore. Note the impressive fireplace. Live jazz every Mon.
▨ Q ✿ ⊨ ◑ ▶ ♠ ≋ P

Onich

Nether Lochaber Hotel (Corran Bar)

Off A82 ☎ (085 53) 235
11–2.30, 5–11 (12.30–2.30, 6.30–11 Sun)
Draught Bass H
Smashing wee public bar tucked in behind the hotel on the slip road down to the Corran ferry.
Q ☎ ⊨ ◑ ▶ ⊟ ♠ P

Join CAMRA — see page 508

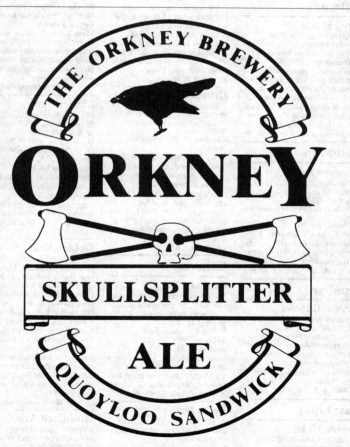

An appropriately titled potent brew from Britain's northernmost brewery

Lothian

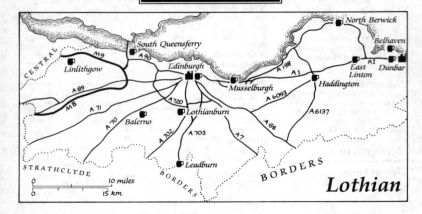

 Belhaven, *Dunbar;* **Caledonian,** *Edinburgh*

Balerno

Grey Horse
22 Main Street (off A70)
☎ (031) 449 3092
11–2.30, 5–11 (closed Sun)
Belhaven 60/-, 80/-
Traditionally-run, wood-panelled gem set in a village increasingly encroached upon by the city suburbs. A fine bank of handpumps dispense the delicious (and cheap) beer. A busy local with a number of rare brewery mirrors. Q ⊞ ♣

Belhaven

Mason's Arms
8 High Street (A1087, off A1, ½ mile W of Dunbar)
☎ (0368) 63700
11 (12.30 Sun)–2.30, 5–11 (closed Sun eve)
Belhaven 80/- H
Friendly locals' bar just up the lane from the brewery. Lovely beaches nearby in this hamlet on the outskirts of Dunbar. Eve meals Thu–Sat. ◑ ▶ ⊞ ♣

Dunbar

Bayswell Hotel
Bayswell Park (off Belhaven Rd, A1087) ☎ (0368) 62225
11–1am (12.30 Sun–12 Sun)
Belhaven St Andrew's Ale H
Small, cosy bar in a clifftop country house hotel with impressive views across the Firth of Forth.
❀ ⇔ ◑ ▶ ⅙ ⇌ (Dunbar)P

East Linton

Crown Hotel
27 Bridge Street (B1377, off A1) ☎ (0620) 860335
11–2.30, 5–11 (11–1am Fri & Sat; 12.30–12 Sun)

Belhaven 80/- H
Cosy wood-panelled locals' bar with a large lounge to the rear. A pair of rare Dudgeon & Co windows remain as a reminder of Belhaven's original name. Beware the keg 60/- and 70/-. Separate games room with pool table.
⊞ ⇔ ◑ ▶

Drover's Inn
5 Bridge Street (B1377, off A1)
☎ (0620) 860298
11–2.30, 5–11 (11–11 summer; 12.30–11 Sun)
Caledonian 80/- H; **guest beers**
Wood-panelled lounge with a marble-topped bar and a distinct 1930s atmosphere. The service is friendly and courteous with a bowl of fruit and mints provided for customers. A rare East Lothian outlet for Worthington White Shield. Highly recommended food. Three guest beers.
⊞ Q ⇔ ◑ ▶

Edinburgh

Bennet's Bar
1 Maxwell Street, Morningside (off A702, Morningside Road, 2 miles from Princes St)
☎ (031) 447 1903
11–2.30, 5–11 (closed Sun)
Belhaven 70/-, 80/-, St Andrew's Ale A
Long-established, 1950s, beer-drinker's boozer at the foot of a Victorian tenement in central Morningside. Avoid the 60/–: it is *not* real ale. Q ⊞ ♣

Bert's Bar
27 William Street (beyond W end of Princes St, parallel with Shandwick Pl)
☎ (031) 225 5748
11–11 (12 Thu–Sat; 12.30–2.30, 6.30–11 Sun)

Alloa Arrol's 80/-; Caledonian 80/-; Ind Coope Burton Ale; Maclay 70/-; Taylor Landlord; Tetley Bitter H
Main bar with a snug and sitting room off, and a very fine ornate brewery mirror. A good example of modern pub architecture, using quality wood and tiling.
Q ◑ ⊞ ⇌ (Haymarket)

Clark's Bar
142 Dundas Street (1 mile N of Princes St, near Canonmills)
☎ (031) 556 1067
11 (12.30 Sun)–11 (11.30 Thu–Sat)
Draught Bass; Caledonian Deuchars IPA; S&N Theakston XB H
Basic, traditional Scottish stand-up boozer with two sitting rooms to the rear, separated by a precipitous stairway. Very busy early evening with a local office crowd. ⊞

Golden Rule
30 Yeaman Place, Fountainbridge (off Dundee St near S&N) ☎ (031) 229 3413
11–11 (12.30–2.30, 6.30–11 Sun)
Draught Bass; Caledonian Deuchars IPA, 80/-; Harviestoun 80/-; Orkney Raven H; **guest beers**
Comfortable, split-level lounge bar with a thriving locals' trade. Has come from nothing to establish itself as one of Edinburgh's premier ale pubs. White Shield available; three guest beers. Live jazz Wed.
Q ◑ ⊞ ⇌ (Haymarket) ♣

Guildford Arms
1 West Register Street (E end of Princes St behind Wimpey)
☎ (031) 556 4312
11–11 (12 Thu–Sat; 12.30–2.30, 6.30–11 Sun)

Belhaven St Andrew's Ale; Caledonian 80/-; Harviestoun 70/-, 80/-; Orkney Dark Island; Taylor Landlord Ⓗ**; guest beers**
One of the city's finest interiors, with an unusual gallery alcove which overlooks the main bar. The famous ceiling is quite superb and there are interesting brewery mirrors too. Close to bus and rail stations. Eight regular and two guest beers.
◖ ≢ (Waverley)

Kay's Bar

39 Jamaica Street West
☎ (031) 225 1858
11–12 (12.30–11 Sun)
Belhaven 80/-; S&N Theakston Best Bitter, XB Ⓗ**; guest beers**
Cosy, convivial, comfortable and consistent New Town bar, tucked behind India Street and featuring clever and interesting bar furniture. Good varied bar lunches. Three guest beers and 50 single malt whiskies.
🚇 Q ◖ ≢ (Waverley)

Leslie's Bar

45 Ratcliffe Terrace
☎ (031) 667 5957
11–11 (12.30 Fri, 11.45 Sat; 12.30–2.30, 6.30–11 Sun)
Draught Bass; Belhaven 80/-; Caledonian 80/- Ⓗ
A real gem of a Victorian pub, complete with a snob screen dividing the saloon from the public bar. The fine interior is somewhat marred by the unfortunate choice of decor but, architecturally, the pub remains one of the best in the city. 🚇 Q ⊞ ♣

Oxford Bar

8 Young Street (between George and Queen St, near Charlotte Sq)
☎ (031) 225 4262
11 (12.30 Sun)–1am
Belhaven 80/- Ⓐ**, St Andrew's Ale** Ⓗ**; guest beer**
Tiny but vibrant New Town drinking shop, retaining signs of its original early 19th-century parlour arrangement. Traditional pub music.
Q ⊞ ≢ (Waverley) ♣

Robbies Bar

367 Leith Walk (A900, ¾ mile from Princes St)
☎ (031) 554 6850
12 (11 Sat)–12 (12.30–11 Sun)
Draught Bass; Caledonian Deuchars IPA, 80/-; Ind Coope Burton Ale; Traquair House Bear Ale Ⓗ**; guest beers**
Victorian-style workingman's bar with interesting woodwork and gantry decor. Original mirrors. White Shield available. ⊞ ♿ ♣

St Vincent Bar

11 St Vincent Street, Stockbridge
☎ (031) 225 7447
12–2.30, 5–11 (11–12 Fri & Sat; 12.30–2.30, 7–11 Sun)
Alloa Arrol's 80/-; Ind Coope Burton Ale; Maclay 80/-; Tetley Bitter Ⓗ**; guest beer**
Traditional bar with a superb gantry and many interesting wall decorations. Hospitable and cosy atmosphere.
Q ◖ 🚇 ♣

Southsider

3–5 West Richmond Street (near Surgeon's Hall, ½ mile from Princes St)
☎ (031) 667 2003
11–11 (12.30–11 Sun)
Maclay 60/- Ⓗ**, 70/-, 80/-** Ⓐ**, Kane's Amber Ale, Scotch Ale** Ⓗ**; guest beers**
Busy Southside lounge bar, popular with students and discerning boozers alike. Impromptu karaoke (late night only). Three guest beers, Worthington White Shield and a few Belgian bottled beers always available. Family room lunchtimes and afternoons.
Q 🍴 ◖ ⊞ ≢ (Waverley) ♣

Stable Bar

30 Frogston Road East, Mortonhall (off B701 – E of A702 – down road by garden centre) OS263685
☎ (031) 664 0773
11–12 (12.30–11 Sun)
Caledonian 80/- Ⓗ
Friendly bar approached through an arch and a cobbled courtyard. Food served all day (except Sun 3–6.30). Adjacent to a camping/caravan park in rural surroundings on the southern edge of the city. Children welcome. Quizzes Fri. 🚇 Q ✿ ◖ ▶ ▲ P

Todd's Tap

42 Bernard Street, Leith
☎ (031) 556 4122
12 (12.30 Sun)–11 (11.30 Thu & Fri, 12 Sat)
Draught Bass; Belhaven 80/-; Ind Coope Burton Ale; Taylor Landlord; Tetley Bitter; Yates Bitter Ⓗ**; guest beers**
Friendly wee howff with a front bar and a back parlour where the unique collection of specially commissioned photographs of extinct city breweries should not be missed. 🚇 Q ◖ ⊞

Winston's

20 Kirk Loan, Corstorphine (off A8)
☎ (031) 334 1196
11–11.30 (12.30–4, 7–11 Sun)
Alloa Arrol's 80/-; Caledonian 70/-; Ind Coope Burton Ale Ⓗ

Small, busy locals' lounge bar housed in an ex-launderette near the zoo in a western suburb of the city. Well worth a visit. ◖

Haddington

Pheasant

72 Market Street (off A1)
☎ (062 082) 6342
11 (12.30 Sun)–11 (12 Thu–Sat)
Belhaven 80/-, St Andrew's Ale; Caledonian 70/-; Ind Coope Burton Ale; Tetley Bitter Ⓗ
Vibrant pub attracting young folk, especially at weekends. The long bar snakes through from the games area to the lounge where Basil (surely a Norwegian Blue) holds court. ◖ ♣

Leadburn

Leadburn Inn

At A703/A701/A6094 jct, 3 miles S of Penicuik
☎ (0968) 72952
11 (12.30 Sun)–11.45
Caledonian 80/- Ⓗ**; guest beers**
Large food-oriented hostelry with 'meals on wheels' –an old railway coach converted into a restaurant. The public bar has two pot-bellied stoves and a picture window on the Pentland Hills. A conservatory links the bar to a plush lounge. Excellent menu with meals available all day till 10pm.
🚇 🍴 ✿ 🛏 ◖ ▶ ⊞ ♣ P

Linlithgow

Four Marys

65 High Street
☎ (0506) 842171
12–2.30, 5–11 (12 Fri; 12–12 Sat; 12.30–2.30, 7–11 Sun)
Belhaven 70/-, 80/-; Caledonian Deuchars IPA; Harviestoun Ptarmigan Ⓗ**; guest beers**
Attractive lounge bar with antique furniture and items reflecting the town's historic past. Good range of constantly changing guest beers and a large choice of malt whiskies. Twice-yearly beer festivals. CAMRA Forth Valley *Pub of the Year* 1992. No food Sun eve. 🍴 ▶ ≢

Red Lion

50 High Street
☎ (0506) 842348
11–11 (12 Thu–Sat; 12.30–11 Sun)
McEwan 70/-, 80/- Ⓐ
Small, friendly bar, popular for pool and darts. Discounts for pensioners. Snacks served all day. ✿ ⊞ ≢ ♣

Lothian

Lothianburn

Steading Inn
118–120 Biggar Road, Hillend (A702, $1/2$ mile S of bypass at city limits) ☎ (031) 445 1128
11–12 (12–11 Sun)
Caledonian 70/-, 80/-, Deuchars IPA; Ind Coope Burton Ale; Tetley Bitter Ⓗ
Former stone-built cottages converted into an attractive bar and restaurant with a new conservatory extension. A very popular eating establishment but the drinking area has been preserved. Close to the Pentland Hills and an artificial ski slope.
🛏 Q ✿ ◖ & P

Musselburgh

Levenhall Arms
10 Ravensheugh Road (off A199 at roundabout near racecourse) ☎ (031) 665 3220
11–11 (1am Fri, 12 Sat; 12–2.30, 6.30–11 Sun)
Broughton Greenmantle Ale;

Ind Coope Burton Ale Ⓗ
Busy public bar where colourful characters mix with the local clientele. Separate games room; regular musical entertainment Sat, Sun and other eves. ⊟ ♠ P

Volunteer Arms (Stagg's)
79–81 North High Street (behind Brunton Hall) ☎ (031) 665 6481
11–11 (closed Sun)
Draught Bass; Caledonian Deuchars IPA, 80/- Ⓗ; guest beer
Established in 1858: an olde-worlde bar with dark wood panelling and a magnificent gantry with four polished casks and brewery mirrors. A busy, friendly local where the clientele mix with theatre-goers. No food. Q ⊟ & ♠ P

North Berwick

Dalrymple Arms
Quality Street ☎ (0620) 2969
11 (12.30 Sun)–11 (12.30 Thu–Sat)

Caledonian 80/- Ⓗ; guest beers
Busy locals' boozer in the middle of a seaside town. The cosy bar has an impressive range of over 30 malt whiskies and an unusual collection of Zippo lighters. Games/TV room at the rear. Three guest beers. Beware the professional Jenga players! 🛏 ⊟ ⇌ ♠

South Queensferry

Hawes Inn
Newhalls Road (B924) ☎ (031) 331 1990
11 (12.30 Sun)–11 (11.45 Fri & Sat)
Alloa Arrol's 80/-; Ind Coope Burton Ale Ⓗ
Splendid country inn standing beneath the world's finest railway bridge. The bar is small and cosy and leads to the larger lounge which houses the food counter. A family room lies at the rear, where a huge Bernard's brewery mirror hangs.
🛏 🛌 ⚒ ◖ ⊟ ⇌ (Dalmeny) ♠ P

TIME FOR THE APPELLATION CONTROLÉE?

Where does the pint in your glass come from? If it's Theakston or Tetley, it must be Yorkshire, everyone knows that - or assumes so.

After all, the pump clips don't tell you that most of Theakston's beers are now produced in Newcastle, at S&N's Tyne Brewery, or that Tetley's Mild and Bitter are brewed at Warrington as well as Leeds. And when S&N spend fortunes portraying Theakston's little Masham brewery in full colour Sunday supplement adverts, well the beer must come from Yorkshire, mustn't it?

S&N and Allied aren't the only brewers playing this little game. For Whitbread it is second nature. Fremlins used to come from Faversham, in the heart of the hop country, yet Whitbread now brew their Kent flagship at Cheltenham. Higsons Bitter, similarly uprooted, has lost all its Merseyside character, now that it is produced in Sheffield.

And that's the point. When a beer is moved to another site (usually to save money), it changes its flavour. Even if the recipe remains the same, the water is different and the yeast reacts differently to the new environment. The original beer has been lost. Sometimes, the new brew can be good, but very often it is inferior.

Perhaps it's time we labelled our beers 'authentically Yorkshire-brewed' or 'genuinely from Kent'. Wine drinkers don't stand for such deceit, why should we?

Strathclyde

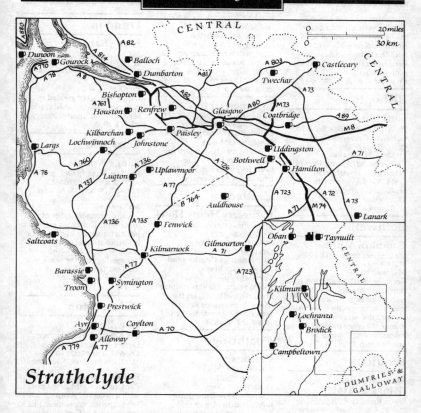

West Highland, *Taynuilt*

Alloway

Bellisle House Hotel (Shanter Bar)
Bellisle Park, Doonfoot Road (A719)
☎ (0292) 42331
11–11 (11–6 winter)
Alloa Arrol's 80/- Ⓔ
Golfers' 19th hole attached to an hotel set in a splendid country park with two golf courses, gardens and a pets corner. Meals available in the cafeteria or hotel. ⌘ Ⓐ P

Auldhouse

Auldhouse Arms
OS624502
☎ (035 52) 63242
12–11 (12 Fri & Sat; 12.30–11 Sun)
Belhaven 80/- Ⓐ
Archetypal village local, consisting of a wood-panelled public bar with several rooms off. Outside the sprawl of East Kilbride, it is very hard to find without a map. The large

switch used to activate the air pressure is off-putting but the beer is genuine.
⌘ Q Ⓓ ▶ Ⓐ ⬥ ♣ P

Ayr

Chestnuts Hotel
52 Racecourse Road (A719)
☎ (0292) 264393
11 (12 Sun)–12
Draught Bass; Broughton Special Ⓗ, **Oatmeal Stout** Ⓐ; **guest beer**
Cosy lounge bar with a vaulted ceiling and a collection of over 300 water jugs. Very good bar meals.
⌘ Q ❀ ⌘ Ⓓ ▶ ⬆ P

Geordie's Byre
103 Main Street
☎ (0292) 264925
11–11 (12 Thu–Sat; 12.30–11 Sun)
Caledonian Deuchars IPA, 80/- Ⓐ; **guest beers**
Friendly, traditional local, convenient for Somerset Park football ground. The back lounge (open weekends) has an interesting array of

Victoriana and bric-a-brac. An occasional 'Poets and Pints' venue. Ⓐ ⬥ ⬆ (Newton) ♣

Balloch

Balloch Hotel
Balloch Road
☎ (0389) 52579
11–11 (including Sun)
Alloa Arrol's 80/-; Ind Coope Burton Ale Ⓗ
Attractive hotel adjacent to the source of the River Leven and the bonnie banks of Loch Lomond. Beer is on tap in the lounge bar only, but is supplied to the public bar.
❀ ⌘ Ⓓ ▶ Ⓐ ⬆ ♣ P

Barassie

Tower Hotel
23 Beach Road (B746)
☎ (0292) 311142
11–12 (12–11 Sun)
Draught Bass; Broughton Greenmantle Ale; Mansfield Riding Mild Ⓗ

381

Strathclyde

Attractive hotel on Troon's North Beach, affording fine views over the Firth of Clyde to Arran. Real ale is sold in both the lounge and public bars. Recently refurbished to a high standard.
Q 🏠 🍴 ◖▶ ◧ 㐧 ≠ ♣ P

Bishopton

Golf Inn
28–30 Old Greenock Road (A8 Glasgow–Greenock Road)
☎ (0505) 862303
11–2.30, 5–12 (11.45 Sat)
Belhaven 80/- Ⓐ; guest beers
A real ale stalwart, where the first CAMRA meeting in Scotland was held in 1974. Three guest beers available; well-stocked off-sales. Q ◧ P

Bothwell

Camphill Vaults
Main Street ☎ (0698) 853526
11 (12.30 Sun)–11.45
McEwan 80/- Ⓐ
Recently-listed, multi-roomed pub in a conservation village, featuring a fine traditional gantry, high quality woodwork and original windows. The lounge is a more modern extension and doubles as a family room. 㐧 ◧ A P

Brodick

Duncans Bar (Kingsley Hotel)
Shore Road ☎ (0770) 2531
11–2.30, 7.30–12 (not Sun–Thu eves in winter; 11–12 summer)
McEwan 70/-, 80/-; S&N Theakston XB Ⓗ
Large, comfortable bar to the side of a sea-shore hotel. The front garden enjoys an excellent view across the bay to Goat Fell. Regular folk and jazz nights in summer.
🍴 㐧 🏠 🍴 ◖▶ ◧ P

Ormidale Hotel
Glencloy Road ☎ (0770) 2293
11.30–2.30 (not Mon–Fri in winter), 4.30–1 (11–1 Sat & Sun)
McEwan 70/- Ⓐ
Splendid sandstone building overlooking the golf course. A small and friendly public bar has an adjoining conservatory giving extra drinking space in summer. A pioneer of real ale on the island and still using the original tall founts. Accommodation available in summer. 🍴 㐧 🏠 🍴 ◖▶ P

Campbeltown

Ardshiel Hotel
Kilkerran Road
☎ (0586) 552133
11–2.30, 5–12
McEwan 80/- Ⓐ; S&N Theakston Best Bitter Ⓗ
Very popular, well-run family hotel on the outskirts of town, on the beautiful South Kintyre peninsula. Excellent home cooking and a wide range of local malt whiskies to sip afterwards at the open fire. Children very welcome; beautiful garden.
🍴 🏠 🍴 ◖▶ P

Commercial Inn
Cross Street ☎ (0586) 553703
11–1am (12.30–1am Sun)
Caledonian Deuchars IPA or 80/- Ⓗ; guest beers
Friendly, family-run pub in the centre of town. Guest beers include Young's Bitter and Taylor Landlord. ◧

Castlecary

Castlecary House Hotel
Main Street (off A80)
☎ (0324) 840233
11–11 (11–2.30, 6–11 Sun)
Draught Bass Ⓗ; Belhaven 80/-; Jennings Cumberland Ale Ⓐ; guest beers
There are three separate drinking areas in this country hotel. The village is on the site of one of the major Roman forts on the Antonine Wall.
🏠 🍴 ◖▶ ◧ 㐧 P

Coatbridge

Carsons
4–6 Whifflet Street
☎ (0236) 22867
11–12 (12.30–12 Sun)
Draught Bass; Broughton Greenmantle Ale Ⓗ
Modern one-bar pub, one of the few 1970s refurbishments which was actually done well: dark wood panels, cask ends and interesting murals. Eve meals finish at 6.30pm; no lunches Sun. ◖▶ ◧ P

Coylton

Finlayson Arms Hotel
24 Hillhead (A70, 4 miles E of Ayr) ☎ (0292) 570298
11–2.30, 5–12 (1am Fri; 11–1am Sat; 12.30–12 Sun)
Broughton Special, Oatmeal Stout Ⓗ
Village inn with a very comfortable lounge serving excellent bar meals. Caravan Club approved site in the hotel grounds. 🍴 Q 🍴 🏠 ◖▶ ◧ A ♣ P

Dumbarton

Stags Head
116 Glasgow Road
☎ (0389) 32642
11–12 (1am Fri & Sat; 11–12 Sun)
Alloa Arrol's 80/-; Ind Coope Burton Ale Ⓐ
Modern, medium-sized, one-roomed, open-plan bar with a friendly atmosphere.
🏠 ◖ ◧ ≠ (East) ♣ P

Dunoon

Lorne Bar
249 Argyll Street
☎ (0369) 5064
11–12 (1am Fri & Sat; 12.30–12 Sun)
McEwan 80/- Ⓐ
Popular no-frills public bar which has never yielded to Americanisation. Meals are served in the smarter lounge.
🍴 ◖▶ ◧ ◧

Fenwick

Kings Arms
89 Main Road (B7061, just off A77) ☎ (056 06) 276464
11.45–2.30, 5–12 (11–12 Fri & Sat; 12.30–12 Sun)
McEwan 80/- Ⓗ
Village inn on the edge of moorland. This listed building has an unusual exterior and a beautiful stained-glass window. The olde-worlde lounge displays the work of a local cartoonist. Children are welcome in the snug.
🍴 🍴 ◖ ♣ P

Gilmourton

Bow Butts
Off A71, half-way between Darvel and Strathaven
OS656400 ☎ (0357) 40333
11–12 (1am Fri; 12.30–11 Sun; closed Tue)
Belhaven 80/- Ⓗ
Remote but well-known pub with a deserved reputation for food. The lounge is more like a restaurant, but the public bar is cosy and traditional.
🍴 🏠 ◖▶ ◧ 㐧 P

Glasgow

Athena Taverna
780 Pollokshaws Road
☎ (041) 424 0858
11–2.30, 5–11 (closed Sun)
Belhaven 80/-; Courage Directors Ⓗ; guest beers
Southside stalwart which always has four guest beers on offer, together with a fine selection of bottled German specialities. A Greek restaurant attached offers high quality at low prices.
Q ◖▶ ≠ (Queens Pk)

Babbity Bowster
16–18 Blackfriars Street
☎ (041) 552 5055
11–12 (12.30–12 Sun)
Maclay 70/-, 80/-, Porter Ⓐ; guest beer
Set in the Merchant City; the owner did an excellent job in converting this building into a well-designed bar. Very popular with the local journalists, the legal profession, and students. Occasional live music during festivals. 🍴 Q 🏠 🍴 ◖▶ ≠ (High St) ↺

382

Blackfriars

36 Bell Street ☎ (041) 552 5924
11–12 (12.30–11 Sun)
**Alloa Arrol's 80/-; Ind Coope
Burton Ale; Maclay 70/-;
Tetley Bitter Ⓐ; guest beers**
Merchant City bar popular
with all types; can get very
busy eves. Hosts regular live
music, plus the 'Comic Club'
on alternate Sats.
◗ ▮ ≹ (High St)

Bon Accord

153 North Street (by M8 near
Mitchell Library)
☎ (041) 248 4427
11–11.45 (6.30–11 Sun)
**Caledonian Deuchars IPA;
McEwan 80/-; Marston's
Pedigree; Taylor Landlord;
S&N Theakston XB; Young's
Bitter; guest beers**
Basic public bar decorated
with mementoes of beer past
and present, plus a plush
lounge at the rear.
Traditionally one of Glasgow's
best-known real ale haunts, it
has fought its way back to pre-
eminence and usually has 12
beers available. ◗ ▮ ⊟ ≹
(Charing Cross/Anderston)
Ө (St Georges Cross)

Boswell Hotel
(The Country Club)

27 Mansionhouse Road,
Langside ☎ (041) 632 9812
11–11 (12.30–11 Sun)
**Draught Bass; Belhaven 80/-;
Caledonian 80/-, Golden
Promise Ⓗ; guest beers**
Split-level pub with a wide
range of guest beers.
Unusually, it offers two real
ciders, plus a wide selection of
foreign bottled beers.
Q ⌥ ✿ ⛵ ◗ ▮ ⊟
≹ (Langside) ♣ ⌂ P ⚲

Brewery Tap

1055 Sauchiehall Street
☎ (041) 339 8866
11 (12 Sat)–11 (12 Fri & Sat; 12.30–11
Sun)
**Alloa Arrol's 80/- Ⓔ; Belhaven
60/- Ⓐ; Caledonian 70/-;
Tetley Bitter Ⓔ; guest beers**
Despite the name, no beer is
brewed here. Usually live
music Fri and Sat nights, and
jazz on Sun afternoons.
Service can be slow, especially
when the pub is busy.
◗ ≹ (Exhibition Centre)
Ө (Kelvinhall)

Mitre

12 Brunswick Street (off
Trongate) ☎ (041) 552 3764
11–12 (12.30–11 Sun)
**Caledonian 70/-; Ind Coope
Burton Ale; Tetley Bitter Ⓗ**
Fine, small and unspoilt pub,
with a mini horseshoe bar,
that provides a welcome
haven from the busy streets.
Fears that new owners would
make changes have happily
proved unfounded. Eve meals

finish at 6.30pm. ◗ ▮ ⊟
≹ (Argyle St) Ө (St Enoch)

Overflow

67 Old Dumbarton Road
☎ (041) 334 4197
11–11 (12 Fri & Sat; 12.30–11 Sun)
**Draught Bass Ⓗ; Broughton
Greenmantle Ale Ⓐ; guest
beer**
A light and airy, open-plan
bar which has been very
popular since becoming a free
house. A welcome new
addition to the *Guide*.
◗ Ө (Kelvinhall)

Station Bar

55 Port Dundas Road,
Cowcaddens ☎ (041) 332 3117
11 (12.30 Sun)–12
**Draught Bass; Caledonian
Deuchars IPA Ⓗ**
Bar where the drabness of the
exterior belies the warm,
friendly atmosphere inside.
Popular with local workers
and memorabilia of past and
present local trades forms the
theme of the decor. ≹
(Queen St) Ө (Cowcaddens)

Tennents

191 Byres Road
11–11 (12 Fri & Sat; 12.30–4, 7–11
Sun)
**Draught Bass; Broughton
Greenmantle Ale, Oatmeal
Stout; Caledonian Deuchars
IPA, Golden Promise; M&B
Highgate Mild Ⓗ; guest beers**
Large corner pub selling ten
permanent and two guest
beers. Local CAMRA *Landlord
of the Year* winner. ◗
≹ (Partick) Ө (Hillhead)

Ubiquitous Chip

12 Ashton Lane
☎ (041) 334 5007
11–11 (12 Fri & Sat; 12.30–11 Sun)
Caledonian 70/-, 80/- Ⓐ
A converted storeroom above
a famous restaurant, retaining
some original features from
the old building, including the
rafters. Pleasantly quiet
during the day, it can become
crowded in the evening.
⛺ Q ◗ ▮ Ө (Hillhead) ⌂

Victoria

157–159 Bridgegate
☎ (041) 552 6040
11–12 (12.30–11 Sun)
**Maclay 70/-, 80/-; guest
beers Ⓐ**
Usually known as 'the Vicky',
this is one of Glasgow's most
famous bars. A very basic
pub, popular with all types,
particularly folk music lovers.
Q ≹ (Argyle St) Ө (St
Enoch)

Gourock

Anchorage Hotel

1 Ashton Road (A770)
☎ (0475) 32202
11–12 (12.45 Fri, 11.45 Sat;

12.30–11.45 Sun)
**Broughton Greenmantle Ale;
Caledonian 80/-; Jennings
Cumberland Ale Ⓗ**
Busy establishment with two
main bars, which can be noisy
at times. Occasional beer
festivals. Good bar food.
Q ⌥ ✿ ⛵ ◗ ▮ ⬥ ≹

Spinnaker Hotel

121 Albert Road (A770)
☎ (0475) 33107
11.30–11.30 (11–12 Thu–Sat; 12.30–11
Sun)
Belhaven 80/- Ⓐ
Small two-bar hotel offering
fine views of the Firth of
Clyde. Q ✿ ⛵ ◗ ▮ ⬥

Hamilton

George

18 Campbell Street (off
Cadzow St) ☎ (0698) 424225
11–11.45 (12.30–2.30, 6.30–11 Sun)
Maclay 80/- Ⓗ
Town-centre lounge with a
dining/meeting/family/func-
tion room at the back. On its
way back to top form after a
dubious interlude. The beer
range may expand in the near
future. Children welcome
until 6pm.
⛺ ◗ ⬥ ≹ (Central)

Houston

Cross Keys

Main Street ☎ (0505) 612209
11–12 (1am Fri, 11.45 Sat)
S&N Theakston Best Bitter Ⓗ
A warm welcome in a family-
run establishment, where a
pool room and restaurant add
to the idyllic atmosphere.
⛺ ✿ ◗ ▮ ⬥ ♣ P

Fox & Hounds

Main Street
☎ (0505) 612248
11–12 (11.45 Sat)
Maclay 70/- Ⓗ
A bar and a cosy lounge
downstairs, decorated with a
hunting theme; a cocktail bar
and restaurant upstairs (real
ale in all bars). Watch that
mynah bird! ◗ ▮ ⊟ P

Johnstone

Coanes

High Street ☎ (0505) 22925
11–11 (12 Thu–Fri, 11.45 Sat; 6.30–11
Sun)
**Draught Bass; Broughton
Greenmantle Ale; Caledonian
Golden Promise; Marston's
Pedigree; Whitbread
Boddingtons Bitter; guest
beer (occasionally) Ⓗ**
Comfortable town-centre
lounge, recently renovated to
include quiet alcoves off the
main bar area; tastefully
decorated with period
pictures and memorabilia. No
food Sun. ◗ ≹ ♣

Strathclyde

Kilbarchan

Trust Inn
8 Low Barholm
☎ (050 57) 2401
5 (11 Thu–Sat)–12 (11.30–2.30; 7–11 Sun)
Ind Coope Burton Ale; Tetley Bitter Ⓗ
Traditional village pub in an area steeped in local weaving history. See the old weaver's cottage nearby. No food Sun.
Ⓓ ▶

Kilmarnock

Gordon's Lounge
17 Fowlds Street
☎ (0563) 42122
11–11 (12 Fri & Sat; 4–11 Sun)
Belhaven 80/- Ⓐ
Town-centre lounge bar attracting a good mix of customers. Deservedly popular for its food and, consequently, it can be very busy at lunchtimes (no meals Sun lunch). Ⓓ ✿ ⅃ ⩵

Hunting Lodge
14 Glencairn Square
☎ (0563) 22920
11–3, 5–12 (11–12 Thu–Sat; 12.30–12 Sun)
Draught Bass; Broughton Greenmantle Ale; Taylor Landlord Ⓗ**; guest beers**
Pub with an old oak-style interior and hunting prints on the walls. It offers a friendly atmosphere, good bar food, and up to four guest beers. Occasional mini-beer festivals are held. ⅃ ✿ ✿ ⓓ ⅃ ⩵ ⚓

Kilmun

Coylet
Loch Eck (A815, 9 miles N of Dunoon)
☎ (036 984) 426
11–2.30, 5–11 (12 Fri & Sat)
McEwan 80/-; Younger No. 3 Ⓐ
Remote roadside pub set amid the splendour of Loch Eck, in the heart of the Cowal peninsula. The water engine was broken by the pressure of the water off the mountain.
⚓ ⅃ ✿ ⅃ ⓓ ▲ P

Lanark

Wallace Cave
Bloomgate ☎ (0555) 3662
11–1am (12.30–11 Sun)
Broughton Greenmantle Ale, Oatmeal Stout Ⓗ
Historic local with attractive brewery windows. The pub name commemorates the escape of William Wallace through the tunnels under the pub. It has a vibrant and friendly public bar at street level and a lounge upstairs.
Ⓓ ⅃ ⩵

Largs

Clachan
14 Bath Street (B7025, just off A78) ☎ (0475) 672224
11–12 (1am Fri & Sat; 12.30–12 Sun)
Belhaven 70/-, 80/- Ⓐ
Cheery and popular, single-bar pub in a side street just behind the seafront. Very busy at weekends with young people. Ⓓ ⅃ ⩵

Sheiling
Main Street ☎ (0475) 676171
11–1am (12.30–12 Sun)
Belhaven 80/- Ⓗ
Busy pub with a small rear lounge. Photographs of Clyde shipping adorn the walls of the public bar. ⅃ ⅃ ⩵

Lochranza

Lochranza Hotel
☎ (077 083) 223
11–1am (including Sun; 11–2.30, 5–1 Nov–Mar)
McEwan 80/- Ⓗ
Family-run hotel on the loch-side, affording views across to Loch Fyne. The friendly public bar can become lively.
⚓ ✿ ⅃ ⓓ ⅃ ⅃ P

Lochwinnoch

Mossend
Largs Road (A760)
☎ (0505) 842672
11–11
Whitbread Castle Eden Ale, Flowers Original Ⓗ
Standard country steakhouse/bar, good for families, and benefiting from convenient road and rail links. Bird sanctuary and a water sports centre nearby.
✿ ⓓ ⅃ ⩵ P

Lugton

Paraffin Lamp
11 Beith Road (A736/B777 jct)
☎ (0505) 85510
11–11 (12–11 Sun)
Whitbread Flowers Original Ⓗ**; guest beer**
Country pub, completely gutted and refurbished to cater for the family and food market, although fine for just a drink. It features pine furniture, flowery wallpaper and Art Deco lampshades. Difficult to reach by public transport. Guest beer is from the Whitbread range.
⅃ ✿ ⓓ ⅃ P

Oban

Oban Inn
1 Stafford Street
☎ (0631) 62484
11–12.45am
McEwan 80/-; Younger No. 3 Ⓐ

Busy pub overlooking the harbour. The public bar has a nautical flavour with wooden benches, while the more restrained lounge upstairs features old stained-glass panels. Q ⓓ ⅃ ⩵

Paisley

Ale House
12 Shuttle Street
☎ (041) 848 7403
12–12 (1am Thu & Fri, 11.45 Sat; 1–11.45 Sun)
Caledonian 70/-, Deuchars IPA, 80/-, Golden Promise; Maclay 70/-, 80/- Ⓗ**; guest beers**
Rising jewel in the crown, formerly known as Chisholms, with friendly staff and a relaxed atmosphere. It has a pool table in the front bar and serves excellent pub grub (Thu–Sat), plus a range of malts. Regular guest ales and frequent mini festivals.
⅃ ⓓ ⩵ (Gilmour St) ♣

Bar Point
42 Wellmeadow Street
☎ (041) 889 5188
11–11 (12 Thu, 1am Fri, 11.45 Sat; 12.30–11 Sun)
Belhaven 80/- Ⓗ
Bright, distinctive one-room lounge with a garden to the rear. Occasional live music/comedians; quiz night Mon. The friendly owners are almost always in attendance to serve the mixed clientele. Excellent food; children allowed in when having meals until 8pm. ✿ ⓓ ♣ ♣

Buddies
23 Broomlands Street
☎ (041) 889 5314
11–12 (11.45 Sat; 12.30–11 Sun)
Marston's Pedigree Ⓗ
Recent decoration does not detract from the character of this fine corner pub, once renowned for its light beer. It has a library, and is Paisley's only chess pub. ⅃ ♣

Bull Inn
7–9 New Street
☎ (041) 887 8545
11–12 (1am Fri, 11.45 Sat; 12–11 Sun)
Belhaven 80/- Ⓐ**; Whitbread Boddingtons Bitter** Ⓗ
Traditional coaching inn on the Paisley Heritage Trail, with wood-panelled walls in the bar and snugs at the back (watch out for the penny farthing on the wall). Food is served 12–2.30, when children are welcome. ⚓ ⓓ
⩵ (Gilmour St/Canal St)

Dusty Miller
31 Causeyside Street
☎ (041) 889 5529
11–11 (12 Thu & Fri, 11.45 Sat; 11–11 Sun)

Ind Coope Burton Ale; Tetley Bitter 🄷
Traditional 'man's bar' on the main thoroughfare in the town centre. Note the displays of trout and salmon flies, which gave rise to the pub's name. Salmon are caught on the nearby River Cart.
⇌ (Gilmour St)

Lord Lounsdale
Lounsdale Road
☎ (041) 889 6263
11–11
Broughton Greenmantle Ale 🄷
Pseudo hunting lodge, complete with fake oak beams and period memorabilia. Nonetheless, it serves excellent lunches and is popular with the locals. Frequent functions, particularly at weekends.
❀ ◖◗ ⊟ ♿ P

RH Finlay's
33 Causeyside Street
☎ (041) 889 9036
11–12 (11.45 Sat; 6.30–11 Sun)
Draught Bass 🄷
Attractive, refurbished town-centre lounge and bar. Recommended for its food; no loud music. Known to local CAMRA members as 'Nancy's'. Q ⊟
⇌ (Gilmour St/Canal St)

Wee Barrel
24 Love Street (on road to Glasgow Airport, follow signs)
☎ (041) 848 1683
11–12 (11.45 Sat; 12.30–11 Sun)
Whitbread Boddingtons Bitter 🄷
Tastefully renovated, this may still be Paisley's cheapest pub. Rod Stewart drinks here occasionally when in town to watch St Mirren (the ground is only a few hundred yards away). ⊟ ⇌ (Gilmour St)

Wee Howff
53 High Street
☎ (041) 889 2095
11–11 (11.30 Fri & Sat; closed Sun)
Ind Coope Burton Ale; Tetley Bitter; guest beer 🄷
Small town-centre pub with many regulars served by friendly and efficient staff. The publican is the first (and only) *Burton Master Cellarman* in Scotland.
⇌ (Gilmour St)

Prestwick

Golf Inn
Main Street
☎ (0292) 77616
11–2.30, 5–11 (11.30 Wed, 12.30 Thu & Fri; 11–12 Sat; 12.30–11 Sun)
Broughton Greenmantle Ale 🄰
Town-centre lounge bar with mock olde-worlde decor, convenient for public transport. The multi-screened video jukebox, plus satellite TV, makes for lively evenings. Children are welcome at lunchtime. ❀ ◖ ♿ ⇌ ♣ P

Parkstone Hotel
Central Esplanade
☎ (0292) 77286
11–2.30, 5–12.30 (1am Fri & Sat)
Belhaven 80/- 🄷
Comfortable lounge bar in a seafront hotel with views across the Firth of Clyde to Arran. It has a slightly genteel atmosphere at times.
♔ Q ❀ 🛏 ◖◗ ♿ ⇌ P

Renfrew

Ferry Inn
2 Clyde Street (A741, at ferry slipway)
☎ (041) 886 2104
11–11 (12 Fri & Sat)
Belhaven 80/-; Marston's Pedigree 🄷
Friendly local displaying pictures of the heyday of Clyde shipbuilding around the walls. The lounge hosts such varied activities as wine tasting and foreign language lessons. Regular mini beer festivals are held. Dogs and cycles welcome. ♔ Q ◗ ♣ P

Saltcoats

Windy Ha'
31 Bradshaw Street
☎ (0294) 63688
11–12 (12.30–11 Sun)
Broughton Greenmantle Ale 🄴
Typical, traditional, West of Scotland, down-to-earth pub, comprising an island bar and a small snug. It holds in-pub and inter-pub competitions in pool, darts, dominoes and football. Possibly the cheapest pint in Ayrshire. ⊟ ⇌ ♣

Symington

Wheatsheaf Inn
Main Street
☎ (0563) 830307
11–2.30, 5–12 (11–12 Fri–Sun)
Belhaven 80/- 🄰
Attractive country pub in a conservation village: a busy locals' public bar, a comfortable lounge and a dining room. Its pleasant beer garden is overlooked by lion sculptures. Renowned for its food. ❀ ◖◗ ⊟ ♿ ▲ P

Taynuilt

Station Tap
6 Fearnoch
☎ (086 62) 246
11–11.30 (1am Fri & Sat; 12.30–1am Sun)
West Highland Heavy, Station Porter, Severe 🄷**; guest beers** (occasionally)
Converted station waiting room with the feel of a century-old pub. Lots of character – and its own brewery.
♔ ♉ ❀ ◖◗ ♿ ▲ ⇌ ⌓ P

Troon

Anchorage Hotel
149 Templehill (B749, follow harbour signs)
☎ (0292) 317448
11–12 (1am Fri & Sat, 11–12 Sun)
Broughton Greenmantle Ale; Caledonian 80/-; Ind Coope Burton Ale 🄷**; guest beers**
The oldest licensed premises in Troon and renowned for its range of beers. Close to Troon marina, it has a nautical theme and affords open views to the Firth of Clyde. Petanque court to the rear. Children are welcome till 9.30. Stocks up to five guest beers and holds occasional mini festivals.
♔ 🛏 ◖◗ ⇌ ♣ P

Twechar

Quarry Inn
Main Street
☎ (0236) 821496
11–11 (1am Fri, 11.30 Sat; 12.30–11 Sun)
Maclay 60/-, 70/-, 80/- 🄷
Traditional and lively village pub in an old mining area. The bar is decorated with many brewery mirrors and warmed by old pot-bellied stoves. Petanque played. ♔ ⊟ ♣ P

Uddingston

Rowan Tree
62 Old Mill Road
☎ (0698) 812678
11–11.45 (12.30–11 Sun)
Maclay 80/- 🄰
Classic Edwardian pub with the finest architecture in Maclay's tied estate, and some splendid mirrors from long-departed breweries. As well as the fine public bar, there is a lounge and a games/function room. ♔ ♉ ◖ ♿ ⇌

Uplawmoor

Uplawmoor Hotel
66 Neilston Road
☎ (050 585) 565
11–11.30 (12 Thu, 12.30 Fri & Sat; 12.30–2.30, 6.30–11 Sun)
S&N Theakston Best Bitter; Younger No. 3 🄷
Picturesque hotel; not readily accessible but well worth the effort. It boasts an excellent restaurant and bar snacks (watch out for Pam's savoury eggs!), and holds occasional mini beer festivals. 🛏 ◖◗ P

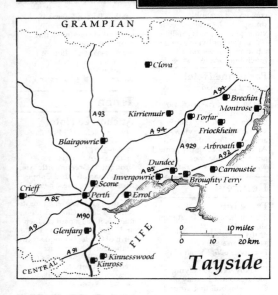

GRAMPIAN

Clova

Brechin
Kirriemuir *Montrose*
A93 *Forfar*
A94 *Friockheim*
Blairgowrie A929 *Arbroath*
A94
Dundee
Invergowrie *Carnoustie*
A85 *Scone* *Broughty Ferry*
Crieff A85 *Errol*
Perth
M90
Glenfarg FIFE
A9
A91 *Kinnesswood*
Kinross
CENTRAL

0   10 miles
0   10   20 km

Tayside

Arbroath

Victoria
15 Catherine Street
☎ (0241) 74589
11–2.30, 5–11 (11–11.45 Fri & Sat; closed
Sun eve)
**Marston's Pedigree; S&N
Theakston Best Bitter** H;
guest beers
Friendly town-centre bar, very
handy for visitors, near the
bus and rail stations. The well-
appointed lounge offers a
selection of guest beers.
Q 🛏 ◑ ⊟ Å ≷ ♣

Blairgowrie

Stormont Arms
Perth Street (A93)
☎ (0250) 873142
11–2.30, 5–11 (11–11.45 Fri & Sat;
12.30–2.30, 5.30–11 Sun)
Belhaven 80/- A
Traditional town bar with a
friendly atmosphere; folk
music on Wed. Pavement
drinking area; limited parking.
❀ ⊟ Å ♣ P

Brechin

Dalhousie Bar
Market Street ☎ (035 62) 2096
11–11 (12.30–11 Sun)
**Draught Bass; Belhaven
80/-** H
Typical market town pub with
an unusual horseshoe bar. A
quiet drinking establishment
which is generally busy at
lunchtimes and early eve. An
ornate brass till hides modern
electronic workings.
Q ◑ ⊟ ♣

Broughty Ferry

Fisherman's Tavern
12 Fort Street (by lifeboat
station) ☎ (0382) 75941
11–12 (12.30–11 Sun)
**Belhaven 80/-; Courage
Directors; McEwan 80/-;
Maclay 80/-; Ruddles
County** H; **guest beers**
Classic small pub, deservedly
popular, with a new
enthusiastic landlord.
Q 🛏 ◑ ⊟ ≷

Old Anchor Inn
Gray Street ☎ (0382) 737899
11.30–11.30 (7–11 Sun)
**Broughton Greenmantle Ale,
Old Jock; Caledonian
Deuchars IPA, 80/-; McEwan
80/-; S&N Theakston Best
Bitter** A
Recently refurbished and
decorated in traditional style,
a one-room bar divided by
partitions. Smoking
restrictions only apply at
lunchtime. Q ◑ ♨ ≷ ✂

Carnoustie

Morven Hotel
West Path ☎ (0241) 52385
11–2.30, 4.30–12 (11–12 summer;
12.30–11 Sun)
**Draught Bass; S&N
Theakston XB** H; **guest beers**
Run by a real ale pioneer, this
hotel has regular guest beers
of a very high quality. The TV
is only on for rugby and
Grand Prix racing. Holds a
beer festival, usually in June.
🛏 ❀ ⊯ ◑ ▶ Å P

Clova

Clova Hotel
Glen Clova, by Kirriemuir
(follow B955 to top of glen)
☎ (057 55) 222
11–11 (12.30–12 Sun)
**Broughton Greenmantle Ale;
Orkney Dark Island** H; **guest
beers**
Haven for walkers, climbers,
pony trekkers and thirsty
tourists. Occasional beer
exhibitions are staged.
🚶 ⚓ ❀ 🛏 ◑ ▶ ⊟ Å P

Crieff

Oakbank Inn
Turret Bridge (A85)
☎ (0764) 2420
11–11 (11.45 Fri & Sat; 12.30–11 Sun)
Ind Coope Burton Ale H
Modern pub, popular with
families. Note the 600-year-old
oak tree in the garden.
Petanque played.
🛏 ❀ ◑ ▶ Å ♣ P

Dundee

Frews Bar
117 Strathmartine Road (opp.
Coldside Library)
☎ (0382) 810975
11–11.45 (12.30–11 Sun)
Draught Bass H
One of the few pubs in the
area to sell bottles of
Worthington White Shield, it
continues its long
commitment to Bass.

Globe Bar
53 Westport (near university)
☎ (0382) 21742
11–12 (12–11 Sun)
**Draught Bass; Caledonian
80/-, Golden Promise;
Whitbread Flowers
Original** H
Bar with an attractive, largely
wood-panelled interior
decorated with items relating
to Dundee's nautical history;
very busy at weekends. The
recent introduction of Scottish
ales is a great improvement.
Holds a children's certificate.
Eve meals finish at 7.30.
◑ ▶ ≷

McGonagall's
142–146 Perth Road (opp. art
college) ☎ (0382) 22392
11–12
McEwan 80/- A; **guest beers** H
Lively bar, a favoured haunt
of art college and university
students. Named after
Dundee's famous (bad) poet,
some of whose works adorn
the walls. Run by one of
Dundee's real ale pioneers.
Always two guest ales. ◑ ≷

Mercantile Bar

100 Commercial Street (near Albert Sq) ☎ (0382) 25500
10–11 (12 Thu–Sat; 7–11 Sun)
Draught Bass; Caledonian 80/-; Ind Coope Burton Ale; McEwan 80/-; Maclay 80/-; S&N Theakston Best Bitter; Younger No. 3 🄷
Tastefully designed city-centre pub in a former department store: split-level with an island bar. The upstairs eating area has a separate no-smoking section. ◑ ◗ ♿ ⇌

Phoenix

103–105 Nethergate (near university) ☎ (0382) 200014
11–12 (12–3, 6.30–11 Sun)
Draught Bass; S&N Theakston Old Peculier; guest beers 🄷
Popular Victorian-style pub on the edge of the city centre. Good range of bottled Belgian beers. Very busy Fri and Sat nights. ◑ ◗ ⇌ ♣

Planet Bar

161 South Road, Lochee (200 yds W of Lochee bypass)
☎ (0382) 623258
11–12 (11 Tue–Thu; 12.30–5.30, 6.30–11 Sun)
Harviestoun Old Manor; McEwan 80/- 🄰**; guest beer** 🄷
An unusual exterior belies the internal decor and convivial atmosphere of this bar. The guest beer is usually from a Scottish independent. ⊞ ♿ P

Royal Oak

167 Brook Street (Blackness Ind. Area, just off Hawkhill)
☎ (0382) 29440
11–12 (closed Sun)
Ind Coope Burton Ale 🄰
Pleasantly uncrowded. Excellent meals, specialising in eastern and Mediterranean cuisine. ⛰ ◑ ◗ ♿

Try also: Tally Ho, Hawkhill; **Mickey Coyle's,** Hawkhill

Errol

Old Smiddy

The Cross ☎ (0821) 642888
11–2.30, 5–11 (11.45 Fri & Sat; 12.30–11 Sun)
Belhaven 80/- 🄷
Medium-sized, country ale and coffee house, with a central fireplace. Regular country/folk music nights.
⛰ ◑ ◗ ♿ P

Forfar

Osnaburg

23 Osnaburg Street
☎ (0307) 63380
11–12 (12.30–11 Sun)
Belhaven 80/- 🄷
Friendly town local in traditional style. Off the town centre, by the indoor swimming pool. ◑ ⊞

Friockheim

Star Inn

14 Gardyne Street (off A932)
☎ (024 12) 248
11–2.30, 5–11 (11–11 Fri–Sun and summer)
McEwan 80/-; S&N Theakston Best Bitter; Younger No. 3 🄷**; guest beers**
Oasis in the centre of Angus: a welcoming inn with a relaxed atmosphere. Serves high tea 4–5.45pm. ⛰ 🐎 🛏 ◑ ◗ ⊞

Glenfarg

Lomond Hotel

Main Street (off M90 between jcts 8 & 9) ☎ (057 73) 474
11–11 (11.45 Sat; 12.30–11 Sun)
Alloa Arrol's 80/-; Marston's Pedigree; Tetley Bitter 🄷
Quiet, 150-year-old coaching inn, eight miles from Perth. Enjoys a good local custom, with a busy seasonal trade. Home of the internationally-famous Glenfarg Village Folk Club (Mon night).
⛰ Q 🛏 ◑ ◗ ♿ P

Invergowrie

Swallow Hotel

Kingsway ☎ (0382) 641122
11–11
Ind Coope Burton Ale 🄰
Upmarket hotel on the outskirts of Dundee.
Q 🐎 🛏 ◑ ◗ ♿ P ⚟

Kinnesswood

Lomond Country Inn

On main street, E side of Loch Leven ☎ (0592) 84253
11–11 (12 Fri & Sat)
Broughton Greenmantle Ale; Harviestoun Ptarmigan; Jennings Bitter 🄷
Pub where the enthusiastic owner enjoys real ale and keeps prices economical. Good views of Loch Leven. Children's licence during mealtimes. The Harviestoun pump may rotate with all of the brewery's ales.
Q ❀ 🛏 ◑ ◗ ♿ ▲ P ⚟

Kinross

Kirklands Hotel

High Street ☎ (0577) 63313
11.30–2.30, 6–11 (11.40 Fri & Sat; 12.30–11 Sun)
Maclay 70/-, 80/- 🄷**; guest beer**
AA and RAC two-star hotel, pleasantly decorated, with pictures of old Kinross and its twin town Gacé in Normandy. Children welcome during mealtimes. 🛏 ◑ ◗ ⊞

Muirs Inn

49 The Muirs (Milnathort road) ☎ (0577) 62270
11–11 (12 Sat; 12.30–11 Sun)
Belhaven 80/-, St Andrew's Ale; Broughton Oatmeal Stout; Caledonian Deuchars IPA; Harviestoun Ptarmigan; Orkney Dark Island 🄷**; guest beers**
Traditional gem of a pub offering guest beers. Well worth seeking out.
Q ❀ ◑ ◗ ⊞ ♿ P

Kirriemuir

White Horse

Bellies Brae ☎ (0575) 72333
11–11 (7–11 only in lounge; 12.30–11 Sun)
Belhaven 80/- 🄷
Pub where ale is served in the lounge which is decorated with stuffed birds and animal heads. Stocks a good range of malts and bottled beers.
⛰ ❀ ⊞ ♣ P

Montrose

George Hotel

George Street ☎ (0674) 75050
11–11 (12–11 Sun)
Allied guest beers 🄷
Comfortable lounge which incorporates an eating area, partly no-smoking. Beers, from the Allied portfolio, at upmarket prices, change regularly. 🛏 ◑ ◗ ⇌ P ⚟

Perth

Greyfriars

South Street ☎ (0738) 33036
11–11 (11–11.45 Fri & Sat; 12.30–11 Sun)
Alloa Arrol's 80/-; Ind Coope Burton Ale 🄷**; guest beers**
Small, friendly city-centre pub, deservedly popular. Four guest beers. Restaurant upstairs. ◑ ◗ ⇌ ♣

Old Ship Inn

Skinnergate ☎ (0738) 24929
11–2.30, 5–11 (11–11 Fri & Sat; closed Sun)
Alloa Arrol's 80/-; Caledonian 70/- 🄷
Despite surrounding improvements, the Old Ship remains unchanged: a traditional bar. Good value lunches are served in the upstairs lounge.
Q ◑ ⊞ ⇌ ♣

Scone

Scone Arms

Perth Road (A94, 2 miles NNE of Perth) ☎ (0738) 51341
11–11 (11.45 Fri & Sat; 12.30–11 Sun)
S&N Theakston Best Bitter, XB; Whitbread Boddingtons Bitter 🄷
Large, family-run, village pub with individual decor. A popular venue for bar meals (eve meals Fri and Sat only) at upmarket prices. ◑ ◗ ⊞ ♣ P

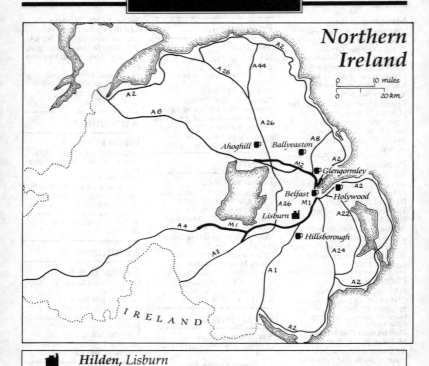

Northern Ireland

0   10 miles
0   20 km

Ahoghill   *Ballyeaston*

Glengormley

Belfast   *Holywood*

Lisburn

Hillsborough

I R E L A N D

Hilden, *Lisburn*

Ahoghill

Rowan Arms
18 The Diamond (take A42 out
of Ballymena) ☎ (0266) 871459
11.30–11 (12.30–2.30, 7–10.30 Sun)
Worthington White Shield
Long-established, family-run
village inn with comfortable
nooks and crannies and local
memorabilia. Q ⊞ ♣

Ballyeaston

Carmichaels (Staffie's)
16 Ballyeaston Village
12–11 (closed Sun)
Worthington White Shield
Traditional one-roomed
country bar of great character
(no draught beer). Q P

Belfast

Kings Head
829 Lisburn Road (A1 opp.
Kings Hall) ☎ (0232) 667805
12–11 (7–10.30 Sun)
Hilden Ale Ⓗ
Newly refurbished bar and
lounge in a pair of Victorian
semis with a modern
conservatory. Right by
Balmoral station. Q ❀ ◑ ⊞
⇌ (Balmoral NIR) P

Kitchen Bar/Parlour Bar
18 Victoria Square/6 Telfair
Street ☎ (0232) 324901
11-30–11 (may be earlier; usually
closed Sun)
S&N Theakston Best Bitter Ⓗ;
guest beers
Two long, narrow,
interconnected, family-run
bars of inspiring and
traditional character in a city-
centre backwater. Super
service, legendary lunches and
folk music played.
Q ◑ ⊞ ⇌ (Central NIR)

Glengormley

Crown & Shamrock
585 Antrim Road (A6, 1¹⁄₂
miles W of centre)
11.30–11 (7–10.30 Sun)
Worthington White Shield
Unspoilt, family-run country
pub with a low-panelled
ceiling to the plain, traditional
bar and intimate sitting room;
an institution. Draught beers
available occasionally.
Q ⊞ P

Whittleys
Kings Moss (B56, 2¹⁄₂ miles
NW of centre) ☎ (0232) 832438
11.30–11 (closed Sun)
Worthington White Shield
Country inn with an old, low-
ceilinged public bar and a
separate modern restaurant.
Q ❀ ◑ ⊞ P

Hillsborough

Hillside
Main Street ☎ (0846) 682765
12–11 (12.30–2.30, 7–10.30 Sun)
Hilden Ale Ⓗ
Marvellous, mellow, multi-
cornered local with a
renowned restaurant above.
Q ❀ ◑ ▶ ⊞

Holywood

Bear Tavern
High Street ☎ (0232) 426837
11.30–11 (1am Fri & Sat; 12.30–2.30,
7–10.30 Sun)
Worthington White Shield
Lively local of Victorian
character with a sloping stone
floor and handsome
appointments in timber and
glass. Parisian-style upstairs
lounge. Draught beers
available occasionally.
◑ ⊞ ♿ ⇌ (NIR)

Join CAMRA —
see page 508

Channel Islands

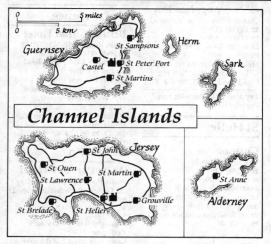

Channel Islands

 Ann Street, St Helier; **Guernsey, Randalls,** St Peter Port

Alderney

St Anne

Coronation Inn
36 High Street
☎ (048 182) 2630
11–2, 5–12 (12–2, 8–12 Sun)
Randalls Best Bitter G
Unspoilt town local with a welcoming atmosphere. Regular charity events.
🍴 Q 🍺 ♣

Georgian House Hotel
Victoria Street
☎ (048 182) 2471
10.30–3, 6.30–12 (12–2, 8–12 Sun)
Ringwood Best Bitter, Old Thumper G
Cosy, wood-panelled lounge bar with an adjoining restaurant, situated in the centre of the main shopping street. Real ale also available from the garden bar in summer. ❀ 🍴 🍺 ◗

Guernsey

Castel

Le Friquet Hotel
Le Friquet ☎ (0481) 56509
10.30–11.45 (closed Sun)
Randalls Best Bitter H
Comfortable lounge in a plush hotel with an excellent restaurant. 🛏 ❀ 🍴 P

Try also: Fleur du Jardin, Kings Mills (Guernsey)

St Martins

Captains Hotel
La Fosse ☎ (0481) 38990
11–11.40 (closed Sun)
Guernsey Real Draught Bitter H
Attractive, L-shaped lounge bar boasting an impressive handpump. No food Tue; eve meals Wed–Sat only. Shove-ha'penny board.
❀ 🍴 ◗ ♣ ♣ P

L'Auberge Divette
Jerbourg ☎ (0481) 38485
10–11.45 (closed Sun)
Guernsey LBA Mild, Real Draught Bitter H
Excellent country pub on a cliff-bound peninsula. Panoramic views from the lounge and large garden. Handy for the cliff paths. Bar billiards. No eve meals Thu.
🍴 🛏 ❀ ◗ ◗ 🍺 ♣ P

Try also: Deerhound Inn, Forest (Guernsey)

St Peter Port

Britannia Inn
Trinity Square
☎ (0481) 721082
10–11.45 (closed Sun)
Ann Street Old Jersey Ale; Guernsey LBA Mild, Britannia, Real Bitter H
Small lounge bar in the old quarter of town, serving no keg bitter. Can get quite smoky.

Drunken Duck
Charotterie ☎ (0481) 725045
10.30–2.30, 4.30–11.45 (10.30–11.45 Fri & Sat; closed Sun)
Ringwood Best Bitter, XXXX Porter, Fortyniner, Old Thumper G; **guest beer** (occasionally)
Local CAMRA *Pub of the Year* 1991: a small, enterprising, two-roomed pub, on the southern edge of town. Impromptu folk night Tue; regular quiz nights. The pub's white cat is often seen in the bar. Occasional ciders. ♣

Golden Lion
Market Street ☎ (0481) 727027
10–11.45 (closed Sun)
Guernsey Real Draught Bitter G
Attractive, bow-fronted pub behind the market. Beer is dispensed by gravity through a handpump from an upstairs cellar! 🍴 ◗ ◗

La Collinette Hotel
St Jacques ☎ (0481) 710331
5–11.45 (closed Sun)
Guernsey Grizzly's H
Comfortable hotel lounge bar not far from Beau Séjour leisure centre. The stuffed bear in the corner of the bar gives the house beer its name.
🛏 ❀ 🛏 ◗ ◗ ♣ P

Rohais Inn
Rohais ☎ (0481) 720060
10–2, 4–11.45 (10–11.45 Sat; closed Sun)
Guernsey LBA Mild H
Friendly local with a large bar on the western outskirts of town. Bar billiards and shove-ha'penny played. Small car park. 🍺 ♣ P

Salerie Inn
Salerie Corner ☎ (0481) 724484
10–2.30, 4.30–11.45 (10–11.45 Sat; closed Sun)
Guernsey LBA Mild, Real Draught Bitter H
Plush lounge with a strong nautical theme. Opposite a public car park. 🍴 ◗ ♣

Ship & Crown
Esplanade (opp. Crown Pier)
☎ (0481) 721368
10–11.45 (closed Sun)
Guernsey Real Draught Bitter H
Busy town pub opposite the main marina for visiting yachts. Decorated with pictures of ships and local shipwrecks. ◗

Thomas de la Rue
The Pollet ☎ (0481) 714990
10–11.45 (closed Sun)
Guernsey Real Draught Bitter H
Split-level lounge bar with a view over the harbour. The famous banknote printer set

Channel Islands

up business here in the 18th century. Its character varies from professional city-type at lunchtime to vibrant disco-bar in the evening. ◁

Try also: **Foresters Arms** (Guernsey); **Prince of Wales**, Smith St (Randalls)

St Sampsons

Pony Inn
Les Capelles
☎ (0481) 44374
10–11.45 (closed Sun)
Guernsey LBA Mild, Real Draught Bitter Ⓗ
Popular pub with three varied bars. Close to Guernsey Candles and Oatlands Craft Centre. Eve meals Fri/Sat only. Shove-ha'penny board.
❀ ◁ ▶ ⊟ ♣ P

Jersey

Grouville

Grouville Tavern
Just off coast road opp. golf course ☎ (0534) 57285
10–11 (11–1, 4.30–11 Sun)
Guernsey Real Draught Bitter Ⓗ
Well modernised, traditional bar with a strong local atmosphere. Comfortable lounge with good food (no meals Sun). ♨ ◁ ▶ ⊟ ♣ P

Seymour Inn
La Rocque (on Gorey coast road) ☎ (0534) 54558
10–11 (11–1, 4.30–11 Sun)
Ann Street Old Jersey Ale; Guernsey LBA Mild, Real Draught Bitter Ⓗ
Popular coastal pub with a real ale bar. Good food, good atmosphere and friendly staff. No meals Sun.
♨ Q ❀ ◁ ▶ ⊟ ♣ P

St Brelade

La Pulente Hotel
La Pulente (southern end of St Ouen's Bay) ☎ (0534) 41760
9am–11pm (11–1, 4.30–11 Sun)
Draught Bass Ⓗ
Situated on the unspoilt western coast with panoramic views. Comfortable lounge and a lively locals' bar serving good value food (no meals Sun). ♨ Q ⌂ ❀ ◁ ▶ ⊟ ♣ P

Olde Smugglers Inn
Ouaisne Bay (close to beach)
☎ (0534) 41510
11–11 (11–1, 4.30–11 Sun)
Draught Bass; Marston's Pedigree Ⓗ
Historic old tavern where a folk club meets on Sun nights. Good food. ♨ Q ⌂ ◁ ▶ P

Try also: **Old Portelet Inn**, Portelet Bay

St Helier

Customs
10 The Esplanade
☎ (0534) 21926
10–11 (11–1, 4.30–11 Sun)
Marston's Pedigree Ⓗ
Lively town pub with live music at weekends and good value food (no meals Sun).
⌂ ◁ ⊟ ♣

Lamplighter
Mulcaster Street
☎ (0534) 23119
10–11 (11–1, 4.30–11 Sun)
Draught Bass Ⓗ
Entertaining, gas-lit town pub with an interesting ambience. The only pub on the island selling real cider. No meals Sun. Q ◁ ♣ ⌁

Peirson
Royal Square
☎ (0534) 22726
10–11 (11–1, 4.30–11 Sun)
Draught Bass Ⓗ
Landmark pub off Royal Square, with a restaurant upstairs. A regular CAMRA meeting place. No food Sun. ◁

Try also: **Cock & Bottle**, Royal Sq; **Dog & Sausage**, Hilgrove St; **Esplanade**, Esplanade; **Exchange**, Grenville St; **Squires**, Seaton Pl

St John

Les Fontaines Tavern
Route du Nord
☎ (0534) 862707
10–11 (11–1, 4.30–11 Sun)
Draught Bass Ⓗ
14th-century granite pub with a traditional locals' bar. Situated on the north coast. No food Sun.
♨ Q ⌂ ❀ ◁ ▶ ⊟ ⌂ ♣

Try also: **St Mary's Country Inn**, St Mary (Bass)

St Lawrence

British Union Hotel
Main Road ☎ (0534) 861070
10.30–11 (11–1, 4.30–11 Sun)
Guernsey LBA Mild, Real Draught Bitter Ⓗ
One of the best pubs on the island: strong local flavour and very friendly staff, especially welcoming of families. Extensive menu (no meals Sun).
♨ Q ⌂ ❀ ◁ ▶ ⊟ ♣

St Martin

Anne Port Bay Hotel
Anne Port (100 yds from bay off Gorey–St Catherine's road)
☎ (0534) 52058
11–2.30, 5–11 (11–11 Sat; 11–1, 4.30–11 Sun)
Draught Bass; Marston's Pedigree Ⓖ
Cosy east coast hotel above a picturesque bay. No lunches Sun. Q ⌂ ⌂ ◁ ▶ P

Royal Hotel
Main Road (next to parish church) ☎ (0534) 56289
11–11 (11–1, 4.30–11 Sun)
Marston's Pedigree Ⓗ
Busy country pub with a good atmosphere in both bars. Good family facilities. The restaurant serves food on Sun.
♨ Q ⌂ ❀ ◁ ▶ ⊟ ⌂ ♣ P

Rozel Bay Inn
Rozel Bay ☎ (0534) 863438
10–11 (11–1, 4.30–11 Sun)
Draught Bass Ⓗ
Traditional pub at the bottom of a valley. Two small, cosy bars. No food Sun.
♨ Q ❀ ◁ ⊟ P

Try also: **Castle Green Hotel**, Gorey

St Ouen

Le Moulin de Lecq
Greve de Lecq Bay (close to beach) ☎ (0534) 482818
11–11 (11–1, 4.30–11 Sun)
Ann Street Old Jersey Ale; Draught Bass; Guernsey LBA Mild, Real Draught Bitter Ⓗ; guest beers
Pub featuring a converted 16th-century working water mill and serving a wide variety of local dishes. Large outdoor area with summer barbecues (including on Sun). No meals Sun eve.
♨ Q ⌂ ❀ ◁ ▶ P

Neighbours

Remember: roads do not end at county boundaries! Check the pages of neighbouring counties for an even bigger choice of great pubs.

Isle of Man

Isle of Man

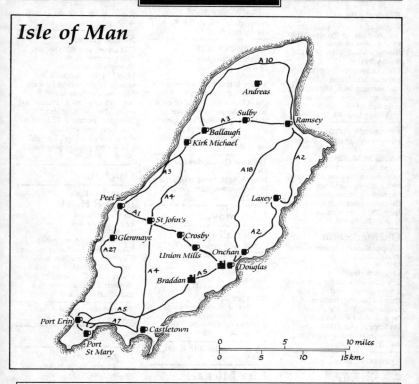

🏭 **Bushy's**, Braddan; **Isle of Man**, Douglas

Sunday hours on the Isle of Man are 12–1.30, 8–10

Andreas

Grosvenor
Kirk Andreas
☎ (0624) 880227
12–2.30, 6–10.45 (12–10.45 Sat)
Okells Bitter Ⓗ
Very attractive, well
maintained house with a first
class pub menu at very
reasonable prices. Quite
modern but retaining a strong
rustic character. Restaurant
open Fri–Sun or by
appointment, except Sun and
Mon in summer.
🛏 ❀ ◖ ◗ 🍴 ♣ P

Ballaugh

Raven Hotel
Ballaugh Bridge
☎ (0624) 897272
12–10.45
**Marston's Pedigree; Okells
Bitter; Whitbread Chester's
Mild** Ⓗ
Friendly village local on the
TT course. An ideal stopping
place for lunch. The outdoor
area is a balcony. ❀ ◖ 🍴 ♣ P

Castletown

Castle Arms (Glue Pot)
The Quayside (opp. the castle)
☎ (0624) 824673
12–10.45
Tetley Bitter Ⓗ
Pub saved from closure by
real ale drinkers and locals.
Very quaint and in a
convenient location.
Q ◖ ≹ (IMR)

Duck's Nest
Station Road ☎ (0624) 823282
12–10.45
**Bushy's Mild, Bitter, Old
Bushy Tail** Ⓗ**; guest beers**
A onetime Castletown
Brewery pub, the 'Duck's'
mirrors the progressive
attitude of its new owners.
The bar has been renovated
without detracting from its
essential layout and character
and the customer can usually
sample a selection of guest
beers imported from the UK.
🛏 ◖ 🍴 ≹ (IMR) ♣

Try also: **Ship Inn** (Okells)

Crosby

Crosby Hotel
Peel Road (A1, 5 miles from
Douglas) ☎ (0624) 851293
12–10.45
Okells Mild, Bitter Ⓗ
Pub situated on the TT course,
a point emphasised by the
bike on display inside.
Spacious bar and lounge.
Outside tables by a wishing
well. Popular for food in
summer. ❀ ◖ 🍴 P

Try also: **Waggon & Horses
(Half Way House)** (Okells)

Douglas

Albert Hotel
Market Place (near bus
station) ☎ (0624) 673632
12–10.45
Okells Mild, Bitter Ⓗ
Fine example of a Manx pub –
a straightforward drinkers'
pub where good quality beers
and atmosphere count for
more than gimmicks. Well
recommended. Snacks
lunchtimes. 🍴 ≹ (IMR) ♣

Isle of Man

Bushy's Pub

Victoria Street (50 yds from sea terminal) ☎ (0624) 675139
12–11.45 (music licence)
Bushy's Mild, Bitter, Old Bushy Tail Ⓗ
Well-known bikers' pub: a popular lunchtime drinking and eating place. The regular evening entertainment is very popular. Site of Bushy's first brewing plant. 🏃 ◐ 🍴 ♣

Foresters Arms

Hope Street ☎ (0624) 676509
11.30–10.45
Okells Mild, Bitter Ⓗ
Good back-street local: a popular social venue for local residents and postmen from the sorting office, as well as the more adventurous yuppy from the nearby financial centre. 🏃 🍴 ⇌ (IMR) ♣

Old Market Inn

Chapel Row (near bus station) ☎ (0624) 675202
12–10.45
Okells Bitter Ⓗ
Friendly back-street pub with a very strong local clientele, though passing trade is welcomed. The Castletown 'wake' was held here. A traditional Douglas local – unfortunately a dying breed. 🏃 🍴 ⇌ (IMR)

Queens Hotel

Queens Promenade ☎ (0624) 675543
11–10.45
Draught Bass; Okells Mild, Bitter Ⓗ
Popular Manx pub with views over Douglas Bay. Beware of passing horse trams when crossing the road! An excellent place to visit or stay for the real ale drinker. Good meals. 🏃 ✿ 🛏 ◐ ⇌ (MER) ♣

Rovers Return (Albion)

Church Street (rear of town hall) ☎ (0624) 676459
12–10.45
Bushy's Mild, Bitter, Old Bushy Tail Ⓗ
Very busy local in the heart of the business centre. Always busy, with a good pub atmosphere. Well worth a visit. Pictures of old pubs in abundance. 🏃 ◐ ⇌ (IMR) ♣

Terminus Tavern

Strathallan Crescent (next to the main Manx Electric Railway terminus) ☎ (0624) 624312
11.30–11
Okells Mild, Bitter Ⓗ
With 1993 the *Year of the Railways* in the IoM, this pub is ideally situated to cater for the many thousands of tourists expected for the event. Good selection of home-cooked foods at reasonable

prices. Park on the promenade. 🏃 ✿ ◐ 🍴 🛏 ♿ ⇌ (MER) ♣

Tramshunters

Harris Promenade
☎ (0624) 626011
12–10.45
Tetley Bitter Ⓗ; **guest beers**
Part of the Sefton Hotel. Two guest beers are available on a regular basis, Flowers being the most popular. The owners have made it more of a traditional pub. Bar billiards. 🛏 ◐ ♣ P

Try also: **Quarterbridge Hotel**, Peel Rd (Okells); **Wheatsheaf**, Lord St (Okells); **Woodbourne**, Alexandra Dr (Okells)

Glenmaye

Waterfall Hotel

In village centre, just off A27
☎ (0624) 842238
11.30–10.45
Okells Bitter Ⓗ
Two-roomed, split-level pub with a pool table downstairs and a fire upstairs. Comfortable and traditional. A mini bus is available for groups of six or more when eating. 🏃 ✿ ◐ ◑

Try also: **Ballacallin Hotel**, Dalby (Okells)

Kirk Michael

Mitre Hotel

Main Road ☎ (0624) 878244
12–10.45
Okells Mild, Bitter Ⓗ
Reputedly the island's oldest pub, situated on the TT course with camping close by. Excellent meals at lunchtimes. Garden at the side. 🏃 ✿ ◐ 🍴 🛏 ♣ P

Laxey

Bridge Inn

New Road ☎ (0624) 862414
12 (11 summer)–10.45
Tetley Bitter Ⓗ
Friendly atmosphere; simple but pleasant decor: a pub of character for the drinker and socialite alike. Friendly, welcoming staff. Keen food prices. 🏃 Q ✿ ◐ 🍴 ⇌ (MER) ♣ P

New Inn

New Road ☎ (0624) 861077
12–10.45
Okells Mild (occasionally), **Bitter** Ⓗ
Pleasant atmosphere, pleasant surroundings and a congenial landlord: a must for those who like a pint in traditional village surroundings. Plain but attractive decor. Soap fans must visit the lounge bar – a super photo collection is on

show. 🏃 ✿ ◐ 🍴 ⇌ (MER) ♣ P

Shore Hotel

Old Laxey ☎ (0624) 861509
12 (11 summer)–10.45
Bushy's Bitter Ⓗ
Harbourside pub with a strong local nautical flavour. Pleasant modern decor without any loss of traditional style. The bar front (from a Douglas church) is 150 years-old. New restaurant. Breakfasts during TT week. Children's garden play area. 🏃 ✿ ◐ 🍴 🛏 ♣ P

Onchan

Creg-ny-Baa (Keppel Hotel)

Mountain Road
☎ (0624) 676948
12–10.45
Okells Bitter; Tetley Bitter Ⓗ
Well-known landmark on the TT course, recently renovated and refurbished. A popular restaurant offers quality meals at modest prices (evenings included). ◐ ♿ 🛏 P

Try also: **Liverpool Arms** (Okells)

Peel

Royal Hotel

Athol Street (opp. bus station)
☎ (0624) 842217
12–10.45
Okells Mild, Bitter Ⓗ
Friendly local with a good bar trade: a 'proper' pub. Note the pub mirror in the front snug. 🍴 🛏 ♣

Whitehouse Hotel

2 Tynwald Road (Douglas St/Atholl St jct)
☎ (0624) 842252
11–10.45
Draught Bass *or* **Marston's Pedigree; Okells Mild, Bitter; Whitbread Chester's Mild** Ⓗ
Comfortable, friendly pub with a cosy snug and separate games and music rooms. Popular with locals. Manx music on Sat nights. Collection of old local pictures. 🏃 Q 🍴 🛏 ♣ P

Port Erin

Falcon's Nest Hotel

Station Road (seafront)
☎ (0624) 834077
11–10.45
Bushy's Old Bushy Tail; Okells Bitter Ⓗ
Although only a small part of a large, rapidly improving, hotel, the lounge bar retains its traditional wood-panelled charm much enjoyed by its regulars. Particularly pleasant views of Port Erin bay. 🏃 🛏 ◐ ⇌ (IMR)

Station Hotel

Station Road ☎ (0624) 832236
11–10.45 (may open later and close 2–4 in winter)
Okells Bitter Ⓗ
Choose between the lively, locals' public bar and the more sedate lounge at the front. Convenient for steam train passengers from Douglas requiring refreshment and/or accommodation. 🏛 🚲 🛏 ◑ ◐ 🍴 ≈ (IMR) ♣ P

Port St Mary

Albert

Atholl Street (opp. harbour)
☎ (0624) 832118
12–10.45
Okells Bitter; Tetley Bitter Ⓗ
Friendly village local well worth a visit: a good example of an unspoilt Manx pub. The roaring coal fire is always a welcoming sight. 🏛 Q 🍴 ♣

Station Hotel

Next to steam railway, ½ mile from centre ☎ (0624) 832249
12–2.30 (not Mon), 4.30–10.45 (12–10.45 Fri & Sat)
Okells Mild, Bitter Ⓗ
Very friendly and comfortable pub, well worth alighting the steam railway for. Good food and conversation. Port St Mary is a sleepy harbour and should not be missed. Lunches Tue–Sat. 🏛 Q 🥄 🌸 ◑ 🍴 ≈ (IMR)

Ramsey

Bridge Inn

Bowring Road
☎ (0624) 813248

12–10.45
Okells Bitter Ⓗ
Down-to-earth drinkers' pub, a plain, pleasant hostelry with an interesting collection of prints of old Ramsey on display. Welcoming atmosphere. The lounge is quiet. Q 🌸 🍴 ≈ (MER) P

Plough

Parliament Street (main shopping street)
☎ (0624) 813323
12–10.45
Okells Mild, Bitter Ⓗ
Well-located, town-centre pub. The lounge is a haven from the traumas of shopping. A good locals' bar.
🏛 🍴 ≈ (MER)

Try also: Central Hotel (Okells); **Royal George** (Okells)

St John's

Central Hotel

Station Road (300 yds from A1, Peel–Douglas road)
☎ (0624) 801372
12–10.45
Okells Bitter Ⓗ
Recently refurbished pub next to the cattle market: a welcome stop-off point for walkers on the Heritage Trail. The annual Tynwald ceremony takes place nearby (5th July). A former Castletown house with tables at the front. 🏛 🌸 ◑ 🍴 ♣ P

Tynwald Hill Inn

Peel Road ☎ (0624) 801249
12–10.45

Okells Mild, Bitter Ⓗ
Large-roomed lounge and bar opposite the famous Tynwald Hill. Popular at lunchtime with excellent lunches served.
◑ 🍴 P

Sulby

Sulby Glen Hotel

Sulby Straight (near Sulby school) ☎ (0624) 897240
12–10.45
Bushy's Old Bushy Tail; Okells Bitter Ⓗ
Friendly pub situated on one of the fastest points of the TT course. Very popular with local people and especially visitors using the nearby campsite. Superb atmosphere during TT week when many use it as a vantage point.
🏛 Q 🌸 🚲 ◑ 🅰 ♣ P

Try also: Ginger Hall (Okells)

Union Mills

Railway Inn

On main road
8–10.30 (closed Sat)
Okells Bitter Ⓖ
The Railway lacks all the 'improvements' now deemed essential to our enjoyment – no pool table, slot machines, jukebox, canned music or chicken and chips. You can enjoy an excellent pint here without these unwelcome distractions, but beware the limited opening hours (standard Sun hours).
Q P

MANX ANGER

In February 1992, Isle of Man Breweries announced that Castletown Bitter would no longer be brewed. Amidst howls of protest, not just from CAMRA members but also from the island's parliament and press, the last link with the Castletown Brewery was severed.

Until a 1986 merger, the island had two breweries, Castletown and Okells, both brewing to the specifications of the 1874 Manx Brewers' Act. The Castletown site was closed, though the bitter was continued at Okells fine, old Falcon brewery. Now all trace of Castletown ales has disappeared and it's not the only cause for concern. Gone, too, is the shortlived Okells 45 premium bitter, and in its place Bass Special Bitter shipped all the way from Tadcaster. The bottling line has also ground to a halt and it has to be asked whether Isle of Man Breweries is really committed to brewing.

THE BREWERIES
Introduction

Thank goodness for the guest beer law and the adventurous landlord. Despite big brewery attempts to sabotage the scheme, many tenants have been positive enough to plump for their own choice of guest ale. And, with free houses becoming more receptive to lesser-known beers, new breweries have been opening up all over the country.

BOOM AND BUST

Finalising this breweries listing proved to be a real headache, as details of yet more new breweries flooded in. Good news has never been so hard to take. As you flick through the following pages, brace yourself for a tough year of tasting ahead. Just when you think you've tried just about all there is, you find yourself back to square one, as over twenty new breweries burst into the Independents section. Some like Branscombe Vale and Judge's are new to the business. Others like Hampshire, Lion's and Black Sheep are run by experienced brewers who have branched out into new enterprises. A few brew pubs have expanded their free trade significantly and have now been included amongst the other commercial breweries, and, to add to the merry confusion, Big End has changed its name to Daleside and Glenny has become Wychwood.

If only it was all good news. As usual, a few favourites have fallen by the wayside. Burts, Isle of Wight brewers since 1840, is now up for sale, and Robinson's closed the Hartleys brewery at Ulverston. Wolverhampton & Dudley (Banks's) has been particularly active. It abandoned the Julia Hanson brewery, agreed a beer swap with Marston's - which will mean the end of the Marston's milds - and bought up the struggling Camerons brewery at Hartlepool. However, the award for

Morland: The Speckled Hen brewery successfully fought off a take-over-and-closure bid from Greene King

thoughtless ambition went to Greene King and its unnecessary and unwelcome bid for Morland. The deal flopped but, ironically, now that the Monopolies and Mergers Commission's pub limit has curbed the voracity of the nationals, it seems that some of the independents we have supported over the years could be picking up where the big boys left off.

INTERNATIONAL INFLUENCES

The Single Market is upon us and international toes are beginning to dip into our brewery waters. The Danes of Faxe Jyske converted their shareholding in Cains into outright ownership and Ruddles, bought and sold by Courage within two years, found itself hitched to Dutch brewers Grolsch. Both new proprietors seem committed to quality ale production, but there are still some less scrupulous American, Australian, Japanese and European giants out there with the awesome spending power to pick up a brewery the size of Bass at any time.

PORTER AND STOUT

From the boardroom to the brewhouse. As new breweries arrive almost weekly, the established concerns have not stood idly by and many have introduced new ales. The latest trend is towards dark beers, with porter and stout the flavours of the month. Even Whitbread got in on the act, producing an anniversary porter for its 250th birthday. There are now over forty real, cask-conditioned stouts and porters brewed around the country, so there's no longer a need to turn to keg Irish stouts whenever you fancy something rich, dark and roasty.

When brewers are looking for the next beer style to promote, perhaps they could consider the 'boy's bitter'. With so much concentration on strong beers, it would be heartening to find more full-flavoured, hoppy beers of low gravity which allow you to lift your head from the pillow the next morning. A beer doesn't have to be powerful to be good.

IT'S IN THE TASTE

All over Britain, specially trained CAMRA activists, organised into official tasting panels, have been soaking their tastebuds in the search for excellence. The tastings have been carried out in pubs, not brewery sample rooms or laboratories, and the findings are therefore representative of the beer quality generally available.

Beer tasting is basically a four-tiered process, although it really begins not with the tongue but with the eye and nose. A beer's condition - the amount of life in it - can be judged often just by looking at it, and its colour can lead you to expect a certain flavour. The next step for our profilers is to assess the aroma. As beer ferments, it produces various scents and tastes, which the brewer harnesses or discards when creating the character of the beer. These may include striking fruit flavours.

A swish around a glass (half-full preferably) allows beer to release its aromas, which often amount to more than just malt and hops. A beer which is off will soon let your nose know.

Step three involves allowing the tongue to examine all the levels of flavour in the beer. The tongue's tastebuds fulfil different functions - detecting salt, sweet, bitter and sour elements - and swirling the beer around your mouth allows you to pick out the dominant characteristics. Finally, unlike in wine tasting, you don't spit out the beer. You need to swallow it in order to assess the finish, or aftertaste, the lingering taste of the beer at the back of the throat. Try these four processes and compare your findings with those of our tasting panels.

FINDING YOUR WAY

With so many new breweries around, not all the beers have been officially sampled this year, and those not surveyed are marked with an asterisk. Beers are listed in the order of their original gravities (a system of gauging the amount of fermentable sugars in the brew before the yeast is added, and also a rough indicator of strength). A more accurate guide to potency is provided by the ABV figure (Alcohol by Volume).

You will notice that some beers have a small tankard next to their names. This denotes that the beer is one of the *Good Beer Guide's Beers of the Year*, one of the finalists at the 1992 *Champion Beer of Britain* awards. These have been chosen by our tasting panels, by votes from the public at local beer festivals and from a poll of CAMRA members. A full list of *Beers of the Year* can be found on page 28.

Breweries are arranged in three groups: Independents, Nationals and Brew Pubs, and a new section has been added this year to provide information on pub-owning groups. Many non-brewing companies are now taking over our pubs, some offering a genuine choice of beers, others simply supplied by one of the national brewers. Pub Groups have become important players in the beer game and companies owning more than twenty-five pubs are listed.

The Independents

ADNAMS

Adnams and Company PLC, Sole Bay Brewery, Southwold, Suffolk, IP18 6JW. Tel. (0502) 722424

East Anglia's seaside brewery, established in 1890. Real ale is available in all its 119 pubs (50 leased from Whitbread in June 1992), as well as over 2,000 free trade outlets, with more than 80% of beer production now sold outside the Adnams estate. Bitter and Broadside are the most widely available.

Mild

(OG 1034, ABV 3.2%) A fine dark mild, malty with subtle hints of hops and fruit. A bitter, malty finish.

Bitter

(OG 1036, ABV 3.6%) A good session beer, refreshingly hoppy throughout, with traces of malt and fruit. Long, dry aftertaste.

Old

(OG 1042, ABV 4.1%) A well-balanced red/brown winter brew. A fine blend of roast grain, malt and fruit is experienced on the palate and in the aroma. A dry, fruity finish lingers.

Extra

(OG 1043, ABV 4.3%) An amber beer, found more easily in Kent and Sussex than in Southwold. Its delicious fruity and bittersweet flavour is complemented by a hoppy aroma and a dry, slightly fruity finish.

Broadside

(OG 1049, ABV 4.4%) A full-bodied beer with a welcoming aroma of fruit and malt. This leads through to a well-balanced blend of malt, hops and fruit, with a bittersweet edge. Dry, faintly fruity finish.

Tally Ho

(OG 1075, ABV 6.2%) A seasonal beer (Christmas) of character: a warm, rich beer with an abundance of fruit in the nose and palate, balanced by malt and a trace of roast grain. Full bittersweet finish.

ALLIED BREWERIES

See page 474.

ALLOA

See Allied Breweries, page 474.

ANN STREET

Ann Street Brewery, Ann Street, St Helier, Jersey, CI. Tel. (0534) 31561

Brewery owning 101 pubs which has, for the first time in over 30 years, started to produce a cask-conditioned beer. Only four of the pubs are beneficiaries at present. Guernsey Brewery beers are also available.

Old Jersey Ale*

(OG 1036, ABV 3.6%)

ANSELLS

See Allied Breweries, page 475.

ARCHERS

Archers Ales Ltd., Station Ind. Estate, London Street, Swindon, Wilts, SN1 5DG. Tel. (0793) 496789

A small brewery, set up in 1979, which has grown very successfully and now supplies 150 free trade outlets from Oxford to Bath (via wholesalers), plus three tied houses. Has increased production by 35 barrels a week through the addition of a new fermenting vessel.

The Independents

Village Bitter (OG 1035, ABV 3.5%) Dry and well balanced, with a full body for its gravity. Malty and fruity in the nose, then a fresh, hoppy flavour with balancing malt, and a hoppy, fruity finish.

Best Bitter (OG 1040, ABV 4%) Slightly sweeter and rounder than Village Bitter, with a malty, fruity aroma and a pronounced bitter finish.

Black Jack Porter (OG 1046, ABV 4.6%) A winter brew: a black beer with intense roast malt dominant on the tongue. The aroma is fruity and there is some sweetness on the palate, but the finish is pure roast grain.

Golden Bitter (OG 1046, ABV 4.7%) A full-bodied, hoppy, straw-coloured brew with an underlying fruity sweetness. Very little aroma, but a strong bitter finish.

Headbanger* (OG 1065, ABV 6.5%) Almost a barley wine in style, enjoying a full flavour. Sweet and powerful, with a pleasant, dry finish.

ARKELL'S

Arkell's Brewery Ltd., Kingsdown, Swindon, Wilts, SN2 6RU. Tel. (0793) 823026

Established in 1843 and now one of the few remaining breweries whose shares are all held by a family; Managing Director, James Arkell, is a great-great-grandson of founder John Arkell. In February 1992, the head brewer, Don Kenchington, retired after 34 years' service. Keen to increase its tied estate, the brewery acquired eight new houses in Cheltenham and Gloucester last year, making a total of 80 tied pubs, most of which serve real ale. Also supplies 60 free trade outlets direct. In tied houses keg 3B is known as North Star Keg.

2B (OG 1032, ABV 3.2%) Well-balanced, pale beer. Essentially bitter, but with a hint of fruit and honey. A most refreshing session or lunchtime beer with good body for its OG.

3B (OG 1040, ABV 4%) An unusual darkish bitter which is coloured by the use of crystal malt, giving a nutty flavour which persists throughout and combines with bitterness in the aftertaste.

Mash Tun Mild (OG 1040, ABV 4%) Initially only produced in winter, but now a year-round brew. An almost black beer with an intense roast flavour which could very nearly be described as a porter. Well worth seeking out.

Kingsdown Ale (OG 1052, ABV 5%) A darker, stronger version of 3B with which it is sometimes parti-gyled. A distinct roast/fruit flavour persists with a lingering dry aftertaste.

Noel Ale (OG 1055, ABV 5.5%) Worth spending Christmas in Swindon for. A sweetish nose followed by a powerful fruit/hop flavour with a lingering bittersweet aftertaste.

ASH VINE

Ash Vine Brewery (South West) Ltd., The White Hart, Trudoxhill, Frome, Somerset, BA11 5DP. Tel. (0373) 836344

Set up in 1987 near Taunton, the brewery moved to the White Hart in January 1989 and bought a second tied house at the same time. These two pubs account for around 10% of the brewery's output, with the rest going to some 80 free trade outlets locally, and nationwide via wholesalers. Two

The Independents

new beers, Trudoxhill and Hop & Glory, were introduced early in 1992 and plans were drawn up to install two new fermenting vessels to cope with increased demand.

Trudoxhill* (OG 1035, ABV 3.3%)

Bitter (OG 1039, ABV 3.8%) A light gold brew with a strong floral hop aroma with malt and fruit undertones. A powerful, bitter hoppiness dominates the taste and leads to a dry, hoppy finish which lasts. An unusual and distinctive, excellent brew.

Challenger (OG 1043, ABV 4.1%) A mid brown beer with a solid malt flavour balanced by a good hoppy bitterness and subtle fruity sweetness. The aroma has similar characteristics, and the finish is dry and bitter. Can be sulphurous.

Tanker (OG 1049, ABV 4.7%) A tawny-coloured beer with a well developed balance of malt, bitter hops, fruit and subtle sweetness. A hoppy aroma and a bitter, dry finish.

Hop & Glory (OG 1059, ABV 5.5%) Copper-coloured beer with malt, hops and fruit in the aroma. Pleasantly bittersweet, with malt and hops in abundance. Similar finish. A complex, warming, satisfying winter ale.

ASTON MANOR **Aston Manor Brewery Company Ltd., 173 Thimblemill Lane, Aston, Birmingham, B7 5HS. Tel. (021) 328 4336**

Founded by ex-Ansells employees in 1983, Aston Manor moved very rapidly into the take-home trade, and discontinued brewing cask ale in 1986. Although still not its main income, the company resumed brewing real ale in 1990 under contract to Chandler's Brewery Company Ltd., and now supplies two local free trade outlets on a regular basis. The brewery site has been doubled in the last year.

Mild (Chandler's Dolly's Dark Mild) (OG 1031, ABV 3%) A roast and hop-flavoured mild with a hint of bitterness and sweetness. Dry, bitter finish.

Bitter (Chandler's JCB) (OG 1036, ABV 3.5%) Mid brown, hoppy and bitter beer with a sweet and bitter aftertaste.

Old Deadlies Winter Ale* (OG 1070, ABV 7.5%)

AYLESBURY (ABC) See Allied Breweries, page 475.

BALLARD'S **Ballard's Brewery Ltd., Unit C, The Old Sawmill, Nyewood, Rogate, Petersfield, Hants, GU31 5HA. Tel. (0730) 821362/821301**

Founded in 1980 at Cumbers Farm, Trotton, the brewery moved in 1985 to the Ballards pub (now the Elsted Inn) and has since relocated to Nyewood (West Sussex, despite the confusing postal address). Supplies 55 free trade outlets and has established a tradition of brewing Christmas ales with different names and appropriate gravities each year: Volcano (OG 1090) for 1990, Gone Fishing (OG 1091) for 1991, etc. A new mild is planned.

Trotton Bitter (OG 1036, ABV 3.5%) A well-flavoured session bitter, amber/tawny in colour. The good balance of malt and hops runs through from the aroma to the finish, with a slight fruitiness also present.

The Independents

Best Bitter (OG 1042, ABV 4.1%) Copper-red, with a malty aroma. Indeed, a notably malty beer altogether, but well-hopped and with a satisfying finish.

Wassail (OG 1060, ABV 5.8%) A strong, full-bodied, fruity beer with a predominance of malt throughout, but also an underlying hoppiness. Tawny/red in colour.

BANKS & TAYLOR

Banks & Taylor Brewery Ltd., The Brewery, Shefford, Beds, SG17 5DZ. Tel. (0462) 815080/816789

Founded in 1981 in a small industrial unit, the brewery has steadily grown to supply ten tied houses and a free trade in the Home Counties and East Anglia; this latter aspect of the business has expanded by leaps and bounds over the last year to its present level of 100-150 outlets. Two more beers (Old Bat and Dragonslayer) have been added to its already extensive range. SOD is often sold under house names.

Shefford Mild* (OG 1035, ABV 3.5%) The new dark mild.

Shefford Bitter (OG 1038, ABV 3.8%) A very drinkable, hoppy beer, with some malt and fruit flavours. Hoppy aroma and a bitter, hoppy aftertaste.

Shefford Pale Ale (SPA) (OG 1041, ABV 4%) A well-balanced beer, with hops and malt present throughout and hints of fruit in the aroma and taste. Dry, bitter aftertaste.

Dragonslayer* (OG 1045, ABV 4.5%) Brewed originally for St George's Day: a straw-coloured, Exmoor Gold-type bitter.

Edwin Taylor's Extra Stout* (OG 1045, ABV 4.5%) A bitter stout.

Shefford Old Dark (SOD) (OG 1050, ABV 5%) Dark, reddish-brown ale with similar characteristics to SOS, but with an added caramel flavouring and often a greater fruity flavour.

Shefford Old Strong (SOS) (OG 1050, ABV 5%) A deceptively drinkable sweetish beer. A hoppy, malty aroma with hints of fruit leads to a well-balanced taste of hops and malt. Sweetish, malty finish with discernible fruit.

2XS* (OG 1058, ABV 5.8%)

Black Bat (OG 1064, ABV 6.4%) A powerful sweet, fruity, malty beer. Fruit and malt dominate the aroma and aftertaste.

Old Bat* (OG 1080, ABV 8%)

BANKS'S

The Wolverhampton & Dudley Breweries PLC, Park Brewery, Lovatt Street, Wolverhampton, W. Midlands, WV1 4NY. Tel. (0902) 711811

Unspoilt by Progress

Wolverhampton & Dudley Breweries was formed in 1890 by the amalgamation of three local companies. Hanson's was acquired in 1943, but the closure of its Dudley brewery was announced in November 1991 with the loss of 11 jobs. Hanson's Mild is now brewed at Wolverhampton, but Hanson's Bitter has been discontinued in cask form. The 150 Hanson's pubs keep their own livery. In January 1992 W&D bought Camerons Brewery and 51 pubs around Blyth and Thirsk from Brent Walker, whose own foray into the brewing industry was short and not very sweet. This brings the tied estate for the whole group to more than 900 houses,

The Independents

most of them serving traditional ales, virtually all through electric, metered dispense. Extensive club trade in cask beer and around 1,850 free trade accounts. In May 1992 W&D entered into a reciprocal trading arrangement with Marston's; Pedigree will now be sold in W&D pubs, with Banks's Mild available in Marston's houses.

Hanson's Mild*
(OG 1036, ABV 3.5%) Not tasted since the move from Dudley.

Mild
(OG 1036, ABV 3.5%) A mid brown, hoppy mild with a strong malty taste. Malt predominates in the aftertaste but roast and caramel are also detectable. Drinks like a dark bitter.

Bitter
(OG 1038, ABV 3.8%) A malty, pale brown bitter with a sharp, dry, hoppy taste.

BASS
See page 478.

BATEMAN

George Bateman & Son Ltd., Salem Bridge Brewery, Mill Lane, Wainfleet, Skegness, Lincs, PE24 4JE. Tel. (0754) 880317

A family-owned and -run brewery which is steadily expanding its sales area to cover nearly the whole of the UK. All its own 66 tied houses serve real ale. Around 400 free trade outlets are supplied directly by the brewery which is planning to increase its brewing capacity to keep up with demand. The award-winning 'Good Honest Ales' are also being exported and Salem Porter has recently been added to the range. CAMRA's bottled 21st Birthday Ale was produced by Bateman.

Dark Mild ⊟
(OG 1033, ABV 3%) Some roast taste and a slight hint of fruit is balanced by a hoppy and bitter flavour and finish. Happily a beer which is enjoying a gentle revival.

XB
(OG 1036, ABV 3.8%) A predominantly hoppy and bitter beer throughout, satisfying and slightly dry. Although popular in the tied estate, it is overshadowed by its heavier brothers in the free trade.

XXXB
(OG 1048, ABV 5%) Although some malt and fruitiness are evident in the aroma and flavour, the hoppy and bitter characteristics always come through. A worthy past winner of CAMRA awards.

Salem Porter* ⊟
(OG 1050, ABV 5.2%) A recent addition to the range.

Victory Ale
(OG 1056, ABV 6%) A warming and powerful, strong beer with malty and sweet flavours masked by a bitter and hoppy presence which gives a lighter, crisper taste, leading the unwary to underestimate its strength.

BATHAM

Bathams (Delph) Ltd., Delph Brewery, Delph Road, Brierley Hill, W. Midlands, DY5 2TN. Tel. (0384) 77229

Small brewery, hidden behind one of the Black Country's most famous pubs, the 'Bull & Bladder'. This family firm has not only managed to survive successfully since 1877, it is now brewing to full capacity and having difficulty maintaining its free trade supplies (around 35 outlets) due to the increased demand in its own eight tied houses. Plans are

The Independents

afoot to buy another couple of pubs and to extend the brewing capacity, but as this represents a major capital investment for the company they will not be rushing into any quick deals.

Mild Ale
(OG 1036.5, ABV 3.6%) A hard-to-find dark brown beer with a caramel and hop taste. Sweetness is well balanced by hop flavour.

Best Bitter ⊞
(OG 1044, ABV 4.3%) A straw-coloured bitter which initially seems very sweet, though a more complex dry, hoppy taste rapidly becomes apparent. A splendid example of the traditional Black Country bitter type.

XXX
(OG 1064, ABV 6.5%) A Christmas ale, mid brown in colour and strong, with a malty, fruity taste. Hop flavour is present but malt predominates through to the aftertaste.

BEER ENGINE
The Beer Engine, Newton St Cyres, Exeter, Devon, EX5 5AX. Tel. (0392) 851282

Successful brew pub now serving an expanding free trade. Stands next to the Barnstaple branch railway line. Owns one other pub, the Sleeper in Seaton. Occasionally produces a bottle-conditioned beer.

Rail Ale
(OG 1037, ABV 3.6%) Yellow-coloured beer with a malty aroma and hoppy flavour. Some bitterness in the aftertaste.

Piston Bitter
(OG 1044, ABV 4.3%) Dark brown in colour; a strong, malty aroma and flavour with a hoppy and malty aftertaste.

Sleeper Heavy
(OG 1055, ABV 5.5%) A pleasant, sweet-tasting beer with a strong fruity taste and aftertaste. Dark brown in colour.

Whistlemas*
(OG 1068, ABV 6.5%) Produced for Christmas.

BELHAVEN
Belhaven Brewery Co. Ltd., Spott Road, Dunbar, Lothian, EH42 1RS. Tel. (0368) 62734

Although established as far back as 1719, making it the oldest brewery in Scotland, Belhaven has changed ownership so often over the last few years that it has been hard to keep track. Currently (since 1989) owned by the London-based property and leisure group, Control Securities PLC, it has managed to continue to produce award-winning beers, with a new brew, St Andrew's Ale, launched in February 1992. All 60 of its tied houses take cask beer, which is also supplied direct to 200 or so free trade outlets. Belhaven is also involved in beer wholesaling.

60/- Ale*
(OG 1032, ABV 2.9%) Dark and malty.

70/- Ale*
(OG 1035, ABV 3.6%) Light and hoppy.

80/- Ale*
(OG 1041, ABV 4.1%) Heavy, full-bodied ale.

St Andrew's Ale*
(OG 1046, ABV 4.5%)

90/- Ale*
(OG 1070, ABV 7.2%) An occasional, rich brew.

BENSKINS
See Allied Breweries, page 475.

BENTLEY
See Whitbread, page 487.

The Independents

BERROW

Berrow Brewery, Coast Road, Berrow, Burnham-on-Sea, Somerset, TA8 2QU. Tel. (0278) 751345

Brewery founded in June 1982 and now supplying pubs and clubs locally, amounting to about 12 free trade outlets.

Best Bitter (BBBB or 4Bs)

(OG 1038, ABV 3.8%) A pleasant, pale brown session beer, with a fruity aroma, a malty, fruity flavour and bitterness in the palate and finish.

Topsy Turvy (TT)

(OG 1055, ABV 6%) An excellent, straw-coloured beer. Its aroma is of malt and hops, which are also evident in the taste, together with sweetness. The aftertaste is malty. Very easy to drink. Beware!

BIG END

See Daleside, page 416.

BIG LAMP

Big Lamp Brewery Company Ltd., 1 Summerhill Street, Newcastle upon Tyne, Tyne & Wear, NE4 6EJ. Tel. (091) 261 4227

Big Lamp was set up in 1982 and changed hands at the end of 1990. Currently supplies one tied house and a growing free trade (about 30 outlets).

Bitter*

(OG 1038, ABV 3.8%) Hoppy but with malty flavours also well represented. Some fruitiness is just detectable throughout and bitterness is present in the taste and aftertaste.

Prince Bishop Ale

(OG 1044, ABV 4.5%) Yellowish, well-hopped and very drinkable beer, with malty, and to a lesser degree, fruity flavours throughout. Bitterness balances the taste and aftertaste.

Summerhill Stout ⊟

(OG 1044, ABV 4.5%) Roast flavours strongly influence this black beer in its aroma, taste and finish, with maltiness also detectable everywhere. Slightly bittersweet.

Winter Warmer

(OG 1048, ABV 4.8%) A welcome new addition to the portfolio, with maltiness and roast dominating the aroma and taste. Bitterness is evident throughout. More of a strong bitter than a winter warmer.

Old Genie

(OG 1070, ABV 8%) An occasional beer. A dark and strong, well-balanced ale. Sweetness dominates the taste and aftertaste, although there are some roast and fruit elements in the aroma.

Blackout

(OG 1100, ABV 11%) An occasional, rare beer. Extremely powerful and aptly-named. Usually brewed for CAMRA beer festivals.

BLACKAWTON

Blackawton Brewery, Washbourne, Totnes, Devon, TQ9 7UF. Tel. (0803) 732339

Situated just outside the village of Washbourne, this small family brewery was only founded in 1977 but it is the oldest in Devon. It originated in the village of Blackawton, but moved to its present site in 1981 and, despite a change of ownership in 1988, retains a loyal local following. Serves around 50 free trade outlets, having no pubs of its own. Brews from traditional ingredients with no additives.

404

The Independents

Bitter	(OG 1037.5, ABV 3.8%) Red in colour, with a malty aroma and a malty and slightly fruity taste. Dry aftertaste.
Devon Gold*	(OG 1040.5, ABV 4.1%) A summer brew, available April-October.
44 Special	(OG 1044.5, ABV 4.5%) Mid brown, malty, slightly fruity-tasting beer with a hint of toffee. Malty aroma and aftertaste. Lacks hoppiness, but is still enjoyable.
Headstrong	(OG 1051.5, ABV 5.2%) Tawny-coloured, malty, aromatic beer. Sweet malty taste and finish.

BLACK SHEEP — **Black Sheep Brewery PLC, Wellgarth, Masham, N. Yorks, HG4 4EN. Tel. (0765) 689227**

New brewery instigated by Paul Theakston, member of Masham's famous brewing family. After raising investment via the Business Expansion Scheme, the company's first brews went on sale in August 1992. The brewery is based in an old maltings.

Best Bitter*	(OG 1038, ABV 3.8%)
Special Bitter*	(OG 1047, ABV 4.4%)

BODDINGTONS — See Whitbread, page 485.

BORDER — See Marston's, page 441.

BRAINS — **SA Brain & Co. Ltd., The Old Brewery, 49 St Mary Street, PO Box 53, Cardiff, S. Glamorgan, CF1 1SP. Tel. (0222) 399022**

A traditional brewery which has been in the Brain family since Samuel Brain and his Uncle Joseph bought the Old Brewery in 1882. Now the largest independent brewery in Wales, supplying cask-conditioned beer to all its 125 tied houses and a substantial free trade. The company has diversified in recent years with interests in hotel, tourism and leisure projects in Wales and the West Country. MA (OG 1035, ABV 3.5%) - a mix of Dark and Bitter - is only available at the Crown Hotel, Skewen.

Dark 🍺	(OG 1035, ABV 3.5%) A full-bodied, dark brown mild with traces of chocolate and fruit and a rounded bittersweet finish.
Bitter	(OG 1035, ABV 3.7%) A distinctively bitter beer, pale, malty and very refreshing, with an intense, dry finish. Commonly known as 'Light'.
SA Best Bitter	(OG 1042, ABV 4.2%) A distinctively full-bodied, malty beer; well-balanced, with a smooth and strong dry finish. A fine premium bitter.

BRAKSPEAR — **WH Brakspear & Sons PLC, The Brewery, New Street, Henley-on-Thames, Oxfordshire, RG9 2BU. Tel. (0491) 573636**

A brewery can be traced back to before 1700 on the present Henley site, but Brakspear came into being in 1799 when Robert Brakspear started up a partnership with Richard Hayward. Robert's son, William Henry, greatly expanded

405

The Independents

the brewery and its trade. It boasts many excellent, unspoilt pubs and all 119 tied houses serve traditional ales. Also supplies over 200 free trade outlets. Bitter is widely available as a guest beer in the South and on Whitbread guest beer lists. Happily, the 27% stake in Brakspear owned by Whitbread has now been reduced to less than 15% without any of the acrimony which followed Whitbread's disposal of shares in Oxfordshire neighbours Morland.

Mild
(OG 1030, ABV 2.8%) Thin beer with a red/brown colour and a sweet, malty, fruity aroma. The well-balanced taste of malt, hops and caramel has a faint bitterness, complemented by a sweet, fruity flavour, having hints of black cherries. The main characteristics extend through to the bittersweet finish.

Bitter
(OG 1035, ABV 3.4%) Amber in colour, with a good fruit, hop and malt nose. The initial taste of malt and the dry, well-hopped bitterness quickly dissolve into a predominantly bitter, sweet and fruity aftertaste.

Special
(OG 1043, ABV 4%) Tawny/amber in colour, its good, well-balanced aroma has a hint of sweetness. The initial taste is moderately sweet and malty, but is quickly overpowered by the dry bitterness of the hops, before a slightly sweet fruitiness. A distinct, dry, malty finish.

Old Ale
(OG 1043, ABV 4%) Red/brown with good body. The strong, fruity aroma is well complemented by malt, hops and roast caramel. Its pronounced taste of malt, with discernible sweet, roast and caramel flavours, gives way to fruitiness. The aftertaste is of bittersweet chocolate, even though chocolate malt is not present.

BRANSCOMBE VALE
Branscombe Vale Brewery, Great Seaside Farm, Branscombe, Seaton, Devon.

Brewery operational from July 1992, founded by two former dairy workers in a National Trust barn.

Brannoc Traditional Ale*
(OG 1040)

BRITISH OAK

British Oak Brewery, Salop Street, Eve Hill, Dudley, W. Midlands, DY1 3AX. Tel. (0384) 236297

Started as a family-run brew pub, in May 1988, and now supplies 20 free trade outlets, as well as a second pub of its own. Also produces traditional cider.

Castle Ruin
(OG 1038, ABV 3.9%) Available April-September: a light, fruity, malty beer with a bitter aftertaste. Pale brown in colour.

Eve'ill Bitter
(OG 1042, ABV 4.1%) A full-bodied darker version of Castle Ruin.

Colonel Pickering's Porter
(OG 1046, ABV 4.4%) Dark, fruity and bitter, a full-bodied, creamy, distinctive beer.

Dungeon Draught
(OG 1050, ABV 4.8%) A mid to dark brown fruity ale with plenty of malt and hops.

Old Jones
(OG 1060, ABV 5.5%) Available September-April; dark, sweet, rich and malty.

The Independents

BROUGHTON

Broughton Brewery Ltd., Broughton, Peeblesshire, Borders, ML12 6HQ. Tel. (089 94) 345

Go-ahead brewery, founded in 1980 by former S&N executive David Younger to brew and distribute real ale in central and southern Scotland (around 220 outlets and two tied houses in Dumfries). While this remains their priority, an increasing amount of bottled beer (not bottle-conditioned) is distributed nationally. The new brew, Scottish Oatmeal Stout, should also be available in bottles soon, but Greenmantle 80/- is no longer brewed. New cellars and extra storage capacity are being added.

Greenmantle Ale (OG 1038, ABV 4%) Beer lacking aroma. Bittersweet in taste, with a hint of fruit, and a very dry finish.

Special Bitter* (OG 1038, ABV 4%) A dry-hopped version of Greenmantle.

Scottish Oatmeal Stout* (OG 1040, ABV 3.8%) A new brew.

Old Jock (OG 1069, ABV 6.7%) Strong, sweetish and fruity in the finish.

MATTHEW BROWN See Scottish & Newcastle, page 484.

BUCKLEY See Crown Buckley, page 416.

BULLMASTIFF

Bullmastiff Brewery, 14 Bessemer Close, off Hadfield Road, Cardiff, S. Glamorgan, CF1 8AQ.

Small brewery set up in Penarth in 1987 by a fanatical home-brewer. Supplies some 40 outlets locally, but not on a regular basis, so the beers are rather hard to find on the brewery's home patch. Much of the production is sold right across the country through wholesalers. Moved to new premises in summer 1992.

Bitter (OG 1035, ABV 3.5%) A pale brown beer with a malty aroma and a bitter finish. A popular session beer.

Ebony Dark (OG 1042, ABV 4%) As its name suggests, a very dark brown beer with a roast malt flavour and aroma. Very drinkable, with a rich, malty aftertaste.

Best Bitter (OG 1043, ABV 4%) A well-balanced, malty, bitter beer with a smooth, fruity finish. Very drinkable.

Son of a Bitch (OG 1062, ABV 6.4%) A full-bodied, notably hoppy, malty beer: a premium bitter with a distinctive aroma and aftertaste.

BUNCES

Bunces Brewery, The Old Mill, Netheravon, Salisbury, Wilts, SP4 9QB. Tel. (0980) 70631

Tony Bunce and his wife welcome visitors (by prior arrangement) to their brewery, which is in a listed building on the Wiltshire Avon. Established in 1984, they deliver cask-conditioned beers to around 40 free trade outlets within a radius of 50 miles, and supply a number of wholesalers. The brewery is currently up for sale.

Vice Beer* (OG 1033, ABV 3.2%) A wheat beer; an occasional brew.

The Independents

Benchmark   (OG 1035, ABV 3.4%) A pleasant, bitter ale of remarkable character, which maintains one's interest for a long time. The taste is malty, the aroma subtle and the very long finish is quite dry on the palate.

Pigswill*   (OG 1040, ABV 3.9%) A beer first brewed for the Two Pigs at Corsham, now generally available.

Best Bitter   (OG 1042, ABV 4.1%) A first-rate beer. The piquant aroma introduces a complex malty and bitter taste with a hint of fruit. Long, fresh, bitter aftertaste.

Old Smokey   (OG 1050, ABV 4.8%) A delightful, warming, dark winter ale, with a roasted malt taste and a hint of liquorice surrounding a developing bitter flavour. Very appealing to the eye.

BURTON BRIDGE

Burton Bridge Brewery, 24 Bridge Street, Burton upon Trent, Staffs, DE14 1SY. Tel. (0283) 510573

Established in 1982, with one tied outlet at the front of the brewery. The adjoining premises, which were acquired recently, are being refurbished into a new brewhouse which should be operational by 1993. This will allow for an extension of the pub into the old brewery premises. Supplies guest beers to around 300 outlets virtually nationwide. Specialises in commemorative bottled beers to order. *Bottle-conditioned beer: Burton Porter* ⊕ *(OG 1045, ABV 4.5%)*

BST Summer Ale*   (OG 1038, ABV 3.8%) Only available during British Summer Time.

XL Bitter   (OG 1040, ABV 4%) A golden/amber, malty drinking bitter, with a dry palate and finish. A faint hoppiness and fruitiness come through in the aroma and taste.

Bridge Bitter   (OG 1042, ABV 4.2%) Again, golden/amber in colour, robust and malty, with a hoppy and bitter palate and aftertaste. Though malt and hops are both present throughout, the dry, hoppy character dominates the finish. Some balancing fruitiness and sweetness.

Burton Porter   (OG 1045, ABV 4.5%) A dark, ruby-red, sweetish porter. The malty, slightly fruity aroma is followed by a roast malt and fruit flavour, and a malty and fairly bitter finish.

Top Dog Stout*   (OG 1050, ABV 5%) A winter brew.

Burton Festival Ale   (OG 1055, ABV 5.5%) Strong, sweetish and full-bodied. The nose is malty and slightly hoppy, and the palate has similar characteristics, with a pronounced fruitiness. Copper-coloured; a little cloying and heavy.

Old Expensive*   (OG 1065, ABV 6.5%) Winter only; a dark, warming beer, also known as OX.

BURTONWOOD

Burtonwood Brewery PLC, Burtonwood Village, Warrington, Cheshire, WA5 4PJ. Tel. (092 52) 25131

A family-run public company, established in 1867 on farmland bought specifically for building a brewery, by James Forshaw who had learnt his trade at Bath Springs Brewery in Ormskirk. Demand for the beers grew steadily and in 1937 the brewery had to be extensively rebuilt. In the eighties Burtonwood embarked on a £6 million extension plan and its new brewhouse was completed in 1990.

The Independents

Supplies real ale to 275 of its 367 tied houses, 138 of which are on long lease from Allied Breweries. Has a 35% stake in the Paramount pub chain and is continuing to develop trading relationships with other pub groups. Also supplies 400 free trade outlets.

Dark Mild (OG 1032, ABV 3.1%) A smooth, dark brown, malty mild with a good roast flavour and some caramel and bitterness. Good dry finish.

Best Bitter (OG 1036, ABV 3.7%) A well-balanced, refreshing and malty bitter, with good hoppiness and a slightly sweet, malty and bitter aftertaste.

James Forshaw's Bitter (OG 1038, ABV 4%) Smooth, hoppy beer, more bitter than Best and now slightly less fruity. Not really different enough from Best to justify appearing on the same bar, especially in low turnover pubs.

BURTS **Burts Brewery Ltd., 119 High Street, Ventnor, Isle of Wight, PO38 1LY. Tel. (0983) 852153**

Brewery founded in 1840 which foundered in 1991 when the Phillips family reluctantly relinquished control. Now no longer brewing, and not much hope for the future.

BUSHY'S **Bushy's Brewery, Mount Murray Brewing Co. Ltd., Mount Murray, Braddan, Isle of Man. Tel. (0624) 661244**

Set up in 1986 as Bushy's Brewpub, in an old Yates Wine Lodge, the production soon merited a separate, self-contained brewery, so it was moved to a converted farm, not far from Douglas. With the closure of the Castletown Brewery and Isle of Man Breweries' reduced production, there is more local demand for Bushy's products and they now supply 12 free trade outlets, as well as their own three tied houses on the island. Sales on the mainland via wholesalers are also increasing. A new mild has been added to the range of beers which are all brewed to the stipulations of the Manx Brewers' Act of 1874.

Dark Mild (OG 1035, ABV 3.7%) With a hoppy aroma, and notes of chocolate and coffee to the malty flavour, this rich, creamy, fruity, very dark brew is reminiscent of a porter.

Best Bitter (OG 1038, ABV 4%) An aroma full of pale malt and hops introduces you to a beautifully hoppy, bitter beer. Despite the predominant hop character, malt is also evident. Fresh and clean tasting.

Piston Brew* (OG 1045, ABV 4.5%) Available during the TT races only.

Old Bushy Tail (OG 1045, ABV 4.6%) An appealing reddish-brown beer with a pronounced hop and malt aroma, the malt tending towards treacle. Slightly sweet and malty on the palate, with distinct orangey tones. The full finish is malty and hoppy, with hints of toffee.

Lovely Jubbely Winter Warmer (OG 1060, ABV 6.2%) A rich, satisfying, mid brown beer with a pronounced aroma of malt and fruit. Sweet and malty on the palate; the finish is balanced with some hop bitterness.

The Independents

BUTCOMBE

Butcombe Brewery Ltd., Butcombe, Bristol, Avon, BS18 6XQ. Tel. (0275) 472240

One of the most successful of the new wave of breweries, set up in 1978 by a former Courage Western MD, Simon Whitmore. Has been brewing to virtual capacity since the 1989 MMC report - 10,000 barrels per year, and there are now plans to acquire a barn adjoining the brewery in order to expand production by as much as 50%. Serves its three houses (which are not tied) and an extensive free trade, mostly around Avon and Somerset.

Bitter

(OG 1039, ABV 4.1%) A pale brown-coloured beer with a pleasant, hoppy/bitter taste, some malt and occasional fruit. It has a hoppy, malty aroma and a bitter finish, which can be very drying. A crisp, refreshing beer.

BUTTERKNOWLE

The Butterknowle Brewery Co., The Old School House, Lynesack, Butterknowle, Bishop Auckland, Co. Durham, DL13 5QF. Tel. (0388) 710109

Launched in August 1990, Butterknowle quickly converted local palates to its beers, and has had much success in beer festivals. Demand continues to grow steadily nationwide, and, with the increase in production, quality has not been forfeited in the process. It now supplies 29 free trade outlets on a regular basis, and over 70 houses with guest beers from its impressive range. The brewery is situated in Victorian buildings once home to the Lynesack National School, and reflects the area's mining history on its attractive point of sale material.

Bitter 🍺

(OG 1036, ABV 3.6%) A pleasant, hoppy, quaffing bitter, with some maltiness in the aftertaste.

Festival Stout

(OG 1038, ABV 3.6%) Originally brewed for the sixth Darlington Spring Festival; a beer with a roast, slightly smoky flavour, a hoppy aroma and a sweetish aftertaste.

Conciliation Ale 🍺

(OG 1042, ABV 4.2%) Butterknowle's flagship brand: a proudly pure, full-flavoured premium ale, well-hopped in both aroma and palate. Flowery and piquant.

Black Diamond

(OG 1050, ABV 4.8%) Actually dark brown in colour and styled as a porter, albeit a strong one. Full in body and flavour, the roast malt being nicely balanced with hops. Sweetish palate, more bitter in the finish.

High Force

(OG 1060, ABV 6.2%) Smooth strong ale, well hopped with some fruity sweetness. A good depth of flavour develops in the aftertaste: a multi-dimensional beer.

Old Ebenezer

(OG 1080, ABV 8%) Splendid, rich and fruity, seasonal barley wine: liquid Christmas cake with a potent punch. Surprisingly moreish, if only in sips!

CAINS

Robert Cain & Co. Ltd., Stanhope Street, Liverpool, Merseyside, L8 5XJ. Tel. (051) 709 8734

When the Higsons brewery in Stanhope Street was closed by Whitbread in early 1990 and all production transferred to Sheffield, the premises were taken on by GB Breweries, which concentrated on canned beer for the take-home trade until producing its first draught ale to much acclaim in March 1991. The brewery then reverted to the old name of

410

The Independents

Robert Cain, a brewery which owned the premises before Higsons bought it in 1923. It is now the only commercial brewery on Merseyside. In January 1992, Cains became a wholly-owned subsidiary of Danish brewers, Faxe Jyske, who had first taken a financial stake in the company the previous summer. However, the future of ale production seems secure; indeed the Formidable Ale has been added to the range and a new mild (Cains Dark) is planned. Supplies a free trade of some 200 outlets (no tied estate).

Traditional Bitter ⊞

(OG 1038, ABV 4%) Darkish, malty, full-bodied and bitter, with a hint of roast malt. Moderate hoppiness and a good bitter aftertaste. A well-balanced, distinctive beer.

Formidable Ale (FA) ⊞

(OG 1048, ABV 5.1%) A well-hopped and bitter beer with some fruit and a strong, dry aftertaste. A pale golden, refreshing beer.

CALEDONIAN

The Caledonian Brewing Company Ltd., Slateford Road, Edinburgh, Lothian, EH11 1PH. Tel. (031) 337 1286

Described by Michael Jackson as a 'living, working museum of beer making', Caledonian operates from a Victorian brewhouse, using the last three direct-fired open coppers in Britain - one of which dates back to 1869 when the brewery was started by George Lorimer and Robert Clark. It was taken over by Vaux of Sunderland in 1919, who continued to brew there until 1987, when, under threat of closure, it was acquired by a management buy-out team. No tied estate, but around 300 free trade outlets are supplied.

60/- Ale*

(OG 1032, ABV 3.3%) A flavoursome light ale.

70/- Ale*

(OG 1036, ABV 3.5%) Soft and malty in flavour.

R&D Deuchars IPA

(OG 1038, ABV 3.8%) A well-hopped session beer, recently added to the range.

80/- Ale*

(OG 1043, ABV 4.2%) Malty and flavoursome, with hops well in evidence.

Porter*

(OG 1043, ABV 4.2%) Dry and nutty.

Golden Promise*

(OG 1048, ABV 4.8%) An organic beer.

Merman XXX*

(OG 1050, ABV 5%) Dark, sweetish heavy beer, based on a Victorian recipe.

Edinburgh Strong Ale or ESA*

(OG 1078, ABV 8%) Rich and deceptively strong.

CAMERONS

The Cameron Brewery Company, Lion Brewery, Hartlepool, Cleveland, TS24 7QS. Tel. (0429) 266666

The future for Camerons looks more rosy than it did a year ago. Having been acquired, along with Tolly Cobbold, in 1989 by leisure group Brent Walker, prospects for the brewery looked very bleak as Brent Walker's financial and business problems continued to grow. Though a management buy-out seemed likely for a while, Brent Walker cynically rejected this option, which would have saved 225 jobs, and sold the brewery instead to Wolverhampton & Dudley Breweries (Banks's and Hansons), who at least plan to continue brewing at Hartlepool, if on a smaller scale. Now sells cask-conditioned ales in 30 of its 51 tied houses and supplies roughly 550 free trade outlets.

411

The Independents

Traditional Bitter (OG 1036, ABV 3.6%) A light beer with a good balance of malt and hops and a true bitter finish. An excellent session beer when in good form but quality does vary.

Strongarm (OG 1040, ABV 3.9%) A pleasant, medium-bodied ale with a lot of character. Darkish in colour, with a full, well-balanced flavour of malt and hops and a dry, bitter finish. Again, quality can vary and there is a trend in some pubs to serve it too cold to be appreciated.

CASTLE EDEN See Whitbread, page 486.

CASTLETOWN See Isle of Man Breweries, page 435.

CHARRINGTON See Bass, page 478.

CHESTER'S See Whitbread, page 487.

CHILTERN **The Chiltern Brewery, Nash Lee Road, Terrick, Aylesbury, Bucks, HP17 0TQ. Tel. (0296) 613647**

Set up in 1980 on a small farm, Chiltern specializes in an unusual range of beer-related products, like beer mustards, Old Ale chutneys, cheeses and malt marmalade. These products are available from the brewery shop and also a dozen other retail outlets. Brewery tours are very popular and plans are being mooted for an on-licence in the dining hall and the brewery shop. The beer itself is regularly supplied to six free trade outlets (no tied houses). Three Hundreds Old Ale is still bottled, but is no longer bottle-conditioned. *Bottle-conditioned beer: Bodgers Barley Wine (OG 1080, ABV 8.5%)*

Chiltern Ale* (OG 1038, ABV 3.7%) A distinctive, tangy light bitter.

Beechwood Bitter* (OG 1043, ABV 4.3%) Full-bodied and nutty.

Three Hundreds Old Ale* (OG 1050, ABV 4.9%) A strong, rich, deep chestnut-coloured beer.

CLARK'S **HB Clark & Co. (Successors) Ltd., Westgate Brewery, Wakefield, W. Yorks, WF2 9SW. Tel. (0924) 373328**

The only brewery in Wakefield, founded in 1905. Ceased brewing during the keg revolution of the sixties and seventies, although it continued to operate as a drinks wholesaler. Resumed cask ale production in 1982 and, within two months, Clark's Traditional Bitter was voted Best Bitter at the Great British Beer Festival in Leeds. The brewer has recently been experimenting with stronger beers, the first of which, T'Owd Dreadnowt (OG 1070), was a special pale ale brewed for the First Merrie City Beer Festival in Wakefield. Supplies real ale to its three tied houses (one up for sale but more to be acquired), and around 25 free trade outlets.

Traditional Bitter (OG 1038, ABV 3.8%) An amber-coloured standard bitter with a pleasing hoppy, fruity aroma. A fine hop flavour is predominant in the palate, with malt and fruit. A good, clean-tasting bitter with a long, hoppy finish.

Burglar Bill (OG 1044, ABV 4.6%) A good, hoppy aroma precedes the excellent, strong hop flavour, combined with rich malt and fruit. A long finish of hops and malt completes this full-bodied, strong bitter.

The Independents

Rams Revenge (OG 1046, ABV 4.8%) A dark brown beer with a reddish hue and a taste dominated by roast malt and caramel. The aroma is fruity, with roast malt, and the finish is dry and malty but short.

Hammerhead (OG 1055, ABV 5.7%) Rich malt in the mouth, but with hop flavour and bitterness to balance. The malty, hoppy aroma is faint, but the finish is long, malty and dry. A robust, strong bitter.

Winter Warmer (OG 1060, ABV 6.4%) A dark brown, powerful strong ale, now increased in gravity. A strong mouth-filling blend of roast malt, hop flavour, sweetness and fruit notes concludes with a satisfying finish of bittersweet roast malt.

COACH HOUSE The Coach House Brewing Company Ltd., Wharf Street, Howley, Warrington, Cheshire, WA1 2DQ. Tel. (0925) 232800

Built in 1991 and run mainly by ex-Greenalls employees. Initial promises of trading agreements with Greenalls and Paramount PLC (the Bass/Burtonwood pub group) unfortunately did not materialise (only 18 Greenalls pubs are supplied), so the brewery has to rely on sales through the free trade. These are growing steadily and the beers can now be found as far afield as Cornwall and Edinburgh, but it is still difficult to find them in their home area. Seasonal beers are company policy, with Blunderbus Old Porter and Squires Gold the first examples.

Coachman's Best Bitter (OG 1037, ABV 3.7%) A fruity and bitter beer. Malt and hop flavours tend to be masked when young. Some sulphur is evident in the nose, and the aftertaste is bitter. Benefits from longer stillaging times, when the dry hopping comes through.

Ostler's SPA* (OG 1038, ABV 4%) A new summer brew.

Squires Gold (OG 1042, ABV 4.2%) The spring beer, golden in colour from the use of amber malt, but with a strong roast coffee flavour, balanced by bitter and hop flavours. The roast carries over to the nose and aftertaste, which also has hints of liquorice. New Zealand hops are used.

Innkeeper's Special Reserve (OG 1045, ABV 4.7%) A darkish best bitter, malty and fruity. As in the bitter, the hops come through in older beer. Some sulphur notes and a little sweetness.

Blunderbus Old Porter ⏛ (OG 1055, ABV 5.2%) A powerful winter porter, reminiscent of Beamish stout. The roast flavour is pronounced, backed up by chocolate and some fruit. Also hints of liquorice, spice and smoke. Despite being massively hopped, the hop flavour is low key. An intense, chewy pint which is surprisingly refreshing and moreish.

COMMERCIAL Commercial Brewing Company, Worth Brewery, Worth Way, Keighley, W. Yorks, BD21. Tel. (0535) 611914

Brewery set up in February 1992, now producing about 20 barrels a week. A very strong winter ale is planned.

Keighlian Best Mild* (OG 1035, ABV 3.5%)

The Independents

Keighlian Bitter*	(OG 1036, ABV 3.6%)
Worth Bitter*	(OG 1045, ABV 4.5%)

COOK'S

Cook's Brewery Co. Bockhampton, 44 Burley Road, Bockhampton, Christchurch, Dorset, BH23 7AJ. Tel. (0425) 73721

After 15 years as a brewing plant engineer, Nigel Cook started brewing in Twickenham in 1988 and selling his polypins to local off-licences. He moved to Dorset in 1989 with plant from the ex-Swannell's brewery in Hertfordshire and went into production there in May 1991. Currently supplies 12 free houses. Yardarm Special is also available in bottles at local off-licences.

Yardarm Special Bitter*	(OG 1052, ABV 5.2%)

CORNISH	See Redruth, page 453.

COTLEIGH

Cotleigh Brewery, Ford Road, Wiveliscombe, Somerset, TA4 2RE. Tel. (0984) 24086

Continued growth has taken this brewery a long way from its first home - a stable block at Cotleigh Farmhouse in 1979. 1985 saw the completion of a purpose-built brewhouse and there was further expansion in 1991 with the purchase of adjoining premises and the doubling of brewing capacity. Most of the beers are seasonal or brewed for special occasions only. Serves 100 outlets, mostly in Devon and Somerset, although the beers are also available across the country. Owns one pub, the Prince of Wales in Holcombe Rogus, Devon (East Devon CAMRA's *Pub of the Year* in 1992).

Harrier SPA	(OG 1036, ABV 3.6%) A straw-coloured beer with a very hoppy aroma and flavour, and a hoppy, bitter finish. Plenty of flavour for a light, low gravity beer.
Nutcracker Mild*	(OG 1036, ABV 3.6%) A dark mild, an occasional brew.
Tawny Bitter	(OG 1040, ABV 3.8%) A mid brown-coloured, very consistent beer. A hoppy aroma, a hoppy but quite well-balanced flavour, and a hoppy, bitter finish.
Aldercote Ale*	(OG 1042, ABV 4.2%) An occasional brew for East-West Ales wholesalers.
Barn Owl Bitter*	(OG 1048, ABV 4.5%) Brewed only occasionally, in aid of the brewery's adopted charity, the Hawk and Owl Trust.
Old Buzzard	(OG 1048, ABV 4.8%) Dark ruby-red beer, tasting strongly of roast malt, balanced with hops. Roast malt again in the finish, with bitterness. Very drinkable once the taste is acquired.
Rebellion*	(OG 1050, ABV 5%) An occasional brew.
Red Nose Reinbeer*	(OG 1060, ABV 5.6%) A dark and warming Christmas brew.

COURAGE	See page 481.

The Independents

CROPTON

Cropton Brewery Co., The New Inn, Cropton, Pickering, N. Yorks, YO18 8HH. Tel. (075 15) 330

Set up in 1984 just to supply the New Inn, the brewery was expanded in 1988 to supply its additive-free beers to a growing local free trade and now sells to around 28 outlets. Scoresby Stout is a new addition to the range.

Two Pints Best Bitter*   (OG 1042, ABV 4.2%) Full-flavoured and distinctive.

Scoresby Stout*   (OG 1044, ABV 4.4%)

Special Strong Bitter*   (OG 1060, ABV 6.4%) A powerful winter ale.

CROUCH VALE

Crouch Vale Brewery Ltd., 12 Redhills Road, South Woodham Ferrers, Chelmsford, Essex, CM3 5UP. Tel. (0245) 322744

Started in 1981 by two CAMRA enthusiasts, Crouch Vale has a single tied house - the Cap & Feathers at Tillingham (national CAMRA *Pub of the Year* 1989), but also supplies some 60 free trade outlets in Suffolk, Essex and Greater London. Continuing growth will mean enlarging the capacity of the brewery and the possible acquisition of an additional tied house. Millennium Ale was introduced in 1991 to celebrate the Battle of Maldon in Essex.

Best Mild   (OG 1036, ABV 3.5%) Dark reddish brown, with a roast aroma and hints of malt and caramel. Good roast flavour, with a sharper bitter aftertaste. Tinged with a lingering dryness.

Woodham IPA   (OG 1036, ABV 3.5%) Amber beer with a fresh, hoppy nose with slight fruitiness. A refreshing lunchtime drink that has a bitter aftertaste to its hoppy, fruity texture.

Best Bitter   (OG 1039, ABV 4%) A rich, balanced red/brown-coloured beer with a hoppy, fruity aroma. The taste is of fruit and malt, with hops, leading to a dry bitter aftertaste.

Millennium Ale   (OG 1041, ABV 4.2%) A wonderful golden beer featuring a strong, hoppy nose with maltiness. A powerful mixture of hops and fruit combines with pale malt to give a final sharp, bitter flavour with malty undertones.

Strong Anglian Special or SAS   (OG 1048, ABV 5%) A tawny-coloured beer with a fruity nose. A balanced brew with a sharp bitterness and a dry aftertaste.

Essex Porter   (OG 1050, ABV 5%) Beer with a dark roast barley aroma and an initially nutty, fruity taste, ending in a bitter, dry aftertaste.

Santa's Revenge   (OG 1055, ABV 5.7%) A Christmas ale, also sold throughout the year under house names. Despite its strength, it is dry and winey, not sweet.

Willie Warmer   (OG l060, ABV 6.5%) A dark red ale, brimming with roast aromas and hints of fruit. The roast and fruit merge pleasantly to give a flavour of balanced sweetness and malt, with pleasant aftertastes.

415

The Independents

CROWN BUCKLEY	**Crown Brewery PLC, Pontyclun, Mid Glamorgan, CF7 9YG. Tel. (0443) 225453**

Buckley, the oldest brewery in Wales (est. 1767) was taken over by Brodian in 1987. This failed to revitalise the ailing brewery which was then bought out by Crown (the former United Clubs Brewery) in 1989 with Harp financial backing, merging the brewing interests and creating a total tied estate of 134 pubs (now reduced to 100). The company has since experienced another massive shake up and is now mostly owned by Guinness. All beer production is carried out at the Llanelli (Buckley) site where money is again being invested in equipment; kegging and bottling are done at Pontyclun, but one site seems almost certain to go in the end. Also has a stake in Llanelli neighbours Felinfoel, although the latter brewery bought back some of its own shares at the time of the Guinness take-over.

Buckley's Dark Mild — (OG 1034, ABV 3.4%) A very dark, malty mild, fairly sweet with traces of chocolate, followed by a nutty bitter finish. Difficult to find in good condition.

Buckley's Best Bitter — (OG 1036, ABV 3.8%) A well-balanced, medium gravity bitter which has a rather sweet, malty flavour and a pleasant, bitter finish.

Special Best Bitter (SBB) — (OG 1036, ABV 3.8%) Distinctively malty and clean tasting, with a pronounced bitter flavour and a rather dry aftertaste. This well-rounded beer is now mainly restricted to former Crown Brewery outlets.

Reverend James Bitter — (OG 1045, ABV 4.5%) A malty, full-bodied bitter with fruity overtones and a bittersweet aftertaste.

DALESIDE	**Daleside Brewery, Camwal Road, Starbeck, Harrogate, N. Yorks, HG1 4PT. Tel. (0423) 880041**

Formerly Big End brewery, founded in 1988 by Bill Witty and Bernard Linley. Moved to new premises in the summer of 1992 and at the same time changed the name of the company and of all the beers, bar one, Monkey Wrench. Supplies around 200 free trade outlets.

Bitter — (OG 1038, ABV 3.7%) Beer with little aroma but a good, smooth balance of malt, hops and bitterness, with fruit notes. A clean-tasting bitter with a long, hoppy finish. Often sold under house names.

Dalesman Old Ale — (OG 1042, ABV 4.2%) Satisfying dark brown strong bitter, with rich malt and roast in the mouth, complemented by hop flavour. Light hop and roast malt finish.

Monkey Wrench — (OG 1056, ABV 5.3%) Powerful strong beer. Tends to lack aroma but is a rich, sweet, malty ale with balancing background bitterness, ending in a roast malt and sweet aftertaste. Can be difficult to find.

DARLEY — See Wards, page 466.

DAVENPORTS — See Allied Breweries, page 476.

The Independents

DENT

Dent Brewery, Hollins, Cowgill, Dent, Cumbria, LA10 5TQ. Tel. (058 75) 326

Set up in a converted barn in March 1990 to supply three local pubs, but now supplying free trade all over northern England. Brewing capacity is due to be doubled to cope with demand. All Dent's beers are brewed using the brewery's own spring water.

Bitter*	(OG 1036, ABV 3.7%)
Ramsbottom Strong Ale*	(OG 1044, ABV 4.5%)

DEVENISH

See Whitbread, page 486.

DONNINGTON

Donnington Brewery, Stow-on-the-Wold, Glos, GL54 1EP. Tel. (0451) 30603

Possibly the most attractive brewery in the country, set in a 13th-century watermill in idyllic surroundings. Bought by Thomas Arkell in 1827, it became a brewery in 1865, and it is still owned and run by the family. Supplies 15 tied houses, and 25 free trade outlets (XXX is only available in a few outlets).

BB (OG 1036, ABV 3.5%) Little aroma, but a pleasing, bitter beer, with a good malt/hop balance. Not as distinctive as it used to be.

XXX (OG 1036, ABV 3.5%) Again, thin in aroma, but flavoursome. More subtle than others in its class. Some fruit and traces of chocolate and liquorice in the taste, with a notably malty finish.

SBA (OG 1042, ABV 4%) Malt dominates over bitterness in the flavour of this premium bitter. Subtle, with just a hint of fruit and a dry, malty finish. Faintly malty aroma.

EARL SOHAM

Earl Soham Brewery, The Victoria, Earl Soham, Woodbridge, Suffolk, IP13 7RL. Tel. (0728) 685758

Established in April 1985 to supply its own pub, the Victoria, and a few years later acquired a second pub, the Tram Depot in Cambridge. This has now been sold to Everards, but it still stocks Victoria Bitter.

Gannet Mild (OG 1032.5) Unusual ale, more like a light porter than a mild, given the bitter finish and roast flavours which compete with the underlying maltiness.

Victoria (OG 1036.5) A characterful, well-hopped malty beer whose best feature is the superbly tangy, hoppy aftertaste.

Albert Ale (OG 1044.5) Hops predominate in every aspect of this beer but especially in the finish which some will find glorious, others astringent. A truly extreme brew.

Jolabrugg (OG 1060) The recipe for this winter-only brew tends to change from batch to batch, but expect something rich, smooth and fruity with a bittersweet aftertaste.

417

The Independents

ELDRIDGE POPE

Eldridge, Pope & Co. PLC, Weymouth Avenue, Dorchester, Dorset, DT1 1QT. Tel. (0305) 251251

Charles and Sarah Eldridge started the Green Dragon Brewery in Dorchester in 1837. By 1880, Edwin and Alfred Pope had bought into the company and it had moved to its present site, next to the railway, its first pubs situated along the line. The brewery is still run by the Pope family. The latest addition to their range, Blackdown Porter, immediately won an award at the Great Western Beer Festival in 1991 and Thomas Hardy Country is another recent award-winner. Thomas Hardy's Ale is notable for being the strongest naturally-conditioned bottled beer. Unfortunately, a cask breather device is used in most of the 180 tied houses; those houses not using the device have been designated 'Traditional Ale Houses'. Free trade extends as far as London, Bristol and Exeter, a total of around 1,000 outlets, some 200 supplied directly by the brewery. *Bottle-conditioned beer: Thomas Hardy's Ale ▣ (OG 1125, ABV 12%)*

Dorchester Bitter	(OG 1033, ABV 3.3%) A well-balanced session beer with a malt and hop flavour and aftertaste. Mainly malty aroma.
EP Best Bitter	(OG 1036, ABV 3.8%) A bland mixture of malt and hops. Difficult to find in cask-conditioned form.
Thomas Hardy Country Bitter	(OG 1040, ABV 4.2%) Mid brown beer which replaced IPA. Hops are dominant throughout, with bitterness coming through in the aftertaste.
Blackdown Porter*	(OG 1042, ABV 4%)
Royal Oak	(OG 1048, ABV 5%) Fruit and malt are prevalent in both aroma and taste. The flavour is balanced, with hops and some sweetness, and there is a fruity finish to this smooth, well-rounded brew.

ELGOOD'S

Elgood & Sons Ltd., North Brink Brewery, Wisbech, Cambs, PE13 1LN. Tel. (0945) 583160

The only brewery left in Cambridgeshire. From its classical Georgian, riverside premises (converted in the 1790s from a mill and granary and acquired by Elgood's in 1878), it supplies all but two of its 49 tied houses with real ale. A mini-brewery has been set up to produce a variety of beers in small volumes to be sold as guests; first off the production line in May 1992 was Black Dog Mild. Serves around 200 free trade outlets in East Anglia.

Black Dog Mild*	(ABV 3.6%)
Cambridge Bitter	(OG 1036, ABV 3.8%) A pleasant but bland beer. The palate has faint traces of malt, hops and fruit. Short, faintly hoppy aftertaste.
Greyhound Strong Bitter or GSB	(OG 1045, ABV 5.2%) A rare brew and, unfortunately, not what it used to be. A pleasant combination of malt, fruit and hops in a faintly bittersweet flavour which leads to a short, dry aftertaste.
Winter Warmer	(OG 1080, ABV 8.2%) A warm red/brown winter ale. Very wine-like with a full, fruity, bittersweet flavour. Good fruity aroma; dry, fruity aftertaste.

The Independents

EVERARDS

Everards Brewery Ltd., Castle Acres, Narborough, Leicester, LE9 5BY. Tel. (0533) 630900

A small brewery, entirely family-owned and -run, which was founded in Leicester in 1849, by the great-great-grandfather of the current chairman, Richard Everard. It transferred all its brewing to Burton upon Trent in 1931, but in 1979 went back to its roots to a new brewery on the outskirts of Leicester. For several years, some of the beers were continued under licence at the Heritage brewery in Burton, but now all beers are brewed in Leicester. Acquired 11 new pubs in 1991, and most of its 142 tied houses sell real ale, some using cask breathers but many offering guest beers. Everards also supplies a widespread free trade.

Mild

(OG 1033, ABV 3.1%) Satisfying, ruby-coloured beer, with an aroma of malt and fruit. Full-bodied malt flavour, with more than a hint of cherries. Long, malty finish.

Beacon Bitter

(OG 1036, ABV 3.8%) Light, golden beer with an aroma of hops and honey. The flavour balances malt and hops and the finish lingers.

Tiger Best Bitter

(OG 1041, ABV 4.2%) Copper-brown, with a malty, hoppy aroma and a soft, malty palate, with plenty of balancing hops and an underlying fruitiness. The finish is long, dry, hoppy and malty. A good, balanced, medium-bodied bitter.

Old Original

(OG 1050, ABV 5.2%) A beer with a smooth, distinctive palate and a faint, hoppy, fruity aroma. Dry, with malt and caramel flavours and some sweetness beneath. The finish is malty and sweetish; the colour is copper-brown.

Old Bill Winter Warmer

(OG 1068, ABV 7.3%) Brewed Dec-Jan. A tawny/red winter ale with a sweet vinous character and an underlying hoppy flavour, which gives some balancing bitterness. The finish is sweet, with a fruity dryness and some malt.

EXE VALLEY

Exe Valley Brewery, Land Farm, Silverton, Exeter, Devon, EX5 4HF. Tel. (0392) 860406

Barron Brewery was set up in 1984 by Richard Barron, and the company name changed when he was joined by Guy Sheppard. At the farm brewery, operating from an old barn (using the farm's own spring water), the production has increased from 12 to 60 barrels a week and, having reached full capacity, expansion is likely in the near future. Some 35 local free trade outlets are supplied on a regular basis (no tied estate).

Bitter

(OG 1039, ABV 4%) Malty, pale brown bitter, with fruity and bittersweet undertones in the aftertaste. A pleasant, malty beer.

Dob's Best Bitter ⊞

(OG 1039, ABV 4.1%) Pale brown bitter with a distinctly hoppy/bitter taste. Pleasant, malty aftertaste.

Devon Glory

(OG 1047, ABV 4.7%) Mid brown, with a malty and fruity aroma. A well-balanced beer with character.

Exeter Old Bitter

(OG 1047, ABV 4.8%) Red/brown-coloured, with a sweet, fruity taste, a fruity aroma and a malty aftertaste.

The Independents

EXMOOR

Exmoor Ales Ltd., Golden Hill Brewery, Wiveliscombe, Somerset, TA4 2NY. Tel. (0984) 23798

When it first started production in 1980, this brewery won immediate national acclaim, with its Exmoor Ale winning the Best Bitter award at CAMRA's Great British Beer Festival. Operating from the former Hancock's Brewery at Wiveliscombe (closed 1959), it now supplies real ale to some 150 pubs in the region and a wholesale network covering virtually the whole country. No houses of its own. A new addition to the range is Exmoor Beast, a winter ale.

Exmoor Ale

(OG 1039, ABV 3.8%) Pale brown beer with a malty aroma and a malty, dry taste. Bitter and malty finish. Very drinkable.

Exmoor Gold

(OG 1045, ABV 4.5%) Yellow/golden in colour, with a malty aroma and flavour, and a slight sweetness and hoppiness. Sweet, malty finish.

Exmoor Stag

(OG 1050, ABV 5.2%) Pale brown beer, with a malty taste and aroma, and a bitter finish. Slightly sweet. Very similar to Exmoor Ale and drinks as easily.

Exmoor Beast*

(OG 1066, ABV 6.6%) A winter brew: October-March.

FEATHERSTONE

Featherstone Brewery, Unit 2, Charnwood Ind. Units, Vulcan Road, Leicester. Tel. (0533) 750952

Commercial brewery spun-off from the success of the Saddle Inn brew pub at Twyford (no longer brews).

Robins Bitter* (OG 1030, ABV 2.6%)

Mild* (OG 1035, ABV 3.6%)

Stout* (OG 1038, ABV 3.8%)

Best Bitter* (OG 1039, ABV 4.1%)

Porter* (OG 1048, ABV 5.1%)

Vulcan Bitter (OG 1048, ABV 5.1%)

ESB* (OG 1057, ABV 7%)

FEDERATION

The Federation Brewery Ltd., Lancaster Road, Dunston Ind. Estate, Dunston, Tyne & Wear, NE11 9JR. Tel. (091) 460 9023

A co-operative, founded in 1919 to discover ways of overcoming the post-war beer shortage, which expanded to supply pubs and clubs through its own depots and wholesalers. 540 member clubs own the brewery and their business accounts for the majority of the brewery's trade. Six pubs are loan-tied to Federation, two taking real ale. Only a very small proportion of the brewery's output is cask-conditioned but a new premium ale, Buchanan's Original, named after a brewery acquired in 1927, has been introduced.

Best Bitter

(OG 1035, ABV 3.6%) Very difficult to find, especially on top form, when it has a pleasant aroma, a bitter flavour and a well-balanced aftertaste, with a hint of fruit throughout. Really an ordinary bitter, not a best.

Special Ale

(OG 1040, ABV 4%) Again, rare and often variable, with malt

420

The Independents

and hop characteristics dominating throughout. Maize is detectable and it lacks finish.

Buchanan's Original*

(OG 1045, ABV 4.4%) A reddish-brown, full-bodied and well-balanced new beer (formerly Buchanan Christmas Ale), which, hopefully, indicates an increasing commitment to real ale from the brewery.

FELINFOEL

The Felinfoel Brewery Co. Ltd., Farmers Row, Felinfoel, Llanelli, Dyfed, SA14 8LB. Tel. (0554) 773357

The Lewis family fights back! This famous Welsh brewery is managing to hang on to its independence despite predators. For a while Crown Buckley held a considerable stake, but, with investment in the latter company by Guinness, the family trust which runs Felinfoel was able to buy back a considerable number of Felinfoel shares, making the Guinness interest in the brewery minimal. Supplies draught ale to most of its 80 houses and serves roughly 400 free trade outlets from Aberystwyth to Hereford and Bristol. Also acts as a wholesaler for other draught ales.

Traditional Bitter

(OG 1033, ABV 3.2%) A very hoppy and moderately malty session beer. Very refreshing, with a hoppy aftertaste. Difficult to find but worth the effort.

Cambrian Best Bitter

(OG 1036, ABV 3.8%) Notably hopped and fairly malty pale brown beer. Somewhat fruity with a pleasantly bitter aftertaste.

Double Dragon 'Premium'

(OG 1048, ABV 5%) A fine, well-balanced, rich bitter with a nutty malt flavour, fruity nose and rounded bittersweet finish.

FLOWERS

See Whitbread, page 486.

FORBES

Forbes Ales, Unit 2, Harbour Road Ind. Estate, Oulton Broad, Lowestoft, Suffolk, NR32 3LZ. Tel. (0502) 587905

Brewery set up in 1988, run by a brewer with a degree in sculpture, supplying beer to a couple of regular free trade outlets. The brewery has the added attraction of tasting rooms and a museum/art gallery. The range of beers and their gravities are often changed and all the beers are brewed to be stronger than even their high gravity suggests. *Bottle-conditioned beer: Black Shuck (OG 1063, ABV 6%)*

Bitter

(OG 1038, ABV 3.9%) An amber beer which is definitely (pleasantly) bitter. Well-balanced from the gentle aroma to the quite strong, hoppy/bitter aftertaste. Hints of fruitiness throughout, too.

Best Bitter*

(OG 1042)

Boadecea

(OG 1045, ABV 4.7%) A fruity, malty beer with some sweetness and hop. Untypically for a Forbes beer, there is not much bitterness. Generally well balanced, with a good amount of body. May also become bottle-conditioned.

Traditional*

(OG 1051)

Black Shuck

(OG 1063, ABV 6%) Winter-only draught version of the bottled beer. A faint, mainly fruity aroma leads on to a strong-tasting, full-bodied, dry stout. The dry, bitter aftertaste is long and satisfying. Very drinkable and moreish.

The Independents

Merry Monarch	(OG 1080) A strong, dark brown winter beer with hops and malt in the nose. Roast malt and fruit are prominent on the tongue, followed by malt in the finish, yet not without some balancing hops and bitterness.

FRANKLIN'S

Franklin's Brewery, Bilton Lane, Bilton, Harrogate, N. Yorks, HG1 4DH. Tel. (0423) 322345

A brewery set up in 1980 by Sean Franklin, who devised a beer to give a similar nose and bouquet to that enjoyed by the wines in which he specialised! Now run by Leeds CAMRA founder-member Tommy Thomas. Supplies around ten free trade outlets and festivals.

Bitter
(OG 1038, ABV 4%) A tremendous hop aroma precedes a flowery hop flavour, combined with malt. Long hop and bitter finish. A fine, unique amber bitter.

Blotto*
(OG 1052, ABV 6%) A seasonal brew.

FREMLINS
See Whitbread, page 487.

FRIARY MEUX
See Allied Breweries, page 475.

FULLER'S

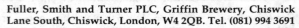

Fuller, Smith and Turner PLC, Griffin Brewery, Chiswick Lane South, Chiswick, London, W4 2QB. Tel. (081) 994 3691

One of the two surviving London independent brewers after the 1960s take-over spree. Uses the CAMRA logo in advertisements for its cask beers; this is not surprising as they are regular CAMRA award-winners. All but three of its 200 tied houses serve real ale and an expanding free trade takes in about 500 outlets, with the brewery having a majority interest in Classic Ales, a London real ale distributor. Brewery redevelopments are still progressing.

Chiswick Bitter
(OG 1034, ABV 3.5%) A distinctively hoppy beer when fresh, with strong maltiness and a fruity character. Finishes with a lasting, dry bitterness and a pleasing aftertaste. *Champion Beer of Britain* 1989.

London Pride ⊕
(OG 1040, ABV 4.1%) An excellent beer with a strong, malty base and a rich balance of well-developed hop flavours and powerful bitterness.

Mr Harry*
(OG 1048, ABV 4.3%) An occasional brew.

ESB ⊕
(OG 1054, ABV 5.5%) A copper-red, strong, robust beer with great character. A full-bodied maltiness and a rich hoppiness are immediately evident and develop into a rich fruitiness with an underlying sweet fullness.

FURGUSONS
See Allied Breweries, page 474.

GALE'S

George Gale & Co. Ltd., The Hampshire Brewery, Horndean, Portsmouth, Hants, PO8 0DA. Tel. (0705) 571212

Hampshire's major brewery, Gale's was founded in 1847. The building was largely destroyed by fire and a new, enlarged brewery was built on the original site in 1869. It grew slowly and steadily during the early 20th century, taking over other small local breweries along the way, and now owns some attractive pubs. Its tied estate was increased

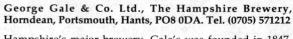

The Independents

by over 50 houses in 1991 after bulk purchases from Allied and Whitbread, and all 154 of its tied houses serve real ale. Gale's also supplies other outlets via the big breweries and brews for Whitbread. *Bottle-conditioned beer: Prize Old Ale ⊕ (OG 1094, ABV 9%)*

XXXL (OG 1032, ABV 2.9%) A pale brown, fairly thin beer which drinks like a light bitter. A low aroma beer, with a sweet and malty middle period leading to a malty sweetness balanced by a little bitterness underneath.

XXXD ⊕ (OG 1032, ABV 2.9%) Although based on a similar recipe to XXXL, this beer is almost black with red hints. Very fruity, with hints of roast malt grain, apricots and caramel, with hops in the bittersweet finish.

BBB or Butser Brew Bitter (OG 1036, ABV 3.6%) Still slightly bland, but an improvement on last year. Golden brown in colour, with little aroma; fairly sweet-tasting, with the sweetness not appearing to come entirely from malt. Some grain and maltiness with bitterness and hop flavour to finish.

Best Bitter (OG 1040, ABV 3.8%) Probably the best balanced beer of the Gale's range: sweet and malty, with some fruit leading to a malty finish with some hop character. A reddish-brown brew.

5X (OG 1044, ABV 4.2%) Available October-March. A very fruity beer, occasionally with liquorice and aniseed as well. There is a winey fruitiness to the nose and some bitterness in the finish.

HSB (OG 1050, ABV 5%) Too sugary-sweet for some palates. A deep brown beer with little aroma but some malt grain and mixed fruit flavours (apples, bananas and damson) leading to a dry, hoppy finish.

Prize Old Ale (OG 1094, ABV 9%) Draught version of the bottle-conditioned beer, available in only a few outlets at Christmastime. Perhaps less full-tasting than from the bottle, with a flavour of woody port and roast malt, which builds up to a slightly bitter finish balanced by tangerines. A very dark brown, vinous brew.

For Whitbread:

Pompey Royal (OG 1043, ABV 4.5%) A brown beer with a hint of redness. Low in aroma, with the flavour dominated by sweetness and pear fruit. The finish can be a little cloying. Becoming harder to find. Perhaps a return to the stronger, original Brickwoods Best recipe would help.

Wethered Winter Royal (OG 1053, ABV 5.5%) Available October-March. A beer with a dry bitterness in the finish: a golden to mid brown brew with an aroma of pear drops. The overall taste is sweet and fruity.

GIBBS MEW

GIBBS MEW

Gibbs Mew PLC, Anchor Brewery, Milford Street, Salisbury, Wilts, SP1 2AR. Tel. (0722) 411911

Established in 1898 by the amalgamation of Salisbury brewers Bridger Gibbs & Sons and Herbert Mew & Co. It is still run by the Gibbs family, brewing with water from its own well, the deepest in the district. Its tied estate has grown considerably in the last ten years and real ale is now supplied to all its 123 pubs. Healthy free trade in southern and south-western England.

The Independents

Chudley Local Line	(OG 1036, ABV 3.5%) A clean-tasting bitter to be savoured. Moderately-hopped and slightly fruity. An ideal lunchtime ale.
Wiltshire Traditional Bitter	(OG 1036, ABV 3.5%) A pleasant enough flavour of malt and hops, but frankly bland and uninspiring. Dry finish.
Premium Bitter	(OG 1042, ABV 4%) A truly bland and uninteresting beer. A small, corky taste and an overbearing sweetness are only tempered by bitterness in the aftertaste. Dwindling availability.
Salisbury Best Bitter	(OG 1042, ABV 4%) A rather chewy, sweet ale, decidedly lacking in bitterness. All the same, a pleasant beer.
The Bishop's Tipple 🍺	(OG 1066, ABV 6.5%) Weaker than the average barley wine, but not lacking in flavour. The full-bodied taste is marvellously malty with a kick that leaves the brain rather less clear than the beer.

GLENNY   See Wychwood, page 471.

GOACHER'S   **P&DJ Goacher, Hayle Mill Cottages, Bockingford, Maidstone, Kent, ME15 6DT. Tel. (0622) 682112**

Kent's most successful small independent brewer, set up in 1983 by Phil and Debbie Goacher, producing all-malt ales with Kentish hops for about 30 free trade outlets in the Maidstone area. The mild is a new addition to the range, introduced in the summer of 1991. Special, a 75%/25% mix of Light and Dark, is also available to pubs for sale under house names. Brewing takes place at a nearby trading estate in Tovil.

Maidstone Real Mild*	(OG 1033, ABV 3.4%)
Maidstone Fine Light*	(OG 1036, ABV 3.7%) Pale, golden brown bitter ale with a strong hoppy aroma and aftertaste. A very hoppy and moderately malty session beer.
Maidstone Best Dark	(OG 1040, ABV 4.1%) Intensely bitter beer, balanced by a moderate maltiness with a complex aftertaste. Lighter in colour than it once was, but still darker than most bitters.
Maidstone Old 1066*	(OG 1066, ABV 6.7%) Black, potent old ale, produced in winter only.

GOLDFINCH   **Tom Brown's Public House and Goldfinch Brewery, 47 High East Street, Dorchester, Dorset, DT1 1HU. Tel. (0305) 264020**

Brewery established in 1987 in a former free house, broadly based on *Tom Brown's Schooldays*. It has expanded from a one-barrel to a four-barrel plant and is still growing. Supplies an increasing free trade.

Tom Brown's Best Bitter	(OG 1039, ABV 4%) A pale-coloured bitter with a fruity nose. The taste is bittersweet, with malt, fruit and some hop. Complex aftertaste.
Flashman's Clout Strong Ale	(OG 1043, ABV 4.5%) A beer with an attractive, honeyed aroma, and, again, a bittersweet taste with malt and fruit. Mid brown in colour, with a predominantly bitter finish.
Old Harry's Midnight Blinder*	(OG 1050, ABV 5%) A new occasional brew.

The Independents

GOOSE EYE

Goose Eye Brewery, Ingrow Bridge, South Street, Keighley, W. Yorks, BD21 5AX. Tel. (0535) 605807

After an absence of three years from the brewing scene, Goose Eye has reopened in a converted carpet warehouse. Bryan Eastell, who ran the brewery for a decade, now has a new partner, Jack Atkinson. The beer (based on the old recipes) is supplied to Bryan's own pub, the Old White Bear at Cross Hills, and some 30 other free trade outlets. A third, medium gravity, beer is planned.

Bitter* (OG 1038)

Pommie's Revenge* (OG 1052)

GRAND METROPOLITAN See Courage, page 481.

GREENALLS See Allied Breweries, page 476.

GREENE KING

Greene King PLC, Westgate Brewery, Westgate Street, Bury St Edmunds, Suffolk, IP33 1QT. Tel. (0284) 763222

East Anglia's largest regional brewery (established 1799), producing cask-conditioned beers at Bury; its Biggleswade brewery is now entirely given over to lager production. Closed the Rayments brewery at Furneux Pelham in 1987, but has appropriated the Rayments name for one of its beers. Acquired 87 Allied pubs in 1990, followed by a further 14 from Courage, all in Kent, in 1991. In May 1992, Greene King announced that it had bought up the Whitbread Investment Company's stake in Morland and was looking for a further 6.7% to take full control and close the Abingdon brewery. The bid flopped disastrously for Greene King and left the company's image badly tarnished. Around 75% of Greene King's 850 tied houses serve real ale, with handpulls now replacing top pressure in most outlets (although a blanket of CO_2 and a cask breather are still sometimes applied). Extensive free trade, but XX Mild is still threatened by declining sales.

XX Mild (OG 1032, ABV 3%) Dark and delicious beer which is sadly difficult to find (it accounts for only 1% of production). Malt dominates the taste but the finish has a pleasing chocolatey dryness.

IPA (OG 1036, ABV 3.6%) When given time to condition in the cask, this is an excellent ale, hoppy on the nose and tongue and with a good bitter finish. If served young, it is often one-dimensional and astringent.

Rayments Special Bitter (OG 1040, ABV 4%) Sweetish beer with malt and fruit dominating the palate and some bitterness on the follow-through. Somewhat underpowered for its strength.

Abbot Ale (OG 1049, ABV 5%) A complex strong ale whose multiplicity of flavours are not always easily kept in balance, but, when on form, a richly satisfying brew.

Winter Ale (OG 1060, ABV 6%) Available November-January and usually served from polypins on the bar. A dark red/brown old ale of substance, like a good wine in many ways. A

The Independents

predominantly fruity nose with some chocolate leads through to a rich blend of fruit, roast malt and some sweetness in the taste. A surprisingly dry aftertaste rounds off this warming brew.

GUERNSEY	**The Guernsey Brewery Co. (1920) Ltd., South Esplanade, St Peter Port, Guernsey, CI. Tel. (0481) 720143**

One of two breweries on this Channel Isle, serving stronger than average real ales in 13 of its 32 tied houses. Free trade takes in some 60 outlets on Alderney, Herm and Jersey. Originally opened as the London Brewery in 1865, it became a Guernsey registered company in 1920 upon the introduction of income tax on the mainland. It was taken over by Jersey's Ann Street Brewery in 1988 and Guernsey real ale is available in selected Ann Street houses. Britannia Bitter is often sold under house names.

LBA Mild (OG 1037, ABV 3.8%) Copper-red in colour, with a complex aroma of malt, hops, fruit and toffee. The rich, mellow flavour combines malt, fruit, hops and butterscotch. The finish has malt and hops. Full-flavoured and surprisingly dry.

Britannia Bitter (OG 1042, ABV 4%) A brewery mix of Mild and Bitter. Amber/tawny in colour, with an aroma of malt, fruit and toffee. Very malty on the palate and again in the finish. Full-bodied and satisfying.

Real Draught Bitter (OG 1045, ABV 4.2%) Golden in colour, with a fine malt aroma. Malt and fruit are strong on the palate and the beer is quite dry for its strength. Excellent, dry malt and hop finish.

GUINNESS See page 482.

HADRIAN **Hadrian Brewery Ltd., Unit 10, Hawick Crescent Ind. Estate, Walker, Newcastle upon Tyne, Tyne & Wear, NE6 1AS. Tel. (091) 276 5302**

Brewery started with a five-barrel plant in 1987 by keen home-brewer Trevor Smith, to serve the North-East's free trade. Has been steadily growing since, and was forced to move to new premises at the end of 1991 in order to expand to a 20-barrel plant. Now supplying adjunct-free beers to 40 free trade outlets as far south as Leeds.

Gladiator Bitter (OG 1039, ABV 4%) A smooth, well-rounded, flavoursome pint, with a nicely balanced aroma, a hoppy/bitter taste, with some underlying fruitiness, and a well-balanced, dry finish.

Centurion Best Bitter (OG 1045, ABV 4.5%) Excellently-balanced beer, enjoying a strong hops and malt presence, and a pleasing, hoppy finish.

Emperor Ale* (OG 1050, ABV 5%) An old ale.

Yule Fuel* (OG 1060, ABV 6%) The Christmas ale.

HALL & WOODHOUSE **Hall & Woodhouse Ltd., The Brewery, Blandford St Mary, Blandford Forum, Dorset, DT11 9LS. Tel. (0258) 452141**

Founded as the Ansty Brewery in 1777 by Charles Hall, whose son, Robert, took Mr GEI Woodhouse into partnership in 1847. Now more usually known as 'Badger's',

The Independents

the brewery serves cask beer in all its 148 houses, although an increasing number now use cask breathers. Free trade to much of southern England (400 outlets), including London and Bedfordshire via wholesalers. Also owns the Gribble Inn brew pub in Oving, West Sussex and sometimes sells its beers in other Badger pubs.

Badger Best Bitter (OG 1041, ABV 4.1%) The taste is strong in hop and bitterness, with a hint of malt and fruit. A hoppy finish with a bitter edge. A fine best bitter.

Hard Tackle* (ABV 4.5%) A full-flavoured, hoppy new beer.

Tanglefoot (OG 1048, ABV 5%) An award-winning, straw-coloured beer with a full fruit character throughout. Malt is also present in the aroma and taste, whilst the finish is bittersweet. Dangerously drinkable.

HALLS See Allied Breweries, page 475.

HAMBLETON

Hambleton Ales, The Brewery, Holme-on-Swale, Thirsk, N. Yorks. Tel. (0845) 567460.

Brewery set up in March 1991 in a Victorian barn on the banks of the River Swale. The production target of 20 barrels a week was achieved six months ahead of schedule and capacity has now been increased to 33 barrels a week. Further expansion will necessitate moving into a purpose-built brewery. Currently serves 20 free trade houses locally on a regular basis and 70 more with guest beers.

Best Bitter* (ABV 3.6%)

Stallion* (ABV 4.2%)

HAMPSHIRE

Hampshire Brewery, 5 Anton Trading Estate, Andover, Hants, SP10 2NJ. Tel. (0264) 336699

A new enterprise, set up by a former Bunces head brewer, Simon Paine, and his partner, Steve Winduss. Started brewing in February 1992 with a new 25-barrel plant, built to their own specification. Their first brew won the *Beer of the Festival* award when it was launched at the Basingstoke Beer Festival. Named after Alfred the Great, whose parliament resided in Andover, the bitter is supplied to carefully targeted pubs and is gaining a reputation for its high hop character.

King Alfred's Hampshire Bitter* (OG 1037, ABV 3.8%) A fruity and deliberately hoppy beer.

HANBY

Hanby Ales, Unit C9, Wem Ind. Estate, Wem, Shropshire, SY4 5SD. Tel. (0939) 232432

Following the closure of Wem Brewery by Greenalls in December 1988, the former head brewer, Jack Hanby, set up his own brewery with a partner. Brewing commenced the following spring and by February 1990 they had moved into a new, larger brewhouse, which was altered and expanded again in 1991 to cope with a larger volume and range of products. The business is supplemented by the supply of soft drinks.

The Independents

Black Magic Mild* (OG 1033, ABV 3.3%)

Drawwell Bitter* (OG 1039, ABV 3.9%)

Treacleminer Bitter* (OG 1046, ABV 4.6%)

Nutcracker Bitter* (OG 1060, ABV 6%)

HANCOCK'S See Bass, page 480.

HANSON'S See Banks's, page 401.

HARDINGTON **Hardington Brewery, Albany Buildings, Dean Lane, Bedminster, Bristol, Avon, BS3 1BT. Tel. (0272) 636194**

Set up in a brewhouse hidden away at the end of a dark tunnel, in April 1991, Hardington's has little connection with the old Somerset brewery of the same name. Demand for its beers has been steadily increasing and it now serves 60 outlets within a 50-mile radius.

Traditional (OG 1038, ABV 3.7%) An amber, clean, refreshing beer. The aroma is hoppy and malty, as is the taste, which has a crisp fruitiness. Long, bitter finish.

Best Bitter (OG 1042, ABV 4.2%) A tawny-coloured, full-flavoured bitter beer with a dry finish and an aroma of malt, hops and citrus fruits. Moreish.

Jubilee (OG 1050, ABV 4.9%) A mid brown, smooth, complex, fruity and warming beer. Beautifully balanced throughout.

Old Lucifer (OG 1054, ABV 6%) Jubilee's even bigger brother. A rich, distinctive, powerful, tawny-coloured dry beer.

HARDYS & HANSONS **Hardys & Hansons PLC, Kimberley Brewery, Kimberley, Nottingham, NG16 2NS. Tel. (0602) 383611**

Established in 1832 and 1847 respectively, Hardys and Hansons were two competitive breweries on opposite sides of the road, sharing the same water supply, until a merger in 1930 produced the present company. Now Nottingham's last independent brewery, the company is controlled by descendants of the original Hardy and Hanson families, who, with the acquisition of 46 new pubs in 1991, are still committed to keeping it that way. Noted for good value beers, but there is still a tendency to spoil them with top pressure in many of the 254 tied houses (this doesn't apply to the strong Kimberley Classic, however).

Best Mild (OG 1035, ABV 3.1%) A dark, sweetish mild, slightly malty. Can have fruity notes.

Best Bitter (OG 1039, ABV 3.9%) Golden/straw-coloured, distinctive, faintly fruity beer. Subtle in aroma; malt is more prominent than hop character and balancing bitterness.

Kimberley Classic* (OG 1047, ABV 4.8%) A light-coloured, deceptively strong beer.

HARTLEYS See Robinson's, page 455.

The Independents

HARVEYS

Harvey & Son (Lewes) Ltd., The Bridge Wharf Brewery, 6 Cliffe High Street, Lewes, E. Sussex, BN7 2AH. Tel. (0273) 480209

Established in the late 18th century by John Harvey, on the banks of the River Ouse, this Georgian brewery was partly rebuilt in 1880 and the Victorian Gothic tower and brewhouse remain a very attractive feature in the town centre. Still a family-run company, offering real ale in all 33 tied pubs and about 350 free trade outlets in Sussex and Kent. A new summer beer was launched in 1991 to celebrate the bicentenary of the publication of *The Rights of Man*, by Tom Paine, who once lived in Lewes. Frequently produces commemorative beers - occasionally on draught.

XX Mild Ale
(OG 1030, ABV 3%) A pleasant, dark brew which is continuing to hold on in a few tied houses. The aroma and taste are malty, with a roast flavour, and the palate is fruity and sweetish. The aftertaste is similar, with lingering malt. Well worth finding.

Sussex Pale Ale
(OG 1033, ABV 3.5%) A very well-hopped, refreshing brew. Hops are in the aroma and palate, with some fruit and sweetness. Hops in the finish, too, with some bitterness. A very good session beer.

Sussex Best Bitter
(OG 1040, ABV 4%) A fine example of a full-bodied southern bitter. Its hoppy aroma gives way to a fruity, sweetish palate. The complex aftertaste features hops, with some bitterness, yet with a lingering sweetness.

XXXX or Old Ale
(OG 1043, ABV 4.3%) Brewed October-May: rich and dark, with lively fruitiness and a caramelly flavour. Mellow and smooth, when on form.

Armada Ale 🍺
(OG 1046, ABV 4.5%) A well-hopped, strong bitter with a powerful finish.

Tom Paine*
(OG 1055, ABV 5.5%) A summer offering, brewed only for the 4th July.

Elizabethan*
(OG 1090, ABV 8.3%) December only, or occasional brews; a silky-smooth barley wine.

HARVIESTOUN

Harviestoun Brewery Ltd., Dollar, Clackmannanshire, Central, FK14 7LX. Tel. (0259) 42141

Hand-built in a 200-year-old stone byre by two home-brew enthusiasts in 1985, this small brewery operates from a former dairy at the foot of the Ochil Hills, near Stirling. Demand for the beer has been such that a new custom-built brew plant was installed in 1991 to treble the capacity and a new brew, Ptarmigan, was also launched that year. With Bavarian hops and Scottish malt giving it an unusual flavour, Ptarmigan was introduced experimentally, but has proved popular enough to become a regular brew. A New Year ale is produced every December with an appropriate OG for each year, so this year's will be 1093. Construction of a new visitor centre on a balcony over the new brewhouse should soon be completed. Currently serves some 40 outlets in central Scotland; no tied houses.

Waverley 70/-*
(OG 1037, ABV 3.8%)

Original 80/-*
(OG 1041, ABV 4.2%)

The Independents

Ptarmigan 85/-*	(OG 1045, ABV 4.6%) The first known 85/- ale.
Old Manor*	(OG 1050, ABV 5.1%) A dark beer with a roast malt flavour.
Nouveau*	(OG 1093, ABV 10.5%) A winter brew for Christmas and the New Year.

HERITAGE

The Heritage Brewery Museum, Anglesey Road, Burton upon Trent, Staffs, DE14 3PF. Tel. (0283) 69226

The brewing company of the Heritage Brewery Museum, based in the former Everards Tiger Brewery which was built in 1881 for Liverpool brewer Thomas Sykes. Thomas Sykes Ale is the speciality brew, sold mostly in corked bottles for celebrations and commemorations, but also available on draught. The beers are sold at the brewery itself, and in the free trade via Lloyds Country Beers.

Bitter*	(OG 1045, ABV 4.2%)
Thomas Sykes Ale*	(OG 1103, ABV 10%)

HESKET NEWMARKET

Hesket Newmarket Brewery, Old Crown Barn, Hesket Newmarket, Cumbria, CA7 8JG. Tel. (069 98) 288

Brewery set up in a barn behind the owners' pub in 1988 and officially opened by telex message from a regular, Chris Bonnington, from Katmandu. Situated in an attractive North Lakes village, most of the beers are named after local fells. The beers are supplied to the Old Crown and to 25 other outlets up and down the country. Brewery tours (including a meal at the inn) are available by prior arrangement.

Great Cockup Porter*	(OG 1035, ABV 2.6%) Long-awaited new brew.
Skiddaw Special Bitter*	(OG 1035, ABV 3.1%) A golden session beer, despite its name.
Blencathra Bitter*	(OG 1035, ABV 3.5%) A ruby-coloured bitter.
Doris's 90th Birthday Ale*	(OG 1045, ABV 4.3%) A fruity premium ale.
Old Carrock Strong Ale*	(OG 1060, ABV 5.9%) A dark red, powerful ale.

HIGHGATE   See Bass, page 479.

HIGSONS   See Whitbread, page 487.

HILDEN

Hilden Brewery, Hilden House, Lisburn, Co. Antrim. Tel. (0846) 663863

Mini brewery in a Georgian country house, set up in 1981 to counter the local all-keg Guinness/Bass duopoly. Presently the only real ale brewery in Northern Ireland, supplying eight free trade outlets and some pubs in England.

Hilden Ale

(OG 1039) An amber-coloured beer with an aroma of malt, hops and fruit. The balanced taste is slightly slanted towards hops, and hops are also prominent in the full, malty finish. Bitter and refreshing.

The Independents

Special Reserve	(OG 1039) Dark red/brown in colour and superbly aromatic - full of dark malts, producing an aroma of liquorice and toffee. Malt, fruit and toffee on the palate, with a sweet, malty finish. Mellow and satisfying. Not regularly available.

HOLDEN'S

Holden's Brewery Ltd., Hopden Brewery, George Street, Woodsetton, Dudley, W. Midlands, DY1 4LN. Tel. (0902) 880051

One of the long-established family breweries of the Black Country, producing a good range of real ales for its 19 pubs and around 40 free trade customers. More tied houses are planned, as finances allow, and with the fourth generation of the Holden family now under tutelage, the future looks optimistic.

Stout	(OG 1036, ABV 3.2%) A dark brown, near black beer, with a bitter, malty flavour. Hints of liquorice in the aftertaste.
Mild ⊲	(OG 1037, ABV 3.6%) A splendid smooth blend of malt, hops and roast flavours. A beer whose full-bodied taste belies its gravity.
Bitter	(OG 1039, ABV 3.9%) Hops and malt predominate in this amber, smooth drink. Pleasantly bitter, with a dry, hoppy, bitter finish.
XB	(OG 1041, ABV 4.1%) Sold mainly as a house beer, under the names of its various outlets. A sweeter, fruitier version of the bitter.
Special	(OG 1051, ABV 4.9%) A pale brown, sweet and malty, strong bitter. Full-bodied, with a bittersweet aftertaste.
XL	(OG 1092, ABV 8.9%) Only available at Christmas: a very strong, sweet and dark ale which drinks and tastes like alcoholic liquorice.

HOLT

Joseph Holt PLC, Derby Brewery, Empire Street, Cheetham, Manchester, M3 1JD. Tel. (061) 834 3285

Successful family brewery, founded in 1849 (not to be confused with Allied's Midlands company Holt, Plant & Deakin). Still producing probably Britain's cheapest pint for its strength in the UK and such is its popularity that it is often delivered in hogsheads (54 gallon barrels). All 102 tied houses serve real ale and only one pub does not sell Mild. The beers are increasingly in demand as guests and free trade is growing all the time, so much so that extensions to the brewery were put in hand in 1992 to cater for the demand.

Mild Ale	(OG 1033, ABV 3.2%) Very dark beer with a complex aroma and taste. Roast malt is prominent, but so are hops and fruit. Strong in bitterness for a mild and has a long-lasting, satisfying aftertaste.
Bitter	(OG 1040, ABV 4%) Tawny beer with a strong hop aroma. Although balanced by malt and fruit, the uncompromising bitterness can be a shock to the unwary and extends into the aftertaste.

HOLTS	See Allied Breweries, page 475.

The Independents

HOME See Scottish & Newcastle, page 484.

HOOK NORTON The Hook Norton Brewery Co. Ltd., The Brewery, Hook Norton, Banbury, Oxfordshire, OX15 5NY. Tel. (0608) 737210

Built by John Harris on the family farm in 1850, Hook Norton remains one of the most delightful traditional Victorian tower breweries in Britain. It retains much of its original plant and machinery, the showpiece being the 25 horsepower stationary steam engine which still pumps the Cotswold well water used for brewing. The brewery boasts some fine old country pubs; all 35 of its tied houses serve real ale, and some 450 free trade outlets are also supplied.

Best Mild (OG 1032, ABV 2.9%) A dark, red/brown mild with a malty aroma and a malty, sweetish taste, tinged with a faint hoppy balance. Malty in the aftertaste. Splendid and highly drinkable.

Best Bitter (OG 1036, ABV 3.3%) An excellently-balanced, golden bitter. Malty and hoppy on the nose and in the mouth, with a hint of fruitiness. Dry, but with some balancing sweetness. A hoppy bitterness dominates the finish.

Old Hooky (OG 1049, ABV 4.3%) An unusual, tawny beer with a strong fruity and grainy aroma and palate, balanced by a hint of hops. Full-bodied, with a bitter, fruity and malty aftertaste.

HOP BACK Hop Back Brewery, 27 Estcourt Road, Salisbury, Wiltshire, SP1 3AS. Tel. (0722) 328594

Originally a brew pub, set up in May 1987 with a five-barrel plant, producing award-winning beers. Moved production to a new brewery at Downton in May 1992 to cope with increased demand but the brewery at the pub will continue to turn out speciality beers. Currently brews around 40 barrels a week, supplying its two tied houses and 12 free trade customers.

GFB (OG 1035, ABV 3.5%) Golden, with the sort of light, clean, tasty quality which makes an ideal session ale. Hoppy aroma and taste, leading to a good dry finish. Refreshing.

Special or Flintnapper (OG 1040, ABV 4%) Medium bitter. Slightly sweet, but with a good balance of malt and hops and a long finish.

Entire Stout (OG 1043, ABV 4.5%) A rich dark stout with a strong roasted malt flavour and a long, smooth and malty aftertaste. A vegan beer.

Summer Lightning ⊲ (OG 1050, ABV 5%) An extremely pleasurable, bitter, straw-coloured beer with a terrific, fresh, hoppy aroma and a well rounded, malty, hoppy flavour with an intense bitterness, which leads to an excellent, long, dry finish.

HOSKINS Hoskins Brewery PLC, Beaumanor Brewery, 133 Beaumanor Road, Leicester, LE4 5QE. Tel. (0533) 661122

Established in 1877 and the smallest remaining tower brewery in the country. Since 1986 has been steadily expanding its tied estate from two to its present 17 outlets, and plans to continue to acquire new houses; all serve real ale and offer guest beers. There has been some rationalisation of the beer range in the last 12 months and Premium is now brewed so rarely that it has been deleted from the list.

The Independents

Beaumanor Bitter   (OG 1039, ABV 3.9%) A very drinkable and refreshing, amber-coloured beer with a thin yet satisfying texture. An aroma of hops and fruit leads on to a hoppy taste and then a long, malty finish.

Penn's Ale   (OG 1045, ABV 4.3%) A full-bodied, easy-drinking beer, golden in colour and with a slightly fruity aroma. Rich, malty and well-balanced in flavour, followed by a clean, dry, crystal malt finish.

Churchill's Pride*   (OG 1050, ABV 4.8%) Launched as a regular brew to replace Premium, but now only an occasional brew for the free trade.

Old Nigel   (OG 1060, ABV 5.7%) Malt and hints of liquorice are present in the robust flavour of this winter beer (December-February). Fruity in aroma and sweet-tasting, with a lasting, pleasantly-fruity finish. Russet in colour.

HOSKINS & OLDFIELD   **Hoskins & Oldfield Brewery Ltd., North Mills, Frog Island, Leicester, LE3 5DH. Tel. (0533) 532191**

Set up by two members of Leicester's famous brewing family, Philip and Stephen Hoskins, in 1984, after the sale of the old Hoskins Brewery. A wide range of beers is produced for a scattered free trade, but local availability is unfortunately limited. Heroes Bitter is produced for the Legendary Yorkshire Heroes pub chain.

HOB Mild   (OG 1035) A dark ruby mild with a chocolate and coffee aroma, and a dry, stout-like flavour. Heavy and creamy, with a lasting, dry, malty finish.

HOB Bitter   (OG 1041) Golden in colour, with an aroma of peardrops. Its flavour is fruity and hoppy, with a harsh, hoppy, but sweet aftertaste.

Little Matty*   (OG 1041) A darker version of HOB Bitter.

Tom Kelly's Stout   (OG 1043) A satisfying stout, dark in colour, with an attractive, golden, creamy head and an aroma of malt and fruit. The flavour is exceedingly bitter but malty and the finish is dry and chocolatey.

Old Navigation Ale   (OG 1071) Ruby/black beer, with an aroma reminiscent of sherry. Sweet and fruity, with a stout-like malt flavour.

Christmas Noggin   (OG 1100) Russet-coloured beer with a spicy, fruity aroma. The taste is of malt and fruit, and the finish balances malt and hops. Sweet but not cloying.

For Legendary Yorkshire Heroes:

Heroes Bitter*   (OG 1037)

HP&D   See Allied Breweries, page 475.

SARAH HUGHES   **Sarah Hughes Brewery, Beacon Hotel, 129 Bilston Street, Sedgley, Dudley, W. Midlands, DY3 1JE. Tel. (0902) 883380**

Brewery reopened in 1988 after lying idle for 30 years, to serve the village pub and a few other outlets. Now produces for the free trade. A Victorian-style conservatory acts as a reception area for brewery visits (always welcome during opening hours). Plans for bottling have not yet got off the ground.

The Independents

Sedgley Surprise	(OG 1048, ABV 5%) A sweet, malty drink with a faint hoppy aftertaste.
Original Dark Ruby Mild ⊆	(OG 1058, ABV 6%) A well-balanced, flavoursome ale with roast, malt, fruit, sweet and bitter flavours all detectable.

HULL

The Hull Brewery Co. Ltd., 144-148 English Street, Hull, Humbs, HU3 2BT. Tel. (0482) 586364

Hull Brewery was resurrected in 1989 after a 15-year gap by two local businessmen in an old fish smokehouse. Originally a mild-only operation, a bitter was introduced in November 1991 and a premium bitter, Guvenor, in the spring of 1992. Plans to develop its own small chain of local pubs took a step forward with the acquisition in May 1992 of the Plimsoll's Ship Hotel. Free trade has grown from a base of serving the Hull club scene to around 95 free trade outlets throughout West Yorkshire and South Humberside.

Mild*	(OG 1033)
Bitter*	(OG 1036)
Guvernor*	(OG 1048)

HYDES' ANVIL

Hydes' Anvil Brewery Ltd., 46 Moss Lane West, Manchester, M15 5PH. Tel. (061) 226 1317

Family-controlled traditional brewery, first established at the Crown Brewery, Audenshaw, Manchester in 1863 and on its present site, a former vinegar brewery, since the turn of the century. It became the Anvil brewery in 1943 and is the smallest of the established Manchester breweries and the only one to produce more than one real mild. Acquired ten pubs from Bass in the summer of 1991; supplies cask ale to all its 60 tied houses. £1 million has been invested to enable the company to brew Harp lager under contract.

Mild	(OG 1032, ABV 3.5%) A light, refreshing, slightly fruity drink with little aftertaste. Fruity aroma, with a hint of malt.
Dark Mild*	(OG 1034, ABV 3.5%) Light with added caramel.
Light	(OG 1034, ABV 3.7%) A lightly-hopped session beer, complex in character, with malt dominating and a brief but dry finish. Available more in southern Manchester than Mild, and vice-versa in northern parts of the city.
Bitter	(OG 1036, ABV 3.8%) A good-flavoured bitter, with a malty nose, fruity background and a malty aftertaste. A hint of bitterness throughout.

IND COOPE   See Allied Breweries, page 474.

ISLAND

The Island Brewery, Manners View, Dodnor Ind. Estate, Newport, Isle of Wight. Tel. (0983) 520123

An ambitious new brewery set up in 1991 by the Hampshire-based soft drinks firm Hartridge's and set to expand following the demise of its only rival on the island, Burts. Owns no pubs, but supplies 60 free trade outlets on the island.

Nipper Bitter*	(OG 1038, ABV 3.8%)

The Independents

Newport Best Bitter*	(OG 1045, ABV 4.5%)
Wight Winter Warmer*	(OG 1060, ABV 6%)

ISLE OF MAN

Isle Of Man Breweries Ltd., Falcon Brewery, Murrays Road, Douglas, Isle of Man. Tel. (0624) 661140

The main brewery on the island, having taken over and closed the rival Castletown brewery in 1986. Although production of Castletown beers was continued for a while, the final death blow was dealt in February 1992 when Castletown Bitter was discontinued. Okells Special Bitter, which was only launched in April 1991 did not survive either, with the brewery keen to supply Bass Special Bitter to its pubs instead. The remaining real ales are produced under the unique Manx Brewers' Act 1874 (permitted ingredients: water, malt, sugar and hops only) at Okell's impressive Victorian tower brewhouse near the centre of Douglas. All but three of its 56 tied houses sell real ale which is also supplied to 12 free trade outlets.

Okells Mild

(OG 1034, ABV 3.4%) A genuine, well-brewed mild ale, with a fine aroma of hops and crystal malt. Reddish-brown in colour, this beer has a full malt flavour with surprising bitter hop notes and a hint of blackcurrants and oranges. Full malty finish.

Okells Bitter

(OG 1035, ABV 3.7%) Golden, malty and superbly hoppy in aroma, with a hint of honey. Rich and malty on the tongue, with a wonderful, dry malt and hop finish. A complex but rewarding beer.

JENNINGS

ESTD. 1828

Jennings Bros PLC, Castle Brewery, Cockermouth, Cumbria, CA13 9NE. Tel. (0900) 823214

Brewery founded in 1828 and on the present site for over 100 years. Whilst the original Mild and Bitter are still in popular demand, the Cumberland Ale and Sneck Lifter, introduced just a few years ago, are increasing in popularity through a fast-growing network of free trade outlets, wholesalers and other brewers across the UK. Real ale is supplied to 90 of its 99 tied houses.

Mild*

(OG 1031, ABV 3.1%) A dark, mellow mild.

Bitter

(OG 1035, ABV 3.4%) An excellent, distinctive, red/brown brew with a hoppy, malty aroma. A good, strong balance of grain and hops in the taste, with a moderate bitterness, developing into a lingering, dry, malty finish.

Cumberland Ale*

(OG 1040, ABV 3.8%) A hoppy, golden bitter.

Sneck Lifter*

(OG 1055, ABV 4.9%) A dark, strong warmer.

JOLLY ROGER

Jolly Roger Brewery, 31-33 Friar Street, Worcester, WR1 2NA. Tel. (0905) 22222

Worcestershire's only brewery, established in 1982 as a brew pub. As demand from the free trade grew, a larger commercial brewery was due to open in Friar Street in 1991, but this was delayed for a year because of planning difficulties. Now owns five tied houses, two of which will continue to operate as brew pubs once the Friar Street site opens. Flagship is the latest addition to the beer range and sedimented bottled beers are planned.

The Independents

Jolly Roger Ale*	(OG 1038, ABV 3.8%) A golden-coloured beer.
Shipwrecked*	(OG 1040, ABV 4%) A dark bitter.
Goodness*	(OG 1042, ABV 4.2%) A stout.
Flagship*	(OG 1052, ABV 5.2%) Chestnut brown and full flavoured.
Winter Wobbler*	(OG 1092, ABV 11%) The seasonal beer - a dark old English ale.

JUDGE'S   **Judge's Brewery, Constable Road, Church Lawford, Rugby, Warwickshire. Tel. (0788) 567243**

Brewery set up by Graham and Ann Judge in early summer 1992.

Barristers Bitter*   (OG 1036)

KELHAM ISLAND   **Kelham Island Brewery, 23 Alma Street, Sheffield, S. Yorks, S3 8SA. Tel. (0742) 781867**

Brewery opened in 1990 at the Fat Cat in Alma Street, using equipment purchased from the former Oxford Brewery and Bakehouse. Now supplies around 45 free houses in Derbyshire, Nottinghamshire and South Yorkshire.

Bitter   (OG 1038, ABV 4%) Beer with a pungent hoppiness in both aroma and taste. Leaves a short but dry and bitter aftertaste. A new brewer's beer that suffers from inconsistency, but promises more.

Celebration*   (OG 1046, ABV 4.7%)

KEYSTONE   **Keystone Brewing Company, Unit 3, Sherburn Enterprise Centre, Aviation Road, Sherburn in Elmet, N. Yorks, LS25. Tel. (0977) 681596**

Brewery set up in January 1992 by a former head barman at the Masons Arms, Cartmel Fell in Cumbria. A premium ale is planned.

Bitter*   (OG 1037, ABV 3.7%)

KING & BARNES   **King & Barnes Ltd., The Horsham Brewery, 18 Bishopric, Horsham, W. Sussex, RH12 1QP. Tel. (0403) 270470**

Long-established brewery, dating back almost 200 years and in the present premises since 1850. It is run by the fifth generation of the King family, having united with the Barnes family brewery in 1906. Its 'Fine Sussex Ales' are served in all 60 country houses (more in the pipeline). Extensive free trade mostly within a radius of 40 miles.

Mild ⏛   (OG 1034, ABV 3.2%) A smooth, malty, dark brown mild, with a bittersweet finish and a fruity, malty aroma. Tends to be displaced by Old Ale in winter.

Sussex Bitter   (OG 1034, ABV 3.5%) A splendid, hoppy, tawny-coloured bitter, with good malt balance and a dry finish.

Broadwood   (OG 1040, ABV 4%) Pale brown with a faint malt aroma. A good marriage of malt and hops is present in the taste, with malt slightly dominating. Also available as a keg beer, though it is usually known then as Ten-Forty.

436

The Independents

Old Ale ⊞   (OG 1046, ABV 4.1%) A classic, almost black old ale. A fruity, roast malt flavour, with some hops, leads to a bittersweet, malty finish. Lovely roast malt aroma. Available October-Easter.

Festive   (OG 1050, ABV 4.8%) Tawny/red with a malty aroma. The flavour is fruity and malty, with a noticeable hop presence. Malt dominates the finish.

LARKINS   **Larkins Brewery Ltd., Larkins Farm, Chiddingstone, Edenbridge, Kent, TN8 7BB. Tel. (0892) 870328**

Larkins Brewery was started by the Dockerty family in 1986, with the purchase of the Royal Tunbridge Wells Brewery, but moved to a converted barn at the owners' farm in 1990. An additional brewing copper and fermenter were acquired in June 1991 to keep up with the growing local free trade - the additive-free beers can now be found in some 65 pubs in the South-East. Only Kent hops are used, some from the farm itself.

Traditional Bitter*   (OG 1035, ABV 3.4%) Beer whose recipe has changed over the last couple of years.

Sovereign Bitter   (OG 1040, ABV 4%) A malty and slightly fruity, bitter ale, with a very malty finish. Copper-red in colour.

Best Bitter   (OG 1045, ABV 4.7%) Full-bodied, slightly fruity and unusually bitter for its gravity. Dangerously drinkable!

Porter Ale   (OG 1055, ABV 5.5%) Each taste and smell of this potent black winter beer reveals another facet of its character. An explosion of roasted malt, bitter and fruity flavours leaves a bittersweet aftertaste.

LEES   **JW Lees & Co. (Brewers) Ltd., Greengate Brewery, PO Box 2, Middleton Junction, Manchester, M24 2AX. Tel. (061) 643 2487**

Family-owned brewery, founded in 1828 by John Lees, a retired cotton manufacturer. The existing brewhouse dates from 1876 but has been expanded in recent years. Serves real ale in all 173 of its tied houses and clubs (mostly in northern Manchester). Free trade in the North-West (about 100 outlets).

GB Mild   (OG 1032, ABV 3%) Malty and fruity in aroma. The same flavours are found in the taste, but do not dominate in a beer with a rounded and smooth character. Dry, malty aftertaste. Low turnover in some outlets.

Bitter   (OG 1038, ABV 4%) Pale beer with a malty, hoppy aroma and a distinctive, malty, dry and slightly metallic taste. Clean, dry Lees finish. Some evidence of a recent increase in hoppiness and bitterness in the flavour.

Moonraker ⊞   (OG 1073, ABV 7.5%) Reddish-brown in colour, having a strong, malty, fruity aroma. The flavour is rich and sweet, with roast malt, and the finish is fruity yet dry. Only available in a handful of outlets.

LINFIT   **Linfit Brewery, Sair Inn, Lane Top, Linthwaite, Huddersfield, W. Yorks, HD7 5SG. Tel. (0484) 842370**

19th-century brew pub which recommenced brewing in 1982, producing an impressive range of ales for sale at the Sair and for a growing free trade as far away as Manchester;

The Independents

serves 12 regular outlets. Occasional batches of bottled beers produced.

Mild (OG 1032, ABV 3%) Roast malt dominates in this straightforward dark mild. Some hop aroma; slightly dry flavour. The finish is malty.

Bitter (OG 1035, ABV 3.5%) Good session beer. A dry-hopped aroma leads to a clean-tasting, hoppy bitterness, balanced with some maltiness. The finish is well balanced, too, but sometimes has an intense bitterness.

Special (OG 1041, ABV 4%) Dry-hopping again provides the aroma for this rich and mellow bitter. Very soft profile and character; fills the mouth with texture rather than taste. Clean, rounded finish.

English Guineas Stout (OG 1050, ABV 5%) A fruity, roasted aroma preludes a smooth, roasted, chocolatey flavour which is bitter but not too dry. Excellent appearance; good, bitter finish.

Old Eli (OG 1050, ABV 5%) Excellent, well-balanced premium bitter with a dry-hopped aroma and a fruity, bitter finish.

Leadboiler (OG 1063, ABV 6%) Flowery and hoppy in aroma, with a very moreish, strong bitter flavour which provides a soft mouthfeel; well-balanced by a prominent maltiness. Rounded, bitter finish.

Enoch's Hammer (OG 1080, ABV 8%) Straw-coloured, vinous bitter with no pretentions about its strength or pedigree. A full, fruity aroma leads on to a smooth, alcoholic, hoppy, bitter taste, with an unexpectedly bitter finish.

Xmas Ale (OG 1082, ABV 8%) A hearty and warming ale. The flavour is strong in roasted malt, with some bitterness. Extremely vinous, with a slightly yeasty, metallic taste. Bitter finish. An adaptation of Enoch's Hammer.

LION'S **Lion's Original Brews Ltd., Griffin Brewery, Belshaw Court, Billington Road, Burnley, Lancs, BB1 5UB. Tel. (0282) 830156**

Brewery which started trading in October 1991. Originally a six-barrel plant, it was expanded during summer 1992. A mild and a premium bitter are under consideration. Supplies around 40 free trade outlets.

Original Bitter* (OG 1038, ABV 4.1%)

Owd Edgar* (OG 1068, ABV 7%) A seasonal brew.

LLOYDS **Lloyds Country Beers Ltd, John Thompson Brewery, Ingleby, Derbyshire, DE7 1HW. Tel. (0332) 863426**

Founded as a home-brew operation at the John Thompson Inn in 1977, Lloyds is the separate business set up to supply the beers to the free trade (over 60 outlets). Also distributes Heritage Bitter from the Heritage Brewery.

Derby Mild* (OG 1033, ABV 3.3%) New to the range.

Classic* (OG 1035 in summer, 1038 in winter, ABV 3.4% and 3.7%)

Derby Bitter or Country Bitter or JTS XXX* (OG 1042, ABV 4.2%) Full and fruity.

The Independents

VIP (Very Important Pint)* (OG 1048, ABV 4.7%) Heavier, darker version of the bitter.

Overdraft* (OG 1067.5, ABV 6.2%)

Skullcrusher* (OG 1067.5, ABV 6.2%) A heavy Christmas beer.

LONGSTONE **Longstone Brewery, Station Road, Belford, Northumberland, NE70 7DT. Tel (0668) 213031**

After a year of difficulty in securing premises, this brewery finally got off the ground in August 1991. A new stronger ale is planned. Supplies seven free trade outlets.

Bitter (OG 1039, ABV 4%) A not unpleasant combination of malt and hop flavours, with a hint of fruit in the aroma. Now finding its way into the limited local free trade.

LORIMER & CLARK See Vaux, page 465, and Caledonian Brewery, page 411.

McEWAN See Scottish & Newcastle, page 483.

THOMAS MCGUINNESS **Thomas McGuinness Brewing Company, 1 Oldham Road, Rochdale, Lancs, OL16 1UA. Tel. (0706) 711476**

A brand new brewery, set up early in 1992 behind the Cask and Feather pub. Starting with one beer and three tied houses, there are plans to expand once the business has been established, with additional brews to serve the free trade.

Best Bitter* (OG 1038, ABV 3.8%)

MACLAY **Maclay & Co. Ltd., Thistle Brewery, Alloa, Clackmannanshire, Central, FK10 1ED. Tel. (0259) 723387**

Family-run business, founded in 1830 by James Maclay and moved to the present Victorian tower brewery in 1869. Still uses traditional brewing methods and direct fired coppers; the beers are produced using only bore-hole water (the only Scottish brewery to do so) without any adjuncts. Porter is no longer produced, but half of the 30 tied houses offer real ale, which is also supplied to 40 free trade outlets.

60/- Ale* (OG 1034, ABV 3.4%) A flavoursome, dark session beer.

70/- Ale* (OG 1036, ABV 3.6%) A well-hopped, quenching beer.

80/- Export* (OG 1040, ABV 4%) Well-balanced and rich.

Kane's Amber Ale* (OG 1040, ABV 4%) New brew in honour of the late Dan Kane, a much-loved Scottish CAMRA activist who died early in 1992.

Scotch Ale* (OG 1050, ABV 5%)

McMULLEN **McMullen & Sons Ltd., The Hertford Brewery, 26 Old Cross, Hertford, Herts, SG14 1RD. Tel. (0992) 584911**

Hertfordshire's oldest independent family brewery, founded in 1827 by Peter McMullen. The Victorian tower brewery, which houses the original oak and copper-lined fermenters still in use today, was built on the site of three wells. Real ale is served in all its 147 pubs in Hertfordshire, Essex and London, and supplied to almost 150 free trade outlets.

439

The Independents

Original AK	(OG 1033, ABV 3.8%) A light bitter with a hoppy aroma. The malty, hoppy flavour is followed by an aftertaste which has bitterness, hoppiness and a touch of malt.
Country Best Bitter	(OG 1041, ABV 4.6%) A predominantly malty beer, although a bitter hoppiness can also be detected. The aroma has hops and malt, and there is a distinctive finish with bitterness, malt and hops.
Stronghart	(OG 1070, ABV 7%) A sweet, rich, dark beer; a single brew for the winter months. It has a malty aroma, with hints of hops and roast malt which carry through to the taste.

For Whitbread:

Wethered Bitter*	(OG 1035, ABV 3.6%)

MALTON

Malton Brewery Company Ltd., Crown Hotel, Wheelgate, Malton, N. Yorks, YO17 0HP. Tel. (0653) 697580

Began brewing in 1985 in a stable block at the rear of Malton's Crown Hotel where the former Grand National winner Double Chance was once stabled, hence the name of the bitter. Steady growth in the sales of their additive-free beers and occasional special brews led to the installation of more fermenting vessels. Supplies 14 free trade outlets regularly as well as guest beers to several pubs in North and West Yorkshire.

Pale Ale	(OG 1034, ABV 3.6%) A fresh, hoppy nose precedes a hoppy, bitter taste with malt embellishments. Dry but bitter, with a clean finish. A light, refreshing, straw-coloured session beer.
Double Chance Bitter	(OG 1038, ABV 4%) An amber brew with a hoppy nose and taste. Dried fruit and a touch of malt in the mouth, but the hops come through to a dry finish.
Pickwick's Porter ⊞	(OG 1042, ABV 4.2%) Meets the perception of a porter better than most that use the title. Lots of malt and roast in the aroma and mouth, but tart, with hints of fruit and chocolate, at the same time. Astringent finish.
Owd Bob	(OG 1055, ABV 5.8%) A winter warmer. A rich aroma of fruit and roast merges into a complex hop, fruit, chocolate and bitter taste and ends in a short, but strong, dry roast finish. Dark chocolate colour with ruby red tints.

MANNS See Courage, page 481.

MANSFIELD

Mansfield Brewery PLC, Littleworth, Mansfield, Notts, NG18 1AB. Tel. (0623) 25691

Founded in 1855, and now one of the country's leading regional brewers, Mansfield stopped brewing cask beer in the early 1970s. It resumed real ale production in 1982 as an experiment and has not looked back since. Its excellent ales are all fermented in traditional Yorkshire squares and have enjoyed steadily rising sales, aided in 1991 by the acquisition of a substantial number of pubs from Courage. Now some 330 of its 448 pubs serve cask beer. Supplies around 650 free trade outlets (particularly East Midlands clubs), and enjoys a reciprocal trading arrangement with Charles Wells.

Old Shilling*	(OG 1030, ABV 3%) Primarily a brew for Boddingtons Pub Company.

The Independents

Riding Dark Mild   (OG 1035, ABV 3.4%) Dark brown in colour, with a hint of red. A predominantly chocolate malt taste and finish, with a dash of fruit, follows a pleasant, roast malt aroma.

Riding Traditional Bitter   (OG 1036, ABV 3.5%) Pale brown, with a malty, hoppy nose. A firm malt background is overlaid with a good bitter bite and hop flavours.

Old Baily   (OG 1045, ABV 4.7%) Resembles a Scotch heavy, but with a fine balance of hop, malt and fruit flavours. Dark copper-red in colour, with an aroma of malt and fruit.

MARSTON MOOR

Marston Moor Brewery, The Crown Inn, Kirk Hammerton, York, N. Yorks, YO5 8DD. Tel. (0423) 330341

Small, but expanding brewery, set up in 1984. Recently increased capacity by almost a third and added two new brews to the range: ESB and the seasonal Black Tom Stout. Supplies its single tied house, the Crown, and a scattered free trade of 20 outlets.

Cromwell Bitter*   (OG 1037.5, ABV 3.7%) A distinctive, bitter beer.

Brewers Pride*   (OG 1042 ABV 4.2%) An amber-coloured, premium beer.

Porter*   (OG 1042, ABV 4.2%) A seasonal brew (October-May), ruby-coloured and stout-like.

Black Tom Stout*   (OG 1045) New winter beer (October-May).

Brewers Droop*   (OG 1050, ABV 5%) A potent, straw-coloured ale.

ESB*   (OG 1050)

MARSTON'S

Marston, Thompson & Evershed PLC, Shobnall Road, Burton upon Trent, Staffs, DE14 2BW. Tel. (0283) 31131

The only brewery still using the unique Burton Union system of fermentation for its stronger ales and Marston's commitment to this method has recently been reinforced with the introduction of new Burton Unions. Real ale is available in most of its 858 pubs, stretching from Yorkshire to Hampshire, and the enormous free trade is helped by many Whitbread houses stocking Pedigree Bitter. The Border beers are the relics of Marston's 1984 take-over of the Border Wrexham brewery. Sadly there are plans to axe both milds, following a deal with Wolverhampton & Dudley, through which Marston's pubs will sell Banks's Mild. W&D outlets will take Pedigree Bitter.

Border Mild   (OG 1031, ABV 3.1%) A thin, dark mild with negligible aroma, a slight malty flavour, with hints of caramel, sulphur and bitterness, and a faint, dry and malty finish.

Mercian Mild   (OG 1032, ABV 3.3%) A copper to dark brown beer, thin, but well balanced. Hints of roast malt and fruit in the taste, and a sweet, mild finish. A quaffing mild.

Border Exhibition   (OG 1034, ABV 3.5%) Originally a light mild when brewed in Wrexham, but now a thinnish, light bitter. A slightly less bitter and more fruity version of Border Bitter. More hoppy of late.

Border Bitter   (OG 1034, ABV 3.6%) Thinnish, light session beer, pale brown in colour, which has a slight, well-balanced, malty, bitter taste, with fruit and hops more pronounced than in previous years. The aftertaste is quite astringent.

The Independents

Burton Best Bitter (OG 1036, ABV 3.7%) An amber/tawny session beer which can often be markedly sulphury in the aroma and taste. At its best, a splendid, subtle balance of malt, hops and fruit follows a faintly hoppy aroma and develops into a balanced, dry aftertaste.

Merrie Monk (OG 1043, ABV 4.5%) A smooth, dark brew. Has a creamy, slightly sweet flavour, with traces of caramel, roast malt and fruit. Sweet, malty finish.

Pedigree Bitter (OG 1043, ABV 4.5%) A famous beer whose quality now varies enormously due to its national availability. Can be less than ordinary and rarely reaches its former heights. Prone to a sulphury aroma when fresh.

Owd Rodger ⊞ (OG 1080, ABV 7.6%) A dark, ruby-red barley wine, with an intense fruity nose before a deep, winey, heavy fruit flavour, with malt and faint hops. The finish is dry and fruity (strawberries). Misunderstood, moreish and strong.

MAULDONS **Mauldons Brewery, 7 Addison Road, Chilton Ind. Estate, Sudbury, Suffolk, CO10 6YW. Tel. (0787) 311055**

Successful brewery, set up in 1982 by former Watney's brewer Peter Mauldon, whose family once had its own brewery. Black Adder received the accolade of CAMRA *Champion Beer of Britain* in 1991, and a new beer, Suffolk Comfort, was added to the sizeable beer list in February 1992, though FA Mild (OG 1034, ABV 3.4%) is now only brewed for festivals. Over 150 free trade outlets in East Anglia and Hertfordshire, and the beers are now becoming more widely available via wholesalers. Provides house beers for local pubs.

Golden Brew* (OG 1034, ABV 3.4%) Summer beer (Easter-September).

Bitter (OG 1037, ABV 3.8%) Malt and fruit are predominant throughout, with little balancing hop or bitterness.

Old Porter (OG 1042, ABV 3.8%) A black beer with malt and roast flavours dominating. Some hop in the finish.

Old XXXX (OG 1042, ABV 4%) Winter ale with a reddish brown appearance. The taste is complex, with fruit, malt, caramel, hop and bitterness all present.

Squires (OG 1044, ABV 4.2%) A best bitter with a good, malty aroma. The taste is evenly balanced between malt and a hoppy bitterness.

Special (OG 1045, ABV 4.2%) By far the most hoppy of the Mauldons beers, with a good, bitter finish. Some balancing malt.

Suffolk Punch (OG 1050, ABV 4.8%) A full-bodied, strong bitter. The malt and fruit in the aroma are reflected in the taste and there is some hop character in the finish. Deep tawny/red in colour.

Black Adder ⊞ (OG 1055, ABV 5.3%) A dark stout. Roast is very strong in the aroma and taste, but malt, hop and bitterness provide an excellent balance and a lingering finish.

Christmas Reserve (OG 1065, ABV 6.6%) A sweet Christmas ale with malt and fruit. Typically for this type of ale, it has little bitterness. Fairly pale in colour for a strong beer, with red tints.

The Independents

MILL

Mill Brewery, Unit 18c, Bradley Lane, Newton Abbot, Devon, TQ12 4JW. Tel. (0626) 63322

Founded in 1983 on the site of an old watermill. Special brews, based on Janner's Old Original, are often sold under local pub names, 'Janner' being the local term for a Devonian. Serves nine regular outlets and the free trade in southern Devon and Torbay.

Janner's Ale

(OG 1038) Pale brown-coloured, bland beer, without any discernible aroma. The flavour is bitter/hoppy and the aftertaste is also bitter, but it lacks balance.

Janner's Old Dark Ale*

(OG 1040) An occasional brew.

Janner's Old Original

(OG 1045) A beer malty and sweet in character, with a slightly 'thick' consistency. Bitter finish.

Janner's Christmas Ale*

(OG 1050) The festive beer.

MINERS ARMS

See Mole's, page 444.

MITCHELL'S

Mitchell's of Lancaster (Brewers) Ltd., 11 Moor Lane, Lancaster, LA1 1QB. Tel. (0524) 60000

The only surviving independent brewery in Lancaster (est. 1880), wholly owned and run by direct descendants of founder William Mitchell. The company is very traditional: many of the casks are still wooden and all the beers are brewed with natural spring well water. Real ale is sold in all but three of its 54 pubs and virtually countrywide in the free trade. Also acts as a beer, cider, wine and minerals wholesaler.

Best Dark Mild

(OG 1034, ABV 3.2%) Black with ruby-red tints. Malty in aroma and taste, with a faint fruitiness. A smooth and highly drinkable mild.

Best Bitter

(OG 1035, ABV 3.6%) A golden bitter with a malty aroma and a superb, dry, malty flavour, with a faint balance of hops. A delicate bitter aftertaste usually demands more of the same.

Olde Priory Porter*

(OG 1036, ABV 3.6%) A new addition to the range.

Fortress*

(OG 1042, ABV 4.2%) Another new brew.

ESB

(OG 1050, ABV 5.2%) Creamy in texture; malty in aroma. The flavour is also malty and fruity, with a hoppy finish.

Single Malt Winter Warmer

(OG 1065, ABV 7.5%) A seasonal brew, mid brown in colour and suggestive of malt whisky in aroma and flavour. Strongly malty throughout, with a subtle bittersweet, hoppy balance in the taste.

MITCHELLS & BUTLERS (M&B)

See Bass, page 479.

The Independents

MOLE'S

Mole's Brewery (Cascade Drinks Ltd.), 5 Merlin Way, Bowerhill, Melksham, Wilts, SN12 6TJ. Tel. (0225) 704734

Established in 1982 by former Ushers brewer Roger Catté (the brewery name came from his nickname), Mole's has remained basically a one-man operation. Serves one tied house and 60 outlets within a 35-mile radius in Wiltshire and Avon, and other parts of the country via beer agencies. Brews under contract for the inoperative Miners Arms brewery and acts as a distributor for other members of the Small Independent Brewers Association (SIBA).

IPA

(OG 1035, ABV 3.5%) A pale brown beer with a trace of maltiness in the aroma. A thin, malty, dry flavour, with little aftertaste. ·

Cask Bitter

(OG 1040, ABV 4%) A pale brown/golden-coloured beer with an aroma of malt, fruit and hops. The taste is malty, with some bitterness; the body is good, with a rounded finish of all the primary flavours. Not too bitter and a little dry.

Brew 97

(OG 1050, ABV 5%) A mid brown, full-bodied beer with a powerful, malty aroma. The strong flavour is sweet and malty, and the full aftertaste has malt and a dry bitterness. A rich, wonderfully warming, malty ale.

XB*

(OG 1060, ABV 6%) A winter ale.

For Miners Arms:

Own Ale

(OG 1038, ABV 3.8%) Pale brown beer with a mostly malty, bitter taste, a malty aroma and a dry finish. Can be slightly lactic.

Guvnor's Special Brew

(OG 1048, ABV 4.8%) A golden, malty brew with a faint, hoppy aroma and a dry, slightly sour palate, with some citrus fruit. A dry, malty, lasting finish.

MOORHOUSE'S

MOORHOUSE'S

Moorhouse's Brewery (Burnley) Ltd., 4 Moorhouse Street, Burnley, Lancs, BB11 5EN. Tel. (0282) 22864

Long-established (1870) producer of hop bitters, which in 1978 began brewing cask beer. Has since had several owners; the latest, Bill Parkinson, took over seven years ago. His investment in a new brewhouse to meet increased demand has been well rewarded and the modern plant is complemented by traditional, turn-of-the-century equipment. The brewery is also building up its tied estate; three new pubs were acquired in 1991, making a total of five, all offering real ale. Also supplies around 120 free trade outlets.

Black Cat Mild*

(OG 1034, ABV 3.2%)

Premier Bitter

(OG 1036, ABV 3.6%) A straw-coloured, clean-tasting bitter with a good balance of flavours and a distinctive, bitter finish. Refreshing.

Pendle Witches Brew

(OG 1050, ABV 5%) Fruit is prominent in the aroma, leading on to a full, malty taste with some of the sweetness more commonly associated with a higher gravity brew.

Owd Ale*

(OG 1065, ABV 6.4%) A winter brew.

444

The Independents

MORLAND

Morland & Co. PLC, PO Box 5, Ock Street, Abingdon, Oxfordshire, OX14 5DD. Tel. (0235) 553377

Old regional brewery, established in 1711, which survived a take-over bid by Greene King in 1992. With the Whitbread Investment Company looking to dispense with its stake in the brewery, Greene King stepped in to buy up all 43.4% of the WIC holding. However, its efforts to pick up a further 6.7% to take overall control and close the brewery were, thankfully, thwarted. Nearly all Morland's 300 pubs serve real ale, but in many cases a cask-breather is used at the licensee's discretion. Morland cask ales are also available in the club and free trade (over 500 outlets).

Original Bitter

(OG 1035, ABV 4%) A light amber beer with malty, hoppy nose with a hint of fruitiness. The distinct, but lightish, malt and hops carry over to the flavour and leave a sweet but dry, hoppy aftertaste.

Old Masters

(OG 1040, ABV 4.6%) A well-balanced tawny/amber beer with not outstandingly strong flavours. The initial aroma of malt and hops leads to a moderately malty but dry and hoppy flavour, with a hint of fruit which can be faintly sulphurous. Dry, bitter finish.

Old Speckled Hen

(OG 1050, ABV 5.2%) Morland's most distinctive beer, deep tawny/amber in colour. A well-balanced aroma of roasted malt and hops is complemented by a good hint of caramel. An initial sweet, malty, fruity, roast caramel taste soon allows the dry hop flavour through, leaving a well-balanced aftertaste.

MORRELLS

Morrells Brewery Ltd., The Lion Brewery, St Thomas Street, Oxford, OX1 1LA. Tel. (0865) 792013

The only brewery in Oxford is still family run, as it has been since 1782. Of its 128 pubs, 50 are within the city limits and all but three outlets serve real ale, though some employ blanket pressure. The decision to cut back on its range of beers in 1991 meant that some of the lower gravity beers were lost. However, both the Mild and Graduate won brewing awards during 1992. Also brews Whitbread's Strong Country Bitter under contract. Around 180 free trade outlets stock the beers.

Bitter

(OG 1036, ABV 3.7%) Golden in colour and light in body, but not in flavour, with a good aroma of hops complemented by malt and fruitiness. An initial dry hop bitterness is well balanced by the flavour of malt which gives way to a nice, refreshing, slightly sweet fruitiness, with a hint of roast caramel. A bittersweet, hoppy finish.

Mild*

(OG 1037, ABV 3.7%)

Varsity

(OG 1041, ABV 4.3%) A tawny/amber beer. Malt, hops and fruit are the main features in aroma and taste, but are well balanced. The slightly sweet, malty, fruity start fades away to a distinctive, bittersweet finish.

Graduate

(OG 1048, ABV 5.2%) An intense malt and roast aroma is complemented by a moderate hoppiness in the taste. Pleasant, bitter finish.

College*

(OG 1073, ABV 7.3%) A winter brew.

For Whitbread:

Strong Country Bitter*

(OG 1037, ABV 3.9%)

The Independents

NETHERGATE

Nethergate Brewery Co. Ltd., 11-13 High Street, Clare, Suffolk, CO10 8NY. Tel. (0787) 277244

Small brewer of award-winning beers, set up in 1986. Only traditional methods are used: no sugars, no colourings and no hop extracts. Brewing capacity has increased by 40% in the last year, the company has acquired its first tied house, the Cambridge Blue in Cambridge, and further expansion is planned. Nearly 140 free trade outlets are supplied, mostly in East Anglia.

IPA

(OG 1036, ABV 3.6%) Superb drinking bitter, much improved from its predecessor (Casks IPA). The lingering hoppy finish is especially fine.

Bitter ⊕

(OG 1039, ABV 4.1%) An enticingly hoppy fragrance leads into a taste which achieves a superb balance between lip-smacking hoppiness, true bitterness and smooth maltiness. The finish is deep and powerfully hoppy.

Old Growler

(OG 1054, ABV 5.5%) Wonderfully complex dark ale. An initially bitter, roasty taste is counterpoised by rich fruit and chocolate flavours. Lots of hops in the follow-through. Based on an old London porter recipe.

NEW FOREST

New Forest Brewery, Old Lyndhurst Road, Cadnam, Hants, SO4 2NL. Tel. (0703) 812766

No longer a brewery, but a wholesaler. Takes Charles Wells ales (Eagle, Bombardier and keg beers) and re-badges them under its own name.

NICHOLSON'S

See Allied Breweries, page 475.

NIX WINCOTT

Nix Wincott Brewery, Three Fyshes Inn, Bridge Street, Turvey, Beds, MK43 8ER. Tel. (023 064) 264

Brewery which began as a brew pub in 1987, but whose beers gained a quick response from the local free trade and wholesalers. In a few years, capacity was doubled. The latest addition to the range is THAT, or Two Henrys Alternative Tipple, which fills the gap in strength between the two other main brews. Currently supplies six outlets regularly, as well as the Three Fyshes.

Two Henrys Bitter

(OG 1039, ABV 4%) Tawny-coloured with faint malt and fruit on the nose. A fruity bitterness leads through to a dry aftertaste.

THAT

(OG 1049, ABV 5%) First brewed in September 1991; a mid brown, well-rounded beer with fruit present throughout. Bittersweet finish.

Old Nix

(OG 1059, ABV 6%) The faintly fruity aroma leads through to a complex flavour of fruit and malt on a bittersweet base. Fruity, bittersweet finish.

Winky's Winter Warmer*

(OG 1059, ABV 6%) A dark Christmas ale.

The Independents

NORTH YORKSHIRE	**North Yorkshire Brewing Co., 84 North Ormesby Road, Middlesbrough, Cleveland, TS7 0DY. Tel. (0642) 226224**

THE NORTH YORKSHIRE BREWING COMPANY

Company started in March 1990 with a purpose-built brewery and an eight-barrel throughput, but demand has been such that a 40-barrel system is planned. A second tied house has been acquired and the company now supplies over 50 free trade outlets with its additive-free beers. Yorkshire Porter is the latest addition to a steadily growing range.

Best Bitter
(OG 1036) Light and very refreshing. Surprisingly full-flavoured for a pale, low gravity beer. A complex, bittersweet mixture of malt, hops and fruit carries through into the aftertaste.

IPA or XXB
(OG 1040, ABV 4.2%) A pleasant, pale brown beer, fruity, malty and hoppy, but without the subtlety of Best Bitter and perhaps a little too sweet. The finish, however, is dry and hoppy.

Yorkshire Porter*
(OG 1040) New brew.

Erimus Dark
(OG 1046) A dark, full-bodied, sweet brew with lots of roast malt and caramel, and an underlying hoppiness. At its best, it is very smooth indeed, with a tight, creamy head and a sweet, malty finish.

Flying Herbert
(OG 1048, ABV 5.2%) A refreshing, red/brown beer with a hoppy aroma. The flavour is a pleasant balance of roast malt and sweetness which predominates over the hops. The malty, bitter finish develops slowly.

Dizzy Dick
(OG 1080) A smooth, strong, dark, aromatic ale with an obvious bite, although too sweet for some. The very full, roast malt and caramel flavour has hints of fruit and toffee. The malty sweetness persists in the aftertaste.

OAK	**Oak Brewing Company Ltd., Phoenix Brewery, Green Lane, Heywood, Gtr. Manchester, OL10 2EP. Tel. (0706) 627009**

Brewery established in 1982, now supplying free trade from West Cheshire to West Yorkshire. The move to its new home in Heywood, from Ellesmere Port, took place in summer 1991.

Hopwood Bitter*
(OG 1034)

Best Bitter
(OG 1038) A tawny, hoppy session beer with some balancing malt in the aroma and taste. A strong, dry and hoppy finish.

Tyke Bitter*
(OG 1042) Originally brewed for the West Riding Brewery (currently inoperative), but available throughout Oak's free trade.

Old Oak Ale
(OG 1044) A well-balanced, brown beer with a multitude of mellow fruit flavours. Malt and hops balance the strong fruitiness in the aroma and taste, and the finish is malty, fruity and dry.

Extra Double Stout*
(OG 1045)

Double Dagger
(OG 1050) A pale brown, malty brew, more pleasantly dry and light than its gravity would suggest. Moderately fruity throughout and a hoppy bitterness in the mouth balances the strong graininess.

The Independents

Porter*   (OG 1050) Now available all year round.

Wobbly Bob   (OG 1060) A red/brown beer with a malty, fruity aroma. Strongly malty and fruity in flavour and quite hoppy, with the sweetness yielding to a dryness in the aftertaste.

OAKHILL   **The Old Brewery, High Street, Oakhill, Bath, Avon, BA3 5AS. Tel. (0749) 840134**

Situated high in the Mendip Hills in Somerset (despite the Avon postal address), the brewery was set up by a farmer in 1984 in an old fermentation room of the original Oakhill brewery (est. 1767), much of which had been destroyed by fire in 1925. Like its predecessor, the present Oakhill brewery uses spring water from the Mendips. The stout, brewed to an old recipe and now renamed Black Magic, was at first an occasional brew, but has earned a permanent place in the beer range. No tied houses, but 70 free trade outlets are supplied in Avon, Somerset, Dorset and Wiltshire, within a 35-mile radius.

Bitter   (OG 1038, ABV 3.8%) Amber-coloured, with a hoppy, malty aroma. Hoppy and bitter in the mouth, with balancing malt. There is a similar balance in the strong finish. Can be sulphury.

Black Magic   (OG 1044, ABV 4%) A black/brown bitter stout with moderate roast malt and a touch of fruit in the nose. Smooth roast malt and bitterness in the taste, with mellow coffee and chocolate. Slightly fruity and sweet. Long lasting, bitter, dry, roast finish.

Yeoman Strong Ale   (OG 1049, ABV 4.8%) A mid brown beer with a hoppy, malty aroma and a malty, fruity, bittersweet taste. The strong finish is fruity, hoppy and dry.

OKELLS   See Isle of Man Breweries, page 435.

OLDHAM   See Whitbread, page 486.

OLD LUXTERS   **Chiltern Valley, Old Luxters Farm Brewery, Hambleden, Henley-on-Thames, Oxfordshire, RG9 6JW. Tel. (049 163) 330**

Brewery set up in a 17th-century barn by David Ealand, owner and producer of Chiltern Valley Wines, with a three and a half barrel plant. The beer first appeared in May 1990 and is now available in seven local free houses. Hambleden is in Buckinghamshire, despite the brewery's postal address.

Barn Ale   (OG 1042.5) Predominantly malty, fruity and hoppy in taste and nose, and tawny/amber in colour. Fairly rich and strong in flavours: the initial, sharp, malty and fruity taste leaves a dry, bittersweet, fruity aftertaste, with hints of black cherry. Can be slightly sulphurous.

OLD MILL   **Old Mill Brewery, Mill Street, Snaith, Goole, Humbs, DN14 9HS. Tel. (0405) 861813**

Small brewery, started in 1983 in a 200-year-old former malt kiln and corn mill. New equipment was installed in 1991 to increase the brew length to 60 barrels to meet demand. Slowly building up its tied estate; now has ten pubs, all serving real ale, and a free trade of around 100 accounts.

The Independents

Traditional Mild   (OG 1034, ABV 3.4%) A dark, red/brown beer, with roast and fruit aromas and taste. A slight sweetness is identifiable in the mouth and finish, to the detriment of the hop presence. Now a thin brew.

Traditional Bitter   (OG 1037, ABV 3.7%) More brown than amber, this beer is also thinner. Malt and hop on the nose; grain and hop taste; the finish is dry and bitter. Softer and more mellow than last year. Possibly better in the free trade than in tied houses.

Bullion   (OG 1044, ABV 4.4%) Beer with a hoppier aroma than before but malt still mixes with ripe fruit in the mouth. The aftertaste has hops and a bittersweet, deep malt lining. Like all Old Mill's beers this year, feels a mite thin and more smooth.

ORKNEY   **The Orkney Brewery, Quoyloo, Sandwick, Orkney, KW16 3LT. Tel. (0856) 84802**

The Orkneys' first brewery in living memory, set up in 1988 by former licensee Roger White. Initially only brewing keg beer for local palates, his personal commitment to real ale has meant that cask ales now represent 90% of sales (mostly to central Scotland). The latest addition to a growing range of additive-free beers is Dragonhead Stout.

Raven Ale   (OG 1038, ABV 3.8%) Still mainly keg on the island, but worth seeking out when in 'real' form. Smooth, mellow and malty, with a distinctive aroma and finish.

Dragonhead Stout*   (OG 1040, ABV 4%)

Dark Island*   (OG 1045, ABV 4.6%)

Skullsplitter*   (OG 1080, ABV 8.5%)

OTTER   **Otter Brewery, Mathayes, Luppitt, Honiton, Devon, EX14 0SA. Tel. (0404) 891289**

New brewery which happily exceeded its owners' expectations at the end of its first year in November 1991. Now the brewing capacity has been doubled with the intention of supplying more local houses. At present 30 pubs take the beers which are brewed using local malt and the brewery's own spring water. Otter Head has recently been introduced and future plans include adding a winter porter to the range.

Bitter ⊕   (OG 1036, ABV 3.6%) Amber/pale brown-coloured beer. Very slightly malty, but a strong hoppy/bitter-tasting beer with a pleasant hoppy, bitter finish.

Otter Ale   (OG 1044, ABV 4.4%) Tawny-coloured with a fruity aroma. Pleasantly sweet and fruity-tasting, yet a bitter beer with a hoppy, bitter aftertaste.

Otter Head   (ABV 5.5%) Tawny-coloured. The fruity, hoppy aroma and flavour make this a very tasty, yet not oversweet beer for the strength.

PACKHORSE   **The Packhorse Brewing Co., The Flour Mills, East Hill, Ashford, Kent, TN24 8PX. Tel. (0233) 638131**

Brews no real ale: a brewery set up in 1991 to brew lagers to the German beer purity law.

The Independents

PALMERS

JC & RH Palmer Ltd., Old Brewery, Bridport, Dorset, DT6 4JA. Tel. (0308) 22396

Thatched brewery in a delightful seaside setting. Brewing has taken place in these former mill buildings since at least 1794, and the Palmer family have been here since the late 1880s. The tied estate is growing slowly but steadily, with cask-conditioned beer in all 68 tied houses, although top pressure and cask breathers are widely in use. About 40 direct free trade outlets, and increasing sales through wholesalers and agents across southern England.

Bridport Bitter or BB
(OG 1032, ABV 3.2%) A light beer with a hoppy aroma, a clean, hoppy taste with some bitterness, and a bitter aftertaste.

Best Bitter or IPA
(OG 1040, ABV 4.2%) A good balance of fruit, bitterness and hop in the taste, with malty undertones, leads to a predominantly bitter finish. A fruity aroma, with some hop.

Tally Ho!
(OG 1046, ABV 4.7%) A dark and complex brew with a malty aroma. The nutty taste is dominated by roast malt, balanced with some bitterness. Malty and bitter aftertaste. Difficult to find, especially in winter.

PARISH

The Parish Brewery, The Old Brewery Inn, High Street, Somerby, Leics, LE14 2PZ. Tel. (066 477) 781

The first brewery to be established in Somerby since the 16th century, Parish started life at the Stag and Hounds, Burrough on the Hill, and moved in July 1990 for greater capacity, following increased sales. Baz's Bonce Blower is the strongest draught beer available all year round in the UK, but production of Porter has ceased. In addition to the Old Brewery Inn, Parish directly supplies half a dozen other outlets.

Mild*
(OG 1034, ABV 3.3%)

Special Bitter or PSB*
(OG 1038, ABV 3.5%)

Somerby Premium Bitter*
(OG 1040, ABV 4%)

Poachers Ale*
(OG 1060, ABV 6.6%) Dark, sweet and malty.

Baz's Bonce Blower or BBB*
(OG 1110, ABV 12%) Rich, black and treacly.

PILGRIM

Pilgrim Brewery, West Street, Reigate, Surrey, RH2 9BL. Tel. (0737) 222651

Surrey brewery which supplies real ale locally and to pubs in London, Kent and Sussex, as well as the Midlands and the North via wholesalers. Currently serves 75 free trade outlets and is increasing brewing capacity to cope with demand. A new premium bitter and a stout have been introduced and the mild has been restyled a porter. Still looking to develop a tied estate through the Pilgrim Taverns subsidiary.

Surrey Pale Ale or SPA
(OG 1037, ABV 3.7%) A well-balanced pale brown bitter with an underlying fruitiness. Hop flavour comes through in the finish. A good session beer.

450

The Independents

Porter (OG 1041, ABV 4%) The new name for XXXX Mild. A dark brown beer with a malty flavour and pleasant fruitiness. A malty sweetness in the finish is balanced by a faint developing hoppiness.

Progress Best Bitter (OG 1041, ABV 4%) Reddish-brown in colour, with a predominantly malty flavour and aroma, although hops are also evident in the taste.

Crusader Premium Bitter ⊄ (OG 1047, ABV 4.7%) Light, golden beer with a malty bitterness. A very drinkable summer brew.

Saracen Stout* (OG 1047, ABV 4.7%) A new occasional stout.

Talisman (OG 1049, ABV 5%) A strong ale with a dark red colour, a fruity, malt flavour and roast overtones. Available all year, but more common in winter.

PITFIELD

PITFIELD'S

Chainmaker Beer Company, Stourbridge Estate, Mill Race Lane, Stourbridge, W. Midlands, DY8 1JN. Tel. (0384) 442040

Following the demise of Premier Ales, the Chainmaker Beer Company was set up in 1991 to continue the production of the Pitfield brands, which had been bought up by Premier in 1989. The new company is closely allied to Wiltshire Brewery and now brews Wiltshire beers under contract, following the end of production at Tisbury. Negotiations are under way to tie the two companies even more closely together. Ten pubs in the Midlands (ex-Premier outlets and Wiltshire acquisitions) are supplied, as well as Wiltshire's southern estate. Only two of the Tisbury beers have survived the move north, and all the Premier brands have now been abandoned.

Mild* (OG 1034)

Bitter* (OG 1036, ABV 3.6%)

ESB (OG 1044, ABV 4.5%) The old Knightly Bitter: a pale brown, malty-flavoured bitter. Quite hoppy and slightly sweet.

Hoxton Heavy (OG 1048, ABV 4.7%) A copper-red beer, quite hoppy in taste and aroma. Slightly sweet.

Dark Star (OG 1050, ABV 4.7%) A malt and roast-flavoured, black beer, slightly fruity, with a hop and bitter finish.

For Wiltshire:

Stonehenge Best Bitter* (OG 1044)

Old Grumble* (OG 1050)

PLASSEY

Plassey Brewery, The Plassey, Eyton, Wrexham, Clwyd, LL13 0SP. Tel. (0978) 780277

Brewery founded in 1985 by former Border brewer, Alan Beresford. Following his death in 1989, it was taken over by another ex-Border man, Ian Dale, in partnership with Tony Brookshaw, owner of the farm on which the brewery is sited. The farm also includes a touring caravan and leisure park, a craft centre and a licensed outlet for Plassey's ales. Cwrw Tudno ('St Tudno's beer'), was produced as a one-off for the first Llandudno Beer Festival in 1990, but proved so popular that it has been continued as a production beer, and a winter ale is planned. The brewery supplies about ten free trade outlets.

Bitter ⏚ (OG 1039, ABV 4%) Excellent, straw-coloured beer, well-hopped and bitter, with blackcurrant fruitiness. Light and refreshing.

Cwrw Tudno (OG 1047, ABV 5%) A well-balanced, hoppy bitter, more fruity than the other beer.

POOLE **The Brewhouse Brewery, 68 High Street, Poole, Dorset, BH15 1DA. Tel. (0202) 682345**

Brewery established in 1981, two years before the Brewhouse pub/brewery was opened. When an extension to the Brewhouse was completed in 1990, the entire brewing operation was transferred there. The Brewhouse pub keeps the beer under blanket pressure, but a dozen free trade outlets also take Poole products. A new premium bitter, Double Barrel (OG 1051, ABV 5.1%), is to be added to the range. This will be supplied in wooden pins and gravity dispensed in selected outlets.

Best Bitter or Dolphin* (OG 1038, ABV 3.8%) An amber-coloured, balanced bitter.

Bosun Bitter* (OG 1045, ABV 4.6%) Amber and rich.

POWELL See Wood, page 469.

PREMIER See Pitfield, page 451.

PRESTON **Preston Brewing Company, Atlas Foundry Estate, Brieryfield Road, Preston, Lancs, PR1 8SR. Tel. (0772) 883055**

Brewery founded by ex-Matthew Brown employee Graham Moss. The first brew was produced in summer 1992 and other beers are planned.

Pride* (OG 1038, ABV 3.8%)

RANDALLS **RW Randall Ltd., Vauxlaurens Brewery, St Julian's Avenue, St Peter Port, Guernsey, CI. Tel. (0481) 720134**

The smaller of Guernsey's two breweries, which was purchased by RH Randall from Joseph Gullick in 1868. He went on to acquire several pubs and hotels and, on his death in 1902, the brewery passed to his son, RW Randall. Successive generations have continued to run the business, except for the period of the German occupation when brewing ceased until after the war. Owns 18 houses, but only four serve real ale.

Best Mild (OG 1035) Copper-red, with a malty and fruity aroma and a hint of hops. The fruity character remains throughout, with a sweetish, malty undertone.

Best Bitter ⏚ (OG 1046) Amber in colour, with a malt and fruit aroma. Sweet and malty both in the palate and finish.

The Independents

RANDALLS (JERSEY)	Randalls Vautier Ltd., PO Box 43, Clare Street, St Helier, Jersey, CI, JE4 8NZ. Tel. (0534) 73541

Brews no real ale but sells Bass and Marston's Pedigree in 13 of its 32 tied houses. No connection with Randalls of Guernsey.

RAYMENTS See Greene King, page 425.

REDRUTH Redruth Brewery Ltd., The Brewery, Redruth, Cornwall, TR15 1AT. Tel. (0209) 212244

The old Cornish Brewery has now reverted to its original name, following a management buy-out from JA Devenish PLC in July 1991. Originally founded in 1792, its time under Devenish management was troubled, culminating in Devenish's decision to opt out of brewing altogether in 1991 after Whitbread offered to supply beer to its pubs. The Redruth brewery has thankfully been saved, but most of the beers have been lost. The only real ale brewed is Cornish Original – for Whitbread to supply to Devenish! Most local pubs are tied to other breweries, giving Redruth no outlets for beers of its own. The management is therefore concentrating on contract packaging and brewing. No tied estate.

For Whitbread:

Cornish Original Bitter* (OG 1036, ABV 3.6%)

REEPHAM Reepham Brewery, Unit 1, Collers Way, Reepham, Norfolk, NR10 4SW. Tel. (0603) 871091

Family brewery, founded in 1983 by a former Watney's research engineer with a purpose-built plant in a small industrial unit. The company was launched on a single beer, Granary Bitter, but now produces quite a range, which varies from year to year. The new Velvet Stout won the *Beer of the Festival* award at CAMRA's 1991 Norwich Beer Festival. Has no tied houses, but supplies real ale to 20 outlets in Norfolk, and more extensively through wholesalers. *Bottle-conditioned beer: Rapier Pale Ale (OG 1044, ABV 4.2%)*

Granary Bitter (OG 1038, ABV 3.8%) This pale brown beer is predominantly hoppy from aroma to aftertaste. Malt and bitterness are also in evidence to balance this good drinking beer.

Dark* (OG 1040, ABV 3.8%) A strong mild.

Velvet Stout ⊟ (OG 1043, ABV 4.2%) A excellent, new sweet stout. A gentle aroma of malt, roast and hop leads into a full-bodied beer with a deep, rounded palate and aftertaste.

Gold* (OG 1044, ABV 4.2%) A pale gold strong ale.

Rapier Pale Ale (OG 1044, ABV 4.2%) A very well-balanced, dry and malty beer, from aroma to aftertaste, with a hint of fruitiness. Very drinkable.

Old Bircham Ale (OG 1046, ABV 4.6%) An amber/tawny beer with good body for its gravity. The fruity aroma precedes a complex, malty, hoppy palate, which also has a sweetness that dies away in the malty, dry finish. A winter brew.

Brewhouse Ale* (OG 1052, ABV 5%) A strong winter ale.

The Independents

REINDEER

The Reindeer Trading Company Ltd., 10 Dereham Road, Norwich, Norfolk, NR2 4AY. Tel. (0603) 666821

Brew pub which opened in 1987 and has doubled its capacity since 1991. Supplies about 20 free trade outlets in the locality, but beers at the pub are stored in cellar tanks under blanket pressure.

Moild*	(OG 1034, ABV 3.6%)
Bevy*	(OG 1037, ABV 4%)
Gnu Bru*	(OG 1042, ABV 4.5%)
Bitter*	(OG 1047, ABV 5%)
Red Nose*	(OG 1057, ABV 6%)
Sanity Claus	(OG 1067, ABV 6.8%) Christmas only.

RIDLEYS

TD Ridley & Sons Ltd., Hartford End Brewery, Chelmsford, Essex, CM3 1JZ. Tel. (0371) 820316

In 1992 Ridleys celebrated 150 years of brewing, in the same buildings on the River Chelmer where Thomas Dixon Ridley began production in 1842. Sadly, the brewery closed three of its pubs in the same year (the first closures for 20 years), although these are now being replaced by acquisitions from the national breweries. The remaining 64 tied houses all sell real ale which is also supplied to over 300 free trade outlets, at the lowest prices in the South-East.

Mild (OG 1034, ABV 3.4%) Dark brown with mixed aromas of roast and caramels. A bitter taste, studded with strong roast flavour; bitter aftertastes. More a bitter with caramel and roast accents than a mild. Found only in a handful of tied pubs.

IPA Bitter 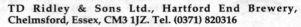 (OG 1034, ABV 3.5%) A hoppy and well-balanced bitter with hints of malt. The dry, bitter aftertaste lingers, with hops and a slight fruit flavour.

Christmas Ale* (OG 1050, ABV 5.1%) The seasonal offering.

RINGWOOD

Ringwood Brewery Ltd., 138 Christchurch Road, Ringwood, Hants BH24 3AP. Tel. (0425) 471177

Hampshire's first new brewery in the real ale revival, founded in 1978 in an old bakery and now housed in attractive 18th-century buildings, formerly part of the old Tunks' brewery. Famous for its award-winning Old Thumper, it has two tied houses and over 200 free trade accounts, from Weymouth to Chichester and the Channel Isles, which the brewery puts down to the efforts of Jersey CAMRA members.

Best Bitter (OG 1038, ABV 4%) A golden brown, moreish beer, with flavours for all. The aroma has a hint of hops and leads to a malty sweetness, which becomes dry, with a hint of orange. Malt and bitterness in the finish.

XXXX Porter (OG 1048, ABV 4.8%) Sadly only available October-March: a rich, dark brew with a strong aroma of roasted malt, hops and fruit. Rich in flavour, with coffee, vanilla, damsons, apples and molasses present. The overall roast maltiness continues into the drying, hoppy, bitter finish.

The Independents

Fortyniner
(OG 1048, ABV 5%) A good premium beer, with malt and hops in good balance. The flavours slowly increase to a fruity finish.

Old Thumper
(OG 1058, ABV 6%) A golden beer with a surprisingly bitter aftertaste, which follows a middle period tasting of a range of fruits. May be a little sweet for some.

RISING SUN

The Rising Sun Inn, Knowle Bank Road, Shraley Brook, Audley, Stoke-on-Trent, Staffs, ST7 8DS. Tel. (0782) 720600

Pub which began brewing in June 1990 and has expanded into the free trade (about a dozen outlets). Plans to brew bottle-conditioned beers, including a fruit beer.

Mild*
(OG 1034, ABV 3.3%)

Sunlight*
(OG 1036, ABV 3.5%) Summer only.

Rising*
(OG 1040, ABV 3.8%)

Setting*
(OG 1045, ABV 4.4%)

Sun Stroke*
(OG 1056, ABV 5.6%)

Total Eclipse*
(OG 1072, ABV 6.8%)

Solar Flare*
(OG 1100, ABV 10%) Winter only.

ROBINSON'S

Frederic Robinson Ltd., Unicorn Brewery, Stockport, Gtr Manchester, SK1 1JJ. Tel. (061) 480 6571

Major family brewery, founded in 1838. Took over Hartleys of Ulverston in 1982, but closed that brewery in October 1991 and is now planning to demolish some of the buildings (including a listed chimney). Only Hartleys XB is still brewed (at Stockport). Most of its 392 tied houses (70 from the Hartleys Cumbrian estate, but most in southern Manchester and Cheshire) sell real ale, though, whereas Best Bitter is widely available, Bitter can be found in only about 20 outlets.

Best Mild
(OG 1032, ABV 3.3%) A pale brown, well-balanced beer, with a sweet aftertaste. A good, refreshing drink.

Dark Best Mild
(OG 1032, ABV 3.3%) Toffee/malt-tasting, with a slight bitterness. Very quaffable, enjoying a fruity/malt aroma and a dry finish. Not commonly available.

Bitter
(OG 1035, ABV 3.5%) Fresh-tasting, with an aniseed tinge. Characteristic aroma and a smooth but brief finish.

Hartleys XB*
(OG 1040, ABV 4%)

Best Bitter
(OG 1041, ABV 4.2%) A golden beer with a good, hoppy nose. A very well-balanced taste precedes a slight, bitter finish.

Old Tom ⊕
(OG 1080, ABV 8.5%) A full-bodied, dark, fruity beer, similar in texture to a barley wine. The aroma is fruity and mouthwatering; the aftertaste is bittersweet. A beer to be sipped respectfully by a roaring winter fire.

The Independents

ROBINWOOD

Robinwood Brewers & Vintners, Robinwood Brewery, Burnley Road, Todmorden, W. Yorks, OL14 8EX. Tel. (0706) 818160

Commenced brewing in 1988 and currently supplies around 200 outlets. Cash-flow problems have been averted by the injection of funds from two new partners. Plans are in hand to increase capacity further and add to the range of bottled beers. *Bottle-conditioned beer: Old Fart (OG 1060, ABV 6%)*

Best Bitter

(OG 1036, ABV 4.1%) Beer with a faint, malty, fruity, sometimes yeasty aroma. The flavour is well-balanced, with a good, malty character which carries through to the finish (moderately bitter).

IPA*

(OG 1040, ABV 4.2%)

Porter*

(OG 1042, ABV 4.2%) An occasional brew.

XB

(OG 1046, ABV 4.7%) Both malt and hops come through in the aroma. The basic malty flavour is overtaken by bitterness and some chocolate. Good body; a malty/bitter finish, with burnt malt detectable at times.

Old Fart

(OG 1060, ABV 6%) Dark brown in colour, with a fruity and slightly malty aroma. There is roasted malt in the vinous, sweet and fruity taste, with some caramel and hoppy bitterness coming through. The finish is malty and dry. Also available as Old XXXX Ale on request.

ROSS

Ross Brewing Company, 36 Gloucester Road, Bishopston, Bristol, Avon, BS7 8AR. Tel. (0272) 427923

Very small Bristol brewery, set up in 1989, the first to brew beer with organic Soil Association barley. The beers are still only available in bottle-conditioned form, but enough interest has been shown in a cask product that suitable premises are being sought to enable the brewery to expand and produce a draught ale. Future plans also include the acquisition of a tied house. The beers are available in ten local free trade outlets and are wholesaled nationally. All are characterised by a certain yeastiness, which is not unpleasant.

Bottle-conditioned beers: Hartcliffe Bitter (OG 1045, ABV 4.5%) An amber/tawny-coloured, solidly malty, bitter beer. Good body, some hoppiness and a slightly sweet flavour. Bitter, malty aftertaste; *Clifton Dark Ale (OG 1045, ABV 4.5%)* A reddish-brown, full-bodied beer. There is a strong roast malt and bitter taste, and a lingering finish with some fruitiness. The aroma is malty. Very moreish; *Saxon Strong Ale (OG 1055, ABV 5.5%)* Unusual and distinctive, brewed to an authentic Saxon recipe which includes honey, apple juice and borrage. Golden brown in colour, with a light, fruity aroma. The taste is sweet but well-rounded and full-bodied, with a hint of honey and herbs. The finish is similar, with a trace of apples.

ROYAL CLARENCE

See Brew Pubs.

456

The Independents

RUDDLES

Ruddles Brewery Ltd., Langham, Oakham, Leicestershire, LE15 7JD. Tel. (0572) 756911

Possibly the best-known brewer of real ale in Britain, founded in 1858, but which lost its independence when it was taken over by Grand Metropolitan in 1986. Ruddles beers subsequently became national brands. Acquired by Dutch lager giants Grolsch in 1992.

Best Bitter

(OG 1037, ABV 3.8%) Thin, with a faint, fruity, malty nose leading into an astringent bitter palate, with little discernible malt or hop presence.

County

(OG 1050, ABV 5%) Copper-coloured, with a fruity, malty aroma and taste; sweetish on the tongue, but with a dry, malty aftertaste. Pleasant, but nothing like the County of old. Lacks hoppiness for a beer of this gravity.

RUDGATE

Rudgate Ales, Unit 2, Centre Park, Marston Business Park, Rudgate, Tockwith, N. Yorks, YO5 8QF. Tel. (0423) 358382

Brewery set up in the armoury building of an old airfield in April 1992.

Viking Bitter*

(OG 1039)

Battleaxe*

(OG 1044)

RYBURN

Ryburn
Brewery

Ryburn Brewery, Mill House, Mill House Lane, Sowerby Bridge, W. Yorks. Tel. (0422) 835413

Founded with a tiny, two-barrel plant in a former dye works, in 1990, but the beers were only available sporadically until 1991 when it began supplying house beers to the Stanley Arms in Stockport on a regular basis. Now also supplies the William IV at Sowerby Bridge and a few other outlets with guest beers. Produces special occasional brews.

Mild*

(OG 1034)

Best Bitter*

(OG 1038)

Stout*

(OG 1040)

Porter*

(OG 1042) A Christmas brew.

Bitter*

(OG 1044)

Stabbers*

(OG 1050)

ST AUSTELL

St Austell Brewery Co. Ltd., 63 Trevarthian Road, St Austell, Cornwall, PL25 4BY. Tel. (0726) 74444

Brewing company set up in 1851 by maltster and wine merchant Walter Hicks. It moved to the present site in 1893 and remains a popular family business, with many of Hicks's descendants employed in all areas of the company. Its 140 tied houses are spread right across Cornwall, nearly all of them serving traditional ale, and some 200 free trade outlets are also supplied. A new visitors' centre has been added.

Bosun's Bitter

(OG 1036, ABV 3.4%) A refreshing session beer, sweetish in aroma and bittersweet in flavour. Lingering, hoppy finish.

XXXX Mild

(OG 1039, ABV 3.6%) Little aroma, but a strong, malty, caramel-sweetish flavour is followed by a good, lingering aftertaste, which is sweet but with a fruity dryness. Very drinkable.

457

The Independents

Tinners Ale (OG 1039, ABV 3.7%) A deservedly-popular, golden beer with an appetising malt aroma and a good balance of malt and hops in the flavour. Lasting finish.

Hicks Special Draught (HSD) (OG 1051, ABV 5%) An aromatic, fruity, hoppy bitter which is initially sweet, has an aftertaste of pronounced bitterness, but whose flavour is fully-rounded.

Winter Warmer* (OG 1060, ABV 6%) Available November-February.

SCOTTIES **Scotties Brewery, Crown Hotel, 151 High Street, Lowestoft, Suffolk, NR32 1HR. Tel. (0502) 569592**

Brewery founded in June 1989 and now supplying beer to about half a dozen free trade outlets. Produced a porter for a short while last year but has no plans to continue with this brew.

Golden Best Bitter (OG 1038.5) As its name suggests, a golden beer which has a distinctly malty taste with some hoppiness, although bitterness is lacking. Neither aroma or aftertaste is strong, but both are well balanced.

Blues and Bloater (OG 1039.5) Not much of anything, really. Its main characteristic is a rather harsh bitterness in the taste and aftertaste, with some astringency.

Dark Oast (OG 1047) A winter beer, red/brown in colour, with less body than its gravity would suggest. The taste has roast malt as its main characteristic, with hoppiness prominent in the aftertaste.

William French (OG 1047) A full and beautifully-balanced beer. A faint, malty aroma leads into a palate with strong malt and hop flavours, and considerable fruitiness. A full and balanced aftertaste, too.

SCOTTISH & NEWCASTLE See page 483.

SELBY **Selby (Middlesbrough) Brewery Ltd., 131 Millgate, Selby, N. Yorks, YO8 0LL. Tel. (0757) 702826**

Old family brewery which resumed brewing in 1972 after a gap of 18 years and is now mostly involved in wholesaling. Real ale is available primarily through its Brewery Tap off-licence in Selby, and not at the company's single house. The ordinary bitter has been discontinued, but the Strong Ale has been reintroduced.

Strong Ale* (OG 1045, ABV 4.5%)

Old Tom* (OG 1069, ABV 6.5%) A distinctive, strong ale.

SHEPHERD NEAME **Shepherd Neame Ltd., 17 Court Street, Faversham, Kent, ME13 7AX. Tel. (0795) 532206**

A fine old brewery retaining many original features, with a visitors' reception centre in a restored medieval hall. Believed to be the oldest continuous brewer in the land (since 1698). The tied estate consists of 314 pubs, the majority selling real ale, which is brewed with only East Kent hops. Free trade runs to about 1,000 outlets, principally in Kent, Essex and London, although this figure includes a sizeable proportion of keg-only business. It is still company policy to

458

The Independents

encourage tenants to keep beers under low blanket pressure. Stock Ale has not been brewed this year, but there are plans for a winter warmer. Offers guest beers to its tenants via a Beer Club.

Master Brew Bitter (OG 1036, ABV 3.8%) A very distinctive bitter, mid brown in colour, with a very hoppy aroma. Well-balanced, with a nicely aggressive bitter taste from its hops, leaving a hoppy/bitter finish, tinged with sweetness.

Best Bitter (OG 1039, ABV 4%) Mid brown, with less marked characteristics than Bitter. However, the nose is very well balanced and the taste enjoys a malty, bitter smokiness. A malty, well-rounded finish.

Spitfire Ale* (OG 1044, ABV 5%) A commemorative brew (Battle of Britain) for the RAF Benevolent Fund's appeal, now a permanent feature.

Bishops Finger* (OG 1053, ABV 5.4%). A well-known bottled beer, introduced in cask-conditioned form in 1989.

SHIPSTONE'S See Allied Breweries, page 476.

SMILES **Smiles Brewing Co. Ltd., Colston Yard, Colston Street, Bristol, Avon, BS1 5BD. Tel. (0272) 297350**

Established in 1977 to supply a local restaurant, and started full-scale brewing early in 1978. Noted for its quality ales and good pub design (winner of CAMRA's 1990 *Best Pub Refurbishment* and 1991 *Best New Pub* awards). Changed hands in 1991 and the new owners are looking for a controlled expansion of the brewery estate. There are no plans to continue brewing Old Vic, the winter beer. Supplies four managed houses and an increasing number of free trade outlets, and the beers are becoming more widely available through wholesalers.

Brewery Bitter (OG 1037, ABV 3.7%) A golden/amber, light beer with plenty of flavour for its gravity. A good mix of malt, bitterness, hops and fruitiness is followed by a pleasant, dry, malty aftertaste. Has a malty, hoppy aroma.

Best Bitter (OG 1041, ABV 4.1%) A copper-brown beer with malt, fruit and some hops in both nose and taste. A well-rounded bitter with a dry, hoppy finish.

Exhibition (OG 1051, ABV 5.2%) A deep red/brown-coloured beer, comprising a complex collection of rich flavours. There is a strong roast malt and fruit presence, with moderate hops and sweetness. Vinous, turning dry and bittersweet towards the finish.

JOHN SMITH'S See Courage, page 481.

SAMUEL SMITH **Samuel Smith Old Brewery (Tadcaster), Tadcaster, N. Yorks, LS24 9SB. Tel. (0937) 832225**

Small company operating from the oldest brewery in Yorkshire, dating from 1758 and once owned by John Smith. Samuel Smith was John's brother and he inherited his business, along with another brother, William, when John died in 1879. William built the new John Smith's brewery in 1884 and the Old Brewery reverted to the late Samuel's heirs,

The Independents

who then proceeded with their own business. Although John Smith's is now Courage-owned, 'Sam's' remains firmly independent. Beers are brewed from well water without the use of any adjuncts and all cask beer is fermented in Yorkshire stone squares and racked into wooden casks provided by the brewery's own cooperage. Real ale is served in the majority of its 200+ tied houses, which include 27 in London, representing good value for the capital. About 200 free trade outlets.

Old Brewery Bitter (OBB) (OG 1037, ABV 3.8%) Malt dominates the nose, the taste and aftertaste, although this is underscored at all stages by a gentle hoppiness. A 'big' beer with loads of flavour, complemented by an attractive amber colour.

Museum Ale (OG 1048, ABV 5.2%) Deep amber in colour, which gives some idea of the fruitiness to be found in the nose, taste and finish. A sweet beer with winey flavours, despite no sugar being used in the brewing process.

SPRINGFIELD See Bass, page 478.

SPRINGHEAD **Springhead Brewery, 25 Main Street, Sutton on Trent, Newark, Notts, NG23 6PF. Tel. (0636) 821000**

Small brewery, in production since May 1991, which installed new plant early in 1992 to expand its capacity to five barrels. A porter and a winter ale may be added.

Bitter* (OG 1040, ABV 4%)

STOCKS **Stocks Brewery, The Hallcross, 33-34 Hallgate, Doncaster, S. Yorks, DN1 3NL. Tel. (0302) 328213**

Brewery founded in December 1981 as a brew pub and now running two other tied houses. Expanding free trade via wholesalers throughout the North; Old Horizontal is particularly popular, especially in the Tap & Spile real ale pub chain. However, overall beer quality has been rather variable recently.

Best Bitter (OG 1038, ABV 3.6%) A clean but thin session beer, this mid brown/tawny ale has a light malt aroma, a malty bitter taste and a moderately dry, bitter finish.

Doncaster Brown Ale* (OG 1044, ABV 4.3%)

Select (OG 1044, ABV 4.3%) A light aroma and thin body for its gravity; malt in the mouth, but a short bitter feel and finish. Variability of colour and condition this year; Best Bitter is the better bet at the moment.

Old Horizontal (OG 1054, ABV 5%) A dark brown beer with red tints, this is the best Stocks brew by far. Can have fruit, roast and chocolate, but malt dominates the taste. Hoppy aroma with roast present; dry and nutty finish. Can be smooth and rich, but varies and is often thin for its gravity.

STONES See Bass, page 480.

STRONG See Whitbread, page 485.

The Independents

SUMMERSKILLS

SEMPER FIDELIS   AD BACCUM

Summerskills Brewery, Unit 15, Pomphlett Farm Ind. Estate, Broxton Drive, Billacombe, Plymouth, Devon, PL9 7BG. Tel. (0752) 481283

Summerskills was initially set up in 1983 in a vineyard, but was only operational for two years. It was relaunched by new owners in 1990, with plant from the old Penrhos brewery, and production has grown at a steady rate. Supplies 20 free trade outlets directly in Plymouth and others nationally via wholesalers. The brewery logo comes from the ship's crest of HMS Bigbury Bay.

Best Bitter

(OG 1042, ABV 4.3%) Mid brown, strong-flavoured beer with a hoppy bitter finish.

Whistle Belly Vengeance

(OG 1046, ABV 4.7%) Mid brown, multi-flavoured beer - predominantly roast malt and hops, with a hoppy bitter finish. Tastes stronger than it is.

TAYLOR

TIMOTHY TAYLOR TRADITIONAL REAL ALES CHAMPIONSHIP BEERS

Timothy Taylor & Co. Ltd., Knowle Spring Brewery, Keighley, W. Yorks, BD21 1AW. Tel. (0535) 603139

The fame of Timothy Taylor's prize-winning ales stretches far beyond West Yorkshire and the brewery's 29 pubs. Founded in 1858, it now offers a wide range of real ales, with Landlord the pride of the pack. A new brewhouse came on stream in spring 1991 and was immediately brewing to capacity. Supplies over 200 free trade outlets.

Dark Mild

(OG 1033, ABV 3.5%) Golden Best with caramel, which can dominate both the aroma and taste. Less sweet, but more burnt than of late, adding a certain dry bitterness to the finish.

Golden Best ⊟

(OG 1033, ABV 3.5%) Amber/gold in colour with a light malt and hop nose. The soft and smooth, malty taste has an overlay of hop this year, before a short malt and hop finish with a hint of bitterness. Darker and sweeter than it was.

Best Bitter

(OG 1037, ABV 4%) An amber/pale brown beer with a fresh, flowery nose. The complex hop and grain taste contains fruit and builds up to a dry, hoppy, bitter finale. Very drinkable.

Landlord ⊟

(OG 1042, ABV 4.3%) A distinctive, multi-layered complex of floral fragrances and fruit, hop and grain tastes. A strong hop finish rounds off a beer which is more bitter now than before. Dry and clean, it leaves you wanting more. Needs maturing.

Porter

(OG 1043, ABV 3.7%) Roast malt and caramel envelope nose and mouth, but sweetness dominates the aftertaste. Now only produced in the winter months.

Ram Tam (XXXX)

(OG 1043, ABV 4.3%) Another winter beer. Lots of caramel, but the underlying Landlord comes through. A dry, hoppy bitterness in the taste and finish. Better than previous years. More like a porter than Taylor's Porter?

TAYLOR WALKER

See Allied Breweries, page 475.

TENNENT CALEDONIAN

See Bass, page 479.

JOSHUA TETLEY See Allied Breweries, page 476.

The Independents

TETLEY WALKER	See Allied Breweries, page 477.

THEAKSTON	See Scottish & Newcastle, page 483.

THOMPSON'S   Thompson's Brewery, 11 West Street, Ashburton, Devon, TQ13 7BD. Tel. (0364) 52478

FINE TRADITIONAL ALES

Started brewing in 1981 for its own pub, the London Inn, which remains its sole tied house. Free trade, however, has been increasing rapidly of late, with 70 outlets throughout the South-West currently supplied, and further growth planned. A major expansion programme is in hand at the brewery, starting with a new brewhouse which opened in early 1992. This now allows a total capacity of 10,000 barrels a year. The beer range tends to change from year to year and 1992 saw the production of a special mild to celebrate CAMRA's 21st birthday.

CAMRA's 21st Birthday Mild*	(OG 1035, ABV 3.6%) A dark, hoppy mild.
Best Bitter	(OG 1040, ABV 4.2%) Amber-coloured beer, with a malty, hoppy and fruity aroma, a strong, hoppy, bitter taste and a dry, bitter finish.
Black Velvet Stout	(OG 1040, ABV 4.2%) A black porter with a strong roast chocolate malt aroma. The flavour and aftertaste have roast malt and bitterness.
IPA	(OG 1044, ABV 4.6%) Pale brown ale with malt and fruit in the aroma and a distinct hoppy, fruity flavour with a dry, bitter finish. A well-rounded beer.
Botwrights Man of War	(OG 1050, ABV 5%) Straw-coloured strong beer featuring a slightly fruity and bitter flavour and finish. Too bland for a winter ale.
Yuletide Tipple	(OG 1050, ABV 5.3%) A fruity, copper-red Christmas beer, enjoying a distinctive contrast of roast and hop flavours, and a bitter finish. Hops and fruit in the aroma.

THWAITES   Daniel Thwaites PLC, PO Box 50, Star Brewery, Blackburn, Lancs, BB1 5BU. Tel. (0254) 54431

Lancashire brewery, founded by excise officer Daniel Thwaites in 1807 and now run by his great-great-grandson who is fiercely proud of the company's tradition and heritage. Still uses shire horse drays and, unusually, produces two milds. Thwaites ales have been regular CAMRA award-winners and were joined by a new stablemate in March 1992, the premium ale, Craftsman. Production has ceased, however, of the winter ale, Daniel's Hammer. Most of the 400 tied houses serve real ale, and a substantial free trade is supplied. The expanding group of managed pubs are run by the subsidiary Thwaites Inns, and the brewery also operates hotels under the name of Shire Inns.

Mild	(OG 1031, ABV 3%) Dark brown/copper beer with a fine malty quality in both aroma and flavour. No perceptible finish.
Best Mild	(OG 1034, ABV 3.2%) A rich, dark mild presenting a smooth, malty flavour and a pleasant, slightly bitter finish.

The Independents

Bitter	(OG 1036, ABV 3.4%) A gently-flavoured, clean-tasting bitter. Malt and hops lead into a full, lingering, bitter finish.
Craftsman*	(OG 1042, ABV 4.2%)

TITANIC

Titanic Brewery, Unit G, Harvey Works, Lingard Street, Burslem, Stoke-on-Trent, Staffs, ST6 1ED. Tel. (0782) 823447

Titanic (est. 1985) has found larger premises since the last edition of this guide, and is now able to keep up with the growing demand for its beers. After a troublesome time in the late eighties, when it ceased trading for a while, the brewery, named in honour of the Titanic's Captain Smith who hailed from Stoke, looks set fair for the future. Some 150 free trade outlets are supplied, and the brewery now runs one pub of its own. *Bottle-conditioned beer: Christmas Ale (Wreckage matured for one year)*

Best Bitter*	(OG 1036, ABV 3.6%) A summer beer, satisfyingly bitter.
Lifeboat Ale	(OG 1040, ABV 4%) A fruity and malty, red/brown, bitter beer, with a slight caramel character. The finish is dry and fruity. Almost like a strong dark mild.
Premium Bitter	(OG 1042, ABV 4.3%) A red/brown beer with a fruity aroma, a malty, fruity taste and aftertaste, and a lingering bitterness.
Captain Smith's Strong Ale	(OG 1050, ABV 5%) Another red/brown beer, but this one is hoppy and bitter with a balancing, malty sweetness. A hoppy aroma; a dry, malty finish. Highly drinkable.
Wreckage*	(OG 1080, ABV 7.8%) A winter brew.

TOLLY COBBOLD

Tollemache & Cobbold Brewery Ltd., Cliff Road, Ipswich, Suffolk, IP3 0AZ. Tel. (0473) 231723

One of the oldest breweries in the country, founded by Thomas Cobbold in 1723 at Harwich. It survived several changes in ownership until, following the Brent Walker take-over in 1989, the Cliff Brewery was closed and production transferred to Camerons in Hartlepool. However, a management buy-out, led by former Tolly directors Brian Cowie and Bob Wales, saved the day and Tolly Cobbold Ipswich-brewed ales were back on sale in September 1990. The new company acquired no pubs from Brent Walker, but secured a five-year trading agreement, supplying a total of over 500 pubs. Opened a brewery tap in June 1992.

Mild	(OG 1032, ABV 3.2%) A malty, dark mild with roasty notes and a hoppy finish to balance the malt. The aroma is mostly of malt.
Bitter	(OG 1035, ABV 3.6%) A light-bodied session bitter with the old Tolly maltiness. Some hoppiness, mainly in the finish, but not a particularly bitter beer.
Original	(OG 1038, ABV 3.8%) A beer with a hoppy and bitter taste, with balancing maltiness. The finish is dry.
Old Strong	(OG 1047, ABV 4.6%) Available November-February. A dark winter ale with a good malt and roast aroma. These characteristics are also evident in the initial flavour, along with caramel. The finish is bittersweet, with a lasting dryness.

The Independents

TRAQUAIR HOUSE	**Traquair House, Innerleithen, Peeblesshire, Borders, EH44 6PW. Tel. (0896) 830371**

Eighteenth-century brewhouse situated in one of the wings of Traquair House, which is over 1,000 years-old and the oldest inhabited house in Scotland. The 20th Laird, Peter Maxwell Stuart, rediscovered the brewery in 1965 and began brewing again using all the original equipment. Today the bottled product, Traquair House Ale (not bottle-conditioned) is exported worldwide, although production is only around 5,000 gallons a year. (It is available on draught only at the White Horse in Parsons Green, London.) Twenty outlets are supplied with the cask-conditioned Bear Ale, but there are no tied houses. The brewery passed to Catherine Maxwell Stuart in 1990.

Bear Ale* (OG 1050, ABV 5%) A strong draught ale.

Traquair House Ale* (OG 1085, ABV 7%) Dark and potent.

TRING **The Tring Brewery Company Ltd., 36 Albert Street, Tring, Herts, HP23 6AU. Tel. (044 282) 3904**

New brewing company, established in summer 1992, which aims to produce bottled, as well as draught, beers.

Ridgeway Bitter* (ABV 3.9%)

TROUGH	**Trough Brewery Ltd., Louisa Street, Idle, Bradford, W. Yorks, BD10 8NE. Tel. (0274) 613450**

Brewery which started in 1981 and has recently enjoyed rapid expansion in the guest beer market, continuing to be popular with the Tap & Spile chain. Otherwise, nearly all Trough's 75 free trade outlets and three tied houses are within a 20-mile range of the brewery. New plant was commissioned in 1992, doubling production capacity. Festival Ale, brewed especially for CAMRA's 1992 Bradford Beer Festival (where it won the *Best Beer* award), is now being marketed in place of Hogshead, which has been dropped.

Bitter (OG 1035, ABV 3.5%) Amber in colour, like all Trough beers. An inviting hop aroma and a fine, strong hop flavour with malt balance, lead to a long, hop and bitter finish with fruit notes. A good, refreshing standard bitter.

Wild Boar (OG 1039, ABV 4%) Only a slight aroma but rich malt, hop and bitter flavours in the mouth, finished by a long, malty and bittersweet aftertaste.

Festival Ale ꒪ (OG 1048, ABV 5%) An excellent new beer with a good hop and fruit aroma. A deceptively strong bitter with a lightness on the palate, yet still packed with flavours of malt, hops and fruit. Long bittersweet and hoppy finish.

TRUMAN See Courage, page 481.

ULEY	**Uley Brewery Ltd., The Old Brewery, Uley, Dursley, Glos, GL11 5TB. Tel. (0453) 860120**

Brewing at Uley began in 1833, but Price's Brewery, as it was then, remained inactive for most of this century. Work

The Independents

commenced on restoring the premises in 1984 and Uley Brewery was reborn in 1985. Demand is still growing for its popular beers and work is in hand to increase brewing capacity by 50%. Has no pubs of its own but serves 30 free trade outlets in the Cotswolds area. Pig's Ear is only brewed to order.

Bitter or Hogshead or UB40 (OG 1040, ABV 4%) Copper-coloured beer with malt, hops and fruit in the aroma and a malty, fruity taste, underscored by a hoppy bitterness. The finish is dry, with a balance of hops and malt.

Old Spot Prize Ale (OG 1050, ABV 5%) A fairly full-bodied, red/brown ale with a fruity aroma, a malty, fruity taste (with a hoppy bitterness), and a strong, balanced aftertaste.

Pig's Ear Strong Beer (OG 1050, ABV 5%) A pale-coloured, light beer, deceptively strong. Notably bitter in flavour, with a hoppy, fruity aroma and a bitter finish.

Pigor Mortis (OG 1058, ABV 5.5%) A winter brew, another beer which belies its strength. No distinct aroma, but a sweet, smooth flavour, with hints of fruit and hops. Dry finish.

USHERS **Ushers Brewery Ltd., Parade House, Trowbridge, Wilts, BA14 8JF. Tel. (0225) 763171**

Along with Ruddles, another recent escapee from the Grand Metropolitan/Courage net. This West Country brewery was founded in 1824, but lost its identity after being swallowed up by Watney in 1960. A successful management buy-out in 1992 has given Ushers back its independence and the once-famous Founders Ale is now brewed again in Wiltshire. The old Pale Ale may also be reintroduced. Supplies real ale to virtually all its 437 tied houses and to Courage/Grand Met Inntrepreneur pubs.

Best Bitter (OG 1037, ABV 3.8%) Cleaner-tasting than its lacklustre Grand Met predecessor, with gentle malt and hops but a harsh bitter dryness. Drinks light for a best bitter but, at the time of sampling, the brewery was still working on the beer.

Founders Ale* (OG 1044, ABV 4.5%)

VAUX **Vaux Breweries Ltd., The Brewery, Sunderland, Tyne & Wear, SR1 3AN. Tel. (091) 567 6277**

First established in 1806 and now one of the country's largest regional brewers, Vaux remains firmly independent. Owns Wards of Sheffield, but sold off Lorimer & Clark in Edinburgh to Caledonian in 1987. Real ale is sold in 257 out of 566 tied houses (which include those run by Vaux Inns Ltd.) and is also provided to 10% of its 700 free trade customers. Sold its four London pubs in 1990 but, otherwise, is looking to increase its tied estate, buying pubs in Yorkshire, the North-West and elsewhere from national brewers. A new strong beer, Vaux Extra Special (OG 1047, ABV 5%) is produced at Wards (see Wards).

Lorimers Best Scotch (OG 1036, ABV 3.6%) Dark, thin and with little aroma, but the roast malt flavour can shine through when the cellar temperature and the pub turnover are right. Unfortunately, it is often served too cold. Intended to be a replica of the original Scottish Scotch; today more of a mild?

The Independents

Bitter* (OG 1036, ABV 3.9%)

Samson (OG 1041, ABV 4.1%) A complex, bittersweet beer with a predominant maltiness. Low in hoppiness and aroma.

Double Maxim (OG 1044, ABV 4.2%) A smooth brown ale, now becoming more common in draught form (keg as well as cask). Malty throughout, with some roast in the flavour. The aftertaste can be pleasantly bitter.

WADWORTH **Wadworth & Co. Ltd., Northgate Brewery, Devizes, Wilts, SN10 1JW. Tel. (0380) 723361**

Delightful market town tower brewery set up in 1885 by Henry Wadworth. Solidly traditional, the brewery still runs horse-drawn drays. The brewery has recently undergone some expansion with the installation of new fermenting vessels to cope with increased demand from the free trade - some 500 outlets are now supplied directly by the brewery, and over 3,000 more via other brewers and wholesalers. Always keen to expand the tied estate (currently 182 houses, all of which offer real ale). 6X remains one of the South's most famous ales, whilst Henry Wadworth IPA is now called Henry's Original IPA.

Henry's Original IPA (OG 1034, ABV 3.8%) A golden brown-coloured beer with a gentle, malty and slightly hoppy aroma, a good balance of flavours, with maltiness gradually dominating, and then a long-lasting aftertaste to match, eventually becoming biscuity. A good session beer, more pleasing than the popular 6X.

6X (OG 1040, ABV 4.3%) Mid brown in colour, with a malty and fruity nose and some balancing hop character. The flavour is similar, with some bitterness and a lingering malty but bitter finish. Full-bodied and distinctive.

Farmer's Glory (OG 1046, ABV 4.5%) Can be delightfully hoppy and fruity, but is variable in flavour and conditioning. The aroma is of malt and it should have a dryish, hoppy aftertaste.

Old Timer (OG 1055, ABV 5.8%) Available in winter only. A rich, copper-brown beer with a strong, fruity, malty aroma. The flavour is full-bodied and complete, with hints of butterscotch and peaches, beautifully balanced by a lasting, malty, dry finish. A classic beer.

PETER WALKER See Allied Breweries, page 477.

WARDS **SH Ward & Co. Ltd., Sheaf Brewery, Ecclesall Road, Sheffield, S. Yorks, S11 8HZ. Tel. (0742) 755155**

Established in 1840, but a subsidiary of Vaux of Sunderland since 1972. Since the closure of the neighbouring Thorne brewery in 1986, Wards has also produced Darley's beers. Real ale is available in half of the 230 tied houses (this figure includes pubs run by Vaux Inns), and the tied estate continues to expand. Supplies some 550 free trade outlets and brews the new Extra Special for Vaux.

Mild (OG 1032, ABV 3.2%) A malty aroma leads to a malty roast taste. A beer which has lost its depth, but keeps an attractive dark brown colour with red undertones. What aftertaste there is can be dry. Sadly one-dimensional lately.

The Independents

Thorne Best Bitter (OG 1037, ABV 3.9%) A beer whose gentle malt aroma is under threat from an increased hoppiness. Is it now dry hopped? A plain mid brown session beer.

Sheffield Best Bitter (OG 1038, ABV 4%) Beer with a notably malty or earthy smell and taste, with hints of fruit and hop; the residual bitterness is heavily edged with sweetness. Can be thin and erratic, and often served too young. In its day, a fine beer.

Kirby Strong Beer (OG 1045, ABV 5%) There are mixed reactions to this red/pale brown beer which is still variable: a malty nose, a malt and bitter taste, and lingering fruit and sweetness. Robust for the gravity, but can be cloying at the finish.

For Vaux:

Extra Special (OG 1047, ABV 5%) A new 'flagship' beer, launched at the 1991 Durham CAMRA Beer Festival. Still relatively rare. A smooth, clean-tasting, malty premium ale with a pleasant hoppy/sweet aftertaste.

WATNEY See Courage, page 481.

WEBSTER'S See Courage, page 481.

WELLS **Charles Wells Ltd., The Eagle Brewery, Havelock Street, Bedford, Beds, MK40 4LU. Tel. (0234) 272766**

Successful, family-owned brewery, established in 1876 and on this site since 1974. Has a tied estate stretching from Lincolnshire to London. While the bulk of the pubs are still centred around Bedford, the purchase in 1991 of 38 pubs from Bass has strengthened its presence in North London and opened up a market in the Coventry area. A new brewhouse and maturation/fermentation block have recently been commissioned. Nearly all 357 pubs serve real ale, but about 50% apply cask breathers.

Eagle IPA (OG 1035, ABV 3.6%) Amber/tawny beer with a distinctive hoppy, slightly citrus nose. A clean hoppy bitterness dominates the flavour and follows through to a dry finish.

Bombardier Best Bitter (OG 1042, ABV 4.2%) Although not as rare as it was, this beer seems to have lost some of its character. A mainly fruity nose precedes a subtle blend of hops and fruit in a mainly bitter flavour. The finish is short, faintly dry and astringent.

WELSH BREWERS See Bass, page 480.

WEM See Greenalls, Pub Groups.

WEST COAST **West Coast Brewing Co. Ltd., 4a Helmshore Walk, Chorlton-on-Medlock, Manchester, M13 9TH. Tel. (061) 273 1053**

Enterprising brewery set up in 1989 by consultant brewer Brendan Dobbin to serve his own pub, the Kings Arms. Outside demand grew (currently supplying 20 free trade outlets) and led to the expansion of the brewery. Dobbin's beers are now also brewed under licence in Bulgaria, Norway and Nigeria! The already extensive beer range is often added to by one-off, humorously-titled brews.

The Independents

Dobbin's North Country (DNC) Dark Mild

(OG 1032, ABV 3%) Very full-flavoured for its gravity; dark and rather fruity.

DNC Best Bitter

(OG 1038, ABV 4%) A pale beer with malt, hops and fruit in the aroma. Fresh, clean taste - hoppy and bitter, with some malt and a dry finish.

DNC Guiltless Stout

(OG 1039, ABV 4%) Very dark in colour, with roast malt predominant in the smell and taste. A long, dry aftertaste.

DNC Big Heavy Jimmie*

(OG 1045, ABV 4.5%) The most recent addition: a pale beer with a greater malt emphasis than is usual for the brewery. A recreation of an old-style Scottish heavy.

DNC Yakima Grande Porter*

(OG 1050, ABV 5.5%) Rich, mellow and dark, brewed with the same American hops as the Pale Ale below.

DNC Ginger Beer*

(OG 1050, ABV 6%) Originally brewed as a strong summer 'refresher', its popularity has led to year-round production.

DNC Yakima Grande Pale Ale

(OG 1050, ABV 6%) A pale beer with a strong, hoppy nose. Hops are also very evident in the flavour. A well-attenuated beer, making it strong and very dry.

DNC Extra Special Bitter

(OG 1060, ABV 7%) A powerful, mid brown beer with a strong, complex aroma, malt and hops on the tongue (with sweetish, fruity undertones), and a full, predominantly bitter, hoppy finish.

DNC Old Soporific

(OG 1084, ABV 10%) Dobbin's new winter offering.

WEST HIGHLAND

West Highland Brewers, Old Station Brewery, Taynuilt, Argyll, Strathclyde, PA35 1JE. Tel. (086 62) 246

Brewery constructed in November 1989 in listed buildings, part of the last remaining station of the Callander and Oban Railway. Owned and run by Dick and Karen Saunders, former Banks & Taylor licensees, the brewery also grows its own hops. The draught Highland Light has been replaced by the stronger, aptly named Station Porter. Has one tied house, the brewery tap, and supplies roughly 12 free trade outlets. The brewery is open to the public and also acts as an informal tourist office. *Bottle-conditioned beer: Severe Beer (OG 1050) Highland Severe bottled*

Highland Heavy*

(OG 1038)

Old Highland Porter*

(OG 1041) Brewed for St Andrew's Day and claimed to be the only 100% Scottish beer produced.

Station Porter*

(OG 1041)

Highland Severe*

(OG 1050)

WETHERED

See Whitbread, page 485.

WHITBREAD

See page 485.

WHITBY'S

Whitby's Own Brewery Ltd., St Hilda's, The Ropery, Whitby, N. Yorks, YO22 4ET. Tel. (0947) 605914

Brewery opened in a former workhouse in 1988 and almost immediately winning an award at the CAMRA Leeds Beer Festival. The beers have continued to win accolades but both

The Independents

Little Waster and Demon have been deleted from the list in the last year. In spring 1992, Whitby's moved 50 yards into newer, larger premises but it is still trying to acquire its first tied house. Free trade (mostly as guest beers) extends from Newcastle upon Tyne to Huddersfield and takes in roughly 50 outlets.

Merryman's Mild* (OG 1036, ABV 3.6%)

Ammonite Bitter (OG 1038, ABV 3.8%) A light, refreshing beer, pleasant and fruity, with a hoppy aftertaste. Difficult to track down, but well worth the effort.

Woblle (OG 1045, ABV 4.5%) A copper-red, full-bodied, malty bitter, with a burnt roast flavour and a dry, hoppy finish.

Force Nine (OG 1055, ABV 5.5%) Strong and dark, with a well-balanced blend of contrasting flavours: sweet and fruity, dry and malty, with a strong, bitter finish. A beer of the winter ale type, excellent in its class.

WICKWAR **The Wickwar Brewing Company, The Old Cider Mill, Station Road, Wickwar, Avon, GL12 8NB. Tel. (0454) 294168**

Launched on the 'Glorious First of May 1990' (guest beer law day) by two Courage tenants, Brian Rides and Ray Penny, with the aim of providing guest ales for their three tenancies. Now producing 30 barrels a week, and still growing, they supply some 35 other outlets, operating from an old cider mill, originally the site of Arnold, Perrett & Co. Ltd. brewery.

Coopers WPA (OG 1036, ABV 3.8%) A yellow/gold, well-balanced, light brew with malt, hops and citrus fruit. Nice dry finish.

Brand Oak Bitter (OG 1039, ABV 4.1%) A tasty balance of hops, malt and fruits comes through in the aroma and in the initially subtle finish, which later asserts a lasting, malty, bitter hoppiness. Full of character; very moreish. Known locally as 'BOB'.

Olde Merryford Ale (OG 1049, ABV 5.1%) A copper-brown, well-balanced beer. Full-flavoured, with a fruity, bitter, dry finish and a hoppy, fruity aroma.

WILSONS See Courage, page 482.

WILTSHIRE **Wiltshire Brewery Co. PLC, Stonehenge Brewery, Church Street, Tisbury, Wilts, SP3 6NH. Tel. (0747) 870666**

No longer brews: the beers are supplied by the Chainmaker Beer Company (see Pitfield, page 451).

WOLVER-HAMPTON & DUDLEY See Banks's, page 401, and Camerons, page 411.

WOOD **The Wood Brewery Ltd., Wistanstow, Craven Arms, Shropshire, SY7 8DG. Tel. (0588) 672523**

Village brewery, founded by the Wood family in 1980, which has enjoyed steady growth in recent years, culminating in a major extension of the brewery during the winter of 1991/92. This additional capacity also allows for the production of Sam Powell beers which were rescued from receivership during the summer of 1991 (Powell's ex-head

The Independents

brewer went to Wood with the beers). Still just one tied house, the Plough next to the brewery, but serving a growing free trade (currently around 75 outlets). Specialises in producing commemorative bottled beers.

Sam Powell Best Bitter* (OG 1034, ABV 3%)

Sam Powell Original Bitter* (OG 1038, ABV 3.5%)

Parish Bitter* (OG 1040, ABV 3.75%) A light, refreshing bitter.

Severn Valley Railway Jubilee* (OG 1041, ABV 3.85%) Occasional brew, only available at SVR pubs.

Special Bitter* (OG 1043, ABV 4%) A full-flavoured, sweetish beer.

Sam Powell Old Sam* (OG 1048, ABV 4.3%)

Wonderful* (OG 1050, ABV 4.75%) Strong and dark.

Christmas Cracker* (OG 1060, ABV 6%) A dark winter warmer (November-January).

WOODFORDE'S Woodforde's Norfolk Ales, Broadland Brewery, Woodbastwick, Norwich, Norfolk, NR13 6SW. Tel. (0603) 720353

Founded in late 1980 in Norwich to bring much-needed choice to a long Watney-dominated region. Moved to a converted farm complex in the picturesque Broadland village of Woodbastwick in 1989. Brews an extensive range of beers which changes from year to year, including several seasonal and occasional brews. Now runs three tied houses, all offering real ale, and supplies 170 free trade outlets in Norfolk, Suffolk and Lincolnshire. *Bottle-conditioned beer: Norfolk Nip (OG 1080, ABV 8.6%) sometimes also on draught*

Mardler's Mild* (OG 1036, ABV 3.5%)

Norfolk IPA* (OG 1036, ABV 3.7%)

Wherry Best Bitter (OG 1039, ABV 4%) This award-winning, amber beer has a distinctly hoppy nose and a well-balanced palate with pronounced bitterness and, usually, a flowery hop character. A long-lasting, satisfying, bitter aftertaste.

Norfolk Porter (OG 1041, ABV 4.3%) Now only brewed occasionally, and light-tasting for its strength and colour, this red/brown beer has a fruity aroma, fleshed out with roast malt and hops. The taste is well balanced, with roast malt and hops; the aftertaste is mainly bitter.

Old Bram* (OG 1044, ABV 4.5%) A roasty, medium dark, winter beer.

Nelson's Revenge* (OG 1045, ABV 4.6%) A new premium bitter.

Norfolk Nog ◲ (OG 1049, ABV 5.1%) A full-bodied red/brown beer with plenty of flavour and aroma. Roast malt balances the sweeter components of the palate. A very good, dark winter brew.

Baldric (OG 1052, ABV 5.5%) The hops and fruit in the aroma are carried through to the palate where they mix with malt and hop bitterness. A dryish aftertaste rounds off this very drinkable, tasty beer. Not as sweet as many beers of this strength.

470

The Independents

Headcracker   (OG 1069, ABV 7.5%) A well-balanced, pale brown beer with a fruity and bitter aftertaste. There is a strong presence of toffee in both the aroma and palate. Not too sweet for a beer of this strength and body. A seasonal brew.

WORLDHAM   **Worldham Brewery, Smith's Farm, East Worldham, Alton, Hampshire, GU34 3AT. Tel. (0420) 83383**

It took 18 months to convert a hop kiln into a 10-barrel brewery, using plant acquired from a number of different breweries. Launched its only beer at the 1991 CAMRA Farnham Beerex and went on to win the *Beer of the Festival* award at the Portsmouth Beerex later that year. Serves around 30 free trade outlets, but this number is steadily expanding, helped by a marketing grant from the Rural Development Commission. Plans are in hand to increase weekly production from 15 to 30 barrels and to brew a higher gravity beer.

Old Dray Bitter   (OG 1042, ABV 4.5%) Mid to deep brown beer, low in aroma and with a dry flavour with some grain. Strong on hops in the slightly cloying finish. A little variable, as might be expected from a new small brewery.

WORTHINGTON See Bass, page 478.

WORTLEY   **Wortley Brewery, Halifax Road, Wortley, Sheffield, S. Yorks, S30 7DB. Tel. (0742) 882245**

South Yorkshire's newest brewery, opened in December 1991 in the cellar of the Wortley Arms Hotel, initially to produce beer for the pub. Fifteen other outlets are now regularly supplied. Survived a brief closure in April 1992, during which all brewing equipment was temporarily removed.

Bitter   (ABV 3.6%) An interesting new beer, rapidly establishing itself in the true free trade. A malty and fruity nose with a strong malt and fruit taste, ending in a gentle bitter finish.

Earls Ale   (ABV 4.2%) A malty base, upon which target hops add a lot of bitterness in the mouth, and a dry yet clean aftertaste. Early days, but this might be a great best bitter in the making.

WYCHWOOD   **The Wychwood Brewery Company, The Two Rivers Brewery, Station Lane, Witney, Oxfordshire, OX8 6BH. Tel. (0993) 702574**

The new name of Glenny Brewery, set up in 1983 in the old maltings of the former Clinch's brewery, and moved to its own premises in 1987. Its first brew was called Eagle Bitter, but the name was changed after a dispute with Charles Wells. Now this beer is known as Shires Bitter. The newest brand, Dr Thirsty's Draught, is aimed primarily at the guest beer market. Runs no pubs of its own, but the number of free trade outlets has increased by a half in the last year, to 92. A summer ale, Fiddler's Elbow, was tested in 1992.

Shires Bitter   (OG 1034, ABV 3.4%) A pleasantly hoppy and malty, light brown session beer, with a roast malt and fruit aroma.

471

The Independents

Best (OG 1042, ABV 4.2%) Mid brown, full-flavoured premium bitter. Moderately strong in hop and malt flavours, with pleasing, fruity overtones which last through to the aftertaste.

Dr Thirsty's Draught* (OG 1050, ABV 5.2%)

Hobgoblin (OG 1058, ABV 6%) Powerful, full-bodied, copper-red, well-balanced brew. Strong in roasted malt, with a moderate, hoppy bitterness and a slight fruity character.

WYE VALLEY

Wye Valley Brewery, 69 St Owen Street, Hereford, HR1 2JQ. Tel. (0432) 274968

Brewery which started production in March 1985 and moved to its present address in October 1986. Going ahead with plans to double capacity to cater for increased sales. A new beer may be introduced at the same time. Runs one tied house (Barrels in Hereford) and supplies 25 other outlets.

Hereford Bitter (OG 1036) Very little nose, but a crisp, dry and truly bitter taste, with a balancing malt flavour. The initial bitter aftertaste mellows to a pleasant, lingering malt.

Hereford Pale Ale or HPA (OG 1040) Beer with a distinctive colour of old pine and a malty nose. On the tongue, it is malty, with some balancing bitterness and a hint of sweetness. Good, dry finish.

Hereford Supreme (OG 1043) This rich, copper-red beer has a good malty, fruity aroma. In the complex variety of flavours, the malt, fruit and bitterness are distinctive. The finish has bitterness but can be cloyingly malty.

Brew 69 (OG 1055) A pale beer which disguises its strength. Has a well-balanced flavour and finish, without the sweetness which normally characterises beer of this strength.

YATES

Yates Brewery, Ghyll Farm, Westnewton, Aspatria, Cumbria, CA5 3NX. Tel. (069 73) 21081

Small, traditional brewery set up in 1986 by Peter and Carol Yates in an old farm building on their smallholding, which itself used to be a brew pub. Brews award-winning beers to its capacity of 34 barrels a week during summer and other peak times, but at present has no plans to expand further. Directly serves 20 free trade outlets.

Bitter (OG 1035, ABV 3.9%) A fruity, bitter, straw-coloured ale with malt and hops in the aroma and a long, bitter aftertaste.

Premium (OG 1048, ABV 5.2%) Available at Christmas and a few other times of the year. Straw-coloured, with a strong aroma of malt and hops, and full-flavoured, with a slight toffee taste. The malty aftertaste becomes strongly bitter.

Best Cellar (OG 1052, ABV 5.4%) Brewed only in winter. An excellent, red/brown beer with a fruity aroma and a sweet, malty flavour, contrasted by a hoppy bitterness. The finish is a bittersweet balance, with grain and some hops.

YOUNGER See Scottish & Newcastle, page 483.

The Independents

YOUNG'S

Young & Co.'s Brewery PLC, The Ram Brewery, High Street, Wandsworth, London, SW18 4JD. Tel. (081) 870 0141

Founded on the banks of the Wandle in 1675 by the Draper family, this brewery was bought by Charles Young and Anthony Bainbridge in 1831. Their partnership was dissolved in 1884 and the business was continued by Charles Young's son and other members of his family. Although now a public company, it is still very much a family affair. The only London brewer not to hitch its drays to the keg revolution in the 1970s, Young's has continued to expand by brewing award-winning beers in the traditional manner. (Some of the deliveries to its 170 pubs are still made by horse-drawn drays.) Young's has also been very selective in its pub acquisitions. Around 600 free trade outlets are supplied, mostly within the M25 ring, though the brewery's presence is extending westward. Special is regularly seen as a guest beer in Courage pubs.

Bitter

(OG 1036, ABV 3.7%) A light and distinctive bitter with well-balanced malt and hop characters. A strong bitterness is followed by a delightfully astringent and hoppy aftertaste.

Porter*

(OG 1040, ABV 4%) A new addition to the range.

Special

(OG 1046, ABV 4.8%) A strong, full-flavoured, bitter beer with a powerful hoppiness and a malty aroma. Hops persist in the aftertaste, with a rich fruitiness and lasting fullness.

Winter Warmer ⅊

(OG 1055, ABV 5%) A dark brown ale with a malty, fruity aroma, a sweet and fruity flavour, with roast malt and some balancing bitterness, and a bittersweet finish, including some lingering malt.

ALLIED BREWERIES

Allied Breweries, 107 Station Street, Burton upon Trent, Staffs, DE14 1BZ. Tel. (0283) 31111

Part of the food and retailing group Allied-Lyons, this brewing conglomerate dates from 1961 and the merger of Ansells, Tetley Walker and Ind Coope. After the number of trading companies under the umbrella had been reduced in recent years, and the retail and production sides split, a merger with Carlsberg was announced in October 1991 to create a new company to be known as Carlsberg-Tetley. The new operation was due to come into effect in March 1992 but has been held up whilst the Office of Fair Trading looks into the matter at CAMRA's request.

This fusion of brewing interests – if it goes ahead – is likely to mean more rationalisation. Already the Romford keg beer brewery has closed and, should Carlsberg's purpose-built Northampton lager brewery be added to a series of breweries whose capacity is already only 72% employed, other sites would be in danger. The greatest threat is to Allied's lager plant at Wrexham, where staffing has already been reduced from 200 to 80 in the last few years, but the word is out that the future of Alloa and possibly even Warrington may not be secure, despite its contract brewing for Greenalls.

Meanwhile, Allied continues to press ahead with the promotion of Tetley Bitter and, lining up alongside Ind Coope Burton Ale on the bar top, it represents Allied's chief national brand. Pubs have been shed to comply with the tied pub limit set by the 1989 Beer Orders, with over 700 pubs leased by Brent Walker, though Allied beers are still supplied to the pubs as part of the contract. Burtonwood also have an agreement to lease 142 Allied pubs and other regional brewers have stepped in to expand their estates.

ALLOA	**Alloa Brewery Company Ltd., Whins Road, Alloa, Clackmannanshire, Central, FK10 3RB. Tel. (0259) 723539**

Allied's Scottish arm, established in 1810, which was taken over by Archibald Arrol in 1866. It fell to Ind Coope & Allsopp's in 1951, becoming part of Allied in the 1961 merger. Took over Drybroughs from Watney in 1987. Deleted Arrol's 70/- in 1989, which was replaced in pubs by Tetley Bitter. Its pubs take Maclay 70/- and 80/- as guest beers, throughout Scotland, and Caledonian 70/- and 80/- in the Edinburgh area. Real ale is available in only 85 of its 350 tied houses, though 130 free trade outlets are supplied with cask beer by the brewery.

Archibald Arrol's 80/-*	(OG 1041, ABV 4.2%) A full-flavoured beer with dry hop character.

FURGUSONS	**Furgusons Plympton Brewery, Valley Road, Plympton, Plymouth, Devon, PL7 3LQ. Tel. (0752) 330171**

Set up in the Halls Plympton depot in 1984, this brewery's business has expanded rapidly over the last four years. It now offers three ales of its own for sale to 29 of Allied's 32 pubs in the area and to free trade in the South-West (about 120 accounts). Brewing capacity was increased by a third in 1991.

Dartmoor Best Bitter (OG 1038, ABV 3.7%) Mid brown to red beer with a sweet, malty flavour and a strong malty aftertaste.

Dartmoor Strong (OG 1044, ABV 4.3%) Mid brown, malty yet bitter-flavoured beer.

Cockleroaster (OG 1060, ABV 5.8%) Winter only. A powerful, golden beer with a strong, near perfect mix of malt and hop flavours, and a fruity note which dominates the aroma. Not overpowering, but distinctive, with a good, hoppy finish.

HP&D **Holt, Plant & Deakin Ltd., Dudley Road, Wolverhampton, W. Midlands, WV2 3AF. Tel. (0902) 450504**

Trades under the name of Holts, but do not confuse it with Manchester's Joseph Holt brewery. A Black Country company set up in 1984 and now running 47 traditional pubs, all serving real ale. Holts Mild and Bitter are brewed by Tetley Walker in Warrington, though Mild may move to Wolverhampton. Some Entire is still produced at the company's old brewery in Oldbury.

Entire (OG 1043, ABV 4.4%) A distinctively hoppy beer with a dry, malty taste.

Deakin's Downfall* (OG 1060, ABV 5.9%) A winter ale.

Plant's Progress* (OG 1060, ABV 5.9%) A second winter brew.

IND COOPE **Ind Coope Burton Brewery Ltd., 107 Station Street, Burton upon Trent, Staffs, DE14 1BZ. Tel. (0283) 31111**

The major brewery in the Allied group which was born of the merger of the adjoining Allsopp's and Ind Coope breweries in 1934. It currently has a capacity of two and a half million barrels a year and brews eight real ales for the South and the Midlands, providing beer for the Ansells, Ind Coope Retail, Taylor Walker and Nicholson's trading divisions.

Ansells is Allied's Midlands and Wales wing, operating some 1,600 pubs, two-thirds selling real ale. Ind Coope Retail controls over 1,400 pubs in the Home Counties, those formerly owned by Aylesbury Brewery (ABC), Benskins, Friary Meux and Halls, whose names are still used on pub livery and signs. Taylor Walker runs 685 pubs and restaurant-pubs in London (including the Muswell's and Exchanges chains), whilst Nicholson's operates 35 upmarket pubs in the capital, all of which sell at least four real ales, including Boddingtons Bitter and other 'guests' like Adnams and Greene King. (£24 million has been earmarked for developing and refurbishing the Nicholson's estate in the next year.) Taylor Walker has also purchased the chain of Firkin brew pubs from Stakis Leisure and now hopes to produce Nicholson's Best Bitter at the Falcon & Firkin (see Brew Pubs).

In the meantime, this beer and Taylor Walker Best Bitter are brewed in Burton, alongside all the other 'local' beers. They are derived from two mashes: ABC, Friary and Taylor

The Nationals

Walker from one, Benskins and Nicholson's from the other. Ind Coope Burton Brewery also brews four beers for Greenalls and Lumphammer (OG 1039) for the Worcestershire-based Little Pub Co. chain.

For Ind Coope Retail:

ABC Best Bitter* (OG 1035, ABV 3.5%) A light, refreshing bitter, owing much of its character to dry hopping.

Friary Meux Best Bitter (OG 1035, ABV 3.5%) Malt just dominates over hops in the aroma and flavour of this tawny beer. A strange, fruity flavour lurks in the background.

Benskins Best Bitter (OG 1035, ABV 3.5%) A hoppy aroma, taste and finish. Can be a bit thin on occasions, when any malt and fruit flavours are lost. Otherwise, it's a pleasant, suppable pint.

Burton Ale (OG 1047, ABV 4.8%) Full of hop and malt flavours with hints of fruit and sweetness. It has a hoppy, malty aroma with a faint smell of fruit and a bitter, hoppy finish. *Champion Beer of Britain* in 1990.

For Ansells:

Ansells Bitter (OG 1035, ABV 3.5%) A pale brown bitter with a malt and hop flavour. A touch of sweetness shows it's aimed at the Midlands market.

Ansells Mild (OG 1035.5, ABV 3.2%) A dark, malty beer with hints of roast and caramel. The aftertaste is also of roast and caramel, overlaid with sweetness.

For Taylor Walker and Nicholson's:

Taylor Walker Best Bitter (OG 1035, ABV 3.5%) Light, malty bitter.

Nicholson's Best Bitter* (OG 1035, ABV 3.5%)

For Greenalls:

Davenports Best Mild* (OG 1034, ABV 3.4%)

Shipstone's Mild* (OG 1034, ABV 3.4%)

Davenports Traditional Bitter* (OG 1037, ABV 3.9%)

Shipstone's Bitter* (OG 1037, ABV 4%)

JOSHUA TETLEY Joshua Tetley & Son Ltd., PO Box 142, The Brewery, Leeds, W. Yorks, LS1 1QG. Tel. (0532) 435282

Yorkshire's best-known brewery, founded in 1822 by maltster Joshua Tetley and now owning 997 pubs, 938 of which serve cask beer. The brewery site covers 20 acres and includes a brewhouse opened in May 1989 to handle the increased demand for Tetley Bitter, Allied's biggest selling cask beer. The massive advertising push for Tetley has been supported by the installation across the country of a special dispense system which recreates the famous Yorkshire tight, creamy head. Versions of both Tetley Bitter and Mild are brewed at the Tetley Walker plant in Warrington, with no point of origin declared on the pump clips.

476

The Nationals

Mild
(OG 1033, ABV 3.2%) Red/brown in colour, with a light hint of malt and caramel in the aroma. A rounded taste of malt and caramel follows, with balancing bitterness, then a generally dry finish. A smooth, satisfying mild.

Bitter
(OG 1035.5, ABV 3.6%) An amber-coloured standard bitter with a faint hoppy aroma. A good, refreshing, smooth balance of hop, bitterness and grain in the mouth, finishing with a long, dry aftertaste. Quality can vary.

TETLEY WALKER Tetley Walker Ltd., Dallam Lane, Warrington, Cheshire, WA2 7NU. Tel. (0925) 31231

Brewery founded by the Walker family in 1852 which merged with Joshua Tetley in 1960. A period of restructuring is now underway at Warrington and all management positions have been transferred to Leeds. Two divisions have been created: one to handle the brewing and wholesaling of Joshua Tetley and Tetley Walker beers, the other to run Joshua Tetley, Tetley Walker and Peter Walker pubs.

Warrington currently brews for the Tetley Walker, Peter Walker, HP&D and Greenalls companies. Of the 784 Tetley Walker houses, over 70% sell real ale. They are split into Tetley and Peter Walker pubs, though some Peter Walker beer is now being sold in Tetley houses. (All 91 Peter Walker tied houses sell cask beer.) The Tetley Mild and Bitter brewed here are versions of the beers from Tetley's Leeds brewery but are sold with identical pump clips. However, in the pub listings, we state Tetley Walker instead of Tetley when we are aware that the beer comes from Warrington and not Leeds.

Tetley Dark Mild
(OG 1032, ABV 2.9%) A smooth, dark, malty mild with balanced roast and caramel flavours, and a hint of fruit and liquorice. Some dryness. Much improved over the last year.

Walker Mild
(OG 1032, ABV 2.9%) Smooth, dark mild with fruit and hints of caramel, roast and bitterness. The malty aftertaste quickly gives way to a faint dryness.

Tetley Mild
(OG 1032, ABV 3.2%) A smooth, malty mild with some fruitiness and bitter notes. The aftertaste is malty, with a little dryness. A refreshing, darkish mild.

Walker Bitter
(OG 1033, ABV 3.3%) A light, refreshing, well-balanced bitter with some hop and a little fruit.

Walker Best Bitter
(OG 1036, ABV 3.3%) A bitter beer with a dry finish. The bitterness is sometimes astringent and can mask other flavours. Reasonably hoppy.

Tetley Bitter
(OG 1036, ABV 3.6%) A fruity session beer with a dry finish. Bitterness tends to dominate malt and hop flavours. Sharp, clean-tasting and popular.

Walker Winter Warmer
(OG 1060, ABV 5.8%) Brewed November–February. A smooth, dark and sweet winter ale, with a strong, fruity flavour, balanced to some degree by a bitter taste and the dry character of the finish. Improves with age as sweetness declines and other flavours emerge. At its best, it is dangerously drinkable.

The Nationals

For HP&D:

HP&D Bitter
(OG 1036, ABV 3.4%) Pale brown, slightly sweet and lightly hoppy beer, brewed not to offend anyone.

HP&D Mild
(OG 1036, ABV 3.4%) An innocuous mild, tasting vaguely of malt and caramel but not much else. May be transferred to HP&D's Wolverhampton brewery.

For Greenalls:

Greenalls Mild
(OG 1032, ABV 3.1%) A dark, malty mild with a faint malt and fruit aroma. Quite fruity, with hints of roast, caramel and a little bitterness. Good when on form but often thin and bland.

Greenalls Bitter
(OG 1036, ABV 3.8%) A well-balanced beer which is quite fruity and well hopped, with a good, dry finish.

Thomas Greenall's Original Bitter
(OG 1045, ABV 4.4%) Astringent bitterness tends to dominate malt and hop flavours; fairly fruity and a little sweet.

BASS

Bass PLC, 66 Chiltern Street, London, W1M 1PR. Tel. (071) 486 4440

Bass Brewers is the country's largest beer company, with an estimated 22% of all production and 23% of sales. Lager accounts for 54% of total sales but Stones Best Bitter, its leading ale brand, ranks number four in the UK market. Worthington Best Bitter is now number five and Draught Bass is increasing its lead as the major premium cask beer. There are currently 11 breweries, with Hope in Sheffield and Heriot in Edinburgh planned for closure, as the company comes to terms with its internal restructuring following the 1989 Beer Orders. The Springfield brewery in Wolverhampton was closed in 1991, its demise announced at the same time as that of the Preston Brook keg beer plant in Cheshire. In addition to the cask beer breweries listed, Bass still runs three keg beer production centres at Alton, Glasgow and Belfast.

One result of these closures has been the transfer of beers. Springfield Bitter is now brewed at Highgate, whilst Charrington IPA has gone back to Cape Hill. However, with the squeeze from the Bass national beers and guest beer arrangements with Young's and Fuller's, this could be the last resting place for Charrington's once-famous London brew. On a more encouraging note, the company may be more positively disposed towards its bottle-conditioned beer, Worthington White Shield, which, having moved only recently from Burton to Sheffield, is soon to be produced in Birmingham.

The company's 5,200 pubs are operated by Bass Taverns. Of these, 2,950 are managed houses. The rest are being transferred to new tied leases, through the Bass Lease Company (responsible for 1,230 pubs), or are tenanted pubs (1,020) controlled by Bass Inns, which are being sold, or transferred to management or tied leases. Bass is well on its way to meeting the pub disposal target of 2,740 set by the Beer Orders.

The Nationals

The Bass organisation is divided into the following companies: Bass Brewers Ltd. (at the Burton address); Bass Brewers South (at the Burton address, with registered companies including Charrington North, Charrington South, Bass South, Bass West and Welsh Brewers); Bass Brewers North (Headingly Office Park, 8 Victoria Road, Leeds, W. Yorks, LS6 1LG. Tel. (0532) 744444, with registered companies including Bass North East, Bass North West, William Stones, Bass Worthington and Bass Mitchells and Butlers); Bass Ireland (Ulster Brewery, Glen Road, Belfast, BT11 8BY. Tel. (0232) 301301); Tennent Caledonian Breweries (110 Bath Street, Glasgow, Strathclyde, G2 2ET. Tel.(041) 552 6552). The following are the group's cask beer breweries.

BURTON

Bass Brewers Ltd., 137 High Street, Burton upon Trent, Staffs, DE14 1JZ. Tel. (0283) 511000

The original home of Bass, producing one of Britain's most famous ales, available throughout its estate and the free trade.

Draught Bass

(OG 1043, ABV 4.4%) Formerly one of Britain's classic beers, this tawny ale can vary widely in character, depending on its age. A fruity and malty aroma and taste are balanced by an underlying hoppy dryness when at its best, though the palate is usually sweetish. The finish is bittersweet, with some lingering malt. Often served too green, but, when it's good, it's still a classic pint.

BIRMINGHAM

Bass Brewers North, Cape Hill Brewery, Smethwick, Birmingham, B16 0PQ. Tel. (021) 558 1481

One of the largest cask beer production centres in the country.

M&B Mild

(OG 1035, ABV 3.4%) A dark brown quaffing mild with a light roast and malt flavour. Dry and hoppy aftertaste.

Charrington IPA*

(OG 1039, ABV 3.6%)

M&B Brew XI

(OG 1040, ABV 4.1%) A sweet, malty beer with a hoppy, bitter aftertaste.

HIGHGATE

Bass Brewers North, Highgate Brewery, Sandymount Road, Walsall, WS1 3AP. Tel. (0922) 23168

Built in 1895 and now a listed building, the Highgate Brewery is the smallest in the Bass group and has remained unchanged for many years. The future of the resurrected Highgate Old is still in some doubt.

M&B Highgate Mild

(OG 1035.5, ABV 3.2%) A well-balanced dark brown mild with a touch of ruby to its colour. Smooth-tasting, with malt, hoppiness and roast flavours. Hints of bitterness and sulphur.

M&B Springfield Bitter

(OG 1036, ABV 3.5%) A sweetish, malty bitter. Highgate's distinctive taste distinguishes it clearly from the Springfield original. The keg version is brewed at Cape Hill.

M&B Highgate Old Ale

(OG 1055.7, ABV 5.3%) November–January only: a dark brown/ruby-coloured strong ale. A full-flavoured, fruity, malty ale with bitterness in the aftertaste.

The Nationals

TADCASTER   **Bass Brewers North, Tower Brewery, Wetherby Road, Tadcaster, N. Yorks, LS24 9SD. Tel. (0937) 832361**

Together with the Cannon Brewery, serves Bass's northern outlets, brewing beers for regional tastes: Light for West Yorkshire, Mild for the Hull area and Special for East Lancashire.

Light   (OG 1031, ABV 3.3%) An amber-coloured mild: a lightly-flavoured blend of malt, sweetness and bitterness. At its best, has a delicate, pleasing, flowery taste, but can too often be bland. A disappointing, short, sweetish finish and little aroma.

Mild XXXX   (OG 1031, ABV 3.3%) A pleasant, smooth, dark mild with a faint aroma of caramel, which leads to a caramel and roast, rich taste, with complementing sweetness and bitterness. A good, long, satisfying, roast malt and caramel-sweet finish.

Special Bitter   (OG 1035, ABV 3.7%) Certainly not special. Pale brown in hue, with little aroma. The generally bland taste has sweetness, malt and a slight bitterness. The poor, sweet and dryish finish can be cloying. Unexciting.

SHEFFIELD: CANNON   **Bass Brewers North, Cannon Brewery, Rutland Road, Sheffield, S. Yorks, S3 8BE. Tel. (0742) 349433**

Stones Best Bitter   (OG 1038, ABV 4.1%) A nice mixture of malt, hop and fruit aromas, with delicate malt on the tongue and a bitter hoppiness. Still a clean hop finish, but the brew is more mellow than before, with the straw colour now more ochre. Has the free trade push compromised the quality, or is it just served too young? Not as good as last year, but still a fine beer.

SHEFFIELD: HOPE   **Bass Brewers North, Hope Brewery, Claywheels Lane, Wadsley Bridge, Sheffield, S. Yorks, S6 1NB. Tel. (0742) 349433**

Bass's specialist bottled beer brewery, soon to be closed. White Shield will be transferred to Cape Hill. *Bottle-conditioned beer: Worthington White Shield* ⊕ *(OG 1051, ABV 5.6%)*

CARDIFF   **Bass Brewers South, Crawshay Street, Cardiff, CF1 1TR. Tel. (0222) 233071**

The Hancock's brewery (founded in 1884) which was taken over by Bass Charrington in 1968 and serves Welsh Brewers, its South Wales trading division. Supplies an extensive free trade, with real ale now becoming more prominent in valleys pubs. Worthington Best Bitter has become a national brand.

Worthington Dark   (OG 1033, ABV 3.3%) A dark brown, creamy mild with some maltiness and a sweet finish. Well worth finding, but low turnover is a cause for concern.

Hancock's HB   (OG 1037, ABV 3.8%) A slightly malty bitter, with a bittersweet aftertaste. A pleasant but not distinctive beer.

Worthington Best Bitter   (OG 1037, ABV 3.8%) A fairly malty, light-coloured beer, with a somewhat bitter finish.

480

The Nationals

COURAGE

Courage Ltd., Ashby House, Bridge Street, Staines, Middlesex, TW18 4XH. Tel. (0784) 466199

1991 was a big year for Courage. Indulging in a pubs-for-breweries swap with Grand Metropolitan (the old Watneys, Manns and Truman breweries), as a means of avoiding the full implications of the 1989 Beer Orders, it divested itself of all its pubs, gaining at the same time all Grand Met's breweries and giving 20% of all UK beer production. The ex-Courage pubs, together with most of Grand Met's pubs, were amalgamated into Inntrepreneur Estates for leasing out on long contracts to existing tenants or other businessmen. These pubs are obliged to take Courage beers for seven years, though this agreement may well continue beyond this time.

1992 was the year that Courage took stock. The brewery closures feared when the deal was announced have yet to materialise, though the future for the old Webster's brewery in Halifax does not look rosy. Webster's Choice has already been killed off by the heavy promotion of Directors, and all non-production staff have been transferred to John Smith's in Tadcaster. Courage did, however, take up the offer for Ruddles from Dutch lager giants Grolsch (see Independents), and the management buy-out of Ushers of Trowbridge also went through, releasing another independent in the West Country (again see Independents). Courage also operates keg beer plants in Mortlake and on the outskirts of Reading.

BRISTOL	**Courage Ltd., Bristol Brewery, Bath Street, Bristol, Avon, BS1 6EX. Tel. (0272) 297222**

The former Georges brewery, now Courage's only real ale brewery in the South, following the closure of traditional breweries in London, Reading and Plymouth, and the buy-out of Ushers. Growing demand for cask beer has resulted in expansion at this plant in recent years, with Best and Directors very well promoted nationally but Bitter Ale somewhat neglected, its sales confined mostly to the West Country and South-East Wales.

Bitter Ale	(OG 1031, ABV 3.2%) A pale, light-bodied bitter, with a delicately hoppy, bitter, malty taste. A dry bitter finish and a hoppy aroma.
Best Bitter	(OG 1039, ABV 4%) A pale brown bitter with a good balance of bitter hops, grainy malt (sometimes fruit), and a slight sweetness. The aroma is malty and hoppy; the finish is bitter and malty.
Directors	(OG 1046, ABV 4.8%) A fine, well-balanced, red/brown malty ale, with ample malt, hops and fruit in the nose. The strong, malty, dry, hoppy taste has a faint fruitiness, and develops into a bitter, dry finish. All too often served below par.

JOHN SMITH'S	**Courage Ltd. Northern Trading, Tadcaster, N. Yorks, LS24 9SA. Tel. (0937) 832091**

A business founded at the Old Brewery in 1758 and taken

The Nationals

over by John Smith (brother of Samuel Smith, see Independents) in 1847. The present brewery was built in 1884 and became part of the Courage empire in 1970. John Smith's Bitter is Courage's best known ale, thanks to extensive television advertising. *Bottle-conditioned beer: Imperial Russian Stout ⊕ (OG 1104), a famous export beer which is now only rarely brewed*

Bitter
(OG 1036, ABV 3.8%) Copper-coloured beer with a pleasant mix of hops and malt in the nose. Malt dominates the taste but hops take over in the finish. The brewery's quality control for this beer is excellent. Widely available nationally.

Magnet
(OG 1040, ABV 4%) A well-crafted beer, almost ruby coloured. Hops, malt and citrus fruit can be identified in the nose and there are complex flavours of nuts, hops and fruit, giving way to a long, malty finish.

FOUNTAIN HEAD
Courage Ltd., Fountain Head Brewery, Ovenden Wood, Halifax, W. Yorks, HX2 0TL. Tel. (0422) 357188

The original Samuel Webster brewery, merged by Watney in 1985 with Wilson's of Manchester, a move which saw the closure of Wilson's own brewery. Webster's Yorkshire Bitter appeared to be threatened by the Grand Met deal, as Courage was already committed to John Smith's Bitter, but the Halifax brew has proved surprisingly resilient and still benefits from a sizeable advertising budget. It may be the one beer to survive if Courage does close the Halifax brewery.

Wilson's Original Mild
(OG 1032, ABV 3%) A malty and fruity aroma leads on to a predominantly malty/caramel flavour, with some bitterness. Thin in body. The aftertaste is slightly malty and bittersweet. Outlets still declining in number.

Webster's Green Label Best
(OG 1034, ABV 3.4%) A faint, hoppy aroma, with a little fruitiness at times. Some sweetness in the malty taste, and a bitter finish. A boy's bitter.

Webster's Yorkshire Bitter
(OG 1037, ABV 3.8%) A disappointing beer with a faintly malty and fruity aroma (sometimes metallic). Often very bland in taste to offend no-one. If you are lucky, it can have a good, fresh, hoppy-bitter flavour and finish (but very rare!).

Wilson's Original Bitter
(OG 1037, ABV 3.8%) A fairly thin, golden beer with a malty and fruity aroma and a flowery hop flavour, which can be very bitter at times. Malty overtones in taste and finish.

GUINNESS

Guinness Brewing (GB), Park Royal Brewery, London, NW10 7RR. Tel. (081) 965 7700

The brewer of the most famous of stouts has breweries around the world, with Guinness also brewed under licence in many more. An excellent bottle-conditioned export stout, brewed in Dublin and once sold as Triple XXX, is no longer available in the UK, where the only 'real' beer available from Guinness is bottle-conditioned *Guinness Original ⊕ (OG 1042)*. Even so, it is difficult for the uninitiated to differentiate at a glance between this naturally-conditioned bottled beer and a pasteurised version which bears the same

The Nationals

name. To clarify the situation, 'real' bottled Guinness is only available in pubs and bars in England and Wales in 275 ml bottles; all bottles in Scotland are pasteurised. In the off-trade, the only real Guinness you may find is in a 550 ml bottle, though these are not so common and should not be confused with the 500 ml pasteurised bottle! However, there are fears that Guinness is preparing to axe all bottle-conditioned versions. If this happens, one of the world's classic real ales will be lost.

All Draught Guinness sold in the UK is keg. In Ireland Draught Guinness (OG 1038, brewed at Arthur Guinness, St James's Gate, Dublin 8) is not pasteurised but is served with gas pressure. Canned 'Draught' Guinness is also pasteurised and produces its tight, creamy head by use of a small plastic sparkler at the bottom of the can.

Guinness is also the largest shareholder in Crown Buckley (see Independents).

SCOTTISH & NEWCASTLE

Scottish & Newcastle Breweries PLC, Abbey Brewery, 111 Holyrood Road, Edinburgh, Lothian, EH8 8YS. Tel. (031) 556 2591

The 1960 merger between Scottish Brewers Ltd. and Newcastle Breweries Ltd. has had a major influence on the British brewing industry. It may not be officially classed as a 'National', because it does not own more than 2,000 pubs, but S&N is a giant brewer in every other way. Its massive free trade presence (particularly through McEwan and Theakston brands) and heavy loan-tieing of 'free' houses, ensure that its influence is significant.

The closure of its Matthew Brown subsidiary in Blackburn in 1991, despite earlier assurances that the brewery was 'sacrosanct', enraged North-Western drinkers. Fears grew for Theakston too, when S&N began to produce Theakston beers at the Tyne Brewery in Newcastle. Today most of Theakston's production comes from Newcastle. On a happier note, Theakston launched a new mild at Masham in 1992.

S&N currently operates a total of 1,957 pubs, over 50% selling cask-conditioned beer, but the future of S&N as a brewing concern has been much questioned, and rumours of links with another major brewery, such as Whitbread, have been heard. Further speculation followed the announcement in February 1992 that S&N was to handle the supply of Whitbread cask beers to the free trade in Scotland. Whitbread's loan-ties with publicans north of the border have also been transferred to S&N. S&N currently has five breweries, including a keg beer plant in Manchester.

FOUNTAIN   **Fountain Brewery, 159 Fountainbridge, Edinburgh, Lothian, EH3 9RZ. Tel (031) 229 9377**

The Scottish production centre, formerly the home of William McEwan & Co. Ltd., founded in 1856. Its beers are sold under two separate names – McEwan and Younger,

The Nationals

depending on the trading area, but such is the promotion of Theakston products that the futures of Scotch Bitter and No. 3 remain in doubt.

McEwan 70/- or Younger Scotch Bitter*
(OG 1036, ABV 3.7%) A well-balanced, sweetish brew, becoming increasingly rare.

McEwan 80/- or Younger IPA*
(OG 1042, ABV 4.5%) Malty and sweet-flavoured, with some graininess and a dry finish.

Younger No. 3*
(OG 1042, ABV 4.5%) Rich and dark.

TYNE
Tyne Brewery, Gallowgate, Newcastle upon Tyne, Tyne & Wear, NE99 1RA. Tel (091) 232 5091

The production centre of Newcastle Breweries Ltd., formed in 1890 as an amalgamation of five local breweries. In recent years it brewed no cask beer, until most of Theakston's production was transferred here (see Theakston, below). No indication is given at the point of sale that Theakston beers are brewed in Newcastle.

Theakston Best Bitter
(OG 1038, ABV 3.8%)

Theakston XB
(OG 1044, ABV 4.5%)

Theakston Old Peculier
(OG 1057, ABV 5.6%)

HOME
Home Brewery PLC, Mansfield Road, Daybrook, Nottingham, NG5 6BU. Tel. (0602) 269741

Founded in 1875 and acquired by S&N in 1986, Home's tied estate offers real ale in 180 of its 400 pubs. Extensive free trade in the Midlands and the North. Now brews the beers from the closed Matthew Brown brewery in Blackburn and these are still sold in 184 of the 403 Matthew Brown pubs in the North-West, although their future is not certain.

Matthew Brown Dark Mild*
(OG 1030.5, ABV 3.1%)

Matthew Brown Bitter*
(OG 1034, ABV 3.5%)

Home Mild
(OG 1036, ABV 3.6%) A notably malty, dark beer, with little aroma. Chocolate and liquorice in the flavour, and an unusually bitter finish for a mild. Slightly acidic and fruity.

Home Bitter
(OG 1038, ABV 3.8%) Again low in aroma. The flavour balances malt and hops well, with a smooth, initial taste and a lingering, dry, bitter finish. Golden/copper in colour.

THEAKSTON
T&R Theakston Ltd., Wellgarth, Masham, Ripon, N. Yorks, HG4 4DX. Tel (0765) 689544

Company formed in 1827 which built this brewery in 1875. Became part of S&N when its parent company, Matthew Brown, was swallowed up. More than £1 million has been spent on this brewery in the last few years, reflecting the 'national' status its brews have been given by S&N. Although Theakston itself runs just ten tied houses, the free trade is enormous and, consequently, most of Theakston's production now takes place in Newcastle. The same pump clips are used for Masham and Newcastle beers, though surely the consumer should be told whether the beer on sale is brewed at Theakston itself or at the S&N Tyne Brewery?

Traditional Mild (OG 1035, ABV 3.5%) A new product, not a copy of the mild brewed at Masham until 1984. Very dark amber in colour, with a mix of malt and hops in the nose. A smooth, full mild with malt and chocolate flavours and a delicate hoppy aftertaste which comes from dry hopping.

Best Bitter (OG 1038, ABV 3.8%) A delicate, straw-coloured beer with a hoppy and fruity nose. There is sharp hoppiness in the flavour, with some hints of malt and fruit, and the finish is dry and lasting.

XB (OG 1044, ABV 4.5%) An impressive aroma of hops and malt, with a hint of orchard fruit, precedes a well-balanced taste where hops slightly outweigh other elements, which include vine fruits. The finish is very dry and slightly unexpected. A well-made beer.

Old Peculier ᛦ (OG 1057, ABV 5.6%) A dark, mysterious-looking brew with just a hint of ruby. Its impressive colour is matched by the rich malt and fruit on the nose. Roast malt and butterscotch stand out in the taste of this full-bodied beer, but there is also some hoppy bitterness and forest fruit notes. Long finish, revealing that hops play an important part in its make up.

WHITBREAD

The Whitbread Beer Company, Porter Tun House, Capability Green, Luton, Beds, LU1 3LS. Tel. (0582) 391166

With only four real ale breweries left to its name, this once famous brewing company (founded 1742) is now divided into separate brewing and retailing wings. Whilst the retailing division has been busy selling and leasing pubs to meet the limit of 4,200 tied pubs set by the Beer Orders, the Whitbread Beer Company has been putting money behind its cask ale portfolio. At the top of the budget has been Boddingtons Bitter, purchased along with the Strangeways Brewery in 1989. Flowers Original is also being heavily promoted.

All this comes after years of brewery closures. The likes of Strong of Romsey, Wethered of Marlow, Fremlins of Faversham, Chester's of Salford and Liverpool's Higsons brewery, together with their distinctive local tastes, have all been sacrificed in the name of rationalisation. The first three breweries' beers were transferred to Cheltenham. The Chester's brews and Higsons Mild and Bitter went to Sheffield. With Strangeways being expanded to cope with the increased demand for Boddingtons Bitter, the only small brewery which Whitbread still owns is Castle Eden.

The result of this centralisation has been a tragic loss of character amongst the beers. The original yeasts have been replaced by a Whitbread strain and party-gyling (making several different brews from one original) has been in force. Furthermore, the low yeast count in the cask, whilst deliberately benefiting the publican by allowing the beer to drop bright quickly, results in little cask-conditioning.

The Nationals

Ironically, some of the beers which Whitbread brought under one roof it has now had to farm out to contract brewers, following its agreement to supply beers for the Devenish pub chain.

In addition to the four cask beer breweries, Whitbread also operates keg beer factories in Magor in South Wales and Samlesbury in Lancashire.

BODDINGTONS **Boddingtons Brewery, PO Box 23, Strangeways, Manchester, M60 3WB. Tel. (061) 828 2000**

Brewery established in 1778 whose Bitter has long been one of Britain's best-known traditional beers. Whitbread acquired the brewery when the Boddingtons company, which had already taken-over and closed Oldham Brewery, retreated to pub owning and other leisure enterprises. Now Whitbread is pushing Boddingtons Bitter relentlessly across the country and has expanded brewing capacity to double production.

Boddingtons Mild (OG 1032, ABV 3%) A thin, dark mild with a malty flavour, somewhat drier in character of late. Short aftertaste. The number of outlets still appears to be in decline.

OB Mild (OG 1032, ABV 3%) Copper-red in colour, with a malty aroma. A smooth roast malt and fruit flavour follows, then a malty aftertaste.

Boddingtons Bitter (OG 1035, ABV 3.8%) A pale beer in which agreeable hoppiness and bitterness can be spoiled by a rather cloying sweetness in flavour and aftertaste.

OB Bitter (OG 1038, ABV 3.8%) Pale beer with an aroma of malt and fruit. The flavour is malty and bitter, with a bittersweet tinge and a dry, malty finish.

CASTLE EDEN **The Brewery, PO Box 13, Castle Eden, Hartlepool, Cleveland, TS27 4SX. Tel. (0429) 836431**

Originally attached to a 17th-century coaching inn, the old Nimmo's brewery (established in 1826) was purchased by Whitbread in 1963. It primarily produces Castle Eden Ale (sadly rare in its native area), the low-alcohol White Label, keg Trophy and keg Scotch Bitter, alongside keg Campbells 70/- and 80/- for the Scottish market. The workforce has been trimmed back but refurbishments are planned and production levels have remained stable. Whitbread has been stressing its commitment to the site (local TV advertisements for the ale) and it may become home to a new porter (OG 1052, ABV 4.6%), which was made available for a limited period in summer 1992 to celebrate 250 years of Whitbread brewing.

Castle Eden Ale (OG 1040, ABV 4.2%) A characteristically sweet north-eastern beer, with a hoppy aroma and a predominantly malty flavour. The bittersweet aftertaste can be a bit cloying. Not bland!

FLOWERS **The Flowers Brewery, Monson Avenue, Cheltenham, Gloucestershire, GL50 4EL. Tel. (0242) 261166**

Brewery established in 1760 by banker John Gardner, which housed the Cheltenham Original Brewery from 1888. It merged in 1958 with Stroud Brewery to form West Country

The Nationals

Breweries Ltd. and was acquired by Whitbread in 1963. Today it is the centre of Whitbread's cask ale production in the South, bearing the name of the old Flowers brewery in Stratford-upon-Avon which Whitbread closed in 1968. In recent years it produced the Wethered, Strong and Fremlins beers, from breweries also closed by Whitbread, though Wethered Bitter (see McMullen), Winter Royal, Pompey Royal (see Gale's) and Strong Country Bitter (see Morrells) are now brewed under contract by other breweries. Some of the capacity created has been used for the brewing of Royal Wessex Bitter for Devenish (though Whitbread have subcontracted Cornish Original back to Redruth, see Independents). A new yeast processing plant has been installed as part of a £1 million investment programme.

West Country Pale Ale (WCPA) (OG 1030, ABV 3%) Hoppy in aroma, but not as distinctive as it used to be. Light, refreshing and hoppy, with a clean, dry finish.

Fremlins Bitter* (OG 1035, ABV 3.5%)

Best Bitter* (OG 1036, ABV 3.5%) Also available in keg form.

Flowers IPA (OG 1036, ABV 3.6%) Pale brown, with little aroma, perhaps a faint maltiness. Moderately dry taste and finish, but no discernible hoppiness. Thin and uninspiring.

Flowers Original (OG 1044, ABV 4.5%) Hoppy aroma and hops in the taste, with some malt and a hint of fruit. A notably bitter finish.

For Devenish:

Royal Wessex Bitter* (OG 1040, ABV 4%)

EXCHANGE **Exchange Brewery, Bridge Street, Sheffield, S. Yorks, S3 8NL. Tel. (0742) 761101**

Whitbread's remaining Yorkshire brewery, built in 1882, once the base of Tennant Brothers Ltd. and taken over in 1962. Now brews beers for sale under the Chester's, Bentley and Higsons dead breweries names. A major refurbishment of the brewhouse has been underway.

Higsons Mild (OG 1032, ABV 3.1%) A thin, uninspiring mild with some malty sweetness and a little bitterness. Also vanilla and papery notes.

Chester's Best Mild (OG 1032, ABV 3.5%) An almost black beer with a faint, malty, fruity nose and a palate dominated by caramel, with some malt and fruit. A sweetish, malty finish. Not the beer which once bore the name.

Chester's Best Bitter (OG 1033, ABV 3.6%) Pale in colour and character. Little discernible aroma; a bitter taste, but with little malt or hop flavour, and a faint, malty, dry finish. Insipid, harsh and uninteresting.

Bentley's Yorkshire Bitter (OG 1036, ABV 3.8%) A resurrection of an old brewery name (closed by Whitbread in 1972) to jump on the Yorkshire Bitter bandwagon.

Trophy (OG 1036, ABV 3.8%) Pale brown and thin, this beer has a light aroma and a moderately sweetish, malty taste with some hops, which also feature in the bitter aftertaste. Overall, a bland and uninteresting session brew.

The Nationals

Higsons Bitter (OG 1037, ABV 3.8%) A moderately fruity bitter with a harsh, artificial bitterness which subsumes any malt and hop taste. Again exhibits papery notes and a dry papery aftertaste.

Wethered Bitter - The archetypal Whitbread 'beer on wheels' : from Marlow to Cheltenham and now brewed at McMullen in Hertford.

ABINGTON PARK BREWERY CO.

Wellingborough Road, Northampton, NN1 4EY. Tel. (0604) 31240

Cobblers Ale (OG 1038)
Dark (OG 1044)
Extra (OG 1048)
Special (OG 1060)

One of the Clifton Inns in-house breweries, a five-barrel plant opened in 1984 in a Victorian-styled pub. Stores beer in cellar tanks under CO₂ at atmospheric pressure. Occasional beers produced in addition to the regulars above.

ALE HOUSE

79 Raglan Road, Leeds, W. Yorks, LS2 9DZ. Tel. (0532) 455447

Meek and Mild (OG 1031)
Monster Mash (OG 1042)
XB (OG 1045)
No. 9 (OG 1046)
Simon's Super Stout (OG 1046)
Brainstormer (OG 1055)
White Rose Ale (OG 1064)
Bye Bye Bitter (OG 1079)
Housewarmer (OG 1079) Brewed at Christmas.

Real ale off-licence next to Leeds University. Started brewing in late 1987 and now offers eight handpumps, with weekly guest beers and four real ciders.

ALFORD ARMS

Frithsden, Hemel Hempstead, Herts, HP1 3DD. Tel. (0442) 864480
Not currently brewing.

ALL NATIONS (Mrs Lewis's)

Coalport Road, Madeley, Telford, Shropshire, TF7 5DP. Tel. (0952) 585747

Pale Ale (OG 1032)

One of four brew pubs left before the new wave arrived. The others are the Blue Anchor, Old Swan and Three Tuns. Still known as Mrs Lewis's, the inn has been in the same family since 1934 and has been brewing for 200 years.

ANCIENT DRUIDS

Napier Street, Cambridge, CB1 1HR. Tel. (0223) 324514

Kite Bitter (OG 1035, ABV 3.5%)
Druid's Special (OG 1047, ABV 4.7%)
Merlin (OG 1055, ABV 6%)
Frostbiter (OG 1068, ABV 7%) Winter only.
Set up in 1984. Uses malt extract.

BIRD IN HAND

Paradise Brewery Ltd., Paradise Park, Hayle, Cornwall, TR27 4HY. Tel (0736) 753365

Bitter (OG 1040)
Artists Ale (OG 1055)
Victory Ale (OG 1070) Winter only.
Unusual brewery in a bird park, founded in 1980.

BLACK HORSE

Dunn Plowman Brewery, 80 South Street, Leominster, Hereford & Worcs, HR6 8JF. Tel. (0568) 615059

Black Horse Bitter (OG 1040, ABV 4%)
Brewery sited in an old bottle store. First brew was in May 1992. A stronger beer for festivals is planned. Hopes to supply other outlets.

BLACK HORSE & RAINBOW

The Liverpool Brewing Company Ltd., 21–23 Berry Street, Liverpool, Merseyside, L1 9DF. Tel. (051) 709 5055

Rainbow Bitter (OG 1038)
Black Horse Bitter (OG 1045)
Winter Bitter (OG 1045)

Five-barrel brewery opened in July 1990. Special brews are produced for events like university graduation and freshers weeks. Uses cellar tanks with a blanket of CO₂. The plant can be viewed from within the pub and from the street.

Brew Pubs

BLUE ANCHOR
50 Coinagehall Street, Helston, Cornwall, TR13 8EL. Tel. (0326) 562821
Medium Bitter (OG 1050)
Best Bitter (OG 1053)
Special Bitter (OG 1066)
Extra Special (OG 1076) Brewed in winter and for Easter.
Historic thatched brew pub, originating as a monks' resting place in the 15th century. Produces powerful ales known locally as 'Spingo' beers.

BORVE BREW HOUSE
Ruthven, Huntly, Grampian, AB5 4SR. Tel. (046 687) 343
Borve Ale (OG 1040, ABV 3.8%)
Bishop Elphinstone Ale (OG 1053, ABV 4.7%) Occasional.
Tall Ships IPA (OG 1053, ABV 5%)
Cairm Porter (OG 1060)
Extra Strong (OG 1085, ABV 10%)
Moved from its original site on the Isle of Lewis in 1988 to a former school on the mainland, now converted to a pub with the brewery adjacent. Supplies about half a dozen free trade outlets.

The Brunswick Inn — A True Free House

BRUNSWICK INN
The Brunswick Brewing Co. Ltd., 1 Railway Terrace, Derby. Tel. (0332) 290677
Celebration Mild (OG 1032)
First Brew (OG 1036)
Second Brew (OG 1042)
Festival (OG 1046) October only.
Old Accidental (OG 1050)
Winter Ale (OG 1051)
New brewery constructed in tower fashion behind Britain's first purpose-built railway hostelry. Supplies two other pubs.

BRYN ARMS
Barry's Brewery, Gellilydan, Blaenau Ffestiniog, Gwynedd, LL41 4EH. Tel. (0766) 85379
Mêl y Moelwyn Bitter (OG 1038, ABV 3.8%)
Free house which began brewing a Yorkshire-style bitter in late summer 1992.

DUKE OF NORFOLK BREWERY
202–204 Westbourne Grove, London, W11. Tel. (071) 229 3551
Broads Bitter (OG 1043)
Norfolk Best (OG 1047)
Dynamite (OG 1054)
Clifton Inns brew pub which began production in November 1989. Beer is brewed from whole malt with no adjuncts. Also produces an occasional Christmas ale and provides cask ales for a couple of other London pubs.

FELLOWS, MORTON & CLAYTON BREWHOUSE COMPANY
54 Canal Street, Nottingham, NG1 7EH. Tel. (0602) 506795
Samuel Fellows Bitter (OG 1040, ABV 4%)
Matthew Clayton's Strong Ale (OG 1050)
Fellows Christmas Cracker (OG 1058)
Clayton's New Year Nectar (OG 1062)
Founded in 1980 as a Whitbread malt extract brew pub, the new tenants are now experimenting with full mash brewing.

FIRST IN, LAST OUT
St Clements Brewery, 14-15 High Street, Old Town, Hastings, E. Sussex, TN34 3EY. Tel. (0424) 425079
Crofters (OG 1040)
Cardinal (OG 1045)
Pub with a brewery installed in 1985.

FLAMINGO BREWERY COMPANY
88 London Road, Kingston upon Thames, KT2 6PX. Tel. (081) 541 3717
Fairfield Bitter (OG 1037)
Royal Charter (OG 1045)
Coronation (OG 1060)
Rudolf's Revenge (OG 1070) Christmas only.
Previously the Flamingo & Firkin, now owned by Saxon Inns. Cellar tanks are used for Fairfield Bitter, which has retailed over the last year at under £1 a pint.

FOX & HOUNDS
Barley Brewery, Barley, Royston, Herts, SG8 8HU. Tel. (0763) 848459
Old Dragon (OG 1039)
Flamethrower (OG 1045+)
Early member of the pub brewing revival, using a 19th-century brewhouse at what used to be the Waggon & Horses before changing its name. Home-brews not always available.

FOX & HOUNDS
Stottesdon, Shropshire, DY14 8TZ. Tel. (074 632) 222
Wust (OG 1037)
Bosting (OG 1043)
Pub which started brewing in the 1970s, though the brewer has now left. The landlord is experimenting with these two brews and hopes to supply the free trade.

FOX & NEWT
9 Burley Street, Leeds, W. Yorks, LS9 1LD. Tel. (0532) 432612

Brew Pubs

Burley Bitter (OG 1036, ABV 3.8%)
Old Willow (OG 1046, ABV 4.6%)
A Whitbread malt extract pub, opened in 1982. Beers kept under a CO_2 blanket in casks.

FROG & PARROT
Division Street, Sheffield, S. Yorks, S1 4GF. Tel. (0742) 721280
Old Croak Ale (OG 1036, ABV 3.3%)
Reckless Bitter (OG 1047, ABV 4.5%)
Roger's Conqueror (OG 1066, ABV 6.1%)
Roger & Out (OG 1125, ABV 16.9%)
Whitbread malt extract brew pub. Roger & Out is listed in the *Guinness Book of Records* as the world's strongest beer and is also sold in nip bottles. Beers are kept under a CO_2 blanket in casks and are made available to four other pubs.

GASTONS BAR
Little Avenham Brewery, 30 Avenham Street, Preston, Lancs, PR1. Tel. (0772) 51380
Clog Dancer (OG 1038, ABV 4%)
Brewery opened in June 1992. A dark beer and a stronger bitter are planned.

GREEN DRAGON
Broad Street, Bungay, Suffolk, NR35 1EE. Tel (0986) 892681
Chaucer Ale (OG 1037, ABV 3.6%)
Bridge Street Bitter (OG 1046, ABV 4.5%)
Dragon Ale (OG 1058, ABV 5.8%)
Pub purchased from Brent Walker in 1991 and refurbished, with a brewery installed in the outbuildings. Only Dragon is kept under a blanket of gas (a CO_2 and nitrogen mix).

GREYHOUND BREWERY COMPANY LTD
151 Greyhound Lane, Streatham Common, London, SW16 5NJ. Tel. (081) 677 9962
XXXP Pedigree Mild (OG 1036, ABV 3.6%)
Special Ale (OG 1038, ABV 3.8%)
Streatham Strong (OG 1048, ABV 4.9%)
Streatham Dynamite (OG 1055, ABV 5.5%)
A Clifton Inns brew pub, set up in 1984. XXXP is the only traditional mild brewed in London, though blanket pressure is used in the cellar tanks. Special beers brewed for bank holidays and other occasions. Supplies three other pubs.

GRIBBLE INN
Oving, Chichester, W. Sussex, PO20 6BP. Tel. (0243) 786893
Harvest Pale (OG 1036, ABV 3.6%)
Gribble Ale (OG 1042, ABV 4.2%)
Reg's Tipple (OG 1055, ABV 5.5%)

Brew pub owned by Hall & Woodhouse which recommenced brewing in autumn 1991 after a gap of 18 months. The beers may sometimes be found in other Hall & Woodhouse pubs.

HAND IN HAND
Kemptown Brewery Company Ltd., 33 Upper St James's Street, Kemptown, Brighton, E. Sussex, BN2 1JN. Tel. (0273) 602521
Mild (OG 1038, ABV 3.5%) Occasional.
Bitter (OG 1040, ABV 4%)
Celebrated Staggering Ale (OG 1050, ABV 5%)
Staggering in the Dark (SID) (OG 1052, ABV 5.2%)
Old Grumpy (OG 1064, ABV 6.4%)
Full mash brewery started in November 1989, taking the name of the old Kemptown Brewery, 500 yards away. Specially constructed behind the pub in the 'tower' tradition. Around ten other outlets supplied.

HEDGEHOG & HOGSHEAD
100 Goldstone Villas, Hove, E. Sussex, BN3 3RX. Tel. (0273) 733660
Brighton Breezy Bitter (OG 1044)
Hogbolter (OG 1059)
Prickletickler (OG 1075) An occasional brew.
Slay Bells (OG 1080) Christmas only.
The first of David Bruce's new ventures, which opened in July 1990. Both casks and tanks are used for storage and blanket pressure is used.

HEDGEHOG & HOGSHEAD
163 University Road, Highfield, Southampton, Hampshire, SO2 1TS. Tel. (0703) 581124
Solent Sunshine (OG 1037) Summer only.
Belcher's Best Bitter (OG 1044)
Hogbolter (OG 1059)
Prickletickler (OG 1075) Winter only.
Slay Bells (OG 1080) Christmas only.
The second in the new chain. Blanket pressure used on cellar tanks. Also supplies beer to Bruce's latest pub, the Water Rat, at Marsh Benham, near Newbury, Berkshire.

HIGHLANDER
North & East Riding Brewers Ltd., 15-16 Esplanade, South Cliff, Scarborough, N. Yorks, YO11 2AF. Tel. (0723) 365627
Mild (OG 1039)
EXB (OG 1040)
No. 68 (OG 1042)
Thistle Scotch Bitter (OG 1042)
Brewery set up behind a Victorian hotel, which used to sell its 'William Clark' Scotch-style beers to the free trade, but now only brews for itself and occasional beer festivals.

JOHN THOMPSON INN
John Thompson Brewery, Ingleby, Derbyshire. Tel. (0332) 862469
JTS XXX (OG 1042, ABV 4.2%)

Brew Pubs

15th-century farmhouse, converted to a pub in 1969. Has brewed since 1977, with its range of other beers supplied to the free trade under the name of Lloyds Country Beers (see Independents), a separate enterprise.

JOLLY ROGER
The Original Hereford Brewing Company, 88 St Owen Street, Hereford, HR1 2QD. Tel. (0432) 274998
Quaff Ale (OG 1038)
Blackbeard (OG 1043)
Old Hereford Bull (OG 1050)
An off-shoot of the well-established Worcester Jolly Roger (see below), established in October 1990. The bar takes the shape of a galleon.

JOLLY ROGER BREWERY AND TAP
50 Lowesmoor, Worcester, WR1 2SG. Tel. (0905) 21540
Quaff Ale (OG 1038, ABV 3.8%)
Severn Bore Special (OG 1048, ABV 4.8%)
Old Lowesmoor (OG 1058, ABV 5.8%)
Winter Wobbler (OG 1093, ABV 11%) The seasonal brew.
Brewery which moved to this site in 1985. Has shared beer production for outside trade with Jolly Roger's commercial brewery (see Independents) but will revert to brew pub status in the future. Some occasional brews. A jug and bottle has been opened.

LASS O'GOWRIE
Charles Street, Manchester, M1 7DB. Tel. (061) 273 6932
LOG 35 (OG 1035)
LOG 42 (OG 1042)
Centurion (OG 1052)
Graduation (OG 1056)
A Whitbread malt extract brew pub, opened in 1983. Beer is stored in cellar tanks without a blanket of gas. Centurion and Graduation are only brewed three or four times a year.

MARISCO TAVERN
Lundy Brewery, Lundy Island, Bristol Channel, EX39 2LY. Tel. (0237) 431831
John 'O's (OG 1035)
Old Light (OG 1040)
Old Light Special (OG 1055) Winter only.
Malt extract beers produced for consumption only on the island. A new brewer was appointed for the 1992 summer season.

MARKET PORTER
9 Stoney Street, Borough Market, London, SE1 9AA. Tel. (071) 407 2495
Bitter (OG 1035)
Special (OG 1048)
Malt extract brew pub.

MASONS ARMS
Lakeland Brewery Company, Strawberry Bank, Cartmel Fell, Grange-over-Sands, Cumbria, LA11 6NW. Tel. (053 95) 68486

Amazon Bitter (OG 1038, ABV 4%)
Great Northern (OG 1047, ABV 5%)
Big Six (OG 1066, ABV 6%)
Famous pub, known for its large selection of bottled beers, which began brewing in May 1990. Beer names are based on books by local author Arthur Ransome. *Bottle-conditioned beers: Great Northern, Big Six and Damson Beer (ABV 9%) – made from the pub's own damsons to a kriek recipe and available from Christmas.*

MINERVA
Nelson Street, Hull, Humbs, HU1 1XE. Tel. (0482) 26909
Pilots Pride (OG 1039)
Joshua Tetley full mash brew pub, set up in 1983 and storing its beer under blanket pressure in cellar tanks.

MIN PIN INN
North Cornwall Brewers, Tregatta Corner, Tintagel, Cornwall, PL34 0DX. Tel. (0840) 770241
Legend Bitter (OG 1035, ABV 3.6%)
Brown Willy Bitter (OG 1055, ABV 4.3%)
Converted farmhouse with possibly the only entirely female-operated brewery in the country (established in 1985). Malt extract used. Closed midweek, November-March.

OLD SWAN (Ma Pardoe's)
Halesowen Road, Netherton, Dudley, W. Midlands, DY2 1BT. Tel. (0384) 253075
Not currently brewing.

ORANGE BREWERY
37–39 Pimlico Road, London, SW1W 8NE. Tel. (071) 730 5984
Pimlico Light (OG 1032, ABV 3%)
SW1 (OG 1039, ABV 3.9%)
Pimlico Porter (OG 1045, ABV 4.3%)
SW2 (OG 1049, ABV 4.9%)
Clifton Inns' first in-house brewery, opened in 1983. The full mash brews are stored with a cask breather. Brews a host of seasonal beers and a lager to the *Reinheitsgebot* German purity law.

PLOUGH INN
Bodicote Brewery, Bodicote, Banbury, Oxfordshire, OX15 4BZ. Tel. (0295) 262327
Bitter (OG 1035, ABV 3.5%)
No. 9 (OG 1045, ABV 4.2%)
Old English Porter (OG 1045, ABV 4.2%)
Triple X (OG 1050, ABV 4.5%) Winter only.
Brewery founded in 1982; the pub has been in the same hands for 34 years. No.9 is now also bottled (not bottle-conditioned).

ROSE STREET BREWERY
55 Rose Street, Edinburgh, Lothian, EH2 2NH. Tel. (031) 220 1227
Auld Reekie 80/- (OG 1043, ABV 4.2%)
Auld Reekie 90/- (OG 1057, ABV 5.3%)
Brew pub founded in 1983, run by Alloa Brewery and now supplying half a dozen other Alloa outlets. Malt extract used.

Brew Pubs

ROYAL CLARENCE
31 The Esplanade, Burnham-on-Sea, Somerset, TA8 1BQ. Tel. (0278) 783138
Pride (OG 1036, ABV 3.6%)
Regent (OG 1050, ABV 5%)
Seaside hotel brewery, now only brewing for itself.

ROYAL INN & HORSEBRIDGE BREWERY
Horsebridge, Tavistock, Devon, PL19 8PJ. Tel. (082 287) 214
Tamar (OG 1039, ABV 3.9%)
Horsebridge Best (OG 1045, ABV 4.5%)
Right Royal (OG 1050) Special occasions only.
Heller (OG 1060, ABV 6%)
15th-century country pub, once a nunnery, which began brewing in 1981. After a change of hands, and a period of inactivity, the single-barrel plant recommenced brewing in 1984.

STAR INN
St Peters Village, Jersey, Channel Islands. Tel. (0534) 485556
Jimmy's Bitter (OG 1039)
SPA (OG 1049)
Half-million pound project by Steve and Sarah Skinner to refurbish and brew at the old Star pub. The first brew appeared in March 1992. Both casks and cellar tanks are used.

STEAM PACKET INN
Racca Green, Knottingley, Pontefract, W. Yorks. Tel. (0977) 677266
Mellor's Gamekeeper (OG 1037)
New brew pub with other beers planned. Has begun to supply some free trade outlets in South Yorkshire.

TALLY HO COUNTRY INN & BREWERY
14 Market Street, Hatherleigh, Devon, EX20 3JN. Tel. (0837) 810306
Dark Mild (OG 1034, ABV 2.8%)
Potboiler's Brew (OG 1036, ABV 3.5%)
Tarka's Tipple (OG 1043, ABV 4.2%)
Nutters (OG 1048, ABV 4.6%)
Janni Jollop (OG 1064, ABV 6.6%) Winter only.
Brew pub whose first beer went on sale at Easter 1990. Full mash, no additives. *Bottle-conditioned beer: Thurgia (OG 1056, ABV 5.7%)*

THREE TUNS BREWERY
Salop Street, Bishop's Castle, Shropshire, SY9 5BW. Tel. (0588) 638797
Light Mild (OG 1035)
XXX Bitter (OG 1042)
Steamer (OG 1045)
Old Scrooge (OG 1055) Winter only.
Jim Wood's (OG 1065)
Historic brew pub which first obtained a brewing licence in 1642. The tower brewery was built in 1888 and is still in use.

WILLY'S
17 High Cliff Road, Cleethorpes, Humbs, DN35 8RQ. Tel. (0472) 602145
Original Bitter (OG 1038, ABV 3.6%)
Burcom Bitter or Mariner's Gold (OG 1044, ABV 4.1%)
Coxswains Special Bitter (OG 1049, ABV 4.7%)
Old Groyne (OG 1060, ABV 5.8%)
Brewery opened in May 1989 to supply this seafront pub and some free trade. Another outlet, SWIGS (Second Willy's In Grimsby), was bought in December 1989.

YORKSHIRE GREY
2 Theobalds Road, London, WC1X 8PN. Tel. (071) 405 8287
City Bitter (OG 1035, ABV 3.2%) Summer only.
Headline Bitter (OG 1037, ABV 3.5%)
Holborn Best Bitter (OG 1047, ABV 4.5%)
Regiment Bitter (OG 1054, ABV 5.1%)
Clifton Inns brew pub on the corner of Gray's Inn Road. CO_2 blanket on cellar tanks, and cask breathers also used.

Brew Pubs

THE FIRKIN PUBS
This highly successful chain of brew pubs was initiated by David Bruce in 1979. In 1988 he sold all the pubs to Midsummer Leisure (later European Leisure), who, in turn, sold them to Stakis Leisure in September 1990. Now the chain has been bought by Allied Breweries, who, it seems, are keen to take some Firkin beer in their Taylor Walker London pubs. Not all the Firkin pubs now brew; some are supplied by the others, so only the actual brew pubs are listed here. All the brews are full mash beers, but most of the pubs use cellar tanks for storage, with the beer kept under a blanket of CO_2. Some of the pubs have taken to serving the beer in plastic beakers. The breweries are often visible from the bar.

FALCON & FIRKIN
360 Victoria Park Road, Hackney, London, E9 7BT. Tel. (081) 985 0693
Falcon (OG 1036, ABV 3.6%)
VP Extra Stout (OG 1042, ABV 3.9%) Winter only.
Hackney (OG 1043, ABV 4.1%)
Flag Porter (OG 1055, ABV 5.4%) Occasional brew.
Dogbolter (OG 1059, ABV 6%)
Slaybells (OG 1080) A Christmas brew.
The largest of the Firkin brew pubs which also supplies cask-conditioned beers for the Flower & Firkin (at Kew Gardens), the Fox & Firkin, the Frigate & Firkin, the Frog & Firkin, the Goose & Firkin and the Pheasant & Firkin. Except for Dogbolter, all other beers are kept in cellar tanks under a nitrogen blanket. *Bottle-conditioned beer: Flag Porter (under contract)*. Plans to supply Nicholson's Best Bitter for Allied's Nicholson's pubs.

FERRET & FIRKIN
114 Lots Road, Chelsea, London, SW10 0RJ. Tel. (071) 352 6645
Ferret Ale (OG 1044, ABV 4.5%)
Dogbolter (OG 1059, ABV 6%)
'The Ferret & Firkin in the Balloon up the Creek', as it is properly known. Opened in 1983.

FLAMINGO & FIRKIN
Becket Street, Derby, DE1 1HT. Tel. (0332) 45948
Special Stout (OG 1042)
Tom Becket (OG 1043)
Dogbolter (OG 1059)
Slaybells (OG 1070) A Christmas beer.
Established in 1988, one of only two Firkins outside London. Beers are kept under a blanket of nitrogen.

FLEA & FIRKIN
137 Grosvenor Street, Manchester, M1 7DZ. Tel. (061) 274 3682
Full Mash Magical Mild (OG 1034, ABV 3.4%)
Scratch Bitter (OG 1037, ABV 3.7%)

Total Eclipse (OG 1043, ABV 4.2%) Summer only.
Grosvenor BB (OG 1043, ABV 4.3%)
Harvest Mouse Wheat Beer (OG 1045, ABV 4.8%)
Stout (OG 1052, ABV 5.1%) Winter only.
Ginger Beer (OG 1057, ABV 6.5%)
Dogbolter (OG 1059, ABV 5.9%)
Opened in 1990 and serves a few other outlets. Strong ales with varying names (ABV 8–9%) are brewed every few months. Scratch, Grosvenor and Dogbolter are cask-conditioned in summer, otherwise all beers are kept in tanks under a blanket of nitrogen and CO_2.

FLOUNDER & FIRKIN
54 Holloway Road, London, N7 8JL. Tel. (071) 609 9574
Bruce's Mild (OG 1036)
Fish T'ale (OG 1036)
Whale Ale (OG 1044)
Bruce's Stout (OG 1050)
Ginger Tom (OG 1050) Summer only.
Dogbolter (OG 1058)
Opened in 1985. Ginger Tom is a hand-pulled ginger beer.

FOX & FIRKIN
316 Lewisham High Street, London, SE13. Tel. (081) 690 8925
Fox Bitter (OG 1044)
Dogbolter (OG 1059)
The second Bruce's pub, opened in 1980. Special brews for the Firkin chain, such as Mild (OG 1041), Porter (OG 1051) and Easter Egg Cracker (OG 1071), are produced here. A light bitter, Vixen Bitter (OG 1036), is occasionally brewed for the Fox at the Falcon & Firkin.

GOOSE & FIRKIN
47–48 Borough Road, London, SE1. Tel. (071) 403 3590
Borough Bitter (OG 1044)
Dogbolter (OG 1059)
The first of the Firkin pubs, still using malt extract in its small cellar brewery. Goose Bitter (OG 1036) is brewed at the Falcon & Firkin.

PHOENIX & FIRKIN
5 Windsor Walk, Camberwell, London, SE5 8BB. Tel. (071) 701 8282
Rail Ale (OG 1037)
Phoenix Bitter (OG 1044)
Midnight Express Stout (OG 1051)
Dogbolter (OG 1059)
An award-winning reconstruction of the burnt-out Denmark Hill railway station, opened in 1984. Midnight Express is a cask-conditioned stout (no blanket pressure), occasionally sold throughout the chain. Plans are in hand to enlarge the premises and store beer in casks, rather than cellar tanks, as at present.

ALLEN PARTNERSHIP LTD
West Hill Place, Balcombe, W. Sussex, RH17 6QY. Tel. (0444) 811559
Company set up in 1988 which now runs 97 managed pubs, many leased from Inntrepreneur, Bass and Allied, some bought from Whitbread. The pubs run from Scotland to the south coast.

BEARDS OF SUSSEX
Stella House, Diplock Way, Hailsham, E. Sussex. Tel. (0323) 847888
Former brewing company which opted out of production in the 1950s. Currently runs 25 pubs in Sussex, selling beer from a range of regional independents.

BODDINGTON PUB COMPANY
West Point, 501 Chester Road, Manchester, M16 9HX. Tel. (061) 876 4292
Famous Manchester brewing name which sold its Strangeways and Higsons breweries to Whitbread in 1989. Had previously taken over and closed the neighbouring Oldham Brewery. Now runs 478 pubs in the North-West, roughly half-managed and half-tenanted, retailing the Boddingtons, Oldham and Higsons beers from Whitbread, as well as Tetley and Theakston brews, and Cains Bitter. A house beer, Old Shilling, is brewed by Mansfield.

CAFE INNS PLC
George House, St Thomas Road, Chorley, Lancs, PR7 1HP. Tel.(025 72) 62424
Eighty-five pubs in the North-West are run by this company, established in 1986. The pubs are mostly tenanted on traditional three-year leases. Shares in a separate operation with Burtonwood Brewery called Vantage Inns which runs 51 pubs.

CENTRIC PUB COMPANY LTD
Star Chambers, 412 Radford Road, Nottingham, NG7 7NP. Tel.(0602) 790066
New pub group, run by a former MD of Mansfield Brewery and established with the leasing of 200 pubs from Bass. All pubs are still supplied with Bass beers. The goal is 400 pubs.

CENTURY INNS LTD
Belasis Business Centre, Coxwold Way, Billingham, Cleveland, TS23 4EA. Tel. (0642) 343426
Company formed in 1991 by Camerons workers with the purchase of 185 pubs from Bass and the intention of providing a north-eastern pub estate for the proposed brewery buy-out which was subsequently scuppered by Brent Walker. More recent purchases have brought the number of pubs up to 283, and most are tenanted. Beer sales are still mostly confined to Bass products, with some Courage and S&N beers.

CHEF & BREWER GROUP LTD
106 Oxford Road, Uxbridge, Middlesex. Tel. (0895) 258233
The managed house division of Grand Metropolitan Estates, operating 1,600 pubs and pub-restaurants, including 330 acquired from Courage in 1991. Pubs are tied to Courage beers until 1995. (See also Inntrepreneur Estates Ltd.)

CONTROL SECURITIES PLC
47-51 Gillingham Street, London, SW1V 1PS. Tel. (071) 828 6405
The retail and property company which owns Belhaven brewery, but which operates many more pubs than that brewery serves. Currently the figure stands at 600 nationwide, all on 20-year leases.

DEAN ENTERTAINMENTS LTD
Dean House, Victoria Road, Kirkcaldy, Fife, KY1 2SA. Tel. (0592) 200417
Scottish-based company owning 25 pubs, two hotels and three discos in the Fife and Tayside area. Fifteen of the pubs came from Tennent Caledonian.

JOHN DEVENISH PLC
Hope Square, Weymouth, Dorset, DT4 8TP. Tel. (0305) 761111
Company founded in 1742 and now the most recent recruit to the family of ex-breweries which only run pubs. Having closed the Weymouth brewery in 1985, it signed a supply deal with Whitbread in 1991, leaving its Redruth brewery to a management buy-out team. Whitbread now supplies Devenish with Royal Wessex Bitter from Cheltenham, as well as Cornish Original, produced for Whitbread by the new regime at Redruth. The 370 pubs (spread across the country: 220 managed, 150 tenanted) also sell national and independent beers. Around 20% of the company is owned by Boddingtons, which failed in its attempt to take complete control just before the Whitbread deal went through. Looking to add 35 pubs a year to the chain which already includes 'specialist ale houses' and 'cheese and ale houses'.

Pub Groups

ENTERPRISE INNS LTD
Friars Gate, Stratford Road, Solihull,
W. Midlands, B90 4BN.
Tel. (021) 733 7700
Midlands-based company founded in 1991
with the purchase of 370 pubs from Bass.
These are now run on a 21-year lease basis,
with beers supplied by Bass. Lessees are
not allowed to buy beers outside the
company, though there are plans to extend
the choice available.

SIR JOHN FITZGERALD LTD
Café Royal Building, 8 Nelson Street,
Newcastle upon Tyne, Tyne & Wear,
NE1 5AW. Tel. (091) 232 0664
Long-established, family-owned company,
dating from the end of the last century. Its
pubs convey a 'free house' image, all 27 (26
managed) being in the North-East.

GRAY & SONS (CHELMSFORD) LTD
Rignals Lane, Galleywood, Chelmsford,
Essex. Tel. (0245) 75181
A brewery which ceased production at its
Chelmsford brewery in 1974, now
supplying its 49 local pubs with beers from
Greene King (IPA and Abbot Ale) and
Ridleys (Mild) instead.

GREENALLS GROUP PLC
Wilderspool House, Greenalls Avenue,
Warrington, Cheshire, WA4 6RH.
Tel. (0925) 51234
An ex-brewing giant which destroyed
many fine independent breweries before
turning its back on brewing in 1991. On a
1980s rampage, Greenalls stormed the
Midlands, taking over and closing the
Wem, Davenports, Simpkiss and
Shipstone's breweries. Its beers are now
brewed by Allied in Warrington and
Burton, and guest beers in its 1,380 pubs in
the North-West and Midlands include
Tetley Bitter, Stones Best Bitter and, in a
few outlets, Cains and Coach House
Bitters. Has recently acquired Allied pubs
in the South. One hundred managed pubs
belong to the Premier House division; the
remainder are part of Greenalls Inns (500
managed, others leased).

GROSVENOR INNS PLC
The Old Schoolhouse, London Road,
Shenley, Herts, WD7 9DX.
Tel. (0923) 855837
Group running 45 pubs in London and the
Midlands, 30 of which are leased from

Inntrepreneur. Formerly Cromwell
Taverns, launched on the USM in May
1992.

HEAVITREE BREWERY PLC
Trood Lane, Matford, Exeter, Devon,
EX2 8YP. Tel. (0392) 58406
West Country brewery which gave up
production in 1970 to concentrate on
running its 120 pubs. Takes its beers
principally from Whitbread, Bass and
Eldridge Pope.

INNTREPRENEUR ESTATES LTD
Mill House, Aylesbury Road, Thame,
Oxfordshire, OX9 3AT.
Tel. (0844) 261526
The pub-owning company formed by
Courage and Grand Metropolitan as part of
the pubs-for-breweries swap in 1991. In the
deal, Courage bought up all Grand Met's
(Watney's) breweries, with most of
Courage's pubs taken over by
Inntrepreneur (330 went directly to Grand
Met). Not all Grand Met pubs were
absorbed into this new company: some are
still operated by the Chef & Brewer
division. Inntrepreneur has led the way
with the long-lease (20 years) as a
replacement for the traditional tenancy. As
a result, many former Courage tenants
have already moved on. The company
currently operates around 7,000 pubs, 4,250
of which it is allowed to keep tied, under
the Government's Beer Orders. The others
(some leased to other pub groups) became
free houses on 1 November 1992. The tied
pubs will take Courage beers until 1998,
after which they will be free, unless
another supply deal is negotiated.

LEISURETIME INNS PLC
Attlee House, St Aldates Courtyard,
Oxford, OX1 1BN.
Tel. (0865) 251681
Company formed in 1988 and now owning
62 pubs within an 80-mile radius of
Oxford. The pubs follow two styles: the
Slug & Lettuce, bare boards, traditional
pub idiom, and the County Taverns, olde-
worlde eating house pattern, with beams
and open fires. Sixty per cent of the estate
is tied to either Courage or Allied, though
the aim is to free the pubs by 1997. All
pubs stock at least two real ales, with Bass
a compulsory guest beer and managers
allowed a choice of others.

PARAGON INNS
29 Ribblesdale Place, Preston, Lancs,
PR1 3NA.
North-western chain of pubs established in
1990 with the purchase of 32 pubs from
S&N.

PARAMOUNT PLC
St Werburgh Chambers, Chester, Cheshire,
CH1 2EP. Tel. (0244) 321171
Pub-owning company part-owned by
Burtonwood (35%) and Bass (15%), whose

Pub Groups

beers are exclusively on sale in the chain of 126 pubs (eight leased, the rest tenanted). The aim is to expand the estate up to 100 miles from Chester and to convert all pubs to cask beer (currently 75% sell real ale). Paramount also owns 50% of another chain, Real Inns (17 pubs); the other 50% belongs to Canadian giants Labatts.

PUBMASTER LTD
Greenbank Offices, Lion Brewery, Hartlepool, Cleveland, TS24 7QF.
Tel. (0429) 266666
Following the break up of the Brent Walker empire, Pubmaster was set up to take over the running of its 1,100 pubs. Brent Walker's experience in the brewing industry was not a happy one. Though Camerons and Tolly Cobbold were purchased from Barclay Brothers in 1989, Tolly was retrieved by a management buy-out in 1990 and Camerons was sold to Wolverhampton & Dudley in 1991, leaving the financially troubled company holding onto pubs from both the old brewery estates. Pubmaster has now leased another 734 pubs from Allied, and is entering into an arrangement with Canadian brewers Labatts to form a pub company called Maple Leaf Inns. Together they hope to take on 1,000 pubs which will operate under the name of Threshold Inns. One notable Pubmaster sub-group is the Tap & Spile chain of 22 real ale pubs.

REGENT INNS PLC
Northway House, 1379 High Road, Whetstone, London, N20 9LP.
Tel. (081) 445 5016
Company founded in 1980 and now owning 35 pubs in London and the Home Counties. Once known as Lockton Inns.

SCORPIO INNS LTD
Zealley House, Greenhills Way, Newton Abbot, Devon, TQ12 3TB.
Tel. (0626) 66117
New pub group running 138 pubs, most leased from Whitbread.

SMITH INNS LTD
Bridge House, Station Road, Scunthorpe, Humbs, DN15 6PY.
Tel.(0724) 861703
Four-year-old company operating 35 managed pubs in Yorkshire, Humberside and Lincolnshire. Twelve pubs are free

houses, the remainder are leased from big brewers and tied to their products. Looking to top the 50-pub mark in the next year.

SURREY FREE INNS PLC
Exchange House, Station Road, Liphook, Hampshire, GU30 7DW.
Tel. (0428) 725248
Established in 1986 to run a series of pubs in the South and now controls 30 outlets which tend to have a commitment to catering. Twenty-eight are managed houses; two are on 20-year leases. Some are Inntrepreneur leases, others private purchases, including former Berni Inns. A company guest beer programme is operated and there is also a house beer known as Auld Soxx (brewer undeclared). Some pubs are free houses. The White Horse at Priors Dean is the most famous acquisition.

THORNABY LEISURE LTD
Enterprise House, Valley Street North, Darlington, Co. Durham, DL1 1GY. Tel. (0325) 489619
Company set up in 1987 which currently has 36 pubs, some bought from S&N. Sixteen pubs are managed, the rest tenanted.

TRENT TAVERNS LTD
PO Box 1061, Gringley on the Hill, Doncaster, S. Yorks, DN10 4ED.
Tel. (0777) 817408
Company set up by a former S&N employee. Sixty-seven pubs in the Midlands and the North are leased from Whitbread.

JD WETHERSPOON ORGANISATION LTD
735 High Road, North Finchley, London, N12 8UA. Tel. (081) 446 9099
Ambitious London-based group which opened its first pub in 1979. Currently owns nearly 50 pubs in and around the capital, all managed, with the goal being 100 pubs in three years' time. Many of the pubs are conversions from shops, including ex-Woolworth stores, giving them an unusual spaciousness. Common names are JJ Moon's and other 'Moon' titles, and there is no music in any of the pubs. Five beers are always sold: Marston's Pedigree, Greene King IPA and Abbot Ale, and S&N Theakston XB and Younger Scotch. Licensees also have a choice from a guest list of over 150 beers.

JAMES WILLIAMS (NARBERTH)
7 Spring Gardens, Narberth, Dyfed, SA67 7BP. Tel. (0834) 860318
Privately-owned concern, founded in 1830 and operating 51 pubs in Dyfed (all tenanted), which has invested heavily in its estate since 1986. Tenants have a choice of selected beers from Brains, Crown Buckley, Felinfoel, Bass, Allied, Courage, Whitbread, Wadworth and Ruddles.

497

The Beers Index

Pedigree, 6X and Landlord are famous beers which need little introduction. But who brews Flying Herbert, Old Buzzard and Viking Bitter? This index is designed to help you match such beers to their breweries. Common beer names like Bitter, Mild, Special and Porter are not featured, as, inevitably, they are already preceded by the name of the brewer.

The Beers Index

The Beers Index

The Beers Index

The Beers Index

The Beers Index

GLOSSARY
Beer language explained

ABV: alcohol by volume. The percentage of alcohol in the beer.

Blanket pressure: a light covering of carbon dioxide added to cask beer to prevent air deteriorating it.
Too much gas can make the beer fizzy, like keg beer.

Bottle-conditioned: a beer which is allowed to continue its fermentation in the bottle and contains a light sediment.

Cask breather: device which allows carbon dioxide into the cask at atmospheric pressure to replace drawn off beer. It is criticised for spoiling the natural maturing process of the beer.

Dry hopping: putting fresh hops into the beer in the cask.

Economiser: a device which directs beer from the drip tray back into the pump for recycling.

Free house: a pub free from any brewery tie and, in theory, able to sell any beer it chooses.

Full mash: mash traditionally produced from malt, not malt extract.

Loan tie: control of a free house, and the tieing of its products, by a brewery, in exchange for the offer of an attractive financial loan.

Malt extract: condensed wort, mostly used in home brewing.

Original gravity: system for discerning the amount of duty payable on a beer, based on the amount of fermentable material it contains prior to yeast being added. Water has a gravity of 1000 degrees, so a beer with an OG of 1040 would have 40 parts of fermentable material before fermentation.

Tenant: licensee who pays a rent and takes beer from the brewery which owns the pub.

Tied house: a pub owned by a brewery and restricted to selling its beer.

Top pressure: means of forcing beer to the point of sale with carbon dioxide.